PRAGATI

PHYSICS

MCQs

(MULTIPLE CHOICE QUESTIONS)

FOR

NEET/JEE (MAINS & ADVANCED) AIPMT/AIIMS/AFMC & OTHER COMPETITIVE EXAMS

J. S. Virdi
M.Sc. M.Phil., B.Ed.
Head, Physics Department,
DPS, R.K. Puram, New Delhi.

Dr. Pradeep Kumar
M.Sc. (Physical Sciences), Ph.D.
Professor
Delhi College of Technology and Management

SALIENT FEATURES OF BOOK

- ★ Authors of Great Repute
- ★ Latest Inputs as per CBSE Syllabus
- ★ Complete Chapterwise MCQs
- ★ More than 4000 MCQs
- ★ Questions from Competitive Exams included
- ★ Latest Papers with Answers included

PRAGATI BOOKS

PP031

Pragati - Physics (MCQs)

First Edition : January 2017

Published By : **Polyplate**

NIRALI PRAKASHAN

Abhyudaya Pragati, 1312, Shivaji Nagar,
Off J.M. Road, PUNE – 411005
Tel - (020) 25512336/37/39, Fax - (020) 25511379
Email : niralipune@pragationline.com

• DISTRIBUTION CENTRES

PUNE

Nirali Prakashan : 119, Budhwar Peth, Jogeshwari Mandir Lane, Pune 411002, Maharashtra
Tel : (020) 2445 2044, 66022708, Fax : (020) 2445 1538
Email : bookorder@pragationline.com, niralilocal@pragationline.com

Nirali Prakashan : S. No. 28/27, Dhyari, Near Pari Company, Pune 411041
Tel : (020) 24690204 Fax : (020) 24690316
Email : dhyari@pragationline.com, bookorder@pragationline.com

MUMBAI

Nirali Prakashan : 385, S.V.P. Road, Rasdhara Co-op. Hsg. Society Ltd.,
Girgaum, Mumbai 400004, Maharashtra
Tel : (022) 2385 6339 / 2386 9976, Fax : (022) 2386 9976
Email : niralimumbai@pragationline.com

• DISTRIBUTION BRANCHES

JALGAON

Nirali Prakashan : 34, V. V. Golani Market, Navi Peth, Jalgaon 425001,
Maharashtra, Tel : (0257) 222 0395, Mob : 94234 91860

KOLHAPUR

Nirali Prakashan : New Mahadvar Road, Kedar Plaza, 1st Floor Opp. IDBI Bank
Kolhapur 416 012, Maharashtra. Mob : 9850046155

NAGPUR

Pratibha Book Distributors : Above Maratha Mandir, Shop No. 3, First Floor,
Rani Jhanshi Square, Sitabuldi, Nagpur 440012, Maharashtra
Tel : (0712) 254 7129

DELHI

Nirali Prakashan : 4593/21, Basement, Aggarwal Lane 15, Ansari Road, Daryaganj
Near Times of India Building, New Delhi 110002
Mob : 08505972553

BENGALURU

Pragati Book House : House No. 1, Sanjeevappa Lane, Avenue Road Cross,
Opp. Rice Church, Bengaluru – 560002.
Tel : (080) 64513344, 64513355,Mob : 9880582331, 9845021552
Email:bharatsavla@yahoo.com

CHENNAI

Pragati Books : 9/1, Montieth Road, Behind Taas Mahal, Egmore,
Chennai 600008 Tamil Nadu, Tel : (044) 6518 3535,
Mob : 94440 01782 / 98450 21552 / 98805 82331,
Email : bharatsavla@yahoo.com

niralipune@pragationline.com | www.pragationline.com

Also find us on f www.facebook.com/niralibooks

PREFACE

The entrance examination scenario has witnessed many changes in the pattern of question papers varying from subjective to multiple choice questions, since the prestigious institutions such as IITs and AIIMS have come into existence.

This book is an attempt to provide an updated and in-depth coverage of the latest syllabus (CBSE) and pattern of question papers for all the Entrance Examinations i.e. JEE-MAINS, MHT-CET, AIPMT, AIIMS, AFMC and other medical and engineering examinations. The book has been shaped entirely according to the student perspective and a sincere effort has been made to present the material in a very functional and practical manner so that students enjoy the learning process as they proceed through the lesson rather than experiencing it as an ordeal. This book will equip the students with the necessary speed, accuracy and confidence for the entrance examinations.

We acknowledge the contribution and support of our families, friends, and of course the contribution of our students who have been a source of inspiration through all the stages of this project. Special thanks and gratitude from the core of our hearts goes to the untiring efforts of our publishers Nirali Prakashan.

Comments and suggestions from the readers of this book will be highly appreciated for the improvement of the book.

J. S. Virdi

Pradeep Kumar

CONTENTS

1

PHYSICAL WORLD AND MEASUREMENT

MULTIPLE CHOICE QUESTIONS

1. One Astronomical Unit (A.U.) is the distance between :
(a) Sun and Pluto
(b) Moon and Earth
(c) Sun and Earth
(d) Mars and Earth

2. The S. I. unit of Planck's constant (h) is :
(a) watt. second (b) J.s
(c) Ws^{-1} (d) Js^{-1}

3. erg cm^{-1} may be a unit of :
(a) force (b) momentum
(c) power (d) acceleration

4. Which of the following physical quantities has neither dimensions nor unit ?
(a) Angle
(b) Luminous intensity
(c) Coefficient of friction
(d) Current

5. Which pair is correct ?
(a) Electric field – Coulomb m^{-1}
(b) Magnetic flux – Weber
(c) Power – Farad
(d) Capacitance – Henry

6. Energy per unit volume expresses :
(a) Pressure (b) Force
(c) Thrust (d) Work

7. The surface tension of Hg is 32 dyne cm^{-1}. In S.I. unit system it will be :
(a) 0.032 (b) 0.32
(c) 3200 (d) 3.20

8. Which one of the following is not measured in units of energy ?
(a) Force × Displacement
(b) Impulse × Time
(c) M.I.× (Angular velocity)^2
(d) Couple of force × Angle turned

9. The dimensions of permeability of free space (μ_0) is : **(I.I.T. 1998)**
(a) $[ML^{-1}T^{-2}A]$ (b) $[MLT^{-2}A^{-2}]$
(c) $[ML^{-1}T^{-2}A^{-2}]$ (d) $[MLTA^{-2}]$

10. The dimensions of $\frac{\varepsilon_0 E^2}{2}$

(where ε_0 = absolute permittivity of free space and E = Electric field intensity) are : **(I.I.T. 2000)**
(a) $[MLT^{-2}]$ (b) $[MLT]$
(c) $[ML^2T^{-1}]$ (d) $[ML^{-1}T^{-2}]$

11. When the unit of force and unit of length are doubled, then the unit of energy will become:
(a) two times (b) one half times
(c) four times (d) three times

12. If $S^2 = at^4$, where 'S' is in meters and '*t*' in seconds, then the unit of 'a' is :
(a) ms^{-2} (b) m^2s^4
(c) ms^2 (d) m^2s^{-4}

13. Identify the pair whose dimensions are equal: **(A.I.E.E.E. 2008)**
(a) Torque and work
(b) Stress and energy
(c) Force and stress
(d) Force and work

14. The physical quantities not having the same dimensions are : **(A.I.E.E.E. 2003)**

(a) Torque and work

(b) Momentum and Planck's constant

(c) Stress and Young's modulus

(d) Speed and $(\mu_0 \varepsilon_0)^{-1/2}$

15. The dimensions of $\frac{1}{\mu_0 \varepsilon_0}$, where symbols have their usual meaning, are : **(A.I.E.E.E. 2003)**

(a) $[L^{-1}T]$ (b) $[L^{-2}T^{2}]$

(c) $[L^{2}T^{-2}]$ (d) $[LT^{-1}]$

16. Which one of the following represents the correct dimensions of coefficient of viscosity (η) ? **(A.I.E.E.E. 2004)**

(a) $[ML^{-1}T^{-2}]$ (b) $[ML^{-1}T^{-1}]$

(c) $[MLT^{-1}]$ (d) $[ML^{-2}T^{-2}]$

17. The terminal velocity (v) of a steel ball of radius (r) falling under gravity through a column of viscous liquid of coefficient of viscosity (η) depends on mass (m) of the ball, and acceleration due to gravity (g). Which of the following relations is dimensionally correct ?

(a) $v \propto \frac{mgr}{\eta}$ (b) $v \propto m g r \eta$

(c) $v \propto \frac{mg}{r\eta}$ (d) $v \propto \frac{\eta mg}{r}$

18. Which of the following relations is dimensionally correct ?

(a) $T = 2\pi\sqrt{R^2 / GM}$

(b) $T = 2\pi\sqrt{R^3 / GM}$

(c) $T = 2\pi\sqrt{\frac{R}{GM}}$

(d) $T = 2\pi\sqrt{\frac{GM}{R^3}}$

19. If $x = at + bt^2$, where x is in metres and t is in seconds, the unit of 'b' will be :

(a) metre (b) ms^{-1}

(c) ms^{-2} (d) m^2s^{-1}

20. The equation of state of a real gas can be expressed as : $\left[P + \frac{a}{V^2}\right](V - b) = RT$, where P is pressure, V is volume and T is absolute temperature, then the dimensions of 'a' and 'b' will be respectively :

(a) $[ML^3 T^0]$ and $[ML^5 T^{-2}]$

(b) $[ML^5 T^{-2}]$ and $[ML^{-3}T]$

(c) $[ML^3 T]$ and $[ML^{-5} T^{-2}]$

(d) $[ML^5 T^2]$ and $[M^0 L^3T^0]$

21. If the velocity of light (c), gravitational constant (G) and Planck's constant (h) are taken as fundamental units, then the dimensions of time are :

(a) $c^{1/2} G^{-1/2} h^{1/2}$ (b) $c^{-3/2} G^{1/2} h^{-1/2}$

(c) $c^{1/2} G^{-3/2} h^{-1/2}$ (d) $c^{-5/2} G^{1/2} h^{1/2}$

22. If the velocity (ν), force (F) and energy (E) are taken as fundamental units, then the dimensional formula for mass will be :

(a) $v^{-2} F^0 E$ (b) $v^0 F E^2$

(c) $vF^{-2} E^0$ (d) $v^{-2} F^0 E$

23. If the velocity (v), acceleration (a) and force (F) are taken as fundamental quantities instead of mass (m), length (L) and time (T), then the dimensions of Young's Modulus will be :

(a) $F a^2 v^{-2}$ (b) $F a^2 v^{-3}$

(c) $F a^2 v^{-4}$ (d) $F a^2 v^{-5}$

24. If m, E, τ and G denote mass, energy, angular momentum and gravitational constant respectively, then the dimensions of $E\tau^2/m^5G^2$ are of :

(a) Angle (b) Mass

(c) Length (d) Time

25. If 'v' is the velocity, 'r' is the radius and 'g' is the acceleration due to gravity, which of the following is dimensionless ?

(a) $\frac{v^2r}{g}$ (b) $\frac{v^2}{rg}$

(c) $\frac{v^2g}{r}$ (d) v^2rg

26. Out of the following pairs, which one doesn't have identical dimensions ?

(A.I.E.E.E. 2005)

(a) M. I and moment of force
(b) Work and torque
(c) Angular momentum and Planck's constant
(d) Impulse and momentum

27. Which of the following units denotes the dimensions ML^2/Q^2, where Q denotes electric charge ? **(A.I.E.E.E. 2006)**

(a) Weber (Wb) (b) Wb m^{-2}
(c) Henry (H) (d) Hm^{-2}

28. The dimensions of magnetic field in M, L, T and C (coulomb) is given as :

(a) $[ML^{-2} C^{-1}]$ (b) $[MLT^{-1} C^{-1}]$
(c) $[ML^2 C^{-2}]$ (d) $[ML^0 T^{-1} C^{-1}]$

29. The speed of gravity waves in water is proportional to $\lambda^a \rho^b g^c$, where λ is wavelength, ρ is density of water and g is the acceleration due to gravity. Which of the following relations is correct ?

(a) a = b = c (b) a ≠ b ≠ c
(c) a ≠ b = c (d) a = b ≠ c

30. A pressure of 10^6 dynes/cm^2 is equivalent to:

(a) 10^5 Nm^{-2} (b) 10^4 Nm^{-2}
(c) 10^6 Nm^{-2} (d) 10^7 Nm^{-2}

31. The unit of potential energy is :

(a) gm cm s^{-2} (b) gm cm^2 s^{-2}
(c) gm cm^2 s^{-1} (d) gm cm s^{-1}

32. The velocity of a body is given by the equation $v = \frac{b}{t} + ct^2 + dt^3$. The dimensions of b are :

(a) $[M^0LT^0]$ (b) $[ML^0T^0]$
(c) $[M^0L^0T]$ (d) $[MLT^{-1}]$

33. The dimensional formula of the ratio of angular to linear momentum is :

(a) $[M^0LT^0]$ (b) $[MLT]$
(c) $[ML^2T^{-1}]$ (d) $[M^{-1}L^{-1}T^1]$

34. The equation of a stationary wave is :

$$y = 2A \sin\left[\frac{2\pi ct}{\lambda}\right] \cos\left[\frac{2\pi x}{\lambda}\right]$$

Which of the following is wrong ?

(a) The unit of ct is same as that of λ.
(b) The unit of x is same as that of λ.
(c) The unit of $\frac{c}{\lambda}$ is same as that of $\frac{x}{\lambda}$.
(d) The unit of $\frac{2\pi c}{\lambda}$ is same as that of $\frac{2\pi x}{\lambda t}$.

35. In the equation $y = a \sin(\omega t + kx)$, the dimensions of ω are :

(a) $[M^0L^0T^{-1}]$ (b) $[M^0LT^{-1}]$
(c) $[ML^0T^0]$ (d) $[M^0L^{-1}T^0]$

36. The dimensional formula of latent heat is :

(a) $[M^0L^2T^{-2}]$ (b) $[MLT^2]$
(c) $[ML^2T^{-2}]$ (d) $[MLT^{-1}]$

37. The dimensional formula of magnetic flux is:

(a) $[ML^2T^{-2}A^{-1}]$ (b) $[ML^0T^{-2}A^{-2}]$
(c) $[M^0L^{-2}T^{-2}A^{-2}]$ (d) $[ML^2T^{-1}A^3]$

38. If the unit of force is kN, unit of time is millisecond and that of power is kW, then the unit of length will be :

(a) 10^{-1} m (b) 10^{-2} m
(c) 10^{-3} m (d) 1m

39. If the unit of force, energy and velocity are 10 N, 100 J and 5 ms^{-1} respectively, the unit of mass is :

(a) 1 kg (b) 2 kg
(c) 3 kg (d) 4 kg

40. A force F is given by $F = at + bt^2$, where t is time. What are the dimensions of 'a' and 'b' ?

(a) $[MLT^{-3}]$ and $[ML^2 T^4]$
(b) $[MLT^{-3}]$ and $[MLT^{-4}]$
(c) $[MLT^{-1}]$ and $[MLT^0]$
(d) $[MLT^{-4}]$ and $[MLT^{-1}]$

41. If area (A), velocity (v) and density (ρ) are taken as fundamental units, what are the dimensions of force ?

(a) $A v^2 \rho$ (b) $A^2 v\rho$

(c) $A v\rho^2$ (d) $A v\rho$

42. The time period of a simple pendulum may depend on mass (m) of the bob, length (l) of the string and acceleration due to gravity (g), i.e. $T \propto m^a l^b g^c$. The values of a, b and c will be :

(a) $0, \frac{1}{2}, -\frac{1}{2}$ (b) $0, -\frac{1}{2}, \frac{1}{2}$

(c) $\frac{1}{2}, 0, -\frac{1}{2}$ (d) $-\frac{1}{2}, 0, \frac{1}{2}$

43. A quantity X is defined by the equation $X = 3\ CB^2$, where C is capacitance in farad, and B represents the magnetic field in tesla. The dimensions of X are :

(a) $[M^2 L^{-2} T]$ (b) $[ML^{-2}T^{-2}A]$

(c) $[ML^2 T^{-2}A]$ (d) $[ML^{-2}]$

44. The dimensions of Boltzmann's constant are:

(a) $[MLT^{-2}K^{-1}]$ (b) $[ML^2T^{-2}K^{-1}]$

(c) $[M^0LT^{-2}K^{-1}]$ (d) $[M^0L^2T^{-2}K^{-1}]$

45. The dimensions of permittivity (ε_0) in vacuum are :

(a) $[M^{-1}L^{-3}T^4A^2]$ (b) $[ML^{-3}T^2A^2]$

(c) $[M^{-1}L^3T^4A^2]$ (d) $[ML^3T^2A^2]$

46. The frequency (υ) of a tuning fork depends upon the length (l) of its prongs, the density (ρ) and Young's modulus of elasticity (Y) of its material. Then for the relation $\upsilon \propto (l)^a (\rho)^b (Y)^c$, the values of a, b and c are :

(a) $1, \frac{1}{2}, -\frac{1}{2}$ (b) $-1, -\frac{1}{2}, \frac{1}{2}$

(c) $\frac{1}{2}, -1, -\frac{1}{2}$ (d) $\frac{1}{2}, -\frac{1}{2}, 1$

47. The dimensions of $\mu_0 I/M.B$, where μ_0 is the magnetic permeability of free space, I is moment of inertia, M is magnetic dipole moment and B is magnetic induction are those of :

(a) $(\text{time})^{1/2}$ (b) (time)

(c) $(\text{time})^2$ (d) $(\text{time})^{3/2}$

48. The velocity (v) of a particle at any time (t) is given by $v = at + \frac{b}{t+c}$. where a, b and c are constants. The dimensions of a, b and c are:

(a) L, T and LT^{-2} (b) LT^2, LT and L

(c) L^2, T and LT^2 (d) LT^{-2}, L and T

49. The frequency (f) of vibration of mass (m) suspended from a spring constant K is given by the relation $f = C\, m^a K^b$, where C is a dimensionless constant. The values of a and b are :

(a) $\frac{1}{2}, \frac{1}{2}$ (b) $-\frac{1}{2}, -\frac{1}{2}$

(c) $\frac{1}{2}, -\frac{1}{2}$ (d) $-\frac{1}{2}, \frac{1}{2}$

50. Which of the following is dimensionally constant ?

(a) Refractive index

(b) Poisson's ratio

(c) Gravitational constant

(d) Relative velocity

51. The dimensions of Stefan's constant are :

(a) $ML^2T^{-2}\theta^{-4}$ (b) $ML^2T^{-2}\theta^4$

(c) $MT^{-3}\theta^{-4}$ (d) $MT^{-2}\theta^4$

52. If M is the mass suspended from a spring of force constant K, then the dimensions of formula $(M/K)^{1/2}$ is same as that for :

(a) Frequency (b) Time period

(c) Velocity (d) Wavelength

53. The time taken by an electron to go to the excited state from ground energy state is one shake. This time in nanosecond will be :

($\because$ 1 shake = 10^{-8} s)

(a) 2 ns (b) 4 ns

(c) 6 ns (d) 10 ns

54. The dimensions of R/L are :

(Since R = Resistance and L = Self Inductance)

(a) $[T^{-2}]$ (b) $[T^{-1}]$
(c) [T] (d) $[ML^{-1}]$

55. The dimensions of power of a lens are :

(a) $[M^0 L^0 T^{-1}]$ (b) $[M^0 L^{-1} T^{-1}]$
(c) $[M^0 L^{-1} T^0]$ (d) $[ML^0 T^0]$

56. The value of 60 joule/min in a system, which has 100 gm, 100 cm and 1 min as fundamental unit is :

(a) 2.16×10^3 (b) 2.16×10^4
(c) 2.16×10^5 (d) 2.16×10^6

57. The velocity of sound in air is 332 ms^{-1}, then its value in kmh^{-1} will be :

(a) 1146 (b) 1195
(c) 1147 (d) 1175

58. If there is a + 50% error in the measurement of the velocity of a body, the error in the measurement of K.E. will be :

(a) 75% (b) 100%
(c) 125% (d) 155%

59. The percentage error in the measurement of mass and speed are 2% and 3% respectively. Then the estimated error in the measurement of K.E. will be :

(a) 4% (b) 6%
(c) 8% (d) 10%

60. If the maximum errors in the measurement of mass and length of a cube are 3% and 2% respectively, then maximum % error in the measurement of density of such a cube will be :

(a) 9% (b) 12%
(c) 13% (d) 14%

61. Error in the measurement of radius of a sphere is 2%. Then the error in the measurement of volume of such a sphere is :

(a) 6% (b) 7%
(c) 8% (d) 9%

62. If the radius of the earth shrinks by $\frac{3}{2}$% (keeping mass same), then the value of acceleration due to gravity changes by :

(a) 4% (b) 3%
(c) 2% (d) 1%

63. The radius of a sphere is (4.6 ± 0.1) cm. The % error in its volume is :

(a) $\frac{0.1}{4.6} \times 100\%$ (b) $3 \times \frac{0.1}{4.6} \times 100\%$

(c) $\left(\frac{0.1}{4.6} \times 100\right)^3 \%$ (d) $\frac{1}{3} \times \frac{0.1}{4.6} \times 100\%$

64. A physical quantity is expressed as $K = M^a L^{-b} T^{-c}$. If the percentage errors in measurement of M, L and T are found to be α %, β % and λ % respectively, then the total percentage error is :

(a) $(\alpha a - \beta b - \lambda c)\%$
(b) $(\alpha a - \beta b + \lambda c)\%$
(c) $(\alpha a + \beta b + \lambda c)\%$
(d) $\alpha a\%$

65. In a physical quantity, errors of measurement in *a, b, c* and *d* are 4%, 2%, 3% and 1% respectively. The percentage error in that physical quantity which can be given by, $z = \frac{a^2 b^3}{c\sqrt{d}}$, will be :

(a) 14.5% (b) 15.5%
(c) 16.5% (d) 17.5%

66. The length of a cube is 2.1×10^{-2} m. The volume in significant figures will be :

(a) $9.2 \times 10^{-6} m^3$ (b) $9.3 \times 10^{-6} m^3$
(c) $9.26 \times 10^{-6} m^3$ (d) $9.261 \times 10^{-6} m^3$

67. The radius of a Cu-wire is 0.14 mm. The area of cross-section of such a wire in $(mm)^2$ with significant figures is :

(a) 0.0616 (b) 0.062
(c) 0.06 (d) 6.16×10^{-2}

68. The least count of a stop watch is 0.1 second. The time for 20 oscillations by the pendulum is found to be 20 secs. The % error in time period is :

(a) 0.25% (b) 0.50%
(c) 0.75% (d) 1.00%

69. Two full turns of the circular scale of a screw gauge cover a distance of 1 mm on its main scale. The total number of divisions on the circular scale are 50. Further it is found that the screw gauge has a zero error of 0.03 mm. While measuring a diameter of a thin wire, a student notes the main scale reading of 3 mm and the number of circular scale divisions in line with the main scale as 35. The diameter of the wire is :

(A.I.E.E.E. 2008)

(a) 3.32 mm (b) 3.37 mm
(c) 3.67 mm (d) 3.38 mm

70. In an experiment, the angles are required to be measured using an instrument. 29 divisions of the main scale coincide with 30 divisions of the vernier scale. If the smallest division of the main scale is half a degree (0.5°), then the least count of the instrument is :

(a) Half minute (b) One degree
(c) Half degree (d) One minute

71. The respective number of significant figures for the numbers 23.023, 0.003 and 2.1×10^{-3} are : **(A.I.E.E.E. 2010)**

(a) 5, 1, 2 (b) 5, 1, 5
(c) 5, 5, 2 (d) 5, 5, 5

72. The S. I. unit of permeability is :

(a) TAm (b) $TA^{-1}m$
(c) Wb $A^{-1}m$ (d) Wb A^{-1} m^{-1}

73. The E.M.F. induced in coil is given by $\varepsilon = \frac{d\phi}{dt}$. Then the dimensions of magnetic flux (ϕ) are :

(a) $[LT^{-2}A^{-1}]$ (b) $[ML^2T^{-2}A^{-1}]$
(c) $[ML^2T^{-2}A]$ (d) $[L^{-1}T^2A^{-1}]$

74. The gravitational constant cannot be expressed as :

(a) Pa m^4 kg^{-2} (b) m^3 kg^{-1} s^{-2}
(c) dyne cm^2 gm^{-2} (d) J m^{-1} kg^{-2}

75. 1 Wb m^{-2} is equal to :

(a) 10^4 gauss (b) 10^{-4} gauss
(c) 10^{-2} gauss (d) 10^2 gauss

76. (Capacitance × Inductance)$^{-1/2}$ has the same unit as :

(a) Velocity
(b) Velocity gradient
(c) Time
(d) Angular frequency

77. Which of the following can be derived by the dimensional method :

(a) $y = a \sin(kx - \omega t)$ (b) $q = q_0 e^{-t/RC}$
(c) $v = \frac{\pi p r^4}{8\eta l}$ (d) $c = \frac{1}{\sqrt{\mu_0 \varepsilon_0}}$

78. When the velocity of light is used as the unit of velocity and one year as the unit of time, then the unit of length is called as :

(a) A.U. (b) Light year
(c) Fermi (d) Shake

79. Bernoulli's equation can be given by :

$$P + \frac{1}{2}\rho v^2 + h\rho g = K \text{ (const.)}$$

The dimensional formula of K is the same as:

(a) Stress
(b) Energy
(c) Momentum
(d) Velocity gradient

80. The ratio of 1 kWh to 1 MeV is :

(a) 2.25×10^{17} (b) 2.25×10^{18}
(c) 2.25×10^{19} (d) 2.25×10^{21}

81. The dimensional formula of solar constant is:

(a) $[ML^2T^{-1}]$ (b) $[M^0LT^{-2}A]$
(c) $[MT^{-3}]$ (d) $[ML^4T^{-1}\theta]$

82. Pascal-second has the dimensions of :

(a) Force
(b) Energy
(c) Pressure
(d) Coefficient of viscosity

83. Banking of a cyclist can be expressed as, $\tan\theta = \frac{rg}{v^2}$. In it, banking angle θ is :

(a) only numerically correct
(b) only dimensionally correct
(c) both numerically and dimensionally correct
(d) neither numerically nor dimensionally correct

84. In the equation $S_n = u + \frac{a}{2}(2n - 1)$. The dimensional formula of S_n is :

(a) $[ML^0T]$ (b) $[ML^{-1}T^{-1}]$
(c) $[M^0LT^{-1}]$ (d) $[M^0LT^0]$

85. The force acting on a body is represented by,

$$F = a\cos bx + c\sin dt$$

where x is the displacement and t is the time. The dimensions of $\frac{a\cdot d}{b\cdot c}$ are :

(a) $[M^0L^0T^0]$ (b) $[M^0L^{-1}T^{-1}]$
(c) $[M^2L^3T^{-3}]$ (d) $[LT^{-1}]$

86. The dimensions of $\frac{e^2}{\varepsilon_0 hc}$ are :

(a) $[M^0L^0T^0A^0]$ (b) $[M^0LTA^0]$
(c) $[M^{-1}L^{-1}T^3A^2]$ (d) $[M^0LT^3A^2]$

87. Which of the following do not have the same dimensions :

(a) $\sqrt{\mu_0\varepsilon_0}$
(b) Frequency × Wavelength
(c) $\sqrt{(\text{Pressure})(\text{Density})^{-1}}$
(d) Angular Frequency × Wave number

88. The electric displacement vector is given by, D = εE where ε = Electric permittivity and E = Electric field. Then the dimensions of D are :

(a) $[ML^{-2}TA]$ (b) $[M^0L^{-2}T^{-1}A]$
(c) $[L^{-2}TA]$ (d) $[ML^3T^0]$

89. The magnetic field force on a point charge is given by $\vec{F} = q(\vec{v}\times\vec{B})$, where q = electric charge, $\vec{v}$ = velocity and $\vec{B}$ = magnetic field. Then the dimensions of $\vec{B}$ are :

(a) $[MLT^{-1}A]$ (b) $[MLT^{-2}A^{-1}]$
(c) $[MT^{-2}A^{-1}]$ (d) $[M^0LT^{-1}]$

90. The initial temperature of a liquid is $T_1 = (80.0 \pm 0{\cdot}1)$°C. After cooling, its temperature becomes $T_2 = (10.0 \pm 0.1)$°C. The fall in temperature is :

(a) (70.0 ± 0.2) °C (b) (70.0 ± 0.1) °C
(c) (70.0 ± 0.3) °C (d) 70.0 °C

91. The sides of a rectangle are 6.01 m and 12 m. The area of rectangle in significant figures is :

(a) 72 m^2 (b) 72.1 m^2
(c) 72.00 m^2 (d) 72.12 m^2

92. The least count of a stop watch is 0.2 second. The time of 20 oscillations of a pendulum is measured to be 25 seconds. The % error in the measurement of time will be :

(a) 1.8% (b) 0.18%
(c) 8% (d) 0.8%

93. The potential energy (U) can be given as $U = \frac{Ky}{y^2 + a^2}$, where y = displacement and a = amplitude. Then, the unit of K is :

(a) ms^{-1} (b) ms
(c) Jm (d) Js^{-1}

94. 1 calorie is a unit of heat and equals 4.2 J. If we use a system for which the unit of mass is α kg, the unit of length is β metre and the unit of time is λ sec, then in this system 1 calorie is equal to :

(a) $\alpha^{-1}\beta^{-2}\gamma^2$ (b) $4.2\,\alpha\beta^2\gamma^2$
(c) $\alpha^2\beta^2\gamma^2$ (d) $4.2\,\alpha^{-1}\beta^{-2}\gamma^2$

95. A resistor of 4 kΩ with tolerance ± 10% is connected with a resistor of 5 kΩ with tolerance ± 10%. The tolerance of such a parallel combination is :

(a) 10% (b) 20%
(c) 30% (d) 40%

96. Let us suppose a new unit of length such that the velocity of light is unity. If light takes 8 minutes and 20 seconds to cover the distance between the sun and the earth, this distance in terms of the new unit is :

(a) 5 (b) 50

(c) 500 (d) 3×10^8

97. What will be the unit of time for a system in which the unit of length is metre, unit of mass is kg and unit of force is kg wt ?

(a) $(9.8)^2$ sec (b) (9.8) sec

(c) $(9.8)^{1/2}$ sec (d) $1/(9.8)^{1/2}$ sec

98. Which of the following is the unit of permeability ?

(a) H m^{-1} (b) Wb A^{-1} m^{-1}

(c) Ω s m^{-1} (d) All of the above

99. Dimensions of which fundamental quantity correspond to that of $[Gh/C^3]^{1/2}$?

(a) Time (b) Length

(c) Mass (d) Temperature

100. Which of the following units denotes the dimensions $[ML^2/Q^2]$, where Q denotes the electric charge ? **(A.I.E.E.E. 2006)**

(a) H (b) H m^{-2}

(c) Wb (d) Wb m^{-2}

101. If the unit of force is 1 kN, the length is 1 km and the time is 100 s, then the unit of mass will be :

(a) 1 kg (b) 10^2 kg

(c) 10^3 kg (d) 10^4 kg

102. If 1 gm cm s^{-1} = x Ns, then x is equal to :

(a) 1×10^{-3} (b) 3.6×10^{-3}

(c) 1×10^{-5} (d) 6×10^{-4}

103. Given that $r = m^2 \sin G.\ t$, where t represents time. If the unit of m is N, then the unit of r is :

(a) N (b) N^2

(c) Ns (d) N^2s

104. $[ML^2T^{-3}A^{-2}]$ is the dimensional formula of :

(a) Electric resistance

(b) Capacitance

(c) Electric potential

(d) Specific resistance

105. The dimensions of thermal conductivity are :

(a) $[ML\,T^{-3}\,K^{-1}]$ (b) $[ML^3\,T^3\,K^2]$

(c) $[ML^3\,T^{-3}\,K^{-2}]$ (d) $[M^2L^3\,T^{-3}\,K^2]$

106. The time dependent of a physical quantity p is given by $p = p_0 \exp(-\alpha t^2)$, where α is constant and t is the time. The constant α :

(a) is dimensionless

(b) has dimension T^{-2}

(c) has dimensions T^2

(d) has dimensions of p

107. The potential energy of a body varies with distance X and is expressed as $U = \left[\left(A\sqrt{X}/X + B\right) + C\right]$. The dimensions of ABC are :

(a) $[M^2L^{11/2}\,T^{-4}]$ (b) $[ML^{7/2}\,T^{-2}]$

(c) $[M^2L^{5/2}\,T^{-4}]$ (d) $[M^3L^{9/2}\,T^{-2}]$

108. One of the following having different dimensions from the remaining three is :

(a) $(\text{Energy/Mass})^{1/2}$

(b) $(\text{Angular frequency/Radius})^{1/2}$

(c) $(\text{Pressure/Density})^{1/2}$

(d) $(\text{Force/Density})^{1/2}$

109. Gravitational constant (G) cannot be expressed as :

(a) Pa m^4 kg^{-2} (b) m^3 kg^{-1} s^{-2}

(c) dyne cm^2 g^{-2} (d) J m^{-1} kg^{-2}

110. The damping force on a body (bob) is proportional to its velocity. The dimension of proportionality constant is :

(a) $[M^2\,T^{-1}]$ (b) $[MLT^{-2}]$

(c) $[MT^{-1}]$ (d) Dimensionless

111. The number of significant figures in $(9.230 + 2.0150) \times 10^6$ is :

(a) 3 (b) 4

(c) 5 (d) 6

112. The heat generated in a circuit depends upon the resistance (R), current (I) and time (T). The errors in measuring these quantities are 1%, 2% and 3% respectively. The error in measurement of heat will be :

(a) 6% (b) 7%

(c) 8% (d) 9%

113. An Aluminium wire increases in length by 3% on heating it upto 20°C. What is the percentage change in the area of cross section of such a wire ?

(a) – 3% (b) 6 %

(c) 9 % (d) 12 %

114. The value of a liquid drop is 1.75 cm^3. Total volume of 50 such drops in the significant figures is :

(a) 0.0616 (b) 0.062

(c) 0.06 (d) 6.16×10^{-2}

115. 45 km min^{-2} = X ms^{-2}, then the value of X is :

(a) 9.5 (b) 4.5

(c) 10.5 (d) 12.5

116. The value of Stefan's constant in C.G.S. system is $\sigma = 5.67 \times 10^{-5}$ erg s^{-1} cm^{-2} K^4. Its value in S. I. system is :

(a) 5.67×10^{-8} J s^{-1} $m^{-2}K^{-4}$

(b) 5.67×10^{-9} J s^{-1} $m^{-2}K^{-4}$

(c) 5.67×10^{8} J s^{-1} $m^{-2}K^{-4}$

(d) 5.67×10^{9} J s^{-1} $m^{-2}K^{-4}$

117. Choose the correct formula for the displacement (y) of a particle executing periodic motion :

(a) $y = r \sin \frac{2\pi}{T} . t$ (b) $y = r \sin v\, t$

(c) $y = r \sin \frac{2\pi}{r} . t$ (d) $y = r \sin \frac{2\pi}{v} . t$

118. The pitch of a screw gauge is 15 mm and there are 100 divisions on the circular scale while measuring a diameter of a thick wire, the main scale 1 mm and 63rd division is on the circular scale. The length of wire is 5.6 cm. Which one is not correct ?

(a) The least count of the screw gauge is 0.001 cm.

(b) The volume of the wire is 0.117 cm^3.

(c) The diameter of the wire is 1.63 m.

(d) The cross-sectional area of the wire is 0.0209 cm^3.

119. The ratio of dimensions of Self Inductance (X_L) and Mutual Inductance is :

(a) $[M^1L^2T^{-2}A^{-2}]$ (b) $[M^1L^{-2}T^{-2}A^{-2}]$

(c) $[M^1L^3T^{-3}A^{-1}]$ (d) Dimensionless

120. Which one has dimensions of time for L-C-R circuit combination ?

(a) R.C (b) $\sqrt{LC}$

(c) $\frac{R}{C}$ (d) $\frac{C}{L}$

121. Pick out the wrong pair : **(A.F.M.C. 2003)**

(a) Charge - coulomb

(b) Temperature - thermometer

(c) Pressure - barometer

(d) Specific gravity – hygrometer

122. Which of the following is the smallest unit ? **(A.F.M.C. 2003)**

(a) millimetre (b) angstrom

(c) fermi (d) metre

123. parsec is the unit of : **(A.I.M.S. 2005)**

(a) Time

(b) Distance

(c) Frequency

(d) Angular acceleration

124. The difference in the length of a mean solar day and a sidereal day is about : **(A.I.I.M.S. 2003)**

(a) 1 min (b) 4 min

(c) 15 min (d) 56 min

125. The unit of Planck's constant in MKS system is : **(H.P.P.M.T. 2008)**
(a) joule/second (b) joule-second
(c) erg/second (d) watt

126. Which is not correct ? **(H.P.P.M.T 2009)**
(a) 1 erg = 10^{-7} joule
(b) 1 eV = 1.6×10^{-19} C
(c) 1 cal = 4186 J
(d) 1 kWh = 3.6×10^6 J

127. The SI unit of magnetic permeability is : **(H.P.P.M.T 2010)**
(a) Am^{-1} (b) Am
(c) Tm/A (d) No unit

128. In a vernier calipers, one main scale division is x cm and n divisions of the vernier scale coincide with $(n - 1)$ divisions of the main scale. The least count in (in cm) of the calipers is : **(A.M.U. 2009)**
(a) $\left(\frac{n-1}{n}\right)x$ (b) $\frac{nx}{(n-1)}$
(c) $\frac{x}{n}$ (d) $\frac{x}{(n-1)}$

129. The unit of magnetic moment is : **(Gujarat C.E.T. 2010)**
(a) Am^{-2} (b) Am^{-1}
(c) TJ^{-1} (d) JT^{-1}

130. A force F is given by $F = at + bt^2$, where t is time. What are the dimensions of a and b ? **(B.H.U. 2005)**
(a) MLT^{-1} and MLT^0
(b) MLT^{-3} and ML^2T^4
(c) MLT^{-4} and MLT^{-1}
(d) MLT^{-3} and MLT^{-4}

131. If C, R, L and I denote capacity, resistance, inductance and electric current respectively, the quantities having the same dimensions of time are : **(E.A.M.C.E.T. 2006)**
(i) CR (ii) L/R
(iii) $\sqrt{LC}$ (iv) LI^2
(a) (i) and (ii) only
(b) (i) and (iii) only
(c) (i) and (iv) only
(d) (i), (ii) and (iii) only

132. The speed of light (c), gravitational constant (G) and Planck's constant (h) are taken as fundamental units in a system. The dimensions of time in this new system should be : **(A.I.I.M.S. 2008)**
(a) $G^{1/2} h^{1/2} c^{-5/2}$ (b) $G^{-1/2} h^{1/2} c^{1/2}$
(c) $G^{1/2} h^{1/2} c^{-3/2}$ (d) $G^{1/2} h^{1/2} c^{1/2}$

133. Dimensions of a and b in equation $\left(P + \frac{an^2}{V^2}\right)(V - nb) = RT$ are : **(H.P.P.M.T 2009)**
(a) ML^3T^{-2} and L^2 (b) ML^5T^{-2} and L^3
(c) ML^2T^{-2} and L^3 (d) None of these

134. If energy E, velocity V and time T are taken as fundamental quantities, the dimensional formula for surface tension is : **(E.A.M.C.E.T. 2009)**
(a) $E^1 V^{-2} T^{-2}$ (b) $E^2 V^1 T^{-2}$
(c) $E^1 V^{-2} T^{-1}$ (d) $E^{-2} V^{-2} T^{-1}$

135. The dimensional formula of $\frac{1}{\mu_0 \varepsilon_0}$ is : **(Gujarat C.E.T. 2010)**
(a) $M^0L^1T^{-1}$ (b) $M^0L^2T^{-2}$
(c) $M^0L^1T^{-2}$ (d) $M^0L^{-2}T^{-2}$

136. A wire has a mass 0.3 ± 0.003 g, radius 0.5 ± 0.005 mm and length 6 ± 0.06 cm. The maximum percentage error in the measurement of its density is : **(I.I.T. - J.E.E. Screening 2004)**
(a) 1 (b) 2
(c) 3 (d) 4

137. A physical quantity $P = \frac{(\sqrt{abc^2})}{d^3 e^{1/3}}$ is determined by measuring a, b, c, d and e

separately with the percentage error of 2%, 3%, 2%, 1% and 6% respectively. Minimum amount of error is contributed by the measurement : **(Kerala P.E.T. 2006)**

(a) *b* (b) *a*
(c) *d* (d) *e*
(e) *c*

138. Two full turns of the circular scale of a screw gauge cover a distance of 1 mm on its main scale. The total number of divisions on the circular scale is 50. Further, it is found that the screw gauge has a zero error of – 0.03 mm. While measuring the diameter of a thin wire, a student notes the main scale reading of 3 mm and the number of circular scale divisions in line with the main scale as 35. The diameter of the wire is :

(A.I.E.E.E. 2008)

(a) 3.38 mm (b) 3.32 mm
(c) 3.73 mm (d) 3.67 mm

139. If the error in the measurement of the radius of a sphere is 2%, then the error in the determination of volume of the sphere will be : **(C.B.S.E. P.M.T. 2008)**

(a) 6% (b) 8%
(c) 2% (d) 4%

140. The percentage errors in the measurement of length and time period of a simple pendulum are 1% and 2% respectively. Then the maximum error in the measurement of acceleration due to gravity is :

(Kerala C.E.T. 2009)

(a) 8% (b) 3%
(c) 4% (d) 6%
(e) 5%

141. If F, T and V denote for force, time and velocity, then the dimensional formula for mass 'M' is **(C.B.S.E. 2002)**

(a) FTV^{-1} (b) $F^{-1}TV$
(c) $F^{-1}T^{-1}V$ (d) $FT^{-1}V^{-1}$

142. Length cannot be measured by

(A.I.E.E.E. 2003)

(a) fermi (b) debye
(c) micron (d) light year

143. Using mass (M), length (L), time (T) and current (A) as fundamental quantities, the dimensional formula of permeability is

(A.I.E.E.E. 2003)

(a) $[M^{-1}LT^{-2}A]$ (b) $[ML^2T^{-2}A^{-1}]$
(c) $[MLT^{-2}A^{-2}]$ (d) $[MLT^{-1}A^{-1}]$

144. The instrument to measure time is

(A.F.M.C. 2003)

(a) barometer (b) chronometer
(c) radiometer (d) none of these

145. The dimensions of $[\mu_0 \varepsilon_0]^{1/2}$ are

(C.B.S.E. 2011)

(a) $[L^{1/2}T^{-1/2}]$ (b) $[L^{-1}T]$
(c) $[LT^{-1}]$ (d) $[L^{1/2}T^{-1/2}]$

146. The dimensional formula of $\frac{a}{b}$ in the equation $P = \frac{a - t^2}{bx}$ where P is pressure, x is distance and t is time is

(J.I.P.M.E.R. 2003)

(a) $[LT^{-3}]$ (b) $[ML^3T^{-1}]$
(c) $[M^2LT^{-3}]$ (d) $[MT^{-2}]$

147. The length, breadth and thickness of a block are given l = 12 cm, b = 6 cm and t = 2.45 cm. The volume of the block according to the idea of significant figures should be **(B.H.U. 2003)**

(a) 1×10^2 cm^3 (b) 2×10^2 cm^3
(c) 1.763×10^2 cm^3 (d) 1×10^3 cm

148. The dimensional formula of light year is

(Manipal 2003)

(a) $[L^{-1}]$ (b) $[T^{-1}]$
(c) $[L]$ (d) $[T]$

149. $[ML^2T^{-3}I^{-1}]$ is the dimensional formula of

(A.F.M.C. 2004)

(a) electric field (b) capacity
(c) potential (d) permittivity

150. What is the unit of $K = \frac{1}{4\pi \varepsilon_0}$?

(A.F.M.C. 2004)

(a) $c^2 N^{-1} m^{-2}$
(b) $NM^2 c^2$
(c) $NM^2 c^2$
(d) unitless

151. Pressure gradient has same dimensions as that of **(A.F.M.C. 2004)**

(a) velocity gradient
(b) potential gradient
(c) energy gradient
(d) none of these

152. The unit of permittivity of free space ε_0 is

(C.B.S.E. 2004)

(a) newton metre^2/coulomb^2
(b) coulomb^2/newton metre ^{2}
(c) coulomb^2/(newton metre)
(d) coulomb/newton metre

153. The velocity v of a particle at time t is given by $v = at + \frac{b}{t + c}$ where a, b, c are constants. The dimensions of a, b and c are respectively.

(a) [L, LT] and [T^2]
(b) [LT^{-2}, L] and [T]
(c) [L^2, T] and [LT^2]
(d) [LT^2, LT] and [L]

154. The physical quantity having the dimensions [$M^{-1} L^{-3}, T^3 A^2$] is **(P.M.T. 2006)**

(a) electromotive force
(b) electrical conductivity
(c) electrical resistivity
(d) electrical resistance

155. The magnetic moment has dimensions of

(A.I.I.M.S. 2006)

(a) [LA] (b) [L^2A]
(c) [LT^{-1} A] (d) [$L^2 T^{-1}$ A]

156. Dimensions of resistance in an electrical circuit in terms of dimension of mass M, length L, time T and current I, would be

(C.B.S.E. 2007)

(a) [$ML^2 T^{-2}$]
(b) [$ML^2 T^{-1} I^1$]
(c) [$ML^2 T^{-3} I^{-2}$]
(d) [$ML^2 T^{-3} I^{-1}$]

157. A force 'F' is given by, $F = at + bt^2$, where t is time. What are the dimensions of 'a' and 'b' ? **(C.B.S.E. 2006)**

(a) [MLT^{-1}] and [MLT^0]
(b) [MLT^{-3}] and [ML^2T^4]
(c) [MLT^{-4}] and [MLT^1]
(d) [MLT^{-3}] and [MLT^{-4}]

158. If the dimensions of a physical quantity are given by $M^a L^b T^c$, then the physical quantity will be **(C.B.S.E. 2009)**

(a) velocity if a = 1, b = 0, c = −1
(b) acceleration if a = 1, b = 1, c = −2
(c) force if a = 0, b = −1, c = −2
(d) pressure if a = 1, b = −1, c = −2

159. The dimensional formula of $\frac{1}{2} \varepsilon_0 E^2$, where ε_0 is the permittivity of free space and E is electric field is **(C.B.S.E. 2010)**

(a) [$ML^2 T^{-1}$] (b) [MLT^{-1}]
(c) [$ML^2 T^{-2}$] (d) [$ML^{-1} T^{-2}$]

160. In an experiment four quantities a, b, c and d are measured with percentage error 1%, 2%, 3% and 4% respectively. Quantity P is calculated as follows,

$P = \frac{a^3b^2}{cd}$. The % error in P is **(NEET 2013)**

(a) 10% (b) 7%
(c) 4% (d) 14%

ANSWER KEY

1. (c)	**2.** (b)	**3.** (a)	**4.** (c)	**5.** (b)	**6.** (a)	**7.** (a)	**8.** (b)	**9.** (b)	**10.** (d)
11. (c)	**12.** (d)	**13.** (a)	**14.** (b)	**15.** (c)	**16.** (b)	**17.** (c)	**18.** (b)	**19.** (c)	**20.** (d)
21. (d)	**22.** (d)	**23.** (c)	**24.** (a)	**25.** (b)	**26.** (a)	**27.** (c)	**28.** (d)	**29.** (d)	**30.** (a)
31. (b)	**32.** (a)	**33.** (a)	**34.** (c)	**35.** (a)	**36.** (a)	**37.** (a)	**38.** (c)	**39.** (d)	**40.** (b)
41. (a)	**42.** (a)	**43.** (d)	**44.** (b)	**45.** (a)	**46.** (b)	**47.** (c)	**48.** (d)	**49.** (d)	**50.** (c)
51. (c)	**52.** (b)	**53.** (d)	**54.** (b)	**55.** (c)	**56.** (d)	**57.** (b)	**58.** (c)	**59.** (c)	**60.** (a)
61. (a)	**62.** (c)	**63.** (b)	**64.** (c)	**65.** (d)	**66.** (c)	**67.** (c)	**68.** (b)	**69.** (d)	**70.** (d)
71. (a)	**72.** (a)	**73.** (b)	**74.** (d)	**75.** (a)	**76.** (b)	**77.** (d)	**78.** (b)	**79.** (a)	**80.** (c)
81. (c)	**82.** (d)	**83.** (b)	**84.** (c)	**85.** (d)	**86.** (a)	**87.** (d)	**88.** (c)	**89.** (c)	**90.** (a)
91. (a)	**92.** (d)	**93.** (c)	**94.** (d)	**95.** (c)	**96.** (c)	**97.** (d)	**98.** (d)	**99.** (b)	**100.** (a)
101. (b)	**102.** (c)	**103.** (b)	**104.** (c)	**105.** (a)	**106.** (b)	**107.** (a)	**108.** (b)	**109.** (d)	**110.** (c)
111. (c)	**112.** (c)	**113.** (a)	**114.** (c)	**115.** (d)	**116.** (a)	**117.** (a)	**118.** (b)	**119.** (d)	**120.** (a) & (b)
121. (a)	**122.** (c)	**123.** (b)	**124.** (b)	**125.** (b)	**126.** (c)	**127.** (c)	**128.** (c)	**129.** (d)	**130.** (d)
131. (d)	**132.** (a)	**133.** (b)	**134.** (a)	**135.** (b)	**136.** (d)	**137.** (b)	**138.** (a)	**139.** (a)	**140.** (e)
141. (a)	**142.** (b)	**143.** (c)	**144.** (b)	**145.** (b)	**146.** (d)	**147.** (b)	**148.** (c)	**149.** (c)	**150.** (b)
151. (d)	**152.** (b)	**153.** (b)	**154.** (b)	**155.** (b)	**156.** (c)	**157.** (d)	**158.** (d)	**159.** (d)	**160.** (d)

✍ ✍ ✍

2

MOTION IN ONE DIMENSION

MULTIPLE CHOICE QUESTIONS

1. A body cannot have :

(a) Zero speed and non-zero acceleration

(b) Non-zero speed and zero acceleration

(c) Constant velocity and a varying speed

(d) Constant speed and a varying velocity

2. Which of the following decreases in motion along a straight line with constant acceleration ?

(a) Speed (b) Acceleration

(c) Displacement (d) Distance

3. A car is moving on the road and rain is falling vertically downwards. Choose the correct answer ?

(a) The rain drops will strike on the behind screen.

(b) The rain drops will strike on the front screen.

(c) The rain drops will strike on both the screens.

(d) None of these.

4. A car travels a distance from A to B with the speed of 40 kmh^{-1} and returns to A with 30 kmh^{-1}. The average speed of the car will be :

(a) 35 kmh^{-1} (b) 24.3 kmh^{-1}

(c) 35.6 kmh^{-1} (d) 10 kmh^{-1}

5. An athlete completes one and half round of circular track of radius R, then the distance and displacement covered by the athlete are:

(a) $2\pi R$ and R (b) $2\pi R$ and 2R

(c) $3\pi R$ and R (d) $3\pi R$ and 2R

6. The slope of velocity-time graph for retarded motion is :

(a) Positive (b) Negative

(c) Zero (d) None of these

7. A body moves along a straight line with an acceleration 3 ms^{-2} for 2 s and then with an acceleration 4 ms^{-2} for 2 s. What is its average acceleration ?

(a) 2.6 ms^{-2} (b) 3.6 ms^{-2}

(c) 4.6 ms^{-2} (d) 5.6 ms^{-2}

8. On displacement-time graph two lines OA and AB make angles 60° and 30° with time axis respectively.

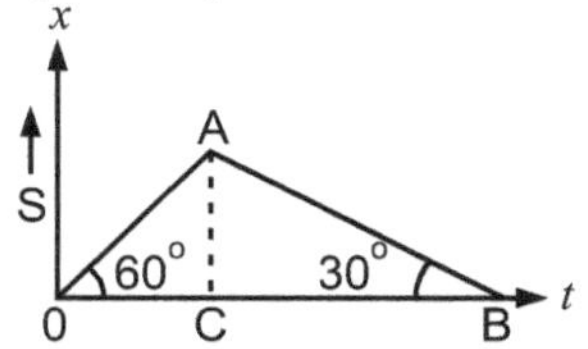

The ratio of velocities represented by them is :

(a) 1 : 2 (b) 1 : 3

(c) 2 : 1 (d) 3 : 1

9. The acceleration due to gravity on the moon is 1.6 ms^{-2}. An inflated balloon is released on the moon. Then

(a) it will move down with acceleration 1.6 ms^{-2}.

(b) it will move up with acceleration 1.6 ms^{-2}.

(c) it will move up with acceleration 9.8 ms^{-2}.

(d) it will burst.

10. A displacement-time graph of a moving particle is shown in figure.

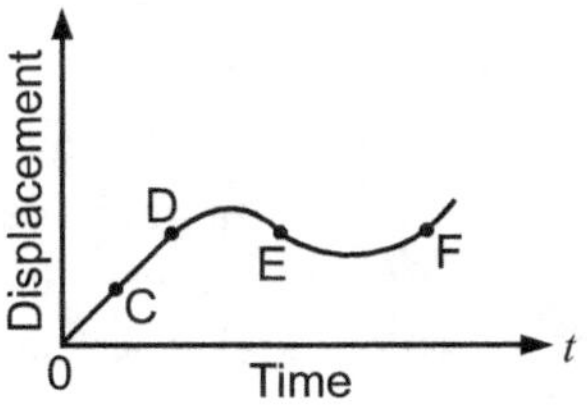

The instantaneous velocity of the particle is negative at the point :

(a) C (b) D

(c) E (d F

11. A particle moves along *x*-axis in such a way that its *x*-co-ordinate varies with time '*t*' according to the equation $x = 6t^2 - 4t + 8$. The velocity-time graph for such a particle should be :

(a)

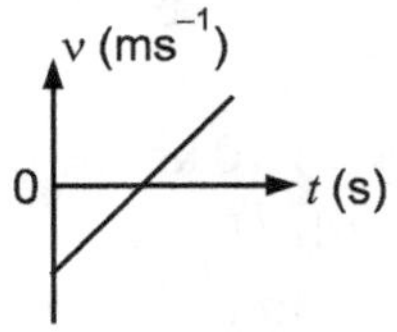

(b)

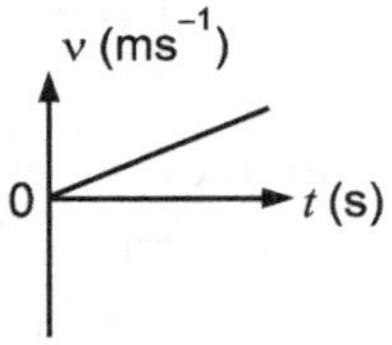

(c)

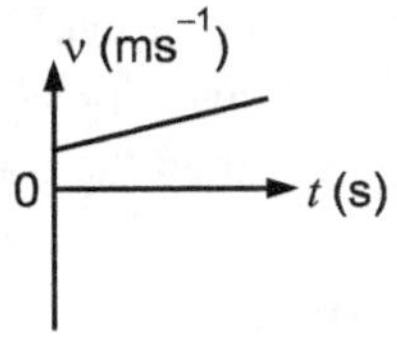

(d)

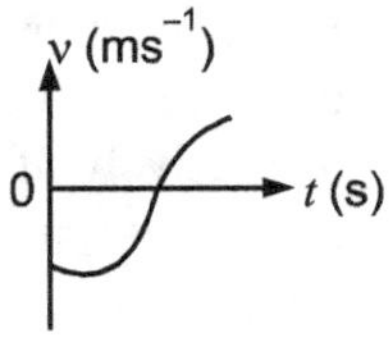

12. The graph below represents motion of a car. The displacement of the car in 20 s is :

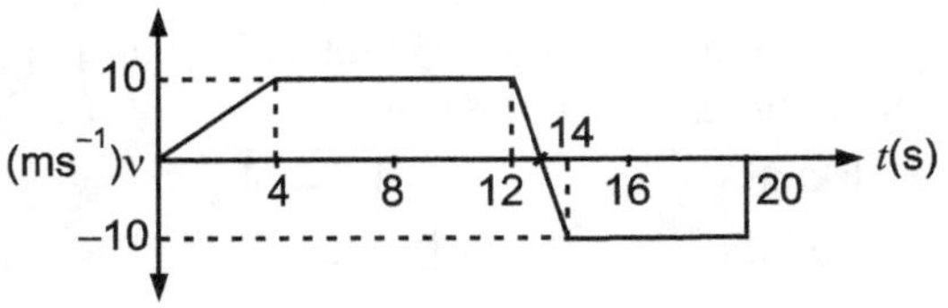

(a) 60 m (b) 20 m

(c) 90 m (d) 10 m

13. Which one of the following time-displacement graphs is not possible in nature?

(a)

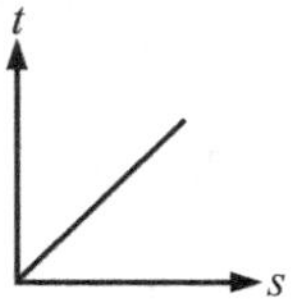

(b)

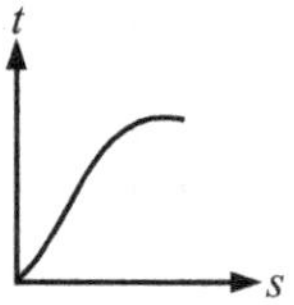

(c)

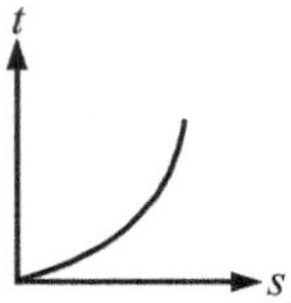

(d)

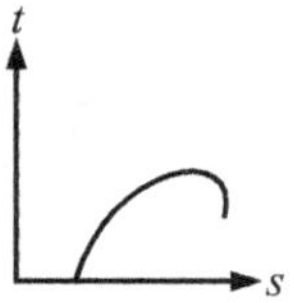

14. A particle moves along the sides AB, BC, CD of a square of side 25 m with the velocity of 15 ms^{-1}. Its average velocity is :

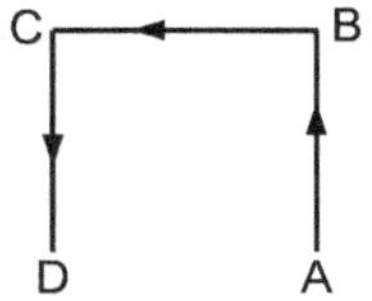

(a) 15 ms^{-1} (b) 7.5 ms^{-1}

(c) 5 ms^{-1} (d) 10 ms^{-1}

15. The displacement of a body is given by $2s = gt^2$, where '*g*' is a constant. The velocity of the body at any time '*t*' is :

(a) gt (b) $gt/2$

(c) $gt^2/2$ (d) $gt^3/2$

16. A ball is thrown vertically upwards. Which of the following graphs represents velocity-time graph of a ball during this flight, ignoring air resistance ?

(a)

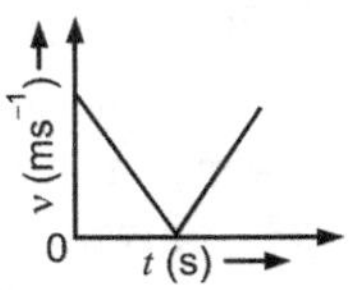

(b)

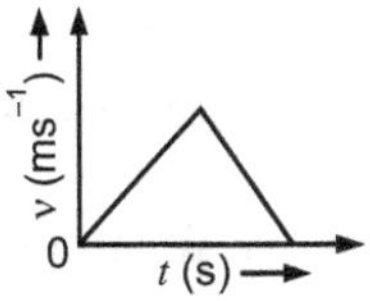

(c)

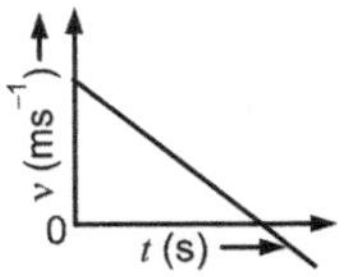

(d)

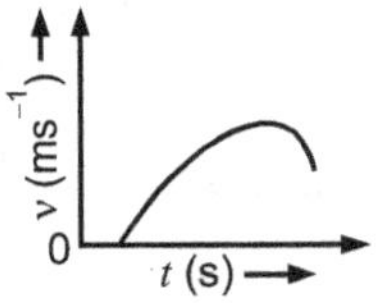

17. In the $S-t$ graph, which of the following regions represents motion when no force is acting on the body ?

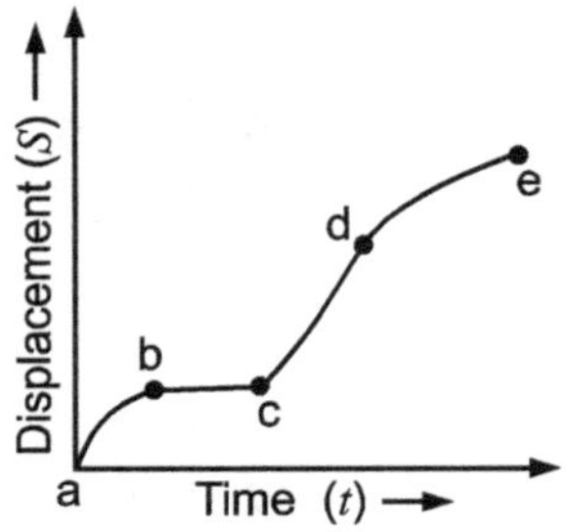

(a) ab (b) bc

(c) cd (d) de

18. Which of the following curves does not represent the motion in one dimension ?

(a) 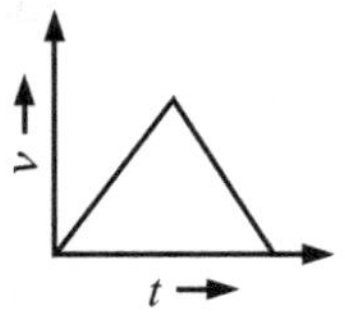

(b) 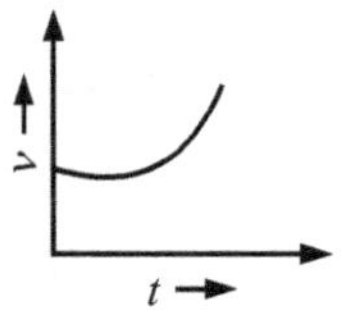

(c) 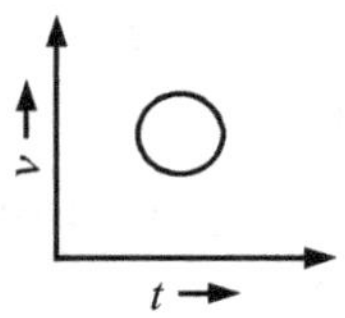

(d) 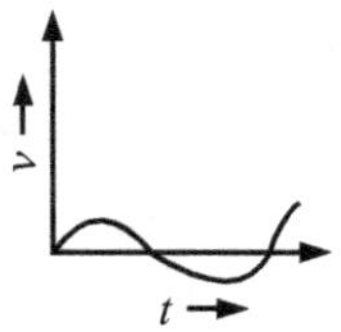

19. A particle moves with constant acceleration and v_1, v_2, and v_3 denote the average velocities in the three successive intervals, t_1, t_2, and t_3 of time. Which of the following relations is correct ?

(a) $\frac{v_1 - v_2}{v_2 - v_3} = \frac{t_1 - t_2}{t_2 + t_3}$ (b) $\frac{v_1 - v_2}{v_2 - v_3} = \frac{t_1 - t_2}{t_1 - t_3}$

(c) $\frac{v_1 - v_2}{v_2 - v_3} = \frac{t_1 - t_2}{t_2 - t_3}$ (d) $\frac{v_1 - v_2}{v_2 - v_3} = \frac{t_1 + t_2}{t_2 + t_3}$

20. A body starts from rest, with uniform acceleration 'a'. This acceleration of a body as a function of time t is given by the equation $a = kt$, where k is constant, then the displacement of the particle in the time interval $t = 0$ to $t = t_1$ will be :

(a) $\frac{1}{2}kt_1^3$ (b) $\frac{1}{3}kt_1^2$

(c) $\frac{1}{4}kt_1^2$ (d) $\frac{1}{6}kt_1^3$

21. A body having uniform acceleration of $10\ ms^{-2}$ has a velocity of $100\ ms^{-1}$. In what time will the velocity of the body be doubled?

(a) 8 s (b) 8.2 s

(c) 10 s (d) 12 s

22. The particle moving with a uniform acceleration along a straight line covers distance 'a' and 'b' in successive intervals of 'm' and 'n' second. The acceleration of the particle is :

(a) $\frac{mn\,(m+n)}{2(b.m - an)}$ (b) $\frac{2(a.n - b.m)}{mn\,(m-n)}$

(c) $\frac{(b.m - a.n)}{m.n\,(m-n)}$ (d) $\frac{2(b.m - a.n)}{m.n\,(m-n)}$

23. A rocket is projected vertically upwards, whose graph is shown. The maximum height attained by the rocket is :

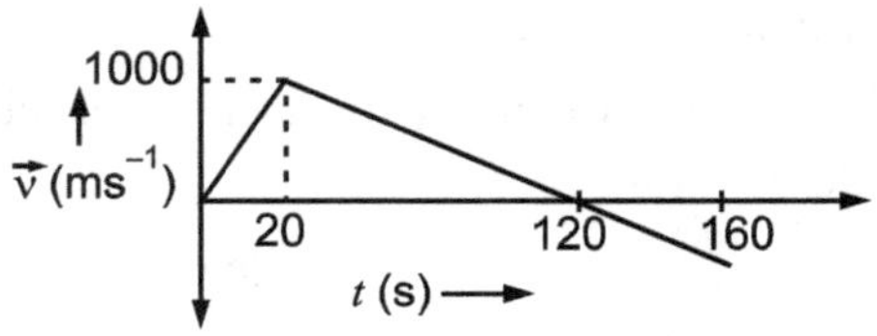

(a) 1 km (b) 10 km

(c) 20 km (d) 60 km

24. A ball is thrown upwards from the ground. It is at a height 100 m in upward and downward journeys at times t_1 and t_2 respectively. If $g = 10\ ms^{-1}$, then the roots of t_1 and t_2 is equal to :

(a) 10 (b) 20

(c) 40 (d) 50

25. Rain is falling vertically downwards with a velocity of $3\ kmh^{-1}$. A man is cyling on the road with the velocity of $4\ kmh^{-1}$. Raindrops fall on the man with the velocity :

(a) $1\ kmh^{-1}$ (b) $1.5\ kmh^{-1}$

(c) $0.5\ kmh^{-1}$ (d) $5\ kmh^{-1}$

26. A woman walks in rain with a velocity of $5\ kmh^{-1}$. The rain drops strike at her at an angle of 45° with the horizontal. The downward velocity of rain drops will be :

(a) $5\ kmh^{-1}$ (b) $1.5\ kmh^{-1}$

(c) $2\ kmh^{-1}$ (d) $2.5\ kmh^{-1}$

27. A car travels equal distances in the same direction with the velocities 60 kmh^{-1}, 20 kmh^{-1} and 10 kmh^{-1} respectively. The average velocity of car during the whole journey is :

(a) 5 ms^{-1} (b) 6 ms^{-1}
(c) 7 ms^{-1} (d) 8 ms^{-1}

28. The acceleration-time graph of a particle is moving along a straight line. At what time does the particle acquire its initial velocity ?

(a) 4 s (b) 6 s
(c) 8 s (d) 10 s

29. A velocity-time graph is given for two particles P_1 and P_2. From the graph which statement is true ?

Relative velocity of particles :

(a) is zero.
(b) is non-zero but constant.
(c) continuously decreases.
(d) continuously increases.

30. For a body, the velocity-time graph is given.

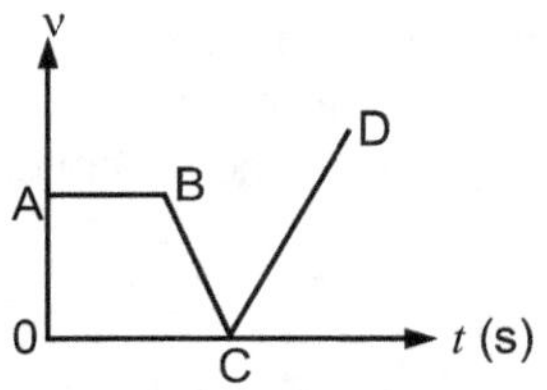

It implies that at BC region :

(a) the force is zero.
(b) there is a force towards motion.
(c) there is a force which opposes motion.
(d) there is only gravitational force.

31. The body starts from rest and moves with a constant acceleration. The ratio of the distance covered in n^{th} second to the distance covered in n seconds is :

(a) $\frac{2}{n}-\frac{1}{n^2}$ (b) $\frac{1}{n^2}-\frac{1}{n}$
(c) $\frac{2}{n^2}-\frac{1}{n}$ (d) $\frac{2}{n}+\frac{1}{n^2}$

32. A body starts from rest with an acceleration a_1. After 2 seconds, another body B starts from rest with an acceleration a_2. If they travel equal distances in the 5th second after starting of body A, then the ratio of their accelerations is $(a_1 : a_2)$ is :

(a) 5 : 9 (b) 1 : 3
(c) 3 : 1 (d) 9 : 5

33. In a motion with constant acceleration, the velocity is reduced to zero in 5 seconds and after covering a distance of 100 m, the distance covered by the particle in the next 5 seconds will be :

(a) Zero (b) 100 m
(c) 250 m (d) 500 m

34. A particle starts with a velocity of 10 ms^{-1} and moves with a constant acceleration till the velocity increases to 50 ms^{-1}. At that instant, the acceleration is suddenly reversed. The velocity of the particle, when it returns to the starting point, will be :

(a) Zero (b) 10 ms^{-1}
(c) 35 ms^{-1} (d) –70 ms^{-1}

35. The $v - t$ graph of a body moving in a straight line is shown.

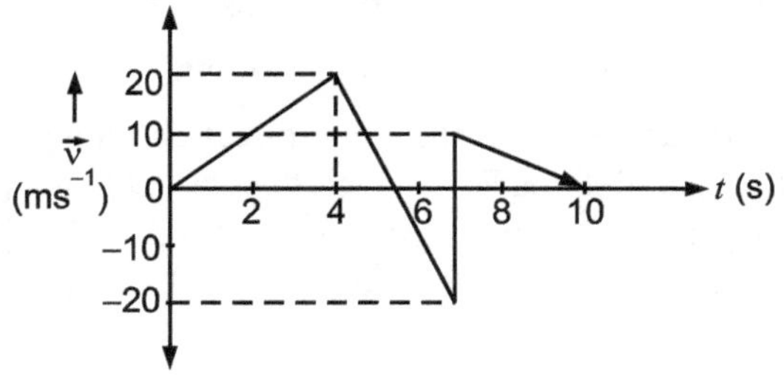

The displacement and distance travelled by the body in 10 seconds are :

(a) 50 m, 90 m (b) 90 m, 90 m
(c) 90 m, 50 m (d) 180 m, 180 m

36. A thief is running away on a straight road in a jeep moving with the speed at 9 ms^{-1}. A policeman catches him on a motorcycle moving at a speed of 10 ms^{-1}. If the instantaneous separation between the jeep and motorcycle is 100 m, the policeman will catch the thief in :

(a) 1 s (b) 19 s
(c) 90 s (d) 100 s

37. A bus is moving with velocity 10 ms^{-1}. A scooterist wishes to overtake the bus in 100 seconds. If bus is at a distance of 1 km from the scooterist, with what velocity should the scooterist catch the bus ?

(a) 50 ms^{-1} (b) 40 ms^{-1}
(c) 30 ms^{-1} (d) 20 ms^{-1}

38. A train accelerating uniformly from rest attains a maximum speed of 40 ms^{-1} in 20 seconds. It travels at speed for 20 s and is brought to rest with uniform retardation in further 40 s. The average velocity during this period is :

(a) 80 ms^{-1} (b) 25 ms^{-1}
(c) 40 ms^{-1} (d) 30 ms^{-1}

39. A 2 m wide truck is moving with a uniform speed of 8 ms^{-1} along a straight road. A pedestrian starts to cross the road with a uniform speed v, when the truck is 4 m away from him. The minimum value of the velocity of pedestrian, so that he can cross the road safely is :

(a) 2.26 ms^{-1} (b) 4.6 ms^{-1}
(c) 3.57 ms^{-1} (d) 1.414 ms^{-1}

40. Two cars move in the same direction along two parallel roads. One of them is 200 m long travelling with a velocity of 7.5 ms^{-1}. How long will it take for the first car to overtake the second car ?

(because the other car is 100 m back moving with 20 ms^{-1})

(a) 6 s (b) 12 s
(c) 18 s (d) 24 s

41. A car is moving along a straight road with uniform acceleration. It passes through two points A and B. These two are separated by a distance with the velocities 30 kmh^{-1} and 40 kmh^{-1} respectively. The velocity of the car midway of A and B is :

(a) 38.35 kmh^{-1} (b) 37.35 kmh^{-1}
(c) 36.35 kmh^{-1} (d) 35.35 kmh^{-1}

42. A honey-bee flies along a line between the points P and Q in 4 s with a velocity of $|(t-2)|$ ms^{-1}. The distance between P and Q in metres is :

(a) 1.4 (b) 2.4
(c) 3.4 (d) 4

43. A car moving with the speed of 40 kmh^{-1} can be stopped by applying brakes after at least 2 m. If the same car is moving with a speed of 80 kmh^{-1}, the minimum stopping distance will be :

(a) 8 m (b) 10 m
(c) 10.2 m (d) 10.26 m

44. The displacement of a particle after time 't' sec. is given by,

$$x = \left(\frac{k}{b^2}\right)(1 - e^{-bt})$$

where b is a constant. The acceleration of a particle will be :

(a) $\frac{-k}{n^2} e^{-bt}$ (b) $\frac{k}{b^2} e^{-bt}$
(c) $-ke^{-bt}$ (d) $k.e^{-bt}$

45. For a particle, the displacement x meter at time t sec. is given by $x^2 = 1 + t^2$. Its acceleration (ms^{-2}) at time t seconds is :

(a) x^{-3} (b) $-t.x^{-3}$
(c) $x^{-1} - t^2x^{-3}$ (d) $x^{-1} - x^{-2}$

46. A person is moving eastward with a speed of 5 ms^{-1} and in 10 s, the speed changes to 5 ms^{-1} northwards. The average acceleration will be : **(I.I.T. 1982)**

(a) Zero
(b) $\frac{1}{\sqrt{2}}$ ms^{-2} towards N–W
(c) $\frac{1}{2}$ ms^{-2} towards N–W
(d) $\frac{1}{2}$ ms^{-2} towards N–E

47. A body covers 200 cm in the first 2 s and 220 m in the next 4 s with deceleration. The velocity of the body at the end of the 7th second is :

(a) 5 cms^{-1} (b) 10 cms^{-1}
(c) 15 cms^{-1} (d) 20 cms^{-1}

48. A particle moving along a straight line has a velocity v ms^{-1}. It covers a distance of z metres and is connected with a relation $v = \sqrt{z + 49}$. When the velocity is 1 ms^{-1}, then its acceleration (in ms^{-2}) is :

(a) 1 (b) 0.75

(c) 0.5 (d) 0.25

49. A particle is moving with initial velocity 4 ms^{-1} till t = 1.55 and then it accelerates at 10 ms^{-2} till t = 3 s. The distance covered by it is :

(a) 17.25 m (b) 23.25 m

(c) 36.25 m (d) 40 m

50. A train starts from a station with an acceleration of 1 ms^{-2}. A passenger is 48 m behind the train and is running with constant velocity 10 ms^{-1} on the platform to catch the train. The time taken by the passenger to catch the train will be :

(a) 4.8 s (b) 8 s

(c) 10 s (d) 12 s

51. Speeds of two identical cars are u and $4u$ at a specific time. If the same deceleration is applied on both the cars, the ratio of the respective distances in which the two cars are stopped from that instant is :

(A.I.E.E.E. 2002)

(a) 1 : 1 (b) 1 : 4

(c) 1 : 8 (d) 1 : 16

52. A car moving with a speed of 50 kmh^{-1}, can be stopped by brakes after at least 6 m. If the same car is moving at the speed of 100 kmh^{-1}, the minimum distance is :

(A.I.E.E.E. 2003)

(a) 6 m (b) 12 m

(c) 18 m (d) 24 m

53. An automobile travelling with a speed of 60 kmh^{-1}, can brake to stop within a distance of 20 m. If the car is going twice as fast i.e. 120 kmh^{-1}, the stopping distance will be : **(A.I.E.E.E. 2004)**

(a) 20 m (b) 40 m

(c) 60 m (d) 80 m

54. The relation between time 't' and distance 'x' is $t = ax^2 + bx$, where a and b are constants. The acceleration is :

(A.I.E.E.E. 2005)

(a) $-2av^3$ (b) $2av^2$

(c) $-2av^2$ (d) $2bv^3$

55. A car starting from rest, accelerates at the rate of 'f' through a distance 'S', then continues at constant speed for time 't' and then decelerates at the rate of $f/2$ to come to rest. If the total distance traversed is 15 s, then : **(A.I.E.E.E. 2005)**

(a) $s = \frac{1}{72}ft^2$ (b) $s = \frac{1}{4}ft^2$

(c) $s = ft$ (d) $s = \frac{1}{6}ft^2$

56. A particle located at $x = 0$ at time $t = 0$, starts moving along the + ve x-direction with a velocity v that varies as $v = \alpha\sqrt{x}$. The displacement of the particle varies with time as : **(A.I.E.E.E. 2007)**

(a) t^3 (b) t^2

(c) t (d) $t^{1/2}$

57. The velocity of a particle is $v = v_0 + gt + ft^2$. If its position is $x = 0$ at $t = 0$, then displacement after unit time ($t = 1$) is :

(a) $v_0 + \frac{g}{2} + f$ (b) $v_0 + 2g + 3f$

(c) $v_0 + \frac{g}{2} + \frac{f}{3}$ (d) $v_0 + g + f$

58. A body is at rest at $x = 0$. At $t = 0$, it starts moving in +ve x-direction with constant acceleration. At the same instant another body passes through $x = 0$ also moving in the positive x-direction with constant speed. The position of the first body is given by $x_1(t)$ after time t and that of the second body by $x_2(t)$ after the same time interval.

Which of the following graphs correctly describes $(x_1 - x_2)$ as a function of time t ?

(a) 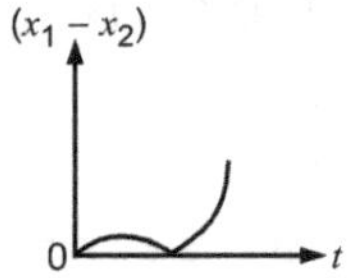

(b) 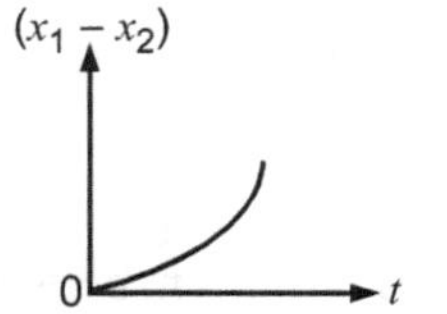

(c) 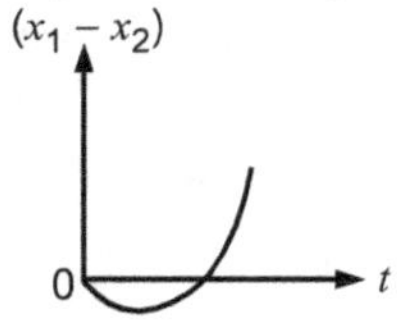

(d) 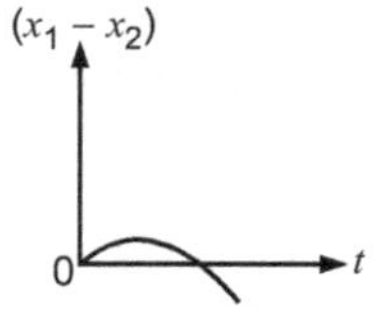

59. If x, v and a denote the displacement, the velocity and the acceleration of a particle executing S.H.M. of time period 'T', then which of the following does not change with time ? **(A.I.E.E.E. 2009)**

(a) $a^2T^2 + 4\pi^2v^2$ (b) $\frac{a.T}{x}$

(c) $aT + 2\pi v$ (d) $\frac{aT}{v}$

60. Consider a rubber ball freely falling from a height h = 4.9 m on to a horizontal elastic plate. Assume that the duration of the collision is negligible and the collision with the plate is totally elastic. Then the velocity as a function of time and the height as a function of time will be : **(A.I.E.E.E. 2009)**

(a) 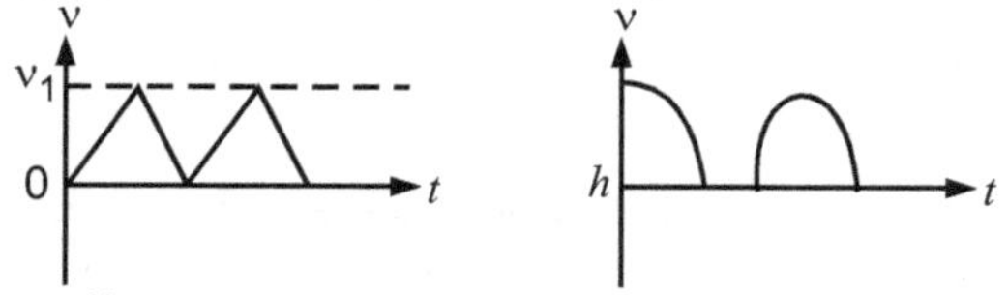

(b) 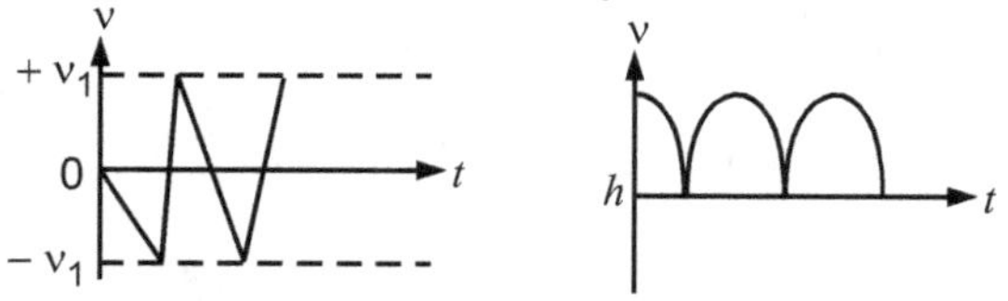

(c) 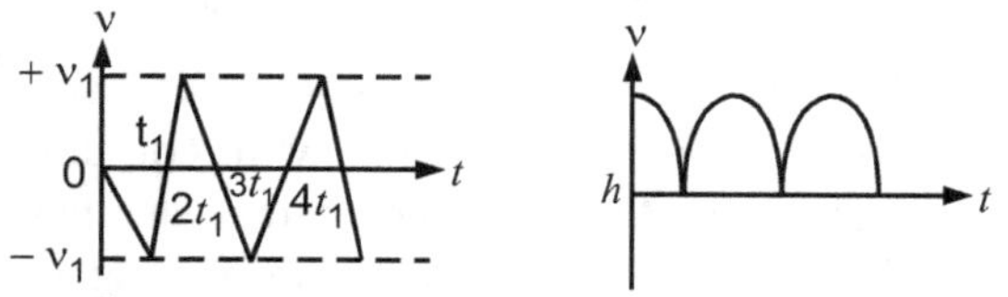

(d) 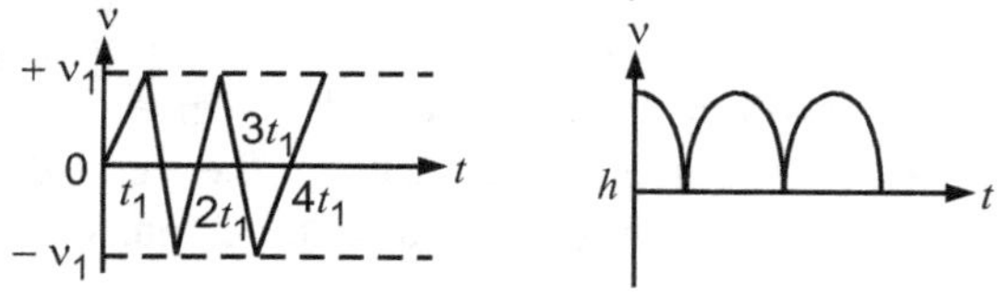

61. A point P moves in counter-clockwise direction on a circular path as shown in the figure. The movement of P is such that it sweeps out a length $s = t^3 + 5$, where S is in meter and t is in seconds. The radius of the path is 20 m. The acceleration of P where t = 2 s is nearly : **(A.I.E.E.E. 2010)**

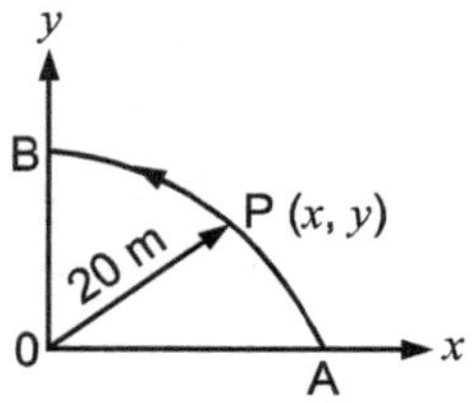

(a) 13 ms^{-2} (b) 12 ms^{-2}

(c) 7.2 ms^{-2} (d) 14 ms^{-1}

62. A particle returns to the starting point after 10 sec. If the rate of change of velocity during the motion is constant in magnitude, then its location after 7 sec. will be same as that after :

(a) 1 sec (b) 2 sec

(c) 3 sec (d) 3.5 sec

63. A body dropped from a height 'h' with initial velocity zero, strikes the ground with the velocity 3 ms^{-1}. Another body from the same height 'h' with an initial velocity with which it strikes the ground will be :

(a) 3 ms^{-1} (b) 4 ms^{-1}

(c) 5 ms^{-1} (d) 12 ms^{-1}

64. A body is projected vertically upwards with a velocity of 10 ms^{-1}. It reaches the maximum height h in time t seconds. In $t/2$, the height gained by it will be :

(a) $h/2$ (b) $2h/5$

(c) $3h/4$ (d) $5h/8$

65. With what speed should a body be thrown upwards so that the distances traversed in 5th second and 6th second are equal ?

(a) 58.4 ms^{-1} (b) 49 ms^{-1}

(c) $\sqrt{98}$ ms^{-1} (d) 98 ms^{-1}

66. A food packet is dropped from a helicopter rising up with a velocity of 4 ms^{-1}. The velocity of the packet after 3 seconds will be:

(a) 20.4 ms^{-1} (b) 25.4 ms^{-1}
(c) 28.4 ms^{-1} (d) 30.4 ms^{-1}

67. A body is dropped from a height of 100 m. At what height will the velocity of the body be equal to one half of the velocity, when it hits the ground ?

(a) 45 m (b) 55 m
(c) 65 m (d) 75 m

68. A parachutist drops freely from an aeroplane for 10 sec. before the parachute opens out. Then he descends with a net retardation of 25 ms^{-2}. If he bails out of the plane at a height of 2.495 m, then his velocity on reaching the ground will be :

($\because g = 10\ ms^{-2}$)

(a) 15 ms^{-1} (b) 20 ms^{-1}
(c) 10 ms^{-1} (d) 5 ms^{-1}

69. A body starts from rest and falls vertically from a height of 19.6 m, then the time taken by the body to fall through the last metre of its fall is :

($\because g = 9.8\ ms^{-2}$)

(a) 2 s (b) 0.05 s
(c) 0.45 s (d) 1.95 s

70. Two bodies begin a free fall from rest, from the same height 2 s apart. How long after the first body begins to fall, will the two bodies be 40 m apart :

($\because g = 10\ ms^{-2}$)

(a) 1 s (b) 2 s
(c) 3 s (d) 4 s

71. A ball is thrown vertically upwards. It was observed at a height '*h*' twice with a time interval Δt. The initial velocity of the ball is:

(a) $\sqrt{8gh + g^2(\Delta t)^2}$

(b) $\sqrt{8gh + \left(\frac{g\Delta t}{2}\right)^2}$

(c) $\frac{1}{2}\sqrt{8gh + g^2(\Delta t)^2}$

(d) $\sqrt{8gh + 4g^2(\Delta t)^2}$

72. A body is thrown vertically upwards with the velocity *v* from a height '*h*' above the ground. The time taken for the body to strike the ground is :

(a) $\sqrt{\frac{2g}{h}}$ (b) $h = vt - \frac{1}{2}gt^2$
(c) $\frac{1}{2}gt^2$ (d) $-h = vt - \frac{1}{2}gt^2$

73. A juggler keeps on moving four balls in air in regular intervals of time. When one ball leaves his hand (speed 20 ms^{-1}), the positions of the other balls will be : ($\because g = 10\ ms^{-2}$)

(a) 10 m, 20 m, 10 m
(b) 15 m, 20 m, 15 m
(c) 5 m, 15 m, 20 m
(d) 5 m, 10 m, 20 m

74. A stone is allowed to fall from the top of a tower 100 m high and at the same time another stone is projected vertically upwards from the ground with the velocity of 254 ms^{-1}. The two stones will meet after :

(a) 4 s (b) 0.4 s
(c) 0.04 s (d) 40 s

75. A stone is dropped from a tower of height '*h*' from rest and simultaneously another stone is projected vertically upwards with an initial velocity. The graph of the distance *S* between the two stones before it hits the ground plotted against time '*t*' will be :

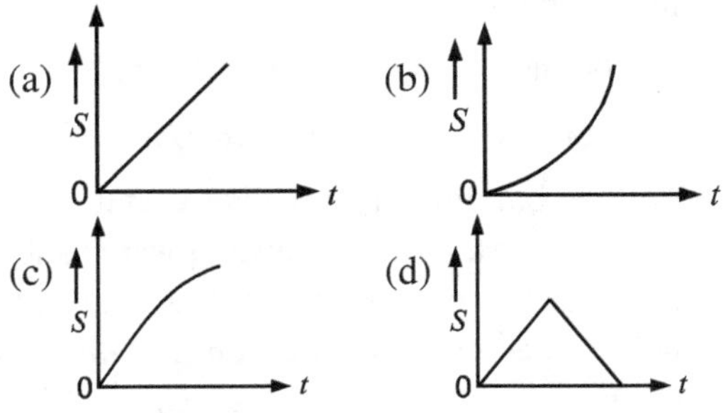

76. The motion of a body falling freely in resistive medium is described by the equation $\frac{dv}{dt}$, where a and b are constant. The velocity of the body at any time t is :

(a) $a(1-b^{2t})$
(b) $\frac{a}{b}(1-e^{-bt})$
(c) $a.b.e^{-1}$
(d) $ab^2(1-t)$

77. A body is dropped from a height 39.2 m. After crossing half the distance, the acceleration due to gravity ceases to act. The body will hit the ground with the velocity :

(a) 1.96 m
(b) 1960 m
(c) 196 m
(d) 19.6 m

78. A stone thrown vertically upwards with the initial velocity u from the top of a tower reaches the ground with a velocity $3u$. The height of the tower is :

(a) $\frac{3u^2}{g}$
(b) $\frac{4u^2}{g}$
(c) $\frac{6u^2}{g}$
(d) $\frac{9u^2}{g}$

79. One body is dropped while a second body is thrown downwards with an initial velocity of 2 ms^{-1} simultaneously. The separation between them is 18 m after a time of

(a) 9 s
(b) 4.5 s
(c) 9.8 s
(d) 18 s

80. A ball is dropped on to the floor from a height of 10 m. It rebounces to a height of 2.5 m. If the ball is in contact with the floor for 0.01 s, what is the average acceleration during contact ?

(a) 700 ms^{-2}
(b) 1400 ms^{-2}
(c) 2100 ms^{-2}
(d) 2800 ms^{-2}

81. From a building, two balls A and B are thrown such that A is thrown upwards and B downwards (both vertically). If v_A and v_B are their respective velocities on reaching the ground, then : **(A.I.E.E.E. 2002)**

(a) $v_B > v_A$
(b) $v_A = v_B$
(c) $v_A > v_B$
(d) Depends on their masses

82. A ball is released from the top of a tower of height 'h' metre. It takes T seconds to reach the ground. What is the position of the ball in T/3 seconds ?

(a) $h/9$ metre from the ground
(b) $7h/9$ metre from the ground
(c) $8h/9$ metre from the ground
(d) $17h/18$ metre from the ground

83. A parachutist after bailing out falls 50 m without friction. When the parachute opens, it decelerates at 2 ms^{-2}. At what height, did he bail out : **(A.I.E.E.E. 2005)**

(a) 293 m
(b) 111 m
(c) 91 m
(d) 182 m

84. A stone dropped from a top of a tower is found to travel $\frac{5}{9}$ of height of the tower during the last second of its fall. The time of fall is :

(a) 2 s
(b) 3 s
(c) 4 s
(d) 5 s

85. A rubber ball is dropped from a height 5 m on a planet, where acceleration due to gravity is not known. On bouncing, it rises to 1.8 m, the ball loses its velocity on bouncing by the factor of :

(a) $\frac{12}{25}$
(b) $\frac{13}{25}$
(c) $\frac{3}{5}$
(d) $\frac{2}{5}$

86. A ball is dropped from the top of a tower 100 m high. At the same time, another ball is thrown upwards with the speed of 50 ms^{-1}. After what time will they cross each other ?

(a) 0.5 s
(b) 1 s
(c) 2 s
(d) 2.5 s

87. An elevator in which a man is standing is moving upwards with a speed of 10 ms^{-1}.

If a coin is dropped by that man from a height 2.45 m, it reaches the floor of the elevator after a time :

(a) $\sqrt{2}$ s (b) $\frac{1}{\sqrt{2}}$ s

(c) 2 s (d) $\frac{1}{2}$ s

88. A man standing at a distance of 7 m from a 11.8 m high building sees a kid slipping from the top floor. With what speed should he run to catch the kid in his arms (height 1.8 m) ?

(a) 4.5 ms^{-1} (b) 4.9 ms^{-1}

(c) 7 ms^{-1} (d) Can't catch

89. A ball is thrown vertically upwards from the top of a tower of height 'h' with the velocity v. The ball strikes the ground after :

(a) $\frac{v}{g}\left[1+\sqrt{1+\frac{2gh}{v^2}}\right]$

(b) $\frac{v}{g}\left[1-\sqrt{1+\frac{2gh}{v^2}}\right]$

(c) $\frac{v}{g}\left[1+\frac{2gh}{v^2}\right]^{1/2}$

(d) $\frac{v}{g}\left[1-\frac{2gh}{v^2}\right]^{1/2}$

90. A stone falls from a balloon that is descending at a uniform rate of 12 ms^{-1}. The displacement of the stone from the point of release after 10 s is :

(a) 725 m (b) 510 m

(c) 490 m (d) 610 m

91. Water drops fall from a tap on the floor 5 m below at regular intervals of time, the first drop striking the floor, when the fifth drop begins to fall. The height at which the third drop will be from the ground, at the instant when the 1st drop strikes the ground will be : ($\because$ $g = 10\ ms^{-2}$)

(a) 1.25 m (b) 2.15 m

(c) 2.73 m (d) 3.75 m

92. A body is falling freely from rest with the velocity v after it falls through a distance 'h'. The distance to fall down further for its velocity to become double is :

(a) h (b) $2\,h$

(c) $3\,h$ (d) $4\,h$

93. Two bodies of different masses are dropped from a height of 16 m and 25 m respectively. The ratio of the time taken by them to reach the ground is :

(a) $\frac{25}{16}$ (b) $\frac{5}{4}$

(c) $\frac{4}{5}$ (d) $\frac{16}{25}$

94. A body is fired vertically upwards. At the maximum height, the velocity of the body is 10 ms^{-1}. The maximum height raised by the body is :

($\because$ $g = 10\ ms^{-2}$)

(a) 4 m (b) 6 m

(c) 8 m (d) 10 m

95. A ball is dropped from a bridge at a height of 176.4 m over a river. After 2 s, another ball is thrown straight downwards. What should be the initial velocity of the second ball so that both hit the water of the river simultaneously ?

(a) 24.5 ms^{-1} (b) 42.5 ms^{-1}

(c) 12.5 ms^{-1} (d) 2.5 ms^{-1}

96. A ball which is at rest is dropped from a height 'h'. As it bounces off the floor, its speed is 80% of what it was just before touching the ground. The ball will then rise nearly to a height of :

(a) 0.94 h (b) 0.80 h

(c) 0.75 h (d) 0.64 h

97. A stone is dropped from a balloon at a height of 300 m from the ground. How long will the stone take to reach the ground ?

(a) 7.12 s (b) 7.75 s

(c) 7.82 s (d) 8.12 s

98. How long will the stone take to reach the ground at a height 300 m when the balloon is ascending with a velocity 5 ms^{-1} ?

(a) 7.12 s (b) 7.26 s

(c) 7.28 s (d) 8.26 s

99. A bomb is dropped from an aeroplane flying horizontally with the velocity of 720 kmh^{-1} at an altitude 980 m. When will the bomb hit the ground ?

(a) 7.2 s (b) 1 s

(c) 0.15 s (d) 14.14 s

100. A bomber plane is flying horizontally with velocity of 600 kmh^{-1} and at a height of 1960 m. When it is vertically above a point A on the ground, a bomb is released from it. The bomb strikes the ground at point B. The distance between A and B is :

(a) 0.33 km (b) 3.33 km

(c) 33.3 km (d) 333 km

101. The figure shows the position-time graph of one dimensional motion of a body of mass 0.4 kg. The magnitude of each impulse is :

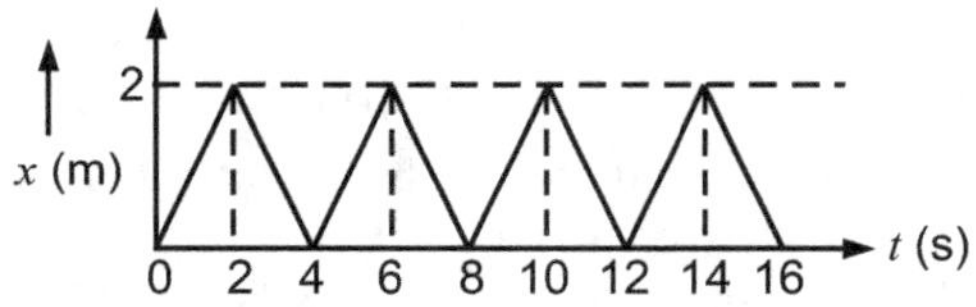

(a) 0.4 Ns (b) 0.8 Ns

(c) 1.6 Ns (d) 0.2 Ns

102. Two trains 121 m and 99 m in length are running in opposite directions with velocities of 40 kmh^{-1} and 32 kmh^{-1}. In what time will they completely cross each other ?

(a) 8 s (b) 9 s

(c) 10 s (d) 11 s

103. A person is going towards east in a car with a velocity 25 kmh^{-1}, a train appears to move towards north with a velocity $25\sqrt{3}$ kmh^{-1}. The actual velocity of the train will be :

(a) 25 kmh^{-1} (b) 50 kmh^{-1}

(c) 5 kmh^{-1} (d) 35 kmh^{-1}

104. Two trains A and B are moving on parallel tracks with velocities of 60 kmh^{-1} and 90 kmh^{-1} respectively but in opposite directions. The relative velocity of : (i) train A w.r.t. train B (ii) and the relative velocity of ground w.r.t. train A will be :

(a) (i) 150 kmh^{-1} (ii) –60 kmh^{-1}

(b) (i) 30 kmh^{-1} (ii) –60 kmh^{-1}

(c) (i) –150 kmh^{-1} (ii) 30 kmh^{-1}

(d) (i) – 30 kmh^{-1} (ii) – 150 kmh^{-1}

105. A man wants to reach at point B on the opposite bank of a river flowing at a speed (u) as shown in the figure. The minimum speed relative to water so that the man can reach point B from point A will be :

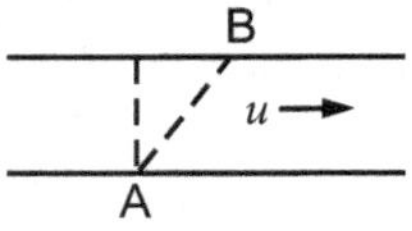

(a) $u\sqrt{2}$ (b) $\frac{u}{\sqrt{2}}$

(c) 2 u (d) $\frac{u}{2}$

106. A boat can travel at a speed of 8 kmh^{-1} in still water. In the flowing water of a stream, it can move at 8 kmh^{-1} relative to water. If the speed of the water stream is 3 kmh^{-1}, how fast can the boat move past a tree on the shore when travelling : (i) up stream (ii) downstream:

(a) 11 kmh^{-1} and 5 kmh^{-1}

(b) 8 kmh^{-1} and 5 kmh^{-1}

(c) 5 kmh^{-1} and 11 kmh^{-1}

(d) 5 kmh^{-1} and 8 kmh^{-1}

ASSERTION AND REASON

Directions for Questions 107 to 111 : Each question contains statement-I as assertion and statement-II as reason and each question also has four alternative choices, in which only one is correct. So you have to choose the correct answer from (a), (b), (c) and (d) given below :

(a) Both Assertion and Reason are true and Reason is correct explanation of Assertion.

(b) Both Assertion and Reason are true, but Reason is not correct explanation of the Assertion.

(c) Assertion is true, but Reason is false

(d) Assertion is false, but Reason is true.

107. (I) The position-time graph of a uniform motion in one dimension of a body can have negative slope.

(II) When the speed of a body decreases with time, then s-*t* graph of body has negative slope.

108. (I) A body moving with a uniform velocity is in equilibrium.

(II) A body can move with a uniform velocity only when a constant force is acting on it.

109. (I) A car moving with a speed of $25 ms^{-1}$ takes a U-turn in 5 seconds without changing its speed. The average acceleration during these 5 seconds is $5\ ms^{-2}$.

(II) $\text{Acceleration} = \frac{\text{Change in velocity}}{\text{Time taken}}$

110. (I) A ball is dropped from a tower of height 90 m. After it falls by half the distance, the acceleration due to gravity ceases to act. The velocity with which it hits the ground is $30\ ms^{-1}$.

$(\because g = 10\ ms^{-2})$

(II) $v^2 = u^2 + 2gh$

111. (I) The relative velocity between two bodies may be equal to the sum of the velocities of two bodies.

(II) Sometimes, the relative velocity between two bodies may also be equal to the differences in the velocities of two bodies.

112. (I) A wheel of radius R rolls forward half a revolution. Then the displacement of the wheel initially in contact with the ground is R .

(II) $\text{Displacement} = \sqrt{x^2 + y^2}$

where x = Horizontal component = πR

y = Vertical Component = 2 R

113. (I) The string of a vibrating simple pendulum is cut when the bob is at extreme position, the bob will follow an elliptical path.

(II) The direction of velocity vector is always perpendicular to the radial length at that instant.

114. (I) The time plotted along x-axis and the acceleration is plotted along y-axis. The area between the graph of x and y gives the distance covered.

(II) Change in velocity is equal to acceleration multiplied by time.

115. (I) A particle moves with uniform velocity, then its acceleration is zero.

(II) $\vec{a} = \frac{d\vec{v}}{dt}$ $\therefore$ $\vec{v}$ is uniform then acceleration is zero.

116. (I) The magnitude of displacement is equal to the distance covered in a given interval of time if the particle moves with a constant speed.

(II) Under uniform velocity, the distance covered is equal to its displacement.

117. When a girl drives a scooty at a speed of $40\ kmh^{-1}$ for the first 0.5 h. and then at a speed of $60\ kmh^{-1}$ for the next 0.5 h., the average speed will be :

(a) $0.5\ kmh^{-1}$ (b) $5\ kmh^{-1}$

(c) $50\ kmh^{-1}$ (d) $48\ kmh^{-1}$

118. The acceleration of a particle varies with time as $a = bt + c$, where b and c are constants. The velocity of the particle which starts from rest after time 't' sec will be :

(a) $bt + \frac{1}{2}ct^2$ (b) $ct + \frac{1}{2}bt^2$

(c) $bt + ct^2$ (d) $ct + bt^2$

119. A car accelerates from rest at a constant rate α for some time, after which it decelerates at a constant rate β to rest. If the total time elapsed is 't' sec, then the maximum velocity acquired by the car is given by :

(a) $\left(\frac{\alpha^2+\beta^2}{\alpha\beta}\right)t$ (b) $\left(\frac{\alpha^2-\beta^2}{\alpha\beta}\right)t$

(c) $\left(\frac{\alpha+\beta}{\alpha\beta}\right)t$ (d) $\left(\frac{\alpha\beta}{\alpha+\beta}\right)t$

120. A stone is dropped into a well in which the water level is at a depth 'h' from the top. If the speed of sound is v, then the time after which the splash is heard will be :

(a) $h\left[\sqrt{\frac{2}{gh}}+\frac{1}{v}\right]$ (b) $h\left[\sqrt{\frac{2}{gh}}-\frac{1}{v}\right]$

(c) $h\left[\frac{2}{g}+\frac{1}{v}\right]$ (d) $h\left[\frac{2}{g}-\frac{1}{v}\right]$

121. A particle moving in a straight line covers half the distance with a speed of 3 ms^{-1}. The other half of the distances covered into two equal time intervals with the speed of 4.5 ms^{-1} and 7.5 ms^{-1} respectively. The average speed during the motion of the particle is :

(a) 2.8 ms^{-1} (b) 3.8 ms^{-1}

(c) 4 ms^{-1} (d) 4.8 ms^{-1}

122. A steamer takes 12 days to reach from port x to port y. Everyday only one steamer sets out from both the ports. How many steamers does each steamer meet in open sea ?

(a) 20 (b) 21

(c) 22 (d) 23

123. The displacement 'x' and time 't' are related as $t = px^2 + qx + r$, where p, q and r are constants, then the relation between velocity 'v' and acceleration 'a' is :

(a) $a \propto v$ (b) $a^2 \propto v$

(c) $a \propto v^3$ (d) $a^2 \propto v^3$

124. The co-ordinates of a moving particle at time 't' are given by $x = ct^3$ and $y = bt^3$. The speed of the particle is :

(a) $3t^2(c+b)$ (b) $3t^2\sqrt{c^2-b^2}$

(c) $t\sqrt{c^2+b^2}$ (d) $3t^2(c^2+b^2)$

125. Two roads cross at right angles at O. A person (A) walking along one of them at 3 ms^{-1} sees another person (B) walking at 4 ms^{-1} along the other road at O, when he is 10 m off. The nearest distance between A and B is :

(a) 7.2 m (b) 7.6 m

(c) 8 m (d) 8.2 m

126. A particle starting from rest moves upto 20 s with a constant acceleration. If S_1 is the distance covered in the last 10 seconds, then:

(a) $S_2 = S_1$ (b) $S_2 = 2S_1$

(c) $S_2 = 3S_1$ (d) $S_2 = 4S_1$

127. A ball is dropped from a height 'd' above the ground. It hits the ground and bounces up vertically to a height $d/2$. Neglecting air resistance, its velocity 'v' varies with the height 'h' above the ground as :

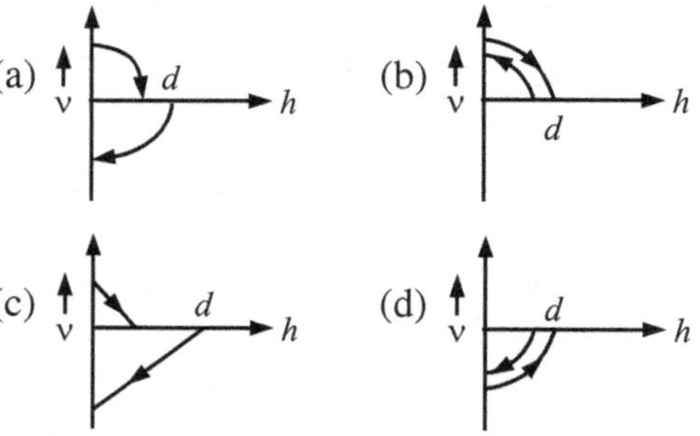

128. From the given $\vec{v} - t$ graph, the distance covered by a car in the last two seconds of its motion is what fraction of the total distance covered by it in all the seven seconds ?

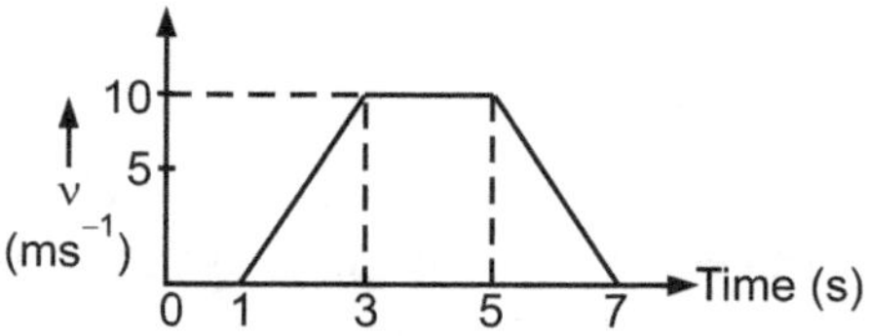

(a) 0.5 (b) 0.25

(c) 0.33 (d) 0.666

129. The acceleration of a particle, starting from rest, varies with time according to the relation $a = -s\omega^2 \sin \omega t$. The displacement of this particle at time t will be :

(a) $s \sin \omega t$ (b) $s\omega \cos t\ \omega t$

(c) $s\omega \sin \omega t$ (d) $\frac{1}{2}(s\omega^2 \sin \omega t)\, t^2$

130. The displacement x of a particle moving in one dimension is related to time by an equation and is given by $t = \sqrt{x} + 3$. The displacement when the velocity is zero is :

(a) 9 m (b) 4 m
(c) 1 m (d) zero

131. Two cars get closer by 8 m every second while travelling in opposite directions. They get closer by 0.8 m while travelling in the same direction. The speed of the two cars will be :

(a) 4 ms^{-1} and 4.4 ms^{-1}
(b) 4.4 ms^{-1} and 3.6 ms^{-1}
(c) 4 ms^{-1} and 3.6 ms^{-1}
(d) 4 ms^{-1} and 3 ms^{-1}

132. The velocity-time graph for a body moving along a straight line is shown in following figure. The displacement of the body in 10 s of its motion will be :

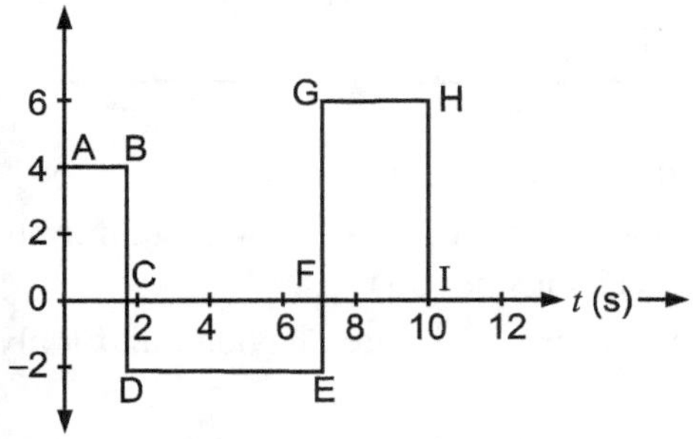

(a) 4 m (b) 6 m
(c) 8 m (d) 10 m

133. A motor of an electro-motive unit (EMU) can give an acceleration of 1 ms^{-2} and breaks give a retardation of 3 ms^{-2}. The shortest time to make a trip between two stations 1215 m apart is :

(a) 113.6 s (b) 56.9 s
(c) 60 s (d) 55 s

134. A metre scale is standing vertically on the earth surface. If now it starts to fall on the earth's surface without slipping, find the velocity with which the free end of the scale strikes the earth :

(a) 9.8 ms^{-1} (b) 5.4 ms^{-1}
(c) 4.5 ms^{-1} (d) 1 ms^{-1}

135. A student not believing his physics teachers explanation of law of gravity, starts his free fall from the top of a 320 m high building with a stop watch. After 5 s, Shaktiman dives off the roof to save the student. What must be the initial velocity of Shaktiman in order that he catches the student just before the ground is reached :

(a) 67.23 ms^{-1} (b) 91.66 ms^{-1}
(c) 102.91 ms^{-1} (d) 105.75 ms^{-1}

136. A car accelerates from rest at a constant rate α for some time, after which it decelerates at a constant rate β to come to rest. If the total time elapsed is t, the distance travelled by the car is :

(a) $\frac{1}{2}\left[\frac{\alpha\beta}{\alpha+\beta}\right]t^2$ (b) $\frac{1}{2}\left[\frac{\alpha+\beta}{\alpha\beta}\right]t^2$

(c) $\frac{1}{2}\left[\frac{\alpha^2+\beta^2}{\alpha\beta}\right]$ (d) $\frac{1}{2}\left[\frac{\alpha^2-\beta^2}{\alpha\beta}\right]t^2$

137. An object is moving with a uniform acceleration which is parallel to its direction of motion. The displacement-velocity graph of this object is :

(a) 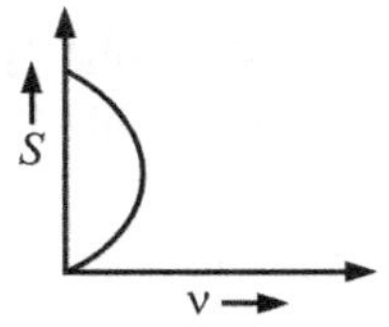

(b) 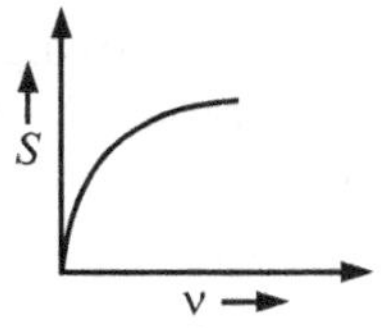

(c) 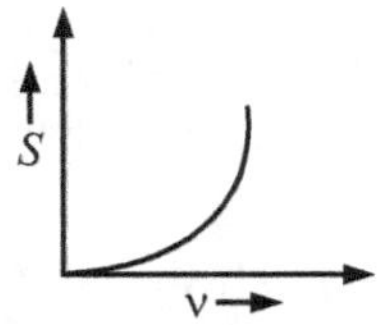

(d) 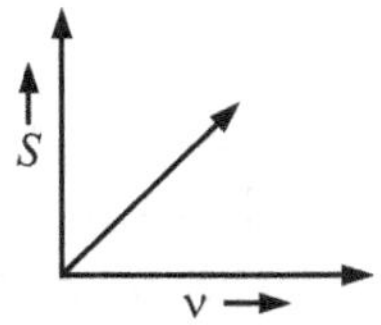

138. A particle moves with an initial velocity v_0 and retardation βv, where v is its velocity at any time 't' :

(a) The particle will stop shortly.
(b) The particle will cover a total distance of $\frac{v_0}{\beta}$.
(c) The particle will continue moving for a very long time.
(d) Both (b) and (c).

139. A ball of density half of that of water falls freely under gravity from a height 19.6 m, and then enters water. Upto what depth will the ball go ? (Neglect air resistance and viscosity effect of water.)

(a) 19.6 m (b) 9.8 m
(c) 4.9 m (d) 39.2 m

140. A balloon is moving upwards with the speed of 5 ms^{-1} when it is at a height of 98 m, a packet is dropped from it. The velocity of the packet, when it strikes the ground is :

(a) 11.1 ms^{-1} (b) 21.1 ms^{-1}
(c) 31.1 ms^{-1} (d) 44.1 ms^{-1}

141. Two bodies begin to fall freely from the same height, the second T *s* after the first. How long after the first body begins to fall, will the distance between the two bodies be equal to ?

(a) $\left(\frac{gT}{l}+\frac{T}{2}\right)$ (b) $\left(\frac{gT^2}{l^2}+\frac{T^2}{2}\right)$
(c) $\left(\frac{l}{gT}+\frac{T}{2}\right)$ (d) $\left(\frac{l^2}{gT^2}+\frac{T^2}{2}\right)$

142. A 120 m long train A is moving in a direction with the speed of 20 ms^{-1}. Another train B moving with 30 ms^{-1} in opposite direction and 130 m long crosses the train A in a time :

(a) 5 s (b) 6 s
(c) 38 s (d) 42 s

143. Two particles are initially located at points A and B at a distance *d* apart. They start moving at time t = 0 second such that the velocity *u* of particle B is always along the horizontal direction and the velocity *v* of A is continuously aimed at B. At t = 0, when will the two particles meet :

(a) $\frac{vd}{v^2-u^2}$ (b) $\frac{d}{u}$
(c) $\frac{u.d}{v^2-u^2}$ (d) $\frac{(v-u)\,d}{v^2}$

144. A particle moves along a line such that its displacement *x* changes with time and is given as:

$$x=\sqrt{at^2+2bt+c}$$

where *a*, *b* and *c* are constants, then the acceleration varies as :

(a) $\frac{1}{x}$ (b) $\frac{1}{x^2}$
(c) $\frac{1}{x^3}$ (d) $\frac{1}{x^4}$

145. The acceleration '*a*' of a particle depends on displacement '*S*' as $a = 5 + S$. Initially $S = 0$ and v = 5. Then the velocity v_1 corresponding to the displacement *S* is given by :

(a) $v = 5 + S$ (b) $v = (5 + S)^{1/2}$
(c) $v=\sqrt{10S+S^2}$ (d) $v = S - 5$

146. Here are two $x - t$ graphs for two particles moving along the *x*-axis as,

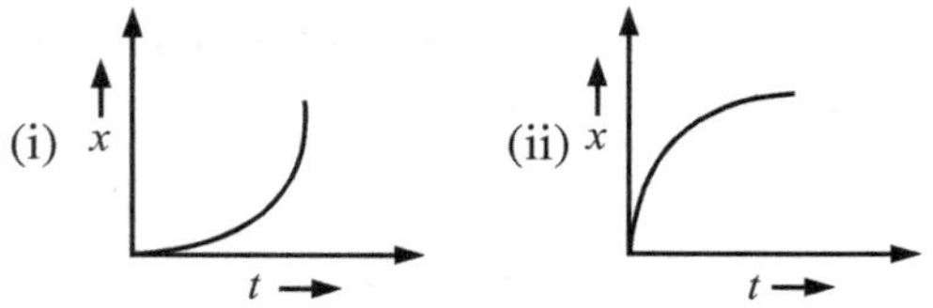

We conclude that :

(a) Both particles are having uniformly accelerated motion.
(b) Both particles are having uniformly retarded motion.
(c) Particle (i) has variable acceleration motion, whereas particle (ii) has variable retarted motion.
(d) Particle (i) is having variable retarded motion, whereas particle (ii) is having variable accelerated motion.

147. A stone is dropped from a building of height '*h*' and it takes time '*t*' on reaching the ground. From the same building, two stones are thrown (one is upwards and other vertically downwards) with the same velocity and they reach the earth's surface after t_1 and t_2 seconds, then :

(a) $t = t_1 - t_2$ (b) $t=\frac{t_1+t_2}{2}$
(c) $t=\sqrt{t_1.t_2}$ (d) $t = t_1^2 . t_2^2$

148. Between two stations, a train accelerates uniformly at first, then moves with constant velocity and finally retards uniformly. If the ratio of time taken is 1 : 8 : 1 and the maximum speed attained is 60 kmh^{-1}, then the average speed over the whole journey is:

(a) 52 kmh^{-1} (b) 48 kmh^{-1}
(c) 54 kmh^{-1} (d) 55 kmh^{-1}

149. Two railway tracks are parallel to E – W direction. Along one track, train A moves with a speed of 30 ms^{-1} from west to east, while along the second track, train B moves with a speed of 48 ms^{-1} from east to west. The relative velocity of train B w.r.t. train A is :

(a) –75 ms^{-1} (b) 75 ms^{-1}
(c) – 78 ms^{-1} (d) 78 ms^{-1}

150. The displacement (in metre) of a particle, moving along x-axis is given by = $18t + 5t^2$. The average velocity between $t = 2$ sec. and $t = 3$ sec. will be :

(a) 40 ms^{-1} (b) 40.8 ms^{-1}
(c) 43.8 ms^{-1} (d) 43 ms^{-1}

151. A proton in a cylotron changes its velocity from 30 kms^{-1} north to 40 kms^{-1} east in 20 s. What is the magnitude of the average acceleration during this time ?

(a) 2.5 kms^{-2} (b) 12.5 kms^{-2}
(c) 22.5 kms^{-2} (d) 32.5 kms^{-2}

152. A train moving with a speed of 36 kms^{-1} takes 14 s to cross a bridge of length 100 m. The length of the train is :

(a) 140 m (b) 40 m
(c) 100 m (d) 360 m

153. A particle is moving in a straight line with retardation proportional to its displacement. Its loss of K.E. for any displacement x is proportional to :

(a) x^2 (b) e^x
(c) x (d) $\log e^x$

154. Metro train starts from rest and in five seconds achieves 108 kms^{-1} speed. After that it moves with a constant velocity and goes to rest after traveling 45 m with uniform retardation. If total distance travelled is 395 m. Then the total time of travelling is :

(a) 9 s (b) 12.2 s
(c) 15.3 s (d) 17.2 s

155. An automobile travelling with a speed of 60 kmh^{-1} can apply brake to stop with a distance of 20 m. If the car is going twice as fast i.e. 120 kmh^{-1}, the stopping distance will be :

(a) 20 m (b) 40 m
(c) 60 m (d) 80 m

156. A body of mass m is accelerated uniformly from rest to a speed v in time T sec. The instantaneous power delivered to the body as a function of time is given by :

(a) $\frac{1}{2}\cdot\frac{mv^2}{T^2}\cdot t^2$ (b) $\frac{1}{2}\cdot\frac{mv^2}{T^2}\cdot t$
(c) $\frac{mv^2}{T^2}\cdot t^2$ (d) $\frac{mv^2}{T^2}\cdot t$

157. A car starting from rest, accelerates at the rate of f through a distance S, then continues at a constant speed for time t and then decelerates at the rate $f/2$ to come to rest. If the total distance is traversed in 15 s, then :

(a) $S = \frac{1}{4}ft^2$ (b) $S = \frac{1}{72}ft^2$
(c) $S = \frac{1}{6}ft^2$ (d) $S = ft$

158. The relation between time t and distance x is $t = ax^2 + bx$, where a and b are constants. The acceleration is :

(a) $2\,av^2$ (b) $-2\,av^3$
(c) $2\,bv^2$ (d) $-2\,abv^2$

159. A parachutist after bailing out falls 50 m without friction. When the parachute opens, it decelerates at 2 ms^{-2}. He reaches the ground with a speed of 3 ms^{-1}. At what height, did he bail out ?

(a) 111 m (b) 293 m
(c) 182 m (d) 91 m

160. A train accelerated uniformly from rest attains a maximum speed of 40 ms^{-1} in 20 s. It travels at this speed for 20 s and is brought to rest with uniform retardation in 40 s. The average velocity during this period is :

(a) $\frac{80}{3}$ ms^{-1} (b) 30 ms^{-1}

(c) 25 ms^{-1} (d) 40 ms^{-1}

161. A scooterist sees a bus 1 km ahead of him moving with a velocity of 10 ms^{-1}. The speed of the scooterist, so that he can overtake the bus in 100 s is :

(a) 10 ms^{-1} (b) 20 ms^{-1}

(c) 30 ms^{-1} (d) 40 ms^{-1}

162. The plotted v – t graph of a moving particle on a straight is given below.

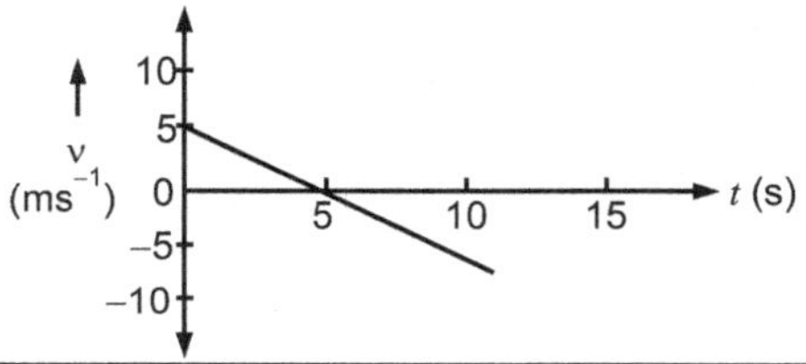

The graph shows that :

(a) The particle has zero displacement.

(b) The particle has never turned around.

(c) The particle has a constant acceleration.

(d) The average speed in time 0 to 5 s is the same as the time 5 to 10 s.

163. A particle is moving with uniform acceleration along a straight line AB. Its speed at A and B is 2 ms^{-1} and 14 ms^{-1} respectively. Then :

(a) The speed of body at mid of AB is 10 ms^{-1}.

(b) The speed at point P such that, AP : PB = 1: 5 is 4 ms^{-1}.

(c) The time to go from A to mid point of AB is double of that to go from mid point to B.

(d) None of the above

ANSWER KEY

1. (c)	**2.** (a)	**3.** (b)	**4.** (b)	**5.** (d)	**6.** (b)	**7.** (b)	**8.** (d)	**9.** (d)	**10.**(c)
11.(a)	**12.**(a)	**13.**(d)	**14.**(c)	**15.**(a)	**16.**(c)	**17.**(b)	**18.**(c)	**19.**(d)	**20.**(d)
21.(c)	**22.**(b)	**23.**(d)	**24.**(b)	**25.**(d)	**26.**(a)	**27.**(a)	**28.**(c)	**29.**(d)	**30.**(c)
31.(a)	**32.**(a)	**33.**(b)	**34.**(d)	**35.**(a)	**36.**(d)	**37.**(d)	**38.**(b)	**39.**(c)	**40.**(d)
41.(d)	**42.**(d)	**43.**(a)	**44.**(c)	**45.**(c)	**46.**(b)	**47.**(b)	**48.**(c)	**49.**(b)	**50.**(b)
51.(d)	**52.**(d)	**53.**(d)	**54.**(a)	**55.**(a)	**56.**(b)	**57.**(c)	**58.**(c)	**59.**(b)	**60.**(c)
61.(d)	**62.**(c)	**63.**(c)	**64.**(c)	**65.**(b)	**66.**(b)	**67.**(d)	**68.**(d)	**69.**(b)	**70.**(c)
71.(c)	**72.**(d)	**73.**(c)	**74.**(a)	**75.**(a)	**76.**(b)	**77.**(d)	**78.**(b)	**79.**(a)	**80.**(c)
81.(b)	**82.**(c)	**83.**(a)	**84.**(b)	**85.**(d)	**86.**(c)	**87.**(b)	**88.**(b)	**89.**(a)	**90.**(d)
91.(d)	**92.**(c)	**93.**(c)	**94.**(d)	**95.**(a)	**96.**(d)	**97.**(b)	**98.**(d)	**99.**(d)	**100.** (b)
101. (b)	**102.** (d)	**103.** (b)	**104.** (a)	**105.** (b)	**106.** (c)	**107.** (c)	**108.** (c)	**109.** (d)	**110.** (a)
111. (b)	**112.** (d)	**113.** (d)	**114.** (d)	**115.** (a)	**116.** (a)	**117.** (c)	**118.** (b)	**119.** (d)	**120.** (a)
121. (d)	**122.** (d)	**123.** (c)	**124.** (d)	**125.** (c)	**126.** (c)	**127.** (a)	**128.** (b)	**129.** (a)	**130.** (d)
131. (b)	**132.** (c)	**133.** (b)	**134.** (b)	**135.** (b)	**136.** (a)	**137.** (c)	**138.** (d)	**139.** (a)	**140.** (d)
141. (c)	**142.** (a)	**143.** (c)	**144.** (c)	**145.** (a)	**146.** (c)	**147.** (c)	**148.** (c)	**149.** (c)	**150.** (d)
151. (a)	**152.** (b)	**153.** (a)	**154.** (d)	**155.** (d)	**156.** (d)	**157.** (b)	**158.** (b)	**159.** (b)	**160.** (c)
161. (b)	**162.** (c) & (d)		**163.** (a) and (c)						

3

KINEMATICS - MOTION IN TWO AND THREE DIMENSIONS

MULTIPLE CHOICE QUESTIONS

1. Given that $\vec{P} + \vec{Q} = \vec{R}$ and $P^2 + Q^2 = R^2$. The angle between $\vec{P}$ and $\vec{Q}$ is :
   (a) 180° (b) 90°
   (c) 45° (c) 0°

2. Three vectors $\vec{A}$, $\vec{B}$ and $\vec{C}$ satisfy the relation $\vec{A}.\vec{B} = 0$ and $\vec{A}.\vec{C} = 0$. The vector $\vec{A}$ is parallel to :
   (a) $\vec{C}$ (b) $\vec{B}$
   (c) $\vec{B}.\vec{C}$ (d) $\vec{B} \times \vec{C}$

3. The cross product of two vectors is not commutative because :
   (a) cos θ = – cos (–θ)
   (b) tan θ = – tan (–θ)
   (c) sin θ = – sin (–θ)
   (d) None of these

4. At what angle should the two unit vectors be inclined so that their resultant is also a unit vector :
   (a) 30° (b) 60°
   (c) 120° (d) 150°

5. Given that $\vec{P}.\vec{Q} = 0$ and $\vec{P} \times \vec{R} = 0$. What is the angle between $\vec{P}$ and $\vec{R}$:
   (a) 135° (b) 180°
   (c) 90° (d) 0°

6. Given that $\vec{P} + \vec{Q} = \vec{R}$ and also $\vec{P} - \vec{Q} = \vec{R}$. The angle between $\vec{P}$ and $\vec{Q}$ will be :
   (a) π/3 (b) π
   (c) 2π/3 (d) 0°

7. A force $\hat{i} + 2\hat{j} - 3\hat{k}$ newton displaces a body from position vector of point (5, 2, –4) m to the position vector (2, 4, –1) m. The work done is :
   (a) 7 J (b) 8 J
   (c) 9 J (d) 10 J

8. If $\vec{A} = -4\hat{i} + 3\hat{j}$ and $\vec{B} = 2\hat{i} + 5\hat{j}$ and $\vec{C} = \vec{A} \times \vec{B}$, then vector $\vec{C}$ makes an angle of:
   (a) 0° with *z*-axis (b) 180° with *z*-axis
   (c) 180° with *y*-axis (d) 45° with *x*-axis

9. If $\vec{A} = 4\hat{i} + 8\hat{j} + 6\hat{k}$ and $\vec{B} = 2\hat{i} + 4\hat{j} + b\hat{k}$ are parallel to each other, then the value of b is :
   (a) 3 (b) –20/3
   (c) –3 (d) 6

10. The area of a triangle formed by the sides $2\hat{i} + \hat{j} - \hat{k}$ and $\hat{i} + \hat{j} + \hat{k}$ is :
    (a) $2\sqrt{3}$ sq. unit (b) $2\sqrt{14}$ sq. unit
    (c) 3 sq. unit (d) $\frac{\sqrt{14}}{2}$ sq. unit

11. The initial velocity of a particle is $\vec{u} = (2\hat{i} + 3\hat{j})$ ms^{-1}. A constant force of $\vec{F} = (4\hat{i} + \hat{j})$ N acts on the particle. If follows that :
    (a) Its velocity is constant
    (b) Its path is a straight line
    (c) It moves in a circular path
    (d) Its path is parabolic

12. A point is shifted from $(7\hat{i} + 7\hat{j} + 8\hat{k})$ m to $(2\hat{i} + 3\hat{j} + 4\hat{k})$ m due to application of force $(5\hat{i} + 4\hat{j} + 10\hat{k})$ N. The gain in K.E. of that point will be :

(a) 81 J (b) 49 J
(c) 11 J (d) 9 J

13. If $\vec{A}$ and $\vec{B}$ are two vectors and θ is the angle between them, then $\vec{A}.\vec{B} = 0$, when :

(a) $\vec{A} = 0$ (b) $\vec{B} = 0$
(c) θ = 90° (d) None of these

14. If $|\vec{A} \times \vec{B}| = 0$ and $\vec{B}.\vec{A} = -AB$, the angle between $\vec{A}$ and $\vec{B}$ is :

(a) 0° (b) 45°
(c) 90° (d) 180°

15. The resultant of three vectors, 3 units in east, 12 units in north and 4 units vertically upwards is :

(a) $\sqrt{24}$ units (b) 13 units
(c) $\sqrt{265}$ units (d) 19 units

16. The resultant of two forces $(\vec{A} + \vec{B})$ and $(\vec{A} - \vec{B})$ is a force $\sqrt{3A^2 + B^2}$. The angle between the two given forces is :

(a) π/4 (b) π/3
(c) π/2 (d) π

17. One of the rectangular components of a velocity of 60 kmph is 30 kmph. The other component will be :

(a) 30 kmph (b) $30\sqrt{3}$ kmph
(c) $30\sqrt{2}$ kmph (d) 0 kmph

18. The angle between *z*-axis and the vector, $\hat{i} + \hat{j} + \sqrt{2}\hat{k}$ is :

(a) 90° (b) 60°
(c) 45° (d) 30°

19. If $\vec{A} = 4\hat{i} - 2\hat{j} + 6\hat{k}$ and $\vec{B} = \hat{i} - 2\hat{j} - 3\hat{k}$, then the angle between $(\vec{A} + \vec{B})$ and *x*-axis is:

(a) $\cos^{-1}\left(\frac{3}{\sqrt{50}}\right)$ (b) $\cos^{-1}\left(\frac{4}{\sqrt{50}}\right)$
(c) $\cos^{-1}\left(\frac{5}{\sqrt{50}}\right)$ (d) $\cos^{-1}\left(\frac{12}{\sqrt{50}}\right)$

20. The X and Y components of force are 2N and –3N. The force is :

(a) $2\hat{i} - 3\hat{j}$ (b) $2\hat{i} + 3\hat{j}$
(c) $-2\hat{i} - 3\hat{j}$ (d) $3\hat{i} + 2\hat{j}$

21. The resultant of which of the following sets of forces can't be zero :

(a) 10, 20, 40 (b) 10, 10, 20
(c) 10, 20, 20 (d) 10, 10, 10

22. The resultant of two forces $(\vec{A} + \vec{B})$ and $(\vec{A} - \vec{B})$ is $\sqrt{A^2 + B^2}$, then the angle between these forces is :

(a) $\cos^{-1}\left[-\frac{(A^2 - B^2)}{(A^2 + B^2)}\right]$

(b) $\cos^{-1}\left[-\frac{(A^2 + B^2)}{(A^2 - B^2)}\right]$

(c) $\cos^{-1}\left[-\frac{(A^2 + B^2)}{2(A^2 - B^2)}\right]$

(d) $\cos^{-1}\left[-\frac{2(A^2 + B^2)}{2(A^2 - B^2)}\right]$

23. If the sum of the two unit vectors is also a unit vector, then the magnitude of their difference is :

(a) $\sqrt{2}$ (b) $\sqrt{3}$
(c) $\sqrt{4}$ (d) $\sqrt{7}$

24. A proton in a cyclotron changes its velocity from 30 km s^{-1} north to 40 km s^{-1} east in 20 s. The average acceleration during this time will be :

(a) 2.5 km s^{-2} at 37° E to S
(b) 2.5 km s^{-2} at 37° E to W
(c) 2.5 km s^{-2} at 37° N to S
(d) 2.5 km s^{-2} at 37° E to N

25. If $\vec{A} + \vec{B} = \vec{C}$ and $A = \sqrt{3}$, $B = \sqrt{3}$ and C = 3, then the angle between $\vec{A}$ and $\vec{B}$ is :

(a) 0° (b) 30°
(c) 60° (d) 90°

26. The resultant of two forces at right angles is 5N. When the angle between them is 120°, the resultant is N. Then the two forces are :

(a) $\sqrt{12}$ N, $\sqrt{13}$ N (b) $\sqrt{20}$ N, $\sqrt{5}$ N
(c) 3 N, 4 N (d) $\sqrt{40}$ N, $\sqrt{15}$ N

27. The resultant of two vectors of magnitude 2A and $\sqrt{2}$A acting at an angle θ is $\sqrt{10}$A. The value of angle θ is :

(a) 30° (b) 45°
(c) 60° (d) 90°

28. The angle between $(\hat{i} + 2\hat{j} + 2\hat{k})$ and $\hat{i}$ is :

(a) 0° (b) π/6
(c) π/3 (d) None of these

29. If $\vec{A} = 4\hat{i} + 6\hat{j}$ and $\vec{B} = 2\hat{i} + 3\hat{j}$, which of the following is correct ?

(a) $\vec{A} \times \vec{B} = 0$
(b) $\vec{A} \cdot \vec{B} = 24$
(c) $\dfrac{|\vec{A}|}{|\vec{B}|} = 0.5$
(d) $\vec{A}$ and $\vec{B}$ are anti parallel

30. If $\vec{A} \cdot \vec{B} = 0$ and $\vec{A} \times \vec{B} = 1$, then $\vec{A}$ and $\vec{B}$ are:

(a) perpendicular unit vectors
(b) parallel unit vectors
(c) parallel
(d) perpendicular

31. Given that $\vec{A} + \vec{B} + \vec{C}$, out of the three vectors, two are equal in magnitude and the magnitude of the third vector is $\sqrt{2}$ times that of either of the two. Then the angles between the vectors $\vec{A}$, $\vec{B}$ and $\vec{C}$ are :

(a) 45°, 45°, 90° (b) 90°, 135°, 135°
(c) 30°, 60°, 90° (d) 45°, 60°, 90°

32. If $\vec{r} = 4\hat{j}$ and $\vec{p} = 2\hat{i} + \hat{j} + \hat{k}$, the angular momentum is :

(a) $4\hat{i} - 8\hat{k}$ (b) $8\hat{i} - 4\hat{k}$
(c) $8\hat{j}$ (d) $9\hat{k}$

33. A force $\vec{F} = (2\hat{i} + 2\hat{j})$ N displaces a particle through $\vec{S} = (2\hat{i} + 2\hat{k})$ m in 16 s. The power produced by $\vec{F}$ is:

(a) 0.25 watt (b) 25 watt
(c) 225 watt (d) 450 watt

34. For what value of m, will $\vec{A} = 2\hat{i} + m\hat{j} + \hat{k}$ be perpendicular to $\vec{B} = 4\hat{i} - 2\hat{j} - \hat{k}$:

(a) 4 (b) 0
(c) 3 (d) 1

35. If momentum $\vec{p} = 2 \cos t\, \hat{i} + 2 \sin t\, 5\hat{j}$, then the angle between force $\vec{F}$ and momentum $\vec{p}$ of the particle is :

(a) 65° (b) 90°
(c) 150° (d) 180°

36. From the given figure, the ratio of tension T_1 and T_2 is :

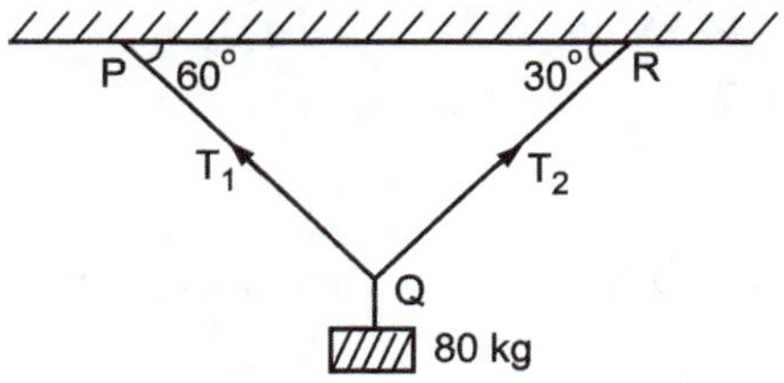

(a) 1 : 1 (b) 1 : $\sqrt{3}$
(c) $\sqrt{3}$: 1 (d) 1 : 3

37. The sum of the magnitudes of two vectors acting at a point is 16 N. The resultant of these forces is perpendicular to the smaller force which has a magnitude of 8 N. The value of the smaller force '*f*' will be (in magnitude)

(a) 2 N (b) 4 N
(c) 6 N (d) 7 N

38. The distance travelled by an object along the axis are given by $x = 3t^3$, $y = 2t^2 + 8t$ and $z = 6t - 5$. The initial velocity of the particle is :

(a) 20 units (b) 10 units
(c) 5 units (d) 13 units

39. From the given figure, three forces are acting along x, y and z axes of a cube. Then the resulting force is :

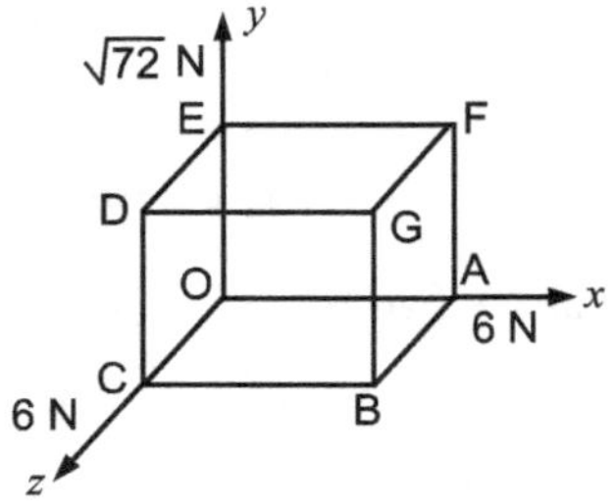

(a) 12 N along OD (b) 12 N along OF
(c) 18 N along OG (d) 12 N along OG

40. From the given figure, the magnitude of displacement vector $\vec{r}$ will be :

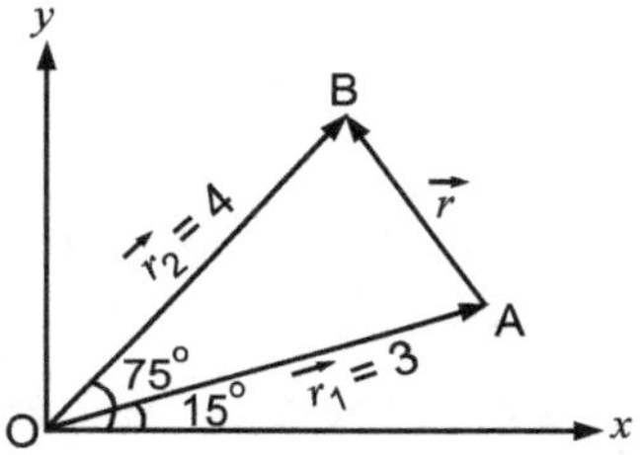

(a) $\sqrt{15}$ (b) 15
(c) $\sqrt{13}$ (d) 17

41. If $\vec{A} \times \vec{B} = \vec{B} \times \vec{A}$, then the angle between $\vec{A}$ and $\vec{B}$ is :

(a) π (b) $\pi/3$
(c) $\pi/2$ (d) $\pi/4$

42. A particle is moving eastwards with a velocity of 5 ms^{-1}. In 10 s, the velocity changes to 5 ms^{-1} northwards. The average acceleration in this time is :

(a) Zero
(b) $\frac{1}{\sqrt{2}}$ ms^{-2} towards N–W
(c) $\frac{1}{\sqrt{2}}$ ms^{-2} towards N–E
(d) $\frac{1}{2}$ ms^{-2} towards N

43. A boat which has speed of 5 km h^{-1} in still water crosses a river of width 1 km along the shortest possible path in 20 minutes. The velocity of the river water is :

(a) 7 km h^{-1} (b) 6 km h^{-1}
(c) 5 km h^{-1} (d) 4 km h^{-1}

44. The given vector $\vec{a}$ is rotated through an angle θ. Then the magnitude of change in vector will be :

(a) $2a \cos \theta/2$ (b) $2a \sin \theta/2$
(c) $2a \cos \theta$ (d) $2a \sin \theta$

45. Two bodies are fired horizontally with different velocities from the same height. Which will reach the ground first ?

(a) Both will reach simultaneously
(b) Faster one
(c) Slower one
(d) Can't be predicted

46. The time of flight of a projectile is related to its horizontal range by the equation $gT^2 = 2R$. The angle of projection is :

(a) 30° (b) 45°
(c) $\sin^{-1} 2$ (d) $\tan^{-1} 2$

47. The range of projectile when launched at an angle θ is same as when launched at angle 2θ. The value of θ is :

(a) 30° (b) 60°
(c) 15° (d) 45°

48. Two projectiles are fired at different angles with the same magnitude of velocity such that they have the same range. The angles which they have been projected with are :

(a) 35° and 75° (b) 10° and 50°
(c) 25° and 65° (d) 40° and 55°

49. A projectile is projected with the K.E. (K). Its range is R. It will have minimum K.E., after covering a horizontal distance equal to:

(a) 3R/4 (b) R/4
(c) R (d) R/2

50. A ball is projected from a point in air and having x and y components of displacement as $x = 6t$ and $y = 8t - 5t^2$. The velocity of projection is :

(a) 4 ms^{-1} (b) 6 ms^{-1}
(c) 8 ms^{-1} (d) 10 ms^{-1}

51. A projectile can have the same range R for two angles of projection. If t_1 and t_2 are the times of flights in the two cases, then $t_1.t_2$ will be equal to :

(a) $t_1.t_2 \propto R$ (b) $t_1.t_2 \propto \frac{1}{R}$

(c) $t_1.t_2 \propto \frac{1}{R^2}$ (d) $t_1.t_2 \propto R^2$

52. A body is projected horizontally from the top of a tower with initial velocity 18 ms^{-1}. It hits the ground at an angle 45°. The vertical component of velocity when it strikes the ground is :

(a) $9\sqrt{2}$ ms^{-1} (b) 9 ms^{-1}

(c) 18 ms^{-1} (d) $18\sqrt{2}$ ms^{-1}

53. Large number of bullets are fired in all directions with the same speed v. The maximum area covered by the bullets on the ground will be :

(a) $\frac{\pi v^2}{g^2}$ (b) $\frac{\pi v^2}{g}$

(c) $\left(\frac{\pi v}{g}\right)^2$ (d) $\frac{\pi^2 v^2}{g}$

54. A projectile is fired with speed 'u' making an angle θ with the horizontal. The potential energy of the projectile at the highest point of trajectory will be :

(a) $\frac{1}{2}mu^2$ (b) $\frac{1}{2}mu^2 \sin 2\theta$

(c) $\frac{1}{2}mu^2 \sin^2\theta$ (d) $\frac{1}{2}mu^2 \cos^2\theta$

55. The trajectory of a projectile as seen from another projectile is a :

(a) Circle (b) Parabola

(c) Straight line (d) Ellipse

56. The maximum height attained by the projectile is increased by 5%. Keeping the angle of projection constant, the percentage increase in the horizontal range will be :

(a) 20% (b) 15%

(c) 10% (d) 5%

57. A ball is projected from the ground with the speed of 10 ms^{-1} making an angle 30° with the horizontal. Another ball is simultaneously released from a point on the vertical line along the maximum height of the projectile. Both balls collide at the maximum height of the projectile. What was the initial height of the second ball ?

(a) 1.0 m (b) 2.0 m

(c) 2.25 m (d) 2.5 m

58. If the range is doubled than the maximum height of a projectile, then θ is :

(a) $\tan^{-1} 4$ (b) $\tan^{-1}\frac{1}{4}$

(c) $\tan^{-1} 1$ (d) $\tan^{-1} 2$

59. A body is projected with an initial velocity $(a\hat{i} + b\hat{j})$ ms^{-1}. If the range of the projectile is doubled, the maximum height reached by it :

(a) $a = 2b$ (b) $b = 4a$

(c) $b = 2a$ (d) $b = a$

60. A rifle fires a bullet with a muzzle speed of 400 ms^{-1} at a small target 400 m away on the ground. The height above the target at which the barrel of the rifle must be aimed for the bullet to hit the target is :

(a) 0.5 m (b) 1 m

(c) 5 m (d) 10 m

61. A fighter plane moves horizontally with a speed of 500 ms^{-1} and a bomb released from it strikes the ground in 10 s. The angle at which the bomb will strike the ground will be ...... ($\because$ g = 10 ms^{-2}) :

(a) $\tan^{-1}\left(\frac{1}{5}\right)$ (b) $\tan\left(\frac{1}{5}\right)$

(c) $\tan^{-1}(1)$ (d) $\tan^{-1}(5)$

62. A body is projected with an initial velocity of $(8\hat{i} + 6\hat{j})$ ms^{-1}. The horizontal range will be :

(a) 9.6 m (b) 14 m

(c) 50 m (d) 74 m

63. Two bodies thrown from the same point at angles 30° and 60° with the horizontal attain the same height. The ratio of their initial velocities is :

(a) 1 : 1 (b) 2 : 1
(c) $1 : \sqrt{3}$ (d) $\sqrt{3} : 1$

64. The projectile is thrown at an angle β with the vertical. It reaches a maximum height H. The time taken to reach the highest point of its path is :

(a) $\sqrt{\frac{H}{g}}$ (b) $\sqrt{\frac{2H}{g}}$
(c) $\sqrt{\frac{H}{2g}}$ (d) $\sqrt{\frac{2H}{g\cos\beta}}$

65. The equation of the projectile is $y = \sqrt{3}x - \frac{gx^2}{2}$. The angle of projection is :

(a) $\tan\theta = \frac{1}{\sqrt{3}}$ (b) $\tan\theta = \sqrt{3}$
(c) π/2 (d) Zero

66. An aeroplane flying horizontally with a speed of 360 km h^{-1} releases a bomb at a height of 490 m from the ground. The bomb will strike the ground in :

(a) 8.2 s (b) 9.2 s
(c) 10 s (d) 10.2 s

67. A particle moves along a parabolic path $y = ax^2$ in such a way that the x-component of velocity remains the same, say c. The acceleration of the particle is :

(a) $ac\hat{k}$ (b) $2ac^2\hat{j}$
(c) $ac^2\hat{k}$ (d) $a^2c\hat{k}$

68. A tennis ball rolls-off the top of a stair-case with a horizontal velocity u ms^{-1}. If the steps are b metre wide and h metre high, the ball will hit the edge of the nth step when :

(a) $n = \frac{2hu}{gb^2}$ (b) $n = \frac{2hu^2}{gb^2}$
(c) $n = \frac{2hu^2}{gb}$ (d) $n = \frac{hu^2}{gb^2}$

69. A marble ball projected horizontally from the top of a table falls at a distance x from the edge of the table. If h is the height of table, then the velocity of projection is :

(a) $gx + h$ (b) ghx
(c) $x \cdot \sqrt{\frac{g}{2h}}$ (d) $h \cdot \sqrt{\frac{g}{2x}}$

70. Two buildings are 40 m apart. With what speed must a ball be thrown horizontally from a window 145 m above the ground in one building so that it will enter a window 22.5 m from the ground of the other building ?

(a) 5 ms^{-1} (b) 8 ms^{-1}
(c) 10 ms^{-1} (d) 16 ms^{-1}

71. A child can jump a maximum horizontal distance 20 m, then the velocity of the child is :

(a) 10 ms^{-1} (b) 14 ms^{-1}
(c) 20 ms^{-1} (d) 24 ms^{-1}

72. A particle starts from the origin of the co-ordinate system at time $t = 0$, and moves in x–y plane with a constant acceleration α in the y-direction. Its equation of motion is $y = \beta x^2$. Its velocity component in the x-direction is :

(a) Variable (b) $\sqrt{\frac{2\alpha}{\beta}}$
(c) $\frac{\alpha}{2\beta}$ (d) $\sqrt{\frac{\alpha}{2\beta}}$

73. A bullet is fired horizontally with a velocity of 80 ms^{-1}. During the first second :

(a) it will fall 9.8 m (b) it will fall $\frac{80}{9.8}$ m
(c) it will not fall at all (d) it will fall 4.9 m

74. For a projectile, the angle of projection is 30°, then how many times is the horizontal range larger than the maximum height ?

(a) 2 (b) 3
(c) $3\sqrt{4}$ (d) $4\sqrt{3}$

75. The kinetic energy of a projectile at the highest point is half of the initial kinetic energy. The angle of projection with the horizontal will be :

(a) 30° (b) 45°
(c) 60° (d) 90°

76. For a projectile, the components of displacement x and y vary with the time in seconds as

$x = 10\sqrt{3}.t$ and $y = 10t - t^2$

The maximum height attained by the ball is :

(a) 100 m (b) 75 m
(c) 50 m (d) 25 m

77. A body P is thrown at an angle of 30° to the horizontal from point 'A'. At the same time, another body is projected from point 'B' vertically upwards, below the highest point. At the highest point 'C', they collide. Then v_2 / v_1 will be :

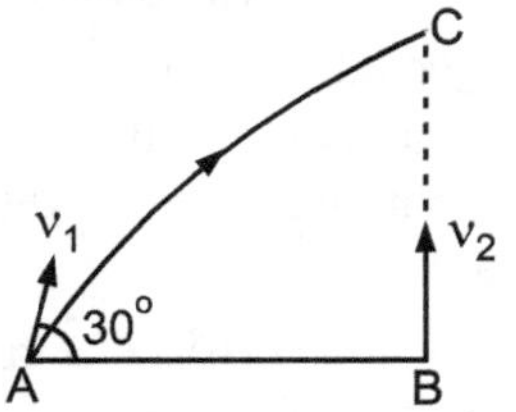

(a) 1 (b) 2
(c) 1/2 (d) 4

78. For a projectile, the horizontal range is $\frac{\sqrt{3}v^2}{2g}$ and vertical range is $\frac{v^2}{8g}$. The angle of projection will be :

(a) 15° (b) 30°
(c) 45° (d) 60°

79. The trajectories of two projectiles are shown in the following figure. If T_1 and T_2 are the time periods and u_1 and u_2 are their speeds of projection, then :

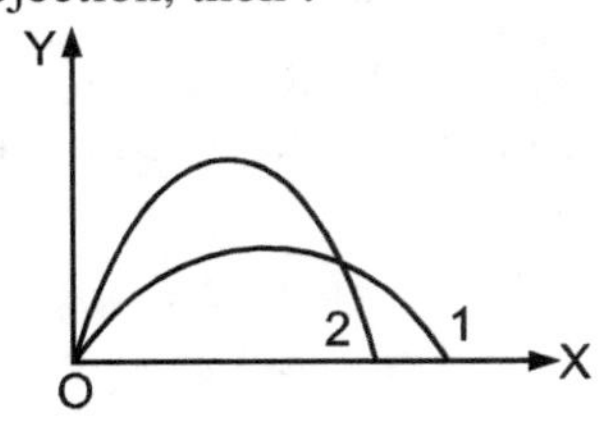

(a) $T_2 > T_1$ (b) $T_1 = T_2$
(c) $u_1 > u_2$ (d) $u_1 < u_2$

80. An aeroplane diving at an angle of 53° with the vertical releases a projectile at an altitude of 730 m. The projectile hits the ground 5 seconds after being released. The speed of the aeroplane is :

(a) 282 ms^{-1} (b) 202 ms^{-1}
(c) 182 ms^{-1} (d) 102 ms^{-1}

81. A particle is projected from point A with the velocity at an angle 45° with the horizontal as shown in the following figure. It strikes the plane BC at right angles. The velocity of the particle at the time of collision is :

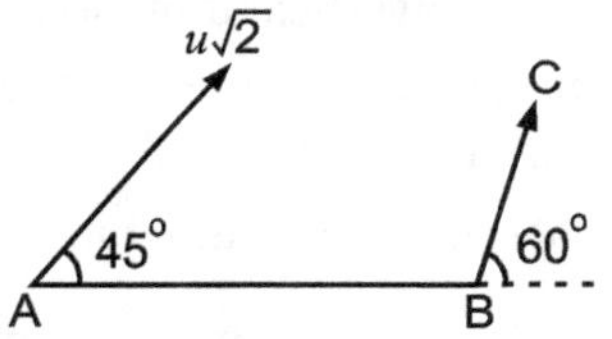

(a) $\frac{\sqrt{3}u}{2}$ (b) $\frac{u}{2}$
(c) $\frac{2u}{\sqrt{3}}$ (d) u

82. A frog finds that he can jump a maximum horizontal distance of 1m. With what speed can he travel along the path, if he spends a negligible time on the ground ?

(a) 2.21 ms^{-1} (b) 3.13 ms^{-1}
(c) 4.42 ms^{-1} (d) 9.8 ms^{-1}

83. The time taken by the projectile to reach from A to B is t, then distance AB is equal to :

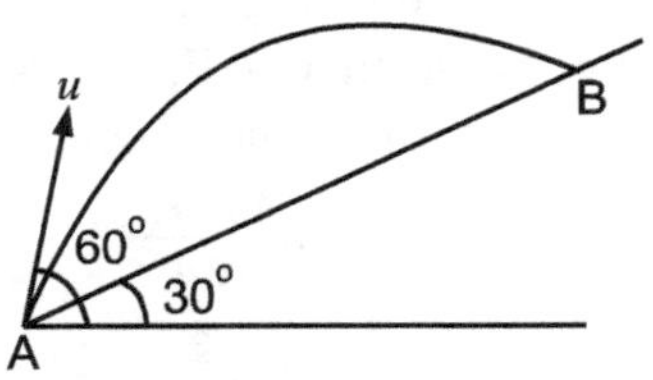

(a) $2ut$ (b) $\sqrt{3}\,ut$
(c) $\frac{\sqrt{3}}{2}ut$ (d) $\frac{ut}{\sqrt{3}}$

84. Two fixed frictionless inclined planes making angles 30° and 60° with the vertical are shown in the figure. Two blocks A and B are placed on the two planes. What is the relative vertical acceleration of A w.r.t. B ?

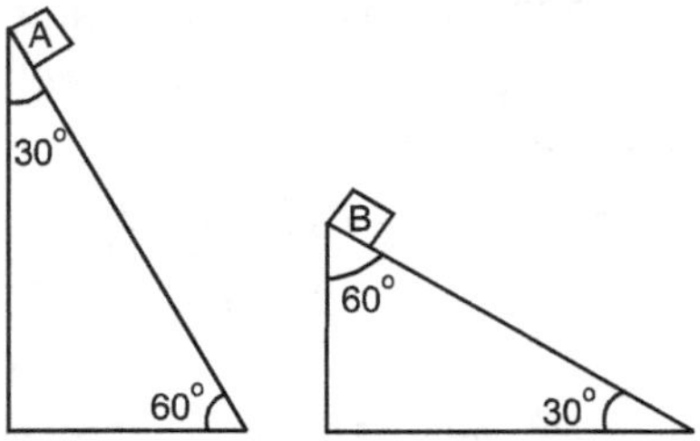

(a) 4.9 ms^{-2} in the horizontal direction
(b) 9.8 ms^{-2} in the vertical direction
(c) Zero
(d) 4.9 ms^{-2} in the vertical direction.

85. A particle of mass m is projected at an angle θ with the x-axis with an initial velocity v_0 in the plane as shown in the figure. At time $t = \frac{v_0 \sin\theta}{g}$, the angular momentum of the particle is :

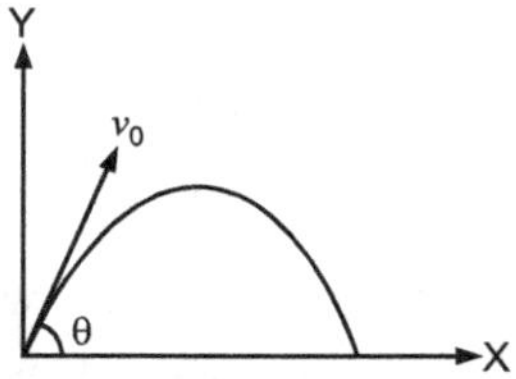

(a) $-mg\, v_0 t^2 \cos\theta\, \hat{j}$
(b) $-mg\, v_0 t \cos\theta\, \hat{k}$
(c) $-mg\, v_0 t^2 \cos\theta\, \hat{k}$
(d) $\frac{1}{2} mg\, v_0 t^2 \cos\theta\, \hat{i}$

86. A particle is projected at 60° to the horizontal with an energy E, the K.E and potential energy at the highest point are :
(a) $\left(\frac{E}{2}, \frac{E}{2}\right)$ (b) $\left(\frac{3E}{4}, \frac{E}{4}\right)$
(c) (E, 0) (d) $\left(\frac{E}{4}, \frac{3E}{4}\right)$

87. A projectile is thrown in the upward direction making an angle of 60° with the velocity of 147 ms^{-1}. Then the time after which its inclination with the horizontal is 45°, will be :
(a) 15 s (b) 10.98 s
(c) 5.49 s (d) 2.745 s

88. The equations of projectile are given by $x = 36t$ m and $2y = 90\,t - 9.8t^2$ m. The angle of projection is :
(a) $\sin^{-1}(4/5)$ (b) $\sin^{-1}(3/5)$
(c) $\sin^{-1}(4/3)$ (d) $\sin^{-1}(3/4)$

89. Two stones are projected with the same speed but make different angles with the horizontal. Their horizontal ranges are equal. The angle of projection of one stone is π/3 and the maximum height reached by it is 102 m. Then the maximum height reached by the other stone will be :
(a) 336 m (b) 224 m
(c) 56 m (d) 34 m

90. A ball is projected from the ground at an angle θ with the horizontal. After 1 s, it moves horizontally. The velocity of projection will be :
(a) $10\sqrt{3}$ ms^{-1} (b) $20\sqrt{3}$ ms^{-1}
(c) $10\sqrt{5}$ ms^{-1} (d) $20\sqrt{2}$ ms^{-1}

91. A body is projected vertically upwards. The time corresponding to height 'h' while ascending and descending are t_1 and t_2 respectively. Then the velocity of projection is :

(∵ g = Acceleration due to gravity)

(a) $g\frac{\sqrt{t_1 \cdot t_2}}{2}$ (b) $\frac{g(t_1 + t_2)}{2}$
(c) $g\, t_1 + t_2$ (d) $\frac{t_1 . t_2}{(t_1 + t_2)}$

92. A projectile is thrown with an initial velocity of $(a\hat{i} + b\hat{j})$ ms^{-1}. If the range of the projectile is doubled, the maximum height reached by it :
(a) $a = 2b$ (b) $b = 4a$
(c) $b = 2a$ (d) $b = a$

93. A shell on striking the ground burst and its fragments fly in all possible directions with speed upto 20 ms^{-1}. The time duration for which a person standing at a distance of $20\sqrt{3}$ m away from it is in danger will be :

(a) $2\sqrt{3}$ s (b) $2(\sqrt{3}-1)$ s

(c) 2 s (d) $\sqrt{3}$ s

94. A shell is fired from a canon with a velocity v at an angle θ with the horizontal. At the highest point, it explodes into two parts of equal masses. One of the pieces retraces its path to the canon. The speed of other piece just after explosion is :

(a) $3v \cos\theta$ (b) $2v\cos\theta$

(c) $\frac{3}{2}v\cos\theta$ (d) $\frac{\sqrt{3}}{2}v\cos\theta$

95. Two stones are projected with the same velocity in magnitude but make different angles with the horizontal. Their ranges are equal. If the angle of projection of one is π/3 and the maximum height is y_1, then the maximum height of the other will be :

(a) $3y_1$ (b) $2y_1$

(c) $\frac{y_1}{2}$ (d) $\frac{y_1}{3}$

96. From a tower, two bodies are projected horizontally with the velocities 10 ms^{-1} and 20 ms^{-1}. They hit the ground in t_1 and t_2 seconds. Then :

(a) $t_1 = t_2$ (b) $t_1 = 2t_2$

(c) $t_2 = 2t_1$ (d) $t_1 = \sqrt{2}t_2$

97. A projectile is fired so as to land at a horizontal distance 1.0 km, but at the maximum height, it explodes in two equal parts. One of them falls vertically down with initial speed zero. At what distance from the launching pad would the other part land ?

(a) 1.0 km (b) 1.2 km

(c) 1.5 km (d) 2.5 km

98. A particle of mass 'm' is projected with a velocity v at an angle of 45° with the horizontal. When the particle is at its maximum height, the magnitude of its angular momentum about the projection is :

(a) Zero (b) $\frac{mv^3}{4\sqrt{2}g}$

(c) $\frac{mv^2}{\sqrt{2}g}$ (d) $m\cdot\frac{mv^2}{\sqrt{2gh^3}}$

99. A particle having a mass 0.5 kg is projected under gravity with a speed of 98 ms^{-1} at an angle of 60°. The magnitude of the change in momentum in kg ms^{-1} of the particle after 10 s is :

(a) 490 (b) 98

(c) 49 (d) 0.5

100. A ball of mass 'm' is thrown vertically upwards. Another ball of mass $2m$ is thrown at an angle θ with the vertical. Both of them stay in air for the same period of time. The heights attained by the two balls are in the ratio of :

(a) 2 : 1 (b) cos θ : 1

(c) 1 : cos θ (d) 1 : 1

101. An aeroplane is flying horizontally with a velocity of 216 kmh^{-1} and at a height of 1960 m. When it is vertically above a point A on the ground, a bomb is released from it. The bomb strikes the ground at point B. The distance AB is :

(a) 1200 m (b) 0.33 km

(c) 3.33 km (d) 33 km

102. The ratio of velocities at points A, B and C in vertical circular motion is :

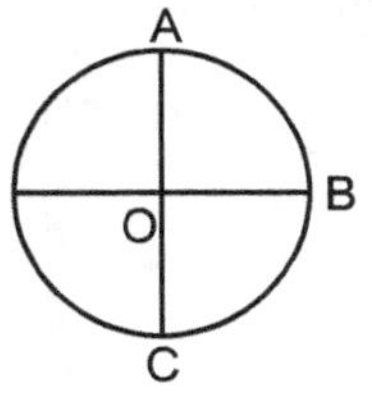

(a) 1 : 2 : 3 (b) 1 : 3 : 5

(c) 1 : 9 : 25 (d) $1:\sqrt{3}:\sqrt{5}$

103. The diameter of a solid disc is 0.5 m and its mass is 16 kg. The torque required to increase its angular velocity from zero to 120 rotations per minute in 8 s will be :

(a) $\frac{\pi}{2}$ Nm (b) π Nm

(c) $\frac{\pi}{4}$ Nm (d) $\frac{\pi}{8}$ Nm

104. The hour hand and the minute hand of a clock coincide at every :

(a) 1 hour (b) 12 hours

(c) $\frac{12}{11}$ hours (d) $\frac{12}{13}$ hours

105. The maximum speed at which a car can take a round of a curve of 36 m radius on a leveled road without skidding is .... ($\mu = 0.4$) :

(a) 4 ms^{-1} (b) 12 ms^{-1}

(c) 15 ms^{-1} (d) 20 ms^{-1}

106. The angular speed of a car increases from 600 rpm to 1200 rpm in 10 s. The angular acceleration of the car is :

(a) 600 rad s^{-2} (b) 60 rad s^{-2}

(c) 60 π rad s^{-2} (d) 2 π rad s^{-2}

107. The speed of revolution of a particle going around a circle is doubled and its angular speed is halved. Then centripetal acceleration will be :

(a) halved (b) doubled

(c) same (d) 4 times

108. A particle is moving along a circular path of radius 6 m with a uniform speed of 8 ms^{-1}. The average acceleration when the particle completes one half of revolution is :

(a) $\frac{32}{3}$ ms^{-2} (b) $\frac{4}{3}$ ms^{-2}

(c) $\frac{64}{3\pi}$ ms^{-2} (d) $\frac{32}{3\pi}$ ms^{-2}

109. A wheel is subjected to uniform angular acceleration about its axis. Initially, its angular velocity is zero. In the first two seconds, it rotates through an angle θ_1, and in the next two seconds, it rotates through an angle θ_2. Then θ_2/θ_1 is :

(a) 1 (b) 2

(c) 3 (d) 4

110. A car is moving with the speed 30 ms^{-1} on a circular path of radius 500 m. Its speed is increasing at the rate of 2 ms^{-2}. The acceleration of car is :

(a) 1.8 ms^{-2} (b) 2 ms^{-2}

(c) 2.7 ms^{-2} (d) 3 ms^{-2}

111. A stone is tied at one end of a 5 m long string and whirled in a vertical circle. The minimum speed required to just cross the top-most position is :

(a) 5 ms^{-1} (b) 7 ms^{-1}

(c) 57 ms^{-1} (d) 75 ms^{-1}

112. A particle of mass m is moving in a circular path of constant radius 'r' such that its centripetal acceleration a_c is varying with time as $a_c = k^2rt^4$, where k is a constant. The power delivered to the particle by the forces acting on it is :

(a) Zero (b) $mk^2r^2t^2$

(c) $\frac{1}{3}mk^2r^2t^2$ (d) $2\,mk^2r^2t^3$

113. A body of mass 1 kg is rotating in a vertical circle of radius 1 m. What will be the difference in its kinetic energy at the top and bottom of the circle ?

($\because$ g = 10 ms^{-2})

(a) 10 J (b) 20 J

(c) 30 J (d) 50 J

114. A mass of 2 kg is whirled in a horizontal circle by means of a string at an initial speed of 5 rpm. Keeping the radius constant, the tension in the string is doubled. The new speed is nearly :

(a) 7 rpm (b) 14 rpm

(c) 10 rpm (d) 20 rpm

115. A mass of 2.9 kg is suspended from a string of length 50 cm and is at rest. Another body of mass 0.1 kg sticks to it. The tension in the string when it makes an angle of 60° with the vertical is :

(a) 130 N (b) 140 N
(c) 145 N (d) 135 N

116. A gramophone record is revolving with an angular velocity ω. A coin is placed at a distance 'R' from the centre of the record. The static coefficient of friction is μ. The coin will revolve with the record if :

(a) $R = \frac{\mu g}{\omega^2}$ (b) $R < \frac{\mu g}{\omega^2}$
(c) $T' = \sqrt{\frac{3}{2}}T$ (d) $T' = \frac{3}{2}T$

117. Certain neutron stars are believed to be rotating about 2 rad s^{-1}. If such a star has a radius of 20 km, the acceleration of an object on the equator of the star will be :

(a) 2×10^4 ms^{-2} (b) 120×10^3 ms^{-2}
(c) 8×10^5 ms^{-2} (d) 4×10^5 ms^{-2}

118. A body tied to a string of length 'l' is revolved in a vertical circle with minimum velocity. When the body reaches the uppermost point, the string breaks and the body moves under the influence of gravitational field of the earth along the parabollic path. The horizontal range AC of the body will be :

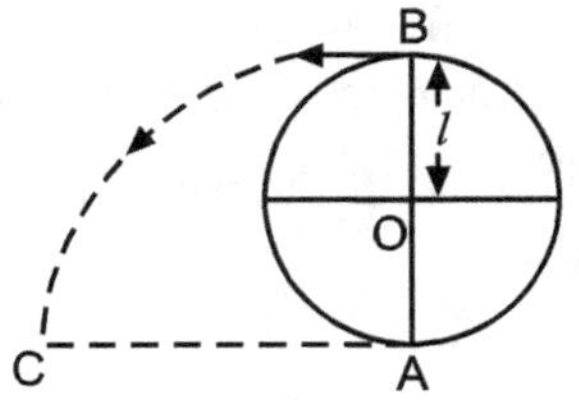

(a) $2l$ (b) $\sqrt{2}l$
(c) l (d) $2\sqrt{2}l$

119. To enable a particle describe a circular path, what should be the angle between its velocity and acceleration ?

(a) 0° (b) 45°
(c) 90° (d) 180°

120. For a car taking a turn on a horizontal surface, the normal reaction of the road on the inner and outer wheels is N_1 and N_2 respectively, then :

(a) $N_1 < N_2$ (b) $N_1 > N_2$
(c) $N_1 = N_2$ (d) None of these

121. A body slides down a frictionless track which ends in a circular loop of diameter D. Then the minimum height 'h' of the body in terms of D so that it may just complete the loop :

(a) $h = \frac{5}{2}D$ (b) $h = \frac{3}{2}D$
(c) $h = \frac{5}{4}D$ (d) $h = 2D$

122. For a dry road, the coefficient of friction is μ. The maximum speed of a car along a circular path is 10 ms^{-1}. If the road becomes wet, the coefficient of friction becomes μ/2, then the maximum permitted speed will be :

(a) 5 ms^{-1} (b) 10 ms^{-1}
(c) $10\sqrt{2}$ ms^{-1} (d) $5\sqrt{2}$ ms^{-1}

123. Two identical bodies A and B are attached at mid point and at one end of a string respectively. The particle moves in concentric circles with the other end of the string as a common centre. The string always remains straight. The ratio of the tensions T_1 and T_2 in the two parts of the string will be :

(a) 1 : 2 (b) 3 : 2
(c) 2 : 3 (d) 1 : 1

124. A particle moves along a circular path of radius r with uniform speed v. The angle described by the particle in one second is given by :

(a) r/v (b) v^2r
(c) v/r^2 (d) v/r

125. The radius of circular path of a particle is doubled, but its frequency of rotation remains unchanged. If the initial centripetal force is F, then the final value of centripetal force will be :

(a) F/2 (b) F
(c) 2F (d) 4F

126. The slope of a smooth banked horizontal road is ρ. If the radius of curvature is 'r', the maximum velocity with which a car can negotiate the curve is given by :

(a) ρrg (b) $\rho/r.g$

(c) $(\rho rg)^{-1}$ (d) $(\rho rg)^{1/2}$

127. The angular speed of the minute hand of a wall clock is :

(a) $\frac{\pi}{1800}$ rad.s^{-1} (b) $\frac{2\pi}{1800}$ rad.s^{-1}

(c) $\frac{\pi}{21600}$ rad.s^{-1} (d) $\frac{2\pi}{2160}$ rad.s^{-1}

128. The angular speed of the hour hand of a clock will be :

(a) $\frac{\pi}{1800}$ rad.s^{-1} (b) $\frac{2\pi}{1800}$ rad.s^{-1}

(c) $\frac{\pi}{21600}$ rad.s^{-1} (d) $\frac{2\pi}{2160}$ rad.s^{-1}

129. The angular speed of the second hand of a clock is :

(a) $\frac{2\pi}{180}$ rad.s^{-1}. (b) $\frac{2\pi}{1800}$ rad.s^{-1}.

(c) $\frac{\pi}{30}$ rad.s^{-1}. (d) $\frac{2\pi}{30}$ rad.s^{-1}.

130. A body of mass m is moving in a horizontal circular path of radius 'r' under a centripetal force of k/r^2. The K.E. of the particle is :

(a) k/r (b) k^2/r

(c) k/r^2 (d) $k/2r$

131. From the given figure, the ends P and Q of an unstrechable string move downwards with uniform speed 'u', Pulleys A and B are fixed. The speed with which the mass 'M' moves upwards will be :

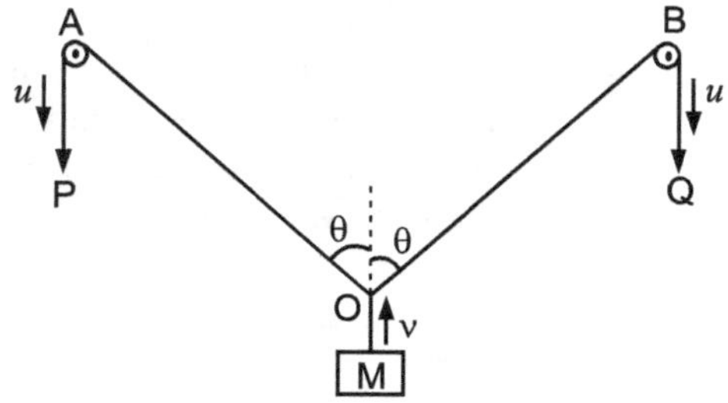

(a) $-u\cos\theta$ (b) $-\frac{\cos\theta}{u}$

(c) $-\frac{u}{\cos\theta}$ (d) $-\frac{1}{u\cos\theta}$

132. A particle has initial velocity 9 ms^{-1} due east and a constant acceleration of 2 ms^{-2} due west. The distance covered by the particle in the 5th second of its motion is :

(a) 0 (b) 2 m

(c) 0.5 m (d) None of these.

133. A cricket ball is thrown up with a speed of 19.6 ms^{-1}. The maximum height it can reach is :

(a) 9.8 m (b) 19.6 m

(c) 29.4 m (d) 39.2 m

134. A particle has an initial velocity $3\hat{i} + 4\hat{j}$ and an acceleration of $0.4\hat{i} + 0.3\hat{j}$. Its speed after 10 seconds is :

(a) 10 units (b) $7\sqrt{2}$ units

(c) 7 units (d) 8.5 units

135. A particle is moving with the velocity $\vec{v} = k(y\hat{i} + x\hat{j})$ where k is a constant. The general equation for its path is :

(a) $y = x^2$ + constant

(b) $y^2 = x$ + constant

(c) xy = constant

(d) $y^2 = x^2$ + constant

136. A force $\vec{F} = 6\hat{i} + 2\hat{j} - 3\hat{k}$ acts on a particle and produces a displacement of $\vec{S} = 2\hat{i} - 3\hat{j} + x\hat{k}$. If the work done is zero, the value of x is :

(a) 1/2 (b) 2

(c) 6 (d) 3

137. An object of mass 3 kg is at rest. Now a force of $\vec{F} = 6t^2.\hat{i} + 4t.\hat{j}$ is applied on the object. Then the velocity of the object at $t = 3$ s is :

(a) $18\hat{i} + 3\hat{j}$ (b) $18\hat{i} + 6\hat{j}$

(c) $3\hat{i} + 18\hat{j}$ (d) $18\hat{i} + 4\hat{j}$

138. Two particles having mass M and m are moving in a circular path of radius R and r. If their time periods are the same, then the ratio of their angular velocities will be :

(a) r/R (b) R/r
(c) 1 (d) $\sqrt{R/r}$

139. If velocity of a projectile is given as $v = 2\hat{i} + 3\hat{j}$ ms^{-1}, then the range is :

(a) 1.2 m (b) 2.4 m
(c) 0.6 m (d) 3.6 m

140. A boy on a cycle pedals around a circle of 20 m radius at a speed of 20 ms^{-1}. The combined mass of the boy and cycle make an angle with the vertical so that he may not fall is : ($\because$ g = 10 ms^{-2})

(a) 60.25° (b) 63.90°
(c) 26.12° (d) 30°

141. A car is moving in a circular horizontal track of radius 10 m with a constant speed of 10 ms^{-1}. A plumb bob is suspended from the roof of the car by a light rigid rod of length 1 m. The angle made by the rod with the track is :

(a) Zero (b) 30°
(c) 45° (d) 60°

142. An electric fan has blades of length 30 cm from the axis of rotation. If the fan is rotating at 120 rpm, the acceleration of a point on the tip of the blade is :

(a) 16000 ms^{-2} (b) 47.4 ms^{-2}
(c) 23.7 ms^{-2} (d) 50.5 ms^{-2}

COMPREHENSION BASED QUESTIONS

Passage - I

A motor cyclist is riding North in still air at 36 kmh^{-1}. The wind starts blowing west wards with velocity 18 km h^{-1}.

143. The direction of apparent velocity of air felt by the rider is :

(a) tan^{-1} (1/2) West of North
(b) tan^{-1} (1/2) North of West
(c) tan^{-1} (1/2) East of North
(d) tan^{-1} (1/2) North of East

144. The distance covered by a motor cyclist in 10 min, when the velocity of wind becomes double but due west, will be :

(a) 1.8 km (b) 2.4 km
(c) 3.6 km (d) 8.5 km

Passage - II

A shot is fired with the velocity of 200 ms^{-1} in a direction making an angle θ = 30° with the vertical.

145. The time taken by the projectile to remain in air is :

(a) 30.30 s (b) 32.32 s
(c) 35.35 s (d) 38.83 s

146. The maximum height attained by the shot is

(a) 1530.5 m (b) 153.05 m
(c) 15.3 m (d) 32 m

147. The horizontal range covered by the fired shot is

(a) 3535 m (b) 1530.5 m
(c) 15.3 m (d) 353.3 m

Passage - III

When a body moves along a circular path, the required centripetal force should be equal to mv^2/r which is provided by the force of friction between the road and tyres of the moving body. To avoid skidding, the speed of the moving body should be $\leq \sqrt{urg}$ and the dependency of friction can be avoided by banking the road suitably by raising the outer edge of road. For safe speed, the outer edge is raised to $\sqrt{\tan \theta . rg}$. The speed limit depends on the mass of the moving body.

Data :

Mass of body	= 800 kg
Wheel base	= 1.1 m
Banking angle	= 30°
Radius of curved road	= 200 m
C.G. point	= 50 cm
μ	= 0.2
g	= 9.8 ms^{-2}

148. To avoid skidding on horizontal curved road, the safe speed is :

(a) 1.98 ms^{-1} (b) 9.8 ms^{-1}
(c) 19.8 ms^{-1} (d) 10 ms^{-1}

149. The safe speed on banked road is :

(a) 9.8 ms^{-1} (b) 19.6 ms^{-1}
(c) 29.4 ms^{-1} (d) 33.6 ms^{-1}

150. At this safe speed, the frictional force is :

(a) Outwards (b) Inwards
(c) Cannot say (d) Zero

ASSERTION AND REASON

Directions for Q. 152 to 158 : In the following questions, statement-I is Assertion followed by statement-II as Reason. For answering a question, you are required to choose the correct one out of the given four options.

A. Statements-I and II, both are true and statement-II is the correct explanation of statement-I.

B. Statement-I and II, both are true and statement-II is not the correct explanation of statement-I.

C. Statement-I is true, but statement-II is false.

D. Statement-I and statement-II both are false.

151. (I) If two balls are released simultaneously from a certain height, one is allowed to fall freely and the other thrown horizontally with some velocity, then both the balls hit the ground together.

(II) In both the cases, the velocity of the balls along the vertical is zero.

(a) A (b) B
(c) C (d) D

152. (I) To keep a body moving with a uniform velocity along a straight line, no external force is required.

(II) According to Newton's First law of motion, a moving body comes to rest only due to the presence of frictional force.

(a) A (b) B
(c) C (d) D

153. (I) It is difficult to move a cycle along the road with its brakes on.

(II) Sliding friction is greater than rolling friction.

(a) A (b) B
(c) C (d) D

154. (I) On a rainy day, it is difficult to drive a car at high speed.

(II) The value of coefficient of friction is lowered due to wetting of the surface.

(a) A (b) B
(c) C (d) D

155. (I) When a stone is moved along a circular path, the centripetal force is balanced by the centrifugal force on it.

(II) It is in accordance with Newton's law of motion.

(a) A (b) B
(c) C (d) D

156. (I) While turning, cyclist lean towards the centre of the curve, while the man sitting in the car leans outwards of the curve.

(II) An acceleration is acting towards the centre of the curve.

(a) A (b) B
(c) C (d) D

157. (I) When a stone tied to a string is revolved along a vertical circle, the string has maximum tendency to break, when the stone is at the lowest point.

(II) Because the tension in the string is maximum at the lowest point.

(a) A (b) B
(c) C (d) D

158. (I) A freely falling body is in the state of weightlessness.

(II) A body becomes conscious about its weight, only when it is opposed.

(a) A (b) B
(c) C (d) D

159. If the radius vector is $-2\hat{i} + \hat{j} + \hat{k}$ and linear momentum is $2\hat{i} + 3\hat{j} - \hat{k}$, then the angular momentum is :

(a) $2\hat{i} + 4\hat{k}$ (b) $-4\hat{i} - 8\hat{k}$

(c) $2\hat{i} - 4\hat{j} + 2\hat{k}$ (d) $4\hat{i} - 8\hat{j}$

160. The resultant of two forces 3P and 2P is R. If the first force is doubled, then the resultant is also doubled. The angle between the two forces is :

(a) 90° (b) 180°

(c) 60° (d) 120°

161. A motor car is moving with the speed 30 ms^{-1} in a circular path of radius 500 m. Its speed is increasing at the rate of 2 ms^{-2}. The resultant acceleration will be :

(a) 2.5 ms^{-2} (b) 2.7 ms^{-2}

(c) 2 ms^{-2} (d) 4.5 ms^{-2}

162. In case of projectile motion of two projectiles A and B projected with the same speed at an angle 15° and 75° respectively to the horizontal, then :

(a) $H_A > H_B$ (b) $H_A < H_B$

(c) $T_A > T_B$ (d) $T_A < T_B$

163. A small sphere is hung by a string fixed to a wall. The sphere is pushed away from the wall by a stick. The force acting on it is shown in the given figure.

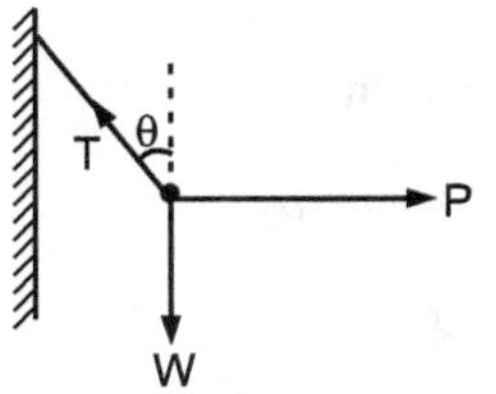

Which of the following is wrong ?

(a) $P = W \tan\theta$ (b) $T^2 = P^2 + W^2$

(c) $\vec{T} + \vec{P} + \vec{W} = 0$ (d) $T = P + W$

164. The X and Y components of $\vec{A}$ have numerical values 6 and 6 respectively and that of $(\vec{A} + \vec{B})$ have 10 and 9. The numerical value of $\vec{B}$ will be :

(a) 2 (b) 3

(c) 4 (d) 5

165. A frictionless track ABCDE ends in a circular loop of radius R as in the given figure. A body slides down the track from point A, which is at a height h = 5 cm.

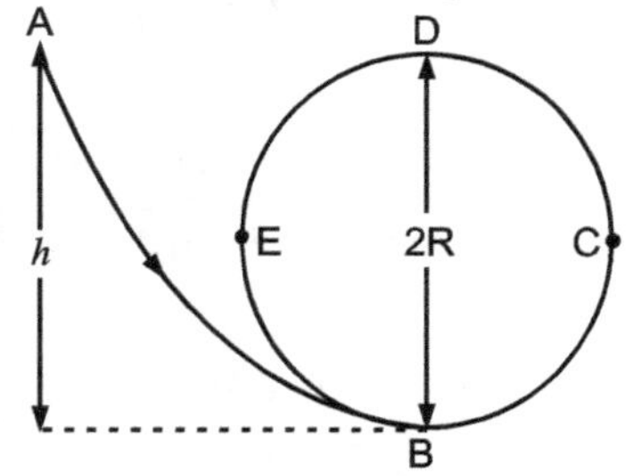

Maximum value of R for the body to successfully complete the loop is :

(a) 2 cm (b) 5 cm

(c) $\frac{15}{4}$ cm (d) $\frac{10}{3}$ cm

166. A point of application of a force $\vec{F} = 5\hat{i} - 3\hat{j} + 2\hat{k}$ is moved from $\vec{r_1} = 2\hat{i} + 7\hat{j} + 4\hat{k}$ or $\vec{r_2} = -5\hat{i} + 7\hat{j} + 3\hat{k}$, then the work done is :

(a) 22 units (b) –22 units

(c) 33 units (d) –33 units

167. A particle is making uniform circular motion with angular momentum J. If its K.E. is made half, then its angular momentum will be :

(a) 2 J (b) 4 J

(c) $\frac{1}{2}$ J (d) $\frac{1}{4}$ J

168. When a body is moving with a constant speed in a horizontal circle, which of the following remains constant ?

(a) Velocity (b) Acceleration

(c) Centripetal force (d) Kinetic energy

169. When water and Hg are rotated in a test tube, then :

(a) Water will be forced to the outer part

(b) Hg will be forced to outer part

(c) Both will be thoroughly mixed up

(d) Hg will be at the top and water at the bottom.

170. When a ceiling fan is switched off, its angular velocity reduces by 50% while it makes 36 rotations. How many more rotations will it make before coming to rest ? (Assume uniform angular retardation)

(a) 36 (b) 48

(c) 18 (d) 12

171. Given that $\vec{A} + \vec{B} = \vec{C}$, $|\vec{A}| = |\vec{C}|$ and $\vec{C} \perp \vec{A}$. Then the angle between $\vec{A}$ and $\vec{B}$ is :

(a) $\pi/4$ (b) $\pi/2$

(c) π (d) $3\pi/4$

172. When a force $\vec{F} = 6\hat{i} - 8\hat{j} + 10\hat{k}$ is applied on a body due to which it accelerates with 1 ms^{-2}, then the mass of the body is :

(a) $10\sqrt{2}$ kg (b) $2\sqrt{10}$ kg

(c) 10 kg (d) 20 kg

173. A particle is projected with a velocity u so that its horizontal range is twice the greatest height attained. The horizontal range is :

(a) u^2/g (b) $2u^2/3g$

(c) $4u^2/5g$ (d) $5u^2/6g$

174. The sum of the magnitude of two forces acting at a point is 18 and the magnitude of their resultant is 12. If the resultant is at 90° with the force of the smaller magnitude, then their magnitudes are :

(a) 3, 15 (b) 4, 14

(c) 5, 13 (d) 6, 12

175. If a body 'A' of mass 'M' is thrown with the velocity v at an angle of 30° to the horizontal and another body 'B' of the same mass is thrown with the same speed at an angle of 60° to the horizontal, the ratio of horizontal range of A to B will be :

(a) 1 : 3 (b) 1 : 1

(c) $1 : \sqrt{3}$ (d) $\sqrt{3} : 1$

176. Two masses M and m are attached to a vertical axis by two weightless threads of combined length 'L'. They are set in rotational motion in a horizontal plane about this axis with constant angular velocity ω. If the tension in the threads is the same during motion, the distance of M from the axis is :

(a) $\frac{M.L}{M+m}$ (b) $\frac{m.L}{M+m}$

(c) $\frac{M+m}{M.L}$ (d) $\frac{M+m}{m.L}$

177. If angular velocity $(\vec{\omega}) = 3\hat{i} - 4\hat{j} + \hat{k}$ and position vector $\vec{r} = 5\hat{i} - 6\hat{j} + 6\hat{k}$, then linear velocity is :

(a) $6\hat{i} + 2\hat{j} - 3\hat{k}$ (b) $6\hat{i} - 2\hat{j} + 8\hat{k}$

(c) $4\hat{i} - 13\hat{j} + 6\hat{k}$ (d) $-18\hat{i} - 13\hat{j} + 2\hat{k}$

178. Radius of curved road on a national highway is R and width of the road is b. The outer edge of the road is raised by h w.r.t. the inner edge so that a car with velocity v can pass safely over it. The value of h is :

(a) $\frac{v^2b}{R.g}$ (b) $\frac{v^2}{Rgb}$

(c) $\frac{v^2R}{g}$ (d) $\frac{v^2b}{R}$

179. For vectors $\vec{A}$ and $\vec{B}$ making an angle 'θ' which one of the following relations is correct ? **(D.C.E. 2009)**

(a) $\vec{A} \times \vec{B} = \vec{B} \times \vec{A}$

(b) $\vec{A} \times \vec{B} = AB \sin\theta$

(c) $\vec{A} \times \vec{B} = AB \cos\theta$

(d) $\vec{A} \times \vec{B} = -\vec{B} \times \vec{A}$

180. If $\hat{i}, \hat{j}$ and $\hat{k}$ represent unit vectors along the x, y and z-axes respectively, then the angle θ between the vectors $\hat{i} + \hat{j} + \hat{k}$ and $\hat{i} + \hat{j}$ is equal to : **(A.M.U. (Med.) 2009)**

(a) $\sin^{-1}\left(\frac{1}{\sqrt{3}}\right)$ (b) $\sin^{-1}\left(\sqrt{\frac{2}{3}}\right)$

(c) $\cos^{-1}\left(\frac{1}{\sqrt{3}}\right)$ (d) 90°

181. Six vectors $\vec{a}$ through $\vec{f}$ have the magnitudes and directions indicated in the figure. **(A.I.P.M.T. (Prelim) 2010)**

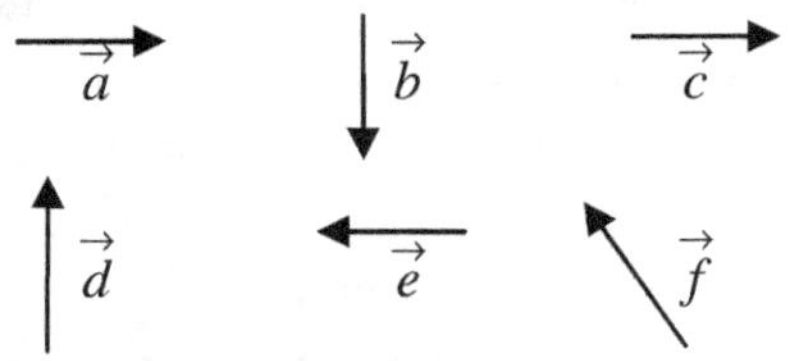

Which of the following statements is true ?

(a) $\vec{b} + \vec{c} = \vec{f}$ (b) $\vec{d} + \vec{c} = \vec{f}$

(c) $\vec{d} + \vec{e} = \vec{f}$ (d) $\vec{b} + \vec{e} = \vec{f}$

182. A car travels 6 km towards north at an angle of 45° to the east and then travels a distance of 4 km towards the north at an angle 135° to the east. How far is the point from the starting point ? What angle does the straight line joining its initial and final position make with the east ? **(A.I.I.M.S. 2008)**

(a) $\sqrt{50}$ km and $\tan^{-1}(5)$

(b) 10 km and $\tan^{-1}(\sqrt{5})$

(c) $\sqrt{52}$ km and $\tan^{-1}(5)$

(d) $\sqrt{52}$ km and $\tan^{-1}(\sqrt{5})$

183. An object moves at a constant speed along a circular path in a horizontal XY plane, with the centre at the origin. When the object is at $x = -2$ m, its velocity is $-(4 \text{ m/s})\hat{j}$. What is the object's acceleration when it is at $y = 2$ m ?

(a) $-(8 \text{ m/s}^2)\hat{j}$ (b) $(8 \text{ m/s}^2)\hat{i}$

(c) $-(4 \text{ m/s}^2)\hat{j}$ (d) $(4 \text{ m/s}^2)\hat{i}$

184. The three initial and final positions of a man on the x-axis are given as : **(D.P.M.T. 2009)**

(i) (−8 m, 7 m)

(ii) (7 m, − 3 m)

(iii) (− 7 m, 3 m)

Which pair gives the negative displacement?

(a) (i) (b) (ii)

(c) (iii) (d) (i) and (iii)

185. A car travelling on a straight path moves with uniform velocity v_1 for some time and with velocity v_2 for the next equal time. The average velocity is given by: **(M.P.P.E.T. 2009)**

(a) $\sqrt{v_1 v_2}$ (b) $\left(\frac{v_1 + v_2}{2}\right)$

(c) $\left(\frac{1}{v_1} + \frac{1}{v_2}\right)^{-1}$ (d) $2\left(\frac{1}{v_1} + \frac{1}{v_2}\right)^{-1}$

186. A body is tied with a string and is given a circular motion with velocity v in radius r. The magnitude of the acceleration is :

(a) v/r (b) v^2/r

(c) v/r^2 (d) v^2/r^2

187. The angular speed of an object trapped in a circular groove of radius 12 cm completes 7 revolutions in 100 seconds : **(H.P.P.M.T. 2009)**

(a) 14 rad s^{-1} (b) 42 rad s^{-1}

(c) 0.44 rad s^{-1} (d) None of these

188. A particle moves in a circle of radius 5 cm with constant speed and time period 0.2π s. The acceleration of the particle is: **(A.I.P.M.T. 2011)**

(a) 15 m/s^2 (b) 25 m/s^2

(c) 36 m/s^2 (d) 5 m/s^2

189. A motor cycle starts from rest and accelerates along a straight path at 2 m/s^2. At the starting point of the motor cycle there is a stationary electric siren. How far has the motor cycle gone when the driver hears the frequency of the siren at 94% of its value when the motor cycle was at rest ? (Speed of sound = 330 m s^{-1}) **(A.I.E.E.E. 2009)**

(a) 49 m (b) 98 m

(c) 147 m (d) 196 m

190. A motor car is moving with a speed of 20 ms^{-1} on a circular track of radius 100 m. If its speed is increasing at the rate of 3 ms^{-1}, its resultant acceleration is : **(Kerala C.E.T. 2009)**

(a) 3 ms^{-2} (b) 5 ms^{-2}
(c) 2.5 ms^{-2} (d) 3.5 ms^{-2}

191. A particle has initial velocity $(3\hat{i} + 4\hat{j})$ and has acceleration $(0.4\hat{i} + 0.3\hat{j})$. Its speed after 10 s is : **(A.I.P.M.T. 2010)**

(a) 7 units (b) $7\sqrt{2}$ units
(c) 8.5 units (d) 10 units

192. When a disc is rotating with angular velocity ω, a particle situated at a distance of 4 cm just begins to slip. If the angular velocity is doubled, at what distance will the particle start to slip ? **(M.H.T.C.E.T. 2010)**

(a) 1 cm (b) 2 cm
(c) 3 cm (d) 4 cm

193. An object moving with a speed of 6.25 m/s, is decelerated at a rate given by **(A.I.E.E.E. 2011)**

$$\frac{dv}{dt} = -2.5\sqrt{v}$$

where v is the instantaneous speed. The time taken by the object, to come to rest, would be :

(a) 8 s (b) 1 s
(c) 2 s (d) 4 s

194. A body is moving with velocity 30 m/s towards east. After 10 seconds its velocity becomes 40 m/s towards north. The average acceleration of the body is : **(A.I.E.E.E. 2011)**

(a) 1 m/s^2 (b) 7 m/s^2
(c) $\sqrt{7}$ m/s^2 (d) 5 m/s^2

195. A body is falling freely under gravity. The distance covered by the body in the first, second and third minute of its motion are in the ratio : **(Kerala C.E.T. 2009)**

(a) 1 : 4 : 9 (b) 1 : 2 : 3
(c) 1 : 3 : 5 (d) 1 : 5 : 6

196. A body starting from rest, accelerates, at a constant rate a m/s^2 for some time after which it decelerates at a constant rate b m/s^2 to come to rest finally. If the total time elapsed is t sec, the maximum velocity attained by the body is given by : **(A.M.U. (Med.) 2009)**

(a) $\frac{ab}{a+b}t$ m/s (b) $\frac{ab}{a-b}t$ m/s
(c) $\frac{2ab}{a+b}t$ m/s (d) $\frac{2ab}{a-b}t$ m/s

197. Which of the following is true regarding projectile motion ? **(D.P.M.T. 2007)**

(a) Horizontal velocity of projectile is constant.
(b) Vertical velocity of projectile is constant.
(c) Acceleration is not constant.
(d) Momentum is constant.

198. The speed of a projectile at its maximum height is half of its initial speed. The angle of projection is: **(A.I.P.M.T. (Mains) 2010)**

(a) 60° (b) 15°
(c) 30° (d) 45°

199. A boy standing at the top of a tower of 20 m height drops a stone. Assuming $g = 10$ ms^{-2}, the velocity with which it hits the ground is : **(A.I.P.M.T. 2011)**

(a) 10.0 m/s (b) 20.0 m/s
(c) 40.0 m/s (d) 5.0 m/s

200. A bullet is to be fired with a speed of 2000 ms^{-1} to hit a target 200 m away on a level ground. If $g = 10$ ms^{-2}, then the gun should be aimed : **(Kerala C.E.T. 2009)**

(a) directly at the target
(b) 5 cm below the target
(c) 5 cm above the target
(d) 2 cm above the target

201. A particle is projected with certain velocity at two different angles of projections with respect to a horizontal plane so as to have same range 'R' on a horizontal plane. If 't_1' and 't_2' is the time taken for the two paths, then which one of the following relations is correct ? **(D.C.E. 2009)**

(a) $t_1t_2 = 2R/g$ (b) $t_1t_2 = R/g$

(c) $t_1t_2 = R/2g$ (d) $t_1t_2 = 4R/g$

202. For an object thrown at 45° to horizontal, the maximum height (H) and horizontal range (R) are related as **(D.C.E. 2009)**

(a) R = 16 H (b) R = 8 H

(c) R = 4 H (d) R = 2 H

203. A person of mass M = 90 kg standing on a smooth horizontal plane of ice throws a body of mass m – 10 kg horizontal on the same surface. If the distance between the person and body after 10 seconds is 10 metres, the K.E. of the person (in joules) is : **(E.A.M.C.E.T. 2008)**

(a) 0.45 (b) 4.5

(c) 0.90 (d) Zero

204. Resultant of non-zero vectors A and B make angle α and β with $\vec{A}$ and $\vec{B}$ respectively. If $|\vec{A}| > |\vec{B}|$ then: **(H.P.P.M.T. 2005)**

(a) $\alpha < \beta$

(b) $\beta > \alpha$

(c) $\frac{\alpha}{\beta} = \frac{|\vec{B}|}{|\vec{A}|}$

(d) No definite inequality can be written between α and β.

205. Three vectors satisfy the relation $\vec{A} \cdot \vec{B} = 0$ and $\vec{A} \cdot \vec{C} = 0$, then $\vec{A}$ is parallel to : **(Punjab C.E.T. 2005)**

(a) $\vec{C}$ (b) $\vec{B}$

(c) $\vec{B} \times \vec{C}$ (d) $\vec{B} \cdot \vec{C}$

206. If the two vectors $\vec{A} = 2\hat{i} + 3\hat{j} + 4\hat{k}$ and $\vec{B} = \hat{i} + 2\hat{j} - n\hat{k}$ are perpendicular, then the value of n is : **(Kerala P.E.T. 2006)**

(a) 1 (b) 2

(c) 3 (d) 4

207. The diagonals of a parallelogram are represented by vectors $\vec{P} = 5\hat{i} - 4\hat{j} + 3\hat{k}$ and $\vec{Q} = 3\hat{i} + 2\hat{j} - \hat{k}$. Then the area of the parallelogram is : **(Kerala P.M.T. 2006)**

(a) $\sqrt{171}$ units (b) $\sqrt{72}$ units

(c) 171 units (d) 72 units

208. Two vectors are perpendicular if : **(D.P.M.T. 2007)**

(a) $\vec{A} \cdot \vec{B} = 1$ (b) $\vec{A} \times \vec{B} = 0$

(c) $\vec{A} \cdot \vec{B} = 0$ (d) $\vec{A} \times \vec{B} = AB$

209. $\vec{A}$ and $\vec{B}$ are two vectors and θ is the angle between them, if $|\vec{A} \times \vec{B}| = \sqrt{3}\,(\vec{A} \cdot \vec{B})$, the value of θ is : **(C.B.S.E. A.I.P.M.T. 2007)**

(a) 45° (b) 30°

(c) 90° (d) 60°

210. Three forces $\vec{A} = (\hat{i} + \hat{j} + \hat{k})$, $\vec{B} = (2\hat{i} - \hat{j} + 3\hat{k})$ and $\vec{C}$ act on a body to keep it in equilibrium. Then $\vec{C}$ is : **(E.A.M.C.E.T. 2008)**

(a) $-(3\hat{i} + 4\hat{k})$ (b) $-(4\hat{i} + 3\hat{k})$

(c) $3\hat{i} + 4\hat{k}$ (d) $2\hat{i} + 3\hat{k}$

211. A bird flies from (–3 m, 4 m, –3 m) to (7 m, –2 m, –3 m) in x, y, z coordinates. The bird's displacement in unit vectors is given by : **(D.P.M.T. 2009)**

(a) $(4\hat{i} + 2\hat{j} - 6\hat{k})$ (b) $(10\hat{i} - 6\hat{j})$

(c) $(4\hat{i} - 2\hat{j})$ (d) $(10\hat{i} + 6\hat{j} - 6\hat{k})$

212. The unit vector parallel to the resultant of the vectors $\vec{A} = 4\hat{i} + 3\hat{j} + 6\hat{k}$ and $\vec{B} = -\hat{i} + 3\hat{j} - 8\hat{k}$ is : **(E.A.M.C.E.T. 2000)**

(a) $\frac{1}{7}(3\hat{i} + 6\hat{j} - 2\hat{k})$

(b) $\frac{1}{7}(3\hat{i} + 6\hat{j} + 2\hat{k})$

(c) $\frac{1}{49}(3\hat{i} + 6\hat{j} - 2\hat{k})$

(d) $\frac{1}{49}(3\hat{i} - 6\hat{j} + 2\hat{k})$

213. If $\vec{a}$ and $\vec{b}$ are two vectors, then the value of $(\vec{a} + \vec{b}) \times (\vec{a} - \vec{b})$ is : **(B.H.U. 2002)**

(a) $2(\vec{b} \times \vec{a})$ (b) $-2(\vec{b} \times \vec{a})$

(c) $(\vec{b} \times \vec{a})$ (d) $\vec{a} \times \vec{b}$

214. Three vectors satisfy the relations $\vec{A} \cdot \vec{B}$ and $\vec{A} \cdot \vec{C} = 0$, then $\vec{A}$ is parallel to :

(Karnataka C.E.T. 2003)

(a) $\vec{B} \times \vec{C}$ (b) $\vec{B} \cdot \vec{C}$

(c) $\vec{C}$ (d) $\vec{B}$

215. If $\vec{A}$ and $\vec{B}$ are non-zero vectors which obey the relation $|\vec{A} + \vec{B}| = |\vec{A} - \vec{B}|$, then the angle between them is :

(Kerala C.E.T. (Medical), 2005)

(a) 0° (b) 60°

(c) 90° (d) 120°

216. The resultant of two forces is 20 N. If one of the force is $20\sqrt{3}$ N and angle between two forces is 30°, then what is the value of second force ? **(A.F.M.C. 2000)**

(a) 10 N (b) 20 N

(c) $20\sqrt{3}$ N (d) $10\sqrt{3}$ N

217. Magnitude of vector which comes on addition of two vectors, $6\hat{i} + 7\hat{j}$ and $3\hat{i} + 4\hat{j}$ is : **(B.H.U. 2000)**

(a) $\sqrt{136}$ (b) $\sqrt{13.2}$

(c) $\sqrt{202}$ (d) $\sqrt{160}$

218. A particle moves with a velocity $6\hat{i} - 4\hat{j} + 3\hat{j}$ m/s under the influence of a constant force $\vec{F} = 20\hat{i} + 15\hat{j} - 5\hat{k}$ N. The instantaneous power applied to the particle is : **(C.B.S.E. 2000)**

(a) 35 J/s (b) 45 J/s

(c) 25 J/s (d) 195 J/s

219. If $|\vec{A} + \vec{B}| = |\vec{A}| + |\vec{B}|$, then angle between $\vec{A}$ and $\vec{B}$ will be : **(C.B.S.E. 2001)**

(a) 90° (b) 120°

(c) 0° (d) 60°

220. If the vectors $\vec{P} = a\hat{i} + a\hat{j} + 3\hat{k}$ and $\vec{Q} = a\hat{i} - 2\hat{j} - \hat{k}$ are perpendicular to each other, then the positive value of a is :

(A.I.I.M.S. 2002)

(a) 3 (b) 2

(c) 1 (d) 0

221. A particle moves from position $\vec{r_1} = 3\hat{i} + 2\hat{j} - 6\hat{k}$ to position $\vec{r_2} = 14\hat{i} + 13\hat{j} + 9\hat{k}$ under the action of force $4\hat{i} + \hat{j} + 3\hat{k}$ N. The work done will be : **(Punjab P.M.T. 2002, 2003)**

(a) 100 J (b) 50 J

(c) 200 J (d) 75 J

222. A person walks first 10 km north and 20 km east, then the resultant vector is :

(A.F.M.C. 2003)

(a) 22.36 km (b) 22.46 km

(c) 25.23 km (d) 20.36 km

223. When $\vec{A} \cdot \vec{B} = -|\vec{A}| \cdot |\vec{B}|$, then :

(Orissa J.E.E. 2003)

(a) $\vec{A}$ and $\vec{B}$ are perpendicular to each other

(b) $\vec{A}$ and $\vec{B}$ act in the same direction

(c) $\vec{A}$ and $\vec{B}$ act in the opposite direction

(d) $\vec{A}$ and $\vec{B}$ can act in any direction.

224. A bus starts from rest with an acceleration of 1 m/s^2. A man who is 40 m behind the bus starts with uniform velocity of 10 m/s. Then minimum time after which the man can catch the bus is **(A.F.M.C. 2001)**

(a) 4 s (b) 10 s
(c) 12 s (d) 8 s

225. If $|\vec{A} + \vec{B}| = |\vec{A}| + |\vec{B}|$, then angle between $\vec{A}$ and $\vec{B}$ will be **(C.B.S.E. 2001)**

(a) 90° (b) 120°
(c) 0° (d) 60°

226. The angle between vectors $\vec{A} = 3\hat{i} + 4\hat{j} + 5\hat{k}$ and $\vec{B} = B\hat{i} + 4\hat{j} - 5\hat{k}$ will be **(C.B.S.E. 2001)**

(a) zero (b) 45°
(c) 90° (d) 180°

227. A force of $(4\hat{i} + 3\hat{j} + 4\hat{k})$ N acts on a body for 4 sec and produces a displacement of $(3\hat{i} + 4\hat{j} + 5\hat{k})$ m. The power delivered is **(C.B.S.E. 2001)**

(a) 4.5 W (b) 6.5 W
(c) 7.5 W (d) 9.5 W

228. A force of $(3\hat{i} + 4\hat{j})$ N acts on a body and displaces it by $(3\hat{i} + 4\hat{j})$ metres. The work done by the force is **(A.I.I.M.S. 2001)**

(a) 10 J (b) 12 J
(c) 16 J (d) 25 J

229. A body of mass 3 kg is at rest. If a force $6t^2\hat{i} + 4t\hat{j}$ is applied on it, the velocity at t = 3 second is **(C.B.S.E. 2002)**

(a) $(18\hat{i} + 3\hat{j})$ (b) $18\hat{i} + 6\hat{j}$
(c) $3\hat{i} + 18\hat{j}$ (d) $18\hat{i} + 4\hat{j}$

230. At the uppermost point of a projectile, its velocity and acceleration are at an angle of **(A.I.I.M.S. 2002)**

(a) 0° (b) 45°
(c) 90° (d) 180°

231. If a ball is thrown vertically upwards with speed u, the distance covered during the last t seconds of its ascent is **(C.B.S.E. 2003)**

(a) $\frac{1}{2}gt^2$ (b) $ut - \frac{1}{2}gt^2$
(c) $(u + gt)^t$ (d) ut

232. A body is moving with uniform acceleration describes 40 m in the first 5 s and 65 m in next 5 s. Its initial velocity will be

(a) 4 m/s (b) 2.5 m/s
(c) 5.5 m/s (d) 11 m/s

233. If $|\vec{A} \times \vec{B}| = \sqrt{3}\, \vec{A} \cdot \vec{B}$, then the value of $|\vec{A} + \vec{B}|$ is **(C.B.S.E. 2004)**

(a) $\left[A^2 + B^2 + \frac{AB}{\sqrt{3}}\right]^{1/2}$
(b) A + B
(c) $[A^2 + B^2 + \sqrt{3}\, AB]^{1/2}$
(d) $[A^2 + B^2 + AB]^{1/2}$

234. Minimum number of unequal vectors which can give zero resultant are **(A.F.M.C. 2005)**

(a) two (b) three
(c) four (d) none of these

235. A force of $-F\hat{k}$ acts on the origin O of the co-ordinate axis system, the torque about the point (1, – 1) is **(A.I.E.E.E. 2006)**

(a) $F(\hat{i} - \hat{j})$ (b) $-F(\hat{i} + \hat{j})$
(c) $F(\hat{i} + \hat{j})$ (d) $-F(\hat{i} - \hat{j})$

236. The vectors $\vec{A}$ and $\vec{B}$ are such that $(\vec{A} + \vec{B}) = (\vec{A} - \vec{B})$. The angle between the two is **(C.B.S.E. 2006)**

(a) 45° (b) 90°
(c) 60° (d) 75°

237. A particle moves along straight line OX at time t (seconds). The distance X (metres) from O is given by $X = 40 + 12t - t^3$. How long the particle travels before coming to rest ? **(C.B.S.E. 2006)**

(a) 16 m (b) 21 m
(c) 40 m (d) 56 m

238. $\vec{A}$ and $\vec{B}$ are two vectors and θ is the angle between them. If $|\vec{A} \times \vec{B}| = \sqrt{3}(\vec{A} \cdot \vec{B})$, the value of θ is **(C.B.S.E. 2007)**

(a) 45° (b) 30°

(c) 90° (d) 60°

239. The distance travelled by a particle starting from rest and moving with an acceleration $\frac{4}{3}$ m/s^2 in the third second is **(C.B.S.E. 2008)**

(a) 4 m (b) $\frac{10}{3}$ m

(c) $\frac{19}{3}$ m (d) 6 m

240. A particle has initial velocity $(3\hat{i} + 4\hat{j})$ and has acceleration $(0.4\hat{i} + 0.3\hat{j})$. Its speed after 10 s is **(C.B.S.E. 2010)**

(a) 8.5 units (b) 10 units

(c) 7 units (d) $7\sqrt{2}$ units

241. A boy standing at the top of a tower of 20 m height drops a stone. Assuming g = 10 m/s^2, the velocity with which it hits the ground is **(C.B.S.E. 2011)**

(a) 10.0 m/s (b) 20.0 m/s

(c) 40.0 m/s (d) 5.0 m/s

242. A missile is fired for maximum range with an initial velocity of 20 m/s. If g = 10 m/s^2, the range of the missile is **(C.B.S.E. 2011)**

(a) 40 m (b) 50 m

(c) 60 m (d) 20 m

243. A body is moving with velocity 30 m/s towards east. After 10 seconds its velocity becomes 40 m/s towards north. The average acceleration of the body is **(C.B.S.E. 2011)**

(a) 1 m/s^2 (b) 7 m/s^2

(c) $\sqrt{7}$ m/s^2 (d) 5 m/s^2

244. The motion of a particle along a straight line is described by equation $X = 8 + 12t - t^3$ where X is in metres and t in seconds. The retardation of the particle, when its velocity becomes zero is **(C.B.S.E. 2012)**

(a) 12 m/s^2 (b) 24 m/s^2

(c) zero (d) 6 m/s^2

245. The horizontal range and the maximum height of a projectile are equal. The angle of projection of the projectile is **(C.B.S.E. 2012)**

(a) θ = 45° (b) $\theta = \tan^{-1}\left(\frac{1}{4}\right)$

(c) $\theta = \tan^{-1}(4)$ (d) $\theta = \tan^{-1}(2)$

246. A particle has initial velocity $(2\hat{i} + 3\hat{j})$ and acceleration $(0.3\hat{i} + 0.2\hat{j})$. The magnitude of velocity after 10 seconds will be **(C.B.S.E. 2012)**

(a) 9 units (b) $9\sqrt{2}$ units

(c) $5\sqrt{2}$ units (d) 5 units

247. A stone falls freely under gravity. It covers distance h_1, h_2 and h_3 in the first 5 s, the next 5 s and the next 5 s respectively. The relation between h_1, h_2 and h_3 is **(NEET 2013)**

(a) $h_1 = \frac{h_2}{3} = \frac{h_3}{5}$

(b) $h_2 = 3h_1$ and $h_3 = 3h_2$

(c) $h_1 = h_2 = h_3$

(d) $h_1 = 2h_2 = 3h_3$

248. The velocity of a projectile at the initial point A is $(2\hat{i} + 3\hat{j})$ m/s. Its velocity (in m/s) at point B is **(NEET 2013)**

(a) $-2\hat{i} + 3\hat{j}$ (b) $2\hat{i} - 3\hat{j}$

(c) $2\hat{i} + 5\hat{j}$ (d) $-2\hat{i} - 3\hat{j}$

249. A uniform force of $(3\hat{i} + \hat{j})$ N acts on a particle of mass 2 kg. Hence the particle is displaced from position $(2\hat{i} + \hat{k})$ metre to position $(4\hat{i} + 3\hat{j} - \hat{k})$ metre. The work done by the force on the particle is **(NEET 2013)**

(a) 6 J (b) 13 J

(c) 15 J (d) 9 J

250. Two forces of 12 N and 8 N act upon a body. The resultant force on the body has a maximum value of **(Manipal 2003)**

(a) 4 N (b) 0 N

(c) 20 N (d) 8 N

251. For a given angle of projection, if the time of flight of a projectile is doubled, the horizontal range will increase

(a) four times (b) thrice

(c) once (d) twice

252. y-component of velocity is 20 and x-component of velocity is 10. The direction of motion of the body with the horizontal at this instant is **(Manipal 2003)**

(a) $\tan^{-1}(2)$ (b) $\tan^{-1}(1/2)$

(c) 45° (d) 0°

253. The maximum range of a gun on horizontal terrain is 16 km. If $g = 10\ m/s^2$, what must be the muzzle velocity of the shell ? **(B.H.U. 2003)**

(a) 200 m/s (b) 100 m/s

(c) 400 m/s (d) 300 m/s

254. The equations of motion of a projectile are given by x = 36t metres and $2y = 96t - 9.8t^2$ metres. The angle of projection is **(J.I.P.M. E.R. 2003)**

(a) $\sin^{-1}\left(\frac{4}{5}\right)$ (b) $\sin^{-1}\left(\frac{5}{3}\right)$

(c) $\sin^{-1}\left(\frac{4}{3}\right)$ (d) $\sin^{-1}\left(\frac{3}{4}\right)$

ANSWER KEY

1. (b)	**2.** (d)	**3.** (c)	**4.** (c)	**5.** (c)	**6.** (c)	**7.** (b)	**8.** (b)	**9.** (a)	**10.** (d)
11. (d)	**12.** (a)	**13.** (c)	**14.** (d)	**15.** (b)	**16.** (b)	**17.** (b)	**18.** (c)	**19.** (c)	**20.** (a)
21. (a)	**22.** (c)	**23.** (b)	**24.** (a)	**25.** (c)	**26.** (c)	**27.** (b)	**28.** (d)	**29.** (a)	**30.** (a)
31. (b)	**32.** (a)	**33.** (a)	**34.** (c)	**35.** (b)	**36.** (c)	**37.** (c)	**38.** (b)	**39.** (d)	**40.** (c)
41. (a)	**42.** (b)	**43.** (d)	**44.** (b)	**45.** (a)	**46.** (b)	**47.** (a)	**48.** (c)	**49.** (d)	**50.** (d)
51. (a)	**52.** (c)	**53.** (a)	**54.** (c)	**55.** (c)	**56.** (d)	**57.** (d)	**58.** (d)	**59.** (c)	**60.** (c)
61. (a)	**62.** (a)	**63.** (c)	**64.** (b)	**65.** (b)	**66.** (c)	**67.** (b)	**68.** (b)	**69.** (c)	**70.** (b)
71. (b)	**72.** (d)	**73.** (d)	**74.** (d)	**75.** (b)	**76.** (d)	**77.** (c)	**78.** (b)	**79.** (c)	**80.** (b)
81. (c)	**82.** (b)	**83.** (d)	**84.** (d)	**85.** (c)	**86.** (d)	**87.** (c)	**88.** (a)	**89.** (d)	**90.** (c)
91. (b)	**92.** (c)	**93.** (b)	**94.** (a)	**95.** (d)	**96.** (a)	**97.** (c)	**98.** (b)	**99.** (c)	**100.** (d)
101. (a)	**102.** (d)	**103.** (c)	**104.** (c)	**105.** (b)	**106.** (d)	**107.** (c)	**108.** (c)	**109.** (c)	**110.** (c)
111. (b)	**112.** (d)	**113.** (b)	**114.** (a)	**115.** (d)	**116.** (b)	**117.** (c)	**118.** (a)	**119.** (c)	**120.** (a)
121. (c)	**122.** (d)	**123.** (b)	**124.** (d)	**125.** (c)	**126.** (d)	**127.** (a)	**128.** (c)	**129.** (c)	**130.** (d)
131. (c)	**132.** (c)	**133.** (b)	**134.** (b)	**135.** (d)	**136.** (b)	**137.** (b)	**138.** (c)	**139.** (a)	**140.** (b)
141. (c)	**142.** (b)	**143.** (a)	**144.** (a)	**145.** (c)	**146.** (a)	**147.** (a)	**148.** (c)	**149.** (d)	**150.** (c)
151. (a)	**152.** (a)	**153.** (a)	**154.** (a)	**155.** (d)	**156.** (c)	**157.** (a)	**158.** (a)	**159.** (b)	**160.** (d)
161. (b)	**162.** (b)	**163.** (d)	**164.** (d)	**165.** (a)	**166.** (b)	**167.** (d)	**168.** (d)	**169.** (b)	**170.** (d)
171. (d)	**172.** (a)	**173.** (c)	**174.** (c)	**175.** (b)	**176.** (b)	**177.** (d)	**178.** (a)	**179.** (d)	**180.** (a)
181. (c)	**182.** (c)	**183.** (a)	**184.** (b)	**185.** (b)	**186.** (b)	**187.** (c)	**188.** (d)	**189.** (b)	**190.** (b)
191. (b)	**192.** (a)	**193.** (c)	**194.** (d)	**195.** (c)	**196.** (a)	**197.** (d)	**198.** (a)	**199.** (b)	**200.** (c)
201. (a)	**202.** (c)	**203.** (a)	**204.** (b)	**205.** (c)	**206.** (b)	**207.** (a)	**208.** (c)	**209.** (d)	**210.** (a)
211. (b)	**212.** (a)	**213.** (a)	**214.** (a)	**215.** (c)	**216.** (b)	**217.** (c)	**218.** (b)	**219.** (c)	**220.** (a)
221. (a)	**222.** (a)	**223.** (c)	**224.** (d)	**225.** (c)	**226.** (c)	**227.** (d)	**228.** (d)	**229.** (c)	**230.** (c)
231. (a)	**232.** (c)	**233.** (d)	**234.** (b)	**235.** (c)	**236.** (d)	**237.** (d)	**238.** (d)	**239.** (b)	**240.** (d)
241. (b)	**242.** (a)	**243.** (d)	**244.** (a)	**245.** (c)	**246.** (c)	**247.** (a)	**248.** (b)	**249.** (d)	**250.** (c)
251. (a)	**252.** (a)	**253.** (c)	**254.** (a)						

4

LAWS OF MOTION

MULTIPLE CHOICE QUESTIONS

1. On a stationary boat, air is blown at the sails from a fan attached to the boat, the boat will:
   (a) remain at rest
   (b) spin around
   (c) move in the direction in which air is blown
   (d) just opposite to the direction of the blown air.

2. A machine gun fires n bullets per second and the mass of each bullet is m. If v is the speed of each bullet, then the force exerted on the gun is :
   (a) mgv (b) mnv
   (c) mv^2g (d) mv^2n

3. A body of mass m has its position x at a time 't' expressed by the equation $x = 3t^{3/2} + 2t^{-1/2}$. The instantaneous force acting on the body is proportional to :
   (a) t (b) t^0
   (c) $t^{3/2}$ (d) $t^{-1/2}$

4. An object of mass m is thrown vertically upwards. At what rate will its momentum change ?
   (a) mgs (b) mg
   (c) mg/s (d) $mg\,(1 + s)$

5. Which of the following statements about friction is true ?
   (a) Frictional force can accelerate a body.
   (b) Friction can be reduced to zero.
   (c) Rolling friction is always lesser than sliding friction.
   (d) Frictional force is proportional to the area of contact between the two surfaces for a given normal force.

6. A lift is moving downwards with an acceleration equal to 'g'. A body of mass 'm' kept on the floor of the lift is pulled horizontally. If the coefficient of friction is μ, then the frictional force is :
   (a) Zero (b) μmg
   (c) mg (d) $2\,\mu mg$

7. If the vector sum of the forces acting on a body at rest is zero, then :
   (a) the body will execute rotatory motion
   (b) the body will execute linear motion
   (c) the body will not roll down
   (d) the body will not execute linear motion.

8. A force of $(\vec{i} + \vec{j})$ N acts on a particle of mass 0.1 kg. If it starts from rest, its position at $t = 1$ sec will be :
   (a) $(\vec{i} + 5\vec{j})$ m (b) $(\vec{i} - \vec{j})$ m
   (c) $(5\vec{i} + 6\vec{j})$ m (d) $(5\vec{i} + 5\vec{j})$ m

9. Three bodies A, B and C have masses of 1 kg, 2 kg and 3 kg respectively. If all the bodies have equal K.E., then which body has greater momentum ?
   (a) A (b) B
   (c) C (d) Can't say.

10. A body of mass M is being pulled by a string of mass m with a force P applied at one end. The force exerted by the string on the body will be :
   (a) $\dfrac{Pm}{(M + m)}$ (b) $\dfrac{PM}{(M + m)}$
   (c) $Pm\,(M + m)$ (d) $\dfrac{P}{(M - m)}$

11. The reference frame attached to the earth can't be an inertial frame because :
(a) Newton's laws are applicable in this frame
(b) the earth is revolving around the sun
(c) the earth is rotating about its axis
(d) both (b) and (c).

12. Compare the impulse exerted on a wall by two objects, a golf ball and lump of mud, both having the same mass and the velocity :
(a) $(\text{Impulse})_{\text{Golf}} > (\text{Impulse})_{\text{Mud}}$
(b) $(\text{Impulse})_{\text{Mud}} > (\text{Impulse})_{\text{Golf}}$
(c) $(\text{Impulse})_{\text{Mud}} = (\text{Impulse})_{\text{Golf}}$
(d) Nothing can be said.

13. If E, G and N represent the magnitudes of electromagnetic, gravitational and nuclear forces between two electrons at 1 mm separation, then :
(a) N = E = G (b) N > G > E
(c) E > G > N (d) E < N < G

14. Two objects x and y are thrown upwards simultaneously with the same speed. The mass of x is greater than that of y. Air exerts equal resistive force on the two objects, then:
(a) x will be higher than y
(b) y will go higher than x
(c) The two objects will reach the same height
(d) None of these.

15. Two blocks of mass $m_1 = 4$ kg and $m_2 = 2$ kg are connected to the ends of a string which passes over a frictionless pulley. If the string is massless, then the total downward thrust on the pulley is nearly :
(a) 27 N (b) 54 N
(c) 0.8 N (d) Zero

16. Block A of mass 2 kg is placed over block B of mass 8 kg. This combination is placed on a rough horizontal surface. If $g = 10$ ms^{-2}, and coefficient of friction between the block B and rough surface is 0.5 and between the blocks A and B is 0.4. When a horizontal force of 10 N is applied on the 8 kg block, then the force of friction between A and B is:
(a) 100 N (b) 50 N
(c) 40 N (d) 20.2 N

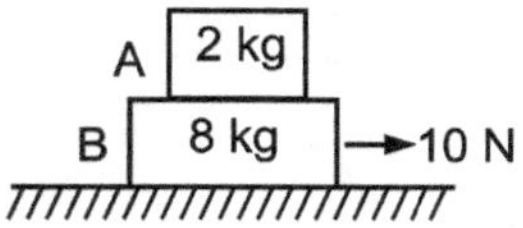

17. A man wants to slide down a rope. The breaking load for the rope is $\left(\frac{2}{3}\right)^{rd}$ of the weight of the man. With what minimum acceleration should the man slide down ?
(a) $g/4$ (b) $g/3$
(c) $2g/3$ (d) $g/6$

18. A rod of length AB = l is slipping with its ends remaining in contact continuously with the frictionless wall and the floor. If at any instant the velocity of end B is 3 ms^{-1} along the x–axis, then the magnitude of velocity of end A will be :
(a) 3 ms^{-1} (b) $\sqrt{3}$ ms^{-1}
(c) 1.5 ms^{-1} (d) 2 ms^{-1}

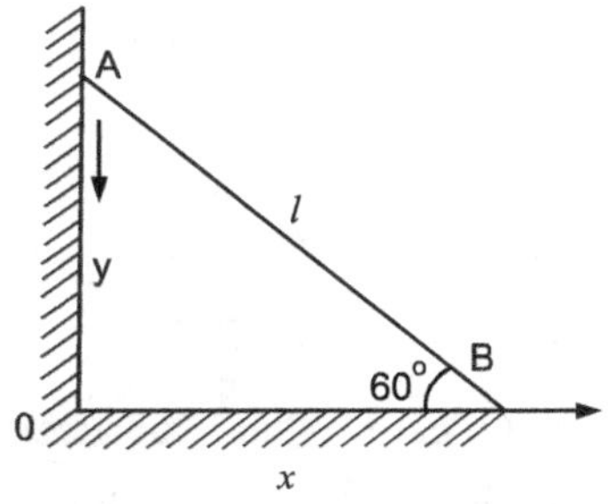

19. Two blocks are in contact on a frictionless table. One has mass m and the other $2m$. A force F is applied on $2m$ and then on m from the right side with the same magnitude. Then the force of contact between m and $2m$ respectively will be :

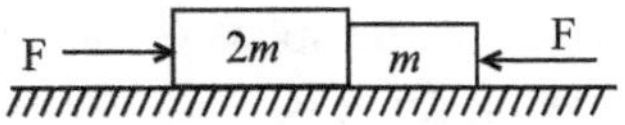

(a) 2 : 1 (b) 1 : 3
(c) 1 : 2 (d) 3 : 1

20. A wooden wedge of mass M and an inclination angle α rests on a smooth floor. A block of mass m is kept on the wedge. A force P is applied on the wedge, such that the block of mass m remains stationary with respect to the wedge. The magnitude of force $\vec{P}$ is :

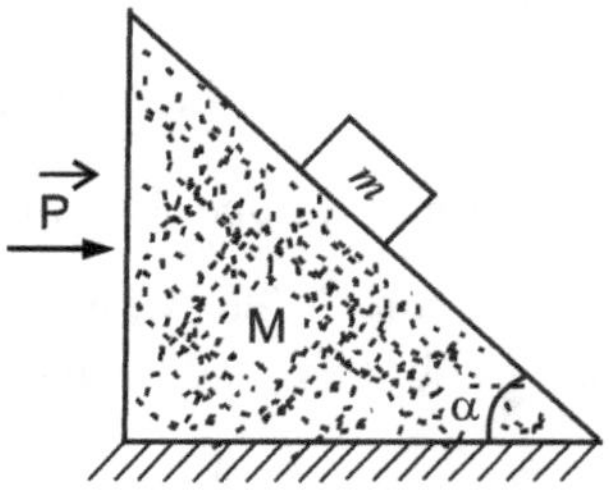

(a) $(M + m)\, g \tan \alpha$

(b) $g \tan \alpha$

(c) $mg \cos \alpha$

(d) $(M + m)\, g \operatorname{cosec} \alpha$

21. A block of mass 10 kg is kept on a horizontal surface. A force F is acted on the block. For what minimum value of F, will the block be lifted up ?

(a) 98 N (b) 49 N

(c) 200 N (d) 9.8 N

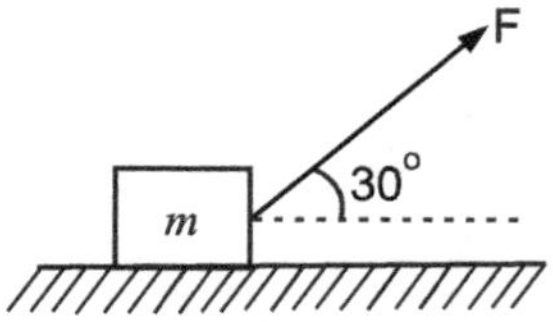

22. The engine of a car produces an acceleration of 6 ms^{-2} in the car. If this car pulls another car of the same mass, then the acceleration would be :

(a) 6 ms^{-2} (b) 12 ms^{-2}

(c) 3 ms^{-2} (d) 1.5 ms^{-2}

23. A machine gun fires n bullets per second each of mass m. If the speed of each bullet is u, then the recoil force is :

(a) nmg (b) nmv

(c) $nmvg$ (d) nmv/g

24. A bag of sand of mass m is suspended by a rope freely. A bullet of mass is fired on it with a velocity v and gets embedded in it. The velocity of the bag finally is :

(a) $\left(\frac{21v}{20}\right)$ (b) $\left(\frac{20}{21}v\right)$

(c) $\frac{v}{20}$ (d) $\frac{v}{21}$

25. A car of mass 120 kg is moving with a uniform velocity of 108 kmh^{-1}. The force required to stop the vehicle in 10 s should be:

(a) 90 N (b) 180 N

(c) 360 N (d) 720 N

26. An astronaut of weight mg is in a rocket accelerating upwards with an acceleration of $4g$. The apparent weight of the astronaut will be :

(a) 5 mg (b) 4 mg

(c) mg (d) Zero

27. The space craft of mass M moving with a velocity 'v', in free space explodes and breaks up into two pieces. After the explosion, a mass m of the space craft is left stationary. The velocity of the other part is :

(a) $\frac{mv}{M - m}$ (b) $\frac{Mv}{M - m}$

(c) $\frac{M + m}{M}$ (d) $\frac{Mv}{M}$

28. An iron nail is dropped from a height h from the level of a sand. If it penetrates through a distance (x) in the sand before coming to rest, then the average force exerted by the sand on the nail is :

(a) $mg\left(\frac{h}{x} + 1\right)$ (b) $mg\left(\frac{x}{h} + 1\right)$

(c) $mg\left(\frac{h}{x} - 1\right)$ (d) $mg\left(\frac{x}{h} - 1\right)$

29. A block of mass M is pulled along a horizontal frictionless surface by a rope of mass m. Force $\vec{P}$ is applied at one end of the rope. The force which the rope exerts on the block is :

(a) $\frac{P}{M(M+m)}$ (b) $\frac{P}{M-m}$

(c) $\frac{Pm}{M-m}$ (d) $\frac{PM}{M+m}$

30. A block of mass m is placed on a smooth inclined plane of inclination θ with the horizontal. The force exerted by the plane on the block has a magnitude :

(a) mg (b) $mg/\cos\theta$

(c) $mg\cos\theta$ (d) $mg\tan\theta$

31. A wooden block of mass 1 kg is attached to the hook of a spring balance. The spring balance is then raised with an acceleration of 9.8 ms^{-2}. The apparent weight of the body is:

(a) 1 kg wt (b) 2 kg wt

(c) 3 kg wt (d) 4 kg wt

32. A block is kept on a frictionless inclined surface with angle of inclination α as shown in figure. The inclined surface is given an acceleration to keep the block stationary. Then $\vec{a}$ is equal to :

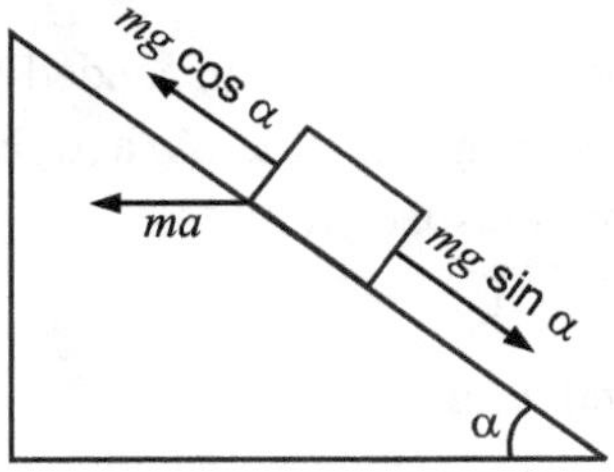

(a) $g\tan\alpha$ (b) g

(c) $g\,\text{cosec}\,\alpha$ (d) $\frac{g}{\tan\alpha}$

33. A bomb of mass 16 kg at rest explodes into two pieces of masses 4 kg and 12 kg. The velocity of the 12 kg mass is 4 ms^{-1}. The kinetic energy of the other mass is :

(a) 288 J (b) 192 J

(c) 96 J (d) 144 J

34. A block of mass m is connected to another block of mass M by a massless spring of constant K. These blocks are kept on a smooth horizontal surface. Initially the blocks are at rest and the spring is unstretched. When a constant force $\vec{F}$ starts acting on the block of mass M to pull it, then the force on the block of mass m is :

(a) $\frac{MF}{(m+M)}$ (b) $\frac{m.F}{M}$

(c) $\frac{(M+m)F}{m}$ (d) $\frac{m.F}{m+M}$

35. A block of mass m is at rest under the action of force F against a wall as shown in the figure. Which of the following statements is correct ?

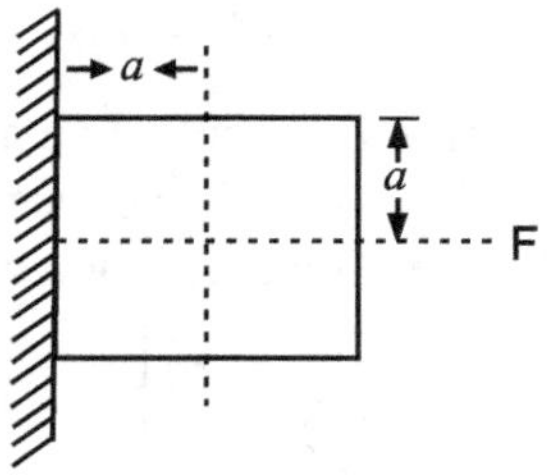

(a) $f = mg$ (where f is the friction force)

(b) F = N (where N is the normal force)

(c) F will not produce torque

(d) N will not produce torque.

36. Two fixed frictionless inclined planes make angles 30° and 60° with the vertical as shown in the figure. Two blocks A and B are placed on these two planes. What is the relative vertical acceleration of A with respect to B ?

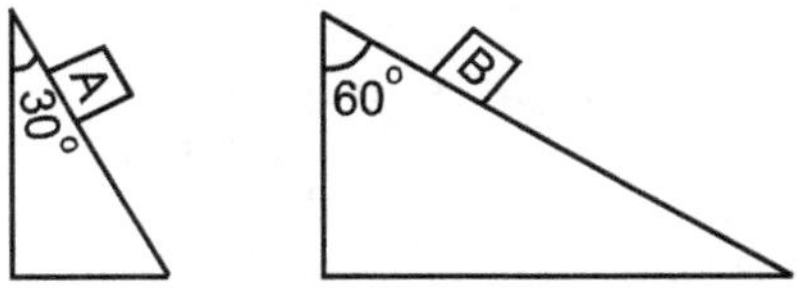

(a) 4.9 ms^{-2} in the horizontal direction

(b) 9.8 ms^{-2} in the vertical direction

(c) Zero

(d) 4.9 ms^{-2} in the vertical direction.

37. A machine-gun mounted on a 2000 kg car on a horizontal frictionless surface fires 10 bullets per second. If 10 gm is the mass of each bullet and 500 ms^{-1}, the velocity of each bullet, then the acceleration of the car will be :

(a) 0.1 ms^{-2} (b) 0.05 ms^{-2}

(3) 0.025 ms^{-2} (d) 0.0167 ms^{-2}

38. Two blocks of masses 1 kg and 2 kg rest on a smooth horizontal table. When the 2 kg block is pulled by a certain force, the tension in the string is 1.5 N. The value of $\vec{F}$ is :

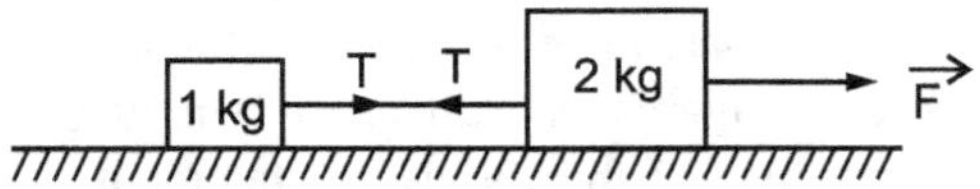

(a) 1.5 N (b) 2.5 N

(c) 3.5 N (d) 4.5 N

39. A horizontal force $\vec{F}$ is applied on a block of mass m placed on a rough inclined plane of inclination θ. The normal reaction N is :

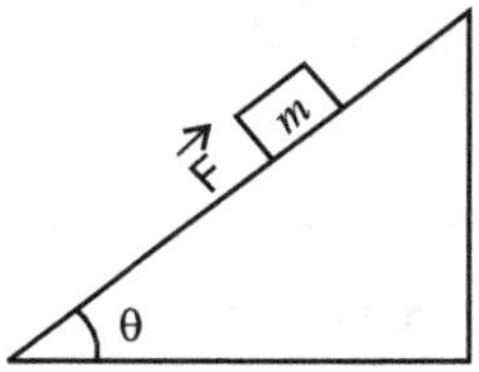

(a) $mg \cos \theta$

(b) $mg \sin \theta$

(c) $mg \cos \theta - F \cos \theta$

(d) $mg \cos \theta + F \sin \theta$

40. The acceleration of the system shown in the given figure is :

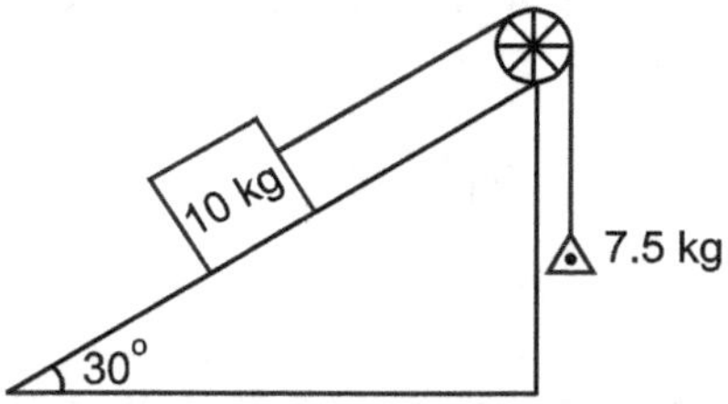

(a) $\frac{35}{17.5} g$ (b) $\frac{7.5}{17.5} g$

(c) $\frac{14.5}{17.5} g$ (d) $\frac{g}{7}$

41. From the given figure, the tension in the massless string for a frictionless pulley will be :

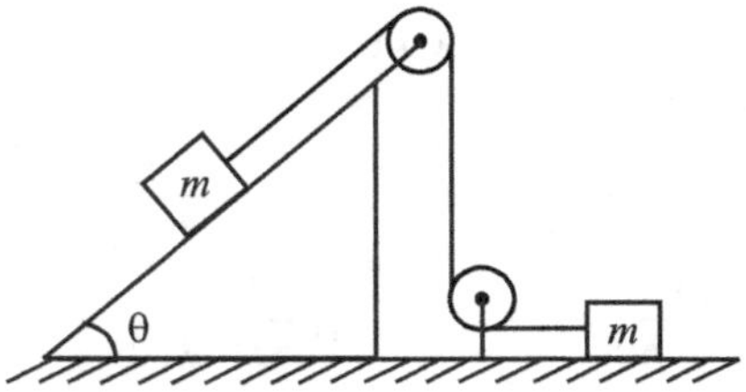

(a) $\frac{2}{3} mg \sin \theta$ (b) $\frac{3}{2} mg \sin \theta$

(c) $\frac{1}{2} mg \sin \theta$ (d) $2\, mg \sin \theta$

42. The acceleration of the 500 gm block in the figure is :

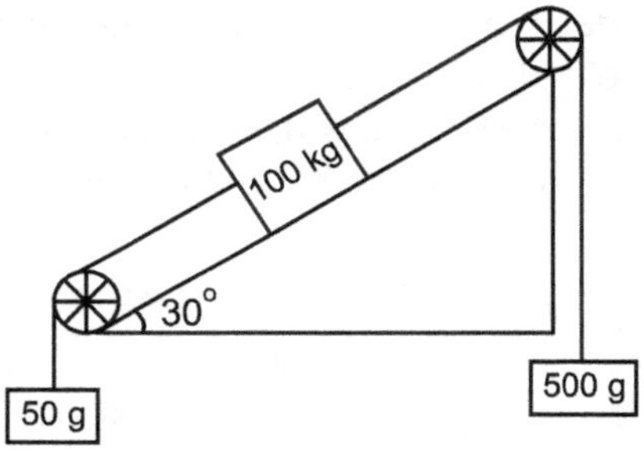

(a) $\frac{6}{13} g$ (b) $\frac{7}{13} g$

(c) $\frac{8}{13} g$ (d) $\frac{9}{13} g$

43. A block of mass 4 kg is suspended through two light spring balances A and B. Then they will read respectively :

(a) 4 kg and 0 kg

(b) 0 kg and 4 kg

(c) 4 kg and 4 kg

(d) 2 kg and 2 kg

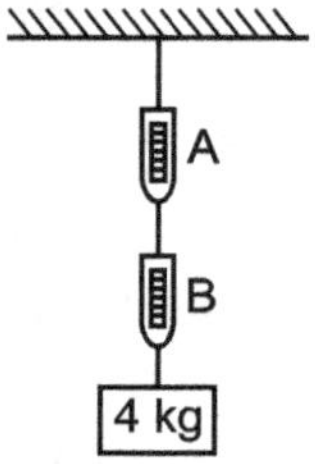

44. From the given figure, calculate the acceleration of 5 kg mass :

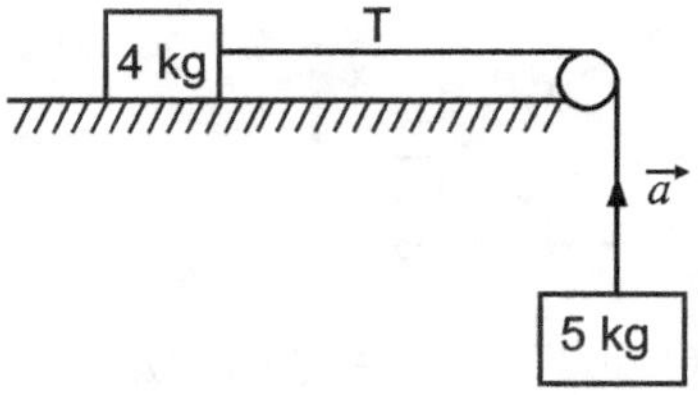

(a) $19.5\ ms^{-2}$ (b) $0.55\ ms^{-1}$
(c) $2.72\ ms^{-2}$ (d) $5.45\ ms^{-2}$

45. A trolley T of mass 5 kg on a horizontal, smooth surface is pulled by a load of 2 kg through a uniform rope ABC of length 2 m and mass 1 kg. As the load falls from BC = 0 to BC = 2 m, its acceleration (in ms^{-2}) changes from :

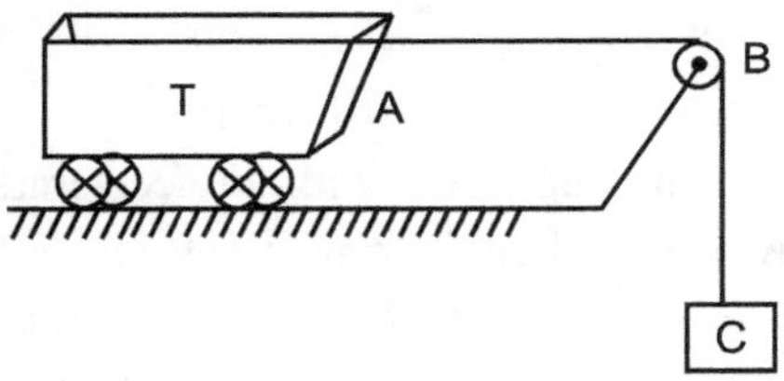

(a) $\frac{20}{6}$ to $\frac{30}{5}$ (b) $\frac{20}{8}$ to $\frac{30}{8}$
(c) $\frac{20}{5}$ to $\frac{30}{6}$ (d) None of these

46. Two blocks of masses M_1 and M_2 are connected with a string passing over a pulley as shown in the figure. The block M_1 lies on a horizontal surface. The coefficient of friction between the block M_1 and the horizontal surface is μ. The system accelerates. What additional mass m should be placed on the block M_1 so that the system does not accelerate ?

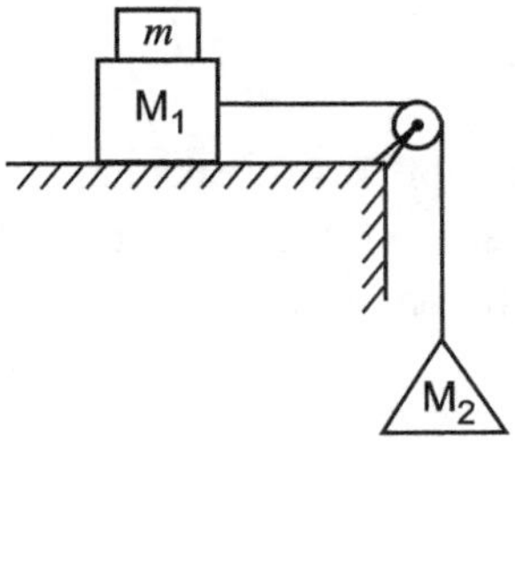

(a) $\frac{M_2 - M_1}{\mu}$ (b) $\frac{M_2}{\mu} - M_1$
(c) $M_2 - \frac{M_1}{\mu}$ (d) $(M_2 - M_1)\mu$

47. Two blocks of masses 6 kg and 3 kg rest on a smooth horizontal surface as shown in figure. The coefficient of friction between A and B is 0.4. The maximum horizontal force which can make them without separation is :

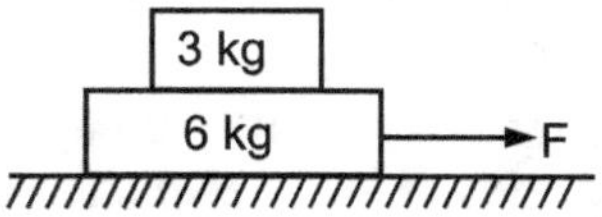

(a) 72 N (b) 40 N
(c) 36 N (d) 20 N

48. Two blocks of mass M = 6 kg and m = 3 kg have coefficient of friction 0.5 between them. The coefficient of friction between M and the surface is 0.4. The maximum horizontal force that can be applied to the mass m so that they move without separation is : ($g = 10\ ms^{-2}$)

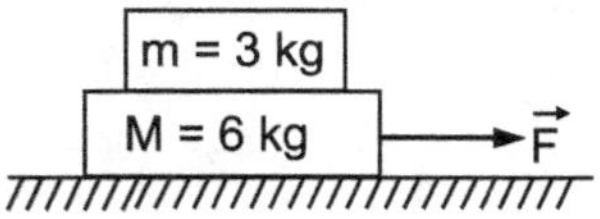

(a) 41 N (b) 61 N
(c) 81 N (d) 101 N

49. Two masses A and B of 10 kg and 5 kg respectively, are connected with a string passing over a frictionless pulley fixed at the corner of a table, $\mu = 0.2$ for block A and the table. The minimum mass of C that may be placed on A to prevent it from moving is equal to :

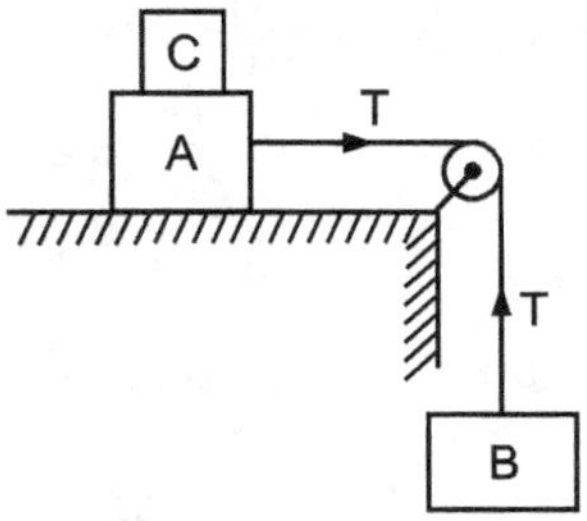

(a) Zero (b) 5 kg
(c) 10 kg (d) 15 kg

50. What is the maximum mass M for which friction force between 2 kg and 3 kg is zero?

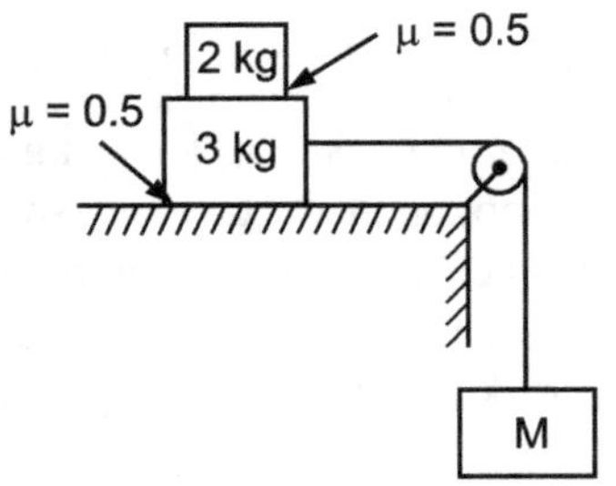

(a) 12.5 kg (b) 1.25 kg
(c) 125 kg (d) None of these

51. A wooden block of mass m resting on a rough horizontal surface is pulled with a force F at an angle θ with the horizontal. If μ is the coefficient of kinetic friction between the block and the surface, then acceleration of the block is :

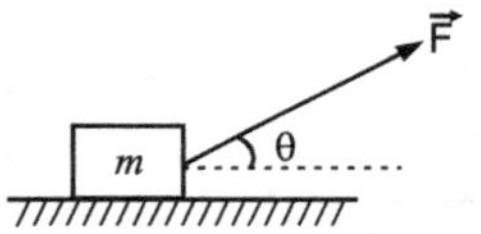

(a) $\mu F \cos\theta$
(b) $\mu F \sin\theta$
(c) $\frac{F \sin\theta}{m}$
(d) $\frac{F}{m}(\cos\theta + \mu \sin\theta) - \mu g$

52. The force acting on the block pushes it, then pushing of the block will be possible along the surface if :

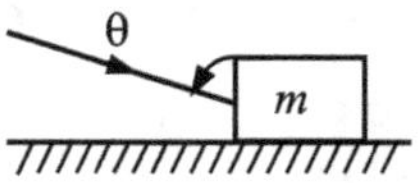

(a) $\tan\theta \geq \mu$ (b) $\cot\theta \geq \mu$
(c) $\tan\frac{\theta}{2} \geq \mu$ (d) $\cot\frac{\theta}{2} \geq \mu$

53. The block of mass m lying on a rough horizontal plane is acted upon by a horizontal force P and another force Q inclined at an angle θ to the vertical. The block will remain in equilibrium if the coefficient of friction between it and the surface is :

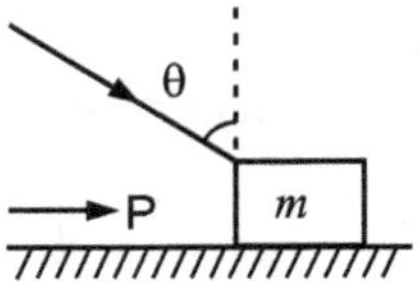

(a) $(P + Q \sin\theta) / (mg + Q \sin\theta)$
(b) $(P \cos\theta + Q) / (mg - Q \sin\theta)$
(c) $(P + Q \cos\theta) / (mg + Q \sin\theta)$
(d) $(P \sin\theta - Q) / (mg - Q \cos\theta)$

54. The minimum velocity (in ms^{-1}) with which a car driver must traverse a flat curve of radius 150 m and coefficient of friction 0.6 to avoid skidding is : **(A.I.E.E.E. 2002)**

(a) 60 ms^{-1} (b) 30 ms^{-1}
(c) 15 ms^{-1} (d) 25 ms^{-1}

55. A lift is moving down with an acceleration 'a'. A man in the lift drops a ball inside the lift. The acceleration of the ball as observed by the man in the lift and a man standing on the ground are respectively :

(A.I.E.E.E. 2002)

(a) g, g (b) $g - a$, $g - a$
(b) $g - a$, g (d) a, g

56. When forces F_1, F_2, F_3 are acting on a particle of mass m such that F_2 and F_3 are mutually perpendicular then, the particle remains stationary. If the force F_1 is now removed, then acceleration of the particle is:

(A.I.E.E.E. 2002)

(a) $\frac{F_1}{m}$ (b) $\frac{F_2 \cdot F_3}{mF_1}$
(c) $\frac{(F_2 - F_3)}{m}$ (d) $\frac{F_2}{m}$

57. If the rope of lift breaks suddenly, the tension exerted by the surface of lift is (a = acceleration of lift)

(a) mg (b) $m(g + a)$
(c) $m(g - a)$ (d) 0

58. A light string passing over a smooth light pulley connects two blocks of masses m_1 and m_2 (vertically). If the acceleration of the system is $g/8$, then the ratio of masses is :

(A.I.E.E.E. 2002)

(a) 8 : 1 (b) 9 : 7

(c) 4 : 3 (d) 5 : 3

59. Three identical blocks of masses m = 2 kg each are drawn by a force F = 10.2 N with an acceleration of 0.6 ms^{-2} on a frictionless surface. What is the tension (in N) in the string between the blocks B and C ?

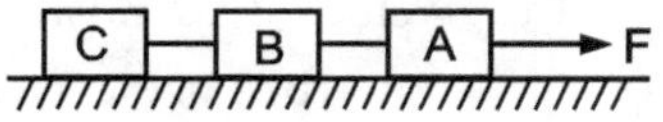

(a) 9.2 N (b) 7.8 N

(c) 4 N (d) 9.8 N

60. Three forces start acting simultaneously on a particle moving with velocity $\vec{v}$ and can be represented by the three sides of a triangle ABC (as shown). The particle will now move with velocity : **(A.I.E.E.E. 2003)**

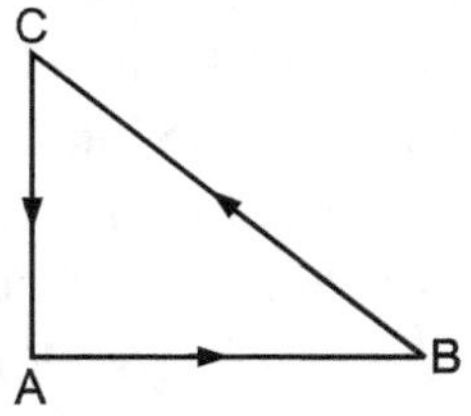

(a) $< \vec{v}$

(b) $> \vec{v}$

(c) $|\vec{v}|$ in the direction of largest force BC

(d) $\vec{v}$, remaining unchanged

61. A spring balance is attached to the ceiling of a lift. A man hangs his bag on the spring and the spring reads 48 N, when the lift is stationary. If the lift moves downwards with an acceleration of 5 ms^{-2}, the reading of the spring balance will be :

(a) 24 N (b) 74 N

(c) 15 N (d) 49 N

62. A horizontal force of 10 N is necessary to hold a block stationary against a wall. The coefficient of friction between the block and the wall is 0.2. The weight of the block is :

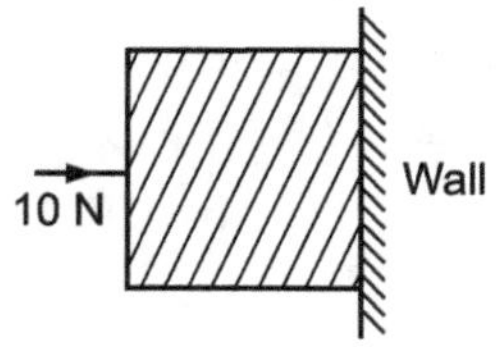

(a) 20 N (b) 50 N

(c) 100 N (d) 2 N

63. A marble block of mass 2 kg lying on ice when given a velocity of 6 ms^{-1} is stopped by friction in 10 s. The coefficient of friction is :

(a) 0.02 (b) 0.03

(c) 0.06 (d) 0.01

64. A block of mass M is pulled along a horizontal frictionless surface by a rope of mass m. If a force P is applied at the free end of the rope, then the force exerted by the rope on the block is :

(a) $\frac{Pm}{M+m}$ (b) $\frac{Pm}{M-m}$

(c) P (d) $\frac{PM}{M+m}$

65. A light spring balance hangs from the hook of the other light spring balance and a block of mass M kg hangs from the former one. Then the true statement about the scale reading is :

(a) Both the scales read M kg each.

(b) The scale of the lower one reads M kg and the upper one zero.

(c) The reading of the two scales can be anything, but the sum of the reading will the M kg.

(d) Both scales read M/2 kg.

66. A rocket with a lift-off mass 3.5×10^4 kg is blasted upwards with an initial acceleration of 10 ms^{-2}. Then the initial thrust of the blast is :

(a) 3.5×10^5 N (b) 7.0×10^5 N

(c) 14×10^5 N (d) 1.75×10^5 N

67. A machine-gun fires a bullet of mass 40 gm with a velocity 1200 ms^{-1}. The man holding it can exert a maximum force of 144 N on the gun. How many bullets can be fired per second at the most ?

(a) 1 (b) 4
(c) 2 (d) 3

68. Two masses m_1 = 5 kg and m_2 = 4.8 kg tied to a string are hanging over a light frictionless pulley. What is the acceleration of the masses when the lift is free to move ? ($\because$ $g = 9.8\ ms^{-2}$)

(a) 0.2 ms^{-2}
(b) 9.8 ms^{-2}
(c) 5 ms^{-2}
(d) 4.8 ms^{-2}

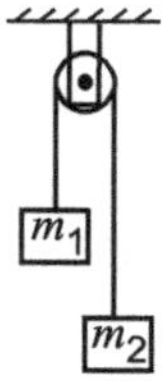

69. A block rests on a rough inclined plane making an angle of 30° with the horizontal. The coefficient of static friction between the block and the plane is 0.8. If the frictional force on the block is 10 N, the mass of the block is : **(A.I.E.E.E. 2004)**

($\because$ $g = 10\ ms^{-2}$)

(a) 2.0 kg (b) 4.0 kg
(c) 1.6 kg (d) 2.5 kg

70. An annular ring with inner and outer radii R_1 and R_2 is rolling without slipping with a uniform angular speed. The ratio of the forces $\frac{F_1}{F_2}$ experienced by the two particles situated on the inner and outer parts of the ring is : **(A.I.E.E.E. 2005)**

(a) 1 (b) $\frac{R_1}{R_2}$
(c) $\frac{R_2}{R_1}$ (d) $\left(\frac{R_1}{R_2}\right)^2$

71. A smooth block is released at rest on a 45° incline and then slides a distance *d*. The time taken to slide is *n* times as much as to slide on a rough inclined than on a smooth incline. The coefficient of friction is :

(A.I.E.E.E. 2005)

(a) $\mu_s = 1 - \frac{1}{n^2}$ (b) $\mu_s = \sqrt{1 - \frac{1}{n^2}}$
(c) $\mu_k = 1 - \frac{1}{n^2}$ (d) $\mu_k = \sqrt{1 - \frac{1}{n^2}}$

72. The upper half of an inclined plane with inclination ϕ is perfectly smooth while the lower half is rough. A body starting from rest at the top will again come to rest at the bottom, then the coefficient of friction for the lower half is given by: **(A.I.E.E.E. 2005)**

(a) 2 tan ϕ (b) tan ϕ
(c) 2 sin ϕ (d) 2 cos ϕ

73. A bullet fired into a fixed target loses half its velocity after penetrating 3 cm. How much further will it penetrate before coming to rest, assuming that it faces constant resistance to motion ? **(A.I.E.E.E. 2005)**

(a) 1.5 cm (b) 1.0 cm
(c) 3.0 cm (d) 2.0 cm

74. A particle of mass 0.3 kg is subjected to a force $F = -kx$ with $k = 15\ Nm^{-1}$. What will be its initial acceleration if it is released from a point 20 cm. away from the origin ?

(A.I.E.E.E. 2005)

(a) 5 ms^{-2} (b) 10 ms^{-2}
(c) 3 ms^{-2} (d) 15 ms^{-2}

75. A block is kept on a frictionless inclined surface with angle of inclination α. The incline is given an acceleration *a* to keep the block stationary. Then *a* is equal to :

(A.I.E.E.E. 2005)

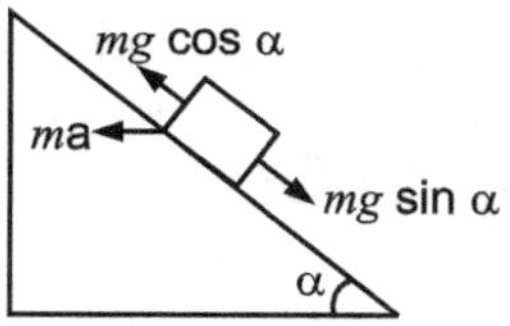

(a) *g* (b) *g* tan α
(c) *g*/tan α (d) *g* cosec α

76. Consider a car moving on a straight road with a speed of 100 ms^{-1}. The distance at which the car can be stopped is .... ($\mu_k = 0{\cdot}5$) : **(A.I.E.E.E. 2005)**

(a) 100 m (b) 400 m
(c) 800 m (d) 1000 m

77. A bullet is fired from a gun. The force on the bullet is given by :

$$F = 600 - 2 \times 20^5 \cdot t$$

where, F is in N and t is in seconds. The force on the bullet becomes zero as soon as it leaves the barrel. The average impulse imparted to the bullet is :

(a) 9 Ns^{-1} (b) Zero
(c) 0.9 Ns^{-1} (d) 1.8 Ns^{-1}

78. A bullet of mass m is fired making an angle θ with the vertical. The bullet is returned to the ground in time 't'. The total change in momentum is :

(a) mgt (b) $mg/2t$
(c) $mgt \cos\theta$ (d) $2\,mgt \cos\theta$

79. A player caught a cricket ball of mass 150 g moving at a rate of 20 ms^{-1}. If the catching process is completed in 0.1 second, the force of the blow exerted by the ball on the hand of the player is : **(A.I.E.E.E. 2006)**

(a) 300 N (b) 150 N
(c) 3 N (d) 30 N

80. A ball of mass 0.2 kg is thrown vertically upwards by applying a force by the hand. If the hand moves 0.2 m while applying the force, the ball goes upto 2 m height further. Find the magnitude of force :
($\because g = 10\ ms^{-2}$) : **(A.I.E.E.E. 2006)**

(a) 22 N (b) 4 N
(c) 16 N (d) 20 N

81. A body of mass m = 3.513 kg is moving along the x-axis with the speed of 5.00 ms^{-1}. The magnitude of its momentum is recorded as : **(A.I.E.E.E. 2006)**

(a) 17.57 kg ms^{-1} (b) 17.6 kg ms^{-1}
(c) 17.565 kg ms^{-1} (d) 17.56 kg ms^{-1}

82. In the given figure, a block of 60 N is placed on a rough surface. The coefficient of friction between the block and the surface is 0.5. What should be the weight W such that the block does not slip on the surface ?

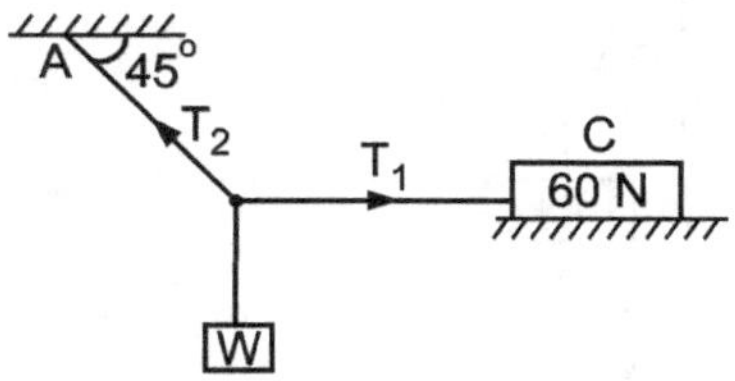

(a) 60 N (b) $\frac{60}{\sqrt{2}}$ N
(c) 30 N (d) $\frac{30}{\sqrt{2}}$ N

83. When a force F acts on a body of mass m, the acceleration produced in the body is $\vec{a}$. If three equal forces $F_1 = F_2 = F_3 = F$ act on the same body as shown in the figure, the acceleration produced is :

(a) $(\sqrt{2} - 1)\,a$ (b) $(\sqrt{2} + 1)\,a$
(c) $\sqrt{2}\,a$ (d) a

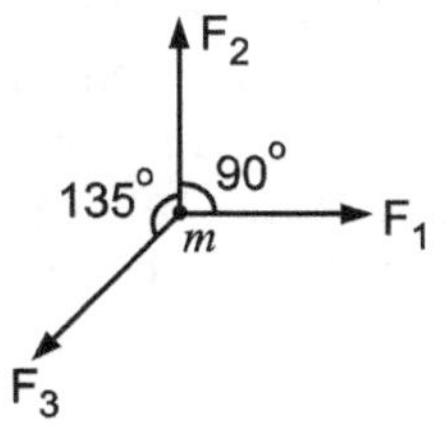

84. Find the tensions T_1 and T_2, when a ball of mass 1 kg is suspended as shown in the figure :

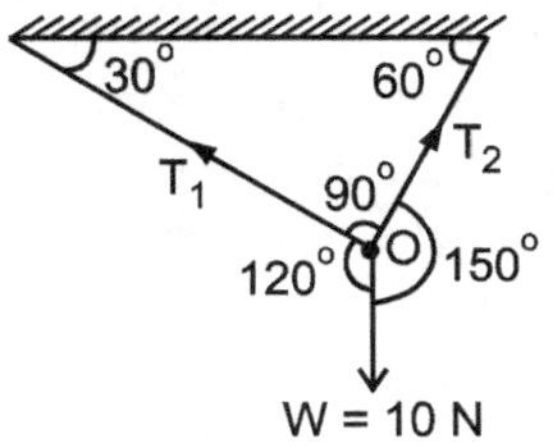

(a) 5 N, zero (b) Zero, 1 N
(c) 5 N, $5\sqrt{3}$ N (d) $5\sqrt{3}$ N, 5 N

85. A 100 kg block is suspended with the help of three massless strings. Then the tension in string C is :

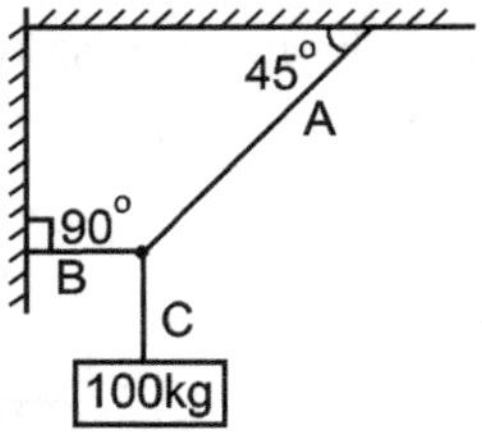

(a) 50 kg N (b) 100 kg N
(c) 200 kg N (d) 20 kg N

86. A block of weight 5 N is pushed against a vertical wall by a force of 12 N. The coefficient of friction between the wall and block is 0.6. The magnitude of the force exerted by the wall on the block is :

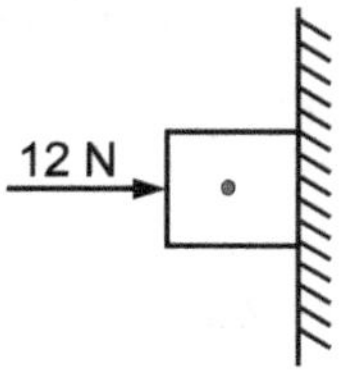

(a) 12 N (b) 5 N
(c) 7.2 N (d) 13 N

87. A plumb bob is hung from the ceiling of a train compartment. The train moves on an inclined track of an inclination 30° with the horizontal. Acceleration of the train up the plane is $a = 9/2$. The angle which the string supporting the bob makes with the normal to the ceiling in equilibrium is :

(a) 30° (b) $\tan^{-1}\left(\frac{2}{\sqrt{3}}\right)$
(c) $\tan^{-1}\left(\frac{\sqrt{3}}{2}\right)$ (d) $\tan^{-1}(2)$

88. A block is placed on a conveyor belt moving horizontally with a constant speed. After 4 s the velocity of the block becomes equal to the velocity of the belt. If $\mu = 0.2$ for the block and the belt, then the velocity of the belt is :

(a) 2 ms^{-1} (b) 4 ms^{-1}
(c) 6 ms^{-1} (d) 8 ms^{-1}

89. A cricket ball of mass 150 gm collides straight with a bat with a velocity of 10 ms^{-1}. The batsman hits it straight back with the velocity of 20 ms^{-1}. If the ball remains in contact with the bat for 0.1 s, then the average force exerted by the bat on the ball is :

(a) 15 N (b) 45 N
(c) 150 N (d) 4.5 N

90. A block moving up an inclined plane of inclination 60° with a velocity of 20 ms^{-1} stops after 2 s. The value of coefficient of friction is : ($\because$ $g = 10$ ms^{-2})

(a) 3 (b) 3.3
(c) 0.27 (d) 0.33

91. A rod of length 'l' and weight W is kept horizontally. A small weight 'w' is hung at its one end. If the system balances on a fulcrum placed at x, then :

(a) $x = l/2$ (b) $x = \frac{w \cdot l}{2(W + w)}$
(c) $x = \frac{w \cdot l}{W}$ (d) None of these.

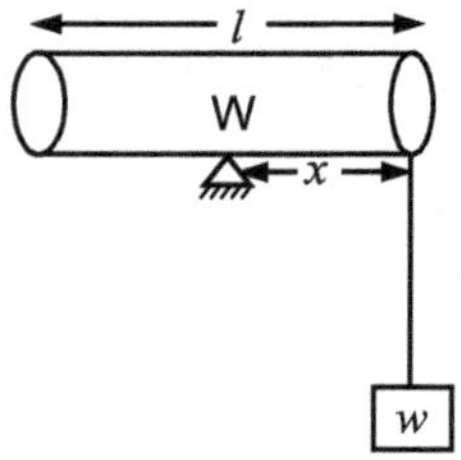

92. A block of weight 100 N is placed on a horizontal plane having coefficient of friction $\mu = 0.25$. The weight of the block B is maximum for the system to be in equilibrium. Then the value of T_1 is :

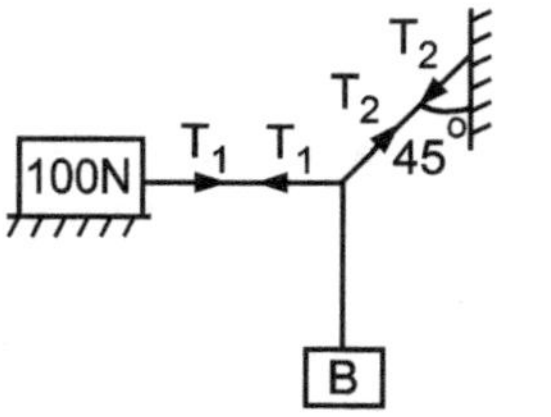

(a) 0.25 N (b) 25 N
(c) 100 N (d) 100.25 N

93. From the given figure, the accelerations of masses are :

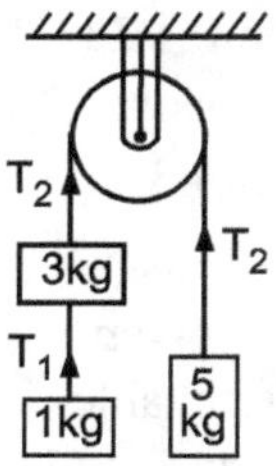

(a) $g/3$
(b) $g/6$
(c) $g/9$
(d) $g/12$

94. A dynamometer D is attached to two blocks of masses 6 kg and 4 kg. Forces of 20 N and 10 N are applied on the blocks as shown in the figure. The dynamometer readings will be :

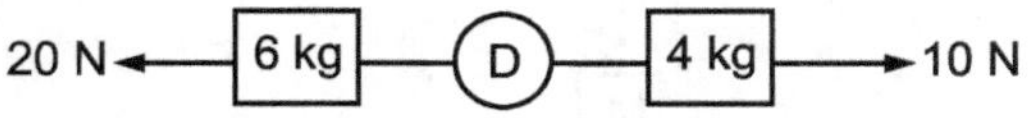

(a) 10 N (b) 20 N
(c) 6 N (d) 14 N

95. From the given figure the tension in the string T_1 is :

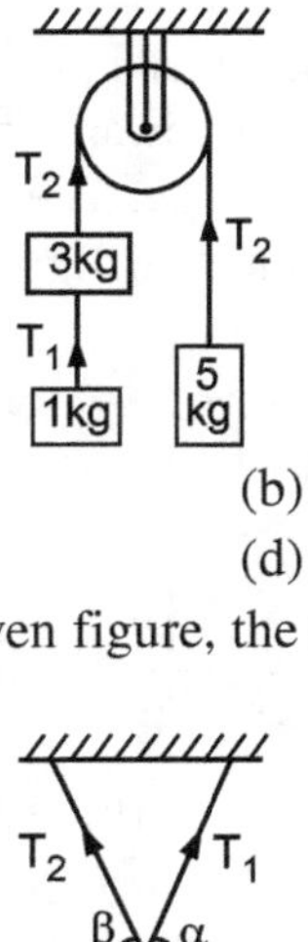

(a) 19.6 N (b) 25 N
(c) 10.6 N (d) 10 N

96. From the given figure, the tension in the two strings is :

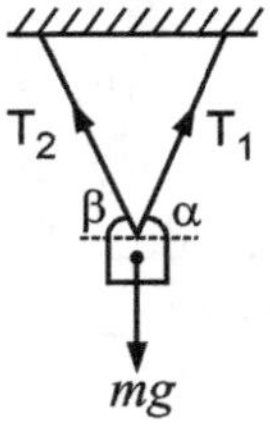

(a) $T_1 = \dfrac{mg\cos\beta}{\sin(\alpha+\beta)} = T_2$

(b) $T_1 = \dfrac{mg\sin\beta}{\sin(\alpha+\beta)} = T_2$

(c) $T_1 = \dfrac{mg\cos\beta}{\sin(\alpha+\beta)}$; $T_2 = \dfrac{mg\cos\alpha}{\sin(\alpha+\beta)}$

(d) None of the above

97. A block of mass 15 kg is resting on a rough inclined plane. The block is tied by a horizontal string and has a tension of 50 N. The coefficient of friction between the surface of contact is : ($\because g = 10\ \text{ms}^{-2}$)

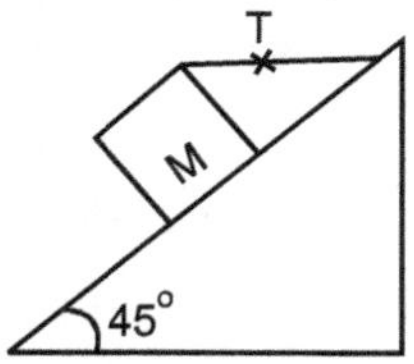

(a) 0.5 (b) 0.75
(c) 0.667 (d) 0.25

98. A spring balance A reads 2 kg with a block *m* suspended from it. A balance B reads 5 kg when a beaker filled with liquid is put on the pan of the balance. The two balances are now so arranged that the hanging mass is inside the liquid as shown in figure. In this situation :

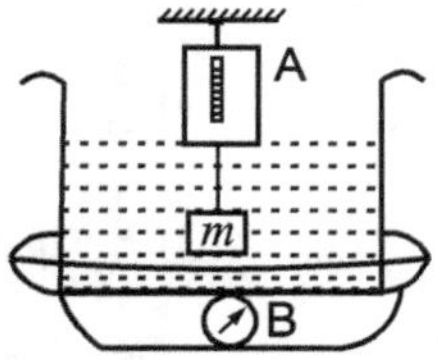

(a) The balance A will read more than 2 kg
(b) The balance B will read more than 5 kg
(c) The balance A will read less than 2 kg and B will read more than 5 kg
(d) The balance A and B will read 2 kg and 5 kg respectively

99. During a red light stop, a 80 kg man and his car collide suddenly with an acceleration of 5 ms^{-1} and time of impact is 0.4 second. The average force on the man will be :

(a) 100 N (b) 200 N
(c) 500 N (d) 1000 N

100. A pendulum bob of mass 50 gm is suspended from the ceiling of an elevator. The tension in the string, if the elevator goes up with the uniform velocity is :

(a) 0.30 N (b) 0.40 N
(c) 0.42 N (d) 0.50 N

101. From the given figure, the reading on the balance is : ($\because g = 10 \text{ ms}^{-2}$)

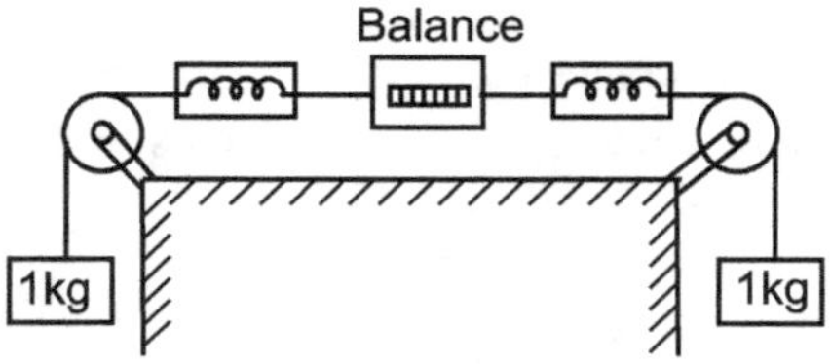

(a) 10 N (b) 20 N
(c) 5 N (d) 0.5 N

102. From the figure, the tension on the string connecting blocks A and B is :

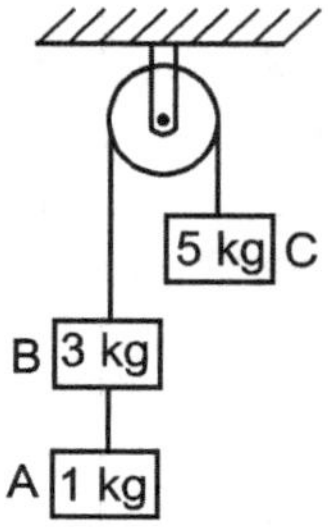

(a) g (b) $\frac{g}{9}$
(c) $\frac{8}{9}g$ (d) $\frac{10}{9}g$

103. A bomb of mass 16 kg at rest explodes into two pieces of masses 4 kg and 12 kg. The velocity of 12 kg mass is 4 ms^{-1}. The kinetic energy of the other mass is :

(a) 96 J (b) 144 J
(b) 288 J (d) 192 J

104. From the given figure, the acceleration of 1 kg mass is :

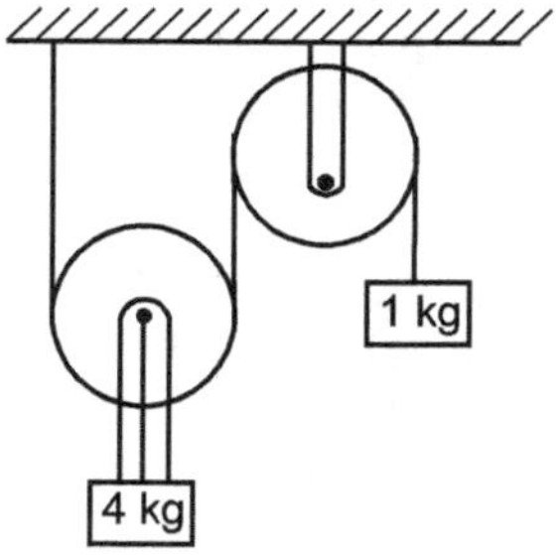

(a) $g/4$ downwards (b) $g/4$ upwards
(c) $g/2$ downwards (d) $g/2$ upwards

105. The length of an elastic string is x, when the tension is 5 N. Its length is y when the tension is 7 N. What will be its length, when the tension is 9 N ?

(a) $2x + y$ (b) $2y - x$
(c) $7y - 5x$ (d) $7y + 5x$

106. In the given figure, the ends P and Q of an unstretchable string move downwards with a uniform speed u. Pulleys A and B are fixed. Mass M moves upwards with a speed :

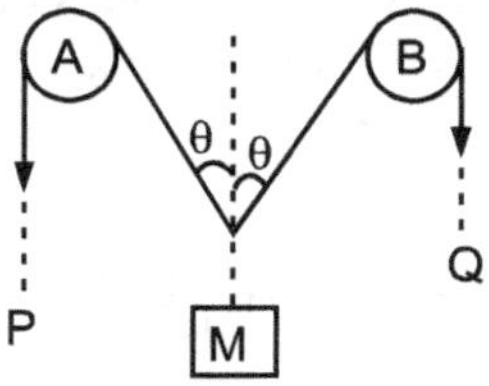

(a) $2u \cos\theta$ (b) $\frac{u}{\cos\theta}$
(c) $\frac{2u}{\cos\theta}$ (d) $u\cos\theta$

107. In the figure, the blocks are initially at rest on the floor and an upward force F = 120 N is applied to the pulley. The acceleration of the two blocks in ms^{-2} will be :

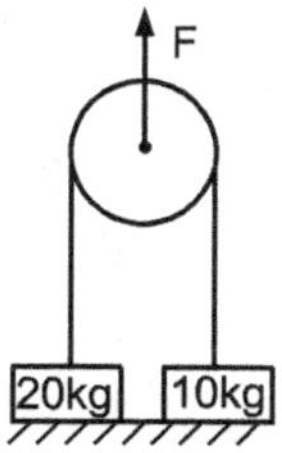

(a) 0, 1 (b) 0, 0
(c) 0.4, 4 (d) None of these

108. Evaluate the acceleration of mass M :

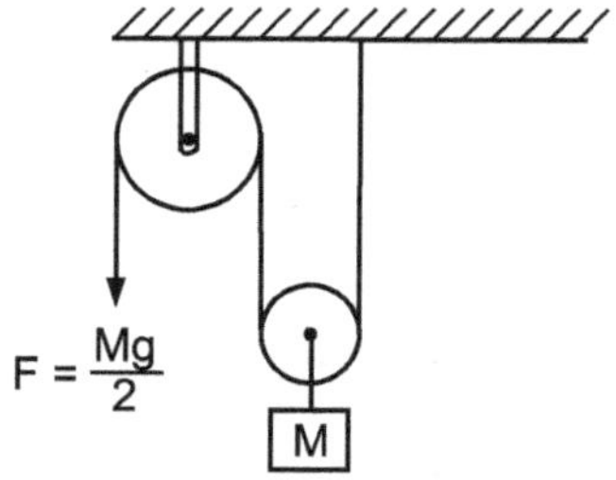

(a) zero (b) 8/2
(c) 8/3 (d) 8/5

109. The tension in the string will be :

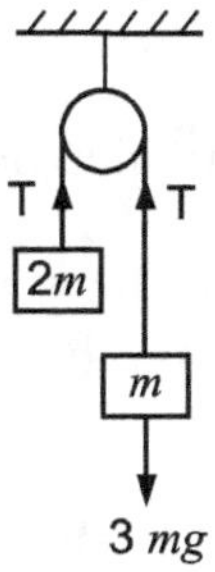

(a) $\frac{10}{3} mg$ (b) $2\ mg$

(c) $3\ mg$ (d) $\frac{10}{7} mg$

110. The value of T_1 and T_2 is :

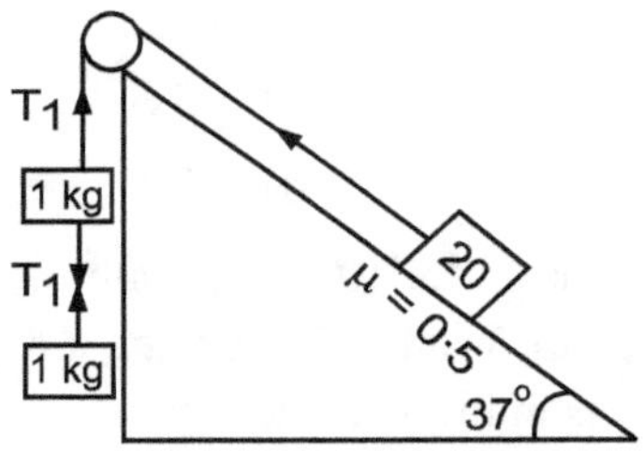

(a) 110 N, 110 N (b) 120 N, 120 N
(c) 110 N, 120 N (d) 120 N, 110 N

COMPREHENSION BASED QUESTIONS

Passage-I

The impulse measures the effect of average force. It is the product of average force and time of impact or the change in momentum. For a given change in momentum, the product of the average force and time of impact is a constant. So we can reduce the average force by increasing the time of impact.

111. A ball of mass 250 gm falls from a height of 5 m above the ground and rebounces upto a height of 2.45 m. The impulse on collision is:

(a) 4.25 kg ms^{-1} (b) 45.2 kg ms^{-1}
(c) 52.4 kg ms^{-1} (d) 54.2 kg ms^{-1}

112. The loss of the energy during impact is :

(a) 75 J (b) 5 J
(c) 57 J (d) 6.38 J

113. The force exerted by the ground on the ball during impact is :

(a) 90.4 N (b) 42.5 N
(c) 84.5 N (d) 45.2 N

114. If the impact lasts for 0.1 s, force by the impinging ball on the ground is :

(a) 45.2 N (b) 45.2 kg wt
(c) 42.5 N (d) 42.5 kg wt

115. A cricket player lowers his hands while catching a ball,

(a) because the ball is heavy
(b) to get injured due to the impact for getting insurance amount
(c) because it increases the time of impact and reduces the average force
(d) for losing the game.

Passage-II

A metallic cube of mass 10 kg is lying on a rough horizontal surface. The coefficient of friction between them is 0.577. When the horizontal surface starts to incline gradually, the cube just begins to slide over it for an angle θ. This angle is called as angle of repose and beyond this inclination angle, the body slides down with some acceleration.

116. The angle of repose in this case is :

(a) 60° (b) 57.7°
(c) 5.7' (d) 30°

117. The minimum force required to move the body up on the inclined plane is :

(a) 100 N (b) 57.7 N
(c) 111.5 N (d) 157.7 N

118. The minimum force required to slide the block on the horizontal surface is :

(a) 57.7 N (b) 100 N
(c) 100 kg (d) 57.7 kg

ASSERTION AND REASON

Directions for Q. 119 to 123 : Question no. 119 to 123 are of Assertion and Reason type. Each of this contains Statement-I (ASSERTION) and Statement-II (REASON) and each question has four alternative choices only one of which is correct. You have to select any one choice from (a), (b), (c) and (d) as given below :

(a) Both, Statement-I and Statement-II are true and the Statement-II is the correct explanation of Statement-I.

(b) Both, Statement-I and Statement-II are true but Statement-II is not the correct explanation of Statement-I.

(c) Statement-I is true, but Statement-II is false.

(d) Statement-I is false, but Statement-II is true.

119. (I) Friction is a self adjusting force.

(II) The magnitude of static friction is equal to the applied force and its direction is opposite to that of the applied force.

120. (I) An electric fan continues to rotate for some time after the current is switched off.

(II) It is because of Inertia of rest.

121. (I) Force is required to move a body along a circle.

(II) When motion is uniform, acceleration is zero.

122. (II) It is impossible to drive a car on a friction-free road.

(II) Friction always opposes motion.

123. (I) The maximum speed with which a car can go round a levelled curved road of radius 10 m without skidding is $\sqrt{10}$ ms^{-1}. ($\because \mu = 0.1$)

(II) For safe driving, the speed of the car should be $v = \sqrt{\mu rg}$

124. The coefficient of friction of a surface is $\frac{1}{\sqrt{3}}$. What should be the angle of inclination so that a body placed on the surface begins to slide down ?

(a) 30° (b) 45°

(c) 60° (d) 90°

125. 300 J of work is done in sliding a 2 kg block up on an inclined plane of height 10 m. Work done against friction is ($\because g = 10$ ms^{-2}) :

(a) 100 J (b) 200 J

(c) 300 J (d) 400 J

126. A ship of mass 3×10^7 kg initially is at rest by a force of 5×10^4 N through a distance of 3 m. Assuming that the resistance due to water is negligible, the speed of the ship is :

(a) 1.5 ms^{-1} (b) 60 ms^{-1}

(c) 0.1 ms^{-1} (d) 5 ms^{-1}

127. A spring of force constant k is cut into two pieces, such that one piece is double the length of the other. Then the long piece will have a force constant of :

(a) $\frac{2}{3}k$ (b) $\frac{3}{2}k$

(c) $3k$ (d) $6k$

128. An ideal spring with spring constant k is hung from the ceiling and a block of mass M is attached to its lower end. The mass is released with the spring initially unstretched. Then the maximum extension in the spring is :

(a) 4 Mg/k (b) 2 Mg/k

(c) Mg/k (d) M$g/2k$

129. A system shown in figure is in equilibrium and at rest. The spring and string are massless. Now the string is cut. The acceleration of mass 2 m and m, just after the string is cut will be :

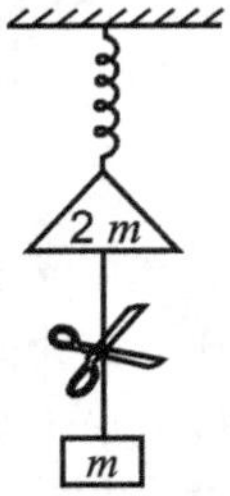

(a) $g/2$ upwards, $g/2$ downwards
(b) g upwards, $g/2$ downwards
(c) g upwards, $2g$ downwards
(d) $2g$ upwards, g downwards

130. A string of negligible mass going over a clamped pulley of mass m supports a pulley of mass M as shown in the figure. The force on the pulley by the clamp is given by :

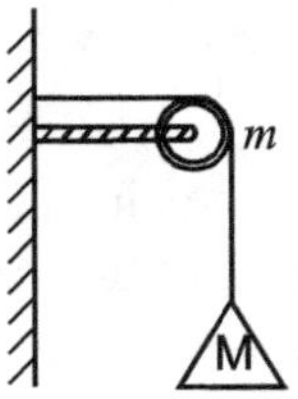

(a) $\sqrt{2}\,Mg$
(b) $\sqrt{2}\,mg$
(c) $\sqrt{(M+m)^2+m^2}\,g$
(d) $\sqrt{(M+m)^2+M^2}\,g$

131. A block of mass 2 kg rests on a rough inclined plane making an angle of 30° with the horizontal. The coefficient of static friction between the block and plane is 0.7. The frictional force on the block is :

(a) 9.8 N (b) $0.7 \times 9.8\sqrt{3}$ N
(c) $98\sqrt{3}$ N (d) $0.7g$ N

132. A weight W rests on a rough horizontal plane. If the angle of friction is θ, the least force that will move the body along the plane will be :

(a) W cos θ (b) W tan θ
(c) W cot θ (d) W sin θ

133. The maximum value of force F, so that the block shown in the arrangement does not move will be :

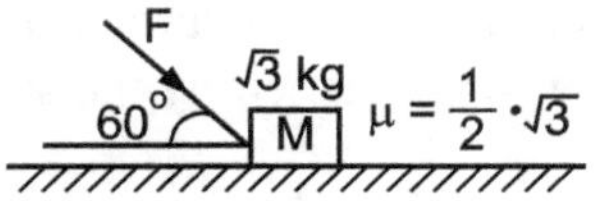

(a) 20 N (b) 10 N
(c) 12 N (d) 15 N

134. An insect crawls up a hemispherical surface very slowly as shown in the given figure. The coefficient of friction between the surface and the insect is 0.33. If the line joining the centre of the hemispherical surface to the insect makes an angle α with the vertical, the maximum possible value of α is given by :

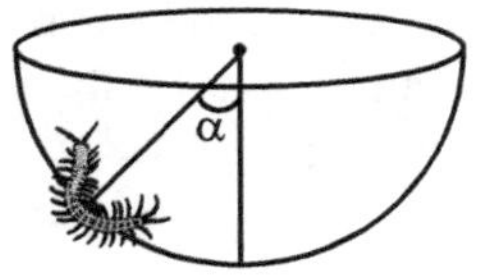

(a) cot α = 3 (b) tan α = 3
(c) sec α = 3 (d) cosec α = 3

135. A solid sphere of mass M is in pure rolling motion on an inclined surface having inclination θ. Then :

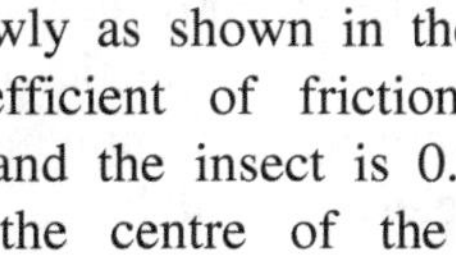

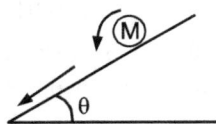

(a) the force of friction on the sphere is, F = μ Mg cos θ
(b) force F is a dissipative force
(c) friction will increase its angular velocity and decrease its linear velocity
(d) If θ decreases, friction will increase.

136. A particle of mass m is moving with velocity v. It is given an impulse such that the velocity becomes v_2. The magnitude of impulse is equal to :

(a) $m(\vec{v}_2 - \vec{v}_1)$ (b) $m(\vec{v}_1 - \vec{v}_2)$
(c) $m \times (\vec{v}_2 - \vec{v}_1)$ (d) $0.5\,m(\vec{v}_2 - \vec{v}_1)$

137. A ball weighing 10 g hits a hard surface vertically with a speed 5 ms^{-1} and rebounds with the same speed. The time of contact between the ball and the surface is 0.01 s. The average force exerted by the surface on the ball is :

(a) 100 N (b) 10 N
(c) 1 N (d) 0.1 N

138. A body of mass 60 kg is dragged with just enough force to start moving it on a rough surface with static and kinetic frictions 0.5 and 0.4 respectively. On applying the same force, the acceleration will be :

(a) 0.98 ms^{-2} (b) 9.8 ms^{-2}
(c) 0.54 ms^{-2} (d) 5.29 ms^{-2}

139. The engine of a car produces an acceleration of 4 ms^{-2} in the car. If the car pulls another car of the same mass, then produced acceleration will be :

(a) 8 ms^{-2} (b) 2 ms^{-2}
(c) 4 ms^{-2} (d) 0.5 ms^{-2}

140. A man fires a bullet of mass 200 g at a speed of 5 ms^{-1}. The gun is of 1 kg mass. By what velocity will the gun rebound ?

(a) 0.1 ms^{-1} (b) 10 ms^{-1}
(c) 1 ms^{-1} (d) 0.01 ms^{-1}

141. The time period of a simple pendulum of length l measured in a lift descending with an acceleration $g/3$ is :

(a) $2\pi\sqrt{\frac{3l}{2g}}$ (b) $2\pi\sqrt{\frac{l}{g}}$
(c) $2\pi\sqrt{\frac{2l}{3g}}$ (d) $2\pi\sqrt{\frac{3l}{4g}}$

142. A 5 kg stationary bomb is exploded in three parts having masses 1 : 1 : 3 respectively. If the parts having same mass move in a perpendicular direction with velocity 39 ms^{-1}, then the velocity of the bigger part will be :

(a) $10\sqrt{2}$ ms^{-1} (b) $\frac{10}{\sqrt{2}}$ ms^{-1}
(c) $13\sqrt{2}$ ms^{-1} (d) $\frac{15}{\sqrt{3}}$ ms^{-1}

143. A given object takes n times more to slide down a 45° rough inclined plane as it takes to slide down a perfectly smooth 45° incline. The coefficient of kinetic friction will be :

(a) $\frac{1}{(1-n^2)}$ (b) $\left(1-\frac{1}{n^2}\right)$
(c) $\left(1-\frac{1}{n^2}\right)^{1/2}$ (d) $\left(\frac{1}{1-n^2}\right)^{1/2}$

144. When the angle of inclinations of an inclined plane is θ, an object slides down with uniform velocity. If the same object is pushed up with an initial velocity on the same inclined plane; it goes up the plane and stops at a certain distance on the plane. Thereafter the body :

(E.A.M.C.E.T. 2006)

(a) slides down the inclined plane and reaches the ground with velocity 'u'
(b) slides down the inclined plane and reaches the ground with velocity less than 'u'
(c) slides down the inclined plane and reaches the ground with velocity greater than 'u'
(d) stays at rest on the inclined plane and will not slide down.

145. A gun fires bullets each of mass 1 g with velocity of 10 ms^{-1} by exerting a constant force of 5 g weight. Then the number of bullets fired per second is : (g = 10 ms^{-2})

(Kerala P.M.T. 2007)

(a) 50 (b) 5
(c) 10 (d) 25

146. Sand is being dropped on a conveyor belt at the rate of M kg/s. The force necessary to keep the belt moving with a constant velocity of v m/s will be : **(C.B.S.E. 2008)**

(a) 2 Mv newton (b) $\frac{Mv}{2}$ newton
(c) Zero (d) Mv newton

147. A block of mass 'm' is resting on a smooth horizontal surface. One end of a uniform rope of mass $\left(\frac{m}{3}\right)$ is fixed to the block, which is pulled in the horizontal direction by applying a force F at the other end. The tension in the middle of the rope is :

(Kerala C.E.T. 2009)

(a) $\frac{8}{7}$F (b) $\frac{1}{7}$F

(c) $\frac{1}{8}$F (d) $\frac{7}{8}$F

148. Impulse means : **(H.P.P.M.T. 2009)**

(a) change in force

(b) change in energy

(c) change in momentum

(d) change in speed

149. A passenger getting down from a moving bus, falls in the direction of the motion of the bus. This is an example of :

(Kerala Engg. 2010)

(a) Moment of inertia

(b) Second law of motion

(c) Third law of motion

(d) Inertia of motion

150. The apparent weight of a person inside a lift is W_1 when lift moves up with a certain acceleration and is W_2 when lift moves down with the same acceleration. The weight of the person when the lift moves up with constant speed is : **(B.H.U. Main 2008)**

(a) $\frac{W_1 + W_2}{2}$ (b) $\frac{W_1 - W_2}{2}$

(c) $2W_1$ (d) $2W_2$

151. A boy of mass 50 kg is standing on a weighing machine placed on the floor of a lift. The machine reads his weight in newtons. What is the reading of the machine if the lift is moving upwards with a uniform speed of 10 m/sec^2 : (g = 10 m/sec^2)

(E.A.M. C.E.T. 2009)

(a) 510 N (b) 480 N

(c) 490 N (d) 500 N

152. A rope of mass 0.1 kg is connected at the same height of two opposite walls. It is allowed to hang under its own weight. At the contact point between the rope and the wall, the rope makes an angle $\theta = 10°$ with respect to the horizontal. The tension in the rope at its mid-point between the walls is :

(D.P.M.T. 2009)

(a) 2.78 N (b) 2.56 N

(c) 2.82 N (d) 2.71 N

153. A pulley of radius 2 m is rotated about its axis by a force F = $(20t - 5t^2)$ newton (where t is measured in seconds) applied tangentially. If the moment of inertia of the pulley about its axis of rotation is 10 kg-m^2, the number of rotations made by the pulley before its direction of motion is reversed is :

(A.I.E.E.E. 2011)

(a) more than 9

(b) less than 3

(c) more than 3 but less than 6

(d) more than 6 but less than 9.

154. A mass m hangs with the help of a string wrapped around a pulley on a frictionless bearing. The pulley has mass m and radius R. Assuming pulley to be a perfect uniform circular disc, the acceleration of the mass m, if the string does not slip on the pulley is :

(A.I.E.E.E. 2011)

(a) $\frac{g}{3}$ (b) $\frac{3}{2}g$

(c) g (d) $\frac{2}{3}g$

155. A mass of 1 kg is just able to slide down the slope of an inclined rough surface when the angle of inclination is 60°. The minimum force necessary to pull the mass up the inclined plane (g = 10 ms^{-2}) is :

(Kerala C.E.T. 2009)

(a) 14.14 N (b) 17.32 N

(c) 10 N (d) 16.66 N

156. A block lying on an inclined plane has a weight of 50 N. It just begins to slide down when the plane makes an angle 30° with the horizontal. The value of coefficient of static friction between the block and the surface is: **(H.P.P.M.T. 2010)**

(a) $\sqrt{3}$ (b) $\frac{1}{\sqrt{3}}$

(c) $\frac{\sqrt{3}}{2}$ (d) $\frac{1}{2}$

157. Two iron blocks of equal masses but with double surface area slide down an inclined plane with friction coefficient μ. If the first block with surface area 'A' experiences a frictional force f, then the second block with surface area 2A will experience a frictional force. **(D.P.M.T. 2009)**

(a) $f/2$ (b) f

(c) $2f$ (d) $4f$

158. A block is lying static on the floor. The maximum value of static frictional force on the block is 10 N. If a horizontal force of 8 N is applied to the block, what will be the frictional force on the block ?

(D.P.M.T. 2009)

(a) 2 N (b) 18 N

(c) 8 N (d) 10 N

ANSWER KEY

1. (a)	**2.** (b)	**3.** (d)	**4.** (b)	**5.** (c)	**6.** (a)	**7.** (d)	**8.** (d)	**9.** (c)	**10.** (b)
11. (d)	**12.** (a)	**13.** (c)	**14.** (a)	**15.** (b)	**16.** (b)	**17.** (b)	**18.** (b)	**19.** (c)	**20.** (a)
21. (c)	**22.** (c)	**23.** (b)	**24.** (d)	**25.** (c)	**26.** (a)	**27.** (b)	**28.** (a)	**29.** (d)	**30.** (c)
31. (b)	**32.** (a)	**33.** (a)	**34.** (d)	**35.** (d)	**36.** (d)	**37.** (c)	**38.** (d)	**39.** (d)	**40.** (d)
41. (c)	**42.** (c)	**43.** (c)	**44.** (d)	**45.** (a)	**46.** (b)	**47.** (c)	**48.** (c)	**49.** (d)	**50.** (b)
51. (d)	**52.** (c)	**53.** (a)	**54.** (b)	**55.** (c)	**56.** (a)	**57.** (d)	**58.** (b)	**59.** (b)	**60.** (d)
61. (a)	**62.** (d)	**63.** (c)	**64.** (d)	**65.** (a)	**66.** (a)	**67.** (d)	**68.** (a)	**69.** (c)	**70.** (b)
71. (c)	**72.** (a)	**73.** (b)	**74.** (b)	**75.** (b)	**76.** (d)	**77.** (c)	**78.** (a)	**79.** (d)	**80.** (a)
81. (a)	**82.** (c)	**83.** (a)	**84.** (c)	**85.** (b)	**86.** (d)	**87.** (b)	**88.** (d)	**89.** (b)	**90.** (c)
91. (b)	**92.** (b)	**93.** (c)	**94.** (d)	**95.** (a)	**96.** (c)	**97.** (a)	**98.** (c)	**99.** (d)	**100.** (d)
101. (a)	**102.** (d)	**103.** (c)	**104.** (d)	**105.** (b)	**106.** (b)	**107.** (b)	**108.** (a)	**109.** (a)	**110.** (c)
111. (a)	**112.** (d)	**113.** (b)	**114.** (c)	**115.** (c)	**116.** (d)	**117.** (c)	**118.** (a)	**119.** (d)	**120.** (c)
121. (c)	**122.** (b)	**123.** (a)	**124.** (a)	**125.** (a)	**126.** (c)	**127.** (b)	**128.** (b)	**129.** (a)	**130.** (d)
131. (a)	**132.** (b)	**133.** (a)	**134.** (a)	**135.**(c, d)	**136.** (a)	**137.** (b)	**138.** (a)	**139.** (b)	**140.** (b)
141. (c)	**142.** (c)	**143.** (b)	**144.** (a)	**145.** (b)	**146.** (b)	**147.** (e)	**148.** (c)	**149.** (d)	**150.** (a)
151. (d)	**152.** (c)	**153.** (c)	**154.** (d)	**155.** (b)	**156.** (b)	**157.** (b)	**158.** (c)		

5

WORK, POWER AND ENERGY

MULTIPLE CHOICE QUESTIONS

1. Two masses of 1 g and 9 g are moving with equal K.E. The ratio of magnitudes of their respective linear momentum is :

(a) 1 : 9 (b) 9 : 1

(c) 1 : 3 (d) 3 : 1

2. When a body is lifted from rest to a height 'h' and the body is in static or dynamic equilibrium, then :

(a) Work done by individual forces must be zero

(b) Net work done is +ve

(c) Net work done is –ve

(d) Net work done is zero.

3. When force retards the motion of a body, the work done is :

(a) zero (b) –ve

(c) +ve (d) None of these

4. A person holds a bucket of weight 60 N. He walks 7 m along a horizontal path and then stairs-up a vertical distance of 5 m. The work done by the person is :

(a) 300 Nm (b) 420 Nm

(c) 720 Nm (d) 820 Nm

5. The momentum of a body decreases by 20%. Then percentage decrease in its K.E. will be :

(a) 40% (b) 20%

(c) 36% (d) 44%

6. The K.E. of a body is increased by 300%. The momentum of the body would increase by :

(a) 50% (b) 100%

(c) 150 % (d) 300%

7. Two bodies of masses M_1 and M_2 have equal K.E. If p_1 and p_2 are their respective momenta then $\frac{p_1}{p_2}$ is equal to :

(a) $\frac{M_1}{M_2}$ (b) $\left(\frac{M_1}{M_2}\right)^2$

(c) $\frac{M_2}{M_1}$ (d) $\left(\frac{M_1}{M_2}\right)^{1/2}$

8. The centripetal acceleration of a particle varies inversely with the square of the radius r of a circular path. The kinetic energy of the particle varies directly as :

(a) r (b) r^2

(c) r^{-1} (d) r^{-2}

9. If a body is placed on another body and is moving with it, then work done by the frictional force on the upper body relative to ground is :

(a) – ve (b) Zero

(c) + ve (d) Unity

10. The K.E. (K) of a particle moving along a straight line depends upon the distance s as $K = as^2$. The force acting on the particle is :

(a) 2 as (b) 2 mas

(c) 2a (d) $\sqrt{as^2}$

11. A body moves a distance of 5 m along a straight line under the action of a force of 10 N. If the work done is 25 J, then the angle between the applied force and direction of displacement will be :

(a) 0° (b) 30°

(c) 60° (d) 90°

12. A 5 kg block of cement of size $(20 \times 10 \times 8)$ cm^3 is lying on the large base. It is now made to stand vertically. Then the amount of work done is : $(g = 10\ ms^{-2})$

(a) 3 J (b) 5 J
(c) 7 J (d) 9 J

13. Force $(\vec{F})$ and displacement $(\vec{S})$ are not equal to zero, but the work done is zero. From this, we can conclude that :

(a) $\vec{F}$ and $\vec{S}$ are in same direction
(b) $\vec{F}$ and $\vec{S}$ are in opposite direction
(c) $\vec{F}$ and $\vec{S}$ are at 90°
(d) $\vec{F}$ and $\vec{S}$ are at 45°

14. A mass M is lowered with the help of a string by a distance 'h' at a constant acceleration $g/2$. The work done by the string will be :

(a) $Mgh/2$ (b) $-Mgh/2$
(c) $3Mgh/2$ (d) $-3Mgh/2$

15. Under the action of force, a 2 kg body moves such that its position x as a function of time 't' is given by $x = \frac{t^3}{3}$ where x is in metre and t is in second. Then the work done by the force in the first two seconds is :

(a) 1.6 J (b) 16 J
(c) 160 J (d) 1600 J

16. A man pumps out 10 m^3 water in 1 sec. from a hand pump. The level of water in the well is 10 m from the ground level. Then the work done by the man is : $(g = 10\ ms^{-2})$

(a) 10^3 J (b) 10^4 J
(c) 10^5 J (d) 10^6 J

17. The displacement x (in metre) of a particle of mass m kg in one dimension under the action of a force is related to the time t in seconds by the equation $t = \sqrt{x} + 3$. The work done by the force in the first six seconds is :

(a) 18 J (b) zero
(c) 4.5 J (d) 36 J

18. The position dependent force $F = (3x^2 - 2x + 7)$ N acts on a body of mass 7 kg and displaces it from $x = 0$ to $x = 5$ m. The work done on the body is x' joule. If both F and x are measured in S.I. units, the value of x' is :

(a) 135 J (b) 235 J
(c) 335 J (d) 3.35 J

19. A 5 kg stone of relative density 3 is resting at the bed of a lake. It is lifted through a height of 5 m in the lake. Then the work done is : $(g = 10\ ms^{-2})$

(a) $\frac{500}{3}$ J (b) 169.9 J
(c) 179.9 J (d) Zero

20. The velocity of a 2 kg body is changed by $(4\hat{i} + 3\hat{j})$. The work done on the body is :

(a) 9 J (b) 11 J
(c) 1 J (d) Zero

21. If a body is thrown upwards with the velocity of 4 ms^{-1}, at what height does its K.E. reduce to half of the initial value ?
$\{\because g = 10\ ms^{-2}\}$

(a) 4 m (b) 2 m
(c) 1 m (d) 0.4 m

22. A car is moving along a straight road with a speed of 72 kmh^{-1}. The coefficient of static friction between the road and tyres is 0.5. The shortest distance in which the car can be stopped is :

(a) 30 m (b) 40 m
(c) 72 m (d) 20 m

23. The potential energy of a certain spring, when stretched through a distance S is 10 J. The amount of work in joule that must be done on this spring to stretch it through an additional distance S will be :

(a) 30 (b) 40
(c) 10 (d) 20

24. A ball is thrown vertically upwards with a velocity of 10 ms^{-1}. It returns to the ground with a velocity of 9 ms^{-1}. The maximum height attained by the ball is :

(a) 5.1 m (b) 4.1 m
(c) 4.61 m (d) 5 m

25. The kinetic energy acquired by a mass m in travelling a certain distance d, starting from rest under the action of a constant force, is directly proportional to :

(a) $\sqrt{m}$

(b) independent of m

(c) $\frac{1}{\sqrt{m}}$

(d) m

26. A bullet fired at a target with a speed of 100 ms^{-1} penetrates one metre into it. If the bullet is fired with the same system at a target of thickness 0.5 m, then it will emerge from it with a velocity of :

(a) $50\sqrt{2}$ ms^{-1} (b) $\frac{50}{\sqrt{2}}$ ms^{-1}

(c) 50 ms^{-1} (d) 10 ms^{-1}

27. A bullet when fired at a target has its velocity decreased to 50% after penetrating 30 cm into it. Then the additional thickness, it will penetrate in cm before coming to rest is :

(a) 10 cm (b) 30 cm

(c) 40 cm (d) 60 cm

28. A 2 kg block drops vertically from a height of 40 cm on a spring whose force constant k is 1.960 Nm^{-1}. Then the maximum compression of the spring is :

(a) 40 cm (b) 25 cm

(c) 10 cm (d) 5 cm

29. Two bodies A and B of equal masses are suspended from two separate springs of spring constant k_1 and k_2 respectively. If the two bodies oscillate vertically such that their maximum velocities are equal, then their ratio of amplitudes of vibration of A to that of B is :

(a) $\frac{k_1}{k_2}$ (b) $\left(\frac{k_1}{k_2}\right)^{1/2}$

(c) $\frac{k_2}{k_1}$ (d) $\left(\frac{k_2}{k_1}\right)^{1/2}$

30. The work done in dragging a stone of mass 100 kg upon an inclined plane 1 in 100 through a distance of 10 m is :

(a) Zero (b) 980 J

(c) 9800 J (d) 98 J

31. At a certain instant, a body of mass 0.4 kg has a velocity of $(8\hat{i} + 6\hat{j})$ ms^{-1}. The kinetic energy of the body is :

(a) 10 J (b) 40 J

(c) 20 J (d) Zero

32. When a man increases his speed by 2 ms^{-1}, he finds that his K.E. is doubled. The original speed of the man is :

(a) $2(\sqrt{2} - 1)$ ms^{-1} (b) $2(\sqrt{2} + 1)$ ms^{-1}

(c) 4.5 ms^{-1} (d) None of these

33. When a body of mass 3 kg is dropped from the top of a tower of height 25 m, then its K.E. after 3 seconds will be :

(a) 1126 J (b) 1048 J

(c) 735 J (d) 1296 J

34. A stone of mass 2 kg is projected upwards with K.E. of 98 J. The height at which its K.E. becomes half of the original value is given by : {$g = 10$ ms^{-2}}

(a) 5 m (b) 2.5 m

(c) 1.5 m (d) 0.5 m

35. A ball whose K.E. is (E), is projected at an angle of 45° to the horizontal. The kinetic energy of the ball at highest point of flight will be :

(a) E (b) $\frac{E}{\sqrt{2}}$

(c) $\frac{E}{2}$ (d) Zero

36. A body of mass 2 kg is thrown up vertically with kinetic energy of 490 J. The height at which the K.E. of the body becomes half of the original value is :

(a) 50 m (b) 12.25 m

(c) 25 m (d) 10 m

37. The potential energy of a particle of mass 5 kg moving in the $x-y$ plane and is given by U = $(-7x + 24y)$ joule, x and y are in metre. If the particle starts from rest from the origin, then the speed of the particle at $t = 2$ s is :

(a) 5 ms^{-1} (b) 0.01 ms^{-1}

(c) 17.5 ms^{-1} (d) 10 ms^{-1}

38. A 50 gm bullet moving with a velocity of 10 ms^{-1} gets embedded into a 950 g stationary body. The loss in K.E. of the system will be :

(a) 95% (b) 100%

(c) 5% (d) 50%

39. A uniform force of 4 N acts on a body of mass 10 kg for a distance of 2.0 m. The K.E. acquired by the body is :

(a) 16 J (b) 32×10^8 erg

(c) 8 J (d) 32 erg

40. The energy required to accelerate a car from rest to 10 ms^{-1} is E. What energy will be required to accelerate the car from 10 ms^{-1} to 20 ms^{-1} ?

(a) E (b) 3 E

(c) 5 E (d) 7 E

41. In the given figure, a particle of mass m is released from A to B. Then :

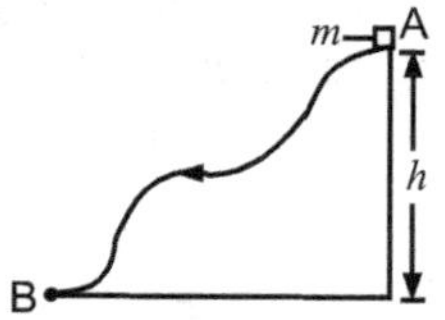

(a) K.E. at B must be mgh

(b) K.E. at B must be zero

(c) K.E. at B must be less than mgh

(d) K.E. at B must not be equal to zero

42. The potential energy of a particle of mass 5 kg moving in the $x-y$ plane is given by U = $(-7x + 24y)$ joule, x and y is in metre. Initially at $t = 0$, the particle is at origin (0, 0) moving with a velocity of $(2.4\hat{i} + 0.7\hat{j})$ ms^{-1}. The magnitude of force on the particle is :

(a) 25 units (b) 24 units

(c) 7 units (d) zero

43. The potential energy as a function of force between two atoms in a diatomic molecule is given by $U(x) = \frac{a}{x^{12}} - \frac{b}{x^6}$, where a and b are positive constants and x is the distance between the atoms. The position of stable equilibrium for the system of the two atoms is given by :

(a) $x = \frac{a}{b}$ (b) $x = \left(\frac{a}{b}\right)^{1/2}$

(c) $x = \frac{\sqrt{3a}}{b}$ (d) $x = \sqrt[6]{\frac{2a}{b}}$

44. A body of mass 4 kg is moving with a momentum of 8 kg-ms^{-1}. A force of 0.2 N acts on it in the direction of motion of the body for 10 s. The increase in K.E. in joule is :

(a) 10 (b) 8.5

(c) 4.5 (d) 4

45. A car is moving with a speed of 100 kmh^{-1}. If the mass of the car is 950 kg, then its kinetic energy is :

(a) 0.367×10^6 J (b) 3.67 J

(c) 3.67 MJ (d) 367 J

46. A machine which is 75% efficient uses 12 J of energy in lifting up a 1 kg mass through a certain distance. The mass is then allowed to fall through that distance. The velocity of the ball at the end of its fall is :

(a) $\sqrt{24}$ ms^{-1} (b) $\sqrt{32}$ ms^{-1}

(c) $\sqrt{18}$ ms^{-1} (d) 3 ms^{-1}

47. Given that the position of the body in metre is a function of time as $x = 2t^4 + 5t + 4$. The mass of the body is 2 kg. The increase in its K.E., one second after the start of motion is :

(a) 168 J (b) 169 J

(c) 32 J (d) 144 J

48. In stable equilibrium position, a body has :

(a) Maximum potential energy
(b) Minimum potential energy
(c) Minimum kinetic energy
(d) Maximum kinetic energy

49. A 3 kg body is dropped from the top of a tower of height 135 m. If $g = 10\ ms^{-2}$, then the K.E. of the body after 3 seconds will be :

(a) 950 J (b) 10 J
(c) 1150 J (d) 1350 J

50. A stone is dropped from the top of a tall building. The ratio of K.E. of the stone at the end of three seconds to the increase in the K.E. of the stone during the next three seconds is :

(a) 1 : 1 (b) 1 : 2
(c) 1 : 3 (d) 1 : 9

51. If g is acceleration due to gravity on the earth's surface, the gain in potential energy of an object of mass 'm' raised from the surface of the earth to a height equal to the radius R of the earth is :

(a) $\frac{mgR}{2}$ (b) 2 mgR
(c) mgR (d) $\frac{1}{4}mgR$

52. A boy of 50 kg finished a long jump at a distance of 8 m. Considering that he moved along a parabolic path and his angle of jump was 45°, his initial kinetic energy will be :

(a) 960 J (b) 1560 J
(c) 2460 J (d) 1960 J

53. A body, constrained to move in the y-direction is subjected to a force $\vec{F} = (-2\hat{i} + 15\hat{j} + 6\hat{k})$ N. The work done by this force in moving the distance 10 m along y-axis will be :

(a) 20 J (b) 150 J
(c) 160 J (d) 190 J

54. Calculate the work done, when a force $\vec{F} = (2\hat{i} + 3\hat{j} - 5\hat{k})$ units acts on a body, producing a displacement $\vec{S} = (2\hat{i} + 4\hat{j} + 3\hat{k})$ units :

(a) 30 units (b) 45 units
(c) 1 unit (d) 72 units

55. A force $\vec{F} = 6\hat{i} + 2\hat{j} - 3\hat{k}$ acts on a particle and produces a displacement $\vec{S} = 2\hat{i} - 2\hat{j} + x\hat{k}$. If work done is zero, then the value of x is :

(a) – 2 (b) 1/2
(c) 6 (d) 2

56. A particle moves under a force F = cx from $x = 0$ to $x = x_1$. The work done is equal to :

(a) Zero (b) cx_1^2
(c) $\frac{cx_1^2}{2}$ (d) $\frac{cx_1^3}{3}$

57. A ball whose K.E. is E, is projected at an angle of 45° to the horizontal. The K.E. of the ball at highest point of its flight will be : **(A.I.E.E.E. 2002)**

(a) E (b) $E/\sqrt{2}$
(c) E/2 (d) Zero

58. Consider the following statements :

(A) Linear momentum of a system of particles is zero.
(B) K.E. of a system of particles is zero. Then :

(a) A does not imply B and B does not imply A.
(b) A implies B, but B does not imply A.
(c) A does not imply B, but B implies A.
(d) A implies B and B implies A.

59. A particle moves in a straight line with retardation proportional to its displacement. Its loss of K.E. for any displacement x is proportional to : **(A.I.E.E.E. 2004)**

(a) x^2 (b) e^x
(c) x (d) $\log_e x$

60. A bomb of mass 16 kg at rest explodes into two pieces of masses 4 kg and 12 kg. The velocity of the 12 kg mass is 4 ms^{-1}. The K.E. of the other mass is : **(A.I.E.E.E. 2006)**

(a) 96 J (b) 144 J
(c) 288 J (d) 192 J

61. A particle is projected at 60° to the horizontal with a kinetic energy (K). The kinetic energy at the highest point is :

(A.I.E.E.E. 2007)

(a) K/2 (b) K
(c) 3K/4 (d) K/4

62. An athlete in the Olympic games covers a distance of 100 m in 10 seconds. His K.E. can be estimated to be in the range :

(A.I.E.E.E. 2007)

(a) 2,000 J – 5000 J
(b) 200 J – 500 J
(c) 2×10^5 J – 3×10^5 J
(d) 20,000 J – 50,000 J

63. A particle is acted upon by a force of constant magnitude which is always perpendicular to the velocity of the particle. The motion of the particle takes place in a plane, it follows that : **(A.I.E.E.E. 2004)**

(a) its velocity is constant.
(b) its acceleration is constant
(c) its kinetic energy is constant
(d) it moves in a straight line

64. A uniform chain of length 2 m is kept on a table such that a length of 60 cm hangs freely from the edge of the table. The total mass of the chain is 4 kg. What is the work done in pulling the entire chain on the table ? **(A.I.E.E.E. 2004)**

(a) 7.2 J (b) 3.6 J
(c) 120 J (d) 1200 J

65. A mass M kg is suspended by a weightless string. The horizontal force that is required to displace it until the string making an angle of 45° with the initial direction is :

(A.I.E.E.E. 2006)

(a) $\sqrt{2}$ Mg (b) Mg $(\sqrt{2} + 1)$
(c) Mg $(\sqrt{2} - 1)$ (d) $\frac{Mg}{\sqrt{2}}$

66. A particle of mass 100 g is thrown vertically upwards with a speed of 5 ms^{-1}. The work done by the force of gravity during the time the particle goes up is : **(A.I.E.E.E. 2006)**

(a) 0.5 J (b) – 0.5 J
(c) – 1.25 J (d) 1.25 J

67. The potential energy of 1 kg particle free to move along the x-axis is given by :

$$V(x) = \left[\frac{x^4}{4} - \frac{x^2}{2}\right] \text{joule}$$

The total mechanical energy of the particle is 2 J. Then maximum speed (in ms^{-1}) is :

(A.I.E.E.E. 2006)

(a) 2 (b) $\frac{3}{\sqrt{2}}$
(c) $\sqrt{2}$ (d) $\frac{1}{\sqrt{2}}$

68. A uniform chain having mass 'M' and length 'L' is lying on a smooth horizontal table with half of its length hanging vertically down. The work done in pulling the chain up the table is :

(a) MgL/2 (b) MgL/4
(c) MgL/8 (d) MgL/16

69. The power of an engine which accelerates a car of mass 800 kg to a speed of 72 km/h from rest in 32 seconds is :

(a) 10 kW (b) 15 kW
(c) 20 kW (d) 5 kW

70. An athelete of mass 60 kg skips at the rate of 20 steps per minute through an average height of 25 cm. The power developed is :

(a) 98 W (b) 49 W
(c) 14 W (d) 21 W

71. A body is dropped from a height 'h'. If it acquires a momentum 'p', then the mass of body is :

(a) $\frac{p}{\sqrt{2gh}}$ (b) $\frac{p^2}{2gh}$

(c) $\frac{2gh}{p}$ (d) $\sqrt{\frac{2gh}{p}}$

72. If the momentum of a body is increased by 50%, its K.E. will increase by :

(a) 25% (b) 50%

(c) 100% (d) 125%

73. If the momentum of a body is increased by 20%, the K.E. will increase by :

(a) 44% (b) 55%

(c) 66% (d) 77%

74. A machine has an efficiency of 25%. Energy is fed into the machine at the rate of 1 kW. The output of the machine is :

(a) 40 W (b) 250 W

(c) 750 W (d) 25 kW

75. A car drives along a straight level frictionless road by an engine delivering constant power. Then velocity is directly proportional to :

(a) t (b) $\frac{1}{\sqrt{t}}$

(c) $\sqrt{t}$ (d) $t^{3/2}$

76. The speed V reached by a car of mass m, driven with constant power P, is given by :

(a) $V = \frac{3xP}{m}$ (b) $V = \sqrt{\frac{3xP}{m}}$

(c) $V = \left(\frac{3xP}{m}\right)^{1/3}$ (d) $V = \left(\frac{3xP}{m}\right)^2$

77. A particle of mass m is moving in a circular path of radius r such that its centripetal acceleration is $a = k^2rt^2$, where k is a constant. The power delivered to the particle by the force acting on it is :

(a) Zero (b) $m\,k^2r^2t^2$

(c) $m\,k^2r^2t$ (d) $m\,k^2rt$

78. Two unequal masses are tied together with a compressed spring. When the cord is burnt with a match stick releasing the string, the two masses fly apart with equal :

(a) K.E. (b) Speed

(c) Momentum (d) Acceleration

79. The human heart discharges 75 cc. of blood through the arteries at each beat against an average pressure of 10 cm of Hg. Assuming that the pulse frequency is 72/min., the rate of working of heart in watt is :
($\delta_{Hg} = 13.6$ g/cc)

(a) 11.9 W (b) 1.19 W

(c) 0.119 W (d) 119 W

80. At her maximum height, a girl in a swing is 3 m above the ground and at the lowest point she is 2 m above the ground. What is her maximum velocity :

(a) $\sqrt{29.4}$ ms^{-1} (b) $\sqrt{9.8}$ ms^{-1}

(c) $\sqrt{19.6}$ ms^{-1} (d) 9.8 ms^{-1}

81. The momentum of a body increases by 20%. The percentage increase in K.E. will be :

(a) 20 (b) 44

(c) 66 (d) 88

82. The kinetic energy of a body is increased by 300%. The percentage increase in the momentum of the body will be :

(a) 50% (b) 100%

(c) 150% (d) 200%

83. In non-relativistic space, if the momentum is increased by 100%, the percentage increase in kinetic energy will be :

(a) 100 (b) 200

(c) 300 (d) 400

84. A man throws a piece of stone to a height of 12 m, where it reaches with a speed of 12 ms^{-1}. If he throws the same stone such that it just reaches this height, the percentage of energy saved is nearly :

(a) 19 (b) 38

(c) 57 (d) 76

85. An engine pumps water continuously through a hole. The speed with which the water passes through the hole nozzle is v and k is mass per unit length of water jet as it leaves the nozzle. The rate at which the kinetic energy is being imparted to water will be :

(a) $\frac{1}{2}kv^2$ (b) $\frac{1}{2}kv^3$

(c) $\frac{v^2}{2k}$ (d) $\frac{v^3}{2k}$

86. The power of a water pump is 200 kW. Then the amount of water that can be raised in 1 min. to a height of 10 m is :

(a) 2000 lit (b) 1000 lit

(c) 100 lit (d) 1200 lit

87. The power of a water jet flowing through an orifice of radius r with the velocity v will be:

(a) zero (b) $500\,\pi\, r^2v^2$

(c) $500\,\pi\, r^2v^3$ (d) $\pi\, r^4v$

88. What power must a sprinter, weighing 80 kg, develop from the start, if he has to impart a velocity of 10 ms^{-1} to his body in 4 seconds ?

(a) 1 kW (b) 2 kW

(c) 3 kW (d) 4 kW

89. The power supplied by a force acting on a particle moving in a straight line is constant. Then the velocity of the particle varies with the displacement x as :

(a) $\sqrt{x}$ (b) x

(c) x^2 (d) $x^{1/3}$

90. A particle of mass m is moving in a circular path of constant radius r such that its centripetal acceleration a_c is varying with time t as $a_c = k^2rt^2$. The power is :

(a) $2\pi\, m\, k^2r^2t$ (b) $mk^2r^2\, t$

(c) $\frac{mk^4r^2t^5}{3}$ (d) Zero

91. Ten litres of water per second is lifted from a well through 20 m and delivered with a velocity of 10 ms^{-1}. Then the power of the motor is :

(a) 1.5 kW (b) 2.3 kW

(c) 3.5 kW (d) 4.5 kW

92. A coolie 1.5 m tall raises a load of 80 kg in 2 second from the ground to his head and then walks a distance of 40 m in another 2 s. The power developed by the coolie is : (g = 10 ms^{-2})

(a) 0.2 kW (b) 0.4 kW

(c) 0.6 kW (d) 0.8 W

93. An engine of 7500 W makes a train move on a horizontal rail with constant velocity of 20 ms^{-1}. The force involved is :

(a) 375 N (b) 400 N

(c) 500 N (d) 275 N

94. A 1 kW motor is used to pump water from a well 10 m deep. The quantity of water pumped out per sec. is nearly :

(a) 1 kg (b) 10 kg

(c) 100 kg (d) 1000 kg

95. An electric motor creates a tension of 9×10^3 N in a hoisting cable and reels it at the rate of 2 ms^{-1}. The power of the electric motor is :

(a) 18 kW (b) 15 kW

(c) 81 kW (d) 225 W

96. A 10 m long iron chain of linear mass density 0.8 kg m^{-1} is hanging freely from a rigid support. The power required to lift the chain up to the point of support in 10 s is : (g = 10 ms^{-2}) **(A.I.E.E.E. 2003)**

(a) 10 W (b) 20 W

(c) 30 W (d) 40 W

97. A body is moved along a straight line by a machine delivering constant power. The distance moved by the body in time 't' is proportional to :

(a) $t^{3/4}$ (b) $t^{3/2}$

(c) $t^{1/4}$ (d) $t^{1/2}$

98. A body of mass m accelerates uniformly from rest to a speed v_1 in time t_1. The instantaneous power delivered to the body as a function of time 't' is : **(A.I.E.E.E. 2004)**

(a) $\frac{mv_1 t}{t_1^2}$ (b) $\frac{mv_1^2 t}{t_1^2}$

(c) $\frac{mv_1 t^2}{t_1}$ (d) $\frac{mv_1^2 t}{t_1}$

99. The body of mass m is accelerated uniformly from rest to a speed v in a time T. The instantaneous power delivered to the body as a function of time t is given by :

(A.I.E.E.E. 2005)

(a) $\frac{1}{2}\frac{mv^2}{T^2}\cdot t$ (b) $\frac{1}{2}\frac{mv^2}{T^2}\cdot t^2$

(c) $\frac{mv^2}{T^2}\cdot t$ (d) $\frac{mv^2}{T^2}\cdot t^2$

100. A block of mass M moving on a frictionless horizontal surface collides with a spring of spring constant K and compresses it by a length L. The maximum momentum of the block after collision is :

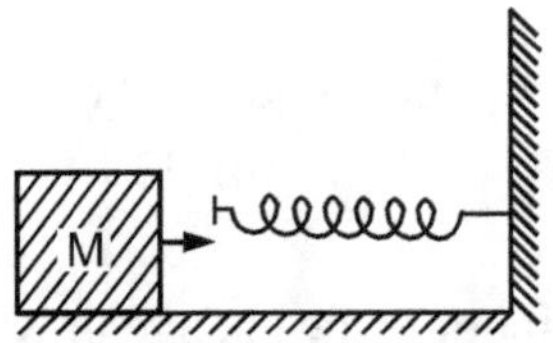

(a) Zero (b) ML^2/K

(c) $\frac{ML^2}{2M}$ (d) $L(\sqrt{MK})$

101. A 2 kg block slides on a horizontal floor with a speed of 4 m/s. It strikes an uncompressed spring and compresses it till the block is motionless. The kinetic force is 15 N and spring constant is 10^5 Nm^{-1}. The spring compresses by :

(a) 8.5 cm (b) 5.5 cm

(c) 2.5 cm (d) 11.0 cm

102. A mass m moves with velocity v and collides inelastically with another identical mass. After collision, the first mass moves with a velocity in a direction perpendicular to the initial direction of motion. Find the speed of the second mass after collision.

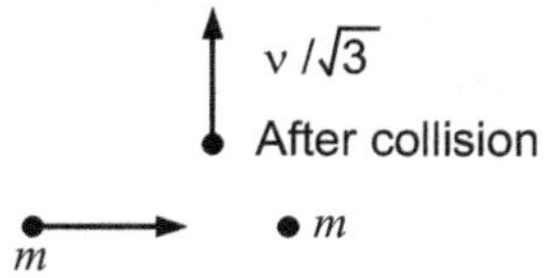

(a) $\frac{2}{\sqrt{3}}v$ (b) $\frac{v}{\sqrt{3}}$

(c) v (d) $\sqrt{3v}$

103. A body of mass 100 gm is rotating in a circular path of radius 'r' with constant speed. The work done in one complete rotation is :

(a) 100 J (b) (r/100) J

(c) (100/r) J (d) zero

104. A rod is elongated by length l, when a body of mass M is suspended from it. The work done is :

(a) Mgl (b) $\frac{1}{2}$Mgl

(c) 2Mgl (d) $\frac{3}{4}$Mgl

105. What is the work done by the force $\vec{F} = (-2\hat{i} + 15\hat{j} + 6\hat{k})$N acting on a body moving through a distance 10 m along the y-axis :

(a) 20 J (b) 150 J

(c) 160 J (d) 190 J

106. A force acting on a particle is N. The work done by this force is zero, when a particle moves on the line. $5 = kx + 3y$. Then the value of k is :

(a) 12 (b) 6

(c) 3 (d) 2

107. A particle moves in the $x-y$ plane under the influence of a force $\vec{F}$ such that its instantaneous momentum is $\vec{p} = (2\cos t)\hat{i} + (2\sin t)\hat{j}$. Then the angle between the force and instantaneous momentum is :

(a) 15° (b) 30°

(c) 45° (d) 90°

108. A truck tows a trailer of mass 1,200 kg at a steady speed of 10 ms^{-1} on a leveled road. The tension in the coupling is 10^3 N. So the power expanded on the trailer is :

(a) 10 W (b) 10^2 W
(c) 10^4 W (d) 10^6 W

109. A bullet fired into a target loses half its velocity after penetrating 25 cm. How much further will it penetrate before coming to rest ?

(a) 8.3 cm (b) 5 cm
(c) 25 cm (d) 75 cm

110. A bob of a simple pendulum of length 'l' is released from its horizontal position and it elastically strikes a block of equal mass lying on a frictionless table. The K.E. of the block will be :

(a) Zero (b) mgl
(c) $mgl/2$ (d) 2 mgl

111. If a man speeds up by 1 ms^{-1}, his kinetic energy increases by 44%. His original speed in ms^{-1} is :

(a) 1 (b) 2
(c) 5 (d) 4

112. An automobile weighing 1200 kg climbs up a hill that rises 1m in 20 seconds. Neglecting frictional effects, the minimum power developed by the engine is 9000 W. Then the velocity of the automobile will be :
($\because g = 10\ ms^{-2}$)

(a) 36 kmh^{-1} (b) 54 kmh^{-1}
(c) 72 kmh^{-1} (d) 90 kmh^{-1}

113. A dam is at a height of 550 m above sea level and supplies water to a power house which is at a height of 50 m above sea level. 2×10^3 kg of water passes through the turbines per second. The maximum electric power (output) of the power house, if the efficiency is 80%, will be :

(a) 8 MW (b) 10 MW
(c) 12.5 MW (d) 16 MW

114. A particle moves in a straight line with retardation proportional to its displacement. Its loss of K.E. for any displacement x is proportional to :

(a) x (b) x^2
(c) x^0 (d) e^x

115. A bullet fired from a gun with a velocity of 10^4 ms^{-1} goes through a bag full of straw. If the bullet loses half of its K.E. in the bag, its velocity when it comes out of the bag will be:

(a) 7071.06 ms^{-1} (b) 707 ms^{-1}
(c) 70.71 ms^{-1} (d) 707.06 ms^{-1}

COMPREHENSION BASED QUESTIONS

Passage - I :

A body of mass 0.8 kg has initial velocity as $\vec{u} = (4\hat{i} + 3\hat{j})\ ms^{-1}$ and final velocity as $\vec{v} = (-6\hat{i} + 2\hat{j})\ ms^{-1}$.

116. The initial K.E. of the body will be :

(a) 2.5 J (b) 5 J
(c) 7.5 J (d) 10 J

117. The final K.E. of the body will be :

(a) 16 J (b) 32 J
(c) 48 J (d) 64 J

118. During the motion, the change in K.E. is :

(a) 11 J (b) 9 J
(c) 6 J (d) 3 J

119. The change in linear momentum is :

(a) 1.06 kg ms^{-1} (b) 10.6 kg ms^{-1}
(c) 106.6 kg ms^{-1} (d) zero

Passage - II :

Two boats A and B set on a parallel course move under their own momentum through the stagnant water of a lake towards each other with the same velocity i.e. 6 ms^{-1}. As soon as they come to rest, a load of 60 kg is shifted from boat A (without any change in velocity of A) into boat B. After that, boat B continues to move in the original direction but with a velocity of 4 ms^{-1}.

120. If the mass of boat A is 500 kg, then the mass of boat B will be :

(a) 270 kg (b) 280 kg
(c) 280.72 kg (d) 300 kg

121. The energy of the boats and the load before they meet will be :

(a) 15.480 kJ (b) 16.587 kJ
(c) 20000 J (d) 20.3 kJ

122. The energy of the boats and the load after they meet will be :

(a) 10.880 kJ (b) 11.880 kJ
(c) 12.880 kJ (d) 12 kJ

123. What is the velocity of boat B w.r.t. boat A after they meet ?

(a) 10 ms^{-1} (b) – 10 ms^{-1}
(c) 2 ms^{-1} (d) – 2 ms^{-1}

ASSERTION AND REASON

Directions for Q. 124 to Q. 131 :

In the following questions, Statement-I is Assertion followed by Statement-II as Reason. For answering a question, you are required to choose the correct one out of the given four options.

(a) Statement-I and II, both are true and Statement-II is the correct explanation of Statement-I.
(b) Statements-I and II, both are true and Statement-II is not the correct explanation of Statement-I.
(c) Statement-I is true and Statement-II is false.
(d) Statement-I and Statement-II both are false.

124. **(I)** $\vec{P} \cdot \vec{Q} = \vec{Q} \cdot \vec{P}$

(II) The dot product of two vectors obeys the commutative law.

125. **(I)** The scalar product of two vectors may be positive, zero or negative.

(II) It will be so, when the angle between the two vectors is < 90°, = 90 or > 90°.

126. **(I)** When a cyclist moves on the road, the work done by the cyclist on the road is zero.

(II) Because the reaction of the road and displacement are perpendicular to each other.

127. **(I)** The kinetic energy, with any reference, must be positive.

(II) Because, in the expression for K.E., the velocity appears with power two

128. **(I)** When the momentum of a body is doubled, its K.E. increases by 300%.

(II) Because K.E. $= \dfrac{p^2}{2m}$

129. **(I)** If a light body and heavy body possess the same momentum, the lighter body will possess more K.E.

(II) The K.E. of a body varies as the square of its velocity.

130. **(I)** The potential energy stored in a spring is positive, when it is compressed and negative when it is stretched.

(II) It is in the accordance with the sign conventions for +ve and – ve work.

131. **(I)** $\vec{P} \times \vec{Q} \neq \vec{Q} \times \vec{P}$

(II) The cross product of two vectors obeys the commutative law.

132. A displacement x in metre of a particle of mass m kg moving in one dimension under the action of a force is related to the time 't' in seconds by the equation $t = \sqrt{x} + 3$. The work done by the force (in joule) in the first six seconds is :

(a) $\frac{9}{2}$ m (b) 18 m
(c) 36 m (d) Zero

133. The velocity of a 2 kg body is changed by $(4\hat{i} + 3\hat{j})$ ms^{-1}. The work done on the body is :

(a) Zero (b) 1 J
(c) 9 J (d) 11 J

134. A body of mass 10 kg is moving on a horizontal surface by applying force 10 N in the forward direction. If the body moves with a constant velocity, the work done by the force of friction for a displacement of 2 m is :

(a) – 20 J (b) 10 J
(c) 20 J (d) – 5 J

135. A force $F = Ay^2 + By + C$ acts on a body in the y-direction. The work done by this force during a displacement from $y = -a$ to $y = a$ is :

(a) $\frac{2Aa^3}{3}$ (b) $\frac{2Aa^3}{3} + 2Ca$
(c) $\frac{2Aa^3}{3} + \frac{Ba^2}{2} + Ca$ (d) Zero

136. A work done in pulling a stone of mass 100 kg upon inclined plane 1 in 100 through a distance of 10 m is :

($\because \vec{g} = 9.8 \text{ ms}^{-2}$)

(a) Zero (b) 98 J
(c) 980 J (d) 9800 J

137. A body of mass 1 kg moves from point A (2m, 3m, 4m) to point B (3m, 2m, 5m) due to the force $\vec{F} = (2\hat{i} - 4\hat{j})$ N acting on it. The work done by the force on the particle during the displacement is :

(a) $(2\hat{i} - 4\hat{j})$ J (b) 2 J
(c) – 2 J (d) zero

138. A spring of spring constant 5×10^3 Nm^{-1} is stretched initially by 5 cm from an unstretched position. Then the work done to stretch it by further 5 cm is :

(a) 12.5 J (b) 18.75 J
(c) 25 J (d) 0.25 J

139. An object of mass m is tied to a string of length L and a variable horizontal force is applied on it, which starts at zero and gradually increases until the string makes an angle θ with the vertical. The work done by the force F is :

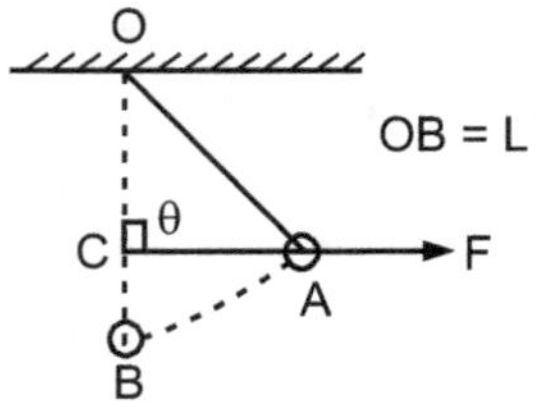

(a) $mgL(1 - \sin\theta)$
(b) mgL
(c) $mgL(1 - \cos\theta)$
(d) $mgL(1 + \cos\theta)$

140. Two blocks each of mass m are connected to a spring of spring constant k as shown in following figure. The maximum displacement in the block is :

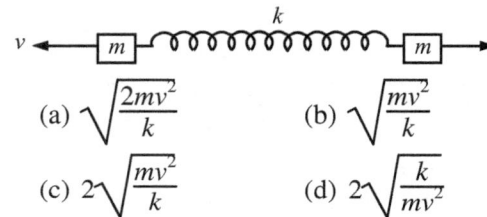

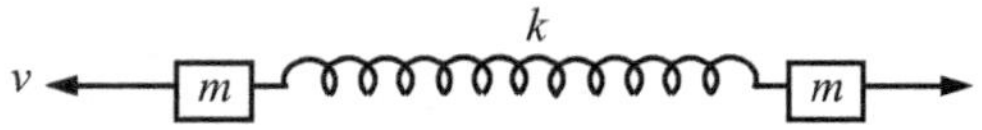

(a) $\sqrt{\frac{2mv^2}{k}}$ (b) $\sqrt{\frac{mv^2}{k}}$
(c) $2\sqrt{\frac{mv^2}{k}}$ (d) $2\sqrt{\frac{k}{mv^2}}$

141. A body of mass m is accelerated uniformly from rest to a speed v in a time T. The instantaneous power delivered to the body as a function of time is given by :

(a) $\frac{1}{2}\frac{mv^2}{T^2} \cdot t^2$ (b) $\frac{1}{2}\frac{mv^2}{T^2} \cdot t$
(c) $2\frac{mv^2}{T^2} \cdot t^2$ (d) $\frac{mv^2}{T^2} \cdot t$

142. Two balls of different masses have the same kinetic energy. The ball having greater momentum, will be :

(a) Both of different mass
(b) Lighter mass ball
(c) Heavier mass ball
(d) None of the above

143. A constant power P is applied to a car starting from rest. If v is the velocity of the car at time t, then :

(a) $v \propto t$ (b) $v \propto \frac{1}{t}$
(c) $v \propto (t)^{1/2}$ (d) $v \propto (t)^{-1/2}$

144. The work done by a particle moving with a velocity of 0.7 c (c = speed of light) in free space and far away from all matter will be :

(a) positive (b) negative

(c) zero (d) infinite

145. The power of a pump which can pump 200 kg of water to a height of 200 m in 10 seconds is : (g = 10 ms^{-2})

(a) 40 kW (b) 4 kW

(c) 80 kW (d) 800 kW

146. A particle of mass 100 g is thrown vertically upwards with a speed of 5 ms^{-1}. The work done by the force of gravity during the time the particle goes up is :

(a) – 0.5 J (b) – 1.25 J

(c) 1.25 J (d) 0.5 J

147. The power applied to a particle varies with time as P = $(3t^2 - 2t + 1)$ watt, where t is in seconds. Find the change in its K.E. between $t = 2$s and $t = 4$s :

(a) 32 J (b) 46 J

(c) 61 J (d) 100 J

148. A body of mass 3 kg acted upon by a constant force is displaced by s metre, given by relation $s = \frac{1}{3}t^2$, where t is in seconds, then the work done by the force in 2 seconds is :

(a) $\frac{8}{3}$ J (b) $\frac{19}{5}$ J

(c) $\frac{5}{19}$ J (d) $\frac{3}{8}$ J

149. A gun of mass 20 kg has a bullet of mass 0.1 kg in it. The gun is free to recoil. 804 J of recoil energy is released on firing the gun. The speed of the bullet (in ms^{-1}) is :

(a) $\sqrt{804 \times 2010}$ (b) $\sqrt{\frac{2010}{804}}$

(c) $\sqrt{\frac{804}{2010}}$ (d) $\sqrt{804 \times 4 \times 10^3}$

150. An engine accelerates a car of mass 800 kg to a speed of 72 kmh^{-1}. If the frictional force is 10 N per ton, the power developed by the engine is :

(a) 10 kW (b) 15 kW

(c) 20 kW (d) 5 kW

151. The $v-t$ graph is given for a particle of mass 2 kg. Then work done by the particle is

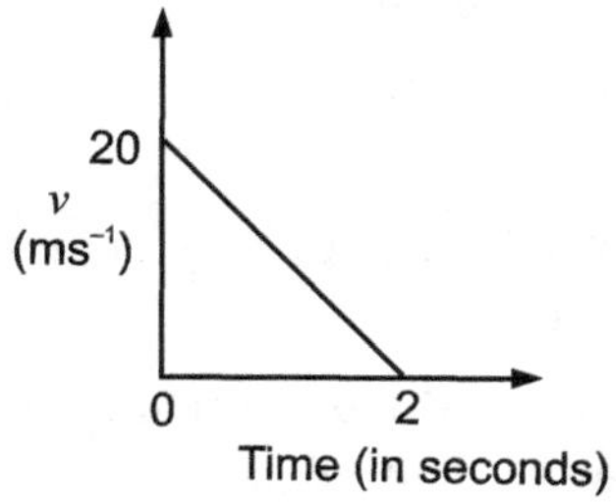

(a) 400 J (b) – 400 J

(c) – 200 J (d) 200 J

152. The potential energy of a long spring when stretched by 2 cm is U. If the spring is stretched by 8 cm, the potential energy stored in it is : **(C.B.S.E. P.M.T. 2006)**

(a) U/4 (b) 4U

(c) 8U (d) 16U

153. Two spheres of same size, one of mass 2 kg and another of mass 4 kg are dropped simultaneously from the top of Qutub Minar (height = 72 m). When they are 1 m above the ground the two spheres have the same : **(C.B.S.E. P.M.T. 2006)**

(a) Momentum (b) Kinetic energy

(c) Potential energy (d) Acceleration

154. Kinetic energy of particles of mass 10 g and 40 g is same, the ratio of their linear momentum is : **(D.P.M.T. 2007)**

(a) 1/4 (b) 1/2

(c) $1/\sqrt{2}$ (d) $\sqrt{2}/1$

155. A body constrained to move in the y-direction is subjected to a force $\vec{F} = 2\hat{i} + 15\hat{j} + 6\hat{k}$ N. The work done by this force in moving the body through a distance of 10 m along y-axis is: **(Kerala P.M.T. 2007)**

(a) 100 J (b) 150 J

(c) 120 J (d) 200 J

156. Identify the false statement from the following : **(Kerala Engg. 2010)**

(a) Work-energy theorem is not independent of Newton's second law.

(b) Work-energy theorem holds in all inertial frames.

(c) Work done by friction over a closed path is zero.

(d) No potential energy can be associated with friction.

157. A body of mass M hits normally a rigid wall with velocity v and bounces back with the same velocity. The impulse experienced by the body is : **(A.I.P.M.T. (Prelims) 2011)**

(a) Mv (b) 1.5 Mv

(c) 2 Mv (d) Zero

158. Work done in increasing the size of a soap bubble from a radius of 3 cm to 5 cm is nearly (surface tension of soap solution = 0.03 Nm^{-1}) : **(A.I.E.E.E. 2011)**

(a) 0.4π mJ (b) 4π mJ

(c) 0.2π mJ (d) 2π mJ

159. A shell of mass 20 kg at rest explodes into two fragments whose masses are in the ratio 2 : 3. The smaller fragment moves with a velocity of 6 ms^{-1}. The kinetic energy of the larger fragment is :

(Karnataka C.E.T. 2007)

(a) 97 J (b) 216 J

(c) 144 J (d) 360 J

160. Mass of M kg is suspended by a weightless string. The horizontal force that is required to displace it until the string makes an angle of 45° with the initial vertical direction is :

(C.P.M.T. 2008)

(a) $Mg(\sqrt{2}+1)$ (b) $Mg\sqrt{2}$

(c) $\frac{Mg}{\sqrt{2}}$ (d) $Mg(\sqrt{2}-1)$

161. An athlete in the Olympic games covers a distance of 100 m in the 10 s. His kinetic energy can be estimated to be in the range :

(A.I.E.E.E. 2008)

(a) 2,000 J - 5,000 J

(b) 200 J - 500 J

(c) 2×10^5 J - 3×10^5 J

(d) 20,000 J - 50,000 J

162. Water falls from a height of 60 m at the rate of 1.5 kg/s to operate a turbine. The losses due to frictional forces are 10% of energy. How much power is generated by the turbine ? ($g = 10$ m/s^2) **(C.B.S.E. 2008)**

(a) 10.2 kW (b) 12.3 kW

(c) 7.0 kW (d) 8.1 kW

163. Two springs P and Q of force constants k_p and k_Q $\left(k_Q = \frac{k_p}{2}\right)$ are stretched by applying forces of equal magnitude. If the energy stored in Q is E, then the energy stored in P is : **(Kerala C.E.T. 2009)**

(a) E (b) 2E

(c) $\frac{E}{8}$ (d) $\frac{E}{2}$

164. If momentum is increased by 20%, then kinetic energy increases by :

(W.B. J.E.E. 2010)

(a) 48% (b) 44%

(c) 40% (d) 36%

165. A bullet hits and gets embedded in a solid block resting on a frictionless surface. In this process, which one of the following is correct ? **(D.C.E. 2009)**

(a) Only momentum is conserved.

(b) Only kinetic energy is conserved.

(c) Neither momentum nor kinetic energy is conserved.

(d) Both momentum and kinetic energy are conserved.

166. A particle of mass m moves in a circular path of radius r under the action of a force $\frac{mv^2}{r}$. The work done during its motion over half of the circumference of the circular path will be : **(M.P.P.E.T. 2009)**

(a) $\left(\frac{mv^2}{r}\right) \times 2\pi r$ (b) $\left(\frac{mv^2}{r}\right) \times \pi r$

(c) $\frac{(2\pi r)}{\left(\frac{mv^2}{r}\right)}$ (d) Zero

167. In an inelastic collision : **(Orissa J.E.E. 2010)**

(a) only momentum is conserved

(b) only kinetic energy is conserved

(c) neither momentum nor kinetic energy is conserved

(d) both momentum and kinetic energy are conserved

168. A block of mass 0.50 kg is moving with a speed of 2.00 ms^{-1} on a smooth surface. It strikes another mass of 1.00 kg and then they move together as a single body. The energy loss during the collision is : **(A.I.E.E.E. 2008)**

(a) 0.34 J (b) 0.16 J

(c) 1.00 J (d) 0.67 J

169. Two bodies A and B have masses 20 kg and 5 kg respectively. Each one is acted upon by a force of 4 kg wt. If they acquire the same kinetic energy in times t_A and t_B, then the ratio $\frac{t_A}{t_B}$ is : **(Kerala 2008)**

(a) $\frac{1}{2}$ (b) 2

(c) $\frac{2}{5}$ (d) $\frac{5}{6}$

170. The object at rest suddenly explodes into three parts with the mass ratio 2 : 1 : 1. The part of equal masses move at right angles to each other with equal speeds. The speed of the third part after the explosion will be: **(E.A.M.C.E.T. 2008)**

(a) 2 v (b) $\frac{v}{\sqrt{2}}$

(c) $\frac{v}{2}$ (d) $\frac{\sqrt{2}}{v}$

171. A shell of mass 200 gm is ejected from a gun of mass of 4 kg by an explosion that generates 1.05 kJ of energy. The initial velocity of the shell is : **(C.B.S.E. 2008)**

(a) 80 ms^{-1} (b) 40 ms^{-1}

(c) 120 ms^{-1} (d) 100 ms^{-1}

172. An ideal spring with spring constant K is hung from the ceiling and a block of mass M is attached to its lower end. The mass is released with the spring initially unstretched. Then the maximum extension in the spring is **(C.B.S.E. 2002)**

(a) $\frac{4\,Mg}{K}$ (b) $\frac{2\,Mg}{K}$

(c) $\frac{Mg}{K}$ (d) $\frac{Mg}{2K}$

173. A car is moving along a straight horizontal road with a speed v_0. If the coefficient of friction between the tyres and the road is μ, the shortest distance in which the car be stopped is **(B.H.U. 2002)**

(a) $\frac{v_0^2}{\mu}$ (b) $\left(\frac{v_0}{\mu g}\right)^2$

(c) $\frac{v_0^2}{\mu g}$ (d) $\frac{v_0^2}{2\mu g}$

174. If kinetic energy of a body is increased by 300 %, then percentage change in momentum will be **(C.B.S.E. 2002)**

(a) 100% (b) 150%

(c) 265% (d) 73.2%

175. If force and displacement of particle in the direction of force are doubled, work would be **(A.F.M.C. 2002)**

(a) double (b) 4 times

(c) half (d) 1/4 times

176. A body of mass M_1 collides elastically with another mass M_2 at rest. There is maximum transfer of energy when **(A.F.M.C. 2002)**

(a) $M_1 > M_2$

(b) $M_1 < M_2$

(c) $M_1 = M_2$

(d) same for all values of M_1 and M_2

177. A machine delivering constant power moves a body along a straight line. The distance moved by the body in time 't' is proportional to **(A.F.M.C. 2002)**

(a) $t^{3/4}$ (b) $t^{3/2}$

(c) $\sqrt{t}$ (d) t

178. An elevator is run by the cables at constant speed. The total work done by the elevator is **(B.H.U. 2003)**

(a) negative

(b) positive

(c) zero

(d) positive or negative depending on the direction of motion

179. A wire suspended vertically from one of its ends is stretched by attaching a weight of 200 N to the lower end. The weight stretches the wire by 1 mm. Then the elastic energy stored in the wire is **(A.F.M.C. 2003)**

(a) 0.2 J (b) 10 J

(c) 20 J (d) 0.1 J

180. A ball is dropped from a height of 20 cm. Ball rebounds to a height of 10 cm. What is the loss of energy ? **(A.F.M.C. 2004)**

(a) 25% (b) 75%

(c) 50% (d) 100%

181. The power of water pump is 2 kW. If $g = 10\ ms^{-2}$, the amount of water it can raise in 1 minute to a height of 10 m is (density of water 1 g/cc) **(Kerala, P.M.T. 2004)**

(a) 2000 lit. (b) 1000 lit.

(c) 100 lit. (d) 1200 lit.

182. A body weighing 100 N is moved up a slope of 50° with the horizontal through a distance of 1 m. The loss of energy due to friction is 20%. The energy gained by the body in joules is **(B.H.U. 2005)**

(a) 80 (b) 100

(c) 100 sin 50° (d) 80 sin 50°

183. An 8 kg metal block of dimensions is 16 cm × 8 cm × 6 cm is lying on a table. If $g = 10\ ms^{-2}$, the minimum amount of work done in making it stand with its length vertical is **(Kerala P.M.T. 2005)**

(a) 0.4 J (b) 6.4 J

(c) 4 J (d) 12.8 J

184. A ball is released from the top of the tower. The ratio of work done by force of gravity in first, second and third second of the motion of the bell is **(Kerala P.M.T. 2005)**

(a) 1 : 2 : 3 (b) 1 : 4 : 9

(c) 1 : 3 : 5 (d) 1 : 5 : 3

185. A particle is displaced from a position $(2\hat{i} - \hat{j} + \hat{k})$ to another position $(3\hat{i} + 2\hat{j} - 2\hat{k})$. The work done by the force in arbitrary unit is **(Kerala 2005)**

(a) 8 (b) 10

(c) 12 (d) 16

186. A uniform metal chain is placed on a rough table such that one end of it hangs down over the edge of the table, when one third of its length hangs over the edge, the chain starts sliding. Then the coefficient of static friction is **(Kerala 2005)**

(a) $\frac{3}{4}$ (b) $\frac{1}{4}$

(c) $\frac{2}{3}$ (d) $\frac{1}{2}$

187. An engine pumps water through a hose pipe. Water passes through the pipe and leaves it with a velocity of 2 m/s. The mass per unit length of water in the pipe is 100 kg/m. What is the power of the engine ? **(C.B.S.E. 2010)**

(a) 100 W (b) 800 W

(c) 400 W (d) 200 W

188. The potential energy of a system increases if work is done **(C.B.S.E. 2011)**

(a) upon the system by a non-conservative force

(b) by the system against a conservative force

(c) by the system against a non-conservative force

(d) upon the system by a conservative force

189. Force F on a particle, moving in a straight line varies with distance d as shown in the figure. The work done on the particle during its displacement of 12 is **(C.B.S.E. 2011)**

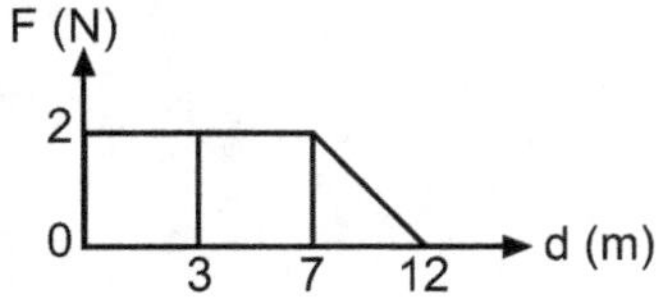

(a) 18 J (b) 21 J

(c) 26 J (d) 13 J

190. Two spheres A and B of masses m_1 and m_2 respectively collide. A is at rest initially and B is moving with velocity v along X-axis. After collision B has a velocity $\frac{v}{2}$ in a direction perpendicular to the original direction. The mass A moves after collision in the direction **(C.B.S.E. 2012)**

(a) $\theta = \tan^{-1}\left(-\frac{1}{2}\right)$ to the X-axis

(b) same as that of B

(c) opposite to that of B

(d) $\theta = \tan^{-1}\left(\frac{1}{2}\right)$ to the X-axis

191. The potential energy of a particle in a force field is $U = \frac{A}{r^2} - \frac{B}{r}$, where A and B are positive constants and r is the distance of particle from the centre of the field. For stable equilibrium, the distance of the particle is **(C.B.S.E. 2012)**

(a) $\frac{B}{A}$ (b) $\frac{B}{2A}$

(c) $\frac{2A}{B}$ (d) $\frac{A}{B}$

192. A uniform force of $(3\hat{i} + \hat{j})$ newton acts on a particle of mass 2 kg. Hence, the particle is displaced from position $(2\hat{i} + \hat{k})$ metre to position $(4\hat{i} + 3\hat{j} - \hat{k})$ metre. The work done by the force on the particle is

(NEET 2013)

(a) 6 J (b) 13 J

(c) 15 J (d) 9 J

193. An explosion breaks a rock into three parts in a horizontal plane. Two of them go off at right angles to each other. The first part of mass 1 kg moves with a speed of 12 ms^{-1} and the second part of mass 2 kg moves with 8 ms^{-1} speed, then its mass is **(NEET 2013)**

(a) 5 kg (b) 7 kg

(c) 17 kg (d) 3 kg

ANSWER KEY

1.(c)	**2.**(d)	**3.**(b)	**4.**(a)	**5.**(c)	**6.**(b)	**7.**(d)	**8.**(d)	**9.**(a)	**10.**(a)
11.(c)	**12.**(a)	**13.**(c)	**14.**(b)	**15.**(b)	**16.**(d)	**17.**(b)	**18.**(a)	**19.**(a)	**20.**(b)
21.(d)	**22.**(b)	**23.**(a)	**24.**(c)	**25.**(b)	**26.**(d)	**27.**(a)	**28.**(c)	**29.**(b)	**30.**(d)
31.(c)	**32.**(b)	**33.**(d)	**34.**(b)	**35.**(c)	**36.**(b)	**37.**(d)	**38.**(a)	**39.**(c)	**40.**(b)
41.(b)	**42.**(a)	**43.**(d)	**44.**(c)	**45.**(a)	**46.**(c)	**47.**(d)	**48.**(b)	**49.**(d)	**50.**(c)
51.(a)	**52.**(d)	**53.**(b)	**54.**(c)	**55.**(d)	**56.**(c)	**57.**(c)	**58.**(c)	**59.**(a)	**60.**(c)
61.(d)	**62.**(a)	**63.**(c)	**64.**(b)	**65.**(c)	**66.**(c)	**67.**(b)	**68.**(c)	**69.**(d)	**70.**(b)
71.(a)	**72.**(d)	**73.**(a)	**74.**(b)	**75.**(c)	**76.**(c)	**77.**(c)	**78.**(c)	**79.**(b)	**80.**(c)
81.(b)	**82.**(b)	**83.**(c)	**84.**(b)	**85.**(b)	**86.**(d)	**87.**(c)	**88.**(a)	**89.**(d)	**90.**(b)
91.(b)	**92.**(c)	**93.**(a)	**94.**(b)	**95.**(a)	**96.**(d)	**97.**(b)	**98.**(b)	**99.**(c)	**100.** (d)
101. (b)	**102.** (a)	**103.** (d)	**104.** (b)	**105.** (b)	**106.** (d)	**107.** (d)	**108.** (c)	**109.** (d)	**110.** (b)
111. (c)	**112.** (b)	**113.** (a)	**114.** (b)	**115.** (a)	**116.** (d)	**117.** (a)	**118.** (c)	**119.** (a)	**120.** (d)
121. (a)	**122.** (b)	**123.** (b)	**124.** (a)	**125.** (a)	**126.** (a)	**127.** (c)	**128.** (a)	**129.** (a)	**130.** (d)
131. (a)	**132.** (d)	**133.** (d)	**134.** (a)	**135.** (b)	**136.** (d)	**137.** (c)	**138.** (b)	**139.** (c)	**140.** (a)
141. (d)	**142.** (c)	**143.** (c)	**144.** (c)	**145.** (a)	**146.** (b)	**147.** (b)	**148.** (a)	**149.** (d)	**150.** (d)
151. (b)	**152.** (d)	**153.** (d)	**154.** (b)	**155.** (b)	**156.** (c)	**157.** (c)	**158.** (a)	**159.** (a)	**160.** (d)
161. (a)	**162.** (d)	**163.** (d)	**164.** (b)	**165.** (a)	**166.** (d)	**167.** (a)	**168.** (d)	**169.** (b)	**170.** (b)
171. (d)	**172.** (b)	**173.** (d)	**174.** (a)	**175.** (b)	**176.** (c)	**177.** (b)	**178.** (b)	**179.** (d)	**180.** (c)
181. (d)	**182.** (d)	**183.** (c)	**184.** (c)	**185.** (a)	**186.** (d)	**187.** (b)	**188.** (b)	**189.** (d)	**190.** (a)
191. (c)	**192.** (d)	**193.** (a)							

6

CENTRE OF MASS AND ROTATIONAL MOTION

MULTIPLE CHOICE QUESTIONS

1. The centre of mass of a system of particles does not depend on :
   (a) mass of the particles
   (b) force on the particles
   (c) position of the particles
   (d) relative distance between the particles

2. The position of the C.M. of a cube of uniform density shall be at :
   (a) the edge of a cube
   (b) the centre of one face
   (c) the centre of intersection diagonals of one face
   (d) the geometric centre of the cube

3. The origin of co-ordinate system lies at the C.M., the sum of the moments of the masses of the system about the centre of mass :
   (a) may be greater than zero
   (b) may be less than zero
   (c) may be equal to zero
   (d) is always zero

4. A uniform metal disc of radius R is taken and out of it a disc of diameter R is cut off from the end. The centre of mass of the remaining part will be :
   (a) $\frac{R}{4}$ from the centre
   (b) $\frac{R}{3}$ from the centre
   (c) $\frac{R}{5}$ from the centre
   (d) $\frac{R}{6}$ from the centre

5. Three particles of masses 1 kg, 2 kg and 3 kg are situated at the corners of an equilateral triangle of side b. The co-ordinates of the C.M. are :
   (a) $\left[0, \frac{7}{12}b, \frac{3\sqrt{3}}{12}b\right]$ (b) $\left[\frac{3\sqrt{3}}{12}b, \frac{7}{12}b, 0\right]$
   (c) $\left[\frac{7}{12}b, \frac{3\sqrt{3}}{12}b, 0\right]$ (d) $\left[\frac{7}{12}b, b, \frac{3\sqrt{3}}{12}b\right]$

6. The position of C.M. of a system consisting of two particles of masses m_1 and m_2 separated by a distance L apart from m will be :
   (a) $\frac{m_1 L}{m_1 + m_2}$ (b) $\frac{m_2 L}{m_1 + m_2}$
   (c) $\frac{m_2 L}{m_1}$ (d) $\frac{L}{2}$

7. A circular ring of mass 6 kg and radius a is placed such that its centre lies at the origin. Two particles of masses 2 kg each are placed at the intersecting points of the circle with +ve x-axis and +ve y-axis. Then the angle made by the position of C.M. of the entire system with the x-axis is :
   (a) 45° (b) 60°
   (c) $\tan^{-1}$ (4/5) (d) 30°

8. Mass is distributed uniformly over a thin square plate. If the two end points of the diagonal are (– 2, 0) and (2, 2), what are the co-ordinates of C.M. of the plate ?
   (a) (2, 1) (b) (2, 2)
   (c) (1, 0) (d) (0, 1)

9. The C.M. of a body :

(a) depends on the choice of the co-ordinate system

(b) is independent on the choice of the co-ordinate system

(c) may or may not depend on the choice of the co-ordinate system

(d) none of these.

10. Four bodies of masses 2, 3, 5 and 8 kg are placed at the four corners of a square of side 2 m. The position of C.M. will be :

(a) $\left[\frac{8}{9}, \frac{13}{9}\right]$ (b) $\left[\frac{7}{9}, \frac{11}{9}\right]$

(c) $\left[\frac{11}{9}, \frac{13}{9}\right]$ (d) $\left[\frac{11}{9}, \frac{8}{9}\right]$

11. A hoop of mass M and radius R is suspended to a peg in a wall. Its moment of inertia about the peg is :

(a) $2\ MR^2$ (b) MR^2

(c) $\frac{MR^2}{2}$ (d) $\frac{3}{2}MR^2$

12. The M.I. of a thin uniform rod of mass M and length L about an axis passing through its centre is $\frac{ML^2}{12}$. Its M.I. about a parallel axis at a distance of $\frac{L}{4}$ from this axis is given by :

(a) $\frac{ML^2}{48}$ (b) $\frac{ML^3}{48}$

(c) $\frac{ML^2}{12}$ (d) $\frac{7\ ML^2}{48}$

13. Moment of inertia of a circular disc about one of its diameter is I. Its M.I. about a tangent parallel to the diameter will be :

(a) 4 I (b) 2 I

(c) $\frac{3}{2}$I (d) 3 I

14. Moment of inertia of a uniform circular disc about a diameter is I. Its M.I. about an axis ⊥ to its plane and passing through a point on its rim will be :

(a) 5 I (b) 3 I

(c) 6 I (d) 4 I

15. Four similar point masses (m each) are symmetrically placed on the circumference of a disc of mass M and radius R. Then, moment of inertia of the system about an axis passing through centre O and perpendicular to the plane of the disc will be:

(a) $MR^2 + 4mR^2$ (b) $MR^2 + \frac{8}{5}mR^2$

(c) $mR^2 + 4\ MR^2$ (d) $\frac{MR^2}{2} + 4mR^2$

16. Two wheels A and B are mounted on the same axle. M.I. of A is 6 kg-m^2 and it is rotating at 600 r.p.m. when B is at rest. What is M.I. of B, if their combined speed is 400 r.p.m. ?

(a) 3 kg-m^2 (b) 4 kg-m^2

(c) 5 kg-m^2 (d) 8 kg-m^2

17. M.I. of a circular loop of radius R about the axis of rotation parallel to the horizontal diameter at a distance R/2 from it is :

(a) MR^2 (b) $\frac{MR^2}{2}$

(c) $2\ MR^2$ (d) $\frac{3}{4}MR^2$

18. Three point masses, each of mass m are placed at the corners of an equilateral triangle of side l. M.I. of this system about an axis along one side of the triangle is :

(a) $3\ ml^2$ (b) $\frac{3}{2}ml^2$

(c) ml^2 (d) $\frac{3}{4}ml^2$

19. Three identical thin rods each of length 'l' and mass M are joined together to form a letter H. What is M.I. of the system about one of the sides of H ?

(a) $\frac{1}{4}Ml^2$ (b) $\frac{1}{3}Ml^2$

(c) $\frac{2}{3}Ml^2$ (d) $\frac{4}{3}Ml^2$

20. Two discs have the same mass and thickness. Their materials have densities d_1 and d_2. The ratio of their moments of inertia about the central axis will be :

(a) $d_1 : d_2$ (b) $d_1 d_2 : 1$

(c) $1 : d_1 d_2$ (d) $d_2 : d_1$.

21. The M.I. of a sphere of mass M and radius R about an axis passing through its centre is $\frac{2}{5}MR^2$. The radius of gyration of the sphere about a parallel axis to the above tangent to the sphere is :

(a) $\frac{7}{5}R$ (b) $\frac{3}{5}R$

(c) $\sqrt{\frac{7}{5}}R$ (d) $\sqrt{\frac{3}{5}}R$

22. A circular plate of uniform thickness has a diameter of 56 cm. A circular portion of diameter 42 cm is removed from one edge. The C.M. of the remaining portion from the centre of plate will be :

(a) 5 cm (b) 7 cm

(c) 9 cm (d) 11 cm

23. A ring, a solid sphere and disc have the same mass and radius. Which of them have the largest M.I. ?

(a) Ring (b) Solid sphere

(c) Disc (d) All of these.

24. Two circular discs have masses in the ratio of 1 : 2 and diameters in the ratio of 2 : 1. The ratio of their M.I. is :

(a) 1 (b) 2

(c) 4 (d) 8

25. If radius of a solid sphere is 35 cm, then the radius of gyration when the axis is along a tangent will be :

(a) $7\sqrt{10}$ cm (b) $7\sqrt{35}$ cm

(c) $\frac{7}{5}$ cm (d) $\frac{2}{5}$ cm

26. Two rings of the same radius and mass are placed in such a manner that their centers are at a common point and their planes are perpendicular to each other. The M.I. of the system about an axis passing through the centre and ⊥ to the plane of one of the rings is :

(a) $\frac{1}{2}mr^2$ (b) mr^2

(c) $\frac{3}{2}mr^2$ (d) $2\,mr^2$

27. The diameter of flywheel increases by 1%. What will be % increase in M.I. about axis of symmetry?

(a) 2% (b) 4%

(c) 1% (d) 0.5%

28. Four point masses each of mass m are at the four corners of a square of side length l. The M.I. of the system about one of its diagonal will be :

(a) $2\,ml^2$ (b) ml^2

(c) $4\,ml^2$ (d) $6\,ml^2$

29. A cricket mat of mass 50 kg is rolled loosely in the form of a cylinder of radius 2 m. Now again it is rolled tightly so that the radius becomes $\frac{3}{4}$ th of its original value. Then the ratio of M.I. of the mat in the two cases will be :

(a) 1 : 3 (b) 4 : 3

(c) 16 : 9 (d) 3 : 5

30. The M.I. of a metre stick of mass 300 gm, about an axis at right angles to the stick and located at the 30 cm mark is :

(a) 8.3×10^5 g-cm^2 (b) 5.8 g-cm^2

(c) 3.7×10^5 g-cm^2 (d) 4.8 g-cm^2

31. One fourth of the disc of mass m is removed. If r is the radius of the disc, the new M.I. of the disc is :

(a) $\frac{3}{2}mr^2$ (b) $\frac{mr^2}{2}$

(c) $\frac{3}{8}mr^2$ (d) $\frac{4}{9}mr^2$

32. Out of two eggs, one is raw and the other is half boiled and they have identical sizes, shapes and weights. The ratio between the M.I. of the raw to the half boiled egg about the central axis is :

(a) One (b) > 1

(c) < 1 (d) None of these

33. A thin rod of length L and mass M is bent at the middle point O at an angle of 60°. The M.I. of rod about an axis passing through O and perpendicular to the plane of the rod will be :

(a) $\frac{ML^2}{6}$ (b) $\frac{ML^2}{12}$

(c) $\frac{ML^2}{24}$ (d) $\frac{ML^2}{3}$

34. The M.I. of a dumb-bell, consisting of point masses $m_1 = 2.0$ kg and $m_2 = 1.0$ kg, fixed to the ends of a rigid massless rod of length L = 0.6 m, about an axis passing through the C.M. and perpendicular to its length is :

(a) 0.72 kg-m^2 (b) 0.36 kg-m^2

(c) 0.27 kg-m^2 (d) 0.24 kg-m^2

35. About which axis in the following figure is the moment of inertia of rectangular lamina maximum ?

(a) 1 (b) 2

(c) 3 (d) 4

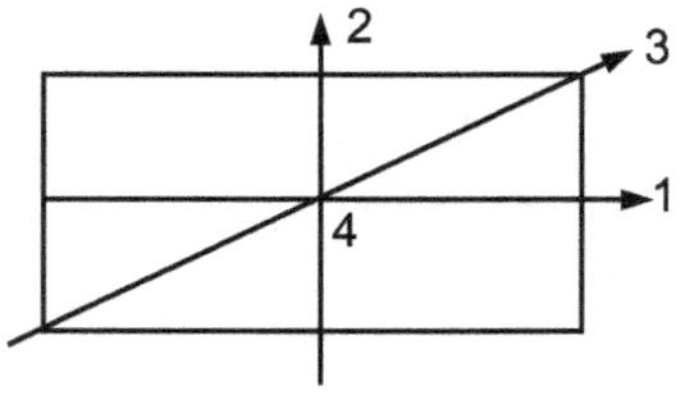

36. Two masses of 200 g and 300 g are attached at the 20 cm and 70 cm marks of a light metre rod respectively. The M.I. of the system about an axis passing through the 50 cm mark will be :

(a) 0.15 kg-m^2 (b) 0.03 kg-m^2

(c) 0.3 kg-m^2 (d) zero

37. Four spheres of diameter $2a$ and mass M are placed with their centres on the four corners of a square of side length b. Then M.I. of the system about an axis along one of the sides of the square is :

(a) $\frac{4}{5}Ma^2 + 2Mb^2$ (b) $\frac{8}{5}Ma^2 + 2Mb^2$

(c) $\frac{8}{5}Ma^2$ (d) $\frac{4}{5}Ma^2 + 4Mb^2$

38. The radius of gyration of a uniform rod of length L about an axis passing through its centre of mass and perpendicular to its length is :

(a) $\frac{L}{\sqrt{12}}$ (b) $\frac{L^2}{12}$

(c) $\frac{L}{\sqrt{3}}$ (d) $\frac{L}{\sqrt{2}}$

39. The M.I. of a solid cylinder of length L and diameter D about an axis passing through its centre of gravity and perpendicular to its geometric axis is :

(a) $M\left[\frac{D^2}{4} + \frac{L^2}{12}\right]$ (b) $M\left[\frac{L^2}{16} + \frac{D^2}{8}\right]$

(c) $M\left[\frac{D^2}{4} + \frac{L^2}{6}\right]$ (d) $M\left[\frac{L^2}{12} + \frac{D^2}{16}\right]$

40. The M.I. of two spheres of equal masses about their diameters are equal. If one of them is solid and the other is hollow, the ratio of their radii is :

(a) $\sqrt{3} : \sqrt{5}$ (b) 3 : 5

(c) $\sqrt{5} : \sqrt{3}$ (d) 5 : 3

41. Three identical particles are fixed to the corners of an isosceles right-angled triangle by means of massless connecting rods. Each of the two equal sides has a length d. The M.I. of this rigid object, when the axis of rotation coincides with the hypotenuse of the triangle is :

(a) $\frac{1}{2}md^2$ (b) $\frac{1}{4}md^2$

(c) md^2 (d) $\frac{3}{4}md^2$

42. Which of the following will have the largest M.I. about an axis passing through the C.G. and perpendicular to the plane of the body ? ($\because$ All have the same mass)

(a) a disc of radius R
(b) a ring of radius R
(c) a square lamina of side 2R
(d) four rods forming a square of side 2R

43. A circular disc A of radius r is made from an iron plate of thickness t and another circular disc B of radius $4r$ and thickness $t/4$. The relation between M.I., I_A and I_B is :

(a) $I_A > I_B$ (b) $I_A = I_B$
(c) $I_A < I_B$ (d) None of them

44. Three point masses m are placed at the vertices of an equilateral triangle of side a. The M.I. of the system about an axis passing through mass m at O and lying in the plane of the triangle and perpendicular to OA is :

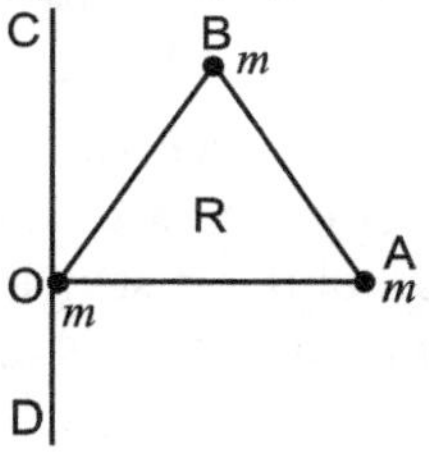

(a) $2\,ma^2$ (b) $\frac{2}{3}ma^2$
(c) $\frac{5}{4}ma^2$ (d) $\frac{7}{4}ma^2$

45. A square plate of side l has mass m. Its M.I. about any one diagonal is :

(a) $\frac{ml^2}{3}$ (b) $\frac{ml^2}{4}$
(c) $\frac{ml^2}{6}$ (d) $\frac{ml^2}{12}$

46. Two circular discs are of the same thickness but diameter of A is twice than that of B. The M.I. of A as compared to that of B is :

(a) twice as large
(b) four times as large
(c) eight times as large
(d) sixteen times as large

47. The moment of inertia of a cylinder about its axis is equal to its M.I. about an axis passing through the C.M. and perpendicular to its length. The ratio of length to radius is :

(a) $1 : 2$ (b) $\sqrt{2} : 1$
(c) $1 : \sqrt{3}$ (d) $\sqrt{3} : 1$

48. A square plate of side A has mass per unit area K. Its M.I. about an axis passing through the centre and perpendicular to its plane is :

(a) $\frac{KA^2}{12}$ (b) $\frac{KA^2}{6}$
(c) $\frac{KA^4}{12}$ (d) $\frac{KA^4}{6}$

49. The M.I. of a solid sphere of density ρ and radius R about its diameter is :

(a) $\frac{10^5}{176}R^3\rho$ (b) $\frac{10^5}{176}R^2\rho$
(c) $\frac{176}{10^5}R^5\rho$ (d) $\frac{176}{10^5}R^2\rho$

50. If M.I. of a disc about an axis tangentially and parallel to its surface be I, then the M.I. about the axis tangentially but perpendicular to the surface will be :

(a) $\frac{6}{5}I$ (b) $\frac{3}{4}I$
(c) $\frac{3}{2}I$ (d) $\frac{5}{4}I$

51. Two identical particles move towards each other with velocity $2v$ and v respectively. The velocity of the centre of mass is :

(A.I.E.E.E. 2002)

(a) v (b) $v/3$
(c) $v/2$ (d) Zero

52. Two spherical bodies of mass M and 5 M and radii R and 2R respectively are released in free space with initial separation between their centres equal to 12R. If they attract each other due to gravity, then the distance covered by the smaller body just before collision is : **(A.I.E.E.E. 2003)**

(a) 4.5 R (b) 7.5 R
(c) 1.5 R (d) 2.5 R

53. A body 'A' of mass M while falling vertically downwards under gravity breaks into two parts; a body 'B' of mass M/3 and a body 'C' of mass 2M/3. The centre of mass of body 'B' and 'C' taken together shifts compared to that of body 'A' towards :

(A.I.E.E.E. 2005)

(a) Depends on height of breaking
(b) Does not shift
(c) Body C
(d) Body B

54. Consider a two particle systems with particles having masses M_1 and M_2. If the first particle is pushed towards the centre of mass through a distance *d*, by what distance should the second particle be moved, so as to keep the centre of mass at the same position ? **(A.I.E.E.E. 2006)**

(a) $\frac{M_1}{M_2} \cdot d$ (b) $\frac{M_2}{M_1} \cdot d$
(c) $\frac{M_1}{M_1 + M_2} \cdot d$ (d) d

55. A circular disc of radius R is removed from a bigger circular disc of radius 2R, such that the circumferences of the disc coincide. The C.M. of the new disc is $\alpha \cdot R$ from the centre of the bigger disc. The value of α is :

(A.I.E.E.E. 2007)

(a) 1/3 (b) 1/2
(c) 1/6 (d) 1/4

56. Moment of inertia of a circular wire of mass M and radius R about its diameter is :

(A.I.E.E.E. 2002)

(a) $\frac{MR^2}{2}$ (b) $\frac{MR^2}{4}$
(c) $2\ MR^2$ (d) MR^2

57. A circular disc X of radius R is made from an iron plate of thickness *t* and another disc Y of radius 4R of thickness $\frac{t}{4}$. Then the relation between their moment of inertia I_x and I_y is : **(A.I.E.E.E. 2003)**

(a) $I_y = I_x$ (b) $I_y = 16\ I_x$
(c) $I_y = 32\ I_x$ (d) $I_y = 64\ I_x$

58. One solid sphere A and another hollow sphere B have the same mass and same outer radii. Their moment of inertia about their diameters are respectively I_A and I_B such that: **(A.I.E.E.E. 2004)**

(a) $I_A = I_B$ (b) $I_A > I_B$
(c) $I_A < I_B$ (d) $\frac{I_A}{I_B} = \frac{\rho_A}{\rho_B}$

Here ρ_A and ρ_B represent their densities.

59. The moment of inertia of a uniform semi-circular disc of mass M and radius R about a line perpendicular to the plane of the disc through the centre is :

(A.I.E.E.E. 2005)

(a) $\frac{MR^2}{4}$ (b) $\frac{2MR^2}{5}$
(c) MR^2 (d) $\frac{MR^2}{2}$

60. Four point masses, each of value M, are placed at the corners of a square ABCD of side L. The M.I. of this system about an axis passing through A and parallel to BD is :

(a) $3\ ML^2$ (b) ML^2
(c) $2\ ML^2$ (d) $\sqrt{3}\ ML^2$

61. For a given uniform square lamina ABCD, whose centre is O :

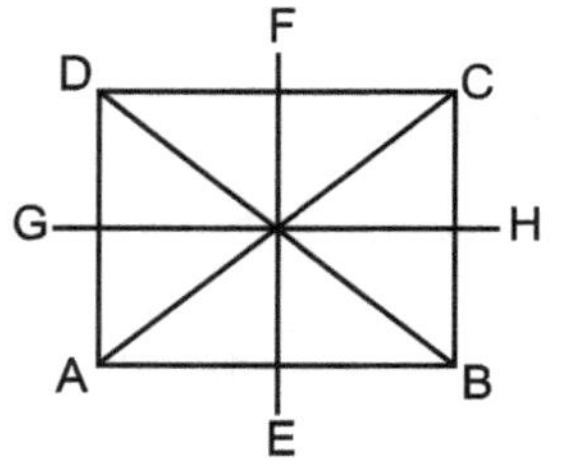

(a) $\sqrt{2}\ I_{AC} = I_{EF}$ (b) $I_{AD} = 3\ I_{EF}$
(c) $I_{AC} = I_{EF}$ (d) $I_{AC} = \sqrt{2}\ I_{EF}$

62. The angular speed of a flywheel making 120 r.p.m. is :

(a) π rad s^{-1} (b) 2π rad s^{-1}
(c) 4π rad s^{-1} (d) $4\pi^2$ rad s^{-1}.

63. A mass is revolving in a circle which is in the plane of the paper. The direction of angular acceleration is :

(a) upwards the radius
(b) towards the radius
(c) tangential
(d) at right angles to the angular velocity.

64. A flywheel of mass 50 kg and radius of gyration about its axis of rotation of 0.5 m is acted upon by a constant torque of 12.5 Nm. Its angular velocity at $t = 5$ seconds is :

(a) 2.5 rad s^{-1} (b) 5 rad s^{-1}
(c) 7.5 rad s^{-1} (d) 10 rad s^{-1}

65. An electric fan with blades of length 30 cm is measured from the axis of rotation. If the fan rotates at 120 r.p.m., the acceleration of a point on the tip of a blade is about :

(a) 4740 ms^{-2} (b) 5055 ms^{-2}
(c) 1600 ms^{-2} (d) 2370 ms^{-2}

66. If a particle moves in the x-y plane, the resultant angular momentum has :

(a) only x-component
(b) only y-component
(c) both x and y components
(d) only z component

67. A flywheel rotating about a fixed axis has a K.E. of 360 J, when its angular speed is 30 rad s^{-1}. The M.I. of the wheel about the axis of rotation is :

(a) 0.6 kg m^2 (b) 0.15 kg m^2
(c) 0.8 kg m^2 (d) 0.75 kg m^2

68. A spherical solid ball of mass 1 kg and radius 3 cm is rotating about an axis passing through its centre with an angular velocity of 50 rad s^{-1}. The K.E. of rotation is :

(a) 4500 J (b) 90 J
(c) $\frac{9}{20}$ J (d) 0.9 J

69. The M.I. of a body about a given axis is 1.2 kg-m^2. Initially, the body is at rest. In order to produce a rotational K.E. of 1500 J, an angular acceleration of 25 rad s^{-2} must be applied about that axis for a duration of :

(a) 4 s (b) 2 s
(c) 8 s (d) 10 s

70. A body of M.I. of 3 kg-m^2 rotating with an angular speed of 2 rad s^{-1} has the same K.E. as a mass of 12 kg moving with the speed of :

(a) 2 ms^{-1} (b) 1 ms^{-1}
(c) 4 ms^{-1} (d) 8 ms^{-1}

71. A mass is whirled in a circular path with a constant angular velocity and its angular momentum is L. If the string is now halved, keeping angular velocity the same, the angular momentum will be :

(a) L/4 (b) L/2
(c) L (d) 2 L

72. Torque required to increase angular velocity of a solid disc of mass 16 kg and diameter 1 m from zero to 120 r.p.m. in 8 seconds is :

(a) $\frac{\pi}{4}$ Nm (b) $\frac{\pi}{2}$ Nm
(c) $\frac{\pi}{3}$ Nm (d) π Nm

73. A solid sphere of mass 1 kg and radius 3 cm is rotating about an axis passing through its centre with an angular velocity 50 rad s^{-1}. Then K.E. of rotation is :

(a) 450 J (b) 45 J
(c) 90 J (d) 0.45

74. A solid cylinder of mass 2 kg and radius 0.2 m is rotating about its own axis without friction with an angular velocity of 3 rad s^{-1}. The angular momentum of the cylinder is :

(a) 0.2 Js (b) 1.12 Js
(c) 0.12 Js (d) 12 Js

75. What is the torque of the force $\vec{F} = (2\hat{i} - 3\hat{j} + 4\hat{k})$ N acting at the point $\vec{r} = (3\hat{i} + 2\hat{j} + 3\hat{k})$ about the origin ?

(a) $-17\hat{i} + 6\hat{j} + 13\hat{k}$ (b) $-6\hat{i} + 6\hat{j} - 12\hat{k}$
(c) $17\hat{i} - 6\hat{j} - 13\hat{k}$ (d) $6\hat{i} - 6\hat{j} + 12\hat{k}$

76. A ring of diameter 0.4 m and of mass 10 kg is rotating about its axis at the rate of 120 r.p.m.. The angular momentum of the ring is :

(a) 60.28 kg m^2s^{-1} (b) 55.26 kg m^2s^{-1}

(c) 40.28 kg m^2s^{-1} (d) 50.26 kg m^2s^{-1}

77. A flywheel of M.I. of 0.4 kg-m^2 and radius 0.2 m is free to rotate about a central axis. If a string is wrapped around it and is pulled with a force of 10N, then its angular velocity after 4s will be :

(a) 10 rad s^{-1} (b) 5 rad s^{-1}

(c) 20 rad s^{-1} (d) 30 rad s^{-1}

78. A stone of mass m is tied to a string of length 'l' rotating along a circular path with constant speed v. The torque on the stone is :

(a) mvl (b) mv/l

(c) mv^2/l (d) Zero

79. In a circular motion, the angle between a particle's linear momentum and angular momentum is :

(a) 0° (b) 45°

(c) 90° (d) 180°

80. A gramophone turn table rotating at 75 r.p.m. slows down uniformly and stops in 5 seconds after the motor is turned off. Its angular acceleration (rad s^{-2}) is :

(a) – 0.42 (b) – 0.89

(c) – 1.57 (d) – 1.96

81. A wheel starts from rest and acquires a rotational speed of 240 r.p.s. in 2 min. Its angular acceleration (in rad s^{-2}) is :

(a) 5 (b) 2

(c) 8 (d) 11

82. When a ceiling fan is switched off, its angular velocity falls to half while it makes 36 rotations. How many more rotations will it make before coming to rest ?

(a) 36 (b) 24

(c) 18 (d) 12

83. A particle starts from rest with an acceleration of 2 rad s^{-2} in a circle of radius 2 m. Its linear speed after 6 s is :

(a) 12 ms^{-1} (b) 24 ms^{-1}

(c) 4 ms^{-1} (d) 2 ms^{-1}

84. A ballet dancer spins with 2.8 r.p.s. with her arms out stretched. When the M.I. about the same axis becomes 0.7I, the new rate of spin is :

(a) 3.2 r.p.s. (b) 4 r.p.s.

(c) 4.8 r.p.s. (d) 5.6 r.p.s.

85. Total K.E. of a sphere of mass M rolling with velocity v is :

(a) 0.7 Mv^2 (b) 0.83 Mv^2

(c) 1.4 Mv^2 (d) 1.42 Mv^2

86. A particle performs circular motion with an angular momentum L. If the frequency of its motion is doubled and its K.E. is halved, the angular momentum will become :

(a) 2 L (b) 4 L

(c) L/2 (d) L/4

87. Four masses each of 2 kg are connected by $\frac{1}{4}$ m spokes to an axle. A force of 24N acts on a lever 1/2 m long to produce angular acceleration α. The magnitude of α in rad s^{-2} is:

(a) 24 (b) 12

(c) 6 (d) 3

88. If the earth were to shrink to half of its present diameter without any change in its mass, the duration of the day will be :

(a) 48 hours (b) 6 hours

(c) 12 hours (d) 24 hours

89. An ice skater spins at 3π rad s^{-1} with her arms extended. If her M.I. with arms folded is 75% of that of the extended arm, her angular velocity, when she folds her arms is:

(a) π rad s^{-1} (b) 2π rad s^{-1}

(c) 3π rad s^{-1} (d) 4π rad s^{-1}

90. A man, 80 kg mass is standing on the rim of a circular platform of mass 200 kg rotating about its axis. The mass of the platform with the man on it rotates at 120 r.p.m.. If the man now moves to the centre of the platform, the rotational speed would become:

(a) 16.5 r.p.m. (b) 25.7 r.p.m.
(c) 32.3 r.p.m. (d) 31.2 r.p.m.

91. A pot-maker rotates a potter wheel of 3m radius by applying a force of 200 N tangentially, because of this, if the wheel completes $\frac{3}{2}$ revolutions, the work done by him will be :

(a) 5654.86 J (b) 4321.32 J
(c) 4197.5 J (d) 5,000 J

92. A body having M.I. 3 kg-m^2 is rotating with angular velocity 3 rad s^{-1}. K.E. of this rotating body is the same as that of a body of mass 27 kg moving with the speed of :

(a) 1 ms^{-1} (b) 0.5 ms^{-1}
(c) 1.5 ms^{-1} (d) 2 ms^{-1}

93. A ring is rolling on a surface without slipping. What is the ratio of its translational K.E. to rotational K.E. ?

(a) 5 : 7 (b) 2 : 5
(c) 2 : 7 (d) 1 : 1

94. A uniform sphere of mass 200 gm rolls without slipping on a plane surface, so that its centre moves at a speed of 2 cm s^{-1}. Its K.E. is :

(a) 5.6×10^{-5} J (b) 5.6×10^{-4} J
(c) 5.6×10^{-3} J (d) 5.6×10^{-2} J

95. A flywheel of radius 2 m and mass 8 kg rotates at an angular speed 4 rad s^{-1} about an axis perpendicular to it through its centre. The K.E. of rotation is :

(a) 128 J (b) 196 J
(c) 256 J (d) 392 J

96. A uniform triangular plate is made to rotate about an axis perpendicular to the plane of paper and (1) passing through '(A)' (2) passing through '(B)', by the application of some force at C (mid-point of AB) as shown in the figure. In which one will the angular acceleration be maximum ?

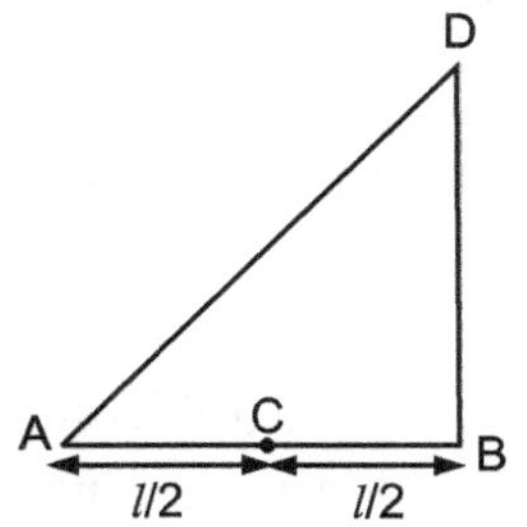

(a) In case (1)
(b) In case (2)
(c) In both the cases
(d) None of the above

97. A thin hollow cylinder is free to rotate about its geometrical axis. It has a mass of 8 kg and radius 20 cm. A rope is wrapped around the cylinder. What force must be exerted along the rope to produce an angular arc of 3 rad s^{-1} ?

(a) 8.4 N (b) 5.8 N
(c) 4.8 N (d) Zero N

98. A string is wrapped around a cylinder of mass M and radius R. The string is pulled vertically upwards to prevent the C.M. from falling as the cylinder unwinds the string. The tension in the string is :

(a) $\frac{Mg}{6}$ (b) $\frac{Mg}{3}$
(c) $\frac{Mg}{2}$ (d) $\frac{2}{3}Mg$

99. An inclined plane makes an angle of 30° with the horizontal. A ring which rolls down to an inclined plane from rest without slipping will have linear acceleration :

(a) $\frac{2}{3}g$ (b) $\frac{g}{2}$
(c) $\frac{g}{3}$ (d) $\frac{g}{4}$

100. A circular disc is rolling on a horizontal plane. Its total K.E. is 150 J. What is its translational K.E. ?

(a) 200 J (b) 100 J

(c) 125 J (d) 2 J

101. A solid sphere of mass 2 kg rolls on a smooth horizontal surface at 10 ms^{-1}. It then rolls up a smooth inclined plane of inclination 30° with the horizontal. The height attained by the sphere before it stops is :

(a) 1.7 m (b) 4.5 m

(c) 5.4 m (d) 7.1 m

102. A flywheel rolls down on an inclined plane. At any time, the ratio of rotational K.E. to total K.E. is :

(a) 1 : 2 (b) 3 : 1

(c) 4 : 3 (d) 1 : 3

103. A rigid body rotates about an axis with variable angular velocity equal to $\alpha - \beta t$ at time t, where α and β are constants. The angle through which it rotates before it comes to rest is :

(a) $\frac{\alpha^2}{2\beta}$ (b) $\frac{\alpha^2 - \beta^2}{2\alpha}$

(c) $\frac{\alpha^2 - \beta^2}{2\beta}$ (d) $\frac{\alpha(\alpha - \beta)}{2}$

104. A loop and a disc have the same mass and roll without slipping with the same linear velocity v. If the total K.E. of the loop is 8J, the K.E. of the disc must be :

(a) 8 J (b) 6 J

(c) 16 J (d) 4 J

105. Two bodies with M.I. I_1 and I_2 ($I_1 > I_2$) have equal angular momenta. If E_1 and E_2 be their K.E. of rotation, then :

(a) $E_1 = E_2$ (b) $E_1 > E_2$

(c) $E_1 < E_2$ (d) $E_1 \geq E_2$

106. A solid sphere rolls down without slipping on a 30° inclined plane. If g = 10 ms^{-2}, the acceleration of the rolling sphere is :

(a) 5 ms^{-2} (b) $\frac{7}{25}$ ms^{-2}

(c) $\frac{25}{7}$ ms^{-2} (d) $\frac{15}{7}$ ms^{-2}

107. The ratio of times taken by a uniform solid sphere and disc of the same mass and the same diameter to roll down through the same distance from rest on a smooth inclined plane is :

(a) 15 : 14 (b) $\sqrt{15} : \sqrt{14}$

(c) $15^2 : 14^2$ (d) $\sqrt{14} : \sqrt{15}$

108. A particle is rotating along a circular path in the x-y plane. The angular momentum vector of the particle will be directed parallel to the:

(a) x-axis (b) y-axis

(c) z-axis (d) None of them

109. The M.I. of a solid cylinder about its axis is I. It is allowed to roll down an inclined plane without slipping. If its angular velocity at the bottom is ω, then K.E. of the cylinder will be :

(a) $\frac{I\omega^2}{2}$ (b) $I\omega^2$

(c) $\frac{3I\omega^2}{2}$ (d) $2\, I\omega^2$

110. A solid sphere rolls down an inclined plane and its velocity at the bottom is v_1. The same sphere slides down the plane (without friction) and its velocity at the bottom is v_2. Which one of the following is correct ?

(a) $v_1 = v_2$ (b) $v_1 = \sqrt{\frac{5}{7}}\, v_2$

(c) $v_1 = \sqrt{\frac{7}{5}}\, v_2$ (d) $v_1 = 3v_2$

111. If $\vec{A} \times \vec{B} = \vec{B} \times \vec{A}$, then the angle between $\vec{A}$ and $\vec{B}$ is :

(a) π (b) $\pi/2$

(c) $\pi/3$ (d) $\pi/4$

112. Let $\vec{F}$ be the force acting on a particle having position vector $\vec{r}$ and $\vec{\tau}$ be the torque of this force about the origin, then : **(A.I.E.E.E. 2003)**

(a) $\vec{r}\cdot\vec{F}=0$ and $\vec{F}\cdot\vec{\tau}\neq 0$

(b) $\vec{r}\cdot\vec{\tau}\neq 0$ and $\vec{F}\cdot\vec{\tau}=0$

(c) $\vec{r}\cdot\vec{\tau}\neq 0$ and $\vec{F}\cdot\vec{\tau}\neq 0$

(d) $\vec{r}\cdot\vec{\tau}=0$ and $\vec{F}\cdot\vec{\tau}=0$

113. A particle performing uniform circular motion has angular momentum L. If its angular frequency is doubled and K.E. is halved, then angular momentum becomes : **(A.I.E.E.E. 2003)**

(a) L/4 (b) 2 L
(c) 4 L (d) L/12

114. A T shaped object with dimensions shown in the figure is lying on a smooth floor. A force $\vec{F}$ is applied at point P parallel to AB, such that the object has only transitional motion without rotation. Find the location of P with respect to C. **(A.I.E.E.E. 2005)**

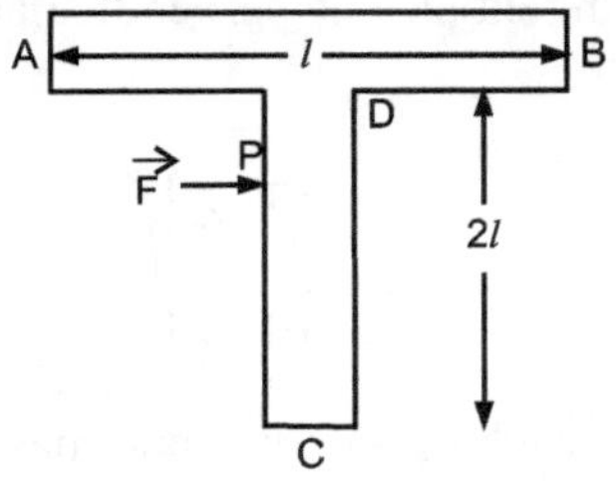

(a) $2l/3$ (b) $3l/2$
(c) $4l/3$ (d) l

115. A force $-F\hat{k}$ acts on O, the origin of the co-ordinate system. The torque about the point (1, – 1) is : **(A.I.E.E.E. 2006)**

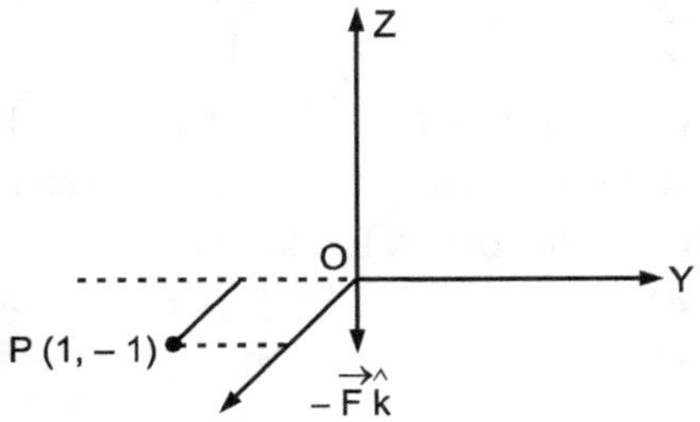

(a) $F(\hat{i}+\hat{j})$ (b) $-F(\hat{i}-\hat{j})$
(c) $F(\hat{i}-\hat{j})$ (d) $-F(\hat{i}+\hat{j})$

116. Angular momentum of the particle rotating with a central force is constant due to : **(A.I.E.E.E. 2000)**

(a) constant force
(b) constant linear momentum
(c) constant torque
(d) zero torque

117. A solid sphere is rotating in free space. If the radius of the sphere is increased keeping the mass same, which one of the following will not be affected ? **(A.I.E.E.E. 2004)**

(a) Momentum of Inertia
(b) Angular momentum
(c) Angular velocity
(d) Rotational K.E

118. A thin circular ring of mass m and radius R is rotating about its axis with constant angular velocity ω. Two objects each of mass M are attached gently to the opposite ends of the diameter of the ring. The ring now rotates with an angular velocity ω', which is equal to : **(A.I.E.E.E. 2006)**

(a) $\dfrac{m\omega}{m+M}$ (b) $\dfrac{m\omega}{m+2M}$
(c) $\dfrac{(m+2M)\,\omega}{m}$ (d) $\left(\dfrac{m-2M}{m+2M}\right)\omega$

119. A uniform round body of radius R, mass M and moment of inertia I rolls down (without slipping) an inclined plane making an angle θ with the horizontal. Then the acceleration is : **(A.I.E.E.E. 2007)**

(a) $\dfrac{g\sin\theta}{1+\dfrac{I}{MR^2}}$ (b) $\dfrac{g\sin\theta}{1+\dfrac{MR^2}{I}}$
(c) $\dfrac{g\sin\theta}{1-\dfrac{I}{MR^2}}$ (d) $\dfrac{g\sin\theta}{1-\dfrac{MR^2}{I}}$

120. A one rupee coin starting from rest rolls down a distance of one metre on an inclined plane at an angle 30° with the horizontal. The time taken is :

($\because g = 9.8\ ms^{-2}$) **(A.I.E.E.E. 2007)**

(a) 0.68 s (b) 0.6 s

(c) 0.5 s (d) 0.7 s

121. A solid sphere rolls down without slipping on an inclined plane at an angle 60° over a distance of 10 m. The acceleration (in ms^{-2}) is :

(a) 4 (b) 5

(c) 6 (d) 7

122. Two spheres each of mass M and radius R/2 are connected with a massless rod of length 2R. What will be the M.I. of the system about an axis passing through the centre of one of the spheres and perpendicular to the rod ?

(a) $\frac{21}{5}MR^2$ (b) $\frac{2}{5}MR^2$

(c) $\frac{5}{2}MR^2$ (d) $\frac{5}{21}MR^2$

123. A uniform rod of mass m and length l is suspended by means of two light inextensible strings as shown in the figure. Tension in one string immediately after the other string is cut is :

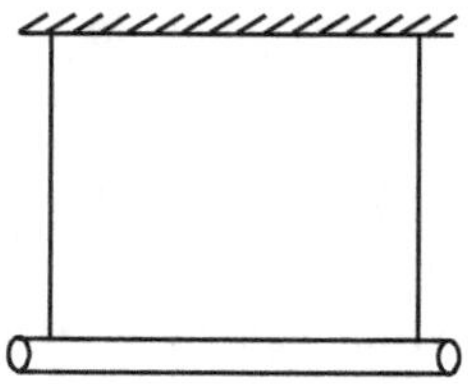

(a) $\frac{mg}{2}$ (b) mg

(c) $2\,mg$ (d) $\frac{mg}{4}$

124. Four holes of radius R are cut from a thin square plate of side 4R and mass M. The M.I. of the remaining portion about the z-axis is :

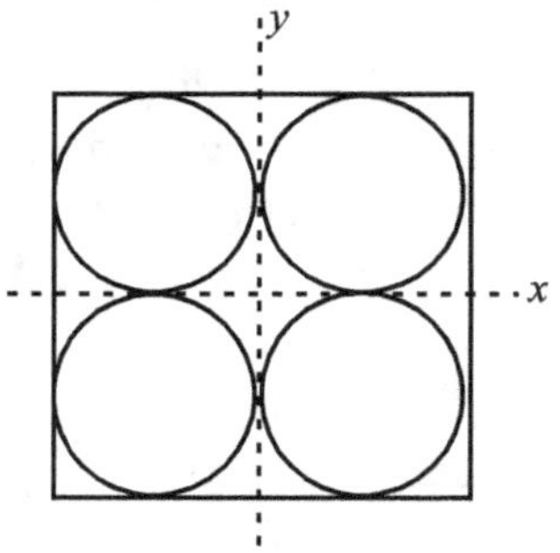

(a) $\frac{\pi}{12}MR^2$ (b) $\left(\frac{4}{3}-\frac{\pi}{4}\right)MR^2$

(c) $\left(\frac{4}{3}-\frac{\pi}{6}\right)MR^2$ (d) $\left(\frac{8}{3}-\frac{10\pi}{16}\right)MR^2$

125. A rectangular block has a square base measuring $a \times a$ and height 'h'. It moves on a horizontal surface in a direction perpendicular to one of its edges. The coefficient of friction is μ. It will topple if :

(a) $\mu > \frac{h}{a}$ (b) $\mu > \frac{a}{h}$

(c) $\mu > \frac{2a}{h}$ (d) $\mu > \frac{a}{2h}$

126. If M.I. of a disc about an axis tangential and parallel to its surface be I, then its M.I. about the axis tangential, but perpendicular to the surface will be :

(a) $\frac{6}{5}I$ (b) $\frac{3}{4}I$

(c) $\frac{3}{2}I$ (d) $\frac{5}{4}I$

127. Three rods each of length L and mass M are placed along the x, y and z axis in such a way that one end of each rod is at the origin. The M.I. of the system about z axis is :

(a) $\frac{ML^2}{3}$ (b) $\frac{2ML^2}{3}$

(c) $\frac{3ML^2}{2}$ (d) $\frac{2ML^2}{12}$

128. A circular disc of mass 0.41 kg and radius 10 m rolls without slipping with a velocity of 2 ms^{-1}. The total K.E. of the disc is :

(a) 0.41 J (b) 1.23 J

(c) 0.82 J (d) 2.45 J

129. Three identical spheres of mass M each are placed at the corners of an equilateral triangle of side $2a$. Taking one of the corners as the origin, the position vector of centre of mass is :

(a) $\sqrt{3}(\hat{i} - \hat{j})$ (b) $\frac{\hat{i}}{\sqrt{3}} + \hat{j}$

(c) $\hat{i} + \hat{j}/3$ (d) $\hat{i} + \hat{j}/\sqrt{3}$

130. A rod of length l is hinged at one end and kept horizontal. It is allowed to fall. The velocity of the other end of the rod is :

(a) $\sqrt{3gl}$ (b) $\sqrt{2gl}$

(c) $2\ Ml^2$ (d) Zero

COMPREHENSION BASED QUESTIONS

Passage I

For a given body, the centre of mass is a point where whole of the mass of the body is supposed to be concentrated. This point may be outside the body. If the body has n number of particles of masses m_1, m_2, m_3...m_n and $\vec{r_1}, \vec{r_2}, \vec{r_3} \ldots \vec{r_n}$, then the centre of mass of body is given by :

$$\vec{r}_{cm} = \frac{m_1\vec{r_1} + m_2\vec{r_2} + \ldots + m_n\vec{r_n}}{m_1 + m_2 + \ldots m_n}$$

or $$\vec{r}_{cm} = \frac{\sum_{i=1}^{n} m_i\vec{r_i}}{\sum_{i=1}^{n} m_i}$$

Read the above passage and answer the following questions

131. Three identical spheres A, B and C, each of radius R are placed touching each other on a horizontal table. The C.M. of the system w.r.t. centre of sphere A will be :

(a) $\frac{1}{3}(\overrightarrow{AB} + \overrightarrow{BC})$ (b) $\frac{3}{2}(\overrightarrow{AB} + \overrightarrow{BC})$

(c) $\frac{(\overrightarrow{AB} + \overrightarrow{AC})}{2}$ (d) $\frac{(\overrightarrow{AB} + \overrightarrow{AC})}{4}$

132. Two particles of masses 100 gm and 300 gm have positions $2\hat{i} + 5\hat{j} + 13\hat{k}$ and $-6\hat{i} + 4\hat{j} - 2\hat{k}$ cm. respectively at a given time. Then the position of centre of mass is :

(a) $-4\hat{i} + \frac{\hat{j}}{4} + \frac{\hat{k}}{4}$ (b) $4\hat{i} + \frac{\hat{j}}{4} - \frac{\hat{k}}{3}$

(c) $-4\hat{i} + \frac{17\hat{j}}{4} + \frac{7\hat{k}}{4}$ (d) $4\hat{i} - \frac{\hat{j}}{4} - \frac{\hat{k}}{3}$

133. Two masses m_1 and m_2 considered to move in a horizontal plane collide, where $m_1 = 85g$ and $m_2 = 200$ g and initially $v_1 = 6.48$ cm s^{-1} and $v_2 = -6.78$ cms^{-1}. The velocity of C.M. will be :

(a) 1.83 cms^{-1} (b) – 1.83 cms^{-1}

(c) 2.83 cms^{-1} (d) – 2.83 cms^{-1}

134. Two charged particles are moving towards each other with velocities v_1 and v_2 due to mutual attraction of force. Then the velocity of C.M. is :

(a) $\left(\frac{v_1 + v_2}{2}\right)$ (b) $\left(\frac{v_1 - v_2}{2}\right)$

(c) v_2 (d) Zero

135. Find C.M. of the following system :

(a) $(0.5x, 0.6x)$

(b) $(0.5x, 0.7x)$

(c) $(0.6x, 0.7x)$

(d) $(0.7x, 0.6x)$

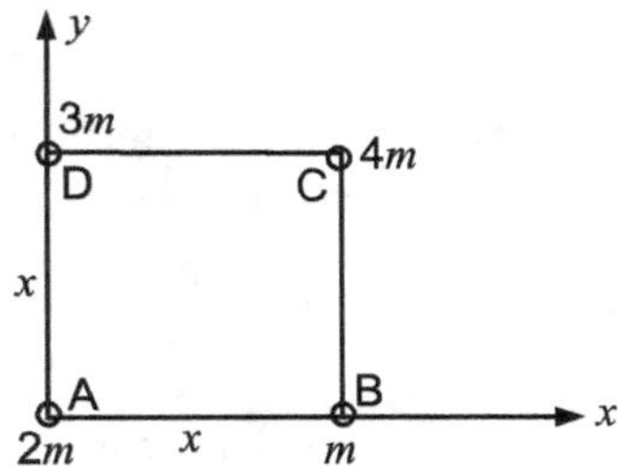

Passage II

The equations for rotational motion can be expressed as :

$$\omega = \omega_0 + \alpha t \quad \text{... (1)}$$

$$\theta = \omega_0 t + \frac{1}{2}\alpha t^2 \quad \text{... (2)}$$

and $$\omega^2 = \omega_0^2 + 2\alpha\theta \quad \text{... (3)}$$

where ω = Final angular velocity

ω_0 = Initial angular velocity

α = Angular acceleration

θ = Angular displacement

t = Time

Linear velocity (v) = Radius (r) × Angular velocity (ω)

Angular velocity (ω) = $\frac{2\pi}{T} = 2\pi f$

Read the above passage and answer the following questions.

136. A flywheel rotating at 420 r.p.m. slows down at a constant rate of 2 rad s^{-2}. How much time is required to stop the flywheel ?

(a) 19.99 s (b) 20.99 s

(c) 21.99 s (d) 22.99 s

137. The speed of a motor increases from 600 r.p.m. to 1200 r.p.m. in 20 s. What is its angular acceleration ?

(a) 4π rad s^{-2} (b) 3π rad s^{-2}

(c) 2π rad s^{-2} (d) π rad s^{-2}

138. From question 137, calculate the number of revolutions made by the motor during this time :

(a) 100 (b) 200

(c) 300 (d) 400

139. The linear velocity of the minute hand of a wall clock with length 6 cm, is :

(a) $\frac{\pi}{100}$ cms^{-1} (b) $\frac{\pi}{200}$ cms^{-1}

(c) $\frac{\pi}{300}$ cms^{-1} (d) 2π cms^{-1}

ASSERTION AND REASON

Directions for Q.140 to Q. 148 : In the following questions, Statement-I is an ASSERTION followed by Statement-II as a REASON

For answering a question, you are required to choose the correct one out of the given four options :

(a) Statement-I and II both are true and Statement II is the correct explanation of Statement-I.

(b) Statement-I and II both are true and Statement-II is not the correct explanation of Statement-I.

(c) Statement-I is true, but Statement-II is false.

(d) Statement-I and Statement-II both are false.

140. (I) The C.M. of a two particle system of unequal masses is closer to the heavier particle.

(II) The C.M. of a two particle system divides the distance between the particles in the inverse ratio of their masses.

141. (I) For a system of particles under a central force field, the total angular momentum is conserved.

(II) The torque acting on such a system is zero.

142. (I) The angular momentum of a body always acts perpendicular to the position vector.

(II) $\vec{L} = \vec{r} \times \vec{p}$

143. (I) The C.M. of a body may lie outside the body.

(II) The C.M. of a body depends on the distribution of mass in the body.

144. **(I)** The torque due to a force always acts perpendicular to the force vector.

(II) Torque $(\vec{\tau}) = \vec{r} \times \vec{F}$

145. **(I)** Moment of inertia of a body depends on its mass and size only.

(II) Irrespective of the location of the axis of rotation, inertness to the rotational motion is determined by the mass and size of the body.

146. **(I)** The angular momentum of a body is equal to twice the product of its mass and areal velocity.

(II) When no external torque acts, the motion of the body takes place in a fixed plane.

147. **(I)** If polar ice melts, days will be shorter.

(II) Moment of inertia decreases and thus angular velocity increases.

148. **(I)** A sphere cannot roll on a frictionless horizontal surface.

(II) The tangential frictional force on the sphere exerts torque and causes it to roll.

149. Two blocks of masses 10 kg and 4 kg are connected by a spring of negligible mass and placed on a frictionless horizontal surface. An impulse gives the velocity of 14 ms^{-1} to the heavier block in the direction of the lighter block. The velocity of C.M. is:

(a) 30 ms^{-1}
(b) 20 ms^{-1}
(c) 10 ms^{-1}
(d) 5 ms^{-1}

150. A smooth sphere A is moving on a frictionless horizontal plane with angular speed ω and centre of mass velocity μ. It collides elastically head on with an identical sphere B at rest. Neglecting friction everywhere, after collision, their angular speeds are ω_A and ω_B, then :

(a) $\omega_A < \omega_B$
(b) $\omega_A = \omega_B$
(c) $\omega_A = \omega$
(d) $\omega_B = \omega$

151. A mass M is moving with a constant velocity parallel to the x-axis. Its angular momentum w.r.t. the origin :

(a) is zero
(b) remains constant
(c) goes on increasing
(d) goes on decreasing

152. A particle of mass m is projected with the velocity v making an angle 45° with horizontal. The magnitude of the angular momentum of the projectile about the point of projection, when the particle is at its maximum height 'h' is :

(a) Zero
(b) $\dfrac{mv^3}{4\sqrt{2}g}$
(c) $\dfrac{mv^2}{\sqrt{2g}}$
(d) $m\sqrt{2gh^3}$

153. The torque $\vec{\tau}$ on a body about a given point is found to be equal to $\vec{A} \times \vec{L}$, where $\vec{A}$ is a constant vector and $\vec{L}$ is the angular momentum of the body about that point. From this, it follows that :

(a) $\dfrac{d\vec{L}}{dt}$ is perpendicular to $\vec{L}$ at all instants of time
(b) The component of $\vec{L}$ in the direction of $\vec{A}$ does not change with time
(c) The magnitude $\vec{L}$ does not change with time
(d) $\vec{A}$ does not change with time

154. The driver of a car suddenly sees a broad wall in front of him. He should :

(a) apply break sharply
(b) turn sharply
(c) (a) and (b) both
(d) none of the above.

155. A cubical block of side L rests on a rough horizontal surface with coefficient of friction μ. A horizontal force F is applied on the block as shown in the figure. If μ is sufficiently high so that the block does not slide before toppling, the minimum force required to topple the block is :

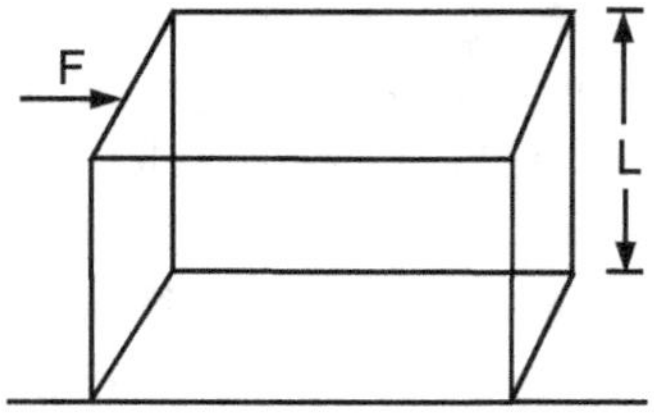

(a) Infinitesimal (b) $mg/4$

(c) $mg/2$ (d) $mg(1-\mu)$

156. Consider a body, consisting of two identical balls, each of mass M connected by a rigid rod of length L. If an impulse I = Mv is imparted to a body at one of its ends, what would be its angular velocity ?

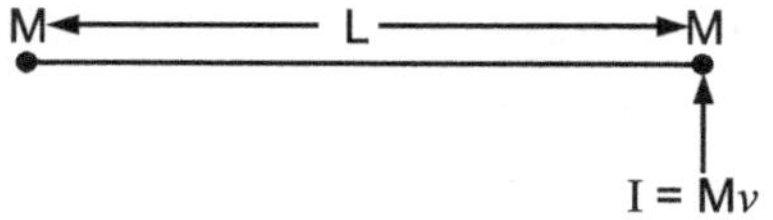

(a) v/L (b) $v/3L$

(c) $2v/L$ (d) $v/4L$

157. A particle undergoes uniform circular motion. About which point on the plane of the circle, will the angular momentum of the particle remain conserved ?

(a) Centre of the circle

(b) Inside the circle

(c) Outside the circle

(d) On the circumference

158. A solid sphere of radius R has M.I. (I). about its geometrical axis. It is melted into a disc of radius r and thickness t. If its M.I. about the tangential axis is also equal to I, then the value of r is equal to :

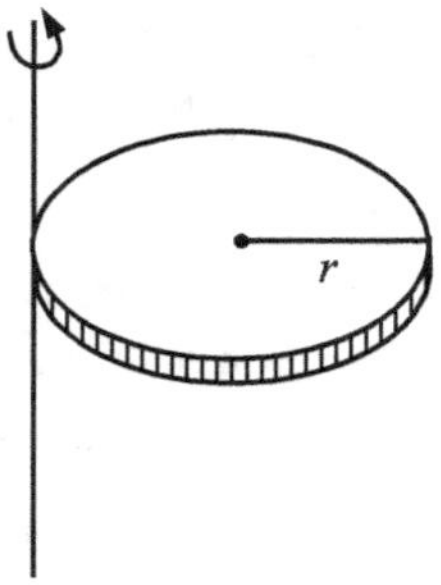

(a) $\frac{2}{\sqrt{15}}R$ (b) $\frac{2}{\sqrt{5}}R$

(c) $\sqrt{\frac{3}{5}}R$ (d) $\frac{1}{\sqrt{5}}R$

159. A disc of mass M and radius R is rolling with angular speed ω on a horizontal plane as shown in the figure. The magnitude of angular momentum of the disc about the origin is :

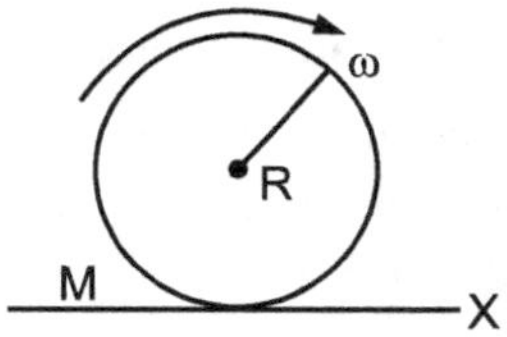

(a) $\frac{MR^2\omega}{2}$ (b) $MR^2\omega$

(c) $\frac{3\,MR^2\omega}{2}$ (d) $2\,MR^2\omega$

160. A wheel has angular acceleration of 3 rad/sec^2 and an initial angular speed of 2 rad/sec. In a time of 2 sec it has rotated through an angle (in radian) of :

(C.B.S.E. AIPMT 2007)

(a) 10 (b) 12

(c) 4 (d) 6

161. A particle of mass m is tied to one end of a string of length l and rotated through the other end along a horizontal circular path with speed v. The work done in half horizontal circle is : **(M.P. P.E.T. 2008)**

(a) Zero (b) $\left(\frac{mv^2}{l}\right)\cdot 2\pi l$

(c) $\left(\frac{mv^2}{l}\right)\pi l$ (d) $\left(\frac{mv^2}{l}\right)l$

162. A wheel has angular acceleration of 3 rad/s^2 and an initial angular speed of 2 rad/s. In a time of 2 s it has rotated through an angle (in radian) of : **(C.P.M.T. 2008)**

(a) 6 (b) 10
(c) 12 (d) 4

163. The radius of the rear wheel of a bicycle is twice that of the front wheel. When the bicycle is moving, the angular speed of the rear wheel compared to that of the front is :

(D.P.M.T. 2009)

(a) greater (b) smaller
(c) same (d) exactly double

164. A thin circular ring of mass M and radius r is rotating about its axis with constant angular velocity ω. Two objects each of mass m are attached gently to the opposite ends of a diameter of the ring. The ring now rotates with angular velocity given by :

(A.I.P.M.T. (Mains) 2010)

(a) $\frac{(M+2m)\,\omega}{2m}$ (b) $\frac{2M\omega}{M+2m}$
(c) $\frac{(M+2m)\,\omega}{M}$ (d) $\frac{M\omega}{M+2m}$

165. A wheel having moment of inertia 2 kg m^2 about its vertical axis rotates at the rate of 60 rotations per minute on this axis. Find torque, which can stop the wheel's rotation in one minute : **(H.P.P.M.T. 2008)**

(a) $\frac{\pi}{18}$ Nm (b) $\frac{2\pi}{15}$ Nm
(c) $\frac{\pi}{12}$ Nm (d) $\frac{\pi}{15}$ Nm

166. On the centre of a frictionless table is a small hole through which a weightless string of length $2l$ is inserted. On the two ends of the string, two balls of the same mass m are attached. Arrangement is made in such a way that half of the string is on the table top and half is hanging below. The ball on the table top is made to move in a circular path with a constant speed v. What is the centripetal acceleration of the moving ball ?

(D.P.M.T. 2009)

(a) mvl (b) g
(c) Zero (d) 2 mvl

167. The angular velocity of the earth is ω_1 and the angular velocity of the hour hand of a clock is ω_2. Then : **(M.H.T.C.E.T. 2009)**

(a) $\omega_2 = \frac{\omega_1}{2}$ (b) $\omega_1 = \frac{\omega_2}{2}$
(c) $\omega_1 = \frac{\omega_2}{4}$ (d) $\omega_1 = \frac{\omega_2}{16}$

168. Consider a two particle system with particles having masses m_1 and m_2. If the first particle is pushed towards the centre of mass through a distance, by what distance should the second particle be moved, so as to keep the centre of mass at the same position ?

(A.I.E.E.E. 2006)

(a) d (b) $\frac{m_2}{m_1}d$
(c) $\frac{m_1}{m_1+m_2}d$ (d) $\frac{m_1}{m_2}d$

169. A thin rod of length L and mass M is bent at its mid-point into two halves so that the angle between them is 90°. The moment of inertia of the bent rod about an axis passing through the bending point and perpendicular to the plane defined by the two halves of the rod is : **(C.B.S.E. 2008)**

(a) $\frac{ML^2}{12}$ (b) $\frac{ML^2}{6}$
(c) $\frac{\sqrt{2}ML^2}{24}$ (d) $\frac{ML^2}{24}$

170. The moment of inertia of a thin uniform rod of length L and mass M about an axis passing through a point at a distance of 1/3 from one of its ends and perpendicular to the rod is: **(M.H.T.C.E.T. 2010)**

(a) $\frac{ML^2}{12}$ (b) $\frac{ML^2}{9}$
(c) $\frac{7\,ML^2}{48}$ (d) $\frac{ML^2}{48}$

171. Moment of inertia of a disc about a diameter is I. Find the moment of inertia of disc about an axis perpendicular to its plane and passing through its rim ?

(M.H.T.C.E.T. 2010)

(a) 6 I (b) 4 I

(c) 2 I (d) 8 I

172. The ratio of the radius of gyration of a circular disc and a circular ring of the same radii about a tangential axis in its own plane is : **(H.P.P.M.T. 2010)**

(a) $1 : \sqrt{2}$ (b) $\sqrt{5} : \sqrt{6}$

(c) 2 : 3 (d) 2 : 1

173. From a circular disc of radius R and mass 9M, a small disc of mass M and radius $\frac{R}{3}$ is removed concentrically. The moment of inertia of the remaining disc about an axis perpendicular to the plane of the disc and passing through its centre is :

(A.I.P.M.T. 2010)

(a) $\frac{40}{9}MR^2$ (b) MR^2

(c) $4\,MR^2$ (d) $\frac{4}{9}MR^2$

174. A thin horizontal circular disc is rotating about a vertical axis passing through its centre. An insect is at rest at a point near the firm of the disc. The insect now moves along a diameter of the disc to reach its other end. During the journey of the insect, the angular speed of the disc :

(A.I.E.E.E. 2011)

(a) First increases and then decreases

(b) Remains unchanged

(c) Continuously decreases

(d) Continuously increases.

175. The moment of inertia of a thin uniform rod of mass M and length L about an axis passing through its mid-point and perpendicular to its length is I_0. Its moment of inertia about an axis passing through one of its ends and perpendicular to its length is :

(A.I.P.M.T. 2011)

(a) $I_0 + \frac{ML^2}{2}$ (b) $I_0 + \frac{ML^2}{4}$

(c) $I_0 + 2ML^2$ (d) $I_0 + ML^2$

176. Three identical spheres, each of mass 3 kg are placed touching each other with their centres lying on a straight line. The centres of the spheres are marked as P, Q and R respectively. The distance of centre of mass of the system from P is : **(Kerala 2008)**

(a) $\frac{PQ + QR + PR}{3}$ (b) $\frac{PQ + PR}{3}$

(c) $\frac{PQ + QR + PR}{9}$ (d) $\frac{PQ + PR}{9}$

177. Two bodies of masses 1 kg and 3 kg have position vectors $\hat{i} + 2\hat{j} + \hat{k}$ and $3\hat{i} - 2\hat{j} + \hat{k}$ respectively. The centre of mass of this system has a position vector :

(A.I.P.M.T. 2009)

(a) $-2\hat{i} - \hat{j} + \hat{k}$ (b) $2\hat{i} - \hat{j} - 2\hat{k}$

(c) $-\hat{i} + \hat{j} + \hat{k}$ (d) $-2\hat{i} + 2\hat{k}$

178. If $\vec{F}$ is the force acting on a particle having position vector $\vec{r}$ and $\vec{\tau}$ is the torque of this force about the origin, then :

(A.I.P.M.T. 2009)

(a) $\vec{r} \cdot \vec{\tau} > 0$ and $\vec{F} \cdot \vec{\tau} < 0$

(b) $\vec{r} \cdot \vec{\tau} = 0$ and $\vec{F} \cdot \vec{\tau} = 0$

(c) $\vec{r} \cdot \vec{\tau} = 0$ and $\vec{F} \cdot \vec{\tau} \neq 0$

(d) $\vec{r} \cdot \vec{\tau} \neq 0$ and $\vec{F} \cdot \vec{\tau} = 0$

179. The magnitude of angular momentum of solid cylinder of M.I. 0.625 kg-m^2 rotating about its axis with angular speed 100 rad s^{-1} is **(H.P.P.M.T. 2009)**

(a) 31.2 kg-m^2 s^{-1} (b) 12.3 kg-m^2 s^{-1}

(c) 62.5 kg-m^2 s^{-1} (d) 2.5 kg-m^2 s^{-1}

180. The moment of inertia of a body initially at rest about a given axis is 1.2 kg-m^2. One applying an acceleration of 25 rad/sec^2, the time it will take to acquire a rotational kinetic energy of 1500 J is : **(H.P.P.M.T. 2010)**

(a) 4 sec (b) 2 sec
(c) 8 sec (d) 10 sec

181. Two bodies rotating with the same angular momentum have M.I. I_1 and I_2 respectively such that ($I_1 > I_2$) with the kinetic energy of rotation as E_1 and E_2 respectively, then : **(M.H.T.C.E.T. 2009)**

(a) $E_2 > E_1$ (b) $E_1 > E_2$
(c) $E_2 = E_1$ (d) $E_1 = 2E_2$

182. A flywheel of moment of inertia 3×10^2 kg-m^2 is rotating with uniform angular speed of 4.6 rad s^{-1}. If a torque of 6.9×10^2 Nm retards the wheel, then the time in which the wheel comes to rest is : **(Kerala Engg. 2010)**

(a) 1.5 s (b) 2 s
(c) 0.5 s (d) 1 s

183. An inclined plane makes an angle of 30° with horizontal. A solid sphere rolling down this inclined plane has a linear acceleration of: **(H.P.P.M.T. 2008)**

(a) $\frac{5g}{14}$ (b) $\frac{2g}{3}$
(c) $\frac{g}{3}$ (d) $\frac{5g}{7}$

184. Angular momentum of a body is defined as the product of **(Kerala 2004)**

(a) mass of angular velocity
(b) centripetal force and radius
(c) linear velocity and angular velocity
(d) moment of inertia and angular velocity

185. The ratio of the radii of gyration of a circular disc to that of a circular ring each of same mass and radius around their respective axes is **(C.B.S.E. 2008)**

(a) $1 : \sqrt{2}$ (b) $\sqrt{2} : 1$
(c) $\sqrt{2} : \sqrt{3}$ (d) $\sqrt{3} : \sqrt{2}$

186. Moment of inertia of a disc about an axis which is tangent and parallel to its plane is I. Then the moment of inertia of disc about a tangent, but perpendicular to its plane will be **(MHT-CET 2005)**

(a) $\frac{31}{4}$ (b) $\frac{31}{2}$
(c) $\frac{51}{6}$ (d) $\frac{61}{5}$

187. By keeping moment of inertia of a body constant, if we double the time period, then angular momentum of body **(MHT-CET 2005)**

(a) remains constant (b) becomes half
(c) doubles (d) quadruples

188. The moment of inertia of a uniform circular disc of radius 'R' and mass 'M' about an axis passing from the edge of the disc and normal to the disc is **(C.B.S.E., P.M.T. 2005)**

(a) $\frac{1}{2}MR^2$ (b) $\frac{7}{2}MR^2$
(c) $\frac{3}{2}MR^2$ (d) MR^2

189. Calculate the M.I. of a thin uniform ring about an axis tangent to the ring and in a plane of the ring if its M.I. about an axis passing through the centre and perpendicular to plane is 4 kg-m^2 **(MHT-CET 2006)**

(a) 12 kg-m^2 (b) 3 kg-m^2
(c) 6 kg-m^2 (d) 9 kg-m^2

190. A uniform disc of mass 2 kg is rotated about an axis perpendicular to the plane of the disc. If radius of gyration is 50 cm, then the M.I. of disc about same axis is **(MHT-CET 2006)**

(a) 0.25 kg-m^2 (b) 0.5 kg-m^2
(c) 2 kg-m^2 (d) 1 kg-m^2

191. A tube of length 'L' is filled completely with an incompressible liquid of mass M and closed at both ends. The tube is then rotated in a horizontal plane about one of its ends with uniform angular velocity ω. The force exerted by the liquid at the other end is **(C.B.S.E. 2006)**

(a) $\frac{ML^2\omega^2}{2}$ (b) $\frac{ML\omega^2}{2}$

(c) $\frac{ML^2\omega}{2}$ (d) $ML\omega^2$

192. The total energy of rolling ring of mass 'm', and radius 'R' is **(MHT-CET 2007)**

(a) $\frac{3}{2}mv^2$ (b) $\frac{1}{2}mv^2$

(c) mv^2 (d) $\frac{5}{2}mv^2$

193. Kinetic energy of a body is 4 J and its moment of inertia is 2 kg-m^2, then angular momentum is **(MHT-CET 2008)**

(a) 2 kg-m^2/s (b) 6 kg-m^2/s

(c) 8 kg-m^2/s (d) 4 kg-m^2/s

194. A thin rod of length L and mass M is bent at its mid-point into two halves so that the angle between them is 90°. The moment of inertia of the bent rod about an axis passing through the bending point and perpendicular to the plane defined by the two halves of the rod is **(C.B.S.E. 2008)**

(a) $\frac{ML^2}{12}$ (b) $\frac{ML^2}{6}$

(c) $\frac{\sqrt{2}\,ML^2}{24}$ (d) $\frac{ML^2}{24}$

195. A thin circular ring of mass M and radius R is rotating in a horizontal plane about an axis vertical to its plane with a constant angular velocity ω. If two objects, each of mass m, be attached gently to the opposite ends of a diametre of the ring, the ring will then rotate with an angular velocity **(C.B.S.E. 2009)**

(a) $\frac{\omega M}{M+2m}$ (b) $\frac{\omega(M+2m)}{M}$

(c) $\frac{\omega M}{M+m}$ (d) $\frac{\omega(M-2m)}{M+2m}$

196. Two particles which are initially at rest, move towards each other under the action of their internal attraction. If their speeds are v and 2v at any instant, then the speed of centre of mass of the system will be **(C.B.S.E. 2010)**

(a) 1.5 v (b) v

(c) 2 v (d) zero

197. If the radius of the earth contracts to half of its present radius, then length of the day will be (if density of the earth remaining same). **(MHT-CET 2011)**

(a) $\frac{3}{4}$ hours (b) 6 hours

(c) 12 hours (d) 24 hours

198. The moment of inertia of a thin uniform rod of mass M and length L about an axis passing through its mid point and perpendicular to its length is I_0. Its moment of inertia about an axis passing through one of its ends and perpendicular to its length is **(C.B.S.E. 2011)**

(a) $I_0 + \frac{ML^2}{2}$ (b) $I_0 + \frac{ML^2}{4}$

(c) $I_0 + 2ML^2$ (d) $I_0 + ML^2$

199. ABC is an equilateral triangle with O as its centre $\vec{F_1}$, $\vec{F_2}$ and $\vec{F_3}$ represent three forces acting along the sides AB, BC, and AC respectively. If the total torque about O is zero, then the magnitude of $\vec{F_3}$ is **(C.B.S.E. 2012)**

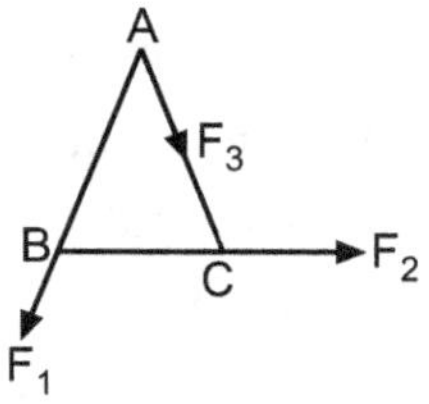

(a) $2(F_1 + F_2)$ (b) $F_1 + F_2$

(c) $F_1 - F_2$ (d) $\frac{F_1 + F_2}{2}$

200. Two persons of masses 55 kg and 65 kg respectively, are at the opposite ends of a boat. The length of the boat is 3.0 m and it weighs 100 kg. The 55 kg man walks upto the 65 kg man and sits with him. If the boat is in still water, the centre of mass of the system shifts by **(C.B.S.E. 2012)**

(a) 0.75 m (b) 3.0 m

(c) 2.3 m (d) zero

201. Moment of inertia of a solid sphere about its diametre is I. If that sphere is recast into 8 identical small spheres, then moment of inertia of such small sphere about its diameter is **(MHT-CET 2012)**

(a) $\frac{I}{8}$ (b) $\frac{I}{16}$

(c) $\frac{I}{24}$ (d) $\frac{I}{32}$

202. Two uniform circular discs A and B of radii R and 4R with thickness X and $\frac{X}{4}$ respectively, rotate about their axes passing through their centres and perpendicular to their planes. If M.I. of first disc is I_A and that of second disc is I_B, then **(MHT-CET 2012)**

(a) $I_A = I_B$

(b) $I_A > I_B$

(c) $I_B > I_A$

(d) Data is insufficient

203. A small object of uniform density rolls up a curved surface with an initial velocity 'v'. It reaches upto a maximum height of $\frac{3v^2}{4g}$ with respect to the initial position. The object is **(NEET 2013)**

(a) solid sphere (b) hollow sphere

(c) disc (d) ring

ANSWER KEY

1. (b)	**2.** (d)	**3.** (d)	**4.** (d)	**5.** (c)	**6.** (b)	**7.** (a)	**8.** (d)	**9.** (b)	**10.** (a)
11. (a)	**12.** (d)	**13.** (d)	**14.** (c)	**15.** (d)	**16.** (a)	**17.** (d)	**18.** (d)	**19.** (d)	**20.** (d)
21. (c)	**22.** (c)	**23.** (a)	**24.** (b)	**25.** (b)	**26.** (c)	**27.** (a)	**28.** (b)	**29.** (c)	**30.** (c)
31. (c)	**32.** (b)	**33.** (b)	**34.** (c)	**35.** (c)	**36.** (b)	**37.** (b)	**38.** (a)	**39.** (d)	**40.** (d)
41. (a)	**42.** (d)	**43.** (c)	**44.** (c)	**45.** (d)	**46.** (d)	**47.** (d)	**48.** (d)	**49.** (d)	**50.** (a)
51. (c)	**52.** (b)	**53.** (b)	**54.** (a)	**55.** (a)	**56.** (a)	**57.** (d)	**58.** (c)	**59.** (d)	**60.** (a)
61. (c)	**62.** (c)	**63.** (c)	**64.** (b)	**65.** (a)	**66.** (d)	**67.** (c)	**68.** (c)	**69.** (b)	**70.** (b)
71. (a)	**72.** (d)	**73.** (d)	**74.** (c)	**75.** (c)	**76.** (d)	**77.** (c)	**78.** (d)	**79.** (c)	**80.** (c)
81. (b)	**82.** (d)	**83.** (b)	**84.** (b)	**85.** (a)	**86.** (d)	**87.** (b)	**88.** (b)	**89.** (d)	**90.** (d)
91. (a)	**92.** (a)	**93.** (d)	**94.** (a)	**95.** (a)	**96.** (b)	**97.** (c)	**98.** (b)	**99.** (d)	**100.** (b)
101. (d)	**102.** (d)	**103.** (a)	**104.** (b)	**105.** (c)	**106.** (c)	**107.** (d)	**108.** (c)	**109.** (c)	**110.** (b)
111. (a)	**112.** (d)	**113.** (a)	**114.** (c)	**115.** (a)	**116.** (d)	**117.** (b)	**118.** (b)	**119.** (a)	**120.** (d)
121. (c)	**122.** (a)	**123.** (d)	**124.** (d)	**125.** (b)	**126.** (a)	**127.** (b)	**128.** (b)	**129.** (c)	**130.** (b)
131. (a)	**132.** (c)	**133.** (d)	**134.** (d)	**135.** (b)	**136.** (c)	**137.** (d)	**138.** (c)	**139.** (c)	**140.** (a)
141. (a)	**142.** (a)	**143.** (a)	**144.** (a)	**145.** (d)	**146.** (b)	**147.** (a)	**148.** (a)	**149.** (c)	**150.** (c)
151. (b)	**152.** (b)	**153.** (a)	**154.** (a)	**155.** (c)	**156.** (a)	**157.** (a)	**158.** (a)	**159.** (c)	**160.** (a)
161. (a)	**162.** (b)	**163.** (b)	**164.** (d)	**165.** (d)	**166.** (b)	**167.** (b)	**168.** (d)	**169.** (a)	**170.** (b)
171. (a)	**172.** (b)	**173.** (a)	**174.** (a)	**175.** (b)	**176.** (a)	**177.** (b)	**178.** (c)	**179.** (c)	**180.** (b)
181. (a)	**182.** (b)	**183.** (a)	**184.** (d)	**185.** (a)	**186.** (d)	**187.** (c)	**188.** (c)	**189.** (b)	**190.** (b)
191. (c)	**192.** (d)	**193.** (b)	**194.** (a)	**195.** (d)	**196.** (a)	**197.** (b)	**198.** (b)	**199.** (b)	**200.** (d)
201. (d)	**202.** (c)	**203.** (c)							

7

GRAVITATION

MULTIPLE CHOICE QUESTIONS

1. Two bodies of masses M_1 and M_2 are initially at rest and a distance K apart. Then they move directly towards one another under the influence of their mutual gravitational attraction. What is the ratio of the distance travelled by M_1 to the distance travelled by M_2 ?

(a) $\frac{M_1}{M_2}$ (b) $\frac{M_2}{M_1}$

(c) 1 (d) $\frac{1}{2}$

2. Two particles of equal masses move in a circle of radius r under the action of their mutual gravitational attraction. If the mass of each particle is M, the speed of each particle is :

(a) $\sqrt{\frac{GM}{r}}$ (b) $\sqrt{\frac{GM}{2r}}$

(c) $\sqrt{\frac{GM}{4r}}$ (d) $\sqrt{\frac{2GM}{r}}$

3. Gravitational force between a point mass m and M separated by a distance is F. Now if a point mass $2m$ is placed next to m in contact with it, the force on M due to m and the total force on m are :

(a) 2F, F (b) F, 2F

(c) F, 3F (d) F, F

4. The gravitational potential at a height h above the earth's surface is -5.12×10^7 J/kg and acceleration due to gravity at this point is 6.4 ms^{-2}. If the radius of the earth is 6400 km, then the value of h is :

(a) 1200 km (b) 1600 km

(c) 1800 km (d) 2400 km

5. The gain in potential energy of an object of mass m raised from the surface of the earth to a height equal to the radius R of the earth is :

(a) $\frac{mgR}{2}$ (b) $2mgR$

(c) mgR (d) $\frac{mgR}{4}$

6. The eccentricity of the earth's orbit is 0.0167. The ratio of its maximum speed in its orbit to its minimum speed is :

(a) 2.507 (b) 1.0339

(c) 8.324 (d) 1.000

7. An earth satellite is moved from one stable circular orbit to a farther circular orbit. Which of the following quantity will increase ?

(a) Linear orbital speed

(b) Gravitational force

(c) Centripetal acceleration

(d) Gravitational potential energy

8. The mass of the earth is 81 times the mass of the moon and the distance between the earth and moon is 60 times the radius of earth. If R is the radius of the earth, then the distance between the moon and the point on the line joining the moon and earth, where the gravitational force becomes zero, is :

(a) 30 R (b) 15 R

(c) 6 R (d) 5 R

9. The ratio of K.E. required to be given to a satellite to escape the earth's gravitational field to the K.E. required to be given so that the satellite moves in a circular orbit just above the earth's atmosphere is :
(a) One (b) Two
(c) Half (d) Infinite

10. Let A be the area swept out by the line joining the earth and the Sun during February 1991. The area swept out by the line during a typical week in February 1991 is :
(a) A (b) 2A
(c) 4A (d) A/4

11. A mass M is split into two parts m and $(M - m)$ which are then separated by a certain distance. The ratio of m/M which maximizes the gravitational force between the parts is :
(a) 1 : 4 (b) 1 : 2
(c) 4 : 1 (d) 2 : 1

12. Two spheres of radii r and $2r$ are touching each other. The force of attraction between them is proportional to :
(a) r^6 (b) r^4
(c) r^2 (d) r^{-2}

13. Suppose a light planet is revolving around a very massive star in a circular orbit of radius r with period of revolution T. If the gravitational force of attraction between them is proportional to $R^{-3/2}$, then T^2 is proportional to :
(a) R^3 (b) $R^{5/2}$
(c) $R^{3/2}$ (d) $R^{7/2}$

14. A uniform ring of mass M and radius R is placed directly above a uniform sphere of mass 8M and of the same radius R. The centre of ring is at a distance from the centre of the sphere. The gravitational attraction between them is :
(a) $\frac{GM^2}{R^2}$ (b) $\frac{3GM^2}{2R^2}$
(c) $\frac{2GM^2}{\sqrt{2}\,R^2}$ (d) $\frac{\sqrt{3}\,GM^2}{R^2}$

15. The sun is about 330 times heavier and 100 times bigger in radius than the Earth. The ratio of mean density of Sun to that of the Earth is :
(a) 3.3×10^{-6} (b) 3.3×10^{-4}
(c) 3.3×10^{-2} (d) 1.3

16. A solid sphere of uniform density and radius r applies a gravitational force $\vec{F_1}$ on a particle placed at P, distance 2R from the centre O of the sphere. A spherical cavity of radius R/2 is now made in the sphere, then this cavitated sphere now applies a gravitational force $\vec{F_2}$ on the same particle P. Then $\vec{F}_1/\vec{F}_2$ is :
(a) $\frac{1}{2}$ (b) $\frac{7}{9}$
(c) 3 (d) 7

17. The acceleration due to gravity on a planet is $1.96\ ms^{-2}$. If it is safe to jump from a height of 3 m on the earth, the corresponding height on the planet will be :
(a) 3 m (b) 6 m
(c) 9 m (d) 15 m

18. If both, the mass and radius of the earth, each decreases by 50%, the acceleration due to gravity would :
(a) remain the same
(b) decrease by 50%
(c) decrease by 100%
(d) increase by 100%

19. The mass of the moon is $\left(\frac{1}{8}\right)^{th}$ that of the earth but gravitational pull is $\left(\frac{1}{6}\right)^{th}$ that of the earth. It is due to the fact that :
(a) Moon is a satellite of the earth
(b) The radius of the earth is 8.6 times that of the moon
(c) The radius of the earth is $\sqrt{8/6}$ of times that the moon
(d) The radius of the moon is 6/8 times that of the earth

20. The gravitational attraction between two bodies increases when their masses are :

(a) reduced and distance is reduced

(b) increased and distance is reduced

(c) reduced and distance is increased

(d) increased and distance is increased

21. If different planets have the same density but different radii, then the acceleration due to gravity on the surface of the planet is related to the radius (R) of the planet as :

(a) $g \propto R^2$ (b) $g \propto R$

(c) $g \propto \frac{1}{R^2}$ (d) $g \propto \frac{1}{R}$

22. A thief stole a box of weight W and while carrying it on his head jumped down from a wall of height *h* on the ground. Before he reaches the ground, he experienced a load :

(a) Zero (b) $\frac{W}{2}$

(c) W (d) 2W

23. The radius of Mars is 3200 km and the mass of the Earth is 10 times the mass of Mars. An object of weight 200 N on earth, will weigh .... on Mars :

(a) 8 N (b) 20 N

(c) 40 N (d) 80 N

24. A man can jump on the earth's surface by 0.5 m maximum. Through what height can the same person jump on the moon, which has a mean density 2/3 of that of the earth and radius 1/4 that of the earth ?

(a) 1.5 m (b) 3 m

(c) 6 m (d) 7.5 m

25. In the above said problem, the ratio of time duration of his jump on the earth to that of his jump on the moon is :

(a) 6 : 1 (b) 1 : 6

(c) $1 : \sqrt{6}$ (d) $\sqrt{6} : 1$

26. Which of the following graphs correctly represents the variation of $\vec{g}$ on the earth ?

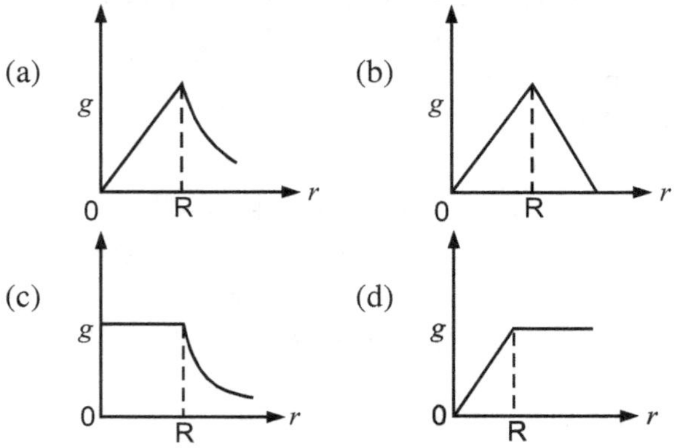

27. At a distance of 320 km from the earth's surface, the value of acceleration due to gravity will be lower than its value on earth's surface by nearly (R_e = 6400 km) :

(a) 2% (b) 6%

(c) 10% (d) 14%

28. If the gravitational force inside the earth's surface varies as x^n, where x is the distance of the body from the surface of the earth, then the value of n will be :

(a) –1 (b) –2

(c) 1 (d) 2

29. If the value of $\vec{g}$ at the earth's surface is 10 ms^{-2}, its value in ms^{-2} at the centre of earth is ..... (R = Radius of earth) :

(a) 5 (b) $\frac{10}{R}$

(c) $\frac{5}{R}$ (d) zero

30. At what height will the weight of the body be same as at the same depth from the surface of the earth ?

(R = Radius of earth)

(a) $\frac{R}{2}$ (b) $\sqrt{5}R - R$

(c) $\frac{\sqrt{5}R - R}{2}$ (d) $\frac{\sqrt{3}R - R}{2}$

31. There is a mine of depth 2 km. In this mine, the conditions as compared to that at the surface are :

(a) Low atmospheric pressure, high $\vec{g}$

(b) High atmospheric pressure, low $\vec{g}$

(c) High atmosphere pressure, high $\vec{g}$

(d) None of these.

32. A clock S is based on oscillation of a spring and a clock P is based on pendulum motion. Both have the same time and are running at the same rate on the earth. On a planet having the same density but twice in radius, which of the following statements is true ?

(a) S will run faster than P

(b) P will run faster than S

(c) Both will show the same time

(d) S will stop and P will become slow

33. An object weighs 10N at the north-pole of the earth. On a geostationary satellite at distance 7R from the centre of the earth (radius of earth is R), the true weight and apparent weight are :

(a) 0 N, 0 N (b) 0.2 N, 0 N

(c) 0.2 N, 9.8 N (d) 0.2 N, 0.2 N

34. If M is the mass of the earth, R is the radius of the earth, then the gravitational potential at a distance r = R/2 from its centre is :

(a) $-\frac{GM}{R}$ (b) $-\frac{3GM}{2R}$

(c) $-\frac{8GM}{11R}$ (d) $-\frac{11GM}{8R}$

35. Suppose the gravitational attraction varies inversely as the distance from the earth. If the orbital velocity of a satellite in such a case varies as the nth power of distance, then n is equal to :

(a) –1 (b) zero

(c) + 1 (d) + 2

36. If a planet whose mass and diameter both are half of the earth, then gravitational potential energy of an object on its surface compared to that on the earth's surface will be :

(a) Same (b) $\frac{1}{2}$

(c) Double (d) $\frac{1}{4}$

37. The distance of a parking satellite from the earth (of radius R) is nearest to :

(a) 5R (b) 6R

(c) 7R (d) 8R

38. At what height from the earth's surface does the value of $\vec{g}$ become half of its original value ?

(R_e = 6400 km)

(a) 3050 km (b) 3240 km

(c) 2650 km (d) zero

39. The satellite is orbiting around the earth with a period T. If the earth suddenly shrinks to half of its orbital radius, the period of revolution of the satellite will be :

(a) $\frac{T}{\sqrt{2}}$ (b) $\frac{T}{2}$

(c) T (d) 2 T

40. A satellite is revolving around the sun in a circular orbit with uniform velocity v. If gravitational field suddenly disappears, the velocity of satellite will be :

(a) Zero (b) v

(c) 2 v (d) Infinity

41. A body is projected vertically upwards with a velocity equal to 1/3 of the escape velocity. The maximum height attained by the body is :

(a) R (b) R/2

(c) R/4 (d) R/8

42. The value of $\vec{g}$ increases by 0.5%, when we go from the equator to the poles, then time period of the pendulum at equator in seconds at the poles will be :

(a) 1.950 s (b) 1.995 s

(c) 2.050 s (d) 2.005 s

43. The speed of the earth's rotation about its axis is W. Its speed is increased to x times to make the effective acceleration due to gravity equal to zero at the equator. Then x is :

(a) 1 (b) 85
(c) 17 (d) 34

44. Which of the following is different from the other ?

(a) Period of satellite orbiting around the earth very near to its surface.
(b) Period of simple pendulum of infinite length.
(c) Period of moon around the earth.
(d) Period of a body in a tunnel passed through the centre of earth.

45. The potential energy of a satellite of mass m and revolving at a height equal to the radius of the earth (6400 km) from the earth's surface is :

(a) mgR (b) 0.67 mgR
(c) –mgR/2 (d) 0.33 mgR

46. Two planets of radii r_1 and r_2 have densities ρ_1 and ρ_2 respectively. The ratio of $\vec{g}$ on them will be :

(a) $r_1\rho_1 : r_2\rho_2$ (b) $r_1\rho_1^2 : r_2\rho_2^2$
(c) $r_1^2\rho_1 : r_2^2\rho_2$ (d) $\rho_2 r_1 : \rho_1 r_2$

47. The escape velocity of a body from the earth's surface is 11.2 kms^{-1}. When it is thrown up with a velocity 4 times of this escape velocity, the velocity of the body, when it has escaped the gravitational pull of the earth, is :

(a) $4v_e$ (b) $3v_e$
(c) $\sqrt{15}\, v_e$ (d) zero

48. The rate of change of weight near the earth's surface varies with height as :

(a) h^{-1} (b) h^0
(c) h (d) $\sqrt{h}$

49. If the earth suddenly shrinks by 1/3 of its original radius, the acceleration due to gravity will be :

(a) $\frac{2}{3}g$ (b) $\frac{3}{2}g$
(c) $\frac{4}{9}g$ (d) $\frac{9}{4}g$

50. A body weighs 700 gm. wt. on the earth's surface. How much will it weigh on the surface of a planet whose mass is 1/7 and radius 1/2 of the earth ?

(a) 50 gm. wt. (b) 200 gm. wt.
(c) 300 gm. wt. (d) 400 gm. wt.

51. If R is the radius of earth and g be the acceleration due to gravity on the earth's surface, the mean density of the earth is :

(a) $\frac{4\pi G}{3g R}$ (b) $\frac{3\pi G}{4g R}$
(c) $\frac{3g}{4\pi RG}$ (d) $\frac{\pi Rg}{12G}$

52. Let F_1 be the magnitude of the force exerted on the moon by the earth and F_2 be the magnitude of force exerted on the earth by the moon due to gravitational attraction, then :

(a) $F_1 > F_2$ (b) $F_1 < F_2$
(c) $F_1 = F_2$ (d) both (b) and (c)

53. Mars has about 1/10 as much mass as the earth and half the diameter. The acceleration of the falling body on Mars in ms^{-2} is about: ($g = 9.8\ ms^{-2}$)

(a) 1.96 (b) 3.92
(c) 4.9 (d) 9.8

54. Two spherical planets A and B have the same mass but densities in the ratio 8 : 1. For them, $\vec{g}$ at the surface of A to its value at the surface of B is : become

(a) 1 : 4 (b) 1 : 2
(c) 4 : 1 (d) 8 : 1

55. A mass m is placed at a point B in the gravitational field of mass M. When the mass m is brought from B near to point A, its gravitational potential energy will :

(a) remain same (b) increase
(c) decrease (d) become zero

56. Two satellites are orbiting around the earth in a circular orbit of the same radius. One of them is 100 times greater in mass than the other. Their periods of revolution are in the ratio :

(a) 1 : 1 (b) 10 : 1
(c) 100 : 1 (d) 1 : 100

57. An artificial satellite revolves around the earth in a circular orbit with the speed v. If m is the mass of the satellite, its total energy is :

(a) $\frac{1}{2}mv^2$ (b) $-\frac{1}{2}mv^2$
(c) $-mv^2$ (d) $\frac{3}{2}mv^2$

58. The gravitational field due to a mass distribution is $E = K/x^3$ in the x-direction (K is a constant). Taking the gravitational potential to be zero at infinity, its value at a distance is :

(a) K/x (b) $K/2x$
(c) K/x^2 (d) $K/2x^2$

59. If a satellite is orbiting the earth very close to its surface, then the orbital velocity mainly depends upon :

(a) the mass of the satellite only
(b) the radius of the earth only
(c) the orbital radius only
(d) the mass of the earth only

60. The escape velocity of a particle of mass m varies directly as :

(a) m^2 (b) m
(c) m^0 (d) m^{-1}

61. The depth from the surface of the earth of radius R at which the acceleration due to gravity will be 75% of the value on the earth surface is :

(a) R/4 (b) R/2
(c) 3R/4 (d) R/8

62. Two equal masses m and m are hung from a balance whose scale pans differ in height by h. If ρ is the mean density of earth, then error in weighing is :

(a) zero (b) $\frac{4\pi G \rho h m}{3}$
(c) $\frac{8\pi G \rho h m}{3}$ (d) $\frac{2\pi G \rho h m}{3}$

63. If a man weighs 90 kg on the earth's surface. The height above the surface of the earth of radius R where the weight is 30 kg is :

(a) 0.73 R (b) $R/\sqrt{3}$
(c) R/3 (d) $\sqrt{3}$ R

64. What will be the effect on the weight of a body placed on the surface of earth, if the earth suddenly starts rotating with half of its angular velocity ?

(a) No effect
(b) Weight reduces
(c) Weight will increase
(d) Weight will become zero

65. The angular velocity of the earth in rad s^{-1}, so that a body of 5 kg weighs zero at the equator is :

(a) 1/1600 rad s^{-1} (b) 1/800 rad s^{-1}
(c) 1/400 rad s^{-1} (d) 1/80 rad s^{-1}

66. The mass of the moon is 7.34×10^{22} kg. If g on the moon is 1.4 ms^{-2}, the radius of the moon is :
($G = 6.67 \times 10^{-11}$ $Nm^2 kg^{-2}$) :

(a) 0.56×10^4 m (b) 1.87×10^6 m
(c) 1.92×10^6 m (d) 1.01×10^8 m

67. At what height in km over the earth's pole, the free fall acceleration decreases by 1% ? (R_e = 6400 km)

(a) 32 (b) 64
(c) 80 (d) 1.253

68. The ratio of acceleration due to gravity at a height h above the surface of the earth and at a depth h below the surface of the earth for $h <<$ radius of earth :
(a) is constant
(b) increases linearly with increasing h
(c) decreases linearly with increasing h
(d) decreases linearly with decreasing h

69. A body situated on the surface of earth at its equator becomes weightless, when the earth has K.E. about its axis as :
(a) mgR (b) $\frac{2}{5}mgR$
(c) $\frac{mgR}{5}$ (d) $\frac{5mgR}{2}$

70. For a body lying on the equator to appear weightless what should be the angular speed of the earth ?
($\because g = 10\ ms^{-2}$ and $R_e = 6400$ km)
(a) 0.125 rad s^{-1}
(b) 1.25 rad s^{-1}
(c) 1.25×10^{-3} rad s^{-1}
(d) 1.25×10^{-2} rad s^{-1}

71. At what height above the earth's surface does the force of gravity decrease by 10% ? (The radius of the earth is 6400 km.)
(a) 345.6 km (b) 687.2 km
(c) 1031.8 km (d) 12836.8 km

72. If $g = 980$ cm s^{-2}, then this value at a height of 64 km from the earth's surface is :
(a) 960.40 cm s^{-2} (b) 984.9 cm s^{-2}
(c) 982.45 cm s^{-2} (d) 977.55 cm s^{-2}

73. The speed of earth's rotation about its axis is ω. Its speed is increased to x-times to make the effective acceleration due to gravity equal to zero at the equator, then x is around:
(a) 1 (b) 8.5
(c) 17 (d) 34

74. If the moon is to escape from the gravitational field of the earth forever, it will require a velocity :
(a) 11.2 km s^{-1} (b) < 11.2 km s^{-1}
(c) > 11.2 km s^{-1} (d) 22.4 km s^{-1}

75. The escape velocity for a body projected vertically upwards from the surface of the earth is 11.2 km s^{-1}. If the body is projected in a direction making an angle of 45° with the vertical, the escape velocity will be :
(a) 11.2 km s^{-1} (b) $11.2 \times \sqrt{2}$ km s^{-1}
(c) 22.4 km s^{-1} (d) $\frac{11.2}{\sqrt{2}}$ km s^{-1}

76. The escape velocity from the earth's surface is 11 km s^{-1}. The escape velocity of a planet having twice the radius and same mean density as the earth would be :
(a) 5.5 km s^{-1} (b) 11 km s^{-1}
(c) 15.5 km s^{-1} (d) 22 km s^{-1}

77. The ratio of the radii of planets P_1 and P_2 is a. The ratio of their accelerations due to gravity is b. Then the ratio of escape velocities for them will be :
(a) ab (b) $\sqrt{ab}$
(c) $\sqrt{a/b}$ (d) $\sqrt{b/a}$

78. The mass of the moon is 1/81 of the earth's mass and its radius is 1/4 that of the earth. If the escape velocity from the earth's surface is 11.2 km s^{-1}, its value for the moon will be:
(a) 0.15 km s^{-1} (b) 5 km s^{-1}
(c) 2.5 km s^{-1} (d) 0.5 km s^{-1}

79. The period of revolution of planet A around the sun is 8 times that of planet B. How many times is the distance A from the sun greater than that of B ?
(a) 2 (b) 3
(c) 1 (d) 5

80. If the radius of earth's orbit is made 1/4, then the duration of a year will become :
(a) 8 times (b) 4 times
(c) $\frac{1}{8}$ times (d) $\frac{1}{4}$ times

81. A planet moves around the sun. At a point P_1 it is close to the sun at a distance d_1 and has speed v_1. At another point P_2 when it is farthest from the sun at a distance d_2, its speed will be :

(a) $\frac{d_2}{d_1} \cdot v_1$ (b) $\frac{d_2^2}{d_1^2} \cdot v_1$

(c) $\frac{d_1^2}{d_2^2} \cdot v_1$ (d) $\frac{d_1}{d_2} \cdot v_1$

82. A planet is revolving round the sun in an elliptical orbit. The work done on the planet by the gravitational force of the sun is zero :

(a) in some parts of the orbit
(b) in any part of the orbit
(c) in no part of the orbit
(d) in one complete revolution

83. A planet is revolving around the sun in an elliptical orbit. Its closest distance from the sun is r and the farthest distance $3r/2$. If the velocity of planet nearest to the sun is v and that farthest from the sun be v_1, then v/v_1 is :

(a) $\frac{2}{3}$ (b) $\frac{3}{2}$

(c) $\frac{4}{9}$ (d) $\frac{9}{4}$

84. A spring balance is graduated on sea level. If a body is weighed with this balance at consecutively increasing heights from the earth's surface, then the weight indicated by the balance :

(a) will go on decreasing continuously
(b) will go on increasing continuously
(c) will remain the same
(d) will increase first and then decrease

85. A satellite is in an orbit around the earth. If its K.E. is doubled, then :

(a) it will rotate with greater speed
(b) it will fall on the earth
(c) it will maintain the orbital path
(d) it will escape out of the earth's gravitational field

86. The gravitational potential energy of a body (in earth's field) is minimum :

(a) from the surface of earth
(b) at infinity
(c) below the earth's surface
(d) between the earth's surface and infinity

87. Height at which the value of $\vec{g}$ will become $\vec{g}/4$ from the earth's surface is :

(a) R (b) 2R

(c) $\frac{3R}{2}$ (d) 4R

88. The acceleration due to gravity near the surface of the planet of radius R and density ρ is proportional to :

(a) ρ/R^2 (b) ρR^2

(c) ρR (d) ρ/R

89. A cosmonaut is orbiting the earth in a space craft at an altitude, h = 630 km with a speed of 8 kms^{-1}. If the radius of the earth is 6370 km, the acceleration of cosmonaut is :

(a) 9.14 ms^{-2} (b) 9.8 ms^{-2}

(c) 10 ms^{-2} (d) 9.88 ms^{-2}

90. A man weighs 80 kg on the earth's surface. The height above the ground, where he will weigh 40 kg is ...... (R_e = 6400 km)

(a) 0.31 R_e (b) 0.41 R_e

(c) 0.51 R_e (d) 0.61 R_e

91. Two spheres of masses m and M are situated in air and the gravitational force between them is F. The space around the masses is now filled with a liquid of specific gravity 3. The gravitational force will now be :

(a) 3F (b) F

(c) F/3 (d) F/9

92. Two particles of masses m_1 and m_2 revolve in a circular path of radii r_1 and r_2 and take same time for one complete revolution. Then ratio of their angular velocities will be:

(a) $m_1 : m_2$ (b) $r_1 : r_2$

(c) 1 : 1 (d) $m_1r_1 : m_2r_2$

93. If the gravitational potential on the earth's surface is v_o, the potential at a point at a distance half of the radius of earth from the centre will be :

(a) $\frac{11}{8}\ v_o$ (b) $\frac{v_o}{2}$

(c) $2\ v_o$ (d) $\frac{8}{11}\ v_o$

94. For a planet revolving around the sun, the velocity vector is normal to the radius vector joining the centres of earth and sun :

(a) Always
(b) Only at the perihelion and aphelion
(c) At four distinct points on its orbit
(d) None of these

95. By what percent does the energy of a satellite be increased to shift it from an orbit of radius r to $3r$?

(a) 22.3% (b) 33.3%
(c) 66.7% (d) 100%

96. The metallic bob of a simple pendulum has relative density ρ. The time period of such a pendulum is T. If this metallic bob is immersed in water, the new time period will be :

(a) $\frac{T(\rho - 1)}{\rho}$ (b) $\frac{T\rho}{(\rho - 1)}$

(c) $T\sqrt{\frac{(\rho - 1)}{\rho}}$ (d) $T\sqrt{\frac{\rho}{(\rho - 1)}}$

97. There is no atmosphere on the moon because :

(a) it is very near to the earth
(b) it does not have its own light
(c) it gets light from the sun
(d) the escape velocity of the gas of moon's atmosphere is less than the r.m.s. velocity on moon.

98. If the earth rotates faster than its present speed, the weight of an object will :

(a) increase at the equator but it will remain same at the poles
(b) decrease at the equator but will remain same at the poles
(c) remain same at the equator but will decrease at the poles
(d) remain same at the equator but will increase at the poles

99. A satellite is moving in a circular orbit at a height 100 km above the earth's surface. A person inside the satellite feels weightlessness because :

(a) $\vec{g} = 0$ at such height
(b) the earth does not exert any force on the person
(c) the centripetal force makes the satellite to move in a circular orbit
(d) the forces due to the earth and moon are almost compensated at such a height

100. If g is the acceleration due to gravity on earth, then increase in potential energy of a body of mass m upto a distance equal to twice of the radius of earth from earth's the surface is :

(a) $\frac{mgR}{2}$ (b) $\frac{2}{3}mgR$

(c) $2mgR$ (d) $\frac{mgR}{4}$

101. Which of the following graph plotted between square of the time period and cube of the distance of the planet from the sun is correct ?

(a)
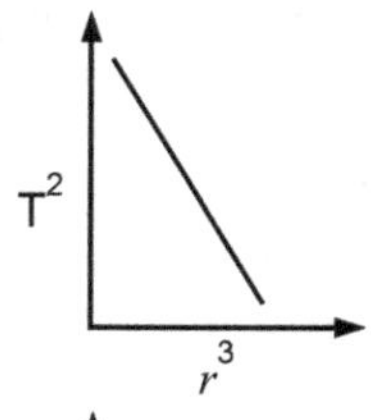

(b)
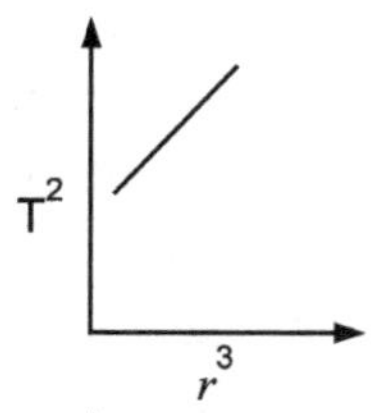

(c)
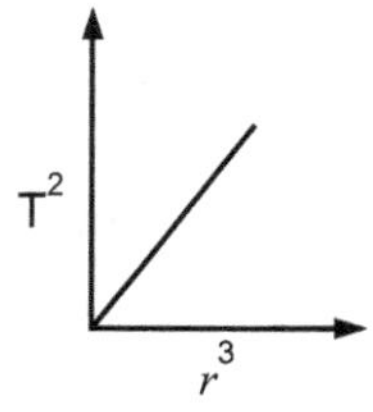

(d)
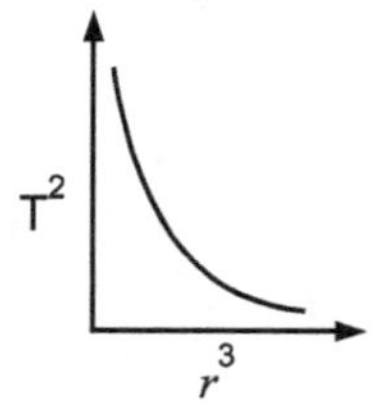

102. Halley's comet has a period of 76 years and a distance of closest approach to the sun is equal to 8.9×10^{10} m. The comet's farthest distance from the sun if the mass of the sun is 2×10^{30} kg and $G = 6.67 \times 10^{11}$ m is :

(a) 2×10^{12} m (b) 2.7×10^{13} m

(c) 5.3×10^{12} m (d) 5.3×10^{13} m

103. A particle of mass m is located at a distance r from the centre of shell of mass M and radius R. The force between the shell and particle is F(r). The plot of F(r) vs. r is :

(a)
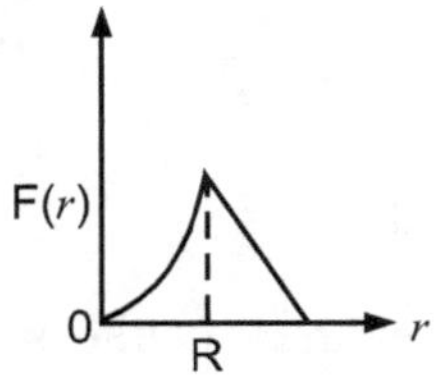

(b)
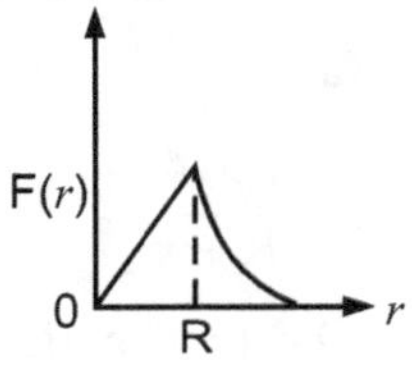

(c)
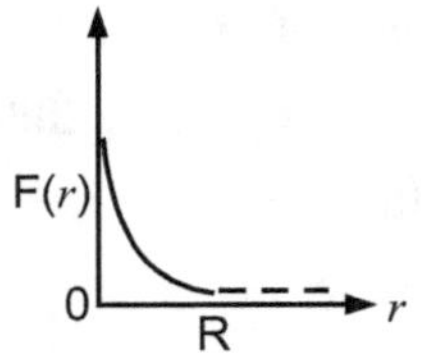

(d)
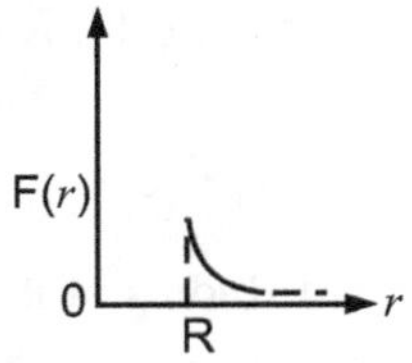

104. If a shell of mass M and radius R has a point mass m placed at a distance r from its centre, the plot between potential energy U(r) vs. r is :

(a)
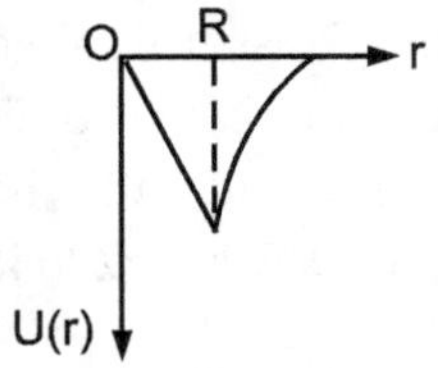

(b)
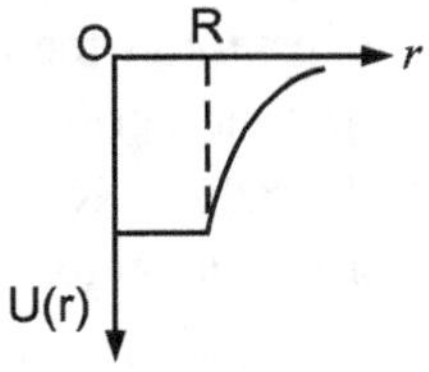

(c)
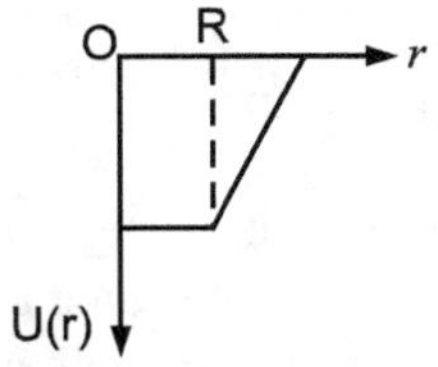

(d)
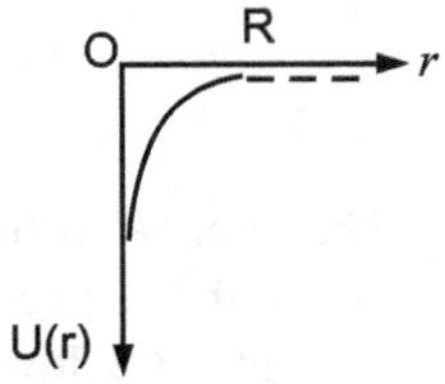

105. Three particles each of mass m rotate in a circle of radius r with uniform angular speed ω under their mutual gravitational attraction. If at any instant, the points are on the vertex of an equilateral triangle of side L, then angular velocity ω is :

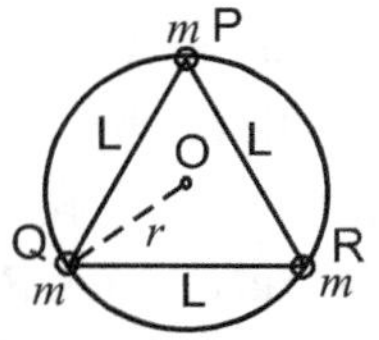

(a) $\sqrt{\frac{2Gm}{L^3}}$ (b) $\sqrt{\frac{3Gm}{L^3}}$

(c) $\sqrt{\frac{5Gm}{L^3}}$ (d) $\sqrt{\frac{Gm}{L^3}}$

106. If gravitational force on a body of mass 1.5 kg at a point is 45 N, then the intensity of gravitational field at that point is :

(a) 67.5 N kg^{-1} (b) 45 N kg^{-1}

(c) 30 N kg^{-1} (d) 15 N kg^{-1}

107. An object weighs 10 N on the north pole of the earth. In a geostationary satellite distant 7R from the centre of earth (of radius R) what will be its true weight ?

(a) 3 N (b) 5 N

(c) 2 N (d) 0.2 N

108. In the above question, the apparent weight of the object is :

(a) 3 N (b) zero

(c) 2 N (d) 0.2 N

109. How much energy will be necessary for making a body of 500 kg to escape from the earth :

(a) $\cong 9.8 \times 10^6$ J (b) $\cong 6.4 \times 10^8$ J

(c) $\cong 3.1 \times 10^{10}$ J (d) $\cong 27.4 \times 10^{12}$ J

110. A particle is projected vertically upwards from the surface of earth of radius R_e, with K.E. equal to half of the minimum value needed for it to escape. The height to which it rises above the earth's surface is :

(a) R_e (b) $2R_e$

(c) $3R_e$ (d) $4R_e$

111. If suddenly the gravitational force of attraction between the earth and a satellite revolving around it becomes zero, then the satellite will : **(A.I.E.E.E. 2002)**

(a) continue to move in its orbit with the same velocity

(b) move tangentially to the original orbit with the same velocity

(c) become stationary in its orbit

(d) move towards the earth

112. Energy required to move a body of mass m from an orbit of radius 2R to 3R is :

(A.I.E.E.E. 2002)

(a) $\frac{GMm}{12R^2}$ (b) $\frac{GMm}{3R^2}$

(c) $\frac{GMm}{8R}$ (d) $\frac{GMm}{6R}$

113. The kinetic energy needed to project a body of mass m from the earth's surface (radius R) to infinity is :

(A.I.E.E.E. 2002, 2004)

(a) $\frac{mgR}{2}$ (b) $2mgR$

(c) mgR (d) $\frac{mgR}{4}$

114. The escape velocity of a body depends upon mass as :

(a) m^0 (b) m^1

(c) m^2 (d) m^3

115. The time period of a satellite of the earth is 5 hours. If separation between the earth and the satellite is increased to 4 times the previous value, the new time period will be :

(A.I.E.E.E. 2003)

(a) 10 hours (b) 80 hours

(c) 40 hours (d) 20 hours

116. Two spherical bodies of masses M and 5M and radii R and 2R respectively are released in free space with initial separation between their centres equal to 12R. If they attract each other due to gravitational force only, then the distance covered by the smaller body just before collision is :

(A.I.E.E.E. 2003)

(a) 2.5R (b) 4.5R

(c) 7.5R (d) 1.5R

117. The escape velocity for a body projected vertically upwards form the earth's surface is 11 km s^{-1}. If the body is projected at an angle of 45° with the vertical, the escape velocity will be : **(A.I.E.E.E. 2003)**

(a) $11\sqrt{2}$ km s^{-1} (b) 22 km s^{-1}

(c) 11 km s^{-1} (d) $\frac{11}{\sqrt{2}}$ km s^{-1}

118. A satellite of mass m revolves around the earth of radius R at a height x from its surface. If g is the acceleration due to gravity on the surface of earth, the orbital speed of the satellite is : **(A.I.E.E.E. 2004)**

(a) gx (b) $\frac{gR}{R-x}$

(c) $\frac{gR^2}{R+x}$ (d) $\left(\frac{gR^2}{R+x}\right)^{1/2}$

119. The time period of an earth's satellite in a circular orbit is independent of :

(A.I.E.E.E. 2004)

(a) The mass of the satellite

(b) Radius of its orbit

(c) Both the mass and radius of the orbit

(d) Neither the mass nor the radius of orbit of the satellite.

120. Suppose the gravitational force varies inversely as the nth power of distance. Then the time period of a planet in circular orbit of radius R around the sun will be proportional to : **(A.I.E.E.E. 2004)**

(a) $(R)^{\frac{n+1}{2}}$ (b) $(R)^{\frac{n-1}{2}}$

(c) R^n (d) $(R)^{\frac{n-2}{2}}$

121. The change in the value of $\vec{g}$ at a height h above the surface of the earth is the same as at depth d below the earth's surface. When both d and h are much smaller than the earth's radius, then which of the following is correct ? **(A.I.E.E.E. 2005)**

(a) $d = 2h$ (b) $d = h$

(c) $d = \frac{h}{2}$ (d) $d = \frac{3h}{2}$

122. A particle of mass 10 g is kept on the surface of a uniform sphere of 100 kg and 20 cm radius. The work done against the gravitational force between them to take the particle far away from the sphere is : ($G = 6.67 \times 10^{-11}$ Nm Kg^{-2})

(A.I.E.E.E. 2005)

(a) 6.67×10^{-9} J (b) 6.67×10^{-10} J

(c) 13.34×10^{-10} J (d) 3.33×10^{-10} J

123. Average density of earth : **(A.I.E.E.E. 2005)**

(a) is directly proportional to g

(b) is inversely proportional to g

(c) doesn't depend on g

(d) is a complex function of g

124. A planet in a distant solar system is 10 times more massive than the earth and its radius is 10 times smaller. The escape velocity from the surface of the planet would be : ($V_e = 11$ km s^{-1}) **(A.I.E.E.E. 2008)**

(a) 0.11 km s^{-1} (b) 1.1 km s^{-1}

(c) 11 km s^{-1} (d) 110 km s^{-1}

COMPREHENSION BASED QUESTIONS

Let g be the value of acceleration due to gravity at a point on the surface of earth of radius R and having mass M, then the relation between them is given by $g = Gm/R^2$. When a body of mass m is placed at a height h from the earth's surface, then the value of g reduces, which is given by $g_h = g\left(1 - \frac{2h}{R}\right)$. Similarly when this body is found at a depth d from the earth's surface, then the value of g also reduces and can be expressed as $g_d = g(1 - d/R)$. So the value of acceleration due to gravity is independent of mass of the body but depends on the height or depth from the surface of the earth.

Read the above passage carefully and answer the following questions :

125. Find the value of $\vec{g}$ at a height of 400 km above the surface of the earth :

($\because$ $g = 9.8$ ms^{-2}, $R_e = 6400$ km)

(a) 4.575 ms^{-2} (b) 8.575 ms^{-2}

(c) 9.575 ms^{-2} (d) 12.57 ms^{-2}

126. Assuming that the earth is a sphere of uniform mass density, how much would a body weigh 800 km below the surface of the earth, if it weighed 360 N on the surface ? (Radius of earth $R_e = 6400$ km)

(a) 115 N (b) 215 N

(c) 315 N (d) 415 N

127. A person has weight 360 N on the surface of the earth. Then his weight at the centre of the earth will be :

(a) zero (b) 180 N

(c) 360 N (d) 540 N

128. At what depth below the surface of earth is the value of g same as that at a height 64 km above the surface of the earth ?

(a) 128 km (b) 32 km

(c) 16 km (d) 8 km

ASSERTION AND REASON

Directions for Q. 129 to Q. 134 : In the following questions, statement-I of assertion is followed by a statement-II of reason. While answering a question, you are required to choose the correct one out of the four given options.

(a) Both statement-I and statement-II are true and statement-II is the correct explanation of statement-I.

(b) Both statement-I and statement-II are true, but statement-II is not the correct explanation of statement-I.

(c) Statement-I is true and statement-II is false.

(d) Statement-I is false and statement-II is true.

129. **(I)** Halley's comet doesn't obey Kepler's Laws of planetary motion.

(II) It does not have elliptical motion.

130. **(I)** If the radius of the earth's orbit around the sun was twice its present value, then the number of days in a year would be 1032 days.

(II) According to Kepler's Laws of planetary motion, $T^2 \propto r^3$.

131. **(I)** The earth without its atmosphere would be inhospitably cold.

(II) All heat would escape in the absence of atmosphere.

132. **(I)** The work done to project a body of mass m from the earth's surface to infinity is mgR.

(II) The required work done is equal to change in potential energy of the mass, which is equal to GMm/R.

133. **(I)** The time period of an earth satellite in a circular orbit is independent of the mass of the satellite.

(II) The time period of satellite of earth in a circular orbit of radius r is given by, $T = 2\pi\sqrt{\dfrac{r^3}{GM}}$

134. **(I)** The time period of pendulum in a satellite orbiting the earth is infinity.

(II) The time period of a simple pendulum is inversely proportional to $\sqrt{g}$.

135. A marble ball A is dropped vertically. Another identical marble ball B is projected horizontally from the same point at the same time, then :

(a) A will reach the ground first
(b) B will reach the ground first
(c) None of the above
(d) Both will reach the ground at the same time

136. If the radius of earth were to shrink by 1%, then acceleration due to gravity on the earth's surface (since mass remains same) :

(a) would decrease
(b) would remain same
(c) would increase
(d) cannot be predicted

137. In a double star system, two stars A and B which have time period T_A and T_B; radii R_A and R_B and masses M_A and M_B respectively. Choose the correct one :

(a) If $T_A > T_B$ then $R_A > R_B$
(b) If $T_A > T_B$ then $M_A > M_B$
(c) $\left(\dfrac{T_A}{T_B}\right)^2 = \left(\dfrac{R_A}{R_B}\right)^3$
(d) $T_A = T_B$

138. Imagine a light planet revolving around a very massive star in a circular orbit of radius R with period of revolution T. If the gravitational force of attraction between the planet and star is proportional to $R^{-5/2}$, then T^2 is proportional to :

(a) R^2 (b) $R^{7/2}$
(c) $R^{3/2}$ (d) $R^{15/4}$

139. If the distance between the earth and the sun were half of its present value, the number of days in a year would have been :

(a) 64.5 (b) 12
(c) 182.5 (d) 730

140. If g be the acceleration due to gravity on the earth's surface, then the gain in the potential energy of an object of mass m raised from the surface of the earth to a height equal to the radius R of the earth is :

(a) $\dfrac{mgR}{2}$ (b) $2\,mgR$
(c) mgR (d) $\dfrac{mgR}{4}$

141. If W_1, W_2 and W_3 represent the work done in moving a particle from A to B along three different paths 1, 2 and 3 respectively in the gravitational field of point mass m. The correct relation between W_1, W_2 and W_3 is :

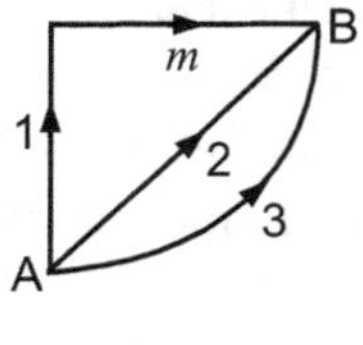

(a) $W_1 > W_2 > W_3$
(b) $W_1 = W_2 = W_3$
(c) $W_1 < W_2 < W_3$
(d) $W_2 > W_1 > W_3$

142. A missile is launched with a velocity less than the escape velocity. The sum of K.E. and P.E. :

(a) is positive

(b) is negative

(c) is zero

(d) may be + ve or – ve depending upon its initial velocity.

143. A geostationary satellite is orbiting in its orbit at a height 36000 km from the earth's surface. Then the time period of a spy satellite orbiting a few hundred km above the earth's surface will be :

(R_e = 6400 km)

(a) $\frac{1}{2}\ h$ (b) $1\ h$

(c) $2\ h$ (d) $4\ h$

144. Two satellites A and B go round a planet P in circular orbits having radii 4R and R respectively. If the speed of the satellite A is $3v$, then the speed of satellite B will be :

(a) $12\ v$ (b) $6\ v$

(c) $\frac{4}{3}\ v$ (d) $\frac{3}{2}\ v$

145. Two small and heavy spheres, each of mass M, are placed a distance r apart on a horizontal surface. The gravitational potential at the mid-point on the line joining the centres of the spheres is :

(A.M.U. (Med.) 2009)

(a) Zero (b) $-\frac{GM}{r}$

(c) $-\frac{2GM}{r}$ (d) $-\frac{4GM}{r}$

146. The heights at which the acceleration due to gravity becomes $\frac{g}{3}$ (where g = acceleration due to gravity on the surface of the earth) is n times the radius R of the earth where n is :

(Manipur M.B.B.S./B.D.S. 2009)

(a) $\sqrt{3}$ (b) $\frac{1}{\sqrt{3}}$

(c) $(\sqrt{3} + 1)$ (d) $(\sqrt{3} - 1)$

147. If g is the acceleration due to gravity on the earth's surface, the gain in potential energy of an object of mass M raised from the surface of the earth to a height equal to the radius R of the earth is :

(a) $MgR/2$ (b) $2MgR$

(c) MgR (d) $MgR/4$

148. A body projected vertically from the earth reaches a height equal to the earth's radius before returning to the earth. The power exerted by the gravitational force is greatest:

(A.I.P.M.T. 2011)

(a) at the highest position of the body.

(b) at the instant just before the body hits the earth.

(c) it remains constant all through

(d) at the instant just after the body is projected.

149. The height at which the acceleration due to gravity becomes $g/9$ (where g = the acceleration due to gravity on the surface of the earth) in terms of R, the radius of the earth is : **(A.I.E.E.E. 2009)**

(a) 2R (b) $\frac{R}{\sqrt{2}}$

(c) $\frac{R}{2}$ (d) $\sqrt{2}R$

150. Two bodies of masses m and $4\ m$ are placed at a distance r. The gravitational potential at a point on the line joining them where the gravitational field is zero is :

(A.I.E.E.E. 2011)

(a) $-\frac{9Gm}{r}$ (b) Zero

(c) $-\frac{4Gm}{r}$ (d) $-\frac{6Gm}{r}$

151. The height vertically above the earth's surface at which the acceleration due to gravity becomes 1% of its value at the surface is : **(W.B.E.E. 2010)**

(R is the radius of the earth).

(a) 8 R (b) 9 R

(c) 10 R (d) 20 R

152. The change in the gravitational potential energy when a body of mass m is raised to a height nR above the surface of the earth is : (here R is the radius of the earth).

(W.B.J.E.E. 2010)

(a) $\left(\frac{n}{n+1}\right) mg\text{R}$ (b) $\left(\frac{n}{n-1}\right) mg\text{R}$

(c) $nmg\text{R}$ (d) $\frac{mg\text{R}}{n}$

153. Two satellites of the earth, S_1 and S_2 are moving in the same orbit. The mass of S_1 is four times the mass of S_2. Which one of the following statements is true ?

(C.B.S.E. A.I.P.M.T. 2007)

(a) The potential energies of earth and satellite in the two cases are equal.

(b) S_1 and S_2 are moving with the same speed.

(c) The kinetic energies of the two satellites are equal.

(d) The time period of S_1 is four times that of S_2.

154. Two satellites of the earth S_1 are S_2 are moving in the same orbit. The mass of S_1 is four times the mass of S_2. Which one of the following statements is true ?

(C.P.M.T. 2008)

(a) The time period of S_1 is four times that of S_2.

(b) The potential energies of the earth and satellite in the two cases are equal.

(c) S_1 and S_2 are moving with the same speed.

(d) The kinetic energies of the two satellites are equal.

155. Kepler's law of area is based on :

(H.P.P.M.T. 2009)

(a) Conservation of energy

(b) Conservation of angular momentum

(c) Conservation of linear momentum

(d) None of these

156. Kepler's second law of planetary motion is a manifestation of the principle of conservation of :

(Manipur MBBS/BDS 2009)

(a) Linear momentum

(b) Energy

(c) Angular momentum

(d) Area

157. Geostationary satellites must always have :

(Manipur MBBS/BDS 2009)

(a) elliptical orbits (b) circular orbits

(c) parabolic orbits (d) hyperbolic orbits

158. A satellite of mass m is moving in a circular orbit of radius R above the surface of a planet of mass M and radius R. The amount of work done to shift the satellite to a higher orbit of radius 2R is : **(M.P.P.E.T. 2009)**

(a) $mg\text{R}$ (b) $\frac{mg\text{R}}{6}$

(c) $\frac{m\text{M}g\text{R}}{(\text{M}+m)}$ (d) $\frac{m\text{M}g\text{R}}{6(\text{M}+m)}$

159. The radii of circular orbits of two satellites A and B of the earth are 4R and R, respectively. If the speed of satellite A is 3V, then the speed of satellite B will be :

(A.I.P.M.T. (Prelim) 2010)

(a) 3V/4 (b) 6V

(c) 12V (d) 3V/2

160. The earth is assumed to be a sphere of radius R. A platform is arranged at a height R from the surface of the earth. The escape velocity of a body from this platform is f v, where v is its escape velocity from the surface of the earth. The value of f is :

(C.B.S.E. P.M.T. 2006)

(a) 1/2 (b) $\sqrt{2}$

(c) $1/\sqrt{2}$ (d) 1/3

161. The orbit of a satellite moving around the earth in the equatorial plane as viewed from the earth appears to be stationary. What is the radius (approximate) of the orbit ? **(S.C.R.A. 2007)**

(a) $(GM/2\omega^2)^{1/.3}$ (b) $(GM/\omega^2)^{1/3}$
(c) $(GM/\omega^2)^{1/2}$ (d) $(2GM/\omega^2)^{1/.3}$

(where G is gravitational constant, M is mass of the earth and ω is the angular velocity of the earth)

162. A satellite is launched in a circular orbit of radius R around the earth. A second satellite is launched into an orbit of radius 1.01 R. The period of the second satellite is longer than the first one (approximate) by : **(Kerala P.E.T. 2007)**

(a) 1.5% (b) 0.5%
(c) 3% (d) 1%

163. If escape velocity from the earth is 11.2 km/s. Then escape velocity from a planet of mass as that of earth but of one fourth its radius is :

(a) 11.2 km/s (b) 22.4 km/s
(c) 5.6 km/s (d) 44.8 km/s

164. If the escape velocity of a planet is 3 times that of the earth and its radius is 4 times that of the earth, then the mass of the planet is : **(Kerala Engg. 2010)**

(a) 1.62×10^{22} kg (b) 0.72×10^{22} kg
(c) 2.16×10^{26} kg (d) 1.22×10^{22} kg

165. The escape velocity from the surface of earth is v_e. The escape velocity from the surface of a planet whose mass and radius are 3 times those of the earth will be **(J.I.P.M.E.R. 2001)**

(a) $3v_e$ (b) $9v_e$
(c) v_e (d) $27v_e$

166. If the gravitational force between two objects were proportional to 1/R (and not as $1/R^2$), where R is separation between them, then a particle in circular orbit under such a force would have its orbital speed v proportional to **(J.I.P.M.E.R. 2001)**

(a) R^1 (b) 1/R
(c) R^0 (d) $1/R^2$

167. If the potential energy of body on a plant is numerically U and the escape velocity for the same body is v_e for same planet, then $\frac{U}{v_e}$ will be **(B.H.U. 2001)**

(a) $m\sqrt{\frac{GM}{2R}}$ (b) $m\sqrt{\frac{GM}{R}}$
(c) $m\sqrt{\frac{2GM}{R}}$ (d) $m\frac{GM}{R}$

168. If the spinning speed of the earth is increased, then the weight of the body at equator **(A.F.M.C. 2002)**

(a) does not change (b) decreases
(c) doubles (d) increases

169. When radius of earth is reduced by 1% without changing the mass, then change in acceleration due to gravity will **(A.F.M.C. 2002)**

(a) decrease by 1% (b) increase by 1%
(c) decrease by 1.5% (d) increase by 2%

170. When body is raised to a height equal to radius of earth, its P.E. changes by **(MHT-CET 2003)**

(a) mgR (b) $\frac{mgR}{2}$
(c) 2mgR (d) $\frac{3}{2}$mgR

171. A plant has twice the radius, but the mean density is $\left(\frac{1}{4}\right)^{th}$ as compared to earth, what is the ratio of escape velocity from earth to that from the plant ? **(MHT-CET 2004)**

(a) 3 : 1 (b) 1 : 2
(c) 1 : 1 (d) 2 : 1

172. When you move from equator to pole, the value of acceleration due to gravity 'g' **(A.F.M.C. 2004)**

(a) increases (b) remains the same
(c) decreases
(d) increases first and then decreases

173. The ratio of acceleration due to gravity of a height 3R above earth's surface to the acceleration due to gravity on the surface of earth is (R = radius of earth).

(MHT-CET 2005)

(a) $\frac{1}{9}$ (b) $\frac{1}{16}$

(c) $\frac{1}{4}$ (d) $\frac{1}{3}$

174. The binding energy of a satellite of mass m in an orbit of radius r is ...... (R = radius of the earth, g = acceleration due to gravity)

(a) $\frac{mgR^2}{r}$ (b) $-\frac{mgR^2}{r}$

(c) $\frac{mgR^2}{2r}$ (d) $-\frac{mgR^2}{2r}$

175. The length of seconds pendulum is 1 m on earth. If mass and diameter of the planet is doubled than that of earth, then length becomes **(A.F.M.C. 2005)**

(a) 1 m (b) 0.5 m

(c) 2 m (d) 4 m

176. What effect occurs on the frequency of a pendulum, if it is taken from the earth's surface to deep into a mine?

(A.F.M.C. 2005)

(a) Increases

(b) First increases, then decreases

(c) Decreases

(d) No effect

177. The gravitational acceleration on the surface of earth of radius R and mean density ρ is

(MHT-CET 2006)

(a) $\left(\frac{4\pi}{3}\right) GR^2\rho$ (b) $\left(\frac{4\pi^2}{3}\right) GR^2\rho$

(c) $\left(\frac{2\pi^2}{3}\right) GR^2\rho$ (d) $\left(\frac{4\pi}{3}\right) GR\rho$

178. The universal gravitational constant has the dimensions **(MHT-CET 2006)**

(a) $[M^1 L^{-3} T^2]$ (b) $[M^{-1} L^3 T^{-2}]$

(c) $[M^{-1} L^{-3} T]$ (d) $[M^1 L^3 T^2]$

179. If the distance between the earth and the sun becomes $\left(\frac{1}{4}\right)^{th}$, then the period of revolution of earth around the sun will become

(MHT-CET 2007)

(a) 330 days (b) 129 days

(c) 365 days (d) 45.6 days

180. Two planets have density in the ratio 2 : 3 and radii in the ratio 1 : 2. Then the ratio of accelerations due to gravity at their surface is **(MHT-CET 2007)**

(a) 1 : 3 (b) 3 : 1

(c) 1 : 9 (d) 9 : 4

181. A particle of mass M is situated at the center of a spherical shell of same mass radius a. The gravitational potential at a point situated at $\frac{a}{2}$ distance from the center will be

(C.B.S.E. 2010)

(a) $-\frac{GM}{a}$ (b) $-\frac{4\,GM}{a}$

(c) $-\frac{3\,GM}{a}$ (d) $-\frac{2\,GM}{a}$

182. If the earth stops rotating, then change in the weight of the body at the north pole will

(MHT-CET 2011)

(a) become zero (b) remain constant

(c) increase (d) decrease

183. A planet moving along an elliptical orbit is closest to the sun of a distance r_1 and farthest away at a distance of r_2. If v_1 and v_2 are the linear velocities at these points respectively, then the ratio $\frac{v_1}{v_2}$ is

(C.B.S.E. 2011)

(a) $\left(\frac{1}{r_2}\right)^2$ (b) $\frac{r_2}{r_1}$

(c) $\left(\frac{r_2}{r_1}\right)^2$ (d) $\frac{r_1}{r_2}$

184. The height at which the weight of a body becomes $1/16^{th}$, its weight on the surface of earth (radius R) is **(C.B.S.E. 2012)**

(a) 4R (b) 5R

(c) 15R (d) 3R

185. A geostationary satellite is orbiting the earth at a height of 5R above the surface of the earth, R being the radius of the earth. The time period of another satellite in hours at a height of 2 R from the surface of the earth is **(C.B.S.E. 2012)**

(a) $\frac{6}{\sqrt{2}}$ (b) 5

(c) 10 (d) $6\sqrt{2}$

186. A spherical planet has a mass M_p and diameter D_p. A particle of mass M falling freely near the surface of this planet will experience an acceleration due to gravity, equal to **(C.B.S.E. 2012)**

(a) $\frac{4GM_pM}{D_p^2}$ (b) $\frac{4GM_p}{D_p^2}$

(c) $\frac{GM_pM}{D_p^2}$ (d) $\frac{GM_p}{D_p^2}$

187. Infinite number of bodies, each of mass 2 kg, are situated on x-axis at distance 1 m, 2 m, 4 m, 8 m, …, respectively, from the origin. The resulting gravitational potential due to the system at the origin will be **(NEET 2013)**

(a) $-\frac{8}{3}G$ (b) $-\frac{4}{3}G$

(c) – 4G (d) – G

ANSWER KEY

1. (b)	**2.** (c)	**3.** (c)	**4.** (b)	**5.** (a)	**6.** (d)	**7.** (d)	**8.** (c)	**9.** (b)	**10.**(d)
11.(b)	**12.**(d)	**13.**(b)	**14.**(d)	**15.**(b)	**16.**(b)	**17.**(d)	**18.**(d)	**19.**(c)	**20.**(b)
21.(b)	**22.**(a)	**23.**(d)	**24.**(b)	**25.**(b)	**26.**(a)	**27.**(c)	**28.**(c)	**29.**(d)	**30.**(c)
31.(b)	**32.**(a)	**33.**(b)	**34.**(d)	**35.**(b)	**36.**(a)	**37.**(c)	**38.**(c)	**39.**(c)	**40.**(b)
41.(d)	**42.**(d)	**43.**(c)	**44.**(c)	**45.**(c)	**46.**(a)	**47.**(c)	**48.**(b)	**49.**(d)	**50.**(d)
51.(c)	**52.**(c)	**53.**(b)	**54.**(c)	**55.**(c)	**56.**(a)	**57.**(b)	**58.**(c)	**59.**(b)	**60.**(c)
61.(a)	**62.**(c)	**63.**(a)	**64.**(b)	**65.**(b)	**66.**(b)	**67.**(a)	**68.**(c)	**69.**(c)	**70.**(c)
71.(a)	**72.**(a)	**73.**(c)	**74.**(a)	**75.**(a)	**76.**(d)	**77.**(b)	**78.**(c)	**79.**(b)	**80.**(c)
81.(d)	**82.**(d)	**83.**(b)	**84.**(a)	**85.**(d)	**86.**(a)	**87.**(a)	**88.**(c)	**89.**(a)	**90.**(b)
91.(b)	**92.**(c)	**93.**(a)	**94.**(a)	**95.**(c)	**96.**(d)	**97.**(d)	**98.**(d)	**99.**(a)	**100.**(b)
101. (c)	**102.** (c)	**103.** (d)	**104.** (b)	**105.** (b)	**106.** (c)	**107.** (d)	**108.** (b)	**109.** (c)	**110.** (a)
111. (b)	**112.** (d)	**113.** (c)	**114.** (a)	**115.** (c)	**116.** (c)	**117.** (c)	**118.** (d)	**119.** (a)	**120.** (a)
121. (a)	**122.** (b)	**123.** (a)	**124.** (d)	**125.** (b)	**126.** (c)	**127.** (a)	**128.** (a)	**129.** (b)	**130.** (a)
131. (a)	**132.** (a)	**133.** (a)	**134.** (a)	**135.** (c)	**136.** (c)	**137.** (d)	**138.** (b)	**139.** (b)	**140.** (a)
141. (b)	**142.** (b)	**143.** (c)	**144.** (b)	**145.** (d)	**146.** (d)	**147.** (c)	**148.** (b)	**149.** (a)	**150.** (a)
151. (b)	**152.** (a)	**153.** (b)	**154.** (c)	**155.** (b)	**156.** (c)	**157.** (a)	**158.** (b)	**159.** (b)	**160.** (c)
161. (b)	**162.** (a)	**163.** (b)	**164.** (c)	**165.** (c)	**166.** (c)	**167.** (a)	**168.** (b)	**169.** (d)	**170.** (b)
171. (c)	**172.** (a)	**173.** (b)	**174.** (c)	**175.** (b)	**176.** (c)	**177.** (d)	**178.** (b)	**179.** (d)	**180.** (a)
181. (c)	**182.** (a)	**183.** (b)	**184.** (d)	**185.** (d)	**186.** (b)	**187.** (c)			

8

PROPERTIES OF BULK MATTER

MULTIPLE CHOICE QUESTIONS

1. Ice floats on oil held in a vessel. When the ice melts, the level of oil :

(a) remains the same (b) goes up

(c) goes down (d) none of these

2. The weight of a rubber tube is W_1 when empty, and W_2 when filled with air at atmospheric pressure. The weight of air in the tube is W. Which one of the following is incorrect :

(a) $W_2 = W_1 + W$ (b) $W_2 < W_1 + \frac{W}{2}$

(c) $W_2 = W_1$ (d) $W_1 < W_2 + \frac{W}{2}$

3. A tank is filled with water to a height of 2 m. A small hole is made in one of the walls of the tank at a depth of 40 cm below the free surface of water. The distance from the foot of the wall at which the water jet coming out through the hole strikes the ground is :

(a) 80 cm (b) 160 cm

(c) 18.3 cm (d) 200 cm

4. A cubic tank of dimensions (1 × 1 × 1) m has water to a height of 40 cm. When a small hole of area 1 cm^2 is made at the bottom, the time taken by the tank to empty the water is :

(a) 23.8 min (b) 7.78 hr

(c) 47.6 min (d) 33.6 min

5. When an air bubble rises from the bottom of a lake to the surface, its radius trebles. If the atmospheric pressure is equal to a column of Hg of height H meter, then the depth of lake (in m) is :

($\because \rho_{Hg} = 13.6$)

(a) 1.91 H (b) 189.6 H

(c) 353.6 H (d) 367.2 H

6. A closed tank filled with water, is given a horizontal acceleration 4.9 ms^{-2}. The pressure at any point 10 cm from the front wall and 20 cm deep is :

(a) 24500 Pa (b) 458.2 Pa

(c) 2020.3 Pa (d) None of these

7. A solid weighs 50 N in air, 40 N in water and 30 N in another liquid. The specific gravity of the liquid is :

(a) 1.2 (b) 0.2

(c) 0.6 (d) 0.8

8. A uniform wire of mass 0.4 kg hangs from the ceiling. A point mass 0.6 kg is attached to its lower end. The ratio of strains at points $\frac{3}{4}l$ from the top and bottom end is :

(a) 9 : 7 (b) 7 : 9

(c) 1 : 1 (d) 3 : 4

9. The breaking force of a wire of diameter D of a material is F. The breaking force for a wire of the same material of radius D is :

(a) F (b) 2 F

(c) F/4 (d) 4 F

10. A wire can be broken by applying a load of 20 kg wt. The force required to break the wire of twice the diameter is :

(a) 20 kg wt (b) 5 kg wt

(c) 80 kg wt (d) 160 kg wt

11. A block hanging from one end of a fixed wire, is stretched by 1 cm. When the block is immersed in a liquid, the wire gets stretched by 0.66 cm. The ratio of relative densities of the block and liquid is :

(a) 3 : 1 (b) 5 : 3
(c) 3 : 2 (d) 4 : 3

12. The breaking stress of a material is 10^6 N/m^2. If the density of the material is 3×10^3 kg m^{-3}, what should be the length of the material so that it breaks by its own weight (g = 10 ms^{-2}) ?

(a) 0.33 m (b) 3.33 m
(c) 33.3 m (d) 333.3 m

13. The bulk modulus of rubber is 9.1×10^8 Nm^{-2}. To what depth should a rubber ball be taken in the lake so that its volume is decreased by 0.1% ?

(a) 25 m (b) 100 m
(c) 200 m (d) 500 m

14. A long spring is stretched by 2 cm and the potential energy is U. If the spring is stretched by 10 cm, then its potential energy will be :

(a) U/25 (b) U/5
(c) 5 U (d) 25 U

15. Young's modulus of brass and steel are 10×10^{10} Nm^{-2} and 2×10^{10} Nm^{-2} and having same length and are extended by 1mm under the same force. The radii of brass and steel wires are R_B and R_S respectively, then :

(a) $R_S = \sqrt{2}R_B$ (b) $R_S = \frac{R_B}{\sqrt{2}}$
(c) $R_S = 4R_B$ (d) $R_S = \frac{R_B}{4}$

16. Two wires of the same material and length but a cross sectional area in the ratio 1 : 2 are used to suspend the same loads. The extensions in them will be in the ratio :

(a) 1 : 2 (b) 2 : 1
(c) 4 : 1 (d) 1 : 4

17. A body of mass 10 kg is attached to a wire of length 0.3 m. Its breaking stress is 4.8×10^7 Nm^{-2}. The area of cross-section of the wire is 10^{-6} m^2. What is the maximum angular velocity with which it can be rotated in the horizontal circle ?

(a) 4 rad s^{-1} (b) 8 rad s^{-1}
(c) 1 rad s^{-1} (d) 2 rad s^{-2}

18. A cable breaks if stretched by more than 2 mm. It is cut into two equal parts. By how much can either part be stretched without breaking ?

(a) 0.25 mm (b) 0.5 mm
(c) 1 mm (d) 2 mm

19. In which case, is there a maximum extension in the wire, if the same force is applied on each wire ?

(a) L = 500 cm; d = 0.5 mm
(b) L = 200 cm ; d = 0.2 mm
(c) L = 300 cm ; d = 0.3 mm
(d) L = 400 cm ; d = 0.1 mm

20. The breaking force for a wire of diameter D of a material is F. The breaking force for a wire of the same material D is :

(a) F (b) 2F
(c) F/4 (d) 4F

21. An iron rod of length 1 m and cross-section 1 cm^2 has a Young's modulus of 10^{12} dyne cm^{-2}. Then the force with which the two ends must be pulled to produce an elongation of 1 mm is equal to :

(a) 10^9 dyne (b) 10^8 dyne
(c) 10^6 dyne (d) 10^{17} dyne

22. A wire of negligible mass, 1 m length and cross-sectional area 10^{-6} is kept on a smooth horizontal table with one end fixed. A ball of mass 1 kg is attached to the other end. The wire and the ball are rotated with an angular velocity 20 rad s^{-1}. If the elongation in the wire is 10^{-3} m, then Young's Modulus of the wire is :

(a) 4×10^{11} Nm^{-2} (b) 6×10^{11} Nm^{-2}
(c) 8×10^{11} Nm^{-2} (d) 10×10^{11} Nm^{-2}

23. The diameter of a brass wire is 0.6 mm and Y is $9 \times 10^6 \times 10^{11}$ Nm^{-2}. The force which will increase its length by 0.2% is about :

(a) 100 N (b) 51 N

(c) 25 N (d) 0 N

24. In steel, the Young's modulus and the strain at the breaking point are 2×10^6 Nm^{-2} and 0.15 respectively. The stress at the breaking point for steel is :

(a) 1.33×10^{11} Nm^{-2}

(b) 1.33×10^{12} Nm^{-2}

(c) 2×10^{10} $N\,m^{-2}$

(d) 3×10^{10} Nm^{-2}

25. A cube of Al of side 0.1 m is subjected to a shearing force of 100 N. The top of the cube is displaced through 0.02 with respect to the bottom face. The shearing strain would be :

(a) 0.02 (b) 0.1

(c) 0.005 (d) 0.002

26. A tensile force of 2×10^3 N doubles the length of a rubber band of cross-sectional area 2×10^{-4} m^2. The Y of the rubber band is:

(a) 4×10^7 Nm^{-2} (b) 2×10^2 Nm^{-2}

(c) 10^7 Nm^{-2} (d) 0.5×10^7 Nm^{-2}

27. Two wires of the same material and length are stretched by the same force. Their masses are in the ratio 3 : 2. Their elongations are in the ratio :

(a) 3 : 2 (b) 9 : 4

(c) 2 : 3 (d) 4 : 9

28. To increase the length by 0.5 mm of a steel wire of length 2 m and area of cross-section 2 mm^2, the force required is

($Y_{steel} = 2.2 \times 10^{11}$ Nm^{-2}) :

(a) 1.1×10^5 N (b) 1.1×10^4 N

(c) 1.1×10^3 N (d) 1.1×10^2 N

29. Two wires of the same length and same material but radii in the ratio of 1 : 2 are stretched by unequal forces to produce equal elongation. The ratio of the two forces is :

(a) 1 : 1 (b) 1 : 2

(c) 2 : 3 (d) 1 : 4

30. A wire of length l and radius r is clamped rigidly at one end. When the other end of the wire is pulled by a force F, its length increases by l. Another wire of the same material of length $4l$, radius $4r$, is pulled by a force 4F. The increase in the length will be:

(a) $l/2$ (b) l

(c) $2l$ (d) $4l$

31. When a weight of 5 kg is suspended from a Cu wire of length 30 m and diameter 0.5 mm, the length of the wire increases by 2.4 cm. If the diameter is doubled, the extension produced is :

(a) 1.2 cm (b) 0.6 cm

(c) 0.3 cm (d) 0.15 cm

32. A one metre long steel wire of cross-sectional area 1 mm^2 is extended by 1 mm. Then work done is

($\because Y_{Steel} = 2 \times 10^{11}$ Nm^{-2}) :

(a) 0.1 J (b) 0.2 J

(c) 0.3 J (d) 0.4 J

33. A wire is stretched 1 mm by a force of 1 kN. How far would a wire of the same material but a length four times the diameter be stretched by the same force ?

(a) 0.5 mm (b) 0.25 mm

(c) 0.125 mm (d) 0.0625 mm

34. A wire extends by 1 mm when a force is applied. Double the force is applied to another wire of same material and length, but half the radius of its cross-section. The elongation of the wire in mm will be :

(a) 8 (b) 4

(c) 2 (d) 1

35. When the tension in a metal wire is T_1, its length is l_1. When tension is T_2, its length is l_2. The natural length of the wire is :

(a) $\frac{T_2}{T_1}(l_1 + l_2)$ (b) $T_1 l_1 + T_2 l_2$

(c) $\frac{l_1 T_2 - l_2 T_1}{T_2 - T_1}$ (d) $\frac{l_1 T_2 + l_2 T_1}{T_2 + T_1}$

36. Two wires of Cu and steel are joined end to end. The area of cross-section of Cu wire is twice that of the steel wire. They are placed under a compressive force F. The ratio of their lengths is
($Y_{Cu} = 2 \times 10^{11}\ Nm^{-2}$,
$Y_{Steel} = 1.1 \times 10^{11}\ Nm^{-2}$):

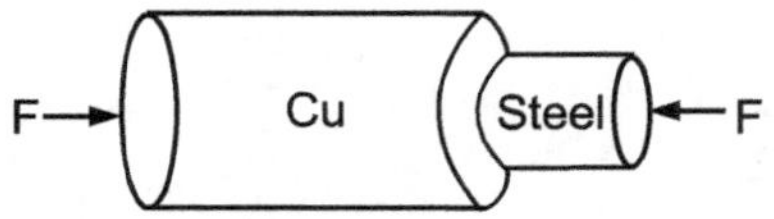

(a) 2 : 1 (b) 1 : 1
(c) 1 : 2 (d) 2

37. A uniform slender rod of length L, cross-sectional area A and Young's modulus Y is acted upon by the forces as shown in figure. The elongation of the rod is :

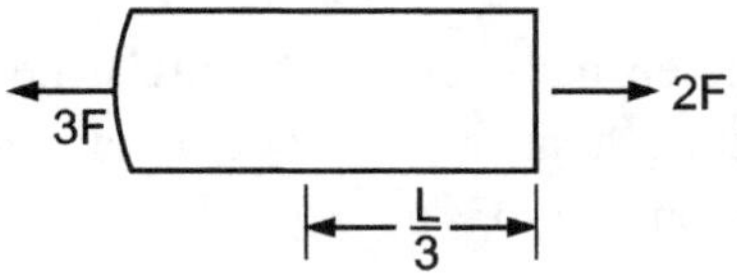

(a) $\frac{3FL}{5\ AY}$ (b) $\frac{2FL}{5AY}$
(c) $\frac{3\ FL}{8\ AY}$ (d) $\frac{8FL}{3AY}$

38. If the Young's modulus of the material is 3 times of its modulus of rigidity, then volume elasticity will be :
(a) Zero (b) Infinity
(c) $2 \times 10^{10}\ Nm^{-2}$ (d) $3 \times 10^{10}\ Nm^{-2}$.

39. If the compressibility of water is σ per unit atmospheric pressure, then the decrease in volume (V) due to the atmospheric pressure P will be :
(a) σ P/V (b) σ PV
(c) $\frac{\sigma}{PV}$ (d) $\frac{\sigma V}{P}$

40. Bulk modulus of water is $2\times10^9\ Nm^{-2}$. The change in pressure required to increase the density of water by 0.1% is :
(a) $2 \times 10^9\ Nm^{-2}$ (b) $2 \times 10^8\ Nm^{-2}$
(c) $2 \times 10^6\ Nm^{-2}$ (d) $2 \times 10^4\ Nm^{-2}$

41. A cube is shifted to a depth of 100 m in a lake. The change in volume is 0.1%. The Bulk modulus of the material is nearly :
(a) 10 Pa (b) 10^4 Pa
(c) 10^7 Pa (d) 10^6 Pa

42. An elastic material of Young's modulus Y is subjected to a stress S. The elastic energy stored per unit volume of the material is :
(a) $\frac{SY}{2}$ (b) $\frac{S^2}{2Y}$
(c) $\frac{S}{2Y}$ (d) $\frac{2S}{Y}$

43. A ball falling in a lake of depth 200 m shows a decrease of 0.1% in its volume at the bottom. The bulk modulus of elasticity of the material of the ball is ($\because g = 10\ ms^{-2}$)
(a) $10^9\ Nm^{-2}$ (b) $2 \times 10^9\ Nm^{-2}$
(c) $3 \times 10^9\ Nm^{-2}$ (d) $4 \times 10^9\ Nm^{-2}$

44. Two wires of the same Young's modulus (Y) and same length 'L' but radii R and 2R respectively are joined end to end and a weight W is suspended from the combination as shown in the given figure. The elastic potential energy of the system is:

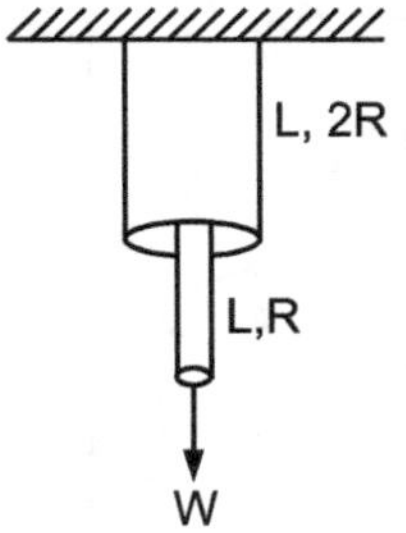

(a) $\frac{3W^2L}{4\pi R^2Y}$ (b) $\frac{3W^2L}{8\pi R^2Y}$
(c) $\frac{5W^2L}{8\pi R^2Y}$ (d) $\frac{W^2L}{\pi R^2Y}$

45. A cube is subjected to a uniform volume compression. If the side of the cube decreases by 1%, the bulk strain is :
(a) 0.01 (b) 0.02
(c) 0.03 (d) 0.06

46. The upper end of a wire of radius 4 mm and length 100 cm is clamped and the other end is twisted through an angle of 30°. The angle of shear is :

(a) 0.012° (b) 0.12°
(c) 1.2° (d) 12°

47. The length of an elastic string is '*a*' metre, when tension is 44 N and '*b*' metre when the tension is 5 N. The length in metres when the tension is 9 N is :

(a) $4a - 5b$ (b) $5b - 4a$
(c) $9b - 9a$ (d) $a + b$

48. A wire is fixed with the upper end is stretched by length *l* by applying a force F. The work done in stretching is :

(a) $\frac{F}{2 \cdot \Delta l}$ (b) $F \cdot \Delta l$
(c) $2F \cdot \Delta l$ (d) $\frac{F \cdot \Delta l}{2}$

49. Two cylinders of the same Young's modulus and same length are joined with their ends. The upper end of A is fixed with a rigid support. Their radii are in the ratio of 1 : 2. If the lower end of B is twisted by an angle θ, the angle of twist of cylinder A is :

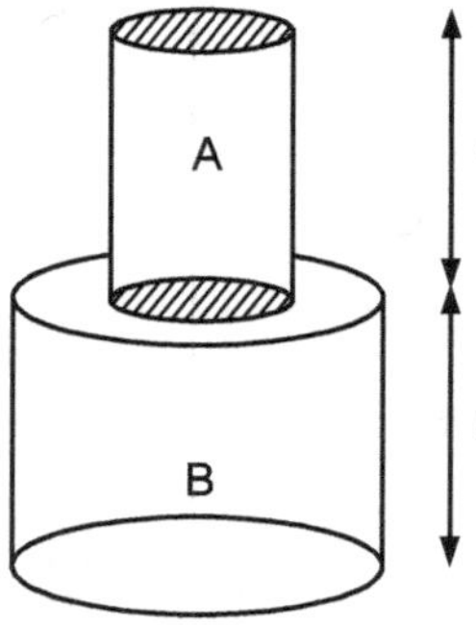

(a) $\frac{15}{16}\theta$ (b) $\frac{16}{15}\theta$
(c) $\frac{16}{17}\theta$ (d) $\frac{17}{16}\theta$

50. If a wire is stretched by hanging a weight from its end, the elastic potential energy per unit volume in terms of longitudinal strain σ and modulus of elasticity Y is :

(a) $\frac{Y\sigma^2}{2}$ (b) $\frac{Y\sigma}{2}$
(c) $\frac{2Y\sigma^2}{2}$ (d) $\frac{Y^2\sigma}{2}$

51. What is the amount of work done in increasing the length of a wire through unity?

(a) $\frac{YL}{2A}$ (b) $\frac{YL^2}{2A}$
(c) $\frac{YA}{2L}$ (d) $\frac{YL}{A}$

52. The upper end of a wire 1 m long and 2 mm radius is clamped. The lower end is twisted through an angle of 45°. The angle of shear is :

(a) 0.09° (b) 0.9°
(c) 9° (d) 90°

53. For a given material, the Young's modulus is 2.4 times that of the modulus of rigidity. Its Poisson's ratio is :

(a) 0.1 (b) 0.2
(c) 0.3 (d) 0.4

54. A water proofing agent changes the angle of contact :

(a) from acute to 90°
(b) from obtuse to 90°
(c) from an acute to obtuse value
(d) from an obtuse to acute value

55. The force required to drag a circular flat plate of radius 5 cm on the surface of water is ....
(Surface Tension of H_2O = 75 dyne/cm) :

(a) 30 dyne (b) 60 dyne
(c) 750 dyne (d) 750 π dyne

56. If C is the radius of the surface of influence of a liquid, then the thickness of the surface film is equal to :

(a) C (b) 2C
(c) $\frac{C}{2}$ (d) Zero

57. Water rises to a height of 10 cm in a capillary tube and Hg falls to a depth of 3.42 cm in the same capillary tube. If the density of Hg is 13.6 and angle of contact is 135°, the ratio of surface tension for H_2O - Hg is :

(a) 1 : 0.5 (b) 1 : 3
(c) 1 : 6.5 (d) 1.5 : 1

58. Liquid rises to a height of 2 cm in a capillary tube. The angle of contact between the solid and the liquid is zero. The tube is depressed more now so that the top of the capillary is only 1 cm above the liquid, then the apparent angle of contact between the solid and the liquid is :

(a) 0° (b) 30°
(c) 60° (d) 90°

59. In a surface tension experiment with a capillary tube, water rises upto 0.1 m. If the same experiment is repeated in an artificial satellite, which is revolving around the earth, H_2O will rise in the capillary tube upto a height of :

(a) 0.1 m (b) 0.2 m
(c) 0.98 m (d) Full tube

60. A drop of liquid pressed between two glass plates spreads into a circle of diameter 10 cm. Thickness of liquid film is 0.5 mm and surface tension is 70×10^{-3} Nm^{-1}. The force required to pull them apart is :

(a) 4.4 N (b) 1.1 N
(c) 2.2 N (d) 3.6 N

61. A water drop is divided into 8 equal droplets. The pressure difference between the inner and outer side of the big drop will be :

(a) same as for the smaller droplet
(b) half of that for the smaller droplet
(c) 1/4 of that for the smaller droplet
(d) twice of that for the smaller droplet

62. A needle is 7.5 mm long. Assuming that the needle is not wetted by water, how heavy can it be that it still floats on water ? (S.T. of H_2O = 70 dyne/cm)

(a) 1.07 gm wt (b) 1.07 N
(c) 1.07 dyne (d) 1.07 kg wt

63. The material of a wire has specific gravity 8. If it is not wetted by water, what is the maximum diameter of the wire that will float on the surface of water ?

(a) 0.75 mm (b) 1.5 mm
(c) 1.5 cm (d) None of these

64. Liquid drops are falling slowly one by one from a vertical glass tube. Then the relation between the weight (W) of drop, surface tension of the liquid drop (T) and radius r of the tube is ($\theta = 0°$) :

(a) $W = \pi r^2 T$ (b) $W = 2\pi r T$
(c) $W = 2\pi r^2 T$ (d) $W = \frac{4}{3}\pi r^3 T$

65. A soap bubble in vacuum has a radius of 3 cm and another soap bubble in vacuum has a radius of 4 cm. If the two bubbles coalesce under isothermal conditions, then the radius of the new bubble is :

(a) 2.3 cm (b) 4.5 cm
(c) 5 cm (d) 7 cm

66. If the diameter of a capillary tube is increased by two times, then the height of liquid rise in it will be :

(a) Two times (b) Half
(c) Remains the same (d) $\frac{1}{4}$th

67. A raft of wood (ρ = 600 kg/m³) of mass 120 kg floats in water. How much weight can be put on the raft to make it just sink ?

(a) 120 kg (b) 200 kg
(c) 40 kg (d) 80 kg

68. A body of density d_1 is counterpoised by Mg of weights of density d_2 in air of density d. Then the true mass of the body is :

(a) M (b) $M\left(1 - \frac{d}{d_2}\right)$
(c) $M\left(1 - \frac{d}{d_1}\right)$ (d) $M\frac{(1 - d/d_2)}{(1 - d/d_1)}$

69. A piece of ice is floating in a beaker containing water. When ice melts, the temperature falls from 20°C to 4°C and the level of water :

(a) remains the same

(b) falls

(c) rises

(d) changes erratically

70. In question 69, if temperature again falls from 4°C to 1°C, then the level of water will:

(a) rise

(b) fall

(c) not change

(d) none of these

71. A rectangular vessel when full of water takes 10 minutes to be emptied through an orifice in its bottom. How much time will it take to be emptied when half filled with H_2O ?

(a) 9 min (b) 7 min

(c) 5 min (d) 3 min

72. In the given stress-strain graph, which part obeys Hooke's Law :

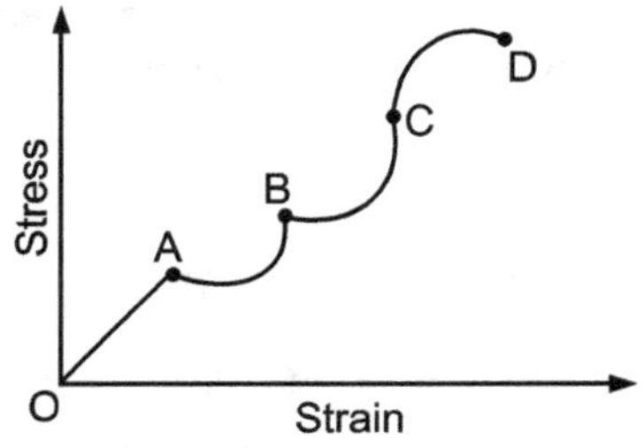

(a) OA (b) AB

(c) BC (d) CD

73. Two forces each of 100 N are applied in opposite directions on the upper and lower faces of a cube of side 20 cm. The upper face is shifted parallel to itself by 0.25 cm. If the sides of the cube were 10 cm, then displacement would be :

(a) 0.25 cm (b) 0.5 cm

(c) 0.75 cm (d) 1 cm

74. A cube of side 10 cm is subjected to a tangential force of 5×10^5 N at the upper face, keeping the lower face fixed. The upper face is displaced by 0.01 radian relative to the lower face along the direction of the tangential force. The shear modulus of the material of the cube is :

(a) 5×10^{10} Nm^{-2} (b) 5×10^{11} Nm^{-2}

(c) 5×10^{12} Nm^{-2} (d) 5×10^{13} Nm^{-2}

75. Equal torsional torque acts on two rods X and Y having equal length. The diameter of rod y is twice the diameter of rod x. If θ_x and θ_y are the angles of twist, then $\frac{\theta_x}{\theta_y}$ is equal to :

(a) 1 (b) 2

(c) 4 (d) 16

76. Young's modulus of the material of wire is 6×10^{12} Nm^{-2} and there is no transverse strain in it, then its modulus of rigidity will be :

(a) 3×10^{12} Nm^{-2} (b) 2×10^{12} Nm^{-2}

(c) 10^{-12} Nm^{-2} (d) None of these

77. The increase in length on stretching a wire is 0.05%. If its Poisson ratio is 0.4, the diameter is reduced by :

(a) 0.01% (b) 0.02%

(c) 0.03% (d) 0.04%

78. Two wires of the same material have their lengths in the ratio 1 : 2 and their diameters in the ratio 2 : 1. If they are stretched by the same force, their elongations will be in the ratio :

(a) 2 : 1 (b) 1 : 4

(c) 1 : 8 (d) 8 : 1

79. A force F is required to break a wire of length l and radius r. What force is required to break a wire of the same material, having twice the length and 6 times the radius ?

(a) F (b) 3 F

(c) 9F (d) 36F

80. When the weight W is suspended from one end with the other end being fixed, then let the elongation produced in it be l. If the same wire goes over a pulley and two weights W each are hung at the two ends, the elongation of the wire will be :

(a) $4l$ (b) $2l$

(c) l (d) $l/2$

81. One end of a uniform rod of mass m_1, uniform area of cross-section A is suspended from the roof and mass m_2 is suspended from the other end. What is the stress at the mid point of the rod ?

(a) $(m_1 + m_2)\, g/\text{A}$ (b) $(m_1 - m_2)\, g/\text{A}$

(c) $\left[\frac{(m_1/2) + m_2}{\text{A}}\right] g$ (d) $\left[\frac{(m_1 + m_2/2)}{\text{A}}\right] g$

82. The upper end of a wire of radius 4 mm and length 100 cm is clamped and its other end is twisted through an angle of 30°. Then angle of shear is :

(a) 12° (b) 0.12°

(c) 1.2° (d) 0.012°

83. A wire is suspended vertically from one of its ends and stretched by attaching a weight of 200 N to the lower end. The wire stretches by 1 mm. Then the elastic energy stored in the wire is : **(A.I.E.E.E. 2003)**

(a) 0.2 J (b) 10 J

(c) 20 J (d) 0.1 J

84. A wire fixed at the upper end, is stretched by a length l by applying a force F. The work done in stretching is :

(A.I.E.E.E. 2004)

(a) $\frac{\text{F}}{2l}$ (b) $\text{F}l$

(c) $2\text{F}l$ (d) $\frac{\text{F}l}{2}$

85. If S is the stress, Y is the Young's modulus of the material of wire, the energy stored in the wire per unit volume is :

(A.I.E.E.E. 2005)

(a) $\frac{2\text{Y}}{\text{S}}$ (b) $\frac{\text{S}}{2\text{Y}}$

(c) $2\text{S}^2\text{Y}$ (d) $\frac{\text{S}^2}{2\text{Y}}$

86. A wire elongates by l mm, when a load W is hung from it. If the wire goes over a pulley and two weights W each are hung at the two ends, the elongation in the wire will be (in mm) : **(A.I.E.E.E. 2006)**

(a) $\frac{l}{2}$ (b) l

(c) $2l$ (d) Zero

87. A cylinder of height 20 m is completely filled with water. The velocity of efflux of water (in ms^{-1}) through a small hole on the side wall of the cylinder near its bottom is :

(A.I.E.E.E. 2002)

(a) 10 (b) 20

(c) 25.5 (d) 5

88. Two wires are made of the same material and have the same volume. However, wire 1 has cross-sectional area 3A. If the length of wire 1 is increased by Δx on applying force F, how much force is needed to stretch wire 2 by the same amount ?

(A.I.E.E.E. 2009)

(a) 4F (b) 6F

(c) 9F (d) F

89. The pressure of a medium is changed from 1.1×10^5 Pa to 1.165×10^5 Pa and change in volume is 10% keeping temperature constant. The bulk modulus of the medium is : **(I.I.T. Screening. 2005)**

(a) 204.8×10^5 Pa (b) 102.4×10^5 Pa

(c) 51.2×10^5 Pa (d) 1.55×10^5 Pa

90. At what speed will the velocity of a stream of water be equal to 20 cm of Hg column ($\because g = 10\ \text{ms}^{-2}$)

(a) $6.4\ \text{ms}^{-1}$ (b) $7.3756\ \text{ms}^{-1}$

(c) $6.4756\ \text{ms}^{-1}$ (d) None of these

91. Water flows through a horizontal pipe of variable cross-section at the rate of 20 litres min. What will be the velocity of water at a point where diameter is 4 cm ?

(a) 0.2639 ms^{-1} (b) 0.5639 ms^{-1}
(c) 0.4639 ms^{-1} (d) 0.3639 ms^{-1}

92. The surface area of an air bubble increases 4 times when it rises from the bottom to the top of a water tank where the temperature is uniform. If the atmospheric pressure is 10 m of water, the depth of the water in the tank is:

(a) 30 m (b) 40 m
(c) 70 m (d) 80 m

93. A cylindrical vessel is filled with equal amounts in weight of Hg on H_2O. The overall height of the two layers is 29.2 cm. Specific gravity of H_2O is 13.6. Then the pressure of the liquid at the bottom of the vessel is :

(a) 29.2 cm of water (b) 13.6 cm of Hg
(c) 4 cm of Hg (d) 15.6 cm of Hg

94. A hydraulic lift is designed to lift cars of maximum mass of 3×10^3 kg. The area of cross-section of the piston carrying the load is 4.25×10^{-12} m^2. The maximum pressure the smaller piston has to bear will be :

(a) 6.92×10^5 Nm^{-2} (b) 7.82×10^7 Nm^{-2}
(c) 9.63×10^9 Nm^{-2} (d) 13.76×10^{11} Nm^{-2}

95. A uniform tapered vessel is filled with a liquid of density 900 kg m^{-3}. The force that acts on the base of the vessel due to the liquid is :

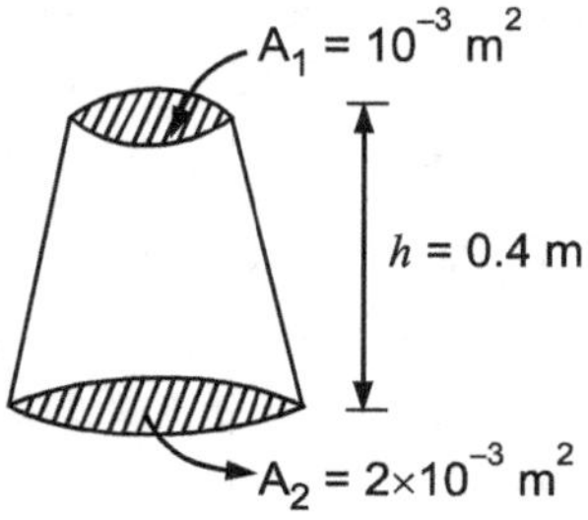

(a) 3.6 N (b) 7.2 N
(c) 9 N (d) 12 N

96. From the given figure, the normal thrust per unit area with the liquid density ρ on the walls of the vessel at point A will be :

(a) ρgh
(b) ρgH
(c) $(H - h) \rho g$
(d) $(H - h) \rho g \cos \theta$

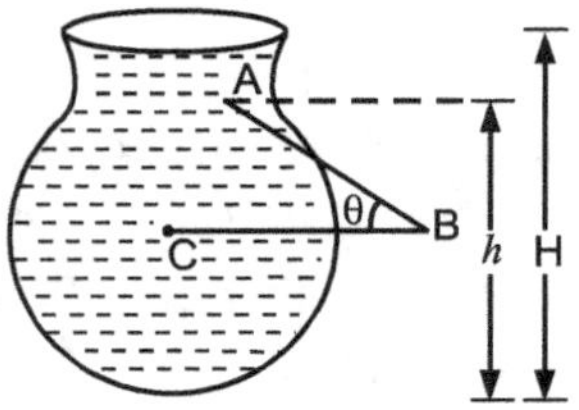

97. When a cubical glass aquarium of side 4 m is half filled, and the water is 2 m deep, it exerts a force F on the wall of the aquarium. The force exerted on the wall of the aquarium when the water is 4 m in depth, will be :

(a) F/2 (b) F
(c) 2F (d) 4F

98. A U-tube is partially filled with water. Oil which does not mix with water is next poured into one side until water rises by 25 cm on the other side. If the density of oil be 0.8, the oil will stand higher than the water level by :

(a) 6.25 cm (b) 12.5 cm
(c) 31.25 cm (d) 62.5 cm

99. The density of ice is 917 kg m^{-3}. What fraction of the volume of an ice piece will be above water, when floating in fresh water ?

(a) 0.083 (b) 0.053
(c) 0.045 (d) 0.043

100. A solid floats with one fourth of its volume above the surface of water, the density of the solid is :

(a) 750 kg m^{-3} (b) 650 kg m^{-3}
(c) 560 kg m^{-3} (d) 450 kg m^{-3}

101. A 25 kg girl wearing high heel shoes balances on a single heel. The heel base is circular with a diameter 1 cm. Then the pressure exerted by the heel on the horizontal floor will be :

(a) 3.12 Nm^{-2} (b) 6.42 Nm^{-2}

(c) 3.12×10^6 Nm^{-2} (d) 6.24×10^6 Nm^{-2}

102. A rectangular plate 3 m × 2m is immersed in water in such a way that its maximum and least depth are 6 m and 4 m respectively from the free surface of water. The total thrust on the plate is :

(a) 294×10^3 N (b) 294 N

(c) 100×10^3 N (d) 400×10^3 N

103. A weightless bag is filled with 5 kg of water and then weighed in water. The reading of the spring balance is :

(a) 5 kg f (b) 2.5 kg f

(c) 1.25 kg f (d) Zero

104. A body of density ρ is dropped from rest at a height h into a lake of water density σ, where σ > ρ. Neglecting all dissipative forces, the maximum depth to which the body sinks before returning to float on the surface will be :

(a) $\frac{h}{(\sigma - \rho)}$ (b) $\frac{h\rho}{\sigma}$

(c) $\frac{h\rho}{(\sigma - \rho)}$ (d) $\frac{h\sigma}{(\sigma - \rho)}$

105. Two cubes each of weight 22 gm. One of them is of iron (σ = 8000 kg m^{-3}) and the other is copper (σ = 3×10^3 kg m^{-3}). When these cubes are weighed in liquid alcohol, then :

(a) iron cube weighs less

(b) copper cube weighs less

(c) both cubes will have equal weight

(d) none of these

106. The spring balance A reads 2 kg with a block of mass M suspended from it. A balance B reads 5 kg when a beaker with liquid is put on the pan of the balance. The two balances are now so arranged that the hanging mass is inside the liquid in a beaker as shown in the given figure :

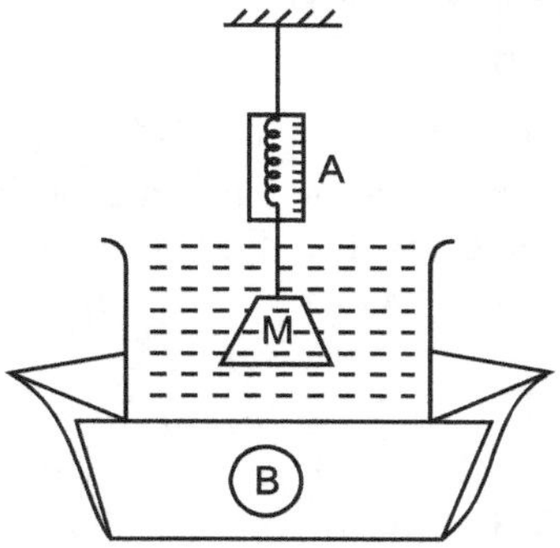

(a) Balance A will read more than 2 kg

(b) Balance B will read less than 2 kg

(c) Balance A will read less than 2 kg and balance B will read more that 5 kg

(d) Balance A will read more than 2 kg and balance B will read less than 5 kg

107. The density of ice is 0.9 gm cc^{-1} and that of sea water is 1.1 gm cc^{-1}. An iceberg of volume V is floating in sea water. The fraction of the iceberg above the water level is :

(a) 1/11 (b) 2/11

(c) 3/11 (d) 4/11

108. The weight of a wooden piece is 6 kg. In the floating state in water, its 1/3 part remains inside the water. On this floating solid, what maximum weight should be applied such that the entire piece of wood is to be sunk in the water ?

(a) 12 kg (b) 10 kg

(c) 14 kg (d) 15 kg

109. A 10 cm long wire is placed horizontally on the surface of water and is gently pulled up with a force of 2×10^{-2} N to keep the wire in equilibrium. The surface tension of water in Nm^{-1} is :

(a) 0.002 (b) 0.001

(c) 0.2 (d) 0.1

110. Surface tension of a soap solution is able to produce a soap bubble of 2 cm diameter. Then the surface energy will be (Surface tension of soap solution is 3.4 dyne/cm) :

(a) $7.6 \times 10^{-6} \pi$ J (b) $15.2 \times 10^{-6} \pi$ J
(c) $1.9 \times 10^{-6} \pi$ J (d) $10^{-4} \pi$ J

111. The surface energy of a liquid drop is U. It splits up into 10^3 equal droplets. Then the surface energy becomes :

(a) U (b) 10 U
(c) 10^2 U (d) 10^3 U

112. Let W be the work done, when a bubble of volume V is formed from a solution. How much work is required to be done to form a bubble of volume 2 V ?

(a) W (b) 2 W
(c) $\sqrt[3]{2}$W (d) $\sqrt[3]{4}$W

113. The amount of work done in blowing a soap bubble such that its diameter increases from d to D (where T is surface tension of the soap bubble) is :

(a) $\pi (D^2 - d^2)$ T (b) $2\pi (D^2 - d^2)$ T
(c) $4\pi (D^2 - d^2)$ T (d) $8\pi (D^2 - d^2)$ T

114. Two large parallel plates are dipped in water vertically with a small separation R. Due to surface tension T, water rises in the gap between the glass plates. If ρ_0 is the atmospheric pressure, then pressure of water just below the water surface in the region between the two plates is :

(a) $\rho_0 - \frac{2T}{R}$ (b) $\rho_0 + \frac{2T}{R}$
(c) $\rho_0 - \frac{4T}{R}$ (d) $\rho_0 + \frac{4T}{R}$

115. When we increase the temperature, then the angle of contact :

(a) decreases (b) increases
(c) remains the same (d) none of these

116. Let h be the height of liquid in a capillary. It will rise to a height more than h :

(a) on the surface of the sun
(b) in a lift moving down with acceleration
(c) at the poles
(d) in a lift moving up with acceleration

117. A rain drop of radius 3 mm has a terminal velocity in air equal to 1 ms^{-1}. The viscous force on it is :

($\because g = 10\ ms^{-2}$)

(a) 101.73×10^{-4} dyne
(b) 101.73×10^{-5} dyne
(c) 16.95×10^{-4} dyne
(d) 16.95×10^{-5} dyne

118. A spherical ball is dropped in a long column of viscous liquid. Which of the following graphs represent the variation of :

(i) gravitational force with time
(ii) viscous force with time
(iii) net force acting on the ball with time

(a) 2, 3, 1 (b) 3, 2, 1
(c) 1, 2, 3 (d) 3, 1, 2

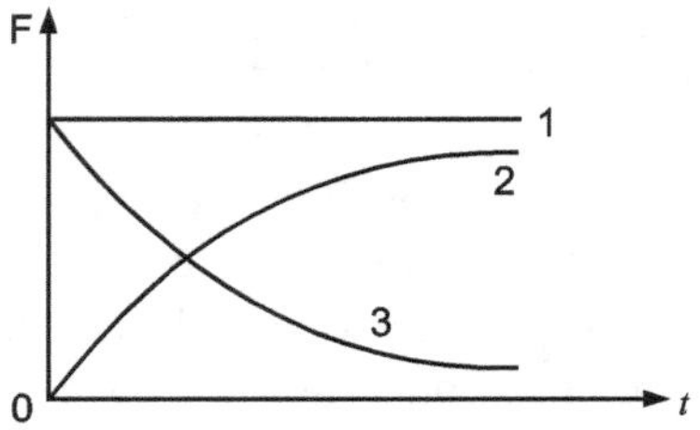

119. If the velocity head of a stream of water is equal to 10 cm, then its speed of flow is ($\because g = 10\ ms^{-2}$) :

(a) 10 ms^{-1} (b) 140 ms^{-1}
(c) 1.4 ms^{-1} (d) 0.1 ms^{-1}

120. Three tubes A, B and C of equal radii, are connected to a horizontal pipe in which a liquid is flowing. The radii of pipe at the joints of A, B and C are 2 cm, 1 cm and 2 cm respectively, then the height of the liquid:

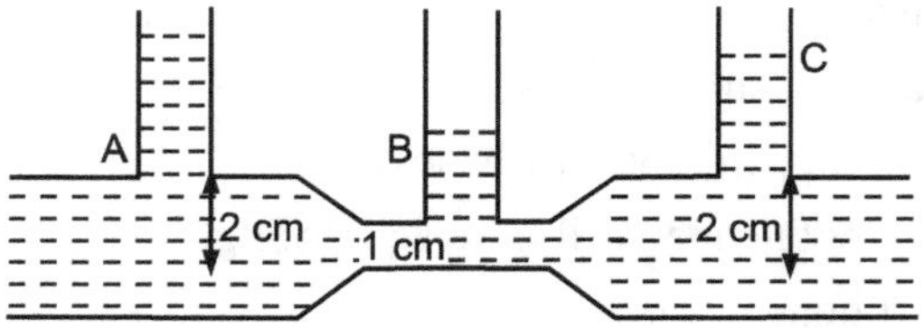

(a) is maximum in A
(b) is equal in A and B
(c) is same in all three
(d) is equal in A and C

121. A liquid is kept in a cylindrical vessel and is rotated about its longest axis. If the radius of the cylinder is 0.05 m and speed of rotation is 2 rad s^{-1}, then the difference in the height of the liquid at the centre and side of the vessel is :

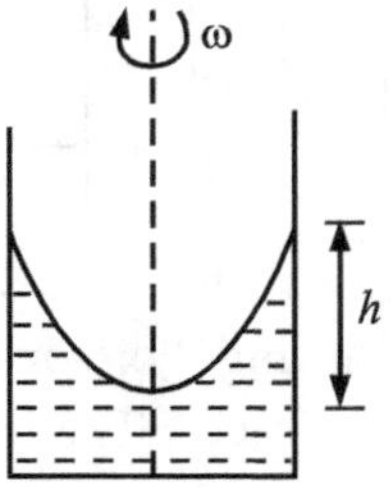

(a) 20 cm (b) 4 cm
(c) 2 cm (d) 0.2 cm

122. There is a hole in the bottom of a tank containing drinking water. If the net pressure at the bottom is 3 atm then velocity of water flowing from the hole is:
(1 atm. $=10^5$ Nm^{-2})

(a) $\sqrt{400}$ ms^{-1} (b) $\sqrt{600}$ ms^{-1}
(c) $\sqrt{60}$ ms^{-1} (d) $\sqrt{6}$ ms^{-1}

123. The speed of a 2 cm radius steel ball in a viscous liquid is 20 cm s^{-1}. Then the speed of a 1 cm radius steel ball in the same liquid will be :

(a) 5 cm s^{-1} (b) 10 cm s^{-1}
(c) 40 cm s^{-1} (d) 80 cm s^{-1}

124. A body of uniform cross-sectional area floats in a liquid of density thrice its value. The portion of exposed height will be :

(a) 2/3 (b) 5/6
(c) 1/16 (d) 9/10

125. A spherical ball of radius R is falling in a liquid of viscosity η with the velocity v. The retarding viscous force acting on the spherical ball is :

(a) directly proportional to radius R and inversely proportional to velocity v
(b) directly proportional to both radius R and velocity v
(c) inversely proportional to both radius R and velocity v
(d) inversely proportional to R, but directly proportional to velocity v.

126. If two soap bubbles of different radii are connected by a tube, then :

(a) air will flow from the bigger bubble to the smaller bubble till the sizes become equal
(b) air will flow from the bigger bubble to the smaller bubble till the sizes are interchanged
(c) air flows from the smaller bubble to the bigger bubble
(d) there is no flow of air

127. A 20 cm long capillary tube is dipped in water. The water rises upto 8 cm. If the entire arrangement is put in a freely falling elevator, the length of the water column in the capillary tube will be :

(a) 4 cm (b) 20 cm
(c) 8 cm (d) 10 cm

128. If the terminal speed of a sphere of gold (ρ_{gold} = kg per m^3) is 0.2 m/s in a viscous liquid ($\rho =$ 1.5 kg per m^3), then find the terminal velocity of sphere of silver (ρ_{silver} = 10.5 mg per m^3) of the same size in the same liquid :

(a) 0.2 ms^{-1} (b) 0.4 ms^{-1}
(c) 0.133 ms^{-1} (d) 0.1 ms^{-1}

129. A jar is filled with two non mixing liquids 1 and 2 having densities ρ_1 and ρ_2 respectively. A solid ball, made up of a material of density ρ_3 is dropped in the jar. It comes to equilibrium in the position shown in the given figure. Which of the following is true for ρ_1, ρ_2 and ρ_3 ?

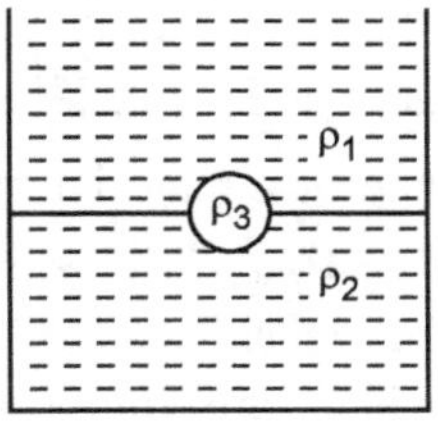

(a) $\rho_1 < \rho_3 < \rho_2$ (b) $\rho_3 < \rho_1 < \rho_2$
(c) $\rho_3 > \rho_2 > \rho_1$ (d) $\rho_1 < \rho_2 < \rho_3$

130. A spherical solid ball of volume V is made of material of density ρ_1. It is falling through a liquid of density ρ_2 ($\rho_2 < \rho_1$). Assume that the liquid applies a viscous force on the ball, that is proportional to the square of its speed v i.e. $\vec{F}_{vis} = -kv^2$ ($k > 0$).
The terminal speed of ball is :

(a) $vg\ (\rho_1 - \rho_2)/k$ (b) $\sqrt{\dfrac{v\,g(\rho_1 - \rho_2)}{k}}$

(c) $\dfrac{vg\rho_1}{k}$ (d) $\sqrt{\dfrac{vg\rho_1}{k}}$

131. A capillary tube A is dipped in water. Another identical tube B is dipped in a soap water solution. Which of the following shows the relative nature of the liquid column in the two tubes ?

(A.I.E.E.E. 2008)

(a)
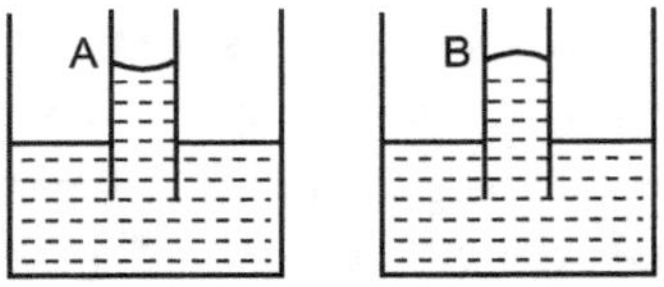

(b)
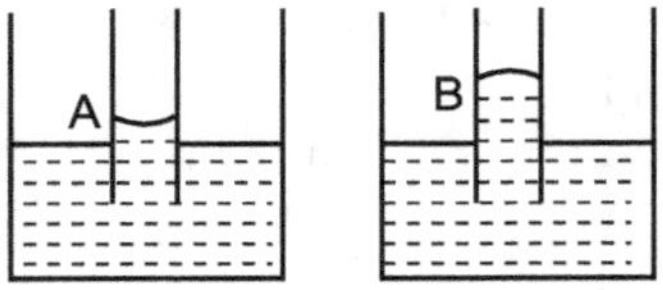

(c)
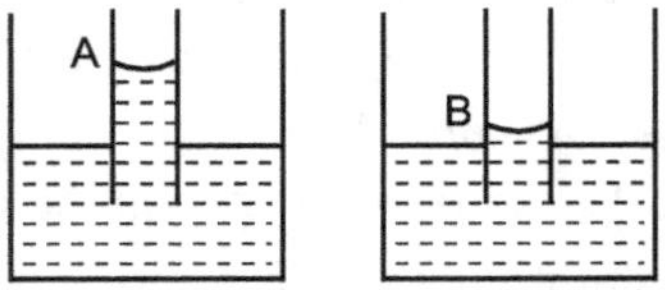

(d)
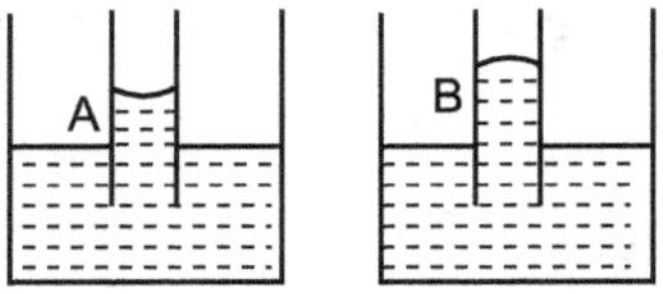

132. A ball is made of a material of density ρ where $\rho_{oil} < \rho < \rho_{water}$ with ρ_{oil} and ρ_{water} representing the densities of oil and water. The oil and water are immiscible. If the above ball is in equilibrium in a mixture of this oil and water, which of the following picture represents its equilibrium position ?

(a)
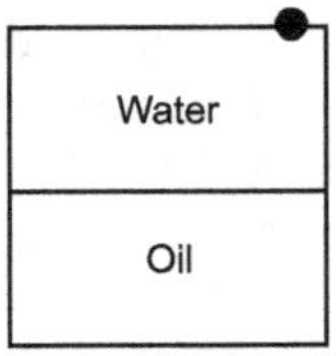

(b)
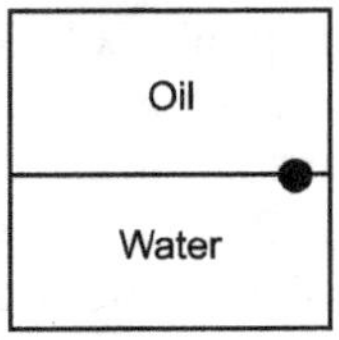

(c)
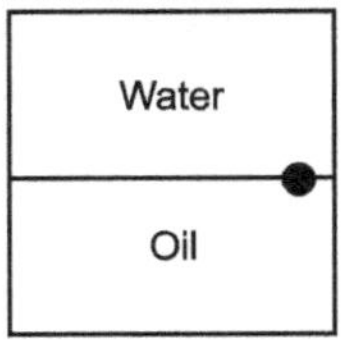

(d)
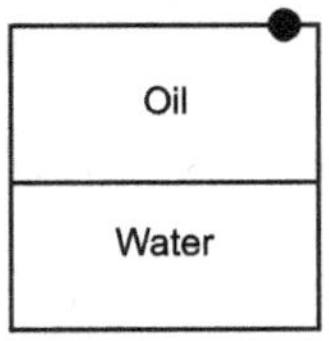

133. A metal wire having Poisson ratio 1/4 is stretched by a force. The ratio of the frictional change in volume to the frictional change in length is :

(a) 1 : 2 (b) 1 : 4
(c) 2 : 1 (d) 5 : 4

134. A viscous liquid flows at a constant rate through a horizontal pipe of radius R. The ratio of velocities at distance R/2 and R/4 from the the centre of the pipe is :

(a) 1 : 2 (b) 1 : 4
(c) 1 : 8 (d) 4 : 5

135. When a capillary tube is immersed in Hg, the depression is found to be h. If the depth of immersion is found to be $h/2$, then what is the angle made by the mercury meniscus with the inner surface of the capillary within the mercury, at the point of contact ?
($\because\ \theta = 135°$)

(a) 135°

(b) $\pi - \sin^{-1}\left(\dfrac{1}{2\sqrt{2}}\right)$

(c) $\dfrac{\pi}{2} + \sin^{-1}\left(\dfrac{1}{2\sqrt{2}}\right)$

(d) $\dfrac{\pi}{2} + \cos^{-1}\left(\dfrac{1}{2\sqrt{2}}\right)$

136. A liquid flowing through a horizontal pipe of a fixed length is subjected to a constant pressure difference. If the average velocity v is plotted against the radius R of the pipe, then which graph represents the variation ?

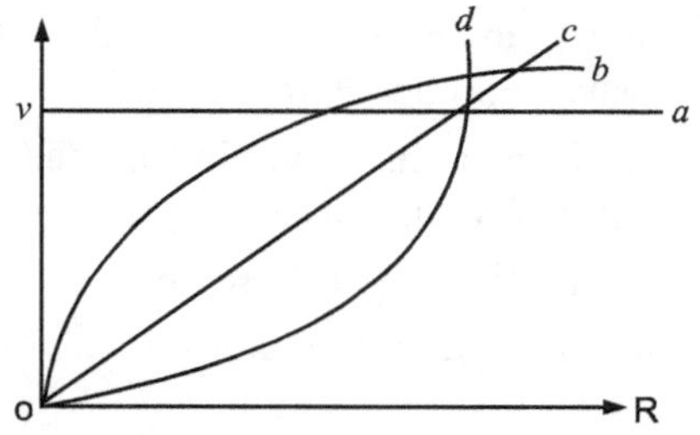

(a) a (b) b

(c) c (d) d

137. Which of the following curves best represents the velocity profile of a laminar flow in a cylindrical pipe?

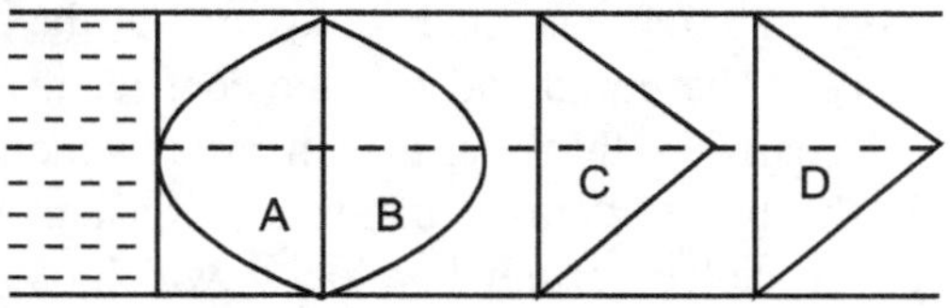

(a) A (b) B

(c) C (d) D

138. A uniform steel wire of density 7800 kg m^{-3} is 2.5 m long and weighs 15.6×10^{-3} kg. It extends by 1.25 mm when loaded by 8 kg. Calculate the value of Young's modulus for steel :

(a) 196×10^{11} N/cm^2

(b) 1.96×10^{11} N/cm^2

(c) 19.6×10^{11} N/cm^2

(d) 0.196×10^{11} N/cm^2

139. Two wires of the same material and length, but diameter in the ratio 1 : 2 are stretched by the same force. The potential energy per unit volume for the wires stretched will be in the ratio :

(a) 16 : 1 (b) 4 : 1

(c) 2 : 1 (d) 6 : 1

140. The diameter of a big drop of water is 2.8 mm. It is broken into 125 equal drops. If the surface tension of water is 75 dyne/km, then the work done is :

(a) zero (b) 19 erg

(c) 46 erg (d) 74 erg

141. A boat having length 3 m and width 2 m is floating on a lake. The boat sinks by 1 cm when a man gets on it. The mass of the man is :

(a) 60 kg (b) 62 kg

(c) 12 kg (d) 128 kg

142. An air bubble of radius 'r' in water is at a depth h, below the water surface at any instant. If P is the atmospheric pressure, d be the density and T is the surface tension of water, then the pressure inside the bubble will be :

(a) $P + hdg - \frac{4T}{r}$ (b) $P + hdg + \frac{2T}{r}$

(c) $P + hdg - \frac{2T}{r}$ (d) $P + hdg + \frac{4T}{r}$

143. A U-tube is such that the diameter of one limb is 0.4 mm and that of the other is d mm. If the surface tension of water contained in that U-tube is 0.07 N/m and the difference in the water levels in the two limbs is 3.6 cm, then the value of d is :

(a) 1.6×10^{-3} m (b) 0.4×10^{-3} m

(c) 8×10^{-3} m (d) 4×10^{-3} m

144. The vertical section of a wing of an aeroplane is shown. The maximum upthrust is in :

(a)  (b) 

(c)  (d) 

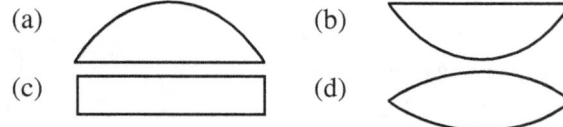

145. At 27°C temperature, the K.E. of an ideal gas is E_1. If the temperature is increased to 327°C, then its K.E. would be :

(a) $E_1/\sqrt{2}$ (b) $E_1/2$

(c) $\sqrt{2}\,E_1$ (d) $2E_1$

146. A vessel contains 1 mole of O_2 gas (Molar mass 32) at a temperature T. The pressure of the gas is P. An identical vessel containing one mole of He gas (Molar mass 4) at temperature 2T has a pressure of :

(a) P/8 (b) P

(c) 2P (d) 8P

147. The v_{rms} of molecules of a gas is 1260 ms^{-1}. The most probable speed of the molecule is :

(a) 1029 ms^{-1} (b) 1161 ms^{-1}
(c) 1671 ms^{-1} (d) 977 ms^{-1}

148. The total K.E. of all molecules of He gas molecules of V volume exerting a pressure P is 1500 J. The total K.E. in joules of all the molecules of N_2 gas having the same volume V and exerting a pressure 2P is :

(a) 3000 (b) 4000
(c) 5000 (d) 6000

149. If the intermolecular forces vanish away, the volume occupied by the molecules contained in 4.5 kg water at STP will be :

(a) 5.6 m^3 (b) 4.5 m^3
(c) 11.2 m^3 (d) 5.6 litres

150. If the pressure in a closed vessel is reduced by drawing out some of the gas, the mean free path of the two molecules :

(a) is increased
(b) is decreased
(c) remains the same
(d) increases or decreases according to the nature of gas

151. The v_{rms} of O_2 gas at 0°C and at atmospheric pressure is :

(a) more than that of air
(b) less than that of air
(c) equal to that of air
(d) none of these

152. There are three beakers A, B and C containing glycerine, water and kerosene respectively. They are stirred vigorously and placed on a table. The liquid which comes to rest at the earliest is :

(a) Glycerine
(b) Water
(c) Kerosene
(d) All of the above at the same time

153. More viscous oil is used in summer than in winter in motor engines due because :

(a) due to rise in temperature in summer, the viscosity of oil decreases
(b) due to rise in temperature in summer, the viscosity of oil increases
(c) surface tension of oil decreases
(d) surface tension of oil increases

COMPREHENSION BASED QUESTIONS

Passage - I

A spherical body of mass m and radius r falls through a viscous medium. If ρ is the density of the spherical body, σ is the density of the liquid and η is the coefficient of viscosity of the liquid, then after some time the body attains a maximum constant velocity called terminal velocity which is given as :

$$v = \frac{2}{9} \times \frac{r^2(\rho - \sigma)g}{\eta}$$

154. The radius of a drop of water falling through air, if it covers 4.1 cm in 4 s with a uniform velocity (ρ_{air} = 0.001293 g cm^{-3} and $\eta_{air} = 1.8 \times 10^{-4}$ poise) is :

(a) 921×10^{-4} cm (b) 92.1×10^{-4} cm
(c) 9.21×10^{-4} cm (d) 0.92×10^{-4} cm

155. A drop of water of diameter 0.02 is falling through a medium of density 1.21×10^{-3}g per cm^3 and coefficient of viscosity is 1.8×10^{-4} poise. The terminal velocity of the drop is :

(a) 1.21 cm s^{-1} (b) 3.21 cm s^{-1}
(c) 4.21×10^{-1} cm s^{-1} (d) 2 cm s^{-1}

156. A ball bearing made of iron of radius 1.5 mm and density 7.85 g cm^{-3} is allowed to fall through a long column of glycerine of density 1.25 g cm^{-3}. It is found to attain a terminal velocity of 2.25 cms^{-1}. The velocity of glycerine in centipoise is :

(a) 1.437 (b) 14.37
(c) 143.7 (d) 1437

157. An air bubble of 1 cm radius rises at a steady rate of 0.2 cms^{-1} through a liquid of density 1.47×10^3 kg m^{-3}. The coefficient of viscosity of the liquid (neglecting density of air) is :

(a) 16.007 Pa (b) 160.07 Pa

(c) 1600.7 Pa (d) Zero

Passage - II

According to Hooke's Law, stress is directly proportional to strain.

i.e. Stress $\propto$ Strain

or Stress = E × Strain

where E is proportionality constant

So,

$$\begin{bmatrix}\text{Coefficient of}\\ \text{elasticity (E)}\end{bmatrix} = \frac{\text{Stress}}{\text{Strain}}$$

where $\text{Stress} = \dfrac{\text{Force (F)}}{\text{Area (A)}}$

and $\text{Strain} = \dfrac{\text{Change in dimension.}}{\text{Original dimension}}$

Then for a uniform cylindrical wire,

$$\begin{bmatrix}\text{Young's modulus}\\ \text{of elasticity (Y)}\end{bmatrix} = \frac{F}{A} \times \frac{l}{\Delta l}\ \text{Nm}^{-2}$$

A structural steel rod has a radius of 10 mm and a length of 1 m. A 100 kN force stretches it along its length.

158. The stress for rod is :

(a) 3.18×10^8 Nm^{-2}

(b) 31.8×10^8 Nm^{-2}

(c) 318×10^8 Nm^{-2}

(d) 0.318×10^8 Nm^{-2}

159. The elongation in the rod is :

(a) 0.1592×10^{-3} m (b) 1.592×10^{-3} m

(c) 15.92×10^{-3} m (d) 159.2×10^{-3} m

160. The strain on the rod is :

(a) 159.2×10^{-3} (b) 15.92

(c) 1.592 (d) 0.1592.

ASSERTION AND REASON

Directions for Q. 161 to 168: In the following questions, a statement-I of assertion is followed by a statement-II of reason. While answering a question, you are required to choose the correct option of the given four options.

(a) Both assertion and reason are true and reason is the correct explanation of assertion.

(b) Both assertion and reason are true, but reason is not the correct explanation of assertion.

(c) Assertion is true, but reason is false.

(d) Both assertion and reason are false.

161. **(I)** Stress is the internal force per unit area of a body.

(II) Rubber is more elastic than steel.

162. **(I)** The size of a H_2 balloon increases as it rises in air.

(II) The material of a balloon can be easily stretched.

163. **(I)** A hydrogen filled balloon stops rising after it has attained a certain height in sky.

(II) The atmospheric pressure decreases with height and becomes zero when maximum height is attained.

164. **(I)** For Reynold's number > 2000, the flow of liquid is turbulent.

(II) Internal forces are dominant compared to the viscous force at such high Reynold's number.

165. **(I)** The velocity of the rain drops increases only upto a limit as they start their journey towards the surface of the earth.

(II) The rain drops attain terminal velocity in the due course of time, while falling through air.

166. **(I)** The upper surface of aeroplane wings is made convex and lower surface is made concave.

(II) The air currents at the loop have a smaller velocity and thus less pressure at the bottom than the top.

167. **(I)** A thin stainless steel needle can lie floating on a still water surface.

(II) Any object floats, when a buoyant force balances the weight of the body.

168. **(I)** The shape of a liquid drop is spherical.

(II) The pressure inside the liquid drop is greater than that outside it.

169. Water contained in a tank K flows through an orifice of diameter 2 cm under a constant pressure difference of 10 cm of water column. The rate of flow of water through the orifice is :

(a) 44 cc/s (b) 4.4 cc/s
(c) 440 cc/s (d) 4400 cc/s

170. A hemispherical bowl floats without sinking in a liquid of density 1.2×10^3 g/m^3. If the outer diameter and the density of bowl are 1 m and 2×10^4 kg/m^3 respectively, the inner diameter of the bowl will be :

(a) 0.94 m (b) 0.97 m
(c) 0.98 m (d) 0.99 m

171. A body of mass 2 kg is floating in water with half of its volume submerged. What would be the force required to wholly submerge it into water?

(a) 2 N (b) 9.8 N
(c) 19.6 N (d) 4.9 N

172. Two substances ρ_1 and ρ_2 are mixed in equal volume and the relative density of the mixture is 4. When they are mixed in equal masses, the relative density of the mixture is 3. The values of ρ_1 and ρ_2 are :

(a) 6, 2 (b) 3, 5
(c) 12, 4 (d) 8, 3

173. Find the density of a block of wood that floats in water with 0.1 of its volume above water :

(a) 0.9 *g/cc* (b) 0.9
(c) 0.1 *g/cc* (d) 0.1

174. The ratio of radii of two wires of the same material is 2 : 1. If these wires are stretched by an equal force, then the ratio of stress produced in them is :

(a) 1 : 2 (b) 1 : 3
(c) 1 : 4 (d) 1 : 5

175. A 5 cm cube has its upper face displaced by a tangential force of 8 N. The modulus of rigidity of the material of the cube is :

(a) 5×10^4 Nm^{-2} (b) 6×10^4 Nm^{-2}
(c) 7×10^4 Nm^{-2} (d) 8×10^4 Nm^{-2}

176. A thick rope of rubber of density $\rho = 1.5 \times 10^3$ kg m^{-3} and $Y = 5 \times 10^6$ Nm^{-2}, 8 m in length is hung from the ceiling of a room. The increase in its length due to its own weight is :

(a) 9.6×10^{-2} m (b) 19.2×10^{-2} m
(c) 9.6×10^{-3} m (d) 9.6 m

177. A 100 N force stretched the length of a hanging wire by 0.5 mm. The force required to stretch a wire of the same material and length but having 4 times the diameter by 0.5 mm is :

(a) 100 N (b) 400 N
(c) 1200 N (d) 1600 N

178. The change in the pressure required to increase the density of water by 0.1% will be

($\because$ $K_{water} = 2 \times 10^9$ Nm^{-2})

(a) 2×10^9 Nm^{-2} (b) 2×10^8 Nm^{-2}
(c) 2×10^6 Nm^{-2} (d) 2×10^4 Nm^{-2}

179. When a wire of length 10 m is subjected to a force of 100 N along its length, the lateral strain produced is 0.01×10^{-3} m. The Poisson's ratio was found to be 0.4. If the area of cross-section of wire is 0.025 m^2, its Young's modulus is : **(E.A.M.S.E.T. 2007)**

(a) 1.6×10^8 N/m^2 (b) 2.5×10^{10} N/m^2
(c) 1.25×10^{11} N/m^2 (d) 16×10^9 N/m^2

180. Write Copper, Steel, Glass and Rubber in order of increasing coefficient of elasticity: **(M.P.P.E.T. 2008)**

(a) Steel, Rubber, Copper, Glass
(b) Rubber, Copper, Glass, Steel
(c) Rubber, Glass, Steel Copper
(d) Rubber, Glass, Copper, Steel

181. Which of the following is not correct ? **(H.P.P.M.T. 2009)**
(a) Spring force is a position dependent only
(b) Spring force is conservative force
(c) Work done in cyclic process by spring force is zero
(d) Work done depends on end point only.

182. A wire of length L and cross-sectional area A is made of material of Young's modulus Y. The work done in stretching the wire by an amount x is given by : **(A.M.U. (Med.) 2009)**
(a) $\frac{YAx^2}{L}$ (b) $\frac{YAx^2}{2L}$
(c) $\frac{YAL^2}{x}$ (d) $\frac{YAL^2}{2x}$

183. Which of the following relation is true ? **(M.H.T.C.E.T. 2010)**
(a) $Y = 2\eta(1 - 2\sigma)$ (b) $Y = 2\eta(1 + 2\sigma)$
(c) $Y = 2\eta(1 - \sigma)$ (d) $(1 + \sigma)2\eta = Y$

184. Which one of the following statements is correct? **(Kerala Engg. 2010)**
(a) In case of shearing stress, there is change in volume.
(b) In case of tensile stress, there is no change in volume.
(c) In case of shearing stress, there is no change in shape.
(d) In case of hydraulic stress, there is no change in volume.

185. A large ship can float but a steel needle sinks because of **(A.F.M.C. 2005)**
(a) Viscosity (b) Surface tension
(c) Density (d) None of these

186. If there were no gravity, which of the following will not be there for a fluid ? **(Karnataka C.E.T. 2006)**
(a) Viscosity
(b) Surface tension
(c) Pressure
(d) Archimedes' upward thrust

187. A piece of solid weighs 120 g in air, 80 g in water and 60 g in a liquid. The relative density of the solid and that of the liquid respectively are : **(Kerala P.E.T. 2007)**
(a) 3, 2 (b) 2, 3/4
(c) 3/2, 2 (d) 3, 3/2

188. Three liquids of equal masses are taken in three identical cubical vessels A, B and C. Their densities are ρ_A, ρ_B and ρ_C respectively. But $\rho_A < \rho_B < \rho_C$. The force exerted by the liquid on the force of the cubical vessel is : **(C.E.T. Karnataka 2010)**
(a) maximum in vessel A
(b) the same in all the vessels
(c) minimum in vessel C
(d) maximum in vessel C

189. At about 4°C, water has maximum : **(H.P.P.M.T. 2010)**
(a) Density (b) Energy
(c) Volume (d) Specific heat

190. The excess pressure inside a spherical drop of water is four times that of another drop. Then their respective mass ratio is : **(Kerala C.E.T. 2009)**
(a) 1 : 16 (b) 8 : 1
(c) 1 : 4 (d) 1 : 64

191. The compressibility of water is 6×10^{-10} N^{-1} m^2. If one litre is subjected to a pressure of 4×10^7 Nm^{-2}, the decrease in its volume is : **(Kerala Engg. 2010)**
(a) 2.4 cc (b) 10 cc
(c) 24 cc (d) 15 cc

192. A solid sphere falls with a terminal velocity 'v' in CO_2 gas. If it is allowed to fall in vacuum, then : **(E.A.M.C.E.T. 2008)**
(a) terminal velocity of sphere = v
(b) terminal velocity of sphere < v
(c) terminal velocity of sphere > v
(d) sphere never attains terminal velocity

193. The main idea of a hydraulic brake is to obtain : **(Manipur M.B.B.S./B.D.S. - 2009)**
(a) a small force by giving a large force
(b) a large force by giving a small force
(c) a large force by giving a large force
(d) a small force by giving a small force.

194. A rain drop with radius 1.5 mm falls from a cloud at a height 1200 m from ground. The density of water is 1000 kg/m^3 and density of air is 1.2 kg/m^3. Assume the drop was spherical throughout the fall and there is no air drag. The impact speed of the drop will be : **(D.P.M.T. 2009)**
(a) 27 km/h (b) 550 km/h
(c) Zero (d) 129 km/h

195. The ratio of radii of two spherical drops is 1 : 2. The ratio of terminal velocities of these drops will be : **(H.P.P.M.T. 2010)**
(a) 4 : 1 (b) 1 : 2
(c) 2 : 1 (d) 1 : 4

196. Water is filled in a cylindrical container to a height of 3 m. The ratio of the cross-sectional area of the orifice and the beaker is 0.1. The square of the speed of the liquid coming out from the orifice is :
($g = 10\ m/s^2$) **(A.I.I.MS. 2008)**
(a) 50 m^2/s^2 (b) 50.5 m^2/s^2
(c) 51 m^2/s^2 (d) 52 m^2/s^2

197. A steel ball of mass m falls in a viscous medium with terminal velocity v. Another steel ball of mass 64 m will fall through the same liquid with terminal velocity :
(Karnataka C.E.T. 2008)
(a) v (b) 4v
(c) 8v (d) 16v

198. Surface tension vanishes at :
(Orissa JEE 2007)
(a) critical temperature
(b) critical velocity
(c) critical pressure
(d) none of these

199. For a liquid which is rising in a capillary, the angle of contact is **(MHT-CET 2005)**
(a) obtuse (b) acute
(c) 180° (d) 90°

200. If a wire having initial diameter of 2 mm produced the longitudinal strain of 0.1%, then the final diameter of wire will be ($\sigma = 0.5$) **(MHT-CET 2005)**
(a) 2.002 mm (b) 1.998 mm
(c) 1.999 mm (d) 2.001 mm

201. For a water does not wet a glass rod, the angle of contact is **(MHT-CET 2006)**
(a) obtuse (b) acute
(c) 0° (d) 90°

202. The bulk modulus of a gas is $6 \times 10^3\ N/m^2$. The additional pressure needed to reduce the volume of the liquid by 10% is
(MHT-CET 2007)
(a) 1200 N/m^2 (b) 600 N/m^2
(c) 2400 N/m^2 (d) 1600 N/m^2

203. Under the action of load F_1, the length of a string is L_1 and that under F_2 is L_2. The original length of the wire is
(MHT-CET 2007)
(a) $\frac{[L_1F_1 - L_2F_2]}{[F_1 + F_2]}$ (b) $\frac{[L_1F_2 - L_2F_1]}{[F_1 - F_2]}$
(c) $\frac{[L_1F_2 - L_2F_1]}{[F_2 - F_1]}$ (d) $\frac{[L_1F_2 - L_2F_1]}{[F_1 + F_2]}$

204. The surface tension of soap solution is 0.035 N/m. The energy needed to increase the radius of the bubble from 4 cm to 6 cm is
(MHT-CET 2007)
(a) 1.5×10^{-3} J (b) 1.5×10^{-2} J
(c) 3×10^{-2} J (d) 1.5×10^{-4} J

205. Poisson's ratio of a material is 0.5, percentage change in its length is 0.04%. What is the change in percentage of diameter ? **(MHT-CET 2008)**
(a) 0.04 % (b) 0.03 %
(c) 0.02 % (d) 0.01 %

206. When the load on a wire is increased slowly from 1 kg wt. to 2 kg wt., the elongation increases from 0.2 mm to 0.3 mm. How much work is done during the extension ? ($g = 9.8\ m/s^2$) **(MHT-CET 2008)**

(a) 1.96×10^{-3} J (b) 19.6×10^{-3} J

(c) 0.196×10^{-3} J (d) 16×10^{-3} J

207. Relation between Y, η and K is **(MHT-CET 2008)**

(a) $\frac{Y}{3} = \frac{3}{K} + \frac{1}{\eta}$ (b) $\frac{9}{Y} = \frac{\eta}{3} + \frac{1}{K}$

(c) $\frac{3}{Y} = \frac{1}{\eta} + \frac{1}{3K}$ (d) $\frac{Y}{3} = \frac{3}{\eta} + \frac{1}{K}$

208. Potential energy of a molecule on the surface of liquid as compared to molecules inside the liquid is **(MHT-CET 2008)**

(a) maximum (b) same

(c) minimum (d) halved

209. When NaCl is dissolved in water, its surface tension **(MHT-CET 2008)**

(a) decreases

(b) increases

(c) first increases and then decreases

(d) no change

210. Two wires are made of the same material and has the same volume. However, wire 1 has cross-sectional area A and wire 2 has cross-sectional area 3 A. If the length of wire 1 increases by Δx on applying force F, how much force is needed to stretch wire 2 by the same amount ? **(A.I.E.E.E. 2009)**

(a) 4F (b) 6F

(c) 9F (d) F

211. The potential energy function for the force between two atoms in a diatomic molecule is approximately given by $U(X) = \frac{a}{X^{12}} - \frac{b}{X^6}$ where a and b are constants and X is the distance between the atoms. If the dissociation energy of the molecule is $D = [U(X = \infty] - U$ at equilibrium], D is **(A.I.E.E.E. 2010)**

(a) $\frac{b^2}{6a}$ (b) $\frac{b^2}{2a}$

(c) $\frac{b^2}{12a}$ (d) $\frac{b^2}{4a}$

212. The load against elongation graph is plotted for four wires of the same material, then the maximum area of cross-section of wire is **(MHT-CET 2011)**

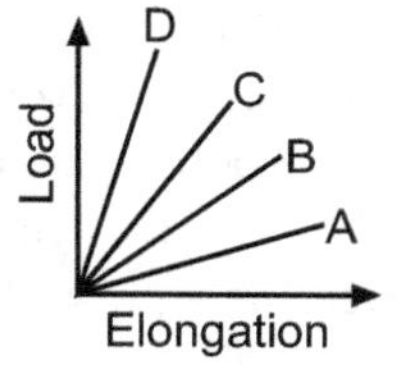

(a) C (b) A

(c) D (d) B

213. The length of material wire is l_1 when the tension in it is T_1 and the length of the wire becomes l_2 when the tension is T_2. Then the natural length of the wire will be **(MHT-CET 2011, 2012)**

(a) $\frac{(l_1 + l_2)}{2}$ (b) $\frac{(l_1 - l_2)}{2}$

(c) $\frac{l_1 T_2 - l_2 T_1}{T_2 - T_1}$ (d) $\frac{l_1 T_2 + l_2 T_1}{T_2 + T_1}$

214. The work done by surface tension on rising water to height of h in a capillary tube of radius r, is

(a) $\frac{2\pi T^2}{Pg}$ (b) $\frac{Pg}{2\pi T^2}$

(c) $\frac{\pi T^2}{Pg}$ (d) $\frac{2\pi T^2}{P}$

215. The S.I. unit of surface tension is **(MHT-CET 2011)**

(a) m/N (b) dyne/cm

(c) J/m^2 (d) J/m

216. Work done in increasing the size of a soap bubble from a radius of 3 cm to 5 cm is nearly ...... (surface tension of soap solution = $0.03\ Nm^{-1}$). **(A.I.E.E.E 2011)**

(a) 0.2π mJ (b) 2π mJ

(c) 0.4π mJ (d) 4π mJ

217. Water is flowing continuously from a tap having an internal diameter 8×10^{-3}. The water velocity as it leaves the distance 2×10^{-1}. The diameter of the water stream at a distance 2×10^{-1} m below the tap is close to **(A.I.E.E.E. 2011)**

(a) 7.5×10^{-3} m (b) 9.6×10^{-3} m
(c) 3.6×10^{-3} m (d) 5.0×10^{-3} m

218. If a ball of steel (density $\rho = 7.88\ cm^{-3}$) attains terminal velocity of 10 cm s^{-1} when falling in water (coefficient of viscosity $\eta_{water} = 8.5 \times 10^{-4}$ Pa.s) then its terminal velocity in glycerine (ρ = 1.2 g cm^{-3}, η = 13.2 Pa.s) would be, nearly

(A.I.E.E.E. 2011)

(a) 6.25×10^{-4} cm s^{-1}
(b) 6.45×10^{-4} cm s^{-1}
(c) 1.5×10^{-5} cm s^{-1}
(d) 1.6×10^{-3} cm s^{-1}

219. Two wires of same material and length are stretched by the same force. If the ratio of radii of the two wires is n : 1, then the ratio of their elongations is **(MHT-CET 2012)**

(a) $n^2 : 1$ (b) $1 : n^2$
(c) 1 : n (d) n : 1

220. A spherical liquid drop of radius 'R' is divided into eight droplets of same size. If surface tension of liquid is T, then the work done in this process will be

(MHT-CET 2012)

(a) $8\pi R^2 T$ (b) $3\pi R^2 T$
(c) $4\pi R^2 T$ (d) $2\pi RT^2$

221. The P.E. of a molecule of a liquid on the surface of the liquid, when compared to the P.E. of molecule inside the liquid is

(MHT-CET 2012)

(a) greater
(b) less
(c) equal
(d) depending on the liquid, sometimes less, sometimes more

ANSWER KEY

1. (c)	**2.** (a)	**3.** (b)	**4.** (c)	**5.** (c)	**6.** (a)	**7.** (a)	**8.** (b)	**9.** (d)	**10.**(c)
11.(a)	**12.**(c)	**13.**(b)	**14.**(d)	**15.**(b)	**16.**(b)	**17.**(a)	**18.**(c)	**19.**(d)	**20.**(d)
21.(b)	**22.**(a)	**23.**(b)	**24.**(d)	**25.**(d)	**26.**(c)	**27.**(c)	**28.**(d)	**29.**(d)	**30.**(b)
31.(b)	**32.**(a)	**33.**(d)	**34.**(a)	**35.**(c)	**36.**(b)	**37.**(d)	**38.**(b)	**39.**(b)	**40.**(c)
41.(d)	**42.**(b)	**43.**(b)	**44.**(c)	**45.**(c)	**46.**(b)	**47.**(b)	**48.**(d)	**49.**(c)	**50.**(a)
51.(c)	**52.**(a)	**53.**(b)	**54.**(c)	**55.**(d)	**56.**(a)	**57.**(c)	**58.**(c)	**59.**(d)	**60.**(c)
61.(b)	**62.**(a)	**63.**(b)	**64.**(b)	**65.**(c)	**66.**(b)	**67.**(d)	**68.**(d)	**69.**(b)	**70.**(a)
71.(b)	**72.**(a)	**73.**(b)	**74.**(a)	**75.**(d)	**76.**(a)	**77.**(b)	**78.**(c)	**79.**(d)	**80.**(c)
81.(c)	**82.**(b)	**83.**(d)	**84.**(d)	**85.**(d)	**86.**(b)	**87.**(b)	**88.**(c)	**89.**(d)	**90.**(b)
91.(a)	**92.**(c)	**93.**(c)	**94.**(a)	**95.**(b)	**96.**(c)	**97.**(d)	**98.**(b)	**99.**(a)	**100.** (a)
101. (c)	**102.** (a)	**103.** (d)	**104.** (c)	**105.** (b)	**106.** (c)	**107.** (b)	**108.** (a)	**109.** (a)	**110.** (b)
111. (b)	**112.** (d)	**113.** (b)	**114.** (a)	**115.** (a)	**116.** (b)	**117.** (a)	**118.** (c)	**119.** (c)	**120.** (d)
121. (c)	**122.** (a)	**123.** (a)	**124.** (a)	**125.** (d)	**126.** (d)	**127.** (b)	**128.** (d)	**129.** (a)	**130.** (b)
131. (d)	**132.** (b)	**133.** (a)	**134.** (d)	**135.** (a)	**136.** (d)	**137.** (b)	**138.** (b)	**139.** (b)	**140.** (d)
141. (a)	**142.** (b)	**143.** (c)	**144.** (a)	**145.** (d)	**146.** (c)	**147.** (a)	**148.** (a)	**149.** (a)	**150.** (a)
151. (b)	**152.** (a)	**153.** (a)	**154.** (c)	**155.** (a)	**156.** (d)	**157.** (d)	**158.** (a)	**159.** (b)	**160.** (c)

161. (c)	**162.** (b)	**163.** (c)	**164.** (a)	**165.** (a)	**166.** (c)	**167.** (c)	**168.** (b)	**169.** (c)	**170.** (c)
171. (c)	**172.** (a)	**173.** (a)	**174.** (c)	**175.** (d)	**176.** (a)	**177.** (d)	**178.** (c)	**179.** (a)	**180.** (d)
181. (d)	**182.** (b)	**183.** (d)	**184.** (a)	**185.** (d)	**186.** (d)	**187.** (d)	**188.** (b)	**189.** (a)	**190.** (d)
191. (c)	**192.** (d)	**193.** (b)	**194.** (b)	**195.** (d)	**196.** (a)	**197.** (d)	**198.** (a)	**199.** (b)	**200.** (c)
201. (a)	**202.** (b)	**203.** (c)	**204.** (a)	**205.** (c)	**206.** (a)	**207.** (c)	**208.** (a)	**209.** (b)	**210.** (c)
211. (d)	**212.** (b)	**213.** (c)	**214.** (a)	**215.** (c)	**216.** (c)	**217.** (c)	**218.** (a)	**219.** (b)	**220.** (c)
221. (a)									

9

HEAT AND THERMODYNAMICS

MULTIPLE CHOICE QUESTIONS

1. In a given process on an ideal gas, $dW = 0$ and $dQ < 0$. For the gas :

(a) the temperature will decrease

(b) the volume will increase

(c) the pressure will remain constant

(d) the temperature will increase

2. A solid cube and a solid sphere have equal surface areas. Both are at the same temperature of 120 °C, then :

(a) both of them will cool down at the same rate

(b) the cube will cool faster than the sphere

(c) the sphere will cool down faster than the cube

(d) whichever of the two is heavier will cool down faster

3. The energy emitted/sec by a black body at 27°C is 10 J. If the temperature of the black body is increased to 327°C, the energy emitted per second will be :

(a) 20 J (b) 40 J

(c) 80 J (d) 160 J

4. At the same temperature, the mean kinetic energies of molecules of hydrogen and oxygen are in the ratio :

(a) 1 : 1 (b) 1 : 16

(c) 8 : 1 (d) 16 : 1

5. Two vessels of different materials are similar in size in every aspect. The same quantity of ice filled in them gets melted in 20 min. and 40 min. respectively. The ratio of thermal conductivities of the metals is :

(a) 5 : 6 (b) 6 : 5

(c) 2 : 1 (d) 1 : 3

6. Two samples, A and B of a gas at the same initial temperature and pressure are compressed from volume V to V/2, A isothermally and B adiabatically. The final pressure of A will be :

(a) greater than that of B

(b) equal to that of B

(c) less than that of B

(d) twice that of B

7. An ideal Carnot engine whose efficiency is 40% receives heat at 500 K. If the efficiency is to be 50%, the intake temperature for the same exhaust temperature is :

(a) 600 K (b) 900 K

(c) 700 K (d) 800 K

8. A steel wire of uniform area 2 mm^2 is heated upto 50°C and is stretched by tying its ends rigidly. The change in tension when the temperature falls from 50°C to 30°C is : ($Y = 2 \times 10^{11}$ N/m^2, $\alpha = 1.1 \times 10^{-5}$/°C)

(a) 1.5×10^{10} N (b) 5 N

(c) 88 N (d) 2.5×10^{10} N

9. A given system undergoes a change in which work done by the system equals decrease in its internal energy. The system must have undergone an :

(a) Isothermal change (b) Isobaric change

(c) Adiabatic change (d) Isochoric change

10. Air in a cylinder is suddenly compressed by a piston, which is then maintained at the same position. With the passage of time :

(a) the pressure increases
(b) the pressure may increase or decrease
(c) the pressure remains the same
(d) the pressure decreases

11. An ideal gas heat engine is operated in a Carnot cycle between 227°C and 127°C. It absorbs 6 kcal of heat at higher temperature. The amount of heat in kcal rejected to the sink is :

(a) 4.8 (b) 2.4
(c) 1.2 (d) 6.0

12. At absolute zero :

(a) All substances exist in solid form
(b) Molecular motion ceases
(c) Water becomes ice
(d) None of these

13. The temperatures T_1 and T_2 of heat reservoirs in the ideal Carnot engine are 1500°C and 500°C respectively. If T_1 increases by 100°C, what will be the efficiency of the engine ?

(a) 62 % (b) 59 %
(c) 95 % (d) 100 %

14. At what temperature will the rms speed of air molecules be double than that at NTP ?

(a) 619°C (b) 719°C
(c) 819°C (d) None of these.

15. The temperature of sink of a Carnot engine is 27°C and its efficiency is 25%. The temperature of the source is :

(a) 227°C (b) 127°C
(c) 27°C (d) 327°C

16. Two spheres of the same material have radii 1 m and 4 m and temperatures 4000 K and 2000 K respectively. The ratio of the energy radiated per second by the first sphere to that by the second is :

(a) 1 : 1 (b) 16 : 1
(c) 4 : 1 (d) 1 : 9

17. Which statement is incorrect :

(a) All reversible cycles have the same efficiency.
(b) A reversible cycle has more efficiency than an irreversible one.
(c) Carnot cycle is a reversible cycle.
(d) Carnot cycle has the maximum efficiency in all cycles.

18. A scientist says that the efficiency of his heat engine which works at source temperature 127°C and sink temperature 27°C is 26%.

(a) It is impossible.
(b) It is possible, but less probable.
(c) It is quite probable.
(d) Data is incomplete.

19. A monoatomic gas of *n* moles is heated from temperature T_1 to T_2 under two different conditions : (i) constant volume (ii) constant pressure. The change in internal energy of the gas :

(a) is more in (i)
(b) is more in (ii)
(c) is same in both cases
(d) is independent of the number of moles

20. The absorptivity of perfectly blackbody is :

(a) Zero (b) 1
(c) Less than 1 (d) Infinity

21. One mole of an ideal monoatomic gas at temperature T_0 expands slowly according to the law P/V = constant. If the final temperature is $2T_0$, heat supplied to the gas is :

(a) $2\,RT_0$ (b) RT_0
(c) $\frac{3}{2}RT_0$ (d) $\frac{1}{2}RT_0$

22. A sample of ideal gas ($\gamma = 1.4$) is heated at constant pressure. If 100 J of heat is supplied to the gas, the work done by the gas is :

(a) 28.57 J (b) 56.54 J
(c) 38.92 J (d) 65.38 J

23. The temperature of a room heated by a heater is 20°C, when outside temperature is −20°C and it is 10°C, when the outside temperature is −40°C. The temperature of the heater is :

(a) 60°C (b) 40°C
(c) 80°C (d) 100°C

24. If gas molecules undergo inelastic collision with the walls of the container, then :

(a) temperature of the gas will increase
(b) temperature of the gas will fall
(c) pressure of the gas will increase
(d) neither the temperature nor the pressure will change

25. In a certain region of space, there are 'n' number of molecules per unit volume. The temperature of the gas is T. The pressure of the gas will be :

(a) $\frac{n'T}{R}$ (b) $\frac{n'T}{K}$
(c) $n'KT$ (d) $n'RT$

26. The molar heat capacity in a process of diatomic gas, if it does work of Q/4 when heat Q is supplied to it is :

(a) $\frac{2}{5}R$ (b) $\frac{10}{3}R$
(c) $\frac{5}{3}R$ (d) $\frac{6}{5}R$

27. Temperature of an ideal gas is 300 K. The change in temperature of the gas when its volume changes from V to 2V in the process $P = \alpha V$ (where α is +ve constant) is :

(a) 900 K (b) 1200 K
(c) 600 K (d) 300 K

28. If pressure and temperature of an ideal gas are doubled and volume is halved, the number of molecules of the gas :

(a) become half
(b) become two times
(c) become 4 times
(d) remain constant

29. PV diagram of a diatomic gas is a straight line passing through origin. The molar heat capacity of the gas in the process will be :

(a) 4R (b) 3R
(c) $\frac{4R}{3}$ (d) 2.5 R

30. Consider a compound slab consisting of two different materials having equal thickness and thermal conductivities k and $2k$ respectively. The equivalent thermal conductivity of the slab is :

(a) $\frac{2}{3}k$ (b) $\sqrt{2}\,k$
(c) $3\,k$ (d) $\frac{4}{3}k$

31. The height of the mercury column in a barometer provided with a brass scale at 0°C is observed to be 75.2 cm at 20°C. If $\alpha_{brass} = 18 \times 10^{-6}$/°C, the true height of the column at 20°C will be :

(a) 75.23 cm (b) 75.24 cm
(c) 75.25 cm (d) 75.26 cm

32. No other thermometer is as suitable as a platinum resistance thermometer to measure temperature in the entire range of :

(a) 0°C to 100°C (b) 100°C to 1500°C
(c) −50°C to 350°C (d) −300°C to 600°C

33. The resistance of a resistance thermometer has values 2.71 and 3.70 Ω at 10°C and 100°C. The temperature at which the resistance is 3.26 Ω is :

(a) 40°C (b) 50°C
(c) 60°C (d) 70°C

34. The temperature range measured by a hydrogen gas thermometer is :

(a) −200°C to 800°C (b) −200°C to 500°C
(c) −260°C to 800°C (d) −260°C to 500°C

35. The temperature at which the reading of the Fahrenheit thermometer will be double than that of Centigrade thermometer is :

(a) 160° (b) 180°
(c) 32° (d) 100°

36. Mercury thermometer can be used to measure temperature upto :

(a) 100°C (b) 212°C
(c) 360°C (d) 500°C

37. The temperature of a substance increases by 27°C. On the Kelvin scale, this increase is equal to :

(a) 300 K (b) 2.46 K
(c) 27 K (d) 7 K

38. The Fahrenheit and Kelvin scales of temperature will give the same reading at :

(a) –40 (b) 313
(c) 574.25 (d) 732.75

39. The reading of the Centigrade thermometer coincides with that of Fahrenheit thermometer in a liquid. The temperature of the liquid is :

(a) –40°C (b) 0°C
(c) 100°C (d) 300°C

40. If the temperature of a patient is 40°C, his temperature on the Fahrenheit scale will be :

(a) 72°F (b) 96°F
(c) 100°F (d) 104°F

41. 10 gm of ice at –20°C is dropped into a calorimeter containing 10 gm of water at 10°C. The specific heat of water is twice that of ice. When equilibrium is reached, the calorimeter will contain :

(a) 20 gm of water
(b) 20 gm of ice
(c) 10 gm ice and 10 gm water
(d) 5 gm ice and 15 gm water

42. 10 litres of a liquid with specific heat 0.2 cal/gm°C has the same thermal capacity as that of 20 litres of liquid with specific heat 0.3. Find the ratio of their densities :

(a) 3 : 1 (b) 1 : 3
(c) 1 : 6 (d) 6 : 1

43. One gm of ice at 0°C is added to 5 gm of water at 10°C. If the latent heat is 80 cal/gm, the final temperature of the mixture is :

(a) 5°C (b) 6°C
(c) –5°C (d) None of these

44. Two spheres A and B have diameters in the ratio 1 : 2, densities in the ratio 2 : 1 and specific heats in the ratio 1 : 3. Find the ratio of their thermal capacities.

(a) 1 : 6 (b) 1 : 12
(c) 1 : 3 (d) 1 : 4

45. If 10 cm of ice at 0°C is mixed with 1 kg of water at 10°C, the resulting temperature will be :

(a) $10 \times 80 = 10\,(10 - t) + 10\,(t - 0)$
(b) $t = 5$°C
(c) $t = 0$°C
(d) $10 \times 80 + 10\,(t - 0) = 10\,(10 - t)$

46. It takes 10 minutes to cool a liquid from 60°C to 59°C. If room temperature is 30°C, then time taken in cooling from 51°C to 49°C is :

(a) 10 min (b) 11 min
(c) 13 min (d) 15 min

47. At some temperature T, a bronze pin is a little large to fit into a hole drilled in a steel block. The change in temperature required for an exact fit is minimum when :

(a) only the block is heated
(b) both block and pin are heated together
(c) both block and pin are cooled together
(d) only the pin is cooled

48. Two rods of same material and length have their radii in the ratio of 3 : 1. The ratio of expansion when the same amount of heat is supplied will be :

(a) 6 : 1 (b) 9 : 1
(c) 3 : 1 (d) 12 : 1

49. Liquid is filled in a flash upto a certain point. When the flask is heated, the level of the liquid :

(a) immediately starts increasing
(b) initially falls and then rises
(c) rises abruptly
(d) falls abruptly

50. A thick and a thin wire of same material and same length are heated from 10°C to 90°C. Which expands more ?

(a) Thick wire

(b) Thin wire

(c) Both show the same expansion

(d) None of these

51. A black body is at a temperature of 2800 K. The energy of radiation emitted by this object with wavelength between 499 nm and 500 nm is U_1, between 999 nm and 1000 nm is U_2 and between 1499 nm and 1500 nm is U_3. The Wien constant $b = 2.80 \times 10^6$ mK. Then :

(a) $U_1 = 0$ (b) $U_3 = 0$

(c) $U_1 > U_2$ (d) $U_2 > U_1$

52. A solid sphere and hollow sphere of the same material and size are heated to the same temperature and allowed to cool in the same surroundings. If the temperature difference between each sphere and its surroundings is T, then :

(a) the hollow sphere will cool at a faster rate for all values of T.

(b) solid sphere will cool at a faster rate for all values of T.

(c) both spheres will cool at the same rate for all values of T.

(d) both spheres will cool at the same rate only for small values of T.

53. If the temperature of the sun is doubled, then:

(a) emission of energy will be doubled

(b) emission of energy will become four times

(c) mostly ultra violet radiation will be emitted

(d) mostly infra red radiation will be absorbed

54. A piece of glass is heated to a high temperature and then allowed to cool. If it cracks, a probable reason is the following property of glass :

(a) Low thermal conductivity

(b) High thermal conductivity

(c) High specific heat

(d) High melting point

55. In winter, an iron chair appears colder than a wooden chair. This is due to :

(a) Conduction (b) Convection

(c) Radiation (d) Boiling

56. To a rough approximation, conductivities of metals are about :

(a) 1000 times as those of liquids and 10,000 times of gases

(b) 10 times as those of liquids and 100 times of gases

(c) 100 times as those of liquids and 1000 times of gases

(d) 10,000 times as those of liquids and 1000 times of gases

57. The thermal conductivity of copper is :

(a) less than that of iron

(b) less than that of Al

(c) less than that of wood

(d) more than that of all the three given above

58. Pure water supercooled to −15°C is contained in a thermally insulated flask. Some ice is thrown into the flask. The fraction of water frozen into ice is :

(a) 3/35 (b) 6/35

(c) 6/29 (d) 2/35

59. A gas in an air tight container is heated from 25°C to 90°C. The density of gas will :

(a) increase slightly

(b) increase considerably

(c) remain the same

(d) decrease slightly

60. Steam is passed through the water contained in a beaker. The water can boil when the steam is at :

(a) atmospheric pressure

(b) pressure higher than the atmosphere

(c) pressure lower than the atmosphere

(d) any pressure

61. A quantity of heat Q is supplied to a monoatomic ideal gas which expands at constant pressure. The fraction of heat that goes into work done by the gas is :

(a) 2/5 (b) 3/5

(c) 2/3 (d) 1

62. The temperature of inside and outside of a refrigerator are 273 K and 303 K respectively. Assuming that the refrigerator cycle is reversible, for every joule of work done, the heat delivered to the surroundings will be nearly :

(a) 10 J (b) 20 J

(c) 30 J (d) 50 J

63. The efficiency of the reversible heat engine is η_r and that of the irreversible heat engine is η_i. Which of the following relations is correct ?

(a) $\eta_r > \eta_i$ (b) $\eta_r < \eta_i$

(c) $\eta_r = \eta_i$ (d) $\eta_r > 1$ and $\eta_i < 1$

64. The efficiency of a Carnot heat engine :

(a) is independent of the temperature of the source and the sink

(b) is independent of the working substance

(c) can be 100%

(d) is not affected by the thermal capacity of the source or the sink

65. We consider a thermodynamic system. If ΔU represents the increase in its internal energy and W the work done by the system, which of the following statements is true :

(a) $\Delta U = -W$ is an isothermal process

(b) $\Delta U = +W$ is an isothermal process

(c) $\Delta U = -W$ is an adiabatic process

(d) $\Delta U = +W$ is an adiabatic process

66. A sink, that is a system where heat is rejected, is essential for the conversion of heat into work. From which law does the above inference follow ?

(a) Zeroth (b) First

(c) Second (d) Third

67. The following sets of values for C_V and C_P of a gas have been reported by different students. The units are cal/gm-mol-K. Which of these sets is most reliable ?

(a) $C_V = 3, C_P = 5$ (b) $C_V = 4, C_P = 6$

(c) $C_V = 3, C_P = 2$ (d) $C_V = 3, C_P = 4.2$

68. $C_P > C_V$ as in the case of C_P:

(a) more heat is required to increase the internal energy

(b) heat is required to do work against external energy

(c) more heat is required to do external work

(d) more heat is required to do external work as well as for increase in internal energy

69. In an isochoric change, there is no :

(a) change in work done

(b) change in volume

(c) change in volume and work done

(d) change in pressure

70. Thermodynamics mostly deals with :

(a) measurement of quantity of heat

(b) transfer of quantity of heat

(c) change of state

(d) conversion of heat into other form of energy

71. When a gas enclosed in a closed vessel was heated so as to increase its temperature by 5°C, its pressure was seen to have increased by 1%. The initial temperature of the gas was nearly :

(a) 500°C (b) 273°C

(c) 227°C (d) 150°C

72. Two rods of lengths d_1 and d_2 and coefficients of thermal conductivities k_1 and k_2 are kept touching each other end to end. The equivalent thermal conductivity is :

(a) $k_1 + k_2$ (b) $k_1d_1 + k_2d_2$

(c) $\frac{d_1k_1 + d_2k_2}{d_1 + d_2}$ (d) $\frac{d_1 + d_2}{(d_1 / k_1 + d_2 / k_2)}$

73. Heat energy absorbed by a system in going through a cyclic process is :

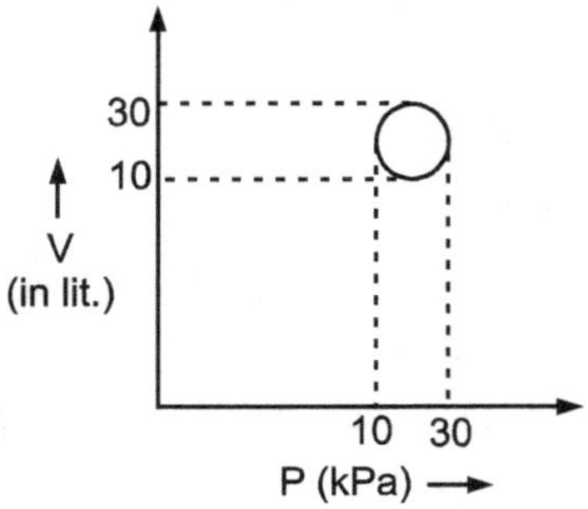

(a) $10^7 \pi$ J (b) $10^4 \pi$ J

(c) $10^2 \pi$ J (d) $10^{-3} \pi$ J

74. Isobaric modulus of elasticity is equal to :

(a) isochoric modulus of elasticity

(b) isothermal modulus of elasticity

(c) zero

(d) infinite

75. If the internal energy does not depend on the path, then the process is called :

(a) Isothermal (b) Adiabatic

(c) Both (a) and (b) (d) None of these

76. P_iV_i and P_fV_f are the initial and final pressures and volumes of a gas in a thermodynamic process respectively. If PV^n = constant, then the amount of work done is :

(a) minimum for $n = \gamma$

(b) minimum for $n = 1$

(c) minimum for $n = D$

(d) minimum for $n = 1/\gamma$

77. The equation of state, corresponding to 8 kg of O_2 is :

(a) PV = RT (b) PV = 8RT

(c) PV = RT/2 (d) PV = RT/4

78. The adiabatic elasticity of hydrogen gas ($\gamma = 1.4$) at NTP is :

(a) 1×10^5 N/m^2 (b) 1×10^{-5} N/m^2

(c) 1.4 N/m^2 (d) 1.4×10^5 N/m^2

79. An engineer claims to have made an engine delivering 10 kW power with fuel consumption of 1 gm/sec. The calorific value of fuel is 2 kcal/gm. This chain is :

(a) Valid

(b) Invalid

(c) Dependent on engine design

(d) Dependent on load

80. For an adiabatic expansion of a perfect gas, the value of $\Delta P/P$ is equal to :

(a) $\frac{\Delta V}{V}$ (b) $\gamma\frac{\Delta V}{V}$

(c) $-\gamma\frac{\Delta V}{V}$ (d) $-\gamma^2\frac{\Delta V}{V}$

81. In the given indicator diagram of an ideal gas, the work done by the gas in the process PQRS is :

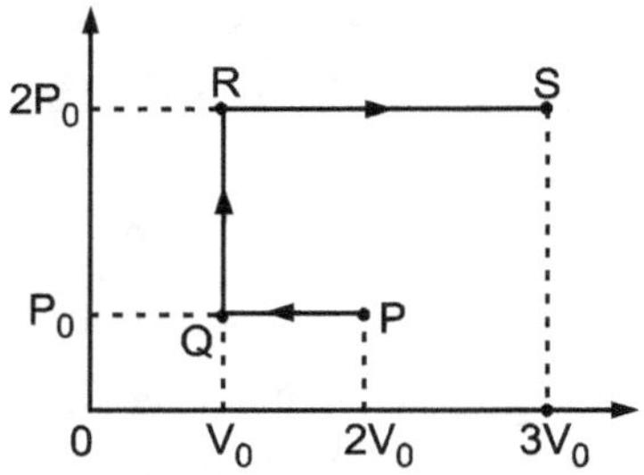

(a) $4 P_0V_0$ (b) $2 P_0V_0$

(c) $3 P_0V_0$ (d) P_0V_0

82. In the given P-V diagram, which one of the following is true ?

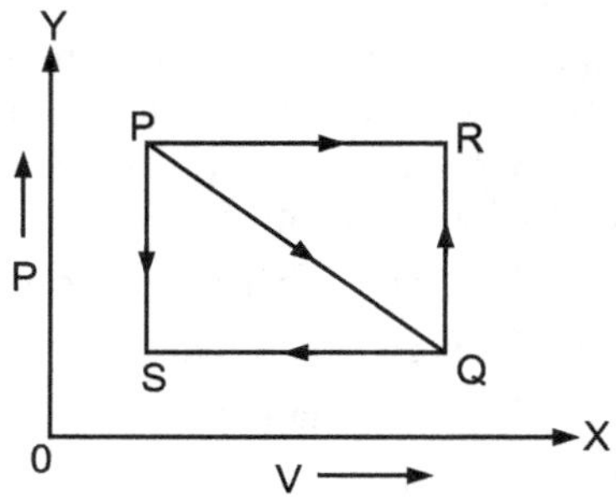

(a) Work done is maximum along PQ
(b) Work done is minimum along PQ
(c) Work done along PRQ = Work done along PSQ
(d) Work done along ADB is minimum

83. In the P-V diagram, work done W_1, W_2 and W_3 are along paths 1, 2 and 3 respectively, then which one is correct ?

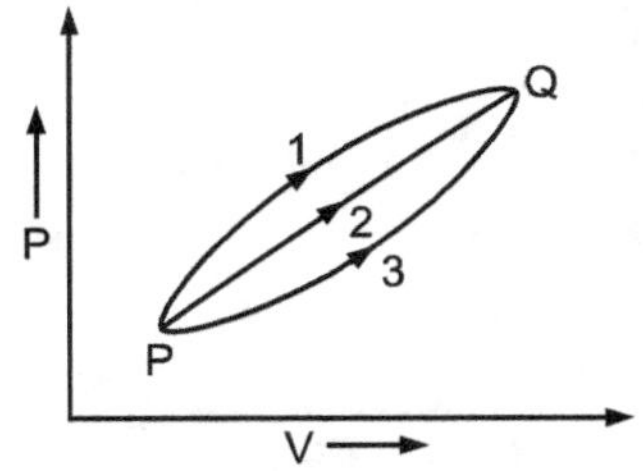

(a) $W_1 < W_2 < W_3$ (b) $W_1 = W_2 = W_3$
(c) $W_1 > W_2 > W_3$ (d) $W_1 = W_2 \neq W_3$

84. For a given cycle, the work done during isobaric process is :

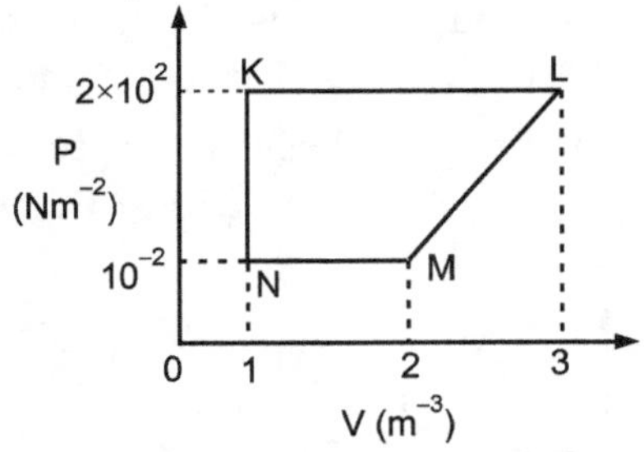

(a) 1600 J (b) 100 J
(c) 400 J (d) 600 J

85. A gas is expanded from volume V_0 to $3V_0$ under various processes as (1) isobaric, (2) isothermal, (3) adiabatic. If ΔU_1, ΔU_2 and ΔU_3 are the changes in internal energy, then :

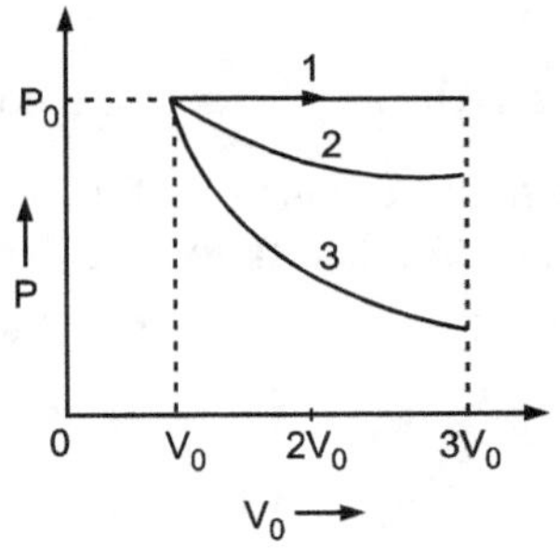

(a) $\Delta U_1 > \Delta U_2 > \Delta U_3$
(b) $\Delta U_1 < \Delta U_2 < \Delta U_3$
(c) ΔU_2
(d) None of these

86. In the above figure, which case has minimum work done ?
(a) 1 (b) 2
(c) 3 (d) 1, 2 and 3 all

87. In a refrigerator, the low temperature coil of the evaporator is at –23°C and compressed gas in condenser has a temperature of 77°C. How much electrical energy is spent in freezing 1 kg of water already at 0°C ?
(a) 13.44×10^4 J (b) 13.44 J
(c) 8×10^5 J (d) 3200 J

88. Heat given to a body which raises its temperature by 1 °C is : **(A.I.E.E.E. 2002)**
(a) Water equivalent
(b) Thermal capacity
(c) Specific heat
(d) Temperature gradient

89. Which statement is incorrect ? **(A.I.E.E.E. 2002)**
(a) All reversible cycles have the same efficiency.
(b) Reversible cycle has more efficiency than the irreversible one.
(c) Carnot cycle is a reversible one.
(d) Carnot cycle has maximum efficiency in all cycles.

90. Cooking gas containers are kept in a lorry moving with uniform speed. The temperature of the gas molecules inside will: **(A.I.E.E.E. 2002)**
(a) increase
(b) decrease
(c) remain same
(d) increase and decrease alternatively

91. At what temperature is the r.m.s. velocity of a hydrogen molecule equal to that of an oxygen molecule at 47°C ?

(A.I.E.E.E. 2002)

(a) 80 K (b) −73 K
(c) 3 K (d) 20 K

92. Even Carnot heat engine cannot give 100% efficiency because we cannot :

(a) prevent radiation
(b) find ideal sources
(c) reach absolute zero temperature
(d) eliminate friction

93. Mole of a gas with $\gamma = 7/5$ is mixed with 1 mole of a gas with $\gamma = 5/3$, then the value of γ for the resulting mixture is :

(A.I.E.E.E. 2002)

(a) 7/5 (b) 2/5
(c) 24/16 (d) 12/7

94. "Heat cannot flow by itself from a body at lower temperature to a body at higher temperature" is the statement or consequence of : **(A.I.E.E.E. 2003)**

(a) Second law of thermodynamics
(b) Conservation law of linear momentum
(c) Conservation law of angular momentum
(d) First law of thermodynamics

95. Which of the following parameters doesn't characterise the thermodynamics state of matter ?

(a) Temperature (b) Pressure
(c) Work (d) Volume

96. Two thermally insulated vessels 1 and 2 are filled with air at temperature (T_1, T_2) respectively. If the wall joining the two is opened, then the temperature inside the vessel at equilibrium will be :

(A.I.E.E.E. 2004)

(a) $T_1 + T_2$

(b) $\dfrac{T_1 + T_2}{2}$

(c) $\dfrac{T_1 T_2 (P_1V_1 + P_2V_2)}{P_1V_1T_2 + P_2V_2T_1}$

(d) $\dfrac{T_2 T_1 (P_1V_1 + P_2V_2)}{P_1V_1T_1 + P_2V_2T_2}$

97. The temperature entropy diagram of a reversible engine-cycle is given in the figure. Its efficiency is : **(A.I.E.E.E. 2005)**

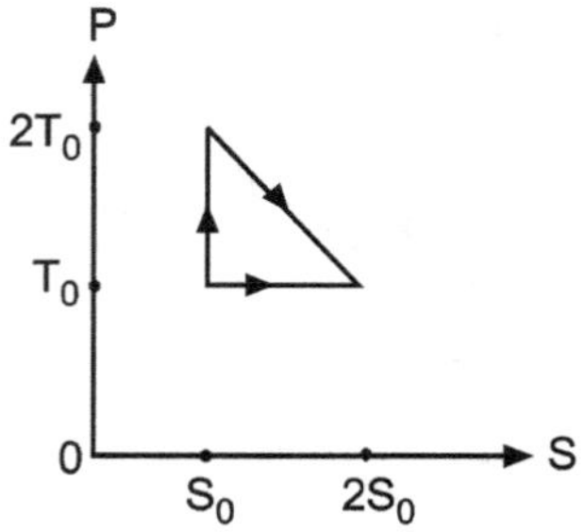

(a) 1/3 (b) 2/3
(c) 1/2 (d) 1/4

98. A system goes from A to B via two processes - I and II as shown in the figure. If ΔU_1 and ΔU_2 are the changes in internal energies for process I and II respectively, then : **(A.I.E.E.E. 2005)**

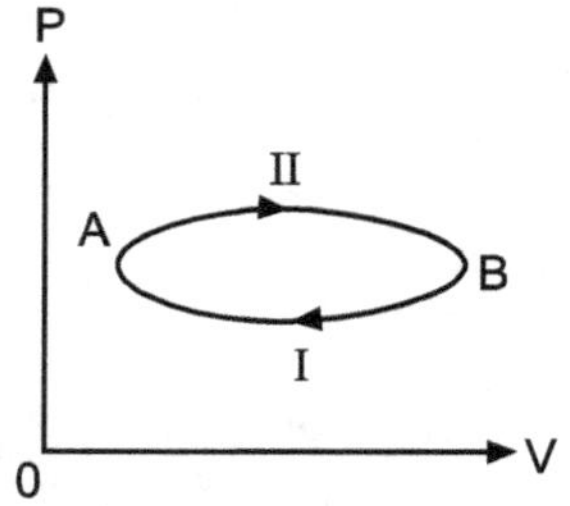

(a) $\Delta U_2 > \Delta U_1$
(b) $\Delta U_2 < \Delta U_1$
(c) $\Delta U_1 = \Delta U_2$
(d) ΔU_1 and ΔU_2 can't be determined

99. A gaseous mixture consists of 16 gm of He and 16 gm of O_2. The ratio of C_p and C_v of the mixture is : **(A.I.E.E.E. 2006)**

(a) 1.4 (b) 1.54
(c) 1.59 (d) 1.62

100. When a system is taken from state i to f along the path iaf, it is found that Q = 50 cal and W = 20 cal. Along the path ibf, Q = 36 cal. W along the path ibf is : **(A.I.E.E.E. 2007)**

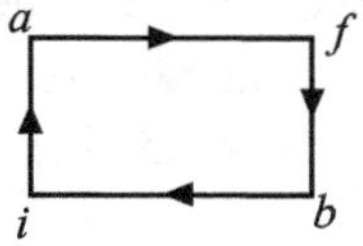

(a) 14 cal (b) 6 cal
(c) 16 cal (d) 66 cal

101. An insulated container of gas has two chambers separated by an insulatory partition. One of the chambers has volume V_1 and contains ideal gas at pressure P_1 and temperature T_1. The other chamber has volume V_2 and contains ideal gas at pressure P_2 and temperature T_2. If the piston is removed without doing any work on the gas, the final equilibrium temperature of the gas in the container will be : **(A.I.E.E.E. 2008)**

(a) $\dfrac{T_1T_2(P_1V_1 + P_2V_2)}{(P_1V_1T_1 + P_2V_2T_2)}$

(b) $\dfrac{T_1T_2(P_1V_1 + P_2V_2)}{(P_1V_1T_2 + P_2V_2T_1)}$

(c) $\dfrac{P_1V_1T_1 + P_2V_2T_2}{P_1V_1 + P_2V_2}$

(d) $\dfrac{P_1V_1T_2 + P_2V_2T_1}{(P_1V_1 + P_2V_2)}$

102. 1 kg of a diatomic gas is at a pressure of 8×10^4 N/m^2. The density of the gas is 4 kg m^{-3}. What is the energy of the gas due to its thermal motion ? **(A.I.E.E.E. 2009)**

(a) 3×10^4 J (b) 5×10^4 J
(c) 6×10^4 J (d) 7×10^4 J

103. A long metallic bar is carrying heat from one of its end to the other end under steady state. The variation of temperature θ along the length x of the bar from its hot end is best described by which of the following ? **(A.I.E.E.E. 2009)**

(a) 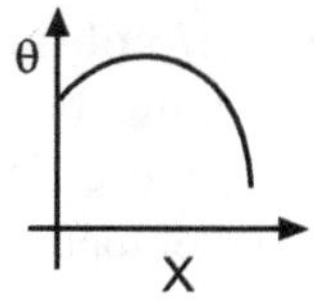

(b) 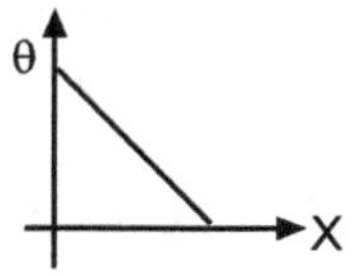

(c) 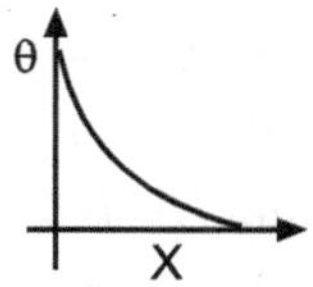

(d) 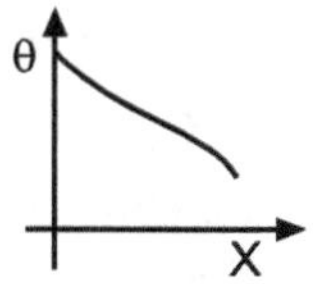

104. A diatomic ideal gas is used in a car engine as the working substance. If during adiabatic expansion part of the cycle, the volume changes from V to 32 V, then the efficiency of the engine is : **(A.I.E.E.E. 2010)**

(a) 0.5 (b) 0.75
(c) 0.99 (d) 0.25

105. One mole of ideal monoatomic gas is heated at a constant pressure of one atmosphere from 0°C to 100°C. Then the change in internal energy is :

(a) 6.56 J (b) 8.32×10^2 J
(c) 12.48×10^2 J (d) 20.8×10^2 J

106. A car tyre has a pressure of 2 atmosphere at 27°C. It suddenly bursts. If $C_P - C_V = 1.4$ for air, then the resulting temperature is :

(a) 27 K (b) 27°C
(c) −27°C (d) 246°C

107. If R is the universal gas constant, the amount of heat needed to raise the temperature of 2 moles of an ideal monoatomic gas from 273 K to 373 K when no work is done is :

(a) 100 R (b) 150 R
(c) 300 R (d) 500 R

108. During thermodynamic process, a gas releases 20 J of heat and 8 J of work is done on the gas. If initial internal energy of the gas was 30 J, what will be its final energy ?

(a) 42 J (b) 12 J
(c) 10 J (d) 18 J

109. A reversible engine converts 1/6 of the heat input into work. When the temperature of the sink is reduced by 62°C, the efficiency of the engine is doubled. The temperature of the source and sink are :

(a) 99°C, 37°C (b) 80°C, 37°C
(c) 95°C, 37°C (d) 90°C, 37°C

110. A certain substance emits only the wavelengths λ_1, λ_2 and λ_3 and λ_4 when it is at a high temperature. When this substance is at a colder temperature, it will absorb only the following wavelength :

(a) λ_1 (b) λ_2
(c) λ_1 and λ_2 (d) λ_1, λ_2, λ_3 and λ_4

111. Two vessels are of different materials and identical in size. The same quantity of ice is melted in them in 20 minutes and 40 minutes respectively. The ratio of thermal conductivities of the metal is :

(a) 5 : 6 (b) 6 : 5
(c) 3 : 1 (d) 2 : 1

112. One end of a cell-rod of length 1.0 m and area of cross-section 10^{-3} m^2 is immersed in boiling water and the other end in ice. If the coefficient of thermal conductivity of cell is 92 cal/s/°C and the latent heat of ice is 8×10^4 cal. kg^{-1}, then the amount of heat for ice which will melt in one minute is :

(a) 9.2×10^{-3} kg (b) 8×10^3 kg
(c) 6.9×10^{-3} kg (d) 5.4×10^{-3} kg

113. Two identical bodies of Fe and Ag are placed in contact as in the given figure. If $k_{Ag} = 11\ k_{Fe}$, then the temperature of their interface will be :

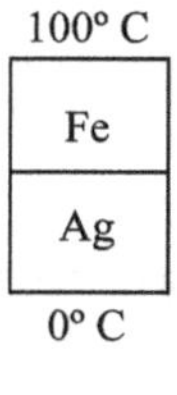

(a) 91.7°C (b) 80°C
(c) 50°C (d) 8.3°C

114. A ball of thermal capacity 10 cal °C^{-1} is heated to a certain temperature in a furnace. It is transferred into a vessel containing water. The water equivalent of the vessel and contents is 200 gm. The temperature of the vessel and its contents rises from 10°C to 40°C. What is the temperature of the furnace?

(a) 640°C (b) 64°C
(c) 600°C (d) 100°C

115. When 300 J of heat is added to 25 gm of sample of a material, then its temperature rises from 25°C to 45°C. The thermal capacity and specific heat of the material are:

(a) 15 J/°C, 600 J/kg °C
(b) 600 J/°C, 15 J/kg °C
(c) 150 J/°C, 60 J/kg °C
(d) None of these

116. A substance of mass m kg requires a power input of P watts to remain in molten state at its M.P. When the power is turned off, the sample completely solidifies in time 't' sec. What is the latent heat of fusion of the substance?

(a) $\frac{P.m}{t}$ (b) $\frac{P.t}{m}$
(c) $\frac{m}{P.t}$ (d) $\frac{t}{P.m}$

117. Two metallic strips each of thickness 't' and length 'L' are riveted together. Their linear expansion coefficients are α_1 and α_2. If they are heated through temperature $\Delta\theta$, the bimetallic strip will bend to form an arc of radius.

(a) $t / [(\alpha_1 + \alpha_2)\Delta T]$
(b) $t / [(\alpha_2 - \alpha_1)\Delta T]$
(c) $t \times (\alpha_1 + \alpha_2)\Delta T$
(d) $t / (\alpha_2 - \alpha_1)\Delta T$

118. Two spheres of radii r_1 and r_2 have densities δ_1 and δ_2 and specific heats C_1 and C_2 respectively. If they are heated to the same temperature. The ratio of their rates of cooling will be :

(a) $\frac{r_2\delta_2 C_2}{r_1\delta_1 C_1}$ (b) $\frac{r_2\delta_2 C_1}{r_1\delta_1 C_2}$

(c) $\frac{r_1\delta_1 C_1}{r_2\delta_2 C_2}$ (d) $\frac{r_2\delta_1 C_2}{r_1\delta_2 C_1}$

119. What is the amount of heat required to raise the temperature of 10 gm of a liquid from 0°C to 10°C, when its specific heat in cal/gm = $0.6\, t^2$, where t is temperature in °C.

(a) 2 kcal (b) 2 cal

(c) 200 cal (d) 60 cal

120. A metal ball immersed in H_2O weighs W_1 at 0°C and W_2 at 50°C. The coefficient of cubical expansion of metal is less than that of water, then :

(a) $W_1 < W_2$ (b) $W_1 > W_2$

(c) $W_1 = W_2$ (d) None of these

121. Two moles of helium are mixed with n moles of hydrogen. The r.m.s. speed of gas molecules in the mixture is $\sqrt{2}$ times the speed of sound in mixture. The value of n is:

(a) 1 (b) 2

(c) 3 (d) 3/2

122. P-V graph for two gases during adiabatic processes shown in plot 1 and 2 should correspond respectively to :

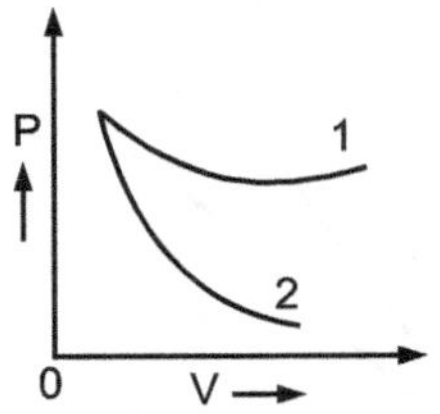

(a) He, O_2 (b) O_2, He

(c) He, Ar (d) O_2, N_2

123. In an adiabatic change, the pressure and temperature of monoatomic gas are related as $P \propto T^{-C}$ where C equals :

(a) 2/5 (b) 5/2

(c) 3/5 (d) 5/3

124. The efficiency of a Carnot engine is 50% and temperature of the sink is 500 K. If temperature of the source is kept constant and its efficiency is raised to 60%, then the required temperature of the sink will be :

(a) 100 K (b) 600 K

(c) 400 K (d) 500 K

COMPREHENSION BASED QUESTIONS

Passage - I

The efficiency of a Carnot heat engine is the ratio of amount of work done to the heat supplied i.e.

$$\eta = \frac{W}{Q_1}$$

But work done $(W) = Q_1 - Q_2$

$$\text{Then efficiency } \eta = \frac{(Q_1 - Q_2)}{Q_1}$$

$$\eta = 1 - \frac{Q_2}{Q_1} \quad \text{But } \frac{Q_2}{Q_1} = \frac{T_2}{T_1}$$

$$\text{then } \eta = 1 - \frac{T_2}{T_1}$$

A Carnot heat engine takes in 100 cal of heat from a reservoir at 427°C and performs 60 J of work. Then,

125. The amount of heat absorbed in joule is :

(a) 420 J (b) 360 J

(c) 180 J (d) 90 J

126. The heat rejected in joule is :

(a) 420 J (b) 360 J

(c) 14.29 J (d) 327 J

127. The efficiency of heat engine is :

(a) 11.29% (b) 12.29%

(c) 13.29% (d) 14.29%

128. The temperature of the cold reservoir is :

(a) 227°C (b) 327°C

(c) 427°C (d) 0°C

Passage - II

According to the principle of calorimetry, when two substances at different temperatures are mixed together, exchange of heat occurs between them till they acquire a common temperature i.e. thermal equilibrium heat gained by one substance is equal to heat lost by the other system.

129. 10 gm of ice at 0°C and water at 100°C are mixed together. Then the temperature would be :

(a) 10°C (b) 5°C

(c) 50°C (d) 40°C

130. Equal mass of ice at 0°C is put in 10 gm of water at 80°C. The final temperature will be:

(a) 10°C (b) 0°C

(c) 40°C (d) 80°C

ASSERTION AND REASON

Directions for Q. 131 to Q. 136 : In the following questions, a statement of assertion (Statement–I) is followed by a statement of reason (Statement–II). While answering a question, you are required to choose the correct one out of the given four options.

(a) Both assertion (Statement-I) and reason (Statement-II) are true and statement-II is the correct explanation of statement-I.

(b) Both assertion (Statement-I) and reason statement-II are true. But statement-II is not correct explanation of statement-I.

(c) Assertion (Statement-I) is true but reason (Statement-II) is false.

(d) Both assertion (Statement-I) and reason (Statement-II) are false.

131. **(I)** The melting of solid causes an increase in the internal energy.

(II) Latent heat is the heat required to melt a unit mass of the solid.

132. **(I)** The isothermal curves intersect each other at a certain point.

(II) The isothermal changes take place slowly, so the isothermal curves have very little slope.

133. **(I)** Air quickly leaking out of a balloon becomes cooler.

(II) The leaking air undergoes adiabatic expansion.

134. **(I)** In adiabatic compression, the internal energy and temperature of the system decreases.

(II) Adiabatic compression is a slow process.

135. **(I)** When a bottle of cold carbonated drink is opened, a slight fog forms around the opening.

(II) Adiabatic expansion of the gas causes lowering of temperature and condensation of water vapours.

136. **(I)** Thermodynamic processes in nature are irreversible.

(II) Dissipative effects cannot be eliminated.

137. In a given process of an ideal gas, $dW = 0$ and $dQ < 0$, then for the gas :

(a) the temperature will decrease

(b) the volume will increase

(c) the pressure will remain constant

(d) the temperature will increase

138. In the following figure, volume (V) and temperature (T) for a perfect gas at two pressures P_1 and P_2, is shown, then :

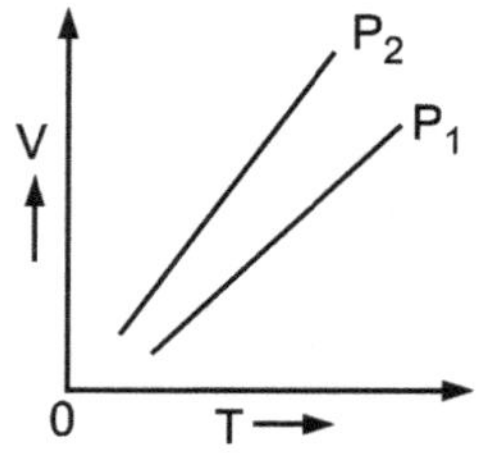

(a) $P_1 > P_2$

(b) $P_1 < P_2$

(c) $P_1 = P_2$

(d) Insufficient information

139. An ideal monoatomic gas is taken round the cycle ABCDA as shown in the P-V diagram. The work-done during the cycle is :

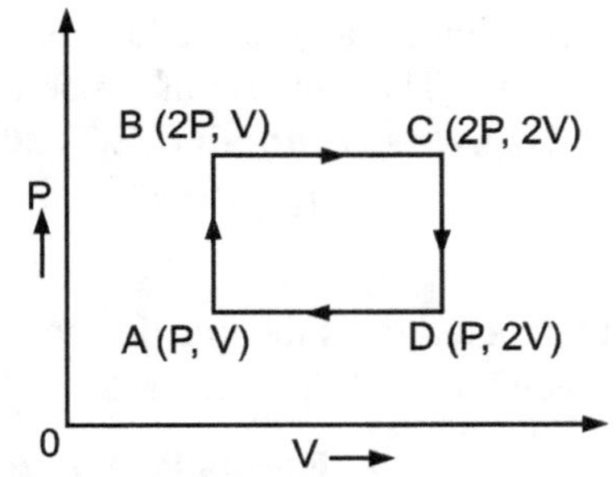

(a) PV (b) 2PV

(c) PV/2 (d) Zero

140. During the melting of a slab of ice at 273 K at atmospheric pressure :

(a) +ve work is done by the ice-water system on the atmosphere

(b) +ve work is done on the ice-water system by the atmosphere

(c) the internal energy of the ice-water system increases

(d) the internal energy of the ice-water system decreases.

141. An ideal gas has a cycle $A \rightarrow B \rightarrow C \rightarrow A$. If the net heat supplied to the gas in the cycle is 5 J, then the work-done by the gas for the process $C \rightarrow A$ is :

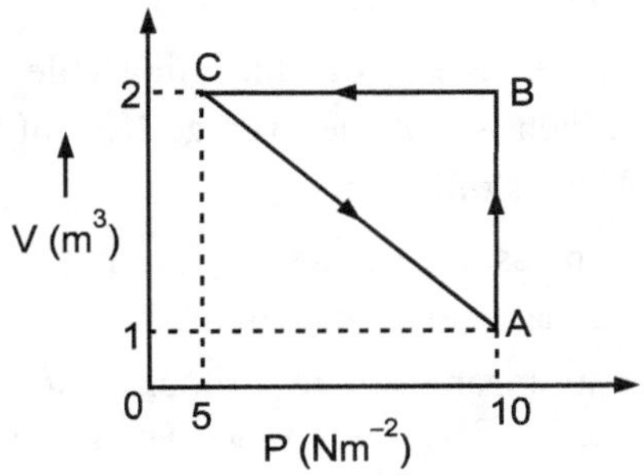

(a) –5 J (b) –10 J

(c) –15 J (d) – 20 J

142. An adiabatic process occurs at constant :

(a) temperature (b) pressure

(c) heat (d) time

143. In a reversible isochoric change :

(a) $\Delta W = 0$ (b) $\Delta Q = 0$

(c) $\Delta T = 0$ (d) $\Delta U = 0$

144. Which of the following graphs correctly represents the variation of $\beta = \frac{dV/dP}{V}$ with P for an ideal gas at constant temperature ?

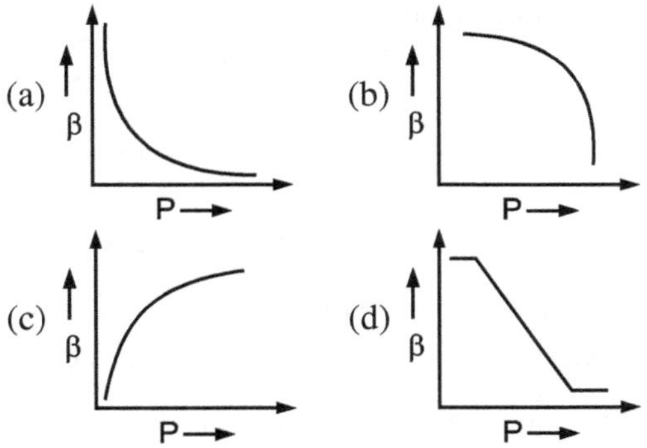

145. The process of production of heat by friction is :

(a) an adiabatic change

(b) an isothermal change

(c) A reversible change

(d) an irreversible change

146. The efficiency of a Carnot heat engine depends on the temperature of :

(a) Source only

(b) Sink only

(c) Source and sink

(d) Working substance

147. According to kinetic theory of gases, Root Mean Square (R.M.S.) velocity of a gas is directly proportional to :

(I.I.I.T. Hyd. 2000)

(a) $\sqrt{T}$ (b) T^2

(c) T (d) $1/\sqrt{T}$

148. The equation of state of some gases can be expressed as :

$$\left(P + \frac{a}{V^2}\right) = \frac{R\theta}{V}$$

where P is the pressure, V the volume, θ the absolute temperature and a and R are constants. The dimensional formula of a is :

(U.P.S.E.A.T. 2002)

(a) $ML^5 T^{-2}$ (b) $M^{-1} L^5 T^{-2}$
(c) $ML^{-1} T^{-2}$ (d) $ML^{-5} T^2$

149. For an ideal gas of diatomic molecules :

(U.P.S.E.A.T. 2002)

(a) $C_p = \frac{5}{2}R$ (b) $C_v = \frac{3}{2}R$
(c) $C_p - C_v = 2R$ (d) $C_p = \frac{7}{2}R$

150. A diatomic gas molecule has translational, rotational and vibrational degrees of freedom, then the ratio $\frac{C_p}{C_v}$ is :

(Punjab P.M.T. 2002)

(a) 1.29 (b) 1.33
(c) 1.4 (d) 1.6

151. Universal gas constant is equal to :

(Orissa J.E.E. 2003)

(a) C_p/C_v (b) $C_p - C_v$
(c) $C_p + C_v$ (d) C_v/C_p

152. A tyre kept outside in sunlight bursts after sometimes because of : **(A.F.M.C. 2005)**

(a) Increase in pressure
(b) Increase in volume
(c) Both (a) and (b)
(d) None of these

153. Gas exerts pressure on the walls of the container because :

(V.G.E.T. - M.A.H.E. Manipal 2005)

(a) Gas has weight
(b) Gas molecules have momentum
(c) Gas molecules collide with each other
(d) Gas molecules collide with the walls of the container

154. An ideal monoatomic gas at 27°C is compressed adiabatically to 8/27 times of its present volume. The increase in temperature of the gas is : **(Punjab C.E.T. 2005)**

(a) 375°C (b) 402°C
(c) 175°C (d) 475°C

155. At what temperature, is the kinetic energy of a gas molecule half of the value at 27°C ?

(Kerala P.M.T. 2007)

(a) 13.5°C (b) 150 K
(c) 75 K (d) 13.5 K

156. Absolute zero is considered at which :

(H.P.P.M.T. 2008)

(a) All molecular motion ceases
(b) Gas becomes liquid
(c) Random motion of molecules occurs
(d) Molecular energy is zero

157. Two vessels A and B having equal volume contain equal masses of hydrogen in A and helium in B at 300 K. Then, mark the correct statement :

(B.H.U. (Screening) 2008)

(a) The pressure exerted by hydrogen is half that exerted by helium.
(b) The pressure exerted by hydrogen is equal to that exerted by helium.
(c) Average K.E. of the molecule of hydrogen is half the average K.E. of the molecules of helium.
(d) The pressure exerted by hydrogen is twice that exerted by helium.

158. The root mean square velocity of gas molecules at 27°C is 1365 m/s. The gas is :

(M.P.P.E.T. 2008)

(a) O_2 (b) He
(c) N_2 (d) CO_2

159. Real gases behave ideally at :

(H.P.P.M.T. 2009)

(a) low pressure and low temperature
(b) high pressure and low temperature
(c) low pressure and high temperature
(d) none of these

160. The mean kinetic energy of one mole of gas per degree of freedom (on the basis of kinetic theory of gases) is : **(D.C.E. 2009)**

(a) $\frac{1}{2}$KT (b) $\frac{3}{2}$KT
(c) $\frac{3}{2}$RT (d) $\frac{1}{2}$RT

161. K.E per unit volume is E. The pressure exerted by the gas is given by :

(M.H.T.C.E.T. 2010)

(a) $\frac{E}{3}$ (b) $\frac{2E}{3}$
(c) $\frac{3E}{2}$ (d) $\frac{E}{2}$

162. Mean free path of a gas molecule is :

(Kerala Engg. 2010)

(a) inversely proportional to number of molecules per unit volume
(b) inversely proportional to diameter of the molecule
(c) directly proportional to the square root of the absolute temperature
(d) directly proportional to the molecular mass

163. A flask is filled with 13 grams of an ideal gas at 27°C. Its temperature is raised to 52°C. The mass of the gas that has to be released to maintain the temperature of the gas in the flask at 52°C and pressure remaining the same is:**(E.A.M.C.E.T. 2000)**

(a) 2.5 grams (b) 2.0 grams
(c) 1.5 grams (d) 1.0 gram

164. How much should the pressure of the gas be increased to decrease the volume by 10% at a constant temperature ?

(E.A.M.C.E.T. 1998)

(a) 10% (b) 9.5%
(c) 11.11% (d) 5.11%

165. A perfect gas at 27°C is heated at constant pressure so as to double its volume. The temperature of the gas will be :

(E.A.M.C.E.T. 1987)

(a) 427°C (b) 457°C
(c) 237°C (d) None of these

166. A thin brass sheet at 10°C and a thin steel sheet at 20°C have the same surface area. The common temperature at which both would have the same area is ..... (Coefficients of linear expansion for brass and steel are 19×10^{-6}/°C and 11×10^{-6}/°C respectively):

(E.A.M.C.E.T. (Med.) A.P. 2003)

(a) – 3.75°C (b) – 2.75°C
(c) 2.75°C (d) 3.75°C

167. A black body is 727°C. It emits energy at a rate which is proportional to:

(C.B.S.E., A.I.P.M.T. 2007)

(a) $(1000)^4$ (b) $(1000)^2$
(c) $(727)^4$ (d) $(727)^2$

168. Hot water cools from 60°C to 50°C in the first 10 minutes and to 42°C in the next 10 minutes. Then the temperature of the surroundings is : **(C.E.T. Karnataka 2010)**

(a) 10°C (b) 15°C
(c) 30°C (d) 20°C

169. The absorptivity of a perfectly black body is:

(Kerala C.E.T. 2009)

(a) 0 (b) 1
(c) less than 1 (d) infinity

170. On a new scale of temperature (which is linear) called the W scale, the freezing and boiling points of water are 39°W and 239°W respectively. What will be the temperature on the new scale, corresponding to a temperature of 39°C on the Celsius scale ?

(C.B.S.E., P.M.T. 2008)

(a) 117° W (b) 200° W
(c) 139° W (d) 78° W

171. 100 g of water is heated from 30°C to 50°C. Ignoring the slight expansion of the water, the change in its internal energy is : **(A.I.E.E.E. 2011)**

(specific heat of water is 4184 J/ kg/ K)

(a) 2.1 kJ (b) 4.2 kJ
(c) 8.4 kJ (d) 84 kJ

172. When a real diatomic gas ($\gamma = 1.4$) is heated at constant pressure, what is the fraction (approximate) of the heat energy supplied which increases the internal energy of the gas ? **(S.C.R.A. 2007)**

(a) 0.2 (b) 0.3
(c) 0.5 (d) 0.7

173. Two moles of oxygen are mixed with eight moles of helium. The effective specific heat of the mixture at constant volume is : **(Kerala P.E.T. 2007)**

(a) 1.3 R (b) 1.4 R
(c) 1.7 R (d) 1.9 R
(e) 1.2 R

174. In an adiabatic process, pressure is increased by $\frac{2}{3}$ %. If $\frac{C_p}{C_v} \cdot \frac{3}{2}$, then the volume decreases by about : **(B.H.U. Screening 2008)**

(a) $\frac{4}{9}$ % (b) $\frac{2}{3}$ %
(c) 4 % (d) $\frac{9}{4}$ %

175. Which one of the following is not correct ? **(H.P.P.M.T. 2009)**

(a) Pressure $\longrightarrow$ Intensive variable
(b) Temperature $\longrightarrow$ Intensive variable
(c) Internal energy $\longrightarrow$ Extensive variable
(d) Volume $\longrightarrow$ Extensive variable

176. If ΔU and ΔW represent the increase in internal energy and work done by the system respectively in a thermodynamical process, which of the following is true ? **(A.I.P.M.T. 2010)**

(a) $\Delta U = -\Delta W$, in an adiabatic process
(b) $\Delta U = \Delta W$, in an isothermal process
(c) $\Delta U = \Delta W$, in an adiabatic process
(d) $\Delta U = -\Delta W$, in an isothermal process

177. If the radius of star is R and it acts as a black body, what would be the temperature of the star, in which the rate of energy production of Q ? **(C.B.S.E. 2012)**

(a) $\left(\frac{a}{4\pi R^2 \sigma}\right)^{1/4}$ (b) $\frac{Q}{4\pi R^2 \sigma}$
(c) $\left(\frac{a}{4\pi^2 \sigma}\right)^{-1/2}$ (d) $\left(\frac{4\pi R^2 Q}{\sigma}\right)^{1/4}$

178. At what temperature does the average translational K.E. of a molecule in a gas become equal to K.E. of an electron accelerated from rest through potential difference of V volt ? All symbols have their usual meaning. **(MHT-CET 2012)**

(a) $\frac{2eVN}{3R}$ (b) $\frac{3R}{2eVN}$
(c) $\frac{NeV}{R}$ (d) $\frac{2NeV}{R}$

179. What will be r.m.s. speed of a gas at 800°K? **(MHT-CET 2012)**

(a) four times the values at 200°K
(b) half the value at 200°K
(c) twice the value at 200°K
(d) same as at 200°K

180. When 1 gm of water at 100°C is completely converted to steam at 100°C, occupies 1650 cc. The increase in the internal energy of the molecules is ...... (atmospheric pressure = 10^5 Pa, L = 540 cal/gm and J = 4.2 J/cal) **(MHT-CET 2011)**

(a) 2103 J (b) 2310 J
(c) 210 J (d) 375 J

181. If a gas expands under isothermal condition, then what happens to r.m.s. velocity ? **(MHT-CET 2011)**

(a) Increases
(b) Decreases
(d) Remains constant
(d) Cannot be predicted

182. The total radiant energy per unit area normal to the direction of incidence, received a distance R from the centre of a star of radius r, whose outer surface radiates as a black body at a temperature T K is given by **(C.B.S.E. 2010)**

(a) $\frac{\sigma r^4 T^4}{r^4}$ (b) $\frac{4\pi\sigma r^4 T^4}{R^4}$

(c) $\frac{\sigma r^4 T^4}{R^2}$ (d) $\frac{\sigma r^2 T^4}{4\pi r^2}$

183. A black body at 227°C radiates heat at the rate of 7 cal/cm^{2}s. At a temperature of 727°C, the rate of heat radiated in the same units will be **(C.B.S.E. 2009)**

(a) 50 (b) 112
(c) 80 (d) 60

184. In thermodynamic processes which of the following statements is not true ? **(C.B.S.E. 2009)**

(a) In an isochoric process pressure remains constant
(b) In an isothermal process the temperature remains constant
(c) In an adiabatic process PV^{γ} = constant
(d) In an adiabatic process the system is insulated from the surroundings.

185. Emissive power of black body is 81 J/m^2, when it is at 300 K and emissivity of ordinary body is 0.8, when it is at 500 K. What is the emissive power of an ordinary body ? **(MHT-CET 2008)**

(a) 500 J/m^{2}s (b) 600 J/m^{2}s
(c) 800 J/m^{2}s (d) 400 J/m^{2}s

186. S.I. unit of Wein's constant is **(MHT-CET 2008)**

(a) mK (b) cal/m^2
(c) J/m^2 (d) K/m

187. Two gases have densities in the ratio 2 : 3 and pressures exerted are in the ratio 3 : 2. Then the ratio of their r.m.s. velocities is **(MHT-CET 2008)**

(a) 2 : 3 (b) 3 : 2
(c) 1 : 3 (d) 6 : 8

188. Kinetic energy per unit volume of a gas is E, then the pressure exerted by the gas is **(MHT-CET 2008)**

(a) 3/2E (b) 2/3E
(c) 1/3E (d) E

189. According to Prevost's theory of heat exchange, the heat exchange shops at **(MHT-CET 2007)**

(a) 0°C (b) – 5°C
(c) – 273°C (d) – 273 K

190. A body radiates heat at the rate of 5 cal/m^{2}s when its temperature is 227°C. The heat radiated by the same body, when its temperature is 727°C is **(MHT-CET 2007)**

(a) 10 cal/m^{2}s (b) 20 cal/m^{2}s
(c) 40 cal/m^{2}s (d) 80 cal/m^{2}s

191. For an ideal gas, $\frac{C_v}{C_p}$ is **(MHT-CET 2007)**

(a) < 1 (b) > 1
(c) = 1 (d) ≥ 1

192. In the condensation of gas the mean K.E. (K) and potential energy (U) of molecules changes; thus **(J.I.P.M.E.R. 2003)**

(a) K increases, U keeps constant
(b) K keeps constant, U decreases
(c) K decreases, U increases
(d) K decreases, U decreases

193. A body cools from 60°C to 50°C in 10 minutes. If the room temperature is 25°C and assuming Newton's law of cooling to hold good, the temperature of the body at the end of the next 10 minutes will be **(J.I.P.M.E.R. 2003)**
(a) 40°C (b) 38.5°C
(c) 45°C (d) 42.85°C

194. The temperature of equal masses of three different liquids A, B and C are 12°C, 19°C and 28°C respectively. The temperature when A and B are mixed is 16°C, when B and C are mixed is 23°C, what is the temperature when A and C are mixed ? **(J.I.P.M.E.R. 2003)**
(a) 28°C (b) 31°C
(c) 20.26°C (d) 19.5°C

195. If a = 0.72, r = 0.24, then value of t is **(MHT-CET 2003)**
(a) 0.02 (b) 0.04
(c) 0.4 (d) 0.2

196. Emissivity of perfectly black body is **(MHT-CET 2003)**
(a) 1 (b) 2
(c) 5 (d) 0

197. If 3 kg of mass is converted into energy, the energy released is **(MHT-CET 2003)**
(a) 9×10^8 J (b) 9×10^{16} J
(c) 27×10^8 J (d) 27×10^{16} J

198. K.E. per unit volume is given by **(MHT-CET 2003)**
(a) $E = \frac{3}{2}P$ (b) $E = \frac{2}{3}P$
(c) $E = \frac{1}{2}mv^2$ (d) none of these

199. Absolute zero is the condition at which **(A.F.M.C. 2003)**
(a) molecular motion ceases
(b) gas becomes liquid
(c) gas cannot be liquefied
(d) random motion of molecules occur

200. A black body is at a temperature 300 K. It emits energy of a rate which is proportional to **(A.I.I.M.S. 2002)**
(a) 300 (b) $(300)^3$
(c) $(300)^2$ (d) $(300)^4$

201. Energy supplied to convert unit mass of substances from solid to liquid state at its melting point is called **(MHT-CET 2003)**
(a) latent heat of fusion
(b) evaporation
(c) solidification
(d) latent heat of fission

202. A unit mass of solid is converted to liquid at its melting point. The heat required for this process is **(MHT-CET 2003)**
(a) specific heat
(b) latent heat of vaporization
(c) latent heat of fusion
(d) external latent heat

203. The dimensions of thermal resistance are **(J.I.P.M.E.R. 2004)**
(a) $[ML^2T^{-2}K^{-2}]$ (b) $[ML^2T^{-3}K]$
(c) $[ML^2T^{-2}K^{-1}]$ (d) $[M^{-1}L^{-2}T^3K]$

204. When water is heated from 0°C to 10°C, its volume **(Kerala P.M.T. 2005)**
(a) increases
(b) does not change
(c) decreases
(d) first decreases and then increases

205. Internal latent heat of ice is **(MHT-CET 2006)**
(a) greater than latent heat
(b) less than latent heat
(c) equal to latent heat
(d) equal to half that of latent heat

206. Pressure at the triple point of water is **(MHT-CET 2007)**
(a) 4 N/m^2 (b) 760 mm of Hg
(c) 5440 Pa (d) 0.544 mm of Hg

207. The two ends of a rod of length L and a uniform cross-sectional area A are kept at two temperatures T_1 and T_2 ($T_1 > T_2$). The rate of heat transfer, $\frac{dQ}{dT}$ through the rod in a steady state is given by **(C.B.S.E. 2009)**

(a) $\frac{dQ}{dT} = \frac{K(T_1 - T_2)}{LA}$

(b) $\frac{dQ}{dT} = KLA\,(T_1 - T_2)$

(c) $\frac{dQ}{dT} = \frac{KLA\,(T_1 - T_2)}{L}$

(d) $\frac{dQ}{dT} = \frac{KLA\,(T_1 - T_2)}{A}$

208. When 1 kg of ice at 0°C melts into water at 0°C, the resulting change in its entropy, taking latent heat of ice to be 80 cal/°C is

(a) 273 cal/K (b) 8×10^4 cal/K

(c) 80 cal/K (d) 293 cal/K

ANSWER KEY

1. (a)	**2.** (a)	**3.** (d)	**4.** (a)	**5.** (c)	**6.** (c)	**7.** (a)	**8.** (c)	**9.** (c)	**10.**(d)
11. (a)	**12.**(b)	**13.**(b)	**14.**(c)	**15.**(b)	**16.**(b)	**17.**(a)	**18.**(a)	**19.**(c)	**20.**(b)
21.(a)	**22.**(a)	**23.**(a)	**24.**(d)	**25.**(c)	**26.**(b)	**27.**(b)	**28.**(a)	**29.**(b)	**30.**(d)
31.(a)	**32.**(d)	**33.**(b)	**34.**(b)	**35.**(a)	**36.**(c)	**37.**(c)	**38.**(c)	**39.**(a)	**40.**(d)
41.(c)	**42.**(a)	**43.**(b)	**44.**(b)	**45.**(c)	**46.**(d)	**47.**(a)	**48.**(b)	**49.**(b)	**50.**(c)
51.(c)	**52.**(c)	**53.**(c)	**54.**(a)	**55.**(a)	**56.**(a)	**57.**(d)	**58.**(b)	**59.**(c)	**60.**(b)
61.(a)	**62.**(a)	**63.**(a)	**64.**(b)	**65.**(c)	**66.**(c)	**67.**(a)	**68.**(b)	**69.**(c)	**70.**(d)
71.(a)	**72.**(d)	**73.**(c)	**74.**(b)	**75.**(c)	**76.**(a)	**77.**(d)	**78.**(d)	**79.**(b)	**80.**(c)
81.(c)	**82.**(d)	**83.**(c)	**84.**(c)	**85.**(a)	**86.**(c)	**87.**(a)	**88.**(b)	**89.**(a)	**90.**(c)
91.(d)	**92.**(c)	**93.**(c)	**94.**(a)	**95.**(c)	**96.**(c)	**97.**(a)	**98.**(c)	**99.**(d)	**100.**(b)
101.(b)	**102.**(b)	**103.**(b)	**104.**(b)	**105.**(c)	**106.**(c)	**107.**(c)	**108.**(d)	**109.** (a)	**110.**(d)
111.(d)	**112.**(c)	**113.**(d)	**114.**(a)	**115.**(a)	**116.**(b)	**117.**(b)	**118.**(a)	**119.** (a)	**120.**(a)
121.(c)	**122.**(b)	**123.**(a)	**124.**(c)	**125.**(a)	**126.**(b)	**127.**(d)	**128.**(b)	**129.** (a)	**130.**(b)
131.(a)	**132.**(d)	**133.**(a)	**134.**(d)	**135.**(a)	**136.**(a)	**137.** (a)	**138.** (a)	**139.** (a)	**140.** b,c
141. (a)	**142.** (c)	**143.** (a)	**144.** (a)	**145.** (d)	**146.** (c)	**147.** (a)	**148.** (a)	**149.** (d)	**150.** (a)
151. (b)	**152.** (a)	**153.** (d)	**154.** (a)	**155.** (b)	**156.** (a)	**157.** (d)	**158.** (b)	**159.** (c)	**160.** (d)
161. (b)	**162.** (a)	**163.** (d)	**164.** (c)	**165.** (d)	**166.** (a)	**167.** (a)	**168.** (a)	**169.** (b)	**170.** (a)
171. (c)	**172.** (d)	**173.** (a)	**174.** (a)	**175.** (d)	**176.** (a)	**177.** (a)	**178.** (a)	**179.** (c)	**180.** (a)
181. (c)	**182.** (c)	**183.** (b)	**184.** (a)	**185.** (a)	**186.** (a)	**187.** (b)	**188.** (b)	**189.** (c)	**190.** (d)
191. (a)	**192.** (b)	**193.** (d)	**194.** (c)	**195.** (b)	**196.** (a)	**197.** (d)	**198.** (a)	**199.** (a)	**200.** (d)
201. (a)	**202.** (c)	**203.** (d)	**204.** (d)	**205.** (a)	**206.** (c)	**207.** (c)	**208.** (d)		

✍ ✍ ✍

10

OSCILLATIONS AND WAVES

MULTIPLE CHOICE QUESTIONS

PART - I

1. A pendulum bob has a speed of 3 ms^{-1} at its lowest position. The pendulum is 0.5 m long. The speed of the bob when the string makes an angle of 60° to the vertical will be ($g = 10\ ms^{-1}$) :

(a) $\frac{1}{3}$ m/s (b) $\frac{1}{2}$ m/s

(c) 2 m/s (d) 3 m/s

2. The time period of a body executing S.H.M. is 0.05 sec and amplitude of vibration is 4 cm. The maximum velocity of the body will be :

(a) 1.6π m/s (b) 2π m/s

(c) 3.1 m/s (d) 4π m/s

3. The acceleration of a particle in S.H.M. is :

(a) always constant

(b) always zero

(c) maximum at extreme position

(d) maximum at mean position

4. The kinetic energy and potential energy of a particle executing S.H.M. will be equal when displacement (amplitude = a) is :

(a) $a\sqrt{2}$ (b) $\frac{a}{2}$

(c) $\frac{a}{\sqrt{2}}$ (d) $\frac{a\sqrt{2}}{2}$

5. A mass m is suspended from a spring of negligible mass. The spring is pulled a little and then released so that the mass executes simple harmonic oscillation with a time period T. If the mass is increased by m, then the time becomes $\left[\frac{5}{4}T\right]$. The ratio of m/M is :

(a) 9/16 (b) 4/5

(c) 5/4 (d) 25/16

6. A large horizontal surface moves up and down in simple harmonic motion with an amplitude of 1 cm. If a mass of 10 kg (which is placed on its surface) is to remain continuously in contact with it, the frequency of SHM should not exceed :

(a) 0.5 Hz (b) 1.5 Hz

(c) 5.0 Hz (d) 10.5 Hz

7. When a particle oscillates simple harmonically, its P.E. varies periodically. If the frequency of oscillation of the particle is n, the frequency of P.E. variation is :

(a) $\frac{n}{2}$ (b) n

(c) $2n$ (d) $4n$

8. The S.H.M. of a particle is given by the equation $y = 3 \sin \omega t + 4 \cos \omega t$. The amplitude is :

(a) 5 (b) 7

(c) 12 (d) 1

9. If the length of second's pendulum is increased by 2%, how many seconds will it lose per day ?

(a) 3927 s (b) 3727 s

(c) 3427 s (d) 864 s

10. The displacement y of a particle executing periodic motion is given by :

$$y = 4\cos^2\frac{t}{2}\sin 1000\,t$$

This expression may be considered to be a result of the superposition of how many independent harmonic motions ?

(a) Five (b) Two

(c) Three (d) Four

11. The percentage change in the time period of a simple pendulum if its length is increased by 4% is :

(a) 2% (b) 4%

(c) 6% (d) No change

12. If the period of oscillation of mass m suspended from a spring is 2 s, then the period of mass $4m$ will be :

(a) 1 s (b) 2 s

(c) 3 s (d) 4 s

13. If the displacement of a particle executing S.H.M. is given by :

$$y = 0.30\sin(220\,t + 0.64)$$

in metres, then the frequency and maximum velocity of the particle is :

(a) 35 Hz, 132 m/s (b) 35 Hz, 66 m/s

(c) 45 Hz, 66 m/s (d) 58 Hz, 113 m/s

14. A particle starts S.H.M. from the mean position. Its amplitude is A and time period T. At the time when its speed is half of the maximum speed, its displacement y is :

(a) $\frac{A}{\sqrt{2}}$ (b) $\frac{A}{2}$

(c) $\frac{A\sqrt{3}}{2}$ (d) $\frac{2A}{\sqrt{3}}$

15. A body executing S.H.M. has a maximum acceleration equal to 24 ms^{-2} and maximum velocity equal to 16 ms^{-1}. The amplitude of S.H.M. is :

(a) $\frac{1024}{9}$ m (b) $\frac{64}{9}$ m

(c) $\frac{32}{3}$ m (d) $\frac{3}{32}$ m

16. A large horizontal surface moves up and down in S.H.M. with an amplitude of 1 cm. If a mass of 10 kg (which is placed on the surface) is to remain continuously in contact with it, the maximum frequency of S.H.M. will be :

(a) 5 Hz (b) 0.5 Hz

(c) 1.5 Hz (d) 10 Hz

17. The period of a simple pendulum is doubled when :

(a) the mass of the bob is doubled

(b) its length is made four times

(c) its length is doubled

(d) the mass of bob and the length of the pendulum is doubled

18. A particle is vibrating in S.H.M. with an amplitude of 4 cm. At what displacement from the equilibrium position is its energy half potential and half kinetic ?

(a) 1 cm (b) $\sqrt{2}$ cm

(c) $2\sqrt{2}$ cm (d) 4 cm

19. A body is executing S.H.M. when its displacement from the mean position is 4 cm and 5 cm, the corresponding velocity of the body is 10 cm/sec and 8 cm/sec. Then the time period of the body is :

(a) $\frac{\pi}{2}$ seconds (b) π seconds

(c) $\frac{3\pi}{2}$ seconds (d) 2π seconds

20. When the displacement is half of the amplitude, then what fraction of the total energy of S.H.M. oscillator is K.E. ?

(a) $\frac{5}{7}^{th}$ (b) $\frac{2}{9}^{th}$

(c) $\frac{2}{7}^{th}$ (d) $\frac{3}{4}^{th}$

21. When the potential energy of a particle executing S.H.M. is one fourth of its maximum value during oscillation, the displacement of the particle, from the equilibrium position in terms of its amplitude a is :

(a) $\frac{a}{4}$ (b) $\frac{a}{3}$

(c) $\frac{a}{2}$ (d) $\frac{2a}{3}$

22. In a simple pendulum, if K.E. is one fourth of the total energy, then the relation between displacement (X) and amplitude (A) is :

(a) X = 2A (b) X = A

(c) $X = \frac{\sqrt{3}}{2}A$ (d) $X = \frac{\sqrt{3}}{4}A$

23. A particle executes S.H.M. with a frequency υ, then the frequency with which its kinetic energy oscillates is :

(a) 4 υ (b) 2 υ

(c) υ (d) υ/2

24. A body is executing S.H.M. of amplitude A. The displacement between maximum K.E. and maximum P.E. position for the particle executing S.H.M. is :

(a) $\pm\frac{A}{2}$ (b) zero

(c) $\pm$ A (d) A^2

25. A particle of mass 10 gm is executing S.H.M. with an amplitude of 0.5 m and periodic time (π/5) seconds. The maximum value of the force acting on the particle is :

(a) 25 N (b) 5 N

(c) 2.5 N (d) 0.5 N

26. The kinetic energy of a particle executing S.H.M. is 16 J when it is in its mean position. If the amplitude of oscillation is 25 cm and mass of the particle is 5.12 kg, then the time period of oscillation is :

(a) $\frac{\pi}{5}$ seconds (b) 2π seconds

(c) 5π seconds (d) 20π seconds

27. The force constant of a weightless spring is 16 Nm^{-1}. A body of mass 1.0 kg suspended from it is pulled down through 5 cm and then released. The maximum kinetic energy of the system (spring + body) will be :

(a) 16×10^{-2} J (b) 8×10^{-2} J

(c) 4×10^{-2} J (d) 2×10^{-2} J

28. A particle of mass 10 gm is executing S.H.M. along a straight line with a period of 2 seconds and amplitude of 10 cm. Its kinetic energy when it is 5 cm from its equilibrium position is :

(a) $0.375\pi^2$ ergs (b) $3.75\pi^2$ cm

(c) $37.5\pi^2$ ergs (d) $375\pi^2$ ergs

29. The period of oscillation of a mass m suspended from a spring is 2 seconds. If along with it another mass 2 kg is also suspended, the period of oscillation increases by one second. The mass m will be:

(a) 2.6 kg (b) 2 kg

(c) 1.6 kg (d) 1 kg

30. Two springs of spring constants 1500 Nm^{-1} and 3000 Nm^{-1} respectively are stretched with the same force. They will have potential energies in the ratio :

(a) 4 : 1 (b) 2 : 1

(c) 1 : 4 (d) 1 : 2

31. When the potential energy of a particle executing S.H.M. is half of the maximum value during oscillations, its displacement from the equilibrium position in terms of its amplitude a is :

(a) $\frac{2a}{3}$ (b) $\frac{a}{\sqrt{2}}$

(c) $\frac{a}{3}$ (d) $\frac{a}{4}$

32. For a particle executing S.H.M. which of the following statements is not correct ?

(a) Total energy of the particle always remains the same.

(b) Restoring force is always directed towards a fixed point.

(c) Restoring force is maximum at the extreme position.

(d) Acceleration of the particle is maximum at the equilibrium position.

33. The kinetic energy of a particle, executing S.H.M. is 16 J, when it is at its mean position. If the amplitude of oscillations is 25 cm and mass of the particle is 5.12 kg, the time period of its oscillations is :

(a) 20π sec (b) 5π sec

(c) 2π sec (d) $\frac{\pi}{5}$ sec

34. Two simple pendulums each of length 0.5 m respectively are given small linear displacements in one direction at the same time. They will again be in the phase when the pendulum of shorter length has completed oscillations :

(a) 5 (b) 3

(c) 2 (d) 1

35. An instantaneous displacement of a simple harmonic oscillator is $x = A\cos\left[\omega t + \frac{\pi}{4}\right]$.

Its speed will be maximum at the time :

(a) $\frac{2\pi}{\omega}$ (b) $\frac{\pi}{\omega}$

(c) $\frac{\pi}{2\omega}$ (d) $\frac{\pi}{4\omega}$

36. A mass m is vertically suspended from a spring of negligible mass. The system oscillates with a frequency (υ). What will be the frequency of the system if a mass 4 m is suspended from the same spring ?

(a) 4υ (b) 2υ

(c) $\frac{\upsilon}{2}$ (d) $\frac{\upsilon}{4}$

37. A spring 40 mm long is stretched by the application of a force. If 10 N force is required to stretch the spring through 1 mm, then work done in stretching the spring through 40 mm is :

(a) 8 J (b) 23 J

(c) 68 J (d) 84 J

38. If a simple pendulum oscillates with an amplitude 50 mm and time period of 2 s, then its maximum velocity is :

(a) 0.8 ms^{-1} (b) 0.16 ms^{-1}

(c) 0.15 ms^{-1} (d) 0.10 ms^{-1}

39. In a sinusoidal wave, the time required for a particular point to move from maximum displacement to zero displacement is 0.170 s. The frequency of the wave is :

(a) 1.47 Hz (b) 0.36 Hz

(c) 0.73 Hz (d) 2.94 Hz

40. To double the frequency of an oscillator, we have to :

(a) double the mass

(b) reduce the mass to half

(c) quadruple the mass

(d) reduce the mass to one fourth

41. The acceleration of a particle performing S.H.M. is 12 cm s^{-2} at a distance of 3 cm from the mean position. Its time period is :

(a) 0.5 second (b) 1.0 second

(c) 2.0 seconds (d) 3.14 seconds

42. A linear oscillator of force constant 2×10^6 Nm^{-1} and amplitude 0.01 m has a total mechanical energy of 160 J. Its :

(a) maximum P.E. is 260 J

(b) maximum P.E. is 100 J

(c) maximum K.E. is 100 J

(d) minimum P.E. is zero.

43. A particle starts S.H.M. from the mean position as shown in the following figure. Its amplitude is a, and time period is T. At what displacement, is its speed half of its maximum speed ?

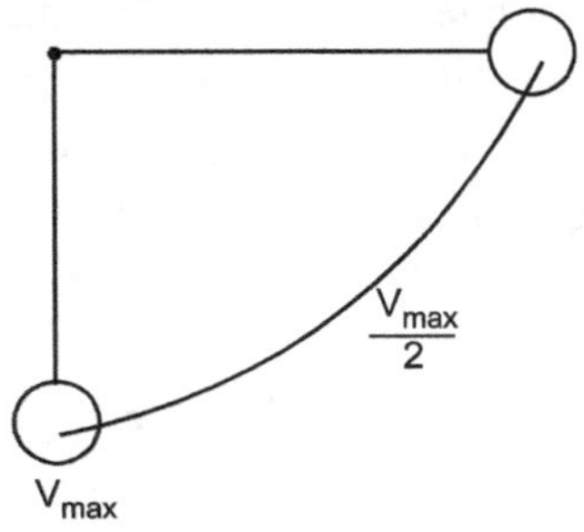

(a) $\frac{\sqrt{3}a}{2}$ (b) $\frac{\sqrt{2}a}{3}$

(c) $\frac{2a}{\sqrt{3}}$ (d) $\frac{3a}{\sqrt{2}}$

44. Two mutually perpendicular simple harmonic vibrations have the same amplitude, frequency and phase. When they superimpose, the resultant form of vibration will be :

(a) A straight line (b) A parabola

(c) A circle (d) an ellipse.

45. A spring having spring constant k is loaded with a mass 'm'. The spring is cut into two equal parts and one of this is loaded again with the same mass. The new spring constant is :

(a) k (b) $2k$

(c) $k/2$ (d) k^2

46. A simple pendulum is suspended from the roof of a trolley which moves in a horizontal direction with an acceleration a, then the time period T is given by $T = 2\pi\sqrt{\frac{l}{g'}}$, where g' is :

(a) g (b) $g - a$

(c) $g + a$ (d) $\sqrt{g^2 + a^2}$

47. The length of the simple pendulum is increased by 1%. Its time period will :

(a) increase by 2% (b) increase by 1%

(c) decrease by 0.5 % (d) increase by 0.5%

48. For a simple pendulum, the graph between length of pendulum (L) and time period (T) will be :

(a) a straight line (b) a hyperbola

(c) a curved line (d) a parabola

49. Two waves of the same frequency and same amplitude respectively, superimpose producing resultant wave of the same amplitude, then the wave differs in phase by:

(a) $\pi/3$ (b) $2\pi/3$

(c) $\pi/4$ (d) Zero

50. A particle with restoring force proportional to displacement and restoring force proportional to velocity is subjected to a force F sin ωt. If the amplitude is maximum for $\omega = \omega_1$ and the energy of the particle is maximum for $\omega = \omega_2$, then :

(a) $\omega_1 = \omega_0$ and $\omega_2 = \omega_0$

(b) $\omega_1 = \omega_0$ and $\omega_2 \neq \omega_0$

(c) $\omega_1 \neq \omega_0$ and $\omega_2 = \omega_0$

(d) $\omega_1 \neq \omega_0$ and $\omega_2 \neq \omega_0$

51. When a particle oscillates simple harmonically, its kinetic energy varies periodically. If frequency of the particle is n, the frequency of the kinetic energy is :

(a) $n/2$ (b) n

(c) $2n$ (d) $4n$

52. How long after the beginning of motion is the displacement of a harmonically oscillating point equal to one half its amplitude, if the period is 24 seconds and the initial phase is zero ?

(a) 12 seconds (b) 2 seconds

(c) 4 seconds (d) 6 seconds

53. The K.E. and P.E. of a particle executing S.H.M. with amplitude A will be equal when its displacement is :

(a) $A\sqrt{2}$ (b) $\frac{A}{2}$

(c) $\frac{A}{\sqrt{2}}$ (d) $A\sqrt{\frac{2}{3}}$

54. A particle of mass 200 gm executes S.H.M. and the restoring force is provided by a spring of force constant 80 Nm^{-1}. The time period of oscillation is :

(a) 0.05 sec (b) 0.314 sec

(c) 0.02 sec (d) 0.15 sec

55. A simple pendulum executing S.H.M. is falling freely along with the support, then :

(a) its periodic time increases

(b) it does not oscillate at all

(c) its periodic time decreases

(d) none of these

56. A particle moves such that its acceleration a is given as $a = -by$ where y is the displacement from equilibrium position and b is constant, then the period of oscillation is:

(a) $2\sqrt{\frac{\pi}{b}}$ (b) $\frac{2\pi}{b}$

(c) $\frac{2\pi}{\sqrt{b}}$ (d) $2\pi\sqrt{b}$

57. A block of mass m, attached to a spring of spring constant k, oscillates on a smooth horizontal table. The other end of the spring is fixed to a wall. The block has a speed v, when the spring is at its natural length. Before coming to an instantaneous rest, if the block moves a distance x from the mean position, then :

(a) $x = v\sqrt{\frac{m}{k}}$ (b) $x = \frac{1}{v}\sqrt{\frac{m}{k}}$

(c) $x = \sqrt{\frac{m}{k}}$ (d) $x = \sqrt{\frac{mv}{k}}$

58. A clock which keeps correct time at 20°C, is subjected to 40°C. If the coefficient of linear expansion of the pendulum is 12×10^{-6} per °C, how much will it gain or lose in time ?

(a) 20.6 seconds/day (b) 20 seconds/day

(c) 10.3 seconds/day (d) 5 seconds/day

59. If a spring extends to x on loading, then the energy stored by the spring is .... (if T is the tension in the spring and k is the spring constant)

(a) $\frac{T^2}{2x}$ (b) $\frac{T^2}{2k}$

(c) $\frac{2T^2}{k}$ (d) $\frac{2k}{T^2}$

60. A particle is performing S.H.M. along the x-axis with amplitude 4 cm and time period 1.2 sec. The minimum time taken by the particle to move from $x = 2$ to $x = 4$ cm and back again is given by :

(a) 0.6 sec (b) 0.4 sec

(c) 0.3 sec (d) 0.1 sec

61. A body executes S.H.M. under the influence of one force with a time period of 3 sec and the same body executes S.H.M. with a time period of 4 seconds under the influence of a second force. When both the forces act simultaneously, the time period of the same body is :

(a) 7 seconds

(b) 5 seconds

(c) $2\sqrt{2}$ seconds

(d) 3.4 seconds

62. A mass m is suspended from two coupled springs connected in series. The force constant for the springs are k_1 and k_2. The time period of the suspended mass will be :

(a) $T = 2\pi\sqrt{\left[\frac{m}{k_1 - k_2}\right]}$

(b) $T = 2\pi\sqrt{\left[\frac{mk_1k_2}{k_1 + k_2}\right]}$

(c) $T = 2\pi\sqrt{\left[\frac{m}{k_1 + k_2}\right]}$

(d) $T = 2\pi\sqrt{\left[\frac{m(k_1 + k_2)}{k_1\,k_2}\right]}$

63. A simple pendulum with a bob of mass m oscillates from A to C and back to A such that PB = H. If the acceleration due to gravity is g, then the velocity of the bob as it passes through B is :

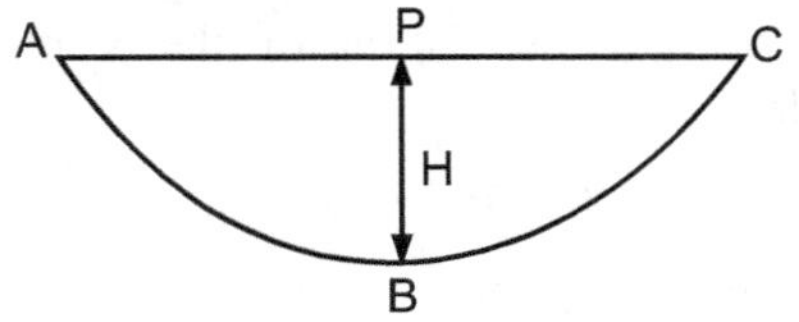

(a) zero (b) 2gH

(c) mgH (d) $\sqrt{2gH}$

64. The average energy in one time period of a simple harmonic oscillator whose amplitude is A, angular velocity ω and mass m is :

(a) $\frac{1}{4}m\omega^2A^2$ (b) $\frac{1}{2}m\omega^2A^2$

(c) $m\omega^2A^2$ (d) zero

65. Two springs of constants k_1 and k_2 have equal highest velocities when executing S.H.M. Then the ratio of their amplitude (given their masses are equal) will be :

(a) k_1/k_2 (b) $(k_1 / k_2)^{1/2}$

(c) k_2/k_1 (d) $(k_2 / k_1)^{1/2}$

66. A vertical mass spring system executes simple harmonic oscillations with a period of 2 seconds. A quantity of this system which exhibits simple harmonic vibration with a period of second is :

(a) Velocity

(b) Potential energy

(c) Phase difference between acceleration and displacement

(d) Difference between kinetic energy and potential energy

67. The total energy of simple harmonic motion is E. What will be the kinetic energy of the particle when displacement is half of the amplitude ?

(a) $3E/4$ (b) $E/2$

(c) $E/4$ (d) $E/3$

68. A particle vibrates in S.H.M. along a straight line. Its greatest acceleration is $5\pi^2$ cms^{-2} and when its distance from the equilibrium position is 4 cm, the velocity of the particle is 3π cms^{-1}. The amplitude and the period of oscillation of the vibrating particle is :

(a) 10 cm, 4 seconds

(b) 5 cm, 2 seconds

(c) 5 cm, 4 seconds

(d) 10 cm, 2 seconds

69. The displacement x of a particle in motion is given in terms of time by,

$x(x-4) = 1 - 5\cos \omega t$. This implies :

(a) The particle executes S.H.M.

(b) The particle executes oscillatory motion which is not S.H.M.

(c) The motion of the particle is neither oscillatory nor simple harmonic.

(d) The particle is not acted upon by a force when it is at $x = y$.

70. The amplitude of a damped oscillator becomes one half in one minute. The amplitude after 3 minutes will be $1/n$ times the original, where n is :

(a) 2×3 (b) 2^3

(c) 3^2 (d) 3×2^2

71. The displacement y (in metres) of a particle performing S.H.M. is related to time t (in second) as $y = 0.05 \cos\left[4\pi t + \frac{\pi}{4}\right]$. The frequency of motion will be :

(a) 2.0 Hz (b) 1.5 Hz

(c) 1.0 Hz (d) 0.5 Hz

72. Two simple harmonic motions act on a particle. These harmonic motions are,

$x = A\cos(\omega t + \delta)$

$y = A\cos(\omega t + \alpha)$

where, $\delta = \alpha + \frac{\pi}{2}$. The resulting motion is :

(a) a circle and the actual motion is counter-clockwise

(b) a circle and the actual motion is clockwise

(c) an ellipse and the actual motion is clockwise

(d) an ellipse and the actual motion is counter-clockwise.

73. If a body is released into a tunnel dug along the diameter of the earth of radius R_0, it executes S.H.M. with time period :

(a) $T = 2\pi\sqrt{\frac{2R_0}{g}}$ (b) $T = 2\pi\sqrt{\frac{R_0}{g}}$

(c) $T = 2\pi\sqrt{\frac{R_0}{2g}}$ (d) 2

74. A simple pendulum of length l has a bob of mass m, with a charge q on it. A vertical sheet of charge, with surface change density σ passes through the point of suspension. At equilibrium, the spring makes an angle θ with the vertical. Its time period of oscillation is T in this position. Then :

(a) $\tan\theta = \frac{\sigma q}{2\varepsilon_0 mg}$ (b) $\tan\theta = \frac{\sigma q}{\varepsilon_0 mg}$

(c) $T > 2\pi\sqrt{\frac{l}{g}}$ (d) $T = 2\pi\sqrt{\frac{l}{g}}$

75. Ratio of average potential energy and kinetic energy in S.H.M. will be :

(a) 1 : 1 (b) 2 : 1

(c) 3 : 2 (d) 2 : 3

76. The bob of a pendulum of length L is pulled aside from its equilibrium position through an angle θ and then released. The bob will then pass through its equilibrium position with a speed v, where v equals :

(a) $\sqrt{2gL(1+\sin\theta)}$

(b) $\sqrt{2gL(1+\cos\theta)}$

(c) $\sqrt{2gL(1-\cos\theta)}$

(d) $\sqrt{2gL(1-\sin\theta)}$

77. Two simple harmonic motions with the same frequency act on a particle at right angles along the x-axis and y-axis. If the two amplitudes are equal and the phase difference is $\frac{\pi}{2}$, the resultant motion will be :

(a) a straight line inclined at 45° to the x-axis

(b) an ellipse with the major axis along the x-axis

(c) an ellipse with the major axis along the y-axis

(d) a circle

78. The bob of a simple pendulum is displaced from its equilibrium position O to a position Q which is at height h above O and the bob is then released. Assuming the mass of the bob to be m and time period of oscillations to be 2.0 seconds, the tension in the string when the bob passes through O is :

(a) $m(g + 2\pi^2 h)$ (b) $m(g + \pi^2 h)$

(c) $m\left[g + \frac{\pi^2}{2}h\right]$ (d) $m\left[\frac{\pi^2}{3}h\right]$

79. A particle has simple harmonic motion. The equation of its motion is $y = 5\sin\left[4t - \frac{\pi}{6}\right]$ where, y is the displacement. If the displacement of the particle is 3 units, then its velocity is :

(a) 16 (b) 20

(c) $\frac{5}{6}\pi$ (d) $\frac{2}{3}\pi$

80. A block is placed on a frictional horizontal surface. The mass of the block is m and springs are attached on either side with force constant k_1 and k_2. If the block is displaced a little and left to oscillate, then the angular frequency of oscillation will be :

(a) $\left[\frac{k_1 k_2}{m(k_1 - k_2)}\right]^{1/2}$ (b) $\left[\frac{k_1 + k_2}{m}\right]^{1/2}$

(c) $\left[\frac{k_1 k_2}{m(k_1 + k_2)}\right]^{1/2}$ (d) $\left[\frac{k_1^2 + k_2^2}{m(k_1 + k_2)}\right]^{1/2}$

81. On a smooth inclined plane, a body of mass M is attached between two springs. The outer ends of the springs are fixed to firm supports. If each spring has force constant k, the period of oscillation of the body (assuming the springs as massless) is :

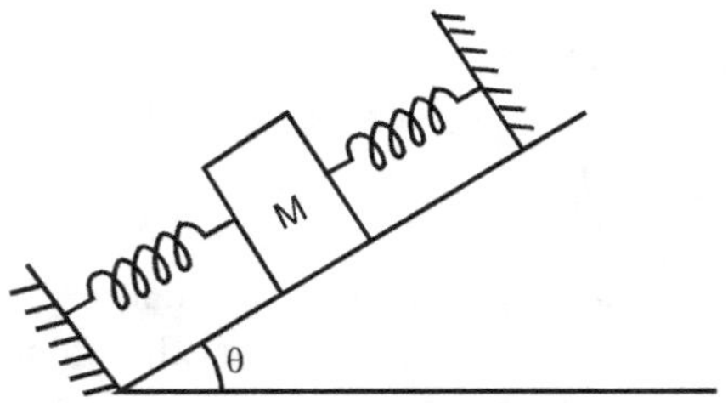

(a) $2\pi\left(\frac{M}{2k}\right)^{1/2}$ (b) $2\pi\left(\frac{2M}{k}\right)^{1/2}$

(c) $2\pi\left(\frac{Mg\sin\theta}{2k}\right)$ (d) $2\pi\left(\frac{2Mg}{k}\right)^{1/2}$

82. What will be the force constant of the spring system shown in the figure ?

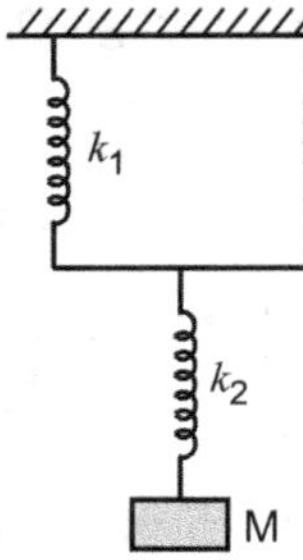

(a) $\frac{k_1}{2} + k_2$ (b) $\left[\frac{1}{2k_1} + \frac{1}{k_2}\right]^{-1}$

(c) $\frac{1}{2k_1} + \frac{1}{k_2}$ (d) $\left[\frac{2}{k_1} + \frac{1}{k_2}\right]^{-1}$

83. A clock which keeps correct time at 20° C is subjected to 40°C. If coefficient of linear expansion of the pendulum is 12×10^{-6} per °C, how much will it gain or lose in time ?

(a) 10.3 seconds/day (b) 20.6 seconds/day

(c) 5 seconds/day (d) 20 minutes/day

84. A particle of mass m is attached to three identical springs A, B and C each of force constant k as shown in the figure below. If the particle of mass m is pushed slightly against the spring A and released, then the time period of oscillation is :

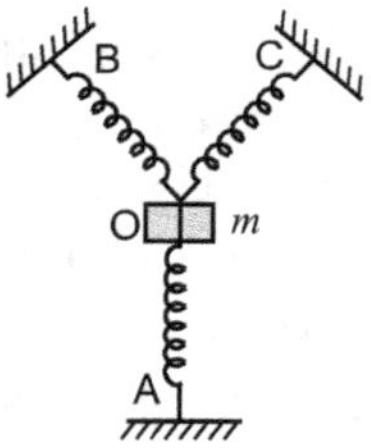

(a) $2\pi\sqrt{\frac{2m}{k}}$ (b) $2\pi\sqrt{\frac{m}{2k}}$

(c) $2\pi\sqrt{\frac{m}{k}}$ (d) $2\pi\sqrt{\frac{m}{3k}}$

85. A pendulum bob carries a charge $- q$. A positive charge $+ q$ is held at the point of support. Then the time period of the bob is :

(a) greater than $2\pi\sqrt{\frac{L}{g}}$

(b) less than $2\pi\sqrt{\frac{L}{g}}$

(c) equal to $2\pi\sqrt{\frac{L}{g}}$

(d) equal to $2\pi\sqrt{\frac{2L}{g}}$

86. A smooth inclined plane having angle of inclination of 30° with the horizontal has a 2.5 kg mass held by a string which is fixed at the upper end. If the mass is taken 2.5 cm up along the surface of the inclined plane, the tension in the spring reduces to zero. If the mass is now released, the angular frequency of oscillation is :

(a) 7 (b) 14

(c) 0.7 (d) 1.4

87. For a particle executing S.H.M., the kinetic energy k is given by $k = k_0 \cos^2 \omega t$. The maximum value of potential energy is :

(a) k_0 (b) zero

(c) $k_0/2$ (d) not obtainable

88. A simple pendulum with length L and mass m of the bob is vibrating with an amplitude a. Then the maximum tension in the string is:

(a) mg (b) $mg\left[1 + \left(\frac{a}{L}\right)^2\right]$

(c) $mg\left[1 + \frac{a}{2L}\right]^2$ (d) $mg\left[1 + \left(\frac{a}{L}\right)\right]^2$

89. Two masses m_1 and m_2 are suspended together by a massless spring of constant k. When the masses are in equilibrium, m_1 is removed without disturbing the system, the amplitude of vibration is :

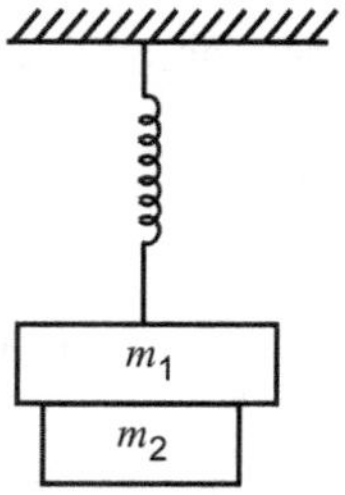

(a) $\frac{m_1 g}{k}$ (b) $\frac{m_2 g}{k}$

(c) $\frac{(m_1 + m_2) g}{k}$ (d) $\frac{(m_2 - m_1) g}{k}$

90. A heavy brass sphere is hung from a spring and it executes vertical vibrations with the period T. The sphere is now immersed in a non-viscous liquid with a density $(1/10)^{th}$ that of brass. When set into vertical vibration with the sphere remaining inside the liquid, the time period will be :

(a) $\sqrt{\frac{9}{10T}}$ (b) $\sqrt{\frac{10}{9T}}$

(c) $\left(\frac{9}{10}\right)T$ (d) unchanged

91. A cylindrical piston of mass M slides smoothly inside a long cylinder closed at one end, enclosing a certain mass of gas. The cylinder is kept with its axis horizontal. If the piston is disturbed from its equilibrium position, it oscillates simple harmonically. The period of oscillations will be :

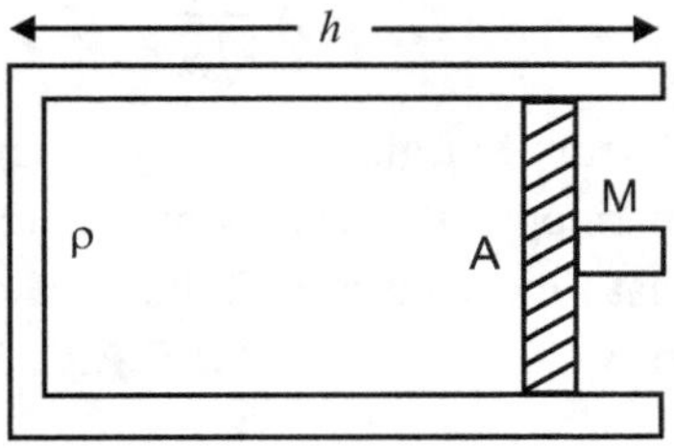

(a) $T = 2\pi\sqrt{\frac{Mh}{\rho A}}$ (b) $T = 2\pi\sqrt{\frac{MA}{\rho h}}$

(c) $T = 2\pi\frac{\sqrt{M}}{\rho A h}$ (d) $T = 2\pi\sqrt{M\rho h A}$

92. Two pendulums of lengths 121 cm and 100 cm start vibrating at the same instant. The two are in the mean position in the same phase. After how many vibrations of the shorter pendulum will the two be in phase in the mean position ?

(a) 10 (b) 11

(c) 20 (d) 21

93. Two particles P and Q describe S.H.M. of the same amplitude a and frequency υ along the same straight line. The maximum distance between the two particles is $\sqrt{2}a$. The initial phase difference between the particles is :

(a) zero (b) $\pi/2$

(c) $\pi/6$ (d) $\pi/3$

94. A simple pendulum is made of a body which a hollow sphere is containing mercury suspended by means of a wire. If a little mercury is drained off, the period of pendulum will :

(a) remain unchanged (b) increase

(c) decrease (d) become erratic

95. A simple harmonic motion has an amplitude A and time period T. The time required by it to travel from $x = A$ to $\frac{A}{2}$ is :

(a) T/6 (b) T/4

(c) T/3 (d) T/2

96. A simple pendulum consisting of a ball of mass m tied to a string of length l is made to swing on a circular arc of angle θ in a vertical plane. At the end of this arc, another ball of mass m is placed at rest. The momentum translated to this ball at rest by the swinging ball is :

(a) Zero (b) $m\theta\sqrt{\frac{l}{g}}$

(c) $m\theta\sqrt{lg}$ (d) $\frac{m}{2}\sqrt{\frac{l}{g}}$

97. Two pendulums begin to swing simultaneously. The first pendulum makes full oscillations. When the first pendulum makes 9 full oscillations, the other makes 7. The ratio of lengths of the two pendulums is:

(a) 9/7 (b) 7/9

(c) 49/81 (d) 81/49

98. Which of the following expressions does not represent SHM ?

(a) $A \cos \omega t$

(b) $A \sin 2\omega t$

(c) $A \sin \omega t + B \cos \omega t$

(d) $A \sin 2\omega t$

99. A mass m = 100 gm is attached at the end of a light spring which oscillates on a frictionless horizontal surface with an amplitude equal to 0.16 m and time period equal to 2 seconds. Initially, the mass is released from rest at $t = 0$ and displacement $x = -0.16$ m. The expression for the displacement of the mass at any time t is :

(a) $x = 0.16 \cos \pi t$

(b) $x = -0.16 \cos \pi t$

(c) $x = 0.16 \cos (\pi t + x)$

(d) $x = -0.16 \cos (\pi t + x)$

100. The P.E. of a particle executing S.H.M. at a distance y from its mean position is :

(a) $\frac{1}{2} m\omega^2 y^2$ (b) $\frac{1}{2} m\omega^2 a^2$

(c) $\frac{1}{2} m\omega^2 (a^2 - y^2)$ (d) zero

101. If a spring has time period T and is cut into n equal parts, the time period of each part will be : **(A.I.E.E.E. 2002)**

(a) $T \cdot \sqrt{n}$ (b) $\frac{T}{\sqrt{n}}$

(c) $n \cdot T$ (d) T

102. A child swinging on a swing in sitting position, stands up, then the time period will: **(A.I.E.E.E. 2003)**

(a) increase

(b) decrease

(c) not change

(d) first increase and then decrease

103. The length of a simple pendulum executing S.H.M. is increased by 21%. The % increase in the time period of pendulum of increased length is : **(A.I.E.E.E. 2003)**

(a) 11% (b) 21%

(c) 42% (d) 10%

104. A particle at the end of a spring executes S.H.M. with a time period t_1, while the corresponding period for another spring is t_2. If the period of oscillation with the two springs in series is T, then :

(A.I.E.E.E. 2004)

(a) $T = t_1 + t_2$ (b) $T^2 = t_1^2 + t_2^2$

(c) $\frac{1}{T} = \frac{1}{t_1} + \frac{1}{t_2}$ (d) $\frac{1}{T^2} = \frac{1}{t_1^2} + \frac{1}{t_2^2}$

105. Two S.H.M.s are represented by the equation $y_1 = 0.1 \sin\left(100\,\pi t + \frac{\pi}{3}\right)$ and $y_2 = 0.1 \cos (\pi t)$. The phase difference of the velocity of particle one w.r.t. the velocity of the second particle is : **(A.I.E.E.E. 2005)**

(a) $-\frac{\pi}{3}$ (b) $\frac{\pi}{6}$

(c) $-\frac{\pi}{6}$ (d) $\frac{\pi}{3}$

106. If S.H.M. is represented by $\frac{d^2x}{dt^2} + \alpha \cdot x = 0$, then its time period is : **(A.I.E.E.E. 2005)**

(a) $2\pi\alpha$ (b) $2\pi\sqrt{\alpha}$

(c) $\frac{2\pi}{\alpha}$ (d) $\frac{2\pi}{\sqrt{\alpha}}$

107. Starting from origin, a body oscillates simple harmonically with a period of 2 s. After what time will its K.E. be 75% of the total energy ? **(A.I.E.E.E. 2005)**

(a) $\frac{1}{12}$ s (b) $\frac{1}{6}$ s

(c) $\frac{1}{4}$ s (d) $\frac{1}{3}$ s

108. The maximum velocity of a particle, executing S.H.M. with an amplitude 7 mm is 4.4 ms^{-1}. The period of oscillation is :

(A.I.E.E.E. 2006)

(a) 100 s (b) 0.01 s

(c) 10 s (d) 0.1 s

109. A particle of mass m executes S.H.M. with amplitude a and frequency υ. The average K.E. during its motion from the position of equilibrium to the end is : **(A.I.E.E.E. 2007)**

(a) $2\pi^2 m a^2 \upsilon^2$ (b) $\pi^2 m a^2 \upsilon^2$

(c) $\frac{m a^2 \upsilon^2}{4}$ (d) $4\pi^2 m a^2 \upsilon^2$

110. The displacement of an object attached to a spring executing S.H.M. is given by $x = 2 \times 10^{-2} \cos \pi t$ metre. The time at which the maximum speed first occurs is :

(a) 0.25 s (b) 0.5 s
(c) 0.75 s (d) 0.125 s

COMPREHENSION BASED QUESTIONS

A particle is executing simple harmonic motion, then the displacement of the particle at any time is given by :

$$y = A \sin \omega t \quad \text{... (1)}$$

where, A is amplitude of S.H.M. and

ω is angular velocity $= \frac{2\pi}{T}$

Then, $y = A \sin \frac{2\pi}{T}$

Therefore, the velocity of that particle,

$$v = \frac{dy}{dt} = A\omega \cos \omega t$$

or $v = A\omega\sqrt{1 - \sin^2 \omega t}$

or $v = A\omega\sqrt{\frac{1 - y^2}{A^2}}$

or $v = \omega\sqrt{A^2 - y^2}$

Then, at mean position i.e. $y = 0$,

$$v = \omega A = V_{max}$$

But at extreme position,

$$y = \pm A$$

then $v = 0$

and acceleration is given by,

$$a = \frac{d^2y}{dt^2} = -\omega^2 y$$

Read the passage and answer the following questions:

111. A point mass describes S.H.M. in a line 4 cm long. Its velocity, when passing through the centre of the line is 12 cms^{-1}. The time period of the point mass is :

(a) 1047 s (b) 104.7 s
(c) 10.47 s (d) 1.047 s

112. The time period of a body executing S.H.M. is 2 seconds. After how much time will its displacement be half of its amplitude :

(a) $\frac{1}{2}$ s (b) $\frac{1}{4}$ s
(c) $\frac{1}{6}$ s (d) $\frac{1}{8}$ s

113. During S.H.M., a particle has an acceleration of 48 cms^{-2}, when displacement from mean position is 12 cm. Then the period of vibration is :

(a) 3.142 s (b) 31.42 s
(c) 314.2 s (d) 3142 s

ASSERTION AND REASON

Directions for Q. 114 to Q. 117 :

In the following questions, a statement of Assertion is followed by a statement of Reason (statement-I and statement-II respectively). While answering a question, you are required to choose the correct one out of the given four responses.

(a) Both the statement-I and statement-II are true and statement-II is the correct explanation of statement-I.

(b) Both statement-I and statement-II are true, but statement-II is not the correct explanation of statement-I.

(c) Statement-I is true, but statement-II is false

(d) Both statement-I and statement-II are false.

114. (I) Water in a U-tube executes S.H.M. The time period for Hg filled upto the same height in the U-tube is greater than in case of water.

(II) The amplitude of an oscillating Hg goes on increasing.

115. (I) The time period of a simple pendulum in a satellite orbiting the earth is infinite.

(II) The time period of a pendulum is inversely proportional to $\sqrt{g}$.

116. (I) The amplitude of an oscillating pendulum decreases gradually with time.

(II) The frequency of the pendulum decreases with time :

117. (I) In S.H.M., the velocity is maximum, when acceleration is minimum.

(II) Displacement and the velocity in S.H.M. differ in phase by $\pi/2$.

118. The function $x = A \sin^2 \omega t + B \cos^2 \omega t + C \sin \omega t \cos \omega t$ represents S.H.M :

(a) for any value of A, B and C (except C = 0)

(b) if A = –B, C = 2B, amplitude = $|\sqrt{2}B|$

(c) if A = B, C = 0

(d) if A = B, C = 2B, amplitude = | B |

119. Three S.H.M.s in the same direction having the same amplitude a and the same period are suspended. If each differs in phase from the next by 45°, then :

(a) the resultant amplitude is $(1+\sqrt{2})\,a$

(b) the phase of the resultant relative to the first is 90°

(c) the energy associated with the resulting motion is $(3+2\sqrt{2})$ times the energy associated with any single motion

(d) the resulting motion is not S.H.M.

120. A particle executes S.H.M. between $x = -a$ and $x = +a$. The time taken for it to go from 0 to $a/2$ is T_1 and to go from $\frac{a}{2}$ to a is T_2, then :

(a) $T_1 > T_2$ (b) $T_1 < T_2$

(c) $T_1 = T_2$ (d) $T_1 = 2T_2$

121. A spring of force constant k is cut into two pieces, such that one is double the length of the other. Then the long piece will have a force constant of :

(a) $\frac{2k}{3}$ (b) $\frac{3k}{2}$

(c) $3k$ (d) $6k$

122. A simple pendulum has a time period T_1, when on the earth's surface, and T_2 when taken to a height R above the earth's surface, then the value of T_1/T_2 is : (R = Radius of earth)

(a) 1 (b) $\sqrt{2}$

(c) 4 (d) 2

123. The mass and the diameter of a planet are twice those of the earth. The period of oscillation of the pendulum on the planet will be (if it is seconds pendulum on earth) :

(a) $\frac{1}{\sqrt{2}}$ s (b) $\sqrt{2}$ s

(c) $2\sqrt{2}$ s (d) $\frac{1}{2}$ s

124. A linear harmonic oscillator of force constant 2×10^6 Nm^{-1} and amplitude 0.01 m has a total mechanical energy of 160 J. Its :

(a) maximum potential energy is 100 J

(b) maximum K.E. is 100 J

(c) minimum potential energy is 160 J

(d) minimum potential energy is 0 J

125. A particle of mass m is executing oscillations about the origin on x-axis. Its potential energy is $U(x) = k\,|x|^3$, where k is +ve constant. If its amplitude is a, then its time period T is :

(a) proportional to $\frac{1}{\sqrt{a}}$

(b) independent of a

(c) proportional to $\sqrt{a}$

(d) proportional to $\sqrt{a^3}$

126. A simple pendulum has time period T_1, the point of suspension is now moved upward according to the relation $y = kt^2$ ($k = 1\ ms^{-2}$), where y is the vertical displacement. Now the time period becomes T_2. The ratio of T_1^2/T_2^2 is .... ($\because$ $g = 10\ ms^{-2}$) :

(a) 6/5 (b) 5/6
(c) 1 (d) 4/5

127. The period of oscillation of a simple pendulum of length 'l' suspended from the roof of a vehicle which moves without friction down an inclined plane of inclination α is given by :

(a) $2\pi\sqrt{\dfrac{l}{g \cos \alpha}}$ (b) $2\pi\sqrt{\dfrac{l}{g \sin \alpha}}$

(c) $2\pi\sqrt{\dfrac{l}{g}}$ (d) $2\pi\sqrt{\dfrac{l}{g \tan \alpha}}$

PART - II

1. Length of a string tied to two riding supports is 40 cm. Maximum wavelength of a stationary wave produced on it is :

(a) 20 cm (b) 40 cm
(c) 120 cm (d) 80 cm

2. 16 tuning forks are arranged in the increasing order of their frequency. Any two consecutive tuning forks when sounded together produce 8 beats/second. If the frequency of the last tuning fork is twice that of the first, the frequency of the first tuning fork is :

(a) 60 (b) 80
(c) 100 (d) 120

3. A transverse wave is represented by the equation :

$$y = y_0 \frac{\sin 2\pi}{\lambda}(Vt - x)$$

For what value of λ is the maximum particle velocity equal to two times the wave velocity ?

(a) $\lambda = 2\pi y_0$ (b) $\lambda = \dfrac{\pi y_0}{3}$

(c) $\lambda = \dfrac{\pi y_0}{2}$ (d) $\lambda = \pi y_0$

4. The equation of a progressive wave is

$$y = a \sin (200\, t - x)$$

where x is in meter, and t is in seconds. The velocity of wave is :

(a) 200 m/s (b) 100 m/s
(c) 50 m/s (d) None of these

5. A cylindrical tube, open at both ends has fundamental frequency f in air. The tube is dipped vertically in water so that half of it is in water. The fundamental frequency of the air column is now :

(a) $\dfrac{f}{2}$ (b) $\dfrac{3f}{4}$

(c) f (d) $2f$

6. A whistle giving out 450 Hz approaches a stationary observer at a speed of 33 m/s. The frequency heard by the observer in Hz is .... (velocity of sound in air = 333 m/s) :

(a) 409 (b) 429
(c) 517 (d) 500

7. If amplitude of two sound waves is a_1 and a_2, then on superposition, the resultant amplitude will be :

(a) $(a_1 + a_2)$ only
(b) $(a_1 - a_2)$ only
(c) Either $(a_1 + a_2)$ or $(a_1 - a_2)$
(d) $\sqrt{a_1^2 + a_2^2 + 2a_1a_2 \cos \phi}$

8. $y = 25 \cos (2\pi t - \pi x)$ is the wave equation. Then the amplitude and frequency respectively are :

(a) 100, 25 (b) 200, 25
(c) 25, 100 (d) 25, 1

9. Which of the following equations represents a wave ?

(a) $y = A \sin \omega t$ (b) $y = A \cos kx$

(c) $y = A \sin (at - bx + c)$

(d) $y = A (\omega t - kx)$

10. A wave is represented by

$$x = 0.4 \cos\left[8t - \frac{y}{2}\right]$$

where x and y are in meters and t in seconds. The speed of the wave is :

(a) 0.5 m/s (b) 8 m/s

(c) 16 m/s (d) 6.1 m/s

11. Equations of two progressive waves at a certain point in a medium are given by,

$$y_1 = a \sin (\omega t + \phi_1)$$

and $$y_2 = a \sin (\omega t + \phi_2)$$

If amplitude and time period of the resultant wave formed by the superposition of these two waves are same as those of either wave, then $(\phi_1 - \phi_2)$ is :

(a) $\pi/3$ (b) $\pi/6$

(c) $\pi/4$ (d) $2\pi/3$

12. Equation of a stationary wave is,

$$y = 10 \sin \frac{\pi x}{4} \cos 20\pi t$$

Distance between two consecutive nodes is:

(a) 4 (b) 2

(c) 1 (d) 8

13. When a stretched wire and tuning fork are sounded together, 5 beats per second are produced. When length of wire is 95 cm or 100 cm, the frequency of fork is :

(a) 90 (b) 100

(c) 105 (d) 195

14. A particle has displacement y given by

$$y = 3 \sin (5\pi t + \phi)$$

where, y is in metres and t is in seconds. What are the frequency and period of motion ?

(a) 0.4 Hz, 2.5 s (b) 2.5 Hz, 0.4 s

(c) 2.5 Hz, 2.5 s (d) 0.4 Hz, 0.4 s

15. If the tension and diameter of a sonometer wire of fundamental frequency n are doubled and density is halved, then its fundamental frequency will become :

(a) $\pi/4$ (b) $\sqrt{2n}$

(c) n (d) $n/\sqrt{2}$

16. A car sounding its horn at 480 Hz moves towards a high wall at a speed of 20 m/s. Then the speed of the reflected sound heard by the man sitting in the car will be nearest to :

(a) 480 Hz (b) 510 Hz

(c) 540 Hz (d) 570 Hz

17. If the equation of sound wave is,

$y = 0.0015 \sin (62.4\,x + 316\,t)$

then, its wave length will be :

(a) 0.2 unit (b) 0.3 unit

(c) 0.1 unit (d) 2 unit

18. Fundamental frequency of a sonometer wire is n. If the length, tension and diameter of wire are tripled, the new fundamental frequency is :

(a) $n/\sqrt{3}$ (b) $n/3$

(c) $n\sqrt{3}$ (d) $n/3\sqrt{3}$

19. The waves $y_1 = a \sin \omega t$ and $y_2 = a \cos \omega t$ are superimposed. Then resultant amplitude is :

(a) a (b) $2a$

(c) $a\sqrt{2}$ (d) $\frac{a}{\sqrt{2}}$

20. The equation of a wave is represented by,

$$y = 10^{-4} \sin\left[100\,t - \frac{x}{10}\right] \text{m}$$

then, the velocity of wave will be :

(a) 100 m/s (b) 4 m/s

(c) 1000 m/s (d) 10 m/s

21. A small piece of cork in a ripple tank oscillates up and down as ripples pass it. If the ripples travelling at 0.5 m/s have a wave-length of 1.5 π cm and the cork vibrates with an amplitude of 5 mm, the maximum velocity of the cork is :

(a) 20 cm/sec (b) 20 m/sec

(c) 0.02 m/sec (d) 200 cm/sec

22. A sound wave of wavelength 90 cm in glass is refracted into air. If the velocity of sound in glass is 5400 *m/s*, the wave length of the wave in the air is :

(a) 55 cm (b) 5.5 cm
(c) 55 m (d) 5.5 m

23. A progressive wave of frequency 500 Hz is travelling with a velocity of 360 m/s. How far apart are the two points 60º out of phase?

(a) 1.2 cm (b) 0.12 cm
(c) 120 cm (d) 12 cm

24. It is possible to distinguish between transverse and longitudinal waves by studying the property of :

(a) Interference (b) Diffraction
(c) Reflection (d) Polarization

25. A light pointer fixed to one prong of a tuning fork touches a vertical plate. The fork is set vibrating and the plate is allowed to fall freely. Eight complete oscillations are counted when the plate falls through 10 cm. What is the frequency of the tuning fork ?

(a) 112 Hz (b) 56 Hz
(c) 8/7 Hz (d) 7/8 Hz

26. Which of the following statements is incorrect ?

(a) Sound travels in a straight line.
(b) Sound travels as a wave.
(c) Sound is a form of energy.
(d) Sound travels faster in vacuum than in air.

27. Two particles P and Q describe S.H.M. of the same amplitude a and frequency υ along a straight line. The maximum distance between the two particles is $a\sqrt{2}$. The initial phase difference between the particles is :

(a) $\pi/3$ (b) $\pi/6$
(c) $\pi/2$ (d) Zero

28. An aeroplane is above the head of an observer and the sound appears to be coming at an angle of 60º with the vertical. If velocity of sound is v, then the speed of aeroplane is :

(a) v (b) $\frac{\sqrt{3}}{2}$ v
(c) $\frac{v}{2}$ (d) 2 v

29. The driver of a car travelling with speed 30 m/s towards a hill sounds a horn of frequency 600 Hz. If the velocity of sound in air is 330 m/s, the frequency of reflected sound as heard by the driver is :

(a) 720 Hz (b) 555.5 Hz
(c) 550 Hz (d) 500 Hz

30. A string of mass 0.2 kg/m has length l = 0.6 m. It is fixed at both ends and stretched such that it has a tension of 80 N. The string vibrates in three segments with amplitude = 0.5 cm. The amplitude of transverse velocity is :

(a) 9.42 m/s (b) 3.14 m/s
(c) 1.57 m/s (d) 6.28 m/s

31. To demonstrate the phenomenon of interference, we need :

(a) two sources which emit radiations of exactly the same frequency
(b) two sources which emit radiations of exactly the same frequency and have a definite phase relationship
(c) two sources which emit radiations of exactly the same frequency and do not have a definite phase relationship
(d) two sources which emit radiations of exactly the same wavelength

32. When two coherent waves interfere, there is:

(a) loss in energy
(b) gain in energy
(c) redistribution of energy which changes with time
(d) redistribution of energy which does not change with time

33. Which is the maximum possible sound level in dB of sound wave in air ? Given that density of air = 1.3 kg/m^3, v = 332 m/s and atmospheric pressure = 1.01×10^5 N/m^2.

(a) 120 dB (b) 60 dB
(c) 190 dB (d) 50 dB

34. If the temperature is raised by 1 K from 300 K, the percentage change in the speed of sound in the gaseous mixture is : (R = 8.31 J/mole-K)

(a) 0.167 % (b) 2 %
(c) 1 % (d) 0.334 %

35. A person hears the sound of a jet aeroplane after it has passed over his head. The angle of the jet plane with the horizontal when the sound appears to be coming vertically downwards is 60°. If the velocity of sound is v, then the velocity of the jet plane should be :

(a) 2 v (b) $\frac{v}{\sqrt{3}}$
(c) $\sqrt{3}$ v (d) v

36. A student sees a jet plane flying from east to west. When the jet is seen just above his head, the sound of the jet appears to reach him making angle 60° with the horizontal from the east. If the velocity of sound is v, then the velocity of the jet plane should be :

(a) 2 v (b) $\frac{v}{\sqrt{3}}$
(c) $\sqrt{3}$ v (d) v

37. An echo is heard when minimum distance of the reflecting surface is :

(a) 10 cm (b) 17 m
(c) 34 m (d) 340 m

38. A sound wave travelling with a velocity v in a medium A reaches a point on the interface of medium A and medium B. If the velocity in the medium B is 2v, the angle of incidence for total interval reflection of the wave will be :

(a) > 15° (b) > 30°
(c) > 45° (d) > 90 °

39. Two sound waves are given by,

$y = a \sin (\omega t - kx)$

$y' = b \cos (\omega t - kx)$

then, the phase difference between the two waves is :

(a) $\pi/2$ (b) $\pi/4$
(c) π (d) $3\pi/4$

40. Three waves of equal frequencies having amplitudes 10 μm, 4 μm and 7 μm arrive at a given point with successive phase difference of $\pi/2$. The amplitude of the resulting wave in μm is given by :

(a) 7 (b) 6
(c) 5 (d) 4

41. The frequency of the note produced by plucking a given string increases as :

(a) the length of the string increases
(b) the tension in the string increases
(c) the tension in the string decreases
(d) the mass per unit length of the string increases

42. With the increase in temperature, the frequency of the sound from an organ pipe :

(a) decreases (b) increases
(c) remains unchanged
(d) changes erratically

43. There are two open organ pipes of exactly the same length and material but different radii. The frequencies of their fundamental notes will be such that :

(a) wider pipe has lower frequency
(b) narrower pipe has lower frequency
(c) both the pipes have same frequency
(d) none of these

44. A stretched string instead of being plucked in the middle is plucked at a point $(1/4)^{th}$ of its length from either of its ends. The frequency of vibration would be :

(a) four times when plucked in the middle
(b) twice when plucked in the middle
(c) eight times when plucked in the middle
(d) same as when plucked in the middle

45. The periodic waves of amplitudes a and b pass through a region at the same time in the same direction. If $a > b$, the difference in the maximum and minimum possible amplitudes is :

(a) $a + b$ (b) $a - b$
(c) $2a$ (d) $2b$

46. If two waves of the same frequency and same amplitude respectively, on superposition produce a resultant disturbance of the same amplitude, the waves differ in phase by,

(a) π (b) $2\pi/3$
(c) $\pi/3$ (d) 3π

47. The displacement of a particle executing periodic motion is given by,

$$y = 4\cos^2(t/2)\sin(1000\,t)$$

This expression may be considered to be a result of superposition of :

(a) two waves (b) three waves
(c) four waves (d) five waves

48. For the production of beats, the two sources must have :

(a) different frequencies and same amplitude
(b) different frequencies
(c) different frequencies, same amplitude and same phase
(d) different frequencies and same phase.

49. 56 tuning forks are so arranged in series that each tuning fork gives 4 beats per second with the previous one. The frequency of the first fork is :

(a) 110 (b) 56
(c) 66 (d) 52

50. The principle of superposition in wave motion tells that, in a motion in which two or more waves are simultaneously producing their displacements in a particle along the same line, then the resultant :

(a) amplitude is the sum of the individual amplitudes
(b) velocity is the sum of the individual velocities
(c) displacement is the sum of the individual displacements
(d) phase is the sum of the individual phases

51. The fundamental frequency of a sonometer wire carrying a block of mass 1 kg and density 1.8 is 266 Hz. When the block is completely immersed in a liquid of density 1.2, then what will be its new frequency ?

(a) 300 Hz (b) 150 Hz
(c) 450 Hz (d) None of these

52. A glass tube of 10 m length is filled with water. The water can be drained out slowly at the bottom of the tube. If a vibrating tuning fork of frequency 500 c/s is brought at the upper end of the tube and the velocity of sound is 330 m/s, then the total number of resonances obtained will be :

(a) 4 (b) 3
(c) 2 (d) 1

53. A uniform wire 20 metre long and weighing 50 N hangs vertically. If $g = 10\text{ m/s}^2$ then the speed of the transverse wave at the middle point of the wire is :

(a) 4 m/s (b) $10\sqrt{2}$ m/s
(c) 10 m/s (d) Zero m/s

54. The end correction of a resonance column is 10 cm. If the shortest length resonating with a tuning fork is 15.0 cm, the next resonating length is :

(a) 31 cm (b) 45 cm
(c) 46 cm (d) 47 cm

55. The speed of longitudinal waves in a thin brass rod is 3480 m/s. If the rod is clamped at one end and gives a fundamental frequency of 435 Hz, the length of the rod is:

(a) 0.5 m (b) 1.0 m
(c) 2.0 m (d) 4.0 m

56. A loaded string of length one metre and weighing 0.5 g is hanging from a tuning fork of frequency 200 Hz and is vibrating in four loops. For the transverse arrangement, the tension is :

(a) 1.25×10^5 dynes (b) 2.5×10^5 dynes
(c) 5×10^5 dynes (d) 10×10^5 dynes

57. A tuning fork of frequency n is held near the open end of a tube which is closed at the other end and the length of the tube is adjusted until resonance occurs. If the two shortest lengths that produce resonance are L_1 and L_2, the speed of the sound is :

(a) $n(L_2 - L_1)$ (b) $n(L_2 - L_1)/2$

(c) $2n(L_2 + L_1)$ (d) $2n(L_2 - L_1)$

58. The fundamental frequency of a string stretched with a weight of 4 kg is 256 Hz. The weight required to produce its octave is:

(a) 4 kg wt (b) 12 kg wt

(c) 16 kg wt (d) 24 kg wt

59. A sonometer wire, 100 cm in length has a fundamental frequency of 330 Hz. The velocity of propagation of transverse waves along the wire is :

(a) 330 m/s (b) 660 m/s

(c) 115 m/s (d) 990 m/s

60. A tuning fork is found to give five beats in three seconds when sounded in conjunction with a stretched string vibrating transversely under a tension of either 10.2 kgf or 9.9 kgf. The frequency of the fork is approximately :

(a) 237 Hz (b) 235 Hz

(c) 223 Hz (d) 225 Hz

61. When two waves of almost equal frequencies n_1 and n_2 are produced simultaneously, then the time interval between successive maxima is :

(a) $\frac{1}{n_1 - n_2}$ (b) $\frac{1}{n_1} - \frac{1}{n_2}$

(c) $\frac{1}{n_1} + \frac{1}{n_2}$ (d) $\frac{1}{n_1 + n_2}$

62. The path difference between two waves

$$y_1 = a_1 \sin\left[\omega t - \frac{2\pi x}{\lambda}\right] \text{ and}$$

$$y_2 = a_2 \cos\left[\omega t - \frac{2\pi x}{\lambda} + \phi\right] \text{ is :}$$

(a) $\frac{\lambda}{2\pi}(\phi)$ (b) $\frac{\lambda}{2\pi}\left[\phi + \frac{\pi}{2}\right]$

(c) $\frac{2\pi}{\lambda}\left[\phi - \frac{\pi}{2}\right]$ (d) $\frac{2\pi}{\lambda}(\phi)$

63. A source of sound emitting a tone of frequency 200 Hz moves towards an observer with a velocity v equal to the velocity of sound. If the observer also moves away from the source with the same velocity v, the apparent frequency heard by the observer is :

(a) 50 Hz (b) 100 Hz

(c) 150 Hz (d) 200 Hz

64. A rocket ship is receding from the earth at a speed of 0.2 c. The ship emits the signal of frequency 4×10^7 Hz. The apparent frequency to an observer on the surface of the earth is :

(a) 3.2×10^7 Hz (b) 4.8×10^7 Hz

(c) 4.0×10^7 Hz (d) 5.3×10^7 Hz

65. If the pressure amplitude in a sound wave is tripled, then the intensity of sound is increased by a factor :

(a) 3 (b) 0

(c) 9 (d) $\sqrt{3}$

66. The intensity of a sound wave gets reduced by 20% on passing through a slab. The reduction in intensity on passage through two such consecutive slabs is :

(a) 40% (b) 36%

(c) 30% (d) 50%

67. When the string of a sonometer of length L between the bridges vibrates in the sound overtone, the amplitude of vibration is maximum at :

(a) L/2

(b) L/4 and 3L/4

(c) L/6, 3L/6 and 5L/6

(d) L/8, 3L/8, 5L/8, 7L/8

68. A wave of frequency 100 Hz is sent along a string towards a fixed end. When this wave travels back after reflection, a node is formed at a distance of 10 cm from the fixed end of the string. The speed of incident (and reflected wave) is :

(a) 40 m/s (b) 20 m/s

(c) 10 m/s (d) 5 m/s

69. In a resonance column experiment, the first resonance is obtained when the level of the water in the tube is at 20 cm from the open end. Resonance will also be obtained when the water level is at a distance of :

(a) 40 cm from the open end

(b) 60 cm from the open end

(c) 80 cm from the open end

(d) 100 cm from the open end

70. A long glass tube is held vertically in water. A tuning fork is struck and held over the tube. Strong resonances are observed at two successive lengths 0.50 m and 0.84 m above the surface of water. If the velocity of sound is 340 m/s, then the frequency of the tuning fork is :

(a) 128 Hz (b) 256 Hz

(c) 384 Hz (d) 500 Hz

71. A uniform rope having mass m hangs vertically from a rigid support. A transverse wave pulse is produced at the lower end. The speed (v) of the wave pulse varies with height h from the lower end as shown in figure :

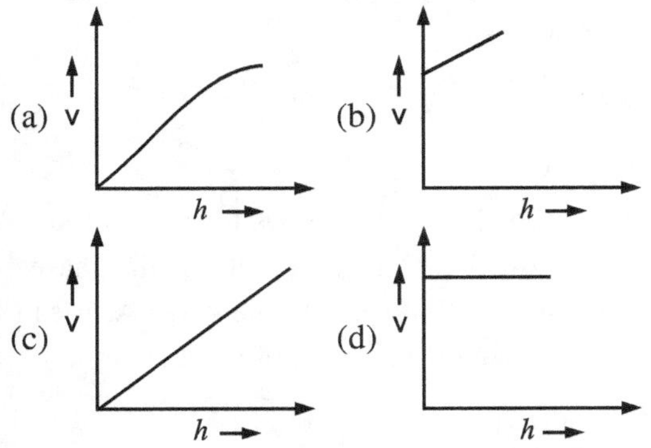

72. An observer starts moving with uniform acceleration 'a' towards a stationary sound source of frequency f_0. As the observer approaches the source, the apparent frequency (f) heard by the observer varies with the time (t) as shown in figure :

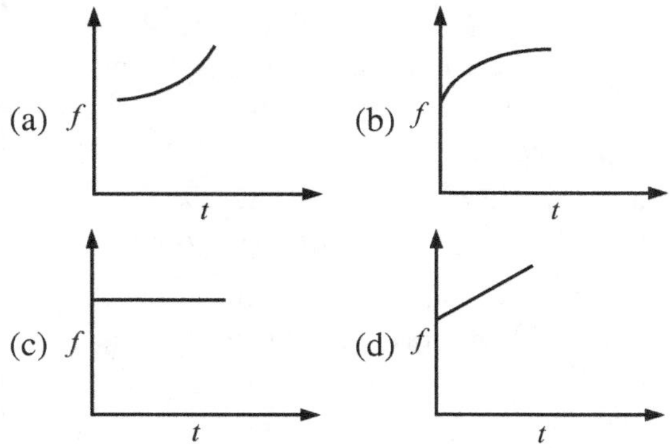

73. Sound of wavelength λ passes through a Quincke's tube which is adjusted to give a maximum intensity I_0. Through what distance should the sliding tube be moved to give an intensity $\frac{I_0}{2}$?

(a) $\frac{\lambda}{2}$ (b) $\frac{\lambda}{3}$

(c) $\frac{\lambda}{4}$ (d) $\frac{\lambda}{8}$

74. In a stationary wave that forms as a result of reflection of waves from an obstacle, the ratio of the amplitude at an antinode to the amplitude at a node is n. The fraction of energy reflected is :

(a) $\left[\frac{n}{n-1}\right]^2$ (b) $\left[\frac{1}{n}\right]^2$

(c) $\left[\frac{n-1}{n}\right]^2$ (d) $\left[\frac{n-1}{n+1}\right]^2$

75. The displacement of a wave travelling in the x-direction is given by :

$$y = 10^{-4} \sin\left(600\,t - 2x + \frac{\pi}{3}\right)$$

where, x and y are in meters and t is in seconds. The speed of the wave motion in m/s is :

(a) 300 (b) 600

(c) 1200 (d) 200

76. An observer moves towards a stationary source of sound with a speed 1/5th of the speed of sound. The wavelength and frequency of sound emitted are λ and f respectively. The apparent frequency and wavelength recorded by the observer are respectively :

(a) $1.2f, 1.2\lambda$ (b) $1.2f, \lambda$

(c) $f, 1.2\lambda$ (d) $0.8f, 0.8\lambda$

77. A wave $y = a \sin(\omega t - kx)$ on a string meets with another wave producing a node at $x = 0$. Then the equation of the unknown wave is :

(a) $y = a \sin(\omega t + kx)$

(b) $y = -a \sin(\omega t + kx)$

(c) $y = a \sin(\omega t - kx)$

(d) $y = -a \sin(\omega t - kx)$

78. The ends of a stretched wire of length (L) are fixed at $x = 0$ and $x = L$. In one experiment, the displacement of the wire is

$$y_1 = A \sin\left(\frac{\pi x}{L}\right) \sin 2\omega t$$

and energy is E_2. Then :

(a) $E_2 = E_1$ (b) $E_2 = 2E_1$

(c) $E_2 = 4E_1$ (d) $E_2 = 16E_1$

79. Two pulses in a stretched string whose centres are initially 8 cm apart are moving towards each other. The speed of each pulse is 2 cm/s. After 2 seconds, the total energy of the pulses will be :

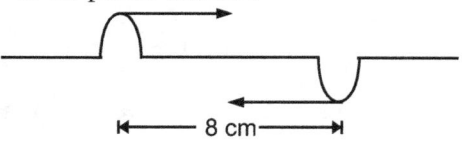

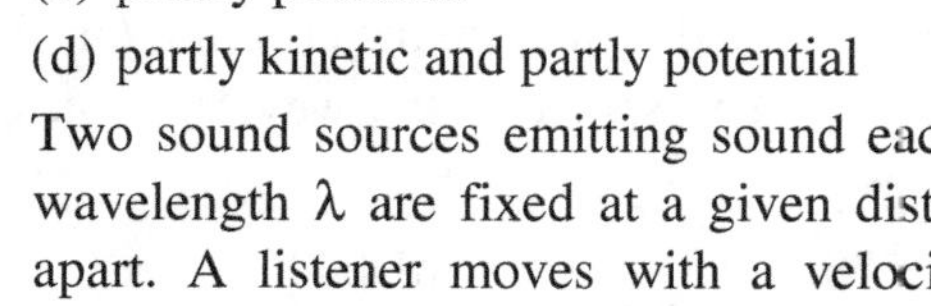

(a) zero

(b) purely kinetic

(c) purely potential

(d) partly kinetic and partly potential

80. Two sound sources emitting sound each of wavelength λ are fixed at a given distance apart. A listener moves with a velocity u along the line joining the two sources. The number of beats heard by him per second is :

(a) $2u/\lambda$ (b) u/λ

(c) $u/3\lambda$ (d) $2\lambda/u$

81. A thin plane membrane separates hydrogen at 7°C, from H_2 at 47°C, both being at the same pressure. If a collimated sound beam travelling from the cooler gas makes an angle of incidence of 30° at the membrane, the angle of refraction is :

(a) $\sin^{-1}\sqrt{\frac{7}{32}}$ (b) $\sin^{-1}\sqrt{\frac{2}{7}}$

(c) $\sin^{-1}\sqrt{\frac{4}{7}}$ (d) $\sin^{-1}\sqrt{\frac{7}{4}}$

82. Two particles P and Q describe S.H.M. of the same amplitude a, and frequency v along the same straight line. The maximum distance between the two particles is $a\sqrt{2}$. The initial phase difference between the particles is :

(a) Zero (b) $\pi/2$

(c) $\pi/6$ (d) $\pi/3$

83. A simple harmonic wave is represented by the relation

$$y(x, t) = a_0 \sin 2\pi\left[vt - \frac{x}{\lambda}\right]$$

If the maximum particle velocity is three times the wave velocity, the wavelength λ of the wave is :

(a) $\pi a_0/3$ (b) $2\pi a_0/3$

(c) πa_0 (d) $\pi a_0/2$

84. The following figure shows four progressive waves A, B, C and D with their phases expressed with respect to the wave A. It can be calculated from the figure that :

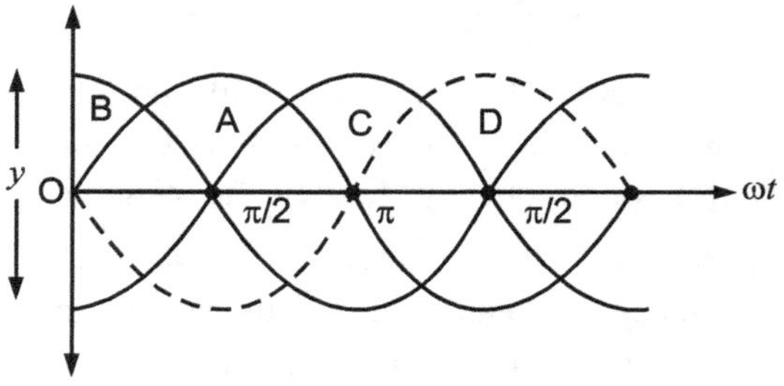

(a) the wave C is ahead by a phase angle of $\pi/2$ and the wave B lags behind by a phase angle of $\pi/2$.
(b) the wave C lags behind by a phase angle of $\pi/2$ and the wave B is ahead by a phase angle of $\pi/2$.
(c) the wave C is ahead by a phase angle of π and the wave B lags behind by a phase angle of π.
(d) the wave C lags behind by a phase angle of π and the wave B is ahead by a phase angle of π.

85. Which of the following does not represent a travelling wave ?
(a) $y = y_m f(x - vt)$
(b) $y = y_m \sin k(x + vt)$
(c) $y = y_m \log(x - vt)$
(d) $y = f(x^2 - vt^2)$

86. The amplitude of a wave disturbance propagating in the positive y - direction is given by,

$y = \frac{1}{1+x^2}$ at $t = 0$ and $y = \frac{1}{1+(x-1)^2}$ at $t = 2$ sec. where, x and y are in m. If the shape of the wave disturbance does not change during the propagation, what is the velocity of the wave ?
(a) 1 m/sec (b) 1.5 m/ sec
(c) 0.5 m/ sec (d) 2 m/ sec

87. If c_0 and c denote the sound velocity and root mean square velocity of a molecule in a gas then :
(a) $c_0 > c$
(b) $c_0 = c$
(c) $c_0 = c\left[\frac{\gamma}{3}\right]^{1/2}$
(d) c_0 and c are not related

88. The difference between the apparent frequency of a source of sound as perceived by the observer during its approach and recession is 2% of the natural frequency of the source. If the velocity of sound in air is 300 m/s, the velocity of the source is :
(a) 12 m/s (b) 1.5 m/s
(c) 3 m/s (d) 6 m/s

89. The frequency of a sonometer wire is 100 Hz. When the weights producing the tension are completely immersed in water, the frequency becomes 80 Hz and on immersing the weights in a certain liquid, the frequency becomes 60 Hz. The specific gravity of the liquid is :
(a) 1.42 (b) 1.77
(c) 1.21 (d) 1.82

90. When a train approaches a stationary observer, the apparent frequency of the whistle is n' and when the same train recedes away from the observer, the apparent frequency is n''. Then the apparent frequency n when the observer moves with the train is :
(a) $n = \frac{n' + n''}{2}$ (b) $n = \sqrt{n' n''}$
(c) $n = \frac{2n' n''}{n' + n''}$ (d) $n = \frac{2n' n''}{n' - n''}$

91. A transverse wave is represented by the equation $y = y_0 \sin \frac{2\pi}{\lambda}(vt - x)$. For what value of λ is the maximum particle velocity equal to two times the wave velocity ?
(a) $\lambda = y_0/2$ (b) $\lambda = \frac{2\pi y_0}{2}$
(c) $\lambda = \pi y_0$ (d) $\lambda = y_0/4$

92. Two whistles A and B produce notes of frequencies 660 Hz and 596 Hz respectively. There is a listener at the mid point of the line joining them. Both the whistle B and the listener start moving with a speed 30 m/s away from whistle A. If the speed of sound is 330 m/s, how many beats will be heard by the listener ?
(a) 2 (b) 4
(c) 6 (d) 8

93. A source of sound 'S' is moving with a velocity 50 m/s towards a stationary observer. The observer measures the frequency of the source as 1000 Hz. What will be the apparent frequency of the source when it is moving away from the observer after crossing him? The velocity of sound in the medium is 350 m/s :

(a) 750 Hz (b) 857 Hz

(c) 1143 Hz (d) 1333 Hz

94. If the tension in the string of a sonometer changes by a small amount from T to T + ΔT, the fundamental frequency of vibration changes from n to $n + \Delta n$, then :

(a) $\frac{\Delta n}{n} = \frac{\Delta T}{T}$ (b) $\frac{\Delta n}{n} = \frac{1}{2}\frac{\Delta T}{T}$

(c) $\frac{\Delta n}{n} = 2\frac{\Delta T}{T}$ (d) $\frac{\Delta n}{n} = -\frac{1}{2}\frac{\Delta T}{T}$

95. If the length of the string between the bridges of a sonometer wire changes by a small amount from L to L + ΔL, the fundamental frequency of vibration changes from n to $n + \Delta n$, then :

(a) $\frac{\Delta n}{n} = \frac{\Delta L}{L}$ (b) $\frac{\Delta n}{n} = -\frac{\Delta L}{L}$

(c) $\frac{\Delta n}{n} = -\frac{1}{2}\frac{\Delta L}{L}$ (d) $\frac{\Delta n}{n} = \frac{1}{2}\left[\frac{\Delta L}{L}\right]$

96. A uniform rope of length 12 metres and mass 6 kg hangs vertically from a rigid support. A block of mass 2 kg is attached to the free end of the rope. A transverse pulse of wavelength 0.06 metre is produced at the lower end of the rope. What is the wavelength of the pulse when it reaches the top of the rope ?

(a) 0.06 metre (b) 0.03 metre

(c) 0.12 metre (d) 0.09 metre

97. In brass, the velocity of a longitudinal wave is 100 times the velocity of a transverse wave. If $Y = 1 \times 10^{11}$ N/mm^2, then stress in the wire is :

(a) 1×10^{13} N / m^2 (b) 1×10^{9} N / m^2

(c) 1×10^{11} N / m^2 (d) 1×10^{7} N / m^2

98. The vibrations of a string of length 60 cm fixed at both ends are represented by the equation, $y = 4 \sin(\pi x/15) \cos(96\pi t)$, where x and y are in cm and t in seconds. The maximum displacement at $x = 5$ cm is :

(a) $2\sqrt{3}$ cm (b) $3\sqrt{2}$ cm

(c) $\sqrt{2}$ cm (d) $\sqrt{3}$ cm

99. Two periodic waves of intensities I_1 and I_2 pass through a region at the same time in the same direction. The sum of the maximum and minimum intensities is :

(a) $(\sqrt{I_1} + \sqrt{I_2})^2$ (b) $(\sqrt{I_1} - \sqrt{I_2})^2$

(c) $I_1 + I_2$ (d) $2(I_1 + I_2)$

100. Consider ten identical sources of sound, all giving the same frequency, but having phase angles which are random. If the average intensity of each source is I_0, the average of the resultant intensity I due to all these ten sources will be :

(a) $I = 100\, I_0$ (b) $I = 10\, I_0$

(c) $I = I_0$ (d) $I = \sqrt{10}\, I_0$

101. When the temperature increases, the frequency of a tuning fork :

(A.I.E.E.E. 2002)

(a) increases (b) decreases

(c) remains the same (d) none of these

102. The length of a string tied to two rigid supports is 40 cm. Maximum length (wavelength) in cm of a stationary wave produced on it is : **(A.I.E.E.E. 2002)**

(a) 20 cm (b) 80 cm

(c) 40 cm (d) 120 cm

103. The displacement y of a particle in a medium can be expressed as, $y = 10^{-6} \sin(100\,t + 20\,x + \pi/4)\, m$, where t is in seconds and x in metres. The speed of the wave is : **(A.I.E.E.E. 2004)**

(a) 2000 ms^{-1} (b) 5 ms^{-1}

(c) 20 ms^{-1} (d) 5π ms^{-1}

104. An observer moves towards a stationary source of sound with a velocity 1/5th of the velocity of sound. The % increase in the apparent frequency is : **(A.I.E.E.E. 2005)**

(a) 5 % (b) 20 %
(c) Zero (d) 0.5 %

105. A whistle producing sound waves of frequencies 9500 Hz and above is approaching a stationary person with speed v ms^{-1}. The velocity of sound in air is 300 ms^{-1}. If the person can hear the frequencies upto a maximum of 10^4 Hz, the maximum value of v upto which he can hear the whistle is : **(A.I.E.E.E. 2006)**

(a) 30 ms^{-1} (b) $15\sqrt{2}$ ms^{-1}
(c) $15/\sqrt{2}$ ms^{-1} (d) 15 ms^{-1}

106. A sound observer attenuates the sound level of 20 dB. The intensity decreases by a factor of : **(A.I.E.E.E. 2007)**

(a) 100 (b) 1000
(c) 10,000 (d) 10

107. The speed of sound in O_2 at a certain temperature is 460 ms^{-1}. The speed of sound in He at the same temperature will be .... (both are ideal)

(a) 330 ms^{-1} (b) 460 ms^{-1}
(c) 500 ms^{-1} (d) 650 ms^{-1}

108. The wave travelling along the x-axis is described by the equation

$$y(x, t) = 0.005 \cos(\alpha x - \beta t).$$

If the wavelength and time period of wave are 0.08 m and 2.05 respectively, then α and β in respective units are:

(a) $\alpha = 12.50\pi$; $\beta = \pi/2.0$

(b) $\alpha = \dfrac{0.08}{\pi}$; $\beta = \dfrac{2}{\pi}$

(c) $\alpha = 25\pi$; $\beta = \pi$

(d) $\alpha = \dfrac{0.04}{\pi}$; $\beta = \dfrac{1.0}{\pi}$

109. Three sound waves of equal amplitudes have frequencies $(\upsilon - 1)$, υ, $(\upsilon + 1)$. They superpose to give beats. The number of beats produced per second will be :

(a) 4 (b) 3
(c) 2 (d) 1

COMPREHENSION BASED QUESTIONS

A harmonic wave function is represented by,

$$y(x, t) = r \sin\left[\frac{2\pi}{\lambda}(vt + x) + \phi\right]$$

where, it represents a periodic wave travelling with velocity v from right to left along x-axis and so is called a harmonic wave. In it y, r, λ, v and ϕ respectively denote displacement at any time 't', amplitude, wavelength, velocity of wave and initial phase of the wave.

Read carefully and answer the following questions :

A transverse harmonic wave on a string is described by $y(x, t) = 5 \sin(25t + 0.005x + \pi/3)$, where x, y are in cm and t in sec. The positive direction of x is from left to right.

110. The above said wave is a :

(a) Stationary wave
(b) Progressive wave
(c) Both (a) and (b)
(d) None of these

111. The speed of the wave is :

(a) 0.5 ms^{-1} (b) 5 ms^{-1}
(c) 50 ms^{-1} (d) 500 ms^{-1}

112. The direction of propagation of the wave is from :

(a) left to right (b) right to left
(c) no direction (d) none of these

113. The amplitude of the wave is :

(a) 0.5 cm (b) 5 cm
(c) 50 cm (d) 500 cm

114. The frequency of the wave is :

(a) 398 Hz (b) 39.8 Hz
(c) 3.98 Hz (d) 0.398 Hz

115. The initial phase at the origin of the wave is:

(a) π radian (b) $\frac{\pi}{2}$ radian

(c) $\frac{\pi}{3}$ radian (d) $\frac{\pi}{4}$ radian

116. The least distance between two successive crests of the wave is :

(a) 1.257 m (b) 12.57 m

(c) 125.7 m (d) 0.1275 m

ASSERTION AND REASON

Directions for Q. 117 to Q. 120: In the following questions, assertion (statement-I) is followed by reasoning (statement-II). While answering a question, you are required to choose the correct one out of the given four responses.

(a) Both statement-I and II are correct and statement-II is the correct explanation of statement-I.

(b) Both statement-I and II are correct, but statement-II is not the correct explanation of statement-I.

(c) Statement-I is true, but statement-II is false.

(d) Both statement-I and statement-II are false.

117. (I) Sound waves cannot propagate through vacuum, but light waves can.

(II) Sound waves cannot be polarised but light waves can.

118. (I) Sound waves move fastest in solids.

(II) Sound waves propagate slightly in vacuum.

119. (I) Speed of wave $= \frac{\text{Wavelength}}{\text{Time period}}$

(II) Wavelength is the distance between the two nearest particles in phase.

120. (I) A tuning fork is in resonance with a closed pipe, but the same cannot be in resonance with an open pipe of the same length.

(II) The above problem is due to end correction.

121. A source of sound of frequency 600 Hz is placed inside water. The speed of sound in water is 1500 ms^{-1} and in air is 300 ms^{-1}. The frequency of the sound recorded by the observer in air will be :

(a) 120 Hz (b) 200 Hz

(c) 600 Hz (d) 3000 Hz

122. The temperature at which the speed of sound in air becomes double of its value at 27°C is:

(a) 54°C (b) 327°C

(c) 927°C (d) –123°C

123. A travelling wave in a stretched string is described by $y = A \sin (kx - \omega t)$. The maximum particle velocity is :

(a) $A\omega$ (b) ω/k

(c) $\frac{d\omega}{dk}$ (d) $\frac{x}{t}$

124. Energy is not carried by :

(a) Transverse progressive waves

(b) Longitudinal progressive waves

(c) Stationary waves

(d) Electromagnetic waves

125. Two pulses in a stretched string, whose centres are 8 cm apart initially, are moving towards each other as shown in the given figure. The speed of each pulse is 2 cms^{-1}. After 2 seconds, the total energy of the pulses will be :

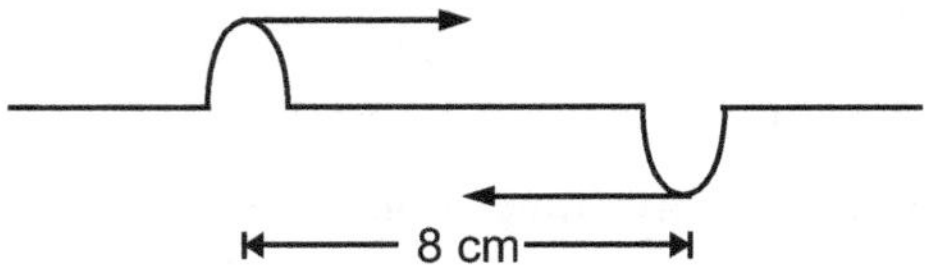

(a) Zero (b) Purely kinetic

(c) Purely potential (d) K.E. and P.E.

126. Two plane harmonic sound waves are expressed by the equations

$$y_1 (x, t) = A \cos (0.5\,\pi x - 100\,\pi t)$$

and $y_2 (x, t) = A \cos (0.46\,\pi x - 92\,\pi t)$

All parameters are in the MKS system. How many times does an observer hear maximum intensity in one second ?

(a) 4 (b) 6

(c) 8 (d) 10

127. The extension in a string is x. The speed of sound in the stretched strings is v. If the extension in the string is increased to 1.5 x, the speed of sound will be :

(a) 1.22 v (b) 0.61 v
(c) 1.5 v (d) 0.75 v

128. If the speed of sound in air is v, the fundamental frequency of a column in a pipe of length L closed at one end is :

(a) v/2L (b) v/L
(c) 3v/L (d) v/4 L

129. As an empty vessel is filled with H_2O, its frequency :

(a) increases (b) decreases
(c) remains same (d) none of these

130. There are three sources of sound of equal intensity with frequency 400, 401 and 402 Hz. Then the speed of sound will be :

(a) 200 ms^{-1} (b) 192 ms^{-1}
(c) 180 ms^{-1} (d) 96 ms^{-1}

131. A particle executes simple harmonic motion with a period of 8 s and amplitude 4 cm. Its maximum speed in cm/s, is :

(J & K C.E.T. 2007)

(a) π (b) $\pi/2$
(c) $\pi/3$ (d) $\pi/4$

132. The displacement of a particle of mass 3 g executing simple harmonic motion is given by $y = 3 \sin (0.2t)$ in SI units. The kinetic energy of the particle at a point which is at a distance equal to (1/3) of its amplitude from its mean position is : **(J & K C.E.T. 2007)**

(a) 12×10^{-3} J (b) 25×10^{-3} J
(c) 0.48×10^{-3} J (d) 0.24×10^{-3} J

133. Two particles A and B execute simple harmonic motion of period T and $\frac{5T}{4}$. They start from mean position. The phase difference between them when the particle A completes an oscillation will be :

(M.P.P.E.T. 2008)

(a) $\pi/2$ (b) 0
(c) $2\pi/5$ (d) $\pi/4$

134. Two simple harmonic motions are represented by

$y_1 = 5 (\sin 2\pi t + \sqrt{3} \cos 2\pi t)$

$y_2 = 5 \sin (2\pi t + \pi/4)$

The ratio of the amplitudes of two SHM's is: **(D.C.E. 2009)**

(a) 1 : 1 (b) 1 : 2
(c) 2 : 1 (d) $1 : \sqrt{3}$

135. A tuning fork of frequency 512 Hz makes 4 beats per second with the vibrating string of a piano. The beat frequency decreases to 2 beats per sec when the tension in the piano string is slightly increased. The frequency of the piano string before increasing the tension was : **(A.I.P.M.T. 2010)**

(a) 510 Hz (b) 514 Hz
(c) 516 Hz (d) 508 Hz.

136. The equation of a simple harmonic wave is given by $y = 5 \sin \frac{\pi}{2}(100t - x)$ where x and y are in metre and time is in second. The period of the wave in second will be :

(Karnataka C.E.T. 2006)

(a) 0.04 (b) 0.01
(c) 1 (d) 5

137. In damped oscillations, the amplitude of oscillation is reduced to one-third of its initial value a_0 at the end of 100 oscillations. When the oscillator completes 200 oscillations, its amplitude must be :

(Kerala P.E.T. 2007)

(a) $a_0/2$ (b) $a_0/6$
(c) $a_0/12$ (d) $a_0/9$

138. A pendulum clock gives correct time at 20°C at a place where g = 10 m/s^2. The pendulum consists of a light steel rod connected to a heavy ball. If it is taken to a different place, where g = 10.01 ms^{-2}, at what temperature the pendulum gives correct time? (α of steel is 10^{-5}/°C) :

(E.M.C.E.T. 2007)

(a) 30°C (b) 60°C
(c) 100°C (d) 120°C

139. A particle of mass m executes simple harmonic motion with amplitude a and frequency υ. The average kinetic energy during its motion from the position of equilibrium to the end is : **(A.I.E.E.E. 2007)**

(a) $2\pi^2 ma^2\upsilon^2$ (b) $\pi^2 ma^2\upsilon^2$
(c) $\frac{1}{4}ma^2\upsilon^2$ (d) $4\pi^2 ma^2\upsilon^2$

140. Which one of the following equations of motion represents simple harmonic motion ?

(A.I.P.M.T. 2009)

(a) Acceleration = $-k(x + a)$
(b) Acceleration = $k(x + a)$
(c) Acceleration = kx
(d) Acceleration = $-k_0x + k_1x^2$

where k, k_0, k_1 and a are all positive.

141. If x, v and a denote the displacement, the velocity and the acceleration of a particle executing simple harmonic motion of time period T, then, which of the following does not change with time ? **(A.I.E.E.E. 2009)**

(a) $a^2T^2 + 4p^2v^2$ (b) aT/x
(c) $aT + 2\pi v$ (d) aT/v

142. The period of oscillation of a mass M suspended from a spring of negligible mass is T. If along with it another mass M is also suspended, the period of oscillation will now be : **(A.I.P.M.T. 2010)**

(a) T (b) $T/\sqrt{2}$
(c) 2T (d) $\sqrt{2}\,T$

143. A simple pendulum is executing SHM with a period of 6 sec between two extreme positions B and C about a point 'O'. If the length of the arc BC is 10 cm, how long will the pendulum take in moving from position C to a position D towards 'O' exactly midway between 'C' and 'O' ?

(E.A.M.C.E.T. 2009)

(a) 0.5 sec (b) 1 sec
(c) 1.5 sec (d) 3 sec

144. A clock pendulum made of invar has a period of 0.5 sec at 20°. If the clock is used in a climate where the temperature averages 30°C, how much time does the clock lose in each oscillation (for invar $\alpha = 9 \times 10^{-7}$/°C and g = constant) : **(E.A.M.C.E.T. 2009)**

(a) 2.25×10^{-6} sec (b) 2.5×10^{-7} sec
(c) 5×10^{-7} sec (d) 1.125×10^{-6} sec

145. A wave travelling along the x-axis is described by the equation

$$y(x, t) = 0.005 \cos(\alpha x - \beta t).$$

If the wavelength and the time period of the wave are 0.08 m and 2.0 s, respectively, then α and β in appropriate units are :

(A.I.E.E.E. 2008)

(a) $\alpha = 12.50\,\pi,\ \beta = \frac{\pi}{2}$

(b) $\alpha = 25.00\,\pi,\ \beta = \pi$

(c) $\alpha = \frac{0.08}{\pi},\ \beta = \frac{2}{\pi}$

(d) $\alpha = \frac{0.04}{\pi},\ \beta = \frac{1}{\pi}$

146. A progressive wave $y = A\sin(kx - \omega t)$ is reflected by a rigid wall at $x = 0$. Then the reflected wave can be represented by :

(Kerala C.E.T. 2009)

(a) $y = A\sin(kx + \omega t)$
(b) $y = A\cos(kx + \omega t)$
(c) $y = -A\sin(kx - \omega t)$
(d) $y = -A\sin(kx + \omega t)$

147. The phase difference between the displacement and acceleration of particle executing SHM in radians is :

(H.P.P.M.T. 2010)

(a) $\pi/4$ (b) $\pi/2$

(c) π (d) 2π

148. A source of sound of frequency 90 Hz is approaching a stationary observer with a speed equal to $1/10^{th}$ speed of sound. The frequency heard by observer will be :

(H.P.P.M.T. 2008)

(a) 80 Hz

(b) 90 Hz

(c) 100 Hz

(d) 120 Hz

149. An observer is approaching a stationary source with a velocity $\frac{1}{4}^{th}$ of the velocity of sound. Then the ratio of the apparent frequency to actual frequency of source is :

(Kerala C.E.T. 2009)

(a) 4 : 5 (b) 5 : 4

(c) 2 : 3 (d) 3 : 2

150. Sound waves travel at 350 m/s through a warm air and at 3500 m/s through brass. the wavelength of a 700 Hz acoustic wave as it enters brass from warm air :

(A.I.P.M.T. 2011)

(a) decreases by a factor 10

(b) increases by a factor 20

(c) increases by a factor 10

(d) decreases by a factor 20

151. A person speaking normally produces a sound of intensity 40 dB at a distance of 1 m. If the threshold intensity of reasonable audibility is 20 dB, the maximum distance at which he can be heard clearly is :

(A.I.I.M.S. 2008)

(a) 4 m (b) 5 m

(c) 10 m (d) 20 m

152. An observer moves towards a stationary source of sound, with a velocity one-fifth of the velocity of sound. What is the percentage increase in the apparent frequency ? **(C.P.M.T. 2008)**

(a) Zero (b) 0.5%

(c) 5% (d) 20%

153. An organ pipe has a fundamental frequency of 100 Hz. Its second overtone is 500 Hz. Find the type of the pipe.

(M.H.T.C.E.T. 2009)

(a) Closed at one end

(b) Closed at both ends

(c) Open at both ends

(d) Sometimes open sometimes closed

154. There are three sources of sound of equal intensity with frequencies 200, 201 and 202 vibrations per second. The number of beats heard per second is : **(H.P.P.M.T. 2006)**

(a) 0 (b) 1

(c) 2 (d) 3

155. A glass tube of length 1.0 m is completely filled with water. A vibrating tuning fork of frequency 500 Hz is kept over the mouth of the tube and the water is drained out slowly at the bottom of the tube. If the velocity of sound in air is 330 ms^{-1}, then the total number of resonances that occur will be :

(Kerala P.E.T. 2008)

(a) 2 (b) 3

(c) 1 (d) 5

ANSWER KEY

Part - I

1. (c)	**2.** (a)	**3.** (c)	**4.** (c)	**5.** (a)	**6.** (c)	**7.** (c)	**8.** (a)	**9.** (d)	**10.**(c)
11.(a)	**12.**(d)	**13.**(b)	**14.**(a)	**15.**(a)	**16.**(c)	**17.**(b)	**18.**(c)	**19.**(b)	**20.**(d)
21.(c)	**22.**(c)	**23.**(b)	**24.**(c)	**25.**(d)	**26.**(a)	**27.**(d)	**28.**(d)	**29.**(c)	**30.**(b)
31.(b)	**32.**(d)	**33.**(d)	**34.**(d)	**35.**(d)	**36.**(c)	**37.**(a)	**38.**(b)	**39.**(a)	**40.**(d)
41.(d)	**42.**(c)	**43.**(a)	**44.**(a)	**45.**(b)	**46.**(d)	**47.**(d)	**48.**(d)	**49.**(b)	**50.**(a)
51.(c)	**52.**(b)	**53.**(c)	**54.**(b)	**55.**(b)	**56.**(c)	**57.**(a)	**58.**(c)	**59.**(b)	**60.**(b)
61.(d)	**62.**(d)	**63.**(d)	**64.**(a)	**65.**(d)	**66.**(d)	**67.**(a)	**68.**(b)	**69.**(a)	**70.**(b)
71.(a)	**72.**(a)	**73.**(a)	**74.**(a)	**75.**(a)	**76.**(d)	**77.**(a)	**78.**(a)	**79.**(a)	**80.**(b)
81.(a)	**82.**(b)	**83.**(a)	**84.**(b)	**85.**(c)	**86.**(b)	**87.**(a)	**88.**(b)	**89.**(a)	**90.**(d)
91.(b)	**92.**(b)	**93.**(b)	**94.**(b)	**95.**(d)	**96.**(a)	**97.**(c)	**98.**(d)	**99.**(b)	**100.** (a)
101. (b)	**102.** (b)	**103.** (d)	**104.** (b)	**105.** (c)	**106.** (d)	**107.** (b)	**108.** (b)	**109.** (b)	**110.** (b)
111. (d)	**112.** (c)	**113.** (a)	**114.** (d)	**115.** (b)	**116.** (c)	**117.** (b)	**118.**b, d	**119.**a, b	**120.** (b)
121. (b)	**122.** (d)	**123.** (c)	**124.** b, c	**125.** (a)	**126.** (a)	**127.** (a)			

Part - II

1. (b)	**2.** (d)	**3.** (d)	**4.** (a)	**5.** (d)	**6.** (d)	**7.** (d)	**8.** (d)	**9.** (c)	**10.** (c)
11. (d)	**12.** (a)	**13.** (d)	**14.** (a)	**15.** (c)	**16.** (c)	**17.** (c)	**18.** (d)	**19.** (c)	**20.** (c)
21. (a)	**22.** (b)	**23.** (b)	**24.** (d)	**25.** (b)	**26.** (d)	**27.** (c)	**28.** (b)	**29.** (a)	**30.** (c)
31. (b)	**32.** (c)	**33.** (c)	**34.** (a)	**35.** (b)	**36.** (d)	**37.** (b)	**38.** (b)	**39.** (a)	**40.** (c)
41. (b)	**42.** (b)	**43.** (d)	**44.** (b)	**45.** (b)	**46.** (b)	**47.** (a)	**48.** (c)	**49.** (a)	**50.** (c)
51. (b)	**52.** (b)	**53.** (c)	**54.** (d)	**55.** (c)	**56.** (c)	**57.** (d)	**58.** (c)	**59.** (b)	**60.** (d)
61. (a)	**62.** (b)	**63.** (d)	**64.** (a)	**65.** (c)	**66.** (b)	**67.** (c)	**68.** (b)	**69.** (b)	**70.** (d)
71. (a)	**72.** (d)	**73.** (d)	**74.** (d)	**75.** (a)	**76.** (b)	**77.** (b)	**78.** (c)	**79.** (b)	**80.** (a)
81. (b)	**82.** (b)	**83.** (b)	**84.** (d)	**85.** (d)	**86.** (c)	**87.** (c)	**88.** (c)	**89.** (b)	**90.** (c)
91. (c)	**92.** (b)	**93.** (a)	**94.** (b)	**95.** (b)	**96.** (c)	**97.** (d)	**98.** (a)	**99.** (d)	**100.** (b)
101. (b)	**102.** (b)	**103.** (b)	**104.** (b)	**105.** (d)	**106.** (a)	**107.** (b)	**108.** (c)	**109.** (c)	**110.**(b)
111.(c)	**112.**(b)	**113.**(b)	**114.**(c)	**115.**(c)	**116.**(b)	**117.**(b)	**118.**(c)	**119.**(b)	**120.**(c)
121. (c)	**122.** (c)	**123.** (a)	**124.** (c)	**125.** (b)	**126.** (a)	**127.** (a)	**128.** (d)	**129.** (a)	**130.** (c)
131. (a)	**132.** (c)	**133.** (a)	**134.** (c)	**135.** (d)	**136.** (a)	**137.** (d)	**138.** (d)	**139.** (b)	**140.** (a)
141. (b)	**142.** (d)	**143.** (b)	**144.** (a)	**145.** (b)	**146.** (d)	**147.** (c)	**148.** (c)	**149.** (b)	**150.** (c)
151. (c)	**152.** (d)	**153.** (a)	**154.** (c)	**155.** (b)					

11

ELECTROSTATICS

MULTIPLE CHOICE QUESTIONS

1. Three charges each equal to q μC are placed at three corners of an equilateral triangle. If the force acting between any two is F, then the net force acting on each will be :

(a) $\sqrt{3}$F (b) $2\sqrt{2}$F

(c) 3F (d) $2\sqrt{3}$F

2. Two identical spheres charged with 200 μC and –200 μC are kept at a distance. The force acting on them is f_1. They are connected using a conductor and then the conductor is removed. The force f_2 acting on them now will be :

(a) equal to f_1 (b) more than f_1

(c) zero (d) infinite

3. Two charges each of 10 μC are placed at the corners of an equilateral triangle of side 8 cm. The field at the third corner is :

(a) 2.43×10^7 Vm^{-1} (b) $5\sqrt{3} \times 10^7$ NC^{-1}

(c) 5.83×10^7 Vm^{-1} (d) $5\sqrt{3} \times 10^8$ NC^{-1}

4. The coulomb force between two α-particles separated by a distance of 8.2 fermi in air is approximately :

(a) 60 N (b) 14 N

(c) 120 N (d) 140 N

5. The four charges, each of value $+q$ are placed at the four corners of a square. How much charge be kept at its centre so that the whole system is in equilibrium ?

(a) $-\frac{q}{4}(1 + 2\sqrt{2})$ (b) $-\frac{q}{8}(1 + 2\sqrt{2})$

(c) $-\frac{q}{2}(1 + 2\sqrt{2})$ (b) $+\frac{q}{4}(1 + 2\sqrt{2})$

6. Two charges $+4q$ and $+q$ are placed at A and B such that AB = 3m. C is the point on the line joining A and B. A third point charge q' is placed at C such that q' is in equilibrium, then AC is :

(a) 2 m (b) 3 m

(c) 1 m (d) 6 m

7. ABC is a right angled triangle, AB = 3 cm, BC = 4 cm, AC = 5 cm and charges +15, +12, and –20 e.s.u are placed at A, B, C respectively. The magnitude of the force experienced by the charge at B in dynes is :

(a) 125 (b) 25

(c) 35 (d) Zero

8. A point charge of 60 stat coulomb is placed at 3 cm in front of earthed metallic plates of large size. Then the force of attraction on the point charge is :

(a) 100 dynes (b) 360 dynes

(c) 400 dynes (d) 180 dynes

9. Three positive charges of equal value q are placed at the vertices of an equilateral triangle. The resulting lines of force should be sketched as in :

(a)

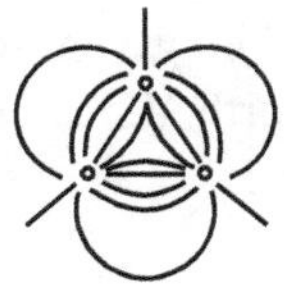

(b)

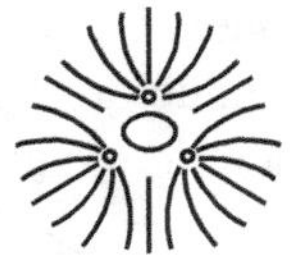

(c)

(d)

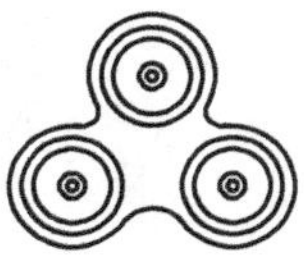

10. The potential of a sphere of radius 2 cm when a charge of 2 coulomb is given to it will be :

(a) 9×10^3 V (b) 9×10^{11} V

(c) 9×10^4 V (d) 9×10^{16} V

11. A uniform electric field pointing in the positive x-direction exists in a region. Let A be the origin, B be the point on the x-axis at $x = +1$ cm and C be the point on the y-axis at $y = +1$ cm. Then the potentials at A, B and C satisfy :

(a) $V_A < V_B$ (b) $V_A > V_B$

(c) $V_A < V_C$ (d) $V_A > V_C$

12. Two small spheres each carrying a charge of q are r metre apart. If one of the spheres is taken around the other in a circular path of radius R meter, the work done will be equal to :

(a) Force between them × R

(b) Force between them × 2R

(c) Force between them × 2 (R – r)

(d) Zero

13. Two point charges placed at a distance of 20 cm in air repel each other with a certain force. When a dielectric slab of thickness 8 cm and dielectric constant K is introduced between these point charges, force of interaction becomes half of its previous value. K is approximately :

(a) 2 (b) 4

(c) $\sqrt{2}$ (d) 1

14. A is a spherical conductor placed concentrically inside a hollow spherical conductor B. Charge +Q is given to the conductor A and B is earthed. Then the electric intensity is not zero :

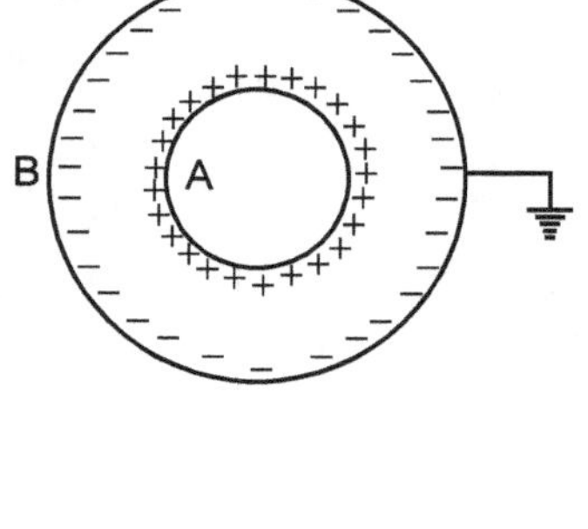

(a) inside A

(b) outside B

(c) on the surface of B

(d) between A and B

15. A is a spherical conductor placed concentrically inside a hollow spherical conductor B. Charge + Q is given to the conductor A and B is earthed. The electrical potential is zero :

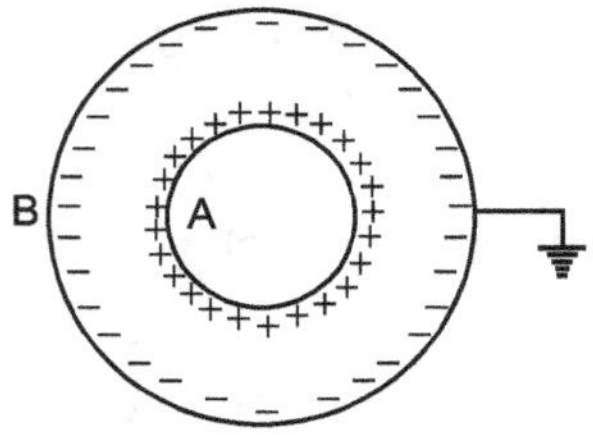

(a) inside A

(b) on the surface of A

(c) outside and on the surface of B

(d) between A and B

16. The radius of the gold nucleus is 6.6×10^{-15} metre and its atomic number is 79. The electric potential at its surface is :

(a) 1.7×10^4 volt (b) 1.7×10^6 volt

(c) 1.7×10^{-4} volt (d) 1.7×10^7 volt

17. The dielectric strength of air at NTP is 3×10^6 volt per metre. Then the maximum charge that can be given to the spherical conductor of radius 3 m is :

(a) 3×10^{-1} C (b) 3×10^{-3} C

(c) 3×10^{-2} C (d) 3×10^{-4} C

18. The dielectric strength of air at NTP is 3×10^6 volt per metre. The maximum potential upto which the spherical conductor of radius 3 m can be charged is :

(a) 9×10^5 volt (b) 9×10^7 volt

(c) 9×10^6 volt (d) 9.3×10^7 volt

19. Two point electric charges of +8 stat coulomb and +32 stat coulomb are placed at A and B such that AB = 120 cm. C is a point on the line joining A and B. The electric intensity at C is zero when :

(a) AC = 40 cm and BC = 80 cm
(b) AC = 120 cm and BC = 240 cm
(c) AC = 80 cm and BC = 40 cm
(d) AC = 240 cm and BC = 120 cm

20. Infinite number of charges each numerically equal to q and of the same sign are placed along the X-axis at $x = 1, x = 2, x = 4, x = 8$ and so on. Then the electrical potential at $x = 0$, due to this set of charges is :

(a) $\frac{2Kq}{3}$ (b) $2Kq$
(c) $\frac{4Kq}{3}$ (d) $\frac{4Kq}{5}$

21. Infinite number of charges each numerically equal to q and of the same sign are placed along the X-axis at $x = 1, x = 2, x = 4, x = 8$ and so on, then electrical intensity at $x = 0$ is:

(a) $\frac{2Kq}{3}$ (b) $2Kq$
(c) $\frac{4Kq}{3}$ (d) $\frac{4Kq}{5}$

22. Infinite number of charges, each numerically equal to q but consecutive charges having opposite sign, are placed along the X-axis at $x = 1, x = 2, x = 4, x = 8$ and so on, then the electrical potential at $x = 0$ due to this set of charges is :

(a) $\frac{2Kq}{3}$ (b) $2Kq$
(c) $\frac{4Kq}{3}$ (d) $\frac{4Kq}{5}$

23. Infinite number of charges, each numerically equal to q but consecutive charges having opposite sign, are placed along the X-axis at $x = 1, x = 2, x = 4, x = 8$ and so on, then the electric field intensity at $x = 0$ due to this set of charges is :

(a) $\frac{2Kq}{3}$ (b) $2Kq$
(c) $\frac{4Kq}{3}$ (d) $\frac{4Kq}{5}$

24. Suppose we have two parallel plates with surface charge densities $\sigma_A = \sigma_B = \sigma$, then the field outside the parallel plates on either side is :

(a) $\frac{\sigma}{4\pi\varepsilon_0}$ (b) $\frac{\sigma}{2\pi\varepsilon_0}$
(c) $\frac{\sigma}{2\varepsilon_0}$ (d) $\frac{\sigma}{\varepsilon_0}$

25. The diagram below shows electric field lines around two isolated point charges P and Q. At X the field strength is zero. Which of the following is true ?

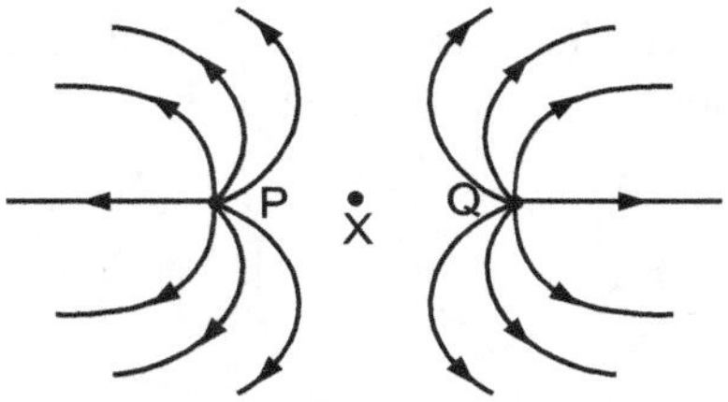

(a) Q is a smaller charge than P because X is closer to P than Q.
(b) Field strength is always proportional to the distance from X.
(c) The potential at Q is less than the potential at P.
(d) The field lines show that both charges are positive.

26. The electric field in region-2 in the figure below is :

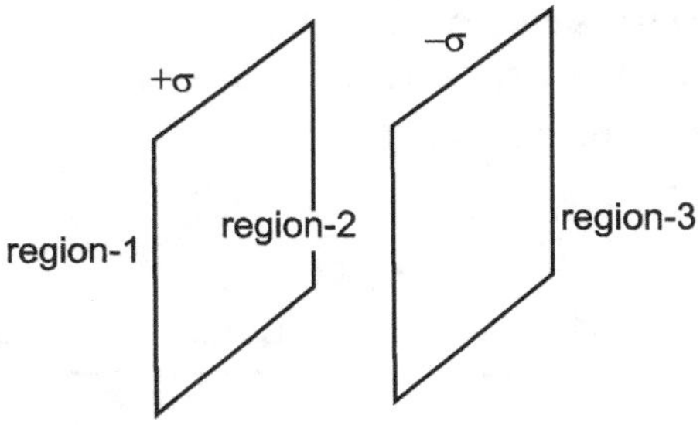

(a) 0 (b) $\frac{\sigma}{4\pi\varepsilon_0}$
(c) $\frac{\sigma}{\varepsilon_0}$ (d) ∞

27. A charge of $q = 8.75\ \mu C$ in an electric field is acted upon by a force of F = 4.5 N. The potential gradient at this point is :

(a) $3.70 \times 10^6\ Vm^{-1}$ (b) $5.14 \times 10^3\ Vm^{-1}$

(c) $5.14 \times 10^4\ Vm^{-1}$ (d) $5.14 \times 10^5\ Vm^{-1}$

28. Solid angle $d\Omega$ is given by :

(a) $\dfrac{dS \sin\theta}{r}$ (b) $\dfrac{dS \cos\theta}{r^2}$

(c) $\dfrac{dS}{r^2 \sin\theta}$ (d) $\dfrac{dS}{r^2 \cos\theta}$

29. Figure shows a charged conductor resting on an insulating stand. If at the point P the charge density is σ, the potential is V and the electric field strength is E, what are the values of these quantities at point Q ?

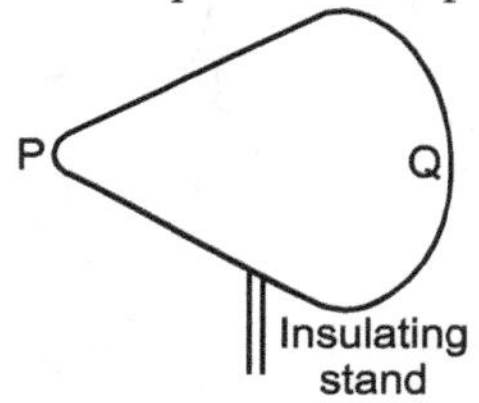

	Charge density	Potential	Electric intensity
(a)	$>\sigma$	$>V$	$>E$
(b)	$>\sigma$	V	$>E$
(c)	$<\sigma$	V	E
(d)	$<\sigma$	V	$<E$

30. An electron is moving round a nucleus in a circular Bohr orbit. Suppose p denotes linear momentum and θ denotes angle of rotation about an axis passing through the nucleus. The configuration of the system essentially remains same or unchanged when θ is increased by some value θ_0 (say). Then p vs θ graph roughly will be :

(a) 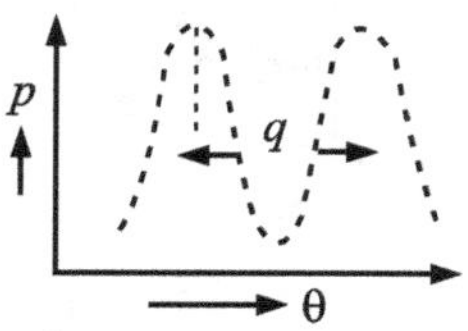

(b) 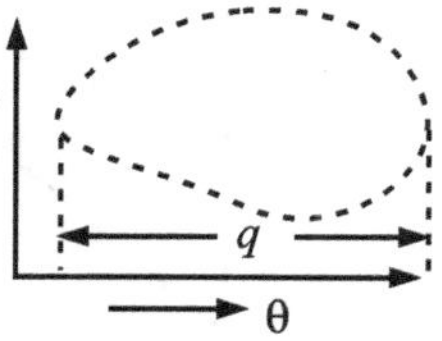

(c) 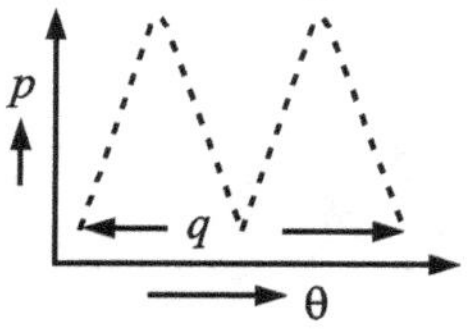

(d) 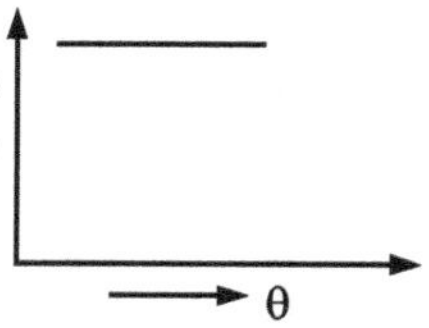

31. If two conducting spheres are separately charged and then brought in contact then :

(a) the total energy of the two spheres is conserved

(b) the total charge on the two spheres is conserved

(c) both the total energy and charge are conserved

(d) the final potential is always the mean of the original potential of the two spheres

32. Two thin spherical conducting shells are a large distance apart. One of the radius 10 cm carries a charge of + 0.5 μC and the other of radius 20 cm carries a charge of + 0.7 μC. The charge on each, when they are connected by a suitable conducting wire, is respectively :

(a) + 0.4 and + 0.8 μC

(b) + 0.425 and + 0.85 μC

(c) + 0.5 and + 0.7 μC

(d) + 0.6 and + 0.6 μC

33. A ring of radius R carries a charge Q, uniformly distributed along its circumference. What is the ratio of the electric field strength at a distance R to that at a distance $R/\sqrt{2}$ along the axis ?

(a) $3\sqrt{3}/8$ (b) $3\sqrt{6}/8$

(c) $3\sqrt{3}/\sqrt{2}$ (d) $2\sqrt{2}/3\sqrt{3}$

34. Three wires of equal length and same material are connected to a battery as shown in the figure. Which one of the following represents the variation of the electric field E inside the conductor with distance x measured along the wire and from the positive terminal of the battery :

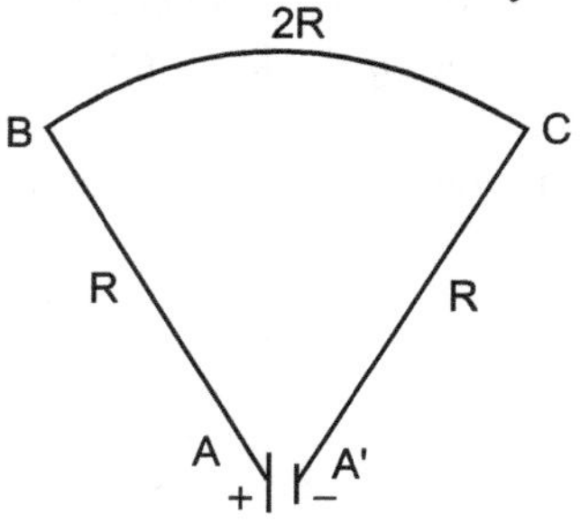

(a) 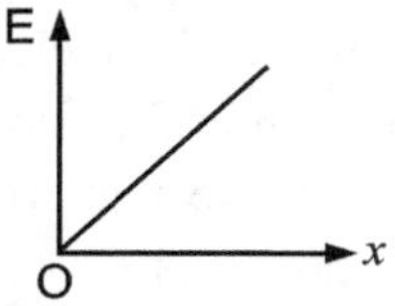

(b) 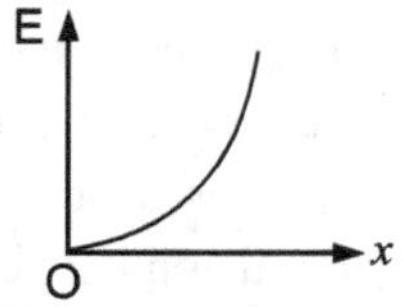

(c) 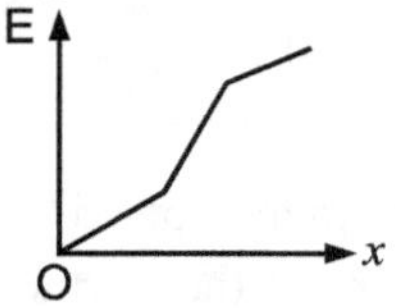

(d) 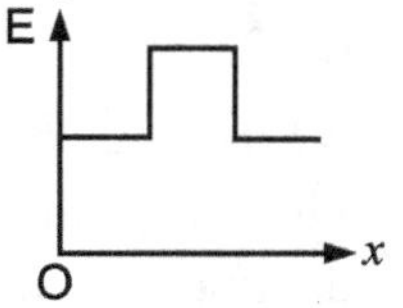

35. Three charges Q, 2Q and 8Q are to be placed on a line whose length is R. What should be the positions where these charges should be placed such that the potential energy of the system is minimum?

(a) Q should be placed in the middle at a distance R / 3 from 2Q.

(b) 2Q should be placed in the middle at a distance 2R / 3 from Q.

(c) 8Q should be placed in the middle at a distance 2R / 3 from Q.

(d) Q should be placed in the middle at a distance 2R / 3 from 2Q.

36. A point charge is placed at X in front of an earthed metal sheet Y. P and Q are two points between X and Y as shown in the figure. If the electric field strength at P and Q are E_P and E_Q, which one of the following statements is correct ?

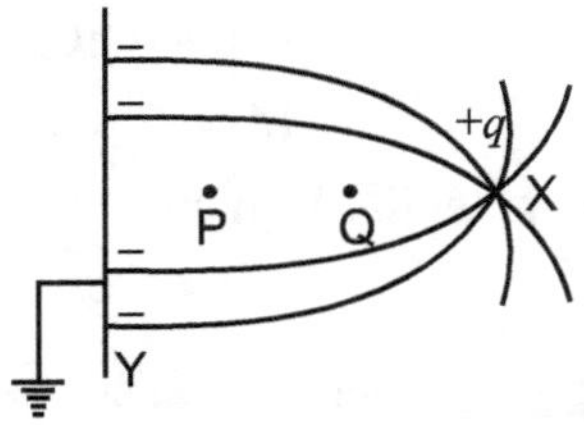

(a) $E_P = E_Q$ (b) $E_P > E_Q$

(c) $E_P < E_Q$ (d) $E_P = 0 = E_Q$

37. The electric field due to an infinite line charge at an external point varies as :

(a) $\frac{1}{r}$ (b) $\frac{1}{r^2}$

(c) $\sqrt{r}$ (d) $1/\sqrt{r}$

38. A ball of mass 1 g and charge 10^{-8} C moves from point A whose potential is 600 V to point B whose potential is zero volt. If velocity of the ball at B is $20\ cms^{-1}$, what is its velocity at A ?

(a) 0.17 ms^{-1} (b) 0.27 ms^{-1}

(c) 0.37 ms^{-1} (d) 0.07 ms^{-1}

39. Suppose we have two parallel plates A and B with uniform charge densities σ_1 and σ_2. Then the field within the plates is :

(a) $\frac{1}{4\pi\varepsilon_0}(\sigma_1 - \sigma_2)$ (b) $\frac{1}{4\varepsilon_0}(\sigma_1 - \sigma_2)$

(c) $\frac{1}{2\varepsilon_0}(\sigma_1 - \sigma_2)$ (d) $\frac{4\pi}{\varepsilon_0}(\sigma_1 - \sigma_2)$

40. A particle of mass 2 g and charge 1μC is held at rest on a frictionless horizontal surface at a distance of 1 m from a fixed charge of 1 mC. If the particle is released, it will be repelled. The speed of the particle when it is at a distance of 10 m from the fixed charge, in ms^{-1} is :

(a) 90 (b) 9

(c) 900 (d) 0.9

41. An electron is moving round a nucleus in circular Bohr orbit. Suppose p denotes linear momentum and θ denotes angle of rotation about an axis passing through the nucleus. The configuration of the system essentially remains unchanged when θ is increased by some value θ_0 (say). Then :

(a) $\theta_0 = \pi$ (b) $\theta_0 = 3\pi$

(c) $\theta_0 = 4\pi$ (d) $\theta_0 = 2\pi$

42. An electron moves along a metal tube with variable cross-section. How will its velocity change when it approaches the neck of the tube ?

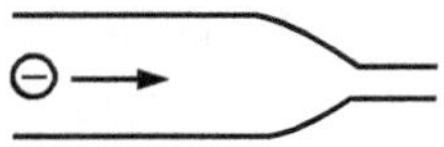

(a) –ve charges will be induced and electron will get decelerated

(b) + ve charges will be induced and electron will get accelerated

(c) Velocity will remain constant as no charges will be induced

(d) No prediction can be made

43. Two insulated charged spheres of radii 70 cm and 75 cm respectively and having equal charge q are connected by a copper wire and then they are separated. Then :

(a) both the spheres will have the same charge q.

(b) the charge on 70 cm sphere will be greater than that on the 75 cm sphere.

(c) the charge on 75 cm sphere will be greater than that on the 70 cm sphere.

(d) both will have zero charge.

44. A thin non-conducting ring of radius R has a linear charge density $\lambda = \lambda_0 \cos\theta$, where λ_0 is the value of λ at $\theta = 0$. The net electric dipole moment for this charge distribution is:

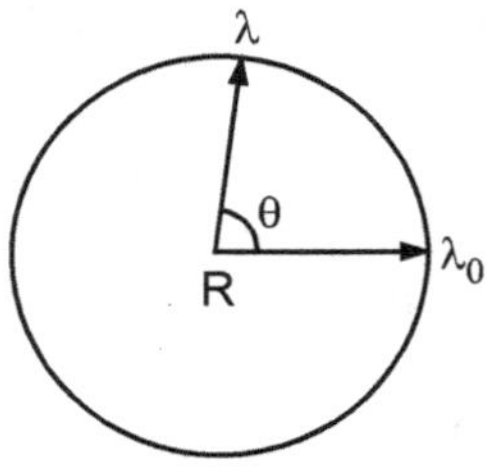

(a) $\pi R^2 \lambda_0$ (b) $2\pi R^2 \lambda_0$

(c) $4\pi R^2 \lambda_0$ (d) $\pi R^2 \lambda_0 / 2$

45. Two completely ionized carbon-12 atoms (q = 6e) are brought to a distance of 10 fermi of each other. What is the force of repulsion ?

(a) 83 N (b) 83 mN

(c) 83 μN (d) 83 nN

46. A solid conducting sphere having charge Q is surrounded by an uncharged concucting hollow spherical shell. Let the potential difference between the surface of the solid sphere and that of the outer surface of the hollow shell be V. If now the shell is given a charge (–3Q), the new potential difference between the same two surfaces is :

(a) V (b) 2V

(c) 4V (d) –2V

47. The excess (equal in number) of electrons that must be placed on each of the two small spheres spaced 3cm apart, so that force of repulsion between the spheres is 10^{-19} N, is :

(a) 25 (b) 225

(c) 625 (d) 1250

48. Find the dipole moment of a charge distributed uniformly over the surface of a spherical shell of radius R. One hemispherical shell has a charge Q while the charge on the other is equal to –Q :

(a) 4QR (b) 2QR

(c) QR (d) QR/2

49. Two completely ionized carbon-12 atoms (q = 6e) are brought to a distance of 10 fermi from each other. If C–12 ions are free to move, what is approximately the initial acceleration of each ?

(a) 4×10^{27} ms^{-2} (b) 4×10^{26} ms^{-2}

(c) 4×10^{25} ms^{-2} (d) 4×10^{28} ms^{-2}

50. A positive charge of 9 μC is fixed at the origin. A second charge q is fixed on the x-axis at $x = a$. A charge q_0 at $x = 3a$ does not experience any net force. What is the value of q ?

(a) –4 μC (b) + 4 μC

(c) + 2 μC (d) – 2 μC

51. The electric potential V in an electric field is given by

$$V = \frac{1}{4\pi\varepsilon_0} \cdot \frac{q}{r} \text{ where } \vec{r} = 2i + 6j + 3k.$$

The electric field at a point is given by :

(a) $\dfrac{1}{2i + 6j + 3k} \cdot \dfrac{1}{4\pi\varepsilon_0}\dfrac{q}{r}$

(b) $\dfrac{1}{4\pi\varepsilon_0}\dfrac{q}{r}\dfrac{2i + 6j + 3k}{49}$

(c) $\dfrac{1}{4\pi\varepsilon_0} \cdot q\dfrac{2i + 6j + 3k}{343}$

(d) $\dfrac{1}{4\pi\varepsilon_0} \cdot \dfrac{q}{r} 2i + 6j + 3k$

52. A sphere of radius R is placed in a uniform electric field E. The total electric flux over the surface of the sphere is given by :

(a) $\pi R^2 E$ (b) $4\pi R^2 E$
(c) $2\pi R^2 E$ (d) Zero

53. A ring made of wire with a radius R = 10 cm is charged negatively and carries a charge $Q = -5 \times 10^{-9}$ C. What are the intensities respectively of an electric field on the axis of the ring at points lying on the axis at a distance of 10 cm and 15 cm from the ring centre ?

(a) 1600 Vm^{-1} and 1150 Vm^{-1}
(b) 1150 Vm^{-1} and 1600 Vm^{-1}
(c) 0 Vm^{-1} and 1600 Vm^{-1}
(d) 1150 Vm^{-1} and 0 Vm^{-1}

54. A long cylindrical wire carries a positive charge of linear density 2.0×10^{-8} cm^{-1}. An electron revolves around it in a circular path under the influence of the attractive electrostatic force. What is the kinetic energy of the electron :

(a) 3×10^{-16} J (b) 3×10^{-17} J
(c) 3×10^{-18} J (d) 3×10^{-15} J

55. Consider a charged filament (charge per unit length λ) of length l. Consider a point P at a distance 'a' from the filament. The electrostatic field at P due to this filament in the limit $a << 1$ will correspond to that due to:

(a) an infinitely long filament
(b) a semi-infinite filament
(c) a point charge
(d) a semi-circular charge (with P as the centre)

56. A uniform electric field exists in the vertically downward direction. Its magnitude is 10 NC^{-1}. What is the increase in electrostatic potential as one goes up through a height of 50 cm ?

(a) 20 V (b) 15 V
(c) 10 V (d) 5 V

57. A non-conducting massless rod of length 10 cm carries two small metallic balls of mass 5 g each. There is a charge of 1 μC on each ball, fixed at each end of the rod. The rod is held in an electrical field of 50 Vm^{-1}, making an angle θ ($\theta << 1$) with the field. When the rod is released, it executes simple harmonic motion. Its time period is :

(a) 2.8 s (b) 0.14 s
(c) 14 s (d) 1.4 s

58. The figure below shows three concentric thin spherical shells A, B and C of radii r_1, r_2 and r_3 respectively. The shells A and C are given charges + q and – q respectively. The shell B is earthed. What is the charge appearing on the surface of B ?

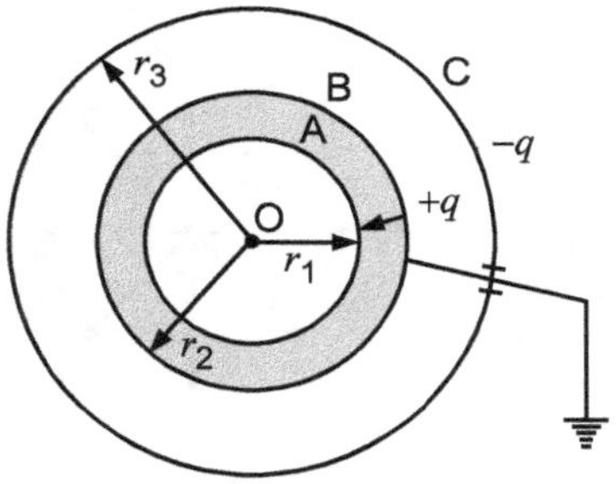

(a) $\frac{-r_1}{r_2}q$ (b) $\frac{r_2}{r_1}q$
(c) $\frac{r_2}{r_3}q$ (d) $\frac{-r_3}{r_2}q$

59. Identical charges $+q$ are placed at the corners of a regular hexagon. The value of the charge Q at the centre of the hexagon to make the whole system of charges at equilibrium is :

(a) 1.83 q (b) –1.83 q
(c) 8.31 q (d) –8.31 q

60. The charge on the uranium nucleus is 1.5×10^{-17} C and the charge on the α-particle is 3.2×10^{-19} C. The electrostatic force between a uranium nucleus and an α-particle separated by 2.0×10^{-13} m is approximately :

(a) 1.1×10^{-33} N (b) 1.1×10^{-20} N
(c) 1.1×10^{-13} N (d) 1.1 N

61. Identify the equipotential surfaces in an electric field due to a point charge and also a region with uniform electric field :

(a)

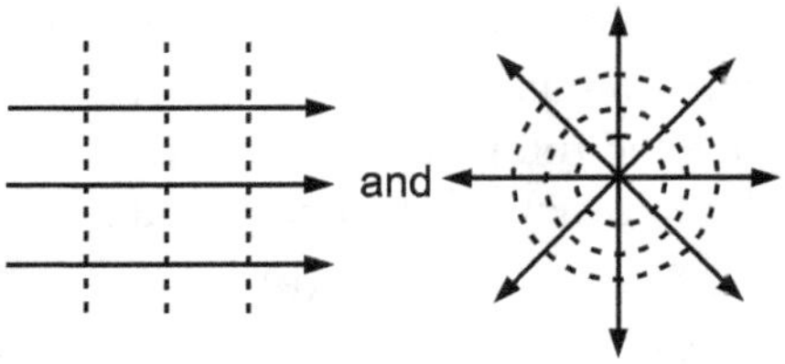

(b)

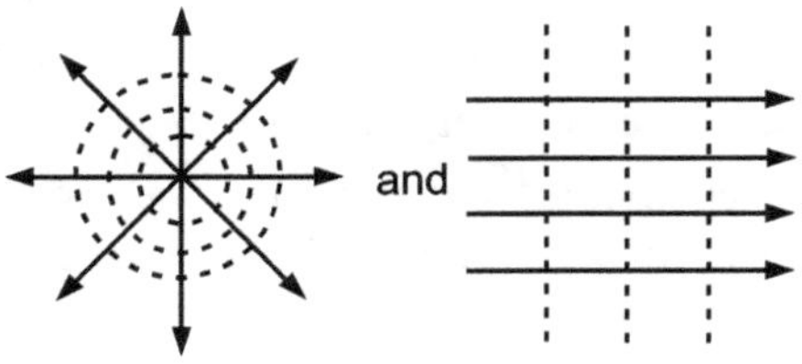

(c)

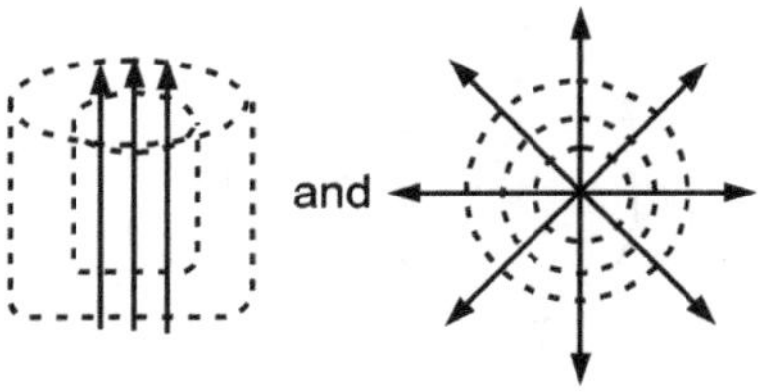

(d)

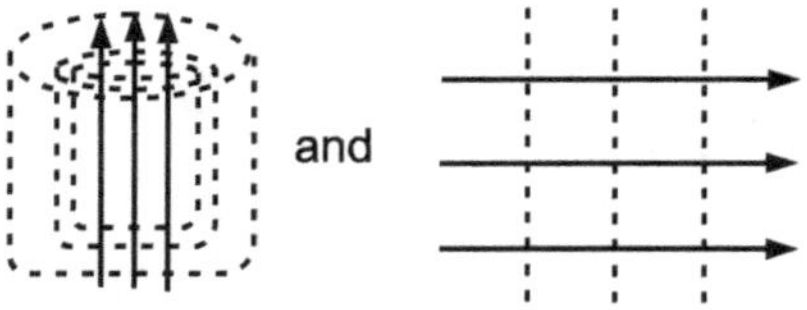

62. Two identical conducting spheres of radius 0.15 m are separated by a distance of 10 m. What is the charge on each sphere if the potentials of the spheres are + 1500 V and – 1500 V respectively ?

(a) 2.6×10^{-6} C (b) 2.6×10^{-7} C

(c) 2.6×10^{-8} C (d) 2.6×10^{-9} C

63. Two charges + 4*q* and + *q* are placed at the ends of a straight line. A charge – *q* is placed at the mid point of this line. Then the charge + *q* will be in :

(a) stable equilibrium

(b) unstable equilibrium

(c) non-equilibrium state

(d) none of the above mentioned states

64. A copper (density of Cu = ρ_C) ball of diameter *d* is immersed in oil of density ρ_0. What is the charge on the ball, if in a homogeneous electric field E directed vertically upward, it is suspended in the oil ?

(a) $\frac{1}{6}\pi d^3 \frac{\rho_c g}{E}\left(1-\frac{\rho_0}{\rho_C}\right)$

(b) $\frac{1}{3}\pi d^3 \frac{\rho_c g}{E}\left(1-\frac{\rho_0}{\rho_C}\right)$

(c) $\frac{1}{2}\pi d^3 \frac{\rho_c g}{E}\left(1-\frac{\rho_0}{\rho_C}\right)$

(d) $\pi d^3 \frac{\rho_c g}{E}\left(1-\frac{\rho_0}{\rho_C}\right)$

65. Electric charges (*q*, *q*, –2*q*) are placed at the corners of an equilateral triangle ABC of side l. The magnitude of the dipole moment of the system is :

(a) 4*ql* (b) $\sqrt{3}\,ql$

(c) 2*ql* (d) *ql*

66. An electric dipole of moment *p* is placed at the origin along the X-axis. The electric field at a point P, whose position vector makes an angle θ with the X-axis, will make an angle ϕ with the X-axis, where $\phi = \theta + \alpha$ with $\alpha = \tan^{-1}\left(\frac{1}{2}\tan\theta\right)$. We have :

(a) $\phi = \theta + 3\alpha$ (b) $\phi = \theta + 2\alpha$

(c) $\phi = \theta + \alpha$ (d) $\phi = \theta$

67. Two charges + *q* and + 2*q* are placed at the ends of a straight line. Where should the third charge (–Q) be placed in the line itself so that it is in stable equilibrium with respect to displacement along the line ?

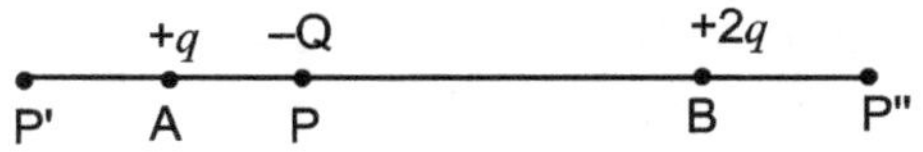

(a) at P

(b) at P'

(c) at P"

(d) None of the above

68. Point charges each of magnitude Q, are placed at the three corners of a square as shown in the figure. What is the direction of the resultant electric field at the fourth corner ?

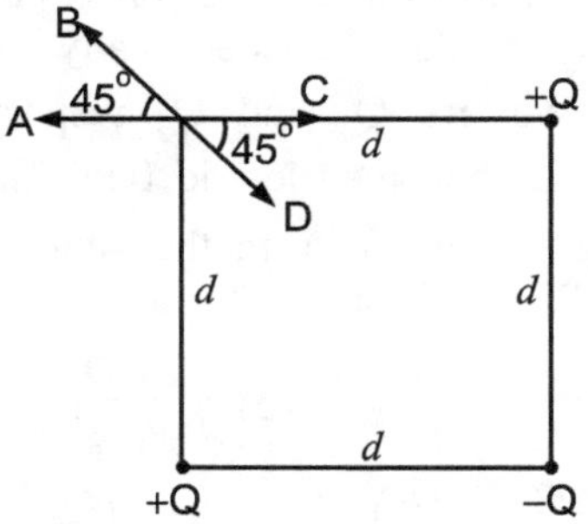

(a) In the direction of A

(b) In the direction of B

(c) In the direction of C

(d) In the direction of D

69. A soap bubble is given a negative charge, then its radius :

(a) decreases

(b) increases

(c) remains uncharged

(d) nothing can be predicted as information is incomplete

70. A proton is released from rest at a distance of 10^{-4} Å from the nucleus of mercury atom (Z = 80). The K.E of the proton when it is far away from the nucleus is :

(a) 12 eV (b) 12 keV

(c) 1.2 MeV (d) 12 MeV

71. Two balls with charges 5 μC and 10 μC are at a distance of 1 m from each other. In order to reduce the distance between them to 0.5 m, the amount of work to be performed is :

(a) 45 J (b) 0.45×10^{-6} J

(c) 1.2×10^{-4} J (d) 0.45 J

72. A cube of side 'a' is placed in a uniform electric field $E = E_0 i$. The total electric flux through the cube is :

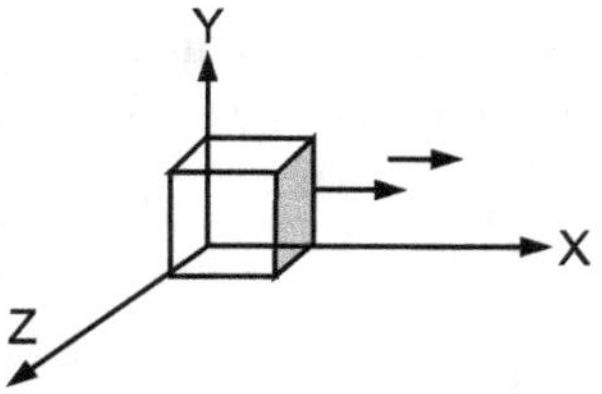

(a) Zero (b) $2a^2\varepsilon_0$

(c) $4a^2\varepsilon_0$ (d) $6a^2\varepsilon_0$

73. A conducting hollow spherical shell having an inner radius 'a' and outer radius 'b' carries a charge Q. If a point charge q is placed at the center of the sphere, then surface charge density at the outer surface is:

(a) $\frac{Q}{4\pi b^2}$

(b) $\frac{-q}{4\pi b^2}$

(c) $\frac{Q+q}{4\pi(b^2-a^2)}$

(d) $\frac{Q+q}{4\pi b^2}$

74. A thin spherical shell of radius 'a' carries a charge 'q'. Concentric with it, is another thin metallic spherical shell of radius b ($> a$). When the outer shell is given a charge Q, the electric field at point C at distance c ($a < c > b$) is :

(a) $\frac{Kq}{a^2}$ (b) $\frac{Kq}{b^2}$

(c) $\frac{Kq}{c^2}$ (d) $\frac{K(q+Q)}{c^2}$

75. Three concentric spherical metallic shells A, B and C of radii a, b and c ($a < b < c$) have charge densities σ, –σ and σ respectively. If the shells A and C are at the same potential, then :

(a) $a + b + c = 0$

(b) $a + c = b$

(c) $a + b = c$

(d) $a = b + c$

76. Two dipoles of dipole moment p each are placed as shown in the figure. Find the force between the two dipoles :

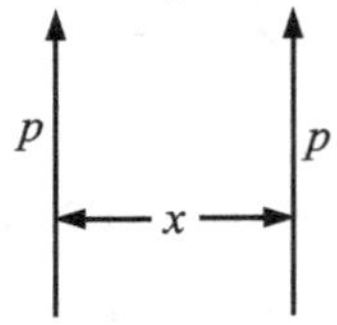

(a) $\frac{3Kp^2}{2x^4}$ (b) $\frac{3Kp^2}{x^4}$

(c) $\frac{3Kp^2}{4x^4}$ (d) $\frac{3Kp^2}{5x^4}$

77. Two vertical metallic plates carrying equal and opposite charges are parallel to each other. A small spherical metallic ball is suspended by a long insulating thread such that it hangs freely in the centre of the two metallic plates. The ball, which is uncharged, is taken slowly towards the positively charged plate and is made to touch the plate. Then the ball will :

(a) Stick to the positively charged plate

(b) Come back to the original position and will remain there

(c) Oscillate between the two plates touching each plate in turn

(d) Oscillate between the plates without touching them

78. An electric dipole is placed along the X-axis at the origin O. A point P is at a distance of 20 cm from this origin such that OP makes an angle $\pi/3$ with the X-axis. If the electric field at P makes an angle θ with the X-axis, the value of θ would be :

(a) $\frac{\pi}{3}$ (b) $2\pi\sqrt{3}$

(c) $\frac{\pi}{3} + \tan^{-1}\left(\frac{\sqrt{3}}{2}\right)$ (d) $\tan^{-1}\left(\frac{\sqrt{3}}{2}\right)$

79. Two thin hollow conducting spheres of radii R_1 and R_2 are placed concentrically; charges on the two are Q_1 and Q_2 respectively. If $R_1 > R_2$ then the electric potential at a point distant r from the centre when $R_1 > r > R_2$ is :

(a) $\frac{1}{4\pi\varepsilon_0}\left(\frac{Q_1}{r}+\frac{Q_2}{r}\right)$ (b) $\frac{1}{4\pi\varepsilon_0}\left(\frac{Q_1}{r}+\frac{Q_2}{R_2}\right)$

(c) $\frac{1}{4\pi\varepsilon_0}\left(\frac{Q_1}{R_2}+\frac{Q_2}{R_2}\right)$ (d) $\frac{1}{4\pi\varepsilon_0}\left(\frac{Q_1}{R_1}+\frac{Q_2}{r}\right)$

80. Two thin hollow conducting spheres of radii R_1 and R_2 are placed concentrically; charges on the two are Q_1 and Q_2 respectively. If $R_1 > R_2$, then the electric field intensity at a point distant r from the centre when $R_1 > r > R_2$ is :

(a) $\frac{1}{4\pi\varepsilon_0}\frac{Q_1}{r^2}$ (b) $\frac{1}{4\pi\varepsilon_0}\frac{Q_2}{r^2}$

(c) $\frac{1}{4\pi\varepsilon_0}\left(\frac{Q_1}{r^2}+\frac{Q_2}{r^2}\right)$ (d) $\frac{1}{4\pi\varepsilon_0}\left(\frac{Q_1}{R_1^2}+\frac{Q_2}{r^2}\right)$

81. A charge Q is distributed uniformly throughout the volume of a non-conducting spherical object of radius R, then the electric potential at a distance r from the centre, when $r < R$ is :

(a) $\frac{1}{4\pi\varepsilon_0}\frac{Q}{K}\left(\frac{3R^2-r^2}{2R^3}\right)$ (b) $\frac{1}{4\pi\varepsilon_0}\frac{Q}{K}\left(\frac{1}{r}\right)$

(c) $\frac{1}{4\pi\varepsilon_0}\frac{Q}{K}\left(\frac{1}{R}\right)$ (d) $\frac{1}{4\pi\varepsilon_0}\frac{Q}{K}\left(\frac{1}{r}+\frac{1}{R}\right)$

82. A positive charge of 9 μC is fixed at the origin. A second charge q is fixed on the x-axis at $x = a$. A charge q_0 at $x = 3a$ does not experience any net force. By displacing q_0 along a small distance Δx along the x-axis and then releasing it, state what kind of equilibrium does q_0 have:

(a) Stable (b) Unstable

(c) Neutral (d) Unpredictable

83. Two point charges $+4q$ and $+q$ are placed at A and B such that AB = 3 metres, C is a point on the line joining A and B such that BC = 1 m and AC = 2 m. A point charge $+q'$ placed at C is in stable equilibrium for a small displacement :

(a) along the line AB

(b) at an angle 45° with AB

(c) normal to the line AB

(d) along all angles with AB

84. ΔABC is a right angled triangle, AB = 3 cm, BC = 4 cm, AC = 5 cm and charges +15, +12, –20 e.s.u are placed at A, B, C respectively. The potential energy of the system is :

(a) 180 ergs

(b) (20 + 15 – 12) ergs

(c) – 60 ergs

(d) $4 \times 5 \times 3$ ergs

85. ΔABC is a right angled triangle, AB = 3 cm, BC = 4 cm, AC = 5 cm and charges +15, +12, –20 e.s.u are placed at A, B, C respectively. The work done in moving the three charges to infinite separation is :

(a) 100 ergs

(b) + 60 ergs

(c) – 60 ergs

(d) (20 + 15 – 12) ergs

86. Two free protons which are separated by a distance of 10^{-10} m, are released, then the kinetic energy of each proton when at infinite separation, is :

(a) 23×10^{-19} J (b) 46×10^{-19} J

(c) 11.52×10^{-19} J (d) 5.6×10^{12} J

87. An electron is accelerated through 1 volt. Its velocity is nearly :

(a) 6×10^5 cm s^{-1} (b) 6×10^4 cm s^{-1}

(c) 6×10^5 m s^{-1} (d) 6×10^6 m s^{-1}

88. Two metal plates have potential difference of 300 V and are 1 cm apart. A charged particle of mass 1.96×10^{-15} kg is held in equilibrium between the plates of the capacitor, then the electric field is :

(a) 300 V m^{-1} (b) 30000 V m^{-1}

(c) 3 V m^{-1} (d) $(30000)^{-1}$ V m^{-1}

89. Two small spheres each carrying a charge of q are r metres apart. If one of the sphere is taken around the other in a circular path of radius R metres, the work done will be equal to :

(a) Force between them × R

(b) Force between them × 2R

(c) Force between them × 2(R - r)

(d) Zero

90. An electron enters with a velocity of 5×10^6 ms^{-1} along the +ve direction of an electric field of intensity 10^3 N C^{-1}. If mass of the electron is 9.1×10^{-31} kg, then the time taken by the electron to come temporarily to rest is :

(a) 5.8×10^{-8} sec (b) Infinite

(c) 1.45×10^{-8} sec (d) 2.9×10^{-8} sec

91. A point charge of 60 stat coulomb is placed 3 cm in front of an earthed metallic plate of large size. Then the force of attraction on the point charge is :

(a) 100 dynes (b) 360 dynes

(c) 400 dynes (d) 180 dynes

92. The electric potential at the surface of an atomic nucleus (Z = 50) of radius 9.0×10^{-13} cm is :

(a) 80 V (b) 8×10^6 V

(c) 9 V (d) 9×10^6 V

93. A hollow metallic sphere of radius 10 cm is given a charge of 3.2×10^{-9} coulomb. The electrical potential at a point 4 cm from the centre is :

(a) 9×10^{-9} V (b) 2.88 V

(c) 288 V (d) Zero

94. Two point charges placed at a distance of 20 cm in air repel each other with a certain force. When a dielectric slab of thickness 8 cm and dielectric constant K is introduced between these point charges, force of interaction becomes $\frac{1}{9}^{\text{th}}$ of its previous value. K is approximately :

(a) 36 (b) 46

(c) 3 (d) 4

95. If the dielectric constant and dielectric strength be denoted by K and X respectively, then the material suitable for use as a dielectric in a capacitor must have :

(a) High K and high X

(b) Low K and high X

(c) High K and low X

(d) Low K and low X

96. The ratio of electric potential due to an electric dipole in the end on position to that in the broad side on position for the same distance from it is :

(a) zero (b) 1

(c) 2 (d) Infinite

97. Three charges +Q each are placed at the corners A, B and C of an equilateral triangle. At the circumcentre O, the electric field will be :

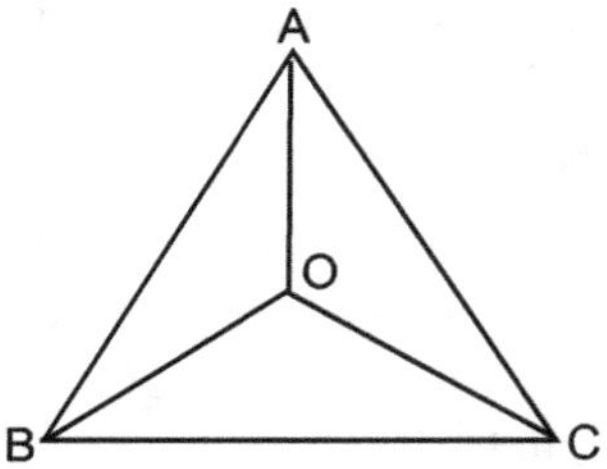

(a) $\frac{1}{4\pi\varepsilon_0}\frac{3Q}{r^3}$ (b) Zero

(c) $\frac{1}{4\pi\varepsilon_0}\frac{Q}{r^2}$ (d) $\frac{1}{4\pi\varepsilon_0}\frac{Q^2}{r^2}$

98. An uncharged metallic sphere is placed inside charged parallel plate sheets as shown in the figure. The lines of force look like :

(a) 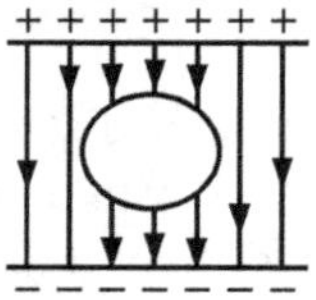

(b) 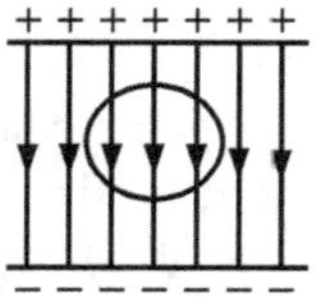

(c) 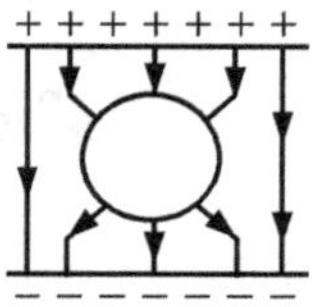

(d) 

99. A particle of mass 2 gm and charge 1μC is held at rest on a frictionless horizontal surface at a distance of 1 metre from a fixed charge of 1 mC. If the particle is released, it will be repelled. The speed of the particle when it is at a distance of 10 m from the fixed charge is :

(a) 100 ms^{-1} (b) 60 ms^{-1}

(c) 90 ms^{-1} (d) 45 ms^{-1}

100. Two metallic charged spheres of radii 20 cm and 10 cm respectively, have 150 micro coulomb positive charge each. The common electric potential after the conducting wire is connected between them, is :

(a) 9×10^6 V (b) 1.8×10^7 V

(c) 4.5×10^6 V (d) 13.5×10^6 V

101. A sphere of 4 cm radius is suspended within a hollow sphere of radius 6 cm. The inner sphere is charged to a potential 3 e.s.u. when the outer sphere is earthed. The charge on the inner sphere is :

(a) 54 esu (b) 1/4 esu

(c) 30 esu (d) 36 esu

102. An electron of mass m_e initially at rest moves through a certain distance in uniform electric field in time t_1. A proton of mass m_p, also initially at rest takes time t_2 to move through an equal distance in this uniform electric field. The ratio of t_2/t_1 is nearly equal to (neglect effect of g) :

(a) 1 (b) $\sqrt{\frac{m_p}{m_e}}$

(c) $\sqrt{\frac{m_e}{m_p}}$ (d) 1836

103. In an electron gun, the electrons are accelerated through a potential difference of V volt. Taking electronic charge and mass to be e and m respectively, the maximum velocity attained by them is :

(a) $\frac{2eV}{m}$ (b) $\sqrt{\frac{2eV}{m}}$

(c) $\frac{2m}{eV}$ (d) $\frac{V^2}{2em}$

104. The electric potential V at any point (x, y, z) all in metres in space is given by $V = 4x^2$. Then the electric field E at point (1, 0, 2) is :

(a) 8 Vm^{-1} along +ve X-direction

(b) 8 Vm^{-1} along – ve X direction

(c) 4 Vm^{-1} along –ve X direction

(d) Zero

105. Two equal positive charges are kept at points A and B. While moving from A to B, the electric potential :

(a) increases continuously

(b) decreases and then increases

(c) decreases continuously

(d) increases and then decreases

106. Three charges of $+2q$, $-q$ and $-q$ are placed at the corners A, B and C of an equilateral triangle of side a as shown in the following figure. Then the dipole moment of this combination is :

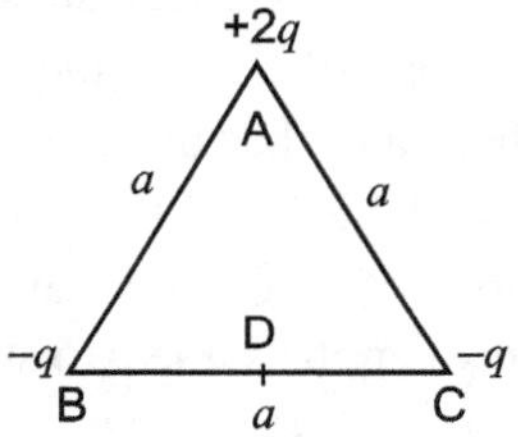

(a) qa (b) $qa\sqrt{3}$

(c) Zero (d) $\frac{2qa}{\sqrt{3}}$

107. Five charges 'q' each are placed at the five corners A, B, C, D and E of a regular hexagon ABCDEF of side 'a', then the electric field intensity at the centre O of the hexagon is :

(a) $\frac{1}{4\pi\varepsilon_0}\frac{q}{a^2}$ along $\overrightarrow{OF}$

(b) $\frac{1}{4\pi\varepsilon_0}\frac{q}{a^2}$ along $\overrightarrow{FO}$

(c) $\frac{1}{4\pi\varepsilon_0}\frac{q}{3a^2}$ along $\overrightarrow{OF}$

(d) $\frac{1}{4\pi\varepsilon_0}\frac{5q}{a^2}$ along $\overrightarrow{OF}$

108. Two small balls having equal charge +Q and mass m equal are suspended by two insulating strings of equal length L from a hook fixed to a stand. The whole setup is in a region outside the gravitational field of earth. In equilibrium, the tension in each string is :

(a) $\frac{1}{4\pi\varepsilon_0}\frac{Q^2}{L^2}$ (b) $\frac{1}{4\pi\varepsilon_0}\frac{Q^2}{2L^2}$

(c) $\frac{1}{4\pi\varepsilon_0}\frac{Q^2}{4L^2}$ (d) $\frac{1}{4\pi\varepsilon_0}\frac{2Q^2}{L^2}$

109. In the electric field of a point charge q, a charge $-q$ is carried from point A to B, C, D, E where all these points on the circle are drawn with the point charge q as centre. The work done is :

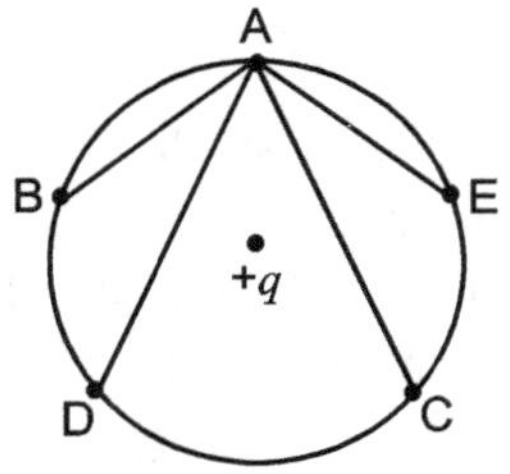

(a) minimum along path AB

(b) minimum along path AD

(c) zero along all the paths

(d) equal along all the paths

110. A charge Q is distributed over two concentric hollow spheres of radii r and R ($> r$) such that the surface densities are equal. The potential at the common centre is:

(a) $\frac{1}{4\pi\varepsilon_0}\frac{Q}{(R^2+r^2)}$ (b) $\frac{1}{4\pi\varepsilon_0}\frac{Q}{R+r}$

(c) Zero (d) $\frac{1}{4\pi\varepsilon_0}\frac{Q(r+R)}{(R^2+r^2)}$

111. Two identical thin rings, each of radius R metres are coaxially placed at distance R metres apart. If Q_1 and Q_2 are respectively the charges uniformly distributed on the two rings, the work done in moving a charge q from the centre of one ring to that of the other is :

(a) Zero

(b) $\frac{1}{4\pi\varepsilon_0}\frac{q(Q_1-Q_2)\cdot(\sqrt{2}-1)}{\sqrt{2}R}$

(c) $\frac{1}{4\pi\varepsilon_0}\frac{\sqrt{2}(Q_1+Q_2)}{R}$

(d) $\frac{1}{4\pi\varepsilon_0}\frac{q(Q_1+Q_2)\cdot(\sqrt{2}+1)}{\sqrt{2}R}$

112. A metal sphere A of radius 'a' is charged to potential V. What will be its potential if it is enclosed by a spherical conducting shell B of radius b and the two are connected by a wire ?

(a) $\frac{a}{b}$V (b) $\frac{a+b}{a}$V

(c) $\frac{b}{a}$V (d) $\frac{b}{a+b}$V

113. In a certain region a uniform electric field $E = E_x\, i$ exists. If a small circle is drawn with the origin as centre cutting the axis at A (a, 0), B (0, a), C (– a, 0) and D (0, – a), the potential is maximum at :

(a) A (b) C

(c) B (d) D

114. Four equal charges of Q each are placed at the four corners of a square of side 'a' metres. The work done in removing a charge – Q coulomb from its centre to infinity is :

(a) Zero (b) $\frac{\sqrt{2}}{4\pi\varepsilon_0}\frac{Q^2}{a}$

(c) $\frac{\sqrt{2}}{\pi\varepsilon_0}\frac{Q^2}{a}$ (d) $\frac{Q^2}{2\pi\varepsilon_0 a}$

115. A hollow charged metallic sphere has radius R. If the p.d. between its centre and a point at a distance 3R from the centre is V, the electric field intensity at a distance 3R from centre is :

(a) $\frac{V}{6R}$ (b) $\frac{V}{4R}$

(c) $\frac{V}{3R}$ (d) $\frac{V}{2R}$

116. Two charged metallic spheres are joined by a very thin metal wire. If the radius of the larger sphere is twice that of the smaller one, the electric field near the larger sphere is :

(a) Twice that near the smaller sphere

(b) Half of that near the smaller sphere

(c) The same as that near the smaller sphere

(d) One fourth of that near the smaller sphere

117. A pendulum bob of mass 80 mg and carrying a charge 2×10^{-8} C is at rest in a horizontal uniform electric field of 20,000 Vm^{-1}. The tension in the thread of the pendulum is :

(a) 2.2×10^{-4} N

(b) 4.4×10^{-4} N

(c) 8.8×10^{-4} N

(d) 17.6×10^{-4} N

118. A solid conducting sphere having a charge Q is surrounded by an uncharged concentric conducting hollow spherical shell. Let the potential difference between the surface of the solid sphere and that of outer surface of the hollow shell be V. If the shell is now given a charge of –3Q, the new potential difference between the same two surfaces is:

(a) V (b) 4V

(c) 2V (d) –2V

119. A point charge at any point on the axis of an electric dipole at some large distance experiences a force F. The force acting on the point when its distance from the dipole is doubled is :

(a) 2F (b) F / 2

(c) F / 4 (d) F / 8

120. An electric dipole placed with its axis at 30° with a uniform electrical field experiences a torque of 0.032 Nm. If the dipole were free to rotate, its potential energy in stable equilibrium would be :

(a) 0.064 J

(b) – 0.064 J

(c) Zero

(d) – 0.16 J

121. As one penetrates a uniformly charged dielectric sphere, the electric field strength :

(a) increases

(b) decreases

(c) remains unchanged

(d) first increases and then decreases

122. The variation of potential with distance r from a fixed point is shown in the figure. The electric field at $r = 5$m is :

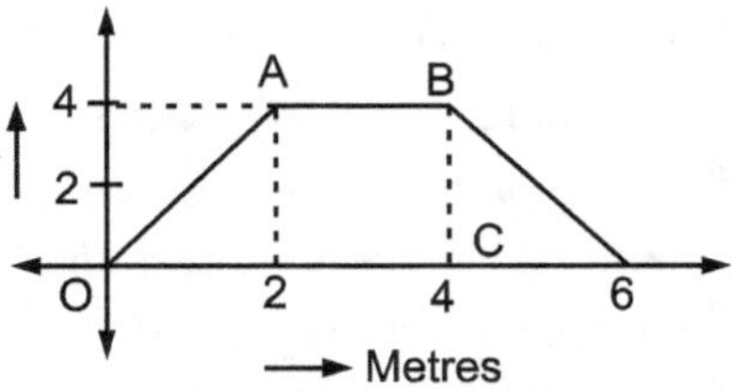

(a) 2 Vm^{-1} (b) – 2 Vm^{-1}
(c) 0.4 Vm^{-1} (d) – 0.4 Vm^{-1}

123. A rectangular sheet of area 30 meter^2 is placed in a uniform electric field of intensity 3000 NC^{-1} such that the normal to the face makes an angle of 60° with the electric intensity. The normal electric flux through the sheet is :

(a) 4.5×10^4 Nm^2C^{-1} (b) 2.25×10^4 Nm^2C^{-1}
(c) 9×10^4 Nm^2 C^{-1} (d) 50 Nm^2 C^{-1}

124. A point charge + q is placed near a surface element of area ds which subtends a solid angle $d\omega$ steradian, then the total normal electric flow through the surface element is :

(a) $\frac{q}{\varepsilon_0}\left(\frac{4\pi}{d\omega}\right)$ (b) $\frac{q}{\varepsilon_0}\left(\frac{d\omega}{4\pi}\right)$

(c) $\frac{q}{\varepsilon_0}ds$ (d) $\frac{q}{\varepsilon_0}d\omega$

125. A sphere of radius R is placed in a uniform electric field E, the total electric flux on the surface of the sphere is given by :

(a) πR^2E (b) $2\pi R^2E$
(c) $4\pi R^2E$ (d) Zero

126. Five thousand lines of induction enter a given closed surface and three thousand lines leave it. Then the charge enclosed within the surface is :

(a) -1.77×10^{-8}C (b) 2000 C
(c) $+1.77 \times 10^{-8}$ C (d) –20000 C

127. Points A and B lie on the equatorial line of a dipole of dipole moment p at a distance d as shown in the figure. What is the work done in moving a charge q from A to B following a semi-circular path in the field of the dipole?

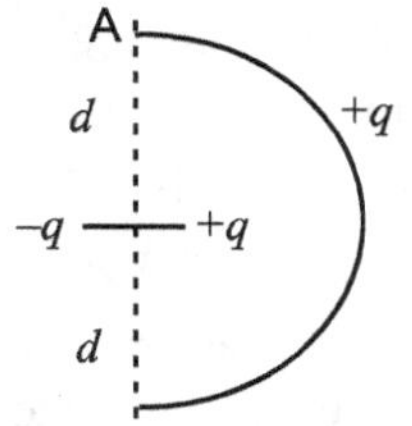

(a) $2q\,E_{eq}$ (b) $-2q\,E_{eq}$
(c) Zero (d) $q^2\,E_{eq}d$

128. A particle of mass 20 gm and a charge 1 C is held at rest on a frictionless horizontal surface at a distance of 1 m from a fixed charge of 1 μC. If the particle is released, it will be repelled. The speed of the particle when it is at a distance of 10 m from the fixed charge is :

(a) 100 ms^{-1} (b) 600 ms^{-1}
(c) 900 ms^{-1} (d) 160 ms^{-1}

129. A square frame of edge 10 cm is placed with its positive normal making an angle of 60° with a uniform electric field of 20 Vm^{-1}. The electric flux through the surface bounded by the frame is :

(a) 0.1 Vm (b) 0.5×10^{-4} Vm
(c) $\sqrt{3} \times 10^{-4}$ Vm (d) 0.1×10^{-4} Vm

130. Two free protons which are separated by a distance of 10^{-10} m, are released, then the K.E. of each proton when at infinite separation, is :

(a) 10.5×10^{-19} J (b) 4.6×10^{-19} J
(c) 11.52×10^{-19} J (d) 5.6×10^{12} J

131. The figure shows a charge q placed at the centre of a hemisphere. A second charge Q is placed at one of the positions A, B, C or D. In which position(s) of the second charge does the electric flux through the hemisphere remain uncharged ?

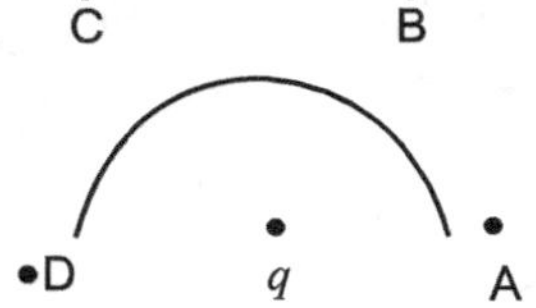

(a) A (b) B
(c) C (d) D

132. Dimensions of atomic polarizability has dimensions as that of :

(a) Dipole moment (b) Charge
(c) Volume (d) Area

133. A parallel plate capacitor is charged upto 100 V. A 2 mm thick plate is inserted between the plates. Then to maintain the same potential difference, the distance between the plates is increased by 1.6 mm. The dielectric constant of the plate is :

(a) 5 (b) 1.25
(c) 4 (d) 2.5

134. Can a sphere of radius 1 m hold a charge of 1 C ?

(a) Yes
(b) No
(c) Depends on the metal of the sphere
(d) Depends upon whether the charge is +ve or –ve

135. When two uncharged metal balls of radius 0.09 mm collide, one electron is transferred between them. The potential difference between them would be :

(a) 16 μV (b) 16 pV
(c) 32 μV (d) 32 pV

136. The field at a distance r from a long string of charge per unit length λ is :

(a) $\frac{K\lambda}{r^2}$ (b) $\frac{K\lambda}{r}$
(c) $\frac{K\lambda}{2r}$ (d) $\frac{2K\lambda}{r}$

137. The electric field outside a charged long straight wire is given by $E = 1000/r\ Vm^{-1}$, and is directed outwards. What is the sign of the charge on the wire if two points A and B are situated such that $r_A = 0.2$ m and $r_B = 0.4$ m? The value of $V_B - V_A$ is :

(a) + charge, – 693.1 Vm^{-1}
(b) – charge, 693.1 Vm^{-1}
(c) + charge, – 96.31 Vm^{-1}
(d) – charge, 96.31 Vm^{-1}

138. The electric potential V at any point (x, y, z) in space is given by $V = 4x^2$ volt. The electric field at the point (1m, 0, 2m) is :

(a) 8 Vm^{-1} along –ve X - direction
(b) 80 Vm^{-1} along –ve X - direction
(c) 0.8 Vm^{-1} along –ve X - direction
(d) 800 Vm^{-1} along –ve X - direction

139. If the potential in the region of the space around the point (–1m, 2m, 3m) is given by $V = 10x^2 + 5y^2 - 3z^2$, the three components of electric field at this point are :

(a) $E_x = 20\ Vm^{-1}$; $E_y = -20\ Vm^{-1}$; $E_z = 18\ Vm^{-1}$
(b) $E_x = 10\ Vm^{-1}$; $E_y = -10\ Vm^{-1}$; $E_z = 9\ Vm^{-1}$
(c) $E_x = 10\ Vm^{-1}$; $E_y = -5\ Vm^{-1}$; $E_z = 3\ Vm^{-1}$
(d) $E_x = 2\ Vm^{-1}$; $E_y = -2\ Vm^{-1}$; $E_z = 18\ Vm^{-1}$

140. A particle of mass m and charge q is placed at rest in a uniform electric field E and then released. The K.E. attained by the particle after moving a distance y is :

(a) qEy^2 (b) qE^2y
(c) qEy (d) q^2Ey

141. A parallel plate capacitor is charged and then isolated. What is the effect on increasing the plate separation?

	Charge	Potential	Capacitance
(a)	constant	constant	decrease
(b)	increase	increase	decrease
(c)	constant	decrease	increase
(d)	constant	increase	decrease

142. A 1 μF capacitor and a 2 μF capacitor are connected in parallel across a 1200 V line. The charged capacitors are then disconnected from the line and from each other. These two capacitors are now connected to each other in parallel with terminals of unlike sign together. The charges on the capacitors will be :

(a) 1800 μC
(b) 800 μC and 400 μC
(c) 400 μC and 800 μC
(d) 800 μC and 800 μC

143. The equivalent capacitance of the combination of three capacitors, each of capacitance C shown in the adjoining diagram between A and B is :

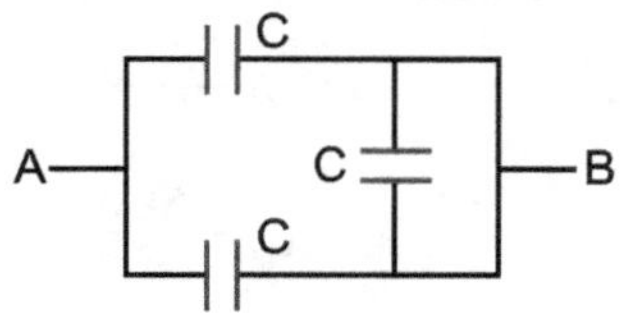

(a) 2C (b) $\frac{3}{2}$C

(c) $\frac{2}{3}$C (d) $\frac{C}{2}$

144. In the adjoining circuit diagram, the potential difference across the plates of capacitor C_1 ($E_1 > E_2$) is :

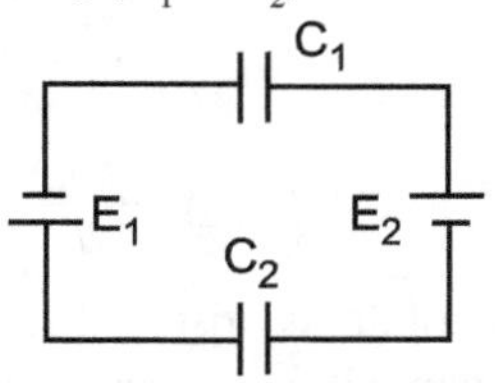

(a) $E_1 + E_2$ (b) $E_1 - E_2$

(c) $\frac{C_2(E_1 - E_2)}{(C_1 + C_2)}$ (d) $\frac{C_2(E_1 + E_2)}{(C_1 + C_2)}$

145. A capacitor A has a capacity of 15μF when it is filled with a medium of dielectric constant 15. Another condenser B has a capacity of 1 μF with air between the plates. Both are charged separately by a battery of 100 V. After charging both are connected in parallel without the battery and the dielectric material is removed. The common potential now is :

(a) 400 V (b) 1200 V

(c) 800 V (d) 1600 V

146. A capacitor of capacitance C is charged to a potential V. The total flux of the electric field over a closed surface enclosing the capacitor is :

(a) $\frac{CV}{2\varepsilon_0}$ (b) $\frac{CV}{\varepsilon_0}$

(c) Zero (d) $\frac{2CV}{\varepsilon_0}$

147. Four capacitors each of 25 μF are connected as shown in the following figure. In the circuit, d.c. voltmeter reads 200 volt. The charge on each plate of the capacitors is :

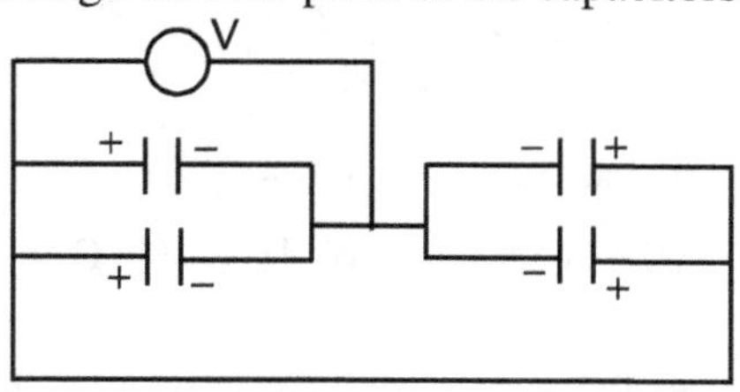

(a) 2×10^{-3} C (b) 2×10^{-2} C

(c) 5×10^{-3} C (d) 5×10^{-2} C

148. A condenser is connected across another charged conductor. The energy in the second condenser will :

(a) be equal to the energy in the initial condenser

(b) be less than that in the initial condenser

(c) be more than that in the initial condenser

(d) be more or less depending upon the capacitance of the second condenser

149. When the key K of a circuit shown is pressed, the pointer of the ammeter A shows:

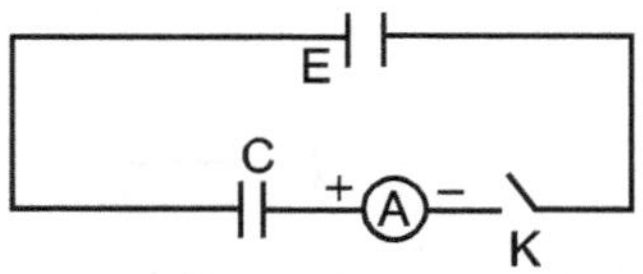

(a) no deflection

(b) constant deflection

(c) erratic deflection

(d) deflection which finally decreases to zero

150. Two condensers of capacity C_1 and C_2 are connected in parallel. If a charge Q is given to the assembly, the charge gets shared. The ratio of the charge on the condenser C_1 to the charge on the condenser C_2 is :

(a) $\frac{1}{C_1C_2}$ (b) $\frac{C_2}{C_1}$

(c) $C_1 C_2$ (d) $\frac{C_1}{C_2}$

151. In the adjoining figure, charge on the 10 μF capacitor is :

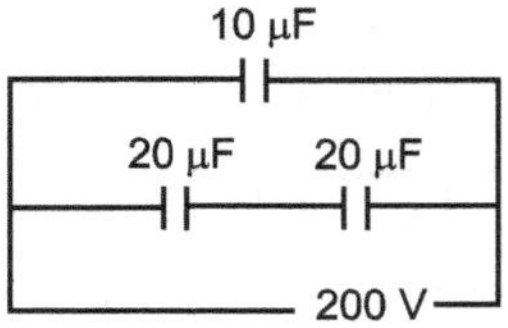

(a) 2×10^{-3} C (b) 16×10^{-4} C
(c) 4×10^{-3} C (d) 8×10^{-4} C

152. Potential difference across C_1 and C_2 when $V_A - V_B = 5$ V are :

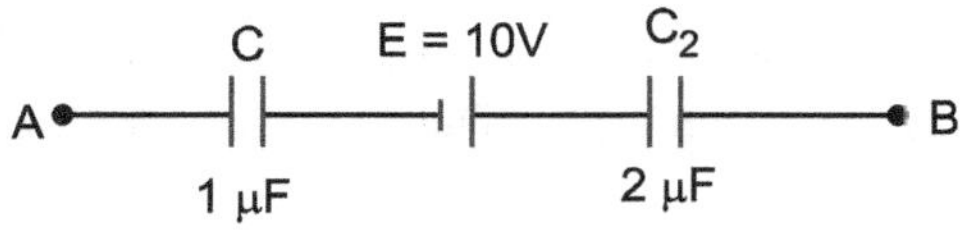

(a) 5 V and 10 V (b) 15 V and 15 V
(c) 10 V and 5 V (d) 7.5 V and 7.5 V

153. Net capacitance between P and Q when A is the area of plates and d is the distance between the plates is :

(a) $\frac{A\varepsilon_0}{d}$ (b) $\frac{2A\varepsilon_0}{d}$
(c) $\frac{3A\varepsilon_0}{d}$ (d) $\frac{4A\varepsilon_0}{d}$

154. Net capacitance between P and Q when A is the area of plates and d is the distance between the plates is :

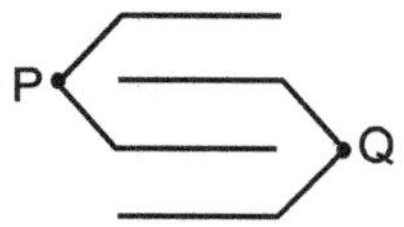

(a) $\frac{3A\varepsilon_0}{2d}$ (b) $\frac{2A\varepsilon_0}{3d}$
(c) $\frac{3A\varepsilon_0}{d}$ (d) $\frac{3A\varepsilon_0}{5d}$

155. Net capacitance between the points P and Q when A is the area of plates and d is the distance between the plates is :

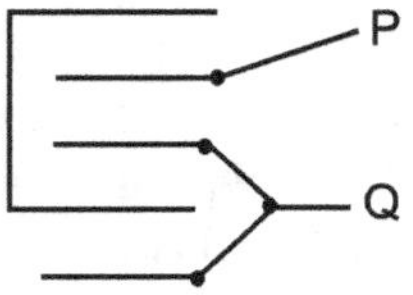

(a) $\frac{A\varepsilon_0}{2d}$ (b) $\frac{5A\varepsilon_0}{3d}$
(c) $\frac{2A\varepsilon_0}{3d}$ (d) $\frac{3A\varepsilon_0}{5d}$

156. Net capacitance between points P and Q when A is the area of plates and d is the distance between the plates is :

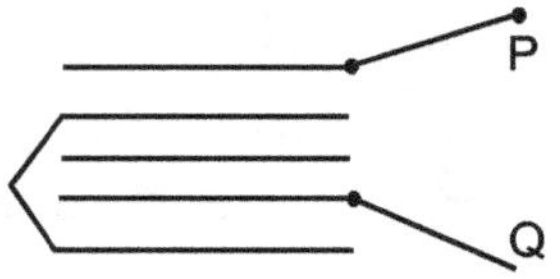

(a) $\frac{4A\varepsilon_0}{2d}$ (b) $\frac{5A\varepsilon_0}{d}$
(c) $\frac{5A\varepsilon_0}{3d}$ (d) $\frac{3A\varepsilon_0}{5d}$

157. A thin metal plate is inserted between the plates of a capacitor of capacitance C in such a way that its edges touch the two plates. Then capacitance becomes :

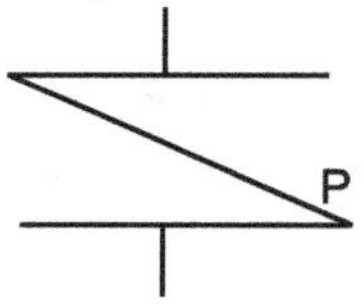

(a) C/2 (b) 2C
(c) 0 (d) Infinity

158. Three dielectric slabs are inserted between the plates as shown. Then the net capacitance between the points P and Q is :

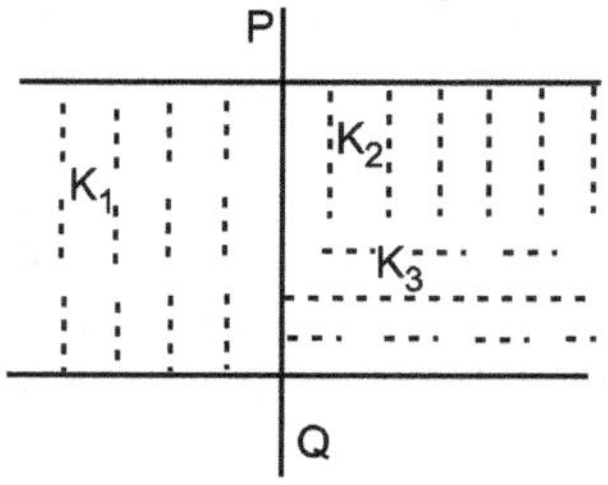

(a) $\frac{A\varepsilon_0}{d}\left(\frac{K_1}{2} + \frac{2K_2K_3}{K_2 + K_3}\right)$

(b) $\frac{A\varepsilon_0}{d}\left(\frac{K_1}{2} + \frac{K_2K_3}{K_2 + K_3}\right)$

(c) $\frac{A\varepsilon_0}{d}\left(2K_1 + \frac{2K_2K_3}{K_2 + K_3}\right)$

(d) $\frac{A\varepsilon_0}{d}(K_1 + K_2 + K_3)$

159. Net capacitance between P and Q when A is the area of the plates and d is the distance between the plates is :

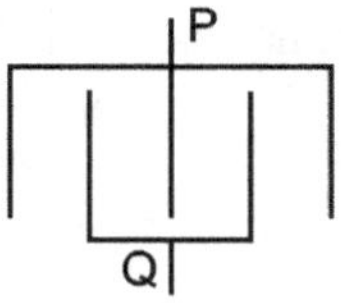

(a) $\frac{4A\varepsilon_0}{d}$ (b) $\frac{5A\varepsilon_0}{d}$

(c) $\frac{5A\varepsilon_0}{3d}$ (d) $\frac{3A\varepsilon_0}{5d}$

160. The figure shows n plates each of area A and separated from one another by a distance 'd'. What is the net capacitance between P and Q ?

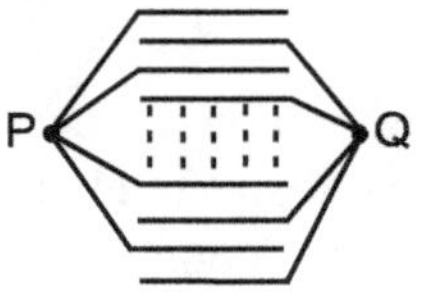

(a) $\frac{A\varepsilon_0}{d}$ (b) $(n-1)\frac{A\varepsilon_0}{d}$

(c) $\frac{nA\varepsilon_0}{d}$ (d) $(n+1)\frac{A\varepsilon_0}{d}$

161. If 100 V of p.d. is applied between A and B in the circuit, the p.d. between C and D is :

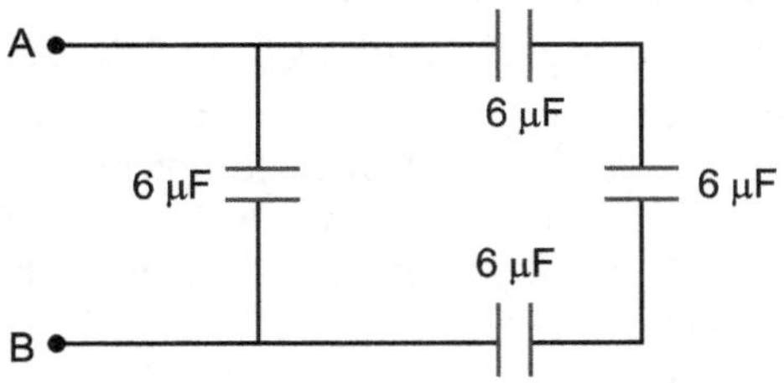

(a) 1.11 V (b) 66.66 V

(c) 33.33 V (d) 100 V

162. The numerical value of charge on either side of the capacitor C shown in the following figure is :

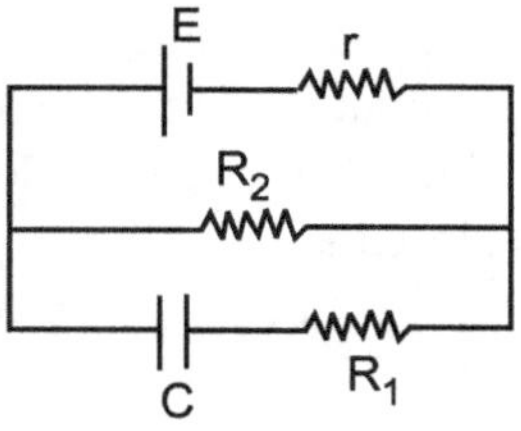

(a) CE (b) $\frac{CER_1}{R_2 + r}$

(c) $\frac{CER_2}{R_2 + r}$ (d) $\frac{CER_1}{R_1 + r}$

163. Two capacitors A and B are connected as shown in figure. The capacitor A has charge q on it, whereas capacitor B is uncharged. When the key K is closed, charge appearing on the capacitor B after a long time is :

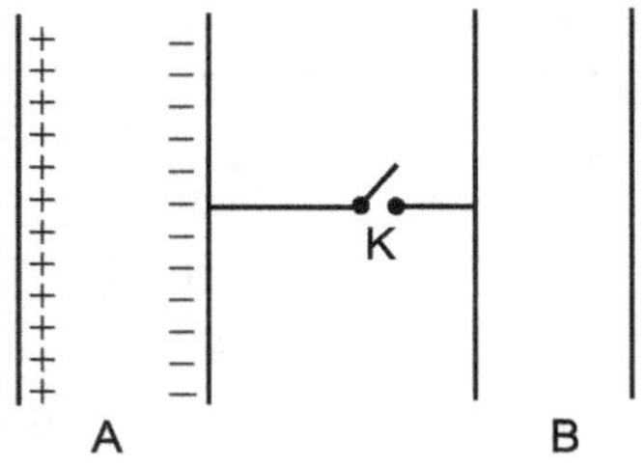

(a) Zero (b) q

(c) $q/2$ (d) $2q$

164. The net capacitance between A and B is :

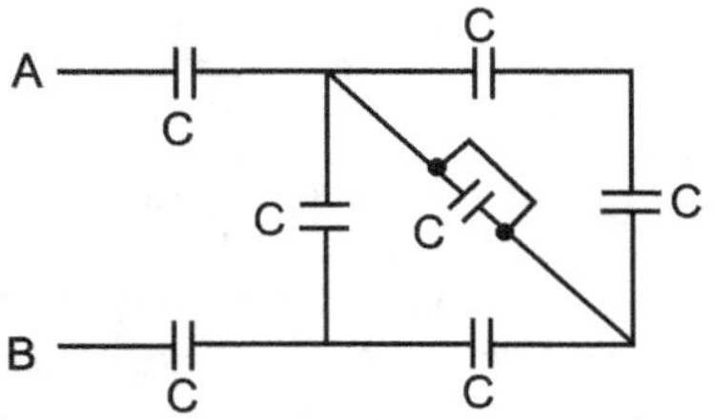

(a) 6 C (b) $\frac{2C}{5}$

(c) $\frac{2C}{3}$ (d) None of these

165. What is the p.d. across 5 μF capacitor ?

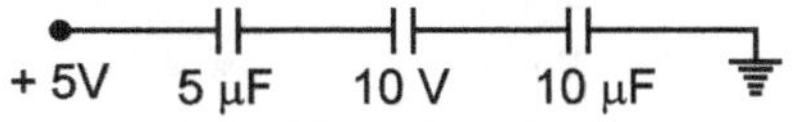

(a) 10 V (b) 12 V

(c) 15 V (d) 5 V

166. A 4 μF capacitor holding a charge of 4×10^{-5} C is connected to a 20 Ω resistor through a switch. Current that flows when the switch is closed is :

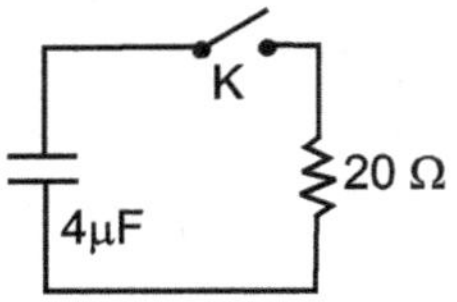

(a) 0 (b) 1.5 A
(c) 1 A (d) 0.5 A

167. A 10 F capacitor is connected as shown in the figure. The charge on this capacitor is approximately :

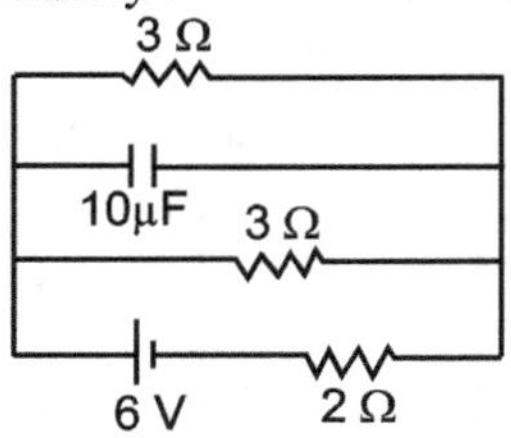

(a) 40 μC (b) 80 μC
(c) 26 μC (d) 8 μC

168. Two condensers of capacity C_1 and C_2 are connected in parallel. If a charge Q is given to the assembly, the charge gets shared. The ratio of the charge on the condenser C_1 to the charge on the condenser C_2 is :

(a) $\frac{C_1}{C_2}$ (b) $\left(\frac{C_2}{C_1}\right)^2$

(c) $C_1^2 C_2^2$ (d) $\frac{1}{C_1 C_2}$

169. A and B are two spherical conductors of the same external size. A is solid and B is hollow. Both are charged to the same potential. If the charges on A and B are Q_A and Q_B, then :

(a) $Q_A > Q_B$ (b) $Q_A = Q_B$
(c) $Q_A < Q_B$ (d) None of these

170. In a charged capacitor, the energy resides in:

(a) The positive charge
(b) Both the positive and negative charge
(c) Electric field between the plates
(d) Around the edge of the capacitor plates

171. The potential gradient at which the dielectric of the condenser just gets punctured, is called :

(a) Dielectric constant
(b) Dielectric strength
(c) Dielectric resistance
(d) Dielectric number

172. The air between the plates of a parallel plate capacitor is replaced by a medium of dielectric constant K. The p.d. between the plates becomes :

(a) K times (b) $\frac{1}{K}$ times

(c) $\sqrt{K}$ times (d) $\frac{1}{\sqrt{K}}$ times

173. In Question No. 172, electric intensity between the plates becomes :

(a) K times (b) $\frac{1}{K}$ times

(c) $\sqrt{K}$ times (d) $\frac{1}{\sqrt{K}}$ times

174. Two insulating charged spheres of radii 20 cm and 25 cm respectively and having an equal charge Q are connected by a copper wire and then they are separated :

(a) Both the spheres will have the same charge Q.
(b) Charge on the 20 cm sphere will be greater than that on the 25 cm sphere.
(c) Charge on the 25 cm sphere will be greater than that on the 20 cm sphere.
(d) Charge on each of the sphere will be 2Q.

175. Two spherical conductors of capacitance 3 μF and 5 μF are charged to potential of 300 V and 500 V. The two are connected resulting in redistribution of charges. The final potential is :

(a) 300 V (b) 425 V
(c) 500 V (d) 400 V

176. In Question No. 175, the final charge on the smaller conductor is :

(a) 900 μC (b) 1275 μC
(c) 2125 μC (d) 2500 μC

177. In Question No. 175, the final charge on the bigger conductor is :

(a) 900 μC (b) 2125 μC

(c) 1275 μC (d) 2500 μC

178. In Question No. 175, the decrease in electrical energy is :

(a) 760×10^{-3} joule (b) 37.5×10^{-3} joule

(c) 722.5×10^{-3} joule (d) Zero

179. A technician has only two capacitors. By using these singly, in series or in parallel, he is able to obtain the capacitance of 3μF, 4μF, 12μF, 16μF. What are the capacitances of capacitors ?

(a) 6 μF and 10 μF (b) 7 μF and 9 μF

(c) 4 μF and 12 μF (d) 4 μF and 16 μF

180. A charged parallel plate capacitor has capacitance C and energy W. When a dielectric slab of dielectric constant 6 is placed between the plates, the capacitance and energy becomes :

(a) 6 C and 6 W

(b) 6 C and W/6

(c) C/6 and W/6

(d) C/6 and 6W respectively

181. Three plates each of area 50 cm² separated from each other by a distance of 3 mm are connected to a source of e.m.f of 120 V. Then the energy stored when the plates are fully charged is :

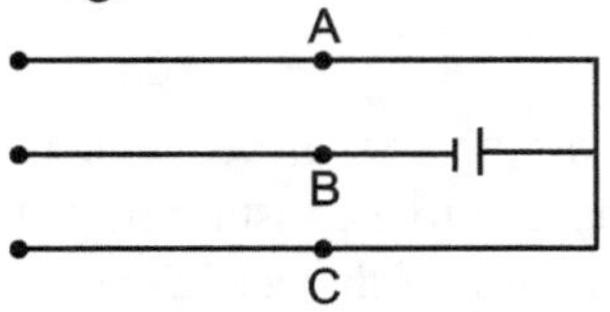

(a) 0.2 J (b) 5 J

(c) 1.6 J (d) 7 J

182. Equivalent capacitance between A and B of the network is :

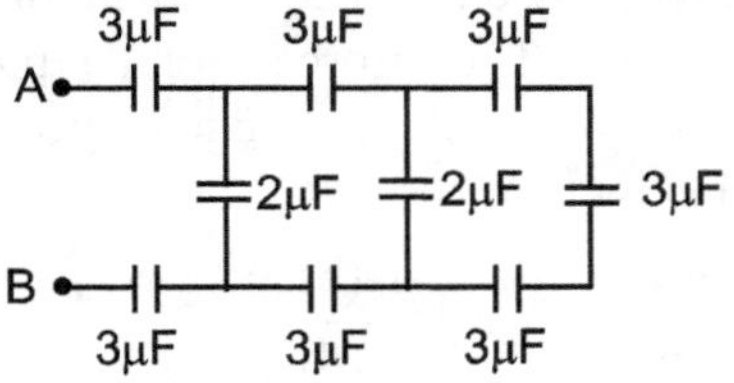

(a) 2 μF (b) 1 μF

(c) 3 μF (d) 1.5 μF

183. Force between the two plates of a capacitor is :

(a) Zero (b) $\frac{Q^2}{2A\varepsilon_0}$

(c) $\frac{2A\varepsilon_0}{Q^2}$ (d) $\frac{2Q^2}{\varepsilon_0}$

184. Two dielectric slabs each of thickness and dielectric constant K_1 and K_2 are inserted between the plates as shown. Then net capacitance between A and B is :

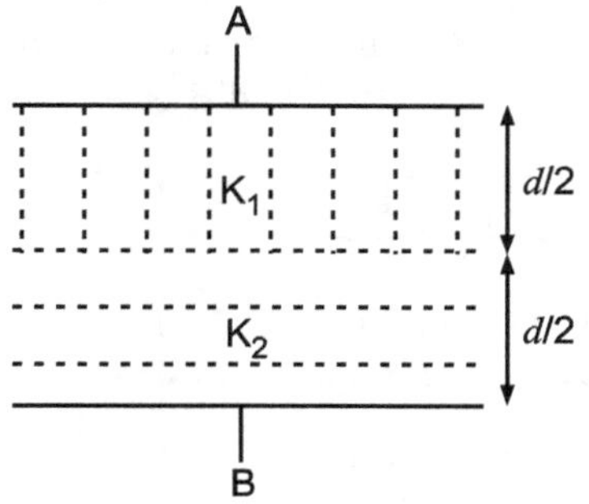

(a) $\frac{K_1K_2}{2}\frac{A\varepsilon_0}{d}$ (b) $\frac{2K_1K_2}{K_1+K_2}\frac{A\varepsilon_0}{d}$

(c) $\frac{K_1+K_2}{2}\frac{A\varepsilon_0}{d}$ (d) $\frac{(K_1+K_2)}{2K_1K_2}\frac{A\varepsilon_0}{d}$

185. Net capacitance between points A and B is :

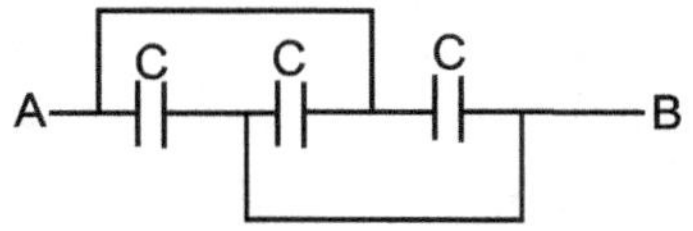

(a) C (b) 2C

(c) 3C (d) $\frac{3C}{2}$

186. Net capacitance between points A and B is :

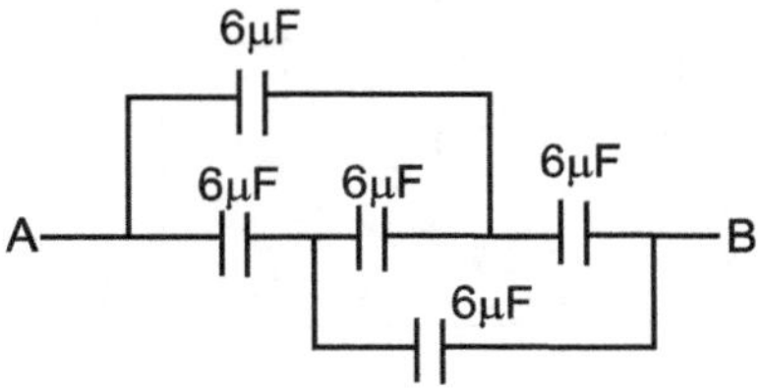

(a) 32 μF (b) 44 μF

(c) 12 μF (d) 6 μF

187. In the circuit shown in the figure, potential difference across the 4.5 μF capacitor is :

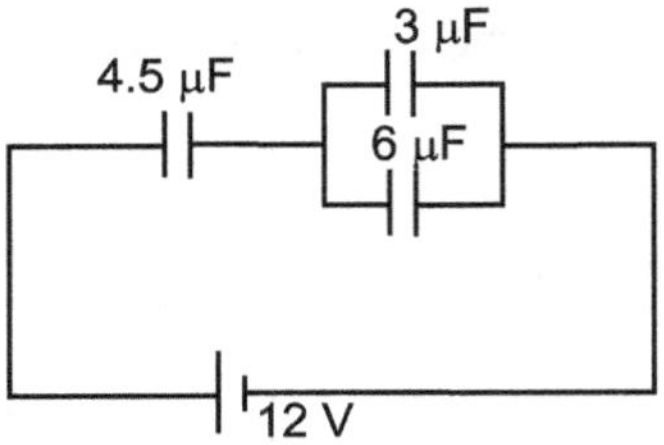

(a) 8/3 V (b) 4 V
(c) 6 V (d) 8 V

188. An infinite number of identical capacitors, each of capacitance 1 μF are connected as shown in the figure. Then the equivalent capacitance between A and B is :

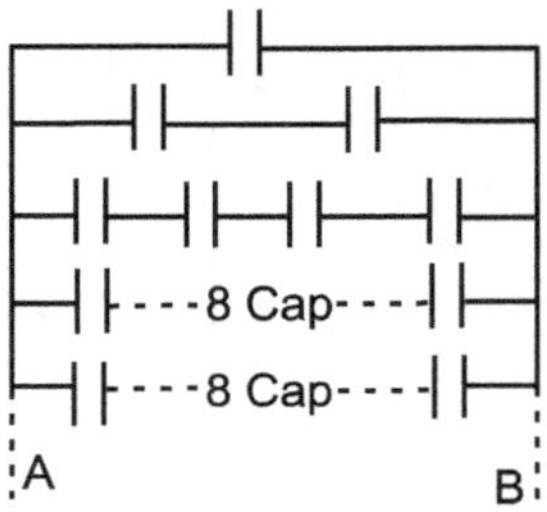

(a) 1 μF (b) 2 μF
(c) 1/2 μF (d) infinite

189. A capacitor when connected in an electrical circuit blocks:

(a) AC only
(b) DC only
(c) Neither AC nor DC
(d) Both AC and DC

190. In the given figure, the correct condition will be :

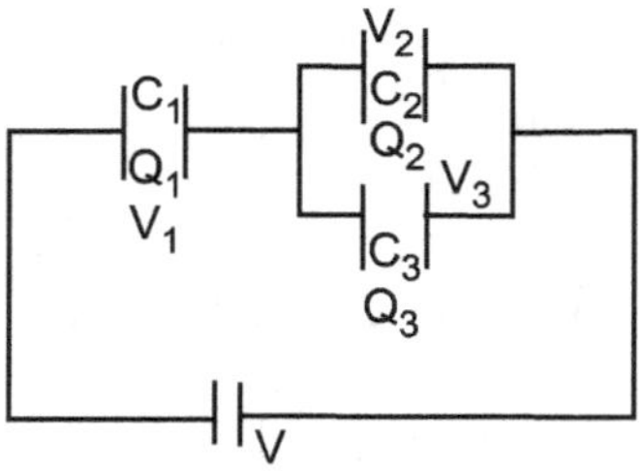

(a) $Q_1 = Q_2 = Q_3$ and $V_1 = V_2 = V_3 = V$
(b) $Q_1 = Q_2 + Q_3$ and $V = V_1 + V_2 + V_3$
(c) $Q_1 = Q_2 + Q_3$ and $V = V_1 + V_2$
(d) $Q_2 = Q_3$ and $V_2 = V_3$

191. The force of attraction between a proton and an electron separated by a distance of 9.6 fermi is approximately :

(a) 2.5 N (b) 3.90 N
(b) 0.320 N (d) 3.40 N

192. Five balls numbered 1 to 5 are suspended using separate threads. Pairs (1, 2), (2, 4) and (4, 1) show attraction, while pairs (2, 3) and (4, 5) show repulsion. Then :

(a) Ball -1 is +vely charged
(b) Ball -1 is neutral
(c) Ball -1 is –vely charged
(d) Ball -1 is –vely and ball –2 is +vely charged

193. When a glass rod rubbed with silk is brought near the gold leaf electroscope, the leaves diverge. The charge on the leaf is :

(a) positive
(b) negative
(c) either positive or negative
(d) equal and opposite

194. Two similar charges of 3 μC and 8 μC are separated by a distance of 7 cm. The null point from 3 μC will be at a distance of :

(a) 2.14 cm (b) 4.5 cm
(c) 2.24 cm (d) 2.65 cm

195. The ratio of the forces between two small spheres charged to a constant potential in air and in a medium of dielectric constant K is :

(a) 1 : K (b) K : 1
(c) $1 : K^2$ (d) $K^2 : 1$

196. Two similar charges each carrying 8.0 μC are separated by a distance of 60 cm of mica (K = 6). The force of repulsion approximately will be equal to 10^{-3} multiplied by :

(a) 18 kg wt (b) 9 kg wt
(c) 6 kg wt (d) 27 kg wt

197. A certain charge Q is divided at first into q and q'. Later on, the charges are placed at certain distance. If the force of interaction between the two charges is maximum, then :

(a) $q/q' = 2$ (b) $q/q' = 1$
(c) $q/q' = 4$ (d) $q/q' = 3$

198. An infinite number of charges each equal to $+q$ are placed at $x = 1, 2, 4, 8$ .... so on. Then potential at $x = 0$ is :

(a) infinite (b) $\frac{q}{4\pi\varepsilon_0}$
(c) 0 (d) $\frac{2q}{4\pi\varepsilon_0}$

199. The value of permittivity (ε_0) of vacuum in S.I. units is :

(a) zero
(b) less than zero
(c) between zero and one
(d) one

200. The dielectric constant K of an insulator can be :

(a) ∞ (b) zero
(e) –2 (d) 6

201. A 800 μF capacitor is charged at a steady rate of 50 c/second. How long will it take to raise its potential to 10 volt ?

(a) 160 seconds (b) 50 seconds
(c) 10 seconds (d) 500 seconds

202. The plates of a capacitor are charged upto 100 V. A 2 mm thick plate is inserted between the plates, then to maintain the same potential difference the distance between the plates of the capacitor is increased by 1.6 mm. The dielectric constant of the plate is :

(a) 5 (b) 1.225
(c) 4 (d) 2.5

203. A capacitor of 100 μF is charged to 400 V and another capacitor of 200 μF is charged to 100 V and then connected in parallel. Then charge from one capacitor flows to other till they attain a p.d. of :

(a) 200 V (b) 500 V
(c) 150 V (d) 250 V

204. Several, charged oil droplets each of radius 'r' and potential 'V' combine together to form a big drop of radius R. Potential of the big drop is then given by :

(a) $\frac{VR^2}{r^2}$ (b) $\frac{Vr^2}{R^2}$
(c) $\frac{Vr^3}{r}$ (d) $\frac{Vr^3}{R}$

205. N drops of mercury of equal radii and possessing equal charges combine to form a big spherical drop, then the capacitance of the bigger drop compared to each individual drop is

(a) N times (b) $N^{2/3}$ times
(c) $N^{1/3}$ times (d) $N^{5/3}$ times

206. Near two charged parallel plates of a capacitor C having frictionless plate, a frictionless dielectric slab S is placed on a frictionless table T as shown in the figure. When the slab is released, then :

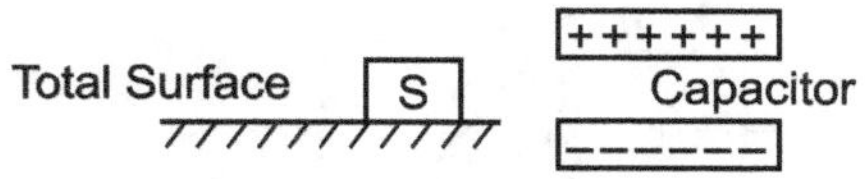

(a) it would stay on the table
(b) it would be pulled by the capacitor and will move out at the other end
(c) it would be pulled inside the capacitor and would come to rest occupying the space between the gap in the plates
(d) none of the above

207. Two conducting plates A and B are placed parallel to each other. Charge Q_1 is given to the plate A and charge Q_2 to the plate B. Then the charges on the inner sides of A and B are :

(a) $\frac{Q_1}{2}$ and $\frac{Q_2}{2}$
(b) $\frac{Q_1 + Q_2}{2}$ and $\frac{-(Q_1 + Q_2)}{2}$
(c) $\frac{Q_1 - Q_2}{2}$ and $\frac{-(Q_1 - Q_2)}{2}$
(d) $\frac{Q_1 + Q_2}{2}$ and $\frac{-(Q_1 + Q_2)}{2}$

208. The potential difference between the points S and Z in the circuit is :

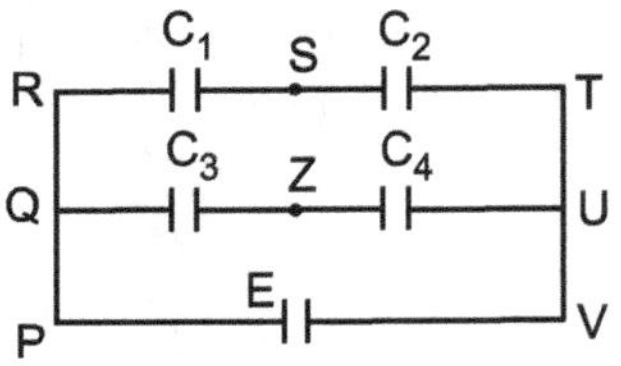

(a) $\frac{C_1C_4E}{(C_2+C_3)(C_2C_3)}$

(b) $\frac{(C_2C_3-C_1C_4)E}{(C_1+C_2)(C_3+C_4)}$

(c) $\frac{(C_2C_3-C_1C_4)E}{C_1+C_2+C_3+C_4}$

(d) $\frac{C_2C_3E}{(C_1+C_4)(C_1C_4)}$

209. Two large parallel conducting plates are situated 10 cm apart. The potential difference between the plates is V. What is the p.d between A and B ?

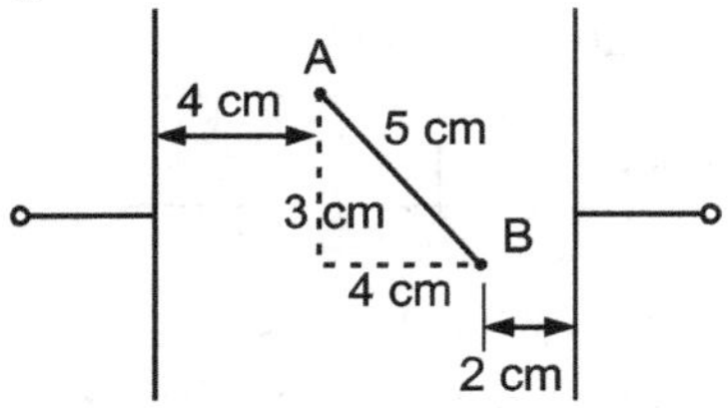

(a) V (b) $\frac{2V}{5}$

(c) V/4 (d) $\frac{3V}{5}$

210. N drops of energy of equal radii and possessing equal charges combine to form a big spherical drop. Then potential of the big drop compared to the individual droplet is :

(a) N times (b) $N^{2/3}$ times

(c) $N^{1/3}$ times (d) $N^{5/3}$ times

211. In question 210, potential energy of the bigger drop compared to the individual droplet is :

(a) N times (b) $N^{2/3}$ times

(c) $N^{1/3}$ times (d) $N^{5/3}$ times

212. Three concentric conducting spherical shells are arranged as shown in the figure. The shell with radius '3*a*' and '*a*' is earthed. Now if the middle sphere is given charge q_0, what are the charges induced on the shell of radius '*a*' and '3*a*' spheres respectively ?

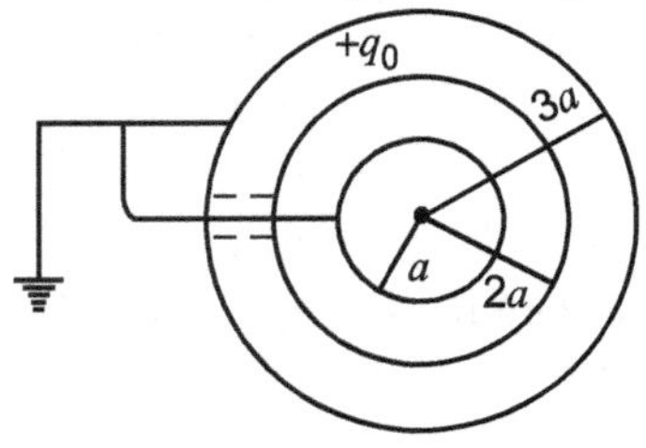

(a) $\frac{-q_0}{4}$ and $\frac{-3q_0}{4}$ (b) $\frac{-3q_0}{4}$ and $\frac{-q_0}{4}$

(c) $\frac{-q_0}{3}$ and $\frac{-2q_0}{3}$ (d) $\frac{-2q_0}{3}$ and $\frac{-q_0}{3}$

213. A bob of mass *m* with a charge *q* is suspended from a string of length *l* inside a parallel plate capacitor whose electric field E is directed downward. The period of oscillation of this pendulum is :

(a) $2\pi\sqrt{\frac{l}{g}}$ (b) $2\pi\sqrt{\frac{l}{g+qE}}$

(c) $2\pi\sqrt{\frac{1}{g+\frac{qE}{m}}}$ (d) $2\pi\sqrt{\frac{l}{g+qEm}}$

214. A thin glass rod is bent into a semicircular ring of radius *r*. A charge +Q is uniformly distributed along one half of the semicircular ring and – Q on the other half as shown in the figure. Electric field E at point P is :

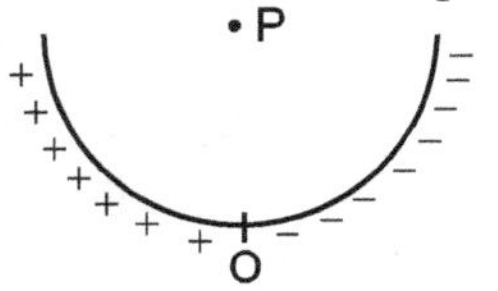

(a) $\frac{3Q^2}{\pi^2\varepsilon_0 r^2}$ (b) $\frac{2Q^2}{\pi^2\varepsilon_0 r^2}$

(c) $\frac{Q}{\pi^2\varepsilon_0 r^2}$ (d) $\frac{Q}{2\pi\varepsilon_0 r^2}$

215. A charge *q* is distributed uniformly over the volume of a ball of radius R. Assume the permittivity to be equal to 1, then electrostatic energy of the ball is :

(a) $\frac{3q^2}{5\pi\varepsilon_0 R}$ (b) $\frac{3q^2}{20\pi\varepsilon_0 R}$

(c) $\frac{3q^2}{10\pi\varepsilon_0 R}$ (d) $\frac{3q^2}{4\pi\varepsilon_0 R}$

216. A charged particle of mass 'm' and charge 'q' is released from rest in an electric field of constant magnitude E. The K.E. of the particle after time t is E_k and the linear momentum is p, then :

(a) $p = q Et^2$ (b) $p = 2qEt$

(c) $E_k = \frac{q^2 E^2 t^2}{2m}$ (d) $E_k = \frac{q^2 E^2 t^2}{m}$

217. An electron has an initial velocity in a different direction from the electric field. The path of the electron is :

(a) a straight line (b) a circle

(c) an ellipse (d) a parabola

218. 20 stat coulomb of charge is divided into two parts so that the two parts repel each other with a maximum force when placed 10 cm apart. Now the work done in decreasing the separation between them to 5 cm will be :

(a) 0.5 mJ (b) 1 μJ

(c) 0.5 nJ (d) 1 pJ

219. A solid conduciting sphere having a charge Q is surrounded by an uncharged spherical shell. Let potential difference between the surface of the solid sphere and outer suface of spherical shell be V. If the shell is now given an addition of charge –3Q, the new potential difference between the same surface is :

(a) V (b) 2 V

(c) 4 V (d) – 2 V

220. A charge q_0 is moved without acceleration from point A to B through a path A → C → B. The potential difference between A and B is :

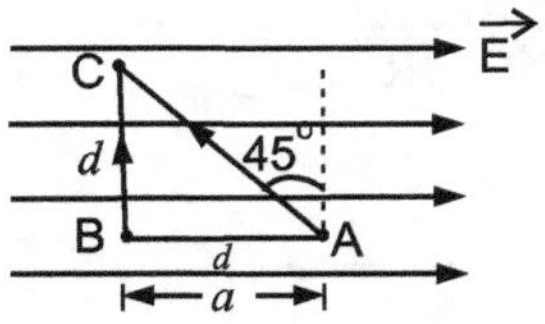

(a) E (AC cos 45° + BC)

(b) $-\vec{E} \times \overrightarrow{BC}$

(c) $\vec{E} \cdot \vec{d} \cos 45°$

(d) $\vec{E} \cdot \vec{d}$

221. A metallic shell has a point charge 'q' kept inside its cavity. Which one of the following diagrams correctly represents the electric lines of forces ? **(I.I.T. 2003 Screening)**

(a)

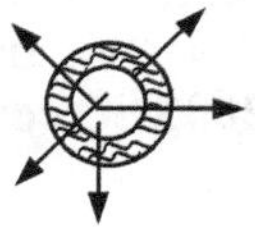

(b)

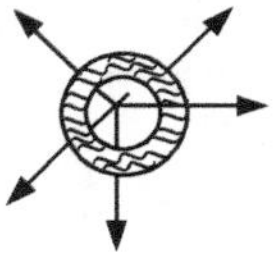

(c)

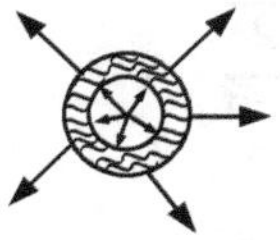

(d)

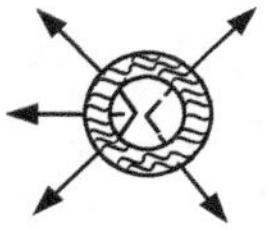

222. The electric potential between a proton and an electron is given by $V = V_0 \, ln \, \frac{r}{r_0}$, where r_0 is a constant. Assuming Bohr's model to be applicable, write the variation of r_n with n, n being the principal quantum number : **(I.I.T. 2003 Screening)**

(a) $r_n \propto n$ (b) $r_n \propto 1/n$

(c) $r_n \propto n^2$ (d) $r_n \propto 1/n^2$

223. What are the charges, if six charges of equal magnitude, 3 positive and 3 negative are to be placed on the PQRSTU corners of a regular hexagon, such that field at the centre is double than of what it would have been if only one +ve charge is placed at R ? **(I.I.T. 2004 Screening)**

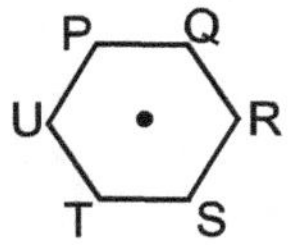

(a) +, +, +, –, –, – (b) –, +, +, +, –, –

(c) –, +, +, –, +, – (d) +, –, +, –, +, –

224. A Gaussian surface in figure is shown by dotted line. The electric field on the surface will be : **(I.I.T. 2004 Screening)**

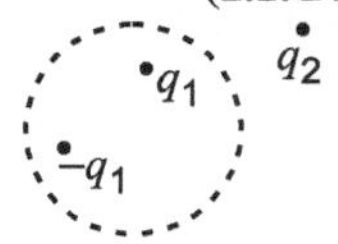

(a) due to q_1 and q_2 only
(b) due to q_2 only
(c) zero
(d) due to all

225. Three infinitely charged sheets are kept parallel to x-y plane having charge densities as shown, then the value of electric field at 'P' is : **(I.I.T. 2005 Screening)**

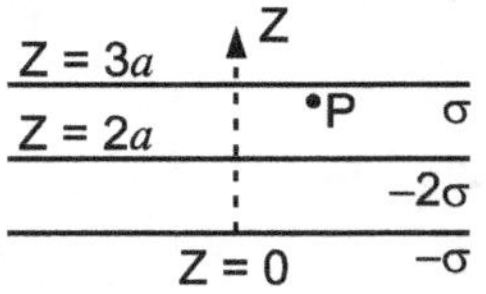

(a) $\frac{-4\sigma}{\varepsilon_0}\hat{k}$ (b) $\frac{4\sigma}{\varepsilon_0}\hat{k}$

(c) $\frac{-2\sigma}{\varepsilon_0}\hat{k}$ (d) $\frac{2\sigma}{\varepsilon_0}\hat{k}$

226. A capacitor C = 4.0 μF is connected through a resistor R = 2.5 MΩ across a battery of negligible internal resistance of voltage 12 volts. The time after which the potential difference across the capacitor becomes three times to that of resistor is ($\log_{10} 2 = 0.693$) : **(I.I.T. 2005 Screening)**

(a) 13.86 sec (b) 6.48 sec
(c) 3.24 sec (d) 20.52 sec

227. The electrostatic potential (ϕ_r) of a spherical symmetric system kept at origin, is shown in the figure and given as : **(I.I.T. 2006)**

$$\phi_r = \frac{q}{4\pi\varepsilon_0 r} \quad (r \geq R_0)$$

$$\phi_r = \frac{q}{4\pi\varepsilon_0 R_0} \quad (r \leq R_0)$$

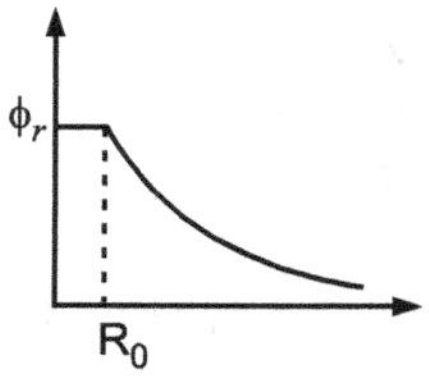

Which of the following option(s) is/are correct ?

(a) For spherical region $r \leq R_0$, the total electrostatic energy stored is zero.
(b) Within $r = 2R_0$, total charge is q.
(c) There will be no charge anywhere except at $r = R_0$.
(d) Electric field is discontinuous at $r = R_0$.

228. A charged ball B hangs from a silk thread S which makes an angle θ with a large charged conducting sheet P, as shown in the figure. The surface charge density σ of the sheet is proportional to : **(A.I.E.E.E. 2005)**

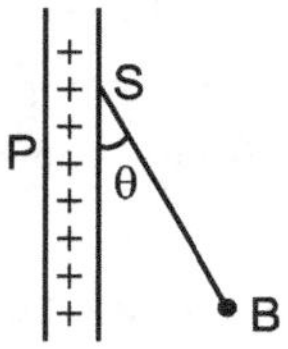

(a) cos θ (b) cot θ
(c) sin θ (d) tan θ

229. Two point charges + 8q and – 2q are located at x = 0 and x = L respectively. The location of a point on the x-axis at which the net electric field due to these two point charges is zero is : **(A.I.E.E.E. 2005)**

(a) $x = 2L$ (b) $x = L/4$
(c) $x = 8L$ (d) $x = 4L$

230. Two thin wire rings each having a radius R are placed at a distance d apart with their axes coinciding. The charges on the two rings are $+q$ and $-q$. The potential difference between the centres of the two rings is : **(A.I.E.E.E. 2005)**

(a) $\frac{QR}{4\pi\varepsilon_0 d^2}$

(b) $\frac{QR}{4\pi\varepsilon_0}\left[\frac{1}{R} - \frac{1}{\sqrt{R^2 + d^2}}\right]$

(c) zero

(d) $\frac{QR}{4\pi\varepsilon_0}\left[\frac{1}{R} + \frac{1}{\sqrt{R^2 + d^2}}\right]$

231. A parallel plate capacitor is made by stacking n equally spaced plates connected alternatively. If the capacitance between any two adjacent plates is C, then the resultant capacitance is : **(A.I.E.E.E. 2005)**

(a) $(n-1)$ C (b) $(n+1)$ C

(c) C (d) nC

232. An electric dipole is placed at an angle of 30° to a non-uniform electric field. The dipole will experience : **(A.I.E.E.E. 2006)**

(a) a torque only

(b) a transitional force only in the direction of the field

(c) a translational force only in the direction normal to the direction of the field

(d) a torque as well as translational force

233. Two insulating plates are both uniformly charged in such a way that the potential difference between them is $V_2 - V_1 = 20$ V. (i.e., plate 2 is at a higher potential). The plates are separated by $d = 0.1$ m and can be treated as infinitely large. An electron is released from rest on the inner surface of plate 1. What is its speed when it hits plate 2 ? **(A.I.E.E.E. 2006)**

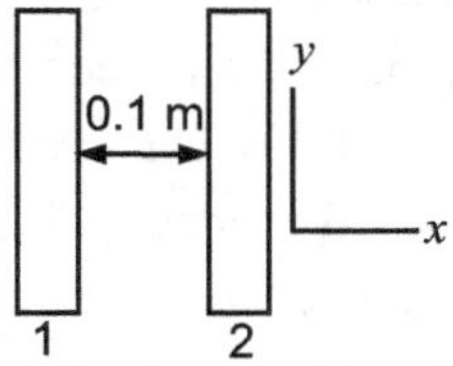

($e = 1.6 \times 10^{-19}$ C, $m_e = 9.11 \times 10^{-31}$ kg)

(a) 32×10^{-19} m/s (b) 2.65×10^{6} m/s

(c) 7.02×10^{12} m/s (d) 1.87×10^{6} m/s

234. Two spherical conductors A and B of radii 1 mm and 2 mm are separated by a distance of 5 cm and are uniformly charged. If the spheres are connected by a conducting wire, then in equilibrium condition, the ratio of the magnitude of the electric fields at the surface of spheres A and B is :

(A.I.E.E.E. 2006)

(a) 1 : 4 (b) 4 : 1

(c) 1 : 2 (d) 2 : 1

235. Ampere second is the unit of :

(MHT-CET 2002)

(a) Capacitance (b) Charge

(c) Energy (d) Power

236. If a 4 μF capacitor is charged to 1 kV, then energy stored in the capacitor is :

(MHT-CET 2003)

(a) 1 J (b) 4 J

(c) 6 J (d) 2 J

237. A cylinder is charged by 10 mC. Length of cylinder is 1 km and radius is 1 mm. Surface density of charge of cylinder is :

(MHT-CET 2004)

(a) 1.59×10^{-4} C/m^2 (b) 1.59×10^{-2} C/m^2

(c) 1.59×10^{-3} C/m^2 (d) 1.59×10^{-5} C/m^2

238. Unit of electric flux is : **(MHT-CET 2005)**

(a) Vm (b) V/m

(c) Nm/C (d) C/Nm

239. A parallel plate capacitor has a capacity C. If a medium of dielectric constant K is introduced between the plates, the capacity of the capacitor becomes :

(MHT-CET 2006)

(a) $\frac{C}{K}$ (b) $\frac{C}{K^2}$

(c) M^2C (d) KC

240. A capacitor of 20 μF is given a potential difference of 500 V and a 10 μF capacitor is charged through a potential difference of 200 V. What is the potential across each when they are connected in parallel ?

(MHT-CET 2008)

(a) 200 V (b) 400 V

(c) 600 V (d) 800 V

241. Two condensers each of capacity 4 μF are connected in series and a third condenser of capacity 4 μF is connected in parallel with the combination. The equivalent capacitance of the arrangement is :

(a) 12 μF (b) 8 μF

(c) 6 μF (d) 2.65 μF

242. Two identical conducting balls A and B have positive charges q_1 and q_2 respectively. But $q_1 \neq q_2$. The balls are brought together so that they touch each other and then kept in their original positions. The force between them is: **(C.E.T. Karnataka 2010)**

(a) zero

(b) same as that before the balls touched

(c) greater than that before the balls touched

(d) less than that before the balls touched

243. In the Davisson and Germer experiment, the velocity of electrons emitted from the electron gun can be increased by :

(A.I.P.M.T. 2011)

(a) increasing the potential difference between the anode and filament

(b) increasing the filament current

(c) decreasing the filament current

(d) decreasing the potential difference between the anode and filament

244. Two identical spheres carrying charge –9 μC and 5 μC respectively are kept in contact and then separated from each other. Point out the true statement from the following. In each sphere : **(Kerala P.M.T. 2007)**

(a) 1.25×10^{13} electrons are in deficit

(b) 1.25×10^{13} electrons are in excess

(c) 2.15×10^{13} electrons are in excess

(d) 2.15×10^{13} electrons are in deficit

245. Two spherical conductors B and C having equal radii and carrying equal charges in them repel each other with a force F, when kept apart at some distance. A third spherical conductor having the same radius as that of B, but uncharged is brought in contact with B and then brought in contact with C, finally removed away from both. The new force of repulsion between B and C is: **(P.M.T. 2008)**

(a) $\frac{F}{4}$ (b) $\frac{3F}{4}$

(c) $\frac{F}{8}$ (d) $\frac{3F}{8}$

246. Two point charges are 3 m apart and their combined charge is 8 μC. The force of repulsion between them is 0.012 N. Charges are : **(C.E.T. Karnataka 2010)**

(a) 4 μC, 4 μC (b) 6 μC, 2 μC

(c) 5 μC, 3 μC (d) 7 μC, 1 μC

247. Four metal conductors having different shapes : (i) A sphere, (ii) Cylindrical, (iii) Pear, and (iv) Lightening conductor are mounted on insulating stands and charged. The one which is best suited to retain the charges for a longer time is :

(C.E.T. Karnataka 2005)

(a) (i) (b) (ii)

(c) (iii) (d) (iv)

248. If σ = surface charge density, ε = electric permittivity, the dimensions of $\frac{\sigma}{\varepsilon}$ are same as: **(U.G.E.T. [M.A.H.E.] - Manipal 2005)**

(a) Electric force

(b) Electric field intensity

(c) Pressure

(d) Electric charge

249. A comb run through one's dry hair attracts small bits of paper. This is due to :

(C.E.T. Karnataka 2006)

(a) Comb is a good conductor

(b) Paper is a good conductor

(c) The atoms in the paper get polarized by the charged comb

(d) The comb possesses magnetic properties.

250. Three concentric metallic spherical shells of radii R, 2R, 3R are given charges Q_1, Q_2, Q_3 respectively. It is found that the surface charge densities on the outer surfaces of the shells are equal. Then, the ratio of the charges given to the shells, $Q_1 : Q_2 : Q_3$ is :

(I.I.T. 2009)

(a) 1 : 2 : 3 (b) 1 : 3 : 5

(c) 1 : 4 : 9 (d) 1 : 8 : 18

251. Two charges +6 μC and +15 μC are placed along the x-axis at $x = 0$ and $x = 2$ m respectively. A negative charge is placed between them such that the resultant force on it is zero. The negative charge is placed at : **(Orissa J.E.E. 2010)**

(a) $x = 0.775$ m
(b) $x = 1.2$ m
(c) $x = 0.5$ m
(d) Position depends on the amount of charge

252. The charged spherical shell does not produce electric field at any : **(Kerala P.M.T. 2004)**

(a) Interior point
(b) Outer point
(c) Beyond 2 metres
(d) Beyond 10 metres

253. An electric dipole of length 1 cm is placed with the axis making an angle of 30° to an electric field of strength 10^4 NC^{-1}. If it experiences a torque of $10\sqrt{2}$ Nm, the potential energy of the dipole is : **(Kerala P.E.T. 2008)**

(a) 0.245 J (b) 2.45 J
(d) 245.0 J (d) 24.5 J

254. Which one of the following is not correct ? **(H.P.P.M.T. 2009)**

(a) A dipole field at larger distances falls off as $\frac{1}{r}$.
(b) For polar molecules, there is a permanent electric dipole moment.
(c) The dipole field at large distance varies as $\frac{1}{r^2}$.
(d) For non-polar molecules, the dipole moment is zero.

255. An electric dipole of dipole moment '$\vec{p}$' is placed in a uniform electric field '$\vec{E}$'. The maximum torque experienced by the dipole is: **(D.C.E. 2009)**

(a) pE (b) p/E
(c) E/p (d) $\vec{p} \cdot \vec{E}$

256. An air capacitor is charged with an amount of charge 'q' and dipped into an oil tank. If the oil is pumped out, the electric field between the plates of the capacitor will: **(D.C.E. 2009)**

(a) increase (b) decrease
(c) remain the same (d) become zero

257. Consider a neutral conducting sphere. A positive point charge is placed outside the sphere. The net charge on the sphere is then: **(I.I.T., J.E.E. 2007)**

(a) Negative and distributed uniformly over the surface of the sphere
(b) Negative and appears only at the point on the sphere closest to the point charge
(c) Negative and distributed non-uniformly over the entire surface of the sphere
(d) Zero

258. Two unlike charges of the same magnitude Q are placed at a distance d. The intensity of the electric field at the middle point in the line joining the two charges is : **(J and K C.E.T. 2007)**

(a) Zero (b) $\frac{8Q}{4\pi\varepsilon_0 d^2}$
(c) $\frac{6Q}{4\pi\varepsilon_0 d^2}$ (d) $\frac{4Q}{4\pi\varepsilon_0 d^2}$

259. **Statement-1:** For practical purpose, the earth is used as a reference at zero potential in electrical circuits and

Statement-2: The electrical potential of a sphere of radius R with charge Q uniformly distributed on the surface is given by $\frac{Q}{4\pi\varepsilon_0 R}$. **(I.I.T. 2008)**

(a) Statement-1 is True, Statement-2 is True; Statement-2 is correct explanation for statement-1.

(b) Statement-1 is True, Statement-2 is True; Statement-2 is not a correct explanation for Statement-1.

(c) Statement-1 is True, Statement-2 is False.

(d) Statement-1 is False, Statement-2 is True.

260. A charge q is placed at the mid-point of the line joining two equal charges of Q. If the whole system is in equilibrium, then the value of q is : **(E.A.M.C.E.T. 2008)**

(a) $-\frac{Q}{2}$ (b) $+\frac{Q}{2}$

(c) $-\frac{Q}{4}$ (d) $+\frac{Q}{4}$

261. The charge given to any conductor resides on its outer surface, because: **(M.P.P.E.T. 2009)**

(a) the free charge tends to be in its minimum potential energy state

(b) the free charge tends to be in its minimum kinetic energy state

(c) the free charge tends to be in its maximum potential energy state

(d) the free charge tends to be in its maximum kinetic energy state

262. Electrostatic field at the surface of a conductor is always : **(H.P.P.M.T. 2005)**

(a) normal to the surface

(b) tangential to the surface

(c) constant throughout the surface

(d) zero

263. The electric field due to an electric dipole at a distance r from its centre in axial position is E. If the dipole is rotated through an angle of 90° about its perpendicular axis, the electric field at the same point will be : **(J and K C C.E.T. 2005)**

(a) E (b) E/4

(c) E/2 (d) 2E

264. Charge q is uniformly distributed over a thin half ring of radius R. The electric field at the centre of the ring is : **(A.I.I.M.S. 2008)**

(a) $\frac{q}{2\pi^2\varepsilon_0 R^2}$ (b) $\frac{q}{4\pi^2\varepsilon_0 R^2}$

(c) $\frac{q}{4\pi\varepsilon_0 R^2}$ (d) $\frac{q}{2\pi\varepsilon_0 R^2}$

265. A water molecule has an electric dipole moment 6.4×10^{-30} cm when it is in vapour state. The distance in metre between the centre of positive and negative charge of the molecule is : **(D.P.M.T. 2009)**

(a) 4×10^{-10} m (b) 4×10^{-11} m

(c) 4×10^{-12} m (d) 4×10^{-13} m

266. Let there be a spherically symmetric charge distribution with charge density varying as $\rho(r) = \rho_0\left(\frac{5}{4} - \frac{r}{R}\right)$ upto r = R, and $\rho(r) = 0$ for r > R, where r is the distance from the origin. The electric field at a distance r (r < R) from the origin is given by : **(A.I.E.E.E. 2010)**

(a) $\frac{\rho_0 r}{4\varepsilon_0}\left(\frac{5}{3} - \frac{r}{R}\right)$ (b) $\frac{4\rho_0 r}{3\varepsilon_0}\left(\frac{5}{4} - \frac{r}{R}\right)$

(c) $\frac{\rho_0 r}{3\varepsilon_0}\left(\frac{5}{4} - \frac{r}{R}\right)$ (d) $4\pi\frac{\rho_0 r}{3\varepsilon_0}\left(\frac{5}{3} - \frac{r}{R}\right)$

267. The electrostatic potential energy between a proton and an electron separated by a distance 1Å is : **(Kerala P.E.T. 2007)**

(a) 13.6 eV (b) 27.2 eV

(c) 14.4 eV (d) 1.44 eV

268. A charge 'Q' is placed at each corner of a cube of side 'a'. The potential at the centre of the cube is : **(E.A.M.C.E.T. 2008)**

(a) $\frac{8Q}{\pi\varepsilon_0 a}$ (b) $\frac{4Q}{4\pi\varepsilon_0 a}$

(c) $\frac{4Q}{\sqrt{3}\pi\varepsilon_0 a}$ (d) $\frac{2Q}{\pi\varepsilon_0 a}$

269. The potential energy of a charged parallel plate capacitor is U_0. If a slab of dielectric constant k is inserted between the plates, then the new potential energy will be : **(M.P.P.E.T. 2009)**

(a) $\frac{U_0}{k}$ (b) $U_0 k^2$

(c) $\frac{U_0}{k^2}$ (d) U_0^2

270. A hollow metal ball 8 cm in diameter is given a charge -4×10^{-8} C. The potential on the surface of the ball is :

(A.M.U.(Med) 2003)

(a) 0 (b) – 90 V
(c) – 9000 V (d) – 900 V

271. The electric potential at a point in free space due to a charge Q coulomb is $Q \times 10^{11}$ volts. The electric field at that point is :

(C.B.S.E.P.M.T. 2008)

(a) $12\pi\varepsilon_0 Q \times 10^{20}$ volt/m
(b) $4\pi\varepsilon_0 Q \times 10^{20}$ volt/m
(c) $12\pi\varepsilon_0 Q \times 10^{22}$ volt/m
(d) $4\pi\varepsilon_0 Q \times 10^{22}$ volt/m

272. Eight charged water drops each with a radius of 1 mm and a charge of 10^{-10} C merge into a single drop. Potential of the big drop will be : **(H.P.P.M.T. 2010)**

(a) 3600 V (b) 900 V
(c) 300 V (d) 150 V

273. Three concentric spherical shells have radii A, B and C (A < B < C) and have surface charge densities σ, $-\sigma$ and σ respectively. If V_A, V_B and V_C denote the potentials of the three shells, then for C = A + B, we have :

(A.I.P.M.T. (Prelims) 2009)

(a) $V_C = V_B \neq V_A$ (b) $V_C \neq V_B \neq V_A$
(c) $V_C = V_B = V_A$ (d) $V_C = V_A \neq V_B$

274. n identical droplets are charged to V volt each. If they coalesce to form a single drop, then its potential will be :

(W.B. J.E.E. 2010)

(a) $n^{2/3}$ V (b) $n^{1/3}$ V
(c) nV (d) V/n

275. The electrostatic potential inside a charged spherical ball is given by $\phi = ar^2 + b$, where r is the distance from the centre; a, b are constants. Then the charge density inside the ball is : **(A.I.E.E.E. 2011)**

(a) $-6a\varepsilon_0$ (b) $-24\pi a\varepsilon_0 r$
(c) $-6a\varepsilon_0 r$ (d) $-24\pi a\varepsilon_0$

276. A parallel plate capacitor is charged and the charging battery is then disconnected. If the plates of the capacitor are moved further apart by means of insulating handles, then which of the following is not correct ?

(A.M.U. (Medical) 2009)

(a) The capacitance decreases.
(b) The charge on the capacitor increases.
(c) The voltage across the plates increases.
(d) The electrostatic energy stored in the capacitor increases.

277. The intensity of electric field between the plates of a charged condenser having charge q and an area a will be : **(H.P.P.M.T. 2010)**

(a) $\frac{qA}{\varepsilon_0}$ (b) $\frac{q}{\varepsilon_0 A}$
(c) $\frac{A}{q\varepsilon_0}$ (d) $\frac{\varepsilon_0 A}{q}$

278. Which one of the following is correct ?

(S.C.R.A. 2007)

If two conducting spheres X and Y are separately charged, and then brought in contact,

(a) only total charge of the two spheres is conserved.
(b) both total electrostatic energy and charge are conserved.
(c) only the total electrostatic energy of the two spheres is conserved.
(d) the total charge of the two spheres becomes half of the original charges of the spheres charged separately.

279. A parallel plate condenser has a uniform electric field E (V/m) in the space between the plates. If the distance between the plates is d (m) and area of each plate is A (m^2), the energy (joules) stored in the condenser is :

(A.I.P.M.T. 2011)

(a) $\frac{E^2 A d}{\varepsilon_0}$ (b) $\frac{1}{2}\varepsilon_0 E^2$
(c) $\varepsilon_0 E A d$ (d) $\frac{1}{2}\varepsilon_0 E^2 A d$

280. An air filled parallel plate condenser has a capacity of 2 pF. The separation of the plates is doubled and the interspace between the plates is filled with wax. If the capacity is increased to 6 pF, the dielectric constant of wax is : **(Karnataka C.E.T. 2005)**

(a) 2 (b) 3

(c) 4 (d) 6

281. Consider a parallel plate capacitor with plate 20 cm by 20 cm and separated by 2 mm. The dielectric constant of the material between the plates is 5. The plates are connected to a voltage source of 500 V. The energy density of the field between the plates will be close to: **(A.M.U. (Medical) 2009)**

(a) $2.65\ J/m^3$ (b) $1.95\ J/m^3$

(c) $1.38\ J/m^3$ (d) $0.69\ J/m^3$

282. A fully charged capacitor C with initial charge q_0 is connected to a coil of self inductance L at $t = 0$. The time at which the energy is stored equally between the electric and the magnetic fields is :

(A.I.E.E.E. 2001)

(a) $\sqrt{LC}$ (b) $\pi\sqrt{LC}$

(c) $\frac{\pi}{4}\sqrt{LC}$ (d) $2\pi\sqrt{LC}$

283. The electric intensity outside a charged sphere of radius R at a distance r (r > R) is

(MHT-CET 2010)

(a) $\frac{\sigma R^2}{\varepsilon_0 r^2}$ (b) $\frac{\sigma r^2}{\varepsilon_0 R^2}$

(c) $\frac{\sigma R}{\varepsilon_0 r}$ (d) $\frac{\sigma r}{\varepsilon_0 R}$

284. Capacity of a capacitor is 48 mF. When it is charged from 0.1 C to 0.5 C, change in energy stored **(MHT-CET 2010)**

(a) 2500 J (b) 2.5×10^{-3} J

(c) 2.5×10^{6} J (d) 2.42×10^{-2} J

285. In a parallel plate capacitor, the capacity increases, if **(MHT-CET 2009)**

(a) area of plates is decreased

(b) distance between the plates is increased

(c) area of plates is increased

(d) dielectric constant is decreased

286. Two positive ions, each carrying a charge q, are separated by a distance d. If F is the force of repulsion between the ions, the number of electrons missing from each ion will be (e being the charge on an electron)

(C.B.S.E., P.M.T. 2010)

(a) $\frac{\sqrt{4\pi\varepsilon_0 Fe^2}}{d^2}$

(b) $\frac{\sqrt{4\pi\varepsilon_0 Fd^2}}{e^2}$

(c) $\frac{4\pi\varepsilon_0 Fd^2}{q^2}$

(d) $\frac{4\pi\varepsilon_0 Fd^2}{e^2}$

287. A series combination of n_1 capacitors, each of value C_1 is charged by a source of potential 4 V. When another parallel combination of n_2 capacitors, each of value C_2 is charged by a source of potential difference V, it has the same (total) energy stored in it as the first combination has. The value of C_2 in terms of C_1 is then

(C.B.S.E., P.M.T. 2010)

(a) $\frac{2n_2}{n_1}C_1$ (b) $\frac{16}{n_1 n_2}C_1$

(c) $\frac{2}{n_1 n_2}C_1$ (d) $\frac{16\,n_2}{n_1}C_1$

288. A charged cylinder of radius 3 mm has surface density of charge $4\ \mu C/m^2$. It is placed in a medium of dielectric constant 6.28. The electric intensity at a point at a distance of 1.5 m from its axis is

(MHT-CET 2011)

(a) 1.44 V/m (b) 2.44 V/m

(c) 3 V/m (d) 0.5 V/m

289. If A is the area of each plate, charge on it is q and potential difference is V, then the distance between the parallel plates of a capacitor is **(MHT-CET 2011)**

(a) $\frac{\varepsilon_0 AV}{2q}$ (b) $\frac{\varepsilon_0 AV}{q}$

(c) $\frac{2\varepsilon_0 AV}{q}$ (d) $\frac{AV}{q}$

290. If n identical capacitors are connected in series and then in parallel, then the ratio of effective capacity in parallel and in series combination i.e. $\frac{C_P}{C_S}$ is **(MHT-CET 2011)**

(a) n (b) 1/n

(c) n^2 (d) $1/n^2$

291. The potential energy of system increases if work is done **(C.B.S.E., P.M.T. 2011)**

(a) upon the system by a non-conservative force

(b) by the system against a conservative force

(c) by the system against a non-conservative force

(d) upon the system by a conservative force

292. A charge Q is enclosed by a Gaussian spherical surface of radius R. If the radius is doubled, then the outward electric flux will

(C.B.S.E., P.M.T. 2011)

(a) increase four times

(b) be reduced to half

(c) remain the same

(d) be doubled

293. Two identical capacitors are first connected in series and then in parallel. The difference between their effective capacities is 3 μF. The capacity of each capacitor is

(MHT-CET 2012)

(a) 3 μF (b) 4 μF

(c) 2 μF (d) 5 μF

294. Van de Graff generator produces

(MHT-CET 2012)

(a) high voltage and high current

(b) high voltage and low current

(c) low voltage and high current

(d) low voltage and low current

295. A, B and C are the points in a uniform electric field. The electric potential is

(NEET 2013)

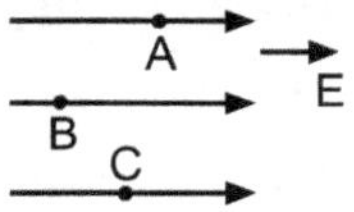

(a) maximum at B

(b) maximum at C

(c) same at all the three points A, B and C

(d) maximum at A

296. Two pith balls carrying equal charges are suspended from a common point by strings of equal length, the equilibrium separation between them is r. Now the strings are rigidly clamped at half the height. The equilibrium separation in between the balls now becomes : **(NEET 2013)**

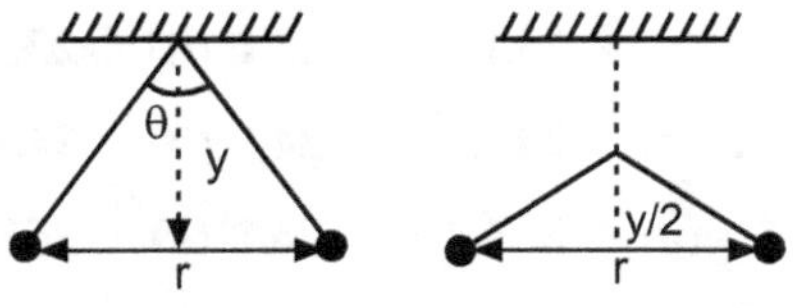

(a) $\left(\frac{r}{3\sqrt{2}}\right)$ (b) $\left(\frac{2r}{\sqrt{3}}\right)$

(c) $\left(\frac{2r}{3}\right)$ (d) $\left(\frac{r}{\sqrt{2}}\right)^2$

ANSWER KEY

1. (a)	**2.** (c)	**3.** (a)	**4.** (b)	**5.** (a)	**6.** (a)	**7.** (b)	**8.** (a)	**9.** (c)	**10.** (b)
11. (b)	**12.** (d)	**13.** (b)	**14.** (d)	**15.** (c)	**16.** (d)	**17.** (b)	**18.** (c)	**19.** (a)	**20.** (b)
21. (c)	**22.** (a)	**23.** (d)	**24.** (d)	**25.** (d)	**26.** (c)	**27.** (d)	**28.** (b)	**29.** (d)	**30.** (d)
31. (b)	**32.** (a)	**33.** (b)	**34.** (d)	**35.** (a)	**36.** (c)	**37.** (a)	**38.** (a)	**39.** (c)	**40.** (a)
41. (d)	**42.** (b)	**43.** (c)	**44.** (a)	**45.** (a)	**46.** (a)	**47.** (a)	**48.** (c)	**49.** (a)	**50.** (a)
51. (c)	**52.** (d)	**53.** (a)	**54.** (b)	**55.** (a)	**56.** (d)	**57.** (c)	**58.** (c)	**59.** (b)	**60.** (d)
61. (b)	**62.** (c)	**63.** (b)	**64.** (a)	**65.** (b)	**66.** (c)	**67.** (d)	**68.** (b)	**69.** (b)	**70.** (d)
71. (d)	**72.** (a)	**73.** (d)	**74.** (d)	**75.** (c)	**76.** (b)	**77.** (c)	**78.** (c)	**79.** (d)	**80.** (b)
81. (a)	**82.** (b)	**83.** (a)	**84.** (c)	**85.** (b)	**86.** (c)	**87.** (c)	**88.** (b)	**89.** (d)	**90.** (d)
91. (a)	**92.** (b)	**93.** (c)	**94.** (a)	**95.** (a)	**96.** (d)	**97.** (b)	**98.** (c)	**99.** (c)	**100.** (a)
101. (d)	**102.** (c)	**103.** (b)	**104.** (b)	**105.** (b)	**106.** (b)	**107.** (a)	**108.** (c)	**109.** (c)	**110.** (d)
111. (b)	**112.** (a)	**113.** (b)	**114.** (c)	**115.** (a)	**116.** (b)	**117.** (c)	**118.** (a)	**119.** (d)	**120.** (b)
121. (b)	**122.** (a)	**123.** (a)	**124.** (b)	**125.** (d)	**126.** (a)	**127.** (c)	**128.** (c)	**129.** (a)	**130.** (c)
131. (a)	**132.** (c)	**133.** (a)	**134.** (b)	**135.** (c)	**136.** (d)	**137.** (a)	**138.** (a)	**139.** (a)	**140.** (c)
141. (d)	**142.** (c)	**143.** (a)	**144.** (d)	**145.** (c)	**146.** (c)	**147.** (c)	**148.** (b)	**149.** (d)	**150.** (d)
151. (a)	**152.** (c)	**153.** (b)	**154.** (c)	**155.** (b)	**156.** (d)	**157.** (d)	**158.** (b)	**159.** (a)	**160.** (b)
161. (c)	**162.** (c)	**163.** (a)	**164.** (b)	**165.** (a)	**166.** (d)	**167.** (c)	**168.** (a)	**169.** (b)	**170.** (c)
171. (b)	**172.** (b)	**173** (b)	**174.** (c)	**175.** (b)	**176.** (b)	**177.** (b)	**178.** (b)	**179.** (c)	**180.** (b)
181. (a)	**182.** (b)	**183.** (b)	**184.** (b)	**185.** (c)	**186.** (d)	**187.** (d)	**188.** (b)	**189.** (b)	**190.** (c)
191. (a)	**192.** (b)	**193.** (a)	**194.** (a)	**195.** (a)	**196.** (d)	**197.** (b)	**198.** (d)	**199.** (c)	**200.** (d)
201. (a)	**202.** (a)	**203.** (a)	**204.** (a)	**205.** (c)	**206.** (c)	**207.** (c)	**208.** (b)	**209.** (b)	**210.** (b)
211. (d)	**212.** (a)	**213.** (c)	**214.** (c)	**215.** (b)	**216.** (c)	**217.** (d)	**218.** (b)	**219.** (a)	**220.** (d)
221. (c)	**222.** (a)	**223.** (c)	**224.** (d)	**225.** (c)	**226.** (a)	**227.** a, b, c, d	**228.** (d)	**229.** (a)	**230.** (b)
231. (a)	**232.** (d)	**233.** (b)	**234.** (d)	**235.** (b)	**236.** (d)	**237.** (c)	**238.** (a)	**239.** (d)	**240.** (b)
241. (c)	**242.** (c)	**243.** (a)	**244.** (b)	**245.** (d)	**246.** (b)	**247.** (a)	**248.** (b)	**249.** (c)	**250.** (b)
251. (a)	**252.** (a)	**253.** (d)	**254.** (a)	**255.** (a)	**256.** (a)	**257.** (d)	**258.** (b)	**259.** (b)	**260.** (c)
261. (a)	**262.** (a)	**263.** (c)	**264.** (a)	**265.** (b)	**266.** (a)	**267.** (c)	**268.** (c)	**269.** (a)	**270.** (c)
271. (d)	**272.** (a)	**273.** (d)	**274.** (a)	**275.** (a)	**276.** (a)	**277.** (b)	**278.** (a)	**279.** (d)	**280.** (d)
281. (c)	**282.** (c)	**283.** (a)	**284.** (a)	**285.** (c)	**286.** (b)	**287.** (b)	**288.** (a)	**289.** (b)	**290.** (c)
291. (d)	**292.** (c)	**293.** (c)	**294.** (b)	**295.** (a)	**296.** (a)				

12

CURRENT ELECTRICITY

MULTIPLE CHOICE QUESTIONS

1. In the circuit shown, each of the resistors r_1 and r_2 has resistance 8 ohm. The cell has e.m.f. 8 V and internal resistance 4 ohm. What is the current in r_2 ?

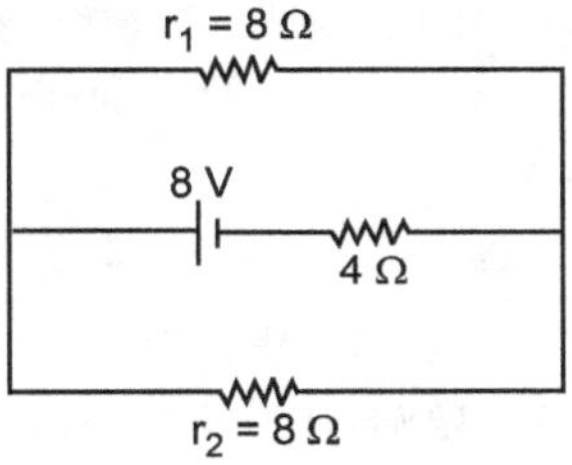

(a) 0.5 A (b) 1.5 A
(c) 1.0 A (d) 2.0 A

2. The resistance of each edge of a wire frame shaped as a cube is r. What is the resistance of the wire frame when the same is measured between a and f ?

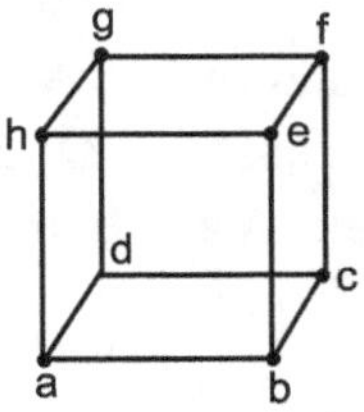

(a) 6/5 r (b) 5/6 r
(c) 7/12 r (d) 5/3 r

3. What will be the equivalent resistance between the two points A and D ?

(a) 10 (b) 20
(c) 30 (d) 40

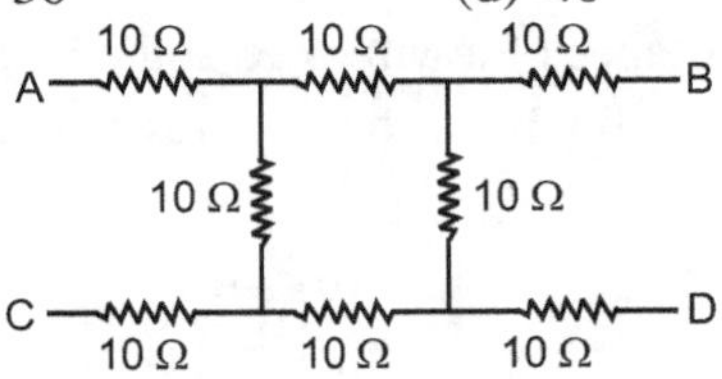

4. What is the equivalent resistance across the terminals A and B ?

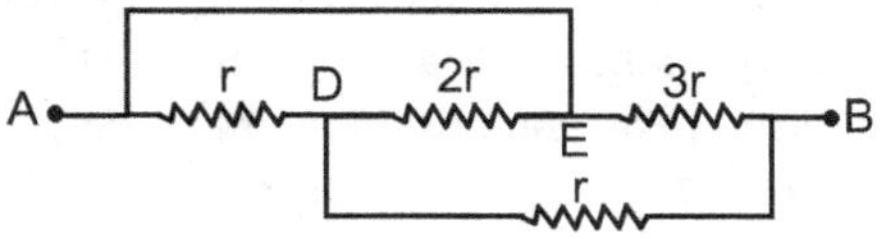

(a) $\frac{15r}{7}$ (b) $\frac{7r}{15}$
(c) $\frac{15r}{14}$ (d) $\frac{8r}{15}$

5. The resistance of a discharge tube is :
(a) ohmic
(b) non-ohmic
(c) both ohmic and non-ohmic
(d) sometimes ohmic, sometimes non-ohmic.

6. Three resistors are connected as shown in figure. The points A and B are connected to a source of direct current. What is the value of the ratio $\left(\frac{i_3}{i_1}\right)$ in terms of (r_1, r_2, r_3) ?

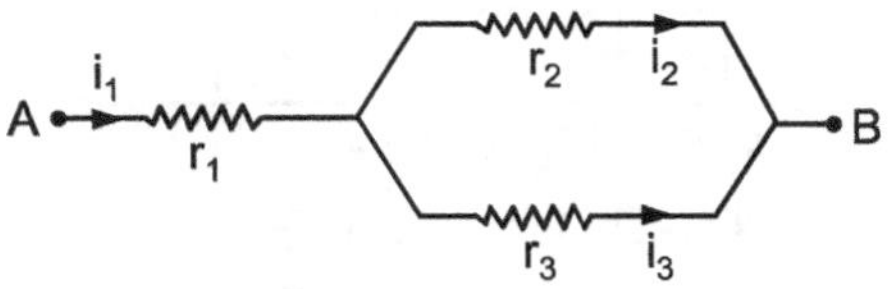

(a) $\frac{r_1}{r_2 + r_3}$ (b) $\frac{r_2}{r_2 + r_3}$
(c) $\frac{r_3}{r_1 + r_2}$ (d) $\frac{r_2}{r_1 + r_3}$

7. A dry cell has an e.m.f. of 1.5 V and internal resistance of 0.05. The maximum current obtained from this cell, for a short time interval is :
(a) 30 A (b) 300 A
(b) 3 A (d) 0.3 A

8. What is the p.d. between the terminals A and B ?

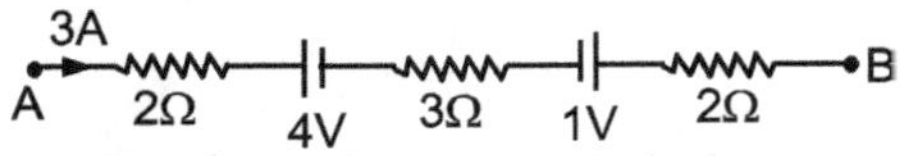

(a) 12 V (b) 24 V
(c) 36 V (d) 48 V

9. In an experiment to measure the internal resistance of a cell by a potentiometer it is found that all the balance points at a length of 2 m when the cell is shunted by a 5 ohm resistance, and is at a length of 3 m when the cell is shunted by a 10 ohm resistance, the internal resistance of the cell is then :

(a) 1.5 Ω (b) 10 Ω
(c) 15 Ω (d) 1 Ω

10. Potential difference across terminals of a cell were measured (in volts) against different currents (in ampere) flowing through the cell. A graph was drawn which came out as a straight line ABC. Using the data given in the graph, what is the value of e.m.f. of the cell ?

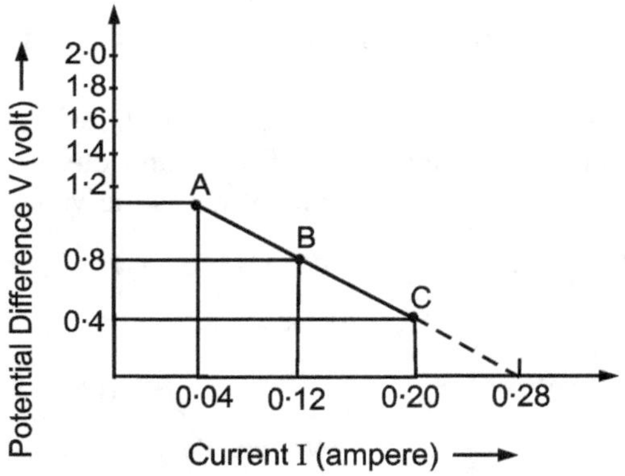

(a) 0.4 V (b) 2.0 V
(c) 1.4 V (d) 0.8 V

11. We are able to obtain fairly large currents in a conductor because :

(a) the electron drift speed is usually very large.
(b) the number density of free electrons as well as the electron drift speeds are very large and these compensate for the very small magnitude of the electron charge.
(c) the number density of free electrons is very high and this can compensate for the low values of electron drift speed and the very small magnitude of the electron charge.
(d) the very small magnitude of the electron charge has to be divided by the still smaller product of the number density and drift speed to get the electron current.

12. Two wires of the metal have the same length but their cross-sections are in the ratio 3 : 1. They are joined in series. The resistance of the thicker wire is 10 Ω. The total resistance of the combination will be :

(a) 40 (b) 40/3
(c) 5/2 (d) 100

13. What is the energy stored in the capacitor ?

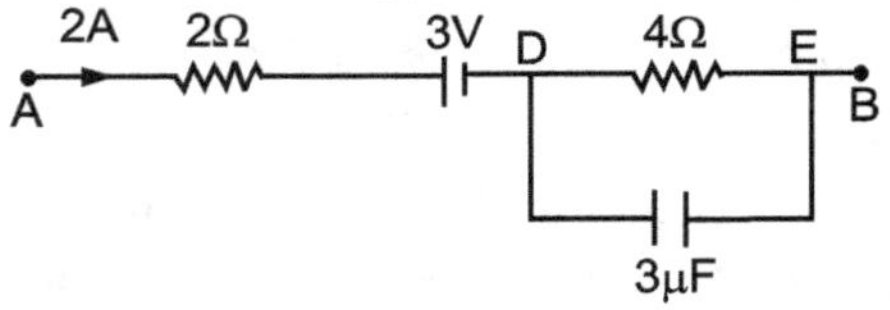

(a) 72 μJ (b) 96 μJ
(c) 96 mJ (d) 96 MJ

14. In the network shown in the figure each of the resistance is equal to 2 Ω. The resistance between the points A and B in the figure is :

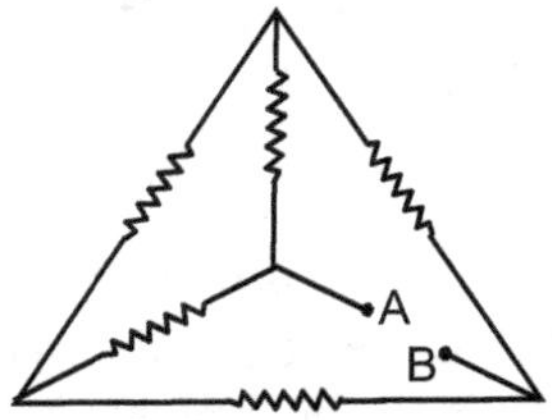

(a) 1 Ω (b) 2 Ω
(c) 3 Ω (d) 4 Ω

15. The resistance of a wire is R. If the length of the wire is doubled, the new resistance will be :

(a) R/2 (b) 4R
(c) 2R (d) R/4

16. In the circuit shown, the current sources are of negligible internal resistances. What is the potential difference between the points B and A ?

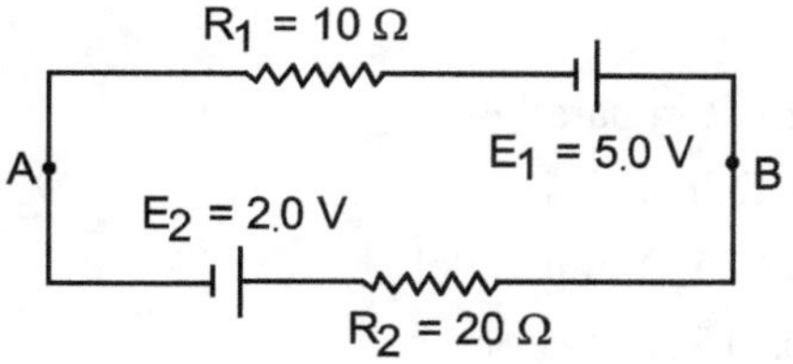

(a) – 4.0 V (b) 4.0 V
(c) – 8.0 V (d) 8.0 V

17. Which of the following has negative temperature coefficient of resistance ?
(a) Fe (b) C
(c) Mn (d) Ag

18. The reciprocal of resistance is called as :
(a) Conductance (b) Resistivity
(c) Specific resistance (d) Voltage

19. A solenoid is at p.d. 60 V and current flowing through it is 15 A, then resistance of coil will be :
(a) 4 Ω (b) 8 Ω
(c) 0.25 Ω (d) 2 Ω

20. A student has 10 resistances of resistance 'r'. The minimum resistance made by him from given resistors is :
(a) 10 r (b) r/10
(c) r/100 (d) r/2

21. Drift velocity is equal to :
(a) *i*/ne (b) *i*/nAe
(c) *i*A/ne (d) nAe*i*

22. What is the potential difference across the points A and B ?

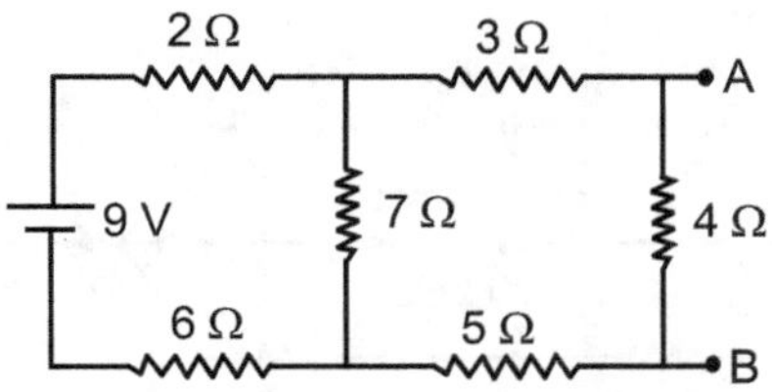

(a) 0.9 V (b) 1.1 V
(c) 1.3 V (d) 0.7 V

23. Which of the following is wrong ?
(a) Ammeter has low resistance and is connected in series.
(b) Ammeter has low resistance and is connected in parallel.
(c) Voltmeter has high resistance and is connected in parallel.
(d) None of the above.

24. A galvanometer of resistance 20Ω gives a full scale deflection with a current of 2 mA. What resistance should be connected in parallel so that it may measure 2A on full scale deflection?
(a) 0.2 Ω (b) 0.4 Ω
(c) 0.02 Ω (d) 0.04 Ω

25. Find the equivalent resistance across the terminals A and B :

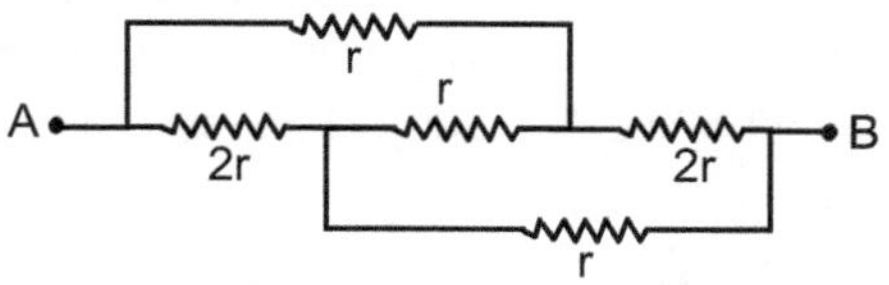

(a) 1.2 r (b) 1.4 r
(c) 1.6 r (d) 1.8 r

26. Equivalent resistance between the ends A and B in the given circuit figure is :

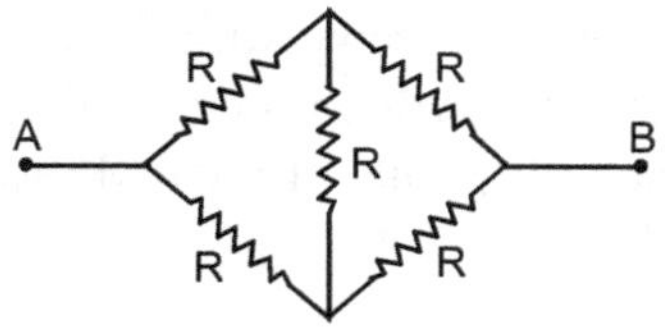

(a) 0 (b) 4R
(c) 5R (d) R

27. A flow of 10^7 electrons per second in a conducting wire constitutes a current of :
(a) 1.6×10^{-26} A (b) 1.6×10^{12} A
(c) 1.6×10^{-12} A (d) 1.6×10^{26} A

28. Identify the set in which all the three materials are good conductors of electricity :
(a) Cu, Ag and Au
(b) Cu, Si and diamond
(c) Cu, Hg and NaCl
(d) Cu, Ge and Hg

29. Six resistors of 3 Ω each are connected along the sides of a hexagon and three resistors of 6 Ω each are connected along AC, AD and AE as shown in the figure. The equivalent resistance between A and B is equal to :

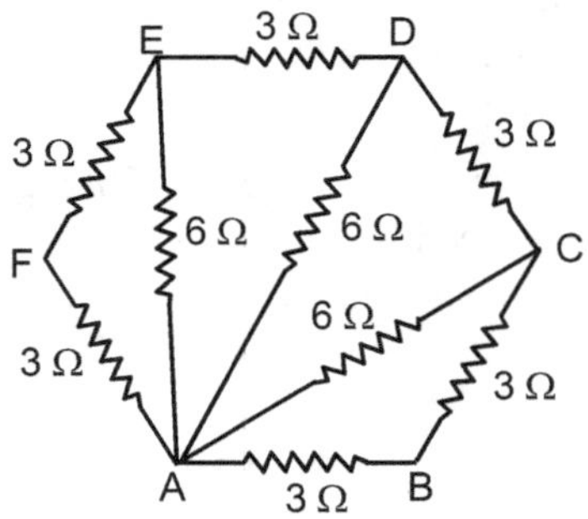

(a) 3 Ω (b) 9 Ω
(c) 2 Ω (d) 16 Ω

30. A wire 50 cm long and 1 mm^2 in cross-section carries a current of 4 A when connected to a 2 V battery. The resistivity of the wire is :

(a) 2×10^{-7} Ω m (b) 5×10^{-7} Ω m
(c) 4×10^{-6} Ω m (d) 1×10^{-6} Ω m

31. Potential difference across terminals of a cell was measured (in volts) against different currents (in ampere) flowing through the cell. A graph was drawn which came out to be a straight line ABC. Using the data given in the graph, the value of internal resistance of the cell is :

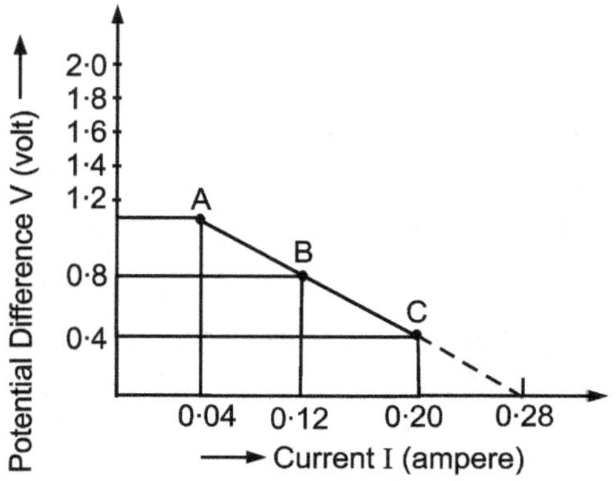

(b) 2 ohm (b) 3 ohm
(c) 5 ohm (d) 4 ohm

32. A galvanometer has 30 divisions and current sensitivity of 20 μA/division. It has a resistance of 25 Ω. To convert it into an ammeter of 1 A range, we should connect a resistance of :

(a) 25 Ω in parallel
(b) 5 Ω in series
(c) 0.015 Ω in parallel
(d) 0.015 Ω in series

33. A parallel combination of three resistors takes a current of 7.5 A from a 30 V supply. If the two resistors are 10 Ω and 12 Ω, find which is the third one ?

(a) 4 Ω
(b) 15 Ω
(c) 12 Ω
(d) 22 Ω

34. Two conductors made of the same material have lengths L and 2L, but have equal resistance. The two are connected in series in a circuit in which current is flowing. Which of the following is correct?

(a) The p.d. across the two conductors is the same.
(b) The electron drift velocity is larger in the conductor of length 2L.
(c) The electric field in the first conductor is twice that in the second.
(d) The electric field in the second conductor is twice that in the first.

35. The total electrical resistance between the points A and B for the circuit figure shown below is :

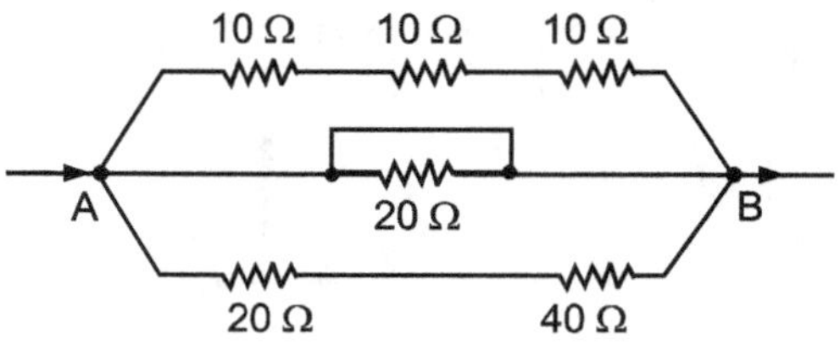

(a) 0 Ω (b) 15 Ω
(c) 30 Ω (d) 100 Ω

36. What is approximately the potential difference across A and B ?

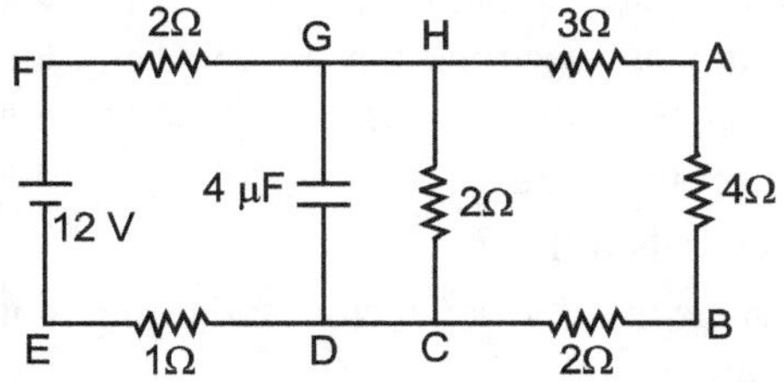

(a) 1 V (b) 2 V

(c) –1 V (d) –2 V

37. A steady current flows in a metallic conductor of non-uniform cross-section. Then which of the following quantities are constant along the conductor ?

(a) Current, current density

(b) Current

(c) Current, current density, electric field

(d) Current, current density, electric field, drift speed

38. The resistivity of alloys is R_{alloy} and the resistivity of constituent metals is R_{metal}. Then, usually :

(a) $R_{alloy} = R_{metal}$

(b) $R_{alloy} < R_{metal}$

(c) $R_{alloy} > R_{metal}$

(d) There is no simple relation between R_{alloy} and R_{metal}

39. A potentiometer wire has length 10 m and resistance 20 Ω. A 2.5 V battery of negligible internal resistance is connected across the wire with an 80 Ω series resistance. The potential gradient on the wire will be :

(a) 2.5×10^{-4} V/cm

(b) 0.62×10^{-4} V/mm

(c) 1×10^{-5} V/mm

(d) 5×10^{-5} V/mm

40. Net resistance between A and B in the given network is :

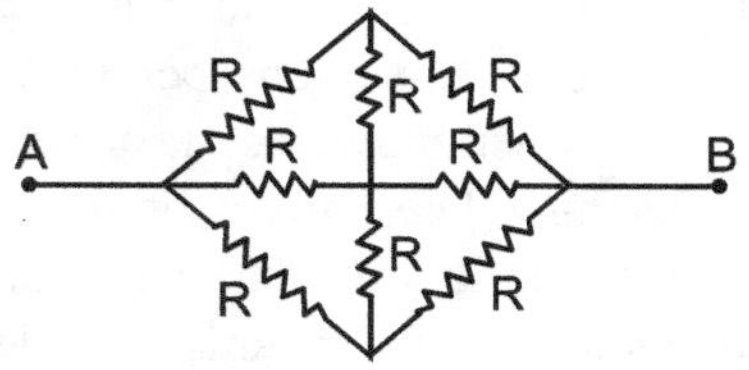

(a) $\frac{2R}{3}$ (b) $\frac{3R}{2}$

(c) $\frac{5R}{3}$ (d) $\frac{3R}{5}$

41. A battery of e.m.f 10 V and internal resistance 0.5 Ω is connected across a variable resistance R. The value of R, for which the power delivered in it is maximum, is given by :

(a) 2.0 Ω (b) 0.25 Ω

(c) 1.0 Ω (d) 0.5 Ω

42. A moving coil galvanometer has a resistance of 900 Ω. In order to send only 10% of the main current through this galvanometer, the resistance of the required shunt is :

(a) 0.9 Ω (b) 100 Ω

(c) 405 Ω (d) 90 Ω

43. What is the energy stored in the capacitor of capacitance 3 μF ?

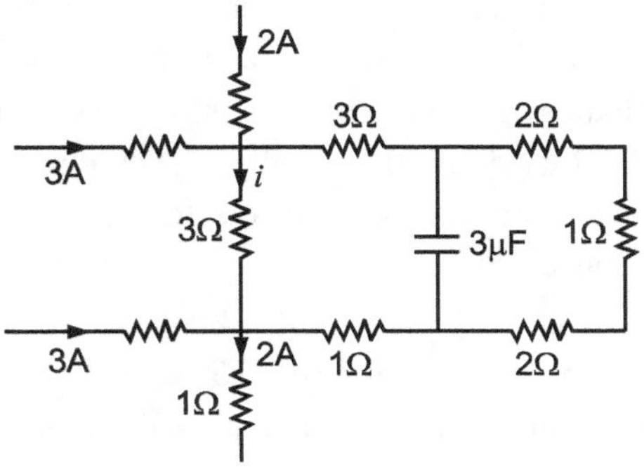

(a) 5.9×10^{-5} J

(b) 5.8×10^{-5} J

(c) 5.7×10^{-5} J

(d) 5.6×10^{-5} J

44. An ionization chamber with parallel conducting plates as anode and cathode, has 5×10^7 electrons and the same number of singly charged positive ions per cm^3. The electrons are moving towards the anode with velocity 0.4 m/s. The current density from anode to cathode is $4\mu\mu A/m^2$. The velocity of positive ions moving towards cathode is :

(a) $0.4\ ms^{-1}$ (b) zero
(c) $1.6\ ms^{-1}$ (d) $0.1\ ms^{-1}$

45. Figure shows a rectangular block with dimensions x, $2x$ and $4x$. Electrical contacts can be made to the block between opposite pairs of faces (for example, between the faces labeled A–A, B–B and C–C). Between which two faces would the maximum electrical resistance be obtained ?

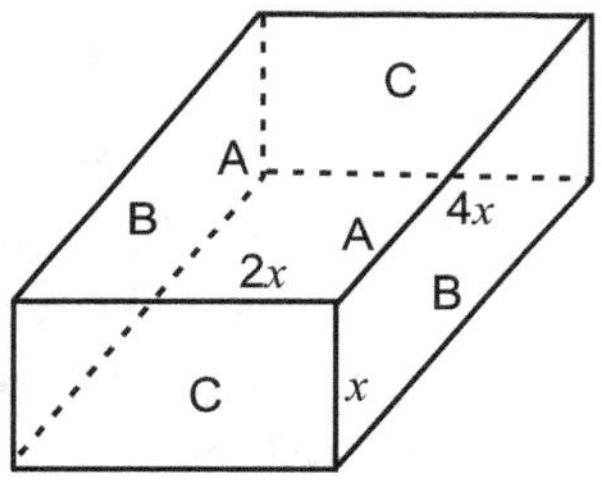

(a) A–A
(b) B–B
(c) C–C
(d) Same for all three pairs

46. In a household, at an instant of time only a 50 watt lamp and a 50 watt electrical appliance are on, both working on the 200 volt domestic supply. The current passing through the only electric meter in the house is :

(a) 20 A (b) 42 A
(c) 30 A (d) 0.5 A

47. Current in a conductor is due to the motion of :

(a) free electrons
(b) positive ions
(c) protons
(d) free electrons and holes

48. Whenever a p.d. is applied across a conductor, the free electrons in it are set into motion. Two velocities are associated with the moving electrons–the drift velocity and average velocity. The fact is that the two are:

(a) actually same
(b) entirely different
(c) same in some conductors and different in others
(d) none of the above

49. Current I flows through a uniform wire of diameter 'd' when the mean drift velocity is v_d. The same current will flow through a wire of diameter $d/2$ made of the same material if the mean drift velocity of the electron is :

(a) $v_d/4$ (b) $v_d/2$
(c) $4v_d$ (d) $2v_d$

50. A metallic block has no potential difference applied across it, then the mean velocity of free electrons is (T = temperature in Kelvin)

(a) proportional to T
(b) proportional to $\sqrt{T}$
(c) zero
(d) finite but independent of T

51. A steady current is passing through a linear conductor of non-uniform cross-section. The net quantity of charge crossing any cross-section per second is :

(a) independent of area of cross-section.
(b) directly proportional to the length of conductor.
(c) directly proportional to the area of cross-section.
(d) inversely proportional to the length of conductor.

52. The diagram below shows a potential divider circuit which, by adjustment of the position of the contact P, can be used to provide a variable potential difference between the terminals A and B. What are the limits of this potential difference ?

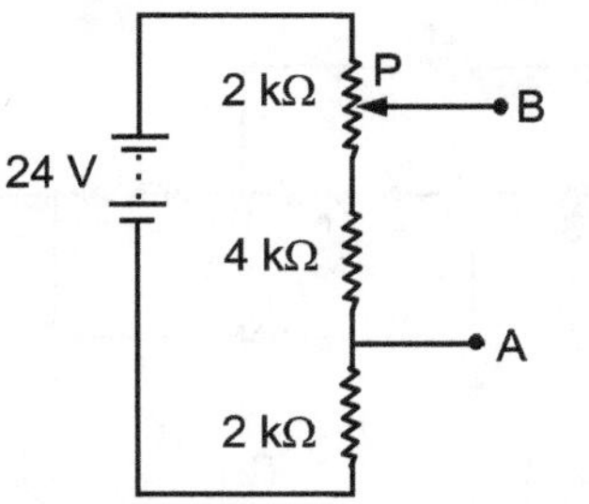

(a) 0 and 18 mV (b) 0 and 20 mV
(c) 0 and 20 V (d) 0 and 18 V

53. The temperature of a metal wire rises when an electric current passes through it, because:
(a) collision of metal atoms with each other releases heat energy.
(b) collision of conduction electrons with each other releases heat energy.
(c) when the conduction electrons fall from higher energy level to a lower energy level, heat energy is released.
(d) collision of conduction electrons with the atoms of the metal gives them energy which appears as heat.

54. Net resistance between A and B in the given network is :

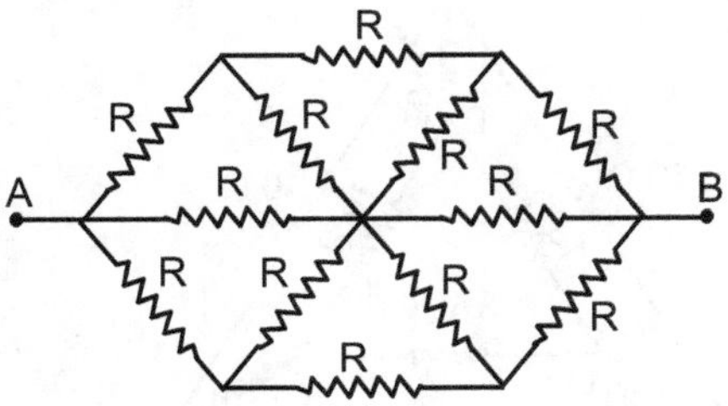

(a) $\frac{5R}{7}$ (b) $\frac{7R}{6}$
(c) $\frac{4R}{5}$ (d) $\frac{6R}{7}$

55. For which of the following dependence of drift velocity v_d on electric field E, is the Ohm's law obeyed?
(a) $v_d \propto E^2$
(b) $v_d \propto E$
(b) $v_d \propto E^{1/2}$
(d) v_d is independent of E

56. In case of liquids, Ohm's law is :
(a) fully obeyed
(b) partially obeyed
(c) there is no relation between current and p.d.
(d) none of these

57. If n, e, τ and *m* are representing electron density, charge on an electron, relaxation time and mass of an electron respectively, then the resistance of wire of length *l* and cross-sectional area A is given by :
(a) $\frac{ml}{ne^2\tau A}$ (b) $\frac{m\tau A}{ne^2 l}$
(c) $\frac{ne^2\tau A}{me}$ (d) $\frac{ne^2 A}{m\tau l}$

58. Two sources of current of equal e.m.f. are connected in series and have different internal resistances R_1 and R_2 ($R_1 > R_2$). What is the external resistance R at which the potential difference across the terminals of one of the sources becomes equal to zero?
(a) $(R_1 - R_2)$ (b) $(R_2 - R_1)$
(c) $\frac{(R_1 + R_2)}{2}$ (d) $(R_1 + R_2)$

59. The electric intensity E, current density J and specific resistance k are related to each other through the relation :
(a) E = J / k (b) E = J k
(c) E = k / J (d) k = J E

60. The specific resistance of a wire varies with its :
(a) length
(b) cross-sectional area
(c) mass
(d) none of these

61. The example of non-ohmic resistance is :
(a) Copper wire
(b) Carbon resistance
(c) Diode
(d) Tungsten wire

62. In the given network, the resistance of all the wires between any two adjacent dots is R. The net resistance between A and B is :

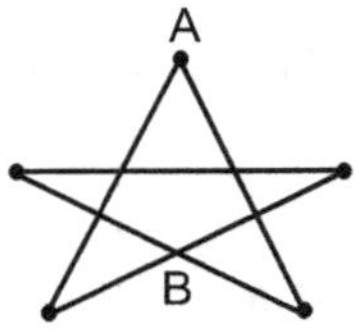

(a) $\frac{5R}{7}$ (b) $\frac{7R}{6}$

(c) $\frac{4R}{5}$ (d) $\frac{7R}{5}$

63. A five-point regular star has been formed from a uniform wire. Calculate the equivalent resistance between points P and Q. Take sin 18° = 1/3, resistance of sections PQ = QR = RS = ST = TU = UV = VW = WX = XY = r :

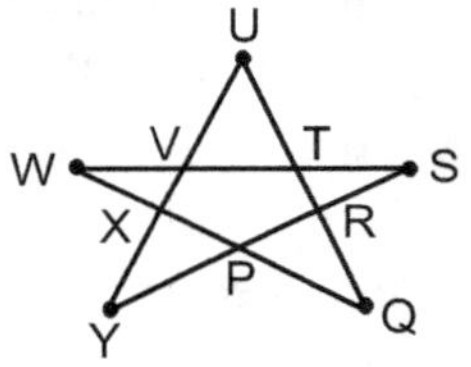

(a) r (b) 2r / 3

(c) 3r / 5 (d) 2r

64. Resistance of a carbon filament bulb and a tungsten filament bulb are measured individually when the bulbs are lit and compared with their respective resistance when cold. Which one of the following statements will be true ?

(a) Resistance of the carbon filament lamp will increase, but that of tungsten will diminish when hot.

(b) Resistance of the tungsten filament lamp will increase, but that of carbon will diminish when hot.

(c) Resistance of both the lamps will increase when hot.

(d) Resistances of both the lamps will decrease when hot.

65. What are the effective resistances between A and B, and D and E respectively ?

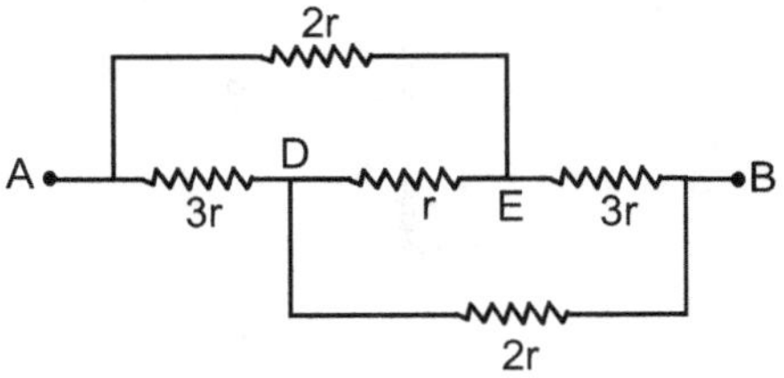

(a) $\frac{10\,r}{7}$ and $\frac{5\,r}{7}$ (b) $\frac{10\,r}{7}$ and $\frac{7\,r}{5}$

(c) $\frac{7\,r}{17}$ and $\frac{8\,r}{7}$ (d) $\frac{17\,r}{7}$ and $\frac{5\,r}{7}$

66. What is immaterial for an electric fuse ?

(a) Its specific resistance

(b) Its radius

(c) Its length

(d) None of these

67. Resistance of a conductor increases with the rise of temperature, because :

(a) Relaxation time decreases

(b) Electron density decreases

(c) Electron mass increases

(d) None of these

68. Net resistance between A and B in the given network is :

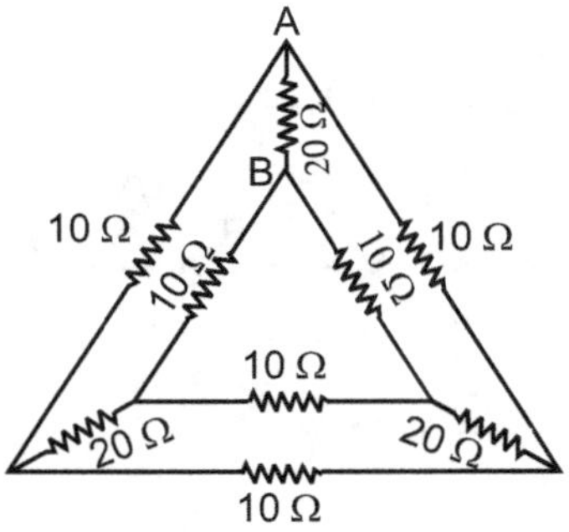

(a) 10 ohm (b) 40 ohm

(c) $\frac{40}{7}$ ohm (d) $\frac{60}{7}$ ohm

69. Constantan wire is used for making standard resistance because it has :

(a) low specific resistance

(b) high specific resistance

(c) negligible temperature coefficient of resistance

(d) both (b) and (c)

70. The temperature coefficient of resistance is positive for :

(a) Carbon (b) Silicon

(c) Germanium (d) Aluminium

71. At a temperature of 0 K, germanium behaves as:

(a) Conductor

(b) Insulator

(c) Superconductor

(d) Ferromagnetic

72. The phenomenon of superconductivity was first discovered by :

(a) Ohm

(b) H. Kammerlingh Onnes

(c) Andre M. Ampere

(d) Kirchhoff

73. Superconductivity is observed because of :

(a) independent electrons which cannot be deflected by ionic vibrations.

(b) mutually coherent electron cloud which cannot be deflected by ionic vibrations.

(c) ionic vibrations that cause deflections, cease leading to nearly zero resistivity.

(d) reasons are not yet known.

74. Specific resistance of all metals is mostly affected by :

(a) volume (b) pressure

(c) temperature (d) magnetic field

75. The current I and voltage V for a given metallic wire at two different temperatures T_1 and T_2 are shown in the figure. It is concluded that :

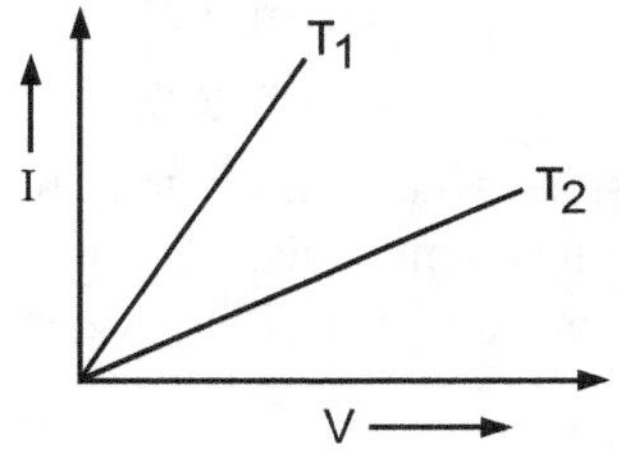

(a) $T_1 > T_2$ (b) $T_1 < T_2$

(c) $T_1 = T_2$ (d) $T_1 = 2T_2$

76. The V-I graph for a conductor at temperatures T_1 and T_2 is as shown in the figure. The term $(T_2 - T_1)$ is proportional to:

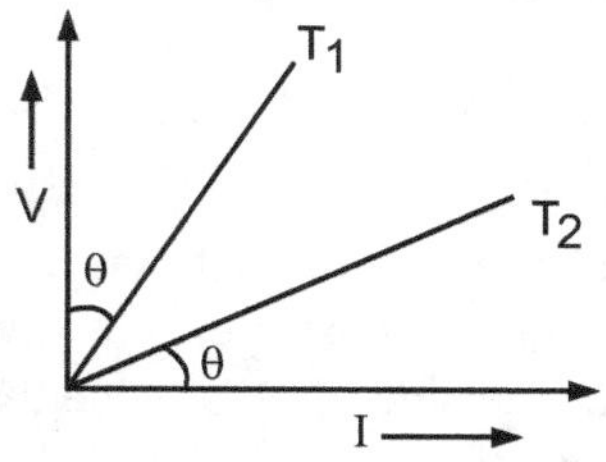

(a) cos 2θ (b) sin 2θ

(c) cot 2θ (d) tan 2θ

77. Which of the following graphs represents an ohmic resistance ?

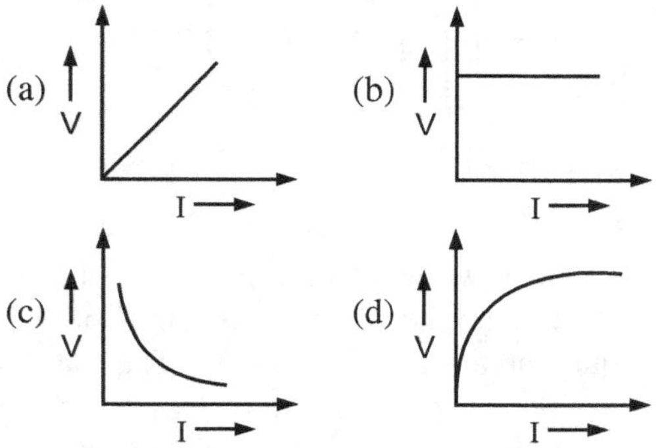

78. The resistance of human body is about (assuming the body to be dry) :

(a) 1 Ω (b) 10 Ω

(c) 10 kΩ (d) 1 kΩ

79. The magnitude of the temperature coefficient of resistivity is often quite large for a semi-conductor. This fact has been used to manufacture thermometers which can detect temperature change of the order of 10^{-3} °C. Such a device is called a :

(a) Semiconductor thermometer

(b) Voltmeter

(c) Thermistor

(d) Potentiometer

80. The gold band on the resistance indicates :

(a) Tolerance

(b) Decimal multiplier

(c) Number at unit's place

(d) Number at ten's place

81. A carbon resistor has a set of coaxial coloured rings in the order brown, violet, brown and silver. The value of resistance (in ohms) is :

(a) $(27 \times 10) \pm 5\%$ (b) $(27 \times 10) \pm 10\%$

(c) $(17 \times 10) \pm 5\%$ (d) $(17 \times 10) \pm 10\%$

82. The figure shows two metal plates A and B which are square in shape and have same thickness t. The side of B is twice that of A. Current flows through them in the direction as shown by the arrow marks. The ratio of resistance of A to that of B is :

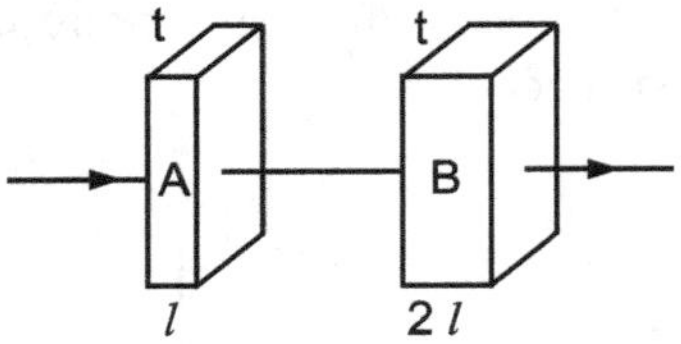

(a) 1 : 2 (b) 2 : 1

(c) 1 : 1 (d) 1 : 4

83. We have two wires of copper, one of length 100 cm and the other of 200 cm. Both have equal area of cross-section. The ratio of specific resistance of the first wire to that of second is :

(a) 1 : 2 (b) 2 : 1

(c) 1 : 1 (d) 1 : 4

84. The masses of three wires of copper are in the ratio of 1 : 3 : 5 and their lengths are in the ratio of 5 : 3 : 1. The ratio of their electrical resistance is :

(a) 1 : 1 : 1 (b) 1 : 3 : 5

(c) 5 : 3 : 1 (d) 125 : 15 : 1

85. The resistance of a wire is R ohm. The wire is stretched 'n' times the original length. Now the resistance of the wire will be :

(a) Same as before (b) nR

(c) R/n (d) n^2R

86. If a copper wire is stretched to make it 0.1 % longer, what is the percentage change in its resistance ?

(a) 0.2% (b) 1.2 %

(c) 0.1% (d) 32%

87. Kirchhoff's first law i.e. at a junction, deals with the conservation of :

(a) Charge (b) Energy

(c) Momentum (d) All of these

88. Kirchhoff's second law is based on the law of conservation of :

(a) Charge (b) Energy

(c) Momentum (d) Current

89. The following figure shows current in a part of an electric circuit. Then current I is:

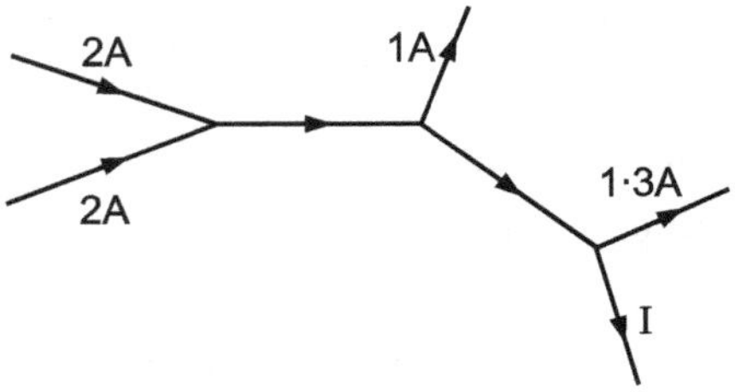

(a) 1.7 A (b) 3.7 A

(c) 1.3 A (d) 1A

90. How many combinations of three equal resistances can be made using all together ?

(a) 2 (b) 4

(c) 6 (d) 9

91. The equivalent resistance between points A and B in the given figure is 1. What is the value of the middle resistance ?

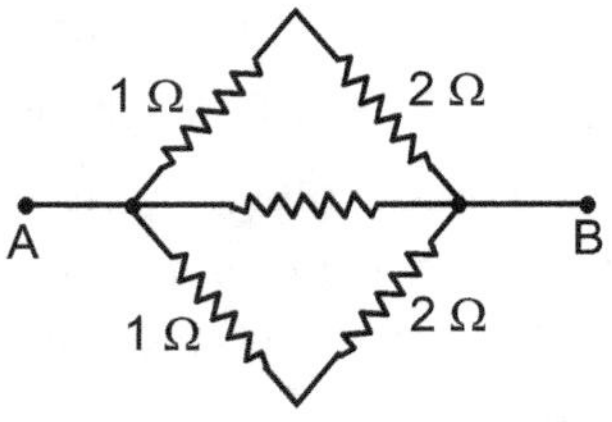

(a) 9 Ω (b) 1 Ω

(c) 6 Ω (d) 3 Ω

92. Two resistors when connected in parallel have an equivalent resistance of 2 Ω and when in series, of 9 Ω. The values of the two resistors are :

(a) 2 Ω and 9 Ω (b) 3 Ω and 6 Ω

(c) 4 Ω and 5 Ω (d) 2 Ω and 7 Ω

93. A current of 2 A flows in a system of conductors shown. The potential difference $V_A - V_B$ will be :

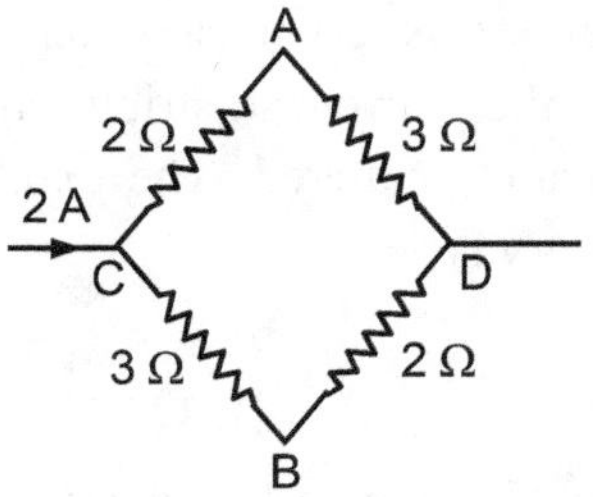

(a) +2 V (b) +1 V
(c) –1 V (d) –2 V

94. The current I in the following circuit is :

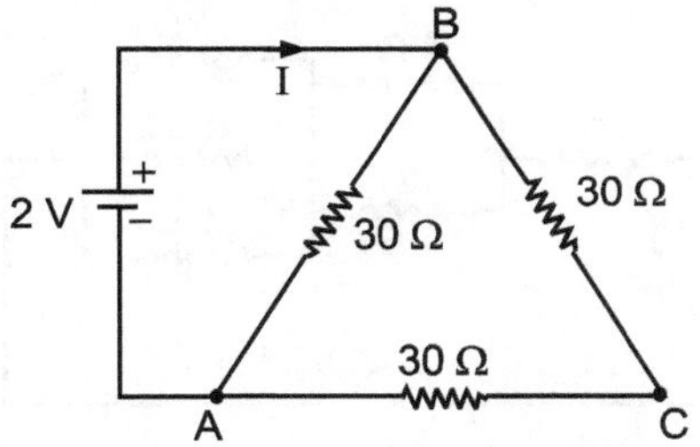

(a) 1/45 A (b) 1/15 A
(c) 1/10 A (d) 1/5 A

95. In the figure below each resistance is of 2 Ω. The total resistance between A and B is :

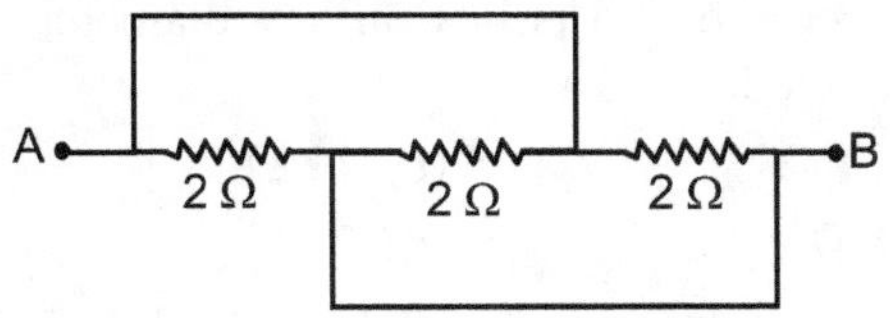

(a) 2/3 Ω (b) 2 Ω
(c) 3/2 Ω (d) 6 Ω

96. The equivalent resistance across P and Q in the given electrical circuit is :

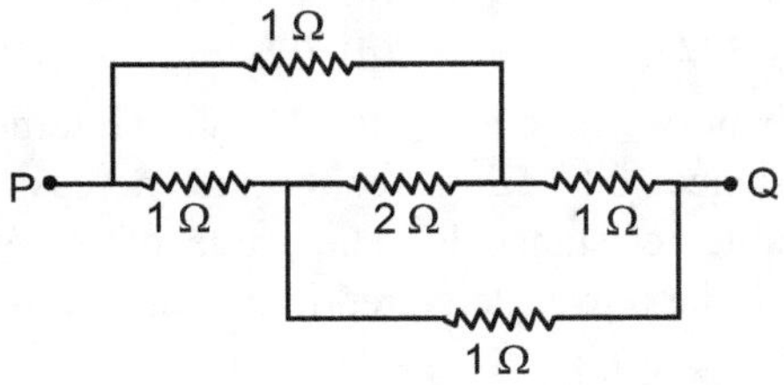

(a) 1 Ω (b) 2/3 Ω
(c) 2 Ω (d) 5 Ω

97. What will be resistance between P and Q in the following circuit diagram ?

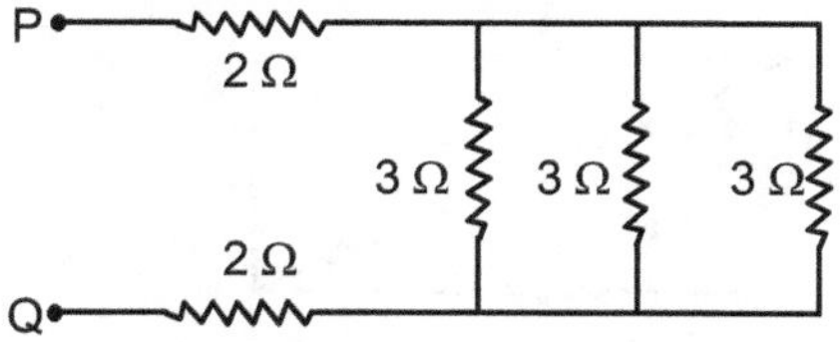

(a) 1/3 Ω (b) 2/3 Ω
(c) 2 Ω (d) 5 Ω

98. The resistance of the following figure between A and B is :

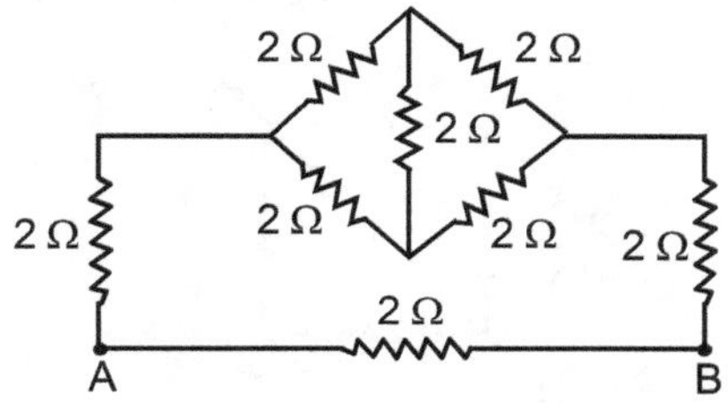

(a) 3/2 Ω (b) 2 Ω
(c) 4 Ω (d) 1 Ω

99. The resistance between A and B in the following circuit is :

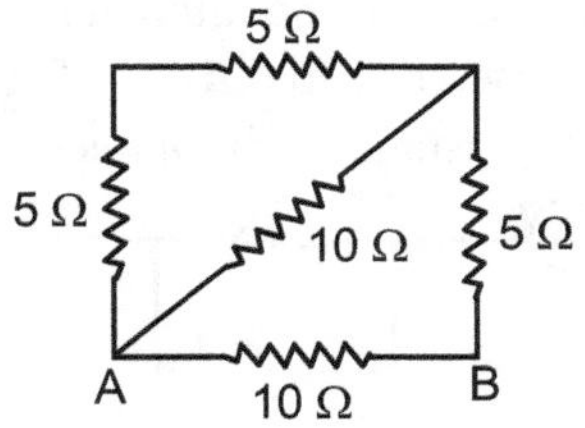

(a) 5 Ω (b) 10 Ω
(c) 20 Ω (d) 40 Ω

100. The following figure shows an infinite ladder network of resistances. The equivalent resistance between points A and B is :

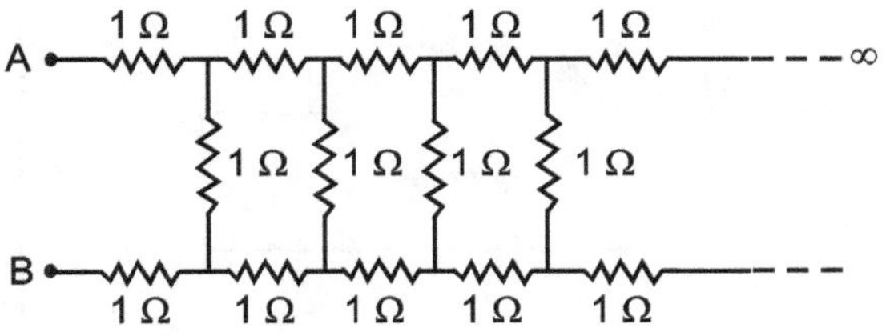

(a) Infinite (b) 3.73 Ω
(c) 2.73 Ω (d) 2/3 Ω

101. In the given figure the equivalent resistance between A and B is :

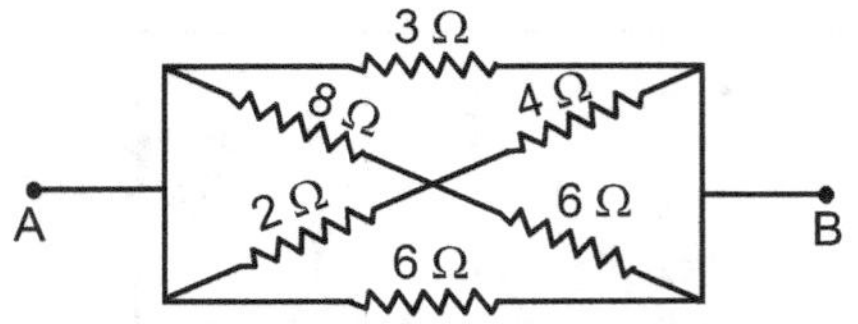

(a) 17/24 Ω (b) 4/3 Ω
(c) 29 Ω (d) 24/17Ω

102. Twelve wires of equal resistance R are connected to form a cube. The effective resistance between the diagonal ends of the figure will be :

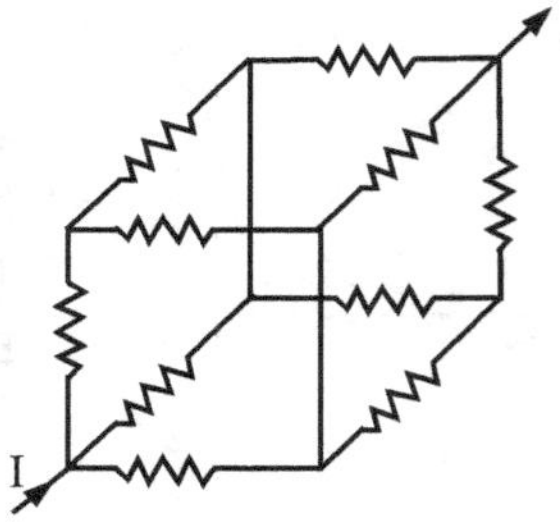

(a) (5/6) R (b) (6/5) R
(c) 3 R (d) 12 R

103. In the circuit shown, the ammeter reads 5 A and the voltmeter reads 20 V. The correct value of the resistance R in ohms is :

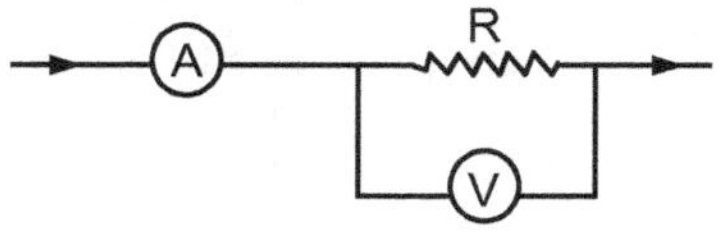

(a) Zero
(b) 4
(c) Slightly less than 4
(d) Slightly greater than 4

104. In the figure shown, potential drop across the 3 Ω resistor is :

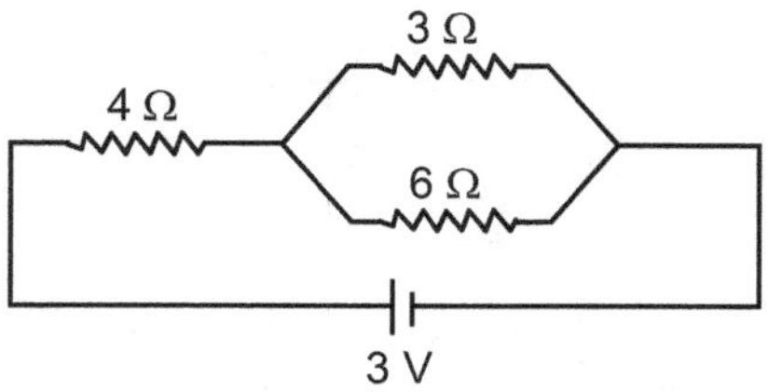

(a) 1 V (b) 1.5 V
(c) 2 V (d) 2.5 V

105. A 12 V battery sends a steady current through a series combination of three resistances of 6 Ω, 8 Ω and 10 Ω. When a second battery is connected across 8 Ω resistance, the current distribution in the circuit remains unaltered. The e.m.f. of the second battery is :

(a) 2 V (b) 4 V
(c) 6 V (d) 8 V

106. The current flowing in the electrical circuit is 1 A. If we replace all the 4 Ω resistances with a 2 Ω resistance, then the value of the current in the circuit will be :

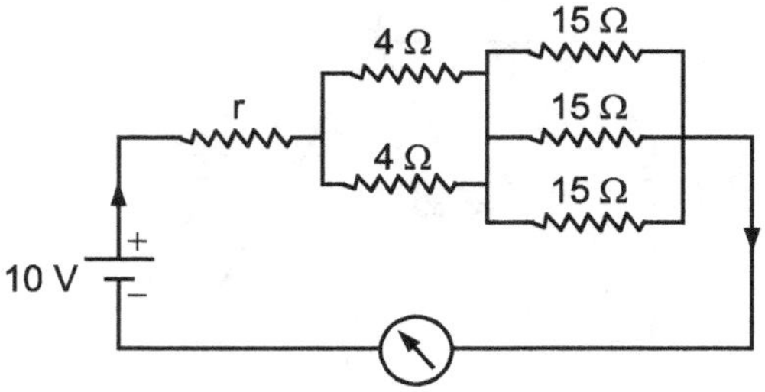

(a) 1.11 A (b) 2.11 A
(c) 3.11 A (d) 4.11 A

107. A wire has resistance 12 ohms. It is bent in the form of a circle. The effective resistance between the two points on any diameter of the circle is :

(a) 24 Ω (b) 12 Ω
(c) 6 Ω (d) 3 Ω

108. The e.m.f. of a cell is 2 V and when it is connected to a wire of 10 Ω resistance, the p.d. across the terminals of the cell is, ... (if the internal resistance of the cell is 10 Ω):

(a) 1 V (b) 2 V
(c) 1.5 V (d) 0.5 V

109. A battery of e.m.f. 10 V and internal resistance 0.5 Ω is connected across a variable resistance R. The value of R, for which the power delivered in it is maximum, is :

(a) 2 Ω (b) 1.5 Ω
(c) 1 Ω (d) 0.5 Ω

110. Net resistance between A and B in the given network is :

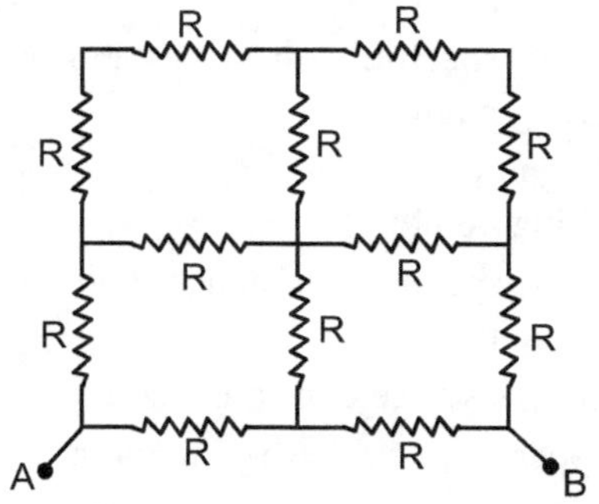

(a) $\frac{5R}{7}$ (b) $\frac{7R}{6}$

(c) $\frac{4R}{5}$ (d) $\frac{5R}{4}$

111. How would you arrange 48 cells each of e.m.f. 2 V and internal resistance 1.5 Ω so as to send maximum current through the external resistance of 2 Ω ?

(a) 2 cells in 24 groups

(b) 4 cells in 12 groups

(c) 8 cells in 6 groups

(d) 3 cells in 16 groups

112. How many dry cells, each of e.m.f. 1.5 V and internal resistance 0.5 Ω, must be joined in series with a resistor of 20 Ω to give a current of 0.6 A in the circuit ?

(a) 2 (b) 8

(c) 10 (d) 12

113. Which of the following instruments is/are based on Wheatstone's bridge ?

(a) Slide wire bridge

(b) Post office box

(c) Potentiometer

(d) Both (a) and (b)

114. In the arrangement of resistances shown in the figure, the potential difference between B and D will be zero when the unknown resistance X is :

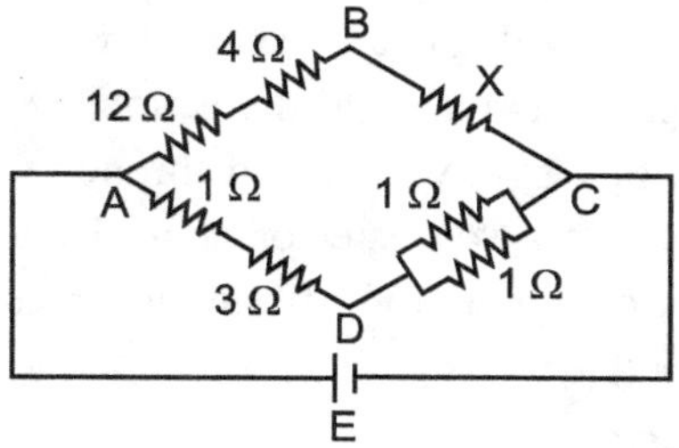

(a) 4 Ω

(b) 2 Ω

(c) 3 Ω

(d) e.m.f. of the cell is required to find out X

115. Shunt is :

(a) Low resistance connected in series

(b) Low resistance connected in parallel

(c) High resistance connected in parallel

(d) High resistance connected in series

116. If the length of the potentiometer wire is decreased, then its sensitivity :

(a) increases

(b) decreases

(c) remains unaffected

(d) either (b) or (c)

117. If the resistance of an ideal voltmeter is R_V and that of an ideal ammeter is R_a then, :

(a) $R_V = 0$; $R_a = \infty$

(b) $R_a = 0$; $R_V = \infty$

(c) Both R_a and R_V are equal to zero

(d) Both R_a and R_V are equal to ∞

118. A galvanometer coil has a resistance of 15 Ω and the meter shows full scale deflection for a current of 4 mA. What should be the resistance of the shunt to be connected in parallel, to convert it into an ammeter of range 0 – 6 A ?

(a) 0.5 Ω

(b) 1 mΩ

(c) 10 mΩ

(d) 1000 mΩ

119. A moving coil galvanometer of resistance 50 Ω gives a full scale deflection, when a current of 0.5 mA is passed through it. To convert it to a voltmeter of range 10 V, the resistance required to be placed in series is :

(a) 10000 Ω (b) 1995 Ω
(c) 19950 Ω (d) 2000 Ω

120. When a current is divided between two resistors according to Kirchhoff's law. then the heat produced is :

(a) zero (b) negligible
(c) minimum (d) maximum

121. Electric bulbs rated 50 watt and 100 watt glowing at full power are used in parallel with a battery of e.m.f. 120 volt and internal resistance 10 ohm. The maximum number of bulbs that can be connected in the circuit when glowing at full power is :

(a) 8 (b) 6
(c) 4 (d) 2

122. The element of an electric heater is made of:

(a) Copper (b) Platinum
(c) Nichrome (d) Tungsten

123. The fuse-wire is made of

(a) Copper (b) Tungsten
(c) Lead – tin alloy (d) Nichrome

124. Net resistance between A and B in the given network is :

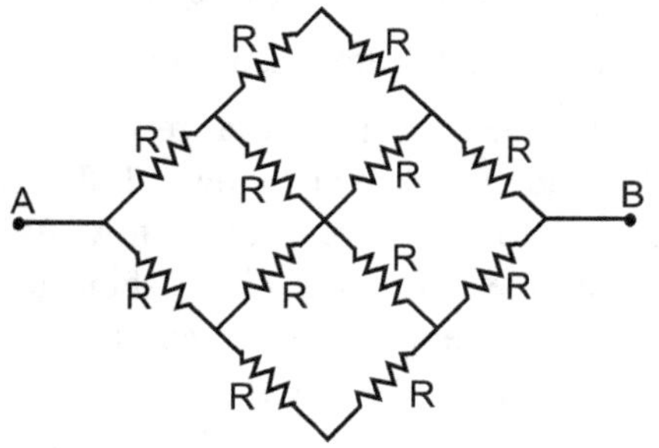

(a) $\frac{5R}{7}$ (b) $\frac{7R}{6}$
(c) $\frac{3R}{2}$ (d) $\frac{5R}{4}$

125. The material of the fuse-wire should have :

(a) a high specific resistance and a high melting point
(b) a low specific resistance and a low melting point
(c) a high specific resistance and a low melting point
(d) a low specific resistance and a high melting point

126. Standard resistance coils are made of :

(a) Copper (b) Platinum
(c) Manganin (d) Nichrome

127. Two electric bulbs whose resistances are in the ratio of 1 : 2 are connected in parallel to a constant voltage source. The powers dissipated in them have the ratio :

(a) 1 : 2 (b) 1 : 1
(c) 2 : 1 (d) 1 : 4

128. If the above two bulbs are connected in series, the power dissipated in them have the ratio :

(a) 1 : 2 (b) 1 : 1
(c) 2 : 1 (d) 1 : 4

129. A heater coil is cut into two parts of equal length and only one of them is used in the heater. The ratio of the heat produced by this half coil to that by the original coil is :

(a) 2 : 1 (b) 1 : 2
(c) 1: 4 (d) 4 : 1

130. Net resistance between A and B in the given network is :

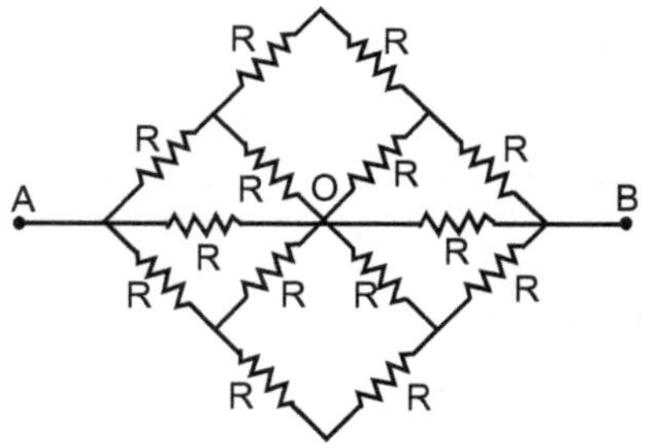

(a) $\frac{5R}{7}$ (b) $\frac{7R}{6}$
(c) $\frac{4R}{5}$ (d) $\frac{6R}{7}$

131. Resistance of one carbon filament and one tungsten lamp are measured individually when the lamps are lit and compared with their respective resistance when cold. Which one of the following statements will be true?

(a) Resistance of the carbon filament lamp will increase, but that of tungsten will diminish when hot.

(b) Resistance of the tungsten filament lamp will increase, but that of carbon will diminish when hot.

(c) Resistance of both the lamps will increase when hot.

(d) Resistance of the lamps will decrease when hot.

132. Two electric bulbs, one of 200 V - 40 W and the other of 200 V - 100 W are connected in a house wiring circuit :

(a) They have equal currents through them.

(b) The resistance of the filaments in both the bulbs is same.

(c) The resistance of the filament in the 40 watt bulb is more than the resistance in the 100 watt bulb.

(d) The resistance of the filament in the 100 watt bulb is more than the resistance in the 40 watt bulb.

133. A 1°C rise in temperature is observed in a conductor by passing a certain current. If the current is doubled, then the rise in temperature is approximately :

(a) 1°C (b) 4°C

(c) 2°C (d) 2.5°C

134. The two bulbs, as in Question 132 above, are connected in series to a 200 volt line. Then :

(a) the potential drop across two bulbs is the same.

(b) the potential drop across the 40 watt bulb is greater than the potential drop across the 100 watt bulb.

(c) the potential drop across the 100 watt bulb is greater than the potential drop across the 40 watt bulb.

(d) the potential drop across both the bulbs is 200 volt.

135. The two electric bulbs have tungsten filament of same length. If one of them gives 60 watt and the other 100 watt then :

(a) 100 watt bulb has thicker filament

(b) 60 watt bulb has thicker filament

(c) Both filaments are of same thickness

(d) It is not possible to get different wattage unless the lengths are different

136. You are given a resistance wire of length 50 m and a battery of negligible resistance. In which of the following cases is largest amount of heat generated ?

(a) When the wire is connected to the battery directly.

(b) When the wire is divided in two parts and both the parts are connected to the battery in parallel.

(c) When the wire is divided in four parts and all the four parts are connected to the battery in parallel.

(d) When only half the wire is connected to the battery.

137. Three equal resistors connected in series across a source e.m.f. together dissipate 10 watt. If the same resistors are connected in parallel across the same e.m.f., the power dissipated will be :

(a) 10 watt (b) 30 watt

(c) 10/3 watt (d) 90 watt

138. Two heating coils, one of fine wire and the other of thick wire of the same material and of the same length, are connected in series and in parallel. Which of the following statement is true ?

(a) In series, fine wire liberates more energy; while in parallel, thick wire will liberate more energy.

(b) In series, fine wire liberates less energy; while in parallel, thick wire will liberate more energy.
(c) Both will liberate equally.
(d) In series, the thick wire will liberate more; while in parallel, it will liberate less energy.

139. A 25 watt, 220 volt bulb and a 100 watt, 220 volt bulb are connected in series across 440 volt line, then :
(a) only 100 watt bulb will fuse
(b) only 25 watt bulb will fuse
(c) none of the bulbs will fuse
(d) both bulbs will fuse

140. A 25 watt, 220 volt bulb and a 100 watt, 220 volt bulb are connected in parallel across a 440 volt line. Then :
(a) only 10 watt bulb will fuse
(b) only 25 watt bulb will fuse
(c) both bulbs will fuse
(d) none of the bulbs will fuse

141. Two resistance thermometers are made, one of platinum wire and the other of germanium. The resistance of both the thermometers is equal at room temperature. The two resistance wires are connected in series and the two resistance wires are heated to 100°C. The potential drop in the two resistances is measured. Which of the following statements is correct ?
(a) The potential drop across the platinum wire is equal to the potential drop across the germanium wire.
(b) The potential drop across the platinum wire is greater than that across germanium wire.
(c) The potential drop across the platinum wire is less than that across germanium wire.
(d) The nature of the potential drop cannot be ascertained unless the magnitude of the current is given.

142. Two identical heaters 220 volt, 1000 watt are placed in series with each other across 220 volt lines, then the combined power is :
(a) 1000 watt (b) 2000 watt
(c) 500 watt (d) 4000 watt

143. An immersion heater is rated 836 watt. It should heat 1 litre of water from 20°C to 40°C in about :
(a) 200 sec (b) 100 sec
(c) 836 sec (d) 418 sec

144. How much electrical energy in kilowatt-hours is consumed in operating ten, 50 watt bulbs for 10 hours per day in a month (30 days) ?
(a) 1500 (b) 15000
(c) 15 (d) 150

145. If current in an electric bulb drops by one percent. then the power decreases by :
(a) 1 percent (b) 2 percent
(c) 4 percent (d) ½ percent

146. An electric kettle has two coils. When one of these is switched on, the water in the kettle boils in 6 minutes. When the other coil is switched on, the water boils in 3 minutes. If the two coils are connected in series, the time taken to boil water in the kettle is :
(a) 3 minutes (b) 6 minutes
(c) 2 minutes (d) 9 minutes

147. An electric kettle has two coils. When one of these is switched on, the water in the kettle boils in 6 minutes. When the other coil is switched on, the water boils in 3 minutes. If the two coils are connected in parallel, the time taken to boil water in the kettle is :
(a) 3 minutes (b) 6 minutes
(c) 2 minutes (d) 9 minutes

148. An electric bulb using a tungsten filament has a working temperature of 2457°C. At this temperature its power consumption is 50 watt. Assume temperature coefficient of resistance for tungsten as 1/273 per °C, then the power consumption at start when temperature of the filament is 0°C is :

(a) 50 watt (b) 2457 watt
(c) 9 watt (d) 500 watt

149. What is immaterial for an electric fuse wire :

(a) Its specific resistance
(b) Its radius
(c) Its length
(d) Current flowing through it

150. An electric bulb is rated 220 V and 100 W. Power consumed by it when operated on 110 V is :

(a) 50 W (b) 75 W
(c) 90 W (d) 25 W

151. According to Joule's law if potential difference across a conductor having a material of specific resistance ρ, remains constant, then heat produced in the conductor is directly proportional to :

(a) ρ (b) ρ^2
(c) $1/\sqrt{\rho}$ (d) $1/\rho$

152. An electric fan and a heater are marked as 100 W - 220 V and 100 W - 220 V respectively. The resistance of the heater is :

(a) zero
(b) greater than that of the fan
(c) less than that of the fan
(d) equal to that of the fan

153. A battery of 20 cells is charged by 220 volt with a charging current of 15 A ampere. If the e.m.f. of each cell is 2 volt and internal resistance is 0.1 ohm, then the series resistance required to be placed in the circuit is :

(a) 12 ohm (b) 14 ohm
(c) 10 ohm (d) 16 ohm

154. In Q. 153, the total power supplied by the charging main is :

(a) 450 watt (b) 3300 watt
(c) 2700 watt (d) 2250 watt

155. In Q. 154, the power wasted as heat is :

(a) 450 watt (b) 600 watt
(c) 3300 watt (d) 2700 watt

156. A Leclanche cell supplies a current of one ampere for one hour, atomic weight of Manganese = 55, Oxygen = 16, Zinc = 65 and electrochemical equivalent of hydrogen = 0.0000104 gm per coulomb. Then the mass of hydrogen liberated is :

(a) 0.03744 gm (b) 1.217 gm
(c) 3.258 gm (d) Indeterminate

157. A Leclanche cell supplies a current of one ampere for one hour, atomic weight of Manganese = 55, Oxygen = 16, Zinc = 65 and electrochemical equivalent of hydrogen = 0.0000104 gm per coulomb. The mass of zinc consumed is :

(a) 0.03744 gm (b) 1.217 gm
(c) 3.258 gm (d) Indeterminate

158. A Leclanche cell supplies a current of one ampere for one hour, atomic weight of Manganese = 55, Oxygen = 16, Zinc = 65 and electrochemical equivalent of hydrogen = 0.0000104 gm per coulomb. The mass of manganese dioxide used is :

(a) 0.03744 gm (b) 1.217 gm
(c) 3.258 gm (d) Indeterminate

159. The Faraday constant is 9.65×10^7 coulomb per kgm equivalent. If the charge on the electron is 1.6×10^{-19} coulomb, then the Avogadro's number is :

(a) 6.03×10^{33} (b) 6.03×10^{26}
(c) 6.03×10^{20} (d) 6.03×10^{18}

160. The main supply voltage to a room is 120 volt. The resistance of the lead wires is 6 ohm. A 60 watt bulb is already giving light. What is the decrease in voltage across the bulb when a 240 watt heater is switched on ?

(a) Zero volt (b) 2.9 volt
(c) 13.3 volt (d) 10.4 volt

161. Three equal resistors are connected as shown in the figure. The maximum power consumed by each resistor is 18 watt. Then maximum power consumed by the combination is :

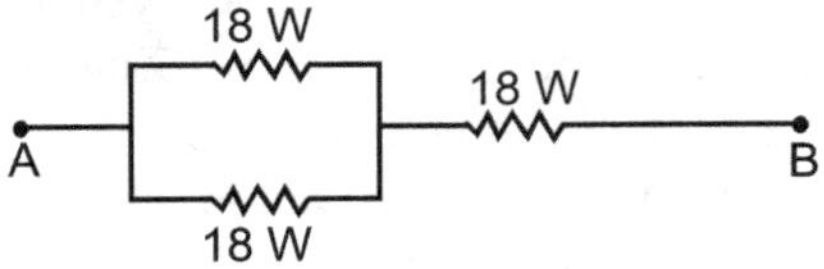

(a) 54 W (b) 27 W
(c) 36 W (d) 12 W

162. Two identical batteries, each of e.m.f. 2 volt and internal resistance 1 ohm are available to produce heat in a resistance R = 0.5 by passing a current through it. The maximum Joulean power that can be developed across R using these batteries is :

(a) 1.28 W (b) 2.0 W
(c) 8/9 W (d) 3/2 W

163. The temperature coefficient of resistance of wire is 0.00125 per °C. At 300 °K its resistance is one ohm. The resistance of the wire will be 2 ohm at :

(a) 1154° K (b) 1100° K
(c) 1400° K (d) 1127° K

164. In the circuit shown, the heat produced in the 5 ohm resistor due to current flowing through it, is 10 calories per second. Then the heat generated in the 4 ohm resistor is :

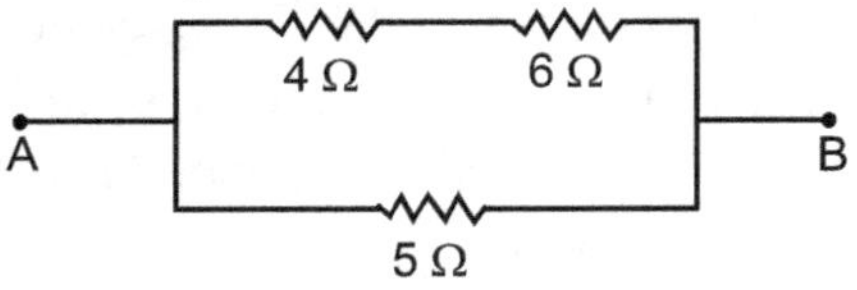

(a) 1 calorie per sec (b) 2 calories per sec
(c) 4 calories per sec (d) 3 calories per sec

165. A Daniel cell has an internal resistance of 2 ohm. Then the ratio of amounts of heat produced in the cell for each gm of zinc consumed in the cell when (i) the cell is short circuited (ii) the terminals of the cell are connected by a resistance of 2 ohm, is :

(a) $\frac{1}{2}:\frac{1}{4}$ (b) $\frac{1}{4}:\frac{1}{2}$
(c) 2 : 4 (d) 1 : 1

166. A cell of e.m.f. E and internal resistance r supplies current for the same time t through external resistance R_1 and R_2 separately. If the heat developed in both cases is the same, then the internal resistance is :

(a) $\frac{1}{r}=\frac{1}{R_1}+\frac{1}{R_2}$ (b) r
(c) $r=\sqrt{R_1R_2}$ (d) $r=R_1R_2$

167. Find the equivalent resistance across the terminal A and B :

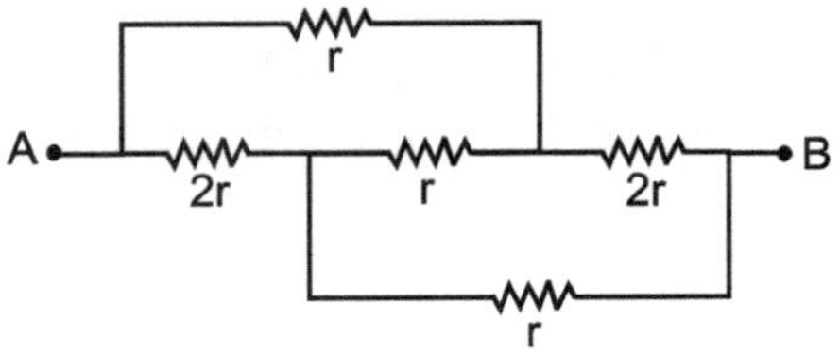

(a) 1.10 r (b) 1.4 r
(c) 2.8 r (d) 1.8 r

168. Potential difference between the points A and B is :

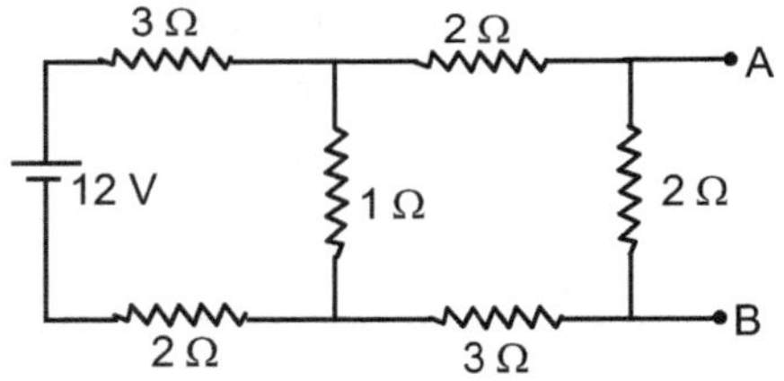

(a) 1.00 V (b) 0.50 V
(c) 1.50 V (d) 2.50 V

169. A charged capacitor of 20 μF capacitance is discharged as shown in the circuit for a period of 80 s, the current was kept constant at 40 μA by continuous adjustment of resistance R. By how much did the potential difference across the capacitor fall during this period of 80 s ?

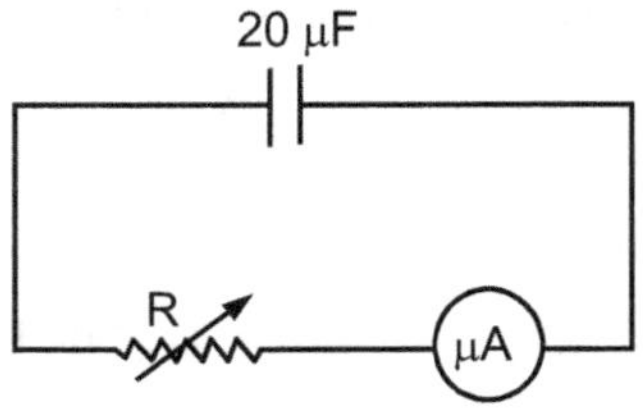

(a) 80 V (b) 160 V
(c) 20 V (d) 40 V

170. What is the equivalent resistance across the terminals A and B ?

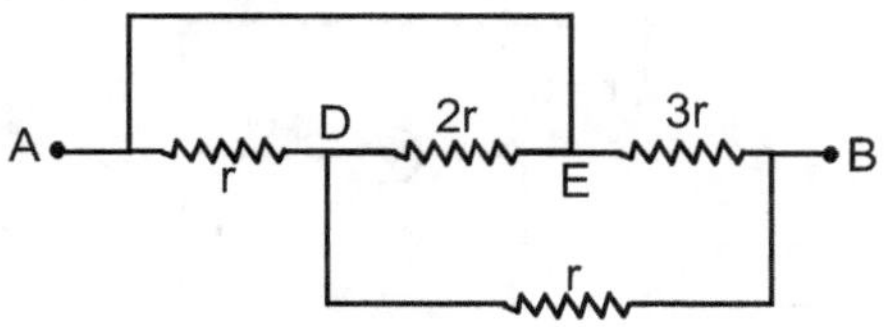

(a) $\frac{15r}{7}$ (b) $\frac{14r}{15}$

(c) $\frac{15r}{14}$ (d) $\frac{21r}{15}$

171. Voltmeters V_1 and V_2 are connected in series across a D.C. line. V_2 reads 80 V and has a per volt resistance of 200 Ω . V_2 has a total resistance of 32 kΩ. What is the line voltage ?

(a) 280 V (b) 240 V

(c) 160 V (d) 200 V

172. A copper wire is stretched to make it 0.1% longer. What is the percentage change in its resistance ?

(a) 0.1 %

(b) 0.4 %

(c) 0.2 %

(d) None of the above

173. When cells are arranged in parallel :

(a) the current capacity decreases

(b) the current capacity increases

(c) the e.m.f. increases

(d) the e.m.f. decreases

174. A standard 40 watt tube-light is in parallel with a room heater both connected to a suitable main A.C. supply line. What will happen when the light is switched off ?

(a) The heater output will be larger.

(b) The heater output will be smaller.

(c) The heater output will remain the same.

(d) None of the above.

175. Assume that each atom of copper contributes one free electron. If the current flowing through a copper wire of 1 mm diameter is 1.1 A, the drift velocity of electrons will be :

(Density of Cu = 9 gm cm^{-3}, At. wt. of Cu = 63)

(a) 0.3 mm/s (b) 0.5 mm/s

(c) 0.1 mm/s (d) 0.2 mm/s

176. There is a current of 1.344 ampere in a copper wire whose area of cross –section normal to the length of the wire is 1 mm^2. If the number of free electrons per cm^3 is 8.4×10^{22}, then the drift velocity would be :

(a) 1.0 mm per sec (b) 1.0 metre per sec

(c) 0.1 mm per sec (d) 0.01 mm per sec

177. A dry cell has an e.m.f. of 1.5 V and an internal resistance of 0.05 Ω. The maximum current obtainable from this cell, for a very short interval is :

(a) 30 A (b) 300 A

(c) 3 A (d) 0.3 A

178. Two cells of same e.m.f. E but of different internal resistances, r_1 and r_2 are connected in series with an external resistance R. The potential drop across the first cell is found to be zero. The external resistance R is :

(a) $r_1 + r_2$ (b) $r_1 - r_2$

(c) $r_2 - r_1$ (d) $r_1 r_2$

179. The smallest resistance obtained by connecting 50 resistances of ¼ ohm each is :

(a) 50/4 ohm (b) 4/50 ohm

(c) 200 ohm (d) 1/200 ohm

180. A 10 m long wire of resistance 20 Ω is connected in series with a battery of e.m.f. 3 V (negligible internal resistance) and a resistance of 10 Ω. The potential gradient along the wire in volt per metre is :

(a) 0.02 (b) 0.1

(c) 0.2 (d) 1.2

181. In the circuit diagram shown below, the magnitude and direction of the flow of current respectively would be :

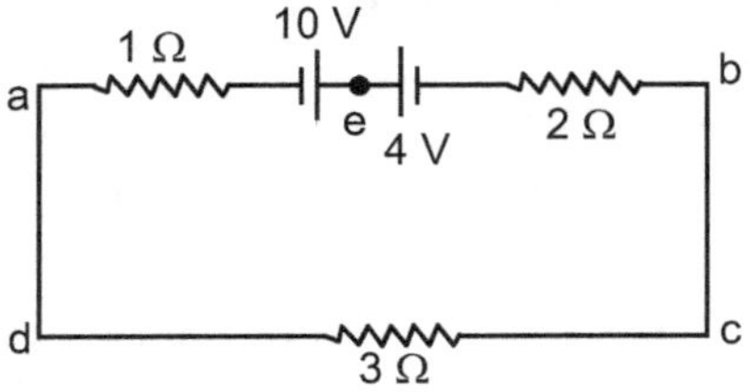

(a) 7/3 amp from a to b via e
(b) 7/3 amp from b to a via e
(c) 1.0 amp from b to a via e
(d) 1.0 amp from a to b via e

182. In the Bohr's model of hydrogen atom, the electron moves around the nucleus in a circular orbit of radius 5×10^{-11} metres. Its time period is 1.5×10^{-16} sec. The current associated with the electron motion is :

(a) Zero (b) 1.6×10^{-19} amp
(c) 0.17 amp (d) 1.07×10^{-3} amp

183. In the circuit shown in the figure the potential difference between points A and B will be :

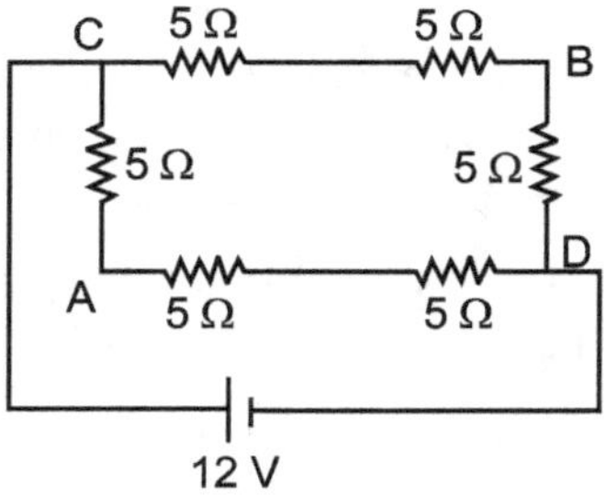

(a) (8/9) V (b) (4/3) V
(c) (2/3)V (d) 2 V

184. In figure current through 3 Ω resistor is 0.8 A, then potential drop across 6 Ω resistor is :

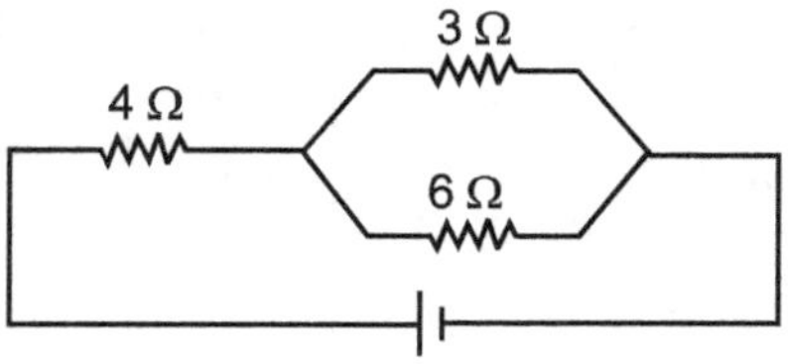

(a) 9.6 V (b) 2.6 V
(c) 4.8 V (d) 1.2 V

185. In the circuit shown in figure the reading of voltmeter is :

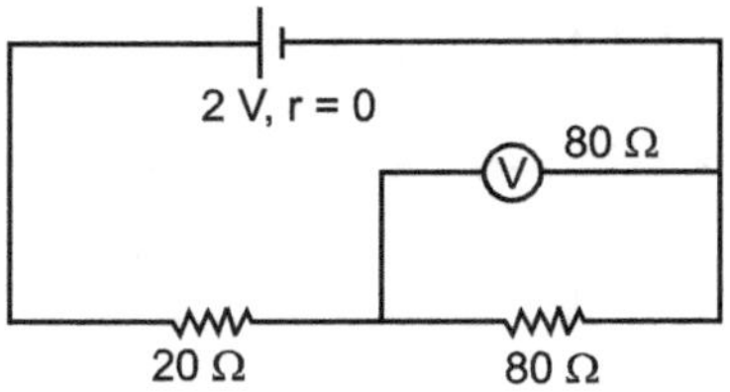

(a) 1.33 V (b) 0.8 V
(c) 2.0 V (d) 1.6 V

186. In the given figure when galvanometer shows no deflection, the current (in amp) flowing through 5 ohm resistance will be :

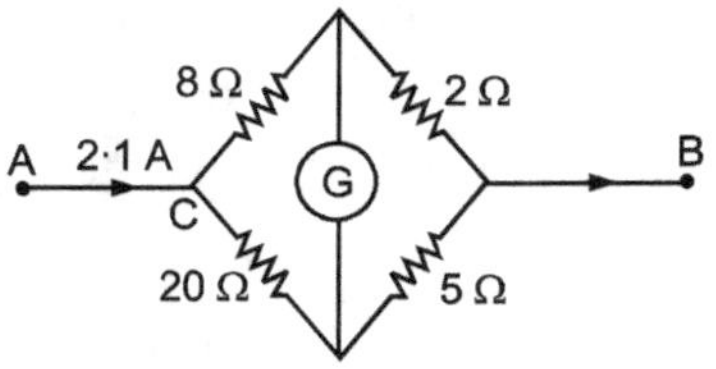

(a) 0.6 (b) 0.5
(c) 1.5 (d) 2.0

187. A copper wire of length l and radius r has a potential V applied across it. The drift speed of the electrons is v_d. If the diameter of the wire is doubled, the electron drift speed becomes :

(a) v_d^2 (b) $v_d/2$
(c) $v_d/3$ (d) v_d

188. A wire has a resistance 10 ohm. It is stretched by one-tenth of its original length. Then its resistance will be :

(a) 10 Ω (b) 12.1 Ω
(c) 0.1 Ω (d) 11 Ω

189. A torch bulb rated as 4.5 W, 1.5 V is connected as shown in figure. The e.m.f. of the cell, needed to make the bulb glow at full intensity is :

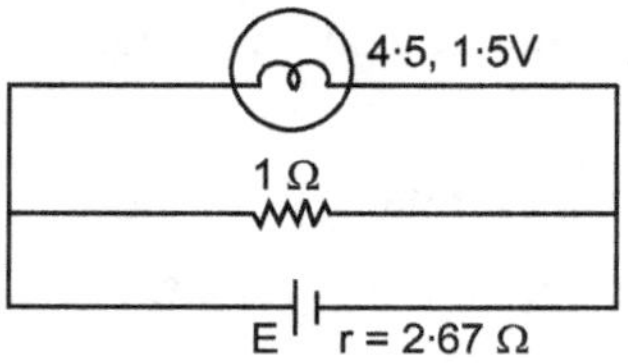

(a) 4.5 V (b) 1.5 V
(c) 2.67 V (d) 13.5 V

190. The potential difference across 8 ohm resistance is 48 V as shown in figure. The value of potential difference across X and Y points will be :

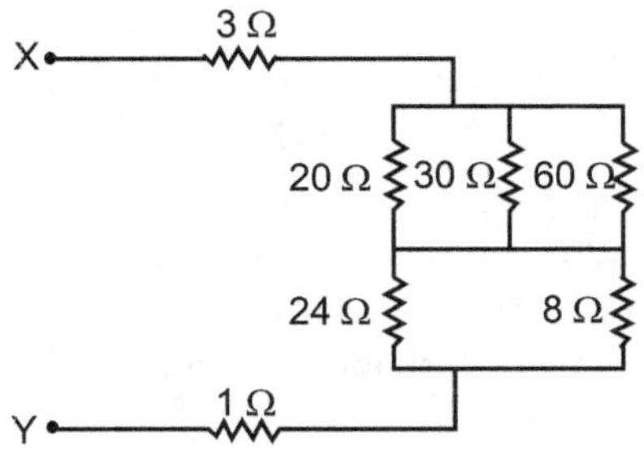

(a) 160 V (b) 128 V
(c) 80 V (d) 62 V

191. A resistance 5Ω is connected in the left gap of a metre bridge and 15Ω in the other gap. The position of balancing point is :

(a) 10 cm (b) 20 cm
(c) 25 cm (d) 75 cm

192. With a potentiometer null points were obtained at 140 cm and 180 cm with cells of e.m.f. 1.1 V and one of unknown value respectively. The unknown e.m.f. is :

(a) 1.1 V (b) 1.8 V
(c) 1.4 V (d) 1.41 V

193. The resistor R_1 dissipates power P when connected to a generator. If a resistor R_2 is inserted in series with R_1, the power dissipated by R_1 :

(a) increases
(b) decreases
(c) remains the same
(d) may decrease or increase depending on the values of R_1 and R_2

194. A certain piece of copper is to be shaped into a conductor of minimum resistance. Its length l and diameter d should be respectively :

(a) l, d (b) $2l, d$
(c) $l/2, 2d$ (d) $2l, d/2$

195. The number of dry cells, each of e.m.f. 1.5 volt and internal resistance 0.5 ohm that must be joined in series with a resistance of 20 ohm so as to send a current of 0.6 ampere through the circuit is

(a) 2 (b) 8
(c) 10 (d) 12

196. A battery of e.m.f. 10 V and internal resistance 0.5 ohm is connected across a variable resistance R. The value of R for which the power delivered in it is maximum is given by :

(a) 2.0 ohm (b) 0.25 ohm
(c) 1.0 ohm (d) 0.5 Ω

197. The resistivity of a potentiometer wire is 40×10^{-8} Ωm and its area of cross section is 8×10^{-6} sq. m. If 0.2 ampere current is flowing through the wire, the potential gradient will be :

(a) 10^{-2} volt / m
(b) 10^{-1} volt / m
(c) 3.2×10^{-2} volt / m
(d) 1 volt / m

198. The resistance of a certain piece of wire is 9. The resistance of a second piece, identical to the first except that its diameter is 3 times as large will be :

(a) 1 Ω (b) 3 Ω
(c) 9 Ω (d) 12 Ω

199. A potentiometer consists of a wire of length 400 cm and of resistance 10 Ω. It is connected to a cell of e.m.f. 2 volt having negligible internal resistance, the potential difference per unit length of the wire is :

(a) 5 volt m^{-1}
(b) 0.5 volt m^{-1}
(c) 50 volt m^{-1}
(d) None

200. What will be the resistance of a semi-circle shown in figure between its two end faces given that radial thickness = 3 cm, axial thickness = 4 cm, inner radius = 6 cm and specific resistance = 4×10^{-6} ohm × cm ?

(a) 7.85×10^{-5} ohm (b) 7.85×10^{-6} ohm

(c) 24.15×10^{-6} ohm (d) $31.45 \times 10^{-6}\ \Omega$

201. A uniform wire of resistance 20 ohm having resistance 1Ω / m is bent in the form of a circle as shown in figure. If the equivalent resistance between M and N is 1.8 Ω, then the length of the shorter section is :

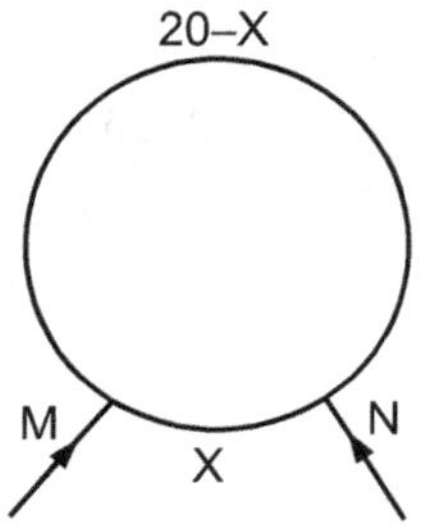

(a) 2 m (b) 5 m

(c) 1.8 m (d) 18 m

202. The net resistance across M and N in the given figure when each resistance is r, is :

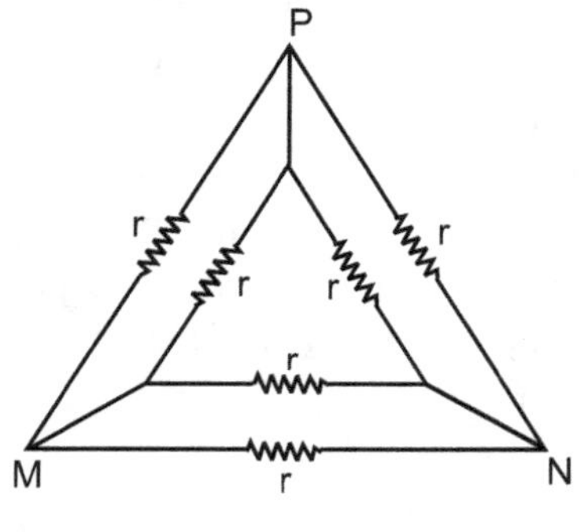

(a) r (b) r/2

(c) r/3 (d) 2r

203. A battery of e.m.f. 10 V is connected to resistances as shown in figure. The potential difference between A and B ($V_A - V_B$) is :

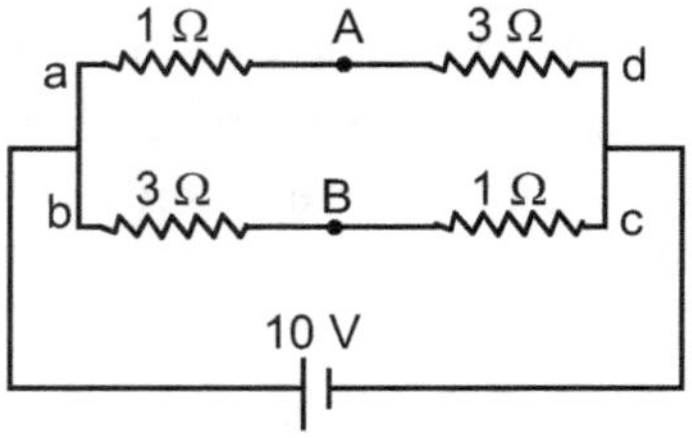

(a) –2 V (b) 2 V

(c) 5 V (d) (20/11) V

204. In the Wheatstone bridge shown, P = 2 Ω, Q = 3 Ω, R = 6 Ω and S = 8 Ω. In order to obtain balance, shunt resistance across S must be :

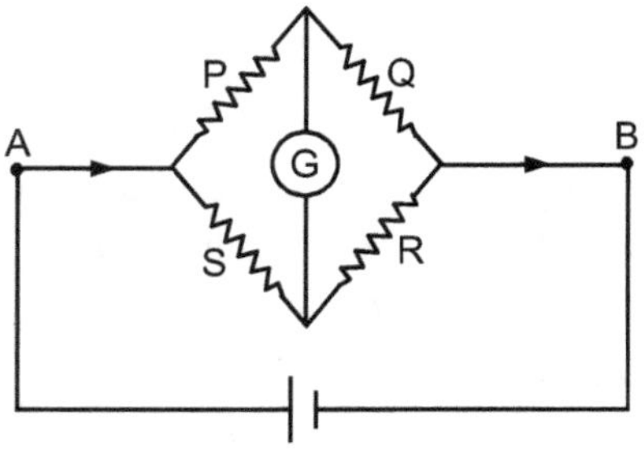

(a) 2 Ω (b) 3 Ω

(c) 6 Ω (d) 8 Ω

205. You are given several identical resistances each of value R = 10 Ω and each capable of carrying a maximum current of one ampere. It is required to make a suitable combination of these resistances of 5 Ω which can carry a current of 4 ampere. The minimum number of resistances of the type R that will be required for this job is :

(a) 4 (b) 10

(c) 8 (d) 20

206. Two wires of same metal have same length, but their cross sections are in the ratio 3 : 1. They are joined in series. The resistance of the thicker wire is 10 Ω. The total resistance of the combination will be :

(a) 5/2 Ω (b) 40/3 Ω

(c) 40 Ω (d) 100 Ω

207. In an experiment to measure the internal resistance of a cell, by a potentiometer, it is found that the balance point is at a length of 2 m, when the cell is shunted by a 5 Ω resistance and is at a length of 3 m when the cell is shunted by a 10 Ω resistance. The internal resistance of the cell is then :

(a) 1.5 Ω (b) 10 Ω

(c) 15 Ω (d) 1 Ω

208. A cylindrical copper rod is reformed to twice its original length with no change in volume. The resistance between its ends before the change was R. Now its resistance will be :

(a) 8R (b) 6R

(c) 4R (d) 2R

209. Two wires A and B of the same material, having radii in the ratio 1 : 2 and carry currents in the ratio 4 : 1. The ratio of drift speed of electrons in A and B is :

(a) 16 : 1 (b) 1 : 16

(c) 1 : 4 (d) 4 : 1

210. The current-voltage graphs for a given metallic wire at two different temperatures T_1 and T_2 are shown in the following figure, then :

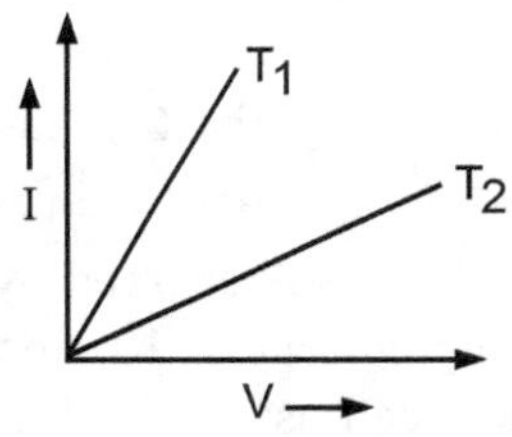

(a) $T_1 > T_2$ (b) $T_1 < T_2$

(c) $T_1 = T_2$ (d) None

211. A cell sends a current through a resistance R for time *t*, next the same cell sends current through another resistance r for the same time *t*. If same amount of heat is developed in both the resistances, then internal resistance of the cell is :

(a) R + r/2

(b) $\sqrt{R - r/2}$

(c) $\sqrt{Rr}$

(d) $\sqrt{R + r/2}$

212. A constant voltage is applied between the two ends of a uniform metallic wire. Some heat is developed in it. The heat developed is doubled if :

(a) both the length and radius of the wire are halved.

(b) both the length and radius of the wire are doubled.

(c) the radius of the wire is doubled.

(d) the length of the wire is doubled.

213. Two heater wires of equal length are first connected in series and then in parallel. The ratio of heat produced in the two cases is :

(a) 2 : 1 (b) 1 : 2

(c) 4 : 1 (d) 1 : 4

214. If the current flowing in a conductor changes by 1%, then power will change by :

(a) 10 % (b) 1 %

(c) 100 % (d) 2 %

215. Seebeck e.m.f. depends on :

(a) temperature of hot junction

(b) temperature of cold junction

(c) neutral temperature

(d) none of these

216. A heater boils 1 kg of water in time t_1 and another heater boils the same water in time t_2. If both are connected in series, the combination will boil the same water in time:

(a) $\dfrac{t_1 t_2}{(t_2 + t_2)}$

(b) $\dfrac{t_1 t_2}{t_1 - t_2}$

(c) $(t_1 + t_2)$

(d) $2\,(t_1 + t_2)$

217. If 2.2 kilowatt power is transmitted through a 10 ohm line at 22,000 volt, the power loss in the form of heat will be :

(a) 0.1 watt (b) 1 watt

(c) 10 watt (d) 100 watt

218. Three equal resistances, each of 10 Ω, are connected as shown in the figure. The maximum power consumed by each resistor is 20 W. Then maximum power consumed by the combination is :

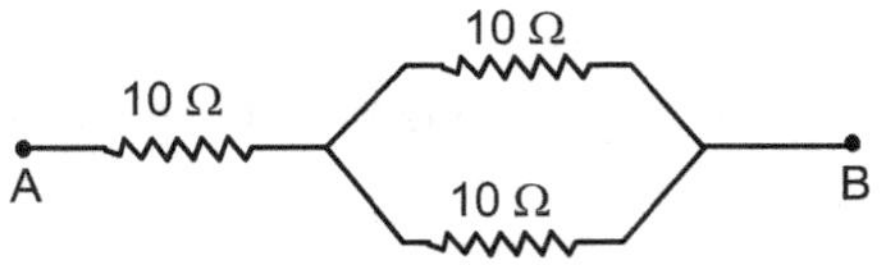

(a) 60 W
(b) 30 W
(c) 15 W
(d) None of the above

219. A condenser of capacity 5 μF is connected to a constant source of e.m.f. 200 volt as shown in figure. What will be the amount of heat produced in R_1 when the key is thrown from contact 1 to 2 ?

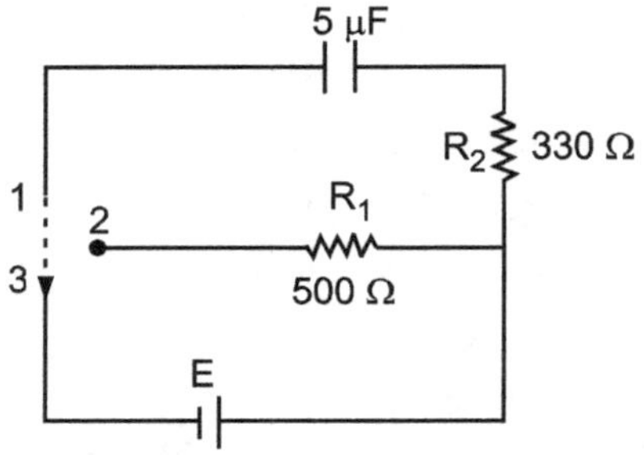

(a) 0.6 J (b) 0.006 J
(c) 6 J (d) 20 J

220. In the given circuit, the battery E_1 has an e.m.f. of 12 volt and zero internal resistance, while the battery E_2 has an e.m.f. of 2 volt. If the galvanometer G reads zero, then the value of the resistance X in ohm is :

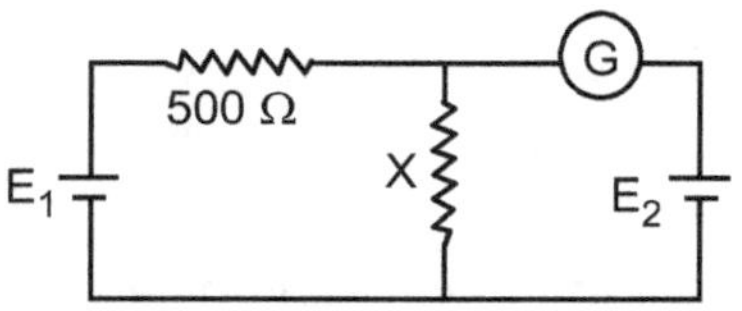

(a) 10 (b) 100
(c) 500 (d) 200

221. In the given circuit, the final voltage drop across the capacitor C is :

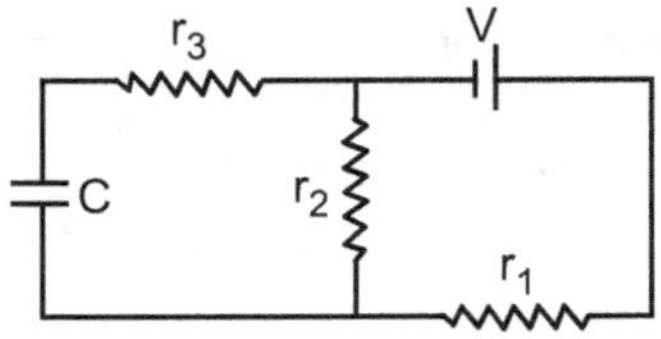

(a) $\frac{Vr_1}{r_1 + r_2}$ (b) $\frac{Vr_2}{r_1 + r_2}$
(c) $\frac{V(r_1 + r_2)}{r_2}$ (d) $\frac{V(r_1 + r_2)}{r_1 + r_2 + r_3}$

222. The equivalent resistance between points A and B in the circuit shown below is :

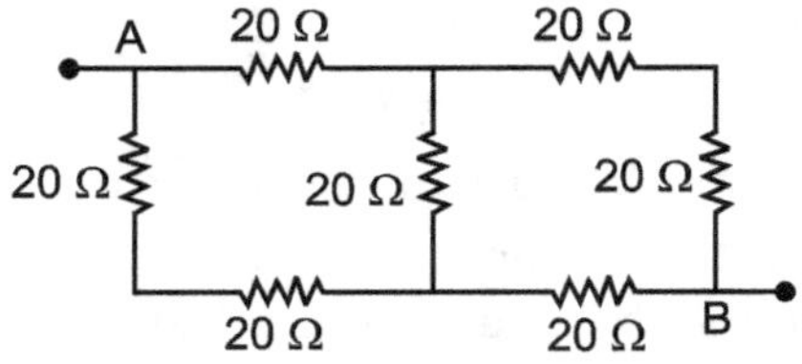

(a) 10 Ω (b) 28 Ω
(c) 20 Ω (d) 14 Ω

223. An electric kettle has two coils. When one of these is switched on, the water in the kettle boils in 2 minutes. When the other coil is switched on, the water boils in 4 minutes. If the two coils are connected in series, the time taken to boil water in the kettle, is :

(a) 3 minutes (b) 6 minutes
(c) 2 minutes (d) 9 minutes

224. A battery of 20 cells is charged by 220 volt with a charging current of 10 ampere if the e.m.f. of each cell is 2 volt and internal resistance is 0.1 ohm. Then the series resistance required to be placed in the circuit is :

(a) 15 ohm (b) 14 ohm
(c) 10 ohm (d) 16 Ω

225. The main supply voltage to a room is 120 volt. The resistance of the lead wires is 40 ohm. A 40 watt bulb is already giving light. What is the decrease in voltage across the bulb when a 240 watt heater is switched on ?

(a) 67.5 V (b) 52.5 V
(c) 40.5 V (d) 10.4 V

226. Express which of the following setups can be used to verify Ohm's law : **(I.I.T. Screening 2003)**

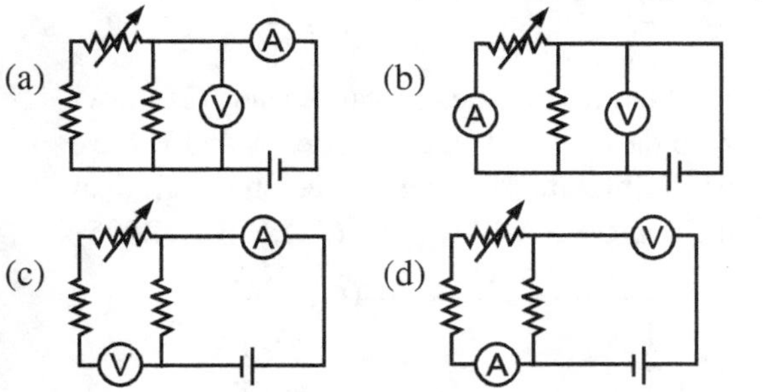

227. In the shown arrangement of the experiment of the metre bridge if length AC corresponds to no deflection in galvanometer is X, what would be its value if the radius of the wire AB is doubled? **(I.I.T. Screening 2003)**

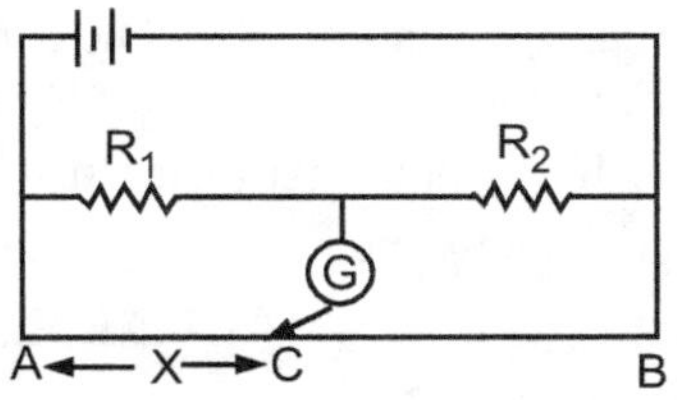

(a) X (b) X/4
(c) 4X (d) 2X

228. The three resistances of equal value are arranged in different combinations as shown below. Arrange them in increasing order of power dissipation : **(I.I.T. Screening 2003)**

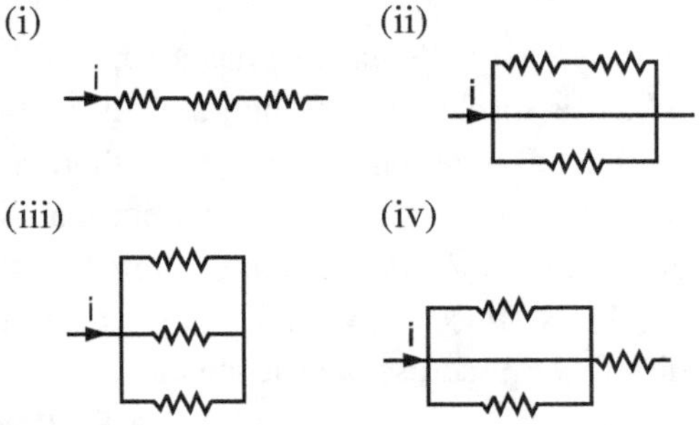

(a) (iii) < (ii) < (iv) < (i)
(b) (ii) < (iii) < (iv) < (i)
(c) (i) < (iv) < (iii) < (ii)
(d) (i) < (iii) < (ii) < (iv)

229. Shown in figure is a Post Office box. In order to calculate the value of external resistance, it should be connected between : **(I.I.T. Screening 2004)**

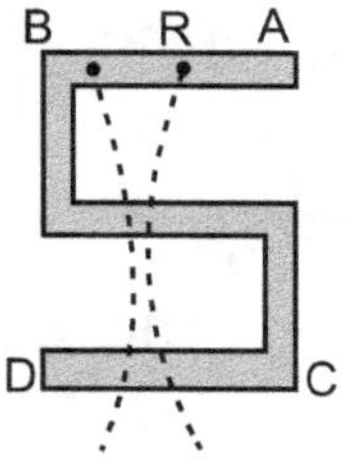

(a) B and C (b) A and D
(c) C and D (d) B and D

230. Six identical resistors are connected as shown in figure. The equivalent resistance will be : **(I.I.T. Screening 2004)**

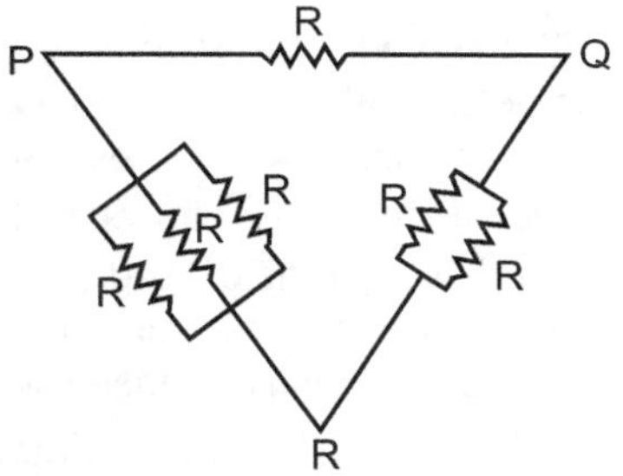

(a) Maximum between P and R
(b) Maximum between Q and R
(c) Maximum between P and Q
(d) All are equal

231. A capacitor is charged using an external battery with a resistance x in series. The dashed line shows the variation of *ln* I with respect to time. If the resistance is changed to 2x, the new graph will be :

(I.I.T. Screening 2004)

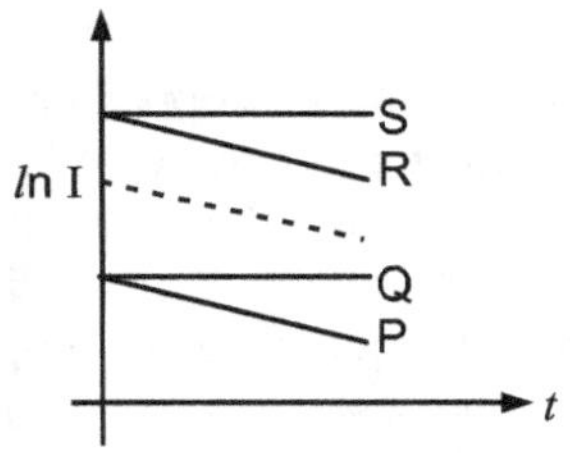

(a) P (b) Q
(c) R (d) S

232. The current in 2 Ω resistor is : **(I.I.T. Screening 2005)**

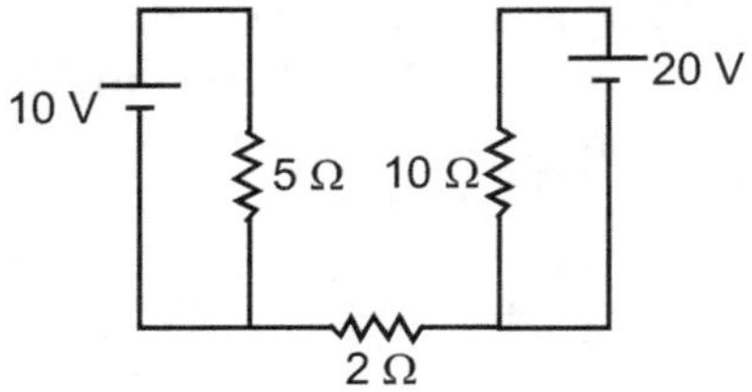

(a) 0 (b) 2 A
(c) 4 A (d) 1 A

233. Which of the following does not have the same dimension ? **(I.I.T. Screening 2005)**
(a) Electric flux, Electric field, Electric dipole moment
(b) Pressure, Stress, Young's modulus
(c) Electromotive force, Potential difference
(d) Heat, Potential energy, Work done

234. A galvanometer with resistance 100 Ω is converted to ammeter with a resistance of 0.1 Ω. The galvanometer shows full scale deflection with a current of 100 μA. Then the minimum current in the circuit for full scale deflection of the galvanometer will be: **(I.I.T. Screening 2005)**
(a) 100.1 mA (b) 10.01 mA
(c) 1.001 mA (d) 0.1001 mA

235. A moving coil galvanometer has 150 equal divisions. Its current sensitivity is 10 divisions per milliampere and voltage sensitivity is 2 divisions per millivolt. In order that each division reads 1 volt, the resistance in ohms needed to be connected in series with the coil will be : **(A.I.E.E.E. 2005)**
(a) 10^3 (b) 10^5
(c) 99995 (d) 9995

236. Two voltmeters one of copper and another of silver, are joined in parallel. When a total charge *q* flows through the voltmeters, equal amount of metals are deposited. If the electrochemical equivalent of copper and silver are z_1 and z_2 respectively, the charge which flows through the silver voltmeter is : **(A.I.E.E.E. 2005)**

(a) $\dfrac{q}{1+\dfrac{z_1}{z_2}}$ (b) $\dfrac{q}{1+\dfrac{z_2}{z_1}}$

(c) $q\dfrac{z_1}{z_2}$ (d) $q\dfrac{z_2}{z_1}$

237. In the circuit, the galvanometer G shows zero deflection. If the batteries A and B have negligible internal resistance, the value of the resistor R will be : **(A.I.E.E.E. 2005)**

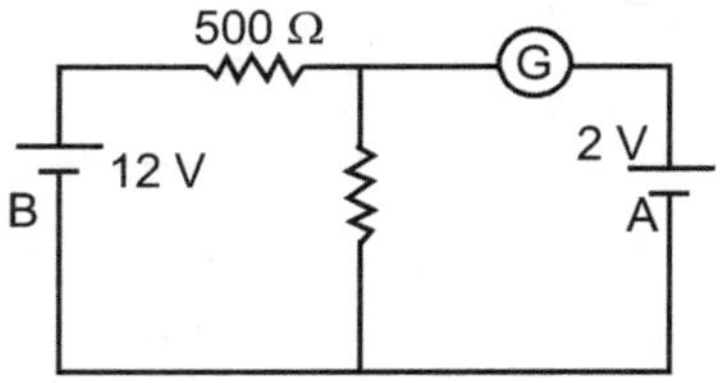

(a) 200 Ω (b) 100 Ω
(c) 500 Ω (d) 1000 Ω

238. Two sources of equal e.m.f. are connected to an external resistance R. The internal resistances of the two sources are R_1 and R_2 ($R_2 > R_1$). If the potential difference across the source having internal resistance R_2 is zero, then : **(A.I.E.E.E. 2005)**

(a) $R = \dfrac{R_2 \times (R_1 + R_2)}{(R_2 - R_1)}$

(b) $R = R_2 - R_1$

(c) $R = \dfrac{R_1 R_2}{(R_1 + R_2)}$

(d) $R = \dfrac{R_1 R_2}{(R_2 - R_1)}$

239. A fully charged capacitor has a capacitance 'C'. It is discharged through a small coil of resistance wire embedded in a thermally insulated block of specific heat capacity 's' and mass '*m*'. If the temperature of the block is raised by 'ΔT', the potential difference V across the capacitance is : **(A.I.E.E.E. 2005)**

(a) $\sqrt{\dfrac{2mC\Delta T}{s}}$ (b) $\dfrac{mC\Delta T}{s}$

(c) $\dfrac{ms\Delta T}{C}$ (d) $\sqrt{\dfrac{2ms\Delta T}{C}}$

240. A heater coil is cut into two equal parts and only one part is now used in the heater. The heat generated will now be : **(A.I.E.E.E. 2005)**

(a) doubled (b) four times
(c) one fourth (d) halved

241. An energy source that will supply a constant current into the load of its internal resistance is : **(A.I.E.E.E. 2005)**

(a) Equal to the resistance of the load
(b) Very large as compared to the load resistance
(c) Zero
(d) Not-zero but less than the resistance of the load.

242. In a potentiometer experiment the balancing point with a cell is at length 240 cm. On shunting the cell with a resistance of 2 Ω, the balancing length becomes 120 cm. The internal resistance of the cell is : **(A.I.E.E.E. 2005)**

(a) 1 Ω (b) 0.5 Ω
(c) 4 Ω (d) 2 Ω

243. The resistance of hot tungsten filament is about 10 times the cold resistance. What will be the resistance of 100 W and 200 V lamp when not in use ? **(A.I.E.E.E. 2005)**

(a) 40 Ω (b) 20 Ω
(c) 400 Ω (d) 200 Ω

244. A material 'B' has twice the specific resistance of 'A'. A circular wire made of 'B' has twice the diameter of a wire made of 'A'. Then for the two wires to have the same resistance, the ratio I_A / I_B of their respective lengths must be : **(A.I.E.E.E. 2005)**

(a) 2 (b) 1
(c) $\frac{1}{2}$ (d) $\frac{1}{4}$

245. The Kirchhoff's first law ($\Sigma i = 0$) and second law ($\Sigma iR = \Sigma E$) where the symbols have their usual meanings, are respectively based on : **(A.I.E.E.E. 2006)**

(a) Conservation of charge, conservation of energy
(b) Conservation of charge, conservation of momentum
(c) Conservation of energy, conservation of charge
(d) Conservation of momentum, conservation of charge

246. In a Wheatstone's bridge, three resistances P, Q and R connected in the three arms and the fourth arm is formed by two resistances S_1 and S_2 connected in parallel. The condition for bridge to be balanced will be : **(A.I.E.E.E. 2006)**

(a) $\frac{P}{Q} = \frac{R}{S_1 + S_2}$ (b) $\frac{P}{Q} = \frac{2R}{S_1 + S_2}$

(c) $\frac{P}{Q} = \frac{R(S_1 + S_2)}{S_1 S_2}$ (d) $\frac{P}{Q} = \frac{R(S_1 + S_2)}{2S_1 S_2}$

247. The current I drawn from the 5 volt source will be : **(A.I.E.E.E. 2006)**

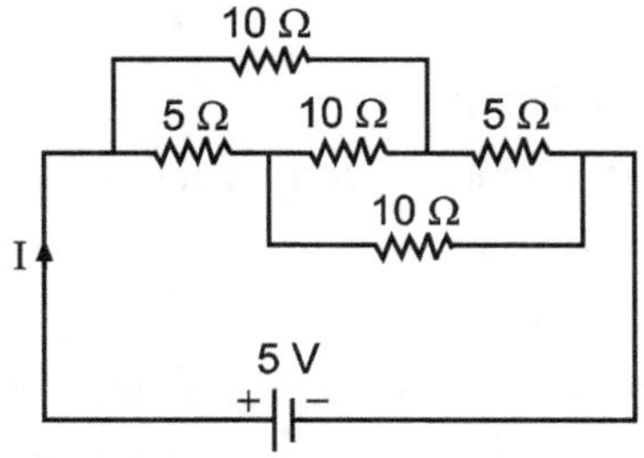

(a) 0.17 A (b) 0.33 A
(c) 0.5 A (d) 0.67 A

248. The resistance of a bulb filament is 100 Ω at a temperature of 100°C. If its temperature coefficient of resistance is 0.005 per °C, its resistance will become 200 Ω at a temperature of : **(A.I.E.E.E. 2006)**

(a) 200°C (b) 300°C
(c) 400°C (d) 500°C

249. A thermocouple is made from two metals, Antimony and Bismuth. If one junction of the thermocouple is kept hot and the other is kept cold then, an electric current will : **(A.I.E.E.E. 2006)**

(a) flow from Antimony to Bismuth at the Cold junction

(b) flow from Antimony to Bismuth at the hot junction

(c) flow from Bismuth to Antimony at the cold junction

(d) not flow through the thermocouple

250. An electric bulb is rated 220 volt 100 watt. The power consumed by it when operated on 110 volt will be : **(A.I.E.E.E. 2006)**

(a) 50 watt (b) 75 watt

(c) 40 watt (d) 25 watt

251. A series combination of two resistors, 1 Ω each, is connected a 12 V battery of internal resistance 0.4 Ω. The current flowing through it is : **(MHT-CET 1999)**

(a) 12 A (b) 6 A

(c) 5 A (d) 3.2 A

252. The alloys constantan and manganin are used to make standard resistances because they have : **(MHT-CET 2000)**

(a) high resistivity

(b) low temperature coefficient of resistance

(c) low resistivity

(d) both (a) and (b)

253. When a wire is stretched and its radius becomes r/2, then the resistance will be : **(MHT-CET 2000)**

(a) 16 R (b) 4 R

(c) 2 R (d) R/2

254. If length of a conductor is doubled by keeping volume constant, then what is its new resistance if initial resistance was 4 Ω ? **(MHT-CET 2002)**

(a) 16 Ω (b) 8 Ω

(c) 4 Ω (d) 2 Ω

255. In a metre bridge, copper strips are used : **(MHT-CET 2002)**

(a) to decrease contact resistance

(b) to reduce thermoelectric effect

(c) to increase grip of wire

(d) to increase length of wire

256. An electric bulb is marked 100 W. If it operates at 220 V, the resistance of bulb will be : **(MHT-CET 2003)**

(a) 200 Ω (b) 100 Ω

(c) 484 Ω (d) 450 Ω

257. In potentiometer experiment, a cell is balanced by length 120 cm. When a cell is shunted by resistance of 5 Ω, the balancing length is 80 cm. The internal resistance of cell is : **(MHT-CET 2004)**

(a) 2.5 Ω (b) 3 Ω

(c) 4 Ω (d) 5 Ω

258. Four resistances arranged to form a Wheatstone's network are 8 Ω, 12 Ω, 6 Ω and 27 Ω. The resistance that should be connected across 27 Ω resistance to balance the bridge is : **(MHT-CET 2004)**

(a) 13.5 Ω (b) 15.5 Ω

(c) 27 Ω (d) 12 Ω

259. In Wheatstone bridge, the resistances in four arms are 10 Ω, 10 Ω, 10 Ω and 20 Ω. To make the bridge balance, resistance connected across 20 Ω is: **(MHT-CET 2006)**

(a) 10 Ω (b) 5 Ω

(c) 20 Ω (d) 40 Ω

260. Sensitivity of the potentiometer can be increased by : **(MHT-CET 2007)**

(a) increasing the length

(b) increasing the potential difference

(c) decreasing the series resistance

(d) increasing the current in the potentiometer

261. S.I. unit of potential gradient is : **(Board Sept. 2008)**

(a) V-cm (b) V/cm
(c) V-m (d) V/m

262. At what temperature will the resistance of a copper wire become three times its value at 0°C ? (Temperature coefficient of resistance for copper = 4×10^{-3} per °C) : **(M.P.C.E.T. 2000)**

(a) 400°C (b) 450°C
(c) 500°C (d) 550°C

263. A car battery has e.m.f. of 12 volt and internal resistance 5×10^{-2} ohm. If it draws 60 ampere current, the terminal voltage of the battery will be : **(C.B.S.E. 2000)**

(a) 5 volt (b) 3 volt
(c) 15 volt (d) 9 volt

264. Given a current carrying wire of non-uniform cross-section. Which of the following is constant throughout the length of the wire ? **(A.I.I.M.S. 2000)**

(a) Current, electric field and drift speed
(b) Drift speed only
(c) Current and drift speed
(d) Current only

265. Three resistors of resistance R each are combined in various ways. Which of the following cannot be obtained ? **(I.I.I.T. Allahabad 2000)**

(a) 3R Ω (b) $\frac{2R}{4}$ Ω
(c) $\frac{R}{3}$ Ω (d) $\frac{2R}{3}$ Ω

266. The resistance of 20 cm long wire is 10 Ω. When the length is changed to 40 cm, the new resistance is : **(C.E.T. Punjab 2000)**

(a) 10 Ω (b) 20 Ω
(c) 30 Ω (d) 40 Ω

267. Number of electrons in 1 mC charge current will be : **(R.P.M.T. 2001)**

(a) 6.25×10^{17} (b) 6.25×10^{15}
(c) 1.6×10^{16} (d) 1.8×10^{-16}

268. In a potentiometer experiment two cells of e.m.f. E_1 and E_2 are used in series and in conjunction and the balancing length is found to be 58 cm of the wire. If the polarity of E_2 is reversed, then the balancing length becomes 29 cm. The ratio $\frac{E_1}{E_2}$ of the e.m.f.s of the two cells is : **(Kerala C.E.T. 2001)**

(a) 1 : 1 (b) 2 : 1
(c) 3 : 1 (d) 4 : 1

269. The colour sequence in a carbon resistor is red, brown, orange and silver. The resistance of the resistor is : **(D.C.E. 2002)**

(a) $21 \times 10^3 \pm 10\%$
(b) $23 \times 10^1 \pm 10\%$
(c) $21 \times 10^3 \pm 5\%$
(d) $12 \times 10^3 \pm 5\%$

270. For two resistance wires joined in parallel, the resultant resistance is 6/5 ohm. When one of the resistance wire breaks, the effective resistance becomes 2 ohm. The resistance of the broken wire is : **(A.I.I.M.S. 2002)**

(a) 3/5 ohm (b) 2 ohm
(c) 6/5 ohm (d) 3 ohm

271. Two wires of the same dimensions but resistivities ρ_1 and ρ_2 are connected in series. The equivalent resistivity of the combination is : **(Karnataka C.E.T. 2003)**

(a) $2(\rho_1 + \rho_2)$ (b) $\sqrt{\rho_1\rho_2}$
(c) $\frac{\rho_1 + \rho_2}{2}$ (d) $\rho_1 + \rho_2$

272. A 6 volt battery is connected to the terminals of a three metre long wire of uniform thickness and resistance of 100 ohm. The difference of potential between two points on the wire separated by a distance of 50 cm will be : **(C.B.S.E. 2004)**

(a) 3 volt (b) 1 volt
(c) 1.5 volt (d) 2 volt

273. Direction: In the following question, a statement of Assertion (A) is given followed by a corresponding statement of Reason (R) just below it.

Assertion: A larger cell has higher e.m.f.

Reason: The e.m.f. of a dry cell is proportional to its size.

Of these statements, mark the correct answer as : **(A.I.I.M.S. 2004)**

(a) Both assertion and reason are true and reason is the correct explanation of assertion.
(b) Both assertion and reason are true, but reason is not the correct explanation of assertion.
(c) Assertion is true, but reason is false.
(d) Both assertion and reason are false.

274. When a metal conductor connected to left gap of a meter bridge is heated, the balancing point : **(J&K C.E.T. 2007)**

(a) shifts towards right
(b) shifts towards left
(c) remains unchanged
(d) remains at zero

275. The Kirchhoff's first law (Σ i = 0) and second law (Σ i/R = Σ E), where the symbols have their usual meanings, are respectively based on: **(A.I.E.E.E. 2006)**

(a) Conservation of charge, conservation of energy
(b) Conservation of charge, conservation of momentum
(c) Conservation of energy, conservation of charge
(d) Conservation of momentum, conservation of charge

276. In a meter bridge experiment, the ratio of the left gap resistance to right gap resistance is 2 : 3, the balance point from left is :

(E.A.M. C.E.T. 2007)

(a) 60 cm (b) 50 cm
(c) 40 cm (d) 20 cm

277. An aluminium (resistivity $\rho = 2.2 \times 10^{-8}$ Ωm) wire of a diameter 1.4 mm is used to make a 4 Ω resistor. The length of the wire is :

(E.A.M. C.E.T. 2007)

(a) 220 m (b) 1000 m
(c) 280 m (d) 1 m

278. Two non-ideal batteries are connected in parallel. Consider the following statements :

(i) The equivalent emf is smaller than either of the two emfs.
(ii) The equivalent internal resistance is smaller than either of the two internal resistances.

Of these statements :

(a) Both (i) and (ii) are correct
(b) (i) is correct, but (ii) is wrong
(c) (ii) is correct, but (i) is wrong
(d) Both (i) and (ii) are wrong

279. The mean free path of electrons in a metal is 4×10^{-8} m. The electric field which can give on an average 2 eV energy to an electron in the metal will be in units V/m :

(A.I.P.M.T. (Prelim.) 2009)

(a) 5×10^{-11} (b) 8×10^{-11}
(c) 5×10^{7} (d) 8×10^{7}

280. A metallic wire of resistance 12 Ω is bent to form a square. The resistance between two diagonal points would be : **(D.C.E. 2009)**

(a) 12 Ω (b) 24 Ω
(c) 6 Ω (d) 3 Ω

281. A uniform wire has resistance 25 Ω. It is bent in the form of a circle. The effective resistance between the two end points on any diameter of the circle is :

(a) 6 Ω (b) 12 Ω
(c) 3 Ω (d) 24 Ω

282. The temperature coefficient of resistivity is negative for : **(H.P.P.M.T. 2010)**

(a) Silver (b) Manganin
(c) Carbon (d) Hard rubber

283. If 10% of the current passes through a moving coil galvanometer of resistance 99 Ω, then the shunt resistance will be : **(H.P.P.M.T. 2010)**

(a) 9.9 Ω (b) 11 Ω

(c) 10 Ω (d) 9 Ω

284. The resistance of ideal voltmeter is : **(Gujarat C.E.T. 2011)**

(a) zero

(b) greater than zero, but of finite value

(c) infinite

(d) 5000 Ω

285. Three resistors are connected so form the sides of a triangle ABC, the resistance of the sides AB, BC and CA are 40 ohms, 60 ohms and 100 ohms respectively. The effective resistance between the points A and B in ohms will be : **(J.I.P.M.E.R. 2002)**

(a) 32 (b) 64

(c) 50 (d) 200

286. A 10 Ω thick wire is stretched so that its length becomes 3 times. Then the new resistance of the wire is : **(A.M.U. (Engg.) 2002)**

(a) 10 Ω (b) 30 Ω

(c) 90 Ω (d) $\frac{10}{9}$ Ω

287. An electric current is passed through a circuit containing two wires of the same material, connected in parallel. If the lengths and radii of the wires are in the ratio of $\frac{4}{3}$ and $\frac{2}{3}$, then ratio of the currents passing through the wires will be: **(A.I.E.E.E. 2004)**

(a) 3 (b) $\frac{1}{3}$

(c) $\frac{8}{9}$ (d) 2

288. An energy source will supply a constant current into the load if its internal resistance is : **(A.I.E.E.E. 2005)**

(a) zero

(b) non-zero but less than the resistance of the load

(c) equal to the resistance of the load

(d) very large as compared to the load resistance

289. A resistor R has power dissipation P with cell voltage E. The resistor is cut in n equal parts and all parts are connected in parallel with same cell. The new power dissipation is: **(Haryana P.M.T. 2005)**

(a) nP (b) nP^2

(c) n^2P (d) n/P

290. A wire P has resistance of 20 ohm. Another wire Q of same material but length twice that of P has resistance of 8 ohm. If r is the radius of cross-section of P, the radius of cross-section of Q is : **(J&K C.E.T. 2007)**

(a) r (b) $\frac{r}{\sqrt{2}}$

(c) $r\sqrt{5}$ (d) 2r

291. In a Wheatstone's network P = 2 Ω, Q = 2 Ω, R = 2 Ω and S = 3 Ω. The resistance with which S is to be shunted in order that the bridge may be balanced is : **(Kerala P.M.T. 2007)**

(a) 1 Ω (b) 2 Ω

(c) 4 Ω (d) 6 Ω

292. **Statement-1:** In a Meter Bridge experiment, null point for an unknown resistance is measured. Now, the unknown resistance is put inside an enclosure maintained at a higher temperature. The null point can be obtained at the same point as before by decreasing the value of the standard resistance.

Statement-2: Resistance of a metal increases with increase in temperature.

(a) Statement-1 is true, Statement-2 is true; Statement-2 is a correct explanation for statement-1.

(b) Statement-1 is true, Statement-2 is true; Statement-2 is not a correct explanation for statement-1.

(c) Statement-1 is true, Statement-2 is false.

(d) Statement-1 is false, Statement-2 is true.

293. This question contains Statement-1 and Statement-2. Of the four choices given after the statements, choose the one that best describes the two statements.

(A.I.E.E.E. 2009)

Statement-1: The temperature dependence of resistance is usually given as $R = R_0 (1 + \alpha\Delta t)$. The resistance of a wire changes from 100 Ω to 150 Ω when its temperature is increased from 27°C to 227°C. This implies that $\alpha = 2.5 \times 10^{-3}/°C$.

Statement-2: $R = R_0 (1 + \alpha\Delta t)$ is valid only when the change in the temperature ΔT is small and $\Delta R = (R - R_0) << R_0$.

(a) Statement-1 is true, Statement -2 is false

(b) Statement-1 is true, Statement-2 is true; Statement-2 is the correct explanation of Statement-1.

(c) Statement-1 is true, Statement-2 is true; Statement-2 is not the correct explanation of Statement-1.

(d) Statement-1 is false, Statement-2 is true.

294. Two different conductors have same resistance at 0°C. It is found that the resistance of the first conductor at t_1°C is equal to the resistance of the second conductor at t_2°C. The ratio of the temperature coefficients of resistance of the conductors, $\frac{\alpha_1}{\alpha_2}$ is : **(Kerala C.E.T. 2009)**

(a) $\frac{t_1}{t_2}$ (b) $\frac{t_2 - t_1}{t_2}$

(c) $\frac{t_2}{t_2 - t_1}$ (d) $\frac{t_2}{t_1}$

295. The external diameter of a 314 m long copper tube is 1.2 cm and the internal diameter is 1 cm. Calculate its resistance if the specific resistance of copper is 2.2×10^{-8} ohm metre :

(A.M.U. (Med.) 2009)

(a) 5.0×10^{-2} ohm (b) 4.4×10^{-2} ohm

(c) 3.14×10^{-2} ohm (d) 2.0×10^{-1} ohm

296. A current of 2 A flows through a 2 Ω resistor when connected across a battery. The same battery supplies a current of 0.5 A when connected across a 9 Ω resistor. The internal resistance of the battery is :

(A.I.P.M.T. (Prelim.) 2011)

(a) 0.5 Ω (b) 1/3 Ω

(c) 1/4 Ω (d) 1 Ω

297. The masses of the three wires of copper are in the ratio 5 : 3 : 1 and their length are in the ratio 1 : 3 : 5. The ratio of their electrical resistances is : **(Gujarat C.E.T. 2011)**

(a) 5 : 3 : 1 (b) $\sqrt{125}$: 15 : 1

(c) 1 : 15 : 125 (d) 1 : 3 : 5

298. The resistance of the series combination of two resistances is *S*. When they are joined in parallel, the total resistance is P. If S = nP, then the minimum possible value of n is :

(A.I.E.E.E. 2004)

(a) 4 (b) 3

(c) 2 (d) 1

299. To draw maximum current from a combination of cells, how should the cells be grouped ? **(A.F.M.C. 2005)**

(a) Series

(b) Parallel

(c) Mixed

(d) Depends upon the relative values of external and internal resistance

300. Potentiometer wire of length 1 m is connected in series with 490 Ω resistance and 2 V battery. If 0.2 mV/cm is the potential gradient, then resistance of the potentiometer wire is : **(D.C.E. 2005)**

(a) 4.9 Ω (b) 7.9 Ω

(c) 5.9 Ω (d) 6.9 Ω

301. A resistance of 2 Ω is connected across one gap of a metre-bridge (the length of the wire is 100 cm) and an unknown resistance, greater than 2 Ω, is connected across the other gap. When these resistances are interchanged, the balance point shifts by 20 cm. Neglecting any corrections, the unknown resistance is : **(I.I.T., J.E.E. 2007)**

(a) 3 Ω (b) 4 Ω
(c) 5 Ω (d) 6 Ω

302. For current entering at A, the electric field at a distance r from A is : **(A.I.E.E.E. 2008)**

(a) $\frac{\rho I}{4\pi r^2}$ (b) $\frac{\rho I}{8\pi r^2}$
(c) $\frac{\rho I}{r^2}$ (d) $\frac{\rho I}{2\pi r^2}$

303. Two sources of equal emf are connected to an external resistance R. The internal resistances of the two sources are R_1 and R_2 ($R_2 > R_1$). If the potential difference across the source having internal resistance R_2, is zero, then : **(A.I.I.M.S. 2008)**

(a) $R = \frac{R_2 \times (R_1 + R_2)}{(R_2 - R_1)}$
(b) $R = R_2 - R_1$
(c) $R = \frac{R_1 R_2}{(R_1 + R_2)}$
(d) $R = \frac{R_1 R_2}{(R_2 - R_1)}$

304. Two resistors of resistances 20 kΩ and 1 MΩ respectively form a potential divider with outer junctions maintained at potentials of + 3 V and – 15 V. Then the potential at the junction between the resistors is : **(Kerala Engg. 2010)**

(a) + 1 V (b) – 0.6 V
(c) 0 V (d) – 12 V
(e) + 12 V

305. A gold wire of resistance 24 Ω is stretched uniformly to a length equal to 4 times its original length. Its new resistance will be : **(Orissa J.E.E. 2010)**

(a) 94 Ω (b) 144 Ω
(c) 288 Ω (d) 384 Ω

306. A circular loop and a square loop are formed from the same wire and the same current is passed through them. Find the ratio of their dipole moments : **(M.H.T. C.E.T. 2010)**

(a) 4 π (b) $\frac{4}{\pi}$
(c) $\frac{2}{\pi}$ (d) 2 π

307. For measurement of potential difference, potentiometer is preferred in comparison to voltmeter because **(MHT-CET 2010)**

(a) potentiometer is more sensitive than voltmeter
(b) the resistance of potentiometer is less than that of voltmeter
(c) potentiometer is cheaper than voltmeter
(d) potentiometer does not take current from the circuit

308. When a resistance of 100 Ω is connected in series with a galvanometer of resistance R, its range is V. To double its range, a resistance of 1000 Ω is connected in series. Find R. **(MHT-CET 2010)**

(a) 700 Ω (b) 800 Ω
(c) 900 Ω (d) 100 Ω

309. The e.m.f. of a thermocouple, cold junction of which is kept at – 300°C is given by $E = 40\ t + \frac{1}{10}\ t^2$. The temperature of inversion of thermocouple will be **(MHT-CET 2010)**

(a) 20°C (b) 400°C
(c) – 200°C (d) – 100°C

310. A student measures the terminal potential difference (V) of a cell (of e.m.f. ε and internal resistance r) as a function of the current (I) flowing through it. The slope and intercept of the graph between V and I, then respectively, equal **(C.B.S.E., P.M.T. 2010)**

(a) – r and ε (b) r and – ε
(c) – ε and r (d) ε and – r

311. Which of the following is correct relation between potential gradient, current I and specific resistance ρ? **(MHT-CET 2011)**

(a) $\frac{A}{I_p}$ (b) $I_p \, l_A$

(c) $\frac{I_p}{A}$ (d) $\frac{I_p}{l_A}$

312. If the temperature of cold junction decreases, then neutral temperature **(MHT-CET 2011)**

(a) increases

(b) decreases

(c) remains constant

(d) may increase or may decrease

313. A current of 2 A flows through a 2 Ω resistor when connected across a battery. The same battery supplies a current of 0.5 A when connected across a 9 Ω resistor. The internal resistance of the battery is **(C.B.S.E., P.M.T. 2011)**

(a) 0.5 Ω (b) 1/3 Ω

(c) 1/4 Ω (d) 1 Ω

314. For a thermocouple, the temperature of inversion is that temperature at which thermo e.m.f. is **(MHT-CET 2012)**

(a) zero

(b) maximum

(c) minimum

(d) none of the above

315. In a Wheatstone's network, the positions of the battery and the galvanometer are interchanged. The balance condition **(MHT-CET 2012)**

(a) remains unaltered

(b) alters

(c) may or may not alter depending on the resistance of the galvanometer and the battery

(d) none of these

316. In the circuit shown, the cells A and B have negligible resistance. For $V_A = 12$ V, $R_1 = 500$ Ω and $R = 100$ Ω, the galvanometer (G) shows no deflection. The value of V_B is **(C.B.S.E., P.M.T. 2012)**

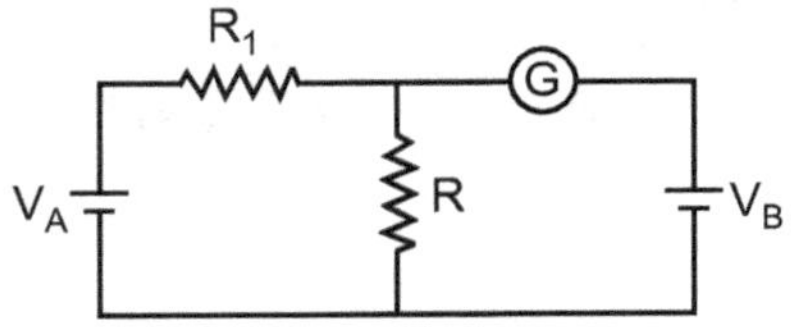

(a) 6 V (b) 4 V

(c) 2 V (d) 12 V

317. If voltage across a bulb rated 220 volt - 100 watt drops by 2.5% of its rated value, the percentage of the rated value by which the power would decrease is

(a) 10% (b) 20%

(c) 2.5% (d) 5%

318. A wire of resistance 4 Ω is stretched to twice its original length. The resistance of stretched wire would be

(a) 4 Ω (b) 8 Ω

(c) 16 Ω (d) 2 Ω

319. The internal resistance of a 2.1 V cell which gives a current of 0.2 A through a resistance of 10 Ω is **(NEET 2013)**

(a) 0.5 Ω (b) 0.8 Ω

(c) 1.0 Ω (d) 0.2 Ω

320. The resistances of the four arms P, Q, R and S in a Wheatstone's bridge are 10 ohm, 30 ohm, and 90 ohm respectively. The e.m.f. and internal resistance of the cell are 7 volt and 5 ohm respectively. If the galvanometer resistance is 50 ohm, the current drawn from the cell will be **(NEET 2013)**

(a) 0.2 A (b) 0.1 A

(c) 2.0 A (d) 1.0 A

ANSWER KEY

1. (c)	**2.** (b)	**3.** (c)	**4.** (c)	**5.** (b)	**6.** (b)	**7.** (a)	**8.** (b)	**9.** (b)	**10.** (c)
11. (c)	**12.** (a)	**13.** (b)	**14.** (b)	**15.** (c)	**16.** (b)	**17.** (b)	**18.** (a)	**19.** (a)	**20.** (b)
21. (b)	**22.** (b)	**23.** (b)	**24.** (c)	**25.** (b)	**26.** (d)	**27.** (c)	**28.** (a)	**29.** (c)	**30.** (d)
31. (c)	**32.** (c)	**33.** (b)	**34.** (a)	**35.** (a)	**36.** (b)	**37.** (b)	**38.** (c)	**39.** (d)	**40.** (a)
41. (d)	**42.** (b)	**43.** (a)	**44.** (d)	**45.** (c)	**46.** (d)	**47.** (a)	**48.** (b)	**49.** (c)	**50.** (c)
51. (a)	**52.** (d)	**53.** (d)	**54.** (c)	**55.** (b)	**56.** (b)	**57.** (a)	**58.** (a)	**59.** (b)	**60.** (d)
61. (c)	**62.** (b)	**63.** (c)	**64.** (b)	**65.** (d)	**66.** (c)	**67.** (a)	**68.** (a)	**69.** (d)	**70.** (d)
71. (b)	**72.** (b)	**73.** (b)	**74.** (c)	**75.** (b)	**76.** (c)	**77.** (a)	**78.** (c)	**79.** (c)	**80.** (a)
81. (d)	**82.** (c)	**83.** (c)	**84.** (d)	**85.** (d)	**86.** (a)	**87.** (a)	**88.** (b)	**89.** (a)	**90.** (b)
91. (d)	**92.** (b)	**93.** (b)	**94.** (c)	**95.** (a)	**96.** (a)	**97.** (d)	**98.** (a)	**99.** (a)	**100.** (c)
101. (b)	**102.** (a)	**103.** (d)	**104.** (a)	**105.** (b)	**106.** (a)	**107.** (d)	**108.** (a)	**109.** (d)	**110.** (d)
111. (c)	**112.** (c)	**113.** (d)	**114.** (b)	**115.** (b)	**116.** (b)	**117.** (b)	**118.** (c)	**119.** (c)	**120.** (d)
121. (c)	**122.** (c)	**123.** (c)	**124.** (c)	**125.** (c)	**126.** (c)	**127.** (c)	**128.** (a)	**129.** (a)	**130.** (c)
131. (b)	**132.** (c)	**133.** (b)	**134.** (b)	**135.** (a)	**136.** (c)	**137.** (d)	**138.** (a)	**139.** (b)	**140.** (c)
141. (b)	**142.** (c)	**143.** (b)	**144.** (d)	**145.** (b)	**146.** (d)	**147.** (c)	**148.** (d)	**149.** (c)	**150.** (d)
151. (d)	**152.** (d)	**153.** (c)	**154.** (b)	**155.** (d)	**156.** (a)	**157.** (b)	**158.** (c)	**159.** (b)	**160.** (d)
161. (d)	**162.** (b)	**163.** (d)	**164.** (b)	**165.** (b)	**166.** (c)	**167.** (b)	**168.** (a)	**169.** (b)	**170.** (c)
171. (b)	**172.** (c)	**173.** (b)	**174.** (c)	**175.** (c)	**176.** (c)	**177.** (a)	**178.** (b)	**179.** (d)	**180.** (c)
181. (d)	**182.** (d)	**183.** (c)	**184.** (c)	**185.** (a)	**186.** (a)	**187.** (d)	**188.** (b)	**189.** (d)	**190.** (a)
191. (c)	**192.** (d)	**193.** (b)	**194.** (c)	**195.** (c)	**196.** (d)	**197.** (a)	**198.** (a)	**199.** (b)	**200.** (b)
201. (a)	**202.** (c)	**203.** (c)	**204.** (d)	**205.** (c)	**206.** (c)	**207.** (b)	**208.** (c)	**209.** (a)	**210.** (b)
211. (c)	**212.** (b)	**213.** (d)	**214.** (d)	**215.** (d)	**216.** (c)	**217.** (a)	**218.** (d)	**219.** (c)	**220.** (b)
221. (b)	**222.** (b)	**223.** (b)	**224.** (d)	**225.** (a)	**226.** (a)	**227.** (a)	**228.** (a)	**229.** (b)	**230.** (c)
231. (b)	**232.** (a)	**233.** (a)	**234.** (a)	**235.** (d)	**236.** (b)	**237.** (b)	**238.** (b)	**239.** (d)	**240.** (a)
241. (b)	**242.** (d)	**243.** (a)	**244.** (a)	**245.** (a)	**246.** (c)	**247.** (c)	**248.** (b)	**249.** (a)	**250.** (d)
251. (c)	**252.** (d)	**253.** (a)	**254.** (a)	**255.** (a)	**256.** (c)	**257.** (a)	**258.** (a)	**259.** (c)	**260.** (a)
261. (d)	**262.** (c)	**263.** (d)	**264.** (d)	**265.** (b)	**266.** (d)	**267.** (b)	**268.** (c)	**269.** (a)	**270.** (d)
271. (c)	**272.** (b)	**273.** (d)	**274.** (a)	**275.** (a)	**276.** (c)	**277.** (c)	**278.** (c)	**279.** (c)	**280.** (d)
281. (a)	**282.** (b)	**283.** (b)	**284.** (c)	**285.** (a)	**286.** (c)	**287.** (b)	**288.** (a)	**289.** (c)	**290.** (c)
291. (d)	**292.** (d)	**293.** (a)	**294.** (d)	**295.** (d)	**296.** (b)	**297.** (c)	**298.** (a)	**299.** (c)	**300.** (a)
301. (a)	**302.** (d)	**303.** (b)	**304.** (c)	**305.** (d)	**306.** (b)	**307.** (d)	**308.** (c)	**309.** (c)	**310.** (a)
311. (c)	**312.** (c)	**313.** (b)	**314.** (a)	**315.** (a)	**316.** (c)	**317.** (d)	**318.** (c)	**319.** (a)	**320.** (b)

13

MAGNETIC EFFECTS OF CURRENT

MULTIPLE CHOICE QUESTIONS

1. Weber/m^2 is equal to : **(A.F.M.C. 1997)**
   (a) Henry (b) Tesla
   (c) Volt (d) All of these

2. Weber/m^2 is the unit of :
   (a) Magnetic induction
   (b) Magnetic field intensity
   (c) Magnetic flux density
   (d) All of these

3. An electron and a proton enter a region of uniform magnetic field in a direction at right-angles to the magnetic field with the same K.E. It describes circles of radius r_e & r_p respectively, then : **(Manipal 1995)**
   (a) $r_e > r_p$ (b) $r_e < r_p$
   (c) $r_e = r_p$ (d) $r_e \geq r_p$

4. Lorentz force is given by : **(M.P.P.E.T. 1994)**
   (a) $\vec{F} = q(\vec{E} + \vec{v} \times \vec{B})$
   (b) $\vec{F} = q(\vec{E} + \vec{v} \times \vec{B})$
   (c) $\vec{F} = q(\vec{E} + \vec{v} \cdot \vec{B})$
   (d) $\vec{F} = q(\vec{E} + \vec{B} \cdot \vec{v})$

5. If a current is passed through a spring then it: **(A.I.E.E.E. 2002, MP P.M.T. 1998)**
   (a) compresses (b) expands
   (c) oscillates (d) rotates

6. In a cyclotron, the angular frequency of the charged particle is independent of : **(C.P.M.T. 1999)**
   (a) Mass (b) Speed
   (c) Charge (d) Magnetic field

7. A proton of mass 1.67×10^{-27} kg and charge 1.6×10^{-19} C is projected with a speed of 2×10^6 ms^{-1} at an angle of 60° to the X-axis. If a uniform magnetic field of 0.14 T is applied along the Y-axis, then the path of the proton is :
   (a) A circle of radius 0.2 m and time period of $2\pi \times 10^{-7}$ sec.
   (b) A circle of radius 0.1 m and time period of 2×10^{-7} sec.
   (c) A helix of radius 0.1 m and time period of $2\pi \times 10^{-7}$ sec.
   (d) A helix of radius 0.12 m and time period of $2\pi \times 10^{-7}$ sec.

8. If a particle of charge 10^{-12} C moving along the x-direction with a velocity of 10^5 m/s experiences a force of 10^{-10} N in the y-direction due to a magnetic field, then the minimum value of the magnetic field is : **(M.P. P.M.T. 1994)**
   (a) 6.25×10^3 Tesla in the z-direction
   (b) 6.25×10^{-3} Tesla in the z-direction
   (c) 10^{-3} Tesla in the z-direction
   (d) 10^{-15} Tesla in the z-direction

9. A proton enters a magnetic field of flux density 1.5 weber/m^2 with a velocity of 2×10^7 ms^{-1} at angle 30° with the field. The force on the proton will be : **(M.P.P.E.T. 1994)**
   (a) 2.4×10^{-12} N (b) 0.24×10^{-12} N
   (c) 24×10^{-12} N (d) 0.024×10^{-12} N

10. The magnetic field dB due to a small current element dl at a distance r and element carrying current i is :

(a) $\vec{dB} = \frac{\mu_0}{4\pi} i \left(\frac{d\vec{l} \times \vec{r}}{r}\right)$

(b) $\vec{dB} = \frac{\mu_0}{4\pi} i^2 \left(\frac{d\vec{l} \times \vec{r}}{r}\right)$

(c) $\vec{dB} = \frac{\mu_0}{4\pi} i^2 \left(\frac{d\vec{l} \times \vec{r}}{r^2}\right)$

(d) $\vec{dB} = \frac{\mu_0}{4\pi} i \left(\frac{d\vec{l} \times \vec{r}}{r^3}\right)$

11. Two straight long wires are set parallel to each other. Each carries a current i in the same direction and the separation between them is $2r$. The intensity of magnetic field at a distance r between the two wires is :

(a) i/r (b) $2\ i/r$
(c) $4\ i/r$ (d) Zero

12. A charge q coulomb moves in a circle at n revolutions per second and the radius of the circle is r metre, then magnetic field at the centre of the circle is : **(C.E.T. 2000)**

(a) $\frac{2\pi q}{nr} \times 10^{-7}\ \frac{\text{newton}}{\text{amp-metre}}$

(b) $\frac{2\pi q}{r} \times 10^{-7}\ \frac{\text{newton}}{\text{amp-metre}}$

(c) $\frac{2\pi\, nq}{r} \times 10^{-7}\ \frac{\text{newton}}{\text{amp-metre}}$

(d) $\frac{2\pi q}{nr}\ \frac{\text{newton}}{\text{amp-metre}}$

13. Two thin long parallel wires separated by a distance b are carrying a current i amp each. The magnitude of the force per unit length exerted by one wire on the other is :

(a) $\frac{\mu_0 i^2}{b^2}$ (b) $\frac{\mu_0 i^2}{2\pi b}$
(c) $\frac{\mu_0 i}{2\pi b}$ (d) $\frac{\mu_0 i}{2\pi b^2}$

14. A conducting circular loop of radius r carries a constant current i. It is placed in a uniform magnetic field B such that B is perpendicular to the plane of the loop. The magnetic force acting on the loop is :

(a) irB (b) $2\pi riB$
(c) Zero (d) πriB

15. An infinitely long straight conductor is bent into a shape as shown below. It carries a current of i ampere and the radius of the circular loop is r metre. Then the magnetic induction at the centre of the circular part is :

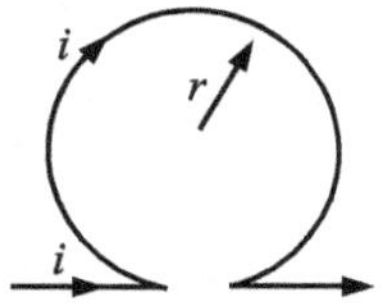

(a) Zero (b) Infinite
(c) $\frac{\mu_0}{4\pi} \cdot \frac{2i}{r} \cdot (\pi + 1)$ (d) $\frac{\mu_0}{4\pi} \cdot \frac{2i}{r} \cdot (\pi - 1)$

16. If an electron describes half a revolution in a circle of radius r in a magnetic field B, the energy acquired by it is :

(a) Zero (b) $\frac{1}{2}\ mv^2$
(c) $\frac{1}{4}\ mv^2$ (d) $\pi r \times Bev$

17. A proton moving with a constant velocity passes through a region of space without any change in its velocity. If E and B represent the electric and magnetic fields respectively, this region of space may have :

(a) $E = 0, B = 0$ (b) $E = 0, B \neq 0$
(c) $E \neq 0, B \neq 0$ (d) All the above

18. Electron and proton of equal momentum enter a uniform magnetic field normal to the lines of force. If the radii of curvature of circular paths are r_e the r_p respectively, then:

(a) $r_e/r_p = 1/1$ (b) $r_e/r_p = m_p/m_e$
(c) $r_e/r_p = \sqrt{m_p/m_e}$ (d) $r_e/r_p = \sqrt{m_e/m_p}$

19. The particles X and Y having equal charges, after being accelerated through the same potential difference, enter a region of uniform magnetic field and describe circular paths of radii R_1 and R_2 respectively. The ratio of mass of X to that of Y is :

(a) $(R_1/R_2)^{1/2}$ (b) R_2/R_1

(c) $(R_1/R_2)^2$ (d) R_1/R_2

20. The field normal to the plane of a wire of n turns and radius r which carries a current i is measured on the axis of the coil at a small distance x from the centre of the coil. This is smaller than the field at the centre by the fraction :

(a) $\frac{3}{2} \cdot \frac{x^2}{r^2}$ (b) $\frac{2}{3} \cdot \frac{x^2}{r^2}$

(c) $\frac{3}{2} \cdot \frac{r^2}{x^2}$ (d) $\frac{2}{3} \cdot \frac{r^2}{x^2}$

21. A circular current carrying coil has a radius R. The distance from the centre of the coil, on the axis where the magnetic induction will be $1/8^{th}$ to its value at the centre of the coil, is :

(a) $R/\sqrt{3}$ (b) $R\sqrt{3}$

(c) $2R\sqrt{3}$ (d) $(2\sqrt{3})R$

22. A current I ampere flows in a circular arc of wire which subtends an angle $(3\pi/2)$ radians at its centre, whose radius is R. The magnetic induction B at the centre is :

(a) $\frac{\mu_0 I}{R}$ (b) $\frac{\mu_0 I}{2R}$

(c) $\frac{2\mu_0 I}{R}$ (d) $\frac{3\mu_0 I}{8R}$

23. An electron is injected into a region of unifrom magnetic flux density, with components of velocity parallel to and normal to the flux. The path of the electron is :

(a) a helix (b) straight line

(c) parabola (d) ellipse

24. The radius of curvature of the path of a charged particle in a uniform magnetic field is directly proportional to :

(a) the charge on the particle

(b) the momentum of the particle

(c) the energy of the particle

(d) the intensity of the field

25. A magnetic needle is kept in a non-uniform magnetic field. It experiences :

(a) a force and torque

(b) a force but not a torque

(c) a torque but not a force

(d) neither a force nor a torque

26. A uniform electric field and a uniform magnetic field are produced, pointed in the same direction. An electron is projected with its velocity pointed in the same direction, then :

(a) the electron will turn to its right

(b) the electron will turn to its left

(c) the electron velocity will increase in magnitude

(d) the electron velocity will decrease in magnitude

27. A proton (mass m and charge $+e$) and an alpha particle (mass $4m$ and charge $+2e$) are projected with the same kinetic energy at right angles to a uniform magnetic field. Which one of the following statements will be true ?

(a) The alpha-particle will be bent in the circular path with a smaller radius than that of the proton.

(b) The radius of the path of the alpha-particle will be greater than that of the proton

(c) The radius of the paths of both the particles will be the same.

(d) None of these.

28. Energy in a current carrying coil is stored in the form of :

(a) Electric field (b) Magnetic field

(c) Dielectric strength (d) Heat

29. A charged particle enters into a magnetic field with a velocity vector making an angle of 30° with respect to the direction of the magnetic field. The path of the particle is :

(a) circular (b) helical

(c) elliptical (d) straight line

30. If the direction of the initial velocity of the charged particle is neither along nor perpendicular to that of the magnetic field, then the orbit will be :

(a) a straight line (b) an ellipse

(c) a circle (d) a helix

31. An electron is moving with a speed of 10^8 ms^{-1} perpendicular to a uniform magnetic field of intensity B. Suddenly the intensity of the magnetic field is reduced to B/2. The radius of the path from the original value of r :

(a) do not change (b) reduces to $r/2$

(c) increases to $2r$ (d) stops moving

32. Two equal electric currents are flowing perpendicular to each other as shown in the figure. AB and CD are perpendicular to each other and symmetrically placed with respect to the currents. Where do we expect the resultant magnetic field to be zero ?

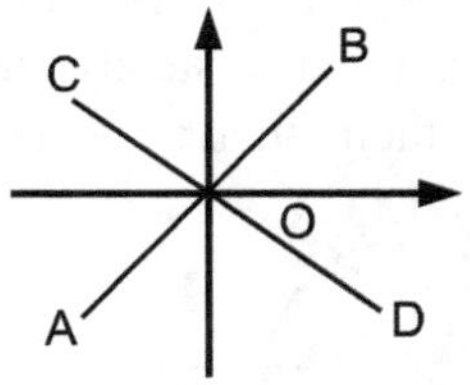

(a) On AB

(b) On CD

(c) On both AB and CD

(d) On both OD and BO

33. A particle of charge $+q$ and mass m moving under the influence of a uniform electric field Ei and a uniform magnetic field Bk follows a trajectory from P to Q as shown in the figure. The velocities at P and Q are vi and vj respectively. Which of the following statement(s) is/are correct ? **(I.I.T. 2000)**

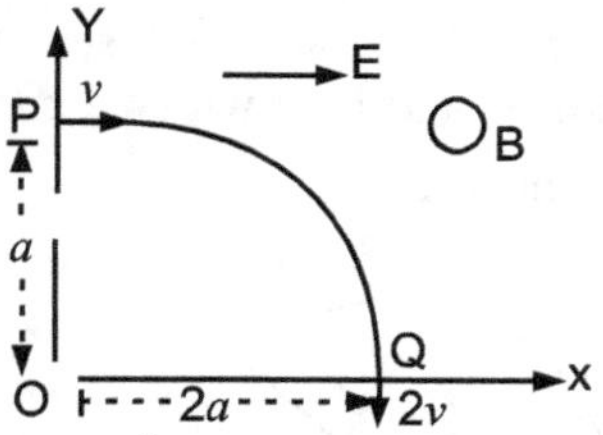

(a) $E = \dfrac{3mv^2}{4qa}$.

(b) Rate of work done by electric field at P is $\dfrac{3mv^2}{4qa}$.

(c) Rate of work done by electric field at P is zero.

(d) Rate of work done by both the fields at Q is zero.

34. If two parallel wires have current I_A and I_B in the same direction, the force between them is :

(a) $\dfrac{\mu_0}{2\pi} \times \dfrac{I_A I_B}{r}$ (b) $\dfrac{I_A I_B}{r}\mu_0$

(c) $\dfrac{\mu_0 I_A}{2\pi(2r)}$ (d) $\dfrac{\mu_0 I_B}{2r}$

35. In the figure, what is the magnetic field induction at point O ?

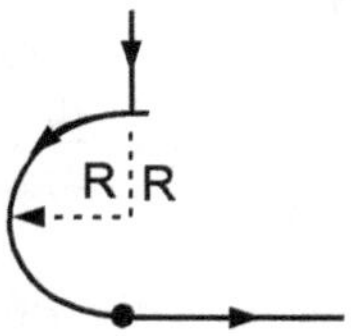

(a) $\dfrac{\mu_0 I}{4\pi R}$ (b) $\dfrac{\mu_0 I}{4R} + \dfrac{\mu_0 I}{2\pi R}$

(c) $\dfrac{\mu_0 I}{4R} + \dfrac{\mu_0 I}{4\pi R}$ (d) $\dfrac{\mu_0 I}{4R^2} + \dfrac{\mu_0 I}{4\pi R}$

36. A current I amp flows in the loop having circular arc of r metre subtending an angle θ. The magnetic field at centre O of circle is:

(a) $\dfrac{\mu_0 I\theta}{4\pi r}$ (b) $\dfrac{2\mu_0 I}{4\pi r^2}\sin\theta$

(c) $\dfrac{2\mu_0 I}{2r}\sin\theta$ (d) $\dfrac{\mu_0 I \sin\theta}{4r}$

37. In the figure, there are two semi-circular rings of radii r_1 and r_2 in which a current I is flowing as shown.

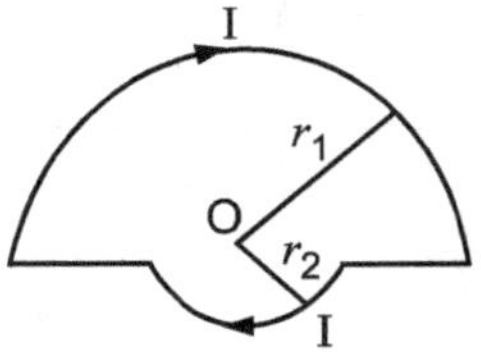

The magnetic induction at the centre O will be :

(a) $\frac{\mu_0 I}{4}(r_1 + r_2)$ (b) $\frac{\mu_0 I}{4}(r_1 - r_2)$

(c) $\frac{\mu_0 I}{4}\left(\frac{r_1 + r_2}{r_1 r_2}\right)$ (d) $\frac{\mu_0 I}{4}\left(\frac{r_1 - r_2}{r_1 r_2}\right)$

38. An infinite straight conductor carrying current 2I is split into a loop of radius r as shown in the figure. The magnetic field at the centre of the coil is :

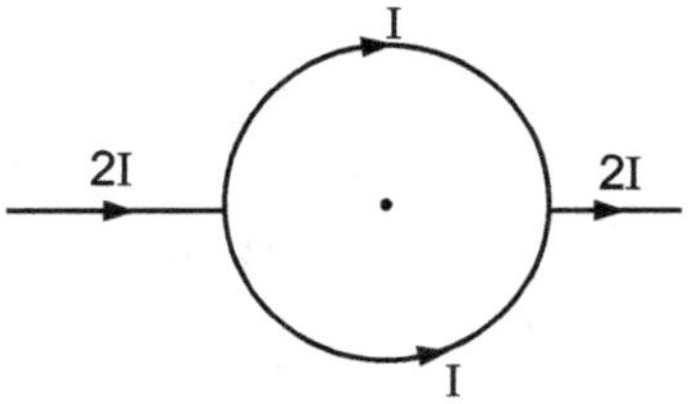

(a) $\frac{\mu_0}{4\pi}\frac{2(\pi + 1)}{r}$ (b) $\frac{\mu_0}{4\pi}\frac{4(\pi + 1)}{r}$

(c) $\frac{\mu_0}{4\pi}\frac{(\pi + 1)}{r}$ (d) Zero

39. An electron and a proton with equal momentum enter perpendicularly into a uniform magnetic field. Then :

(A.I.E.E.E. 2000)

(a) the path of the proton shall be more curved than that of the electron.

(b) the path of the proton shall be less curved than that of the electron.

(c) both will be equally curved.

(d) path of both particles will be a straight line.

40. A particle of mass m and charge q is placed at rest in a uniform electric field E and then released. The K.E. attained by the particle after moving a distance y is :

(a) $q\text{E}y^2$ (b) $q\text{E}y$

(c) $q\text{E}^2y$ (d) $q^2\text{E}y$

41. A wire carrying current I is shaped as shown below. Section AB is a quarter circle of radius r. **(Karnataka C.E.T. 2002)**

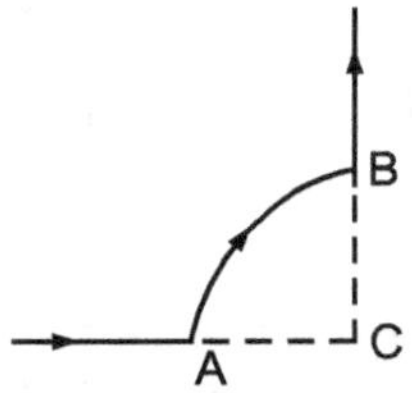

The magnetic field is directed :

(a) along the bisecter of the angle ACB away from AB.

(b) perpendicular to the plane of paper and directed into the paper.

(c) at an angle to the plane of paper.

(d) along the bisector of the angle ACB towards AB.

42. Two insulated rings, one of slightly smaller diameter than the other are suspended along their common diameter as shown. Initially the planes of the rings are mutually perpendicular. When a steady current is set up in each of them, then : **(I.I.T. 1995)**

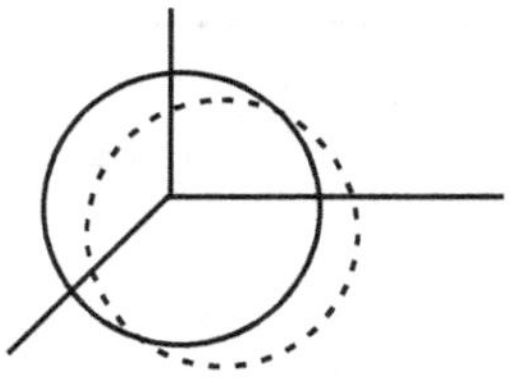

(a) the two rings rotate into a common plane.

(b) the inner ring oscillates about its initial position.

(c) the outer ring stays stationary, while the inner ring moves into the plane of the outer ring.

(d) the inner ring stays stationary, while the outer ring moves into the plane of the inner ring.

43. A wire of length l is formed into a circular loop of one turn and is suspended in magnetic field B. When a current I is passed through the loop, the torque experienced by it is :

(a) $\frac{1}{4\pi}$ BIl (b) $\frac{1}{4\pi}$ B^2 Il

(c) $\frac{1}{4\pi} l^2 IB$ (d) $\frac{1}{4}\pi BI^2 l$

44. A deutron of K.E. 50 keV is describing a circle of radius 0.5 metre in a plane perpendicular to the magnetic field $\vec{B}$. The kinetic energy of the proton that describes a circular orbit of radius 0.5 metre in the same plane with the same $\vec{B}$ is :

(a) 200 keV (b) 100 keV

(c) 50 keV (d) 25 keV

45. A long straight wire along z-axis carries a current I in the –ve z-direction. The magnetic field vector $\vec{B}$ at a point having co-ordinates (x, y) in the $-z = 0$ plane is :

(I.I.T. Screening 2002)

(a) $\frac{\mu_0}{2\pi} \frac{I(y\hat{i} - x\hat{j})}{x^2 + y^2}$ (b) $\frac{\mu_0}{2\pi} \frac{I(y\hat{i} - x\hat{j})}{x^2 - y^2}$

(c) $\frac{\mu_0}{2\pi} \frac{I(x\hat{i} - y\hat{i})}{2\pi(x^2 + y^2)}$ (d) $\frac{\mu_0}{2\pi} \frac{I(x\hat{j} - \hat{y})}{(x^2 + y^2)}$

46. A square frame of side l carrying a current I produces a field B at its centre. The same current is passed through a circular coil having the same perimeter as the square. The field at the centre of the circular coil is B'. The ratio of B'/B is :

(a) $\frac{\pi^2}{8\sqrt{2}}$ (b) $\frac{8\pi^2}{\sqrt{2}}$

(c) $\frac{3\pi}{8\sqrt{2}}$ (d) $\frac{\pi^2}{4\sqrt{2}}$

47. A proton of mass 1.67×10^{-27} kg is projected with a speed of 2×10^6 ms^{-1} at an angle of 60° to the x-axis. If a uniform magnetic field of 0.104T is applied along the y-axis, the path of the proton is : **(I.I.T. 1995)**

(a) a circle of radius 0.2 m and time period $2\pi \times 10^{-7}$s

(b) a helix of radius 0.2 m and time period $2\pi \times 10^{-7}$ s

(c) a circle of radius 0.1 m and time period $2\pi \times 10^{-7}$s

(d) a helix of radius 0.1 m and time period $2\pi \times 10^{-7}$s

48. Two parallel wires in free space are 10 cm apart and each carries a current of 10 A in the same direction. The force experienced per unit length of each wire is :

(C.B.S.E. P.M.T. 1997)

(a) 2×10^{-4} N attractive

(b) 2×10^{-4} N repulsive

(c) 2×10^{-7} N attractive

(d) 2×10^{-7} N repulsive

49. The magnetic field density B at a distance 'r' from a long straight rod carrying a steady current varies with r as :

(a)

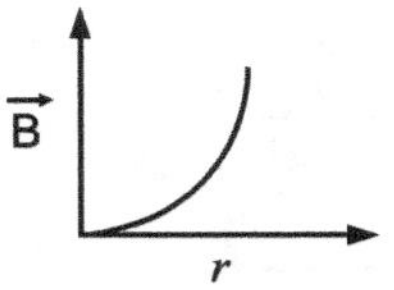

(b)

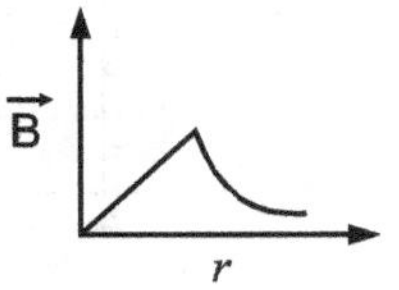

(c)

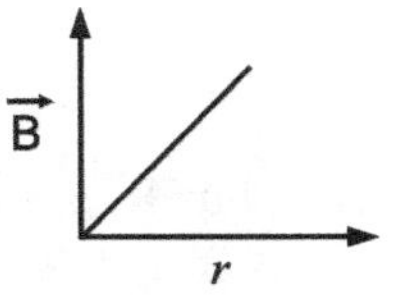

(d)

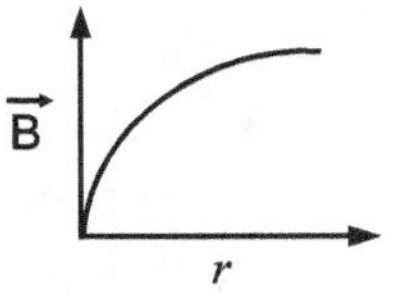

50. An electron is revolving around a proton in a circular path of diameter 1Å. It produces a magnetic field of 14T at the proton. Then angular speed of the electron is :

(a) 8.8×10^{16} rad s^{-1}

(b) 4.4×10^{16} rad s^{-1}

(c) 1.1×10^{16} rad s^{-1}

(d) 2.2×10^{16} rad s^{-1}

51. Two infinitely long conducting wires carry current as shown in the figure. If the wire carrying current along x-direction produces a magnetic field B at point $(-2a, -a, 0)$, then the resultant magnetic field at point P is : **(I.I.T. 2004)**

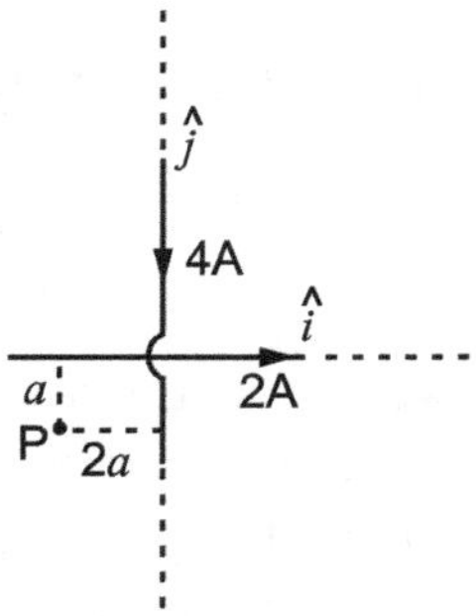

(a) $-2.0\,B\,\hat{k}$ (b) $-1.5\,B\,\hat{k}$

(c) Zero (d) $1.5\,B\,\hat{k}$

52. A wire ABC carrying current I is bent as shown in the figure and placed in a uniform magnetic field B. Let length AB = l and $\angle ABC = 45°$, then ratio of force on AB and on BC is :

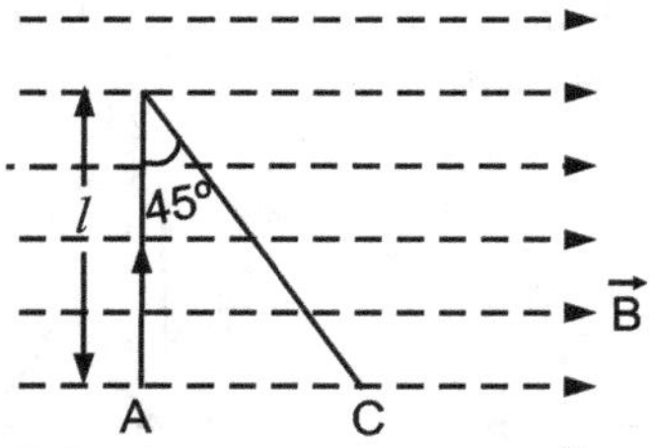

(a) $\dfrac{1}{\sqrt{2}}$ (b) $\dfrac{2}{3}$

(c) $\sqrt{2}$ (d) 1

53. A long copper tube of inner radius R carries a current I. The magnetic field B inside the tube is :

(a) $\dfrac{\mu_0 I}{2\pi R}$ (b) $\dfrac{\mu_0 I}{2R}$

(c) Zero (d) $\dfrac{\mu_0 I}{4\pi R}$

54. Two parallel wires P and Q carrying the same amount of current directed perpendicularly outward to the plane of the paper are '$2a$' distance apart as shown in the figure. The variation of magnetic field B along the line XX' is given by : **(I.I.T. 2003)**

(a)

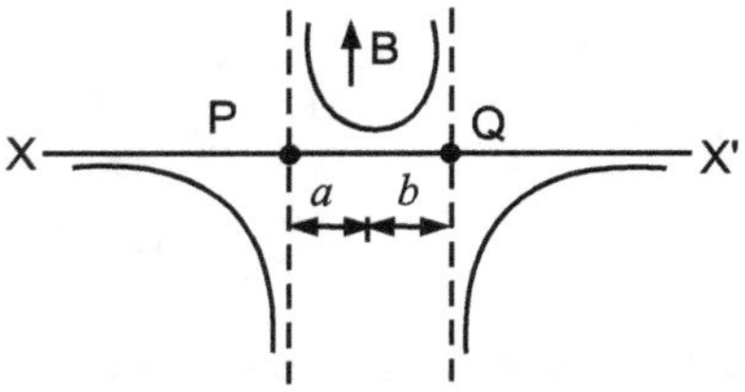

(b)

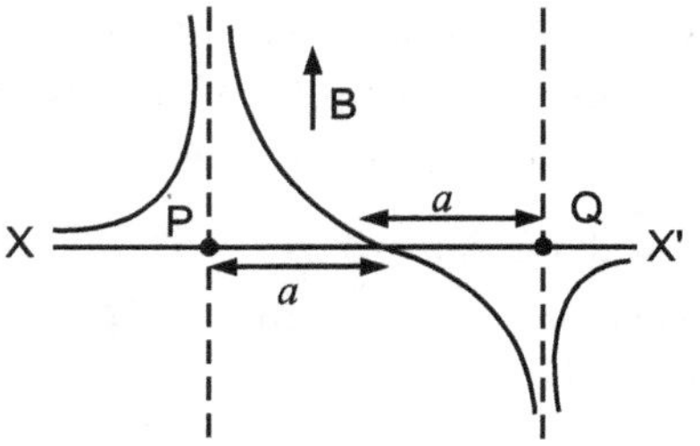

(c)

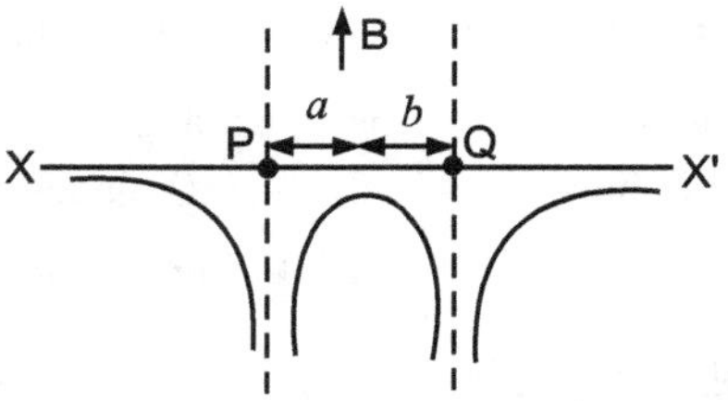

(d)

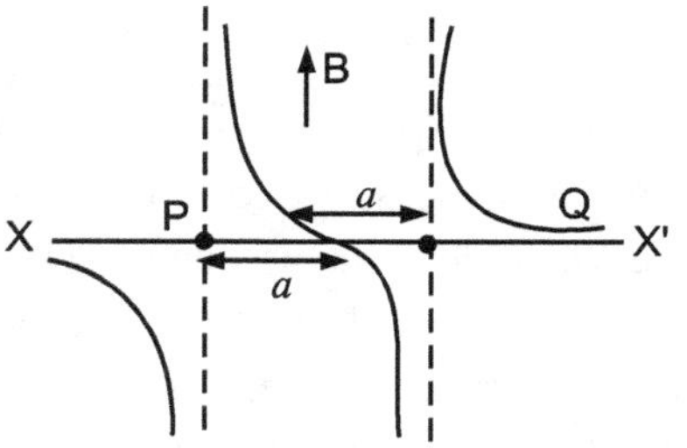

55. An electron is falling vertically through the earth's magnetic field. In which direction, is it likely to deflect ?

(a) Due South (b) Due West

(c) Due East (d) Due North

56. A rectangular loop of 2 cm × 1.5 cm is placed in a magnetic field of 0.025 Tesla such that the face of the loop is parallel to the magnetic field. If the number of turns in the coil is 1600 and carries a current of 50 mA, then torque on the coil is :

(a) 4.8×10^{-3} Nm (b) 4.8 Nm
(c) 4.8×10^{-2} Nm (d) 4.8×10^{-4} Nm

57. A proton beam is heading towards you through a magnetic field directing downwards. The proton beam will deflect towards your :

(a) right
(b) left
(c) vertically upward
(d) vertically downward

58. Four wires each of length 'l' are bent into four shapes P, Q, R and S and suspended in a uniform magnetic field. When the same current is passed through each of the four loops, then which statement is true ?

(M.H.P.E.T. 1998)

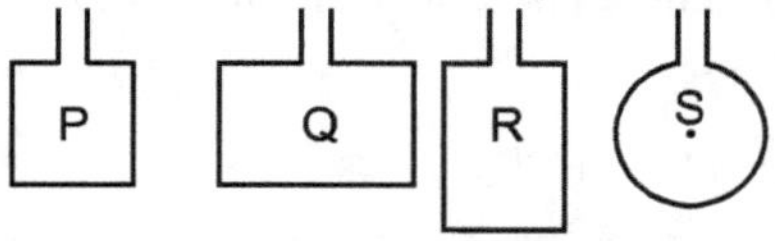

(a) couple on the loop Q will be highest
(b) couple on the loop P will be highest
(c) couple on the loop R will be highest
(d) couple on the loop S will be highest

59. Two identical coils are placed with their planes at right angles such that their centres coincide with each other. If the same current flows through the two wires, then what is the ratio of magnitude of the resultant magnetic field at the centre and the field due to one coil along its axis ?

(a) 2 : 1 (b) $1 : \sqrt{2}$
(c) $\sqrt{2} : 1$ (d) 1 : 1

60. A current of 1 A is flowing in an equilateral triangle of side 4.5×10^{-2} m. The magnetic field at the centroid of the triangle is :

(Roorkee 1991)

(a) 4×10^{-5} T (b) 3×10^{-5} T
(c) 10^{-5} T (d) $2\sqrt{3} \times 10^{-5}$ T

61. A rectangle coil carrying a current of 0.1 A and having 20 turns of 10 cm × 5 cm is suspended at one side as shown in the figure. Torque on the loop if it is mounted with its plane at an angle of 30° to the direction of a uniform magnetic field of 0.5 Tesla is :

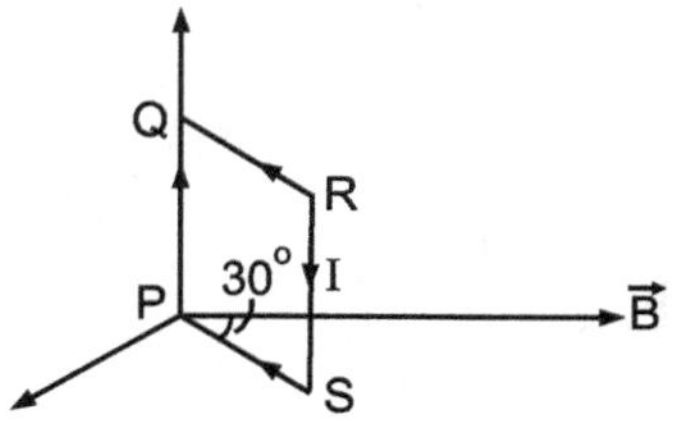

(a) 4.33×10^{-3} Nm (b) 2.5×10^{-3} Nm
(c) 0.33×10^{-2} Nm (d) $4\sqrt{2} \times 10^{-3}$ Nm

62. A cyclotron has frequency 10 MHz and radius of its D is 60 cm. The magnitude of the operating magnetic field is :

(a) 0.96 T (b) 0.656 T
(c) 0.56 T (d) 0.256 T

63. In Q.62, the kinetic energy of the beam produced by the cyclotron is :

(a) 7.412 MeV (b) 4.712 MeV
(c) 2.471 MeV (d) 2.741 MeV

64. If the torsional constant of the suspension of the two moving coil galvanometers has same value and rest of the parameters are as under:

Meter A : N = 30, A = 1.5×10^{-3} m^3, B = 0.25 T, R = 20,

Meter B : N = 35, A = 2×10^{-3} m^3, B = 0.25 T, R = 30

Then $\frac{(\text{Current sensitivity})_A}{(\text{Current sensitivity})_B}$ is :

(a) $\frac{28}{27}$ (b) $\frac{9}{28}$
(c) $\frac{27}{28}$ (d) $\frac{9}{14}$

65. In Q.64, value of $\frac{(\text{Voltage senstivity})_A}{(\text{Voltage sensitivity})_B}$ is :

(a) $\frac{28}{27}$ (b) $\frac{9}{28}$
(c) $\frac{27}{28}$ (d) $\frac{9}{14}$

66. Two protons move parallel to each other with an equal velocity of 300 kms^{-1}. If the two protons are moving at a perpendicular separation of 6 m, then magnetic induction due to one on the other proton will be :

(a) $\vec{B} = \frac{\mu_0}{4\pi}\frac{e(\vec{v}\times\vec{r})}{r^3}$

(b) $\vec{B} = \frac{\mu_0}{4\pi}\frac{e(\vec{v}\times\vec{r})}{r^2}$

(c) $\vec{B} = \frac{\mu_0}{4\pi}\frac{e(\vec{v}\cdot\vec{r})}{r^2}$

(d) $\vec{B} = \frac{\mu_0}{4\pi}\frac{(\vec{v}\times\vec{r})}{r^3}$

67. In Q.66, the force of magnetic interaction $\vec{F}_m$ is given by :

(a) $\frac{\mu_0}{4\pi}\frac{e^2}{r^2}\times(-v^2\vec{r})$ (b) $\frac{\mu_0}{4\pi}\frac{e^2}{r^2}\times(-v^2\vec{r})$

(c) $\frac{\mu_0}{4\pi}\frac{e^2}{r^3}\times(-v^2\vec{r})$ (d) $\frac{\mu_0}{4\pi}\frac{e^2}{r^3}\times(v^2)$

68. In Q.66, force of electric interaction $\vec{F}_e$ is given by :

(a) $\frac{e^2}{r^3}\vec{r}$ (b) $K\frac{e^2}{r^2}\vec{r}$

(c) $\frac{e^2}{r^2}$ (d) $\frac{1}{4\pi\varepsilon_0}\frac{e^2}{r^3}\vec{r}$

69. In Q.66, the ratio of force of magnetic interaction to the electric interaction of the protons is :

(a) 10^{-6} (b) 10^{6}

(c) 10^{-12} (d) 10^{-11}

70. Helium nucleus travelling along a curved path in the magnetic field has velocity v. The velocity of protons moving in the same magnetic field along the same curved path will be :

(a) v (b) $\frac{v}{2}$

(c) $2v$ (d) $4v$

71. A particle of mass m having charge q and kinetic energy E is shot into the region of a magnetic field between the two parallel plates r distance apart. What should be the value of B so that the particle misses collision with the opposite plates ?

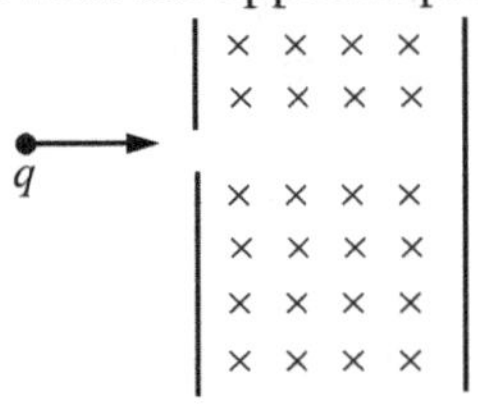

(a) $\frac{\sqrt{2mE}}{qr^2}$ (b) $\frac{\sqrt{2mEr}}{q}$

(c) $\frac{qr}{\sqrt{2mE}}$ (d) $\frac{\sqrt{2mE}}{qr}$

72. A particle of charge q coulomb moves in a circle of radius r metres, at n revolutions per second. The magnetic field intensity at the centre is :

(a) $\frac{2\pi q}{r}$ NA^{-1} m^{-1}

(b) $\frac{2\pi q}{nr}\times 10^{-7}$ NA^{-1} m^{-1}

(c) $\frac{2\pi nq}{r}\times 10^{-7}$ NA^{-1} m^{-1}

(d) $\frac{2\pi q}{r}\times 10^{-7}$ NA^{-1} m^{-1}

73. A current carrying wire is stretched horizontally carrying current along West to East. The direction of a magnetic field 1 m above the wire will be :

(a) West to East (b) North to South

(c) East to West (d) South to North

74. Two concentric circular wires carrying currents I_1, and I_2 have their radii in the ratio 1 : 2 and produce magnetic field at the common centre in the ratio of 1 : 3, then value of ratio $\frac{I_1}{I_2}$ is :

(a) $\frac{1}{4}$ (b) $\frac{1}{3}$

(c) $\frac{1}{6}$ (d) $\frac{1}{2}$

75. The wire loop ABCD is formed by joining two semicircular wires of radii R_1 and R_2 as shown. The magnitude of the magnetic field at common centre 'O' is given by :

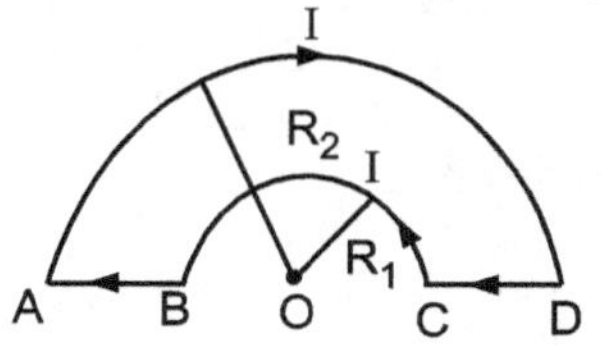

(a) $\frac{\mu_0 I}{4}\left[\frac{R_1}{R_2}-\frac{1}{R_1}\right]$ (b) $\frac{\mu_0 I}{R_1}$

(c) $\frac{\mu_0 I}{4}\left[\frac{1}{R_1}-\frac{1}{R_2}\right]$ (d) $\mu_0 I\left[\frac{1}{R_2}-\frac{1}{R_2}\right]$

76. On connecting a battery to the two corners of a diagonal of a square conductor frame of side 'a', the magnitude of the magnetic field at the centre will be :

(a) Zero (b) $\frac{\mu_0}{\pi a}$

(c) $\frac{2\mu_0}{\pi a}$ (d) $\frac{4\mu_0 I}{\pi a}$

77. The orbital speed of an electron orbiting around the nucleus in a circular orbit of radius 50 mm is 2.2×10^6 ms^{-1}. Then the magnetic dipole moment of an electron is :

(a) 1.6×10^{-19} Am^2 (b) 8.8×10^{-24} Am^2

(c) 5.3×10^{-21} Am^2 (d) 8.8×10^{-16} Am^2

78. Earth's magnetic field at a place is 7×10^{-5} Tesla. This field is to be neutralized by the magnetic field produced at the centre of a circular loop 50 cm in radius. Then the current required to be passed through the loop is :

(a) 0.56 A (b) 5.6 A

(c) 2.8 A (d) 56 A

79. A wire of length l carrying current I is first bent to a circular loop of one turn. The same wire is now wound more sharply to three turns of smaller circular loops. The magnetic field produced at the centre with same current I is :

(a) unaltered

(b) nine times of the first value

(c) one third of its first value

(d) three times of its first value

80. A current of I ampere flows along the inner core of a coaxial cable and returns along the outer conductor. Then the magnetic induction at a distance 'r' metre from the axis is :

(a) zero (b) infinite

(c) $\frac{\mu_0}{4\pi}\frac{2I}{r}$ (d) $\frac{\mu_0}{2}\frac{I}{r}$

81. Two straight long current carrying conductors LOM and NOK carrying current I_1 and I_2 respectively are placed perpendicular to each other. The magnetic field intensity produced at point P at a distance 'a' from 'O' in the direction perpendicular to the plane LMNK is :

(a) $\frac{\mu_0}{2\pi a}\left(I_1^2 + I_2^2\right)^{1/2}$ (b) $\frac{\mu_0}{2\pi a}(I_1 + I_2)^{1/2}$

(c) $\frac{\mu_0}{2\pi a}(I_1 - I_2)^{1/2}$ (d) $\frac{\mu_0}{2\pi a}\left(\frac{I_1 I_2}{I_1 + I_2}\right)^{1/2}$

82. The deflection in a moving coil galvanometer is reduced to half when shunted with a 40 Ω resistance. The resistance of the galvanometer is :

(a) 80 Ω (b) 40 Ω

(c) 15 Ω (d) 20 Ω

83. A 100 turn rectangular coil 24 cm × 30 cm is placed in a uniform magnetic field of 4×10^{-4} Tesla and its plane parallel to the lines of induction. A current of 0.4 A flows in the coil. The torque acting on the coil when 24 cm side is (i) perpendicular and (ii) parallel to the field are respectively :

(a) 115.2×10^{-5} Nm and Zero Nm

(b) 115.2×10^{-5} Nm and 115.2×10^{-5} Nm

(c) Zero Nm and 115.2×10^{-5} Nm

(d) 230.4×10^{-5} Nm and 230.4×10^{-5} Nm

84. A, B and C are long parallel straight wires in air, carrying currents 20 A, 40 A and 60 A respectively. Force on the conductor B is :

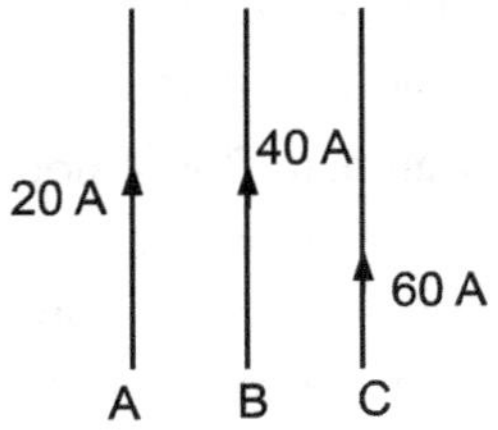

(a) to the left
(b) to the right
(c) perpendicularly outward to the plane of the paper
(d) perpendicularly inward to the plane of the paper

85. Three infinite long straight conductors K, L and M carrying currents 1 A, 2 A and 3 A respectively are placed as shown in the figure. The resultant force on wire L will be:

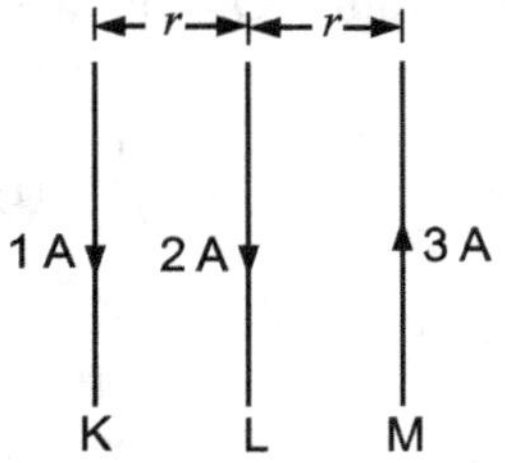

(a) Towards K
(b) Towards M
(c) Zero
(d) Perpendicularly outward to the plane of the paper

86. A circular coil of radius R is placed in a uniform magnetic field with its plane perpendicular to the magnetic field 'B'. If current I is made to flow through the coil as shown in the figure, then the torque experienced by the coil is :

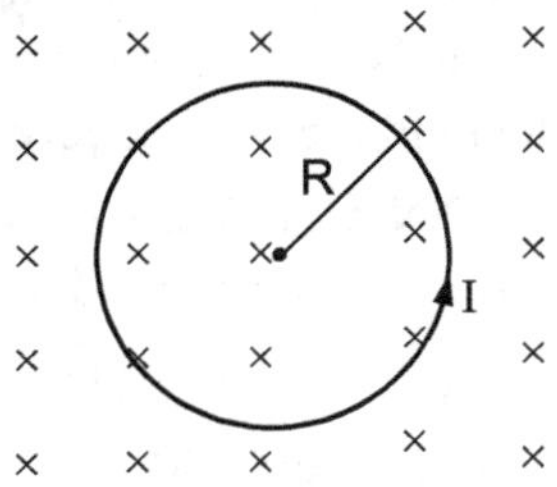

(a) $BI\left(\frac{\pi R^2}{2}\right)$ (b) $BI\pi R^2$
(c) Zero (d) $\frac{BI\pi R^2}{\sqrt{2}}$

87. A straight wire of length l has a magnetic moment M. It is bent in L-shape. The new magnetic moment is :

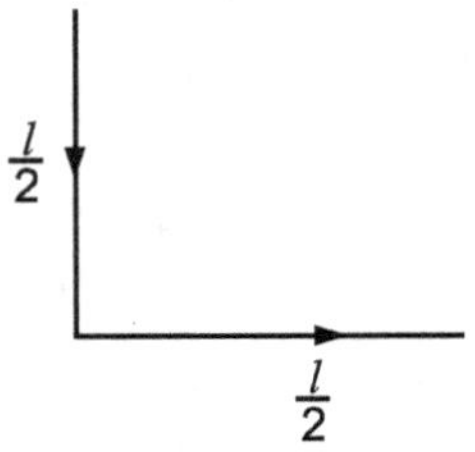

(a) M (b) $\frac{M}{\sqrt{2}}$
(c) 2 M (d) $\frac{M}{2}$

88. An alpha particle, an electron, a proton and a neutron enter a region of uniform magnetic field with equal velocities. The path followed by the particles is labeled as A, B, C and D as shown in the figure. Then track of electron is :

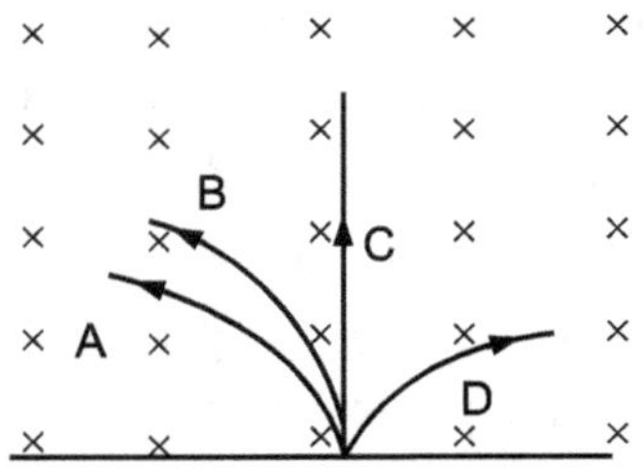

(a) A (b) B
(c) C (d) D

89. In Q. 88, trajectory of neutron is :
(a) A (b) B
(c) C (d) D

90. In Q. 88, trajectory of proton is :
(a) A (b) B
(c) C (d) D

91. In Q. 88, trajectory of α-particle is :
(a) A (b) B
(c) C (d) D

92. The radius of current of the track of a charged particle in a uniform magnetic field is directly proportional to :

(a) the charge on the particle
(b) the momentum of the particle
(c) the energy of the particle
(d) the intensity of magnetic field

93. Two long parallel wires separated by a distance 'x' are carrying a current I ampere each. Force per unit length experienced by each other is :

(a) $\frac{\mu_0 I}{4\pi x}$ (b) $\frac{\mu_0 I}{2\pi x}$
(c) $\frac{\mu_0 I^2}{x^2}$ (d) $\frac{\mu_0 I^2}{2\pi x^2}$

94. A circuit is in the form of a regular hexagon of side 'a'. If current flowing through the hexagon is I, then the magnetic field intensity produced at the centre is given by :

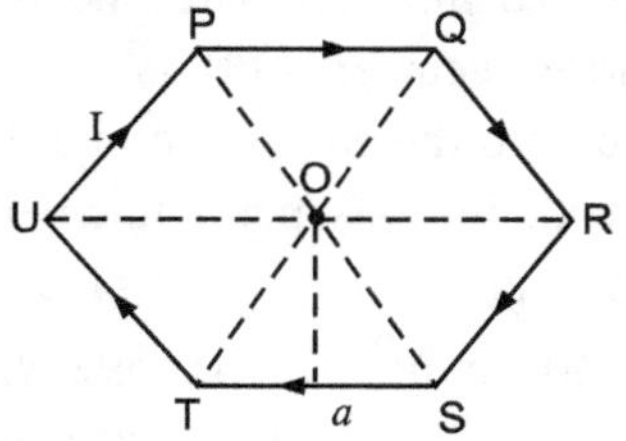

(a) $\frac{\mu_0 I}{2\sqrt{3}\pi a}, \odot$ (b) $\frac{\mu_0 I}{2\sqrt{3}\pi a}, \otimes$
(c) $\frac{\sqrt{3}\mu_0 I}{\pi a}, \odot$ (d) $\frac{\sqrt{3}\mu_0 I}{\pi a}, \otimes$

95. A particle of mass m = 1.6×10^{-27} kg and charge q = 1.6×10^{-19} C enters a region of uniform magnetic field of 1 Tesla along the direction shown in the figure. The speed of the particle is 10^7 ms^{-1}. If the particle leaves the region of the field at the point F, then angle θ is : **(Roorke 1992, I.I.T. 1994)**

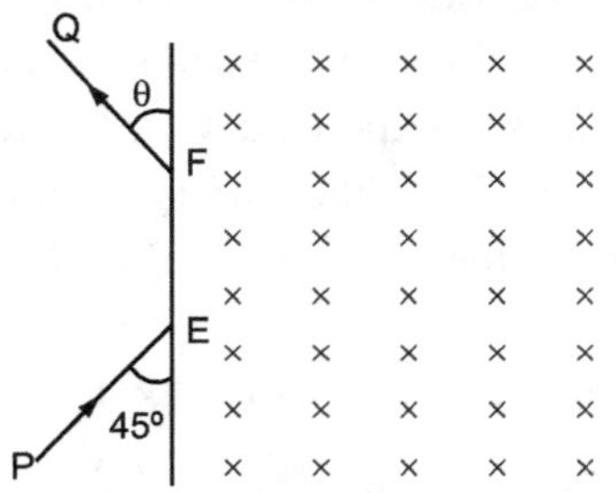

(a) 30° (b) 60°
(c) 45° (d) 15°

96. In Q. 95, distance EF is :

(a) 0.1414 m (b) 2.82 m
(c) 1.414 m (d) 0.707 m

97. Force on each segment AB, BC, CD and DE of the wire shown below is :

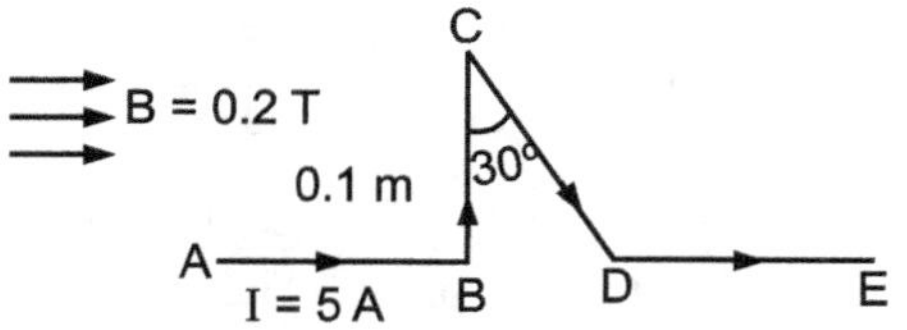

(a) 0 N, 0.1 N, 0.091 N, 0 N
(b) 0.1 N, 0 N, 0.91 N, 0 N
(c) 0.1 N, 0 N, 0 N, 0.91 N
(d) 0 N, 0.1 N, 0.05 N, 0N

98. A copper rod weighing 100 gm rests on two parallel rails 40 cm apart and carries a current of 5 amp. from one rail to another. The limiting coefficient between the rails and the copper rod is 0.4. The smallest magnetic field applied perpendicular to the plane of rails that would cause the rod to slide is :

(a) 0.98 T (b) 0.196 T
(c) 19.6 T (d) 4 T

99. A coil having N turns is wound tightly in the form of a spiral with inner and outer radii a and b respectively. When a current I passes through the coil, the magnetic field at the centre is : **(I.I.T. Screening 2001)**

(a) $\frac{2\mu_0 NI}{a}$ (b) $\frac{\mu_0 NI}{b}$
(c) $\frac{2\mu_0 NI}{2(b-a)} \log\frac{b}{a}$ (d) $\frac{\mu_0 NI}{(b-a)} \log\frac{b}{a}$

100. Two particles X and Y, having equal changes after being accelerated through the same potential difference enter a region of uniform magnetic field and describe circular paths of radii R_1 and R_2 respectively. The ratio of the mass of X to Y is : **(I.I.T. 1998)**

(a) $\left(\frac{R_1}{R_2}\right)^{1/2}$ (b) $\frac{R_2}{R_1}$
(c) $\left(\frac{R_1}{R_2}\right)^2$ (d) $\frac{R_1}{R_2}$

101. Two particles P and Q of masses m_P and m_Q respectively and having the same charge are moving in a plane :

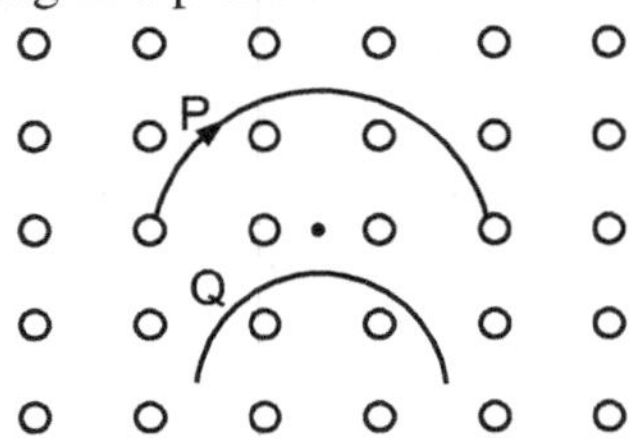

A uniform magnetic field exists perpendicular to this plane. The speeds of particles are v_P and v_Q respectively and the trajectories are as shown in the figure, then

(I.I.T. Screening 2001)

(a) $m_P v_P < m_Q v_Q$ (b) $m_P v_Q < m_Q v_P$

(c) $m_P = m_Q$ and $v_P = v_Q$ (d) $m_P v_P > m_Q v_Q$

102. A proton, a deuteron and an α-particle having the same K.E. are moving in circular orbits in the given magnetic field B. If R_p, R_d and R_α denote the radii of orbits of the particles respectively then: **(I.I.T. 1997)**

(a) $R_p = R_d = R_\alpha$ (b) $R_\alpha = R_p < R_d$

(c) $R_\alpha > R_d > R_p$ (d) $R_\alpha = R_d < R_p$

103. A magnetic field of 0.004 $\hat{k}$ T exerts a force of $(4i + 3j) \times 10^{-10}$ N on a particle having charge of 10^{-9} C and moving in xy plane. The velocity of the particle is :

(a) $(75\,i + 100\,j)$ ms^{-1}

(b) $(-75\,i + 100\,j)$ ms^{-1}

(c) $(75\,i - 100\,j)$ ms^{-1}

(d) $(-75\,i - 100\,j)$ ms^{-1}

104. Two solenoids A and B of equal length but different numbers of turns, are arranged coaxially as shown in the figure.

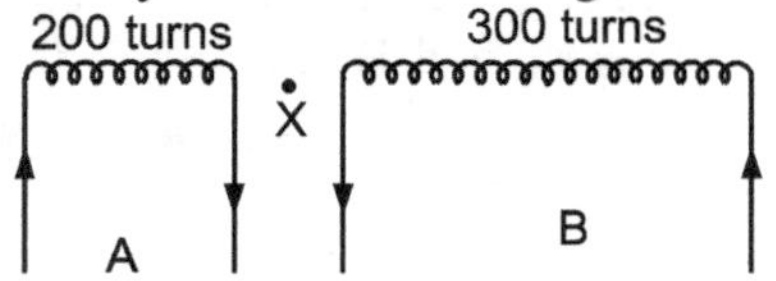

Solenoid A has 200 turns and B has 300 turns. If current flowing through solenoid B is 1 A, then what must be the current flowing through A such that the resultant magnetic field at the pt 'X' midway between the two solenoids is zero :

(a) $\frac{2}{3}$ A (b) $\frac{3}{2}$ A

(c) $\frac{4}{3}$ A (d) 1 A

105. A proton and an α-particle enter a uniform magnetic field perpendicularly with the same speed. If proton takes 25 μs to make 5 revolutions, then the periodic time for the α-particle is :

(a) 10 μs (b) 5 μs

(c) 50 μs (d) 25 μs

106. A solenoid of length 0.4 m and having 500 turns of wire carries a current of 3 A. A thin coil having 10 turns of wire and of radius 0.01 m carries a current of 0.4 A. The torque required to hold the coil in the middle of the solenoid with its axis perpendicular to the axis of the solenoid is : **(I.I.T. 1994)**

(a) 5.92×10^{-6} Nm (b) 0.1592 Nm

(c) 3.7×10^{-6} Nm (d) 0.137 Nm

107. A wire is bent to form a closed regular hexagon of each side 10 cm. If the wire carries a current of 5 A, then magnetic field produced at the centre is :

(a) 3.46×10^{-5} T (b) 1.5×10^{-5} T

(c) 12×10^{-5} T (d) 10^{-5} T

108. A solenoid is 0.4 metre long and 5 cm in diameter and has three layers of turns, each layer carrying 450 turns and current I ampere. A wire of length 2 cm placed in the middle of the solenoid and perpendicular to its axis, experiences a force of 2.7×10^{-4} N. When the wire is in series with the solenoid, then current I in the wire is :

(I.I.T. 1997)

(a) 3.56 A (b) 1.78 A

(c) 0.89 A (d) 0.49 A

109. Two long straight parallel wires are 2 metres apart, perpendicular to the plane of the paper as shown in the figure. The wire A carries a current of 9.6 A directed into the plane of the paper. The wire B carries current such that the magnetic field intensity at P is zero. The magnitude and direction of the current in B is :

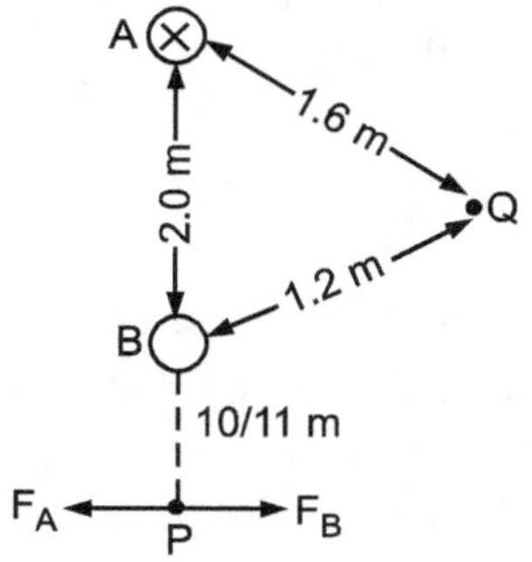

(a) 2 A (b) 3 A
(c) 2.5 A (d) 4 A

110. In Q. No. 109, magnetic field intensity at S is :

(a) 2×10^{-6} T (b) 10^{-6} T
(c) 4×10^{-6} T (d) 2×10^{-5} T

111. In Q. 109, force per unit length on wire B is:

(a) 14.4×10^{-7} N (b) 57.6×10^{-7} N
(c) 28.8×10^{-7} N (d) $3\pi \times 10^{-7}$ N

112. A circular coil of 200 turns, with radius 2.0 cm and carrying current of 0.2 amp is in a magnetic field of 1.2 Tesla. Torque exerted by the field on the dipole is :

(a) 0.3 Nm (b) 0.6 Nm
(c) 1.5 Nm (d) 0.15 Nm

113. In Q. No. 112, how much work must an external agent do to turn it from $\theta = 0$ to $\theta = 180°$?

(a) 0.3 J (b) 0.6 J
(c) 1.5 J (d) 0.15 J

114. There is magnetic field acting in a plane perpendicular to the sheet of paper in the downward direction (figure). Particles in vacuum move in the plane of paper from left to right. The path indicated by an arrow could be travelled by :

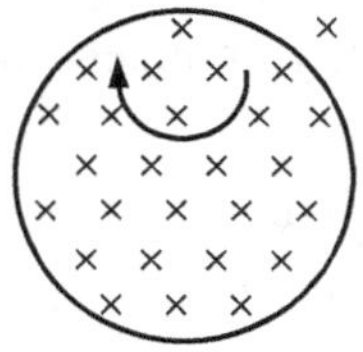

(a) Proton (b) Neutron
(c) Electron (d) α -particle

115. Two long straight conductors carry equal currents I and are separated by a distance *r*. They exert a force F on each other. If the current in each wire is doubled and the separation between them is halved, the magnetic force will become :

(a) F / 8 (b) F / 2
(c) 2F (d) 8F

116. The magnetic moment of a current loop is given by :

(a) A (b) Am^2
(c) Am^{-1} (d) Am^{-2}

117. A proton charge (+ e coulomb) enters in a magnetic field of strength B Tesla making an angle 30° with the direction of magnetic field with speed *v*. The magnetic force on the proton is :

(a) evB (b) Zero
(c) ∞ (d) $evB/2$

118. A moving charge produces :

(a) electric and magnetic fields both
(b) electric field only
(c) magnetic field only
(d) neither electric nor magnetic field

119. A charged particle enters at 30° to the magnetic field. Its path becomes :

(a) circular
(b) helical
(c) elliptical
(d) straight line

120. A uniform electric field and a uniform magnetic field are produced, pointed in the same direction. An electron is projected with its velocity pointed in the same direction:

(a) the electron will turn to its left
(b) the electron will turn to its right
(c) the electron velocity will increase in magnitude
(d) the electron velocity will decrease in magnitude

121. A copper rod carries a direct current. The magnetic field due to the current will be :

(a) only inside the rod
(b) only outside the rod
(c) both inside and outside the rod
(d) neither inside nor outside the rod

122. Two parallel wires A and B carry currents of 10 and 2 amp respectively in opposite directions. The distance between the wires is 10 cm. If the wire A is infinitely long and the wire B has a length of 2 metres, then the force acting on B will be :

(a) 8×10^{-5} N (b) 4×10^{-5} N
(c) $8\pi \times 10^{-7}$ N (d) 4×10^{-7} N

123. A conducting circular loop of radius r carries a constant current i. It is placed in a uniform magnetic field B such that B is perpendicular to the plane of loop. The magnetic force acting on the loop is :

(a) Bir (b) $2\pi irB$
(c) 0 (d) πirB

124. Two concentric coils carry the same current flowing in opposite directions such that the diameter of the outer is double than that of the inner one. The magnetic field produced by the smaller coil at the centre is T, the magnetic field at the common centre is :

(a) T (b) T/2
(c) 2T (d) 4 T

125. An electron revolves in a circular path with a frequency 6×10^{15} per second. The current in the loop will be :

(a) 0.96 mA (b) 0.96 μA
(c) 28.8 A (d) 2.88 A

126. A charged particle is whirled in a horizontal circle on a frictionless table by attaching it to a string fixed at one point. If a magnetic field is switched on in the vertical direction, the tension in the string :

(a) will increase
(b) will decrease
(c) will remain the same
(d) may increase or decrease

127. An electron describes half a revolution in a circular path of radius r inside a magnetic field of strength B. The energy gained by the electron is :

(a) Zero (b) $Bev \times \pi r$
(c) $\frac{1}{4}mv^2$ (d) $Bev.2r$

128. If n is the number of turns per unit length and current flowing through a solenoid is i, then the magnetic field near the edges of the solenoid is :

(a) $\mu_0 ni$ (b) $\frac{\mu_0 ni}{2}$
(c) $\frac{\mu_0 ni}{2\pi}$ (d) $\frac{\mu_0 ni}{4}$

129. A stream of electrons is projected horizontally to the right. A straight conductor carrying a current is supported parallel to the electron stream and above it. If the current in the conductor is from left to right, then what will be the effect on the electron stream ?

(a) The electron stream will be speeded up towards the right.
(b) The electron stream will be retarded.
(c) The electron stream will be pulled upward.
(d) The electron stream will be pulled downward.

130. The torque acting on a rectangular loop having area A, carrying current i and placed in a magnetic field B with which the loop makes an angle θ is given by :

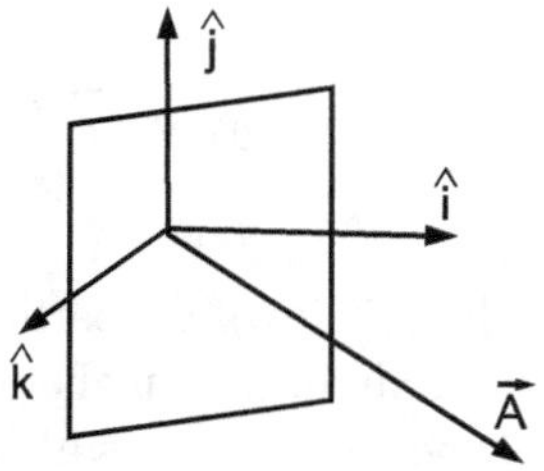

(a) $Bi\,A\hat{i}$ (b) $Bi\,A\sin\theta\hat{k}$

(c) $Bi\,A\cos\theta\,\hat{j}$ (d) $Bi\,A\tan\theta\hat{k}$

131. A proton moving with a constant velocity passes through a region of space without change in its velocity. If E and B represent electric and magnetic fields respectively, this region of space may not have :

(a) $E = 0, B = 0$ (b) $E = 0, B \neq 0$

(c) $E \neq 0, B = 0$ (d) $E \neq 0, B \neq 0$

132. Currents of 10 A and 2 A are passed through two parallel wires A and B respectively in opposite directions. If the wire A is infinitely long and length of wire B is 2 m, the force on conductor B, which is situated at a distance of 10 cm from A, will be :

(a) 8×10^{-5} N (b) 5×10^{-5} N

(c) $8\pi \times 10^{-7}$ N (d) $4\pi \times 10^{-7}$ N

133. A positively charged particle projected towards east is deflected towards north by a magnetic field. The field may be :

(a) towards west (b) towards south

(c) upward (d) downward

134. A charged particle moves along a circle under the action of possible constant electric and magnetic fields. Which of the following are possible ?

(a) $E = 0, B = 0$ (b) $E = 0, B \neq 0$

(c) $E \neq 0, B = 0$ (d) $E \neq 0, B \neq 0$

135. A rectangular loop carrying a current *i* is situated near a long straight wire such that the wire is parallel to one of the sides of the loop and is B in the plane of the loop. If a steady current I is established in the wire, as shown in figure, the loop will :

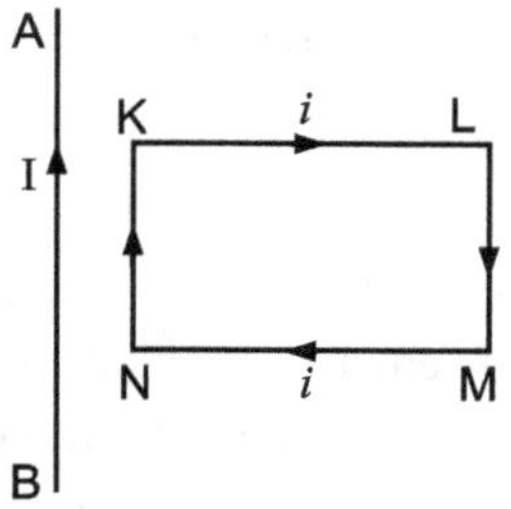

(a) rotate about an axis parallel to the wire

(b) move away from the wire

(c) move towards the wire

(d) remain stationary

136. In the given figure, PQ is a long current-carrying wire which is placed near a current-carrying coil. The direction of the force acting on PQ will be :

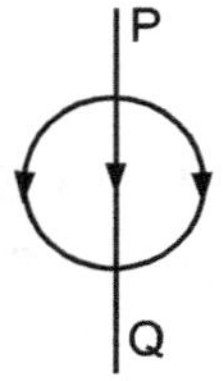

(a) parallel to PQ towards P

(b) parallel to PQ towards Q

(c) perpendicular to PQ towards right

(d) perpendicular to PQ towards left

137. A charged particle moves in a gravity free space with change in velocity. Which of the following is possible?

(a) $E = 0, B = 0$ (b) $E = 0, B \neq 0$

(c) $E \neq 0, B = 0$ (d) $E \neq 0, B \neq 0$

138. A straight wire of diameter 0.5 mm carrying a current of 1 ampere is replaced by another wire of 1 mm diameter carrying the same current. The strength of the magnetic field far away is :

(a) twice the earlier value

(b) one-half of the earlier value

(c) one-quarter of the earlier value

(d) same as the earlier value

139. Which of the following particles will have minimum frequency of revolution when projected with the same velocity perpendicular to a magnetic field ?

(a) Electron (b) Proton

(c) He^+ (d) Li^+

140. The magnetic field of a given length of wire carrying a current for a single turn circular coil at centre is B, then its value for two turns for the same wire when the same current passes through it is : **(CBSE 2002)**

(a) B/4 (b) B/2

(c) 2B (d) 4B

141. A helium nucleus makes a full rotation in a circle of radius 0.8 m in 2 s. The value of the magnetic field B at the centre of the circle will be :

(a) $10^{-19}/\mu_0$ (b) $10^{-19}\mu_0$

(c) $2 \times 10^{-19}\mu_0$ (d) $2 \times 10^{-19}/\mu_0$

142. The magnetic flux density B at a distance r from a long straight wire carrying a steady current varies with r as shown in figure :

(a)

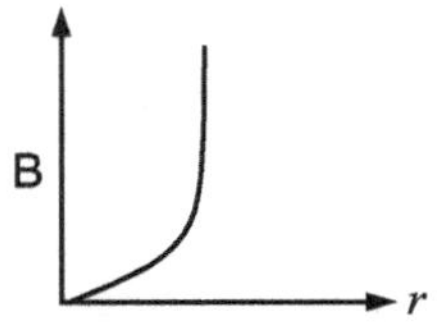

(b)

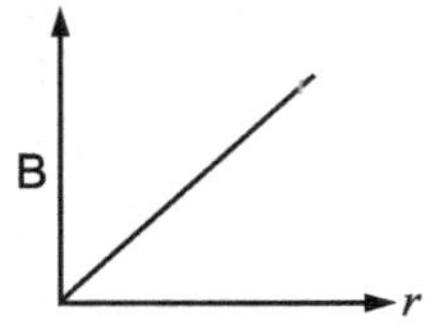

(c)

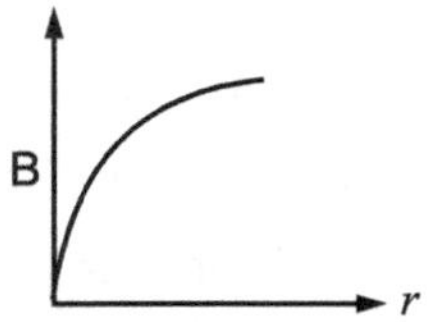

(d)

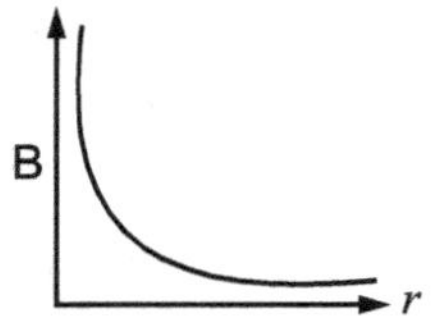

143. In a certain region of space, electric field $\vec{E}$ and magnetic field $\vec{B}$ are perpendicular to each other and an electron enters in a region perpendicular to the directions of both $\vec{B}$ and $\vec{E}$ both and moves undeflected, then velocity of the electron is :

(a) $\frac{|\vec{E}|}{|\vec{B}|}$ (b) $\vec{E} \times \vec{B}$

(c) $\frac{|\vec{B}|}{|\vec{E}|}$ (d) $\vec{E} \cdot \vec{B}$

144. Which of the following particles will experience maximum magnetic force (magnitude) when projected with the same velocity perpendicular to a magnetic field?

(a) Electron (b) Proton

(c) He^+ (d) Li^{++}

145. A current of 50 mA flows in a rectangular coil of effective area 75×10^{-3} m^2. If the coil is in equilibrium in a field of 40 G, then the torque is :

(a) 150 Nm (b) 1.5×10^{-5} Nm

(e) 1.5×10^{7} Nm (d) 1.5×10^{-3} Nm

146. A cyclotron can be used to accelerate

(a) α-particles (b) β-particles

(c) neutrons (d) positrons

147. Magnetic effect of current was discovered by :

(a) Faraday (b) Oersted

(c) Ampere (d) Bohr

148. Two streams of protons move parallel to each other in the same direction. They will :

(a) attract each other

(b) repel each other

(c) neither attract nor repel

(d) rotate

149. Two particles X and Y having equal charges, after being accelerated through the same potential difference, enter a region of uniform magnetic field and describe circular paths of radii R_1 and R_2 respectively. The ratio of the mass of X to that of Y is :

(a) $(R_1 / R_2)^{1/2}$ (b) R_1 / R_2

(c) $(R_1 / R_2)^2$ (d) R_2 / R_1

150. A coil having N-turns is wound tightly in the form of a spiral with inner and outer radii 'a' and 'b' respectively. When current 'I' passes through the coil, the magnetic field at the centre is :

(a) $\frac{\mu_0 NI}{b}$ (b) $\frac{\mu_0 NI}{a}$

(c) $\frac{\mu_0 NI}{2(b-a)} \log_e \frac{b}{a}$ (d) $\frac{\mu_0 NI}{b-a} \log_e \frac{b}{a}$

151. A rectangular coil has 100 turns each of area 50 cm^2. It is capable of rotation about an axis joining the mid point of the two opposite sides. When a current of 5 A is passed through it, while its plane is at right angles to a uniform magnetic field, it experiences a torque of 5 Nm. The magnetic field will be :

(a) T (b) 2 T

(c) 0.5 T (d) 1.5 T

152. A particle carrying a charge 100 times the charge on an electron is revolving once per second on a circular path of radius 0.8 m. The value of the magnetic field produced at the centre will be :

(a) $10^{-7}/\mu_0$ (b) $10^{-17}\mu_0$

(c) $10^{-6}\mu_0$ (d) $10^{-7}\mu_0$

153. A circular coil A has a radius R and the current flowing through it is I. Another circular coil B has a radius 2R and if 2I is the current flowing through it, then the magnetic fields at the centre of the circular coil are in the ratio of (i.e. B_1 to B_2) :

(a) 4 : 1 (b) 2 : 1

(e) 3 : 1 (d) 1 : 1

154. An electric current 'i' enters and leaves a uniform circular wire of radius a through diametrically opposite points. A charged 'q' moving along the axis of the circular wire passes through its centre at speed 'v'. The magnetic force acting on the particle when it passes through the centre has a magnitude :

(a) $qv\frac{\mu_0 i}{2a}$ (b) $qv\frac{\mu_0 i}{2\pi a}$

(c) $qv\frac{\mu_0 i}{a}$ (d) Zero

155. Two thin, long, parallel wires separated by a distance b are carrying a current of i each. The magnitude of the force per unit length exerted by one wire on the other is :

(a) $\frac{\mu_0 i^2}{b^2}$ (b) $\frac{\mu i^2}{2\pi b}$

(c) $\frac{\mu_0 i}{2\pi b}$ (d) $\frac{\mu_0 i}{2\pi b^2}$

156. Two long parallel wires P and Q are held perpendicular to the plane of the paper with a distance of 5 m between them. If P and Q carry current of 2.5 A and 5 A respectively in the same direction, then the magnetic field at a point half-way between the wires is:

(a) $\frac{\mu_0}{\pi}$ (b) $\frac{\mu_0}{2\pi}$

(c) $\frac{\sqrt{3}\mu_0}{\pi}$ (d) $\frac{3\mu_0}{2\pi}$

157. Which of the following particles will describe the smallest circle when projected with the same velocity perpendicular to a magnetic field ?

(a) Electron (b) Proton

(c) He^+ (d) Li^+

158. A particle of mass m and charge q moves with a constant velocity v along the positive x-axis. It enters a region containing a uniform magnetic field B directed along the negative z-axis, extending from $x = a$ to $x = b$. The minimum value of v required so that the particle can just enter the region $x > b$ is : **(I.I.T. Screening 2002)**

(a) $\frac{qbB}{m}$ (b) $\frac{q(b-a)B}{m}$

(c) $\frac{qbB}{m}$ (d) $\frac{q(b+a)B}{2m}$

159. A circular loop of area 1 cm^2, carrying a current of 10 A, is placed in a magnetic field of 0.1 T perpendicular to the plane of the loop. The torque on the loop due to the magnetic field is :

(a) Zero (b) 10^{-4} Nm

(c) 10^{-2} Nm (d) 1 Nm

160. A long straight wire carries a current i. A particle having charge q and mass m, kept at a distance X_o from the wire as shown in the figure is projected towards it with a speed v. What is the minimum separation (X_{min}) between the wire and the particle ?

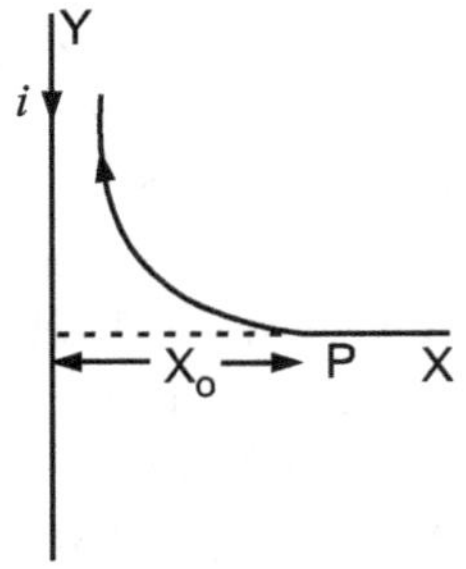

(a) $X_{min} = 2X_o\, e^{\left(\frac{-2\pi mv}{\mu_0 qi}\right)}$

(b) $X_{min} = X_o\, e^{\left(\frac{-2\pi mv}{\mu_0 qi}\right)}$

(c) $X_{min} = \dfrac{X_o\, e^{\left(\frac{-2\pi mv}{\mu_0 qi}\right)}}{2}$

(d) $X_{min} = \dfrac{X_o\, e^{\left(\frac{-2\pi mv}{\mu_0 qi}\right)}}{8}$

161. Two ions have equal masses but one is singly-ionized and the other is doubly-ionized. They are projected from the same place in a uniform magnetic field with the same velocity perpendicular to the field then:

(a) both ions will go along circles of equal radii

(b) the circle described by the singly-ionized charge will have a radius double that of the other circle

(c) the two circles do not touch each other

(d) the two circles intersect each other

162. Find the magnetic induction of the field at the point O of a loop with current I, whose shape is illustrated in the figure. The radii a and b as well as the angle ϕ are known:

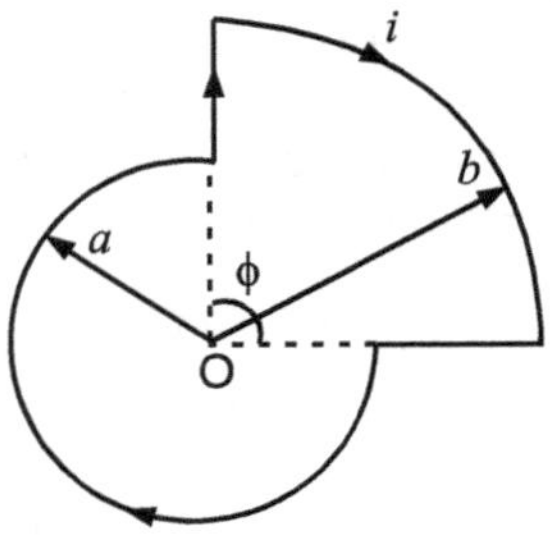

(a) $\frac{\mu_0 I}{4\pi}\left(\frac{2\pi-\phi}{a}+\frac{\phi}{b}\right)$ (b) $\frac{\mu_0 I}{4\pi a}$

(c) $\frac{\mu_0 I}{4\pi a}\left(\frac{3\pi}{4a}+\frac{\sqrt{2}}{b}\right)$ (d) None

163. Find the magnetic induction of the field at the point O of a loop with current I, whose shape is illustrated in figure. The radius a and side b are known :

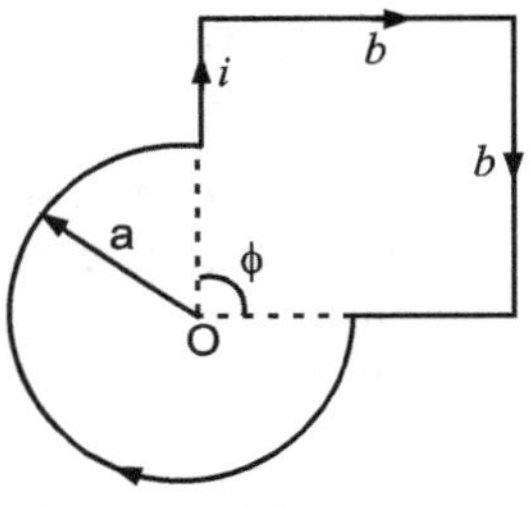

(a) $\frac{\mu_0 I}{4\pi}\left(\frac{2\pi-\phi}{a}+\frac{\phi}{b}\right)$ (b) $\frac{\mu_0 I}{4\pi a}$

(c) $\frac{\mu_0 I}{4\pi}\left(\frac{3\pi}{4a}+\frac{\sqrt{2}}{b}\right)$ (d) None

164. For a positively charged particle moving in the x-y plane initially along the x-axis, there is a sudden change in its path due to the presence of electric and/or magnetic fields beyond P. The curved path is shown in the x-y plane and is found to be non-circular. Which one of the following combinations is possible ? **(I.I.T. Screening 2003)**

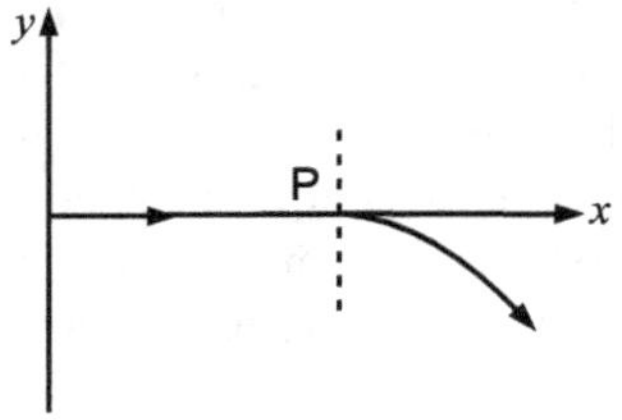

(a) $\vec{E} = 0;\ \vec{B} = b\hat{i} + c\hat{k}$

(b) $\vec{E} = a\hat{i};\ \vec{B} = c\hat{k} + a\hat{i}$

(c) $\vec{E} = 0; \vec{B} = c\hat{j} + b\hat{k}$

(d) $\vec{E} = a\hat{i}; \vec{B} = c\hat{k} + b\hat{j}$

165. A conducting loop carrying a current I is placed in a uniform magnetic field pointing into the plane of the paper as shown. The loop will have a tendency to : **(I.I.T. Screening 2003)**

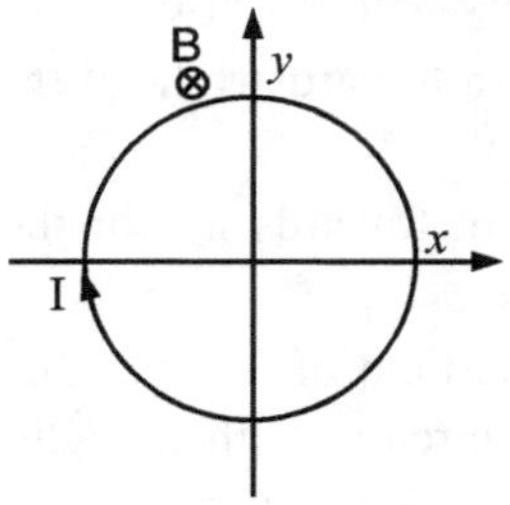

(a) contract
(b) expand
(c) move towards +ve x-axis
(d) move towards –ve x-axis

166. A current carrying loop is placed in a uniform magnetic field in four different orientations, (i), (ii), (iii) and (iv). Arrange them in the decreasing order of potential energy: **(I.I.T. Screening 2003)**

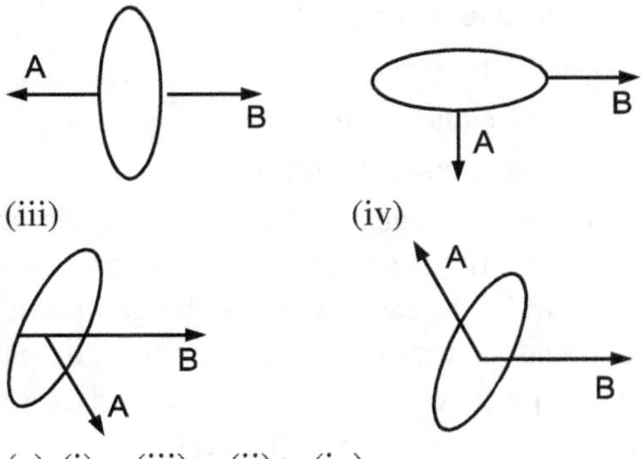

(a) (i) > (iii) > (ii) > (iv)
(b) (i) > (ii) > (iii) > (iv)
(c) (i) > (iv) > (ii) > (iii)
(d) (iii) > (iv) > (i) > (ii)

167. An electron travelling with a speed u along the positive x-axis enters into a region of magnetic field where $B = B_0k$ $(x > 0)$. It comes out of the region with speed v, then: **(I.I.T. Screening 2004)**

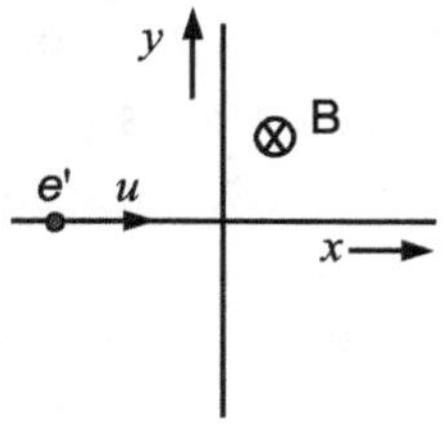

(a) $v = u$ at $y > 0$ (b) $v = u$ at $y < 0$
(c) $v > u$ at $y > 0$ (d) $v > u$ at $y < 0$

168. A cylindrical conducting rod is kept with its axis along the positive z-axis, where a uniform magnetic field exists parallel to the z-axis. The current induced in the cylinder is: **(I.I.T. 2005)**

(a) zero
(b) clockwise as seen from + z-axis
(c) anti-clockwise as seen from + z-axis
(d) opposite to the direction of magnetic field

169. In the given diagram, a line of force of a particular force field is shown. Out of the following options, it can never represent : **(I.I.T. 2006)**

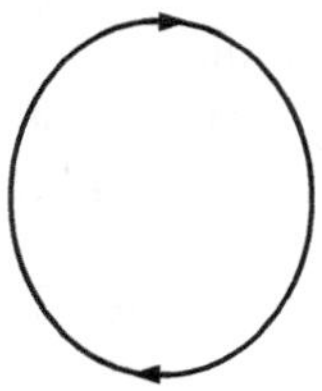

(a) an electrostatic field
(b) a magnetostatic field
(c) a gravitational field of a mass at rest
(d) an induced electric field

170. An infinite current carrying wire passes through point O and perpendicular to the plane containing a current carrying loop ABCD is shown in the figure. Choose the correct option(s) : **(I.I.T. 2006)**

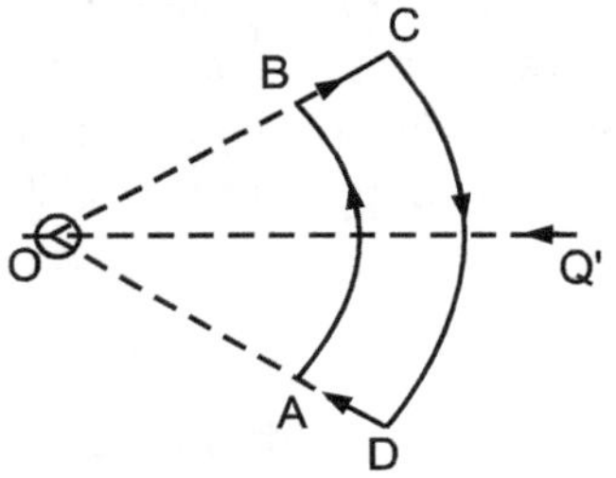

(a) Net force on the loop is zero.
(b) Net torque on the loop is zero.
(c) As seen from O, the loop rotates clockwise.
(d) As seen from O, the loop rotates anticlockwise.

171. One conducting U tube can slide inside another as shown in figure, maintaining electrical contacts between the tubes. The magnetic field B is perpendicular to the plane of the figure. If each tube moves towards the other at a constant speed v, then the emf induced in the circuit in terms of B, l and v, where l is width of each tube, will be: **(A.I.E.E.E. 2005)**

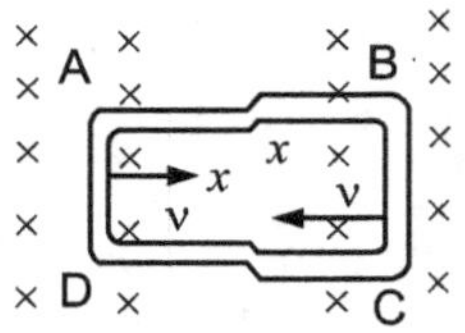

(a) Blv (b) $-Blv$
(c) Zero (d) $2\,Blv$

172. Two thin, long parallel wires separated by a distance 'd' carry a current of 'i' in the same direction. They will : **(A.I.E.E.E. 2005)**

(a) attract each other with a force of $\frac{\mu_0 i^2}{2\pi d}$.
(b) repel each other with a force of $\frac{\mu_0 i^2}{2\pi d}$.
(c) attract each other with a force of $\frac{\mu_0 i^2}{(2\pi d)^2}$.
(d) repel each other with a force of $\frac{\mu_0 i^2}{(2\pi d)^2}$.

173. Two concentric coils each of radius equal to 2π cm are placed at right angles to each other. 3 ampere and 4 ampere are the currents flowing in each coil respectively. The magnetic induction in Wb/m^2 at centre of the coils will be ($\mu_0 = 4\pi \times 10^{-7}$ Wb/A-m): **(A.I.E.E.E. 2005)**

(a) 12×10^{-5} (b) 10^{-5}
(c) 5×10^{-5} (d) 7×10^{-5}

174. A uniform electric field and a uniform magnetic field are acting along the same direction in a certain region. If an electron is projected along the direction of the fields with a certain velocity, then : **(A.I.E.E.E. 2005)**

(a) its velocity will decrease
(b) its velocity will increase
(c) it will turn towards right of the direction of motion
(d) it will turn towards left of the direction of motion

175. A charged particle of mass m and charge q travels on a circular path of radius r that is perpendicular to a magnetic field B. The time taken by the particle to complete one revolution is : **(A.I.E.E.E. 2005)**

(a) $\frac{2\pi mq}{B}$ (b) $\frac{2\pi q^2 B}{m}$
(c) $\frac{2\pi qB}{m}$ (d) $\frac{2\pi m}{qB}$

176. A magnetic needle is kept in a non-uniform magnetic field. It experiences : **(A.I.E.E.E. 2006)**

(a) a torque, but not a force
(b) neither a force nor a torque
(c) a force and a torque
(d) a force, but not a torque

177. In a region, steady and uniform electric and magnetic fields are present. These two fields are parallel to each other. A charged particle is released from rest in this region. The path of the particle will be a : **(A.I.E.E.E. 2006)**

(a) Circle (b) Helix
(c) Straight line (d) Ellipse

178. Needles N_1, N_2 and N_3 are made of a ferromagnetic, a paramagnetic and a diamagnetic substance respectively. A magnet when brought close to them will : **(A.I.E.E.E. 2006)**

(a) attract all three of them
(b) attract N_1 and N_2 strongly, but repel N_3

(c) attract N_1 strongly, N_2 weakly and repel N_3 weakly

(d) attract N_1 strongly, but repel N_2 and N_3 weakly

179. Which of the following units denotes the dimensions ML^2/Q^2, where Q denotes the electric charge :

(a) weber (Wb)

(b) Wb/m^2

(c) henry (H)

(d) H/m^2

180. A long solenoid has 200 turns per cm and carries a current *i*. The magnetic field at its centre is 6.28×10^{-2} weber/m^2. Another long solenoid has 100 turns per cm and it carries a current *i*/3. The value of the magnetic field at its centre is : **(A.I.E.E.E. 2006)**

(a) 1.05×10^{-4} weber/m^2

(b) 1.05×10^{-2} weber/m^2

(c) 1.05×10^{-5} weber/m^2

(d) 1.05×10^{-3} weber/m^2

ANSWER KEY

1. (b)	**2.** (d)	**3.** (b)	**4.** (a)	**5.** (a)	**6.** (b)	**7.** (c)	**8.** (c)	**9.** (a)	**10.** (d)
11. (d)	**12.** (c)	**13.** (b)	**14.** (c)	**15.** (d)	**16.** (a)	**17.** (d)	**18.** (a)	**19.** (c)	**20.** (a)
21. (b)	**22.** (d)	**23.** (a)	**24.** (b)	**25.** (a)	**26.** (d)	**27.** (c)	**28.** (b)	**29.** (b)	**30.** (d)
31. (c)	**32.** (a)	**33.**(a&d)	**34.** (a)	**35.** (c)	**36.** (a)	**37.** (c)	**38.** (d)	**39.** (c)	**40.** (b)
41. (b)	**42.** (a)	**43.** (c)	**44.** (b)	**45.** (a)	**46.** (a)	**47.** (d)	**48.** (a)	**49.** (d)	**50.** (b)
51. (a)	**52.** (d)	**53.** (c)	**54.** (c)	**55.** (b)	**56.** (d)	**57.** (a)	**58.** (d)	**59.** (c)	**60.** (a)
61. (a)	**62.** (b)	**63.** (a)	**64.** (d)	**65.** (c)	**66.** (a)	**67.** (c)	**68.** (d)	**69.** (a)	**70.** (c)
71. (d)	**72.** (c)	**73.** (b)	**74.** (c)	**75.** (c)	**76.** (a)	**77.** (b)	**78.** (d)	**79.** (b)	**80.** (a)
81. (a)	**82.** (b)	**83.** (b)	**84.** (b)	**85.** (a)	**86.** (c)	**87.** (b)	**88.** (d)	**89.** (c)	**90.** (a)
91. (b)	**92.** (b)	**93.** (d)	**94.** (d)	**95.** (c)	**96.** (a)	**97.** (a)	**98.** (b)	**99.** (c)	**100.** (c)
101. (d)	**102.** (b)	**103.** (b)	**104.** (b)	**105.** (a)	**106.** (a)	**107.** (a)	**108.** (b)	**109.** (b)	**110.** (a)
111. (c)	**112.** (d)	**113.** (a)	**114.** (c)	**115.** (d)	**116.** (b)	**117.** (d)	**118.** (a)	**119.** (b)	**120.** (d)
121. (b)	**122.** (a)	**123.** (c)	**124.** (b)	**125.** (a)	**126.** (d)	**127.** (a)	**128.** (b)	**129.** (c)	**130.** (c)
131. (c)	**132.** (a)	**133.** (d)	**134.** (b)	**135.** (c)	**136.** (d)	**137.** (c)	**138.** (d)	**139.** (d)	**140.** (d)
141. (b)	**142.** (d)	**143.** (a)	**144.** (d)	**145.** (b)	**146.** (a)	**147.** (b)	**148.** (b)	**149.** (c)	**150.** (c)
151. (b)	**152.** (b)	**153.** (d)	**154.** (d)	**155.** (b)	**156.** (b)	**157.** (a)	**158.** (b)	**159.** (a)	**160.** (b)
161. (b)	**162.** (a)	**163.** (c)	**164.** (b)	**165.** (b)	**166.** (c)	**167.** (b)	**168.** (a)	**169.** a,c	**170.**a, c
171. (d)	**172.** (a)	**173.** (c)	**174.** (a)	**175.** (d)	**176.** (c)	**177.** (c)	**178.** (c)	**179.** (c)	**180.** (b)

14

MAGNETISM

MULTIPLE CHOICE QUESTIONS

1. An electromagnet uses :

(a) Soft iron core (b) Steel core
(c) Nickel core (d) Copper core

2. Permeability of a material is 0.872. This material is then : **(P.M.T. C.B.S.E. 2000)**

(a) Ferromagnetic (b) Paramagnetic
(c) Diamagnetic (d) None of these

3. Susceptibility is large and + ve for :

(a) Paramagnetic (b) Diamagnetic
(c) Ferromagnetic (d) None of these

4. Susceptibility is small and + ve for :

(a) Paramagnetic (b) Diamagnetic
(c) Ferromagnetic (d) None of these

5. Susceptibility is small and –ve for :

(a) Paramagnetic (b) Diamagnetic
(c) Ferromagnetic (d) None of these

6. At a place horizontal component of earth's magnetic field is equal to the vertical component, then the place is situated at : **(P.B.C.E.T. 1999)**

(a) Poles (b) Equator
(c) At latitude 45° (d) None of these

7. At a place horizontal component of earth's magnetic field is equal to the vertical component, ther the place is situated at :

(a) poles (b) equator
(c) where dip is 45° (d) where dip is 60°

8. At a place horizontal component of earth's magnetic field is $\sqrt{3}$ times the vertical component, then the angle of dip at the given place is : **(D.C.E. 1998)**

(a) 45° (b) 30°
(c) 60° (d) 15°

9. For soft iron in comparison to steel :

(a) hysteresis loss is more
(b) hysteresis loss is same
(c) hysteresis loss is less
(d) hysteresis loss is negligible

10. A bar magnet is suspended freely, its neutral points shall lie :

(a) on the axial line
(b) inside its magnet
(c) on the equatorial line
(d) anywhere around the magnet

11. A bar magnet is placed on the table, its neutral points shall lie :

(a) on the axial line
(b) inside the magnet
(c) on the equatorial line
(d) anywhere around the magnet

12. A magnetic needle suspended by a silk thread is vibrating in the earth's magnetic field. If temperature of the needle is increased by 800°C then : **(M.N.R. 1995)**

(a) its time period increases
(b) its time period decreases
(c) its time period remains unchanged
(d) it stops vibrating

13. When a diamagnetic liquid is poured into a U-tube and one arm of the U-tube is placed between the two poles of a strong magnet, then the level of the liquid in the arm where B is applied will :

(a) fall
(b) rise
(c) oscillate
(d) remain unchanged

14. A bar magnet has a magnetic moment of 5×10^{-5} weber-metre. It is suspended in a magnetic field of $8\pi \times 10^{-4}$ T. The magnet vibrates with the period of vibration equal to 15 seconds. The moment of inertia of the magnet is : **(B.S.E. 2001)**

(a) 11.25 kg-m^2 (b) 5.62 kg-m^2
(c) 0.7 kg-m^2 (d) 22.5 kg-m^2

15. The hysteresis cycle for a material of permanent magnet is :

(a) tall and wide
(b) short and wide
(c) tall and narrow
(d) short and narrow

16. The unit of intensity of magnetisation is :

(a) ampere-m^2 (b) $\frac{\text{ampere}}{\text{metre}}$
(c) ampere-metre (d) weber per metre

17. Magnetic lines of force due to a bar magnet do not intersect because :

(a) a point always has a single net magnetic field
(b) the lines diverge from a single point
(c) the lines have similar charges and so repel each other
(d) None of these

18. The angle of dip at a place on the earth surface gives :

(a) direction of magnetic field
(b) horizontal component of earth's magnetic field
(c) vertical component of earth's magnetic field
(d) location of geographic poles

19. Relation between $\vec{H}$, $\vec{I}$ and $\vec{B}$ is :

(a) $B = \mu_0 (H + I)$ (b) $B = \mu_0 H$
(c) $B = \mu_0 I$ (d) $B = \frac{\mu_0 H}{I}$

20. At a place the angle of dip is 30°. If the horizontal component of earth's field is H, then the net field intensity at the place will be :

(a) H/2 (b) $2H/\sqrt{3}$
(c) $H/\sqrt{2}$ (d) $H/\sqrt{3}$

21. A bar magnet is placed on the table with its South pole facing the geographic North, its neutral points will lie :

(a) on the axial line
(b) on the equatorial line
(c) inside the magnet
(d) none of these

22. A bar magnet of length 10 cm and having a pole strength equal to 10^{-3} weber is kept in the magnetic field having magnetic induction equal to $4\pi \times 10^{-3}$ T. If the magnet makes an angle of 30° with the magnetic field, then torque on the dipole is :

(a) $2\pi \times 10^{-7}$ Nm (b) 0.5×10^{2} Nm
(c) $2\pi \times 10^{-5}$ Nm (d) 0.5 Nm

23. A point near the equator has : **(A.I.E.E.E. 2002)**

(a) $B_V >> B_H$ (b) $B_H >> B_V$
(c) $B_V = B_H$ (d) $B_V = B_H = 0$

24. Two magnets of magnetic moments M and 2M are placed in a vibration magnetometer with the like poles together. The time period of the combination is T_1. When the same magnets are placed with opposite poles together and made to oscillate with the time period T_2, then : **(A.F.M.C. 2002)**

(a) $T_2 > T_1$ (b) $T_2 < T_1$
(c) $T_2 = T_1$ (d) T_2 is infinite

25. The magnetic field of a tangent galvanometer is deflected by an angle 30° due to the current flowing through it. The horizontal component of earth's magnetic field is 0.34×10^{-4} T along the plane of the coil. The magnetic intensity due to the current flowing is : **(A.I.I.M.S. 2002)**

(a) 1.96×10^{-5} T (b) 1.96×10^{5} T
(c) 1.96×10^{-4} T (d) 1.96×10^{4} T

26. Due to earth's magnetic field, charged particles of cosmic rays in the atmosphere :
(a) require greater K.E. to reach the equator than the pole.
(b) can never reach the pole.
(c) can never reach the equator.
(d) require less K.E. to reach the equator than the pole.

27. From which of the following substances, the magnetic susceptibility is independent of temperature ? **(C.B.S.E. 2001)**
(a) Diamagnetic
(b) Ferromagnetic
(c) Paramagnetic
(d) Diamagnetic and ferromagnetic

28. A bar magnet of magnetic moment M is placed in magnetic field of induction B. Then torque on it is given by :
(E.A.M.C.E.T. 1995; M.P.P.M.T. 2001)
(a) $\vec{M} . \vec{B}$ (b) $-\vec{M} . \vec{B}$
(c) $\vec{M} \times \vec{B}$ (d) $\vec{B} \times \vec{M}$

29. A magnetic field of 1600 Am^{-1} produces magnetic flux of 2.4×10^{-5} weber in an iron bar of cross section 0.2 cm^2. The susceptibility of iron is : **(B.H.U. 2002)**
(a) 596 (b) 1788
(c) 298 (d) 894

30. The hysteresis cycle for the material of transformer core is :
(a) tall and wide
(b) short and narrow
(c) tall and narrow
(d) short and wide

31. The area of B-H hysteresis loop is an indication of :
(a) the permeability of the medium.
(b) the retentivity of the medium.
(c) the energy dissipated per cycle.
(d) the susceptibility of the medium.

32. Ferromagnetic materials have their properties due to :
(a) vacant inner subshells
(b) partially filled inner subshells
(c) filled inner subshells
(d) none of these

33. A line joining places of zero dip is called :
(a) Aclinic (b) Isoclinic
(c) Isodynamic (d) Isogonal

34. A line joining places of zero declination is called :
(a) Agonic (b) Isoclinic
(c) Isodynamic (d) Isogonal

35. A line joining places of equal declination is called :
(a) Aclinic (b) Isoclinic
(c) Isodynamic (d) Isogonal

36. A line joining places of equal horizontal field is called :
(a) Aclinic (b) Isodynamic
(c) Isoclinic (d) Isogonal

37. A line joining places of equal dip is called :
(a) Aclinic (b) Isoclinic
(c) Isodynamic (d) Isogonal

38. Ferromagnetism is not found in :
(a) conductor (b) liquid and gases
(c) semiconductor (d) liquids

39. The declination at a place is 10° west to north. The direction in which a ship should steer so that it reaches a place due east is :
(a) 70° due east (b) 100° due east
(c) 110° due west (d) 100° due west

40. Magnetic field does not interact with :
(a) stationary electric charges
(b) moving electric charges
(c) stationary permanent magnet
(d) moving permanent magnet

41. A dip needle in a place perpendicular to magnetic meridian will remain :
(a) vertical
(b) in any direction
(c) horizontal
(d) at 45° with the horizontal

42. The period of oscillation of a magnet in a vibration magnetometer is 2 seconds. The period of oscillation of a magnet whose magnetic moment is four times that of the first magnet is :
(a) 4 seconds (b) 1 second
(c) 8 seconds (d) 0.25 seconds

43. At a certain place a magnet makes 30 oscillations per minute. At another place where the magnetic field is doubled, its time period is :
(a) $\sqrt{2}$ seconds (b) $2\sqrt{2}$ seconds
(c) 4 seconds (d) $\frac{1}{2}$ second

44. At a certain place the angle of dip is 30° and the horizontal component of earth's magnetic field is 0.50 gauss. The earth's total magnetic field is :
(a) $\sqrt{3}$ (b) $\frac{1}{\sqrt{3}}$
(c) 1 (d) $\frac{1}{2}$

45. A magnet is placed on a piece of cork which floats on water, then the cork :
(a) is likely to rotate
(b) moves bodily
(c) has rotational and translation motion
(d) has neither rotational nor translational motion

46. Two isolated point poles of strength 30 A- m and 60 A-m are placed at a distance of 0.3 metre. Then the force of repulsion is :
(a) 2 dynes (b) 2×10^{-3} newton
(c) 3×10^{-5} newton (d) 2×10^{-4} newton

47. A bar magnet 8 cm long is placed in the magnetic meridian with N-pole facing geographic north. Two neutral points separated by a distance of 6 cm are obtained on the equatorial axis of the magnet. If $B_H = 3.2 \times 10^{-5}$ Tesla, then the pole strength of the magnet is :
(a) 5 ab-amp-cm (b) 10 ab-amp-cm
(c) 20 ab-amp-cm (d) 2.5 ab-amp-cm

48. A thin bar magnet of length $2l$ and breadth $2b$, pole strength p and magnetic moment M is divided into four equal parts with length and breadth of each part being half of the original magnet. Then the pole strength of each part is :
(a) p (b) 2p
(c) p/2 (d) p/4

49. The angle of dip at a place is 60°. A magnetic needle oscillates in a horizontal plane at this place with the time period T. If the same needle is made to oscillate in a vertical plane coinciding with the magnetic meridian, then the time period will be :
(a) T (b) 2T
(c) $T/\sqrt{3}$ (d) $T/\sqrt{2}$

50. A dip needle vibrates in the vertical plane perpendicular to the magnetic meridian with the time period 2 seconds. When the same needle is allowed to vibrate in the horizontal plane, then also its time period is 2 seconds, then angle of dip at the place is :
(a) 45° (b) 60°
(c) 0° (d) 30°

51. Two bar magnets of magnetic dipole moments M_1 and M_2 when placed with their axes along the same straight line with their centres r distance apart are found to experience a force 8 N. If the same magnets along the same axis are $2r$ distance apart, then force between them is :
(a) 0.5 N (b) 2 N
(c) 4 N (d) 1 N

52. The tangent galvanometer coil has radius 16 cm. When current of 40 mA is passed through it, the galvanometer shows a deflection of 45°. If earth's horizontal component of magnetic field is 0.36×10^{-4} T, then number of turns in the coil of the galvanometer is :

(a) 220 turns (b) 225 turns
(c) 229 turns (d) 235 turns

53. The direction of magnetic lines of force due to a bar magnet is : **(A.F.M.C. 1995)**

(a) from North to South
(b) from South to North
(c) South to North inside the magnet and North to South outside the magnet
(d) across the bar magnet

54. A circular coil carrying current I is placed in earth's magnetic field such that its magnetic dipole moment is pointing towards North-West. The neutral points are located on a line passing through the centre of the coil and pointing towards : **(P.B.C.E.T. 1999)**

(a) North (b) East
(c) North-East (d) South-East

55. Magnetic dipole moment is a vector quantity directed from : **(A.I.E.E.E. 2002)**

(a) South to North (b) West to East
(c) North to South (d) East to West

56. Two identical magnets of dipole moment M and 2M are first placed one over another with similar poles together. The time period of oscillations is T_1. When the polarity of one of the magnets is reversed, then the time period is T_2. Then **(C.B.S.E. 2002)**

(a) $T_1 = T_2$ (b) $T_1 < T_2$
(c) $T_2 < T_1$ (d) $T_2 = \infty$

57. When 3 amp current is passed through a tangent galvanometer, it gives a deflection of 60°. For 30° deflection, the current must be :

(a) 1 amp (b) 3 amp
(c) 1.3 amp (d) $2\sqrt{3}$ amp

58. If a magnet is placed vertically on the horizontal board, number of neutral points obtained on the board is :

(a) four (b) one
(c) three (d) two

59. Which of the followings is correct ?

(a) Magnetic length = Geometric length
(b) Geometric length = $\frac{10}{19}$ of magnetic length
(c) Magnetic length = 0.8 times the geometric length
(d) Geometric length = 0.8 times the magnetic length

60. To shield an instrument from an external magnetic field, it may be placed in an enclosure made up of :

(a) Soft iron (b) Wood
(c) Copper (d) Ebonite

61. The short bar magnets with magnetic moments 400 ab-amp-cm^2 and 800 ab-amp-cm^2 are placed with axis along same straight line such that similar poles face each other. The centers of two magnets are 20 cm from each other. Then force between them is:

(a) 6 dyne repulsive
(b) 12 dyne repulsive
(c) 800 dyne repulsive
(d) 400 dyne repulsive

62. A bar magnet P in the vibration magnetometer has time period 2 seconds. When an identical bar Q of same mass and size is placed on the top of P, then time period is unchanged. Which of the following statements is true ?

(a) Q is a bar magnet identical to P and similar poles of P and Q are placed together.
(b) Q is not a bar magnet
(c) Q is a diamagnetic bar of same dipole moment.
(d) Q is a bar magnet placed with opposite poles of P and Q together.

63. A bar magnet 8 cm long is placed in the magnetic meridian with the N-pole pointing towards geographical North. Two neutral points separated by a distance of 6 cm are obtained on the equatorial line of the magnet. If horizontal component of earth's magnetic field at the place is $B_H = 0.32 \times 10^{-5}$ T, then the pole strength of the magnet is :

(a) 5 ab-amp-cm (b) 2.5 ab-amp-cm
(c) 20 ab-amp-cm (d) 10 ab-amp-cm

64. A magnet used in vibration magnetometer is heated so as to reduce its magnetic moment by 19%. Then periodic time of the oscillation will :

(a) decrease by 11% (b) decrease by 19%
(c) increase by 11% (d) increase by 19%

65. A steel wire of length l has a magnetic dipole moment M. When it is bent into a semicircular arc, the new magnetic moment is :

(a) M (b) $2\,M/\pi$
(c) M/l (d) $M \times l$

66. A dip needle arranged to move freely in the magnetic meridian dips by an angle ϕ. If the vertical plane in which the needle moves is rotated through an angle α to the magnetic meridian, then the needle will dip by an angle :

(a) ϕ (b) α
(c) more than ϕ (d) less than ϕ

67. Two bar magnets of same mass, length and breadth but having magnetic moments M and 2M are joined together pole to pole and suspended by a string. The time period of the assembly in the magnetic field of strength H is 3 seconds. If now the polarity of one of the magnet is reversed and combination is again made to oscillate in the same field, then the time period is :

(a) 3 seconds (b) $3\sqrt{3}$ seconds
(c) $\frac{3}{\sqrt{3}}$ seconds (d) $\frac{1}{\sqrt{3}}$ seconds

68. Points A and B are situated along the extended axis of a 2 cm long bar magnet at a distance x and $2x$ centimeters respectively from the pole nearer to the points. The ratio of magnetic field at A and B will be :

(a) 8 : 1 approx (b) 4 : 1 exactly
(c) 4 : 1 approx (d) 8 : 1 exactly

69. At a place of latitude 5°, the angle of dip is nearly :

(a) 5° (b) 10°
(c) 7.5° (d) 2.5°

70. Two short bar magnets with pole strengths of 900 ab-amp-cm and 100 ab-amp-cm are placed with their axes in the same vertical line with similar poles facing each other. Each magnet has a length of 1 cm when the separation between the nearer poles is 1 cm, the weight of the upper magnet is supported by the repulsive force between the magnets. If g is 1000 cms^{-2}, then the mass of the upper magnet is :

(a) 55 gm (b) 100 gm
(c) 77.5 gm (d) 45 gm

71. The ratio of magnetic potentials due to magnetic dipole in the end on position to that in the broad side on position for the same distance from it is :

(a) zero (b) ∞
(c) 1 (d) 2

72. The magnetic potential at a point distance 10 cm from the middle point of a magnetic dipole on a line inclined at an angle of 60° with the axis is 3 C.G.S e.m.u. Then the magnetic moment of the magnet is :

(a) 300 ab-amp-cm^2 (b) 600 ab-amp-cm^2
(c) 60 ab-amp-cm^2 (d) 30 ab-amp-cm^2

73. Two short bar magnets with magnetic moment 400 ab-amp-cm^2 and 800 ab-amp-cm^2 are placed with their axes in the same straight line with similar poles facing each other and with their centres at a distance of 20 cm from each other. Then the force of repulsion is :

(a) 12 dynes (b) 6 dynes
(c) 400 dynes (d) 200 dynes

74. The correct value of dip angle at a place is 45°. If the dip circle is rotated by 45° out of the meridian, then the tangent of the angle of apparent dip at the place is :

(a) 1 (b) 1/2

(c) $1/\sqrt{2}$ (d) $\sqrt{2}$

75. A magnet is suspended in such way that it oscillates in a horizontal plane. It makes 20 oscillations per minute at a place where dip angle is 30° and 15 oscillations per minute at a place where dip angle is 60°. Ratio of total earth's magnetic field at two places is :

(a) $3\sqrt{3} : 8$ (b) $16 : 9\sqrt{3}$

(c) 4 : 9 (d) $2\sqrt{3} : 9$

76. A vibration magnetometer consists of two identical bar magnets placed one over another such that they are mutually perpendicular and bisect each other. The time period of oscillations in a horizontal magnetic field is 4 seconds. If one of the magnet is taken away, the new value of the period is :

(a) 2 seconds (b) 6.72 seconds

(c) 3.36 seconds (d) 1 second

77. If δ_1 and δ_2 are the angles of dip observed in two vertical planes at right angles to each other and δ is the true value of dip then :

(a) $\tan^2 \delta = \tan^2 \delta_1 + \tan^2 \delta_2$

(b) $\cot^2 \delta = \cot^2 \delta_1 + \cot^2 \delta_2$

(c) $\tan^2 \delta = \dfrac{\tan^2 \delta_1 + \tan^2 \delta_2}{\tan^2 \delta_1 \ \tan^2 \delta_2}$

(d) $\cot^2 \delta = 1 + \cot^2 \delta_1 \cot^2 \delta_2$

78. A compass needle placed at a distance r from a short magnet in tan A position shows deflection of 60°. When the distance is increased to $r(3)^{1/3}$, then deflection of compass needle is :

(a) 30° (b) $60 \times (3)^{1/3}$

(c) $60 \times (3)^{1/3}$ (d) 45°

79. The time period of vibration of a dip needle vibrating in the magnetic meridian in the vertical plane is 3 seconds and when made to vibrate in the horizontal plane in the magnetic meridian, it vibrates with the time period of $3\sqrt{2}$ seconds. Then the angle of dip is :

(a) 15° (b) 30°

(c) 45° (d) 60°

80. Two tangent galvanometers having coils of the same radius are connected in series. When current is made to flow through them, they show deflection of 60° and 45° respectively. The ratio of number of turns in the coils is :

(P.E.T.M.P. 1995, D.C.E. 1998)

(a) $\dfrac{4}{\sqrt{3}}$ (b) $\dfrac{\sqrt{3}}{1}$

(c) $\dfrac{\sqrt{3}-1}{\sqrt{3}+1}$ (d) $\dfrac{1}{\sqrt{3}+1}$

81. A circular coil of radius 0.314 m and having 100 turns is placed in magnetic meridian such that its axis is in the magnetic meridian. A dip needle is suspended at the centre of the coil with its axis of rotation horizontal and in the plane of the coil. When the current flows through the coil, angle of dip is found to be 30°. The angle of dip becomes 60° when direction of current is reversed. Assuming magnetic field due to the coil is smaller than the earth's magnetic field ($H = 3 \times 10^{-5}$ T), the current in the coil is :

(a) 0.75 A (b) 0.5 A

(c) 0.25 A (d) 1 A

82. Two magnets are held together in a vibration magnetometer and are allowed to oscillate in the earth's magnetic field. With like poles placed together, it makes 12 oscillations per minute. When unlike poles are placed together, it makes 4 oscillations per minute. The ratio of magnetic moments of two magnets is :

(a) 3 : 5 (b) 5 : 4

(c) 3 : 1 (d) 1 : 5

83. Two identical bar magnets of dipole moment 1.0 A-m^2 are placed at a distance of 2 m with their axes perpendicular to each other. The resultant magnetic field at a point midway between the dipole is : **(Roorkee 1995)**

(a) 2×10^{-7} T (b) 10^{-7} T

(c) $\sqrt{2} \times 10^{-7}$ T (d) $\sqrt{5} \times 10^{-7}$ T

84. When a thin rectangular magnet is suspended freely, it oscillates with the time period of 4 seconds. Now if the magnet is cut into two halves along the line perpendicular to its axis and one half is made to oscillate in earth's magnetic field, then time period is :

(a) 0.25 seconds (b) 2 seconds

(c) 4 seconds (d) 0.5 seconds

85. Two bar magnets of equal dipole moment M each are placed at 30° with each other as shown in following figure. The resultant magnetic moment is :

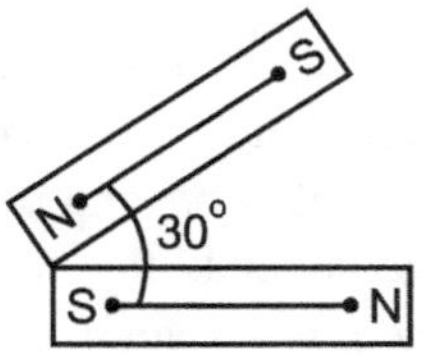

(a) M (b) $M\sqrt{2-\sqrt{3}}$

(c) $\sqrt{2}$ M (d) $\sqrt{3}$ M

86. Two magnets of magnetic moment μ and 2μ are placed with the same poles in the same direction in a vibration magnetometer. The time period noted is T. Then they are oppositely placed and made to vibrate. The time period noted is T′. Then :

(a) $T' = T$ (b) $T' > T$

(c) $T' < T$ (d) Not predictable

87. A wire of length $2l$ having magnetic moment μ is bent into a semi-circle. The magnetic moment now will be :

(a) $\frac{2\mu}{\pi}$ (b) $2\pi\mu$

(c) $\frac{\mu}{2\pi}$ (d) $\frac{\mu}{2\pi + 1}$

88. A magnet starts 10 revolutions per minute at a place where angle of dip is 45° and total intensity of the field is 0.4 C.G.S unit. At another place where angle of dip is 60° and the intensity of the field is 0.5 C.G.S unit, same magnet will make revolution per second equal to :

(a) 0.15 (b) 0.125

(c) 1 (d) 0.715

89. An electromagnet has a solenoid winding 250 mm long with a total of 750 turns. What is the magnetic induction B near the centre of the winding and far from any poles if the current is 0.8 A ? (The iron has relative permeability of 350.)

(a) 1.055 T (b) 10.55 T

(c) 105.5 T (d) 0.1055 T

90. A magnet is suspended in such a way that it oscillates in the horizontal plane. It makes 20 oscillations per minute at a place where dip angle is 30° and 15 oscillations per minute at a place where dip angle is 60°. The ratio of total earth's magnetic field at the two places is :

(a) $3\sqrt{3} : 8$

(b) $16 : 9\sqrt{3}$

(c) $4 : 9$

(d) $2\sqrt{3} : 9$

91. A bar magnet A of magnetic moment M_A is found to oscillate at a frequency twice that of magnet B of magnetic moment M_B when placed in a vibrating magnetometer. Then we can say that :

(a) $M_A = 2M_B$ (b) $M_A = 8M_B$

(c) $M_A = 4M_B$ (d) $M_B = 8M_A$

92. The ratio of magnetic moments of two short magnets which give null deflection in tan B position at 12 cm and 18 cm from the centre of a deflection magnetometer is :

(a) 4 : 9 (b) 27 : 8

(c) 8 : 27 (d) 2 : 3

93. The period of oscillation of a magnet in a vibration magnetometer is 2 seconds. The period of oscillation of a magnet whose magnetic moment is four times that of the first magnet is :

(a) 1 second (b) 4 seconds
(c) 8 seconds (d) 0.5 seconds

94. Two bar magnets of same mass, same length and breadth, but having magnetic moments M and 2M are joined together pole to pole and suspended by a string. The time period of the assembly in a magnetic field of strength H is 3 seconds. If now the polarity of one of the magnets is reversed and the combination is again made to oscillate in the same field, the time of oscillation is :

(a) 5 seconds (b) $3\sqrt{3}$ seconds
(c) 3 seconds (d) 6 seconds

95. A current of 3 ampere is flowing in a plane circular coil of radius 4 cm and number of turns 20. The coil is placed in a uniform magnetic field of magnetic induction 0.5 Tesla. Then the dipole moment of the coil is :

(a) 3000 amp-metre^2 (b) 0.3 amp-metre^2
(c) 75 amp-metre^2 (d) 300 amp-metre^2

96. A hydrogen atom is paramagnetic. A hydrogen molecule is :

(a) diamagnetic
(b) paramagnetic
(c) ferromagnetic
(d) anti-ferromagnetic

97. At a certain place, horizontal component of earth's magnetic field is $\sqrt{3}$ times the vertical component. The angle of dip at the place is :

(a) 75° (b) 60°
(c) 45° (d) 30°

98. At a place of latitude 5°, the angle of dip is nearly :

(a) 5° (b) 10°
(c) 2.5° (d) 7.5°

99. At a certain place a magnet makes 30 oscillations per minute. At another place where the magnetic field is doubled, its time period will be :

(a) 4 seconds (b) 2 seconds
(c) 1/2 second (d) $\sqrt{2}$ seconds

100. Points A and B are situated perpendicular to the axis of a 2 cm long bar magnet at large distance X and 3X from its centre on opposite sides. The ratio of the magnetic fields at A and B will be approximately equal to :

(a) 1 : 9 (b) 2 : 9
(c) 27 : 1 (d) 9 : 1

101. At a certain place the angle of dip is 30° and the horizontal component of earth's magnetic field is 0.50 oersted. The earth's total magnetic field is :

(a) 3 (b) 1
(c) $1/\sqrt{3}$ (d) 1/2

102. The period of oscillation of a bar magnet in a vibration magnetometer is 4 seconds. The time period of oscillation of a bar magnet of same dimensions and mass, but whose magnetic moment is sixteen times that of the first magnet is :

(a) 1 second (b) 4 seconds
(c) 2 seconds (d) 1/4 second

103. The isoclinic lines are loci of equal

(a) dip angle (b) declination angle
(c) B_H (d) B_V

104. The isodynamic lines are loci of equal :

(a) dip angle (b) declination angle
(c) B_H (d) B_V

105. A compass needle is placed at the magnetic pole, then the compass needle :

(a) points South-North
(b) points East-West
(c) becomes vertical
(d) may stay in any direction

106. A piece of cork with a magnet placed on it, floats on water. Then the cork :

(a) rotates
(b) moves bodily
(c) has rotational and translational motion
(d) has neither rotational nor translational motion

107. The time period of oscillation of a magnet in vibration magnetometer is 1.5 s. The time period of oscillation of another magnet similar in size, shape and mass but having one fourth magnetic moment than that of the first magnet oscillating at the same place will be :

(a) 0.75 s (b) 1.5 s
(c) 3.0 s (d) 6.0 s

108. Consider the following statements :

Assertion (A) : The poles of magnets cannot be separated by breaking it into two pieces.

Reason (R) : The magnetic moment will be reduced to half when a magnet is broken into two equal parts. Of these statements,

(a) both A and R are true and R is the correct explanation of A.
(b) both A and R are true and R is not the correct explanation of A.
(c) A is true, but R is false.
(d) A is false, but R is true.

109. Force between two identical bar magnets whose centres are r m apart is 4.8 N when their axes are in the same line. If separation is increased to $2r$, the force between them is reduced to :

(a) 2.4 N (b) 0.6 N
(c) 1.2 N (d) 0.3 N

110. A magnet when placed perpendicular to a uniform field of strength 10^{-4} Wb/m^2 experiences a couple of moment 4×10^{-5} N/m. What is its magnetic moment?

(a) 0.4 Am^2 (b) 0.04 Am^2
(c) 0.2 Am^2 (d) 0.16 Am^2

111. Two small bar magnets are placed in a line at a certain distance d apart. If the length of each magnet l is negligible as compared to d, the force between them will be inversely proportional to :

(a) d (b) d^2
(c) $\frac{1}{d^2}$ (d) d^4

112. A small bar magnet A oscillates in a horizontal plane with a period T. Another bar magnet B of same size as A is oscillated at the same place. If the magnetic moment of B is four times that of A, the period of B will be :

(a) T/4 (b) T/2
(c) 2T (d) 4T

113. A magnetic needle oscillates in a horizontal plane with a period T at a place where the angle of dip is 60°. When the same needle is made to oscillate in a vertical plane coinciding with the magnetic meridian, its period will be :

(a) $T/\sqrt{2}$ (b) T
(c) $\sqrt{2}$ T (d) 2T

114. A bar magnet of length 10 cm and having the pole strength equal to 10^{-3} Wb is kept in a magnetic field having magnetic induction $B = 4\pi \times 10^{-3}$ T. It makes an angle of 30° with the direction of magnetic field B. The torque in newton-metre is :

(a) $2\pi \times 10^{-7}$ (b) 0.5
(c) $2\pi \times 10^{-5}$ (d) 5×10^{-3}

115. To increase the sensitivity of MCG, we must decrease : **(MHT-CET 2006)**

(a) Area of coil
(b) Torsional constant
(c) Magnetic field
(d) Number of turns

116. The magnetic field at the centre of the MCG is 0.25 T. The coil has an area of 0.2 m^2 and has 28 turns. If the sensitivity of the MCG is to be increased by 25%, the number of turns of the coil should be........ (Assume all other things remaining constant)

(MHT-CET 2007)

(a) 30 (b) 32

(c) 35 (d) 38

117. Tangent galvanometer shows a deflection of 45° for some current. When the current is reduced to $1/\sqrt{3}$ times the original, what is the deflection ? **(MHT - CET 2008)**

(a) Increases by 15° (b) Decreases by 15°

(c) Increases by 30° (d) Decreases by 30°

118. The tangent galvanometer is set into magnetic meridian : **(Board March 2009)**

(a) to minimize error due to parallax.

(b) to produce strong magnetic field.

(c) to make magnetic field due to current carrying coil, exactly parallel to horizontal component of earth's magnetic field.

(d) to make magnetic field due to current carrying coil, exactly perpendicular to horizontal component of earth's magnetic field.

119. Consider a point on an equatorial axis of a short bar magnet. The direction of magnetic field at that point is:

(a) anti-parallel to magnetic moment.

(b) parallel to magnetic moment.

(c) perpendicular to magnetic moment.

(d) arbitrary depended on a distance of a point from centre of the magnet.

120. A wire of length L m carrying a current 'i', is bent in the form of a circle. The magnitude of magnetic moment is :

(MHT-CET 2006)

(a) $\frac{iL}{4\pi}$ (b) $\frac{i^2L}{4\pi}$

(c) $\frac{iL^2}{4\pi}$ (d) $\frac{iL^2}{4}$

121. A bar magnet of moment M is divided into two equal parts by cutting it perpendicular to its length. The magnetic moment of each piece will be : **(Board Feb. 2008)**

(a) Zero (b) M/2

(c) M (d) 2 M

122. Magnetic potential at a point due to a short magnetic dipole of moment 2 Am^2 at a distance of 100 cm along a line making an angle of 60° with the axis is :

(Board Sept. 2008)

(a) $\sqrt{3} \times 10^{-7}$ J/Am (b) 1×10^{-7} J/Am

(c) $\sqrt{3} \times 10^{-11}$ J/Am (d) 1×10^{-9} J/Am

123. An electron beam travels with a velocity of 1.6×10^7 ms^{-1} perpendicular to magnetic field of intensity 0.1 T. The radius of the path of the electron beam is :

($m_e = 9 \times 10^{-31}$ kg)

(E.A.M.C.E.T. 2007)

(a) 9×10^{-5} m (b) 9×10^{-2} m

(c) 9×10^{-4} m (d) 9×10^{-3} m

124. The earth's magnetic field is about :

(H.P.P.M.T. 2009)

(a) 8.7×10^{-2} T (b) 2.7×10^{-10} T

(c) 3.6×10^{-5} T (d) 10^{-8} T

125. If two parallel wires carry current in opposite directions : **(D.C.E. 2009)**

(a) the wires attract each other

(b) the wires repel each other

(c) the wires experience neither attraction nor repulsion

(d) the forces of attraction or repulsion do not depend on current direction

126. Under the influence of a uniform magnetic field, a charged particle moves with constant speed v in a circle of radius R. The time period of rotation of the particle :

(A.I.P.M.T. Prelim 2009)

(a) depends on R and not on v

(b) is independent of both v and R

(c) depends on both v and R

(d) depends on v and not on R

127. Magnetic field at the centre of circular coil of radius R due to current I flowing through it is B. The magnetic field at a point along the axis at distance R from the centre is :

(C.E.T. Karnataka 2010)

(a) $\sqrt{8}$ B (b) $\frac{8}{\sqrt{8}}$

(c) $\frac{B}{4}$ (d) $\frac{B}{2}$

128. Two wires A and B are of lengths 40 cm and 30 cm. A is bent into a circle of radius *r* and B into an arc of radius *r*. A current I_1 is passed through A and I_2 through B. To have the same magnetic inductions at the centre, the ratio of $I_1 : I_2$ is : **(E.A.M.S.E.T. 2007)**

(a) 3 : 4 (b) 3 : 5

(c) 2 : 3 (d) 4 : 3

129. Two concentric coils each of radius equal to 2π cm are placed at right angles to each other. 3 A and 4 A are the currents flowing in each coil respectively. The magnetic induction in Wb/m^2 at the centre of the coils will be : ($\mu_0 = 4\pi \times 10^{-7}$ Wb/Am)

(A.I.I.M.S. 2008)

(a) 12×10^{-5} (b) 10^{-5}

(c) 5×10^{-5} (d) 7×10^{-5}

130. Two long parallel wires carry currents i_1 and i_2 such that $i_1 > i_2$. When the currents are in the same direction, the magnetic field at a point midway between wires is 6×10^{-6} T. If the direction of i_2 is reversed, the field becomes 3×10^{-5} T. The ratio $\frac{i_1}{i_2}$ is

(Kerala C.E.T. 2009)

(a) $\frac{1}{2}$ (b) 2

(c) $\frac{-2}{3}$ (d) $\frac{3}{2}$

131. A cyclotron is used to accelerate protons, deuterons, α-particles etc. If the energy attained after acceleration, by the protons is E, the energy attained by α-particles shall be: **(A.M.U. (Medical) 2009)**

(a) 4E (b) 2E

(c) E (d) E/4

132. A 2μC charge moving around a circle with a frequency of 6.25×10^{12} Hz produces a magnetic field 6.28 Tesla at the centre of the circle. The radius of the circle is :

(Kerala Engg. 2010)

(a) 2.25 m (b) 0.25 m

(c) 13.0 m (d) 1.25 m

133. To produce a magnetic field of π Tesla at the centre of a circular loop of a diameter 1 m, the current flowing through the loop is:

(H.P.P.M.T. 2010)

(a) 5×10^6 A (b) 10^7 A

(c) 2.5×10^6 A (d) 2×10^6 A

134. Relative permittivity and permeability of a material are ε_r and μ_r, respectively. Which of the following values of these quantities are allowed for a diamagnetic material ?

(A.I.E.F.E. 2008)

(a) $\varepsilon_r = 1.5, \mu_r = 1.5$ (b) $\varepsilon_r = 0.5, \mu_r = 1.5$

(c) $\varepsilon_r = 1.5, \mu_r = 0.5$ (d) $\varepsilon_r = 0.5, \mu_r = 0.5$

135. In an A.C. generator : **(H.P.P.M.T. 2009)**

(a) magnetic energy is converted into mechanical energy

(b) mechanical energy is converted into magnetic energy

(c) electrical energy is converted into mechanical energy

(d) heat energy is converted into mechanical energy

136. A moving coil galvanometer can be converted into ammeter by introducing a :

(H.P.P.M.T. 2009)

(a) shunt resistance in series

(b) high resistance in parallel

(c) shunt resistance in parallel

(d) high resistance in parallel

137. A galvanometer of resistance 100 Ω is converted to a voltmeter of range 10 V by connecting a resistance of 10 kΩ. The resistance required to convert the same galvanometer to an ammeter of range 1 A is **(Kerala Engg. 2009)**

(a) 0.4 Ω (b) 0.3 Ω
(c) 1.2 Ω (d) 0.1 Ω

138. A galvanometer has a coil of resistance 100 ohm and gives a full scale deflection for 30 mA current. It is to work as a voltmeter of 30 volt range, the resistance required to be added will be : **(A.I.P.M.T. (Prelim) 2010)**

(a) 900 Ω (b) 1800 Ω
(c) 500 Ω (d) 1000 Ω

139. Which of the following is not correct ? **(H.P.P.M.T. 2009)**

(a) For diamagnetic material, susceptibility is negative.
(b) For paramagnetic material, susceptibility is positive and small.
(c) For ferromagnetic material, susceptibility is large and positive.
(d) For paramagnetic material, susceptibility is negative.

140. If a diamagnetic substance is brought near the north or the south pole of a bar magnet. It is : **(A.I.P.M.T. (Prelim) 2009)**

(a) repelled by the North Pole and attracted by the South Pole.
(b) attracted by the North Pole and repelled by the South Pole.
(c) attracted by both the poles.
(d) repelled by both the poles.

141. The area enclosed by a hysteresis loop is a measure of: **(Gujarat C.E.T. 2011)**

(a) Retentivity (b) Susceptibility
(c) Permeability (d) Energy loss

142. Resultant force acting on diamagnetic material in a magnetic field is in the direction **(Gujarat C.E.T. 2011)**

(a) from stronger to the weaker part of the magnetic field.
(b) from weaker to the stronger part of the magnetic field.
(c) perpendicular to the magnetic field.
(d) making 60° to the magnetic field.

143. Magnetic moment of deuteron is : **(Karnataka C.E.T. 2008)**

(a) –ve almost the same as that of an electron
(b) +ve same as that of a proton
(c) +ve less than that of a proton
(d) zero

144. Isogonic lines are those for which : **(M.P.P.E.T. 2009)**

(a) declination is the same at all places on the line
(b) angle of dip is the same at all places on the magnetic field is the same
(c) the value of horizontal, component of earth's magnetic field is the same
(d) all of the above.

145. A short bar magnet experiences a torque of magnitude 0.64 J when it is placed in a uniform magnetic field of 0.32 T, making an angle of 30° with the direction of the field. The magnetic moment of the magnet is : **(Gujarat C.E.T. 2010)**

(a) 6 Am^2 (b) 4 Am^2
(c) 2 Am^2 (d) None of these

146. The earth's magnetic field inside an iron box as compared to that outside the box is :

(a) less (b) more
(c) zero (d) same

147. A dip needle arranged to move freely in the magnetic meridian dips by an angle θ. If the vertical plane in which the needle moves is rotated through an angle α to the magnetic meridian, then the needle will dip by an angle: **(B.H.U. Screening 2008)**

(a) θ (b) α
(c) more than θ (d) less than θ

148. The angle of dip at a place is 37° and the vertical component of the earth's magnetic field is 6×10^{-5} T. The earth's magnetic field at this place is : (tan 37° = 3/4)

(Kerala C.E.T. 2009)

(a) 7×10^{-5} T (b) 6×10^{-5} T
(c) 5×10^{-5} T (d) 10^{-4} T

149. A solenoid has core of a material with relative permeability 500 and its windings carries a current of 1 *A*. The number of turns of the solenoid is 500 per metre. The magnetization of the material is nearly

(Kerala Engg. 2010)

(a) 2.5×10^3 Am^{-1} (b) 2.5×10^5 Am^{-1}
(c) 2.0×10^3 Am^{-1} (d) 2.0×10^5 Am^{-1}

150. A moving charge will produce :

(H.P.P.M.T. 1999; A.F.M.C. 2000; C.E.T. J & K 2000; C.E.T. J & K 2002)

(a) only a magnetic field
(b) only an electric field
(c) both electric and magnetic fields
(d) none of the fields

151. An electron moving towards the east enters a magnetic field directed towards the north. The force on the electron will be directed :

(M.P.C.E.E.T. 2000)

(a) vertically upward
(b) vertically downward
(c) towards the west
(d) towards the south

152. A long wire A carries a current of 10 ampere. Another long wire B, which is parallel to A and separated by 0.1 m from A, carries a current of 5 ampere in the opposite direction to that in A. What is the magnitude and nature of the force experienced per unit length of B ? ($\mu_0 = 4\pi \times 10^{-7}$ Wb/Am) ?

(M.P.C.E.E.T. 2000)

(a) Repulsive force of 10^{-4} N/m
(b) Attractive force of 10^{-4} N/m
(c) Repulsive force of $2\pi \times 10^{-5}$ N/m
(d) Attractive force of $2\pi \times 10^{-5}$ N/m

153. Two wire lopes of different radii are placed in a plane such that they are concentric. The current in outer loop is clockwise and is increasing with time. The current in the inner loop is : **(H.P.P.M.T. 2000)**

(a) Clockwise
(b) Anticlockwise
(c) Zero
(d) Clockwise or anticlockwise depending on the loop radii.

154. If an electron enters a magnetic field with its velocity pointing in the same direction as the magnetic field, then : **(M.P.P.M.T. 2000)**

(a) the electron will turn to its right
(b) the velocity of the electron will increase
(c) the electron will turn to its left
(d) the velocity of the electron will remain unchanged

155. The cyclotron is used to accelerate :

(P.M.T. Delhi 2000)

(a) Protons only (b) Electrons only
(c) α-particles only (d) Both (a) and (c)

156. The magnetic field due to a large solenoid of N turns due to current flowing through it is :

(I.I.I.T. Alla. 2001)

(a) directly proportional to N
(b) inversely proportional to N
(c) directly proportional to N^2
(d) independent of N

157. A proton and an alpha particle are separately projected in a region where a uniform magnetic field exists. Their initial velocities are perpendicular to direction of magnetic field. If both the particles move around magnetic field in circles of equal radii, the ratio of momentum of proton to alpha particle (P_P/P_α) is : **(M.P.C.E.E.T. 2001)**

(a) 1 (b) 1/2
(c) 2 (d) 1/4

158. Magnetic field induction at one end on the axis of a long solenoid having n turns per unit length and carrying current of i ampere is : **(U.P.C.P.M.T. 2001)**

(a) $\frac{1}{2}\mu_0 ni$ (b) $2\mu_0 ni$

(c) $\mu_0 ni$ (d) $\mu_0 n \pi i$

159. If the current is doubled, the deflection is also doubled in : **(Orissa J.E.E. 2002)**

(a) a tangent galvanometer

(b) a moving coil galvanometer

(c) both (a) and (b)

(d) none of these

ANSWER KEY

1. (a)	**2.** (d)	**3.** (c)	**4.** (a)	**5.** (b)	**6.** (d)	**7.** (c)	**8.** (b)	**9.** (c)	**10.** (c)
11. (d)	**12.** (d)	**13.** (a)	**14.** (c)	**15.** (b)	**16.** (c)	**17.** (a)	**18.** (a)	**19.** (a)	**20.** (b)
21. (a)	**22.** (a)	**23.** (b)	**24.** (a)	**25.** (a)	**26.** (c)	**27.** (a)	**28.** (c)	**29.** (a)	**30.** (c)
31. (c)	**32.** (b)	**33.** (a)	**34.** (a)	**35.** (d)	**36.** (b)	**37.** (b)	**38.** (a)	**39.** (b)	**40.** (a)
41. (a)	**42.** (b)	**43.** (a)	**44.** (b)	**45.** (a)	**46.** (b)	**47.** (a)	**48.** (c)	**49.** (c)	**50.** (a)
51. (a)	**52.** (c)	**53.** (c)	**54.** (c)	**55.** (a)	**56.** (b)	**57.** (a)	**58.** (b)	**59.** (c)	**60.** (b)
61. (b)	**62.** (b)	**63.** (a)	**64.** (c)	**65.** (b)	**66.** (c)	**67.** (b)	**68.** (a)	**69.** (b)	**70.** (a)
71. (b)	**72.** (b)	**73.** (a)	**74.** (d)	**75.** (b)	**76.** (c)	**77.** (b)	**78.** (a)	**79.** (d)	**80.** (b)
81. (a)	**82.** (b)	**83.** (d)	**84.** (b)	**85.** (b)	**86.** (b)	**87.** (a)	**88.** (a)	**89.** (a)	**90.** (b)
91. (c)	**92.** (c)	**93.** (a)	**94.** (c)	**95.** (b)	**96.** (a)	**97.** (d)	**98.** (b)	**99.** (d)	**100.** (c)
101. (c)	**102.** (a)	**103.** (a)	**104.** (c)	**105.** (d)	**106.** (a)	**107.** (c)	**108.** (b)	**109.** (d)	**110.** (a)
111. (d)	**112.** (b)	**113.** (a)	**114.** (a)	**115.** (b)	**116.** (c)	**117.** (b)	**118.** (d)	**119.** (a)	**120.** (c)
121. (b)	**122.** (b)	**123.** (c)	**124.** (c)	**125.** (b)	**126.** (b)	**127.** (b)	**128.** (c)	**129.** (c)	**130.** (d)
131. (c)	**132.** (d)	**133.** (c)	**134.** (c)	**135.** (d)	**136.** (c)	**137.** (d)	**138.** (a)	**139.** (d)	**140.** (d)
141. (d)	**142.** (a)	**143.** (b)	**144.** (a)	**145.** (b)	**146.** (c)	**147.** (c)	**148.** (d)	**149.** (b)	**150.** (c)
151. (b)	**152.** (a)	**153.** (b)	**154.** (d)	**155.** (d)	**156.** (a)	**157.** (b)	**158.** (a)	**159.** (b)	

15

ELECTROMAGNETIC INDUCTION AND ALTERNATING CURRENTS

MULTIPLE CHOICE QUESTIONS

1. Average value of current in one complete cycle of A.C. is :

(a) $0.707\ I_0$ (b) $0.636\ I_0$

(c) $\frac{I_0}{\sqrt{2}}$ (d) Zero

2. Frequency of household A.C. in India is :

(a) 220 V (b) 220 Hz

(c) 50 Hz (d) 60 Hz

3. S.I. unit of magnetic flux density is :

(a) weber (b) tesla

(c) maxwell (d) gauss

4. S.I. unit of magnetic flux is :

(a) weber (b) tesla

(c) maxwell (d) gauss

5. A magnet is falling vertically through a metallic ring as shown in figure, its acceleration will be :

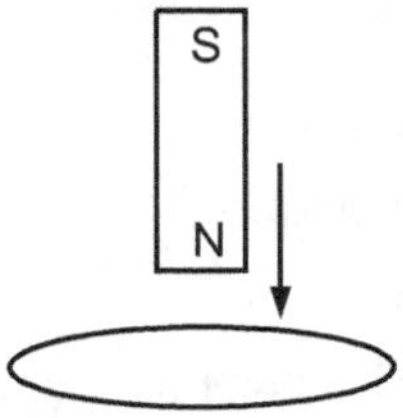

(a) greater than g (b) equal to g

(c) less than g (d) none of these

6. Current from A to B in the straight wire is decreasing. The direction of induced current in the circular loop is :

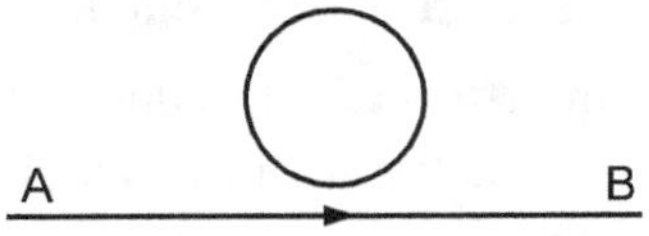

(a) anticlockwise (b) clockwise

(c) no current flows (d) none of these

7. A pure/ideal inductor is one which has zero :

(a) inductance (b) resistance

(c) conductance (d) capacitance

8. An e.m.f. of 7V is produced in a coil, when current flowing through the coil changes from 8 A to 7 A in 1 millisecond. The coefficient of self induction of the coil is :

(a) 7×10^{-2} H (b) 7×10^{-5} H

(c) 7×10^{3} H (d) 7×10^{-3} H

9. 1 weber is equal to :

(a) 10^{-4} tesla (b) 10^{4} gauss

(c) 10^{4} maxwell (d) 10^{8} maxwell

10. Magnetic flux linked with a coil is given by ϕ (in weber) $= 10t^2 + 4t + 7$. The e.m.f. induced in the coil at $t = 0.75$ seconds is :

(a) 19 V (b) 20 V

(c) 14 V (d) 21 V

11. In Q. 10, how much is the current flowing through the coil at $t = 0.75$ sec if resistance of the coil is 20 Ω :

(a) 0.95 A (b) 0.85 A

(c) 0.2 A (d) 2 A

12. Transformer can be used on :

(a) A.C. only

(b) D.C. only

(c) A.C. and D.C. both

(d) none of these

13. In a step-up transformer :

(a) current decreases

(b) voltage decreases

(c) power increases

(d) power decreases

14. In the given figure two bulbs B_1 and B_2, resistor R and inductor L are connected as shown. When the switch S is switched ON then :

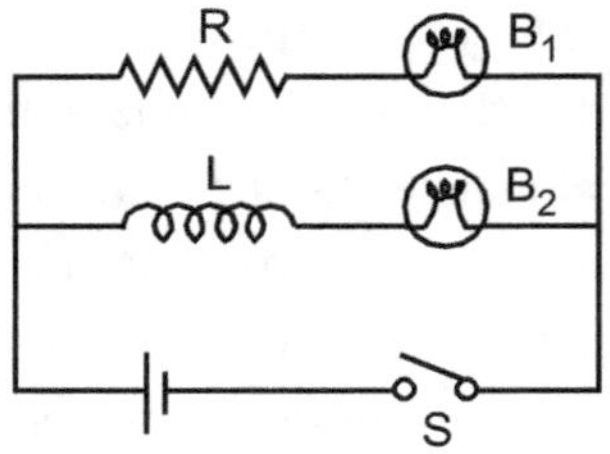

(a) B_1 glows instantly and B_2 glows with some delay

(b) B_2 glows instantly and B_1 glows with some delay

(c) B_1 and B_2 both glow instantly

(d) B_1 and B_2 both glow with the same brightness

15. If the number of turns in the coil and the length of the coil is also doubled. then coefficient of self induction of the coil :

(a) remains unchanged

(b) becomes 4 times

(c) becomes 2 times

(d) becomes half

16. Armature current in the D.C. motor is maximum when the motor :

(a) has picked up maximum speed

(b) has just switched OFF

(c) has just switched ON

(d) has some intermediate speed

17. A long solenoid of cross section A, length l and turns N_1 has wound about its centre a small coil of turns N_2. Then the mutual inductance of the two coils is :

(a) $\frac{\mu_o N_1^2 N_2}{l}$ (b) $\frac{\mu_o N_1^2 N_2 A}{l}$

(c) $\frac{\mu_o N_1 N_2 A}{l}$ (d) $\mu_o A N_1 N_2 l$

18. A series combination of pure inductor L and pure resistance R is connected to a battery of e.m.f. E and negligible internal resistance, then the current flowing in the circuit depends upon :

(a) L, R and E (b) L and R

(c) E and R (d) E and L

19. An electric motor runs on D.C. source of e.m.f. 200 V and draws current of 10 A. If the efficiency is 40%, then the resistance of the armature is :

(a) 5 Ω (b) 120 Ω

(c) 12 Ω (d) 160 Ω

20. A current from A to B is increasing in magnitude. What is the direction of the induced current in the loop ?

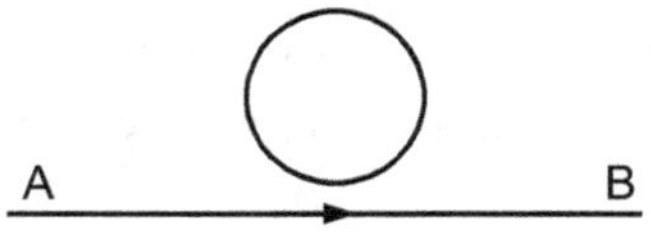

(a) clockwise

(b) anticlockwise

(c) no current is induced

(d) none of these

21. Coils in the resistance boxes are made up of doubled insulated wire, this is to :

(a) decrease the resistance of wire

(b) increase the resistance of wire

(c) increase the induction effect at the time of make and break of the circuit

(d) nullify the effect of self-induced e.m.f. in the coil at the time of make and break of the circuit

22. The magnetic flow passing perpendicular to the plane of the coil and directed into the paper is varying according to the relation $\phi_B = (6t^2 + 7t + 1)$ milli weber.

Magnitude of e.m.f. induced in the loop at $t = 2$ seconds is :

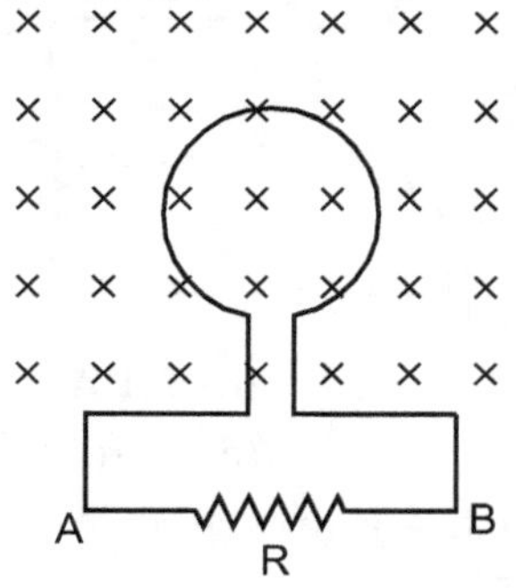

(a) –19 mV (b) + 19 mV
(c) 31 mV (d) – 31 mV

23. In Q. 22, the direction of current through resistor R is :
(a) A to B (b) B to A
(c) No current flows (d) None of these

24. A copper disc of radius 0.1 m is rotated about its centre with 10 revolutions per second in a uniform magnetic field of 0.1 Tesla with its plane perpendicular to the field. The e.m.f. induced between the centre and the circular edge of the disc is:
(a) 20π volts (b) 2π volts
(c) $\pi \times 10^{-2}$ volts (d) $2\pi \times 10^{-1}$ volt

25. When a current in a coil changes from 2 amp to 6 amp in 0.05 sec, an e.m.f. of 8 volt is induced in the coil. The coefficient of self induction of the coil is :
(a) 0.1 H (b) 0.2 H
(c) 0.4 H (d) 2 H

26. A 50 Hz A.C. current of crest value 1 A flows through the primary of a transformer. If the mutual inductance between the primary and secondary is 1.5 H, the crest voltage induced in the secondary is :
(a) 300 V (b) 73 V
(c) 150 V (d) 230 V

27. In the LCR series circuit the voltmeter across 'R' and ammeter readings are :

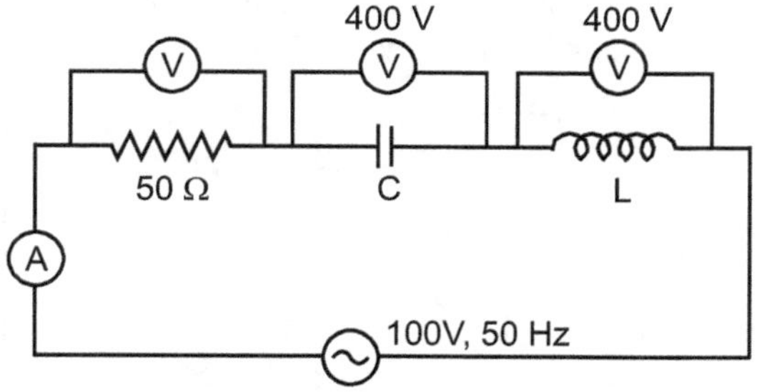

(a) V = 100 V, I = 1 A
(b) V = 100 V, I = 2 A
(c) V = 100 V, I = 5 A
(d) V = 100, I = 3 A

28. What value of inductance of a coil is connected with a capacitor of 0.3 pF so that the oscillating frequency is 1 MHz ?
(a) 42.5 mH (b) 84.5 H
(c) 84.5 mH (d) 42.5 H

29. A resistor of 40 Ω, capacitor of 10 μF and inductor of 1 H are connected in series with 220 V, 50 Hz source of alternating current. The reactance of the circuit is given by :
(a) 4.47 Ω (b) 4.47 H
(c) Zero (d) 84.7 Ω

30. A transformer has 5 turns in its primary coil and 4 turns in its secondary coil. If the supply voltage is 240 V to the primary, the ratio of current in the primary to the secondary windings is : **(C.P.M.T. 2000)**
(a) 5 : 4 (b) 5 : 9
(c) 4 : 5 (d) 9 : 5

31. Lenz's law is a consequence of the law of conservation of :
(a) charge (b) energy
(c) mass (d) momentum

32. PQ is the boundary of the region where uniform magnetic field is acting. A semicircular conductor XYZ of radius r is rotated with constant angular speed with its centre lying on the boundary PQ and plane lying in the plane of the paper. Which of the following graphs represents the variation of induced e.m.f. with time ?

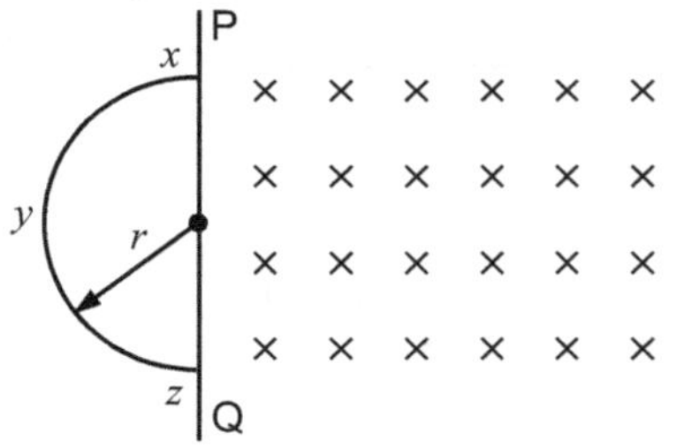

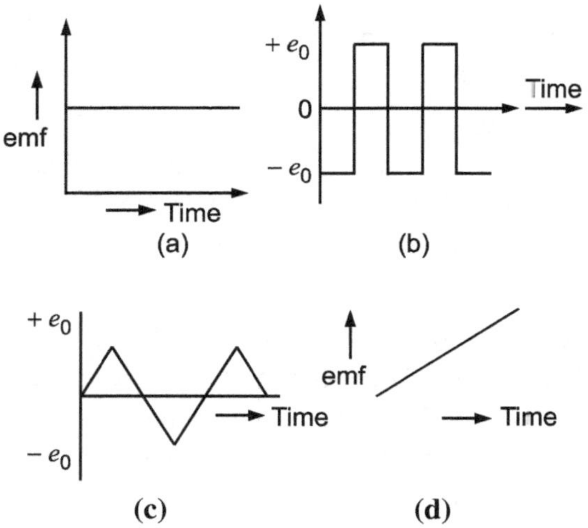

33. Force required to move a rod with a constant speed of 2 ms^{-1} in the circuit shown is : (B = 0.15 T and R = 3 Ω)

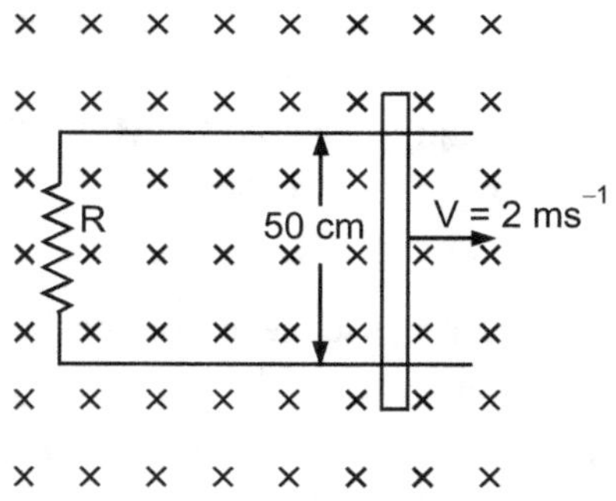

(a) 3.75×10^{-3} N
(b) 3.75×10^{-4} N
(c) 3.75×10^{-2} N
(d) 3.75×10^{2} N

34. An ideal inductance of 2 H is connected as shown in the figure. When key K is pressed, the value of current in 20 Ω resistance at steady state is :

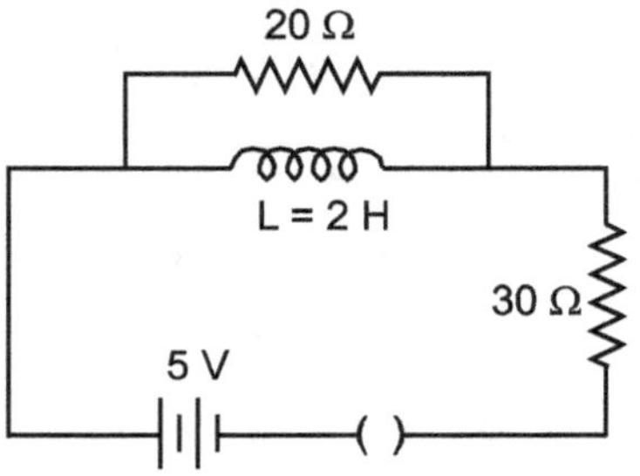

(a) 0.25 A (b) 0.1 A
(c) 10 A (d) Zero

35. Which quantity is increased in step down transformer?

(a) Power (b) Current
(c) Voltage (d) Frequency

36. The number of turns in the primary and the secondary of a transformer are N_P and N_S and the resistance of the secondary circuit is R_S, then equivalent resistance of the load from the point of view of primary circuit is :

(a) $R_S\left(\frac{N_P}{N_S}\right)^2$ (b) $R_S\left(\frac{N_P}{N_S}\right)$
(c) $R_S\left(\frac{N_S}{N_P}\right)^2$ (d) $R_S\left(\frac{N_S}{N_P}\right)$

37. Power factor of LR circuit in A.C. is : **(A.I.E.E.E. 2002)**

(a) $\frac{R}{\sqrt{R^2+\omega^2L^2}}$ (b) Zero
(c) $\frac{R}{\sqrt{\omega L+R}}$ (d) $\frac{1}{\sqrt{R^2+\omega^2L^2}}$

38. In an A.C. e.m.f. and current are given by the equation E = 200 sin 314t and I = 50 sin $\left(314\,t+\frac{\pi}{3}\right)$ respectively. Then power factor of the circuit is : **(C.P.T. 1996)**

(a) $\frac{1}{4}$ (b) $\frac{\sqrt{3}}{2}$
(c) $\frac{1}{2}$ (d) $\frac{1}{\sqrt{3}}$

39. In the circuit shown, current through the inductor is 0.8 A and through the capacitor is 0.6 amp. The current drawn from the source is :

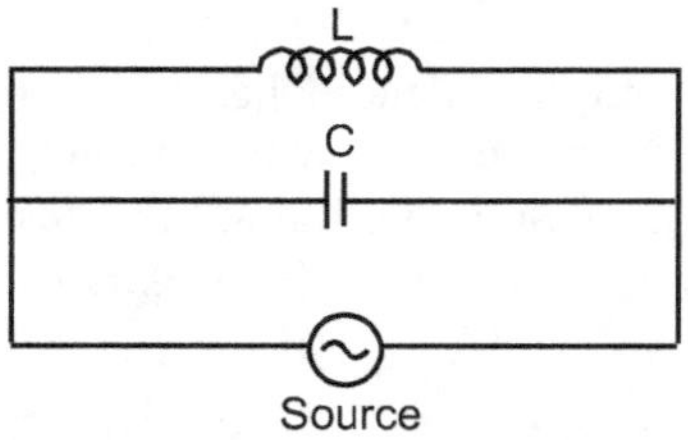

(a) 0.1 A (b) 0.2 A

(c) 1.4 A (d) 1 A

40. At resonance the peak value of current in L-C-R series circuit is :

(a) $\frac{E_o}{R}$

(b) $\frac{E_o}{\sqrt{2}\sqrt{R^2+\left(\omega^2L^2-\frac{1}{\omega^2C^2}\right)}}$

(c) $\frac{E_0}{\sqrt{R^2+\left(\omega L-\frac{1}{\omega C}\right)^2}}$

(d) $\frac{E_o}{\sqrt{2}R}$

41. The instantaneous current and voltage in an A.C. circuit is given by I = 4 sin ωt and $E = 150\cos\left[\omega t+\frac{\pi}{3}\right]$ respectively, then the phase difference between voltage and current in the circuit is given by :

(a) $\frac{5\pi}{6}$ (b) $\frac{2\pi}{3}$

(c) $\frac{7\pi}{6}$ (d) $\frac{\pi}{3}$

42. Amplitude of current oscillations in LCR circuit is maximum, when ω is :

(a) $\sqrt{LC}$ (b) $\frac{1}{\sqrt{LC}}$

(c) 0 (d) ∞

43. In LCR circuit, R = 100 Ω, L = 8 henry and C = 0.5 μF are connected in series, the resonance frequency is :

(a) 600 radian per sec

(b) 500 radian per sec

(c) 600π radian per sec

(d) 250π radian per sec

44. The inductance between the points A and B is : **(A.I.E.E.E. 2002)**

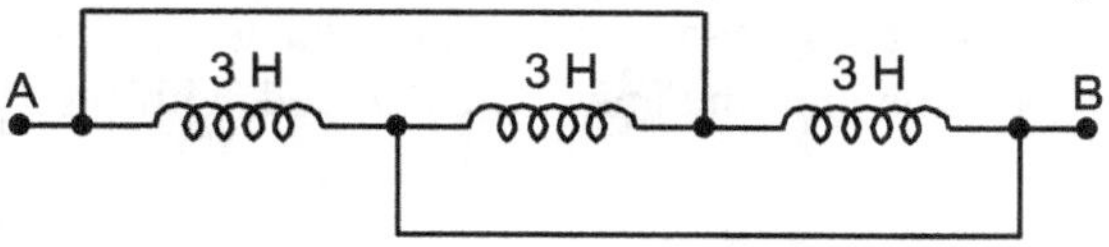

(a) 3 H (b) 1 H

(c) 9 H (d) 0.66 H

45. In an a.c. circuit current and voltage are given by $I = 100\sin\left(314t+\frac{\pi}{3}\right)$ ampere, $E = 100\sin 314t$ volt.

The power dissipated in the circuit is :

(a) 100 watt (b) 2500 watt

(c) 500 watt (d) 104 watt

46. Current through 20 Ω resistor in the given circuit is :

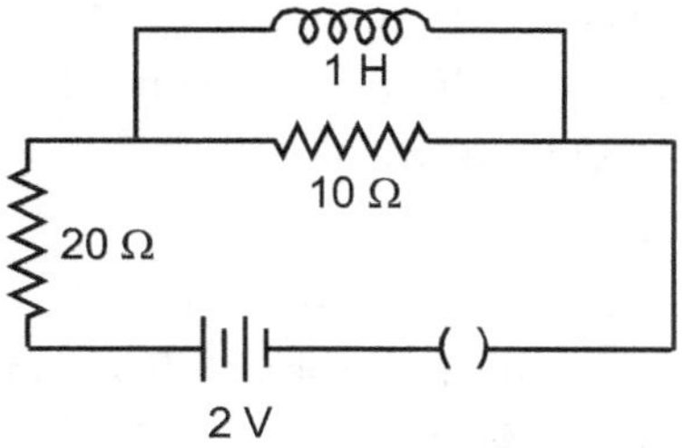

(a) 0.3 A (b) 0.2 A

(c) 0.1 A (d) 0.66 A

47. Current in a coil is increased from 1 A to 11 A in 4 milliseconds. If the inductance of the coil is 40 mH, then e.m.f. induced in the coil during this process is :

(a) 40 volt (b) 0.4 volt

(c) 100 volt (d) 440 volt

48. Average power dissipation in a pure capacitor in a.c. circuit is : **(C.P.M.T. 1998)**

(a) $\frac{1}{2}CV^2$ (b) $2CV^2$

(c) Zero (d) CV^2

49. Two inductors each of inductance L are connected in series with opposite magnetic flux. What is the resultant inductance ?

(D.P.M.T. 2000)

(a) 3 L (b) 2 L
(c) L (d) Zero

50. Current of 1 amp flows through a coil of N turns. The magnetic flux linked with the coil is :

(a) $\frac{N}{L}$ (b) L
(c) NL (d) N^2L

51. The output voltage of an ideal transformer connected to a 240 V a.c. mains is 24 V. When the transformer is used to light a bulb with rating 24 V, 24 W. Then current in the primary coil of the circuit is :

(C.B.S.E/P.M.T. 2000)

(a) 0.1 A (b) 0.2 A
(c) 0.3 A (d) Zero

52. An alternating e.m.f., E (in volt) = 200 sin 100t is connected to 1 μF capacitor through an a.c. ammeter. The current in the ammeter is :

(a) 20 mA (b) 80 mA
(c) 10 mA (d) 40 mA

53. A straight conductor of length 0.4 is moved with a speed of 7 m/s perpendicular to a magnetic field of induction 0.9 weber per m^2. The induced e.m.f. across the conductor is : **(C.B.S.E. 1995)**

(a) 25.2 V (b) 1.26 V
(c) 5.04 V (d) 2.52 V

54. What is the unit of self inductance of a coil ?

(D.P.M.T. 2000)

(a) volt s^{-1} A^2 (b) volt s A^{-1}
(c) volt s^{-1} A^{-1} (d) volt s^{-1} A

55. The power factor of an a.c. circuit having L and R connected in series to an a.c. source of angular frequency ω is given by :

(A.I.E.E.E. 2002)

(a) $\frac{\sqrt{R^2+\omega^2 L^2}}{R}$ (b) $\frac{R}{\sqrt{R^2+\omega^2L^2}}$

(c) $\frac{\omega L}{R}$ (d) $\frac{R}{\omega L}$

56. A long straight solenoid has 800 turns per meter and current flowing through it is 1.6 A. Magnetic induction at the ends of the solenoid on its axis is : **(M.P.C.E.E. 1999)**

(a) 4×10^{-4} T (b) 0.16×10^{-2} T
(c) 0.8×10^{-4} T (d) 32×10^{-4} T

57. When current changes from +2 A to –2 A in 0.05 sec, an e.m.f. of 8 V is induced in a coil. The coefficient of self inductance of the coil is : **(A.I.E.E.E. 2003)**

(a) 0.2 H (b) 0.4 H
(c) 0.1 H (d) 0.8 H

58. A current carrying loop behaves as a small magnet. If A is the area of the loop and M is the magnetic dipole moment, then current flowing through the loop is :

(M.P.P.M.T. 1998)

(a) M/A (b) MA^2
(c) A/M (d) MA

59. A cylindrical magnet is placed near a circular coil as shown in the figure below :

(P.M.T. 1995)

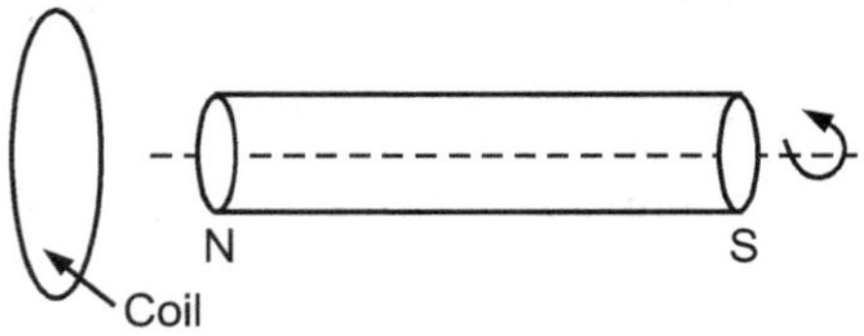

When the magnet is rotated about its own axis, then induced current in the coil is :

(a) zero
(b) anticlockwise
(c) clockwise
(d) depends upon the speed of rotation (ω)

60. The armature of DC motor has 20 Ω resistance. It draws current of 1.5 amp, when run by 220 volts d.c. supply. The value of back e.m.f. induced in it will be :

(a) 190 V (b) 170 V
(c) 150 V (d) 160 V

61. In an ideal parallel LC circuit, the capacitor is charged by connecting it to a d.c. source, which is then disconnected from the source. The current in the circuit :

(a) oscillates instantly
(b) becomes zero instantly
(c) decays monotonically
(d) grows monotonically

62. A rectangular loop PQRS is moved with velocity v in the magnetic field as shown in the figure below.

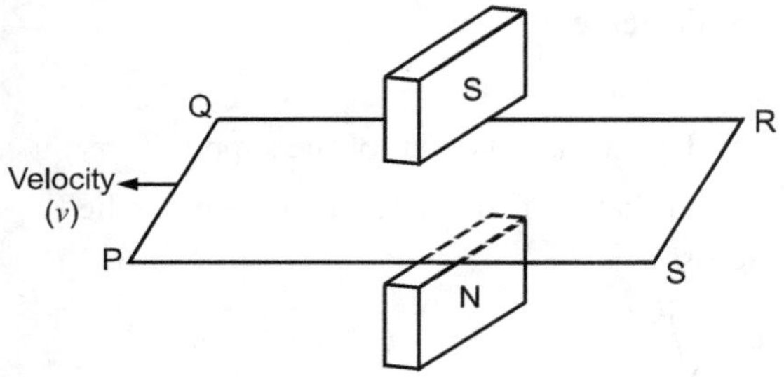

When the edge PQ enters the magnetic field at $t = 0$, which one of the following graphs represents the induced e.m.f. in the coil ?

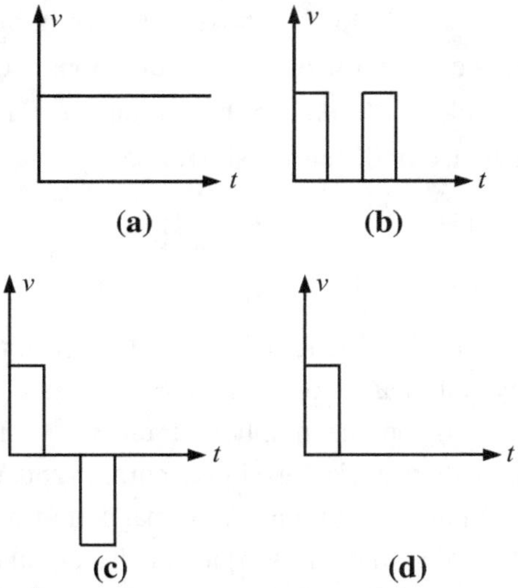

63. An area 0.5 m^2 is situated in a uniform magnetic field of 4 weber m^{-2} making an angle of 60° with the field. The magnetic flux linked with the area would be :

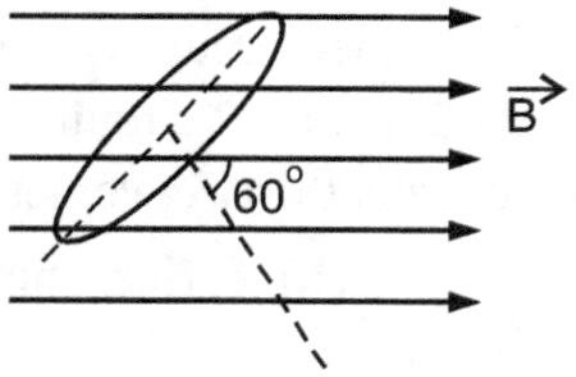

(a) $\sqrt{3}$ weber (b) 2.0 weber
(c) 1.0 weber (d) 0.5 weber

64. When a magnet is moved with its north pole towards a coil placed in a closed circuit, then the nearest face of the coil :

(a) shows south polarity
(b) shows north polarity
(c) shows on polarity
(d) shows sometimes north and sometimes south polarity.

65. A conducting square loop of side L and resistance R moves in its plane with uniform velocity v perpendicular to one of its sides. A magnetic induction B, constant in time and space, pointing perpendicular and into the plane of the loop, exists everywhere with half the loop outside the field as shown in the figure below. The induced e.m.f. is :

(A.I.E.E.E. 2002)

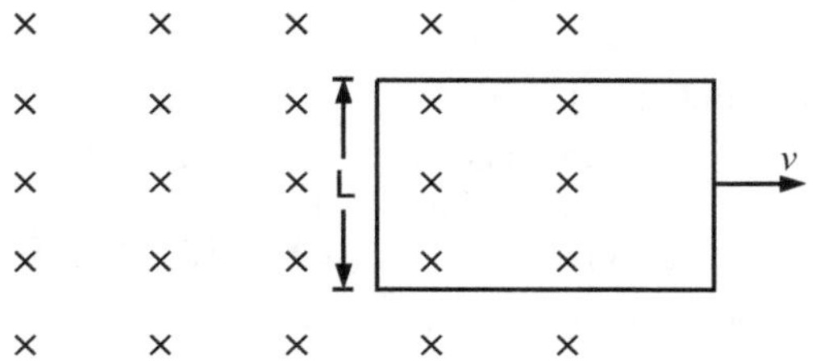

(a) BvR (b) $\frac{BvL}{R}$
(c) BvL (d) $\frac{BvL}{2}$

66. When an alternating voltage $V = V_0 \sin(100t)$ is applied across a circuit, then the phase difference between voltage V and current I in the circuit is observed to be $\frac{\pi}{4}$ as shown in the figure. If the circuit is possibly a series R-C, L-C or R-L circuit, then the relationship between the two elements is : **(I.I.T. Screening 2003)**

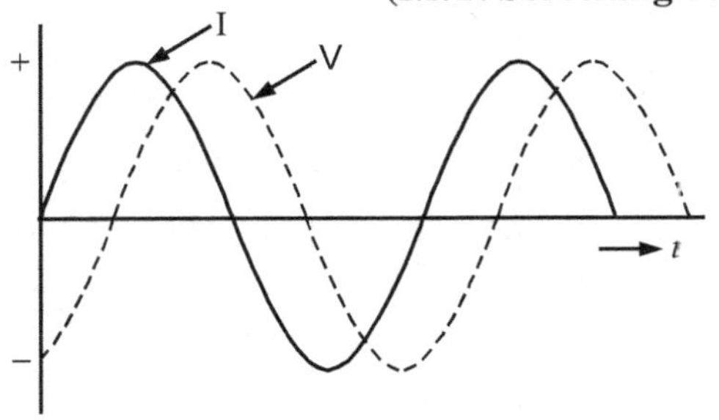

(a) R = 1 kΩ, C = 10 μF
(b) R = 1 kΩ, L = 1 H
(c) R = 1 kΩ, C = 1 μF
(d) R = 1 kΩ, L = 10 H

67. Two circular coils can be arranged in any of three situations as shown in the figure. Their mutual inductance will be : **(I.I.T. Screening 2001)**

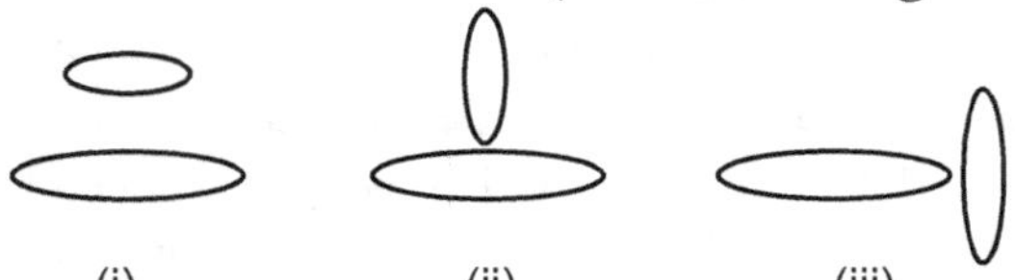

(a) Maximum in case (i)
(b) Maximum in case (ii)
(c) Maximum in case (iii)
(d) Same in all cases

68. If two coils are placed close to each other, then mutual inductance of pair of coils depends upon : **(A.I.E.E.E. 2003)**
(a) the material of wires of two coils
(b) the rate at which current is changing in the coil
(c) relative position and orientation of the two coils
(d) the current in the two coils

69. A 220 V, 1000 W bulb is connected across a 110 V mains supply. The power consumed will be : **(A.I.E.E.E. 2003)**
(a) 250 W (b) 750 W
(c) 1000 W (d) 500 W

70. A bulb is connected in series with an inductor and 6 V d.c. supply, soft iron core is inserted in the coil. During this process intensity of bulb :

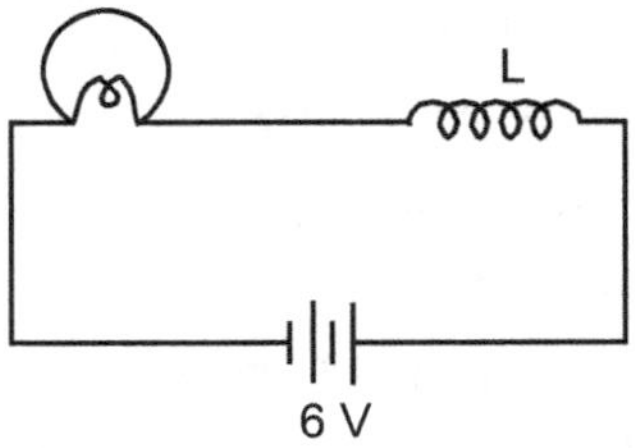

(a) remains unchanged
(b) decreases
(c) increases
(d) depends upon e.m.f. of the supply.

71. Power factor of LR - circuit with a.c. applied across it is :
(a) $\frac{R}{\sqrt{\omega L}}$ (b) $\sqrt{R^2 + \omega^2 L^2}$
(c) $\frac{R}{\sqrt{\omega^2 L^2 + R^2}}$ (d) Zero

72. An alternating e.m.f. of $E = 100 \sin (100\, \pi t)$ is connected to a choke of negligible resistance and current oscillations of amplitude 1 A are to be produced. The inductance of the choke should be :
(a) 100 H (b) $\frac{1}{\pi}$ H
(c) 1 H (d) π H

73. A wire of fixed length l can be formed into many circular loops of varying radii r depending on the number of turns n. The loop so formed is carrying a current and is placed normally in a uniform magnetic field B. In order that the torque on the circular loop formed be maximum; the number of turns n must be equal to:
(a) 1 (b) 4
(c) 8 (d) ∞

74. The bob of a simple pendulum is replaced by a magnet. The oscillations are set along the length of the magnet. A copper coil is added so that one pole of the magnet passes in and out of the coil. The coil is short-circuited. Then which one of the following happens ?
(a) Period decreases
(b) Period does not change
(c) Oscillations are damped
(d) Amplitude increases

75. A 3 metre long conductor is moved at right angles to a magnetic field of intensity 10^{-3} tesla at 10^2 m sec^{-1}. The potential difference across the conductor is :
(a) 3 V (b) 0.3 V
(c) 0.03 V (d) 3×10^{-3} V

76. In an a.c. circuit, the instantaneous values of e.m.f. and current are $E = 200 \sin 314t$ volts and $I = \sin\left(314\,t + \frac{\pi}{3}\right)$ ampere. The average power consumed in watt is :
(a) 200 (b) 100
(c) 0 (d) 50

77. When 100 volt d.c. is applied across a coil, current of 1 amp flows through it. When 100 volt a.c. at 50 Hz is applied to the same coil, only 0.5 ampere current flows. The impedance of the coil is: **(C.M.E.T. 1995)**
(a) 100 Ω (b) 200 Ω
(c) 300 Ω (d) 400 Ω

78. A transformer steps down 200 volt to 22 volt to operate a device with an impedance of 220 ohm. Then the current drawn from the mains by the primary of the transformer, is :
(a) 1 amp (b) 0.1 amp
(c) 0.01 amp (d) 0.001 amp

79. The coefficient of mutual inductance between the two coils depends upon :
(a) Medium between coils only
(b) Separation between two coils only
(c) Both (a) and (b)
(d) None of these

80. For series LCR circuit the wrong statement is : **(Rajasthan C.E.T. 1997)**
(a) Applied e.m.f. and potential difference across resistance are in the same phase.
(b) Applied e.m.f. and potential difference at inductor coil have phase difference of $\frac{\pi}{2}$.
(c) Potential difference across capacitor and inductor have phase difference of $\frac{\pi}{2}$.
(d) Phase difference and the potential difference between resistor and capacitor is $\frac{\pi}{2}$.

81. A step-up transformer operates on a 200 volt line and supplies a current of 2 ampere. The ratio of primary and secondary windings is 1 : 5. The output voltage in the secondary is :
(a) 200 volt (b) 40 volt
(c) 1000 volt (d) Zero volt

82. In Q. No. 81, if the efficiency is 100%, then the current in the primary coil is :
(a) 10 ampere (b) 0.4 ampere
(c) 2 ampere (d) Zero ampere

83. An a.c. expressed by $E(t) = E_0 \cos \omega t$ is applied across a pure inductance. The phase difference between voltage and the applied a.c. is :
(a) 0 (b) $-\frac{\pi}{4}$
(c) $-\frac{\pi}{2}$ (d) $\frac{\pi}{2}$

84. In a step-up transformer the turns ratio is 1 : 2. A leclanche cell (e.m.f. = 1.5 V) is connected across the primary. The voltage developed in the secondary would be :
(a) 3.0 volt (b) 0.7 volt
(c) 1.5 volt (d) Zero

85. The equation of an alternating current is $I = 50\sqrt{2} \sin 400 \pi t$ amp, then the frequency and the root mean square value of the current are respectively :

(a) 200 hertz, 50 amp

(b) 400 hertz, $50\sqrt{2}$ amp

(c) 200 hertz, $50\sqrt{2}$ amp

(d) 50 hertz, 200 amp

86. A dynamo is sometimes said to generate electricity. It actually acts as a source of :

(a) charge (b) magnetism

(c) e.m.f. (d) energy

87. A step-down transformer is used to reduce the voltage from 110 V to 11 V. The current in primary and secondary is 2 A and 18 A respectively. The efficiency of the transformer is : **(CET 2000)**

(a) 100% (b) 90%

(c) 80% (d) 60%

88. The power factor of a pure resistive and pure inductive circuit have a ratio of :

(a) 1

(b) 0

(c) ∞

(d) Finite positive number

89. A coil has an area of 0.05 m^2 and it has 800 turns. After placing the coil in a magnetic field of strength 4×10^{-5} Wb/m^2, it is rotated through 90° in 0.1 sec. The average e.m.f. induced in the coil is : **(C.P.M.T. 2001)**

(a) 0.026 V (b) 0.056 V

(c) 0.046 V (d) 0.016 V

90. In a region of uniform magnetic induction $B = 10^{-2}$ tesla, a circular coil of radius 30 cm and resistance π^2 ohm is rotated about an axis which is perpendicular to the direction of B and which forms a diameter of the coil. If the coil rotates at 200 r.p.m. the amplitude of the alternating current induced in the coil is : **(Premedical Dental 1990)**

(a) $4\pi^2$ mA (b) 30 mA

(c) 6 mA (d) 200 mA

91. A circular coil of radius r and n turns lies on a horizontal table. On top of it a long straight wire, electrically insulated from the coil, is placed bisecting the coil as shown in figure. The wire carries a current $I_0 \sin \omega t$, the induced e.m.f. in the coil is : (where E_0 is constant). **(A.I.E.E.E. 2008)**

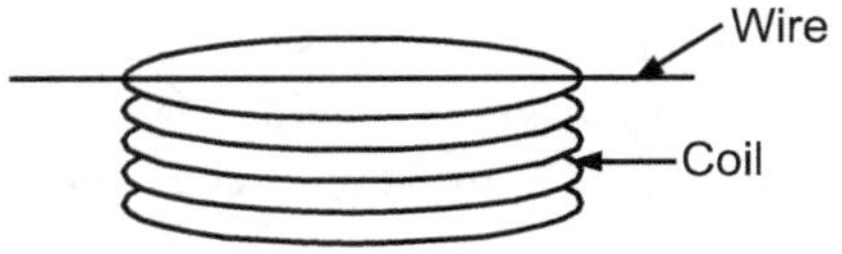

(a) E_0 (b) $E_0 \cos \omega t$

(c) $E_0 \sin \omega t$ (d) Zero

92. In a step-down transformer the turns ratio is 3 : 1. A cell of e.m.f. 1.5 volt is connected across the primary. The voltage across the secondary is :

(a) 1.5 V (b) 4.5 V

(c) Zero (d) 0.5 V

93. When 100 volt d.c. is applied across a solenoid. a current 1.0 amp flows in it. When 100 volt a.c. is applied across the same coil, the current drops to 0.5 amp. If the frequency of a.c. source is 50 Hz, the impedance and inductance of the solenoid are : **(C.P.M.T. 1990)**

(a) 200 ohm and 0.55 henry

(b) 100 ohm and 0.86 henry

(c) 300 ohm and 1.0 henry

(d) 100 ohm and 0.93 henry

94. A generator produces a voltage that is given by $V = 240 \sin 120t$ volt, where t is in seconds. The frequency and r.m.s. voltage are : **(M.P.P.M.T. 1990)**

(a) 60 Hz and 240 volt

(b) 19 Hz and 120 volt

(c) 19 Hz and 170 volt

(d) 754 Hz and 170 volt

95. In an a.c. circuit the potential V and the current I are given respectively by V = 100 sin (100 t) volt and

$I = 100 \sin\left(100t + \frac{\pi}{3}\right)$ milliampere. The power dissipation in the circuit will be : **(C.P.M.T. 1991)**

(a) 10.4 watt (b) 10 watt
(c) 2.5 watt (d) 5 watt

96. If you are not to develop eddy currents in the core of the transformer then it can be obtained :

(a) by increasing the number of turns in the secondary coil
(b) by taking a laminated core
(c) by making a step-down transformer
(d) by using a weak-alternating current at high potential

97. Which of the following plots may represent the reactance of a series LC combination ?

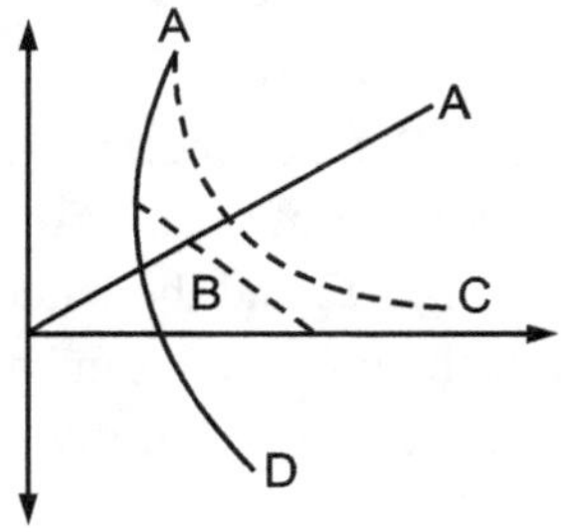

(a) A (b) B
(c) C (d) D

98. An e.m.f. of 1.0 V is applied in a circuit containing 5 H inductance and 10 ohm resistance. The ratio of current at t = infinite and t = 1 sec is :

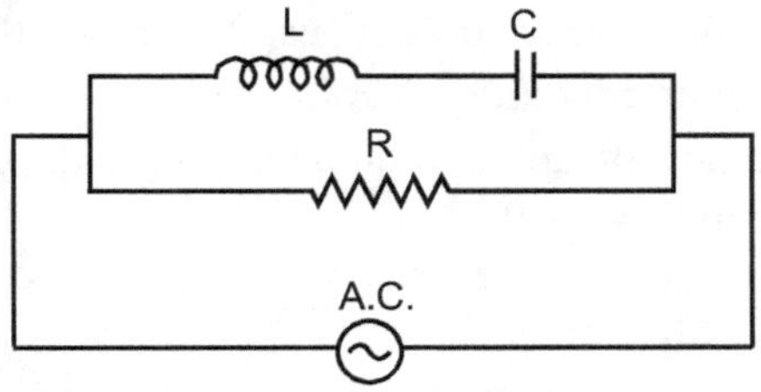

(a) e^{-1} (b) $1 - e^{-1}$
(c) $\frac{e^{1/2}}{e^{1/2} - 1}$ (d) $\frac{e^2}{e^2 - 1}$

99. With increase in frequency of an a.c. supply the inductive reactance :

(a) decreases
(b) increases, and is directly proportional to frequency
(c) increases as square of frequency
(d) decreases inversely with frequency

100. Alternating current instead of direct current is used in long distance electric transmission because : **(N.D.A. 2004)**

(a) it is easy to generate
(b) rectification is possible
(c) energy losses are minimum
(d) it causes fewer accidents.

101. A certain choke coil of negligible resistance draws a current of 8 A, when connected to a supply of 100 volts, at 50 Hz. A certain non-inductive resistance, under the same conditions at 40 Hz, the total current they will take if joined in series is :

(a) 1.06 amp (b) 10.6 amp
(c) 0.106 amp (d) None of these

102. An alternating voltage is given by $E = E_1 \sin \omega t + E_2 \cos \omega t$. Then the root mean square value of voltage is given by : **(A.I.E.E.E. 2007)**

(a) $\sqrt{E_1^2 + E_2^2}$ (b) $\sqrt{E_1 E_2}$
(c) $\sqrt{\frac{E_1 E_2}{2}}$ (d) $\sqrt{\frac{E_1^2 + E_2^2}{2}}$

103. In an a.c. circuit, e.m.f. and current are given by, $E = 200 \sin 314\, t$, $I = \sin\left(314\, t + \frac{\pi}{3}\right)$. Average power consumption in the circuit will be :

(a) 200 W (b) 100 W
(c) 50 W (d) 25 W

104. A dynamo works on the principle of :

(a) Electrostatic induction
(b) Optical induction
(c) Electromagnetic induction
(d) None of the above

105. An inductor has a resistance R and inductance L. It is connected to an a.c. source of e.m.f. E_V and angular frequency ω, then the current I_V in the circuit is given by :

(a) $I_V = \frac{E_V}{\omega L}$

(b) $I_V = \frac{E_V}{R}$

(c) $I_V = \frac{E_V}{\sqrt{R^2 + \omega^2 L^2}}$

(d) $I_V = \sqrt{\left(\frac{E_V}{R}\right)^2 + \left(\frac{E_V}{\omega L}\right)^2}$

106. A step-up transformer operates on a 230 V line and supplies a load of 2 ampere. The ratio of the primary and secondary windings is 1 : 25. The current in the primary is :

(C.B.S.E. 1998)

(a) 15 A (b) 25 A
(c) 12.5 A (d) 50 A

107. A player with a 3 metre long iron rod runs towards east with a speed of 30 km/hr. The horizontal component of earth's magnetic field is 4×10^{-5} weber/m^2. If he is running with a rod in horizontal and vertical positions, then the potential difference induced between the two ends of the rod in the two cases will be :

(a) Zero in vertical position and 10^{-3} volt in horizontal position
(b) 10^{-3} volt in vertical position and zero in horizontal position
(c) Zero in both positions
(d) 10^{-3} volt in both positions

108. A transformer is a device which converts :

(N.C.E.R.T. 1999)

(a) small current at low voltage to high current at high voltage
(b) large current at low voltage to low current at high voltage
(c) small current at high voltage to small current at low voltage
(d) large current at high voltage to low current at low voltage

109. An average induced e.m.f. of 1V appears in a coil when the current in it is changed from 10 A in one direction to 10 A in opposite direction in 0.5 sec. Self-inductance of the coil is : **(C.P.M.T. 2001)**

(a) 25 mH (b) 75 mH
(c) 50 mH (d) 100 mH

110. Which of the following does alternating current show ? **(J.I.P.M.E.R. 1998)**

(a) Chemical effect (b) Magnetic effect
(c) Heating effect (d) All of these

111. An alternating current source of frequency 100 Hz is joined to a combination of a resistance, a capacitance and a coil in series. The potential across the coil, the resistor and the capacitor is 46, 8 and 40 volt, respectively. The electromotive force of alternating current source in volt is :

(M.P.P.E.T. 1995)

(a) 94 (b) 14
(c) 10 (d) 76

112. Two coils A and B are connected in series to a supply of 240 V r.m.s. and 50 cps. The resistance of A is 5 Ω and the inductance of B is 0.02 H. If the power consumed is 3 kW and the power factor is 0.75, the resistance of coil B is :

(a) 5.8 Ω (b) 0.58 Ω
(c) 58 Ω (d) 0.058 Ω

113. The coil of a dynamo is rotating in a magnetic field. The developed induced e.m.f. changes and the number of magnetic lines of force also changes. Which of the following conditions is correct ?

(a) Lines of force minimum, but induced e.m.f. is zero.
(b) Lines of force maximum, but induced e.m.f. is zero.
(c) Lines of force maximum, but induced e.m.f. is not zero.
(d) Lines of force maximum, and induced e.m.f. is also maximum.

114. A coil has 2000 turns and area of 70 cm^2. The magnetic field perpendicular to the plane of the coil is 0.3 Wb/m^2 and takes 0.1 sec to rotate through 180°. The value of induced e.m.f. will be :

(a) 8.4 volt (b) 84 volt

(c) 42 volt (d) 4.2 volt

115. You have two copper cables of equal length for carrying current. One of them has a single wire of area of cross-section A, the other has ten wires of cross-section A/10 each. Which of them will be suitable for transporting a.c. and d.c. ?

(a) Only single strand for d.c., either for a.c.

(b) Only single strand for a.c., either for d.c.

(c) Either for d.c. and only multiple strands for a.c.

(d) Only single strand for d.c. and only multiple strands for a.c.

116. The overall efficiency of a transformer is 90%. The transformer is rated for an output of 9000 watt. The primary voltage is 100 volt. The ratio of turns in the primary to secondary coil is 5 : 1. The iron losses at full load are 700 watt. The primary voltage is 1000 volt. The primary coil has resistance of 1 ohm. Then the voltage in the secondary coil is :

(a) 1000 volt (b) 5000 volt

(c) 200 volt (d) Zero volt

117. A resistor, an inductor and a capacitor are connected in series to an a.c. power supply. When measured with the help of an a.c. voltmeter, the voltage across them is found to be 80 V, 30 V and 90 V respectively. What is the supply voltage ?

(a) 200 V (b) 100 V

(c) 140 V (d) $\frac{200}{\sqrt{2}}$ V

118. The p.d. across an instrument in an a.c. circuit of frequency f is V and the current flowing through it is I such that V = 5 cos $2\pi ft$ volts and I = 2 sin $2\pi ft$ amps. The power dissipated in the instrument is :

(a) 0 watts (b) 10 watts

(c) 5 watts (d) 2.5 watts

119. The instantaneous voltage across a pure capacitor :

(a) leads current in phase by $\frac{\pi}{2}$

(b) lags behind the current in phase by $\frac{\pi}{2}$

(c) is in phase with the current

(d) lags behind current in phase by an angle depending on frequency

120. At low frequency a condenser offers :

(a) high impedance

(b) low impedance

(c) zero impedance

(d) impedance of condenser is independent of frequency

121. A 750 Hz, 20 volt source is connected to a resistance of 100 ohm, an inductance of 0.1803 H and a capacitance of 10 μF, all in series. The time in which the resistance (thermal capacity = 2 joule/°C) will get heated by 10°C is :

(a) 348 seconds (b) 328 seconds

(c) 248 seconds (d) 228 seconds

122. In general, in an alternating current circuit :

(a) the average value of current is zero

(b) the average value of square of the current is zero

(c) average power dissipation is zero

(d) the phase difference between voltage and current is zero

123. The north pole of a long horizontal bar magnet is being brought closer to a vertical conducting plane along the perpendicular direction. The direction of the induced current in the conducting plane will be :

(a) horizontal (b) vertical

(c) clockwise (d) anticlockwise

124. The device that does not work on the principle of mutual induction is :

(a) induction coil (b) motor

(c) tesla coil (d) transformer

125. A step down transformer of transformation ratio 3 has an efficiency of 80%. The input power of 360 W is at a voltage of 120 V. The input current is :

(a) 3 A (b) 0.33 A

(c) 2.4 A (d) 0.24 A

126. A capacitive circuit has zero resistance. When a.c. voltage is applied across this circuit, then the current leads the applied a.c. voltage by an angle :

(a) 30° (b) 45°

(c) 90° (d) 0°

127. The peak value of an alternating e.m.f. E given by $E = E_0 \cos \omega t$ is 10 volt and its frequency is 50 Hz. At a time $t = \frac{1}{600}$ sec, the instantaneous value of the e.m.f. is :

(M.P.P.M.T. 1990)

(a) 10 volt (b) $5\sqrt{3}$ volt

(c) 5 volt (d) 1 volt

128. A wire coil carries the current I. The potential energy of the coil does not depend upon :

(a) the value of I

(b) the number of turns in the coil

(c) whether the coil has an iron core or not

(d) the resistance of the coil

129. In an a.c. circuit, the potential difference across an inductor and resistor joined in series are respectively 16 V and 20 V. The total potential difference across the circuit is: **(A.F.M.C. Pune 1998)**

(a) 20.0 V (b) 25.6 V

(c) 31.9 V (d) 53.5 V

130. A magnetic field of 2×10^{-2} T acts at right angles to a coil of area 100 cm^2 with 50 turns. The average e.m.f. induced in the coils is 0.1 V, when it is removed from the field in time *t*. The value of *t* is :

(C.P.M.T. 2001)

(a) 0.01 sec (b) 0.1 sec

(c) 0.5 sec (d) 1 sec

131. A capacitor is a perfect insulator for :

(a) direct current

(b) alternating current

(c) effective voltage

(d) none of these

132. An inductance of 0.2 H and a resistance of 100 Ω are connected in series with an a.c. supply of 220 volts - 50 Hz. Phase lag of current from e.m.f. applied is :

(a) $\tan^{-1}(0.4\pi)$ (b) $\tan^{-1}(\pi)$

(c) $\tan^{-1}(4\pi)$ (d) $\tan^{-1}(0.2\pi)$

133. A capacitor of 2μF draws a current of 4 mA when connected across an a.c. of 300 Hz. The voltage drop across capacitor is :

(a) 1.06 V (b) 1.5 V

(c) 2.1 V (d) 6.6 V

134. A coil of area 80 square cm and 50 turns is rotating with 2,000 revolutions per minute about an axis perpendicular to a magnetic field of 0.05 tesla. The maximum value of the e.m.f. developed in it is :

(a) 200π volt (b) $\frac{10\pi}{3}$ volt

(c) $\frac{4\pi}{3}$ volt (d) $\frac{2}{3}$ volt

135. Power factor is defined as :

(a) Apparent power / True power

(b) True power / Apparent power

(c) True power × Apparent power

(d) None of these

136. The magnitude of the potential difference across the secondary of a transformer does not depend on : **(BHU 2000)**

(a) the potential difference in the primary

(b) the number of turns in primary

(c) the number of turns in the secondary

(d) the resistance of the primary and the secondary

137. A capacitor has a resistance of 1200 mega ohm and capacitance of 22 microfarad. When connected to an a.c. supply of frequency 80 hertz, then the alternating voltage supply required to drive a current of 10 virtual ampere is :

(a) $904\sqrt{2}$ (b) 904 volt

(c) $\frac{904}{\sqrt{2}}$ (d) 452 volt

138. An e.m.f. of 1.5 V is applied in a circuit containing 5 henry inductance and 10 Ω resistance. The ratio of current at time $t = \infty$ and $t = 1$ sec is :

(a) $\frac{e^{1/2}}{e^{1/2}-1}$ (b) $\frac{e^2}{e^2-1}$

(c) e^{-1} (d) $1 - e^{-1}$

139. A square metal wire loop of side 10 cm and resistance 1 Ω is moved with a constant velocity v_o in a uniform magnetic field of induction B = 2T as shown in the figure. The magnetic field lines are perpendicular to the plane of the loop directed into the plane of the page. The loop is connected to a network of resistors each of value 3 Ω. The resistance of lead wires ND and MB are negligible. What should be the speed of the loop v_o so as to have a steady current of 1 mA in the loop ?

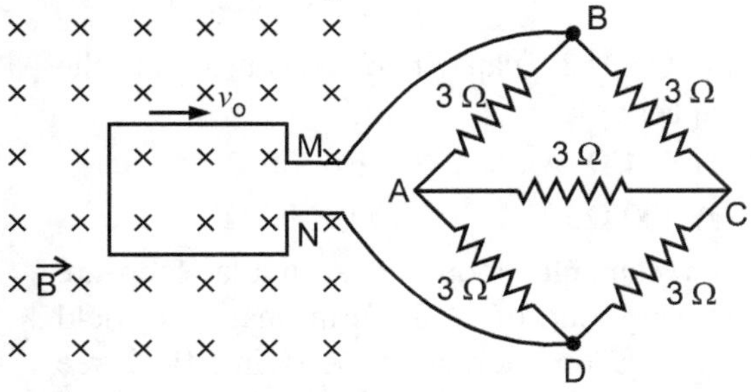

(a) 0.2 m/s (b) 2 m/s

(c) 2 cm/s (d) 0.2 cm/s

140. A short circuited coil is placed in a time varying magnetic field. Electric power is dissipated due to the current induced in the coil. If the number of turns were to be quadrupled and the wire radius halved, the electrical power dissipated would be :

(a) quadrupled (b) halved

(c) doubled (d) the same

141. An ideal coil of 10 H is connected in series with a resistor of 5 Ω and a source of e.m.f. of 5 volt. Current flowing through the circuit after 2 seconds when the circuit is switched ON is :

(a) e (b) $1 - e^{-1}$

(c) e^{-1} (d) $1 - e$

142. Two different coils have self inductance L_1 = 1 mH and L_2 = 4 mH. The current in the first coil is increased at constant rate. The current in the second coil is also increased at constant rate and at the same rate. At a particular instant power flowing through the coil is same. At this instant the induced voltage, induced current and energy in the first coil are V_1, I_1 and e_1 respectively. Similarly, in the second coil these are V_2, I_2 and e_2 respectively. Then :

(a) $\frac{e_2}{e_1} = \frac{1}{4}$ (b) $\frac{I_1}{I_2} = 4$

(c) $\frac{V_1}{V_2} = \frac{1}{4}$ (d) All of these

143. As shown in figure M and N are two co-axial conducting loops separated by some distance. When the switch S is closed, a clockwise current I_M flows in M as seen by the eye E and an induced current I_{N_1} flows in N. The switch remains closed for a long time, when S is opened, a current I_{N_2} flows in coil N. Then direction of I_{N_1} and I_{N_2} as seen by the eye E will be :

(I.I.T. Screening 2002)

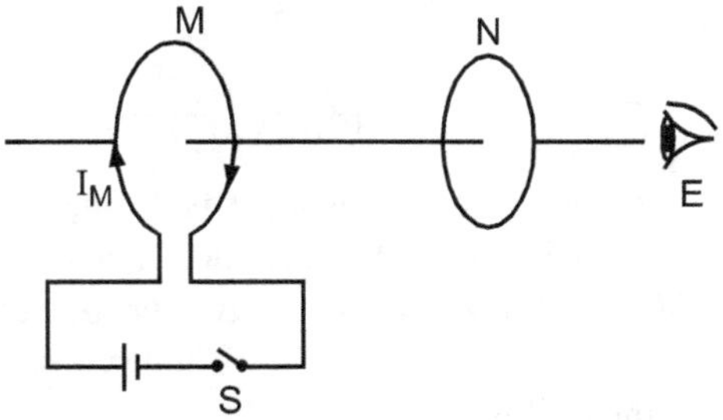

(a) Both anticlockwise

(b) Both clockwise

(c) Clockwise and anticlockwise respectively
(d) Anticlockwise and clockwise respectively

144. The equivalent inductance between A and B shown in the network will be :

(A.I.E.E.E. 2002)

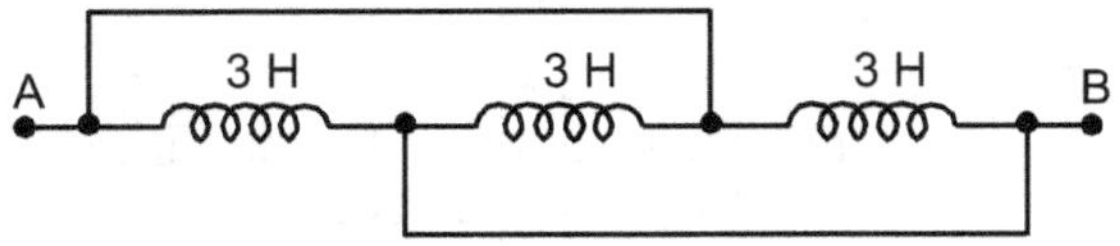

(a) 9 H (b) 3 H
(c) 1 H (d) 2 H

145. A 220V, 1000 watt bulb is connected across a 110V mains supply. The power consumed will be :
(a) 250 W (b) 750 W
(c) 500 W (d) 250 W

146. A gramophone disc of brass having a diameter of 30 cm rotates horizontally at the rate of 100 revolutions in 3 minutes. If the vertical component of earth's magnetic field is 0.01 T, then e.m.f. induced between the centre and rim of the disc is :
(a) 48×10^{-4} V (b) 12.85×10^{-4} V
(c) 24.7×10^{-4} V (d) 36×10^{-2} V

147. A circuit containing resistance R_1, inductance L_1 and capacitance C_1 connected in series resonate at the same frequency υ as a second combination of R_2, L_2 and C_2. If the two circuits are connected in series, then the circuit will resonate at :
(a) υ (b) 2υ
(c) $\sqrt{\frac{L_2C_2}{L_1C_1}}$ (d) $\sqrt{\frac{L_2C_1}{L_1C_2}}$

148. A coil of negligible resistance is connected in series with 90 Ω resistance across a 120 V – 60 Hz a.c. A voltmeter placed across resistor reads 36 V. Then voltage across the coil is :
(a) 114 V (b) 36 V
(c) 84 V (d) 72 V

149. In Q 148 self inductance of the coil will be :
(a) 90 H (b) 1 H
(c) 0.76 H (d) 1.5 H

150. The capacitor of an oscillatory circuit of negligible resistance is enclosed in a container. When the container is evacuated, the frequency of the circuit is 150 kHz and when the container is filled with a gas, the frequency changes by 100 Hz. The dielectric constant of the gas is :
(a) 2 (b) 1.53
(c) 1.0012 (d) 3

151. A coil wound uniformly has self inductance 1.8×10^{-4} H and resistance 6 Ω. The coil is broken into two identical parts. The two parts are then connected in parallel across a 12 V battery of negligible internal resistance. The current through battery at steady state is :
(a) 8 A (b) 16 A
(c) 4 A (d) 5 A

152. A 120 V, 60 Hz a.c. power is connected 800 Ω non-inductive resistance and unknown capacitance in series. The voltage drop across the resistance is found to be 102 V, then voltage drop across capacitor is:
(a) 8 V (b) 102 V
(c) 63 V (d) None of these

153. In Q 152, capacitive reactance of the capacitor is :
(a) 494 Ω (b) 300 Ω
(c) 400 Ω (d) 590 Ω

154. A rectangular loop and a circular loop are moving out of a uniform magnetic field region acting normal to loops in a field free region with a constant velocity. In which loop do you expect the induced e.m.f. to be constant during the passage out of the field region ?
(a) Rectangular loop
(b) Circular loop
(c) In both loops
(d) None of the above

155. An iron bar falling vertically through the hollow region of a thick cylindrical shell and made of copper experiences a retarding force because the iron bar :

(a) induces current in the cylinder

(b) is a magnet

(c) is a positively charged conductor

(d) is a negatively charged conductor

156. Self-induction is also called :

(a) Inertia of rest

(b) Inertia of motion

(c) Inertia of current

(d) Inertia of elasticity

157. A square of side l made from a wire is placed at the centre of a larger square side L made from a similar wire (but L >> l). The planes of two squares are coplanar and their centres coincide. If a current passing through a square of side L is I, then their mutual inductance is given by :

(a) $\frac{2\sqrt{2}\,\mu_0}{\pi L}$ (b) $\frac{\sqrt{2}\,\mu_0 l^2}{\pi L}$

(c) $\frac{2\sqrt{2}\,\mu_0 l^2}{\pi L}$ (d) $\frac{\pi L}{\sqrt{2}\,\mu_0 l^2}$

158. A thin semicircular conducting ring of radius 'a' is falling with its plane vertical in a horizontal magnetic field as shown in the figure. At the position PQR, the speed of the ring is v. What is the potential difference developed across the ring at the position PQR ? **(I.I.T. 1996)**

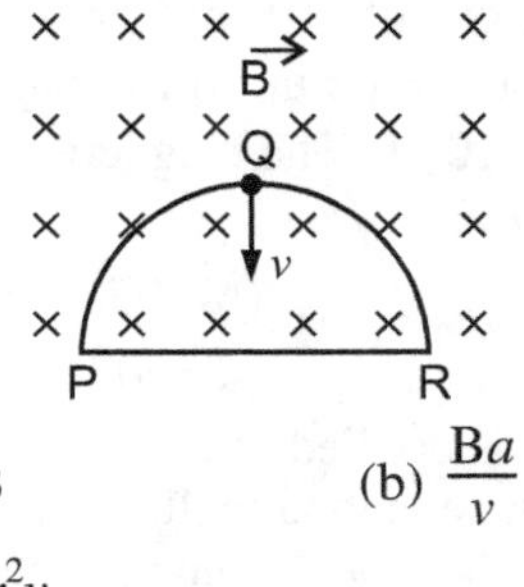

(a) vaB (b) $\frac{Ba}{v}$

(c) $\frac{B\pi r^2 v}{2}$ (d) $2Bav$

159. The time required for a current to attain the maximum value in a d.c. circuit containing Land R depends upon :

(a) R only

(b) L only

(c) L/R

(d) The applied potential difference

160. Mutual inductance of pair of coils is 0.005 H. The current in the first coil according to equation $I = I_0 \sin \omega t$, where $I_0 = 10$ A and $\omega = 100\pi$ radian per second. The maximum value of e.m.f. in the second coil (in volt) is :

(a) 4π (b) π

(c) 5π (d) 2π

161. The peak value of an alternating e.m.f. E is given by $E = E_0 \cos \omega t$ is 10V and its frequency is 50 Hz. At the time $t = \frac{1}{600}$ sec, the instantaneous value of the e.m.f. is :

(a) 10 V (b) $5\sqrt{3}$ V

(c) 5 V (d) 1 V

162. An electric current I flowing through a folded circular copper wire as shown in the figure. The magnetic induction at the centre of the loop will be : **(N.S.E.P. 2000)**

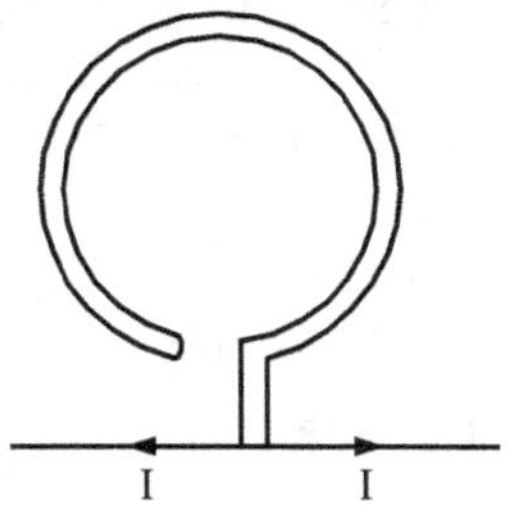

(a) $\frac{\mu_0 I}{r}$ (b) $\frac{\mu_0 I}{2r}$

(c) zero (d) $\frac{2\mu_0 I}{r}$

163. Along the axis of a circular coil, a cylindrical magnet is kept. If the magnet is rotated about this axis, then :

(a) both e.m.f. and a current will be induced in the coil

(b) neither e.m.f. nor current will be induced in the coil

(c) a current will be induced in the coil

(d) no current will be induced in the coil

164. A capacitor C, an inductor L and a.c. ammeters A_1, A_2 and A_3 are connected in the circuit as shown. When the frequency of the oscillator is increased, then at resonance frequency, the reading of ammeter :

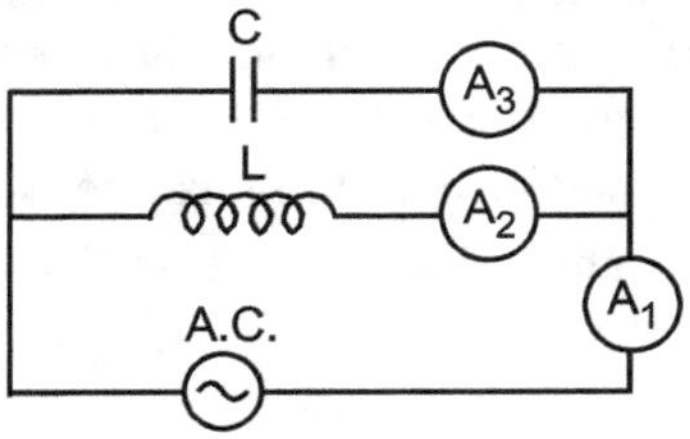

(a) A_3 is zero (b) is the same
(c) A_1 is zero (d) A_2 is zero

165. A solenoid (air core) is 20 cm long and has a cross-section of 4 cm^2 and 400 turns. Then the coefficient of self induction is approximately : **(J.I.P.M.E.R. 2001)**
(a) 4×10^{-4} H (b) 40 H
(c) 4×10^{-5} H (d) 4 H

166. When 100 volt d.c. is applied across a solenoid, a current of 1.0 amp flows in it. When 100 volt a.c. is applied across the same coil, the current drops to 0.5 amp. If the frequency of a.c. source is 50 Hz, the impedance and inductance of the solenoid are :
(a) 100 ohm and 0.86 henry
(b) 100 ohm and 0.93 henry
(c) 200 ohm and 0.55 henry
(d) 200 ohm and 1.0 henry

167. A step-down transformer reduced 220 V to 110 V. The primary coil draws current of 5 amp and secondary supplies 9 ampere. The efficiency of the transformer is :
(a) 70% (b) 60%
(c) 80% (d) 90%

168. The efficiency of a transformer is 90%. The transformer is rated for an output of 9000 W. The applied voltage is 1000 volt. The transformation ratio is 5 : 1. The iron losses at full load are 700 W. The primary coil has a resistance of 1 Ω. The voltage in the secondary coil is :
(a) 5000 V (b) 200 V
(c) 1000 V (d) 0 V

169. Radio frequency choke is :
(a) Air cored
(b) Air as well as iron cored
(c) Iron cored
(d) None of these

170. Roselyn has a coil of 3 mH and wishes to construct a circuit whose resonance frequency is 1000 kHz. The value of capacitor she must use is about (1 picofarad = 10^{-12} F) :
(a) 8.5 picofarad (b) 0.8 picofarad
(b) 85 picofarad (d) 850 picofarad

171. The coefficient of induction of a choke coil is 0.1 H and resistance is 12 Ω. If it is connected to an alternating current source of frequency 60 Hz, the power factor of the circuit is :
(a) 0.30 (b) 0.32
(c) 0.24 (d) 0.28

172. An aeroplane is flying horizontally with a velocity of 360 km/hr^{-1}. The distance between the tips of the wings of aeroplane is 50 m. The vertical component of earth's magnetic field is 4×10^{-4} Wb/m^{-2}. The induced e.m.f. is :
(a) 2 millivolts (b) 2 μ volts
(c) 200 V (d) 2 V

173. A square coil of 10 m^2 area is placed perpendicular to the uniform magnetic field of induction 10^3 T. The magnetic flux linked with the coil is :
(a) 20 Wb (b) 10^4 Wb
(c) 0 (d) 10 Wb

174. A 20 V a.c. is applied to a circuit consisting of a resistance and a coil with negligible resistance. If the voltage across the resistance is 12 V, the voltage across the coil is :
(a) 6 V (b) 8 V
(c) 10 V (d) 16 V

175. A d.c. motor draws a current of 1.5 amp, when run by 220 volts d.c. supply. If it has 20 Ω resistance, then value of back e.m.f. induced in it will be :

(a) 150 V (b) 170 V
(c) 180 V (d) 190 V

176. An inductor of negligible resistance whose reactance is 22 Ω at 200 Hz is connected to a 200 volt, 50 Hz power line. The value of inductance is :

(a) 0.0175 henry (b) 0.175 henry
(c) 1.75 henry (d) 17.5 henry

177. An inductor, a capacitor and a resistor are connected in series to an a.c. supply. When measured with an a.c. voltmeter, the potential difference across the inductor, capacitor and resistor are respectively 60 volt, 90 volt and 40 volt. Then the supply voltage is : **(D.C.E., 2002)**

(a) 130 volt (b) 50 volt
(c) 190 volt (d) 100 volt

178. The core of the transformer is laminated to reduce :

(a) copper losses (b) iron losses
(c) eddy current losses (d) hysteresis losses

179. A coil has 2000 turns and area of 70 cm^2. The magnetic field perpendicular to the plane of the coil is 0.3 Wb/m^3 and takes 0.1 sec to rotate through 180°. The value of induced e.m.f. will be :

(a) 8.4 volt (b) 84 volt
(c) 42 volt (d) 4.2 volt

180. The magnetic flux linked with a coil of 100 turns is 5 Wb when current passing is 50 A. The self inductance of the coil is :

(a) 0.1 H (b) 10 H
(c) 1 H (d) 0.01 H

181. A.C. cannot be measured by direct current ammeter because :

(a) A.C. is virtual
(b) A.C. cannot pass through direct current ammeter
(c) A.C. changes its direction
(d) Average value of current for complete cycle is zero

182. A current carrying coil is subjected to a uniform magnetic field. The coil will orient so that its plane becomes :

(a) inclined at 45° to the magnetic field
(b) inclined at any arbitrary angle to the magnetic field
(c) parallel to the magnetic field
(d) perpendicular to the magnetic field

183. A transformer has 100 windings in the primary and 200 windings in the secondary. The primary is connected to a.c. supply of 120 volts at 10 amp. Check the correct situation for this transformer out of the following :

(a) The secondary voltage is 240 volts and current 10 ampere.
(b) The secondary voltage is 240 volts and current 5 ampere.
(c) The secondary voltage is 60 volts and current 10 ampere.
(d) The secondary voltage is 240 volts and current 20 ampere.

184. A coil of inductance 0.20 H is connected in series with a switch and a cell of e.m.f. 1.6 V. The total resistance of the circuit is 4.0 ohm. What is the initial rate of growth of current when the switch is closed ?

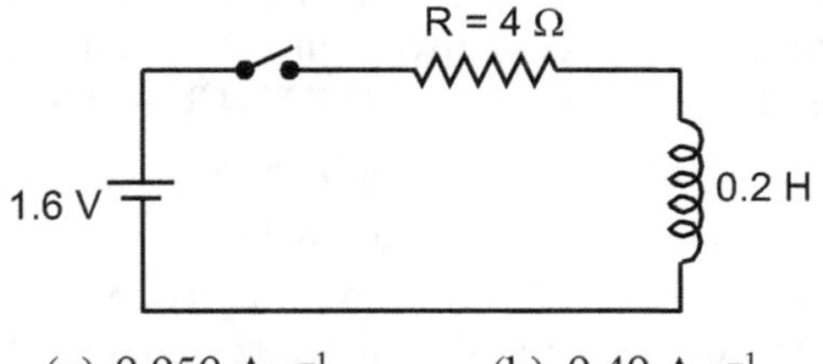

(a) 0.050 A s^{-1} (b) 0.40 A s^{-1}
(c) 0.13 A s^{-1} (d) 80 A s^{-1}

185. A conducting rod of 2 m is moving with a velocity of 1 m/sec perpendicular to a magnetic field of 0.5 Weber/m^2. The e.m.f. induced in it will be :

(a) 0.5 volt (b) 1 volt
(c) 0.1 volt (d) 2 volt

186. A rectangular coil of 20 turns and area of cross-section 25 cm^2 has a resistance of 100 Ω. If a magnetic field which is perpendicular to the plane coil changes at a rate of 1000 tesla per sec, the current in the coil is :

(a) 5.0 amp (b) 0.5 amp

(c) 50 amp (d) 1.0 amp

187. The voltage of an a.c. supply varies with time (t) as V = 120 sin 100 πt cos 100πt. The maximum voltage and frequency respectively are :

(a) 60 V, 200 Hz (b) 60 V, 100 Hz

(c) 120 V, 100 Hz (d) $\frac{120}{\sqrt{2}}$ V, 100 Hz

188. In the induction coil, across secondary coil, the output voltage is practically :

(MHT - CET 2005)

(a) unidirectional, high, intermittent

(b) directional, low, intermittent

(c) unidirectional, high, constant

(d) unidirectional, low, constant

189. A wire of length 2.5 km and resistance 35 Ω has fallen from a height of 10 m in the earth's horizontal field of 2×10^{-5} T. The current through the coil is :

(MHT-CET 2006)

(a) 0.02 A (b) 0.002 A

(c) 0.2 A (d) 2 A

190. E.m.f. is given by e = 200 sin 50 t. The r.m.s. value of current in a circuit of resistance 50 Ω is : **(MHT-CET 2002)**

(a) 0.02828 (b) 0.2828

(c) 2.828 (d) 28.28

191. A rod of length l is rotated about its one end perpendicular to the magnetic field of induction B. The emf induced in the rod is :

(MHT-CET 2007)

(a) $Bl^2\omega$ (b) 0.5 $Bl^2\omega$

(c) $Bl\omega$ (d) 0.5 $Bl\omega$

192. Henry is equivalent to : **(Board Feb. 2008)**

(a) ampere/second (b) ampere-second

(c) ohm/second (d) ohm-second

193. In LCR series circuit, at resonance, the power factor is : **(Board March 2008)**

(a) 0 (b) 0.5

(c) 1 (d) ∞

194. The north pole of a bar magnet is moved towards a coil along the axis passing through the centre of the coil and perpendicular to the plane of the coil. The direction of the induced current in the coil when viewed in the direction of the motion of the magnet is **(E.A.M.C.E.T. 2008)**

(a) clockwise

(b) anti-clockwise

(c) no current in the coil

(d) either clockwise or anti-clockwise

195. A transformer has 1500 turns in the primary coil and 1125 turns in the secondary coil. If the voltage in the primary coil is 200 V, then the voltage in the secondary coil is :

(E.A.M.C.E.T., 2008)

(a) 100 V (b) 150 V

(c) 200 V (d) 250 V

196. Which types of losses do not occur in the transformer ? **(M.P.P.E.T. 2008)**

(a) Iron losses (b) Copper losses

(c) Mechanical losses (d) Flux leakage

197. Lenz's law is a consequence of the law of conservation of : **(M.P.P.E.T., 2009)**

(a) charge (b) mass

(c) momentum (d) energy

198. A coil of metal is kept stationary in a non-uniform magnetic field :

(A.M.U. Medical 2009)

(a) An emf and current are both induced in the coil.

(b) A current is induced, but no emf is induced in the coil.

(c) An emf is induced, but no current is induced in the coil.

(d) Neither emf nor current is induced in the coil.

199. Magnetic flux of 10 μWb is linked with a coil, when a current of 2 mA flows through it. What is the self inductance of the coil ?

(Gujarat, C.E.T. 2011)

(a) 10 mH (b) 5 mH

(c) 15 mH (d) 20 mH

200. A circuit area 0.01 m^2 is kept inside a magnetic field which is normal to its plane. The magnetic field changes from 2 tesla to 1 tesla in 1 millisecond. If the resistance of the circuit is 2 Ω, the amount of heat evolved is : **(Orissa J.E.E. 2007)**

(a) 5 J (b) 50 J

(c) 0.05 J (d) 0.5 J

201. The primary and secondary coils of a transformer have 50 and 1500 turns respectively. If the magnetic flux $\phi = \phi_0 + 4t$, where ϕ is in weber, t is time in seconds and ϕ_0 is a constant, the output voltage across the secondary coil is :

(C.B.S.E.A.T.P.M.T., 2007)

(a) 120 volts (b) 220 volts

(c) 30 volts (d) 90 volts

202. Current in a coil changes from 2 A to 4 A in 0.05 sec. If the average emf in the coil is 8 V, then the self inductance in the coil will be : **(H.P.P.M.T. 2008)**

(a) 0.2 H (b) 0.1 H

(c) 0.8 H (d) 0.4 H

203. What should be the value of self inductance of an inductor that should be connected to 220 V, 50 Hz supply so that a maximum current of 0.9 A flows through it ?

(Gujarat C.E.T. 2011)

(a) 11 H (b) 2 H

(c) 1.1 H (d) 5 H

204. A conducting ring of radius 1 metre is placed in an uniform magnetic field B of 0.01 tesla oscillating with frequency 100 Hz with its plane at right angles to B. What will be the induced electric field ?

(A.I.I.M.S. 2005)

(a) π volt/m (b) 2 volt/m

(c) 10 volt/m (d) 62 volt/m

205. An infinite long cylindrical conducting wire is kept parallel to uniform magnetic field along positive z-axis. The current induced on the surface of the conducting rod is :

(I.I.T. 2005)

(a) along the direction of magnetic field

(b) zero

(c) circulates in clockwise direction when viewed from z-axis

(d) circulates in anticlockwise direction when viewed from z-axis.

206. A rectangular loop of length 'l' and breadth 'b' is placed at a distance of x from an infinitely long wire carrying current 'I' such that the direction of current is parallel to breadth. If the loop moves away from the current wire in a direction perpendicular to it with a velocity 'v', the magnitude of the emf in the loop is (μ_0 = permeability of free space) : **(E.A.M.C.E.T. 2006)**

(a) $\frac{\mu_0 i v}{2\pi x}\left(\frac{l+b}{b}\right)$ (b) $\frac{\mu_0 i^2 v}{4\pi^2 x}\log\left(\frac{b}{l}\right)$

(c) $\frac{\mu_0 i l b v}{2\pi x\,(l+x)}$ (d) $\frac{\mu_0 i l b v}{2\pi}\log\left(\frac{x+l}{x}\right)$

207. One end each of a resistance 'r', capacitance C and resistance '2r' are connected together. The other ends are respectively connected to the positive terminals of the batteries P, Q, R having e.m.f.s. E, E and 2E respectively. The negative terminals of the batteries are then connected together. In this circuit, with steady current the potential drop across the capacitance is **(E.A.M.C.E.T. 2006)**

(a) $\frac{E}{3}$ (b) $\frac{E}{2}$

(c) $\frac{2E}{3}$ (d) E

208. 200 V ac source is fed to series LCR circuit having $X_L = 50\ \Omega$, $X_C = 50\ \Omega$, $R = 25\ \Omega$. Potential drop across the inductor is :

(Karnataka, C.E.T. 2008)

(a) 100 V (b) 200 V

(c) 400 V (d) 10 V

209. Two coaxial solenoids are made by winding thin insulated wire over a pipe of cross-sectional area A = 10 cm^2 and length = 20 cm. If one of the solenoids has 300 turns and the other 400 turns, their mutual inductance is :

$(\mu_0 = 4\pi \times 10^{-7}\ T\ mA^{-1})$

(A.I.E.E.E. 2008)

(a) $2.4\pi \times 10^{-4}$ H (b) $2.4\pi \times 10^{-5}$ H

(c) $4.8\pi \times 10^{-4}$ H (d) $4.8\pi \times 10^{-5}$ H

210. A rectangular, a square, a circular and an elliptical loop, all in the *(x–y)* plane, are moving out of a uniform magnetic field with a constant velocity $\vec{v} = \upsilon\hat{i}$. The magnetic field is directed along the negative z-axis direction. The induced emf, during the passage of these loops, out of the field region, will not remain constant for :

(A.I.P.M.T. Prelim 2009)

(a) the circular and the elliptical loops

(b) only the elliptical loop

(c) any of the four loops

(d) the rectangular, circular and elliptical loops

211. The resonance frequency of a circuit consisting of a coil of inductance 2 μH and a capacitor of 2 μF is

(Manipur M.B.B.S./B.D.S. 2009)

(a) $\frac{10^6}{4\pi}$ Hz (b) $\frac{10^6}{2\pi}$ Hz

(c) $\frac{10^{-6}}{4\pi}$ Hz (d) $\frac{2 \times 10^{-6}}{\pi}$ Hz

212. The average induced e.m.f. in a coil in which the current changes from 0 to 2 A in 0.05 sec is 8 V. The self-inductance of the coil is : **(H.P.P.M.T. 2010)**

(a) 0.1 H (b) 0.2 H

(c) 0.4 H (d) 0.8 H

213. An ac voltage is applied to a resistance R and an inductor L in series. If R and the inductive reactance are both equal to 3 Ω, the phase difference between the applied voltage and the current in the circuit is :

(Gujarat C.E.T. 2011)

(a) $\pi/6$ (b) $\pi/4$

(c) $\pi/2$ (d) 0

214. A coil has an inductance of 0.7 H and is joined in series with a resistance of 220 Ω. When an alternating emf of 220 V at 50 cps is applied to it, then the wattless component of the current in the circuit is :

(B.H.U. Screening 2008)

(a) 5 A (b) 0.5 A

(c) 0.7 A (d) 7 A

215. If the current in an inductor is tripled, by what factor does the stored energy change ?

(Manipur M.B.B.S./B.D.S., 2009)

(a) 4.5 (b) 2

(c) $\frac{1}{9}$ (d) 9

216. A transformer is used to light a 100 W and 110 V lamp from a 220 V main supply. If the main current is 0.5 A, then the efficiency of the transformer is nearly :

(Kerala Engg. 2010)

(a) 89% (b) 100%

(c) 95% (d) 91%

217. A transformer of efficiency 90% draws an input power of 4 kW. An electrical appliance connected across the secondary draws a current of 6 A. The impedance of the device is : **(Kerala C.E.T. 2009)**

(a) 60 Ω (b) 50 Ω

(c) 80 Ω (d) 100 Ω

218. The surface of a metal is illuminated with the light of 400 nm. The kinetic energy of the ejected photoelectrons was found to be 1.68 eV. The work function of the metal is (hc = 1240 eV nm) : **(A.I.E.E.E., 2009)**

(a) 3.09 eV (b) 1.41 eV

(c) 1.51 eV (d) 1.68 eV

219. A 50 Hz ac current of peak value 2 A flows through one of the pair of coils. If the mutual inductance between the pair of coils is 150 mH, then the peak value of voltage induced in the second coil is :

(Kerala Engg. 2010)

(a) 30 πV (b) 60 πV

(c) 15 πV (d) 300 πV

220. Average power in LCR circuits depends upon **(MHT-CET 2010)**

(a) current

(b) phase difference only

(c) e.m.f.

(d) current, e.m.f. and phase difference

221. A transformer is having 2100 turns in primary and 4200 turns in secondary. An a.c. source of 120 V, 10 A is connected to its primary. The secondary voltage and current are **(MHT-CET 2010)**

(a) 240 V, 5 A (b) 120 V, 10 A

(c) 240 V, 10 A (d) 120 V 20 A

222. When the number of turns and length of a solenoid are doubled keeping the area of cross-section same, the inductance becomes

(MHT-CET 2010)

(a) half (b) zero

(c) two times (d) four times

223. If the current through the coil changes from + 2 A to – 2 A in 0.05 sec and 8V e.m.f. is developed in the coil, then the self inductance of the coil is **(MHT-CET 2011)**

(a) 0.05 H (b) 0.1 H

(c) 0.2 H (d) 0.4 H

224. An e.m.f. $e = 200\sqrt{2}\sin(100t)$ is applied across capacitor of capacitance 2 μF then current through capacitor is

(MHT-CET 2011)

(a) 4 mA (b) 40 mA

(c) 2 mA (d) 3 mA

225. In LCR series circuit power factor at resonance is **(MHT-CET 2011)**

(a) less than one

(b) greater than one

(c) unity/one

(d) cannot be predicted

226. The current in a coil varies with time as shown in the figure. The variation of induced e.m.f. with time would be

(C.B.S.E., P.M.T. 2011)

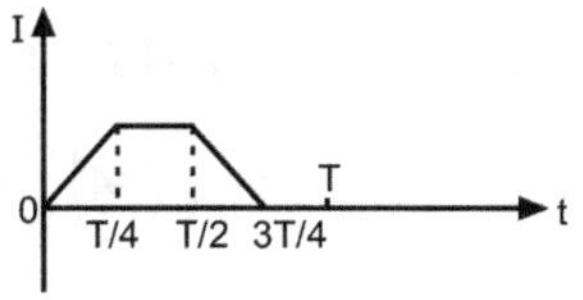

(a)

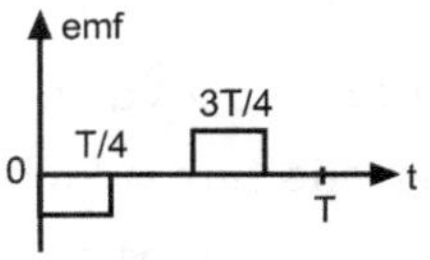

(b)

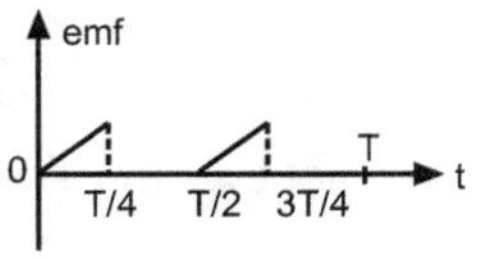

(c)

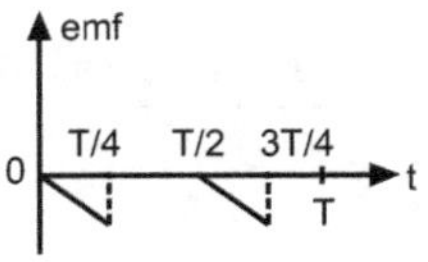

(d)

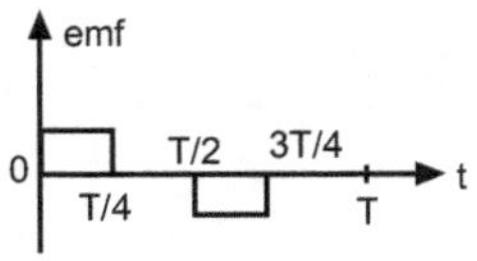

227. In series LCR circuit at resonance.

(MHT-CET 2012)

(a) current is maximum and voltage is minimum

(b) current is maximum and voltage is maximum

(c) current is minimum and voltage is maximum

(d) current is minimum and voltage is minimum

228. The self inductance of coil of 400 turns is 8 mH. If current of 5 mA flows in it, then flux associated with the coil is

(MHT-CET 2012)

(a) $\left(\frac{\mu_0}{4\pi}\right)$ (b) μ_0

(c) $\frac{\mu_0}{100\,\pi}$ (d) $\left(\frac{4\pi}{\mu_0}\right)$

229. In LCR series circuit an a.c. e.m.f. of 2 volt and frequency 50 Hz is applied across the combination. If resistance is 4 Ω, capacitance is 8 μF and inductance is 10^{-2} H, then the voltage across inductor will be **(MHT-CET 2012)**

(a) $\left(\frac{3}{5}\text{ V}\right)$ (b) $\left(\frac{5}{3}\text{ V}\right)$

(c) $\left(\frac{2}{3}\text{ V}\right)$ (d) (0.02 V)

230. A coil of resistance 400 Ω is placed in a magnetic field. If the magnetic flux o (Wb) linked with the coil varies with time t (s) is, $\phi = 50\,t^2 + 4$. The current in the coil at t = 2 s is **(C.B.S.E., P.M.T. 2012)**

(a) 1 A (b) 0.5 A

(c) 0.1 A (d) 2 A

231. In an electrical circuit R, L, C and a.c. voltage source are all connected in series. When I is removed from the circuit, the phase difference between the voltage and the current in the phase difference is again $\frac{\pi}{3}$. The power factor of the circuit is

(C.B.S.E., P.M.T. 2012)

(a) $\frac{\sqrt{3}}{2}$ (b) $\frac{1}{2}$

(c) $\frac{1}{\sqrt{2}}$ (d) 1

232. A coil of self-inductance L is connected in series with a bulb B and an AC source. Brightness of the bulb decreases when

(NEET 2013)

(a) number of turns in the coil are reduced

(b) a capacitance of reactance $X_C = X_L$ is included in the same circuit

(c) an iron rod is inserted in the coil

(d) frequency of the AC source is decreased

233. A wire loop is rotated in a magnetic field. The frequency of change of direction of the induced e.m.f. is

(a) twice per revolution

(b) four times per revolution

(c) six times per revolution

(d) once per revolution

ANSWER KEY

1. (b)	**2.** (c)	**3.** (b)	**4.** (a)	**5.** (c)	**6.** (a)	**7.** (b)	**8.** (d)	**9.** (d)	**10.**(a)
11.(a)	**12.**(a)	**13.**(a)	**14.**(a)	**15.**(c)	**16.**(c)	**17.**(c)	**18.**(c)	**19.**(c)	**20.**(a)
21.(d)	**22.**(d)	**23.**(a)	**24.**(c)	**25.**(a)	**26.**(a)	**27.**(b)	**28.**(c)	**29.**(a)	**30.**(c)
31.(b)	**32.**(b)	**33.**(a)	**34.**(b)	**35.**(b)	**36.**(a)	**37.**(a)	**38.**(c)	**39.**(b)	**40.**(a)
41.(a)	**42.**(b)	**43.**(b)	**44.**(b)	**45.**(b)	**46.**(c)	**47.**(c)	**48.**(c)	**49.**(b)	**50.**(c)
51.(a)	**52.**(a)	**53.**(d)	**54.**(b)	**55.**(b)	**56.**(c)	**57.**(c)	**58.**(a)	**59.**(a)	**60.**(a)
61.(a)	**62.**(c)	**63.**(c)	**64.**(b)	**65.**(c)	**66.**(a)	**67.**(a)	**68.**(c)	**69.**(a)	**70.**(b)
71.(c)	**72.**(b)	**73.**(a)	**74.**(c)	**75.**(b)	**76.**(d)	**77.**(b)	**78.**(c)	**79.**(c)	**80.**(c)
81.(c)	**82.**(a)	**83.**(d)	**84.**(d)	**85.**(a)	**86.**(c)	**87.**(b)	**88.**(c)	**89.**(d)	**90.**(c)
91.(d)	**92.**(c)	**93.**(a)	**94.**(c)	**95.**(c)	**96.**(b)	**97.**(d)	**98.**(d)	**99.**(b)	**100.** (c)
101. (b)	**102.** (d)	**103.** (c)	**104.** (c)	**105.** (c)	**106.** (d)	**107.** (b)	**108.** (b)	**109.** (a)	**110.** (c)
111. (c)	**112.** (a)	**113.** (b)	**114.** (b)	**115.** (c)	**116.** (c)	**117.** (b)	**118.** (a)	**119.** (b)	**120.** (a)
121. (a)	**122.** (a)	**123.** (d)	**124.** (b)	**125.** (a)	**126.** (c)	**127.** (b)	**128.** (d)	**129.** (b)	**130.** (b)
131. (a)	**132.** (a)	**133.** (a)	**134.** (c)	**135.** (b)	**136.** (d)	**137.** (b)	**138.** (b)	**139.** (c)	**140.** (d)
141. (b)	**142.** (d)	**143.** (d)	**144.** (c)	**145.** (a)	**146.** (c)	**147.** (a)	**148.** (a)	**149.** (c)	**150.** (c)
151. (a)	**152.** (c)	**153.** (a)	**154.** (a)	**155.** a, b	**156.** (d)	**157.** (c)	**158.** (d)	**159.** (c)	**160.** (c)
161. (b)	**162.** (c)	**163.** (b)	**164.** (d)	**165.** (a)	**166.** (c)	**167.** (d)	**168.** (b)	**169.** (a)	**170.** (a)
171. (a)	**172.** (d)	**173.** (b)	**174.** (d)	**175.** (d)	**176.** (a)	**177.** (b)	**178.** (c)	**179.** (b)	**180.** (a)
181. (d)	**182.** (d)	**183.** (b)	**184.** (d)	**185.** (b)	**186.** (b)	**187.** (b)	**188.** (a)	**189.** (a)	**190.** (a)
191. (b)	**192.** (d)	**193.** (c)	**194.** (b)	**195.** (b)	**196.** (c)	**197.** (d)	**198.** (d)	**199.** (b)	**200.** (b)
201. (a)	**202.** (a)	**203.** (c)	**204.** (b)	**205.** (b)	**206.** (c)	**207.** (a)	**208.** (b)	**209.** (a)	**210.** (a)
211. (a)	**212.** (b)	**213.** (b)	**214.** (b)	**215.** (d)	**216.** (d)	**217.** (d)	**218.** (b)	**219.** (a)	**220.** (d)
221. (a)	**222.** (c)	**223.** (b)	**224.** (b)	**225.** (c)	**226.** (a)	**227.** (a)	**228.** (c)	**229.** (d)	**230.** (b)
231. (d)	**232.** (d)	**233.** (d)							

16

WAVE OPTICS

MULTIPLE CHOICE QUESTIONS

1. Two coherent waves are represented by $y_1 = a_1 \cos \omega t$ and $y_2 = a_2 \sin \omega t$. The resultant intensity due to interference will be:
   (a) $(a_1 + a_2)$ (b) $(a_1 - a_2)$
   (c) $(a_1^2 + a_2^2)$ (d) $(a_1^2 - a_2^2)$

2. When light passes from one medium into another medium, then the physical property which does not change, is : **(P.M.T. 1990)**
   (a) Velocity (b) Wavelength
   (c) Frequency (d) Refractive index

3. Which of the following has the minimum wavelength ? **(A.I.E.E.E. 2003)**
   (a) γ-rays (b) X-rays
   (c) Cosmic rays (d) Ultra violet rays

4. Newton gave corpuscular theory on the basis of : **(A.I.E.E.E. 2003)**
   (a) Newton's rings
   (b) Rectilinear motion
   (c) Certain corpuscles
   (d) Wavefront

5. Idea of quantum nature of light emerged to explain :
   (a) Interference
   (b) Diffraction
   (c) Radiation spectrum of a black body
   (d) Polarization

6. A very thin film in reflected white light appears :
   (a) Coloured (b) White
   (c) Black (d) Red

7. At first diffraction pattern is obtained using red light, now if white light is used for diffraction pattern then diffraction pattern will : **(A.I.I.M.S. 2001)**
   (a) shrink (b) enlarge
   (c) centre white (d) none of these

8. The colour of bright fringe nearest central achromatic fringe in the interference pattern with white light will be :
   (a) Violet (b) Red
   (c) Green (d) Yellow

9. Light appears to travel in straight lines since:
   (a) it is not absorbed by the atmosphere
   (b) it is reflected by the atmosphere
   (c) its wavelength is very small
   (d) its velocity is very large

10. Which of the following phenomena is not common to sound and light waves ?
    (a) Interference (b) Diffraction
    (c) Coherence (d) Polarization

11. The correct formula for fringe visibility is :
    (a) $V = \frac{I_{max} - I_{min}}{I_{max} + I_{min}}$ (b) $V = \frac{I_{max} + I_{min}}{I_{max} - I_{min}}$
    (c) $V = \frac{I_{max}}{I_{max}}$ (d) $V = \frac{I_{min}}{I_{max}}$

12. In Young's experiment, monochromatic light is used to illuminate the two slits A and B. Interference fringes are observed on a screen placed in front of the slits. Now if a thin glass plate is placed normally in the path of the beam coming from the slit A, then :

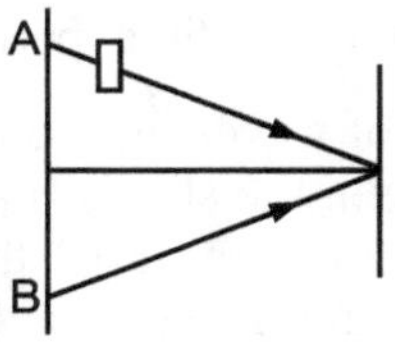

(a) the fringes will disappear

(b) the fringe width will increase

(c) the fringe width will decrease

(d) there will be no change in fringe width

13. Which out of the following, cannot produce two coherent sources ?

(a) Lloyd's mirror

(b) Fresnel's Biprism

(c) Young's double slit

(d) Prism

14. In the figure below, a wavefront AB moving in air is incident on a plane glass surface XY. Its position CD after refraction through a glass slab is shown in the same figure. The refractive index of the glass with respect to air will be equal to :

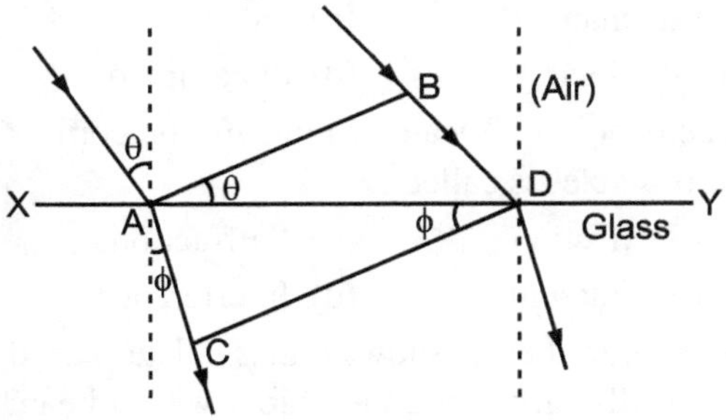

(a) BD/AC (b) AB/CD

(c) BD/AD (d) AC/AD

15. C.V. Raman got Nobel Prize for his experiment on : **(A.F.M.C. 2001)**

(a) Dispersion of light

(b) Reflection of light

(c) Deflection of light

(d) Scattering of light

16. The velocity of light is maximum in : **(D.C.E. 1990)**

(a) Diamond (b) Water

(c) Vacuum (d) Glass

17. The device which produces highly coherent sources is :

(a) Fresnel's biprism

(b) Young's double slit

(c) Laser

(d) Lloyd's mirror

18. In two separate set-ups of Young's double slit experiment using light of same wavelength, fringes of equal width are observed. If ratio of slit separation in the two is 2 : 3, the ratio of the distance between source and screen placed in the two set-ups is :

(a) 2 : 3 (b) 3 : 2

(c) 4 : 9 (d) 9 : 4

19. Wavelength of a monochromatic light is 5000 angstrom. Then its wave number is : **(A.I.I.M.S. 1991)**

(a) 5000×10^{-10} metre^{-1}

(b) 2×10^{5} metre^{-1}

(c) 2×10^{6} metre^{-1}

(d) 2×10^{4} metre^{-1}

20. A ray of light is incident on the surface of a glass plate at an angle of incidence equal to Brewster's angle ϕ. If μ represents the refractive index of glass with respect to air, then the angle between the reflected and the refracted rays is : **(A.I.E.E.E. 2003)**

(a) $90 + \phi$

(b) $\sin^{-1}(\mu \cos \phi)$

(c) 90°

(d) $90° - \sin^{-1}\left(\frac{\sin \phi}{\mu}\right)$

21. The maximum intensity produced by two coherent sources of intensity I_1 and I_2 will be:

(a) $I_1 + I_2$ (b) $I_1^2 + I_2^2$

(c) $I_2 + I_2 + 2\sqrt{I_1 I_2}$ (d) Zero

22. The correct relation between the size of the obstacle and wavelength of light in order to observe the diffraction event is :

(a) $\frac{a}{\lambda} = 1$ (b) $\frac{a}{\lambda} = 0$

(c) $\frac{a}{\lambda} = \infty$ (d) $\frac{a}{\lambda} = 150$

23. Two coherent light sources S_1 and S_2 ($\lambda = 6000$ Å) are 1 mm apart from each other. The screen is placed at a distance of 25 cm from the sources. The width of the fringes on the screen should be :

(a) 0.015 cm (b) 0.025 cm

(c) 0.010 cm (d) 0.030 cm

24. Wave nature of light follows because :

(a) light rays travel in a straight line

(b) light exhibits the phenomenon of reflection and refraction

(c) light exhibits the phenomenon of interference

(d) light causes the phenomenon of photo-electric effect

25. Two waves originating from S_1 and S_2 having zero phase difference and common wavelength λ will show complete destructive interference at a point P if $S_1P - S_2P =$

(a) 5λ (b) $\frac{3\lambda}{4}$

(c) $\frac{4\lambda}{2}$ (d) $\frac{11\lambda}{2}$

26. Newton's Corpuscular theory states that velocity of light in rarer medium as compared to that in a denser medium is :

(a) less

(b) more

(c) sometimes less, sometimes more

(d) much less

27. Light propagates approximately rectilinearly because of its : **(A.I.I.M.S. 2002)**

(a) Frequency (b) Wavelength

(c) Velocity (d) Wave nature

28. In Young's double slit experiment carried out with light of wavelength $\lambda = 5000$ Å, the distance between the slits is 0.2 mm and the screen is at 200 cm from the slits. The central maximum is at $x = 0$. The third maximum (taking the central maximum as zeroth maximum) will be at x equal to :

(D.C.E. 1992)

(a) 1.67 cm (b) 1.5 cm

(c) 0.5 cm (d) 5.0 cm

29. The fringe width at a distance of 50 cm from the slits in Young's experiment for light of wavelength 6000 Å is 0.048 cm. The fringe width at the same distance for $\lambda = 5000$ Å will be :

(a) 0.04 cm (b) 0.4 cm

(c) 1.4 cm (d) 0.45 cm

30. In Young's double slit experiment, the separation, between the slit is halved and the distance between the slits and screen is doubled. Then the fringe width is :

(a) unchanged (b) halved

(c) doubled (d) quadrupled

31. The bending of beam of light around corners of obstacles is called :

(a) Reflection (b) Diffraction

(c) Refraction (d) Interference

32. The figure below shows a glass plate placed vertically on a horizontal table with a beam of unpolarized light falling on its surface at the polarizing angle of 57° with the normal. The electric vector in the reflected light on the screen S, will vibrate with respect to the plane of incidence in a :

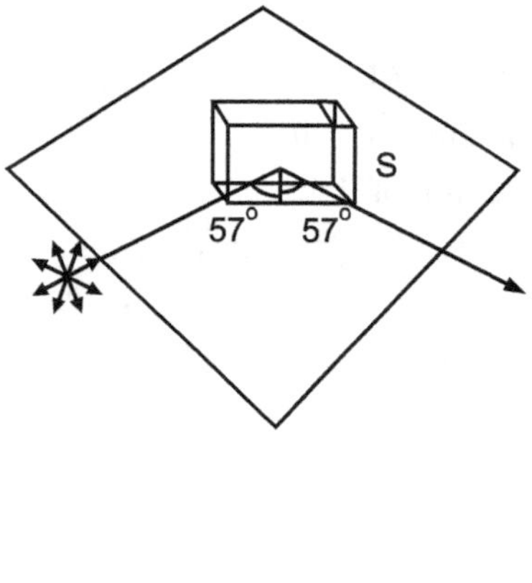

(a) vertical plane
(b) horizontal plane
(c) plane making an angle of 45° with the vertical
(d) plane making an angle of 57° with the horizontal

33. The fringe width β of the fringes produced in Young's double slit experiment is :

(Haryana C.E.T. 1991)

(a) $\beta = \frac{\lambda D}{d}$
(b) $\beta = D\frac{d}{\lambda}$
(c) $\beta = \frac{\lambda d}{D}$
(d) $\beta = \lambda d^2 / D^2$

34. Huygens' concept of secondary wave :
(a) allows us to find the focal length of a thick lens
(b) is a geometrical method of finding a wavefront
(c) is used to determine the velocity of light
(d) is used to explain polarization

35. Pick out the longest wavelength from the following types of radiations :

(C.B.S.E. P.M.T. 1990)

(a) Blue light
(b) Gamma rays
(c) X-rays
(d) Red light

36. When a cotton cloth is put in front of eyes and a distant lighting bulb is viewed, then multiple bulbs are seen in a rectangular pattern around the bulb. The reason for this is :
(a) sight illusion
(b) A large number of holes in the cloth
(c) the small holes in the cloth behave like slits for light due to which a diffraction pattern is observed
(d) the size of the cloth is equal to that of the bulb

37. Two beams of light having intensities I and 4I interfere to produce a fringe pattern on a screen. The phase difference between the beams is $\pi/2$ at point A and π at point B. Then the difference between the resultant intensities at A and B is :

(I.I.T. Screening 2001)

(a) 2I
(b) 4I
(c) 5I
(d) 7I

38. The correct curve between the energy of photon (E) and its wavelength (λ) is :

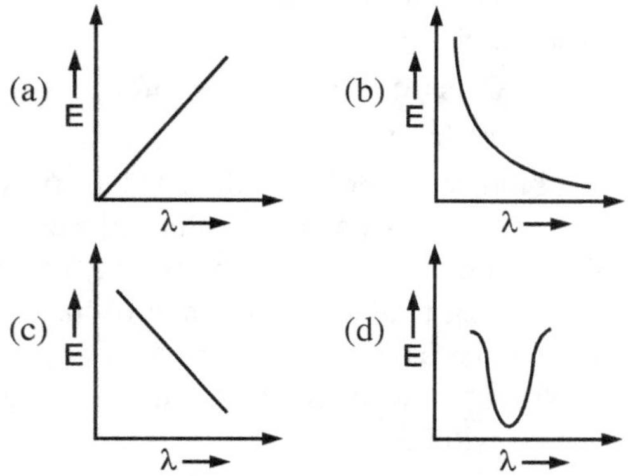

39. A single slit of width d is placed in the path of a beam of wavelength λ. The angular width of the principal maximum obtained is:

(Haryana CET 1991)

(a) d/λ
(b) $\pm\lambda/d$
(c) $2\lambda/d$
(d) $2d/\lambda$

40. The displacements of interfering waves are $Y_1 = 4 \sin \omega t$ cm and $Y_2 = 3 \sin (\omega t + \pi/2)$ cm respectively. The amplitude of the resultant will be :
(a) 5
(b) 7
(c) 1
(d) 0

41. To observe diffraction, the size of an aperture : **(C.P.M.T. 1991)**
(a) should be of the same order as of wavelength
(b) should be much larger than the wave-length
(c) has no relation to wavelength
(d) should be exactly $\lambda/2$

42. In Young's double slit experiment, the seventh maximum with wavelength λ_1 is at a distance d_1 and the same maximum with wavelength λ_2 is at a distance d_2. Then $d_1/d_2 =$

(a) $\frac{\lambda_1}{\lambda_2}$ (b) $\frac{\lambda_2}{\lambda_1}$

(c) $\frac{\lambda_1^2}{\lambda_2^2}$ (d) $\frac{\lambda_2^2}{\lambda_1^2}$

43. In Huygen's theory, the locus of all points in the same phase of vibration is :

(a) A half period zone (b) vibrator

(c) A wavefront (d) a ray

44. In a biprism experiment, the 5th dark fringe is obtained at a point. If a thin transparent film is placed in the path of one of the waves, then the 7th bright fringe is obtained at the same point. The thickness of the film in terms of wavelength λ and refractive index μ will be

(a) $\frac{15\lambda}{(\mu-1)}$ (b) $1.5(\mu-1)\lambda$

(c) $2.5(\mu-1)\lambda$ (d) $\frac{2.5\lambda}{(\mu-1)}$

45. In a double slit interference experiment, the distance between the slits is 0.05 cm and screen is 2 m away from the slits. The wavelength of light is 0.8×10^{-5} cm. The distance between successive fringes is :

(A.I.E.E.E. 2003)

(a) 0.24 cm (b) 3.2 cm

(c) 1.28 cm (d) 0.32 cm

46. Which of the following statements is wrong?

(a) Infrared photon has more energy than the photon of visible light.

(b) Photographic plates are sensitive to ultraviolet rays.

(c) Photographic plates can be made sensitive to infrared rays.

(d) Infrared rays are invisible but can cast shadows like visible light rays.

47. In a medium, the source and the observer are both moving in the same direction with the same speed v. The apparent frequency υ' is then related to the frequency υ by (speed of sound in the medium = c)

(Haryana C.E.T. 1994)

(a) $\upsilon' = \left(\frac{1-v/c}{1+v/c}\right)\upsilon$ (b) $\upsilon' = \upsilon$

(c) $\upsilon' = \sqrt{1+\frac{v^2}{c^2}}\,\upsilon$ (d) $\upsilon' = \left(\frac{1-v/c}{1+v/c}\right)\upsilon$

48. Light of wavelength 6000 Å is incident normally on a slit of width 24×10^{-5} cm. The angular position of second minimum from central maximum will be :

(a) 0° (b) 15°

(c) 30° (d) 60°

49. Instead of using two slits, if we use two separate identical sodium lamps in Young's experiment, which of the following will occur ?

(a) General illumination

(b) Widely separate interference

(c) Very bright maximum

(d) Very dark minimum

50. Oil floating on water looks coloured due to interference of light. The approximate thickness of oil for such effect to be visible is : **(C.P.M.T. 1990)**

(a) 100 Å (b) 1000 Å

(c) 1 mm (d) 1 cm

51. In the ideal double-slit experiment, when a glass-plate (refractive index 1.5) of thickness t is introduced in the path of one of the interfering beams (wavelength λ), the intensity at the position where the central maximum occurred previously remains unchanged. The minimum thickness of the glass-plate is : **(I.I.T. Screening 2002)**

(a) 2λ (b) $2\lambda/3$

(c) $\lambda/3$ (d) λ

52. In Young's experiment, two coherent sources are placed 0.90 mm apart and the fringes are observed 1 m away. If it produces the second dark fringe at a distance of 1 mm from the central fringe, the wavelength of monochromatic light used will be : **(C.B.S.E. P.M.T. 1992)**

(a) 60×10^{-4} cm (b) 10×10^{-4} cm

(c) 10×10^{-5} cm (d) 6×10^{-5} cm

53. A red piece of paper when illuminated by green light appears :

(a) Blue (b) Yellow

(c) Green (d) Black

54. In a biprism experiment, by using light of wavelength 5000 Å, 5 mm wide fringes are obtained on a screen 1.0 m away from the coherent sources. The separation between the two coherent sources is :

(a) 1.0 m (b) 0.1 mm

(c) 0.05 mm (d) 0.01 mm

55. Two sources of light of wavelengths 2500 Å and 3500 Å are used in Young's double slit experiment simultaneously. Which orders of fringes of two wavelength patterns coincide?

(a) 3rd order of 1st source and 5th of the 2nd

(b) 7th order of 1st and 5th order of the 2nd

(c) 5th order of 1st and 3rd order of the 2nd

(d) 5th order of 1st and 7th order of the 2nd

56. In Young's double slit experiment, carried out with light of wavelength $\lambda = 5000$ Å, the distance between the slits is 0.2 mm and the screen is at 200 cm from the slits. The central maxima is at $x = 0$. The third maxima (taking central maxima as zeroth maxima) will be at x equal to: **(C.E.T. 2001)**

(a) 1.67 cm (b) 1.5 cm

(c) 0.5 cm (d) 5.0 cm

57. v_O and v_E represent the velocities, μ_0 and μ_E the refractive indices of ordinary and extraordinary rays for a double refracting crystal. then : **(K.E.T. 2002)**

(a) $v_O \le v_E$, $\mu_O \ge \mu_E$, if the crystal is calcite

(b) $v_O \ge v_E$, $\mu_O \ge \mu_E$, if the crystal is quartz

(c) $v_O \ge v_E$, $\mu_O \le \mu_E$, if the crystal is calcite

(d) $v_O \le v_E$, $\mu_O \le \mu_E$, if the crystal is quartz

58. The correct curve between refractive index μ and wavelength λ will be :

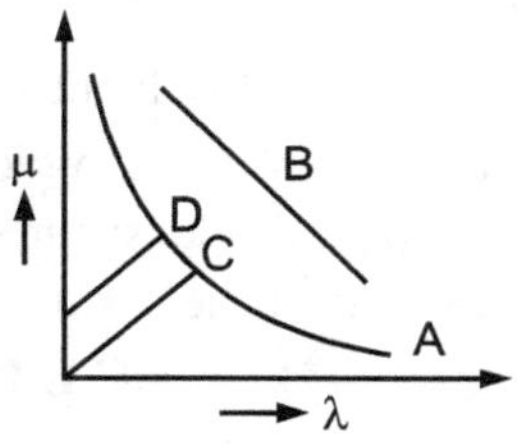

(a) A (b) D

(c) B (d) C

59. The position of the direct image obtained at O, when a monochromatic beam of light is passed through a plane transmission grating at normal incidence is shown in the figure below. The diffracted images A, B and C correspond to the first, second and third order diffraction when the source is replaced by another source of shorter wave length.

(M.P.C.E.T. 2002)

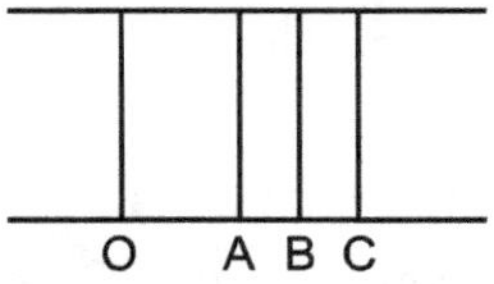

(a) All the four will shift in the direction C to O.

(b) All the four will shift in the direction O to C.

(c) The images C, B and A will shift towards O.

(d) The images C, B and A will shift away from O.

60. Golden view of sea shell is due to :

(a) Diffraction (b) Dispersion

(c) Polarization (d) Reflection

61. Two independent waves are expressed as $Y_1 = a_1 \sin \omega_1 t$. Is interference possible with these ?

(a) Yes

(b) No

(c) Sometimes possible and sometimes not

(d) Nothing can be predicted

62. The limit of resolution of an optical instrument arises an account of :

(a) Interference (b) Diffraction

(c) Polarization (d) None of these

63. When light travels from an optically rarer medium to an optically denser medium, the velocity decreases because of change in : **(N.C.E.R.T. 1990)**

(a) Wavelength (b) Frequency

(c) Amplitude (d) Phase

64. The axes of two Nicol prisms are parallel to one another. One of the two Nicols is rotated through an angle of 60°. The ratio of the intensity of transmitted light before and after rotation is :

(a) 1 : 2 (b) 2 : 1

(c) 4 : 1 (d) 1 : 4

65. The first diffraction minima due to a single slit diffraction is at $\theta = 30°$ for a light of wavelength 500 Å. The width of the slit is : **(C.E.T. 2002)**

(a) 5×10^{-5} cm (b) 1.0×10^{-5} cm

(c) 2.5×10^{-5} cm (d) 1.25×10^{-5} cm

66. Light of wavelength 6.5×10^{-7} m is made incident on two slits 1 mm apart. The distance between the third dark fringe and fifth bright fringe on a screen distant 1 m from the slits will be : **(A.I.E.E.E. 2006)**

(a) 0.325 mm (b) 0.65 mm

(c) 1.625 mm (d) 3.25 mm

67. If a plate of mica of thickness t and refractive index μ is introduced in the path of one of the coherent waves in an interference experiment, the fringe pattern will shift by : **(Raj. C.E.T. 1997)**

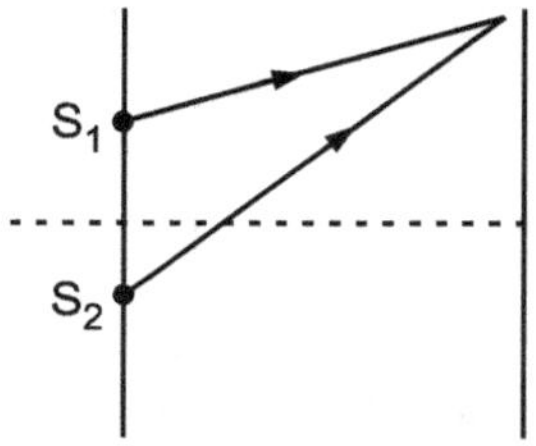

(a) $\frac{d}{D}(\mu - 1)$ (b) $\frac{D}{d}(\mu - 1)\,t$

(c) $\frac{d}{(\mu - 1)D}$ (d) $\frac{D}{d}(\mu - 1)$

68. Two coherent sources of intensities I_1 and I_2 produce an interference pattern. The maximum intensity in the interference pattern will be :

(a) $I_1 + I_2$ (b) $I_1^2 + I_2^2$

(c) $(I_1 + I_2)^2$ (d) $(\sqrt{I_1} + \sqrt{I_2})^2$

69. The Young's double slit experiment is performed with blue and green light of wavelengths 4360Å and 5460Å respectively. If x is the distance of 4th maxima from the central one, then :

(a) x (blue) = x (green)

(b) x (blue) > x (green)

(c) x (blue) < x (green)

(d) x (blue) x (green) = 5460/4360

70. The difference between light waves and sound waves is :

(a) Light waves in air are transverse, while sound waves in air are longitudinal.

(b) Light waves in air are longitudinal, while sound waves in air are transverse.

(c) Light waves in air may be longitudinal or transverse, but sound waves in air are always longitudinal.

(d) Light waves in air are transverse only, while sound waves in air may be longitudinal or transverse

71. A ray of light is incident on the surface of a glass plate at an angle of incidence equal to Brewster's angle ϕ. If μ represents the refractive index of glass with respect to air, then the angle between the reflected and refracted rays is : **(C.P.M.T. 1990)**

(a) $90° + \phi$ (b) $\sin^{-1}(\mu \cos \phi)$

(c) 90° (d) $0° - \sin^{-1}\left(\frac{\sin \phi}{\mu}\right)$

72. If you have been sitting in sun for 2.5 hours, the area of your body exposed normally to sun rays is 1.3 m^2. The intensity of sun rays is 1.1 kW/m^2. If your body completely absorbs the sun rays, then the momentum transferred to your body will be (in kg. m/s)

(a) 0.043 (b) 0.037

(c) 0.61 (d) 0.91

73. In Young's double slit experiment, the fringe width is found to be 0.4 mm. If the whole apparatus is immersed in water of refractive index 4/3, without disturbing the geometrical arrangement, the new fringe width will be :

(a) 0.30 mm (b) 0.40 mm

(c) 0.53 mm (d) 450 microns

74. In Young's double slit experiment, the two slits are 0.2 mm apart. The interference fringes for light of wavelength 6000 Å are formed on the screen 80 cm away. The distance of the fifth dark fringe, from the central fringe, will be :

(C.B.S.E. P.M.T. 1990, A.I.E.E.E. 2003)

(a) 6.8 mm (b) 7.8 mm

(c) 9.8 mm (d) 10.8 mm

75. In Young's experiment, the distance between two slits is $d/3$ and the distance between the screen and the slits in 3 D. The number of fringes in 1/3 m on the screen, formed by monochromatic light of wavelength 3λ, will be :

(a) $\frac{d}{9D\lambda}$ (b) $\frac{d}{27D\lambda}$

(c) $\frac{d}{81D\lambda}$ (d) $\frac{d}{D\lambda}$

76. In Young's experiment, two coherent sources are placed 0.90 mm apart and fringes are observed one metre away. If it produces a second dark fringe at a distance of 1 mm from the central fringe, the wavelength of monochromatic light used would be :

(a) 60×10^{-4} cm (b) 10×10^{-4} cm

(c) 10×10^{-5} cm (d) 6×10^{-5} cm

77. For what value of angle of incidence a ray incident on a glass plate ($\mu = 1.5$) will the reflected ray and the refracted ray be perpendicular to each other ?

(a) $\angle i = 45^\circ$ (b) $\angle i = 30^\circ$

(c) $\angle i = 40^\circ$ (d) $\angle i = 57^\circ$

78. What should be the refractive index of a transparent medium to be invisible in vacuum ?

(a) 1 (b) < 1

(c) > 1 (d) None of these

79. A ray of light from a denser medium strikes a rarer medium as shown in the figure below. The reflected and refracted rays make an angle of 90° with each other. The angles of reflection and refraction are r and r' respectively. The critical angle would be :

(A.I.E.E.E. 2004)

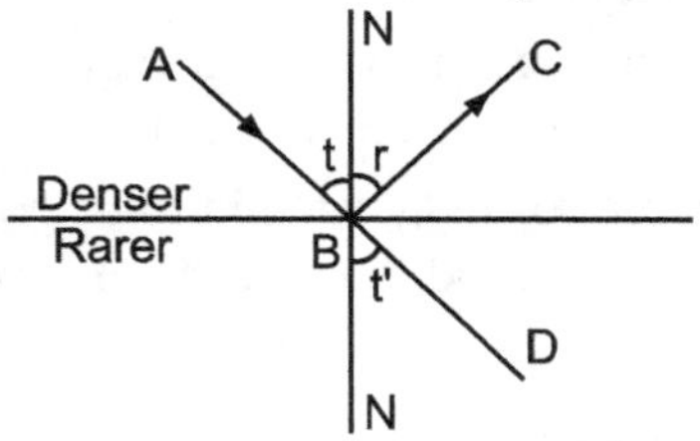

(a) $\sin^{-1}(\tan r)$ (b) $\tan^{-1}(\sin r)$

(c) $\sin^{-1}(\tan r')$ (d) $\tan^{-1}(\tan r)$

80. A ray of light consisting of two wavelengths 4000 Angstrom and 5000 Angstrom falls from air on a quartz surface. The angle of incidence is 30°, and the indices of refraction for the two wavelengths are respectively 1.47 and 1.46. The angle between the two refracted beams will be :

(a) 0° (b) 45°

(c) 90° (d) 0.14°

81. A beam of monochromatic light is refracted from vacuum into a medium of refractive index 1.5. The wavelength of refracted light will be :

(a) dependent on intensity of refracted light

(b) same

(c) smaller

(d) larger

82. The light waves from two coherent sources of the same intensity (I) produce interference. At minimum, intensity of light is zero, what is the intensity of light at the maximum ?

(a) I (b) 4I
(c) I^2 (d) $4I^2$

83. The limit of resolution of eye is approximately :

(a) 1° angle (b) 1' angle
(c) 1 mm (d) 1 cm

84. Interference was observed in an interference chamber, when air was present. If the chamber is evacuated and the same light is used, then we will see : **(BHU 2002)**

(a) no interference
(b) interference with dark bands
(c) interference with bright bands
(d) interference in which breadth of the fringe will be slightly increased

85. Two sources of light are said to be coherent if the waves produced by them have the same :

(a) wavelength
(b) amplitude
(c) wavelength and a constant phase difference
(d) amplitude and same wavelength

86. The interfering fringes formed by a thin oil film on water are seen in yellow light of a sodium lamp. We find the fringes :

(a) coloured
(b) black and white
(c) yellow and black
(d) coloured without yellow

87. Two coherent monochromatic light beams of intensities I and 4I are superposed. The maximum and minimum possible intensities in the resulting beam are :

(a) 5I and I (b) 9I and I
(c) 5I and 3I (d) 9I and 3I

88. In a certain double slit experimental arrangement, interference fringes of width 1.0 mm each are observed when light of wavelength 5000 Å is used. Keeping the set-up unaltered, if the source is replaced by another of wavelength 6000 Å, the fringe width will be :

(a) 0.5 mm (b) 1.0 mm
(c) 1.2 mm (d) 1.5 mm

89. The equations of waves emitted by S_1, S_2, S_3 and S_4 are respectively $Y_1 = 20 \sin (100 \pi t)$, $Y_2 = 20 \sin (200 \pi t)$, $Y_3 = 10 \cos (100 \pi t)$ and $Y_4 = 20 \cos (100 \pi t)$. The phenomenon of interference will be produced by :

(a) Y_1 and Y_2
(b) Y_2 and Y_3
(c) Y_1 and Y_3
(d) Interference is not possible

90. When light wave suffers reflection at the interface from air to glass, the change in phase of the reflected light is equal to : **(C.E.T. 1991)**

(a) 0 (b) $\pi/2$
(c) π (d) 2π

91. Find the thickness of a plate which will produce a change in optical path equal to half the wavelength of the light passing through it, normally. The refractive index of the plate is μ : **(M.P.C.E.T. 2000)**

(a) $\dfrac{\lambda}{4(\mu - 1)}$ (b) $\dfrac{2\lambda}{4(\mu - 1)}$
(c) $\dfrac{\lambda}{(\mu - 1)}$ (d) $\dfrac{\lambda}{2(\mu - 1)}$

92. In Young's double slit experiment; if the monochromatic source of light is replaced by white light, then one sees :

(a) no interference fringe pattern
(b) coloured fringes
(c) black and white fringes
(d) white central fringe surrounded by a few coloured fringes on either side

93. A thin sheet of glass ($\mu = 1.5$) of thickness 6 microns introduced in the path of one of the interfering beams in a double slit experiment shifts the central fringe to a position previously occupied by the fifth bright fringe. Then the wavelength of light used is:

(a) 6000 Å (b) 3000 Å
(c) 4500 Å (d) 7500 Å

94. If the ratio of amplitude of two waves is 4 : 3, then the ratio of maximum and minimum intensity is : **(A.F.M.C. 1997)**

(a) 16 : 18 (b) 18 : 16
(c) 49 : 1 (d) 94 :1

95. When a thin film of thickness t is placed in the path of a light wave emerging out of source S_1, then increase in the length of the optical path will be :

(a) $(\mu - 1)$ t (b) $(\mu + 1)$ t
(c) μt (d) μ/t

96. In a Young's double slit experiment, the source, slit S and the two slits A and B are horizontal with slit A above slit B. The fringes are observed on a vertical screen K. The optical path length from S to B is increased very slightly (by introducing a transparent material of higher refractive index) and the optical path length from S to A is not changed, as a result the fringe system on K moves :

(a) vertically downwards slightly
(b) vertically upwards slightly
(c) horizontally, slightly to the left
(d) horizontally, slightly to the right

97. A thin oil layer floats on water, a ray of light making an angle of incidence of 40° shines on the oil layer. The angle of refraction of light ray water surface is :
($\mu_{oil} = 1.45$, $\mu_{water} = 1.33$)

(Chd. C.E.T. 1991)

(a) 36.1° (b) 44.5°
(c) 26.8° (d) 28.9°

98. Light is incident normally on a diffraction grating through which the first order diffraction is seen at 32°. The second order diffraction will be seen at :

(a) 48°
(b) 64°
(c) 80°
(d) There is no second order diffraction in this case

99. Light of wavelength 6328 Å is incident normally on a slit of width 0.12 mm. The angular width of central maximum on a screen distant 9 m will be : **(K.E.T. 2000)**

(a) 0.36° (b) 0.28°
(c) 0.82° (d) 0.09°

100. Two slits separated by a distance of 1 mm are illuminated with red light of wavelength 6.5×10^{-7} metre. The interference fringes are observed on a screen placed one metre from the slits. The distance between the third fringe and fifth bright fringe on the same side of the centre is equal to :

(N.C.E.R.T. 1992)

(a) 0.65 mm (b) 1.63 mm
(c) 3.25 mm (d) 4.8 mm

101. Sodium light ($\lambda = 6 \times 10^{-7}$ m) is used to produce interference pattern. The observed fringe width is 0.12 mm. The angle between the two interfering wave trains is :

(a) 5×10^{-1} radian (b) 5×10^{-3} radian
(c) 1×10^{-2} radian (d) 1×10^{-3} radian

102. White light is incident on a soap film of thickness 5×10^{-5} cm and refractive index 1.33. Which wavelength is reflected maximum in the visible region ?

(D.C.E 2000)

(a) 26000 Å (b) 8866 Å
(c) 5320 Å (d) 3800 Å

103. Which one of the following phenomena is not explained by Huygens' construction of wavefront ?

(a) Refraction (b) Reflection
(c) Diffraction (d) Origin of spectra

104. In Young's experiment for interference of light with two slits, reinforcement takes place when $\sin\theta = \frac{m\lambda}{d}$, d is :

(a) distance from slits to the screen
(b) distance between dark and bright fringes
(c) distance between slits
(d) width of mth fringe

105. A beam of unpolarized light passes through a tourmaline crystal A and then through another such crystal B, oriented so that its principal plane is parallel to A. The intensity of emergent light is I_0. Now B is rotated by 45° about the ray. The emergent light will have intensity :

(a) $\frac{I_0}{2}$ (b) $\frac{I_0}{\sqrt{2}}$
(c) $\frac{I_0^2}{\sqrt{2}}$ (d) $2 I_0$

106. Huygen's wave theory of light cannot explain:

(a) Diffraction
(b) Interference
(c) Polarization
(d) Photoelectric effect

107. A Fresnel's biprism is used to form the interference fringes. The distance between the source and the biprism is 20 cm and that between the biprism and the screen is 80 cm. If λ = 6563 Angstrom and the separation between the virtual sources is 3.6 mm, then the fringe width is :

(a) 1.82 cm (b) 0.182 cm
(c) 0.0182 cm (d) 0.00182 cm

108. The Fraunhofer 'diffraction' pattern of a single slit is formed in the focal plane of a lens of focal length 1 m. The width of the slit is 0.3 mm. If third minimum is formed at a distance of 5 mm from central maximum, the wavelength of light will be :

(a) 5000 Å (b) 2500 Å
(c) 7500 Å (d) 8500 Å

109. Which of the following is conserved when light waves interfere with each other ?

(A.I.E.E.E. 2002)

(a) Energy (b) Intensity
(c) Amplitude (d) Momentum

110. Monochromatic light of wavelength 5×10^{-7} m illuminates a pair of narrow slits 1 mm apart. The separation of bright lines in the interference pattern formed on a screen 2 metres away is : **(Chd. C.E.T. 1991)**

(a) 0.1 mm (b) 0.25 mm
(c) 0.4 mm (d) 1.0 mm

111. The ratio of intensities of consecutive maxima in the diffraction pattern due to a single slit is :

(a) 1 : 4 : 9 (b) 1 : 2 : 3
(c) $1 : \frac{4}{9\pi^2} : \frac{4}{25\pi^2}$ (d) $1 : \frac{4}{\pi^2} : \frac{9}{\pi^2}$

112. A laser is a coherent source because it consists of :

(a) many values of wavelengths
(b) uncoordinated waves of particular wavelength
(c) coordinated waves of many wavelengths
(d) coordinated waves of a particular wavelength

113. In Young's experiment, the wavelength of red light is 7.8×10^{-7} m and that of the blue light is 5.2×10^{-7} m. The value of n for which $(n + 1)^{th}$ blue bright band coincides with n^{th} red bright band is :

(M.H.C.E.T. 2000)

(a) 4 (b) 3
(c) 2 (d) None of these

114. In a Fresnel biprism experiment, the two positions of lens give separation between the slits as 16 cm, and 9 cm respectively. The actual distance of separation between the slits is : **(M.N.R. 1999)**

(a) 12.5 cm (b) 12.0 cm
(c) 15 cm (d) 14 cm

115. Path difference between two interfering waves at a point on the screen is $\lambda/8$. The ratio of intensity at this point and that at the central fringe will be :

(a) 0.8537 (b) 8.53
(c) 85.3 (d) 853

116. Time taken by sunlight to pass through a window of thickness 4 mm whose refractive index is 3/2 is : **(K.E.T. 1997)**

(a) 2×10^{-4} sec (b) 2×10^{8} sec
(c) 2×10^{-11} sec (d) 2×10^{11} sec

117. Two sources of waves are called coherent if: **(A.I.I.M.S. 2000)**

(a) both have the same amplitude of vibrations.
(b) both produce waves of the same wavelength.
(c) both produce waves of the same wavelength having constant phase difference.
(d) both produce waves having the same velocity.

118. Which of the following statements is correct?

(a) Diffraction is because of interference of light from same source; whereas interference is due to light from two isolated sources.
(b) Diffraction is due to interaction of light from the same wavefront; whereas interference is due to interaction of two waves derived from the same source.
(c) Diffraction is due to interference of waves derived from the same source; whereas interference is bending of light from the same source.
(d) Diffraction is due to reflected waves; whereas interference is due to transmitted waves, from a source.

119. A slit of width 12×10^{-7} m is illuminated by light of wavelength 6000 Å. The angular width of the central maximum is approximately :

(a) 30° (b) 60°
(c) 90° (d) 0°

120. Velocity of light cannot be determined by :

(a) Fizeau's toothed wheel method
(b) Foucault's rotatory mirror method
(c) Nicol rotatory mirror method
(d) Fresnel's biprism

121. In Young's double slit experiment, one slit is covered with red filter and another slit is covered by green filter, then interference pattern will be :

(a) Red (b) Green
(c) Yellow (d) Invisible

122. Which of the following statements is correct about the biological importance of ozone layer ? **(C.B.S.E. 2001)**

(a) It stops ultraviolet rays.
(b) It reflects radiowaves.
(c) It reduces green house effect.
(d) It controls O_2/H_2 ratio is atmosphere.

123. The direction of the motion of wavefront of a wave is: **(Raj. C.E.T. 1997)**

(a) parallel (b) perpendicular
(c) opposite (d) at angle of θ

124. Light of wavelength 6000×10^{-10} metre is incident on a slit. The first minimum of the diffraction pattern is observed to lie at a distance of 6 mm from the central maximum on a screen placed at distance of 2 metres from the slit. Then the width of the slit is :

(a) 2.0 cm (b) 0.2 cm
(c) 0.02 cm (d) 0.01 cm

125. If the distance between slits of Young's double slit experiment is reduced to half, then the fringe width will become : **(BHU 2002)**

(a) half (b) two times
(c) four times (d) constant

126. If yellow light emitted by sodium lamp in Young's double slit experiment is replaced by monochromatic blue light of the same intensity then :

(a) fringe width will decrease
(b) fringe width will increase
(c) fringe width will remain unchanged
(d) fringes will become less intense

127. A narrow monochromatic beam of light of intensity I is incident on a glass plate. Another identical glass plate is kept close to the first one and parallel to it. Each plate reflects 25% light incident on it and transmits the remaining. The ratio of minimum to maximum intensity in the interference pattern formed by the two beams obtained after one reflection from each plate is :

(a) $\frac{1}{49}$ (b) $\frac{16}{25}$
(c) $\frac{1}{81}$ (d) $\frac{1}{25}$

128. In a Young's double slit experiment, the angular width of a fringe formed on a distant screen is 0.1°. The wavelength of light used is 6000 Å. Then spacing between the slits is:

(a) 3.44×10^{-2} m (b) 3.44×10^{-4} m
(c) 1.72×10^{-2} m (d) 1.72 mm

129. In a Young's double slit experiment, two slits 2 mm apart are illuminated with a mixture of two wavelengths $\lambda_1 = 6{,}000 \times 10^{-10}$ m and $\lambda_2 = 7{,}500$ Å. The minimum distance at which the common bright fringe on a screen 2.5 m from the slits with a bright fringe from one interference pattern coinciding with bright fringe from the other is :

(a) 1.75 mm (b) 2.5 mm
(c) 3.75 mm (d) 1.5 mm

130. Radar operates at wavelength 50 cm. If the beats frequency between the transmitted signal and the signal reflected from the aircraft ($\Delta\upsilon$) is 1 kHz, then velocity of the aircraft will be :

(a) 700 km/hr (b) 1,000 km/hr
(c) 800 km/hr (d) 900 km/hr

131. In a Young's double slit experiment, the incident sodium light is composed of two wavelengths 5,890 Å and 5896 Å. The distance between the slits is 1 mm and the screen is placed 1 m away from the slits. The order up to which fringes can be seen is: **(Roorkee 1997)**

(a) 1697 (b) 589
(c) 1284 (d) 698

132. In Q. 131, how far from the central maxima can the last fringe be observed ?

(a) 0.75 m (b) 0.85 m
(c) 0.92 m (d) 1.0 m

133. Wavelength of light received from the far off star is 0.5% more than that coming from a source on the earth. The velocity of the star is : **(Roorkee 1994)**

(a) $1.5 \times 10^{8}\ ms^{-1}$ (b) $3 \times 10^{10}\ ms^{-1}$
(c) $1.5 \times 10^{6}\ ms^{-1}$ (d) $1.5 \times 10^{10}\ ms^{-1}$

134. The thinnest film of oil having refractive index 1.4 floating on water surface in which green light of wavelength 5,000 Å in air is eliminated by the destructive interference of white light incident normally on the film is :

(a) 2,000 Å (b) 1,290 Å
(c) 1,790 Å (d) 1,000 Å

135. In Q. 134, if the oil film was on a glass of refractive index 1.6, then maximum thickness of the oil film will be:

(a) 893 Å (b) 700 Å
(c) 850 Å (d) 875 Å

136. In Young's double slit experiment fringes of angular width 0.20° are obtained with light of wavelength 5,890 Å. If the fringes of angular width 10% greater are to be obtained, then wavelength used should be :

(a) 5,896 Å (b) 6,000 Å
(c) 6,279 Å (d) 6,479 Å

137. In a single slit diffraction pattern, first minima obtained with red light of wavelength 6,600 Å coincides with first maxima of some other wavelength λ, then value of λ is:

(a) 5,500 Å (b) 4,400 Å
(c) 5,000 Å (d) 4,800 Å

138. A beam of light is sent through three polaroids placed in a line. First and the third polaroids are so placed to transmit maximum intensity of light. The middle polaroid has its axis 60° with the other two polaroids. The intensity of light transmitted is :

(a) 0.75 I_0 (b) 0.025 I_0
(c) 0.25 I_0 (d) 0.0625 I_0

139. If the two coherent sources of intensity ratio β interfere, then ratio $\frac{I_{max} - I_{min}}{I_{max} + I_{min}}$ will be :

(a) β (b) $\frac{2\beta}{\beta + 1}$
(c) $\frac{2\sqrt{\beta}}{\beta + 1}$ (d) $\frac{\sqrt{\beta}}{\beta + 1}$

140. A beam of plane polarized light falls normally on a polarizer of cross-sectional area 3×10^{-4} m^2 which rotates about the axis of the ray with an angular velocity 31.4 radians per sec. If the flux of energy of the incident light is 10^{-3} watt, then energy of light passing through the polarizer per revolution will be :

(a) 2×10^{-4} J (b) 3×10^{-4} J
(c) 4×10^{-4} J (d) 10^{-4} J

141. In Young's double slit experiment, 12 fringes are obtained to be formed in a certain segment of the screen when light of 600 nm is used. If wavelength of light is changed to 400 nm, number of fringes obtained in the same segment of the screen is given by : **(I.I.T. 2001)**

(a) 12 (b) 15
(c) 18 (d) 21

142. A parallel beam of monochromatic unpolarized light is incident on a transparent dielectric plate of refractive index μ. Reflected beam is completely polarized. If angle of incidence is 30º, then μ will be :

(a) $\frac{1}{3}$ (b) 1.5
(c) $\sqrt{\frac{1}{3}}$ (d) $\sqrt{\frac{4}{3}}$

143. Electromagnetic waves are transverse in nature is evident by : **(A.I.E.E.E. 2002)**

(a) Interference (b) Diffraction
(c) Polarization (d) Reflection

144. A beam of monochromatic blue light of wavelength 4200 Å in air travels in water with refractive index 4/3. Wavelength of light in water will be :

(a) 4000 Å (b) 5500 Å
(c) 3000 Å (d) 3150 Å

145. Newton gave the corpuscular theory on the basis of : **(A.F.M.C. 2001)**

(a) Newton's rings
(b) Rectilinear motion
(c) Certain corpuscles
(d) Wavefront

146. In Young's double slit experiment, a thin glass sheet of refractive index 1.5 is introduced in the path of one of the interfering beams. By doing so, the central fringe shifts to a position occupied by the fifth bright fringe. Wavelength of light used is :

(a) 4000 Å (b) 5000 Å
(c) 6000 Å (d) 7000 Å

147. A limit on the performance of resolving instrument is set by : **(D.C.E. 2001)**

(a) Quantum nature of light
(b) Interference of light
(c) Diffraction of light
(d) Polarization of light

148. Doppler shift for the light of wavelength 6000 Å emitted from the sun is 0.04 Å. If radius of the sun is 7×10^8 m, then time period of rotation of the Sun will be :

(a) 30 days (b) 365 days
(c) 24 hours (d) 25 days

149. In Young's Double slit experiment, the distance between the slits is 1 mm and that between slit and screen is 1 metre and 10th fringe is 5 mm away from the central bright fringe, then wavelength of light used will be:

(a) 5000 Å (b) 6000 Å
(c) 7000 Å (d) 8000 Å

150. In Young's double slit experiment, 12 fringes are obtained to be formed in a certain segment of the screen when light of wavelength 600 nm is used. If the wavelength of light is changed to 400 nm, number of fringes observed in the same segment of the screen is given by :

(I.I.T. Screening 2001)

(a) 12 (b) 18
(c) 24 (d) 30

151. Two beams of light having intensities I and 4I interfere to produce a fringe pattern on a screen. The phase difference between the beams is $\pi/2$ at point A and π at point B. Then the difference between the resultant intensities at A and B is :

(a) 2I (b) 4I
(c) 5I (d) 7I

152. Frequency of the signal emitted by a rocket is 4×10^7 Hz. If apparent frequency observed on earth is 3.2×10^7 Hz, then velocity with which the rocket is moving away is :

(a) 0.5 c (b) 0.3 c
(c) 0.4 c (d) 0.2 c

153. In a Young's double slit experiment using red and blue lights of wavelength 600 nm and 480 nm respectively, the value of n for which the nth red fringe coincides with $(n + 1)^{th}$ blue fringe is :

(a) 5 (b) 4
(c) 3 (d) 2

154. If there is zero absorption in the polarizer, and intensity of plane polarized light coming out of polarizer is A^2, then intensity of incident beam will be :

(a) A^2 (b) $A^2/2$
(c) $2A^2$ (d) None of these

155. A small aperture is illuminated with a parallel beam of $\lambda = 628$ nm. The emergent beam, has an angular divergence of 2°. The size of the aperture is :

(a) 9 μm (b) 18 μm
(c) 27 μm (d) 36 μm

156. A mixture of yellow light of wavelength 3800 Å and blue light of wavelength 4000 Å is incident normally on air film 0.00010 mm thickness. The colour of the reflected light is:

(a) Red (b) Blue
(c) Violet (d) Grey

157. The path difference between two wavefronts emitted by coherent sources of wavelength 5460 Å is 2.1 micron. The phase difference between the wavefronts at that point is :

(a) 7.692 (b) 7.692 π
(c) 7.692/π (d) 7.692/3π

158. In Young's double slit experiment, fringe width is found to be 0.4 mm. If the whole apparatus is immersed in water of refractive index 4/3 without disturbing the geometrical arrangement, new fringe width will be :

(Roorkee 1995)

(a) 0.30 mm (b) 0.40 mm
(c) 0.50 mm (d) 0.45 mm

159. A thin film ($\mu = 1.6$) of thickness 10^{-3} mm is introduced in the path of one of the two interfering beams. The central fringe moves to a position occupied by the 10th bright fringe earlier. The wavelength of light is :

(a) 600 Å (b) 6000 Å

(c) 60 Å (d) 660 Å

160. In Young's experiment, wavelength of red light is 7.8×10^{-8} cm and that of blue light is 5.2×10^{-8} cm. Value of n for which $(n + 1)^{th}$ blue bright line coincides with n^{th} red fringe is :

(a) 1 (b) 2

(c) 3 (d) 4

161. The equations of displacement of two waves are given as $Y_1 = 10 \sin (3\pi t + \pi/3)$

$Y_2 = 5 (\sin 3\pi t + \cos 3\pi t)$, then what is the ratio of their amplitudes ? **(A.I.I.M.S. 1997)**

(a) 1 : 2 (b) 2 : 1

(c) 1 : 1 (d) None of these

162. In Young's double slit experiment, ratio of intensities of a bright band and a dark band is 16 : 1. The ratio of amplitudes is :

(a) 16 (b) 5/3

(c) 4 (d) 1/4

163. Doppler shift is given by :

(a) $\Delta\lambda = \pm 2\frac{v_s}{c}\lambda$ (b) $\Delta\lambda = \pm\frac{v_s}{c}\lambda$

(c) $\Delta\lambda = \pm\frac{c\lambda}{v_s}\lambda$ (d) $\Delta\lambda = \pm v_s\lambda_c$

164. Two waves $Y_1 = A_1 \sin (\omega t - \beta_1)$ and $Y_2 = A_2 \sin (\omega t - \beta_2)$ superimpose to form a resultant wave whose amplitude is :

(a) $\sqrt{A_1^2 + A_2^2 + 2A_1A_2 \cos (\beta_1 - \beta_2)}$

(b) $\sqrt{A_1^2 + A_2^2 + 2A_1A_2 \sin (\beta_1 - \beta_2)}$

(c) $A_1 + A_2$

(d) $| A_1 + A_2 |$

165. A light source approaches the observer with velocity 0.5 cms^{-1}. Doppler shift for light of wavelength 550.0. Å is :

(a) 617 Å (b) 1833 Å

(c) 5500 Å (d) 6160 Å

166. Of the two slits producing interference in Young's experiment, one is covered with glass so that light intensity passing is reduced to 50%. Which of the following is correct ?

(a) Intensity of fringes remains unaltered.

(b) Intensity of bright fringe decreases and that of dark fringe increases.

(c) Intensity of bright fringe increases and that of dark fringe decreases.

(d) Intensity of both bright and dark fringes decreases.

167. The order of magnitude of thickness of oil layer so that this layer appears coloured due to interference of light :

(a) 1 μm (b) 1 cm

(c) 10 Å (d) 100 Å

168. A parallel beam of monochromatic unpolarized light is incident on a transparent dielectric plate of refractive index $\frac{1}{\sqrt{3}}$. The reflected beam is completely polarized. Then the angle of incidence is :

(a) 30° (b) 60°

(c) 45° (d) 75°

169. Ordinary light is :

(a) Plane polarized

(b) Circularly polarized

(c) Elliptically polarized

(d) Unpolarized

170. Light incident on a glass slab at polarizing angle suffers a deviation of 22°, then angle of refraction in glass shall be :

(a) 34° (b) 22°

(c) 12° (d) 56°

ANSWER KEY

1. (c)	**2.** (c)	**3.** (a)	**4.** (b)	**5.** (c)	**6.** (c)	**7.** (c)	**8.** (a)	**9.** (c)	**10.**(d)
11.(a)	**12.**(d)	**13.**(d)	**14.**(d)	**15.**(d)	**16.**(c)	**17.**(c)	**18.**(a)	**19.**(c)	**20.**(c)
21.(c)	**22.**(a)	**23.**(a)	**24.**(c)	**25.**(d)	**26.**(a)	**27.**(d)	**28.**(b)	**29.**(a)	**30.**(d)
31.(b)	**32.**(a)	**33.**(a)	**34.**(b)	**35.**(d)	**36.**(c)	**37.**(b)	**38.**(b)	**39.**(b)	**40.**(a)
41.(a)	**42.**(a)	**43.**(c)	**44.**(d)	**45.**(d)	**46.**(a)	**47.**(b)	**48.**(c)	**49.**(a)	**50.**(b)
51.(a)	**52.**(d)	**53.**(d)	**54.**(b)	**55.**(b)	**56.**(b)	**57.**(a)	**58.**(a)	**59.**(c)	**60.**(c)
61.(b)	**62.**(b)	**63.**(a)	**64.**(c)	**65.**(b)	**66.**(c)	**67.**(b)	**68.**(d)	**69.**(c)	**70.**(a)
71.(c)	**72.**(a)	**73.**(a)	**74.**(d)	**75.**(c)	**76.**(d)	**77.**(d)	**78.**(a)	**79.**(a)	**80.**(d)
81.(c)	**82.**(b)	**83.**(b)	**84.**(d)	**85.**(c)	**86.**(c)	**87.**(b)	**88.**(c)	**89.**(c)	**90.**(c)
91.(b)	**92.**(d)	**93.**(a)	**94.**(c)	**95.**(a)	**96.**(a)	**97.**(d)	**98.**(d)	**99.**(a)	**100.** (b)
101. (b)	**102.** (c)	**103.** (d)	**104.** (c)	**105.** (a)	**106.** (d)	**107.** (c)	**108.** (a)	**109.** (a)	**110.** (d)
111. (c)	**112.** (d)	**113.** (c)	**114.** (b)	**115.** (a)	**116.** (c)	**117.** (c)	**118.** (b)	**119.** (b)	**120.** (d)
121. (d)	**122.** (a)	**123.** (a)	**124.** (c)	**125.** (c)	**126.** (a)	**127.** (a)	**128.** (b)	**129.** (c)	**130.** (d)
131. (a)	**132.** (d)	**133.** (c)	**134.** (c)	**135.** (a)	**136.** (d)	**137.** (b)	**138.** (d)	**139.** (c)	**140.** (d)
141. (a)	**142.** (c)	**143.** (b)	**144.** (d)	**145.** (b)	**146.** (c)	**147.** (c)	**148.** (d)	**149.** (a)	**150.** (b)
151. (b)	**152.** (d)	**153.** (b)	**154.** (c)	**155.** (d)	**156.** (b)	**157.** (b)	**158.** (a)	**159.** (a)	**160.** (b)
161. (c)	**162.** (b)	**163.** (b)	**164.** (a)	**165.** (b)	**166.** (b)	**167.** (a)	**168.** (a)	**169.** (d)	**170.** (a)

17

RAY OPTICS

MULTIPLE CHOICE QUESTIONS

1. Two mirrors are kept at 60° to each other and a body is placed in the middle. The total number of images formed is : **(A.I.I.M.S. 1997)**

(a) Six (b) Five
(c) Four (d) Three

2. Plane mirrors A and B are kept at an angle θ with respect to each other. Light falls on A, is reflected, then falls on B and is reflected. The emergent ray is opposite to the incident direction. Then angle θ is equal to :

(a) 30° (b) 60°
(c) 90° (d) 45°

3. Two plane mirrors are at right angles to each other. A man stands between them and combs his hair with his right hand. How many of the images will be seen in using his right hand ?

(a) 1 (b) 2
(c) 3 (d) None of these

4. The image of an object formed by a device is always virtual and small. The device may be : **(C.P.M.T. 1993)**

(a) a glass plate (b) concave lens
(c) convex lens (d) concave mirror

5. A small object is 10 cm in front of a plane mirror. If you stand 30 cm behind the object and look at its image, at what distance must you focus your eyes ?

(a) 50 cm (b) 40 cm
(c) 30 cm (d) 10 cm

6. How many images will be formed if two mirrors are fitted on adjacent walls and one mirror on the ceiling ? **(A.F.M.C. 1994)**

(a) 5 (b) 7
(c) 11 (d) 2

7. A converging lens has a focal length in air = 20 cm. When it is immersed in a liquid of refractive index less than the refractive index of the material of the lens, the focal length of lens in the liquid :

(a) = 20 cm (b) > 20cm
(c) < 20 cm (d) Changes the sign

8. The lens shown in the figure is made of two different materials. A point object is placed on the axis. How many images will the object form ?

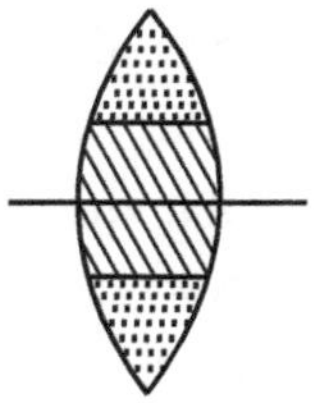

(a) One
(b) Two
(c) Three
(d) No image

9. The refractive index of an equilateral prism is $\sqrt{3}$. What is the angle of minimum deviation of the prism ? **(Karnataka 1992)**

(a) 45° (b) 37°
(c) 60° (d) 30°

10. A convergent beam is incident on a convex lens L as shown in the figure. The image formed is :

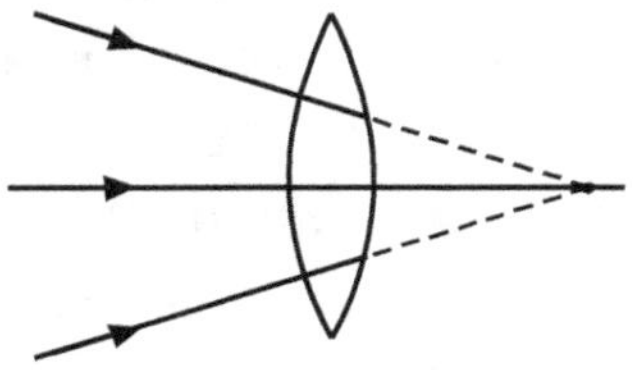

(a) real, erect and enlarged
(b) real, erect and diminished
(c) virtual, erect and diminished
(d) virtual, erect and enlarged

11. A 9 cm high image of an object is formed on a screen by a convex lens. When the lens is displaced towards the screen, again a 4 cm high image is formed on the screen. The height of the object is : **(C.P.M.T. 1993)**

(a) 6 cm (b) 6.25 cm
(c) 6.5 cm (d) None of these

12. Radius of curvature of concave mirror is 40 cm and size of the image is twice as that of the object. The object distance is : **(A.F.M.C. 1996)**

(a) 20 cm (b) 30 cm
(c) 60 cm (d) 40 cm

13. A thin lens, made of glass of refractive index 1.5, has a front surface + 11 D power and back surface –6 D. If this lens is submerged in a liquid of refractive index 1.6, the resulting power of the lens is :

(a) –1 dioptre (b) +1 dioptre
(c) –5 dioptre (d) +5 dioptre

14. A double convex lens of refractive index μ_1 is immersed in a liquid of refractive index μ_2. This lens will act as :

(a) diverging lens if $\mu_1 > \mu_2$
(b) diverging lens if $\mu_1 < \mu_2$
(c) converging lens if $\mu_1 = \mu_2$
(d) converging lens if $\mu_1 < \mu_2$

15. If a diverging lens is to be used to form an image which is one fourth of the size of the object, where must the object be placed :

(a) f (b) 2f
(c) 3f (d) 4f

16. As an object gets closer to the focal point of a converging lens from infinity, its image :

(a) becomes smaller
(b) remains the same size
(c) gets farther from the lens
(d) gets closer to the lens

17. In order to increase the magnifying power of a microscope, the focal power of the :

(a) objective and the eye-piece should be small.
(b) objective should have small focal length and the eye-piece should have large focal length.
(c) both should have large focal lengths.
(d) the objective should have large focal length and eye-piece should have small focal length.

18. A beam of light is partially reflected and partially refracted from a surface. The angle between the reflected and the refracted light is 90°. The angle of refraction is 30°. Then the angle of incidence must be : **(Karnataka 1994)**

(a) 78° (b) 50°
(c) 60° (d) 75°

19. Critical angle for total internal reflection will be smallest for light travelling from : **(A.F.M.C. 1994)**

(a) Water to glass (b) Glass to air
(c) Glass to water (d) Water to air

20. A convex lens of focal length 2 m has an object placed, at a distance of 0.5 m from it. The image formed is :

(a) real, at a distance of 2/3 m from the lens
(b) virtual, at a distance of 2/3 m from the lens
(c) real, at a distance of 0.4 m from the lens
(d) virtual, at a distance of 0.04 m from the lens

21. The focal length of a convex lens depends upon : **(A.F.M.C. 1994)**

(a) frequency of the light ray
(b) wavelength of the light ray
(c) both (a) and (b)
(d) none of these

22. A convergent lens is placed inside a vessel filled with liquid is shown in the figure below. The lens has focal length +20 cm when in air, and its material has refractive index 1.5. If the liquid has refractive index 1.6, the focal length of the system is

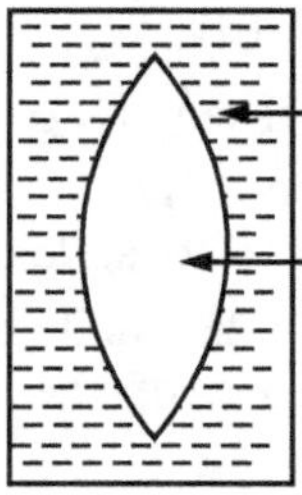

(a) + 80 cm (b) –80 cm
(c) –160 cm (d) –100 cm

23. A 1.7 m tall person stands 1.6 m in front of a vertical plane mirror. The height of his image will be :
(a) 1.6 m (b) 1.7 m
(c) 0.85 m (d) 3.4 m

24. A convergent lens is placed inside a vessel filled with liquid. The lens has focal length +20 cm when in air, and its material has refractive index 1.5. If the liquid has refractive index 1.33, the new focal length of the lens is : **(P.M.T. M.P. 1999)**
(a) + 80 cm (b) –80 cm
(c) –160 cm (d) –100 cm

25. A plane glass slab is kept over various coloured letters. The letter which appears least raised is : **(B.H.U. 1998)**
(a) Blue (b) Violet
(c) Green (d) Red

26. The sun (diameter = D) subtends an angle θ radians at the pole of a concave mirror of focal length f. The diameter of the image of the sun formed by the mirror is : **(I.I.T. 1993)**
(a) $f\theta$ (b) $2f\theta$
(c) $f^2\theta/D$ (d) $D\theta$

27. A light beam passes from air into liquid and is deviated by 15° when the angle of incidence is 60°. What is the index of refraction of the liquid ?
(a) $\frac{2}{\sqrt{3}}$ (b) $\frac{\sqrt{3}}{2}$
(c) $\frac{\sqrt{2}}{3}$ (d) $\sqrt{\frac{3}{2}}$

28. A lens is placed between a source of light and a wall. It forms images of area A_1 and A_2 on the wall, for its two different positions. The area of source is :
(a) $\frac{A_1 + A_2}{2}$ (b) $\left[\frac{1}{A_1} + \frac{1}{A_2}\right]^{-1}$
(c) $\sqrt{A_1 A_2}$ (d) $\left[\frac{\sqrt{A_1} + \sqrt{A_2}}{2}\right]^2$

29. Which source is associated with a line emission spectrum ?
(a) Red traffic light (b) Sun
(c) Electric fire (d) Neon street light

30. How should people wearing their spectacles work with a microscope ?
(a) They should keep on wearing their spectacles.
(b) They should take off their spectacles.
(c) They may either put on their spectacles or they may take off their spectacles; it makes no difference.
(d) They cannot use the microscope at all.

31. A mark 'A' placed on the surface of a glass sphere is viewed through glass from a point directly opposite. Radius of sphere = 10 cm. Refractive index of glass is 1.5. Which one of the following statements is correct ?
(a) The image formed is real and at a distance of 0.4 m from the eye.
(b) The image formed is virtual and at a distance of 0.2 m from the eye.
(c) The image formed is virtual and at a distance of 0.3 m from the centre of the sphere.
(d) The image formed is real and at a distance of 0.2 m from point A.

32. Immiscible transparent liquids A, B, C, D and E are placed in a rectangular container of glass with the liquids making layers according to their densities. The refractive index of the liquids is shown in the following figure. The container is illuminated from the side and a small piece of glass having refractive index 1.61 is gently dropped into the liquid layers. The glass piece, as it descends downwards, will not be visible in (Refer figure) :

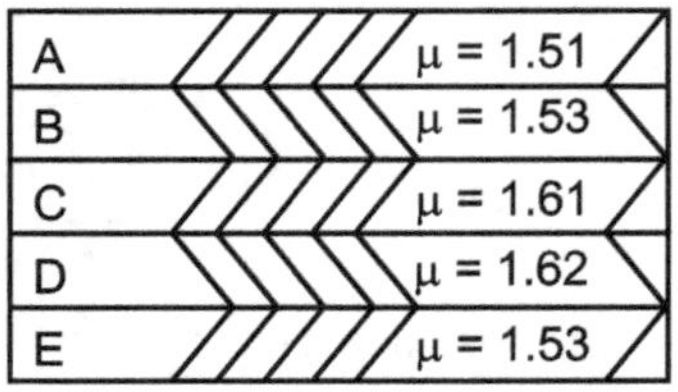

(a) Liquid A and B only

(b) Liquid C only

(c) Liquids D and E

(d) Liquids A, B, D and E

33. A convex lens of glass is immersed in water. Compared to its power in air, its power in water will : **(Karnataka 1993)**

(a) diminish

(b) increase

(c) remain the same

(d) diminish for red light and increase for blue light

34. The focal length of a convex lens is 30 cm and the size of the image is half of the object. The object distance is :

(A.F.M.C.1995)

(a) 60 cm (b) 90 cm

(c) 30 cm (d) 40 cm

35. A lens behaves as a converging lens in air and a diverging lens in water. The refractive index of the material is :

(a) equal to unity

(b) equal to 1.33

(c) between unity and 1.33

(d) greater than 1.33

36. In the displacement method of finding focal length of a convex lens, I_1 and I_2 are the sizes of the images respectively for the two positions of the lens. The size of the object is :

(a) $\sqrt{I_1 / I_2}$ (b) $\sqrt{I_2 / I_1}$

(c) $\sqrt{I_1 I_2}$ (d) $I_1 I_2$

37. f_V and f_R are the focal lengths of a convex lens for violet and red light, respectively, and F_V and F_R are the focal lengths of a concave lens for violet and red light, respectively. Which one of the following relations is correct ?

(CPMT 1998; CBSE 1996)

(a) $f_V < f_R$ and $F_V > F_R$

(b) $f_V > f_R$ and $F_V < F_R$

(c) $f_V < f_R$ and $F_V < F_R$

(d) $f_V > f_R$ and $F_V > F_R$

38. A thin convex lens of focal length 30 cm and refractive index 1.5 is placed on a horizontal plane mirror. It is found that an object, at a height '*h*' above the lens, has no parallax with its image. Then *h* is :

(a) 60 cm (b) 30 cm

(c) 45 cm (d) 20 cm

39. Time taken by the sunlight to pass through a window of thickness 4 mm whose refractive index is 1.5 is : **(C.B.S.E. 1983)**

(a) 2×10^{11} seconds (b) 2×10^{8} seconds

(c) 2×10^{-11} seconds (d) 2×10^{-8} seconds

40. Two lenses, whose powers are +2D and –4D respectively, are placed in contact. The power of the combination is :

(A.F.M.C. Pune 1998)

(a) – 2D (b) – 4D

(c) + 2D (d) + 4D

41. A double convex lens of refractive index μ_1 is immersed in a liquid of refractive index μ_2. This lens will act as a :

(a) diverging lens if $\mu_1 > \mu_2$

(b) diverging lens if $\mu_1 < \mu_2$

(c) converging lens if $\mu_1 = \mu_2$

(d) converging lens if $\mu_1 < \mu_2$

42. How many images will be formed if two mirrors are fitted on adjacent walls and one mirror on the ceiling? **(A.F.M.C. 1994)**

(a) 7 (b) 2

(c) 5 (d) 11

43. A telescope has an objective of focal length 50 cm and an eye-piece of focal length 5 cm. It is focused for distinct vision on a scale 200 cm away from the objective. Then the optical length of the telescope is :

(a) 200/3 cm (b) 25/6 cm

(c) 425/6 cm (d) 375/6 cm

44. A concave mirror is placed on a horizontal table with its axis directed vertically upwards. Let P be the pole of the mirror and C its centre of curvature. A point object is placed at C. It has a real image also located at C. If the mirror is now filled with water, the image will be : **(I.I.T.1998)**

(a) real and located at a point between C and P

(b) virtual and located at a point between C and P

(c) real and located at a point between C and infinity

(d) real and will remain at C

45. A parallel beam of light in air is incident on a glass sphere of refractive index 1.5 and diameter 20 cm parallel to its horizontal diameter. The rays converge to a point at the distance of d from the centre of the sphere, then d is : **(Karnataka 1995)**

(a) 20 cm (b) 15 cm

(c) 10 cm (d) 5 cm

46. A convex spherical surface forms an inverted image of an object. The object is placed in air and its image is formed in glass (μ = 1.5). If the object and image distance from the spherical surface is 0.2 m and 0.3 m respectively, the magnification is :

(a) 1.5 (b) 0.67

(c) 1 (d) 0.45

47. To get three images of a single object, one should have two plane mirrors at an angle of: **(Karnataka 1992)**

(a) 50° (b) 60°

(c) 30° (d) 90°

48. The focal length of a concave mirror is f and the distance from the object to the principal focus is p. Then the ratio of the size of the image to the size of the object is :

(a) $\frac{f^2}{p^2}$ (b) $\sqrt{\frac{f}{p}}$

(c) $\frac{f}{p}$ (d) $\frac{f+p}{p}$

49. Resolving power of a microscope depends upon : **(M.P.P.E.T. 1995)**

(a) the focal length and aperture of the eye lens

(b) the focal lengths of the objective and the eye lens

(c) the apertures of the objective and the eye lens

(d) the wavelength of light illuminating the object

50. A convex lens of focal length f is placed somewhere in between an object and a screen. The distance between an object and the screen is x, if the magnification produced by the lens is m, the focal length of the lens is :

(a) $\frac{(m-1)^2}{m}$ (b) $\frac{(m+1)^2}{m}$

(c) $\frac{mx}{(m-1)^2}$ (d) $\frac{mx}{(m+1)^2}$

51. An equiconvex lens is cut into two halves by a plane AB as shown in figure. The focal length of each half so obtained is :

(a) f (b) f/2

(c) 2f (d) 3f/2

52. A double convex lens of focal length 6 cm is made of glass of refractive index 1.5. The radius of curvature of one surface, which is double than that of the other surface, will be:

(a) 3 cm (b) 6 cm
(c) 8 cm (d) 9 cm

53. A rectangular block of glass (refractive index 3/2) is kept in water (refractive index 4/3). The critical angle for total internal reflection is : **(I.I.T.1994)**

(a) $\sin^{-1}$ (8/9) for a ray of light passing from water to glass
(b) $\sin^{-1}$ (8/9) for a ray of light passing from glass to water
(c) $\sin^{-1}$ (8/9) for a ray of light passing from glass to air
(d) $\sin^{-1}$ (2/9) for a ray of light passing from glass to air

54. The refractive index of water and glass with respect to air are 1.3 and 1.5 respectively. What will be the refractive index of glass with respect to water ? **(A.F.M.C. 1994)**

(a) 15/13 (b) 13/15
(c) 2 (d) 3

55. A convex lens of focal length 20 cm produces a real image twice the size of the object. Then the distance of the real object from the lens is :

(a) 20 cm (b) 30 cm
(c) 10 cm (d) 60 cm

56. Which of the following statements is not correct ?

(a) A double convex air bubble in water will act like a concave lens.
(b) A divergent lens causes parallel rays to come to a focus.
(c) A ray of light passing through a lens is bent towards the thicker part of the lens.
(d) All the statements are correct.

57. While taking photographs with a camera if one wants that every object beyond one metre should be in focus, one should :

(a) give short exposure without changing aperture
(b) reduce the aperture and increase the time of exposure
(c) increase the aperture and reduce the time of exposure
(d) give long exposure without changing the aperture

58. Total internal reflection can occur when light passes from : **(Delhi P.M.T. 1993)**

(a) a rarer medium to a denser medium
(b) one medium to another of equal refractive index
(c) a denser to a rarer medium
(d) one medium to another of equal absorption coefficient

59. A lense behaves as a converging lens in air and a diverging lens in water. The refractive index of the lens material is :

(C.P.M.T. 2001)

(a) equal to 1.33
(b) equal to unity
(c) greater than 1.33
(d) between unity and 1.33

60. Two thin lenses of focal length f_1 and f_2 respectively are placed in contact. The effective focal length of the combination is given by :

(a) $\frac{f_1}{f_1 + f_2}$ (b) $\frac{f_2}{f_1 + f_2}$
(c) $\frac{f_1 f_2}{f_1 + f_2}$ (d) $\frac{f_1 + f_2}{f_1 f_2}$

61. A concave lens made of water (μ = 1.33) is placed inside a glass slab (μ = 1.5) for an object placed within the focus and twice the focus, the image formed is :

(a) virtual
(b) real, inverted and magnified
(c) virtual, inverted and magnified
(d) real, inverted and diminished

62. Which of the following forms a virtual and erect image for all positions of the object ? **(I.I.T. 1996)**

(a) Concave lens

(b) Convex lens

(c) Concave mirror

(d) None of these

63. A Plano-convex lens of focal length 60 cm is silvered on its plane face. An object is placed at a distance of 60 cm from it. The distance of the image from it, is :

(a) 50 cm (b) 55 cm

(c) 60 cm (d) $\frac{300}{7}$ cm

64. A convex lens of focal length 1.0 m and a concave lens of focal length 0.25 m are 0.75 m apart. A parallel beam of light is incident on the convex lens. The beam emerging after refraction from both the lenses is :

(a) parallel to the principal axis

(b) convergent

(c) divergent

(d) none of the above

65. The focal length of combination of lenses formed with lenses having powers of + 2.50 D and – 3.75 D will be : **(Raj. P.M.T. 1997)**

(a) – 20 cm (b) – 40 cm

(c) – 60 cm (d) – 80 cm

66. A luminous object is kept at a fixed distance from a screen and with the help of a convex lens, an image is obtained on the screen. The lens is then moved till another image is obtained on the screen. If the sizes of the images are 2 cm and 8 cm and the distance between the object and the screen is 90 cm, then size of the object is : **(C.P.M.T. 1998)**

(a) 2 cm (b) 8 cm

(c) 4 cm (d) 6 cm

67. A lens is made of two types of transparent materials indicated by different shades. A point object is placed on its axis. The object will form : **(K.E.T. 2002)**

(a) 1 image (b) 2 images

(c) 3 images (d) 9 images

68. In the method of displacement, to determine the focal length of a convex lens, the distance between the object and the screen is D and real images of an object are formed on the screen for two positions of the lens which are separated by a distance x. The ratio of the sizes of the two images will be :

(a) $\sqrt{D/x}$ (b) $\left(\frac{D-x}{D+x}\right)^2$

(c) D^2/x^2 (d) D/x

69. A lamp hanging 4 metres above the table is lowered by 1 metre. How much percent is the increase in the illumination on the table?

(a) 25% (b) 52%

(c) 77.7% (d) No increase

70. In optical-fibres, the following principle is used : **(Punjab C.E.T. 1998)**

(a) Total internal reflection

(b) Scattering

(c) Successive reflection

(d) Refraction

71. The magnifying power of an astronomical telescope is 8 and the distance between the two lenses is 54 cm. The focal length of the eye-lens and objective lens will be respectively :

(a) 6 cm and 48 cm

(b) 48 cm and 6 cm

(c) 8 cm and 64 cm

(d) 64 cm and 8 cm

72. A convergent beam is incident on a concave lens as shown in the figure. Which of the following statements is not correct ?

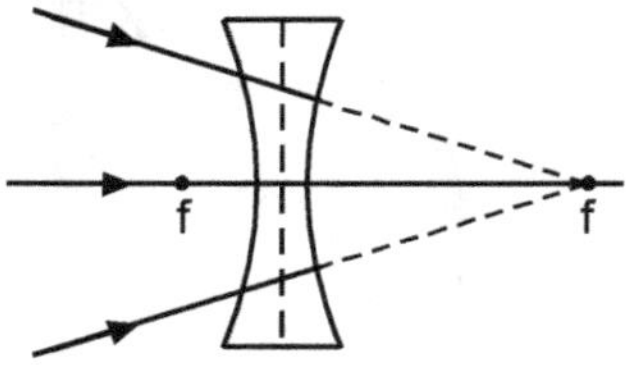

(a) The image formed is real.
(b) The image formed is virtual.
(c) The image formed is erect.
(d) The image formed is magnified.

73. A plane mirror produces a magnification of :
(a) – 1
(b) + 1
(c) zero
(d) between 0 and + ∞

74. If f_V and f_R denote the focal length of a simple convex lens corresponding to violet and red colours respectively, which of the following is correct ?
(a) $f_V > f_R$
(b) $f_V < f_R$
(c) $f_V = f_R$
(d) It will depend upon the nature of glass

75. A convex lens forms a real image of a point object placed on its principal axis. If the upper half of the lens is painted black, the image will : **(M.P.P.E.T. 1995)**
(a) be shifted downwards
(b) be shifted upwards
(c) not be shifted
(d) be shifted on the principal axis

76. In the human eye, the focusing is done by :
(a) to and fro movement of the eye-lens
(b) to and fro movement of the retina
(c) change in the convexity of the lens
(d) change in the refractive index of the eye fluids

77. The speed of light in air is 3×10^8 ms^{-1}. What will be its speed in diamond whose refractive index is 2.4 ? **(Karnataka 1993)**
(a) 3×10^8 ms^{-1}
(b) 1.25×10^8 ms^{-1}
(c) 332 ms^{-1}
(d) 7.2×10^8 ms^{-1}

78. A vessel of depth $2d$ cm is half filled with a liquid of refractive index μ_1 and the upper half with a liquid of refractive index μ_2. The apparent depth of the vessel seen perpendicularly is :
(a) $d\left(\frac{\mu_1\mu_2}{\mu_1+\mu_2}\right)$ (b) $d\left(\frac{1}{\mu_1}+\frac{1}{\mu_2}\right)$
(c) $2d\left(\frac{1}{\mu_1}+\frac{1}{\mu_2}\right)$ (d) $2d\frac{1}{\mu_1\mu_2}$

79. A thin lens has focal length f and its aperture has diameter d. It forms an image of intensity I. Now the central part of the aperture upto diameter $d/2$ is blocked by an opaque paper. The focal length and the image intensity will change to :
(a) f/2 and 1/2 (b) f and 1/4
(c) 3f/4 and 1/2 (d) f and 3/4

80. An object is placed 12 cm to the left of a converging lens of focal length 8 cm. Another converging lens of 6 cm focal length is placed at a distance of 30 cm to the right of the first lens. The second lens will produce : **(K.E.T. 2002)**
(a) a real enlarged image
(b) a real inverted image
(c) no image
(d) a virtual enlarged image

81. With fixed positions of the object and the image pins in the displacement method, the second position of the lens can be obtained only when the distance D between the object pin and image pin is :
(a) less than 4f (b) equal to 4f
(c) more than 4f (d) 3f or 4f

82. A concave lens has a focal length of 20 cm. A convergent beam of light converges to a point 20 cm behind the concave lens on the principal axis. The image is formed at :

(a) infinity (c) 10 cm
(b) 20 cm (d) 40 cm

83. You are supplied with four convex lenses of focal lengths 100 cm, 25 cm, 3 cm and 2 cm. For an astronomical telescope with maximum magnifying power, you will use lenses of focal lengths :

(a) 100 cm and 25 cm
(b) 100 cm and 3 cm
(c) 25 cm and 3 cm
(d) 100 cm and 2 cm

84. The curved face of a plano-convex lens is silvered. If μ is the refractive index and R the radius of curvature of its curved surface, then the system behaves like a concave mirror of radius :

(a) $R(\mu - 1)$ (b) $R\mu$
(c) $\frac{R}{(\mu - 1)}$ (d) $\frac{R}{\mu}$

85. Light of a certain colour has 2000 waves to the millimeter in air. What will be the wavelength of this light in a medium of refractive index 1.25 ?

(a) 1000 Å (b) 2000 Å
(c) 3000 Å (d) 4000 Å

86. A Plano-convex lens is made of refractive index 1.6. The radius of curvature of the curved surface is 60 cm. The focal length of the lens is : **(C.P.M.T. 2001)**

(a) 200 cm (b) 100 cm
(c) 50 cm (d) 400 cm

87. The distance between an object and a divergent lens is 'm' times the focal length of the lens. The linear magnification produced by the lens will be equal to :

(a) m (b) $\frac{1}{m}$
(c) $(m + 1)$ (d) $\frac{1}{m+1}$

88. A point source of light is placed 4 m below the surface of water of refractive index 5/3. The minimum diameter of the disc, which should be placed over the source, on the surface of water to cut off all light coming out of the water is : **(C.B.S.E. 1994)**

(a) Infinite (b) 6 m
(c) 4 m (d) 3 m

89. A needle 10 cm long is placed along the axis of a convex lens of focal length 10 cm such that the middle point of the needle is at 20 cm distance from the lens. The length of the image of needle is

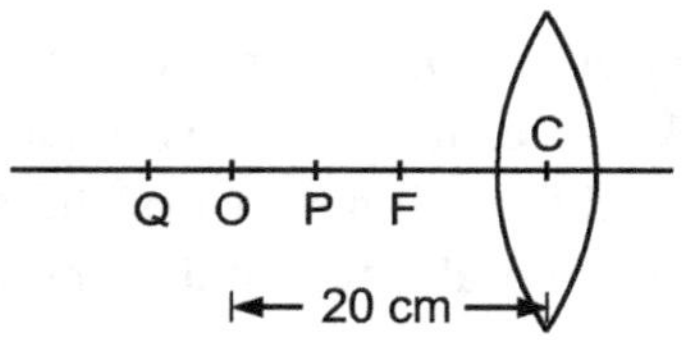

(a) 13.33 cm (b) 20 cm
(c) 1 cm (d) 10 cm

90. Two thin lenses, when in contact, produce a combination of power +10 D. When they are 0.25 m apart, they produce power of +6 dioptre. Focal lengths of the two lenses are : **(I.I.T. 1997)**

(a) 12.5 cm and 50 cm
(b) 25 cm and 110 cm
(c) 25 cm and 50 cm
(d) 12.5 cm and 72.5 cm

91. A ray of light is incident at an angle of 60° on one face of a prism which has an angle of 30°. The ray emerging out of the prism makes an angle of 30° with the incident ray. Then angle of emergence is :

(a) 60° (b) 30°
(c) 90° (d) 0°

92. In Q. 91, refractive index of the material of the prism is :

(a) 1.73 (b) 1.5
(c) 1.2 (d) 1.6

93. A convex mirror and a concave mirror each of focal length 5 cm, are placed at a distance 15 cm apart facing each other. A point object is placed midway between them. If reflection first takes place at the concave mirror and then at the convex mirror, the final image is formed at :

(a) 15 cm behind the convex mirror

(b) 10 cm from the concave mirror and between the 2 mirrors

(c) at the pole of the concave mirror

(d) at the pole of the convex mirror

94. The diameter of a plano convex lens is 6 cm and thickness at the centre is 3 mm. The speed of light in the material of the lens is 2×10^8 ms^{-1}. Focal length of the lens is :

(a) 10 cm (b) 20 cm

(c) 15 cm (d) 30 cm

95. A convex lens of focal length 1.0 m and a concave lens of focal length 0.25 m are kept 0.75 m apart. A parallel beam of light first passes through a convex lens and then through the concave lens. The image formed will be :

(a) virtual, at a distance of 0.25 m from the concave lens and between the two lenses

(b) real, at a distance of 0.25 m from the concave lens and between the two lenses

(c) at a point midway between the two lenses

(d) at infinity

96. A right angled prism (45° - 90° - 45°) of refractive index μ has a plate of refractive index μ_1 ($\mu_1 < \mu$) cemented to its diagonal face. The system is placed in air. A ray is incident on face AB as shown in the figure. The angle of incidence at face AB for which the ray strikes the diagonal face at critical angle is :

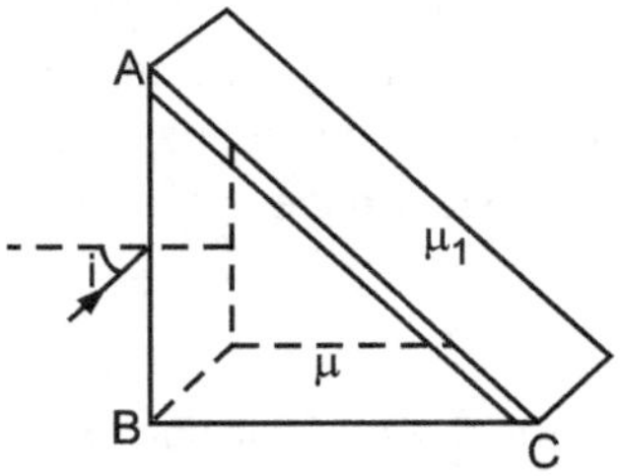

(a) $i = \sin^{-1}\left[\sqrt{\mu^2 - \mu_1^2} - \mu_1\right]$

(b) $i = \sin^{-1}[\mu^2 - \mu_1^2]$

(c) $i = \sin^{-1}\left[\frac{\sqrt{\mu^2 - \mu_1} - \mu_1}{\sqrt{2}}\right]$

(d) $i = \sin^{-1}\left[\sqrt{2}\sqrt{\mu^2 - \mu_1} - \sqrt{2}\mu_1\right]$

97. In Q. 96, if μ =1.352, then angle of incidence at face AB for which the refracted ray passes undeviated through the diagonal face is :

(a) 45° (b) 53°

(c) 73° (d) 30°

98. A pile 4 m high stands in the lake, such that it appears 1 m above the surface of water. If refractive index of water is $\mu = \frac{4}{3}$ and sun rays make an angle of 45° with the water surface, then length of the shadow of pile on the bed of the lake will be :

(a) 1 m (b) 1.88 m

(c) 2.88 m (d) 0.88 m

99. If a glass slab is placed on the letters of different colours, then which colour will appear most raised ?

(a) Red (b) Green

(c) Blue (d) Yellow

100. A ray of light is incident normally on one of the faces of a prism of apex angle 30° and refractive index $\sqrt{2}$. The angle of deviation for the ray of light is :

(a) 45° (b) 30°

(c) 60° (d) 15°

101. A bulb is situated at the base of a swimming pool of depth 10 m. If the refractive index of water is 1.33, then the surface area of water illuminated will be :

(a) 300 m^2 (b) 404 m^2
(c) 150 m^2 (d) 270 m^2

102. A thin rod of length f/3 is placed along the optic axis of a concave mirror of focal length f such that its image, which is real and elongated, just touches the rod. Then magnification of the mirror is :

(a) 1.5 (b) 2
(c) 3 (d) 2.5

103. A plano convex lens has thickness 4 cm. When placed on a horizontal table with the curved surface in contact with it, the apparent depth of the bottom-most point of the lens is found to be 3 cm. Now, if the lens is inverted such that the plane surface is on the table, the apparent depth of the centre of the plane face is found to $\frac{25}{8}$ cm. The focal length of the lens is :

(a) 15 cm (b) 25 cm
(c) 45 cm (d) 75 cm

104. A convex lens and a concave lens having focal lengths 30 cm and 20 cm are placed 10 cm apart. The distance of a source of light at which it must be placed for this system to give a parallel beam of rays, is :

(a) 10 cm (b) 20 cm
(c) 30 cm (d) ∞

105. If a plane mirror approaches us with a speed of 20 cm /sec, then our image in the plane mirror will approach us with a speed of :

(a) 10 cm/sec (b) 20 cm/sec
(c) 30 cm/sec (d) 40 cm/sec

106. On heating a liquid, the refractive index generally :

(a) decreases
(b) increases
(c) does not change
(d) increases or decreases depending upon rate of heating

107. Light from a sodium lamp (λ = 6000 Å) passes through a tank of glycerin (refractive index 1.6) 20 m long in time t_1. If it takes time t_1 to traverse the same tank, when filled with air (μ = 1), what is the difference between t_2 and t_1 ?

(a) 2×10^{-3} s (b) 3×10^{-8} s
(c) 4×10^{-8} s (d) 5×10^{-8} s

108. If a plane mirror is rotated by an angle θ about an axis while passing through the point where the incident ray, reflected ray and the normal meet with each other, then the reflected ray is rotated by an angle :

(a) θ (b) 2θ
(c) 3θ (d) 4θ

109. A plastic hemisphere has a radius of curvature of 8 cm and refractive index of 1.6. On the axis halfway between the plane surface and the spherical surface (4 cm from each) is a small flaw. How far from the surface does the flaw appear to be when viewed along the axis of the spherical surface ?

(a) – 3.25 cm (b) + 3.25 cm
(c) – 2.25 cm (d) + 2.25 cm

110. When a concave mirror is immersed in water:

(a) its focal length increases
(b) its focal length decreases
(c) its focal length remains unchanged
(d) it loses its reflecting power

111. At what angle of incidence should a beam of light strike the surface of water of a still pond if the angle between the refracted ray and the reflected ray is to be 90° (refractive index of water 1.33) ?

(a) $\theta = \tan^{-1}(13.3)$ (b) $\theta = \tan^{-1}(1.33)$
(c) $\theta = \tan^{-1}(1/1.33)$ (d) $\theta = \tan^{-1}(0.133)$

112. Ratio of refractive index of blue light to red light in air is :

(a) equal to unity (b) less than unity
(c) greater than unity (d) Any of these

113. A bi-convex lens (μ = 1.5) of focal length 0.2 m acts as a divergent lens of power one dioptre when immersed in a liquid. The refractive index of the liquid is :

(a) 1.33 (b) 1.67
(c) 1.25 (d) 1.2

114. An object 5 cm tall is placed 1 m from a concave spherical mirror which has a radius of curvature of 20 cm. The size of the image is :

(a) 0.11 cm (b) 0.50 cm
(c) 0.55 cm (d) 0.60 cm

115. A graph drawn with object distance along abscissa and image distance as ordinate for a convex lens is :

(a) a straight line
(b) a circle
(c) a parabola
(d) a rectangular hyperbola

116. A person can't see objects beyond 25 cm. The power of the lens to correct the vision will be :

(a) –4 D (b) –2 D
(c) –1 D (d) +2 D

117. If for a concave mirror, an object is placed at a distance d_1 from it's focus and image is formed at a distance d_2 from the focus, then focal length of the mirror is given by :

(a) $d_1 + d_2$ (b) $d_1 - d_2$
(c) $d_1 d_2$ (d) $\sqrt{d_1 d_2}$

118. The sun subtends an angle of 30' on the earth surface. A convex lens of focal length 200 cm is used to form its image. The diameter of the image of the solar disc is ?

(a) 3.48 cm (b) 0.87 cm
(c) 1.74 cm (d) 200 cm

119. A ray of light passes from a medium of refractive index $\sqrt{2}$ into another medium having refractive index 1. What is the critical angle of incidence :

(a) 30° (b) 45°
(c) 60° (d) 90°

120. Two plane mirrors A and B are aligned parallel to each other as shown in the figure. A ray of light is incident at an angle of 30° just inside one end of A. Plane of incidence coincides with the plane of the figure. The maximum number of times the ray undergoes reflections (including the first one) before it emerges out is :

(I.I.T. Screening 2002)

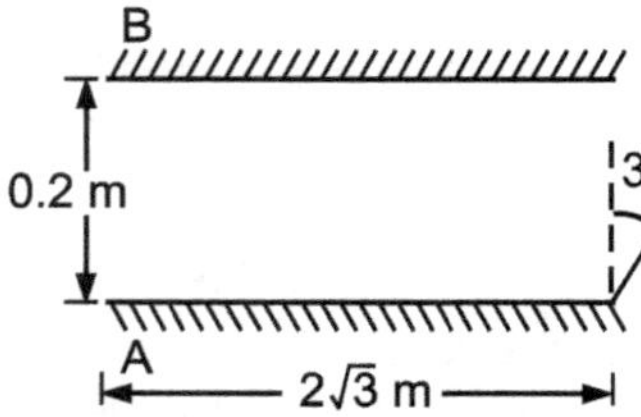

(a) 28 (b) 30
(c) 32 (d) 34

121. By looking at an empty glass along the path shown dotted in the figure (angle θ), one sees the lower left hand corner figure. Now when the glass is filled with water of refractive index (4/3), one sees the middle of the bottom of the glass again looking along angle θ. Given the diameter of the base of glass is 5 cm, what is the height of the glass (y) ?

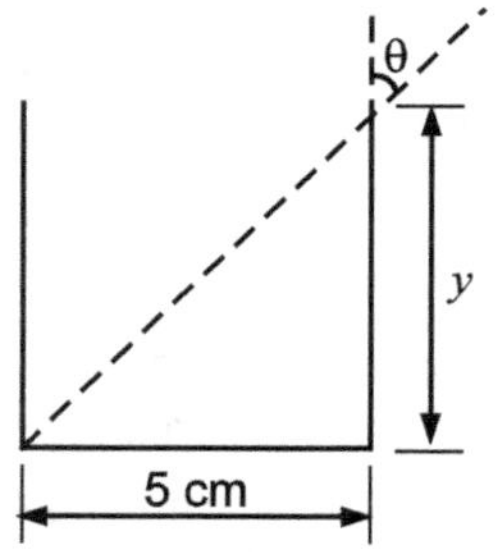

(a) 1.48 cm (b) 2.96 cm
(c) 6.66 cm (d) 5.9 cm

122. Dispersion can be explained with the help of:

(a) Cauchy's formula
(b) Snell's law
(c) Internal reflection
(d) Any of these

123. A convex lens of focal length 40 cm is held coaxially above a concave mirror of focal length 18 cm. A luminous point object placed *d* cm above the lens on its axis gives rise to an image coincident with itself. Then *d* is :

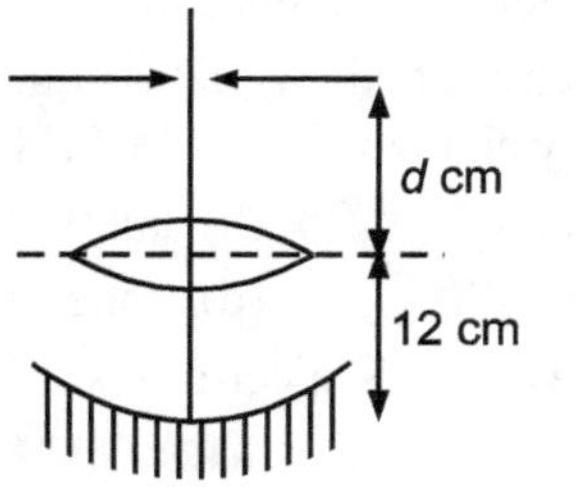

(a) 15 cm (b) 18 cm
(c) 40 cm (d) 30 cm

124. A person stands straight in front of a mirror at a distance of 30 cm away from it. He sees his erect image whose height is $1/5^{th}$ of his real height. The mirror he is using is :
(a) plane mirror
(b) concave mirror
(c) convex mirror
(d) plano-concave mirror

125. The wavelength of light diminishes 'μ' times in a medium. A diver from inside water (μ = 1.33) looks at an object whose natural colour is green. He sees the objects as :
(a) green (b) blue
(c) yellow (d) red

126. A ray of light is incident normally on one face of the prism as shown below. If $\theta = 45°$, then refractive index of the material of the prism is :

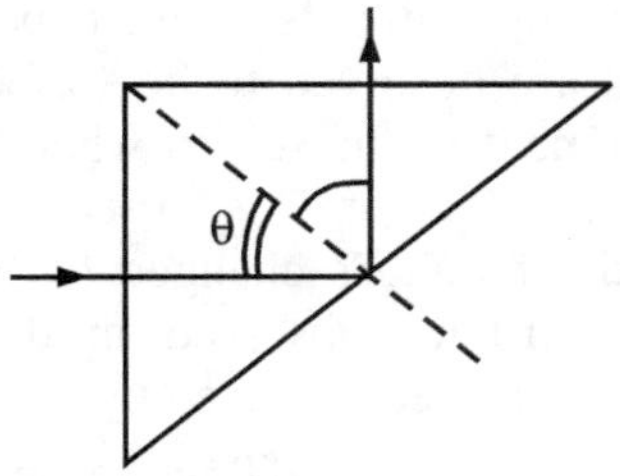

(a) 1 (b) $<\sqrt{2}$
(c) equal to $\sqrt{2}$ (d) $>\sqrt{2}$

127. Two identical double convex lenses X and Y, have the same focal length, but the radii of curvature differ so that $R_x = 0.9\ R_y$. If $\mu_x = 1.54$, what is the refractive index of the material of the other lens?
(a) 1.3 (b) 1.4
(c) 1.5 (d) 1.6

128. The resolution limit of the eye is 1 minute. At a distance of *x* cm from the eye, two persons stand with a lateral separation of 3 m. For the two persons just to be resolved by the naked eye, *x* should be :
(a) 30 km (b) 20 km
(c) 15 km (d) 10 km

129. A liquid of R.I. 1.6 is introduced between two identical plano-convex lenses in two ways P and Q as shown in the figure. If the lens material has R.I. 1.5, the combination is:

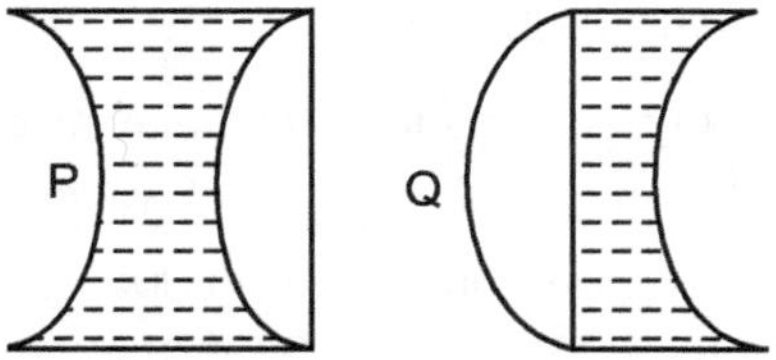

(a) convergent in both
(b) divergent in both
(c) convergent in Q only
(d) convergent in P only

130. An observer can see through a pin hole at the top end of a thin rod of height *h* placed as shown in the figure. Beaker height is 3*h* and its radius is *h*. When the beaker is filled with a liquid upto a height 2*h*, he can see the lower end of the rod. Then refractive index of the liquid is : **(I.I.T. Screening 2002)**

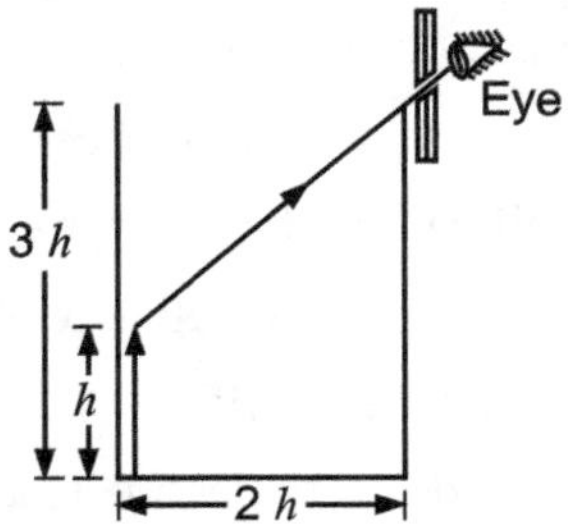

(a) $\frac{3}{2}$ (b) $\frac{\sqrt{3}}{2}$

(c) $\frac{5}{2}$ (d) $\sqrt{\frac{5}{2}}$

131. An air bubble in water behaves as :

(a) a plane mirror

(b) a converging lens

(c) a concave mirror

(d) a diverging lens

132. An air bubble inside a glass slab (μ = 1.5) appears at 6 cm when viewed from one side and 4 cm when viewed from the opposite side. The thickness of the slab is :

(a) 10 cm

(b) 6.67 cm

(c) 15 cm

(d) None of the above

133. When a ray is refracted from one medium into another medium, the wavelength changes from 6000 Å to 4000 Å. The critical angle for a ray from the second medium will be :

(a) $\cos^{-1}(2/3)$ (b) $\sin^{-1}(2/5)$

(c) $\tan^{-1}(3/2)$ (d) $\sin^{-1}(2/\sqrt{13})$

134. A spherical convex surface separates object and image space of refractive index 1.0 and 1.33. If radius of curvature of the surface is 0.1 m, its power is :

(a) 2.48 D (b) – 2.48 D

(c) 3.3 D (d) – 3.3 D

135. Resolving power of a telescope depends on :

(H.P.M.T. 1999, 2000)

(a) the magnification of eye piece

(b) the focal length of objective lens

(c) diameter of objective lens

(d) refractive index of objective lens

136. In a compound microscope, the intermediate image is: **(I.I.T. Screening 2000)**

(a) virtual, erect and magnified

(b) real, erect and magnified

(c) real, inverted and magnified

(d) virtual, erect and reduced

137. The velocity of light in vacuum can be changed by changing : **(A.F.M.C. 2000)**

(a) frequency (b) amplitude

(c) wavelength (d) none of these

138. The nature of Sun's spectrum is:

(M.P.C.E.E.T. 2000)

(a) continuous spectrum with absorption lines

(b) line spectrum

(c) the spectrum of the Helium atom

(d) band spectrum

139. The angle of prism is 5° and its refractive indices for red and violet colours are 1.5 and 1.6 respectively. The angular dispersion produced by the prism is:

(M.P.P.M.T. 2000)

(a) 7.75° (b) 0.5°

(c) 5° (d) 0.17°

140. The magnifying power of telescope can be increased by

(I.I.I.T. Alla. 2000, D.C.E. 2001)

(a) increasing focal length of eyepiece

(b) keeping lenses at least distance of distinct vision

(c) increasing focal length of objective

(d) decreasing focal length of eyepiece

141. In a Young's double slit experiment, 12 fringes are observed to be formed in a certain segment of the screen when light of wavelength 600 nm is used. If the wavelength of light is changed to 400 nm, number of fringes observed in the same segment of the screen is given by

(I.I.T Screening 2001)

(a) 12 (b) 18

(c) 24 (d) 30

142. Two lenses of power 2.5 D and 1.5 D are joined together. The power of the new lens formed is **(B.V.T. M.B.B.S. 2001)**

(a) 1.0 D (b) $\frac{5}{3}$ D

(c) $\frac{3}{5}$ D (d) 4.0 D

143. In the Young's double slit experiment, for which colour the fringe width is least? **(M.P.C.E.E.T. 2001)**

(a) Red (b) Green

(c) Blue (d) Yellow

144. Dispersion of light occurs due to: **(I.I.I.T. Alla. 2001)**

(a) side of the prism

(b) wavelength

(c) angle of incidence

(d) angle of prism

145. A convex lens produces a real image m times the size of the object. What will be the distance of the object from the lens ? **(J.I.P.M.E.R. 2002)**

(a) $\left(\frac{m+1}{m}\right)f$ (b) $(m-1)f$

(c) $\left(\frac{m-1}{m}\right)f$ (d) $\frac{m+1}{f}$

146. Two thin lenses of focal lengths f_1 and f_2 are in contact. The focal length of this combination is : **(C.P.M.T. 1982)**

(a) $\frac{f_1f_2}{f_1-f_2}$ (b) $\frac{f_1f_2}{f_1+f_2}$

(c) $\frac{2f_1f_2}{f_1-f_2}$ (d) $\frac{2f_1f_2}{f_1+f_2}$

147. The angle of prism is 30°. The rays incident at 60° at one refracting face suffer a deviation at 30°. The angle of emergence is : **(M.P. P.M.T. 2002)**

(a) 0° (b) 30°

(c) 60° (d) 90°

148. Huygen's principle of secondary wavelets may be used to: **(Kerala C.E.T. Engg. 2002)**

(a) find the velocity of light in vacuum

(b) explain the particle behaviour of light

(c) find the new position of a wavefront

(d) explain photo-electric effect

149. Magnifying power of an astronomical telescope for normal vision with usual notation is : **(D.C.E. 2002)**

(a) $-f_o/f_e$ (b) $-f_o \times f_e$

(c) $-f_e/f_o$ (d) $-f_o + f_e$

150. The power of lens, a short sighted person uses is –2 diopter. Find the maximum distance of an object, which he can see without spectacle : **(J & K.C.E.T. 2002)**

(a) 25 cm (b) 50 cm

(c) 100 cm (d) 10 cm

151. What is the difference between soft and hard X-rays ? **(A. F. M.C. 2002)**

(a) Velocity (b) Intensity

(c) Frequency (d) Polarisation

152. Brilliance of diamond is due to : **(A.I.I.M.S. 2002)**

(a) Shape

(b) Cutting

(c) Reflection

(d) Total internal reflection

153. A ray of light travels from an optically denser to a rarer medium. The critical angle for the two media is C. The maximum possible deviation of the ray will be : **(Karnataka C.E.T. 2002)**

(a) 2C (b) $\frac{\pi}{2}-C$

(c) $\pi - C$ (d) $\pi - 2C$

154. Light appears to travel in straight lines because : **(Karnataka C.E.T. 2002)**

(a) light consists of very small particles

(b) the frequency of light is very small

(c) the velocity of light is different for different colours

(d) the wavelength of light is very small

155. To increase both the resolving power and magnifying power of a telescope :

(Karnataka C.E.T. 2002)

(a) the focal length of the objective has to be increased

(b) both the focal length and aperture of objective has to be increased

(c) the wavelength of light has to be decreased

(d) the aperture of the objective has to be increased

156. The resolving power of a telescope whose lens has a diameter of 1.22 m for a wavelength of 5000 Å is :

(Kerala C.E.T. (Med) 2002)

(a) 2×10^5 (b) 2×10^6

(c) 2×10^4 (d) 2×10^2

157. Two waves have their amplitudes in the ratio of 1 : 9. The maximum and minimum intensities, when they interfere, are in the ratio: **(Kerala C.E.T. (Med) 2002)**

(a) $\frac{25}{16}$ (b) $\frac{16}{25}$

(c) $\frac{1}{9}$ (d) $\frac{10}{8}$

158. The focal length of a convex lens is (f). An object is placed at a distance x from its first focal point. The ratio of the size of the real image to that of the object is :

(Haryana C.E.E.T. 2002)

(a) f/x^2 (b) x^2/f

(c) f/x (d) x/f

159. The final image formed by a microscope is :

(A.M.U. (Engg.) 2002)

(a) Virtual and magnified

(b) Real and magnified

(c) Real and diminished

(d) Virtual and diminished.

160. The velocity of light in a medium of refractive index 3/2 is :

(A.M.U. (Engg.) 2002)

(a) 2×10^8 m/s (b) 4×10^8 m/s

(c) 5×10^5 m/s (d) 9×10^5 m/s

161. When the distance between the slits of Young's double slit experiment is reduced to half, then the fringe width will become :

(B.H.U. 2002)

(a) constant (b) four times

(c) two times (d) half

162. To get three images of a single object, one should have two plane mirrors at an angle of: **(A.I.E.E.E. 2003)**

(a) 30° (b) 60°

(c) 90° (d) 120°

163. Huygen's wave theory of light could not explain : **(A.F.M.C. 2003)**

(a) Diffraction

(b) Interference

(c) Polarization

(d) Photoelectric effect

164. Prof. C.V. Raman was awarded the Nobel prize for : **(A.F.M.C. 2003)**

(a) Dispersion of light

(b) Scattering of light

(c) Refraction of light

(d) Reflection of light

165. Polarization of light takes place due to many processes. Which of the following will not cause polarization ?

(Kerala C.E.T. (Engg.) 2003)

(a) Reflection (b) Absorption

(c) Scattering (d) Diffraction

166. The power of an achromatic convergent lens of two lenses is +2 D. The power of convex lens is +5 D. The ratio of dispersive power of convex and concave lenses will be :

(Punjab C.E.E.T. 2003)

(a) 5 : 3 (b) 3 : 5

(c) 2 : 5 (d) 5 : 2

167. A prism of refractive index $\sqrt{2}$ has a refracting angle of 60°. At what angle a ray must be incident on it so that it suffers a minimum deviation ? **(B.H.U. 2003)**

(a) 45° (b) 60°
(c) 90° (d) 180°

168. A short linear object of length b lies along the axis of a concave mirror of focal length at distance u from the pole of the mirror. What is the size of image ? **(B.H.U. 2003)**

(a) $\left(\frac{f}{u-f}\right)b$ (b) $\left(\frac{f}{u-f}\right)^2 b$

(c) $\left(\frac{f}{u-f}\right)b^2$ (d) $\left(\frac{f}{u-f}\right)$

169. The rectilinear propagation of light in a medium is due to : **(D.C.E. 2003)**

(a) its short wavelength
(b) its high frequency
(c) its high velocity
(d) the refractive index of medium

170. The wavelength of sodium light in air is 5890 Å. The velocity of light in air is 3×10^8 ms^{-1}. The wavelength of light in a glass of refractive index 1.6 would be close to : **(D.C.E. 2003)**

(a) 5890 Å (b) 3681 Å
(c) 9424 Å (d) 15078 Å

171. A pencil of light is incident on a plane mirror and when reflected back it forms a real image. The pencil of light incident on the plane mirror is : **(D.C.E. 2003)**

(a) parallel (b) convergent
(c) divergent (d) none of these

172. The light gathering power of a camera lens depends on: **(D.C.E. 2003)**

(a) its diameter only
(b) ratio of focal length and diameter
(c) product of focal length and diameter.
(d) wavelength of light used

173. In diffraction from a single slit, the angular width of the central maximum does not depend on :

(a) wavelength of light used
(b) width of slit
(c) distance of slits from screen
(d) ratio of λ and slit width

174. Illumination of the Sun at noon is maximum because : **(Manipal 2003)**

(a) scattering is reduced at noon
(b) refraction of light is minimum at noon
(c) rays are incident almost normally
(d) the sun is nearer to earth at noon

175. A nicol prism is based on the action of :
(A.M.U. (Med) 2003)

(a) Double refraction (b) Refraction
(c) Dichroism (d) Both (a) and (c)

176. A source of light suspended above a circular table at a height equal to the radius of the table gives an intensity I at the centre of the table. The intensity at the edge of the table would be : (assuming illuminance remains the same) **(A.M.U. (Med). 2003)**

(a) 0.25 I (b) 0.5 I
(c) 0.7 I (d) 2.8 I

177. The angle of incidence at which reflected light is totally polarized for reflection from air to glass (refractive index *n*) is :
(A.I.E.E.E. 2004)

(a) $\sin^{-1}$ (n) (b) $\sin^{-1}$ (1/n)
(c) $\tan^{-1}$ (1/n) (d) $\tan^{-1}$ (n)

178. In the human eye, the focusing is done by:
(N.D. A. 2004)

(a) to and fro movement of the eye lens
(b) to and from movement of the retina
(c) change in the convexity of the eye lens
(d) change in the refractive index of the eye fluids

179. An object is immersed in a fluid. In order that the object becomes invisible, it should :

(Kerala P.M.T. 2004)

(a) behave as a perfect reflector
(b) absorb all light falling on it
(c) have refractive index one
(d) have refractive index exactly matching with that of the surrounding fluid

180. When light is incident on a diffraction grating, the zero order principal maximum will be : **(Karnataka C.E.T. 2004)**

(a) spectrum of the colours
(b) white
(c) one of the component colours
(d) absent

181. A thin glass (refractive index 1.5) lens has optical power of –5 D in air. Its optical power in a liquid medium with refractive index 1.6 will be : **(A.I.E.E.E. 2005)**

(a) 25 D (b) – 25 D
(c) 1 D (d) – 1 D

182. Refractive index of material is equal to tangent of polarising angle. It is called :

(A.I.E.E.E. 2004)

(a) Brewster's law (b) Lambert's law
(c) Malus's law (d) Bragg's low

183. Which of the following is not a property of light ? **(A.F.M.C. 2005)**

(a) It requires a material medium for propagation.
(b) It can travel through vacuum.
(c) It involves transportation of energy.
(d) It has finite speed.

184. What causes change in the colours of the soap or oil films for the given beam of light?

(A.F.M.C. 2005)

(a) Angle of incidence
(b) Angle of reflection
(c) Thickness of film
(d) None of these

185. What happens to the fringe pattern when the Young's double slit experiment is performed in water instead of air ? **(A.F.M.C. 2005)**

(a) Shrinks
(b) Disappears
(c) Remains unchanged
(d) Gets enlarged

186. Sir C.V. Raman was awarded Nobel Prize for his work connected with which of the following phenomenon of radiation ?

(A.F.M.C. 2005)

(a) Scattering (b) Diffraction
(c) Interference (d) Polarization

187. An object is placed at a distance equal to focal length of convex mirror. If the focal length of the mirror is f, then the distance of the image from the pole of the mirror is :

(A.F.M.C. 2005)

(a) less than f (b) equal to f
(c) more than f (d) infinity

188. Ability of the eye to see objects at all distances is called : **(A.F.M.C. 2005)**

(a) Binocular vision (b) Myopia
(c) Hypermetropia (d) Accommodation

189. The wave theory of light, in its original form, was first postulated by,

(Karnataka C.E.T. 2005)

(a) Isaac Newton
(b) Christian Huygens
(c) Thomas Young
(d) Augustin Jean Fresnel

190. Which of the following is wrong statement ?

(Karnataka C.E.T. 2005)

(a) D = 1/f, where f is the focal length and D is called the refractive power of a lens.
(b) Power is called a dioptre when f is in metres.
(c) Power is called a dioptre and does not depend on the system of unit used to measure f.
(d) D is positive for convergent lens and negative for divergent lens.

191. Two coherent sources of intensity ratio β interfere. Then the value of $\frac{I_{max} - I_{min}}{I_{max} + I_{min}}$ is : **(A.F.M.C. 2005)**

(a) $\frac{1+\beta}{\sqrt{\beta}}$ (b) $\sqrt{\left(\frac{1+\beta}{\beta}\right)}$

(c) $\frac{1+\beta}{2\sqrt{\beta}}$ (d) $\frac{2\sqrt{\beta}}{1+\beta}$

192. Two thin lenses of focal lengths f_1 and f_2 are in contact and coaxial. The power of the combination is **(C.B.S.E. P.M.T. 2008)**

(a) $\sqrt{\frac{f_2}{f_1}}$ (b) $\frac{f_1 + f_2}{2}$

(c) $\frac{f_1 + f_2}{f_1 f_2}$ (d) $\sqrt{\frac{f_1}{f_2}}$

193. If the fringe width X = 0.4 mm, the distance between 6th bright band and the 4th dark band on the same side is : **(M.H.T. C.E.T. 2009)**

(a) 1 mm (b) 0.5 mm

(c) 1.5 mm (d) 2.5 mm

194. A red flower kept in green light will appear : **(M.P.P.E.T. 2009)**

(a) red (b) yellow

(c) black (d) white

195. The magnifying power of a telescope is m. If the focal length of the eye-piece is halved, then its magnifying power is .... **(Gujarat C.E.T. 2010)**

(a) $\frac{1}{2m}$ (b) 4m

(c) 2m (d) $\frac{m}{2}$

196. A plane mirror produces a magnification of .... **(Gujarat C.E.T. 2010)**

(a) zero (b) infinite

(c) – 1 (d) + 1

197. Light enters from air into a medium of R.I. 1.5. The percentage change in its wavelength is **(MHT-CET 2007)**

(a) 66.66% (b) 50%

(c) 33.33% (d) 25%

198. Time taken by the light to travel through 5 cm of glass is same as that through X cm of air. R.I. of glass is 1.5, then X is **(MHT-CET 2007)**

(a) 7.5 cm (b) 1.33 cm

(c) 9 cm (d) 6 cm

199. Light enters glass from water, then **(MHT-CET 2008)**

(a) wavelength remains same

(b) wavelength decreases

(c) frequency increases

(d) wavelength increases

200. Light is incident on a substance of refractive index at an angle of 45°. What is the ratio of width of beam in air to the medium ? **(MHT-CET 2008)**

(a) $\sqrt{3} : \sqrt{2}$ (b) $1 : \sqrt{1.5}$

(c) $1 : 2\sqrt{2}$ (d) $\sqrt{2} : \sqrt{3}$

201. The nature of light waves is similar to **(MHT-CET 2009)**

(a) alpha rays (b) gamma rays

(c) cathode rays (d) cosmic rays

202. If the critical angle for total internal reflection, from a medium to vacuum is 30°, then velocity of light in the medium is **(MHT-CET 2009)**

(a) 6×10^8 m/sec (b) 3×10^8 m/sec

(c) 2×10^8 m/sec (d) 1.5×10^8 m/sec

203. If light travels from vacuum to water, its wavelength **(MHT-CET 2010)**

(a) increases

(b) remains constant

(c) decreases

(d) may increase or decrease

204. A light of wavelength 6000 Å travels from rarer medium to denser medium of refractive index 1.5. If its frequency in rarer medium is 5×10^{14} Hz, then its frequency in denser medium will be **(MHT-CET 2010)**

(a) 3.3×10^{14} Hz

(b) 5×10^{14} Hz

(c) 2.5×10^{7} Hz

(d) 7.5×10^{14} Hz

205. A lens having focal length and aperture of diameter d forms an image of intensity I. Aperture of diameter d/2 in centre region of lens is covered by a black paper. Focal length of lens and intensity of image now will be respectively **(A.I.P.M.T. 2010)**

(a) f and 3I/4 (b) f/2 and I/2

(c) f and I/4 (d) 3f/4 and I = 2

206. The tourmaline crystal **(MHT-CET 2011)**

(a) absorbs ordinary light and transmits extra ordinary light.

(b) absorbs extra ordinary light and transmits ordinary light.

(c) absorbs both ordinary and extra ordinary light.

(d) transmits both ordinary and extra ordinary light.

207. The angle of refraction is found to be half the angle of refraction. Then refractive index of medium is **(MHT-CET 2011)**

(a) $\cos^{-1}\left(\frac{\mu}{2}\right)$ (b) $\cos^{-1}(\mu)$

(c) $2\sin^{-1}(\mu)$ (d) $2\cos^{-1}\left(\frac{\mu}{2}\right)$

208. In Nicol prism Canada balsam acts as an …… medium for the extra ordinary ray.

(MHT-CET 2012)

(a) optically rarer (b) optically denser

(c) opaque (d) none of these

209. A light ray is travelling from air to medium, c is velocity of light in air and v is velocity of light in medium. The reflected and refracted rays are perpendicular to each other. The angle of polarization is

(MHT-CET 2012)

(a) $\theta = \tan^{-1}\left(\frac{v}{c}\right)$

(b) $\theta = \cos^{-1}\left(\frac{v}{c}\right)$

(c) $\theta = \text{con}^{-1}\left(\frac{v}{c}\right)$

(d) $\theta = \sin^{-1}\left(\frac{v}{c}\right)$

210. A plano convex lens fits exactly into a plano concave lens. Their plane surfaces are parallel to each other. If lenses are made of different materials of refractive indices μ_1 and μ_2 and R is the radius of curvature of the curved surface of the lenses, then the focal length of the combination is

(NEET 2013)

(a) $\frac{R}{2(\mu_1 - \mu_2)}$ (b) $\frac{R}{(\mu_1 - \mu_2)}$

(c) $\frac{2R}{(\mu_1 - \mu_2)}$ (d) $\frac{R}{2(\mu_1 + \mu_2)}$

211. For a normal eye, the cornea of eye provides a converging power of 40 D and the least converging power of the eye lens behind the cornea is 20D. Using this information the distance between the retina and the cornea eye lens can be estimated to be

(NEET 2013)

(a) 2.5 cm (b) 1.67 cm

(c) 1.5 cm (d) 5 cm

212. For minimum intensity the phase difference between the two waves is

(MHT-CET 2011)

(a) $2\pi n$ (b) $(2n - 1)\pi$

(c) $(2n + 3)\pi$ (d) πn

213. Two waves of amplitudes A_1 and A_2 superimpose with each other such that $A_1 > A_2$. The difference between maximum and minimum amplitudes is

(MHT-CET 2011)

(a) A_1 (b) $2A_2$

(c) $2A_1$ (d) A_2

214. In a single slit diffraction pattern intensity and width of fringes are of

(MHT-CET 2011)

(a) unequal width

(b) equal width

(c) equal width and equal intensity

(d) unequal width and unequal intensity

215. If path difference between waves is $\frac{11\lambda}{4}$ then the phase difference between two waves will be **(MHT-CET 2012)**

(a) $\frac{11\pi}{2}$ (b) $\frac{5\pi}{2}$

(c) $\frac{13\pi}{2}$ (d) $\frac{7\pi}{2}$

216. Resolving power of telescope can be increased by **(MHT-CET 2012)**

(a) increasing diameter of the objective of the telescope

(b) decreasing diameter of the objective of the telescope

(c) increasing the wavelength of light

(d) none of these

217. In the experiment of interference, p is the number of bright bands for a light of wavelength λ_1. If source of light is replaced by λ_2 then the number of bright bands will be **(MHT-CET 2012)**

(a) $\frac{p\lambda_2}{\lambda_1}$ (b) $\frac{p\lambda_1}{\lambda_2}$

(c) $p\lambda_1$ (d) $p\lambda_2$

218. In Young's double slit experiment, the slits are 2 mm apart and are illuminated by photons of two wavelengths $\lambda_1 = 12{,}000\ \text{Å}$ and $\lambda_2 = 10{,}000\ \text{Å}$. At what minimum distance from the common central bright fringe on the screen 2 m from the slit will a bright fringe from one interference pattern coincide with a bright fringe from the other?

(NEET 2013)

(a) 6 mm (b) 4 mm

(c) 3 mm (d) 8 mm

219. A parallel beam of fast moving electrons is incident normally on a narrow slit. A fluorescent screen is placed at a large distance from the slit. If the speed of the electrons is increased, which of the following statements is correct ?

(NEET 2013)

(a) The angular width of the central maximum of the diffraction pattern will increase.

(b) The angular width of the central maximum of the diffraction pattern will decrease.

(c) The angular width of the central maximum will decrease.

(d) Diffraction pattern is not observed on the screen in the case of electrons.

ANSWER KEY

1. (b)	**2.** (c)	**3.** (a)	**4.** (b)	**5.** (a)	**6.** (b)	**7.** (b)	**8.** (b)	**9.** (c)	**10.**(b)
11.(a)	**12.**(b)	**13.**(c)	**14.**(b)	**15.**(c)	**16.**(c)	**17.**(a)	**18.**(c)	**19.**(b)	**20.**(b)
21.(c)	**22.**(c)	**23.**(b)	**24.**(a)	**25.**(d)	**26.**(a)	**27.**(d)	**28.**(c)	**29.**(d)	**30.**(b)
31.(c)	**32.**(b)	**33.**(a)	**34.**(b)	**35.**(c)	**36.**(c)	**37.**(c)	**38.**(b)	**39.**(c)	**40.**(a)
41.(b)	**42.**(a)	**43.**(c)	**44.**(a)	**45.**(b)	**46.**(c)	**47.**(d)	**48.**(c)	**49.**(d)	**50.**(d)
51.(c)	**52.**(d)	**53.**(b)	**54.**(a)	**55.**(b)	**56.**(b)	**57.**(b)	**58.**(c)	**59.**(d)	**60.**(c)
61.(b)	**62.**(a)	**63.**(c)	**64.**(a)	**65.**(d)	**66.**(c)	**67.**(b)	**68.**(b)	**69.**(c)	**70.**(a)
71.(a)	**72.**(b)	**73.**(a)	**74.**(b)	**75.**(c)	**76.**(c)	**77.**(b)	**78.**(b)	**79.**(d)	**80.**(a)
81.(c)	**82.**(a)	**83.**(d)	**84.**(d)	**85.**(d)	**86.**(b)	**87.**(d)	**88.**(d)	**89.**(a)	**90.**(a)
91.(d)	**92.**(a)	**93.**(d)	**94.**(d)	**95.**(d)	**96.**(c)	**97.**(c)	**98.**(c)	**99.**(a)	**100.** (d)
101. (b)	**102.** (a)	**103.** (d)	**104.** (d)	**105.** (d)	**106.** (a)	**107.** (c)	**108.** (b)	**109.** (a)	**110.** (c)
111. (b)	**112.** (c)	**113.** (b)	**114.** (c)	**115.** (d)	**116.** (c)	**117.** (d)	**118.** (c)	**119.** (b)	**120.** (b)
121. (b)	**122.** (a)	**123.** (a)	**124.** (c)	**125.** (b)	**126.** (d)	**127.** (d)	**128.** (d)	**129.** (a)	**130.** (d)
131. (d)	**132.** (c)	**133.** (b)	**134.** (a)	**135.** (c)	**136.** (c)	**137.** (d)	**138.** (a)	**139.** (b)	**140.** (c)
141. (b)	**142.** (d)	**143.** (c)	**144.** (b)	**145.** (a)	**146.** (b)	**147.** (a)	**148.** (c)	**149.** (a)	**150.** (b)
151. (c)	**152.** (d)	**153.** (b)	**154.** (d)	**155.** (b)	**156.** (b)	**157.** (a)	**158.** (c)	**159.** (a)	**160.** (a)
161. (c)	**162.** (c)	**163.** (d)	**164.** (b)	**165.** (d)	**166.** (b)	**167.** (a)	**168.** (b)	**169.** (c)	**170.** (b)
171. (b)	**172.** (a)	**173.** (c)	**174.** (c)	**175.** (d)	**176.** (d)	**177.** (d)	**178.** (c)	**179.** (d)	**180.** (b)
181. (c)	**182.** (a)	**183.** (a)	**184.** (c)	**185.** (a)	**186.** (a)	**187.** (a)	**188.** (d)	**189.** (b)	**190.** (c)
191. (d)	**192.** (c)	**193.** (a)	**194.** (c)	**195.** (c)	**196.** (d)	**197.** (c)	**198.** (a)	**199.** (d)	**200.** (d)
201. (b)	**202.** (d)	**203.** (c)	**204.** (d)	**205.** (a)	**206.** (a)	**207.** (a)	**208.** (a)	**209.** (c)	**210.** (b)
211. (a)	**212.** (b)	**213.** (b)	**214.** (d)	**215.** (a)	**216.** (a)	**217.** (b)	**218.** (a)	**219.** (b)	

18

ELECTRONS AND PHOTONS (DUAL NATURE OF MATTER AND RADIATIONS)

MULTIPLE CHOICE QUESTIONS

1. In Millikan's oil drop experiment, a drop of radius *r*, carrying a charge *q* is in equilibrium between the plates at a potential difference V. Then, another drop of radius 2*r* will be stationary at a potential difference 4 V if it carries a charge : **(B.H.U. 2000)**

(a) $q/2$ (b) $2q$

(c) $4q$ (d) $q/4$

2. If the energy of a photon of wavelength of 6000 Å is 3.32×10^{-19} J, the photon energy for a wavelength of 4000 Å will be :

(a) 4.98×10^{-19} J (b) 4.44×10^{-19} J

(c) 2.22×10^{-19} J (d) 1.11×10^{-19} J

3. Photoelectrons are emitted from a metal surface only when : **[Delhi P.M.T. 1994]**

(a) metal is initially charged

(b) wavelength of incident light is less than some maximum limit

(c) frequency of incident light is less than some minimum value

(d) incident angle should be greater than the critical angle.

4. When UV rays are incident on a photosensitive surface, then photoelectric effect does not occur. It occurs by the incidence of: **(C.B.S.E. 2002)**

(a) X-rays

(c) Infrared rays

(b) Radiowave

(d) Green house effect

5. The acceleration of an electron in an electric field of magnitude 50 V /cm, when *e/m* value of the electron is 1.76×10^{11} C/kg, is : **(C.P.M.T. 2001)**

(a) 6.2×10^{13} (b) 5.4×10^{12}

(c) 8.8×10^{14} (d) Zero

6. The work function of a substance is 4.0 eV. The longest wavelength of light that can show photoelectron emission from this substance is approximately : **(I.I.T. 1998)**

(a) 540 nm (b) 400 nm

(c) 310 nm (d) 220 nm

7. In a discharge tube at 0.02 mm, there is a formation of : **(C.B.S.E. P.M.T. 1996)**

(a) CDS (b) FDS

(c) Both space (d) None of these

8. If Planck's constant is denoted by h and the electronic charge by e, then photoelectric effect allows the determination of **(C.B.S.E. 1993)**

(a) only h (b) only e

(c) both h and e (d) only h/e

9. The specific charge of a particle is :

(a) ratio of its charge to mass

(b) ratio of its mass to charge

(c) its charge in coulomb

(d) none of the above

10. Two photons of energies twice and thrice the work function of a metal are incident on the metal surface. Then the ratio of maximum velocities of the photoelectrons emitted in the two cases respectively, is :

(E.A.M.C.E.T. 2002)

(a) $\sqrt{2} : 1$ (b) $1 : \sqrt{2}$

(c) $\sqrt{3} : 3$ (d) $\sqrt{3} : \sqrt{2}$

11. Photoelectrons are being obtained by irradiating zinc by a radiation of 3100 Å. In order to increase the kinetic energy of ejected photoelectrons :

(a) the wavelength of radiation should be decreased

(b) the wavelength of incident radiation should be increased

(c) the intensity of radiation should be increased

(d) both wavelength and intensity of radiation should be increased

12. The specific charge of an electron is :

(M.P.P.M.T. 1998)

(a) 1.6×10^{-19} coulomb

(b) 5.7×10^{-12} kg/C

(c) 1.76×10^{11} C/kg

(d) 9.1×10^{-31} kg

13. Which of the following statement is correct?

(C.B.S.E. P.M.T. 1997)

(a) Photocurrent increases with increase in applied voltage.

(b) Photocurrent increases with increase in frequency of light.

(c) Photocurrent increases with increase in intensity of light.

(d) None of these.

14. By increasing the frequency of incident light work function will : **(A.I.I.M.S. 2001)**

(a) remain same

(b) decrease

(c) increase

(d) none of the above

15. The de Broglie wavelength of a particle moving with a velocity 2.25×10^8 m/s is equal to the wavelength of a photon. The ratio of kinetic energy of the particle to the energy of the photon is :

(E.A.M.C.E.T. 2003)

(a) 3/8 (b) 5/8

(c) 7/8 (d) 1/8

16. Photo electrons are emitted when :

(a) a zinc plate is heated

(b) a zinc plate is hammered

(c) a zinc plate is irradiated with light

(d) a zinc plate is subjected to a very high pressure

17. The stopping potential as a function of frequency of incident radiation is plotted for two different photoelectric surfaces A and B as shown in the figure. The graphs show that the work function of A is :

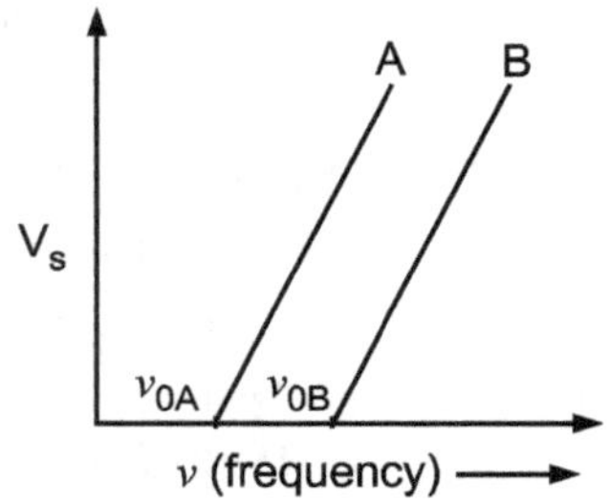

(a) same as that of B

(b) smaller than that of B

(c) greater than that of B

(d) no comparison can be done from the given graphs

18. An electric field of intensity 6×10^4 volt/m is applied perpendicular to the direction of motion of the electron. A magnetic field of intensity 8×10^{-2} T is applied perpendicular to both the electric field and direction of motion of the electron. What is the velocity of the electron if it passes undeflected ?

(a) 7.5×10^5 m/s (b) 7.5×10^{-5} m/s

(c) 6×10^4 m/s (d) 8×10^{-2} m/s

19. A proton and an alpha particle are accelerated to the same potential. Their de Broglie wavelengths are in the ratio of :

(a) $\sqrt{2} : 1$ (b) $4 : 1$

(c) $2 : 1$ (d) $2\sqrt{2} : 1$

20. Cathode rays are :

(a) a stream of neutral particles

(b) a stream of negative charges

(c) a stream of positive charges

(d) none of these

21. If an electron has no initial velocity in a direction other than that of an electric field, then trajectory of the electron is

(a) a straight line (b) a parabola

(c) an ellipse (d) a circle

22. The work function of a photosensitive surface is 5.18 eV. The photoelectrons are emitted when light of wavelength 2000 Å falls on it. The potential difference applied to stop the fastest photoelectron is :

(a) 1.0 V (b) 2.24 V

(c) 2.4 V (d) 4.8 V

23. UV radiation of 7.2 eV is incident on a photosensitive surface. If the work function of the surface is 5.4 eV, then the maximum velocity of the emitted photoelectrons is nearly :

(a) 2×10^6 m/sec (b) 10×10^5 m/sec

(c) 4×10^6 m/sec (d) 8×10^5 m/sec

24. The cathode rays travel with the speed :

(a) equal to 3×10^8 m/s

(b) less than 3×10^8 m/s

(c) greater than 3×10^8 m/s

(d) may be less than, greater than or equal to 3×10^8 m/s.

25. Photons of energy 8 eV is incident on a photosensitive surface of threshold frequency 1.6×10^{15} Hz. If $h = 6 \times 10^{-34}$ Js, then kinetic energy (in eV) of the photoelectrons emitted is : **(C.B.S.E. 1999)**

(a) 6 (b) 1.6

(c) 1.2 (d) 2

26. Photon P has twice the wavelength of photon Q, then energy of photon A is :

(a) Four times that of Q

(b) Twice that of Q

(c) Thrice that of Q

(d) Half that of Q

27. Modern theory for nature of light states that light has : **(M.P.P.M.T. 1998)**

(a) particle nature only

(b) wave nature only

(c) both wave and particle (dual) nature

(d) neither particle nature nor wave nature

28. The electrons are emitted in the photoelectric effect from a metal surface :

(a) at a rate that is independent of the nature of the metal

(b) with a maximum velocity proportional to the frequency of incident radiation

(c) only if the frequency of the incident radiation is above a certain threshold value

(d) only if the temperature of the surface is high

29. The maximum kinetic energy of photoelectrons emitted from a surface when photons of energy 6 eV fall on it is 4 eV. The stopping potential is : **(I.I.T. 1997)**

(a) 2 V (b) 4 V

(c) 6 V (d) 10 V

30. Which one of the following statements about photon is incorrect ?

(a) Energy of photons is $h\upsilon$.

(b) Momentum of photon is $h\upsilon$.

(c) Rest mass of photon is zero.

(d) Photons exert no pressure.

31. Radiations of wavelength 1100 Å incident on a metal surface which has a negligible work function. Then the kinetic energy of the photoelectrons emitted is :

(a) 11.25 eV (b) 1.125 eV

(c) 112.5 eV (d) 1125 eV

32. A metal having work function 3.31 eV is illuminated by light of $\lambda = 3 \times 10^{-7}$ m. What is the threshold frequency of photoelectric emission ?

(a) 2.4×10^{15} Hz (b) 3.2×10^{15} Hz
(c) 0.8×10^{15} Hz (d) 1.6×10^{15} Hz

33. In a mass spectrograph, an ion X of mass number 24 and charge + e and another ion Y of mass number 22 and charge + 2e, enter a perpendicular magnetic field with the same velocity. The ratio of the radii of their circular paths in the field will be :

(a) 11/22 (b) 24/11
(c) 22/11 (d) 11/2

34. A particle of mass M initially at rest decays into two particles of masses m_1 and m_2 having some velocities. The ratio of the de Broglie wavelengths of the particles is :

(I.I.T. 1999)

(a) $\frac{m_2}{m_1}$ (b) $\frac{m_1}{m_2}$
(c) 1:1 (d) $\sqrt{\frac{m_2}{m_1}}$

35. Threshold wavelength of surface X is 2300 Å. When irradiated by UV light of wavelength 1800 Å, the maximum kinetic energy of the photoelectrons is :

(a) ≈ 5 foot pound (b) ≈ 5 joule
(c) ≈ 5 ergs (d) ≈ 1.5 eV

36. An electron at rest is accelerated through 200 volts and gains a velocity 8.4×10^6 m/s. Then *e/m* of the electron is :

(a) 1.76×10^9 C/kg (b) 1.76×10^{11} C/kg
(c) 76×10^{13} C/kg (d) 76×10^{18} C/kg

37. Cathode of a photocell having cathode with work function W_1 and current I_1, is changed with some other material with work function W_2 and current I_2. When ($W_2 > W_1$), then

(a) $I_1 > I_2$ (b) $I_1 < I_2$
(c) $I_2 = I_1$ (d) None of these

38. *e/m* value of electron is :

(Delhi P.M.T. 1992)

(a) 1.6×10^{10} C/kg
(b) 9.11×10^{-20} kg
(c) 1.76×10^{11} C/kg
(d) 1.62×10^{-31} C/kg

39. In the photoelectric effect, the velocity of ejected electrons depends upon the nature of the target and

(a) the intensity of the incident light
(b) the polarization of incident light
(c) the time for which the light has been incident
(d) the frequency of the incident light

40. When light falls on a metal surface, the maximum kinetic energy of the emitted photoelectrons depends upon :

(a) frequency of incident light
(b) velocity of the incident light
(c) intensity of the incident light
(d) the time for which light falls on the metal

41. Three particles having charges in the ratio of 1 : 2 : 3 produce the same point on the photographic film in the Thomson's experiment. Their masses are in the ratio of :

(a) 1 : 2 : 3 (b) 2 : 3 : 1
(c) 3 : 2 : 1 (d) 1 : 3 : 2

42. For a photosensitive surface, a graph of stopping potential V_s vs frequency (υ) is plotted and is as shown in the figure. The slope of the line equals :

(A.I.I.M.S. 2000; M.P.P.E.T. 1999)

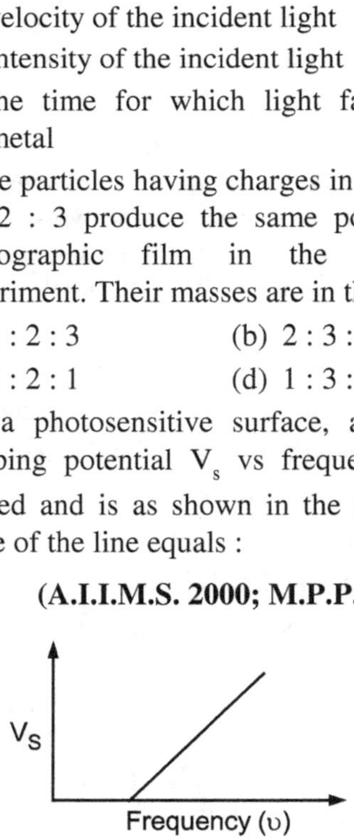

(a) V_s (b) e/h
(c) h/e (d) he

43. If λ is the de Broglie wavelength for a proton accelerated through a potential difference of 100 V, the de Broglie wavelength for an α-particle accelerated through the same potential difference will be: **(E.A.M.C.E.T. 2002)**

(a) $\lambda / 2$ (b) $\lambda / \sqrt{2}$

(c) $2\sqrt{2}\,\lambda$ (d) $\lambda / 2\sqrt{2}$

44. When highly energetic cathode rays are suddenly stopped by a solid target of high melting point, it produces :

(a) X - rays (b) α - rays

(c) β - rays (d) γ - rays

45. The maximum energy of the electron released in photoelectric effect is independent of :

(a) intensity of incident light

(b) nature of the cathode rays

(c) frequency of incident light

(d) none of these

46. In J. J. Thomson's method, magnetic field B, velocity v of the electrons and electric field E were in mutually perpendicular directions. This velocity selector allows particles of velocity v to travel undeflected when :

(a) $v = B^2 / E$ (b) $v = B / E$

(c) $v = E / B$ (d) $v = B.E$

47. The quantization of charge is proved by the experiment of : **(D.P.M.T. 1996)**

(a) Millikan's oil drop method

(b) Compton scattering

(c) Raman's scattering

(d) Davisson Germer

48. Energy of electron can be increased by :

(a) allowing them to fall from a height

(b) passing them through a lead block

(c) passing them through a high magnetic field

(d) moving them through an electric potential

49. The momentum of a particle of mass m and charge q is equal to that of a photon of wavelength λ. Then the speed of the particle is given by :

(a) $\dfrac{mh}{\lambda}$ (b) $\dfrac{h}{m\lambda}$

(c) $\dfrac{h\lambda}{qm}$ (d) $qh\lambda$

50. Wave nature of matter is not apparent to our daily observations because :

(a) wavelength of waves associated with a heavy mass is very small

(b) wavelength of the waves associated with a heavy mass is very large

(c) small bodies travel with large velocities

(d) none of the above

51. Kinetic energy of a particle becomes 4 times. Then how many times will its de Broglie wavelength become :

(a) 1/4 (b) 1/2

(c) 2 (d) 4

52. When light of wavelength less than 6000 Å is incident on a metal, then an electron is emitted. The approximate work function of the metal is : **(D.P.M.T. 2000)**

(a) 1 eV (b) 2 eV

(c) 4 eV (d) 6 eV

53. A cathode emits 1.8×10^{17} electrons per second when heated. When 400 volts is applied to the anode, all the electrons emitted reach the anode. The maximum anode current is :

(a) 10^{-11} A (b) 29 mA

(c) 10^{11} A (d) 11.6 A

54. A photon in motion has a mass equal to :

(a) $h\upsilon/c^2$ (b) $h\upsilon$

(c) $c/h\upsilon$ (d) h/λ

55. The K.E of the most energetic photoelectrons emitted from a photosensitive surface is doubled, when the wavelength of the incident radiation is reduced from λ_1 to λ_2. Then work function of the metal is : **(C.E.T. 1998)**

(a) $\frac{hc}{\lambda_1\lambda_2}(\lambda_1 - \lambda_2)$ (b) $\frac{hc}{\lambda_1\lambda_2}(\lambda_1 + \lambda_2)$

(c) $\frac{hc}{\lambda_1\lambda_2}(2\lambda_1 - \lambda_2)$ (d) $\frac{hc}{\lambda_1\lambda_2}(2\lambda_2 - \lambda_1)$

56. A radio transmitter operates at a frequency of 880 kHz and a power of 10 kW. The number of photons emitted per second is :

(a) 1.72×10^{31} (b) 13.27×10^{34}

(c) 13.27×10^{24} (d) 13.27×10^{44}

57. The function of a photoelectric cell is to transform light energy into :

(a) sound energy (b) heat energy

(c) magnetic energy (d) electrical energy

58. Cathode rays can be deflected by :

(a) Electric field only

(b) Magnetic field only

(c) Both magnetic and electric field

(d) None of these

59. If the momentum of a particle is doubled, then the wavelength associated with the particle will : **(Delhi P.M.T. 1999)**

(a) remain unchanged (b) become half

(c) become double (d) none of these

60. Cathode rays enter a magnetic field making an oblique angle with the lines of magnetic induction. Then their path in the magnetic field is a :

(a) straight line (b) helix

(c) circle (d) parabola

61. If threshold wavelength of a material is 350 nm, then which one of the following sources will show photoemission ?

(a) A 200 W fluorescent bulb

(b) A 200 W infrared bulb

(c) A ruby laser source of 0.5 W

(d) An ultraviolet lamp of 0.5 W

62. When a monochromatic source of light is at a distance of 0.2 m from a photoelectric cell, the cut off voltage and the saturation current are 0.6 V and 18 mA respectively. If the same source is placed 0.6 m away from the cell, then : **(I. I.T. 1992)**

(a) the saturation current will be 2.0 mA

(b) the stopping potential will be 1.8 V

(c) the stopping potential will be 0.2 V

(d) the saturation current will be 6.0 mA

63. In which of the following devices light energy is converted into electrical energy ?

(a) Discharge tube (b) Thermocouple

(c) Pyrometer (d) Photo cell

64. The work required to move an electron between the plates, whose potential difference is 3 million volts, is :

(a) 5.6×10^{6} J (b) 4.8 J

(c) 4.8×10^{-19} J (d) 4.8×10^{-13} J

65. The number of electrons ejected depends on:

(a) the frequency

(b) the intensity

(c) both on intensity and frequency

(d) neither intensity nor frequency of the radiations

66. Two electron beams having velocities in the ratio of 2 : 1 are subjected separately to identical magnetic fields. What is the ratio of the deflections produced ?

(a) 1 : 4 (b) 4 : 1

(c) 1 : 2 (d) 2 : 1

67. Who suggested first that matter behaves like a wave ?

(a) G.P. Thomson (b) de Broglie

(c) Huygens (d) Rutherford

68. The idea of quantum nature of light has emerged in an attempt to explain :

(a) the interference of light

(b) radioactivity

(c) thermionic emission

(d) the thermal radiations of a black body

69. Which of the following is correct ? **(C.B.S.E. 1997)**

(a) The photocurrent increases if the intensity of incident light is increased.

(b) The photocurrent is proportional to the applied voltage.

(c) The stopping potential increases if the intensity of the incident light is increased.

(d) The current in a photocell increases with increasing frequency.

70. The work function of photosensitive surface is 2.3 eV. What is the maximum wavelength for the light that will cause photoelectrons to be emitted from the surface ?

(a) 53.8 Å (b) 5.38 Å

(c) 5380 Å (d) 538 Å

71. Gases begin to conduct electricity at low pressures because :

(a) atoms break up into electrons and positive ions.

(b) electrons in atoms can move freely at low pressure.

(c) colliding electrons acquire higher K.E. leading to ionization of atoms.

(d) none of these.

72. A beam of α-particles passes undeflected through crossed electric and magnetic fields with $E = 6.6 \times 10^6$ NC^{-1} and B = 1.2 T. Then speed of α - particles in m/s will be :

(a) 1.1×10^6 (b) 5.5×10^6

(c) 7.8×10^6 (d) 1.8×10^6

73. When light of wavelength 2537 Å is incident over a photosensitive surface, stopping voltage 0.24 volt is required to stop the fastest photoelectron. The threshold frequency for the surface is :

(Raj. P.E.T. 1996)

(a) 2.248×10^{15} Hz

(b) 1.414×10^{14} Hz

(c) 1.124×10^{15} Hz

(d) None of the above

74. Cathode ray :

(a) is a beam of negatively charged ions towards the anode.

(b) is a beam of electrons emitted by the cathode.

(c) is a beam of atoms moving towards the cathode.

(d) is electromagnetic wave.

75. A photocell is illuminated by source placed 1 m away. When the same source of light is placed 2 m away, the electrons emitted by the photocathode :

(a) are one-quarter in number

(b) are half in number

(c) each carries one quarter of their previous momentum

(d) each carries one quarter of their previous energy

76. Wavelength associated with an electron of energy 100 eV is :

(a) 0.12 Å (b) 12.0 Å

(c) 1.2 Å (d) 6.3 Å

77. The maximum velocity of photoelectrons emitted from a metal surface is 1.76×10^6 ms^{-1}. If the e/m ratio of an electron is 1.76×10^{11} C kg^{-1}, then the stopping potential of the metal is : **(B.H.U. 2000)**

(a) 8.8 V (b) 17.6 V

(c) 2.2 V (d) 4.4 V

78. In an oscilloscope the focusing of beam on the screen is achieved by :

(a) convex lenses (b) magnetic field

(c) electric potential (d) all of the above

79. Which of the following is not a property of the cathode ray ? **(C.B.S.E. P.M.T. 2002)**

(a) It casts sharp shadow.

(b) It produces heating effect.

(c) It produces fluorescence.

(d) It does not deflect in electric field.

80. With the increase in the number of incident photons : **(C.B.S.E. P.M.T. 2000)**

(a) Photoelectric current decreases.

(b) kinetic energy of photoelectrons decreases.

(c) photoelectric current increases.

(d) kinetic energy of photoelectrons increases.

81. The de Broglie wavelength of a proton of energy 1 keV is about (in mm) :

(a) 10^{-3} (b) 10^{-4}

(c) 10^{-1} (d) None of these

82. Stopping potential will increase when : **(A.I.I.M.S. 2001)**

(a) frequency of incident light is decreased

(b) frequency of incident light is increased

(c) intensity of incident light is increased

(d) intensity of incident light is decreased

83. When the energy of the incident radiation is increased by 20%, then K.E of the photoelectrons emitted from a metal increases from 0.5 eV to 0.8 eV. The work function of the metal is :

(a) 1.0 eV (b) 1.3 eV

(c) 0.65 eV (d) 1.5 eV

84. If frequency of the waves emitted from a radio station is 6 Mega Hertz. Then wavelength of the waves will be :

(a) 24 m (b) 12 m

(c) 6 m (d) 50 m

85. If kinetic energy of the emitted electrons is zero for the incident light of wavelength 686 nm on Cesium, and if work function of Cesium is 1.81 eV, then wavelength of radiations emitting electrons having energy 1.81 eV, will be :

(a) 1372 nm (b) 2058 nm

(c) 342 nm (d) 686 nm

86. The rest mass of photons is :

(a) Zero (b) $h\upsilon$

(c) $h\upsilon/c$ (d) $h\upsilon^2/c$

87. Resistance of discharge tube is :

(a) ohmic (b) non-ohmic

(c) zero (d) none of these

88. On increasing the potential difference between the cathode and anode, the photo-current :

(a) first increases and then remains constant

(b) remains constant

(c) decreases

(d) first increases and then decreases

89. Frequency of a photon, having energy 100 eV is : **(A.F.M.C. 2000)**

(a) 2.42×10^{12} Hz (b) 2.42×10^{9} Hz

(c) 2.42×10^{26} Hz (d) 2.42×10^{16} Hz

90. The frequency and intensity of the incident beam of light falling on the photosensitive surface is doubled. This will :

(a) double the maximum kinetic energy of the photoelectrons and the photoelectric current.

(b) increase the maximum kinetic energy of the photoelectrons, and would decrease the photoelectric current by a factor of two.

(c) increase the maximum kinetic energy of the photoelectrons by a factor of two and will have no effect on the magnitude of the photoelectric current produced.

(d) not produce any effect on the kinetic energy of the emitted electrons, but will increase the photoelectric current by a factor of two.

91. A metal plate gets heated, when cathode rays strike against it, due to : **(C.P.M.T. 2000)**

(a) linear velocity of cathode rays

(b) angular velocity of cathode rays

(c) kinetic energy of cathode rays

(d) potential energy of cathode rays

92. Doubly ionized helium atoms and hydrogen ions are accelerated from rest through the same potential drop. The ratio of the final velocities of the helium and the hydrogen ions is : **(C.B.S.E. 1994)**

(a) $\frac{1}{2}$ (b) 2

(c) $\frac{1}{\sqrt{2}}$ (d) $\sqrt{2}$

93. The threshold wavelength for photoelectric emission from a material is 5200 Å. Photoelectrons will be emitted when this material is illuminated with monochromatic radiations from a :

(a) 50 watt ultraviolet lamp

(b) 1 watt ultraviolet lamp

(c) 50 watt infrared lamp

(d) I watt infrared lamp

94. de-Broglie wavelength associated with thermal neutrons at room temperature of 27°C is :

(a) 1.452×10^{-10} m (b) 2.57×10^{-10} m

(c) 0.452×10^{-10} m (d) 3.452×10^{-10} m

95. de-Broglie wavelength associated with an electron moving with velocity 0.5 c is

(a) 10^{-12} m (b) 1.2×10^{-12} m

(c) 4.2×10^{-12} m (d) 3.6×10^{-12} m

96. Sodium and copper have work function 2.3 eV and 4.5 eV respectively. The ratio of their wavelengths is approximately :

(a) 4 : 1 (b) 1 : 4

(c) 1 : 2 (d) 2 : 1

97. Two identical photosensitive surfaces are radiated by frequencies f_1 and f_2. If the velocity of photoelectrons of mass m_e emitted by the surface is v_1 and v_2 respectively, then : **(A.I.E.E.E. 2003)**

(a) $v_1 - v_2 = \frac{2h}{m_e}(f_1 - f_2)^{1/2}$

(b) $v_1^2 + v_2^2 = \frac{2h}{m_e}(f_1 + f_2)$

(c) $v_1 + v_2 = \frac{2h}{m_e}(f_1 + f_2)^{1/2}$

(d) $v_1^2 - v_2^2 = \frac{2h}{m_e}(f_1 - f_2)$

98. If n_r and n_b are the number of photons emitted by a red bulb and blue bulb respectively of equal power in a given time, then :

(a) $n_r = n_b$

(b) $n_r > n_b$

(c) $n_r < n_b$

(d) Information is insufficient

99. If the distance of 100 watt lamp is increased from a photo cell, saturation current I in the photocell varies with the distance d as : **(A.F.M.C. 2000)**

(a) $I \propto \frac{1}{d^2}$ (b) $I \propto d$

(c) $I \propto d^2$ (d) $I \propto d^{-1}$

100. Two identical metal plates show photoelectric effect. Light of wavelength λ_1 falls on plate - 1 and λ_2 falls on plate - 2 and $\lambda_1 = 2\lambda_2$. The maximum kinetic energy of the photoelectrons is K_1 and K_2 respectively. Then :

(a) $K_1 > 2K_2$ (b) $K_1 < (K_2/2)$

(c) $2K_1 = K_2$ (d) $K_1 = 2K_2$

101. In a Millikan's oil drop experiment, one of the drop falls at speed v without field and rises at speed 2v with field E applied. If the field is $\frac{E}{2}$, then the drop will :

(a) rise with speed v/2

(b) rise with the speed 3v/2

(c) fall with speed v/4

(d) remain stationary

102. Radiations of wavelength 6,000 Å are incident on a metal surface having a work function of 1.2 eV, then stopping potential for the ejected electron is :

(a) 0.47 volt (b) 3.7 volt

(c) 0.7 volt (d) 0.87 V

103. Light of wavelength $\lambda = 4,000$ $\mathring{A}$ and intensity 100 watt/m^2 is incident on a metal plate of threshold frequency 5.5×10^{14} Hz. The maximum number of photons incident per m^2 per second is :

(C.B.S.E. mains 20004)

(a) $1.35 \times 10^{+19}$ (b) $2 \times 10^{+7}$

(c) $2 \times 10^{+20}$ (d) 6×10^{22}

104. In Q. 103, the maximum K.E. of ejected photoelectrons will be :

(a) 2×10^{-7} J (b) 2×10^{-20} J

(c) 6×10^{-19} J (d) 1.35×10^{-19} J

105. X-ray tube operates at 10 kV. The ratio of X-ray wavelength to that of the de Broglie wavelength is :

(a) 4.7 (b) 6.87

(c) 10.062 (d) 8.34

106. In a photoelectric set up, the radiations from the Balmer series hydrogen atom are incident on a metal surface of work function 2 eV. The wavelength of incident radiations lies between 450 nm to 700 nm. The maximum K.E. of photoelectron is

(given $\frac{hc}{e} = 1242$ eV – nm)

(a) 0.55 eV (b) 2 eV

(c) 10.2 eV (d) 0.25 eV

107. According to Einstein's photoelectric equation, the plot of K.E. of the emitted photoelectrons from a photosensitive surface verses frequency of incident radiations gives a straight line. Then the slope of this line :

(A.I.E.E.E. 2004)

(a) depends upon intensity of radiations and metal used

(b) is same for all metals and independent of intensity

(c) depends on nature of metal

(d) depends on intensity of radiations

108. If a photon and electron have the same de-Broglie wavelength, then among both who has greater total energy ?

(a) Electron

(b) Photon

(c) Both have the equal energy

(d) Insufficient information

109. In Q. 108, who has greater K.E. ?

(a) Electron

(b) Photon

(c) Both have the same K.E.

(d) Insufficient information

110. Lights of two different frequencies, whose photons have energies 2 eV and 10 eV respectively, successively illuminate a metal of work function 1 eV. The ratio of the maximum speeds of the emitted electrons will be :

(a) 1 : 5 (b) 3 : 1

(c) 1 : 9 (d) 1 : 3

111. If the work function of a metal is 5 eV and photons of energy 20 eV are incident on the surface, then the stopping potential of the surface is :

(a) 25 V (b) 20 V

(c) 15 V (d) 5 V

112. A uniform electric field and a uniform magnetic field are produced pointing in the same direction. An electron is projected with its velocity pointed in the same direction, then :

(a) the electron velocity will decrease in magnitude

(b) the electron velocity will increase in magnitude

(c) the beam will turn to its left

(d) the electron will turn to its right

113. The work function of aluminium is 4.2 eV. If two photons, each of energy 3.5 eV, strike an electron of aluminium, then the emission of electron will :

(a) depend upon the density of the surface

(b) be possible

(c) not be possible

(d) data is incomplete

114. The phenomenon of discharge through gases at low pressure can be explained on the basis of :

(a) wave nature of electron
(b) wave nature of light
(c) dual nature of light
(d) collision between the charged particles emitted from the cathode and the atoms of the gas in the discharge tube

115. For light of wavelength 5000 Å, the photon energy is nearly 2.5 eV. For X-ray of wavelength 1 Å, the photon energy will be close to :

(a) $[2.5 \times (5000)^2]$ eV (b) $[2.5 \times 5000]$ eV
(c) $[2.5/5000]$ eV (d) $[2.5/(5000)^2]$ eV

116. A metal surface is illuminated by a light of given intensity and frequency to cause photoemission. If the intensity of illumination is reduced to one fourth of its original value, then the maximum kinetic energy of the emitted photoelectrons would become :

(a) Four times the original value
(b) Twice the original value
(c) 1/6th of original value
(d) Unchanged

117. The photoelectric threshold wavelength of certain metal is 3000 Å. When radiation of 2000 Å is incident on the metal, then :

(a) electrons will be emitted
(b) positrons will be emitted
(c) protons will be emitted
(d) electrons will not be emitted

118. If the work function for a certain metal is 3.2×10^{-19} joule and it is illuminated with light of frequency $f = 8 \times 10^{14}$ Hz, the maximum kinetic energy of the photoelectron would be :

(a) 2.1×10^{-19} joule (b) 8.5×10^{-19} joule
(c) 5.3×10^{-19} joule (d) 3.2×10^{-19} joule

119. If h is Planck's constant, the momentum of a photon of wavelength 0.01 Å is :

(a) $h \times 10^{12}$ (b) $h \times 10^{2}$
(c) h (d) $h \times 10^{-2}$

120. Cesium photocell with a steady potential difference of 90 volt across it is illuminated by a small bright light placed one metre away. When the same light is placed two metres away, then electrons crossing the photocell :

(a) are half as numerous
(b) are one quarter as numerous
(c) each carries one quarter of their previous energy
(d) each carries one quarter of their previous momentum

121. Which of the following statement is not correct ?

(a) The magnitude of photoelectric current depends upon the time for which light is incident.
(b) Photoelectron emission takes place when the frequency of radiation is more than a certain critical frequency called the threshold frequency.
(c) The magnitude of photoelectric current is directly proportional to the intensity of incident radiation.
(d) Photoelectron's velocity can be increased by increasing the frequency of incident light.

122. The work function :

(a) depends upon the frequency of incident radiation
(b) is the same for all metals
(c) is different for different metals
(d) depends upon the intensity of incident light

123. Charge to mass ratio of Helium nucleus having mass 4 a.m.u. is :

(a) 2.7×10^{4} C/kg (b) 5.4×10^{5} C/kg
(c) 4.8×10^{7} C/kg (d) 2.4×10^{7} C/kg

124. In photoelectric emission, the number of electrons ejected per second :
(a) is proportional to the intensity of light
(b) is proportional to the wavelength of light
(c) is proportional to the frequency of light
(d) is proportional to the work function of the metal

125. Ultraviolet radiation of 6.2 eV falls on an aluminium surface (work function 4.2 eV). The kinetic energy in joule of the fastest electron emitted is approximately :
(a) 3×10^{-15} (b) 4×10^{-11}
(c) 3×10^{-19} (d) 3×10^{-21}

126. In a discharge tube, Crooke's dark space is formed at a pressure of :
(a) 5.0 mm of Hg (b) 0.5 mm of Hg
(c) 2.0 mm of Hg (d) 3.0 mm of Hg

127. Sodium surface is subjected to ultra violet and infrared radiation separately and the stopping potential is determined. Then the stopping potential :
(a) is equal in both cases
(b) more when ultra violet light is used
(c) more when infrared light is used
(d) may be more or less for ultraviolet light depending on its intensity as compared to infrared light

128. The de Broglie wavelength of 500 eV electron is
($m_e = 9.0 \times 10^{-31}$ kg, h = 6.62×10^{-34} J-s) :
(a) 0.55 Å (b) 55 Å
(c) 5.5 Å (d) 550 Å

129. Light of frequency υ is incident on a substance of threshold frequency υ_0 ($\upsilon_0 < \upsilon$). The energy of the emitted photoelectron will be **(M.P.C.E.E.T. 2000)**
(a) $h(\upsilon - \upsilon_0)$ (b) h/υ
(c) $hc(\upsilon - \upsilon_0)$ (d) h/υ_0

130. No photoelectrons are emitted from a surface when light of wavelength 4600 Å is incident on it. The photoelectric emission may take place if the :
(a) wavelength of light is decreased
(b) intensity of light is increased
(c) frequency of light is decreased
(d) in all the above cases

131. Which of the following statements is not true?
(a) Photons of visible light have less energy than infrared photons.
(b) Infrared rays are invisible.
(c) Photographic plates are sensitive to infrared rays.
(d) Photographic plates are sensitive to ultraviolet rays.

132. In photoelectric effect, the number of electrons emitted is proportional to the :
(a) work function of cathode
(b) velocity of incident beam
(c) frequency of incident beam
(d) intensity of incident beam

133. Which of the following is not a correct statement ?
(a) Cathode rays have momentum and energy.
(b) Cathode rays are positively charged particles.
(c) The nature of cathode rays is the same for all gases.
(d) Cathode rays travel in a straight line.

134. A mono energetic electron beam with electron speed of 5.28×10^6 m/s is subjected to a magnetic field of 1.2×10^{-4} T normal to the beam velocity. What is the radius of the circle traced by the beam, given e/m for electron is 1.76×10^{11} C/kg :
(a) 15 cm (b) 20 cm
(c) 25 cm (d) 30 cm

135. If cut-off wavelength for a metal surface is 6600 Å, then its work function will be :
(a) 13.6 eV (b) 1.36 eV
(c) 1.88 eV (d) 3.0 eV

136. If the K.E of the most energetic photoelectrons emitted from a photosensitive surface becomes four times when the wavelength of the incident radiation is reduced from λ_1 to λ_2, then work function of the metal is :

(a) $\frac{hc}{\lambda_1\lambda_2}(\lambda_1 - \lambda_2)^2$ (b) $\frac{hc}{\lambda_1\lambda_2}(\lambda_1 + \lambda_2)^2$

(c) $\frac{hc}{\lambda_1\lambda_2}(2\lambda_1 - \lambda_2)$ (d) $\frac{1}{3}\frac{hc}{\lambda_1\lambda_2}(4\lambda_2 - \lambda_1)$

137. When light of wavelength 2537 Å is incident over the photosensitive surface, the stopping voltage of 0.24 volt is required to stop the fastest photoelectron. The threshold frequency for the surface is :

(a) 2.248×10^{15} Hz (b) 1.414×10^{14} Hz

(c) 1.124×10^{15} Hz (d) None of these

138. In Millikan's oil drop experiment, a drop of charge Q and radius r is kept constant between two plates of potential difference of 800 volt. The charge on the other drop of radius $3r$ which is kept constant with a potential difference of 3200 volt is

(B.H.U. 2000)

(a) Q/2 (b) 2Q

(c) 4Q (d) Q/4

139. When a monochromatic source of light is at a distance of 0.2 m from a photoelectric cell, the cut off voltage and the saturation current are 0.6 V and 18 mA respectively. If the same source is placed 0.6 m away from the cell, then :

(a) the saturation current will be 2.0 mA

(b) the stopping potential will be 1.8 V

(c) the stopping potential will be 0.2 V

(d) the saturation current will be 6.0 mA

140. In a photoelectric experiment, the anode potential is plotted against plate current. Hence, from the figure :

(I.I.T. 2004 Screening)

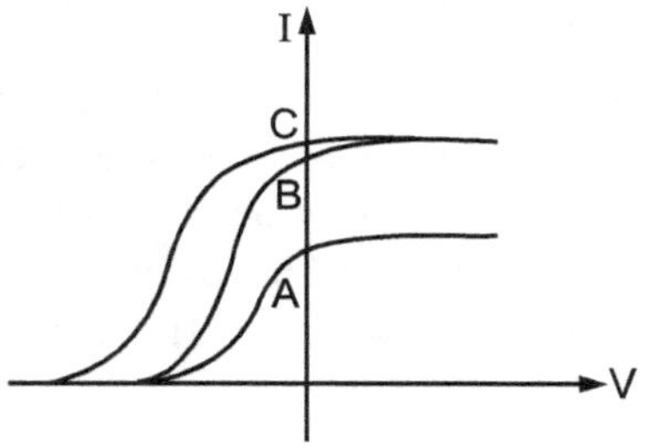

(a) A and B will have different intensities, while B and C will have different frequencies

(b) B and C will have different intensitie,s while A and C will have different frequencies

(c) A and B will have different intensities, while A and C will have equal frequencies

(d) A and B will have equal intensities, while B and C will have different frequencies

141. A proton has kinetic energy E = 100 keV which is equal to that of a photon. The wavelength of photon is λ_2 and that of proton is λ_1. The ratio λ_1/λ_2 is proportional to : **(I.I.T. 2004 Screening)**

(a) E^2 (b) $E^{1/2}$

(c) E^{-1} (d) $E^{-1/2}$

142. A photon of energy 10.2 eV collides inelastically with a hydrogen atom in ground state. After a certain time interval of a few micro seconds, another photon of energy 15.0 eV collides inelastically with the same hydrogen atom, then the observation made by a suitable detector is :

(I.I.T. Screening 2005)

(a) 1 photon with energy 10.2 eV and an electron with energy 1.4 eV

(b) 2 photons with energy 10.2 eV

(c) 2 photons with energy 1.4 eV

(d) 1 photon with energy 3.4 eV and 1 electron with energy 1.4 eV

143. The graph between $1/\lambda$ and stopping potential (V) of three metals having work functions ϕ_1, ϕ_2 and ϕ_3 in an experiment of photoelectric effect is plotted as shown in the following figure. Which of the following statement(s) is/are correct ? [Here λ is the wavelength of the incident ray.]

(I.I.T. 2005 screening)

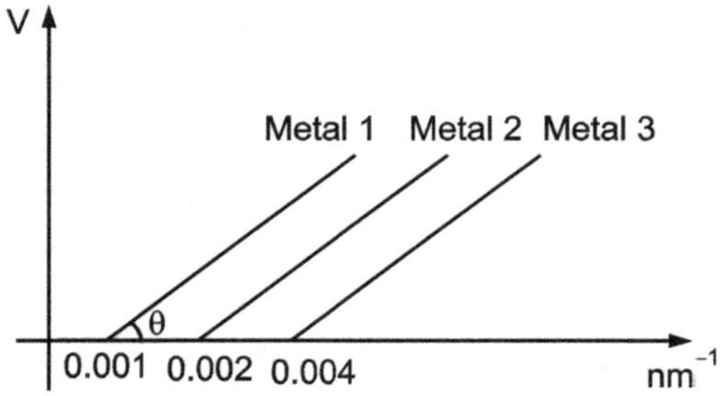

(a) Ratio of work functions $\phi_1 : \phi_2 : \phi_3 = 1 : 2 : 4$

(b) Ratio of work functions $\phi_1 : \phi_2 : \phi_3 = 4 : 2 : 1$

(c) $\tan\theta$ is directly proportional to hc/e, where h is Planck's constant and c is the speed of light.

(d) the violet colour light can eject photo-electrons from metals 2 and 3.

144. The intensity of gamma radiation from a given source is I. On passing through the lead of thickness 36 mm, it is reduced to $\frac{I}{8}$. The thickness of lead which will reduce the intensity to $\frac{I}{2}$ will be: **(A.I.E.E.E. 2005)**

(a) 6 mm (b) 9 mm

(c) 18 mm (d) 12 mm

145. A photocell is illuminated by a small bright source placed 1 m away. When the same source of light is placed $\frac{1}{2}$ m away, the number of electrons emitted by photo-cathode would : **(A.I.E.E.E., 2005)**

(a) decrease by a factor of 4

(b) increase by a factor of 4

(c) decrease by a factor of 2

(d) increase by a factor 2

146. If the kinetic energy of a free electron is doubled, its de Broglie wavelength changes by the factor : **(A.I.E.E.E., 2005)**

(a) $\frac{1}{2}$ (b) 2

(c) $\frac{1}{\sqrt{2}}$ (d) $\sqrt{2}$

147. The time by a photoelectron to come out after the photon strikes is approximately :

(A.I.E.E.E., 2006)

(a) 10^{-1} s (b) 10^{-4} s

(c) 10^{-10} s (d) 10^{-16} s

148. The threshold frequency for a metallic surface corresponds to an energy of 6.2 eV, and the stopping potential for a radiation incident on this surface 5 V. The incident radiation lies in : **(A.I.E.E.E., 2006)**

(a) X-ray region

(b) Ultra-violet region

(c) Infrared region

(d) Visible region

149. The anode voltage of a photocell is kept fixed. The wavelength λ of the light falling on the cathode is gradually changed. The plate current I of the photocell varies as follows : **(A.I.E.E.E., 2006)**

(a)
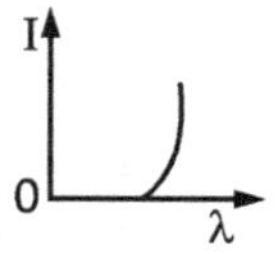

(b)
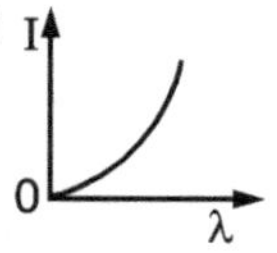

(c)
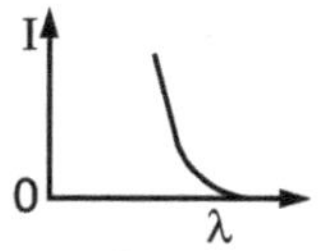

(d)
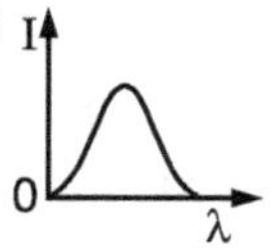

150. The 'rad' is the correct unit used to report the measurement of : **(A.I.E.E.E., 2006)**

(a) the rate of decay of radioactive source

(b) the ability of a beam of gamma ray photons to produce ions in a target

(c) the energy delivered by radiation to a target.

(d) the biological effect of radiation.

151. In an X-ray tube, electrons bombarding the anode produce X-rays of wavelength 1 Å. The energy of an electron, when it hits the anode is : **(MHT - CET 1999)**

(a) 19.8×10^{-6} J (b) 16.3×10^{-16} J

(c) 13.7×10^{-16} J (d) 9.8×10^{-16} J

152. The radius of a circular path of an electron, when subjected to a perpendicular magnetic field is : **(MHT - CET 2000)**

(a) $\frac{Be}{mv}$ (b) $\frac{mE}{B}$

(c) $\frac{me}{B}$ (d) $\frac{mv}{Be}$

153. A charged particle is projected in a chamber with velocity v. It moves undeflected. What can be definitely said about the field ? **(MHT - CET 2001)**

(a) Only $\vec{E}$ is present

(b) Only $\vec{B}$ is present

(c) Both $\vec{E}$ and $\vec{B}$ are present

(d) None of these

154. Mutually perpendicular electric and magnetic fields are given by, E = 1500 V/m and B = 0.04 T. Then velocity is given by : **(MHT - CET 2004)**

(a) 60 m/s (b) 3.75×10^6 m/s

(c) 3.75×10^4 m/s (d) 60×10^4 m/s

155. When light of 2.5 eV falls on a metal surface, maximum kinetic energy of electron is 1.5 eV. If incident relation of 4 eV falls on same metal surface, maximum kinetic energy of electrons is doubled. The work function of metal is : **(MHT - CET 2004)**

(a) 1 eV (b) 4 eV

(c) 1.5 eV (d) 0.5 eV

156. Photoelectric emission takes place : **(MHT - CET 2004)**

(a) when incident wavelength is greater than threshold wavelength

(b) when incident wavelength is less than threshold wavelength

(c) when incident frequency is greater than threshold frequency

(d) at any frequency

157. An electron is projected in a perpendicular uniform magnetic field of 3×10^{-3} T. If the electron moves in circle of radius 4 mm, then linear momentum of electron is : **(MHT - CET 2005)**

(a) 1.92×10^{-21} kg m/s

(b) 1.92×10^{-24} kg m/s

(c) 1.2×10^{-21} kg m/s

(d) 3.2×10^{-21} kg m/s

158. The radiations of 1 eV and 2.5 eV are incident on a metal having a work function of 0.5 eV. The ratio of their maximum velocities is : **(MHT - CET 2006)**

(a) $\frac{1}{2}$ (b) $\frac{1}{4}$

(c) $\frac{2}{5}$ (d) $\sqrt{\frac{5}{2}}$

159. When temperature of a metal increases : **(MHT - CET 2007)**

(a) K.E. of the electrons increases

(b) K.E. of the electrons decreases

(c) All the electrons are ejected from the atom

(d) All the atoms are ionized

160. A charge q and mass m is fired perpendicular to a magnetic field (B) with a velocity v. The frequency of revolution of the charge is : **(MHT - CET 2007)**

(a) $\frac{2\pi}{Bq}$ (b) $\frac{2\pi Bq}{m}$

(c) $\frac{2\pi m}{Bq}$ (d) $\frac{Bq}{2\pi m}$

161. The stopping potential of a photoelectric diode is 9 volts. $e/m = 1.8 \times 10^{11}$ C kg^{-1}, then what is its velocity ? **(MHT - CET 2008)**

(a) 1.8×10^6 m/s (b) 1.8×10^5 m/s

(c) 2.1×10^5 m/s (d) 1.8×10^4 m/s

162. An electron enters in a magnetic field of induction 2mT with velocity of 1.8×10^7 m/s. The radius of a circular path is : **(MHT - CET 2008)**

(a) 5.1 cm (b) 5.1 mm

(c) 5 km (d) 2.1 cm

163. de Broglie's equation states the : **(B.H.U. 2000)**

(a) Particle nature (b) wave nature

(c) Dual nature (d) none of these.

164. The difference between soft and hard X-rays is of : **(M.P.P.M.T. 2000)**

(a) velocity (b) frequency

(c) intensity (d) polarization

165. The work functions of metals A and B are in the ratio 1 : 2. If light of frequencies f and $2f$ are incident on metal surfaces of A and B respectively, then the ratio of the maximum kinetic energies of photoelectrons emitted is ... : (f is greater than threshold frequency of A, $2f$ is greater than threshold frequency of B) **(E.A.M.C.E.T. 2000) (M.P. 1986)**

(a) 1 : 1 (b) 1 : 2

(c) 1 : 3 (d) 1 : 4

166. A ball of mass m travelling with a certain velocity has a kinetic energy K. Then the de Broglie wavelength associated with ball is : **(I.I.I.T. Alla. 2001)**

(a) $\frac{h}{\sqrt{2\,Km}}$

(b) $\sqrt{\frac{h}{2\,Km}}$

(c) $\frac{h}{2\,Km}$

(d) It is only associated with atomic particles.

167. Work functions of three metals A, B and C are 4.5 eV, 4.3 eV and 3.5 eV respectively. If a light of wavelength 4000 Å is incident on the metals then : **(I.I.I.T. Alla. 2001)**

(a) photoelectrons are emitted from A

(b) photoelectrons are emitted from B

(c) photoelectrons are emitted from C

(d) photoelectrons are emitted from all the metals.

168. Rutherford's X-ray scattering by particles concluded that : **(A.F.M.C. 2001)**

(a) electrons revolve around nucleus

(b) electrons are scattered in space

(c) there is heavy mass at centre

(d) velocity of all electrons is same.

169. The most important characteristics of electron in the production of X-rays is : **(A.F.M.C. 2001)**

(a) Charge of electron

(b) Mass of electron

(c) Revolution of electron around the nucleus

(d) Speed of electron

170. Photons of energy 6 eV are incident on a metal surface whose work function is 4 eV. The minimum kinetic energy of the emitted photoelectrons will be : **(M.P.C.E.T. 2001)**

(a) 0 eV (b) 1 eV

(c) 2 eV (d) 10 eV.

171. Planck's constant has same dimensions as : **(U.P.C.P.M.T. 2001)**

(a) Angular momentum

(b) Linear momentum

(c) Work

(d) Coefficient of viscosity.

172. The mass of photon at rest is : **(J.I.P.M.E.R. 2002)**

(a) 1.67×10^{-35} kg (b) 9×10^{-31} kg

(c) one a.m.u. (d) zero.

173. When X-rays pass through a strong uniform magnetic field, then they: **(M.P.P.E.T. 2002)**

(a) do not get deflected at all

(b) get deflected in the direction of the field

(c) get deflected in the direction opposite to the field

(d) get deflected in the direction perpendicular to the field.

174. 1 atomic mass unit is equivalent to : **(C.B.S.E. 1992, M.P.P.E.T. 2002)**

(a) 39 MeV (b) 93 MeV

(c) 139 MeV (d) 931.5 MeV.

175. In Thomson experiment of finding e/m for electrons, beam of electrons is replaced by that of muons (particles with same charge as that of electrons, but mass 208 times that of electrons). No deflection condition in this case is satisfied if : **(Orissa J.E.E. 2002)**

(a) B is increased 208 times

(b) E is increased 208 times

(c) B is increased 14.4 times

(d) None of these.

176. Photoelectric effect can be explained by assuming that light : **(J & K. C. E. T. 2002)**

(a) is a form of transverse wave

(b) is a form of longitudinal wave

(c) can be polarised

(d) consists of quanta.

177. The stopping potential depends on : **(J & K. C. E. T. 2002)**

(a) intensity of incident light

(b) frequency of incident light

(c) both (a) and (b)

(d) neither (a) and (b)

178. The value of Plank's constant is : **(C.B.S.E. 2002)**

(a) 6.63×10^{-34} J/sec

(b) 6.63×10^{-34} kg-m^2/s

(c) 6.63×10^{-34} kg-m^2

(d) 6.63×10^{-34} kg-m^2/s.

179. In photoelectric effect, the number of photoelectrons emitted is proportional to : **(C.E.T. J & K 2000)**

(a) intensity of incident beam

(b) frequency of incident beam

(c) velocity of incident beam

(d) work function of photocathode.

180. An X-ray (gamma ray) is :

(a) an energetic neutron emitted by a nucleus

(b) an energetic electron emitted by a nucleus

(c) an energetic photon emitted by a nucleus

(d) an energetic proton emitted by a nucleus

ANSWER KEY

1. (b)	**2.** (a)	**3.** (b)	**4.** (a)	**5.** (c)	**6.** (c)	**7.** (a)	**8.** (d)	**9.** (a)	**10.**(b)
11.(a)	**12.**(c)	**13.**(c)	**14.**(a)	**15.**(a)	**16.**(c)	**17.**(b)	**18.**(a)	**19.**(d)	**20.**(b)
21.(a)	**22.**(a)	**23.**(d)	**24.**(b)	**25.**(d)	**26.**(d)	**27.**(c)	**28.**(c)	**29.**(b)	**30.**(d)
31.(a)	**32.**(c)	**33.**(b)	**34.**(c)	**35.**(d)	**36.**(b)	**37.**(c)	**38.**(c)	**39.**(d)	**40.**(a)
41.(a)	**42.**(c)	**43.**(c)	**44.**(a)	**45.**(a)	**46.**(c)	**47.**(a)	**48.**(d)	**49.**(b)	**50.**(a)
51.(b)	**52.**(b)	**53.**(b)	**54.**(a)	**55.**(d)	**56.**(a)	**57.**(d)	**58.**(c)	**59.**(b)	**60.**(b)
61.(d)	**62.**(a)	**63.**(d)	**64.**(d)	**65.**(b)	**66.**(c)	**67.**(b)	**68.**(d)	**69.**(a)	**70.**(c)
71.(c)	**72.**(b)	**73.**(c)	**74.**(b)	**75.**(a)	**76.**(c)	**77.**(a)	**78.**(c)	**79.**(d)	**80.**(c)
81.(a)	**82.**(b)	**83.**(a)	**84.**(d)	**85.**(c)	**86.**(a)	**87.**(b)	**88.**(a)	**89.**(d)	**90.**(b)
91.(c)	**92.**(c)	**93.** (a &b)	**94.**(a)	**95.**(c)	**96.**(d)	**97.**(d)	**98.**(b)	**99.**(a)	**100.** (b)
101. (a)	**102.** (d)	**103.** (c)	**104.** (d)	**105.** (c)	**106.** (a)	**107.** (b)	**108.** (a)	**109.** (b)	**110.** (d)
111. (c)	**112.** (a)	**113.** (c)	**114.** (d)	**115.** (b)	**116.** (d)	**117.** (a)	**118.** (a)	**119.** (a)	**120.** (b)
121. (c)	**122.** (c)	**123.** (c)	**124.** (a)	**125.** (c)	**126.** (b)	**127.** (b)	**128.** (a)	**129.** (a)	**130.** (a)
131. (a)	**132.** (d)	**133.** (b)	**134.** (c)	**135.** (c)	**136.** (d)	**137.** (c)	**138.** (d)	**139.** (a)	**140.** (a)
141. (b)	**142.** (a)	**143.** (a &c)	**144.** (d)	**145.** (b)	**146.** (c)	**147.** (c)	**148.** (b)	**149.** (c)	**150.** (d)
151. (a)	**152.** (d)	**153.** (c)	**154.** (c)	**155.** (a)	**156.** (c)	**157.** (b)	**158.** (a)	**159.** (a)	**160.** (d)
161. (a)	**162.** (a)	**163.** (c)	**164.** (b)	**165.** (b)	**166.** (a)	**167.** (d)	**168.** (c)	**169.** (d)	**170.** (a)
171. (a)	**172.** (d)	**173.** (a)	**174.** (d)	**175.** (c)	**176.** (d)	**177.** (c)	**178.** (d)	**179.** (a)	**180.** (c)

19

ATOMS, MOLECULES AND NUCLEI

MULTIPLE CHOICE QUESTIONS

1. A hydrogen atom does not emit X-rays since:

(a) it is too small in size

(b) its energy levels are too far apart

(c) it has single electron

(d) its energy levels are too close to each other

2. Values of Z and A in the reaction

$_{92}U^{235} + {}_0n^1 \rightarrow {}_{54}Xe^{140} + {}_ZSr^A + 2\,{}_0n^1$ are :

(a) 37, 93 (b) 38, 94

(c) 38, 95 (d) 39, 92

3. Mass defect per nucleon is called :

(a) Packing fraction

(b) Excitation energy

(c) Binding energy

(d) Ionization energy

4. Complete the equation for the following fission process :

$_{92}U^{235} + {}_0n^1 \rightarrow \ldots\ldots\ldots\ldots + {}_{38}Kr^{90} + \ldots\ldots$

(C.B.S.E. Med. 1998)

(a) $_{54}Xe^{143} + 3\,{}_0n^1$ (b) $_{54}Xe^{142} + {}_0n^1$

(c) $_{57}Xe^{142}$ (d) $_{54}Xe^{145}$

5. Emission of β rays in a radioactive decay results in a daughter element representing a :

(a) change in charge but not in mass

(b) change in mass but not in charge

(c) change in both

(d) change in neither

6. The binding energy per nucleon of a stable nucleus is :

(a) 8 eV (b) 8 keV

(c) 8 MeV (d) 8 BeV

7. Density of nuclear matter is nearly :

(a) 10^3 kg/m^3 (b) 10^{10} kg/m^3

(c) 10^{17} kg/m^3 (d) 10^{24} kg/m^3

8. If wavelength of the energy emitted when electron comes from 4th orbit to 2nd orbit in hydrogen atom is 20,397 units, then the wavelength λ of energy for the same transition in He^+ is : **(A.I.I.M.S. 1997)**

(a) 5,099 units (b) 20,497 units

(c) 40,994 units (d) 81,988 units

9. In Bohr's model of atom, stationary orbits are postulated :

(a) to meet the condition that the atom is not ionized

(b) to meet the condition that the electrons moving in the stationary orbits do not radiate energy

(c) to meet the condition for the dynamical equilibrium of the electron

(d) in accordance with classical theory of electromagnetism

10. In which of the following processes, maximum energy will be released?

(C.P.M.T. 1999; D.C.E. 1996)

(a) Combustion of 1 gram coal

(b) Fission of 1 g of U-235

(c) Fusion of 1 g of hydrogen nuclei

(d) Decay of 1 g of radioactive substance

11. It is possible to understand nuclear fission on the basis of the : **(C.B.S.E. Med. 2000)**
(a) independent particle model of the nucleus
(b) meson theory of the nuclear forces
(c) proton-proton cycle
(d) liquid drop model of the nucleus

12. In the nuclear reaction ${}_6C^{11} \rightarrow {}_5B^{11} + \beta^+ + X$, where X stands for : **(C.B.S.E. Med. 2000)**
(a) an electron (b) a proton
(c) a neutron (d) none of these

13. a.m.u cannot be expressed in :
(a) joule (b) erg
(c) electron volt (d) dyne

14. The binding energies per nucleon of deuteron (${}_1H^2$) and helium (${}_2He^4$) nuclei are 1.1 MeV and 7 MeV respectively. If two deuterons fuse together to form a helium nucleus, then energy produced is :
(C.B.S.E. 2000, C.P.M.T. 2001)
(a) 5.9 MeV (b) 23.6 MeV
(c) 26.9 MeV (d) 32.4 MeV

15. The size of atom is nearly :
(a) 10^{-14} m (b) 10^{-6} m
(c) 10^{-8} m (d) 10^{-10} m

16. Half-life of a radioactive element is determined by : **(A.F.M.C. 2001)**
(a) atomic number (b) mass number
(c) temperature (d) none of these

17. If the radioactive decay constant of radium is 1.17×10^{-4} per year, then it's half life period is approximately equal to :
[A.I.I.M.S. 1998]
(a) 2520 years (b) 5923 years
(c) 7010 years (d) 8900 years

18. Which of the following radiation series is found in the visible region ?
(A.F.M.C. 1998)
(a) Lyman (b) Paschen
(c) Pfund (d) Balmer

19. In an atom the two electrons move around the nucleus in circular orbits of radii R and 2R. The ratio of the squares of their time periods is :
(a) 1 : 4 (b) 1 : 8
(c) 4 : 1 (d) 8 : 1

20. Which of the following substances is best moderator for fast neutrons ?
(a) Graphite (b) Heavy water
(c) Cadmium (d) Uranium

21. In radio therapy, X-rays are used to :
(a) detect fault in radio receiving circuits
(b) detect heart disease
(c) treat cancer
(d) detect bone fracture

22. Maximum penetrating power is that of :
(A.F.M.C. 2000)
(a) α -rays (b) X-rays
(c) γ-rays (d) β -rays

23. Relation between Half life period (T) and decay constant (λ) of a radioactive isotope is : **(C.B.S.E. P.M.T. 2000)**
(a) $\lambda = \dfrac{1}{\log_e 2T}$ (b) $\lambda = \dfrac{T}{\log_e 2}$
(c) $\lambda = \dfrac{\log_e 2}{T}$ (d) $\lambda = \dfrac{T}{2}$

24. Mass number of the resulting nucleus when a nucleus with mass number 10 is bombarded by an alpha particle is :
(a) 6 (b) 7
(c) 14 (d) 13

25. The nuclear process ${}_1H^1 + {}_1H^1 + {}_1H^2 \rightarrow {}_2He^4 + {}_1e^0$ + Energy, will require :
(C.P.M.T. 1994)
(a) low temperature and low pressure
(b) high temperature and normal pressure
(c) high pressure and normal temperature
(d) high temperature and high pressure

26. If v_1 and v_4 are the speeds of the electron in the states n = 1 and n = 4 respectively of the Bohr model of the atom, then the ratio v_1 to v_4 is :
(a) 1/4 (b) 4
(c) 2 (d) 1/2

27. Minimum value of excitation potential of Bohr's first orbit in hydrogen atom is :
(a) 13.6 V (b) 3.4 V
(c) 10.2 V (d) 3.6 V

28. The main source of energy in stars is :
(a) Nuclear fusion
(b) Nuclear fission
(c) Gravitational contraction
(d) Burning of coal

29. The mass defect of a helium nucleus is 0.0303 a.m.u. The binding energy per nucleon of helium nucleus is then: **(C.P.M.T. 1999)**
(a) 28 MeV (b) 7 MeV
(c) 4 MeV (d) 1 MeV

30. 1 Becquerel equals how many radioactive disintegrations per second ?
(a) 10^6
(b) 3.7×10^{10}
(c) 1
(d) None of the above

31. Which of the following is a correct statement ? **[I.I.T. 1998]**
(a) Protons and neutrons have exactly same mass.
(b) Alpha particles are singly ionized helium atoms.
(c) Gamma rays are high energy neutrons.
(d) Beta rays are same as cathode rays.

32. For the fission of $_{92}U^{235}$ we need :
(a) fast neutrons (b) slow neutrons
(c) fast protons (d) fast ions

33. If in 40 days $\left(\frac{1}{16}\right)^{th}$ of the original amount of a radioactive substance is left, then half life of the substance is : **(D.P.M.T. 2000)**
(a) 5 days (b) 20 days
(c) 15 days (d) 10 days

34. In the Bohr model of a hydrogen atom, the required centripetal force is given by the Coulomb force of attraction between the proton and the electron. If a_0 is the radius of the orbit in its ground state, m is the mass of electron, e is the charge on electron and ε_0 is the permittivity of free space, then speed of the electron is : **(C.B.S.E. P.M.T.1998)**
(a) $\sqrt{\frac{4\pi\varepsilon_0 a_0 m}{e}}$ (b) $\frac{e}{\sqrt{\varepsilon_0 a_0 m}}$
(c) Zero (d) $\frac{e}{\sqrt{4\pi\varepsilon_0 a_0 m}}$

35. The band spectra (characteristic of molecular species) is due to emission of radiation in :
(a) all the three states (b) gaseous state
(c) liquid state (d) solid state

36. Fast moving neutrons can be slowed down by :
(a) elastic collisions with heavy nuclei
(b) passing them through water
(c) using lead shielding
(d) applying strong electric field

37. Ar-40, Ca-40, and K-40 are :
(a) isotopes of each other
(b) isotones of each other
(c) isobars of each other
(d) none of these

38. In the given nuclear reaction, number of α and β-particles emitted in the radioactive decay of $_{90}X^{200} \rightarrow {}_{80}Y^{168}$ are : **(C.B.S.E. 1995)**
(a) 6 and 8 (b) 8 and 8
(c) 8 and 6 (d) 6 and 6

39. If original amount of the radioactive specimen is 10.38 gm and its half life is 3.8 days, then substance left after 19 days will be :

(a) 0.151 g (b) 0.32 g

(c) 1.51 g (d) 0.16 g

40. The energy difference between the first two levels of hydrogen atom is 10.2 eV. For another element of mass number 20 and atomic number 10 , it will be :

(a) 0.102 eV (b) 0.51 eV

(c) 2040 eV (d) 1020 eV

41. In nuclear fission :

(a) whole mass of nucleus is converted into energy

(b) two light nuclei fuse together to form a heavy nucleus

(c) a heavy nucleus emits some radiations spontaneously

(d) a heavy nucleus breaks into two lighter nuclei

42. Which statement is correct ? **(I.I.T. 1998)**

(a) Gamma rays are high energy neutrons.

(b) α-particles are singly ionized helium atoms.

(c) Protons and neutrons have exactly same mass.

(d) Beta rays are same as cathode rays.

43. The electron emitted in β radiation originates from : **(I.I.T. Screening 2001)**

(a) inner orbits of atoms

(b) free electrons existing in nuclei

(c) decay of a neutron in a nucleus

(d) photon escaping from the nucleus

44. The transition from the state n = 4 to n = 3 in a hydrogen-like atom results in ultraviolet radiation. Infrared radiation will be obtained in the transition : **(I.I.T. Screening 2001)**

(a) $2 \rightarrow 1$ (b) $3 \rightarrow 2$

(c) $4 \rightarrow 2$ (d) $5 \rightarrow 4$

45. How much energy will approximately be released if all the atoms of 1 kg of deuterium could undergo fusion?

(a) 2×10^7 kWh (b) 9×10^{13} J

(c) 6×10^{27} calorie (d) 9×10^{13} MeV

46. The ratio of the areas of the circular orbits of an electron for the first excited state in a hydrogen atom to that for the ground state is:

(a) 4 : 1 (b) 16 : 1

(c) 2 : 1 (d) 3 : 1

47. Thermal neutron has average K.E of the order of :

(a) 0.003 keV (b) 0.03 keV

(c) 3.0 keV (d) 0.3 eV

48. When two deuterons fuse to form a helium nucleus ($_2He^4$), then energy released (Binding energy per nucleus for $_1H^2$ and $_2He^4$ are 1.1 MeV and 7.0 MeV respectively) is :

(a) 8.1 MeV (b) 11.6 MeV

(c) 23.6 MeV (d) 24.3 MeV

49. The ratio of longest wavelength and the shortest wavelength observed in the five spectral series of emission spectrum of hydrogen is :

(a) 960 : 11 (b) 25 : 1

(c) 4 : 3 (d) 525 : 376

50. When a thermal neutron strikes a $_{92}U^{235}$ nucleus, then the process that takes place is : **(A.F.M.C. 1998)**

(a) Fusion of neutron (b) Fission of U^{235}

(c) Fusion of U^{235} (d) None of above

51. The energy produced in the Sun is due to : **(A.F.M.C. 1998)**

(a) Fusion reaction

(b) Fission reaction

(c) Chemical reaction

(d) Motion of electrons and ions

52. If the magnitude of charge of proton and electron in a hydrogen atom were doubled, the energy emitted in the transition from n = 2 to n = 1 would change by a factor of :

(a) 8 (b) 4
(c) 1/4 (d) 16

53. In a nuclear reaction, there is conservation of : **(A.I.I.M.S. 1997)**

(a) mass only
(b) energy only
(c) momentum only
(d) mass, energy and momentum

54. Light consisting of a continuous range of wavelengths is passed through hydrogen gas whose atoms are in the ground state. The absorption spectrum produced will have dark lines corresponding to the :

(a) Paschen series (b) Balmer series
(c) Pfund series (d) Lyman series

55. In an atom having mass M, atomic number Z and mass number A, mass defect is given by:

(a) M.A.Z.
(b) M (A – Z)
(c) $[Zm_p + (A - Z)\, m_n] - M$
(d) $[Zm_p + (A - Z)\, m_n + Zm_e] - M$

56. The ratio of minimum to maximum wavelength in Balmer series is :

(a) 3 : 4 (b) 1 : 4
(c) 5 : 36 (d) 5 : 9

57. Boron rods in a nuclear reactor are used as :

(a) Moderators (b) Control rods
(c) Coolants (d) Protective shield

58. Heavy water is used as a moderator in nuclear reactors. The function of the moderator is : **(C.B.S.E. 1994)**

(a) to slow down the neutrons to thermal energies
(b) to cool the reaction
(c) to absorb neutrons and stop chain reaction
(d) to control the energy released in the reactor

59. What was the fissionable material used in the bomb dropped at Nagasaki (Japan) in the year 1945 ?

(a) Uranium (b) Neptunium
(c) Plutonium (d) Cadmium

60. Half life of a radioactive substance is 20 minutes. How much is the time interval between 33% decay and 67% decay ? **(A.I.I.M.S. 2000)**

(a) 20 minutes (b) 25 minutes
(c) 30 minutes (d) 40 minutes

61. In the second orbit of hydrogen atom, angular momentum for an electron as per Bohr's model of atom will be : **(A.I.I.M.S. 2000)**

(a) π / h (b) $2\pi h$
(c) h / π (d) $2h/\pi$

62. If the wavelength of K α-line in copper is 1.54 Å, then ionization energy of K electron in copper is :

(a) 10×10^{-16} J
(b) 17×10^{-16} J
(c) 12.9×10^{-16} J
(d) 11.2×10^{-17} J

63. For the statements below, choose the correct choice :

(I) The spectrum of α-emission radioactive decay is discrete.
(II) The spectrum of β-emission radioactive decay is continuous. **(A.M.U. 1999)**

(a) (I) is true, but (II) is false.
(b) (II) is true, but (I) is false.
(c) (II) is true.
(d) (I) is true.

64. Equation $4\,{}_1H^1 \rightarrow {}_2He^4 + 2\,{}_1e^0 + 26$ MeV represents:

(a) α-decay (b) β-decay
(c) γ-decay (d) Fusion

65. When the number of nucleons in nuclei increases, then binding energy per nucleon must :

(a) increase

(b) decrease

(c) first increase and then decrease

(d) remain unchanged

66. Half lives of two radioactive substances are 40 and 20 minutes respectively and initially samples were having equal number of nuclei. After 80 minutes ratio of the remaining numbers of nuclei will be :

(C.B.S.E. Med. 1998)

(a) 4 : 1 (b) 1 : 16

(c) 8 : 1 (d) 16 : 1

67. By emitting an α -particle Rn decays into Po with half life of 4 days. A sample contains 6.4×10^{10} atoms of Rn. After 12 days, the number of atoms left in the sample are :

(M.P. Engg. 1999)

(a) 2.1×10^{10} (b) 0.8×10^{10}

(c) 3.2×10^{10} (d) 0.53×10^{10}

68. If the radius of second stationary orbit of electron in Bohr's atoms is R, then radius of third orbit will be :

(a) R/3 (b) 9 R

(c) 2.25 R (d) 3 R

69. Energy released in the fission of ${}_{92}U^{235}$ nucleus is 200 MeV. If a reactor fuel is ${}_{92}U^{235}$ and operating at power level 5 watt, then fission rate will be about :

(a) 1.5×10^{16} sec^{-1} (b) 1.5×10^{17} sec^{-1}

(c) 1.5×10^{10} sec^{-1} (d) 1.5×10^{11} sec^{-1}

70. If ionization energy of the hydrogen atom is 13.6 eV, then the wavelength of the first line of Lyman series is :

(a) 22.20 Å (b) 1.22 Å

(c) 122 Å (d) 1216 Å

71. When potential difference of 42000 volts is used in X-ray tube to accelerate electrons, then the X-ray radiation produced of maximum frequency is :

(a) 10^{18} Hz (b) 10^{19} Hz

(c) 10^{20} Hz (d) 10^{6} Hz

72. After five half lives what will be the fraction of initial radioactive substance left ?

(a) $(1/2)^{15}$ (b) $(1/2)^{4}$

(c) $(1/2)^{5}$ (d) $(1/2)^{10}$

73. Radioactive decay constant for radium is 1.07×10^{-4} per year, then its half life period will be : **(A.I.I.M.S. 1998)**

(a) 2520 years (b) 6476 years

(c) 7000 years (d) 8900 years

74. Binding energy per nucleon for O^{16} is 7.99 MeV and it is 7.95 MeV for O^{17}. Energy required to remove one neutron from O^{17} is : **(I.I.T. 1995)**

(a) 15.94 MeV (b) 0.04 MeV

(c) 7.31 MeV (d) 0.06 MeV

75. If binding energy for deuterium is 2.23 MeV, then mass defect in a.m.u. is :

(a) 0.0024 (b) 0.0012

(c) –0.0012 (d) 0.0036

76. We use Molybdenum as a target element for production of X-rays because it is :

(a) a heavy element with high melting point

(b) an element having high thermal conductivity

(c) a heavy element and can easily absorb high velocity electrons

(d) a heavy element and can easily deflect electrons

77. Which one of the following processes is not related to radioactive disintegration ?

(a) Positron emission (b) Electron capture

(c) α-decay (d) Nuclear fusion

78. If a nucleus ${}_{Z}X^{A}$ emits an α-particle and the resultant nucleus emits a β^{+} particle, then atomic charge and mass numbers of the final nucleus will be :

(a) Z – 2, A – 4 (b) Z – 1, A – 4

(c) Z – 3, A – 4 (d) Z, A – 2

79. Transitions from the state n = 4 to n = 3 in a hydrogen like atom results in ultraviolet radiations. Infrared radiations will be obtained in the transition :

(I.I.T. Screening 2000)

(a) 5 to 4 (b) 4 to 2
(c) 3 to 2 (d) 2 to 1

80. According to Bohr's postulates, which of the following quantities takes discrete values ?
(a) Potential energy
(b) Kinetic energy
(c) Momentum
(d) Angular momentum

81. Control rods in a nuclear reactor are made up of :
(a) Cadmium (b) Graphite
(c) Uranium (d) Copper

82. In Bohr's model, the atomic radius of the first orbit is r_0, then the radius of the third orbit is : **(A.I.I.M.S. 1997)**
(a) $r_0/9$ (b) r_0
(c) $9r_0$ (d) $3r_0$

83. Fissionable isotope is :
(a) ${}_6C^{13}$ (b) ${}_8O^{17}$
(c) ${}_{92}U^{235}$ (d) ${}_{92}U^{238}$

84. X-ray region lies between :
(a) visible and ultraviolet regions
(b) short radio waves and visible region
(c) short radio waves and long radio waves
(d) gamma rays and ultraviolet region

85. If the decay constant of ${}_{80}Po^{206}$ is λ, then its half life and mean life are :
(a) $\frac{1}{\lambda}$ and $\frac{\log_e 2}{\lambda}$ respectively
(b) $\frac{1}{\lambda}$ and $\frac{\lambda}{\log_e 2}$ respectively
(c) $\frac{\log_e 2}{\lambda}$ and $\frac{1}{\lambda}$ respectively
(d) $\frac{1}{\lambda}$ and $\frac{2}{\log_e \lambda}$ respectively

86. According to Bohr's model of atom principal quantum number (n) and radius of the orbit (r) are related as :

(A.I.I.M.S. 1999)

(a) $r \propto n$ (b) $r \propto n^2$
(c) $r \propto \frac{1}{n}$ (d) $r \propto \frac{1}{n^2}$

87. A radioactive nucleus undergoes a series of decay as shown :

$$A \xrightarrow{\alpha} A_1 \xrightarrow{\beta} A_2 \xrightarrow{\alpha} A_3 \xrightarrow{\gamma} A_4$$

If the mass number and atomic number of A are 180 and 72 respectively, then these numbers for A_4 are :
(a) 174, 71 (b) 180, 70
(c) 172, 69 (d) 170, 69

88. Which of the following sources give discrete emission spectrum ?
(a) Candle
(b) Mercury vapour lamp
(c) Sun
(d) Incandescent bulb

89. In the disintegration chain,

${}_{92}U^{238} \xrightarrow{\alpha} X \xrightarrow{\beta} {}_ZY^A$, the values of Z and A will be :
(a) Z = 91, A = 234 (b) Z = 92, A = 236
(c) Z = 90, A = 234 (d) Z = 88, A = 232

90. Which of the following statements is true ?
(a) The Balmer series is a line spectrum in the ultraviolet region.
(b) The spectral series formulae can be derived from the Rutherford's model of hydrogen atom.
(c) The Lyman series is a continuous spectrum.
(d) The Paschen series is a line spectrum in the infrared region.

91. The ionization energy of hydrogen atom is 13.6 eV. According to Bohr's theory, the energy corresponding to a transition between the 3rd and 4th orbit is :
(a) 1.51 eV (b) 3.4 eV
(c) 0.65 eV (d) 0.85 eV

92. The source of energy in nuclear reactor is :
(a) Nuclear fission
(b) Nuclear fusion
(c) Solar cell
(d) Spontaneous radioactive decay

93. We use radio isotopes as tracers because :
(a) They emit α , β and γ rays.
(b) They can not be distinguished from normal atoms easily.
(c) Their chemical properties are different.
(d) They can be detected accurately in small quantities.

94. The frequency of K_α line for gold atoms (Z for gold is 79) is :
(a) 3×10^{10} Hz (b) 6×10^{19} Hz
(c) 1.5×10^{19} Hz (d) 3×10^{19} Hz

95. Ionization energy of an electron present in the second Bohr's orbit of hydrogen atom is:
(D.P.M.T. 2000)
(a) 1.5 eV (b) 3.4 eV
(c) 54.4 eV (d) 13.6 eV

96. Half life of a radioactive specimen is 2.3 days. λ for this substance will be :
(A.F.M.C. 1997)
(a) 0.3 (b) 1.0
(c) 1.6 (d) 2.3

97. A radioactive substance has a half-life of 60 minutes. During 3 hours the fraction of atom that have decayed would be :
(a) 25.1% (b) 8.5%
(c) 12.5% (d) 87.5%

98. The Rydberg constant R for hydrogen is :
(a) $R = \left(\frac{1}{4\pi\varepsilon_0}\right)^2 \frac{2\pi^2 me^4}{c^2h^2}$
(b) $R = \left(\frac{1}{4\pi\varepsilon_0}\right) \frac{2\pi^2 me^4}{ch^2}$
(c) $R = \left(\frac{1}{4\pi\varepsilon_0}\right) \frac{2\pi^2 me^2}{ch^2}$
(d) $R = \left(\frac{1}{4\pi\varepsilon_0}\right)^2 \frac{2\pi^2 me^4}{ch^3}$

99. Rutherford and Geiger - Marsden's experiments on scattering alpha particles from metal foils suggest that :
(a) The positive charges in an atom are evenly distributed throughout the atom.
(b) Neutrons exist in the nucleus.
(c) The electrons form a hard, impenetrable shell around the nucleus.
(d) An extremely small, positively charged nucleus exists.

100. The function of heavy water in a nuclear reactor is :
(a) To control the energy released in the reactor.
(b) To absorb neutrons and stop chain reaction.
(c) To cool the reactor.
(d) To slow down the neutrons to thermal energies.

101. One gram of uranium releases
(a) 9×10^{12} J (b) 9×10^{13} J
(c) 9×10^{10} J (d) 9×10^{11} J

102. The wavelength λ_e of an electron and λ_p of a photon of same energy E are related by
(NEET 2013)
(a) $\lambda_p \propto \lambda_e$ (b) $\lambda_p \propto \sqrt{\lambda_e}$
(c) $\lambda_p \propto \frac{1}{\sqrt{\lambda_e}}$ (d) $\lambda_p \propto \lambda_e^2$

103. I. Orbiting speed of electron decreases as it shifts to discrete orbits away from the nucleus.
II. Radii of allowed orbits of electron are proportional to the principal quantum number.
III. Frequency with which electron orbits around the nucleus in discrete orbits is inversely proportional to the principal quantum number.
IV. Binding force with which the electron is bound to the nucleus increases as it shifts to outer orbits.

Which of the above statements are true regarding Bohr's model of hydrogen atom?

(a) I and III (b) II and IV

(c) I, II and III (d) II, III and IV

104. The difference in angular momentum associated with the electron in the two consecutive orbits of hydrogen atom is :

(a) $(n-1)\frac{h}{2\pi}$ (b) $\frac{h}{2\pi}$

(c) $\frac{h}{\pi}$ (d) $\frac{h}{2}$

105. If λ_1 and λ_2 are the wavelengths of characteristic X-rays and gamma rays respectively, then the relation between them is :

(a) $\lambda_1 = \frac{1}{\lambda_2}$ (b) $\lambda_1 = \lambda_2$

(c) $\lambda_1 > \lambda_2$ (d) $\lambda_1 < \lambda_2$

106. Which of the followings is correct ?

(a) ${}_{84}Pb^{214} \rightarrow {}_{82}Pb^{210} + {}_1H^1$

(b) ${}_{90}Th^{214} \rightarrow {}_{91}Pa^{234} + {}_2He^4$

(c) ${}_{92}U^{238} \rightarrow {}_{90}Th^{234} + {}_2He^4$

(d) None of these

107. Binding energies per nucleon for Li^7 and He^4 are 5.60 MeV and 7.06 MeV respectively. Then energy of reaction $Li^7 + H^1 \rightarrow He^4$ is :

(a) 8.4 MeV (b) 2.4 MeV

(c) 19.6 MeV (d) 17.3 MeV

108. Penetrating power of X-rays depends on :

(a) current flowing in the filament

(b) applied potential difference

(c) nature of the target

(d) all of the above

109. Which of the following transitions in a hydrogen atom emits the photon of highest frequency ? **(C.B.S.E. Med. 2000)**

(a) n = 1 to n = 2 (b) n = 2 to n = 1

(c) n = 2 to n = 6 (d) n = 6 to n = 2

110. What are the limits of Lyman series in the hydrogen spectrum ?

(a) 911 Å to 1215 Å

(b) 0 to infinity

(c) 500 Å to 1000 Å

(d) 1000 Å to 1500 Å

111. Binding energy per nucleon is maximum in :

(a) ${}_{56}Ba^{141}$ (b) ${}_{26}Fe^{56}$

(c) ${}_2He^4$ (d) ${}_{92}U^{234}$

112. Half life period of a radioactive element X is same as the mean life of other radioactive element Y. Initially both of them have same number of atoms. Then : **(I.I.T. Dec. 98)**

(a) X will decay at a faster rate than Y

(b) Y will decay at a faster rate than X

(c) X and Y both will decay at the same rate

(d) Initial decay rate of X and Y were same

113. Atomic weight of Boron is 10.81 and it has two isotopes ${}_5B^{10}$ and ${}_5B^{11}$. Then the ratio of ${}_5B^{10}$ and ${}_5B^{11}$ in nature would be :

(C.B.S.E. Med 1998)

(a) 15 : 16 (b) 81 : 12

(c) 19 : 81 (d) 10 : 11

114. What percent of original radioactive substance is left after 5 half-life times ?

(A.F.M.C. 2001)

(a) 20% (b) 3%

(c) 5% (d) 10%

115. X-rays and γ-rays having same energies can be distinguished by :

(a) their ionizing power

(b) their velocity

(c) method of production

(d) their intensity

116. Which of the following transitions gives an absorption line of least frequency ?

(a) n = 8 to n = 3 (b) n = 2 to n = 1

(c) n = 1 to n = 2 (d) n = 3 to n = 8

117. If the speed of X-rays, light and radio waves in vacuum are represented by v_X, v_L and v_R respectively, then :

(a) $v_X > v_L > v_R$ (b) $v_L > v_X > v_R$

(c) $v_L = v_R = v_X$ (d) $v_L > v_R > v_X$

118. Thermal neutron is captured by ${}_{92}U^{236}$. Fission of ${}_{92}U^{236}$ occurs by : **(I.I.T. 1994)**

(a) ${}_{92}U^{236} \rightarrow {}_{50}Sn^{144} + {}_{42}Mo^{80} + 6n + Q$

(b) ${}_{92}U^{236} \rightarrow {}_{56}Xe^{144} + {}_{36}Ko^{80} + 3n + Q$

(c) ${}_{92}U^{236} \rightarrow {}_{50}Te^{144} + {}_{42}Mo^{80} + 3n + Q$

(d) ${}_{92}U^{236} \rightarrow {}_{56}Ba^{144} + {}_{36}Ko^{80} + 3n + Q$

119. When an electron jumps from the fourth orbit to second orbit of a hydrogen atom, we get : **(C.B.S.E. Med. 2000)**

(a) second line of Paschen series

(b) second line of Balmer series

(c) first line of Pfund series

(d) second line of Lyman series

120. In a Coolidge tube the energy of a photon of characteristic X-ray comes from :

(a) the kinetic energy of the ions of the target

(b) an electronic transition of the target atom

(c) the kinetic energy of the striking electron

(d) the kinetic energy of the free electrons of the target

121. The absorption coefficient of X-rays for a given wavelength is larger for :

(a) Copper (b) Lithium

(c) Lead (d) Aluminium

122. Rydberg constants for helium R_{He} and for hydrogen R_H are related as :

(a) $R_{He} > R_H$ (b) $R_{He} = R_H$

(c) $R_{He} < R_H$ (d) $R_{He} = R_H/2$

123. An electron has energy −13.6 eV in the lowest (n = 1) orbit in hydrogen atom. Energy required to ionize a hydrogen atom which is in the first excited level is : **(M.P. Engg. Test 2000)**

(a) 1.9 eV (b) 10.2 eV

(c) 13.6 eV (d) 3.4 eV

124. The momentum of an electron revolving in second orbit of hydrogen atom will be : **(M.P. Engg. Test 1999)**

(a) $2\pi h$ (b) πh

(c) $\frac{h}{\pi}$ (d) $\frac{2h}{\pi}$

125. The mass of photon in the visible, microwave and X-rays region decreases in the following order :

(a) Microwave > visible > X-rays

(b) Microwave > X-rays > visible

(c) X-rays > visible > microwave

(d) X-rays > microwave > visible

126. Electron in a hydrogen atom makes a transition from an excited state to the ground state. Which of the following statement is true ? **(I.I.T. 1999)**

(a) It's kinetic energy decreases, potential energy increases and total energy also increases.

(b) It's kinetic energy decreases and total energy increases.

(c) It's kinetic energy increases, potential energy decreases and total energy also decreases.

(d) It's kinetic energy, potential energy and total energy all increase.

127. Best nuclear fuel out of the following is :

(a) Uranium 236 (b) Thorium 236

(c) Neptunium 293 (d) Plutonium 239

128. What will happen if X-rays are allowed to fall on the surface of a zinc plate ?

(a) Electrons come out of the surface.

(b) Photons come out of the surface.

(c) Neutrons come out of the surface.

(d) X-rays are reflected by the surface.

129. If the principal quantum number n = 3, then the possible values of orbital quantum number *l* will be : **(M.P. Engg. 2001)**

(a) 0, 1, 2 (b) −1, 0, +1

(c) 1, 2, 3 (d) 0, 1, 2, 3

130. Liquid drop model of the nucleus was given by :

(a) Chadwick (b) Thomson
(c) Fermi (d) Bohr

131. Binding energy per nucleon v/s mass number curve for various nuclei is shown in the figure below. P, Q, R and S are the four nuclei indicated in the curve. Process in which energy is released will be :

(I.I.T. 1998)

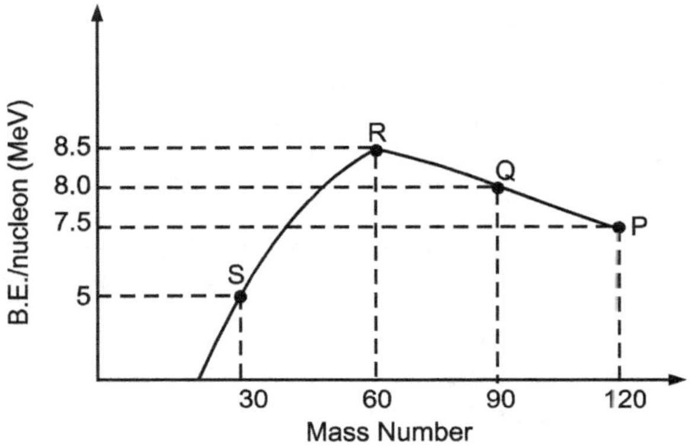

(a) $R \rightarrow 2S$ (b) $P \rightarrow 2R$
(c) $Q \rightarrow R + S$ (d) $P \rightarrow Q + S$

132. In an X-ray tube, electrons are accelerated by applying a high voltage V. If e is the electronic charge and h the Planck's constant, the highest frequency f_{max} of the emitted X-rays is given by :

(a) $f_{max} = \frac{eV}{h}$ (b) $f_{max} = \frac{2eh}{V}$
(c) $f_{max} = \frac{1}{2}\frac{e^2h^2}{V^2}$ (d) $f_{max} = \frac{2e^2h^2}{V^2}$

133. A nucleus ruptures into two nuclear parts which have their velocity ratio equal to 1 : 2. What will be the ratio of their nuclear size (nuclear radius) ?

(a) $1 : 2^{1/3}$ (b) $2^{1/3} : 1$
(c) $3^{1/2} : 1$ (d) $1 : 3^{1/2}$

134. In Bohr's model of hydrogen atom centripetal force is given by Coulomb's force of attraction between a proton and electron. Let a_0 be the radius of ground state orbit, m be mass, e be the charge on an electron and ε_0 be the permittivity of free space. Then speed of the electron is given by : **(C.B.S.E. Med. 1998)**

(a) $\sqrt{\frac{a_0 m}{\varepsilon_0 e}}$ (b) $\sqrt{\frac{em}{a_0 \varepsilon_0}}$
(c) $\frac{e}{\sqrt{4\pi \varepsilon_0 a_0 m}}$ (d) $\frac{\sqrt{4\pi \varepsilon_0 a_0 m}}{e}$

135. The amount of $_{84}P^{240}$ required to provide a source of α-particles of 5 millicurie strength when half life of P_0 is 138 days will be :

(a) 1.11×10^{-3} gm (b) 2×10^{-6} gm
(c) 1.11×10^{-6} gm (d) 2.7×10^{-6} gm

136. If one gm of U^{238} emits 1.24×10^4 α-particles per sec, then half life of U^{238} is :

(a) 4.259×10^{10} years (b) 2.25×10^{10} years
(c) 3.870×10^{3} years (d) 5.8×10^{10} years

137. If 200 MeV energy is released in the fission of a single nucleus of $_{92}U^{235}$, then how many fissions per second must occur to produce power of 1 kW ?

(a) 2.73×10^{10} (b) 3.12×10^{13}
(c) 3.12×10^{10} (d) 2.73×10^{13}

138. At any instant there are 25% undecayed nuclei in a sample. After 10 seconds number of decayed nuclei reduces to 12.5%. Then mean life of nuclei approximately will be :

(I.I.T. 1996)

(a) 20 sec (b) 10 sec
(c) 14.43 sec (d) 17 sec

139. Half lives of two radioactive specimens are 1620 years and 810 years respectively. Emission of α- and β-particles takes place simultaneously. One fourth of the undecayed substance will be left after :

(I.I.T. 1995)

(a) 1080 years (b) 1040 years
(c) 980 years (d) 940 years

140. If half life of radium is 1,500 years, then one gram of radium loses one milligram in :

(a) 2 years (b) 3 years
(c) 4 years (d) 1 year

141. If energy released per fission of U^{235} is 185 MeV in a nuclear reactor and the reactor requires 2 kg of U^{235} for 30 days to meet the demand, then the output power of the reactor is approximately :

(a) 5,800 MW (b) 580 MW
(c) 58 MW (d) 58 kW

142. When an electron makes a transition from n_1 to n_2 such that its time period increases eight times, then possible values of n_1 and n_2 are :

(a) $n_1 = 6, n_2 = 3$ (b) $n_1 = 2, n_2 = 4$
(c) $n_1 = 4, n_2 = 2$ (d) $n_1 = 3, n_2 = 6$

143. Graph drawn between log $\left(\frac{R}{R_0}\right)$ and mass number (A) will be : (where R is radius of the nucleus)

(a) a parabola (b) a straight-line
(c) a circle (d) an ellipse

144. An atom is made up of a proton and an imaginary particle of double the mass of e^- but having same charge as one electron. Apply Bohr's theory and consider all possible transitions of this imaginary particle to the 1st excited level. The longest wavelength emitted in terms of Rydberg's constant will be : **(I.I.T. Screening 2000)**

(a) $\frac{36}{5R}$ (b) $\frac{18}{5R}$
(c) $\frac{9}{5R}$ (d) $\frac{4}{R}$

145. A radioactive sample at any instant has its disintegration rate 5,000 disintegrations per minute. After 5 minutes, the rate is 1250 disintegrations per minute. Then the decay constant per minute is : **(A.I.E.E.E. 2003)**

(a) 0.1 log 2 (b) 0.8 log 2
(c) 0.4 log 2 (d) 0.2 log 2

146. The wavelength of 1st line of Balmer series is x and the 2nd line of Balmer series is 4861 Å, then value of x is

(a) 4101 Å (b) 4340 Å
(c) 1216 Å (d) 6562 Å

147. An electron emitted in β-radiation originates from **(I.I.T. 2001)**

(a) inner orbit of atoms
(b) proton escaping from the nucleus
(c) decay of neutron in a nucleus
(d) free electron existing in nuclei

148. The activity of a radioactive sample at a certain time is 4,750 disintegrations per minute. Five minutes later the activity becomes 2700 disintegrations per minute. Then the decay constant of the sample is :

(Roorkee 1986)

(a) 0.1131 per minute (b) 1.113 per minute
(c) 0.2262 per minute (d) 2.62 per minute

149. In Q.148 half life of the sample is :

(Roorkee 1986)

(a) 12 minutes (b) 18 minutes
(c) 6.13 minutes (d) 2.7 minutes

150. If the atom $_{100}Fm^{257}$ follows the Bohr model and the radius of $_{100}Fm^{257}$ is n times the Bohr radius, then n is :

(I.I.T. Screening 2003)

(a) 1/4 (b) 4
(c) 200 (d) 100

151. The binding energy of electron in H-atom is 13.6 eV, the energy required to remove the electron from the 1st excited state of Li^{++} is :

(a) 3.4 eV (b) 30.6 eV
(c) 122.4 eV (d) 13.6 eV

152. Energy in the Sun is generated mainly by :

(a) Fusion of radioactive material
(b) Fusion of helium atoms
(c) Chemical reaction
(d) Fusion of hydrogen atoms

153. In nuclear fusion :

(a) a heavy nucleus breaks into two lighter nuclei
(b) a light nucleus breaks by bombardment of thermal neutrons
(c) a heavy nucleus breaks by bombardment of thermal neutrons
(d) two light nuclei fuse together to form a heavy nucleus and other possible products

154. Out of the following spectral series of hydrogen spectrum, the one which lies wholly in the ultraviolet region is :

(a) Lyman series (b) Paschen series

(c) Brackett series (d) Balmer series

155. Characteristic X-ray radiation is emitted when :

(a) the valence electrons in the target atom are removed as a result of the collision

(b) the bombarding electrons knock out electrons from the inner shell of the target atoms and one of the outer electrons falls into this vacancy

(c) the source of electrons emits a monoenergetic beam

(d) the electrons are accelerated to a fixed energy

156. Range of nuclear force is about :

(a) 7.2×10^{-4} m (b) 1.5×10^{-15} m

(c) 1.6×10^{-19} m (d) 6.6×10^{-34} m

157. If multiplication factor is greater than unity in a nuclear fission reaction involving neutron capture; then :

(a) process stops after some time

(b) process cannot stop

(c) explosion may result

(d) explosion cannot take place

158. The half-life period of a radioactive substance is 5 minutes. The amount of substance decayed in 20 minutes will be :

(a) 93.75% (b) 75%

(c) 25% (d) 6.25%

159. If elements with principal quantum number $n > 4$ were not allowed in nature, the number of possible elements would be :

(a) 64 (b) 60

(c) 32 (d) 4

160. In the reactions

${}_7N^{14} + {}_2He^4 \to X + {}_1H^1$, X represents :

(a) ${}_4N^{17}$ (b) ${}_8He^{17}$

(c) ${}_8F^{17}$ (d) ${}_8O^{17}$

161. What happens when high speed electrons hit a target of high atomic number ?

(a) Heat is produced and simultaneously continuous and characteristic X-rays are produced.

(b) Only continuous and characteristic X-rays are produced.

(c) Only continuous X-rays are produced.

(d) Only heat is produced.

162. In obtaining X-ray photograph of our hand, we use the principle of :

(a) Ionization produced by the X-rays

(b) Photoelectric effect

(c) Image formation by optical system

(d) Shadow photography

163. Number of α and β particles emitted in the nuclear reaction ${}_{90}Th^{238} \to {}_{84}Bi^{212}$ are :

(a) 4 α and 1 β (b) 4 α and 2 β

(c) 3 α and 7 β (d) 4 α and 5 β

164. The half life of radium is 1,600 years. The fraction of a sample of radium that would remain after 6,400 years is :

(a) $\frac{1}{12}$ (b) $\frac{1}{16}$

(c) $\frac{1}{14}$ (d) $\frac{1}{18}$

165. Binding energies of ${}_1H^2$, ${}_2He^4$, ${}_{26}Fe^{56}$ and ${}_{92}U^{235}$ are 2.22, 28.3, 492 and 1786 MeV respectively. Most stable nuclei of these is :

(a) ${}_1H^2$ (b) ${}_2He^4$

(c) ${}_{26}Fe^{56}$ (d) ${}_{92}U^{235}$

166. 1 gram of radioactive element reduces to 1/3 gram at the end of 2 days. Then the mass of the element remaining at the end of 6 days is (in gm) :

(a) 1/9 (b) 1/6

(c) 1/ 27 (d) 1/12

167. A nucleus ruptures into two nuclear parts which have their velocity ratio as 2 : 1. Ratio of their nuclear size will be :

(a) $1 : 2^{1/3}$ (b) $2^{1/3} : 1$

(c) $3^{1/2} : 1$ (d) $1 : 3^{1/2}$

168. A particle having velocity equal to 1/10th of light will cross the nucleus in about :
(a) 10^{-34} sec (b) 10^{-22} sec
(c) 10^{-19} sec (d) 10^{-15} sec

169. What is binding energy of hydrogen nucleus?
(a) Zero (b) 13.6 eV
(c) More than 13.6 eV (d) Infinite

170. An isobar is produced in :
(a) β emission
(b) α emission
(c) Proton emission
(d) Deuteron emission

171. When hydrogen atom is in its first excited level, its radius is :
(a) half of the radius of hydrogen atom in its ground state
(b) same as radius of hydrogen atom in its ground state
(c) twice of the radius of hydrogen atom in its ground state
(d) four times as the hydrogen atom in its ground state.

172. Atomic weight of Boron is 10.81. Boron has two isotopes $_5B^{10}$ and $_5B^{11}$. Ratio of $_5B^{10}$ and $_5B^{11}$ in nature is :
(a) 19 : 81 (b) 81 : 19
(c) 10 : 11 (d) 11 : 10

173. In the disintegration series
$_{92}U^{238} \xrightarrow{\alpha} X \xrightarrow{-\beta} {_Z}Y^A$ the value of Z and A respectively will be :
(a) 92, 236 (b) 88, 230
(c) 90, 234 (d) 91, 234

174. r_1 and r_2 are the radii of atomic nuclei of mass numbers 64 and 27 respectively. The ratio (r_1/r_2) is :
(a) 64 / 27 (b) 27 / 64
(c) 4/3 (d) 1

175. Which of the following transitions in a hydrogen atom emits the photons of highest frequency ?
(a) n = 3 to n = 7 (b) n = 2 to n = 1
(c) n = 6 to n = 2 (d) n = 1 to n = 3

176. An atom of mass number 17 and atomic number 8 captures an α-particle and then emits a proton. Then mass number and atomic number of the resulting product will be :
(a) 20, 9 (b) 21, 10
(c) 20, 10 (d) 21, 9

177. Half-lives of two radioactive substances A and B are respectively 20 minutes and 40 minutes. Initially, the samples of A and B have equal number of nuclei. After 80 minutes, the ratio of remaining number of nuclei of A and B is :
(a) 1 : 16 (b) 4 : 1
(c) 1 : 4 (d) 1 : 1

178. A particle, which can easily penetrate a nucleus, is :
(a) Proton (b) Electron
(c) α-particle (d) Neutron

179. The absorption transitions between the first and the fourth energy states of hydrogen atom are 3. The emission transitions between these states will be :
(a) 3 (b) 4
(c) 5 (d) 6

180. If a proton is completely converted into energy, then energy released will be about :
(a) 13.6 MeV (b) 931 MeV
(c) 931 joules (d) 931 calories

181. If an element X decays into $_{88}Ra^{238}$ with the emission of a positron and three alpha particles, then atomic number and mass number of initial element will be :
(a) 90, 238 (b) 93, 240
(c) 88, 228 (d) None of these

182. If the atom $_{100}Fm^{257}$ follows the Bohr model and the radius of $_{100}Fm^{257}$ is n times the Bohr radius, then n is

(I.I.T. 2003 Screening)

(a) 100 (b) 200
(c) 4 (d) 1/4

183. For uranium nucleus how does its mass vary with volume ? **(I.I.T. 2003 Screening)**

(a) $m \propto V$ (b) $m \propto 1/V$
(c) $m \propto \sqrt{V}$ (d) $m \propto V^2$

184. A nucleus with mass number 220 initially at rest emits an α-particle. If the Q value of the reaction is 5.5 MeV, calculate the kinetic energy of the α-particle :

(I.I.T. 2004 Screening)

(a) 4.4 MeV (b) 5.4 MeV
(c) 5.6 MeV (d) 6.5 MeV

185. A 280 days old radioactive substance shows an activity of 6,000 dps. 140 days later its activity becomes 3,000 dps. What was its initial activity ? **(I.I.T. 2004 Screening)**

(a) 20,000 dps (b) 24,000 dps
(c) 12,000 dps (d) 6,000 dps

186. The atomic number (Z) of an element whose K_α wavelength λ is 11. The atomic number of an element whose K_α wavelength is 4λ is equal to : **(I.I.T. 2005 Screening)**

(a) 6 (b) 11
(c) 44 (d) 4

187. Given is a sample of Radium-226 having half-life of 4 days. Find the probability that a nucleus disintegrates after 2 half lives :

(I.I.T. 2006 Screening)

(a) 1 (b) 1/2
(c) 1.5 (d) 3/4

188. In hydrogen-like atom (Z = 11), n^{th} line of Lyman series has wavelength λ equal to the de-Broglie's wavelength of electron in the level from which it originated. What is the value of n ? **(I.I.T. 2006 Screening)**

(a) 24 (b) 23
(c) 25 (d) 26

189. Match the following columns :

Column I	Column II
(i) Nuclear fusion	(P) Converts some matter into energy
(ii) Nuclear fission	(Q) Generally possible for nuclei with low atomic number
(iii) β-decay	(R) Generally possible for nuclei with higher atomic number
(iv) Exothermic nuclear reaction	(S) Essentially proceeds by weak nuclear forces.

(a) i $\rightarrow$ P, Q, ii $\rightarrow$ P, R, iii $\rightarrow$ S, P, iv$\rightarrow$ P, Q, R
(b) i $\rightarrow$ P, Q, R, ii $\rightarrow$ P, R, iii $\rightarrow$ Q, P, iv $\rightarrow$ P, R
(c) i $\rightarrow$ Q, R, ii $\rightarrow$ P, Q, iii $\rightarrow$ S, P , iv $\rightarrow$ R, Q
(d) i $\rightarrow$ P,Q, ii $\rightarrow$ S, P, iii $\rightarrow$ P, Q, R, iv $\rightarrow$ P, Q

190. Starting with a sample of pure ^{66}Cu, 7/8 of it decays into Zn in 15 minutes. The corresponding half-life is :

(A.I.E.E.E. 2005)

(a) 10 minutes (b) 15 minutes
(c) 5 minutes (d) $7\frac{1}{2}$ minutes

191. If radius of $_{13}Al^{27}$ nucleus is estimated to be 3.6 Fermi, then the radius of $_{52}Te^{125}$ nucleus is nearly : **(A.I.E.E.E. 2005)**

(a) 6 fermi (b) 8 fermi
(c) 4 fermi (d) 5 fermi

192. The diagram shows the energy levels for an electron in a certain atom. Which transition shown represents the emission of a photon with the most energy ? **(A.I.E.E.E. 2005)**

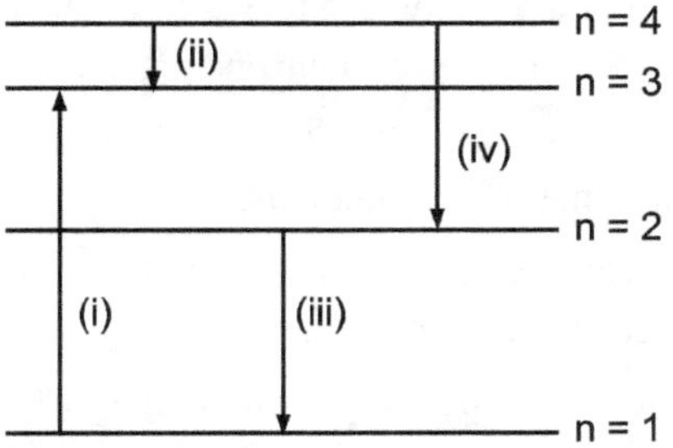

(a) (iii) (b) (iv)
(c) (i) (d) (ii)

193. A nuclear transformation is denoted by X(n, α) ${}^{7}_{3}$Li. Which of the following is the nucleus of element X ? **(A.I.E.E.E. 2005)**

(a) ${}_{6}C^{12}$ (b) ${}_{5}B^{10}$
(c) ${}_{5}B^{9}$ (d) ${}_{4}Be^{11}$

194. An alpha nucleus of energy $\frac{1}{2}mv^2$ bombards a heavy nuclear target of charge Ze. Then the distance of closest approach for the alpha nucleus will be proportional to : **(A.I.E.E.E. 2006)**

(a) $\frac{1}{Ze}$ (b) v^2
(c) $\frac{1}{m}$ (d) $\frac{1}{v^4}$

195. The energy spectrum of β-particles [number N(E) as a function of β-energy E] emitted from a radioactive source is : **(A.I.E.E.E. 2006)**

(a)
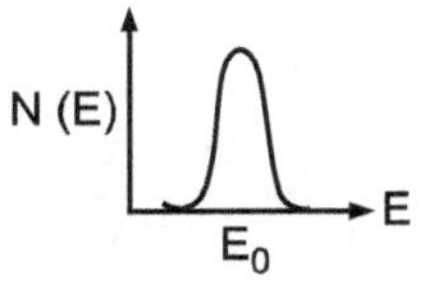

(b)
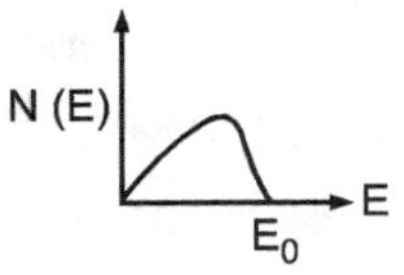

(c)
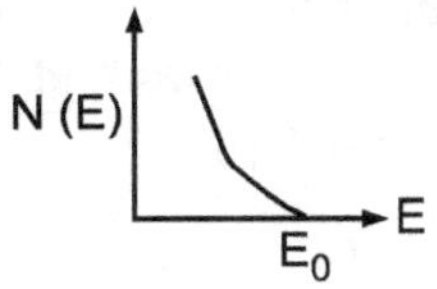

(d)
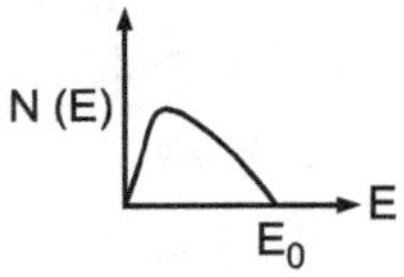

196. When ${}_{3}Li^{7}$ nuclei are bombarded by protons and the resultant nuclei are ${}_{4}Be^{8}$, then the emitted particles will be :

(a) Neutrons (b) Alpha particles
(c) Beta particles (d) Gamma photons

197. If the binding energy per nucleon in ${}_{3}Li^{7}$ and ${}_{2}He^{4}$ nuclei are 5.60 MeV·and 7.06 MeV respectively, then in the reaction

$$p + {}_{3}Li^{7} \rightarrow {}_{2}He^{4}$$

energy of proton must be: **(A.I.E.E.E. 2006)**

(a) 39.2 MeV (b) 28.24 MeV
(c) 17.28 MeV (d) 1.46 MeV

198. The radius of a nucleus is : **(MHT - CET 1999)**

(a) directly proportional to its mass number
(b) inversely proportional to its atomic weight
(c) directly proportional to the cube root of its mass number
(d) none of these

199. Charge on an α-particle is: **(MHT - CET 2000)**

(a) 1.6×10^{-19} C (b) 3.2×10^{-19} C
(c) 16×10^{-20} C (d) 4.8×10^{-19} C

200. Unit of 'λ' in radioactivity is : **(MHT - CET 2002)**

(a) m
(b) (unit of half-life)$^{-1}$
(c) (year)$^{-1}$
(d) sec

201. What is the amount of energy released, when 3 kg mass is annihilated? **(MHT - CET 2003)**

(a) 22×10^{16} J (b) 18×10^{16} J
(c) 27×10^{16} J (d) 9×10^{16} J

202. In Bohr atom, the angular velocity of electron is : **(MHT - CET 2004)**

(a) inversely proportional to n^2
(b) inversely proportional to n^3
(c) directly proportional to n
(d) independent of n

203. Plank's constant has same dimensions as : **(MHT - CET 2004)**

(a) Energy
(b) Angular momentum
(c) Mass
(d) Force

204. Which of the following transitions of electron in H atom give the highest frequency for photon emission? **(MHT - CET 2006)**

(a) $n_1 = 1$ to $n_2 = 2$ (b) $n_1 = 2$ to $n_2 = 1$
(c) $n_1 = 2$ to $n_2 = 5$ (d) $n_1 = 5$ to $n_2 = 2$

205. The magnitude of the P.E. of the electron in the first orbit of the Bohr's atom is E. Its K.E. is : **(MHT - CET 2007)**

(a) E (b) 2E
(c) E/2 (d) E/4

206. Radius of nth Bohr's orbit is directly proportional to : **(MHT - CET 2007)**

(a) n (b) $\sqrt{n}$
(c) n^{-1} (d) n^2

207. What is the ratio of orbital magnetic moment and linear momentum of an electron in Bohr's atom? **(MHT - CET 2008)**

(a) e/2m (b) e/m
(c) 2e/m (d) m/2e

208. If F is the force between two electrons placed at a distance of 1 m, then Rydberg's constant is : **(MHT - CET 2008)**

(a) $\frac{m\pi F}{h^3 c}$ (b) $\frac{2m\pi^2 F}{h^3 c}$
(c) $\frac{2m\pi^2 F^2}{h^3 c}$ (d) $\frac{m\pi F^2}{h^3 c}$

209. If the velocity of an electron in its first orbit of hydrogen atom is 2.1×10^6 m/s, then its velocity in the third orbit is : **(MHT - CET 2008)**

(a) 7×10^6 m/s (b) 7×10^5 m/s
(c) 7×10^4 m/s (d) 2×10^4 m/s

210. Find the wrong statement : **(T.N.P.C.E.E. 2002)**

(a) Half-life of neutron is 13 minutes.
(b) The stability of a nucleus is determined by the number of neutrons present in it.
(c) Both fast and slow neutrons are capable of penetrating a nucleus.
(d) A free neutron decays into a proton, an electron and positron.

211. In nuclear fission the percentage of mass converted into energy is about : **(Karnataka C.E.T. 2002)**

(a) 0.01 % (b) 10%
(c) 1% (d) 0.1%

212. The SI unit of radioactivity is : **(Karnataka C.E.T. 2002)**

(a) Rutherford (b) Roentgen
(c) Becqueral (d) Curie

213. Function of controlling rod in nuclear reactor is to : **(C.E.T. Chandigarh 2002)**

(a) Attenuate neutron
(b) Speed up the neutrons
(c) Absorb neutrons
(d) Slow down the neutrons

214. In the fission process represented by reaction: **(Haryana C.E.E.T. 2002)**
${}_{92}U^{235} + {}_0n^1 \longrightarrow {}_{56}Ba^{144} + {}_{36}Kr^{235} + 3{}^0n_1$ if ${}_{92}U^{235} = 235.95$ amu ${}_{56}Ba^{144} = 143.28$ amu and ${}_{56}Kr^{89} = 88.99$ amu and ${}_0n^1 = 1.01$ amu, then the energy released is :

(a) 100 MeV (b) 190 MeV
(c) 250 MeV (d) 30 MeV

215. A radioactive element has half life of 3.6 days. In what time will it be left $1/32^{nd}$ undecayed ? **(Manipal 2002)**

(a) 4 days (b) 12 days
(c) 18 days (d) 24 days

216. A nuclear reaction given by, **(C.B.S.E. 2003)**

$_{Z}X^{A} \longrightarrow {}_{Z+1}Y^{A} + {}_{-1}e^{0} + \bar{\upsilon}$ represents :

(a) γ-decay (b) Fusion

(c) Fission (d) β-decay

217. The mass number of a nucleus is : **(C.B.S.E. 2003)**

(a) always more than its atomic number

(b) sometimes equal to its atomic number

(c) sometimes less than and sometimes more than its atomic number

(d) always less than its atomic number

218. Which one of the following is most fissionable ? **(A.F.M.C. 2003)**

(a) Uranium (b) Plutonium

(c) Thorium (d) None

219. A radioactive substance has an average life of 5 hours. In a time of 4 hours : **(Orissa. J.E.E. 2003)**

(a) half of the active nuclei decay

(b) less than half of the active nuclei decay

(c) more than half of the active nuclei decay

(d) all active nuclei decay

220. Shorter wavelength is of : **(Punjab P.M.T. 2003)**

(a) infrared rays (b) γ–rays

(c) visible light (d) X-rays

221. A nucleus represented by the symbol $^{A}_{Z}X$ has: **(C.B.S.E. 2004)**

(a) Z protons and A – Z neutrons

(b) Z protons and A neutrons

(c) A protons and Z – A neutrons

(d) Z neutrons and A – Z protons

222. The Bohr model of atoms : **(C.B.S.E. 2004)**

(a) uses Einstein's photo-electric equation

(b) predicts continuous emission spectra for atoms

(c) predicts the same emission spectra for all types of atoms

(d) assumes that angular momentum of electrons is quantized

223. When temperature of a metal increases **(MHT-CET 2007)**

(a) K.E. of the electrons increases

(b) K.E. of the electrons decreases

(c) All the electrons are ejected from the atom

(d) All the atoms are ionized

224. An electron is fired through a region of crossed electric and magnetic field (0.05 T). The electric field is formed between two plates separated by a distance of 2 mm having a P.D. of 125 V. The speed of the electron is **(MHT-CET 2007)**

(a) 12.5×10^6 m/s (b) 1250 km/s

(c) 125 km/s (d) 1.25×10^7 m/s

225. A charge q and mass m is fired perpendicular to a magnetic field (B) with a velocity V. The frequency of revolution of the charge is **(MHT-CET 2007)**

(a) 2π/Bq (b) 2πBq/m

(c) 2πm/Bq (d) Bq/2πm

226. The stopping potential of a photoelectric diode is 9 volts, $e/m = 1.8 \times 10^{11}$ C kg^{-1}, then what is its velocity? **(MHT-CET 2008)**

(a) 1.8×10^6 m/s (b) 1.8×10^5 m/s

(c) 2.1×10^5 m/s (d) 1.8×10^4 m/s

227. An electron enters in a magnetic field of induction 2 mT with velocity of 1.8×10^7 m/s. The radius of circular path is **(MHT-CET 2008)**

(a) 5.1 cm (b) 5.1 mm

(c) 5 km (d) 2.1 cm

228. In photoelectric effect, if the intensity of light is doubled, then maximum kinetic energy of photoelectrons will be **(MHT-CET 2009)**

(a) double (b) half

(c) four times (d) no change

229. The de-Broglie wavelength of an electron in the ground state of hydrogen atom is **(MHT-CET 2010)**

(a) πr^2 (b) $2\pi r$

(c) πr (d) $\sqrt{2}\pi r$

230. Calcium plate has maximum possible radiation of wavelength 1 of 400 nm to eject electrons. Its work function is **(MHT-CET 2010)**

(a) 2.3 eV (b) 3.1 eV

(c) 4.5 eV (d) 1.8 eV

231. Two particles of same charge are accelerated to same potential difference and they enter perpendicular to uniform magnetic field and move in circular paths of radii r_1 and r_2. Ratio of their masses is **(MHT-CET 2011)**

(a) $r_1 : r_2$ (b) $r_2^2 : r_1^2$

(c) $r_2 : r_1$ (d) $r_1^2 : r_2^2$

232. If the wavelength λ of photon decreases, then momentum and energy of photon **(MHT-CET 2011)**

(a) both increase

(b) both decrease

(c) momentum increases and energy decreases

(d) momentum decreases and energy increases

233. The de-Broglie's wavelength in 1st Bohr's orbit is **(MHT-CET 20011)**

(a) πr (b) $2\pi r$

(c) $3\pi r$ (d) $\pi r/2$

234. In Millikan's experiment, an oil drop having charge q and mass m, gets accelerated by applying a potential difference V in between two plates separated by a distance 'd'. The acceleration is **(MHT-CET 2012)**

(a) qVd (b) $q\frac{d}{V}$

(c) $\frac{qm}{Vd}$ (d) $\frac{qV}{md}$

235. The de-Broglie wavelength λ associated with charged particle of charge q, mass m and potential difference V is **(MHT-CET 2012)**

(a) $\frac{h}{\sqrt{2\,mqV}}$ (b) $\frac{h^2}{\sqrt{2mqV}}$

(c) $\frac{h}{\sqrt{mqV}}$ (d) $\frac{h}{\sqrt{2qV}}$

236. If a charged particle of charge q and mass m moves in a circular path in a magnetic field of induction B, under a potential of V volts, then radius of circular path is **(MHT-CET 2012)**

(a) $\sqrt{\frac{2\,mV}{q}}$ (b) $\frac{B}{1}\sqrt{\frac{2\,mV}{q}}$

(c) $\frac{1}{B}\sqrt{\frac{2\,mV}{q}}$ (d) $\frac{1}{B^2}\sqrt{\frac{2\,mV}{q}}$

237. For photoelectric emission from certain metal, the cutoff frequency is υ. If radiation of frequency 2υ impinges on the metal plate, the maximum possible velocity of the emitted electron will be (m is the electron mass) **(NEET 2013)**

(a) $\sqrt{\frac{h\upsilon}{m}}$ (b) $\sqrt{\frac{2h\upsilon}{m}}$

(c) $2\sqrt{\frac{h\upsilon}{m}}$ (d) $\sqrt{\frac{h\upsilon}{(2m)}}$

ANSWER KEY

1. (d)	**2.** (b)	**3.** (a)	**4.** (a)	**5.** (a)	**6.** (c)	**7.** (c)	**8.** (a)	**9.** (b)	**10.**(c)
11.(d)	**12.**(d)	**13.**(d)	**14.**(b)	**15.**(a)	**16.**(b)	**17.**(b)	**18.**(d)	**19.**(b)	**20.**(b)
21.(c)	**22.**(c)	**23.**(c)	**24.**(b)	**25.**(d)	**26.**(a)	**27.**(c)	**28.**(a)	**29.**(a)	**30.**(c)
31.(d)	**32.**(b)	**33.**(d)	**34.**(d)	**35.**(b)	**36.**(b)	**37.**(c)	**38.**(c)	**39.**(b)	**40.**(d)
41.(d)	**42.**(d)	**43.**(c)	**44.**(d)	**45.**(b)	**46.**(b)	**47.**(b)	**48.**(c)	**49.**(b)	**50.**(b)
51.(a)	**52.**(d)	**53.**(d)	**54.**(d)	**55.**(c)	**56.**(d)	**57.**(b)	**58.**(a)	**59.**(c)	**60.**(a)
61.(c)	**62.**(b)	**63.**(b)	**64.**(d)	**65.**(c)	**66.**(a)	**67.**(b)	**68.**(c)	**69.**(d)	**70.**(d)
71.(b)	**72.**(c)	**73.**(b)	**74.**(b)	**75.**(a)	**76.**(a)	**77.**(d)	**78.**(b)	**79.**(a)	**80.**(d)
81.(a)	**82.**(c)	**83.**(c)	**84.**(d)	**85.**(c)	**86.**(b)	**87.**(c)	**88.**(b)	**89.**(a)	**90.**(d)
91.(c)	**92.**(a)	**93.**(d)	**94.**(c)	**95.**(b)	**96.**(a)	**97.**(d)	**98.**(d)	**99.**(d)	**100.** (d)
101. (b)	**102.** (d)	**103.** (a)	**104.** (b)	**105.** (c)	**106.** (c)	**107.** (d)	**108.** (b)	**109.** (b)	**110.** (a)
111. (b)	**112.** (b)	**113.** (c)	**114.** (b)	**115.** (c)	**116.** (d)	**117.** (c)	**118.** (a)	**119.** (b)	**120.** (b)
121. (c)	**122.** (a)	**123.** (d)	**124.** (c)	**125.** (c)	**126.** (c)	**127.** (d)	**128.** (b)	**129.** (a)	**130.** (b)
131. (b)	**132.** (a)	**133.** (b)	**134.** (c)	**135.** (c)	**136.** (a)	**137.** (b)	**138.** (c)	**139.** (a)	**140.** (a)
141. (c)	**142.** (a&c)	**143.** (b)	**144.** (b)	**145.** (c)	**146.** (d)	**147.** (c)	**148.** (a)	**149.** (c)	**150.** (a)
151. (b)	**152.** (d)	**153.** (d)	**154.** (a)	**155.** (b)	**156.** (b)	**157.** (c)	**158.** (d)	**159.** (b)	**160.** (d)
161. (a)	**162.** (d)	**163.** (b)	**164.** (b)	**165.** (c)	**166.** (c)	**167.** (a)	**168.** (b)	**169.** (b)	**170.** (d)
171. (d)	**172.** (a)	**173.** (d)	**174.** (c)	**175.** (b)	**176.** (a)	**177.** (c)	**178.** (d)	**179.** (d)	**180.** (b)
181. (d)	**182.** (d)	**183.** (a)	**184.** (b)	**185.** (b)	**186.** (a)	**187.** (b)	**188.** (b)	**189.** (a)	**190.** (c)
191. (a)	**192.** (a)	**193.** (b)	**194.** (c)	**195.** (d)	**196.** (d)	**197.** (c)	**198.** (c)	**199.** (b)	**200.** (b)
201. (c)	**202.** (b)	**203.** (b)	**204.** (b)	**205.** (c)	**206.** (d)	**207.** (a)	**208.** (c)	**209.** (b)	**210.** (d)
211. (d)	**212.** (c)	**213.** (c)	**214.** (b)	**215.** (c)	**216.** (d)	**217.** (b)	**218.** (b)	**219.** (c)	**220.** (b)
221. (a)	**222.** (d)	**223.** (a)	**224.** (b)	**225.** (d)	**226.** (a)	**227.** (a)	**228.** (d)	**229.** (b)	**230.** (b)
231. (d)	**232.** (a)	**233.** (b)	**234.** (d)	**235.** (a)	**236.** (c)	**237.** (b)			

20

SOLIDS AND SEMICONDUCTOR DEVICES

MULTIPLE CHOICE QUESTIONS

1. In a P-type semiconductor the majority carriers of current are: **(C.B.S.E. Med 1999)**
   (a) Electrons (b) Protons
   (c) Holes (d) Neutrons
2. The dopant to be added to germanium to make it N-type is: **(Karnataka Engg. 2000)**
   (a) Indium (b) Arsenic
   (c) Iodine (d) Aluminium
3. Energy gap of silicon is 1.14 eV. Maximum wavelength at which silicon will begin absorbing energy is:
   (a) 19526 Å (b) 12521 Å
   (c) 10888 Å (d) 6896 Å
4. Indium when added as impurity to silicon, gives :
   (a) P-type semiconductor
   (b) N-type semiconductor
   (c) Conductor
   (d) Insulator
5. Electrical conductivity of a semiconductor : **(P.M.T. M.P. 1993)**
   (a) does not depend on temperature
   (b) increases with rise in temperature
   (c) decreases with rise in temperature
   (d) none of these
6. Resistance decreases with increase in temperature in :
   (a) Copper (b) Aluminium
   (c) Tungsten (d) Germanium
7. In the terminology of semiconductor, what is a hole ? **(D.P.M.T. 2000)**
   (a) Space which was previously occupied by an electron.
   (b) A hole in a space-time distribution of the universe.
   (c) Space which is negatively charged.
   (d) Dense area in space which even absorbs light i.e. a black hole.
8. Number of atoms per unit cell in B.C.C. are: **(C.B.S.E. P.M.T. 2002)**
   (a) 1 (b) 2
   (c) 4 (d) 9
9. On subtracting 010101 from 101010, we get:
   (a) 001011 (b) 001100
   (c) 010101 (d) 011111
10. The forbidden energy gap in germanium and silicon in eV is : **(M.P. Engg. 2001)**
    (a) 0.7, 1.1 respectively
    (b) 1.1, 0.7 respectively
    (c) 1.0, 0 respectively
    (d) 0, 1.1 respectively
11. Pt and Ge are heated upto 3000°C and after that they are cooled. In the process of heating :
    (a) resistance of Ge will decrease and of Pt will increase
    (b) resistance of Ge and Pt (both) will decrease
    (c) resistance of Ge will increase and of Pt will decrease
    (d) resistance of Ge and Pt (both) will increase

12. In a P-type semiconductor: **[A.I.I.M.S. 1997]**
(a) majority carriers are negative ions
(b) majority carriers are holes
(c) majority carriers are electrons
(d) none of these

13. In a pure silicon, number of electrons and holes per unit volume are 1.5×10^{16} /m^3. If Si is doped with Boron in such a way that on doping hole density increases to 4.5×10^{22} /m^3. Then electron density in doped semiconductor will be :
(a) 7×10^9/m^3 (b) 3×10^9/m^3
(c) 5×10^9/m^3 (d) 1×10^9/ m^3.

14. Which one of the following statements is incorrect ? **(S.C.R.A. 2000)**
(a) A P-N junction diode symbol shows an arrow identifying the direction of current (forward) flow.
(b) An ideal diode is an open switch.
(c) A diode does not obey Ohm's law.
(d) An ideal diode is an ideal one-way conductor.

15. Holes exist in :
(a) semiconductors (b) insulators
(c) conductors (d) none of these

16. In a P- type silicon semiconductor doping is done at an average of one indium atom per 5×10^7 silicon atoms. If the number density of atoms in silicon specimen is 5×10^{28} atoms/m^3, then number of indium atoms in silicon per cm^3 will be :
(a) 2.5×10^{30} atoms/cm^3
(b) 2.5×10^{36} atoms/cm^3
(c) 1.0×10^{15} atoms/cm^3
(d) 1.0×10^{13} atoms/cm^3

17. For Ge, forbidden energy gap in joules is : **(M.P. Engg. 2000)**
(a) 1.76×10^{-19} (b) 1.12×10^{-19}
(c) 1.6×10^{-19} (d) Zero

18. For a crystal system, $a = b = c$, $\alpha = \beta = \gamma \neq 90°$, then the system is : **(B.H.U. 2000)**
(a) Cubic system
(b) Orthorhombic system
(c) Tetragonal system
(d) Rhombohedral system

19. Energy bands in solids are a consequence of: **(D.C.E. 2001)**
(a) Ohm's law
(b) Heisenberg's uncertainty principle
(c) Pauli's exclusion principle
(d) Bohr's theory

20. In an insulator, forbidden energy gap is of the order of :
(a) 5 eV (b) 1 eV
(c) 0.1 eV (d) 0.75 eV

21. The thickness of P-N junction is of the order of : **(B.I.T. 1990)**
(a) 10^{-8} cm (b) 10^{-6} cm
(c) 1 mm (d) 10^{-12} cm

22. Resistivity of a semiconductor is given by :
(a) $e^{-1} (n_e \mu_e + n_h \mu_h)$
(b) $e (n_e \mu_e + n_h \mu_h)^{-1}$
(c) $e^{-1} (n_e \mu_e + n_h \mu_h)^{-1}$
(d) $e (n_e \mu_e + n_h \mu_h)$

23. Which of the following, when used as dopant in silicon, produces N-type semiconductor ? **(C.B.S.E. Med 1999)**
(a) As (b) Al
(c) B (d) In

24. The nature of binding for a crystal with alternate and evenly spaced positive and negative ions is : **(C.B.S.E. Med 2000)**
(a) ionic (b) dipolar
(c) covalent (d) metallic

25. In a P-N junction diode :
(a) forward current is independent of the bias voltage
(b) reverse bias current is independent of the bias voltage

(c) current in the reverse bias condition is small

(d) forward bias current is small as compared to reverse bias current

26. Thermionic current is proportional to : **(Raj. Med 2001)**

(a) $T^{1/2}$ (b) $T^{3/2}$

(c) T^2 (d) T

27. The forbidden energy band gap is maximum in : **(A.I.E.E.E. 2002)**

(a) semiconductors

(b) super conductors

(c) insulators

(d) metals

28. Number of atoms per unit cell of a face centered cubic crystal is : **[B.H.U. 1995]**

(a) 1 (b) 4

(c) 3 (d) 2

29. Number of atoms in a unit cell of a simple cubic crystal is :

(a) 1 (b) 2

(c) 3 (d) 4

30. In a P-N-P transistor, the collector current is 10 mA. If 90% of the holes reach the collector, then emitter current will be : **[I.I.T. 1992]**

(a) 13 mA (b) 12 mA

(c) 11 mA (d) 10 mA

31. Which of the following statements is incorrect ? **(B.H.U. 2000)**

(a) In an amorphous material each grain is composed of a single representative unit.

(b) In liquid crystals periodicity is maintained in only one or two dimensions.

(c) A single representative unit spread out in whole of the material in ordered regular arrays gives a single crystal.

(d) A polycrystalline solid is composed of grains in which regular periodicity is broken inside the grains, but regularity is maintained at grain boundaries.

32. Electrical conductivity of a semiconductor increases when electromagnetic radiations of wavelength shorter than 2480 nm is incident on it. Band gap for the semiconductor is : **[I.I.T. 1997]**

(a) 1.1 eV (b) 0.9 eV

(c) 0.7 eV (d) 0.5 eV

33. In a common base amplifier, the phase difference between input signal voltage and output voltage is : **[C.B.S.E. 1990]**

(a) 0 (b) $\pi/4$

(c) $\pi/2$ (d) π

34. The forward biased diode is : **[C.B.S.E. Med 2000]**

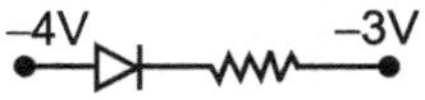

(a)

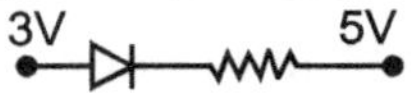

(b)

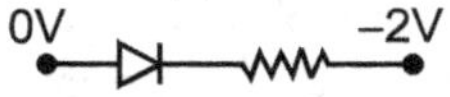

(c)

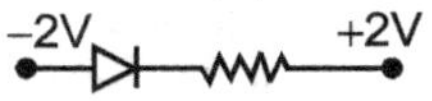

(d)

35. When a P-N junction is forward biased, then which of the following circuits gives the correct direction of current inside the semiconductor ? **[C.B.S.E. Med 1999]**

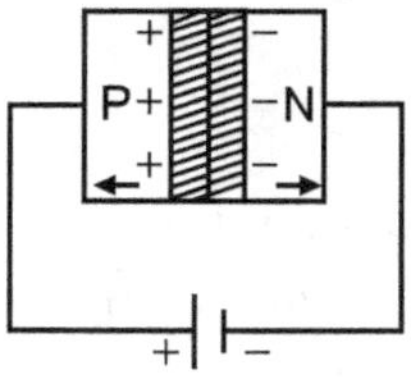

(a)

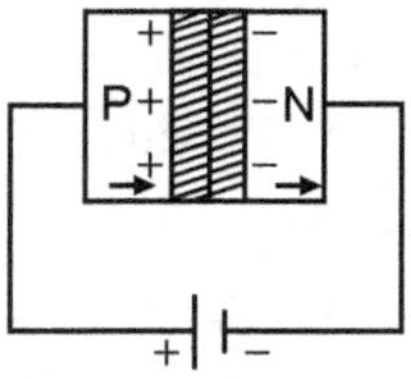

(b)

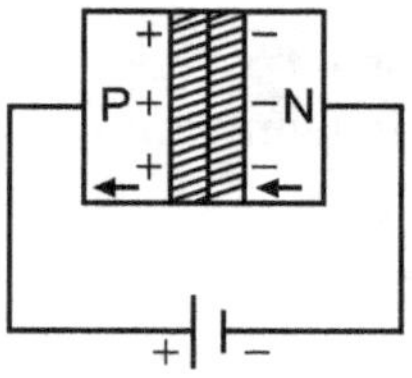

(c)

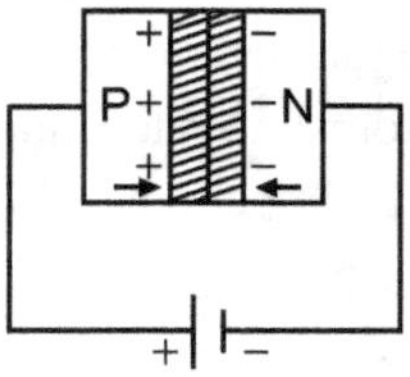

(d)

36. For triode, which one is the correct relation? **(D.P.M.T. 2001)**

(a) $\mu = 2g_m \times r_p$ (b) $\mu = \frac{g_m}{r_p}$

(c) $\mu = g_m \times r_p$ (d) None of these

37. Rectifier is used to convert : **(Haryana Engg. 2000)**

(a) high voltage to low voltage
(b) direct current to alternating current
(c) alternating current to direct current
(d) low voltage to high voltage

38. Symbol below represents : **[C.B.S.E. 1996]**

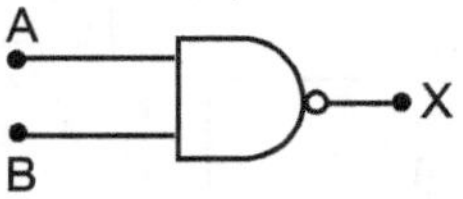

(a) NAND (b) NOR
(c) AND (d) OR

39. In a half wave rectifier which one of the output waveforms given below is true ?

(a) 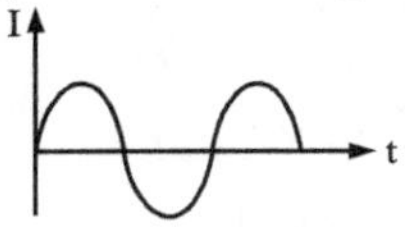
(b) 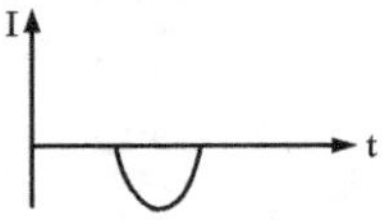
(c) 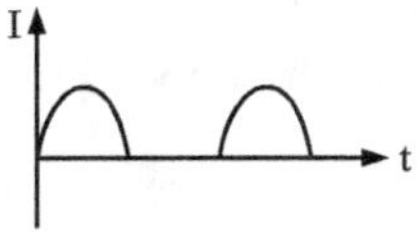
(d) 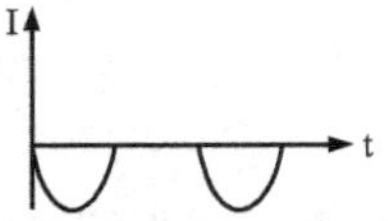

40. When the resistance between the P and N sections of a junction diode is high, then the diode acts as a :

(a) Transistor (b) Capacitor
(c) Resistor (d) None of these

41. To obtain a P-type Germanium semiconductor, germanium should be doped with : **[C.B.S.E. 1991]**

(a) Indium (b) Arsenic
(c) Antimony (d) Phosphorus

42. A P-type semiconductor is a : **[I.I.T. 1988]**

(a) Germanium crystal doped with phosphorus
(b) Germanium crystal doped with boron
(c) Silicon crystal doped with boron
(d) Silicon crystal doped with aluminium

43. On doping, the resistivity of Ge :

(a) increases
(b) increases or decreases depending upon the nature of dopant
(c) remains unchanged
(d) decreases

44. Which of the following semiconductor diodes is reverse biased ? **(D.P.M.T. 2000)**

(a) 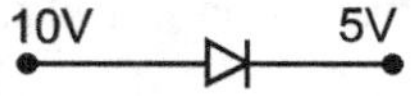

(b) 

(c) 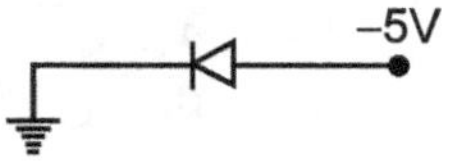

(d) 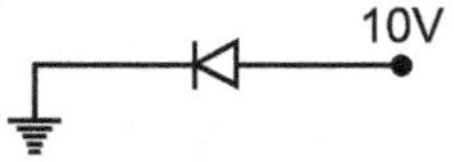

45. The correct symbol for zener diode is :

(a) 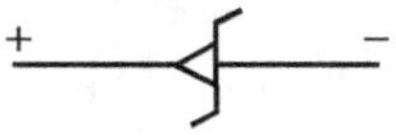
(b) 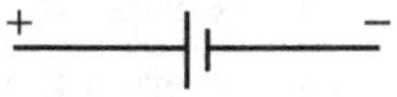
(c) 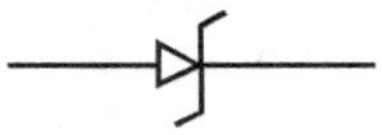
(d) 

46. Truth table below is for which gate ? **[C.B.S.E. MED 2000]**

P	Q	R
0	0	0
1	0	0
0	1	0
1	1	1

(a) NAND (b) OR
(c) NOR (d) AND.

47. Which of the following graphs, shows the V-I characteristics for a P-N junction diode?

(a) 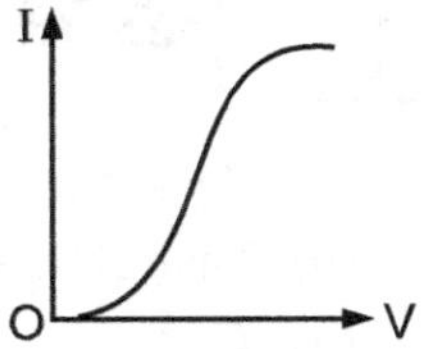
(b) 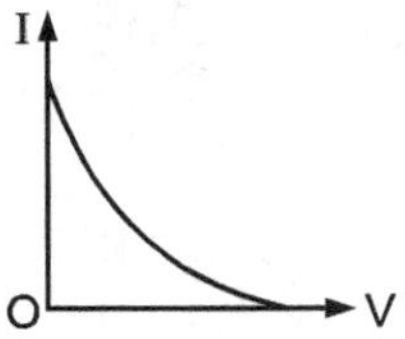
(c) 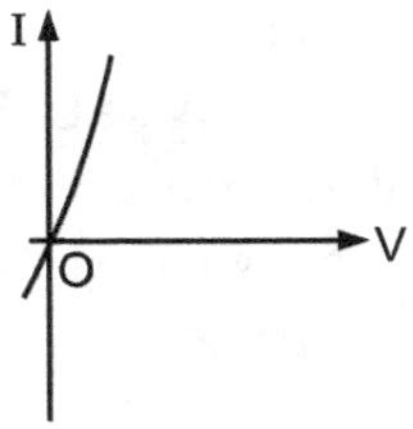
(d) 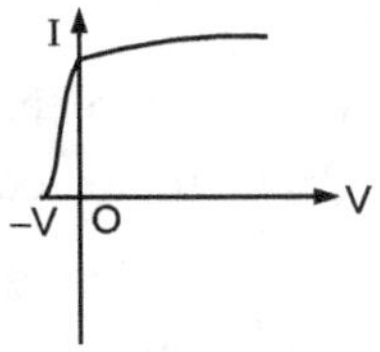

48. Transfer ratio β of a transistor is 50. Input resistance of the transistor when used in common emitter configuration is 1 kΩ. Peak value of the collector ac current for an ac input voltage of 0.01 V peak is :

[C.B.S.E. Med 1998]

(a) 1000 μA (b) 500 μA
(c) 0.250 μA (d) 0.01 μA

49. The width of a depletion layer in a P-N junction :

(a) increases when forward biased
(b) decreases when reverse biased
(c) increases when reverse biased
(d) is independent of voltage

50. In the circuit shown below potential difference between A and B is :

[P.E.T. MP 1996]

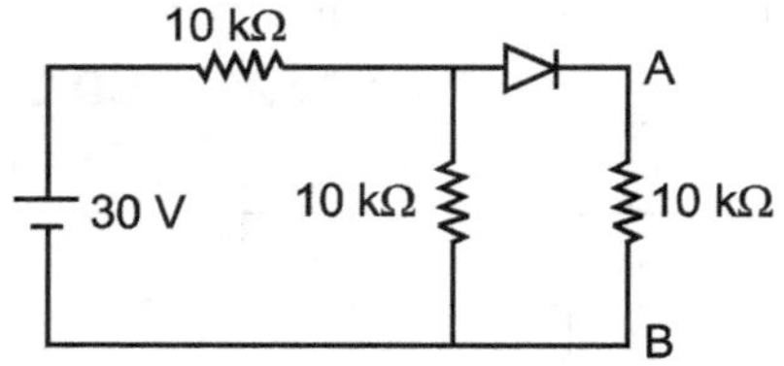

(a) 0 (b) 5 volt
(c) 10 volt (d) 15 volt

51. A full wave rectifier along with input and output is shown below. Contribution due to the diode D_1 will be : **[I.I.T. 1996]**

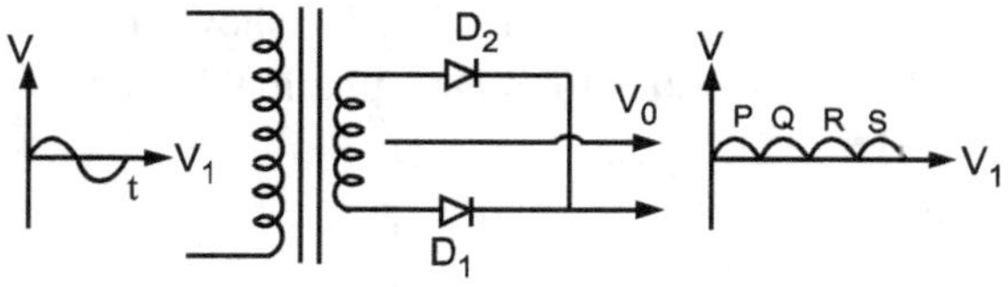

(a) P and R (b) Q and R
(c) P (d) R

52. The transistors provide good power amplification when they are used in :

(A.M.U. 1999)

(a) Common base configuration
(b) Common collector configuration
(c) Common emitter configuration
(d) None of these

53. Packing fraction of a simple cubic unit cell in cubic crystal is : **[A.F.M.C. 1997]**

(a) $\pi/8$ (b) $\pi/6$
(c) $\pi\sqrt{3}/8$ (d) $\pi/\sqrt{3}$

54. In the circuit, transistor has a current gain (β) = 100. What should be the base resistor R_B ? Neglect V_{BE}, so that $V_{CE} = 5$ V :

[C.B.S.E. 1994]

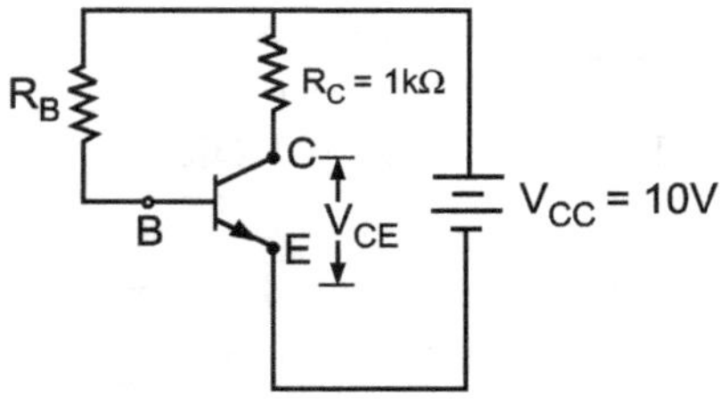

(a) 200 kΩ (b) 1 MΩ
(c) 500 kΩ (d) 2 kΩ

55. Consider the following events :

(i) Positive voltage on the anode attracting the electrons
(ii) Heating the cathode
(iii) Electrons passing the minimum potential near the cathode
(iv) Secondary electrons

The correct sequence in which these events occur inside an operating diode valve is :

(a) (i), (ii), (iii), (iv) (b) (ii), (i), (iii), (iv)
(c) (ii), (iii), (iv), (i) (d) (iv), (ii), (iii), (i)

56. A solar cell can be made from :

[Kurukshetra 1996]

(a) a thin wafer of Si doped with As
(b) a thin wafer of germanium
(c) a thin wafer of pure gallium arsenide
(d) none of these

57. In case of NPN transistor, emitter current is always greater than collector current, because : **[A.I.I.M.S. 1983]**

(a) collector side is reverse biased and emitter side is forward biased
(b) collector being reverse biased, attracts more electrons

(c) some electrons are lost in base

(d) collector side is forward biased and emitter side is reverse biased

58. In a P-N junction when diode is not connected to any circuit : **[I.I.T. 1998]**

(a) there is an electric field at the junction from N-side to P-side

(b) potential on P-side is higher than on N-side

(c) potential is same everywhere

(d) electric field at the junction is from P-side to N-side

59. In which of the following circuits diodes is forward biased ? **(Raj. Med. 2001)**

(a) 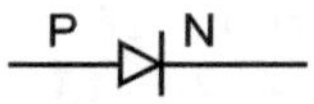

(b) 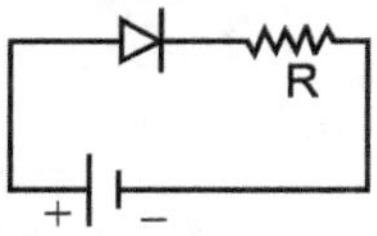

(c) 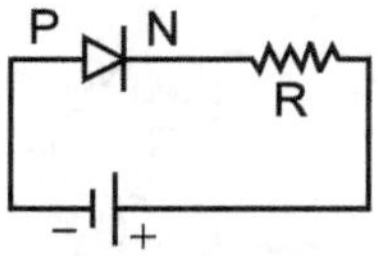

(d) None of these

60. A common emitter transistor has current gain 80. What is the change in collector current, when the change in base current is 250 μA : **[C.B.S.E. Med. 2000]**

(a) 250/80 μA (b) (250 + 80) μA

(c) (250 – 80) μA (d) 80 × 250 μA

61. Of the following options, the correct arrangement of semiconductors in the order of their increasing energy gap is :

[M.P. Med. 1993]

(a) Silicon, Germanium, Tellurium

(b) Germanium, Silicon, Tellurium

(c) Tellurium, Germanium, Silicon

(d) Tellurium, Silicon, Germanium

62. When we add binary numbers 111 and 111 we get the binary number :

(a) 222 (b) 1000

(c) 1110 (d) 000

63. At the junction of a P-N diode we get :

[C.B.S.E. Med 2002]

(a) high potential at N side and low potential at P side

(b) high potential at P side and low potential at N side

(c) P and N both are at same potential

(d) undetermined

64. In the study of transistor as an amplifier, if $\alpha = I_c / I_e$ and $\beta = I_c / I_b$, where I_c, I_b and I_e are the collector, base and emitter currents, then : **[C.B.S.E. P.M.T. 2000]**

(a) $\alpha = \beta + 1$ (b) $\alpha + \beta = 1$

(c) $\dfrac{\alpha}{\alpha + 1} = \beta$ (d) $\alpha = \dfrac{\beta}{1 + \beta}$

65. Forward biasing of a P-N junction diode is used in which of the following devices ?

(D.P.M.T. 2000)

(a) Rectifier (b) Tank circuit

(c) Transistor (d) All of these

66. Which of the following is reverse-biased ?

[D.C.E. 2001]

(a) 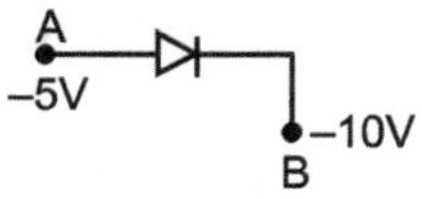

(b) 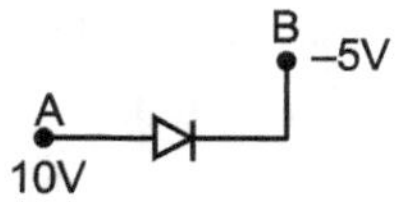

(c) 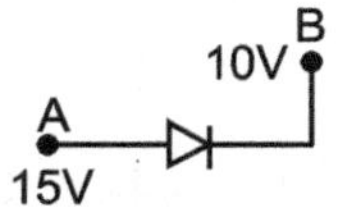

(d) 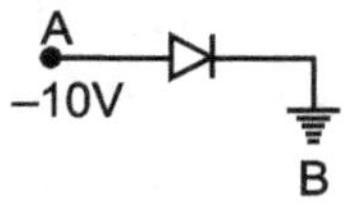

67. A pure semiconductor has: **[C.P.M.T. 1980]**

(a) a finite resistance which decreases with temperature

(b) a finite resistance which increases with temperature

(c) an infinite resistance at 0°C

(d) a finite resistance which does not depend on temperature

68. Reverse bias applied to a junction diode :

(C.B.S.E. Med 2003)

(a) lowers the potential barrier

(b) raises the potential barrier

(c) increases the majority carrier current

(d) increases the minority carrier current

69. In the middle of the depletion layer of a reverse biased P-N junction, the : **[A.I.E.E.E. 2003]**

(a) Electric field is zero

(b) Potential is maximum

(c) Electric field is maximum

(d) Potential is zero

70. Two identical P-N junctions are connected in series with a battery in three ways as shown in the figure below. Potential drop across two P-N junctions is equal in : **[I.I.T. 1989]**

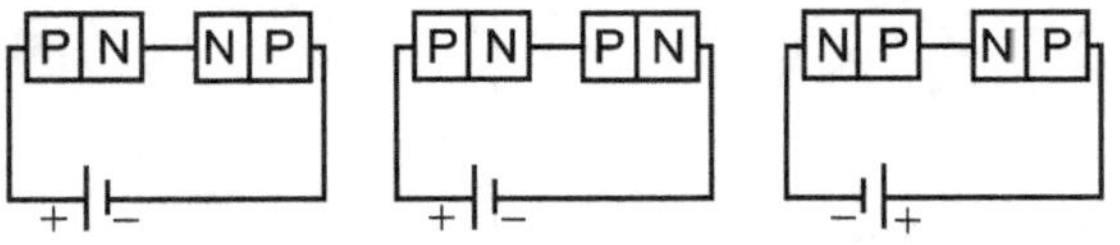

(i) (ii) (iii)

(a) Circuit (i) and circuit (ii)

(b) Circuit (i) only

(c) Circuit (i) and circuit (iii)

(d) Circuit (ii) and circuit (iii)

71. If on increasing temperature the resistance decreases, then it is : **[D.C.E. 2001]**

(a) insulator

(b) semiconductor

(c) superconductor

(d) none of the above

72. When we add two binary numbers 101010 and 010101, we get a binary number :

(a) 110111 (b) 100000

(c) 111111 (d) 010000

73. Barrier potential of a P-N junction diode does not depend on : **(C.B.S.E. Med 2003)**

(a) Diode design (b) Temperature

(c) Forward bias (d) Doping density

74. An N-P-N transistor conducts when : **(C.B.S.E. Med 2003)**

(a) collector is positive and emitter is negative with respect to base

(b) collector is positive and emitter is at same potential as the base

(c) both collector and emitter are negative with respect to base

(d) both collector and emitter are positive with respect to base

75. Combinations of NAND gates shown below are equivalent to :

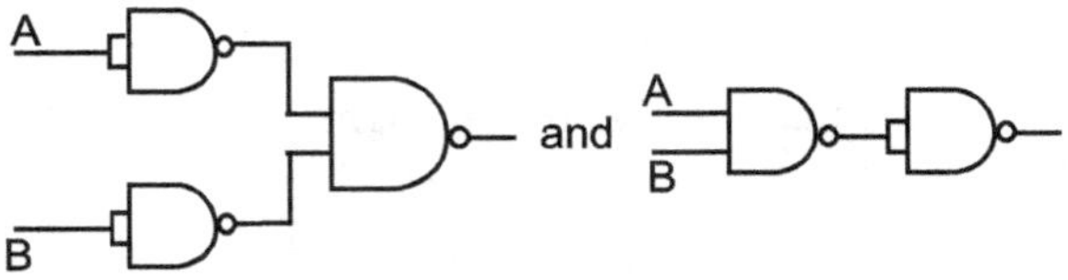

(a) AND and OR gates respectively

(b) OR and NOT gates respectively

(c) AND and NOT gates respectively

(d) OR and AND gates respectively

76. The following combination of gates is equivalent to : **(A.M.U. 1999)**

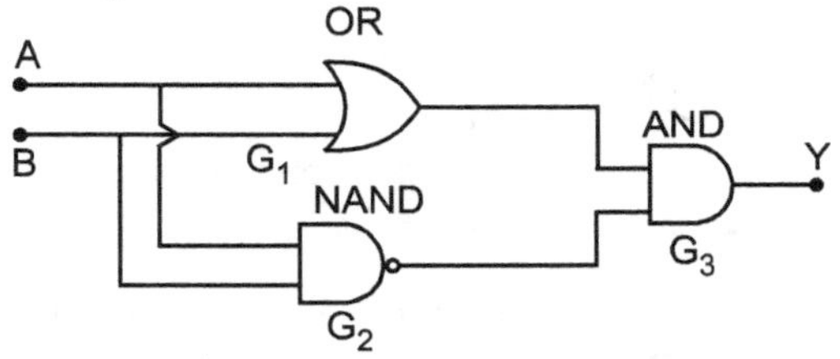

(a) XOR (b) OR

(c) NAND (d) None of these

77. Relation between two current gains (α and β) of a transistor is : **[C.B.S.E. 1997]**

(a) $\alpha = \frac{1-\beta}{\beta}$ (b) $\alpha = \frac{\beta}{1-\beta}$

(c) $\alpha = \frac{\beta}{1+\beta}$ (d) $\alpha = \frac{1+\beta}{\beta}$

78. Which one of the following is the best conductor of electricity ? **[D.P.M.T. 1983]**

(a) Silver (b) Iron

(c) Copper (d) Gold

79. In an insulator, the forbidden energy gap between the valence band and conduction band is of the order of

(a) 1 MeV (b) 2 MeV

(d) 5 eV (d) 5 MeV

80. A semiconductor is cooled from θ_1°C to θ_2 °C. Its resistance will : **(M.P. C.E.T. 1999)**
(a) first decrease and then increase
(b) not change
(c) decrease
(d) increase

81. The depletion layer in a P-N junction contains charges that are :
(a) mobile donor and acceptor ions
(b) fixed donor and acceptor ions
(c) mostly majority carriers
(d) mostly minority carriers

82. Germanium and Copper are cooled to 70 K from room temperature, then resistance of :
(a) Copper increases while that of Germanium decreases
(b) Copper decreases while that of Germanium increases
(c) Both decreases
(d) Both increases

83. The grid voltage of any triode valve is changed from −1 volt to −3 volt and the mutual conductance is 3×10^{-4} mho. The change in plate current will be :
(a) 0.8 mA (b) 0.6 mA
(c) 0.4 mA (d) 1 mA

84. An N-type and a P-type silicon can be obtained by
(a) Boron and Phosphorus respectively
(b) Sodium and Radium respectively
(c) Phosphorus and Boron respectively
(d) Sodium and Manganese respectively

85. A CE amplifier is designed with a transistor having $\alpha = 0.99$. Input impedance is 1 kΩ and load is 10 kΩ . Voltage gain will be :
(a) 9900 (b) 99000
(c) 99 (d) 990

86. GaAs is a :
(a) bad conductor
(b) metallic conductor
(c) elemental semiconductor
(d) alloy semiconductor

87. The energy gap between conduction band and valence band is of the order of 0.07 eV. It is a : **(A.F.M.C. 2000)**
(a) conductor (b) insulator
(c) alloy (d) semiconductor

88. A change in 100 μA in the base current of a common emitter NPN transistor causes a change of 10 mA in the collector current, then current gain of the transistor will be : **(N.C.E.R.T.)**
(a) 125 (b) 100
(c) 50 (d) 75

89. In the figure given below, is a

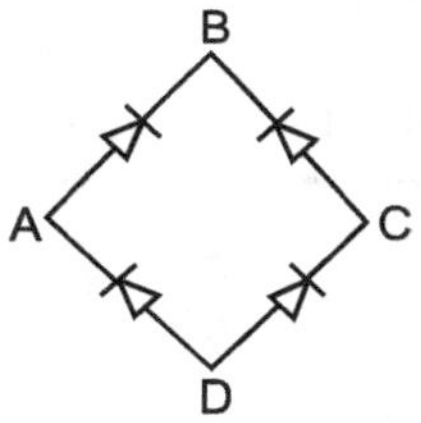

(a) half wave rectifier
(b) Bridge rectifier
(c) diode
(d) none of these

90. A silicon P-N junction is formed by adding phosphorus and indium atoms as impurities. The depletion layer of the junction has :
(a) P^+ ions on P-side and In^+ ions on N-side
(b) P^+ ions on N-side and In^+ ions on P-side
(c) In^- ions on N-side and P^+ ions on P-side
(d) In^- ions on P-side and P^+ ions on N-side

91. In a P-N junction diode width of the depletion layer : **[I.I.T. 1994]**
(a) increases when reverse bias is applied
(b) decreases when reverse bias is applied
(c) increases when forward bias is applied
(d) does not depend on biasing

92. Decimal number 15 is equivalent to the binary number :
(a) 110001 (b) 000101
(c) 101101 (d) 001111

93. Decimal number 37 is equivalent to the binary number :

(a) 110011 (b) 110101
(c) 101101 (d) 100101

94. An N-type semiconductor is : **[A.F.M.C. 1988]**

(a) positively charged
(b) negatively charged
(c) neutral
(d) none of these

95. When a junction diode is forward biased,

(a) majority-carrier current decreases to zero
(b) minority-carrier current decreases to zero
(c) potential barrier increases
(d) potential barrier decreases

96. An NPN transistor is connected in a circuit as shown below. It is a :

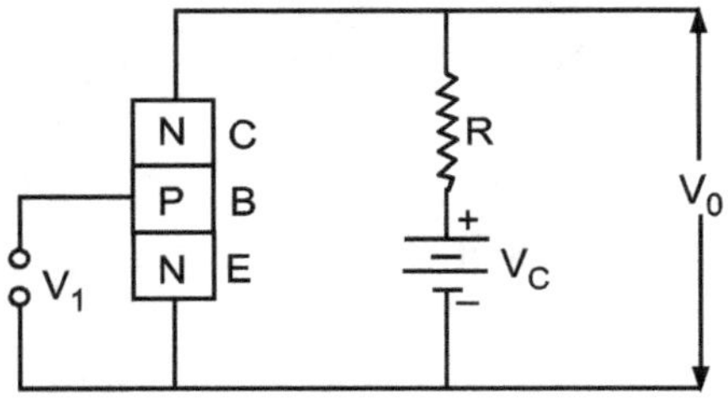

(a) Circuit of common emitter amplifier
(b) Circuit of common collector amplifier
(c) Circuit of a common base amplifier
(d) None of these

97. The number of donors per unit volume in a P-N junction is N_d and the number of acceptors is N_a. If the depletion layer has a width X_1 in the P-side and width X_2 in the N-side, then

(a) $N_d X_1 = N_a X_2$
(b) $X_1 = X_2$
(c) $N_a X_1 = N_d X_2$
(d) $X_1 . \sqrt{N_d} = X_2 . \sqrt{N_a}$

98. Electrical conductivities of Ge and Na are σ_1 and σ_2 respectively. If both of them are heated then :

(a) σ_1 increases and σ_2 decreases
(b) σ_1 decreases and σ_2 increases
(c) σ_1 and σ_2 both increase
(d) σ_1 and σ_2 both decrease

99. Two amplifiers having gains 10 and 20 are cascaded with each other. If a signal of 10 mV is applied at the input, output signal will be : **[N.C.E.R.T.]**

(a) 200 mA (b) 100 mV
(c) 300 mA (d) 2 V

100. At 0°K, intrinsic semiconductor behaves as :

(a) a semiconductor
(b) a perfect insulator
(c) a perfect conductor
(d) a superconductor

101. Zener diode is used :

(a) as an oscillator
(b) as a voltage regulator
(c) as an amplifier
(d) as a rectifier

102. Zener diode is :

(a) forward biased
(b) reverse biased
(c) sometimes forward biased and sometimes reverse biased
(d) none of the above

103. P-type semiconductor has acceptor level 57 eV above the valence band. The maximum wavelength of light required to create a hole is :

(a) 217.1 Å (b) 57×10^{20} Å
(c) 57×10^{-3} Å (d) 11.6×10^{-33} Å

104. When an N-type semiconductor is heated then :

(a) number of electrons and holes remains same
(b) number of electrons and holes increases equally
(c) number of electrons increases, while that of holes decreases
(d) number of holes increases, while that of electrons decreases

105. In the biasing of P-N junction diode as shown in the figure, which is correct ?

[C.B.S.E. PMT 2002]

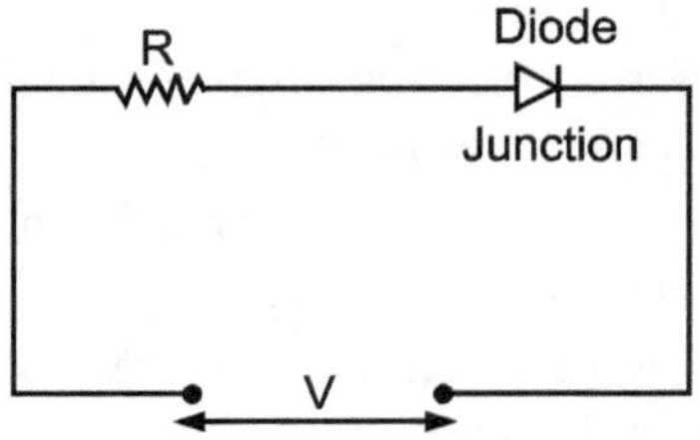

(a) In forward bias, the voltage across R is V.

(b) In reverse bias, the voltage across R is V.

(c) In forward bias, the voltage across R is 2V.

(d) In reverse bias, the voltage across R is 2V.

106. Relation between lattice parameters and interfacial angles in a triclinic system is :

[E.A.M.C.E.T. 1995]

(a) $a \neq b \neq c$

(b) $a = b = c, \alpha = \beta = \gamma = 90°$

(c) $a = b \neq c, \alpha = \beta = \gamma = 90°$

(d) $a \neq b \neq c$ and $\alpha \neq \beta \neq \gamma = 90°$

107. Energy band diagrams for three different samples of Si are shown below,

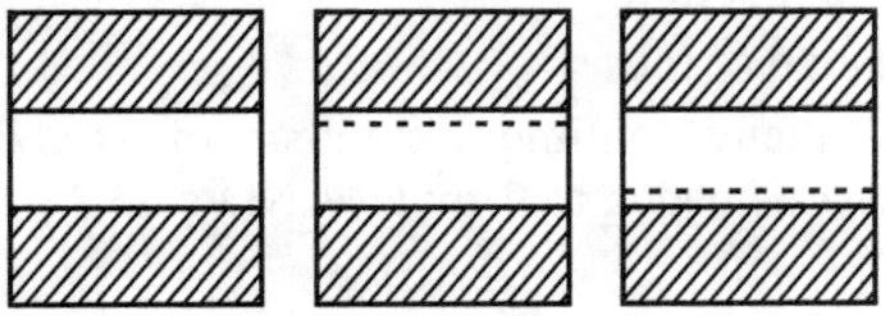

(i) (ii) (iii)

Select the correct statement :

(a) Sample (i), is undoped, sample (ii) is doped with 3rd group dopant and sample (iii) is doped with fifth group dopant.

(b) Sample (i) is undoped, sample (ii) is doped with fifth group dopant and sample (ii) is doped with third group dopant.

(c) Sample (i) is doped, samples (ii) and (iii) are undoped.

(d) Sample (i) is undoped and samples (ii) and (iii) are doped with third group impurity.

108. The typical ionization energy of a donor in silicon is :

(a) 0.05 eV (b) 0.001 eV

(c) 10.0 eV (d) 1.0 eV

109. With the increase in temperature, the width of the forbidden gap will : **[Manipal 2002]**

(a) decrease (b) increase

(c) remain same (d) become zero

110. Following is the relation between current and charge, $J = AT^2e^{\phi_o/V}$ then value of V will be : **[D.P.M.T. 2001]**

(a) V / KT (b) KV / T

(c) KT (d) VT / K

111. A semiconductor is damaged by a strong current, because of : **[Delhi P.M.T. 1999]**

(a) decrease in electrons

(b) lack of free electrons

(c) excess of electrons

(d) none of these

112. Some donor atoms are added to a pure germanium semiconductor to produce N-type semiconductor of conductivity 5 siemen/cm. Then number density of the donor atoms will be :

(Given $\mu_e = 3900\ cm^2/V\text{-}S$)

(a) $5 \times 10^{15}\ /cm^3$ (b) $6 \times 10^{15}\ /cm^3$

(c) $8 \times 10^{15}\ /cm^3$ (d) None of these

113. What is the voltage gain in a common emitter amplifier where input resistance is 5 Ω, load resistance is 40 Ω and current gain is 60 ?

(a) 240 (b) 48

(c) 840 (d) 480

114. Sodium has body centered packing. When the distance between two nearest atoms is 3.7 Å, then lattice parameter is : **[C.B.S.E. 1999]**

(a) 3.3 Å (b) 4.3 Å
(c) 4.8 Å (d) 4.4 Å

115. Read the following statements carefully;

(A) The resistivity of a semiconductor decreases with the increase in its temperature.

(B) In a conducting solid, the rate of collision between free electrons and ions increases with the increase in its temperature.

(a) Both (A) and (B) are true.
(b) (A) is true, but (B) is false.
(c) (A) is false, but (B) is true.
(d) (A) is true and (B) is the correct reason for (A).

116. When the conductivity of a semiconductor is only due to breaking of covalent bonds, the semiconductor is called :

(a) P-type (b) N-type
(c) Intrinsic (d) Extrinsic

117. Truth table given below is for which gate? **[C.B.S.E. 1998]**

A	B	X
0	0	1
0	1	1
1	0	1
1	1	0

(a) XOR (b) NOR
(c) NAND (d) OR

118. P-N junction diode is used as : **[A.I.I.M.S. 1999]**

(a) an oscillator (b) a rectifier
(c) a modulator (d) an amplifier

119. When donor impurity is added to a semiconductor at room temperature, then :

(a) number of electrons decreases, number of holes increases
(b) number of electrons remains unaltered, number of holes increases
(c) number of electrons increases, number of holes remains unaltered
(d) number of electrons increases, number of holes decreases

120. Boolean algebra is essentially based on : **[A.I.I.M.S. 1999]**

(a) Symbol (b) Logic
(c) Numbers (d) Truth

121. The electrical circuits used to smoothen the output current obtained from a rectifier is called :

(a) Oscillator circuit
(b) Full wave rectifier circuit
(c) Amplifier circuit
(d) Filter circuit

122. Cause of potential barrier in a P-N junction diode is : **[C.B.S.E. 1998]**

(a) Concentration of positive and negative ions near the junction
(b) Concentration of positive charges near the junction
(c) Concentration of negative charges near the junction
(d) None of these

123. How many minimum number of NAND gates are needed to form an AND gate ?

(a) 2 (b) 3
(c) 4 (d) 5

124. Select the incorrect statement : **[I.I.T. 1997]**

(a) Doping pure Si with trivalent dopant gives P-type semiconductor.
(b) Resistance of intrinsic semiconductors decreases with increase in temperature.
(c) Majority carriers in N-type semiconductor are holes.
(d) P-N junction acts like a semiconductor diode.

125. A half wave rectifier is used to rectify 50 Hz a.c. Number of pulses of rectified signal obtained in one second will be :

[S.C.R.A. 1998]

(a) 100 (b) 50
(c) 25 (d) 75

126. A charge of 7.89 mA in emitter current produces a charge of 7.8 mA in collector current. Then charge in base current is :

[N.C.E.R.T.]

(a) 7.8 mA (b) 8.89 mA
(c) 0.09 mA (d) 0.9 mA

127. When a silicon junction diode is forward biased by applying a voltage of 0.9 V; then current through the diode is 55 mA at 27° C. Then d.c resistance of the circuit will be

(a) 5.3 ohm (b) 12.8 ohm
(c) 16.4 ohm (d) 23.8 ohm

128. Circuit shown in the figure below contains two bodies each with a forward resistance of 50 Ω and with infinite backward resistance. If the battery voltage is 6 Ω, then current through 100 Ω resistance is : **[I.I.T. 1997]**

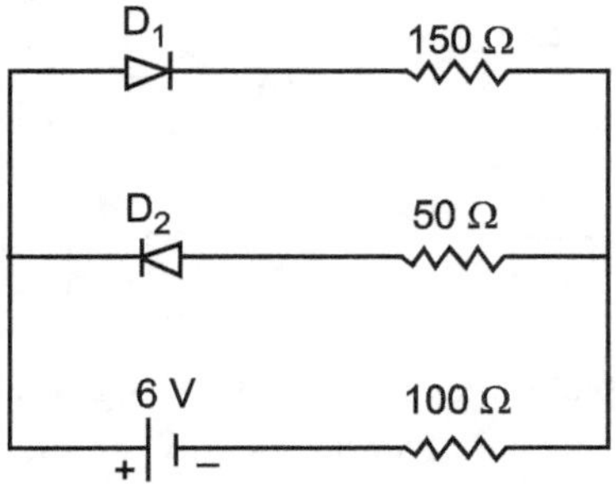

(a) 0.02 A (b) 0.0 A
(c) 0.04 A (d) 0.036 A

129. In the circuit given below, V(*t*) is the sinusoidal voltage source, voltage drop V_{AB} (*t*) across the resistance R :**[I.I.T. 1993]**

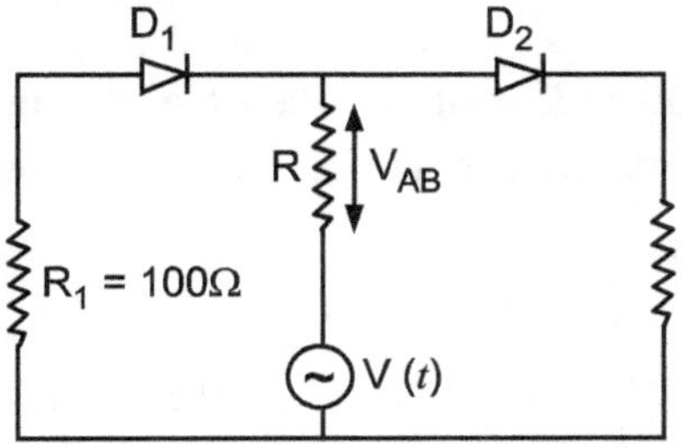

(a) is half wave rectified
(b) is full wave rectified
(c) has the same peak value in the positive and negative half cycle
(d) has different peak value during positive and negative half cycle

130. If internal resistance of a cell is negligible, then current flowing through the cell is :

[C.B.S.E. 2001]

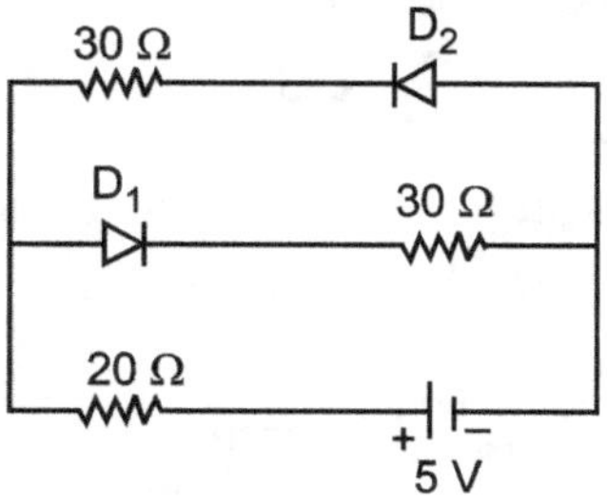

(a) 0.06 A (b) 0.1 A
(c) 0.08 A (d) 0.02 A

131. A transistor is used in the common-emitter mode as an amplifier. Then : **[I.I.T. 1998]**

(a) the base-emitter junction is forward-biased
(b) the base-emitter junction is reverse-biased
(c) the input signal is connected in series with the voltage applied to bias the base-emitter junction
(d) the input signal is connected in series with the voltage applied to bias the base-collector junction

132. The output of the combination of two basic gates shown below is :

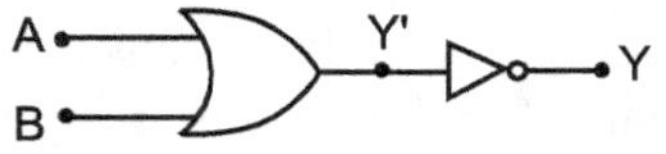

(a) $Y = \overline{A + B}$ (b) $Y = \overline{A} + \overline{B}$

(c) $Y = \overline{A.B}$ (d) $Y = \overline{A} . \overline{B}$

133. The combination of the two basic gates shown below represents :

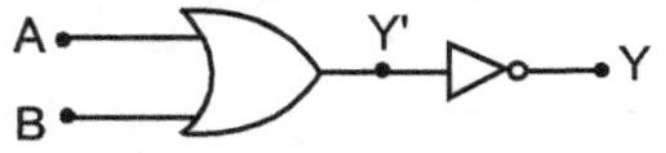

(a) NOR gate (b) NAND gate
(c) XOR gate (d) NOT gate

134. The output of combination of the two basic gates shown below is :

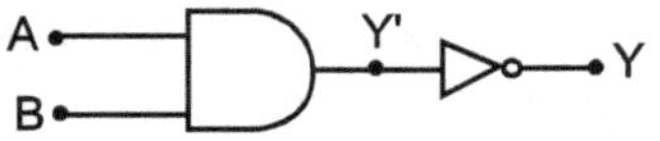

(a) $Y = \overline{A + B}$ (b) $Y = \bar{A} + \bar{B}$

(c) $Y = \overline{A.B}$ (d) $Y = \bar{A} . \bar{B}$

135. The combination of the two basic gates shown below represents :

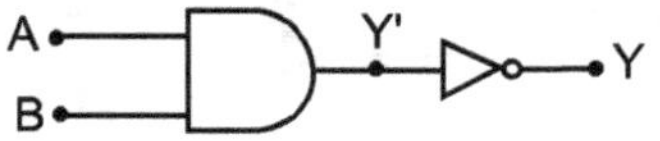

(a) NOR gate (b) NAND gate

(c) XOR gate (d) NOT gate

136. Which of the following truth tables is true ?

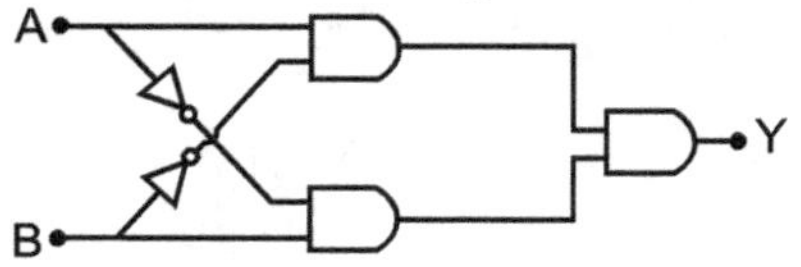

(a)

A	B	Y
0	0	0
1	0	1
0	1	1
1	1	0

(b)

A	B	Y
0	0	0
1	0	0
0	1	1
1	1	1

(c)

A	B	Y
0	0	0
1	0	1
0	1	1
1	1	1

(d)

A	B	Y
0	0	1
1	0	1
0	1	0
1	1	0

137. In the following common emitter configuration, an NPN transistor with current gain $\beta = 100$ and $V_i = 1$ mV are used. The output voltage of the amplifier will be :

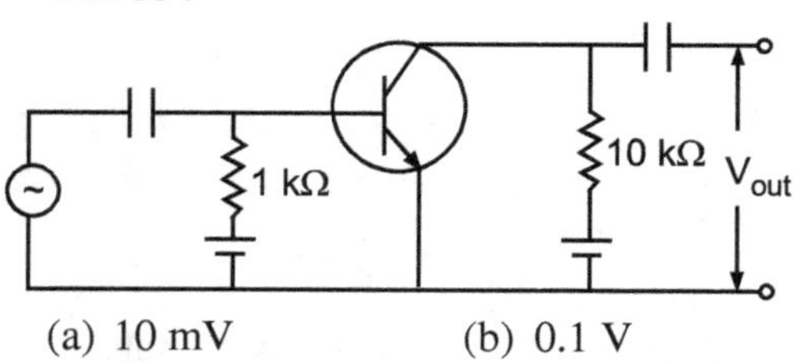

(a) 10 mV (b) 0.1 V

(c) 1.0 V (d) 10 V

138. In figure, the input is across the terminals A and C and the output is across B and D. Then the output is

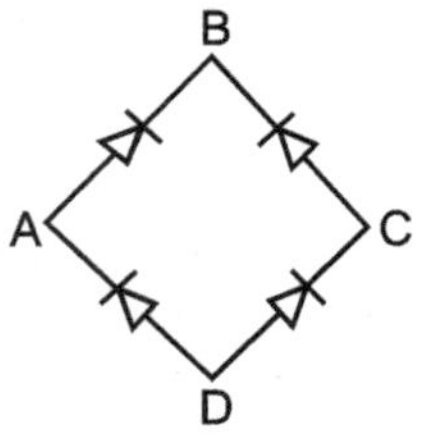

(a) Zero

(b) The same as the input

(c) Full wave rectified

(d) Half wave rectified

139. In a P-N junction a square input signal of 10 V is applied, then the value of output signal across R_L will be

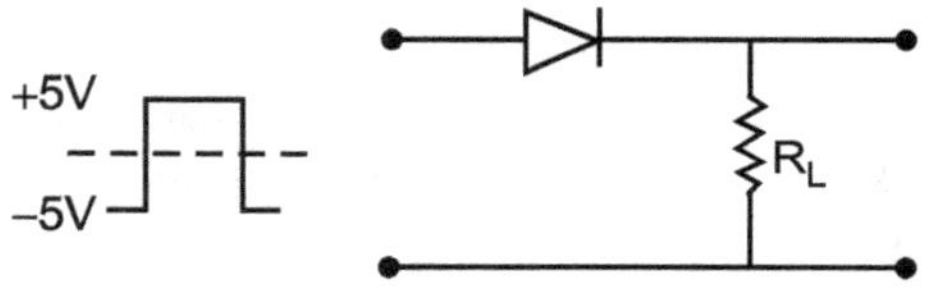

(a) 

(b) 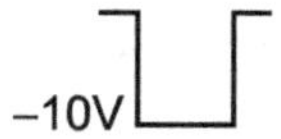

(c) 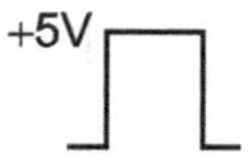

(d) 

140. The depletion layer in Si diode is 1 μm wide and the knee potential is 0.6 V, then the electric field in the depletion layer will be :

(a) Zero (b) 0.6 V/m

(c) 6×10^4 V/m (d) 6×10^5 V/m

141. The energy of a photon of sodium light of $\lambda = 5890$ Å equals the band gap of a semiconductor material, then the maximum energy required to create the electron-hole pair is :

(a) 1.05 eV (b) 2.10 eV

(c) 4.2 eV (d) 5.89 eV

142. If a zener diode (V_Z = 5 V and I_Z = 10 mA) is connected in series with a resistance and 20 V is applied across the combination, then the maximum resistance one can use without spoiling Zener action is:

(a) 20 kΩ (b) 15 kΩ
(c) 10 kΩ (d) 1.5 kΩ

143. A junction diode is connected to a 10 V source and 10^3 Ω rheostat. The slope of load line on the characteristic curve of the diode will be :

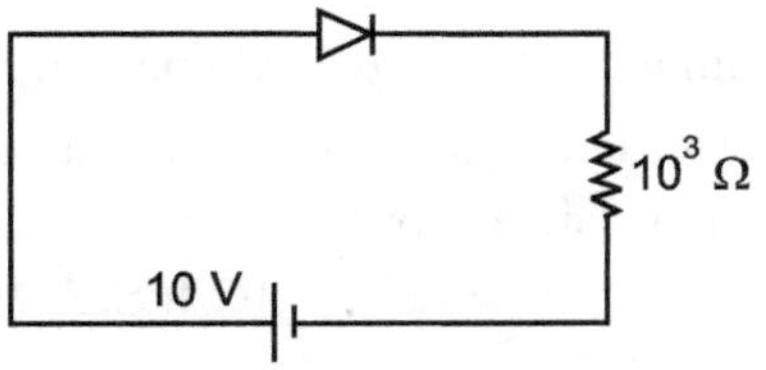

(a) 10^{-2} A/V (b) 10^{-3} A/V
(c) 10^{-4} A/V (d) 10^{-5} A/V

144. The transfer ratio β of transistor is 50. The load input resistance of a transistor when used in common emitter configuration is 1 kΩ. The peak value of collector a.c. current for a peak value a.c. input voltage of 0.01 V is :

(a) 0.01 μA (b) 0.25 μA
(c) 250 μA (d) 500 μA

145. To get an output Y = 1 from circuit of figure, the input must be

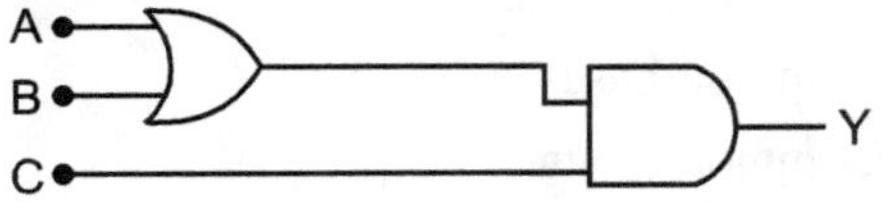

	A	B	C
(a)	1	1	0
(b)	1	0	0
(c)	1	0	1
(d)	0	1	1

146. What is the output of the combination of the gates shown in figure :

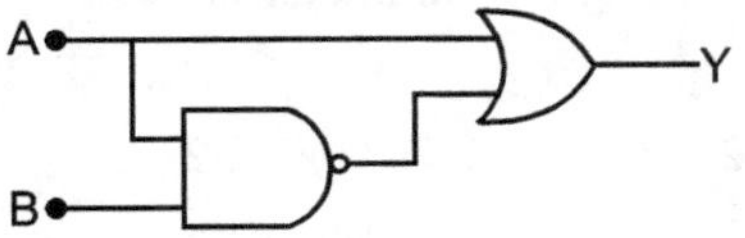

(a) $A + \overline{A \cdot B}$ (b) $A \cdot B + \bar{A} \cdot \bar{B}$

(c) $(A + B) \cdot \overline{(A \cdot B)}$ (d) $(A + B)(\bar{A} + \bar{B})$

147. In the circuit shown in figure, the transistor used has a current gain β = 100.

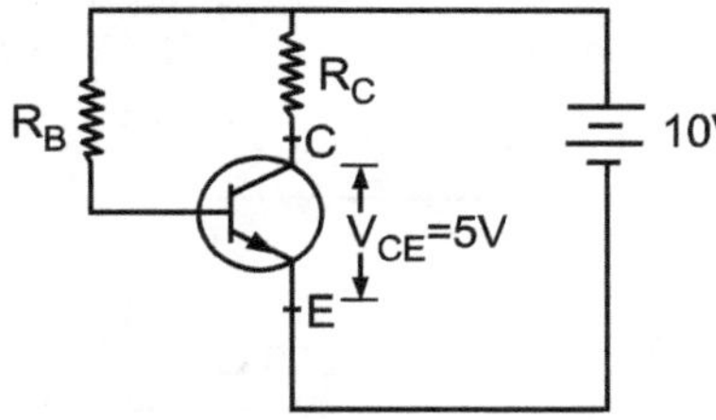

Load resistor R_C = 1 kΩ, bias resistor R_B = 200 kΩ, V_{CC} = 10 V, V_{CE} = 5 V and V_{BE} is negligible. What are the values of collector current I_C and base current I_B ?

(a) I_C = 5 mA, I_B = 500 mA
(b) I_C = 5 mA, I_B = 50 μA
(c) I_C = 2 mA, I_B = 200 mA
(d) I_C = 2 mA, I_B = 20 μA

148. When a transistor amplifier having current gain of 75 is given an input signal,

$V_I = 2 \sin (157\,t + \pi/2)$,

The output signal is found to be,

$V_O = 200 \sin [157\,t + 3\pi/2]$

The transistor is connected as :

(a) a common collector amplifier
(b) a common base amplifier
(c) a common emitter amplifier
(d) an oscillator

149. The voltage-current characteristic of an ideal P-N junction diode is given by,

$I = I_o [e^{eV/KT} - 1]$

where the drift current I_o equals 10 μA. If the temperature T is 300 K, the voltage V_o for which $e^{eV/KT} = 100$ is :

(a) 0.2 V (b) 0.12 V
(c) 0.24 V (d) 0.3 V

150. The type of bonds in a silicon crystal is :

(a) covalent (b) Van der Waals
(c) ionic (d) metallic

151. Circuit shown in the figure below contains two diodes each with a forward resistance of 200 Ω and with infinite backward resistance. If the battery voltage is 6 V, then current through 100 Ω resistance is :

[I.I.T. 1997]

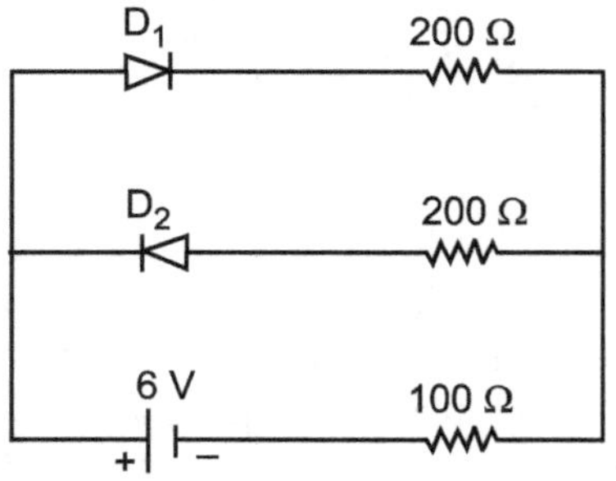

(a) 0.012 A (b) 0.0 A
(c) 0.03 A (d) 0.036 A

152. The combination of the two basic gates shown below represents

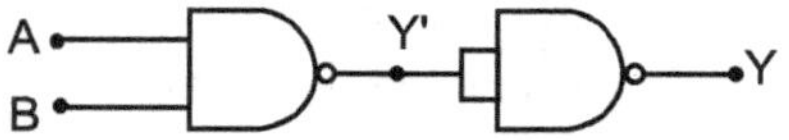

(a) NAND gate (b) AND gate
(c) NOT gate (d) XOR gate

153. If there are 4 atoms per unit cell in a solid, the crystal is : **[C.E.T. 1999]**

(a) Tetragonal
(b) Simple cubic
(c) Body-centered cubic
(d) Face-centered cubic

154. In the circuit given below, V(t) is the sinusoidal voltage source, voltage drop V_{AB} (t) across the resistance R :

[I.I.T. 1993]

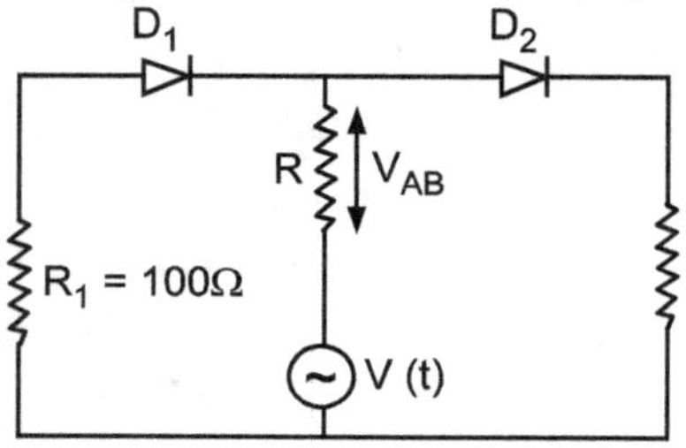

(a) is half wave rectified
(b) is full wave rectified
(c) has the same peak value in the positive and negative half cycle
(d) has different peak value during positive and negative half cycle

155. The impurity atoms with which pure silicon should be doped to make a P-type semiconductor are those of :

[C.E.T. 1998; I.I.T. 1988]

(a) Phosphorus (b) Arsenic
(c) Antimony (d) Aluminium

156. In BCC structure of lattice constant a, the minimum distance between atoms is :

[C.B.S.E. 2001]

(a) $\frac{\sqrt{3}a}{2}$ (b) $\sqrt{2}$ a

(c) $\frac{a}{\sqrt{2}}$ (d) $\frac{a}{2}$

157. An oscillator is an amplifier with :

[C.B.S.E. 1995; Pre-Medical/Dental, 1994]

(a) a large gain
(b) negative feedback
(c) positive feedback
(d) no feedback

158. In which of the transistor configurations, the voltage gain is highest ?

(a) Common-base
(b) Common-emitter
(c) Common-collector
(d) Same in all the three

159. On subtracting 010111 from 101010 we get:

(a) 001011 (b) 001100
(c) 010011 (d) 011111

160. For an FCC unit cell, the ratio of the radius of atoms to lattice parameter is :

[C.E.T. 1998]

(a) 1 : 2 (b) 1 : $2\sqrt{2}$
(c) 2 : 1 (d) 1 : 4

161. A P-type semiconductor is
(a) a silicon crystal doped with arsenic impurity
(b) a silicon crystal doped with antimony impurity
(c) a germanium crystal doped with boron impurity
(d) a germanium crystal doped with phosphorus impurity

162. The main difference between conductors, semiconductors and insulators is because of:
(a) Work function
(b) Binding energy of electrons
(c) Width of forbidden energy gap
(d) Mobility of electrons

163. Sodium has body centered packing. If the distance between the two nearest atoms is 3.7 A, then lattice parameter is :
(a) 3.9 A (b) 3.3 A
(c) 4.8 A (d) 4.3 A

164. Which of the following gates will have an output of 1 ?

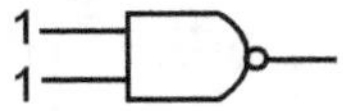

(A)

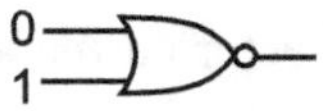

(B)

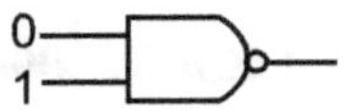

(C)

(D)

(a) D (b) A
(c) B (d) C

165. The diode used in the circuit shown in figure has a constant voltage drop of 0.5 volt at all currents and a maximum power rating of 100 mW. What should be the value of the resistor R connected in series with the diode for obtaining maximum current ?

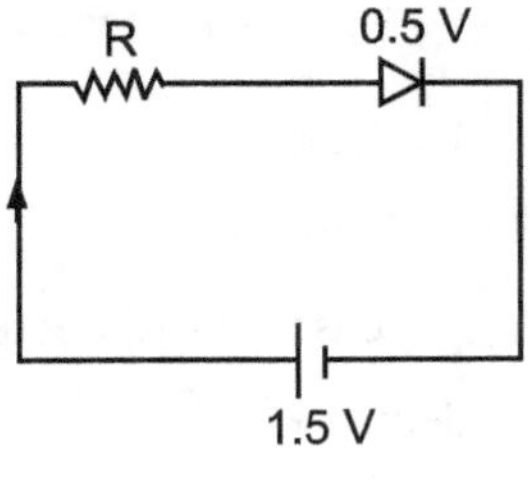

(a) 5 Ω (b) 5.6 Ω
(c) 6.76 Ω (d) 10 Ω

166. Polycrystals :
(a) are in fact amorphous in nature
(b) have orderly arrangement throughout their bodies
(c) do not have orderly arrangement throughout their bodies
(d) none of the above

167. A transistor is used in the common-emitter mode as an amplifier. Then : **[I.I.T. 1998]**
(a) the base-emitter junction is forward-biased
(b) the base-emitter junction is reverse-biased
(c) the input signal is connected in series with the voltage applied to bias the base-emitter junction
(d) the input signal is connected in series with the voltage applied to bias the base-collector junction

168. An N-type and a P-type silicon can be obtained by doping pure silicon with :
(a) sodium and magnesium respectively
(b) phosphorus and boron respectively
(c) boron and phosphorus respectively
(d) indium and sodium respectively

169. Collector current in a PNP transistor is 10 mA. If 90% of holes are able to reach the collector, then base current will be :

[I.I.T. 1992]

(a) 1 mA (b) 11 mA
(c) 10 mA (d) 3 mA

170. Diode used in the figure below has the constant voltage drop of 0.5 V at all currents. Maximum power rating of this diode is 100 mW. What should be the value of R so as to get the maximum current in the circuit ?

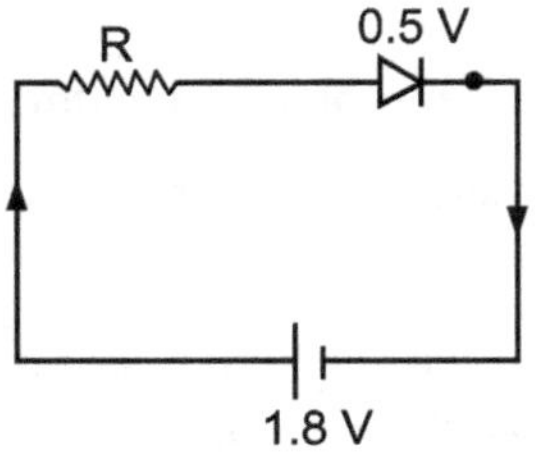

(a) 5.6 ohms (b) 6.9 ohms
(c) 15.3 ohms (c) 6.5 ohms

171. In a common emitter amplifier $(I_c/I_e) = 0.98$, then current gain is : **[D.C.E. 2001]**
(a) 49 (b) 4.9
(c) 98 (d) 9.8

172. Transfer ratio β of a transistor is 50. Input resistance of the transistor when used in CE mode is 1 kΩ. For an input peak voltage of 0.01 volts, the peak value of collector current will be :
(a) 500 μA (b) 100 μA
(c) 25 μA (d) 1.0 μA

173. In a pure silicon, number of electrons and holes per unit volume are $1.5 \times 10^{16}/m^3$. If Si is doped with boron in such a way that on doping hole density increases to $4.5 \times 10^{22}/m^3$, then electron density in doped semiconductor will be :
(a) $7 \times 10^9/m^3$ (b) $3 \times 10^9/m^3$
(c) $5 \times 10^9/m^3$ (d) $1 \times 10^9/ m^3$

174. The electrical conductivity of a semi-conductor increases when electromagnetic radiation of wavelength shorter than 2480 mm is incident on it. The band gap in (eV) for the semiconductor is :

[A.I.E.E.E. 2005]
(a) 1.1 eV (b) 2.5 eV
(c) 0.5 eV (d) 0.7 eV

175. In a common base amplifier, the phase difference between the input signal voltage and output voltage is : **[A.I.E.E.E. 2005]**
(a) $\frac{\pi}{4}$ (b) π
(c) 0 (d) $\frac{\pi}{2}$

176. In a full wave rectifier circuit operating from 50 Hz mains frequency, the fundamental frequency in the ripple would be :
(a) 50 Hz (b) 25 Hz
(c) 100 Hz (d) 70.7 Hz

177. If the ratio of the concentration of electrons to that of holes in a semiconductor is $\frac{7}{5}$ and the ratio of currents is $\frac{7}{4}$, then what is the ratio of their drift velocities ?

[A.I.E.E.E. 2006]
(a) $\frac{4}{7}$ (b) $\frac{5}{8}$
(c) $\frac{4}{5}$ (d) $\frac{5}{4}$

178. In a common base mode of a transistor, collector current is 5.488 mA for an emitter current of 5.60 mA. The value of the base current amplification factor (β) will be :

[A.I.E.E.E. 2006]
(a) 48 (b) 49
(c) 50 (d) 51

179. If the lattice constant of this semiconductor is decreased, then which of the following is correct ? **[A.I.E.E.E. 2006]**

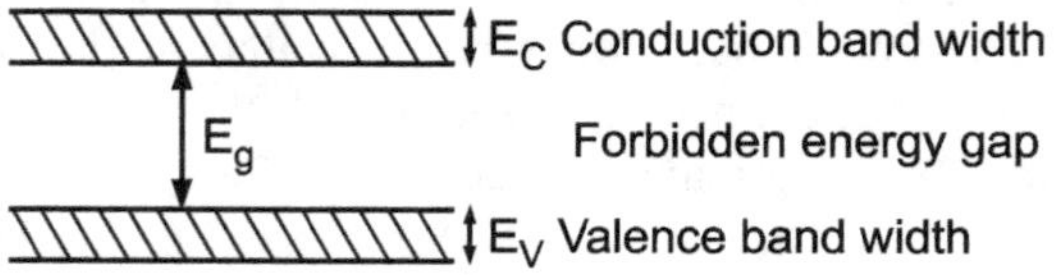

(a) All E_c, E_g, E_v decrease
(b) All E_c, E_g, E_v increase
(c) E_c, and E_v increase, but E_g decreases
(d) E_c, and E_v decrease, but E_g increases

180. In the following, which one of the diodes is reverse biased ? **[A.I.E.E.E. 2006]**

(a) 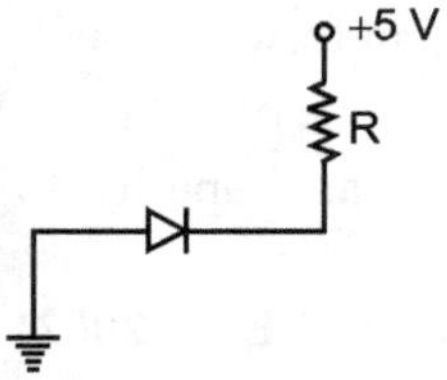

(b) 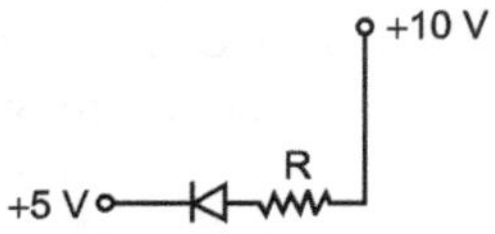

(c) 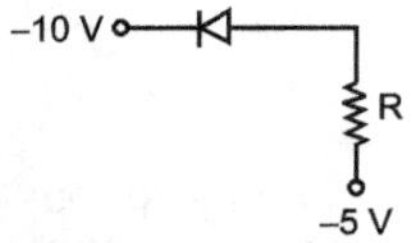

(d) 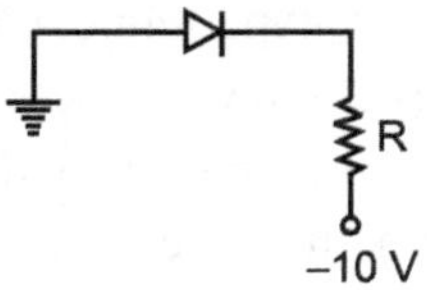

181. The circuit has two oppositely connected ideal diodes in parallel. What is the current flowing in the circuit ? **[A.I.E.E.E. 2006]**

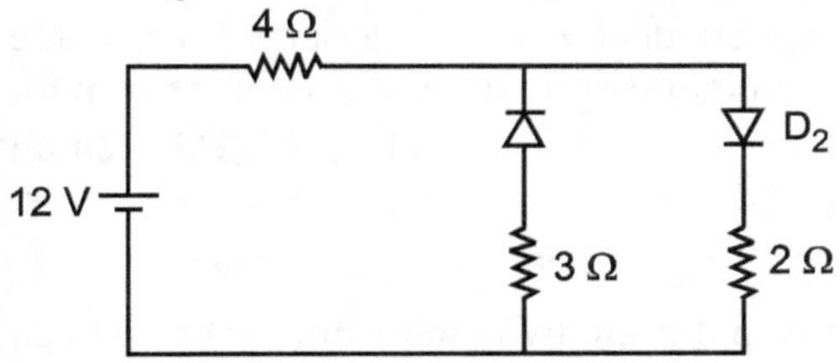

(a) 1.33 A (b) 1.71 A
(c) 2.00 A (d) 2.31 A

182. The impurity added in Germanium crystals to make n-type semiconductor is: **(B.H.U. 2000)**

(a) Aluminium (b) Gallium
(c) Iridium (d) Phosphorus

183. The energy gap between conduction band and valence band is of the order of 0.07 eV. It is : **(A.F.M.C. 2000)**

(a) Insulator (b) Conductor
(c) Semiconductor (d) Alloy

184. At 0 K, intrinsic semiconductor behaves as : **(M.P. C.E.T. 2000)**

(a) a perfect conductor
(b) a superconductor
(c) a semiconductor
(d) a perfect insulator

185. For germanium crystal, the forbidden energy gap in joules is : **(M.P.C.E.T. 2000)**

(a) 1.12×10^{-19} (b) 1.15×10^{-19}
(c) 1.6×10^{-19} (d) Zero

186. The diffusion current in a P-N junction is : **(H.P.P.M.T. 2000)**

(a) from n-side to p-side
(b) from p-side to n-side
(c) from n-side to p-side, if forward Biased.
(d) from p-side to n-side, if reverse biased.

187. Heat in metal is produced due to : **(C.E.T. 2000)**

(a) collision of electrons with electrons
(b) collision of conduction electrons with atoms
(c) collision of conduction electrons with protons
(d) In all these ways as mentioned in above options

188. In diode when there is saturation current, the plate resistance is : **(Haryana P.M.T. 2000)**

(a) zero
(b) infinite
(c) finite but constant
(d) Data are insufficient

189. In a p-type semiconductor : **(Haryana P.M.T. 2000)**

(a) major current carriers are electrons
(b) major current carriers are mobile negative ions
(c) major current carriers are mobile holes
(d) the number of mobile holes exceeds the number of mobile acceptors

190. Forbidden energy band gap in semiconductor is : **(R.P.M.T. 2001)**

(a) 1 eV (b) 6 eV
(c) 0 eV (d) 3 eV

191. Zener breakdown will occur, if : **(R.P.M.T. 2001)**

(a) impurity level is low
(b) impurity level is high
(c) impurity is less in n-side
(d) impurity is less in p-side.

192. GaAs is : **(R.P.M.T. 2001)**
(a) element semiconductor
(b) alloy semiconductor
(c) band conductor
(d) metallic semiconductor

193. Diode is used as a : **(R.P.M.T. 2001)**
(a) Rectifier (b) Amplifier
(c) Detector (d) Modulator.

194. At absolute zero, Si acts as : **(A.I.E.E.E. 2002)**
(a) Non-metal (b) Metal
(c) Insulator (d) None of these

195. When the P-end of the P-N junction is connected to the negative terminal of the battery and the N-end to the positive terminal of the battery, then the P-N junction behaves like : **(M.P.P.M.T. 2002)**
(a) a conductor (b) an insulator
(c) a superconductor (d) a semiconductor

196. The dominant contribution to current comes from holes in case of : **(Orissa J.E.E. 2002)**
(a) Metals
(b) Intrinsic semiconductors
(c) P-type extrinsic semiconductors
(d) N-type extrinsic semiconductors

197. The valence band and conduction band of a solid overlap at low temperature, the solid may be : **(Orissa J.E.E. 2002)**
(a) a metal (b) a semiconductor
(c) an insulator (d) none of these

198. A logic gate having two inputs A and B and output C has the following truth table : **(U.P.S.E.A.T. 2002)**

A	B	C
1	1	0
1	0	1
0	1	1
0	0	1

(a) OR (b) AND
(c) NOT (d) NAND

199. The P-N junction diode works as insulator, if connected : **(J & K.C.E.T. 2002)**
(a) to a.c. (b) in forward bias
(c) in reverse bias (d) none of these

200. When arsenic is added as an impurity to silicon, the resulting material is : **(J & K.C.E.T. 2002)**
(a) N-type conductor
(b) N-type semiconductor
(c) P-type conductor
(d) P-type semiconductor

201. Which of the following is not an amorphous substance ? **(J & K.C.E.T. 2002)**
(a) Glass (b) Polymers
(c) Copper (d) Rubber

202. Superconductivity was observed when the temperature of mercury was cooled down to: **(T.N.P.C.E.E. 2002)**
(a) 14.2 K (b) 4.2 K
(c) 4.2° C (d) 14.2° C

203. If A and B are two inputs in AND gate, then AND gate has an output of 1 when the values of A and B are: **(T.N.P.C.E.E. 2002)**
(a) A = 0, B = 0 (b) A = 1, B = 1
(c) A = 1, B = 0 (d) A = 0, B = 1

204. What will be the input of A and B for the Boolean expression $\overline{A+B} \cdot \overline{A \cdot B} = 1$: **(T.N.P.C.E.E. 2002)**
(a) 0, 0 (b) 0, 1
(c) 1, 0 (d) 1, 1

205. Which of the following is correct for Tetragonal system ? **(B.C.E.C.E. 2002)**
(a) $a = b \neq c$ and $\alpha = \beta = \gamma = 90°$
(b) $a \neq b = c$ and $\alpha = \beta = \gamma = 90°$
(c) $a \neq b \neq c$ and $\alpha = \beta = \gamma = 90°$
(d) $a = b = c$ and $\alpha = \beta = \gamma = 90°$

206. The least doped region in a transistor is : **(Kerala C.E.T. (Med.) 2002)**
(a) emitter
(b) collector
(c) base
(d) either emitter or collector

207. NAND gate is : **(Kerala C.E.T. (Engg.) 2003)**
(a) a basic gate
(b) not a universal gate
(c) a basic universal gate
(d) a universal gate
(e) only an input logic gate

208. In junction diode, the holes are because of : **(P.M.T. Punjab 2003)**
(a) missing electrons (b) extra electrons
(c) protons (d) neutrons

209. Boron is added as an impurity to silicon. The resulting material is : **(H.P.P.M.T. 2006)**
(a) N-type semiconductor
(b) N-type conductor
(c) P-type semiconductor
(d) P-type conductor

210. When germanium is doped with phosphorus what type of semiconductor is produced ? **(Orissa J.E.T. 2006)**
(a) N-type (b) P-type
(c) Both (a) and (b) (d) None of these

211. If α and β are the current gain in the CB and CE configurations respectively of the transistor circuit, then $\frac{\beta - \alpha}{\alpha\beta}$ = **(Kerala P.E.T. 2006)**
(a) ∞ (b) 1
(c) 2 (d) 0.5

ANSWER KEY

1. (c)	**2.** (b)	**3.** (c)	**4.** (a)	**5.** (b)	**6.** (d)	**7.** (a)	**8.** (b)	**9.** (c)	**10.**(a)
11.(a)	**12.**(b)	**13.**(c)	**14.**(d)	**15.**(a)	**16.**(c)	**17.**(a)	**18.**(d)	**19.**(c)	**20.**(a)
21.(b)	**22.**(c)	**23.**(a)	**24.**(a)	**25.**(c)	**26.**(c)	**27.**(c)	**28.**(b)	**29.**(a)	**30.**(c)
31.(d)	**32.**(d)	**33.**(a)	**34.**(c)	**35.**(b)	**36.**(c)	**37.**(c)	**38.**(a)	**39.**(c)	**40.**(b)
41.(a)	**42.**(d)	**43.**(d)	**44.**(c)	**45.**(c)	**46.**(d)	**47.**(a)	**48.**(b)	**49.**(c)	**50.**(c)
51.(a)	**52.**(c)	**53.**(b)	**54.**(a)	**55.**(b)	**56.**(b)	**57.**(c)	**58.**(a)	**59.**(c)	**60.**(d)
61.(c)	**62.**(c)	**63.**(a)	**64.**(d)	**65.**(a)	**66.**(d)	**67.**(a)	**68.**(b)	**69.**(c)	**70.**(d)
71.(a)	**72.**(c)	**73.**(a)	**74.**(a)	**75.**(d)	**76.**(a)	**77.**(c)	**78.**(a)	**79.**(c)	**80.**(d)
81.(b)	**82.**(b)	**83.**(b)	**84.**(c)	**85.**(d)	**86.**(d)	**87.**(a)	**88.**(b)	**89.**(b)	**90.**(d)
91.(a)	**92.**(d)	**93.**(d)	**94.**(c)	**95.**(d)	**96.**(a)	**97.**(c)	**98.**(a)	**99.**(d)	**100.** (b)
101. (b)	**102.** (b)	**103.** (a)	**104.** (b)	**105.** (a)	**106.** (d)	**107.** (b)	**108.** (a)	**109.** (a)	**110.** (c)
111. (c)	**112.** (c)	**113.** (d)	**114.** (b)	**115.** (a)	**116.** (c)	**117.** (c)	**118.** (b)	**119.** (d)	**120.** (b)
121. (d)	**122.** (a)	**123.** (a)	**124.** (c)	**125.** (b)	**126.** (c)	**127.** (c)	**128.** (a)	**129.** (d)	**130.** (b)
131. (a, c)	**132.** (a)	**133.** (a)	**134.** (c)	**135.** (b)	**136.** (a)	**137.** (c)	**138.** (c)	**139.** (c)	**140.** (d)
141. (b)	**142.** (d)	**143.** (b)	**144.** (d)	**145.** (c, d)	**146.** (a)	**147.** (b)	**148.** (c)	**149.** (b)	**150.** (a)
151. (a)	**152.** (b)	**153.** (d)	**154.** (d)	**155.** (d)	**156.** (a)	**157.** (c)	**158.** (b)	**159.** (c)	**160.** (b)
161. (c)	**162.** (c)	**163.** (d)	**164.** (d)	**165.** (a)	**166.** (c)	**167.** (a, c)	**168.** (b)	**169.** (a)	**170.** (c)
171. (a)	**172.** (a)	**173.** (c)	**174.** (c)	**175.** (c)	**176.** (c)	**177.** (d)	**178.** (b)	**179.** (d)	**180.** (a)
181. (c)	**182.** (d)	**183.** (c)	**184.** (d)	**185.** (b)	**186.** (b)	**187.** (b)	**188.** (b)	**189.** (c)	**190.** (a)
191. (b)	**192.** (b)	**193.** (a)	**194.** (c)	**195.** (b)	**196.** (c)	**197.** (a)	**198.** (d)	**199.** (c)	**200.** (b)
201. (c)	**202.** (b)	**203.** (b)	**204.** (a)	**205.** (a)	**206.** (c)	**207.** (d)	**208.** (a)	**209.** (c)	**210.** (a)
211. (b)									

21

ELECTROMAGNETIC WAVES AND COMMUNICATION SYSTEMS

MULTIPLE CHOICE QUESTIONS

1. The velocity of light in vacuum can be changed by changing : **(A.F.M.C 2000)**

(a) frequency (b) amplitude

(c) wavelength (d) none of these

2. Ozone layer in the atmosphere extends from about :

(a) 10-20 km above the ground

(b) 20-50 km above the ground

(c) 50-80 km above the ground

(d) 80-100 km above the ground

3. Which one of the following sequences of electromagnetic waves is in order of increasing frequency?

(a) Gamma rays, visible light, ultraviolet rays

(b) Gamma rays, ultraviolet rays, radio waves

(c) Microwaves, ultraviolet rays, X-rays

(d) Radiowaves, visible light and infrared radiation

4. The frequency of an electromagnetic wave which will be most appropriate to observe a particle of radius 3×10^{-4} cm will be of the order of : **(C.B.S.E. 1993)**

(a) 10^{15} (b) 10^{14}

(c) 10^{13} (d) 10^{12}

5. The waves of wavelength of 10^{-3} m and above are called :

(a) Radio waves (b) Radar waves

(c) T.V. waves (d) Sonar waves

6. According to Maxwell's hypothesis, a changing electric field gives rise to : **(A.I.I.M.S. 1998)**

(a) electric current (b) emf

(c) pressure radiant (d) magnetic field

7. The minimum wavelength of the emitted X-rays obtained when the accelerating potential difference in X-ray tube at the anode is V volt is : **(Kar. C.E.T. 2004)**

(a) e V / hc. (b) hc / e V

(c) eV / h (d) h / eV

8. The number of microwave radio frequency carrier waves transmitted by a television signal transmitter is:

(a) four (b) three

(c) two (d) one

9. The limit of ground wave transmission is roughly :

(a) 1500 MHz (b) 15000 MHz

(c) 1500 Hz (d) 1500 kHz

10. Dimensional formula of $\varepsilon_0 \frac{d\phi_E}{dt}$ is same as of:

(a) Capacitance (b) Potential

(c) Charge (d) Current

11. The amplitudes of electric and magnetic fields related to each other as :

(a) $E_0 = B_0$ (b) $E_0 = cB_0$

(c) $E_0 = B_0/c$ (d) $E_0 = c/B_0$

12. If the energies of red and blue photons of light are represented by ε_r and ε_b, then :

(a) $\varepsilon_r = \varepsilon_b$ (b) $\varepsilon_r > \varepsilon_b$

(c) $\varepsilon_r < \varepsilon_b$ (d) $\varepsilon_r = \varepsilon_b/2$

13. Dimensions of $1/(\mu_0 \varepsilon_0)$ is :

(a) L^2/T^2 (b) T^2/L^2

(c) T/L (d) L/T

14. If the magnetic monopoles could exist then which of the following Maxwell's equations is required to be modified ?

(a) $\oint \vec{E}.d\vec{S} = \frac{q}{\varepsilon_0}$

(b) $\oint \vec{B}.d\vec{S} = 0$

(c) $\oint \vec{E}.d\vec{l} = -\frac{d}{dt}\int \vec{B}.d\vec{S}$

(d) $\oint \vec{B}.d\vec{l} = \mu_0 \varepsilon_0 \frac{d}{dt}\int \vec{E}.d\vec{S} + \mu_0 I$

15. Ozone layer above earth's atmosphere will :

(a) prevent infrared rays reflected from earth from escaping earth's atmosphere.

(b) prevent ultraviolet rays from sun.

(c) prevent infrared radiations from sun reaching earth.

(d) reflect back radiowaves.

16. The frequency of visible light is of the order of :

(a) 10^8 Hz (b) 10^{20} Hz

(c) 10^{10} Hz (d) 10^{15} Hz

17. Which of the following can be expressed in coulomb :

(a) $\oint \vec{B}.d\vec{l}$ (b) $\oint \vec{E}.d\vec{l}$

(c) $\oint_S \varepsilon_0 \vec{E}.d\vec{S}$ (d) $\oint_S \frac{\vec{B}}{\mu_0} \cdot d\vec{S}$

18. A plane electromagnetic wave of wave intensity 6 W / m^2 strikes a small mirror of area 30 cm^2, held perpendicular to the approaching wave. The momentum transferred in kg-ms^{-1} by the wave to the mirror each second will be :

(a) 3.6×10^{-8} (b) 4.8×10^{-7}

(c) 1.2×10^{-10} (d) 2.4×10^{-9}

19. Radiowaves with frequencies higher than television signals are :

(a) Macrowaves (b) Microwaves

(c) Cable waves (d) Television waves

20. The frequencies of X-rays, γ-rays and ultraviolet rays are respectively a, b and c. Then: **(CBSE PMT 2000)**

(a) a < b, b > c (b) a > b, b > c

(c) a > b, b < c (d) a < b, b < c

21. A magnetic field is produced by :

(a) a changing electric field

(b) a moving charge

(c) both (a) and (b)

(d) none of these

22. In a plane e.m. wave, the electric field oscillates sinusoidally at a frequency of 2.5×10^{10} Hz and amplitude 480 V/m. The amplitude of the oscillating magnetic field will be : **(DCE 1998)**

(a) 1.6×10^{-6} Wb/m^2

(b) 1.6×10^{-7} Wb/m^2

(c) 1.52×10^{-8} Wb/m^2

(d) 1.52×10^{-7} Wb/m^2

23. The electromagnetic radiations are in descending order of wavelengths in the following sequence :

(a) Infrared waves, radiowaves, X-rays, visible light rays

(b) Radiowaves, infrared waves, visible light rays, X-rays

(c) Radiowaves, visible light rays, infrared waves, X-rays

(d) X-rays visible light rays, infrared waves, radiowaves

24. A plane electromagnetic wave is incident on a material surface. The wave delivers momentum p and energy E :

(a) $p \neq 0, E \neq 0$ (b) $p = 0, E = 0$

(c) $p = 0, E \neq 0$ (d) $p \neq 0, E = 0$

25. The ozone layer blocks :

(a) X-rays

(b) Cosmic rays

(c) Ultraviolet radiations

(d) Infrared radiations

26. The T.V. transmission tower in Delhi has a height of 240 m. The distance upto which the broadcast can be received (taking the radius of earth to be 6.4×10^6 m) is :

(a) 100 km (b) 60 km

(c) 55 km (d) 50 km

27. An electromagnetic wave going through vacuum is described by $E = E_0 \sin(kx - \omega t)$ and $B = B_0 \sin(kx - \omega t)$:

(a) $E_0 k = B_0 \omega$ (b) $E_0 \omega = B_0 k$

(c) $E_0 B_0 = \omega k$ (d) None of these

28. Which of the following pairs of space and time varying electric field E and magnetic field B would generate a plane electromagnetic wave propagating in the Z-direction ?

(a) E_X, B_Z (b) $E_X\ B_Y$

(c) E_X, B_X (d) E_Z, B_X

29. According to Ampere's law $\oint \vec{B}.d\vec{l}$ is equal to :

(a) $\mu_0 I$ (b) $\mu_0\left[I - \varepsilon_0 \frac{\partial \phi_E}{\partial t}\right]$

(c) $\mu_0\left[I + \varepsilon_0 \frac{\partial \phi_E}{\partial t}\right]$ (d) None of these

30. If ε_0 and μ_0 represent the absolute permittivity and absolute permeability of free space and ε and μ represent the absolute permittivity and absolute permeability of a medium, then refractive index of the medium is given by :

(I.I.T. Screening 2004)

(a) $\sqrt{\frac{\mu_0 \varepsilon_0}{\varepsilon}}$ (b) $\sqrt{\frac{\varepsilon}{\mu_0 \varepsilon_0}}$

(c) $\sqrt{\frac{\varepsilon \mu}{\varepsilon_0 \mu_0}}$ (d) $\sqrt{\frac{\varepsilon_0 \mu_0}{\varepsilon \mu}}$

31. Waves most suitable for telecommunication are:

(a) Microwaves (b) Visible light

(c) Ultraviolet light (d) Infrared waves

32. An oscillating charge between the two plates of an electric field emits :

(a) I R radiations

(b) Electromagnetic waves

(c) X-rays

(d) Mechanical waves

33. The audio waves after being converted into electrical waves cannot be transmitted as such because :

(a) they are heavily absorbed by the atmosphere.

(b) the height of antenna has to be increased several times.

(c) they travel with the speed of sound.

(d) the frequency is not constant.

34. A lamp emits monochromatic green light in all directions. If lamp is 3% efficient in converting electrical power to electromagnetic waves and consumes 100 W of power, then amplitude of the electric field associated with the electromagnetic radiation at a distance of 5 m from the lamp will be :

(a) 2.68 V / m (b) 5.36 V / m

(c) 1.34 V /m (d) 4.02 V /m

35. S.I unit of displacement current is :

(a) $A\ s^{-1}$ (b) C

(c) C–m (d) A

36. A compass needle lies between the two parallel plates of a capacitor. The capacitor is connected to source of emf. The compass needle :

(a) deflects and remains deflected as long as the battery is connected.

(b) deflects for a very short time and then comes back to the original position.

(c) deflects and gradually comes to the original position in a time which is large compared to the time constant.

(d) does not deflect.

37. The conduction current in an ideal case through a circuit is zero when charge on capacitor is :

(a) zero

(b) maximum

(c) dependent on value of C and R

(d) any transient value

38. γ-rays and X-rays are both electromagnetic waves. Which of the following statements is true for these rays ?

(a) X-rays in general have larger wavelength than γ-rays.

(b) X-rays in general have same frequency as γ - rays.

(c) X-rays in general have smaller wavelength then γ-rays.

(d) X-rays in general have same wavelength as γ-rays.

39. If a source is transmitting electromagnetic waves of frequency 8.2×10^6 c/s, then wavelength of the these electromagnetic waves transmitted from the source will be :

(a) 50.9 m (b) 40.5 m

(c) 42.3 m (d) 36.6 m

40. If a T.V. tower has a height of 320 m and radius of the earth be 6400 km, then the distance upto which the signal can reach is about :

(a) 20 km (b) 40 km

(c) 64 km (d) 80 km

41. The area to be covered for a T.V. telecast is doubled, then the height of transmitting antenna will have to be :

(a) halved (b) doubled

(c) quardupled (d) kept unchanged

42. If the range of the T.V. telecast is to be doubled, then the height of the transmitting antenna will have to be :

(a) halved (b) doubled

(c) quardupled (d) kept unchanged

43. According to Gauss's theorem of electrostatics :

(a) $\oint \vec{E}.d\vec{S} = p$ (b) $\oint \vec{E}.d\vec{S} = \frac{q}{\varepsilon_0}$

(b) $\oint \vec{E}.d\vec{S} = 0$ (d) $\oint \vec{E}.\,d\vec{S} = \infty$

44. According to Gauss's theorem of magnetism:

(a) $\oint \vec{B}.d\vec{S} = p$ (b) $\oint \vec{B}.d\vec{S} = \frac{q}{\varepsilon_0}$

(b) $\oint \vec{B}.d\vec{S} = 0$ (d) $\oint \vec{B}.d\vec{S} = \infty$

45. The wavelength of microwaves is :

(a) larger than the wavelength of red light.

(b) larger than the wavelength of radio waves.

(c) smaller than the wavelength of violet light.

(d) smaller than the wavelength of yellow light.

46. An oscillating charge with a frequency of 1000 Hz would radiate electromagnetic waves of wavelength :

(a) 400 km (b) 300 km

(c) 200 km (d) 100 km

47. For a linearly polarized plane electromagnetic wave:

(A) The electric energy and the magnetic energy have equal average values.

(B) The electric field and the magnetic field have equal average values.

Of these two statements :

(a) B is false, but A is true.

(b) Both A and B are false.

(c) A is false, but B is true.

(d) Both A and B are true.

48. Radio waves detected from distant stars have a wavelength of about 0.20 m. If the speed of the wave is 3×10^8 ms^{-1}, then the frequency of the waves will be :

(D.C.E. 1997)

(a) 1.5×10^9 Hz (b) 6.7×10^{-9} Hz

(c) 1.5×10^4 Hz (d) 6.7×10^{-10} Hz

49. In an electromagnetic wave the average energy density associated with electric field is :

(a) $CV^2 / 2$ (b) $Q^2 / 2C$

(c) $\varepsilon_0^2 / 2E$ (d) $\varepsilon_0 E^2 / 2$

50. In an experiment, the electric field was found to oscillate with an amplitude of 18 V/m. The magnitude of the oscillating magnetic field will be :

(a) 11×10^{-11} T (b) 6×10^{-8} T

(c) 9×10^{-9} T (d) 4×10^{-6} T

51. Television signals have frequency range of :

(a) 10-50 MHz (b) 50-100 MHz

(c) 100-200 MHz (d) 10-50 kHz

52. In vacuum, the velocity of light does not depend upon :

(a) direction of propagation of light

(b) colour of light

(c) speed of source

(d) all of the above

53. The energy contained in a small volume through which an electromagnetic wave is passing oscillates with :

(a) the frequency of the wave

(b) half the frequency of the wave

(c) double the frequency of the wave

(d) zero frequency

54. If μ_0 is the permeability and k_0 is the dielectric constant of a medium, its refractive index is given by:

(a) $\frac{1}{\sqrt{\mu_0 k_0}}$ (b) $\frac{1}{\mu_0 k_0}$

(c) $\sqrt{\mu_0 k_0}$ (d) $\mu_0 k_0$

55. Microwaves are used in :

(a) Radar

(b) Radio transmission

(c) Laser

(d) Solar cell

56. The sun delivers 10^3 W/m^2 of electromagnetic flux to the earth's surface. The total power that is incident on a roof of dimensions 8 m × 20 m, will be :

(a) 2.56×10^4 W (b) 6.4×10^5 W

(c) 4.0×10^5 W (d) 1.6×10^5 W

57. In an electromagnetic wave, the oscillating electric field and magnetic field are :

(a) perpendicular to each other

(b) opposite to each other

(c) parallel to each other

(d) inclined at an angle of 45°

58. Which of the following is the infrared wavelength?

(a) 10^{-4} cm (b) 10^{-5} cm

(c) 10^{-6} cm (d) 10^{-7} cm

59. Maxwell's equations describe the fundamental laws of : **(A.I.E.E.E. 2003)**

(a) electricity only

(b) magnetism only

(c) both of electricity and magnetism

(d) mechanics only

60. Microwaves have frequencies :

(a) lower than radio waves

(b) equal to radio waves

(c) higher than radio waves

(d) none of the above

61. An electric field $\vec{E}$ and a magnetic field $\vec{B}$ exist in a region. The fields are not perpendicular to each other because:

(a) an electromagnetic wave may be passing through the region.

(b) an electromagnetic wave is certainly passing through the region.

(c) this is not possible.

(d) no electromagnetic wave is passing through the region

62. Green house effect keeps the atmosphere warm by trapping :

(a) infrared rays close to the earth's surface.

(b) ultraviolet rays close to the earth's surface.

(c) X-rays close to the earth's surface.

(d) visible light.

63. Red light differs from yellow light in its :
(a) velocity (b) frequency
(c) intensity (d) all of these

64. The process of superimposing signal wave on the high frequency carrier wave is known as :
(a) Modulation (b) Detection
(c) Transmission (d) Reception

65. Which of the following statements is correct in relation to electromagnetic waves in an isotropic medium?
(a) For a given amplitude of $\vec{E}$, the intensity increases as the first power of frequency f.
(b) For cylindrical wavefronts, the amplitude of the waves varies in proportion to $1/r^2$, where r is the radius of the wavefront.
(c) Energy due to electric field is equal to that due to magnetic field.
(d) Electric vector and magnetic vector $\vec{B}$ are in plane.

66. Ozone layer absorbs radiations of wavelength less than :
(a) 300 nm (b) 400 nm
(c) 500 nm (d) 600 nm

67. Which of the following statements is incorrect about electromagnetic waves :
(a) They travel with the same speed in all media.
(b) They are produced by accelerating charges.
(c) They travel with the velocity of light in vacuum.
(d) They are transverse in nature.

68. In an electromagnetic wave, the electric and magnetic fields are 100 V/m and 0.265 A/m. The maximum energy flow is :
(a) 46.7 W /m^2 (b) 76.5 W /m^2
(c) 26.5 W /m^2 (d) 36.5 W /m^2

69. The concept of displacement current was first given by :
(a) Gauss (b) Maxwell
(c) Coulomb (d) Bose

70. Which of the following has the longest wavelength?
(a) γ-rays (b) Radio waves
(c) X-rays (d) Infrared rays

71. Which of the following statements is correct?
(A) X-rays in vacuum travel faster than light waves in vacuum.
(B) The energy of X-rays photon is greater than that of a light photon.
(C) Light can be polarized but X-rays cannot.
(a) A and B (b) B and C
(c) A, B and C (d) B only

72. If v_g, v_x and v_m are the speeds of gamma rays, X-rays and microwaves respectively in vacuum, then : **(D.P.M.T. 1994)**
(a) $v_g > v_x < v_m$ (b) $v_g = v_x = v_m$
(c) $v_g < v_x < v_m$ (d) $v_g > v_x > v_m$

73. A free electron is placed in the path of a plane electromagnetic wave. The electron will start moving:
(a) along the plane of electric field.
(b) along the magnetic field.
(c) along the direction of propagation of the wave.
(d) in a plane containing the magnetic field and the direction of propagation.

74. Given the wave function (in S.I. units) for a wave to be,

$$\phi(x, t) = 10^3 \sin \pi (3 \times 10^6 x - 9 \times 10^{14} t).$$

The speed of the wave is :
(a) 3×10^6 m/s (b) 3×10^7 m/s
(c) 3×10^8 m/s (d) 9×10^{14} m/s

75. A parallel plate capacitor consists of two circular plates each of radius 12 cm and separated by 5.0 mm. The capacitor is being charged by an external source. The charging current is constant and is equal to 0.15 A. The rate of change of potential difference between the plates will be :

(a) 1.873×10^7 V/ s (b) 1.873×10^8 V/s

(c) 1.873×10^9 V/s (d) 1.873×10^{10} V/s

76. The sun radiates electromagnetic energy at the rate of 3.9×10^{26} W. Its radius is 6.96×10^8 m. The intensity of sun light (in W/m^2) at the solar surface will be :

(a) 4.2×10^6 (b) 4.2×10^7

(c) 5.6×10^6 (d) 5.6×10^7

77. An electromagnetic wave travelling through vacuum represented by $E = E_0 \sin (kx - \omega t)$. Which of the following is/are independent of the wavelength ?

(a) k (b) k/ω

(c) $k\omega$ (d) ω

78. In A.M., carrier frequency is in :

(a) Mega hertz (b) Kilo hertz

(c) Milli hertz (d) Giga hertz

79. The wavelength of waves transmitted by a 50 Hz transmission line is :

(a) 6×10^3 m (b) 6×10^4 m

(c) 6×10^5 m (d) 6×10^6 m

80. The unit of $\mu_o\, \varepsilon_0$ is :

(a) m/s (b) m^2/s^2

(c) s/m (d) s^2/m^2

81. A flood light is covered with a filter that transmits red light. The electric field of the emerging beam is represented by a sinusoidal plane wave

$E_x = 36 \sin (1.20 \times 10^7 x - 3.6 \times 10^{15}\, t)$ V/m

The average intensity of beam in watt/(metre)^2 will be:

(a) 6.88 (b) 3.44

(c) 1.72 (d) 0.86

82. E.M. waves do not transport :

(a) magnetic field (b) charge

(c) energy (d) electric field

83. In an amplitude modulated wave for audio-frequency of 500 cycles/second, the appropriate carrier frequency will be :

(a) 50 cycles/sec (b) 100 cycles/sec

(c) 500 cycles/sec (d) 50,000 cycles/sec

84. If the electric amplitude of the wave is 5 Vm^{-1}, the magnetic amplitude of this wave is :

(a) 5 A Wb/m^2

(b) 1.67×10^{-10} Wb/m^2

(c) 1.67×10^{-8} Wb/m^2

(d) 5×10^{-10} Wb/m^2

85. Which of the following pairs of space and time varying electric (E) and magnetic (B) fields would generate a plane electromagnetic wave travelling along the X-direction ?

(a) E_X , B_Z (b) E_Y , B_Z

(c) E_Z , B_X (d) E_Y , B_X

86. An accelerating proton produces :

(a) α-rays (b) γ-rays

(c) β-rays (d) E.M. rays

87. Speed of electromagnetic wave is the same :

(a) for all wavelengths

(b) for all frequencies

(c) in all media

(d) for all intensities

88. The average temperature on the surface of the earth in the absence of atmosphere would be :

(a) lower (b) higher

(c) unchanged (d) 0°C

89. Low lying clouds reflect :

(a) IR radiations (b) UV radiations

(c) All radiations (d) X-ray radiations

90. Dimensions of $\varepsilon_0\, \mu_0$ are :

(a) $L\, T^{-1}$ (b) $L^{-1}\, T$

(c) $L^2\, T^{-2}$ (d) $L^{-2} T^2$

91. The dimensions of $\frac{1}{2}\varepsilon_0 E^2$ (ε_0 = permittivity of free space; E = electric field) is :

(I.I.T 2000)

(a) MLT^{-1} (b) ML^2T^{-2}

(c) $ML^{-1}T^2$ (d) ML^2T^{-1}

92. If $\vec{E}$ and $\vec{B}$ represent electric and magnetic field vectors of the electromagnetic waves, then the direction of propagation of the electromagnetic waves is that of :

(a) $\vec{E}$ (b) $\vec{B}$

(c) $\vec{E}\times\vec{B}$ (d) $\vec{B}\times\vec{E}$

93. Which of the following has minimum wavelength? **(C.B.S.E. 2001)**

(a) X-rays (b) Ultraviolet rays

(c) γ-rays (d) Cosmic rays

94. Infrared spectrum lies between :

(C.E.T 1998)

(a) Radio wave and microwave region

(b) Microwave and visible region

(c) Visible and ultraviolet region

(d) Ultraviolet and X-ray region

95. Which of the following statements is wrong?

(a) Ultraviolet rays have a wavelength longer than infra-red rays.

(b) Infrared rays travel with the same velocity as visible light.

(c) Infrared rays can be focussed by a lens and can be reflected by a mirror just as visible light.

(d) Infrared rays have more heating power than visible light rays.

96. Which of the following is independent of wavelength ?

(a) k (b) ω

(c) ωk (d) k/ω

97. Let $[\varepsilon_0]$ denote the dimensional formula of the permittivity of the vacuum and $[\mu_0]$ that of the permeability of the vacuum. If M = mass, L = length, T = time and I = electric current, then :

(a) $[\varepsilon_0] = M^{-1}L^{-3}T^2I$

(b) $[\varepsilon_0] = M^{-1}L^{-3}T^4I^2$

(c) $[\mu_0] = MLT^{-2}I^{-2}$

(d) $[\mu_0] = ML^2T^{-1}I$

98. A uniform but time-varying magnetic field B(t) exists in a circular region of radius a and directed into the plane of the paper as shown. **(I.I.T 2000)**

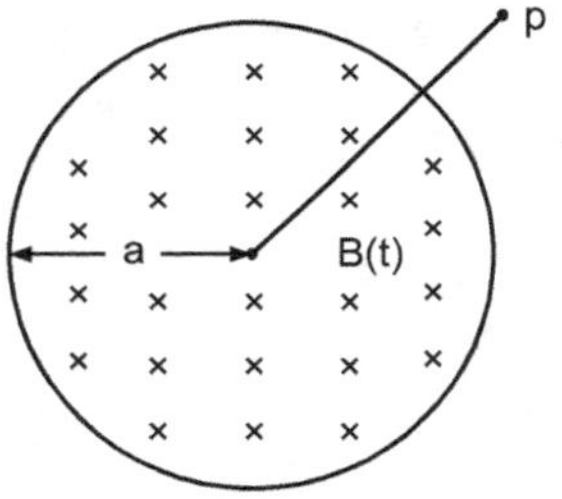

The magnitude of the induced electric field at point P at a distance r from the centre of the circular region :

(a) is zero (b) decreases as 1/r

(c) increases as r (d) decreases as 1/2

99. Electromagnetic waves travel in a medium at a speed of $1.5\times10^8\ ms^{-1}$. The relative permeability of the medium is 1.0. The relative permittivity of the medium is

(a) 1.5 (b) 2

(c) 3 (d) 4

100. We can produce a displacement current of 1 A between the plates of capacitor of $1\mu F$ by :

(a) increasing voltage between the plates at the rate $10^6\ Vs^{-1}$.

(b) decreasing voltage between the plates at the rate $10^6\ Vs^{-1}$.

(c) both (a) and (b).

(d) current cannot be produced between the plates of the capacitor.

101. The electric field of a plane electromagnetic wave in vacuum is given by $E_x = 0$:

$E_y = 0.5 \cos\left[2\pi \times 10^8 \left(t - \frac{x}{c}\right)\right]$, $E_z = 0$, the direction of propagation of the electromagnetic wave is along

(a) positive x-axis (b) negative x-axis

(c) positive y-axis (d) negative y-axis

102. In Q. 101, wavelength of the wave is :

(a) $(3/2\pi)$ m (b) $(30/2\pi)$ units

(c) 3 units (d) 1.5 units

103. Magnetic field component associated with the electromagnetic wave given in Q. 101 will be :

(a) $B_x = \frac{0.5}{3 \times 10^8} \cos\left[2\pi \times 10^8 \left(t - \frac{x}{c}\right)\right]$;

$B_y = 0;\ B_z = 0$

(b) $B_x = 0,\ B_y = 0.5 \cos\left[2\pi \times 10^8 \left(t - \frac{x}{c}\right)\right]$;

$B_z = 0$

(c) $B_x = 0;\ B_y = 0;$

$B_z = \frac{0.5}{3 \times 10^8} \cos\left[2\pi \times 10^8 \left(t - \frac{x}{c}\right)\right]$

(d) $B_x = 0;\ B_y = 0;$

$B_z = 0.5 \cos\left[2\pi \times 10^8 \left(t - \frac{x}{c}\right)\right]$

104. A capacitor of 4μF is charged to 20V and then suddenly short circuited by a coil of negligible resistance and inductance 16 μH. The maximum amplitude of the current oscillations will be :

(a) 5 A (b) 2 A

(c) 10 A (d) 4 A

105. In Q. 104, maximum frequency of current oscillations will be approximately :

(a) 1.99×10^4 Hz (b) 10^4 Hz

(c) 2×10^6 Hz (d) 9×10^6 Hz

106. A parallel plate capacitor of plate area 50 cm^2 and plate separation 3.0 mm is charged initially to 80μC. Due to radioactive source nearby, the medium between plates becomes slightly conducting and the plates start losing charge initially at the rate of 1.5×10^{-8} Cs^{-1}. Magnitude and direction of displacement current will be :

(a) 1.5×10^{-8} A (b) 3×10^{-8} A

(c) 10^{-2} A (d) 1.3×10^{-2} A

107. Energy stored in a 30 cm length of a laser beam operating at 5 mW is :

(a) 10^{-12} J (b) 12×10^{-12} J

(c) 5×10^{-12} J (d) 5×10^{-12} erg

108. A plane e.m. wave propagating along x-direction has a wavelength of 6 mm. The electric field is in the y-direction and its maximum magnitude is 33 Vm^{-1}. Equations for electric field and magnetic fields as function of x and t are

(a) $E_x = 33 \sin \pi \times 10^{11} \left(t - \frac{x}{c}\right)$ and

$B_z = 33 \sin \pi \times 10^{11} \left(t - \frac{x}{c}\right)$

(b) $E_y = 33 \sin \pi \times 10^{11} \left(t - \frac{x}{c}\right)$ and

$B_x = 1.1 \times 10^{-7} \sin \pi \times 10^{11} \left(t - \frac{x}{c}\right)$

(c) $E_y = 33 \sin \pi \times 10^{11} \left(t - \frac{x}{c}\right)$ and

$B_z = 33 \sin \pi \times 10^{11} \left(t - \frac{x}{c}\right)$

(d) $E_y = 33 \sin \pi \times 10^{11} \left(t - \frac{x}{c}\right)$ and

$B_z = 1.1 \times 10^{-7} \sin \pi \times 10^{11} \left(t - \frac{x}{c}\right)$

109. The wave emitted by any atom or molecule has $\lambda = 5.9 \times 10^{-7}$ cm, it must have some finite total length. For sodium light if this length (called coherence length) is 2.4 cm, then number of oscillations in this length are:

(a) 4.068×10^6 Hz (b) 2.3×10^3 Hz

(c) 3×10^{-11} Hz (d) 1.5×10^8 Hz

110. In Q. 109 the coherence time will be :
(a) 10^{-11} sec (b) 10^{-6} sec
(c) 8×10^{-11} sec (d) 10^{-2} sec

111. A lamp emits monochromatic green light in all directions. If lamp is 3% efficient in converting electrical power to electromagnetic waves and consumes 100 W of power, then amplitude of the electric field associated with the electromagnetic radiation at a distance of 5 m from the lamp will be :
(a) 2.68 V / m (b) 5.36 V / m
(c) 1.34 V /m (d) 4.02 V /m

112. The correct statement about electromagnetic waves is :
(a) They are supersonic waves.
(b) They are electric charged particles.
(c) They travel with the speed of light.
(d) They can only be produced in laboratory.

113. Wavelength of X-rays is of order :
(a) 10 A (b) 1 A
(c) 100 A (d) 1000 A

114. Which of the following electromagnetic waves are useful for telecommunication ?
(a) Infrared waves (b) Ultraviolet rays
(b) Radiowaves (d) Microwaves

115. Ozone layer blocks the radiations of wavelength :
(a) less than 3×10^{-7} m
(b) equal to 3×10^{-7} m
(c) greater than 3×10^{-7} m
(d) all of these

116. The phase and orientation of the magnetic vector associated with electromagnetic oscillations differ respectively from those of the corresponding electric vector by :
(a) Zero and zero (b) Zero and π /2
(c) π /2 and π /2 (d) π /2 and zero

117. Which of the following radiations form the part of electromagnetic spectrum?
(a) Alpha rays (b) Beta rays
(c) Cathode rays (d) Gamma rays

118. Radio transmitter works at a frequency of 880 kHz and power of 10 kW. The number of photons per second emitted is :
(a) 0.075×10^{-34} (b) 1.7×10^{31}
(c) 1327×10^{34} (d) 13.27×10^{34}

119. The stratosphere in the atmosphere extends from about :
(a) 10-20 km above the ground
(b) 20-50 km above the ground
(c) 50-80 km above the ground
(d) 80-100 km above the ground

120. The distance upto which T.V. signals can be received depends upon :
(a) radius of the earth
(b) height of the antenna
(c) radius of the earth and also height of the antenna
(d) none of the above.

121. In a plane e.m. wave, the electric field oscillates sinusoidally at a frequency of 2.5×10^{10} Hz and amplitude 480 V/m. The amplitude of the oscillating magnetic field will be :
(a) 1.6×10^{-6} Wb/m^2
(b) 1.6×10^{-7} Wb/m^2
(c) 1.52×10^{-8} Wb/m^2
(d) 1.52×10^{-7} Wb/m^2

122. Radiowaves received by a radio telescope from distant stars may have a wavelength of about 2 m. If the speed of the wave is 3×10^8 m/s, then frequency of the wave will be :
(a) 1.5×10^{10} Hz (b) 1.5×10^8 Hz
(c) 6.7×10^{-10} Hz (d) 6.7×10^{-9} Hz

123. A lamp emits monochromatic green light in all directions. If lamp is 6% efficient in converting electrical power to electromagnetic waves and consumes 100 W of power then amplitude of the electric field associated with the electromagnetic radiation at a distance of 5 m from the lamp will be :
(a) 3.79 V / m (b) 5.36 V / m
(c) 1.34 V /m (d) 4.02 V / m

124. A T.V. tower has a height of 100 m. The average population density around the tower is 1000 km^{-2} and radius of the earth is 6.37×10^6 m. The population covered is :

(a) 4×10^6 (b) 6×10^4
(c) 8×10^6 (d) 16×10^4

125. Radiowaves of constant amplitude can be generated with :

(a) Filter (b) Rectifier
(c) FET (d) Oscillator

126. Which of the following have zero average value in a plane electromagnetic wave?

(a) Electric energy (b) Magnetic energy
(c) Magnetic field (d) Electric field

127. The name of the source and the spectral range of few wavelengths of electro-magnetic spectrum are given. Which of the following statements is wrong?

(a) 5800 Å from ionized gases and illuminated bodies, visible range
(b) 200 m oscillating electric circuits, radio waves
(c) 0.6 Å fast electrons striking heavy target, X-rays
(d) 1.2 Å sun light, ultra-violet rays

128. The area to be covered for T.V. telecast is doubled, then the height of transmitting antenna will have to be :

(a) halved (b) doubled
(c) quadrupled (d) kept unchanged

129. Transmission of T.V. signals from the surface of the moon can be received on earth. But transmitted T. V. signals from Delhi cannot be received beyond a 110 km distance. The reason is :

(a) There is no atmosphere on the moon.
(b) Strong gravitational effect on T.V. signals.
(c) T. V. signals travel along a straight line, they do not follow the curvature of earth.
(d) There is atmosphere around the earth.

130. If the range of the T.V. telecast is to be made three times, then the height of transmitting antenna will have to be :

(a) halved (b) doubled
(c) nine times (d) kept unchanged

131. In an electromagnetic wave the average energy density associated with electric field is :

(a) $CV^2 / 2$ (b) $Q^2 / 2C$
(c) $\varepsilon_0^2 / 2E$ (d) $B^2 / 2\mu_0$

132. For telecommunication through artificial satellites, the waves used are :

(a) Microwaves
(b) Radiowaves
(c) A.M.
(d) Of frequencies of the order of 10^{16} Hz

133. Microwaves are electromagnetic waves with frequency, in the range of :

(a) Micro hertz (b) Mega hertz
(c) Giga hertz (d) Hertz

134. Which of the following layers disappear at night ?

(a) F_1 - layer (b) F_2 - layer
(c) D - layer (d) E - layer

135. The sun delivers 10^3 W/m^2 of electromagnetic flux to the earth's surface. The total power that is incident on a roof of dimensions 10 m × 30 m, will be :

(a) 2.56×10^4 W (b) 6.4×10^5 W
(c) 4.0×10^5 W (d) 3×10^5 W

136. In an electromagnetic wave, the electric and magnetic fields are 200 V/m and 0.53 A/m. The maximum energy flow is :

(D.P.M.T. 1997)

(a) 46.7 W/m^2 (b) 76.5 W/m^2
(c) 106 W/m^2 (d) 100 W/m^2

137. Given the wave function (in S.I. units) for an electromagnetic wave to be,

$\phi(x, t) = 10^3 \sin \pi (3 \times 10^6 x - 9 \times 10^{16} t)$.

The speed of the wave is :

(a) 3×10^6 m/s (b) 3×10^7 m/s
(c) 3×10^8 m/s (d) 9×10^{14} m/s

138. A particle of charge $- 16 \times 10^{-18}$ coulomb moving with velocity 10 ms^{-1} along the x-axis enters a region where a magnetic field of induction B of magnitude 10 V/m is along the negative z-axis. If the charged particle continues moving along the x-axis, the magnitude of B is : **(A.I.E.E.E. 2003)**

(a) 10^{-3} Wb/m^2 (b) 10^3 Wb/m^2

(c) 10^5 Wb/m^2 (d) 10^{16} Wb/m^2

139. The speed of electromagnetic waves in vacuum : **(Kerala P.M.T. 2004)**

(a) depends upon the source of radiation

(b) increases as we move from γ-rays to radiowaves

(c) decreases as we move from γ-rays to radio waves

(d) is same for all of them

140. Which of the following values is equal to velocity of light ? **(J & K C.E.T. 2007)**

(a) $\frac{\sqrt{\mu_0}}{\varepsilon_0}$ (b) $\frac{1}{\sqrt{\mu_0 \varepsilon_0}}$

(c) $\sqrt{\mu_0 \varepsilon_0}$ (d) $\sqrt{\frac{\mu_0}{\varepsilon_0}}$

141. (i) The wavelength of microwaves is greater than that of UV-rays.

(ii) The wavelength of IR rays in lesser than that of UV-rays.

(iii) The wavelength of microwaves is lesser than that of IR rays.

(iv) Gamma ray has shortest wavelength in the electromagnetic spectrum.

(Kerala P.E.T. 2007)

Of the above statements :

(a) (i) and (ii) are true

(b) (ii) and (iii) are true

(c) (iii) and (iv) are true

(d) (i) and (iii) are true

142. Biological importance of ozone layer is that it: **(H.P.P.M.T. 2008)**

(a) reduces greenhouse effect

(b) stops the ultraviolet rays

(c) reflects radio waves

(d) contracts O_2/H_2 ratio in atmosphere

143. The velocity of electromagnetic radiation in a medium of permittivity ε_0 and permeability μ_0 is given by, **(C.B.S.E. P.M.T. 2008)**

(a) $\sqrt{\mu_0 \varepsilon_0}$ (b) $\frac{1}{\sqrt{\mu_0 \varepsilon_0}}$

(c) $\sqrt{\frac{\mu_0}{\varepsilon_0}}$ (d) $\sqrt{\frac{\varepsilon_0}{\mu_0}}$

144. The radiation pressure (in N/m^2) of the visible light is of the order of :

(D.P.M.T. 2009)

(a) 10^{-2} (b) 10^{-4}

(c) 10^{-6} (d) 10^{-8}

145. The wavelength of X-rays is of the order of :

(Manipur M.B.B.S./B.D.S. 2009)

(a) 1 cm (b) 1 micron

(c) 1 Å (d) 1 m

146. Electromagnetic wave consists of periodically oscillating electric and magnetic vectors : **(C.E.T. Karnataka 2010)**

(a) in mutually perpendicular planes but vibrating in phase.

(b) in randomly oriented planes but vibrating in phase.

(c) in mutually perpendicular planes but vibrating with a phase difference of π/2.

(d) in mutually perpendicular planes but vibrating with a phase difference of π.

147. A plane electromagnetic wave travelling along the X-direction has a wavelength of 3 mm. The variation in the electric field occurs in the Y-direction with an amplitude 66 Vm^{-1}. The equations for the electric and magnetic fields as a function of x and t are ...... respectively. **(Kerala P.E.T. 2008)**

(a) $E_y = 33 \cos \pi \times 10^{11}\left(t - \frac{x}{c}\right)$,

$B_z = 1.1 \times 10^{-7} \cos \pi \times 10^{11}\left(t - \frac{x}{c}\right)$

(b) $E_y = 11 \cos 2\pi \times 10^{11}\left(t - \frac{x}{c}\right)$,

$B_y = 11 \times 10^{-7} \cos 2\pi \times 10^{11}\left(t - \frac{x}{c}\right)$

(c) $E_x = 33 \cos \pi \times 10^{11}\left(t - \frac{x}{c}\right)$,

$B_x = 11 \times 10^{-7} \cos \pi \times 10^{11}\left(t - \frac{x}{c}\right)$

(d) $E_y = 66 \cos 2\pi \times 10^{11}\left(t - \frac{x}{c}\right)$,

$B_z = 2.2 \times 10^{-7} \cos 2\pi \times 10^{11}\left(t - \frac{x}{c}\right)$

(e) $E_y = 66 \cos \pi \times 10^{11}\left(t - \frac{x}{c}\right)$,

$B_y = 2.2 \times 10^{-7} \cos \pi \times 10^{11}\left(t - \frac{x}{c}\right)$

148. The maximum electron density in the ionosphere in the morning is 10^{10} m^{-3}. At noon time, it increases to 2×10^{10} m^{-3}. Find the ratio of critical frequency at noon and the critical frequency in the morning : **(Gujarat C.E.T. 2009)**

(a) 2.00 (b) 2.82

(c) 4.00 (d) 1.414

149. A plane electromagnetic wave of frequency 30 MHz travels in the free space along the *x*-direction. The electric field component of the wave at a perpendicular point of space and time is E = 6 V/m along *y*-direction. Its magnetic field component B at this point would be : **(D.C.E. 2009)**

(a) 2×10^{-8} T along *z*-direction

(b) 6×10^{-8} T along *x*-direction

(c) 2×10^{-8} T along *y*-direction

(d) 6×10^{-8} T along *z*-direction

150. The refractive index and the permeability of a medium are 1.5 and 5×10^{-7} Hm^{-1} respectively. The relative permittivity of the medium is nearly : **(Kerala C.E.T. 2009)**

(a) 25 (b) 15

(c) 81 (d) 6

151. The magnetic field in a plane electromagnetic field is given by

$B_y = 2\times10^{-7} \sin (0.5\times 10^3 z + 1.5 \times 10^{11} t)$T.

The expression for the electric field may be given by : **(A.M.U. (Medical) 2009)**

(a) $E_y = 2 \times 10^{-7} \sin (0.5 \times 10^3 z + 1.5 \times 10^{11} t)$ V/m

(b) $E_x = 2 \times 10^{-7} \sin (0.5 \times 10^3 z + 1.5 \times 10^{11} t)$ V/m

(c) $E_y = 60 \sin (0.5 \times 10^3 z + 1.5 \times 10^{11} t)$ V/m

(d) $E_x = 60 \sin (0.5 \times 10^3 z + 1.5 \times 10^{11} t)$ V/m

152. A layer of ionosphere does not reflect waves with frequencies greater than 10 MHz; then maximum electron density in this layer is: **(Gujarat C.E.T. 2009)**

(a) 1.23×10^{11} m^{-3} (b) 1.23×10^{13} m^{-3}

(c) 1.23×10^{10} m^{-3} (d) 1.23×10^{12} m^{-3}

153. A point source of electromagnetic radiation has an average power output of 1500 W. The maximum value of electric field at a distance of 3 m from this source in Vm^{-1} is : **(Kerala C.E.T. 2009)**

(a) 500 (b) 100

(c) $\frac{500}{3}$ (d) $\frac{250}{3}$

154. The electric field of an electromagnetic wave in free space is given by

$\vec{E} = 10 \cos (10^7 t + kx) \hat{j}$ V/m,

where *t* and *x* are in seconds and metres respectively. It can be inferred that : **(A.I.P.M.T. (Mains) 2010)**

(i) the wavelength λ is 188.4 m

(ii) the wave number k is 0.33 rad/m

(iii) the wave amplitude is 10 V/m

(iv) the wave is propagating along +*x*-direction

Which one of the following pairs of statements is correct ?

(a) (iii) and (iv) (b) (i) and (ii)

(c) (ii) and (iii) (d) (i) and (iii)

155. Which of the following has maximum energy? **(R.P.M.T. 2001)**

(a) Radiowaves

(b) Infrared rays

(c) Ultraviolet rays

(d) Microwaves

156. In T.V. broadcasting both picture and sound are transmitted simultaneously. In this : **(T.N.P. C.E.E. 2002)**

(a) audio signal is frequency modulated and video signal is amplitude modulated.

(b) both audio and video signals are frequency modulated.

(c) audio signal is amplitude modulated and video signal is frequency modulated.

(d) both audio and video signals are amplitude modulated.

157. For sky wave propagation of a 10 MHz signal, what should be the minimum electron density in ionosphere ?

(a) $\sim 1.2 \times 10^{12}\ m^{-3}$ (b) $\sim 10^{6}\ m^{-3}$

(c) $\sim 10^{14}\ m^{-3}$ (d) $\sim 10^{22}\ m^{-3}$

158. Sky wave propagation is used in :

(a) Radio communication

(b) Satellite communication

(c) TV communication

(d) Both TV and satellite communication

159. The principle used for the transmission of light signals through the optical fibre is : **(Kerala P.M.T. 2007)**

(a) Reflection

(b) Refraction

(c) Interference

(d) Total internal reflection

160. The sky wave propagation is suitable for radio waves of frequency

(a) Upto 2 MHz

(b) From 2 MHz to 20 MHz

(c) From 2 MHz to 30 MHz

(d) From 2 MHz to 50 MHz

161. Modulation is the process of superposing : **(Kerala P.M.T. 2007)**

(a) low frequency audio signal on high frequency radio waves.

(b) low frequency radio signal on low frequency audio waves.

(c) high frequency radio signal on low frequency audio signal.

(d) high frequency audio signal on low frequency radio waves.

162. In satellite communication : **(Kerala P.E.T. 2008)**

(i) the frequency used lies between 5 MHz and 10 MHz.

(ii) the uplink and downlink frequencies are different.

(iii) the orbit of geostationary satellite lies in the equatorial plane at an inclination of 0°.

In the above statements :

(a) Only (ii) and (iii) are true

(b) All are true

(c) Only (ii) is true

(d) Only (i) and (ii) are true

163. Which of the following statements is wrong? **(Kerala P.E.T. 2009)**

(a) Ground wave propagation can be sustained at frequencies 500 kHz to 1500 kHz.

(b) Satellite communication is useful for the frequencies above 30 MHz.

(c) Sky wave propagation is useful in the range of 30 to 40 MHz.

(d) Space wave propagation takes place through tropospheric space.

164. Ionosphere is used for : **(M.H.T. C.E.T. 2009)**

(a) Sky waves (b) Space waves

(b) Ground waves (d) All

165. A typical optical fibre consists of a fine core of a material of refractive index μ_1, surrounded by a glass or plastic cladding with refractive index μ_2 : **(D.C.E. 2009)**

(a) μ_2 is slightly less than μ_1.

(b) μ_2 is slightly higher than μ_1.

(c) μ_2 should be equal to μ_1.

(d) The difference $\mu_2 - \mu_1$ should be strictly equal to 1.

166. Which one of the following is a full duplex transmission system?

(Gujarat C.E.T. 2010)

(a) Telephone

(b) Walky-talky (wireless used in the Army)

(c) T.V.

(d) Radio

167. The frequency band used in the downlink of satellite communication is :

(Kerala Engg. 2010)

(a) 9.5 to 2.5 GHz (b) 896 to 901 MHz

(c) 3.7 to 4.2 GHz (d) 3.7 to 4.2 MHz

168. What fraction of the surface area of Earth can be covered to establish communication by one geostationary satellite ?

(Gujarat C.E.T. 2011)

(a) $\frac{1}{2}$ (b) $\frac{1}{3}$

(c) $\frac{1}{4}$ (d) $\frac{1}{8}$

ANSWER KEY

1. (d)	**2.** (b)	**3.** (c)	**4.** (b)	**5.** (a)	**6.** (d)	**7.** (a)	**8.** (c)	**9.** (d)	**10.**(d)
11.(b)	**12.**(c)	**13.**(a)	**14.**(b)	**15.**(b)	**16.**(d)	**17.**(c)	**18.**(c)	**19.**(a)	**20.**(a)
21.(c)	**22.**(a)	**23.**(b)	**24.**(a)	**25.**(c)	**26.**(c)	**27.**(a)	**28.**(b)	**29.**(a)	**30.**(c)
31.(a)	**32.**(b)	**33.**(a)	**34.**(a)	**35.**(d)	**36.**(b)	**37.**(b)	**38.**(a)	**39.**(d)	**40.**(c)
41.(b)	**42.**(c)	**43.**(b)	**44.**(c)	**45.**(a)	**46.**(b)	**47.**(d)	**48.**(a)	**49.**(d)	**50.**(b)
51.(c)	**52.**(d)	**53.**(c)	**54.**(c)	**55.**(a)	**56.**(d)	**57.**(a)	**58.**(a)	**59.**(c)	**60.**(c)
61.(d)	**62.**(a)	**63.**(b)	**64.**(a)	**65.** (c & d)	**66.**(b)	**67.**(a)	**68.**(c)	**69.**(b)	**70.**(b)
71.(c)	**72.**(b)	**73.**(a)	**74.**(c)	**75.**(c)	**76.**(d)	**77.**(b)	**78.**(b)	**79.**(d)	**80.**(d)
81.(c)	**82.**(b)	**83.**(d)	**84.**(c)	**85.**(b)	**86.**(d)	**87.**(d)	**88.**(a)	**89.**(a)	**90.**(d)
91.(c)	**92.**(c)	**93.**(c)	**94.**(b)	**95.**(a)	**96.**(d)	**97.**(b)	**98.**(b)	**99.**(d)	**100.** (c)
101. (a)	**102.** (c)	**103.** (c)	**104.** (c)	**105.** (a)	**106.** (a)	**107.** (c)	**108.** (d)	**109.** (a)	**110.** (c)
111. (a)	**112.** (c)	**113.** (b)	**114.** (d)	**115.** (a)	**116.** (b)	**117.** (d)	**118.** (b)	**119.** (b)	**120.** (c)
121. (a)	**122.** (b)	**123.** (a)	**124.** (a)	**125.** (d)	**126.** (c, d)	**127.** (d)	**128.** (b)	**129.** (c)	**130.** (c)
131. (d)	**132.** (d)	**133.** (c)	**134.** (b)	**135.** (d)	**136.** (c)	**137.** (c)	**138.** (b)	**139.** (d)	**140.** (b)
141. (d)	**142.** (b)	**143.** (b)	**144.** (c)	**145.** (c)	**146.** (a)	**147.** (d)	**148.** (d)	**149.** (a)	**150.** (d)
151. (d)	**152.** (d)	**153.** (b)	**154.** (d)	**155.** (c)	**156.** (a)	**157.** (a)	**158.** (a)	**159.** (d)	**160.** (c)
161. (a)	**162.** (a)	**163.** (c)	**164.** (a)	**165.** (a)	**166.** (a)	**167.** (c)	**168.** (b)		

QUESTION PAPERS OF PREVIOUS YEARS EXAMS
NEET 2013

1. In an experiment four quantities a, b, c and d are measured with percentage error 1%, 2%, 3% and 4% respectively. Quantity P is calculated as follows,

$P = \frac{a^3b^2}{cd}$ · Then % error in P is :

(a) 14% (b) 10%

(c) 7% (d) 4%

2. The velocity of a projectile at the initial point A is $(2\hat{i} + 3\hat{j})$ m/s. Its velocity (in m/s) at point B is :

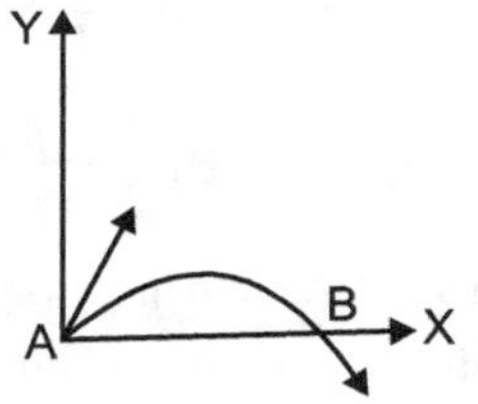

(a) $-2\hat{i} + 3\hat{j}$ (b) $2\hat{i} - 3\hat{j}$

(c) $2\hat{i} + 3\hat{j}$ (d) $-2\hat{i} - 3\hat{j}$

3. A stone falls freely under gravity. It covers distances h_1, h_2 and h_3 in the first 5 seconds, the next 5 seconds and the next 5 seconds respectively. The relation between h_1, h_2 and h_3 is

(a) $h_1 = \frac{h_2}{3} = \frac{h_3}{5}$

(b) $h_2 = 3h_1$ and $h_3 = 3h_2$

(c) $h_1 = h_2 = h_3$

(d) $h_1 = 2h_2 = 3h_3$

4. Three blocks with masses m, $2m$ and $3m$ are connected by strings as shown in figure. After an upward force F is applied on block m, the masses move upward at constant speed v. What is the net force on the block of mass $2m$? (g is the acceleration due to gravity)

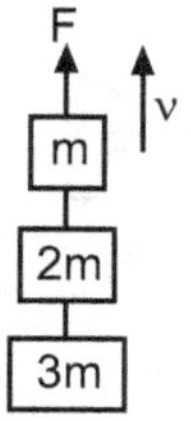

(a) 2 mg

(b) 3 mg

(c) 6 mg

(d) Zero

5. The upper half of an inclined plane of inclination θ is perfectly smooth while lower half is rough. A block starting from rest at the top of the plane will again come to rest at the bottom, if the coefficient of friction between the block and lower half of the plane is :

(a) $\mu = \frac{2}{\tan\theta}$ (b) $\mu = 2\tan\theta$

(c) $\mu = \tan\theta$ (d) $\mu = \frac{1}{\tan\theta}$

6. A uniform force of $(3\hat{i} + \hat{j})$ newton acts on a particle of mass 2 kg. Hence, the particle is displaced from position $(2\hat{i} + \hat{k})$ metre to position $(4\hat{i} + 3\hat{j} - \hat{k})$ metre. The work done by the force on the particle is :

(a) 6 J (b) 13 J

(c) 15 J (d) 9 J

7. An explosion breaks a rock into three parts in a horizontal plane. Two of them go off at right angles to each other. The first part of mass 1 kg moves with a speed of 12 ms^{-1} and the second part of mass 2 kg moves with 8 ms^{-1} speed. If the third part flies off with 4 ms^{-1} speed, then its mass is :

(a) 5 kg (b) 7 kg

(c) 17 kg (d) 3 kg

8. A rod PQ of mass M and length L is hinged at end P. The rod is kept horizontal by a massless string tied to point Q as shown in figure. When string is cut, the initial angular acceleration of the rod is :

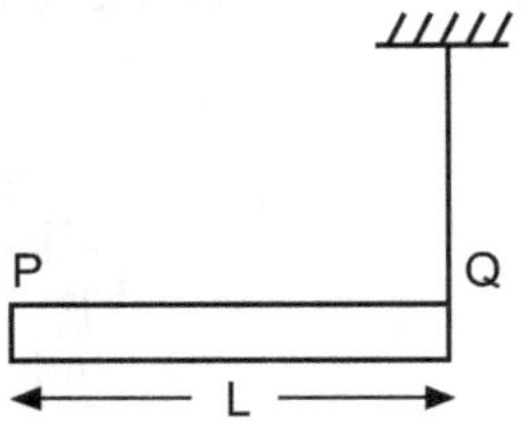

(a) $\frac{g}{L}$ (b) $\frac{2g}{L}$

(c) $\frac{2g}{3L}$ (d) $\frac{3g}{2L}$

9. A small object of uniform density rolls up a curved surface with an initial velocity 'v'. It reaches up to a maximum height of $\frac{3v^2}{4g}$ with respect to the initial position. The object is :

(a) Solid sphere (b) Hollow sphere

(c) Disc (d) Ring

10. A body of mass 'm' is taken from the earth's surface to the height equal to twice the radius (R) of the earth. The change in potential energy of body will be :

(a) $\frac{2}{3}mg\text{R}$ (b) $3\,mg\text{R}$

(c) $\frac{1}{3}mg\text{R}$ (d) $mg2\text{R}$

11. Infinite number of bodies, each of mass 2 kg are situated on x-axis at distance 1 m, 2 m, 4 m, 8 m, ... respectively, from the origin. The resulting gravitational potential due to this system at the origin will be :

(a) $-\frac{8}{3}$G (b) $-\frac{4}{3}$G

(c) – 4G (d) – G

12. The following four wires are made of the same material. Which of these will have the largest extension when the same tension is applied ?

(a) Length = 100 cm, diameter = 1 mm

(b) Length = 200 cm, diameter = 2 mm

(c) Length = 300 cm, diameter = 3 mm

(d) Length = 50 cm, diameter = 0.5 mm

13. The wettability of a surface by a liquid depends primarily on :

(a) Surface tension

(b) Density

(c) Angle of contact between the surface and the liquid

(d) Viscosity

14. The molar specific heats of an ideal gas at constant pressure and volume are denoted by C_p and C_v respectively. If $\gamma = \frac{C_p}{C_v}$ and R is the universal gas constant, then C_v is equal to :

(a) $\frac{R}{(\gamma - 1)}$ (b) $\frac{(\gamma - 1)}{R}$

(c) γR (d) $\frac{1+\gamma}{1-\gamma}$

15. A piece of iron is heated in a flame. It first becomes dull red, then becomes reddish yellow and finally turns to white hot. The correct explanation for the above observation is possible by using :

(a) Wien's Displacement Law

(b) Kirchhoff's Law

(c) Newton's Law of cooling

(d) Stefan's Law

16. A gas is taken through the cycle A → B → C → A, as shown. What is the net work done by the gas ?

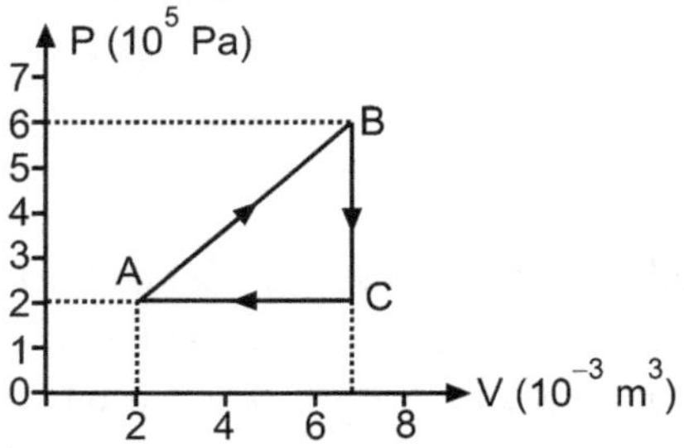

(a) 1000 J (b) Zero

(c) – 2000 J (d) 2000 J

17. During an adiabatic process, the pressure of a gas is found to be proportional to the cube of its temperature. The ratio of $\frac{C_p}{C_v}$ for the gas is :

(a) 2 (b) $\frac{5}{3}$

(c) $\frac{3}{2}$ (d) $\frac{4}{3}$

18. In the given (V-T) diagram, what is the relation between pressures P_1 and P_2 ?

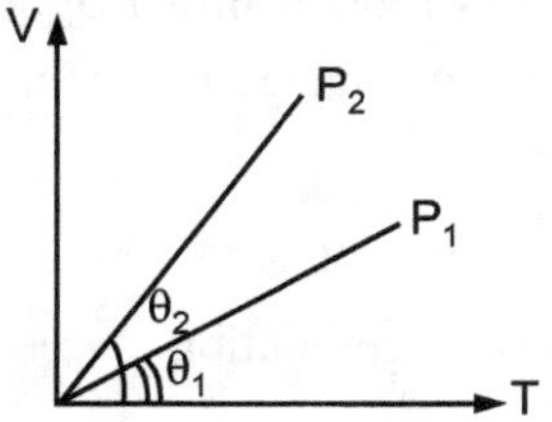

(a) $P_2 > P_1$

(b) $P_2 < P_1$

(c) Cannot be predicted

(d) $P_2 = P_1$

19. The amount of heat energy required to raise the temperature of 1 g of Helium at NTP, from T_1 °K to T_2 °K is :

(a) $\frac{3}{2} N_a K_B (T_2 - T_1)$ (b) $\frac{3}{4} N_a K_B (T_2 - T_1)$

(c) $\frac{3}{4} N_a K_B \frac{T_2}{T_1}$ (d) $\frac{3}{8} N_a K_B (T_2 - T_1)$

20. A wave travelling in the +ve x-direction having displacement along y-direction as 1 m, wavelength 2π m and frequency is $\frac{1}{\pi}$ Hz is represented by :

(a) $y = \sin(2\pi x - 2\pi t)$

(b) $y = \sin(10\pi x - 20\pi t)$

(c) $y = \sin(2\pi x + 2\pi t)$

(d) $y = \sin(x - 2t)$

21. If we study the vibration of a pipe open at both ends, then the following statement is not true :

(a) Odd harmonics of the fundamental frequency will be generated.

(b) All harmonics of the fundamental frequency will be generated.

(c) Pressure change will be maximum at both ends.

(d) Open end will be antinode.

22. A source of unknown frequency gives 4 beats/s, when sounded with a source of known frequency 250 Hz. The second harmonic of the source of unknown frequency gives five beats per second, when sounded with a source of frequency 513 Hz. The unknown frequency is :

(a) 246 Hz (b) 240 Hz

(c) 260 Hz (d) 254 Hz

23. Two pith balls carrying equal charges are suspended from a common point by strings of equal length, the equilibrium separation between them is *r*. Now the strings are rigidly clamped at half the height. The equilibrium separation between the balls now becomes :

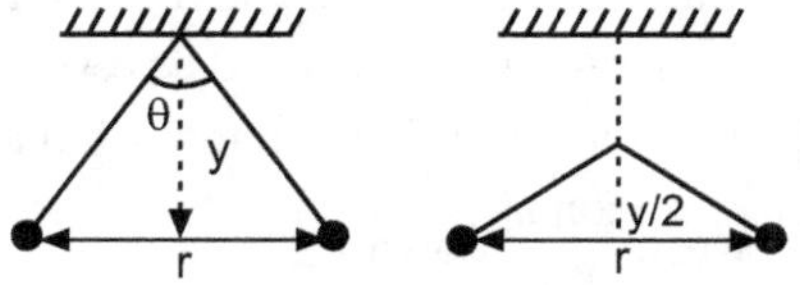

(a) $\frac{r}{\sqrt[3]{2}}$ (b) $\left(\frac{2r}{\sqrt{3}}\right)$

(c) $\left(\frac{2r}{3}\right)$ (d) $\left(\frac{r}{\sqrt{2}}\right)^2$

24. A, B and C are three points in a uniform electric field. The electric potential is :

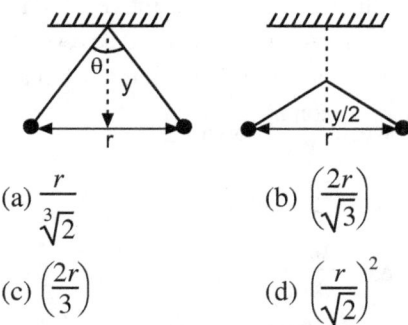

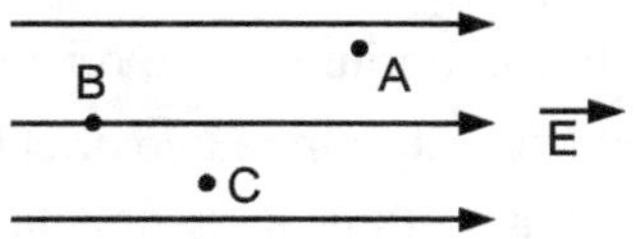

(a) Maximum at B

(b) Maximum at C

(c) Same at all the three points A, B and C

(d) Maximum at A

25. A wire of resistance 4 Ω is stretched to twice its original length. The resistance of stretched wire would be :

(a) 4 Ω (b) 8 Ω

(c) 16 Ω (d) 2 Ω

26. The internal resistance of a 2.1 V cell which gives a current of 0.2 A through a resistance of 10 Ω is :

(a) 0.5 Ω (b) 0.8 Ω

(c) 1.0 Ω (d) 0.2 Ω

27. The resistances of the four arms P, Q, R and S in a Wheatstone's bridge are 10 ohm, 30 ohm, 30 ohm and 90 ohm, respectively. The e.m.f. and internal resistance of the cell are 7 volt and 5 ohm respectively. If the galvanometer resistance is 50 ohm, the current drawn from the cell will be :

(a) 0.2 A (b) 0.1 A

(c) 2.0 A (d) 1.0 A

28. When a proton is released from rest in a room, it starts with an initial acceleration a_0 towards west. When it is projected towards north with a speed v_0, it moves with an initial acceleration $3a_0$ towards west. The electric and magnetic fields in the room are :

(a) $\frac{ma_0}{e}$ west, $\frac{2ma_0}{ev_0}$ down

(b) $\frac{ma_0}{e}$ east, $\frac{3ma_0}{ev_0}$ up

(c) $\frac{ma_0}{e}$ east, $\frac{3ma_0}{ev_0}$ down

(d) $\frac{ma_0}{e}$ west, $\frac{2ma_0}{ev_0}$ up

29. A current loop in a magnetic field :

(a) can be in equilibrium in one orientation.

(b) can be in equilibrium in two orientations, both the equilibrium states are unstable.

(c) can be in equilibrium in two orientations; one stable, while the other is unstable.

(d) experiences a torque whether the field is uniform or non-uniform in all orientations.

30. A bar magnet of length 'l' and magnetic dipole moment 'M' is bent in the form of an arc as shown in figure. The new magnetic dipole moment will be :

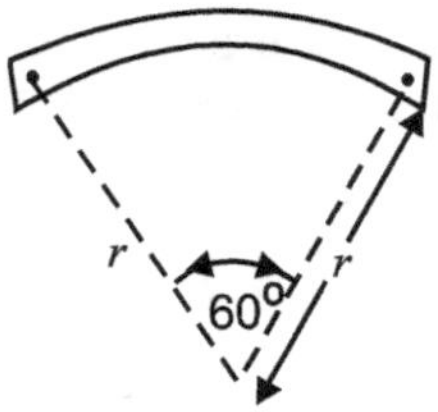

(a) $\frac{3}{\pi}$M (b) $\frac{2}{\pi}$M

(c) $\frac{M}{2}$ (d) M

31. A wire loop is rotated in a magnetic field. The frequency of change of direction of the induced e.m.f. is :

(a) twice per revolution

(b) four times per revolution

(c) six times per revolution

(d) once per revolution

32. A coil of self-inductance L is connected in series with a bulb B and an AC source. Brightness of the bulb decreases when :

(a) number of turns in the coil is reduced

(b) a capacitance of reactance $X_C = X_L$ is included in the same circuit

(c) an iron rod is inserted in the coil

(d) frequency of the AC source is decreased

33. The condition under which a microwave oven heats up a food item containing water molecules most efficiently is :

(a) The frequency of the microwaves has no relation with natural frequency of water molecules.

(b) Microwaves are heat waves, so always produce heating.

(c) Infra-red waves produce heating in a microwave oven.

(d) The frequency of the microwaves must match the resonant frequency of the water molecules.

34. Ratio of longest wavelengths corresponding to Lyman and Balmer series in hydrogen spectrum is :

(a) $\frac{3}{23}$ (b) $\frac{7}{29}$

(c) $\frac{9}{31}$ (d) $\frac{5}{27}$

35. The half life of a radioactive isotope 'X' is 20 years. It decays to another element 'Y' which is stable. The two elements 'X' and 'Y' were found to be in the ratio 1 : 7 in a sample of a given rock. The age of the rock is estimated to be :

(a) 60 years (b) 80 years

(c) 100 years (d) 40 years

36. A certain mass of Hydrogen is changed to Helium by the process of fusion. The mass defect in fusion reaction is 0.02866 u. The energy liberated per u is :

(given 1 u = 931 MeV)

(a) 26.7 MeV (b) 6.675 MeV

(c) 13.35 MeV (d) 2.67 MeV

37. For photoelectric emission from certain metal the cut-off frequency is υ. If radiation of frequency 2υ impinges on the metal plate, the maximum possible velocity of the emitted electron will be : (m is the electron mass)

(a) $\sqrt{\frac{h\upsilon}{m}}$ (b) $\sqrt{\frac{2h\upsilon}{m}}$

(c) $2\sqrt{\frac{h\upsilon}{m}}$ (d) $\sqrt{\frac{h\upsilon}{(2m)}}$

38. The wavelength λ_e of an electron and λ_p of a photon of same energy E are related by :

(a) $\lambda_p \propto \lambda_e$ (b) $\lambda_p \propto \sqrt{\lambda_e}$

(c) $\lambda_p \propto \frac{1}{\sqrt{\lambda_e}}$ (d) $\lambda_p \propto \lambda_e^2$

39. A plano-convex lens fits exactly into a plano-concave lens. Their plane surfaces are parallel to each other. If lenses are made of different materials of refractive indices μ_1 and μ_2 and R is the radius of curvature of the curved surface of the lenses, then the focal length of the combination is :

(a) $\frac{R}{2(\mu_1 - \mu_2)}$ (b) $\frac{R}{(\mu_1 - \mu_2)}$

(c) $\frac{2R}{(\mu_2 - \mu_1)}$ (d) $\frac{2R}{2(\mu_1 + \mu_2)}$

40. For a normal eye, the cornea of eye provides a converging power of 40 D and the least converging power of the eye lens behind the cornea is 20 D. Using this information, the distance between the retina and the cornea-eye lens can be estimated to be:

(a) 2.5 cm (b) 1.67 cm

(c) 1.5 cm (d) 5 cm

41. In Young's double slit experiment, the slits are 2 mm apart and are illuminated by photons of two wavelengths $\lambda_1 = 12000$ Å and $\lambda_2 = 10000$ Å. At what minimum distance from the common central bright fringe on the screen 2 m from the slit will a bright fringe from one interference pattern coincide with a bright fringe from the other?

(a) 6 mm (b) 4 mm

(c) 3 mm (d) 8 mm

42. A parallel beam of fast moving electrons is incident normally on a narrow slit. A fluorescent screen is placed at a large distance from the slit. If the speed of the electrons is increased, which of the following statements is correct ?

(a) The angular width of the central maximum of the diffraction pattern will increase.

(b) The angular width of the central maximum will decrease.

(c) The angular width of the central maximum will be unaffected.

(d) Diffraction pattern is not observed on the screen in the case of electrons.

43. In a n-type semiconductor, which of the following statement is true ?

(a) Electrons are minority carriers and pentavalent atoms are dopants.

(b) Holes are minority carriers and pentavalent atoms are dopants.

(c) Holes are majority carriers and trivalent atoms are dopants.

(d) Electrons are majority carriers and trivalent atoms are dopants.

44. In a common emitter (CE) amplifier having a voltage gain G, the transistor used has transconductance 0.03 mho and current gain 25. If the above transistor is replaced with another one with transconductance 0.02 mho and current gain 20, the voltage gain will be :

(a) 1.5 G (b) $\frac{1}{3}$ G

(c) $\frac{5}{4}$ G (d) $\frac{2}{3}$ G

45. The output (X) of the logic circuit shown in figure will be :

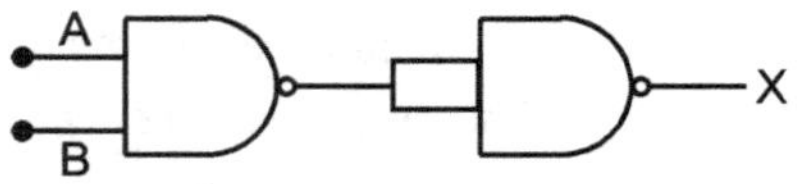

(a) $X = \overline{A \cdot B}$ (b) $X = A \cdot B$

(c) $X = \overline{A + B}$ (d) $X = \bar{\bar{A}} \cdot \bar{\bar{B}}$

ANSWER KEY

1. (a)	**2.** (b)	**3.** (a)	**4.** (d)	**5.** (b)	**6.** (d)	**7.** (a)	**8.** (d)	**9.** (c)	**10.** (a)
11. (c)	**12.** (d)	**13.** (c)	**14.** (a)	**15.** (a)	**16.** (a)	**17.** (c)	**18.** (b)	**19.** (d)	**20.** (d)
21. (c)	**22.** (d)	**23.** (a)	**24.** (a)	**25.** (c)	**26.** (a)	**27.** (a)	**28.** (a)	**29.** (c)	**30.** (a)
31. (a)	**32.** (c)	**33.** (d)	**34.** (d)	**35.** (a)	**36.** (b)	**37.** (b)	**38.** (d)	**39.** (b)	**40.** (b)
41. (a)	**42.** (b)	**43.** (b)	**44.** (d)	**45.** (b)					

✍ ✍ ✍

1. A conducting sphere of radius R is given a charge Q. The electric potential and the electric field at the centre of the sphere respectively are :

(a) $\frac{Q}{4\pi\varepsilon_o R}$ and zero

(b) $\frac{Q}{4\pi\varepsilon_o R}$ and $\frac{Q}{4\pi\varepsilon_o R^2}$

(c) Both are zero

(d) Zero and $\frac{Q}{4\pi\varepsilon_o R^2}$

2. If n_1, n_2 and n_3 are the fundamental frequencies of three segments into which a string is divided, then the original fundamental frequency n of the string is given by :

(a) $\frac{1}{\sqrt{n}} = \frac{1}{\sqrt{n_1}} + \frac{1}{\sqrt{n_2}} + \frac{1}{\sqrt{n_3}}$

(b) $\sqrt{n} = \sqrt{n_1} + \sqrt{n_2} + \sqrt{n_3}$

(c) $n = n_1 + n_2 + n_3$

(d) $\frac{1}{n} = \frac{1}{n_1} + \frac{1}{n_2} + \frac{1}{n_3}$

3. Copper of fixed volume 'V' is drawn into wire of length 'l'. When this wire is subjected to a constant force 'F', the extension produced in the wire is 'Δl'. Which of the following graphs is a straight line ?

(a) Δl versus l^2 (b) Δl versus $1/l^2$

(c) Δl versus l (d) Δl versus $1/l$

4. A thermodynamic system undergoes cyclic process ABCDA as shown in figure. The work done by the system in the cycle is :

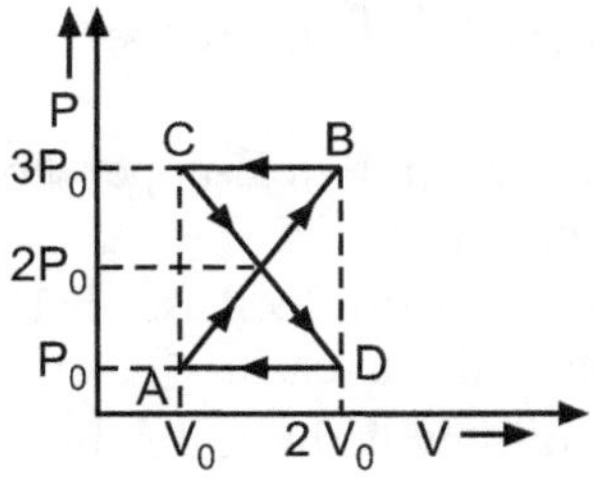

(a) $2P_0V_0$ (b) $\frac{P_0V_0}{2}$

(c) Zero (d) P_0V_0

5. Two thin dielectric slabs of dielectric constants K_1 and K_2 ($K_1 < K_2$) are inserted between plates of a parallel plate capacitor, as shown in the figure. The variation of electric field 'E' between the plates with distance 'd' as measured from plate P is correctly shown by :

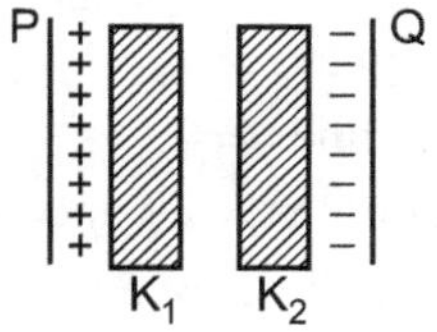

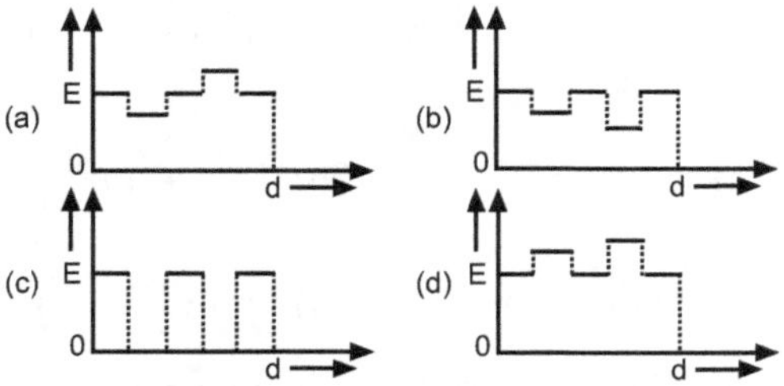

6. The resistances in the two arms of the meter bridge are 5 Ω and R Ω, respectively. When the resistance R is shunted with an equal resistance, the new balance point is at $1.6l_1$. The resistance 'R', is :

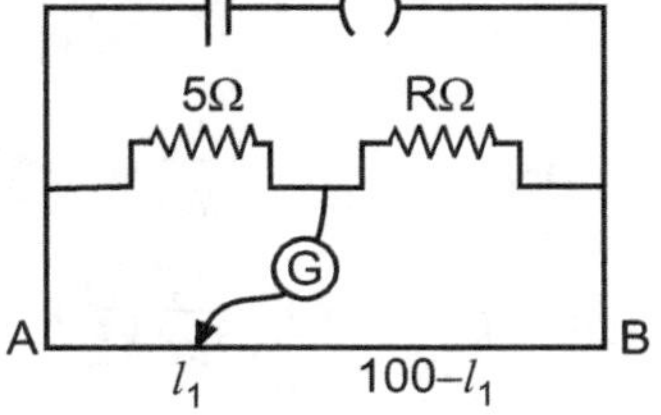

(a) 15 Ω (b) 20 Ω

(c) 25 Ω (d) 10 Ω

7. A thin semicircular conducting ring (PQR) of radius 'r' is falling with its plane vertical in a horizontal magnetic field B, as shown in figure. The potential difference developed across the ring when its speed is v, is :

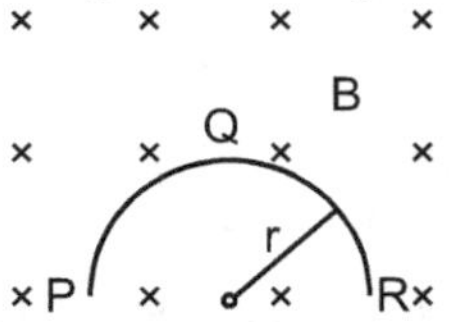

(a) $Bv\pi r^2/2$ and P is at higher potential
(b) πrBv and R is at higher potential
(c) $2rBv$ and R is at higher potential
(d) Zero

8. A particle is moving such that its position coordinates (x, y) are :

(2m, 3m) at time t = 0,
(6m, 7m) at time t = 2 s and
(13m, 14m) at time t = 5 s.

Average velocity vector ($\vec{V}_{av}$) from t = 0 to t = 5 s is :

(a) $\frac{7}{3}(\hat{i} + \hat{j})$ (b) $2(\hat{i} + \hat{j})$
(c) $\frac{11}{5}(\hat{i} + \hat{j})$ (d) $\frac{1}{5}(13\hat{i} + 14\hat{j})$

9. Two identical long conducting wires AOB and COD are placed at right angles to each other, with one above other such that 'O' is their common point for the two. The wires carry I_1 and I_2 currents, respectively. Point 'P' is lying at distance 'd' from 'O' along a direction perpendicular to the plane containing the wires. The magnetic field at the point 'P' will be :

(a) $\frac{\mu_o}{2\pi d}(I_1 + I_2)$ (b) $\frac{\mu_o}{2\pi d}(I_1^2 - I_2^2)$
(c) $\frac{\mu_o}{2\pi d}\left(I_1^2 + I_2^2\right)^{1/2}$ (d) $\frac{\mu_o}{2\pi d}\left(\frac{I_1}{I_2}\right)$

10. A system consists of three masses m_1, m_2 and m_3 connected by a string passing over a pulley P. The mass m_1 hangs freely and m_2 and m_3 are on a rough horizontal table (the coefficient of friction = μ). The pulley is frictionless and of negligible mass. The downward acceleration of mass m_1 is :
Assume $m_1 = m_2 = m_3 = m$)

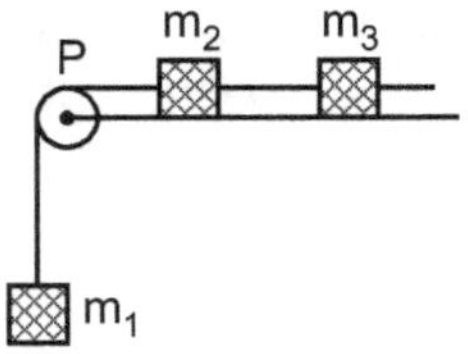

(a) $\frac{2g\mu}{3}$ (b) $\frac{g(1-2\mu)}{3}$
(c) $\frac{g(1-2\mu)}{2}$ (d) $\frac{g(1-g\mu)}{9}$

11. In an ammeter 0.2% of main current passes through the galvanometer. If resistance of galvanometer is G, the resistance of ammeter will be :

(a) $\frac{499}{500}G$ (b) $\frac{1}{500}G$
(c) $\frac{500}{499}G$ (d) $\frac{1}{499}G$

12. Following figures show the arrangement of bar magnets in different configurations. Each magnet has magnetic dipole moment $\vec{m}$. Which configuration has highest net magnetic dipole moment ?

(1) 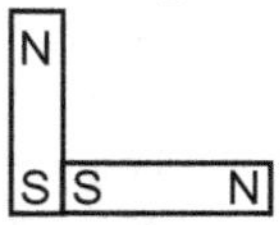

(2) 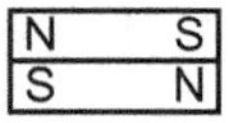

(3) 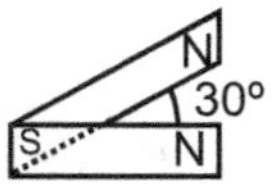

(4) 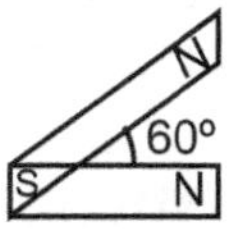

(a) (2) (b) (3)
(c) (4) (d) (1)

13. If the focal length of objective lens is increased, then magnifying power of :
(a) microscope and telescope both will increase.
(b) microscope and telescope both will decrease.
(c) microscope will decrease but that of telescope will increase.
(d) microscope will increase but that of telescope decrease.

14. The angle of a prism is 'A'. One of its refracting surfaces is silvered. Light rays falling at an angle of incidence 2A on the first surface returns back through the same path after suffering reflection at the silvered surface. The refractive index μ, of the prism is :

(a) 2 cos A (b) $\frac{1}{2}$ cos A

(c) tan A (d) 2 sin A

15. The oscillation of a body on a smooth horizontal surface is represented by the equation,

$X = A \cos(\omega t)$

where X = displacement at time t

ω = frequency of oscillation

Which one of the following graphs shows correctly the variation 'a' with 't' ?

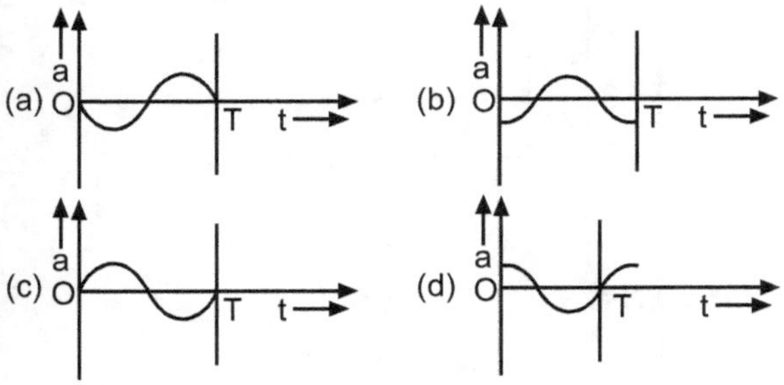

Here a = acceleration at time t

T = time period

16. The given graph represents V-I characteristic for a semiconductor device.

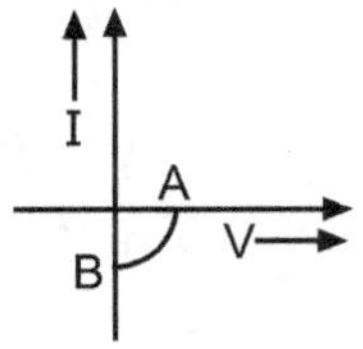

Which of the following statements is correct?

(a) It is for a solar cell and points A and B represent open circuit voltage and current, respectively.

(b) It is for a photodiode and points A and B represent open circuit voltage and current respectively.

(c) It is for a LED and points A and B represent open circuit voltage and short circuit current respectively.

(d) It is V-I characteristic for solar cell where point A represents open circuit voltage and point B short circuit current.

17. Dependence of intensity of gravitational field (E) of earth with distance (r) from centre of earth is correctly represented by :

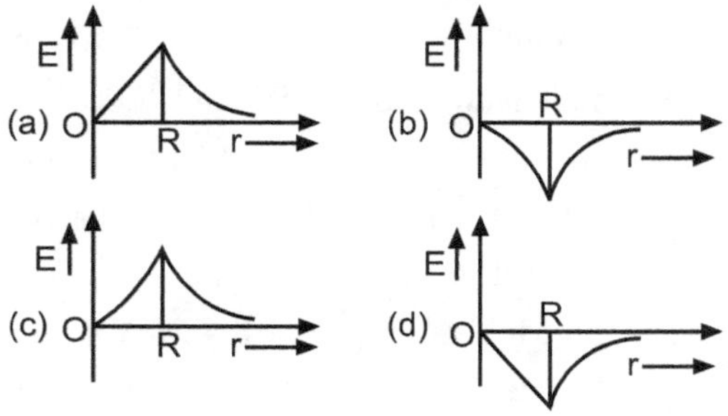

18. The number of possible natural oscillations of air column in a pipe closed at one end of length 85 cm whose frequencies lie below 1250 Hz are : (velocity of sound = 340 ms^{-1})

(a) 5 (b) 7

(c) 6 (d) 4

19. Two cities are 150 km apart. Electric power is sent from one city to another city through copper wires. The fall of potential per km is 8 volt and the average resistance per km is 0.5 Ω. The power loss in the wire is :

(a) 19.2 kW (b) 19.2 J

(c) 12.2 kW (d) 19.2 W

20. A beam of light of λ = 600 nm from a distant source falls on a single slit 1 mm wide and the resulting diffraction pattern is observed on a screen 2 m away. The distance between first dark fringes on either side of the central bright fringe is :

(a) 1.2 mm (b) 2.4 cm

(c) 2.4 mm (d) 1.2 cm

21. If force (F), velocity (v) and time (T) are taken as fundamental units, then the dimensions of mass are :

(a) $[F\, v\, T^{-2}]$ (b) $[F\, v^{-1}\, T^{-1}]$

(c) $[F\, v^{-1}\, T]$ (d) $[F\, v\, T^{-1}]$

22. The barrier potential of a p-n junction depends on :

(1) type of semiconductor material

(2) amount of doping

(3) temperature

Which one of the following is correct ?

(a) (2) only (b) (2) and (3) only

(c) (1), (2) and (3) (d) (1) and (2) only

23. The binding energy per nucleon of ${}^7_3Li$ and ${}^4_2He$ nuclei are 5.60 MeV and 7.06 MeV, respectively. In the nuclear reaction ${}^7_3Li + {}^1_1H \rightarrow {}^4_2He + {}^4_2He + Q$, the value of energy Q released is :

(a) –2.4 MeV (b) 8.4 MeV

(c) 17.3 MeV (d) 19.6 MeV

24. If the kinetic energy of the particle is increased to 16 times its previous value, the percentage change in the de-Broglie wavelength of the particle is :

(a) 75 (b) 60

(c) 50 (d) 25

25. Light with an energy flux of 25×10^4 Wm^{-2} falls on a perfectly reflecting surface at normal incidence. If the surface area is 15 cm^2, the average force exerted on the surface is :

(a) 2.50×10^{-6} N (b) 1.20×10^{-6} N

(c) 3.0×10^{-6} N (d) 1.25×10^{-6} N

26. In a region, the potential is represented by $V(x, y, z) = 6x - 8xy - 8y + 6yz$, where V is in volts and x, y, z are in metres. The electric force experienced by a charge of 2 coulomb situated at point (1, 1, 1) is :

(a) 30 N (b) 24 N

(c) $4\sqrt{35}$ N (d) $6\sqrt{5}$ N

27. A speeding motor cyclist sees traffic jam ahead of him. He slows down to 36 km/hr. He finds that traffic has eased and a car moving ahead of him at 18 km/hr is honking at a frequency of 1392 Hz. If the speed of sound is 343 m/s, the frequency of the honk as heard by him will be :

(a) 1372 Hz (b) 1412 Hz

(c) 1454 Hz (d) 1332 Hz

28. The ratio of the accelerations for a solid sphere (mass 'm' and radius 'R') rolling down an incline of angle 'θ' without slipping and slipping down the incline without rolling is :

(a) 2 : 3 (b) 2 : 5

(c) 7 : 5 (d) 5 : 7

29. The force 'F' acting on a particle of mass 'm' is indicated by the force-time graph shown below. The change in momentum of the particle over the time interval from zero to 8 s is :

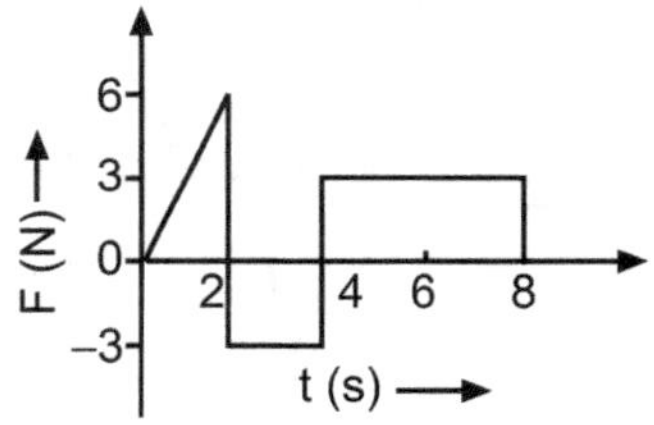

(1) 20 Ns (b) 12 Ns

(c) 6 Ns (d) 24 Ns

30. In the Young's double-slit experiment, the intensity of light at a point on the screen where the path difference is λ is K, (λ being the wavelength of light used). The intensity at a point where the path difference is λ/4, will be :

(a) K/4 (b) K/2

(c) Zero (d) K

31. A balloon with mass 'm; is descending down with an acceleration 'a' (where a < g). How much mass should be removed from it so that its starts moving up with an acceleration 'a' ?

(a) $\frac{2\,ma}{g-a}$ (b) $\frac{ma}{g+a}$

(c) $\frac{ma}{g-a}$ (d) $\frac{2\,ma}{g+a}$

32. A potentiometer circuit has been set up for finding the internal resistance of a given cell. The main battery, used across the potentiometer wire, has an e.m.f. of 2.0 V and a negligible internal resistance. The potentiometer wire itself is 4 m long. When the resistance R, connected across the given cell, has values of

(i) infinity (ii) 9.5 Ω,

the 'balancing lengths', on the potentiometer wire are found to be 3 m and 2.85 m, respectively.

The value of internal resistance of the cell is:

(a) 0.95 Ω (b) 0.5 Ω

(c) 0.75 Ω (d) 0.25 Ω

33. A monoatomic gas at a pressure P, having a volume V expands isothermally to a volume 2V and then adiabatically to a volume 16V. The final pressure of the gas is :

(take $\gamma = 5/3$)

(a) 32 P (b) P/64

(c) 16 P (d) 64 P

34. A certain number of spherical drops of a liquid of radius 'r' coalesce to form a single drop of radius 'R' and volume 'V'. If 'T' is the surface tension of the liquid, then :

(a) energy $= 3VT\left(\frac{1}{r}+\frac{1}{R}\right)$ is absorbed.

(b) energy $= 3VT\left(\frac{1}{r}-\frac{1}{R}\right)$ is released.

(c) energy is neither released nor absorbed.

(d) energy $= 4VT\left(\frac{1}{r}-\frac{1}{R}\right)$ is released.

35. A body of mass (4m) is lying in x-y plane at rest. It suddenly explodes into three pieces. Two pieces, each of mass (m) move perpendicular to each other with equal speeds (v). The total kinetic energy generated due to explosion is :

(a) $\frac{3}{2}mv^2$ (b) $2\ mv^2$

(c) $4\ mv^2$ (d) mv^2

36. Hydrogen atom in ground state is excited by a monochromatic radiation of $\lambda = 975$ Å. Number of spectral lines in the resulting spectrum emitted will be :

(a) 2 (b) 6

(c) 10 (d) 3

37. A black hole is an object whose gravitational field is so strong that even light cannot escape from it. To what approximate radius would earth (mass = 5.98×10^{24} kg) have to be compressed to be a black hole ?

(a) 10^{-6} m (b) 10^{-2} m

(c) 100 m (d) 10^{-9} m

38. A projectile is fired from the surface of the earth with a velocity of 5 ms^{-1} and angle θ with the horizontal. Another projectile fired from another planet with a velocity of 3 ms^{-1} at the same angle follows a trajectory which is identical with the trajectory of the projectile fired from the earth. The value of the acceleration due to gravity on the planet is (in ms^{-2}) is : (given g = 9.8 ms^{-2})

(a) 5.9 (b) 16.3

(c) 110.8 (d) 3.5

39. Certain quantity of water cools from 70°C to 60°C in the first 5 minutes and to 54°C in the next 5 minutes. The temperature of the surroundings is :

(a) 20°C (b) 42°C

(c) 10°C (d) 45°C

40. A solid cylinder of mass 50 kg and radius 0.5 m is free to rotate about the horizontal axis. A massless string is wound round the cylinder with one end attached to it and other hanging freely. Tension in the string required to produce an angular acceleration of 2 revolutions s^{-2} is :

(a) 50 N (b) 78.5 N

(c) 157 N (d) 25 N

41. Steam at 100°C is passed into 20 g of water at 10°C. When water acquires a temperature of 80°C, the mass of water present will be :
[Take specific heat of water = 1 cal g^{-1} °C^{-1} and latent heat of steam = 540 cal g^{-1}]
(a) 31.5 g (b) 42.5 g
(c) 22.5 g (d) 24 g

42. A radio isotope 'X' with a half life 1.4×10^9 years decays to 'Y' which is stable. A sample of the rock from a cave was found to contain 'X' and 'Y' in the ratio 1 : 7. The age of the rock is :
(a) 3.92×10^9 years (b) 4.20×10^9 years
(c) 8.40×10^9 years (d) 1.96×10^9 years

43. A transformer having efficiency of 90% is working on 200 V and 3 kW power supply. If the current in the secondary coil is 6A, the voltage across the secondary coil and the current in the primary coil respectively are :
(a) 450 V, 15 A (b) 450 V, 13.5 A
(c) 600 V, 15 A (d) 300 V, 15 A

44. When the energy of the incident radiation is increased by 20%, the kinetic energy of the photoelectrons emitted from a metal surface increased from 0.5 eV to 0.8 eV. The work function of the metal is :
(a) 1.0 eV (b) 1.3 eV
(c) 1.5 eV (d) 0.65 eV

45. The mean free path of molecules of gas, (radius 'r') is inversely proportional to :
(a) r^2 (b) r
(c) $\sqrt{r}$ (d) r^3

ANSWER KEY

1. (a)	**2.** (d)	**3.** (a)	**4.** (c)	**5.** (a)	**6.** (a)	**7.** (c)	**8.** (c)	**9.** (c)	**10.** (b)
11. (d)	**12.** (b)	**13.** (c)	**14.** (a)	**15.** (d)	**16.** (d)	**17.** (c)	**18.** (c)	**19.** (a)	**20.** (c)
21. (c)	**22.** (c)	**23.** (c)	**24.** (a)	**25.** (d)	**26.** (c)	**27.** (b)	**28.** (d)	**29.** (b)	**30.** (b)
31. (d)	**32.** (b)	**33.** (b)	**34.** (b)	**35.** (a)	**36.** (a)	**37.** (b)	**38.** (d)	**39.** (d)	**40.** (c)
41. (c)	**42.** (b)	**43.** (a)	**44.** (a)	**45.** (a)					

✍✍✍

CBSC AIMPT 2015

1. If energy (E), velocity (v) and time (T) are chosen as the fundamental quantities, the dimensional formula of surface tension will be

(a) $[Ev^{-2}T^{-1}]$ (b) $[Ev^{-1}T^{-2}]$

(c) $[Ev^{-2}T^{-2}]$ (d) $[E^{-2}v^{-1}T^{-3}]$

2. A ship A is moving Westwards with a speed of 10 km h^{-1} and a ship B 100 km South of A, is moving Northwards with a speed of 10 km h^{-1}. The time after which the distance between them becomes shortest is

(a) 0 h (b) 5 h

(c) $5\sqrt{2}$ h (d) $10\sqrt{2}$ h

3. A particle of unit mass undergoes one-dimensional motion such that its velocity varies according to $v(x) = \beta x^{-2n}$ where, β and n are constants and x is the position of the particle. The acceleration of the particle as a function of x, is given by

(a) $-2n\beta^2 x^{-2n-1}$ (b) $-2n\beta^2 x^{-4n-1}$

(c) $-2\beta^2 x^{-2n+1}$ (d) $-2n\beta^2 e^{-4n+1}$

4. Three blocks A, B and C of masses 4 kg, 2 kg and 1 kg respectively, are in contact on a frictionless surface, as shown. If a force of 14 N is applied on the 4 kg block, then the contact force between A and B is

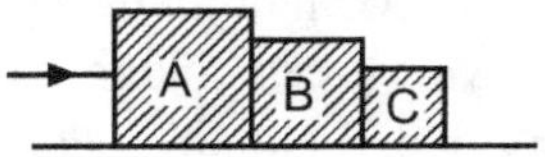

(a) 2 N (b) 6 N

(c) 8 N (d) 18 N

5. A block A of mass m_1 rests on a horizontal table. A light string connected to it passes over a frictionless pulley at the edge of table and from its other end another block B of mass m_2 is suspended. The coefficient of kinetic friction between the block and the table is μ_k. When the block A is sliding on the table, the tension in the string is

(a) $\frac{(m_2 + \mu_k m_1)g}{(m_1 + m_2)}$ (b) $\frac{(m_2 - \mu_k m_1)g}{(m_1 + m_2)}$

(c) $\frac{m_1 m_2 (1 + \mu_k)g}{(m_1 + m_2)}$ (d) $\frac{m_1 m_2 (1 - \mu_k)g}{(m_1 + m_2)}$

6. Two similar springs P and Q have spring constants K_P and K_Q, such that $K_P > K_Q$. They are stretched, first by the same amount (case a), then by the same force (case b). The work done by the springs W_P and W_Q are related as, in case (a) and case (b), respectively

(a) $W_P = W_Q$; $W_P > W_Q$

(b) $W_P = W_Q$; $W_P = W_Q$

(c) $W_P > W_Q$; $W_Q > W_P$

(d) $W_P < W_Q$; $W_Q < W_P$

7. A block of mass 10 kg, moving in x-direction with a constant speed of 10 ms^{-1}, is subjected to a retarding force F = 0.1x J/m during its travel from x = 20 m to 30 m. Its final KE will be

(a) 475 J (b) 450 J

(C) 275 J (d) 250 J

8. A particle of mass m is driven by a machine that delivers a constant power k watts. If the particle starts from rest, the force on the particle at time t is

(a) $\sqrt{\frac{mk}{2}}\, t^{-1/2}$ (b) $\sqrt{mk}\, t^{-1/2}$

(c) $\sqrt{2mk}\, t^{-1/2}$ (d) $\frac{1}{2}\sqrt{mk}\, t^{-1/2}$

9. Two particles of masses m_1, m_2 move with initial velocities u_1 and u_2. On collision, one of the particles get excited to higher level, after absorbing energy E. If final velocities of particles are v_1 and v_2, then we must have

(a) $m_1^2 u_1 + m_2^2 u_2 - E = m_1^2 v_1 + m_2^2 v_2$

(b) $\frac{1}{2} m_1 u_1^2 + \frac{1}{2} m_2 u_2^2 = \frac{1}{2} m_1 v_1^2 + \frac{1}{2} m_2 v_2^2 - E$

(c) $\frac{1}{2} m_1 u_1^2 + \frac{1}{2} m_2 u_2^2 - E = \frac{1}{2} m_1 v_1^2 + \frac{1}{2} m_2 v_2^2$

(d) $\frac{1}{2} m_1^2 u_1^2 + \frac{1}{2} m_2^2 u_2^2 + E = \frac{1}{2} m_1^2 v_1^2 + \frac{1}{2} m_2^2 v_2^2$

10. A rod of weight w is supported by two parallel knife edges A and B and is in equilibrium in a horizontal position. The knives are at a distance d from each other. The centre of mass of the rod is at distance x from A. The normal reaction on A is

(a) $\frac{wx}{d}$ (b) $\frac{wd}{x}$

(c) $\frac{w(d-x)}{x}$ (d) $\frac{w(d-x)}{d}$

11. A mass m moves in a circle on a smooth horizontal plane with velocity v_0 at a radius R_0. The mass is attached to a string which passes through a smooth hole in the plane as shown.

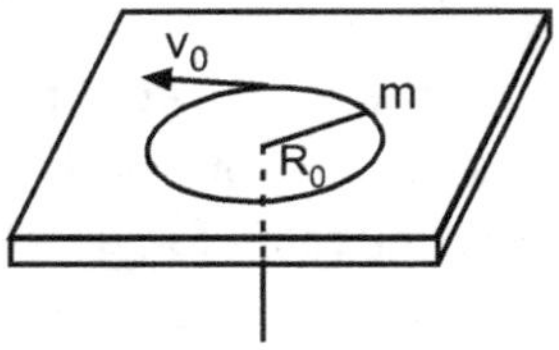

The tension in the string is increased gradually and finally m moves in a circle of radius $\frac{R_0}{2}$. The final value of the kinetic energy is

(a) mv_0^2 (b) $\frac{1}{4}mv_0^2$

(c) $2\,mv_0^2$ (d) $\frac{1}{2}mv_0^2$

12. Three identical spherical shells, each of mass m and radius r are placed as shown in figure. Consider an axis XX', which is touching to two shells and passing through diameter of third shell.

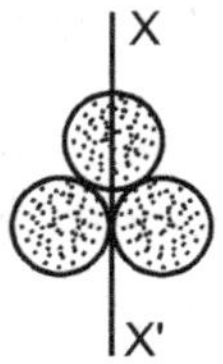

Moment of inertia of the system consisting of these three spherical shells about XX' axis is

(a) $\frac{11}{5}mr^2$ (b) $3\,mr^2$

(c) $\frac{16}{5}mr^2$ (d) $4\,mr^2$

13. Kepler's third law states that square of period of revolution (T) of a planet around the sun, is proportional to third power of average distance r between the sun and planet i.e. $T^2 = Kr^3$, here K is constant.

If the masses of the sun and planet are M and m respectively, then as per Newton's law of gravitation, force of attraction between them is $F = \frac{GMm}{r^2}$, here G is gravitational constant.

The relation between G and K is described as

(a) $GK = 4\pi^2$ (b) $GMK = 4\pi^2$

(c) $K = G$ (d) $K = \frac{l}{G}$

14. Two spherical bodies of masses M and 5M and radii R and 2R are released in free space with initial separation between their centres equal to 12R. If they attract each other due to gravitational force only, then the distance covered by the smaller body before collision is

(a) 2.5R (b) 4.5R

(c) 7.5R (d) 1.5R

15. On observing light from three different stars P, Q and R, it was found that intensity of violet colour is maximum in the spectrum of P, the intensity of green colour is maximum in the spectrum of R and the intensity of red colour is maximum in the spectrum of Q. If T_P, T_Q and T_R are the respective absolute temperatures of P, Q and R, then it can be concluded from the above observations that

(a) $T_P > T_Q > T_R$ (b) $T_P > T_R > T_Q$

(c) $T_P < T_R < T_Q$ (d) $T_P < T_Q < T_R$

16. The approximate depth of an ocean is 2700 m. The compressibility of water is 45.4×10^{-11} Pa^{-1} and density of water is 10^3 kg / m^3. What fractional compression of water will be obtained at the bottom of the ocean?

(a) 0.8×10^{-2} (b) 1.0×10^{-2}

(c) 1.2×10^{-2} (d) 1.4×10^{-2}

17. The two ends of a metal rod are maintained at temperatures 100°C and 110°C. The rate of heat flow in the rod is found to be 4.0 J/s. If the ends are maintained at temperatures 200°C and 210°C, the rate of heat flow will be

(a) 44.0 J/s (b) 16.8 J/s

(c) 8.0 J/s (d) 4.0 J/s

18. A wind with speed 40 m/s blows parallel to the roof of a house. The area of the roof is 250 m^2. Assuming that the pressure inside the house is atmospheric pressure, the force exerted by the wind on the roof and the direction of the force will be

($\rho_{air} = 12\ kg/m^3$)

(a) 4.8×10^5 N, downwards

(b) 4.8×10^5 N, upwards

(c) 2.4×10^5 N, upwards

(d) 2.4×10^5 N, downwards

19. Figure below shows two paths that may be taken by a gas to go from a state A to a state C.

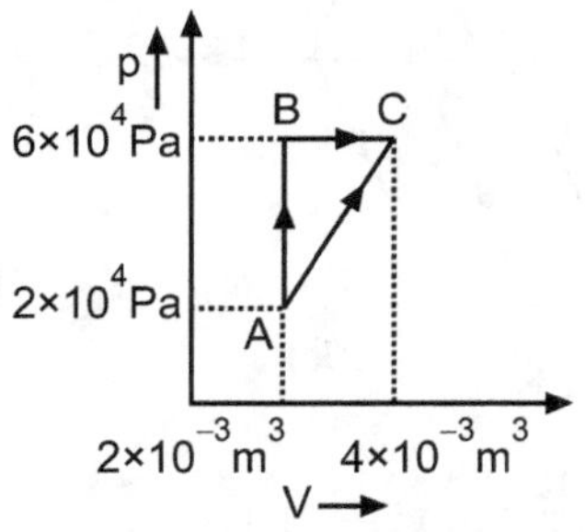

In process AB, 400 J of heat is added to the system and in process BC, 100 J of heat is added to the system. The heat absorbed by the system in the process AC will be

(a) 380 J (b) 500 J

(c) 460 J (d) 300 J

20. A Carnot engine, having an efficiency of $\eta = \frac{1}{10}$ as heat engine, is used as a refrigerator. If the work done on the system is 10 J, the amount of energy absorbed from the reservoir at lower temperature is

(a) 100 J (b) 99 J

(c) 90 J (d) 1 J

21. One mole of an ideal diatomic gas undergoes a transition from A to B along a path AB as shown in the figure.

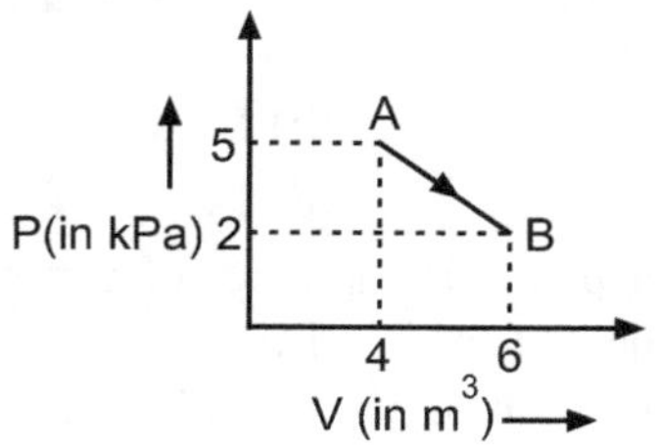

The change in internal energy of the gas during the transition is

(a) 20 kJ (b) – 20 kJ

(c) 20 J (d) – 12 kJ

22. The ratio of the specific heats $\frac{C_P}{C_V} = \gamma$ in terms of degrees of freedom (n) is given by

(a) $\left(1 + \frac{1}{n}\right)$ (b) $\left(1 + \frac{n}{3}\right)$

(c) $\left(1 + \frac{2}{n}\right)$ (d) $\left(1 + \frac{n}{2}\right)$

23. When two displacements represented by $y_1 = a \sin(\omega t)$ and $y_2 = b \cos(\omega t)$ are superimposed, the motion is

(a) not a simple harmonic

(b) simple harmonic with amplitude $\frac{a}{b}$

(c) simple harmonic with amplitude $\sqrt{a^2 + b^2}$

(d) simple harmonic with amplitude $\frac{(a + b)}{2}$

24. A particle is executing SHM along a straight line. Its velocities at distances x_1 and x_2 from the mean position are v_1 and v_2, respectively. Its time period is

(a) $2\pi\sqrt{\frac{x_1^2 + x_2^2}{v_1^2 + v_2^2}}$ (b) $2\pi\sqrt{\frac{x_2^2 - x_1^2}{v_1^2 - v_2^2}}$

(c) $2\pi\sqrt{\frac{v_1^2 + v_2^2}{x_1^2 + x_2^2}}$ (d) $2\pi\sqrt{\frac{v_1^2 - v_2^2}{x_1^2 - x_2^2}}$

25. The fundamental frequency of a closed organ pipe of length 20 cm is equal to the second overtone of an organ pipe open at both the ends. The length of organ pipe open at both the ends is

(a) 80 cm (b) 100 cm
(c) 120 cm (d) 140 cm

26. A parallel plate air capacitor of capacitance C is connected to a cell of emf V and then disconnected from it. A dielectric slab of dielectric constant K, which can just fill the air gap of the capacitor, is now inserted in it. Which of the following is incorrect?

(a) The potential difference between the plates decreases K times
(b) The energy stored in the capacitor decreases K times
(c) The change in energy stored is $\frac{1}{2}CV^2\left(\frac{1}{K}-1\right)$
(d) The charge on the capacitor is not conserved

27. The electric field in a certain region is acting radially outward and is given by E = Ar. A charge contained in a sphere of radius 'a' centred at the origin of the field will be given by

(a) $4\pi\varepsilon_0 Aa^2$ (b) $A\varepsilon_0 a^2$
(c) $4\pi\varepsilon_0 Aa^3$ (d) $\varepsilon_0 Aa^3$

28. A potentiometer wire has length 4 m and resistance 8 Ω. The resistance that must be connected in series with the wire and an accumulator of emf 2 V, so as to get a potential gradient 1 mV per cm on the wire is

(a) 32 Ω (b) 40 Ω
(c) 44 Ω (d) 48 Ω

29. A, B and C are voltmeters of resistance R, 1.5 R and 3R respectively as shown in the figure. When some potential difference is applied between X and Y, the voltmeter readings are V_A, V_B and V_C respectively. Then,

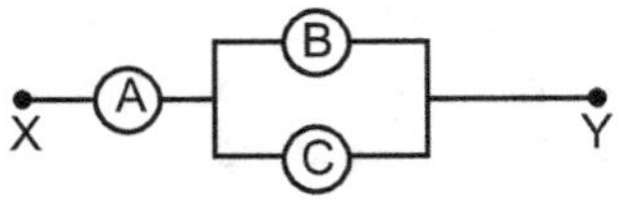

(a) $V_A = V_B = V_C$ (b) $V_A \neq V_B = V_C$
(c) $V_A = V_B \neq V_C$ (d) $V_A \neq V_B \neq V_C$

30. Across a metallic conductor of non-uniform cross-section, a constant potential difference is applied. The quantity which remains constant along the conductor is

(a) current density (b) current
(c) drift velocity (d) electric field

31. A wire carrying current I has the shape as shown in adjoining figure. Linear parts of the wire are very long and parallel to X-axis while semicircular portion of radius R is lying in Y-Z plane. Magnetic field at point O is

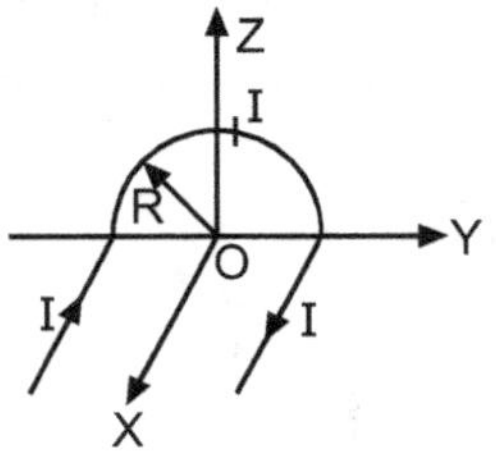

(a) $B = \frac{\mu_0}{4\pi}\frac{I}{R}(\pi\hat{i} + 2\hat{k})$

(b) $B = -\frac{\mu_0}{4\pi}\frac{I}{R}(\pi\hat{i} - 2\hat{k})$

(c) $B = -\frac{\mu_0}{4\pi}\frac{I}{R}(\pi\hat{i} + 2\hat{k})$

(d) $B = \frac{\mu_0}{4\pi}\frac{I}{R}(\pi\hat{i} - 2\hat{k})$

32. An electron moving in a circular orbit of radius r makes n rotations per second. The magnetic field produced at the centre has magnitude

(a) $\frac{\mu_0 ne}{2\pi r}$ (b) zero
(c) $\frac{\mu_0 n^2 e}{r}$ (d) $\frac{\mu_0 ne}{2r}$

33. A conducting square frame of side 'a' and a long straight wire carrying current I are located in the same plane as shown in the figure. The frame moves to the right with a constant velocity 'v'. The emf induced in the frame will be proportional to

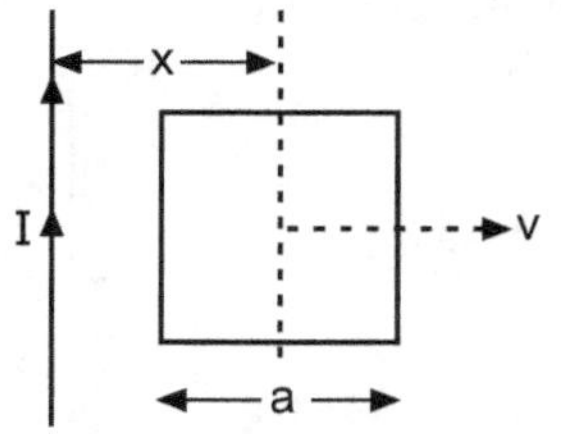

(a) $\frac{1}{x^2}$ (b) $\frac{1}{(2x-a)^2}$

(c) $\frac{1}{(2x+a)^2}$ (d) $\frac{1}{(2x-a)(2x+a)}$

34. A resistance 'R' draws power 'P' when connected to an AC source. If an inductance is now placed in series with the resistance, such that the impedance of the circuit becomes 'Z', then the power drawn will be

(a) $P\left(\frac{R}{Z}\right)^2$ (b) $P\sqrt{\frac{R}{Z}}$

(c) $P\left(\frac{R}{Z}\right)$ (d) P

35. A radiation of energy `E' falls normally on a perfectly reflecting surface. The momentum transferred to the surface is

(c = velocity of light)

(a) $\frac{E}{c}$ (b) $\frac{2E}{c}$

(c) $\frac{2E}{c^2}$ (d) $\frac{E}{c^2}$

36. Two identical thin plano-convex glass lenses (refractive index 1.5) each having radius of curvature of 20 cm are placed with their convex surfaces in contact at the centre. The intervening space is filled with oil of refractive index 1.7. The focal length of the combination is

(a) – 20 cm (b) – 25 cm

(c) – 50 cm (d) 50 cm

37. For a parallel beam of monochromatic light of wavelength 'λ' diffraction is produced by a single slit whose width 'a' is of the order of the wavelength of the light. If `D' is the distance of the screen from the slit, the width of the central maxima will be

(a) $\frac{2D\lambda}{a}$ (b) $\frac{D\lambda}{a}$

(c) $\frac{Da}{\lambda}$ (d) $\frac{2Da}{\lambda}$

38. In a double slit experiment, the two slits are 1 mm apart and the screen is placed 1 m away. A monochromatic light of wavelength 500 nm is used. What will be the width of each slit for obtaining ten maxima of double slit within the central maxima of single slit pattern?

(a) 0.2 mm (b) 0.1 mm

(c) 0.5 mm (d) 0.02 mm

39. The refracting angle of a prism is A, and refractive index of the material of the prism is cot (A/2). The angle of minimum deviation is

(a) 180° – 3A (b) 180° – 2A

(c) 90° – A (d) 180° + 2A

40. A certain metallic surface is illuminated with monochromatic light of wavelength λ. The stopping potential for photoelectric current for this light is $3V_0$. If the same surface is illuminated with light of wavelength 2λ, the stopping potential is V_0. The threshold wavelength for this surface for photoelectric effect is

(a) 6λ (b) 4λ

(c) $\frac{\lambda}{4}$ (d) $\frac{\lambda}{6}$

41. Which of the following figures represent the variation of particle momentum and the associated de-Broglie wavelength?

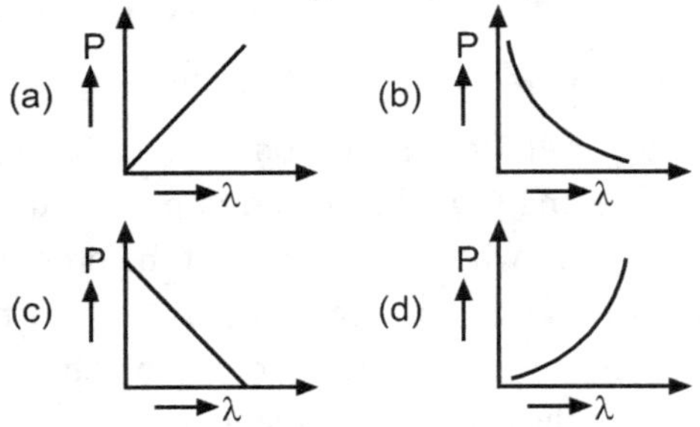

42. Consider 3rd orbit of He^+ (Helium), using non-relativistic approach, the speed of electron in this orbit will be (given $K = 9 \times 10^9$ constant, Z = 2 and h (Planck's constant) = 6.6×10^{-34} J-s)

(a) 2.92×10^6 m/s (b) 1.46×10^6 m/s

(c) 0.73×10^6 m/s (d) 3.0×10^8 m/s

43. If radius of the $^{27}_{13}Al$ nucleus is taken to be R_{Al}, then the radius of $^{125}_{53}Te$ nucleus is nearly

(a) $\left(\frac{53}{13}\right)^{\frac{1}{3}} R_{Al}$ (b) $\frac{5}{3} R_{Al}$

(c) $\frac{3}{5} R_{Al}$ (d) $\left(\frac{13}{53}\right)^{\frac{1}{3}} R_{Al}$

44. If in a p-n junction, a square input signal of 10 V is applied as shown,

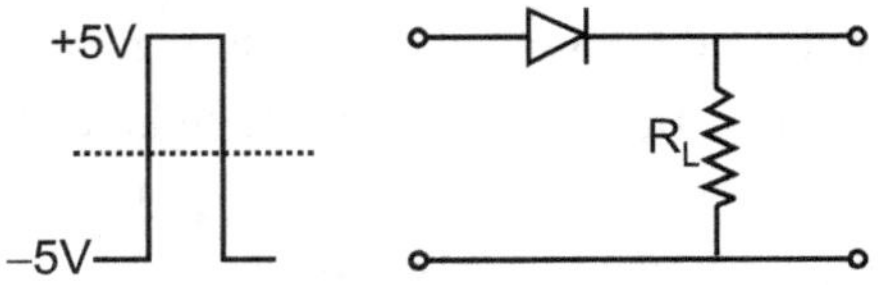

then the output across R_L will be

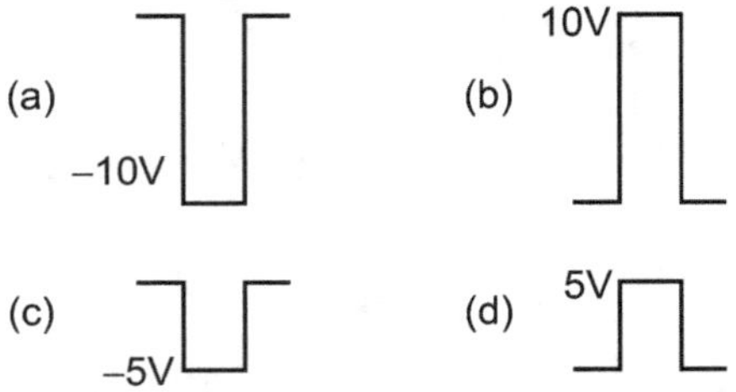

45. Which logic gate is represented by the following combination of logic gates ?

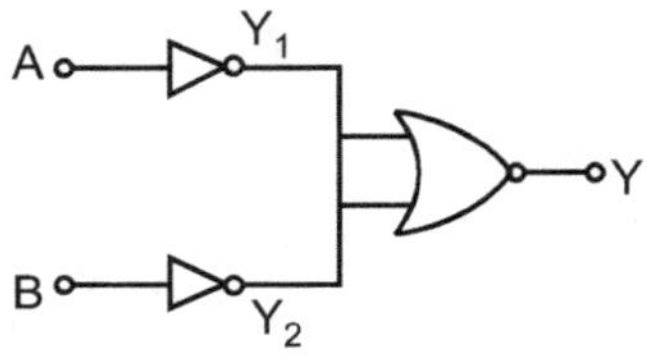

(a) OR (b) NAND

(c) AND (d) NOR

ANSWER KEY

1. (c)	**2.** (b)	**3.** (b)	**4.** (b)	**5.** (c)	**6.** (c)	**7.** (a)	**8.** (a)	**9.** (c)	**10.** (d)
11. (c)	**12.** (d)	**13.** (b)	**14.** (c)	**15.** (b)	**16.** (c)	**17.** (d)	**18.** (c)	**19.** (c)	**20.** (c)
21. (b)	**22.** (c)	**23.** (c)	**24.** (b)	**25.** (c)	**26.** (d)	**27.** (c)	**28.** (a)	**29.** (a)	**30.** (b)
31. (c)	**32.** (d)	**33.** (d)	**34.** (a)	**35.** (b)	**36.** (c)	**37.** (a)	**38.** (a)	**39.** (b)	**40.** (b)
41. (b)	**42.** (b)	**43.** (b)	**44.** (d)	**45.** (c)					

✍ ✍ ✍

CBSC AIPMT 2015 (JULY)

1. The cylindrical tube of a spray pump has radius R, one end of which has n fine holes, each of radius r. If the speed of the liquid in the tube is v, the speed of the ejection of the liquid through the holes is

(a) $\frac{vR^2}{n^2r^2}$ (b) $\frac{vR^2}{nr^2}$

(c) $\frac{vR^2}{n^3r^2}$ (d) $\frac{v^2R}{nr}$

2. Point masses m_1 and m_2 are placed at the opposite ends of a rigid rod of length L and negligible mass. The rod is to be set rotating about an axis perpendicular to it. The position of point P on this rod through which the axis should pass, so that the work required to set the rod rotating with angular velocity ω_0 is minimum, is given by

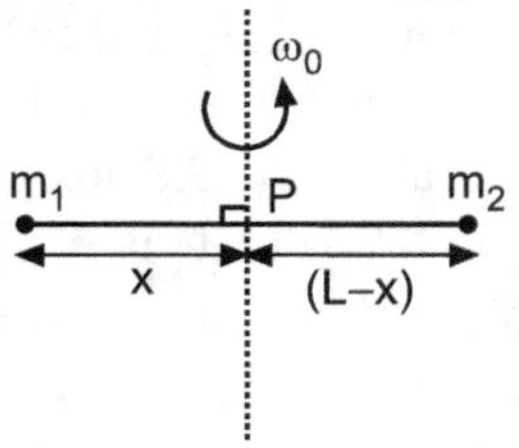

(a) $x = \frac{m_1 L}{m_1 + m_2}$ (b) $x = \frac{m_1}{m_2}L$

(c) $x = \frac{m_2}{m_1}L$ (d) $x = \frac{m_2 L}{m_1 + m_2}$

3. A proton and an alpha particle both enter a region of uniform magnetic field B, moving at right angles to the field B. If the radius of circular orbits for both the particles is equal and the kinetic energy acquired by proton is 1 MeV, the energy acquired by the alpha particle will be

(a) 4 MeV (b) 0.5 MeV

(c) 1.5 MeV (d) 1 MeV

4. A plank with a box on it at one end is gradually raised about the other end. As the angle of inclination with the horizontal reaches 30°, the box starts to slip and slides 4.0 m down the plank in 4.0 s. The coefficients of static and kinetic friction between the box and the plank will be, respectively

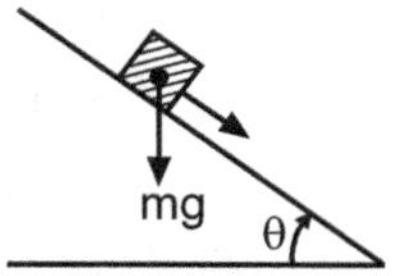

(a) 0.6 and 0.6 (b) 0.6 and 0.5

(c) 0.5 and 0.6 (d) 0.4 and 0.3

5. An ideal gas is compressed to half its initial volume by means of several processes. Which of the process results in the maximum work done on the gas?

(a) Adiabatic (b) Isobaric

(c) Isochoric (d) Isothermal

6. A ball is thrown vertically downwards from a height of 20 m with an initial velocity v_0. It collides with the ground, loses 50 % of its energy in collision and rebounds to the same height. The initial velocity v_0 is

(Take, $g = 10\ ms^{-2}$)

(a) $14\ ms^{-1}$ (b) $20\ ms^{-1}$

(c) $28\ ms^{-1}$ (d) $10\ ms^{-1}$

7. In the spectrum of hydrogen, the ratio of the longest wavelength in the Lyman series to the longest wavelength in the Balmer series is

(a) $\frac{4}{9}$ (b) $\frac{9}{4}$

(c) $\frac{27}{5}$ (d) $\frac{5}{27}$

8. A source of sound S emitting waves of frequency 100 Hz and an observer O are located at some distance from each other. The source is moving with a speed of $19.4\ ms^{-1}$ at an angle of 60° with the source. observer line as shown in the figure.

The observer is at rest. The apparent frequency observed by the observer (velocity of sound in air is 330 ms^{-1}), is

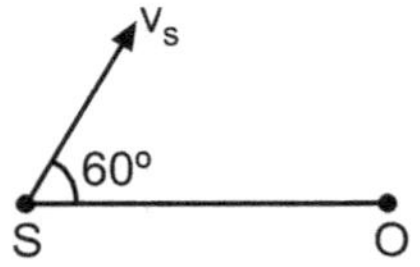

(a) 100 Hz (b) 103 Hz
(c) 106 Hz (d) 97 Hz

9. If dimensions of critical velocity v_c of a liquid flowing through a tube are expressed as $[\eta^x \rho^y r^z]$, where η, ρ and r are the coefficient of viscosity of liquid, density of liquid and radius of the tube respectively, then the values of x, y and z are given by

(a) 1, – 1, – 1 (b) – 1, – 1, 1
(c) – 1, – 1, – 1 (d) 1, 1, 1

10. 4.0 g of a gas occupies 22.4 L at NTP. The specific heat capacity of the gas at constant volume is 5.0 JK^{-1} mol^{-1}. If the speed of sound in this gas at NTP is 952 ms^{-1}, then the heat capacity at constant pressure is (Take gas constant R = 8.3 JK^{-1} mol^{-1})

(a) 8.0 JK^{-1} mol^{-1}
(b) 7.5 JK^{-1} mol^{-1}
(c) 7.0 JK^{-1} mol^{-1}
(d) 8.5 JK^{-1} mol^{-1}

11. If vectors $A = \cos \omega t\,\hat{i} + \sin \omega t\,\hat{j}$ and $B = \cos \frac{\omega t}{2}\,\hat{i} + \sin \frac{\omega t}{2}\,\hat{j}$ are functions of time, then the value of t at which they are orthogonal to each other, is

(a) $t = \frac{\pi}{4\omega}$ (b) $t = \frac{\pi}{2\omega}$

(c) $t = \frac{\pi}{\omega}$ (d) $t = 0$

12. In the given figure, a diode D is connected to an external resistance R = 100 Ω and an e.m.f of 3.5 V. If the barrier potential developed across the diode is 0.5 V, the current in the circuit will be

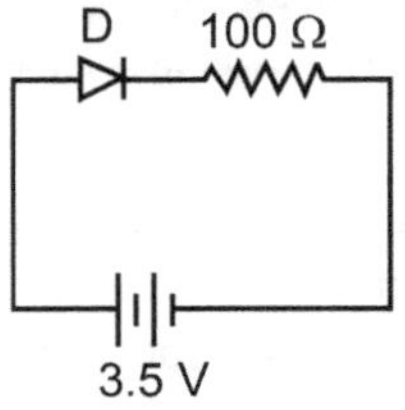

(a) 30 mA (b) 40 mA
(c) 20 mA (d) 35 mA

13. If potential (in volts) in a region is expressed as V (x, y, z) = 6xy – y + 2yz, the electric field (in N/C) at point (1, 1, 0) is

(a) $-(3\hat{i} + 5\hat{j} + 3\hat{k})$

(b) $-(6\hat{i} + 5\hat{j} + 2\hat{k})$

(c) $-(2\hat{i} + 3\hat{j} + \hat{k})$

(d) $-(6\hat{i} + 9\hat{j} + \hat{k})$

14. A remote sensing satellite of earth revolves in a circular orbit at a height of 0.25×10^6 m above the surface of earth. If earth's radius is 6.38×10^6 m and g = 9.8 ms^{-2}, then the orbital speed of the satellite is

(a) 7.76 kms^{-1} (b) 8.56 kms^{-1}
(c) 9.13 kms^{-1} (d) 6.67 kms^{-1}

15. Two metal wires of identical dimensions are connected in series. If σ_1 and σ_2 are the conductivities of the metal wires respectively, the effective conductivity of the combination is

(a) $\frac{2\sigma_1\sigma_2}{\sigma_1 + \sigma_2}$ (b) $\frac{\sigma_1 + \sigma_2}{2\sigma_1\sigma_2}$

(c) $\frac{\sigma_1 + \sigma_2}{\sigma_1\sigma_2}$ (d) $\frac{\sigma_1\sigma_2}{\sigma_1 + \sigma_2}$

16. A satellite S is moving in an elliptical orbit around the earth. The mass of the satellite is very small as compared to the mass of the earth. Then,

(a) the angular momentum of S about the centre of the earth changes in direction, but its magnitude remains constant.
(b) the total mechanical energy of S varies periodically with time.

(c) the linear momentum of S remains constant in magnitude.

(d) the acceleration of S is always directed towards the centre of the earth.

17. Two particles A and B, move with constant velocities v_1 and v_2. At the initial moment, their position vectors are r_1 and r_2 respectively. The condition for particles A and B for their collision is

(a) $\frac{r_1 - r_2}{|r_1 - r_2|} = \frac{v_2 - v_1}{|v_2 - v_1|}$

(b) $r_1 \cdot v_1 = r_2 \cdot v_2$

(c) $r_1 \times v_1 = r_2 \times v_2$

(d) $r_1 - r_2 = v_1 - v_2$

18. Two stones of masses m and 2m are whirled in horizontal circles, the heavier one in a radius $\frac{r}{2}$ and the lighter one in radius r. The tangential speed of lighter stone is n times that of the value of heavier stone when they experience same centripetal forces. The value of n is

(a) 2 (b) 3

(c) 4 (d) 1

19. A parallel plate air capacitor has capacity C, distance of separation between plates is d and potential difference V is applied between the plates. Force of attraction between the plates of the parallel plate air capacitor is

(a) $\frac{C^2V^2}{2d}$ (b) $\frac{CV^2}{2d}$

(c) $\frac{CV^2}{d}$ (d) $\frac{C^2V^2}{2d^2}$

20. The position vector of a particle R as a function of time is given by

$$R = 4\sin(2\pi t)\,\hat{i} + 4\cos(2\pi t)\,\hat{j}$$

where R is in metre, t is in seconds and $\hat{i}$ and $\hat{j}$ denote unit vectors along x and y-directions, respectively. Which one of the following statements is wrong for the motion of particle?

(a) Acceleration is along – R.

(b) Magnitude of acceleration vector is $\frac{v^2}{R}$, where v is the velocity of particle.

(c) Magnitude of the velocity of particle is 8 m/s.

(d) Path of the particle is a circle of radius 4 m.

21. A series R-C circuit is connected to an alternating voltage source. Consider two situations :

1. When capacitor is air filled.
2. When capacitor is mica filled.

Current through resistor is i and voltage across capacitor is V then

(a) $V_a < V_b$ (b) $V_a > V_b$

(c) $i_a > i_b$ (d) $V_a = V_b$

22. A string is stretched between fixed points separated by 75.0 cm. It is observed to have resonant frequencies of 420 Hz and 315 Hz. There are no other resonant frequencies between these two. The lowest resonant frequency for this strings is

(a) 155 Hz (b) 205 Hz

(c) 10.5 Hz (d) 105 Hz

23. The coefficient of performance of a refrigerator is 5. If the temperature inside freezer is – 20°C, the temperature of the surroundings to which it rejects heat is

(a) 31°C (b) 41°C

(c) 11°C (d) 21°C

24. A photoelectric surface is illuminated successively by monochromatic light of wavelength λ and $\frac{\lambda}{2}$. If the maximum kinetic energy of the emitted photoelectrons in the second case is 3 times that in the first case, the work function of the surface of the material is

(h = Planck's constant, c = speed of light)

(a) $\frac{hc}{2\lambda}$ (b) $\frac{hc}{\lambda}$

(c) $\frac{2\,hc}{\lambda}$ (d) $\frac{hc}{3\lambda}$

25. In an astronomical telescope in normal adjustment a straight black line of length L is drawn on inside part of objective lens. The eye-piece forms a real image of this line. The length of this image is I. The magnification of the telescope is

(a) $\frac{L}{l} + 1$ (b) $\frac{L}{l} - 1$

(c) $\frac{L+1}{L-1}$ (d) $\frac{L}{l}$

26. Two slits in Young's experiment have widths in the ratio 1: 25. The ratio of intensity at the maxima and minima in the interference pattern $\frac{I_{max}}{I_{min}}$ is

(a) $\frac{9}{4}$ (b) $\frac{121}{49}$

(c) $\frac{49}{121}$ (d) $\frac{4}{9}$

27. Two vessels separately contain two ideal gases A and B at the same temperature, the pressure of A being twice that of B. Under such conditions, the density of A is found to be 1.5 times the density of B. The ratio of molecular weight of A and B is

(a) $\frac{2}{3}$ (b) $\frac{3}{4}$

(c) 2 (d) $\frac{1}{2}$

28. A circuit contains an ammeter, a battery of 30 V and a resistance 40.80 Ω all connected in series. If the ammeter has a coil of resistance 480 Ω and a shunt of 20 Ω, then reading in the ammeter will be

(a) 0.5 A (b) 0.25 A

(c) 2 A (d) 1 A

29. The value of coefficient of volume expansion of glycerin is $5 \times 10^{-4}\ K^{-1}$. The fractional change in the density of glycerin for a rise of 40°C in its temperature is

(a) 0.015 (b) 0.020

(c) 0.025 (d) 0.010

30. The heart of a man pumps 5 L of blood through the arteries per minute at a pressure of 150 mm of mercury. If the density of mercury is $13.6 \times 10^3\ kg/m^3$ and $g = 10\ m/s^2$, then the power of heart in watt is

(a) 1.70 (b) 2.35

(c) 3.0 (d) 1.50

31. A beam of light consisting of red, green and blue colours is incident on a right angled prism. The refractive index of the material of the prism for the above red, green and blue wavelengths are 1.39, 1.44 and 1.47, respectively.

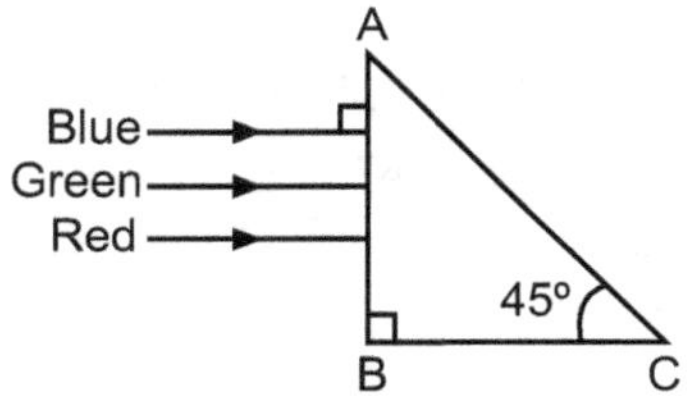

The prism will

(a) separate the blue colour part from the red and green colours.

(b) separate all the three colours from one another.

(c) not separate the three colours at all.

(d) separate the red colour part from the green and blue colours.

32. A rectangular coil of length 0.12 m and width 0.1 m having 50 turns of wire is suspended vertically in a uniform magnetic field of strength 0.2 Wb/m^2. The coil carries a current of 2 A. If the plane of the coil is inclined at an angle of 30° with the direction of the field, the torque required to keep the coil in stable equilibrium will be

(a) 0.15 Nm (b) 0.20 Nm

(c) 0.24 Nm (d) 0.12 Nm

33. An electron moves on a straight line path XY as shown. The abcd is a coil adjacent in the path of electron. What will be the direction of current, if any, induced in the coil?

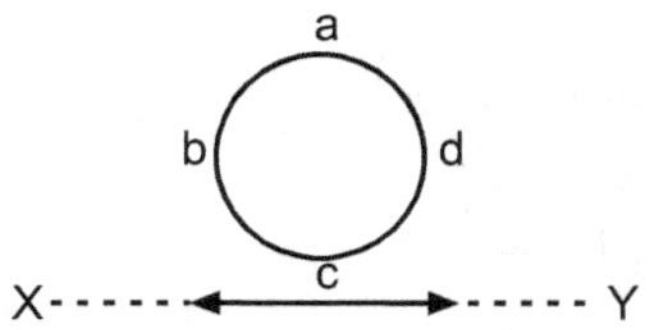

(a) abcd
(b) adcb
(c) The current will reverse its direction as the electron goes past the coil
(d) No current induced

34. A nucleus of uranium decays at rest into nuclei of thorium and helium. Then,
(a) the helium nucleus has more kinetic energy than the thorium nucleus.
(b) the helium nucleus has less momentum than the thorium nucleus.
(c) the helium nucleus has more momentum than the thorium nucleus.
(d) the helium nucleus has less kinetic energy than the thorium nucleus.

35. A force $F = \alpha\hat{i} + 3\hat{j} + 6\hat{k}$ is acting at a point $r = 2\hat{i} - 6\hat{j} - 12\hat{k}$. The value of α for which angular momentum about origin is conserved is
(a) -1 (b) 2
(c) 0 (d) 1

36. Water rises to a height 'h' in capillary tube. If the length of capillary tube above the surface of water is made less than 'h', then
(a) water rises upto the tip of capillary tube and then starts overflowing like a fountain.
(b) water rises upto the top of capillary tube and stays there without overflowing.
(c) water rises upto a point a little below the top and stays there.
(d) water does not rise at all

37. A particle is executing a simple harmonic motion. Its maximum acceleration is α and maximum velocity is β. Then, its time period of vibration will be
(a) $\frac{\beta^2}{\alpha^2}$ (b) $\frac{\alpha}{\beta}$
(c) $\frac{\beta^2}{\alpha}$ (d) $\frac{2\pi\beta}{\alpha}$

38. The energy of the EM waves is of the order of 15 keV. To which part of the spectrum does it belong?
(a) X-rays (b) Infrared rays
(c) Ultraviolet rays (d) y-rays

39. Light of wavelength 500 nm is incident on a metal with work function 2.28 eV. The de-Broglie wavelength of the emitted electron is
(a) $< 2.8 \times 10^{-10}$ m (b) $< 2.8 \times 10^{-9}$ m
(c) $\geq 2.8 \times 10^{-9}$ m (d) $\leq 2.8 \times 10^{-12}$ m

40. At the first minimum adjacent to the central maximum of a single slit diffraction pattern, the phase difference between the Huygen's wavelet from the edge of the slit and the wavelet from the midpoint of the slit is
(a) $\frac{\pi}{4}$ radian (b) $\frac{\pi}{2}$ radian
(c) π radian (d) $\frac{\pi}{8}$ radian

41. On a frictionless surface, a block of mass M moving at speed v collides elastically with another block of same mass M which is initially at rest. After collision the first block moves at an angle θ to its initial direction and has a speed $\frac{v}{3}$. The speed of the second block after the collision is
(a) $\frac{2\sqrt{2}}{3}v$ (b) $\frac{3}{4}v$
(c) $\frac{3}{\sqrt{2}}v$ (d) $\frac{\sqrt{3}}{2}v$

42. A potentiometer wire of length L and a resistance r are connected in series with a battery of e.m.f. E_0 and a resistance r_1. An unknown e.m.f. is balanced at a length l of the potentiometer wire. The e.m.f. E will be given by

(a) $\frac{LE_0r}{lr_1}$ (b) $\frac{E_0r}{(r+r_1)}\cdot\frac{l}{L}$

(c) $\frac{E_0l}{L}$ (d) $\frac{LE_0r}{(r+r_1)l}$

43. The Young's modulus of steel is twice that of brass. Two wires of same length and of same area of cross-section, one of steel and another of brass are suspended from the same roof. It we want the lower ends of the wires to be at the same level, then the weight added to the steel and brass wires must be in the ratio of

(a) 1 : 2 (b) 2 : 1

(c) 4 : 1 (d) 1 : 1

44. The input signal given to a CE amplifier having a voltage gain of 150 is $V_i = 2\cos\left(15t+\frac{\pi}{3}\right)$. The corresponding output signal will be

(a) $300\cos\left(15t+\frac{\pi}{3}\right)$

(b) $75\cos\left(15t+\frac{2\pi}{3}\right)$

(c) $2\cos\left(15t+\frac{5\pi}{3}\right)$

(d) $300\cos\left(15t+\frac{4\pi}{3}\right)$

45. An automobile moves on a road with a speed of 54 kmh^{-1}. The radius of its wheels is 0.45 m and the moment of inertia of the wheel about its axis of rotation is 3 kg-m^2. If the vehicle is brought to rest in 15 s, the magnitude of average torque transmitted by its brakes to the wheel is

(a) 6.66 kg m^2 s^{-2} (b) 8.58 kg m^2 s^{-2}

(c) 10.86 kg m^2 s^{-2} (d) 2.86 kg m^2 s^{-2}

ANSWER KEY

1. (b)	**2.** (d)	**3.** (d)	**4.** (b)	**5.** (a)	**6.** (b)	**7.** (d)	**8.** (b)	**9.** (a)	**10.** (a)
11. (c)	**12.** (a)	**13.** (b)	**14.** (a)	**15.** (a)	**16.** (d)	**17.** (a)	**18.** (a)	**19.** (b)	**20.** (c)
21. (b)	**22.** (d)	**23.** (a)	**24.** (a)	**25.** (d)	**26.** (a)	**27.** (b)	**28.** (a)	**29.** (b)	**30.** (a)
31. (d)	**32.** (b)	**33.** (c)	**34.** (a)	**35.** (a)	**36.** (a)	**37.** (d)	**38.** (a)	**39.** (b)	**40.** (c)
41. (a)	**42.** (b)	**43.** (b)	**44.** (d)	**45.** (a)					

✍ ✍ ✍

NEET 2016

1. A capacitor of $2\mu F$ is charged as shown in the figure. When the switch S is turned to position 2, the percentage of its stored energy dissipated is

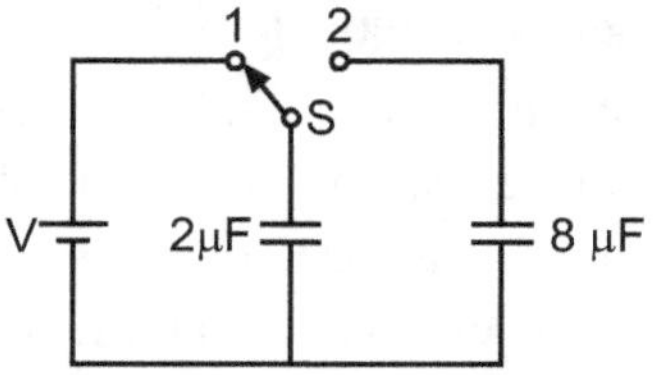

(a) 20% (b) 75%
(c) 80% (d) 0%

2. To get output 1 for the following circuit, the correct choice for the input is

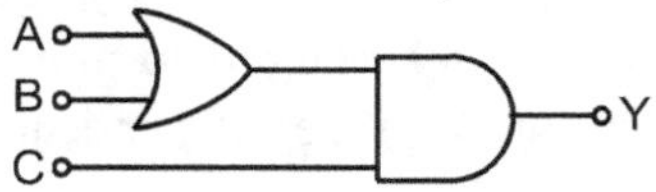

(a) A = 1, B = 0, C = 0
(b) A = 1, B = 1, C = 0
(c) A = 1, B = 0, C = 1
(d) A = 0, B = 1, C = 0

3. A potentiometer wire is 100 cm long and a constant potential difference is maintained across it. Two cells are connected in series first to support one another and then in opposite direction. The balance points are obtained at 50 cm and 10 cm from the positive end of the wire in the two cases. The ratio of emf is

(a) 5 : 4 (b) 3 : 4
(c) 3 : 2 (d) 5 : 1

4. When a metallic surface is illuminated with radiation of wavelength λ, the stopping potential is V. If the same surface is illuminated with radiation of wavelength 2λ, the stopping potential is $\frac{V}{4}$. The threshold wavelength for the metallic surface is

(a) 5λ (b) $\frac{5}{2}\lambda$
(c) 3λ (d) 4λ

5. Two non-mixing liquids of densities ρ and $n\rho$ $(n > 1)$ are put in a container. The height of each liquid is h. A solid cylinder of length L and density d is put in this container. The cylinder floats with its axis vertical and length pL $(p < 1)$ in the denser liquid. The density d is equal to

(a) $\{2 + (n + 1)p\}\rho$ (b) $\{2 + (n - 1)p\}\rho$
(c) $\{1 + (n - 1)p\}\rho$ (d) $\{1 + (n + 1)p\}\rho$

6. Out of the following options which one can be used to produce a propagating electromagnetic wave?

(a) A stationary charge
(b) A chargeless particle
(c) An accelerating charge
(d) A charge moving at constant velocity

7. The charge flowing through a resistance R varies with time t as $Q = at - bt^2$, where a and b are positive constants. The total heat produced in R is

(a) $\frac{a^3R}{3b}$ (b) $\frac{a^3R}{2b}$
(c) $\frac{a^3R}{b}$ (d) $\frac{a^3R}{6b}$

8. At what height from the surface of earth the gravitation potential and the value of g are -5.4×10^7 J kg^{-2} and 6.0 ms^{-2} respectively? (Take the radius of earth as 6400 km.)

(a) 1600 km (b) 1400 km
(c) 2000 km (d) 2600 km

9. Coefficient of linear expansion of brass and steel rods are α_1 and α_2. Lengths of brass and steel rods are l_1 and l_2 respectively. If $(l_2 - l_1)$ is maintained same at all temperatures, which one of the following relations holds good ?

(a) $\alpha_1 l_2^2 = \alpha_1 l_1^2$ (b) $\alpha_1^2 l_2 = \alpha_2^2 l_1$
(c) $\alpha_1 l_1 = \alpha_2 l_2$ (d) $\alpha_1 l_2 = \alpha_2 l_1$

10. The intensity at the maximum in a Young's double slit experiment is I_0. Distance between two slits is d = 5λ, where λ is the wavelength of light used in the experiment. What will be the intensity in front of one of the slits on the screen placed at a distance D = 10 d ?

(a) $\frac{I_0}{4}$ (b) $\frac{3}{4} I_0$

(c) $\frac{I_0}{2}$ (d) I_0

11. Given the value of Rydberg's constant is 10 m^{-1}, the wave number of the last line of the Balmer series in hydrogen spectrum will be:

(a) $0.5 \times 10^7 \text{ m}^{-1}$ (b) $0.25 \times 10^7 \text{ m}^{-1}$

(c) $2.5 \times 10^7 \text{ m}^{-1}$ (d) $0.025 \times 10^4 \text{ m}^{-1}$

12. The ratio of escape velocity at earth (v_e) to the escape velocity at a planet (v_p) whose radius and mean density are twice as that of earth is

(a) $1 : 2\sqrt{2}$ (b) 1 : 4

(c) $1 : \sqrt{2}$ (d) 1 : 2

13. A long solenoid has 1000 turns. When a current of 4 A flows through it, the magnetic flux linked with each turn of the solenoid is 4×10^{-3} Wb. The self-inductance of the solenoid is

(a) 3 H (b) 2 H

(c) 1 H (d) 4H

14. A car is negotiating a curved road of radius R. The road is banked at angle θ. The coefficient of friction between the tyres of the car and the road is μ_s. The maximum safe velocity on this road is

(a) $\sqrt{gR\left(\frac{\mu_s + \tan\theta}{1 - \mu_s \tan\theta}\right)}$

(b) $\sqrt{\frac{g}{R}\left(\frac{\mu_s + \tan\theta}{1 - \mu_s \tan\theta}\right)}$

(c) $\sqrt{\frac{g}{R^2}\left(\frac{\mu_s + \tan\theta}{1 - \mu_s \tan\theta}\right)}$

(d) $\sqrt{gR^2\left(\frac{\mu_s + \tan\theta}{1 - \mu_s \tan\theta}\right)}$

15. The magnetic susceptibility is negative for

(a) paramagnetic material only.

(b) ferromagnetic material only.

(c) paramagnetic and ferromagnetic materials.

(d) diamagnetic material only.

16. A siren emitting a sound of frequency 800 Hz moves away from an observer towards a cliff at a speed of 15 ms^{-1}. Then, the frequency of sound that the observer hears in the echo reflected from the cliff is

(Take, velocity of sound in air = 330 ms^{-1})

(a) 800 Hz (b) 838 Hz

(c) 885 Hz (d) 765 Hz

17. A body of mass 1 kg begins to move under the action of a time dependent force $F = (2t\hat{i} + 3t^2\hat{j})$ N, where $\hat{i}$ and $\hat{j}$ are unit vectors along X and Y axis. What power will be developed by the force at the time (t)?

(a) $(2t^2 + 4t^4)$ W (b) $(2t^3 + 3t^4)$ W

(c) $(2t^3 + 3t^5)$ W (d) $(2t + 3t^3)$ W

18. From a disc of radius R and mass M, a circular hole of diameter R, whose rim passes through the centre is cut. What is the moment of inertia of the remaining part of the disc about a perpendicular axis, passing through the centre ?

(a) $13 MR^2/32$ (b) $11 MR^2/32$

(c) $9 MR^2/32$ (d) $15 MR^2/32$

19. In a diffraction pattern due to a single slit of width a, the first minimum is observed at an angle 30° when light of wavelength 5000 Å is incident on the slit. The first secondary maximum is observed at an angle of

(a) $\sin^{-1}\left(\frac{2}{3}\right)$ (b) $\sin^{-1}\left(\frac{1}{2}\right)$

(c) $\sin^{-1}\left(\frac{3}{4}\right)$ (d) $\sin^{-1}\left(\frac{1}{4}\right)$

20. A square loop ABCD carrying a current i, is placed near and coplanar with a long straight conductor XY carrying a current I, the net force on the loop will be

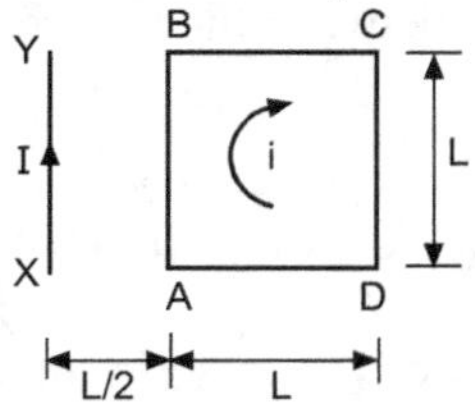

(a) $\frac{\mu_0 Ii}{2\pi}$ (b) $\frac{2\mu_0 IiL}{3\pi}$

(c) $\frac{\mu_0 IiL}{2\pi}$ (d) $\frac{2\mu_0 Ii}{3\pi}$

21. A black body is at a temperature of 5760 K. The energy of radiation emitted by the body at wavelength 250 nm is U_1, at wavelength 500 nm is U_2 and that at 1000 nm is U_3. Wien's constant, $b = 2.88 \times 10^6$ nmK. Which of the following is correct?

(a) $U_3 = 0$ (b) $U_1 > U_2$

(c) $U_2 > U_1$ (d) $U_1 = 0$

22. An air column, closed at one end and open at the other, resonates with a tunning fork when the smallest length of the column is 50 cm. The next larger length of the column resonating with the same tunning fork is

(a) 100 cm (b) 150 cm

(c) 200 cm (d) 66.7 cm

23. The molecules of a given mass of a gas have r.m.s. velocity of 200 ms^{-1} at 27°C and 1.0×10^5 Nm^{-2} pressure. When the temperature and pressure of the gas are respectively, 127°C and 0.05×10^5 Nm^{-2}, the r.m.s. velocity of its molecules in ms^{-1} is

(a) $\frac{400}{\sqrt{3}}$ (b) $\frac{100\sqrt{2}}{3}$

(c) $\frac{100}{3}$ (d) $100\sqrt{2}$

24. Consider the junction diode as ideal. The value of current flowing through AB is

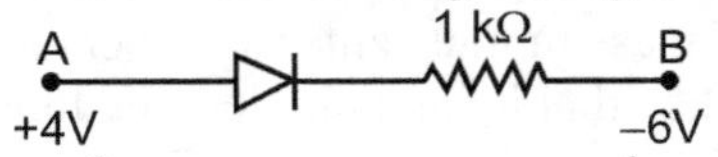

(a) 10^{-2} A (b) 10^{-1} A

(c) 10^{-3} A (d) 0 A

25. If the magnitude of sum of two vectors is equal to the magnitude of difference of the two vectors, then the angle between these vectors is

(a) 90° (b) 45°

(c) 180° (d) 0°

26. An astronomical telescope has objective and eyepiece of focal lengths 40 cm and 4 cm respectively. To view an object 200 cm away from the objective, the lenses must be separated by a distance

(a) 46.0 cm (b) 50.0 cm

(c) 54.0 cm (d) 37.3 cm

27. An n-p-n transistor is connected in common emitter configuration in a given amplifier. A load resistance of 800 Ω is connected in the collector circuit and the voltage drop across it is 0.8V. If the current amplification factor is 0.96 and the input resistance of the circuits is 192 Ω, the voltage gain and the power gain of the amplifier will respectively be

(a) 3.69, 3.84 (b) 4, 4

(c) 4, 3.69 (d) 4, 3.84

28. A gas is compressed isothermally to half its initial volume. The same gas is compressed separately through an adiabatic process until its volume is again reduced to half. Then

(a) compressing the gas through adiabatic process will require more work to be done.

(b) compressing the gas isothermally or adiabatically will require the same amount of work.

(c) which of the case (whether compression through isothermal or through adiabatic process) requires more work will depend upon the atomicity of the gas.

(d) compressing the gas isothermally will require more work to be done.

29. A long straight wire of radius a carries a steady current I. The current is uniformly distributed over its cross-section. The ratio of the magnetic fields B and B' at radial distances $\frac{a}{2}$ and 2a respectively, from the axis of the wire is

(a) $\frac{1}{2}$ (b) 1

(c) 4 (d) $\frac{1}{4}$

30. Match the corresponding entries of Column 1 with Column 2. [Where m is the magnification produced by the mirror]

Column 1	Column 2
(A) $m = -2$	(a) Convex mirror
(B) $m = -\frac{1}{2}$	(b) Concave mirror
(C) $m = +2$	(c) Real image
(D) $m = +\frac{1}{2}$	(d) Virtual image

(a) A → a and c; B → a and d; C → a and b; D → c and d

(b) A → a and d; B → b and c; C → b and d; D → b and c

(c) A → c and d; B → b and d; C → b and c; D → a and d

(d) A → b and c; B → b and c; C → b and d; D → a and d

31. If the velocity of a particle is $v = At + Bt^2$, where A and B are constants, then the distance travelled by it between 1s and 2s is

(a) 3A + 7B (b) $\frac{3}{2}A + \frac{7}{3}B$

(c) $\frac{A}{2} + \frac{B}{3}$ (d) $\frac{3}{2}A + 4B$

32. A disc and a sphere of same radius but different masses roll off on two inclined planes of the same altitude and length. Which one of the two objects gets to the bottom of the plane first?

(a) Sphere

(b) Both reach at the same time

(c) Depends on their masses

(d) Disc

33. Two identical charged spheres suspended from a common point by two massless strings of lengths l, are initially at a distance d ($d << l$) apart because of their mutual repulsion. The charges begin to leak from both the spheres at a constant rate. As a result, the spheres approach each other with a velocity v. Then, v varies as a function of the distance x between the sphere, as

(a) $v \propto x$ (b) $v \propto x^{-1/2}$

(c) $v \propto x^{-1}$ (d) $v \propto x^{1/2}$

34. A particle moves so that its position vector is given by $r = \cos \omega t \, \hat{x} + \sin \omega t \, \hat{y}$, where ω is a constant.

Which of the following is true?

(a) Velocity and acceleration both are parallel to r.

(b) Velocity is perpendicular to r and acceleration is directed towards the origin.

(c) Velocity is perpendicular to r and acceleration is directed away form the origin.

(d) Velocity and acceleration both are perpendicular to r.

35. A piece of ice falls from a height h so that it melts completely. Only one-quarter of the heat produced is absorbed by the ice and all energy of ice gets converted into heat during its fall. The value of h is ... [Take latent heat of ice = 3.4×10^5 J/kg and g = 10 N/kg]

(a) 544 km (b) 136 km

(c) 68 km (d) 34 km

36. A uniform circular disc of radius 50 cm at rest is free to turn about an axis which is perpendicular to its plane and passes through its centre. It is subjected to a torque which produces a constant angular acceleration of 2.0 rad/s^2. Its net acceleration in m/s^2 at the end of 2.0 s is approximately

(a) 7.0 (b) 6.0

(c) 3.0 (d) 8.0

37. What is the minimum velocity with which a body of mass m must enter a vertical loop of radius R so that it can complete the loop?

(a) $\sqrt{2gR}$ (b) $\sqrt{3gR}$

(c) $\sqrt{5gR}$ (d) $\sqrt{gR}$

38. A small signal voltage $V(t) = V_0 \sin \omega t$ is applied across an ideal capacitor C. Then
(a) Over a full cycle the capacitor C does not consume any energy from the voltage source.
(b) current I(t) is in phase with voltage V(t).
(c) current I(t) leads voltage V(t) by 180°.
(d) current I(t), lags voltage V(t) by 90°.

39. A uniform rope of length L and mass m_1 hangs vertically from a rigid support. A block of mass m_2 is attached to the free end of the rope. A transverse pulse of wavelength λ_1 is produced at the lower end of the rope. The wavelength of the pulse when it reaches the top of the rope is λ_2. The ratio λ_2 / λ_1 is
(a) $\sqrt{\frac{m_1 + m_2}{m_2}}$ (b) $\sqrt{\frac{m_2}{m_1}}$
(c) $\sqrt{\frac{m_1 + m_2}{m_1}}$ (d) $\sqrt{\frac{m_1}{m_2}}$

40. An inductor 20 mH, a capacitor 50 μF and a resistor 40 Ω are connected in series across a source of emf V = 10 sin 340 t. The power loss in AC circuit is
(a) 0.67 W (b) 0.76 W
(c) 0.89 W (d) 0.51 W

41. An electron of mass m and a photon have same energy E. The ratio of de-Broglie wavelengths associated with them is
(a) $\left(\frac{E}{2m}\right)^{1/2}$ (b) $c(2mE)^{1/2}$
(c) $\frac{1}{c}\left(\frac{2m}{E}\right)^{1/2}$ (d) $\frac{1}{c}\left(\frac{E}{2m}\right)^{1/2}$
(c being velocity of light)

42. When an α-particle of mass m moving with velocity v bombards on a heavy nucleus of charge Ze, its distance of closest approach from the nucleus depends on m as
(a) $\frac{1}{\sqrt{m}}$ (b) $\frac{1}{m^2}$
(c) m (d) $\frac{1}{m}$

43. A refrigerator works between 4°C and 30°C. It is required to remove 600 calories of heat every second in order to keep the temperature of the refrigerated space constant. The power required is
(Take, 1 cal = 4.2 joules)
(a) 23.65 W (b) 236.5 W
(c) 2365 W (d) 2.365 W

44. A particle of mass 10 g moves along a circle of radius 6.4 cm with a constant tangential acceleration. What is the magnitude of this acceleration, if the kinetic energy of the particle becomes equal to 8×10^{-4} J by the end of the second revolution after the beginning of the motion?
(a) 0.15 m/s^2 (b) 0.18 m/s^2
(c) 0.2 m/s^2 (d) 0.1 m/s^2

45. The angle of incidence for a ray of light at a refracting surface of a prism is 45°. The angle of prism is 60°. If the ray suffers minimum deviation through the prism, the angle of minimum deviation and refractive index of the material of the prism respectively, are
(a) $30°; \sqrt{2}$ (b) $45°; \sqrt{2}$
(c) $30°; \frac{1}{\sqrt{2}}$ (d) $45°; \frac{1}{\sqrt{2}}$

ANSWER KEY

1. (c)	**2.** (c)	**3.** (c)	**4.** (c)	**5.** (c)	**6.** (c)	**7.** (d)	**8.** (d)	**9.** (c)	**10.** (c)
11. (b)	**12.** (a)	**13.** (c)	**14.** (a)	**15.** (d)	**16.** (b)	**17.** (c)	**18.** (a)	**19.** (c)	**20.** (d)
21. (c)	**22.** (b)	**23.** (a)	**24.** (a)	**25.** (a)	**26.** (c)	**27.** (d)	**28.** (a)	**29.** (b)	**30.** (d)
31. (b)	**32.** (a)	**33.** (b)	**34.** (b)	**35.** (b)	**36.** (d)	**37.** (c)	**38.** (a)	**39.** (a)	**40.** (d)
41. (d)	**42.** (d)	**43.** (b)	**44.** (d)	**45.** (a)					

NEET 2016 (JULY)

1. Planck's constant (h), speed of light in vacuum (c) and Newton's gravitational constant (G) are three fundamental constants. Which of the following combinations of these has the dimension of length?

(a) $\frac{\sqrt{hG}}{c^{3/2}}$ (b) $\frac{\sqrt{hG}}{c^{5/2}}$

(c) $\sqrt{\frac{hc}{G}}$ (d) $\sqrt{\frac{Gc}{h^{3/2}}}$

2. Two cars P and Q start from a point at the same time in a straight line and their positions are represented by $x_P(t) = at + bt^2$ and $x_Q(t) = ft - t^2$. At what time do the cars have the same velocity?

(a) $\frac{a-f}{1+b}$ (b) $\frac{a+f}{2(b-1)}$

(c) $\frac{a+f}{2(1+b)}$ (d) $\frac{f-a}{2(1+b)}$

3. In the given figure, $a = 15\ m/s^2$ represents the total acceleration of a particle moving in the clockwise direction in a circle of radius R = 2.5 m at a given instant of time. The speed of the particle is

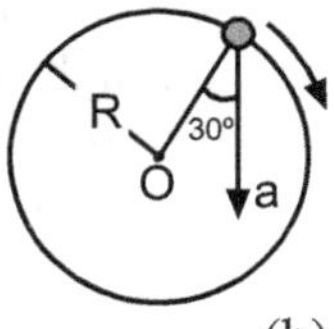

(a) 4.5 m/s (b) 5.0 m/s
(c) 5.7 m/s (d) 6.2 m/s

4. A rigid ball of mass m strikes a rigid wall at 60° and gets reflected without loss of speed as shown in the figure. The value of impulse imparted by the wall on the ball will be

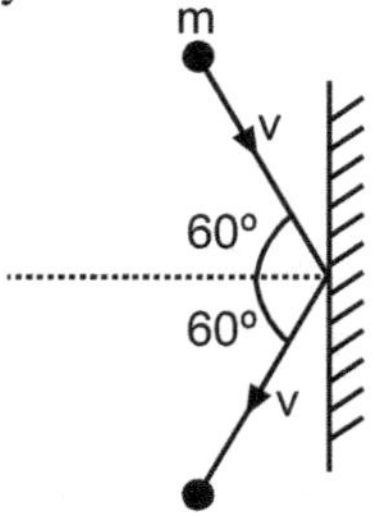

(a) mv (b) 2mv
(c) mv/2 (d) mv/3

5. A bullet of mass 10 g moving horizontal with a velocity of 400 m/s strikes a wood block of mass 2 kg which is suspended by light inextensible string of length 5 m. As a result, the centre of gravity of the block is found to rise a vertical distance of 10 cm. The speed of the bullet after it emerges of horizontally from the block will be

(a) 100 m/s (b) 80 m/s
(c) 120 m/s (d) 160 m/s

6. Two identical balls A and B having velocities of 0.5 m/s and – 0.3 m/s respectively collide elastically in one dimension. The velocities of B and A after the collision respectively will be

(a) – 0.5 m/s and 0.3 m/s
(b) 0.5 m/s and – 0.3 m/s
(c) – 0.3 m/s and 0.5 m/s
(d) 0.3 m/s and 0.5 m/s

7. A particle moves from a point $(-2\hat{i} + 5\hat{j})$ to $(4\hat{j} + 3\hat{k})$ when a force of $(4\hat{i} + 3\hat{j})$ N is applied. How much work has been done by the force?

(a) 8 J (b) 11 J
(c) 5 J (d) 2 J

8. Two rotating bodies A and B of masses m and 2m with moments of inertia I_A and I_B $(I_B > I_A)$ have equal kinetic energy of rotation. If L_A and L_B are their angular momenta respectively, then

(a) $L_A = \frac{L_B}{2}$ (b) $L_A = 2L_B$

(c) $L_B > L_A$ (d) $L_A > L_B$

9. A solid sphere of mass m and radius R is rotating about its diameter. A solid cylinder of the same mass and same radius is also rotating about its geometrical axis with an angular speed twice that of the sphere. The ratio of their kinetic energies of rotation $(E_{sphere} / E_{cylinder})$ will be

(a) 2 : 3 (b) 1 : 5
(c) 1 : 4 (d) 3 : 1

10. A light rod of length l has two masses m_1 and m_2 attached to its two ends. The moment of inertia of the system about an axis perpendicular to the rod and passing through the centre of mass is

(a) $\frac{m_1 m_2}{m_1 + m_2} l^2$ (b) $\frac{m_1 + m_2}{m_1 m_2} l^2$

(c) $(m_1 + m_2) l^2$ (d) $\sqrt{m_1 m_2}\, l^2$

11. Starting from the centre of the earth having radius R, the variation of g (acceleration due to gravity) is shown by

(a)
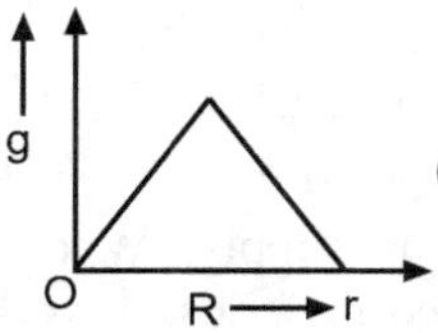

(b)
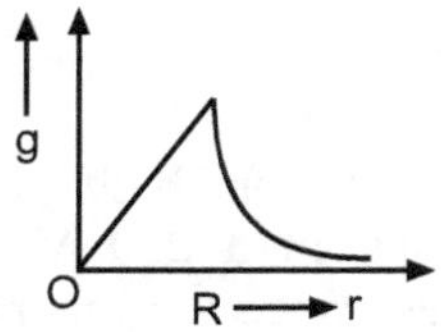

(a)
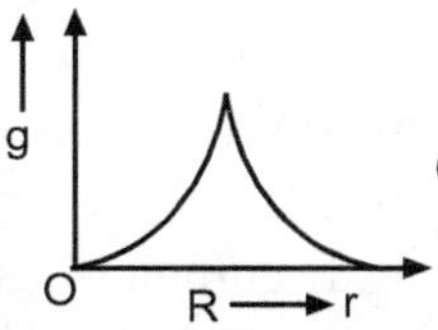

(b)
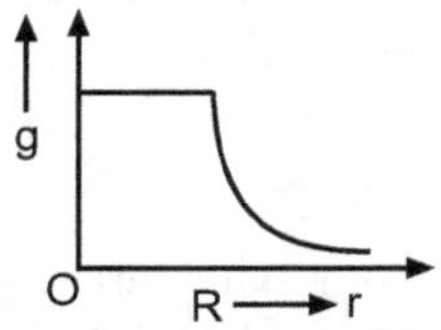

12. A satellite of mass m is orbiting the earth (of radius R) at a height h from its surface. The total energy of the satellite in terms of g_0, the value of acceleration due to gravity at the earth's surface is

(a) $\frac{mg_0R^2}{2(R + h)}$ (b) $-\frac{mg_0R^2}{2(R + h)}$

(c) $\frac{2mg_0R^2}{R + h}$ (d) $-\frac{2mg_0R^2}{R + h}$

13. A rectangular film of liquid is extended from (4 cm × 2 cm) to (5 cm × 4 cm). If the work done is 3×10^{-4} J, the value of the surface tension of the liquid is

(a) 0.250 Nm^{-1} (b) 0.125 Nm^{-1}

(c) 0.2 Nm^{-1} (d) 8.0 Nm^{-1}

14. Three liquids of densities ρ_1, ρ_2 and ρ_3 (with $\rho_1 > \rho_2 > \rho_3$), having the same value of surface tension T, rise to the same height in three identical capillaries. The angles of contact θ_1, θ_2 and θ_3 obey

(a) $\frac{\pi}{2} > \theta_1 > \theta_2 > \theta_3 \geq 0$

(b) $0 \leq \theta_1 < \theta_2 < \theta_3 < \frac{\pi}{2}$

(c) $\frac{\pi}{2} < \theta_1 < \theta_2 < \theta_3 < \pi$

(d) $\pi > \theta_1 > \theta_2 > \theta_3 > \frac{\pi}{2}$

15. Two identical bodies are made of a material for which the heat capacity increases with temperature. One of these is at 100°C, while the other one is at 0°C. If the two bodies are brought into contact, then assuming no heat loss, the final common temperature is

(a) 50°C

(b) more than 50°C

(c) less than 50°C, but greater than 0°C

(d) 0°C

16. A body cools from a temperature 3T to 2T in 10 minutes. The room temperature is T. Assume that Newton's law of cooling is applicable. The temperature of the body at the end of the next 10 minutes will be

(a) $\frac{7}{4}$T (b) $\frac{3}{2}$T

(c) $\frac{4}{3}$T (d) T

17. One mole of an ideal monoatomic gas undergoes a process described by the equation pV^3 = constant. The heat capacity of the gas during this process is

(a) $\frac{3}{2}$R (b) $\frac{5}{2}$R

(c) 2 R (d) R

18. The temperature inside a refrigerator is t_2 °C and the room temperature is t_1 °C. The amount of heat delivered to the room for each joule of electrical energy consumed ideally will be

(a) $\frac{t_1}{t_1 - t_2}$ (b) $\frac{t_1 + 273}{t_1 - t_2}$

(c) $\frac{t_2 + 273}{t_1 - t_2}$ (d) $\frac{t_1 + t_2}{t_1 + 273}$

19. A given sample of an ideal gas occupies a volume V at a pressure p and absolute temperature T. The mass of each molecule of the gas is m. Which of the following gives the density of the gas?

(a) p/(kT) (b) pm/(kT)

(c) p/(kTV) (d) mkT

20. A body of mass m is attached to the lower end of a spring whose upper end is fixed. The spring has negligible mass. When the mass m is slightly pulled down and released, it oscillates with a time period of 3 s. When the mass m is increased by 1 kg, the time period of oscillations becomes 5 s. The value of m in kg is

(a) $\frac{3}{4}$ (b) $\frac{4}{3}$

(c) $\frac{16}{9}$ (d) $\frac{9}{16}$

21. The second overtone of an open organ pipe has the same frequency as the first overtone of a closed pipe L metre long. The length of the open pipe will be

(a) L (b) 2L

(c) L/2 (d) 4L

22. Three sound waves of equal amplitudes have frequencies (n – 1), n, (n + 1). They superimpose to give beats. The number of beats produced per second will be

(a) 1 (b) 4

(c) 3 (d) 2

23. An electric dipole is placed at an angle of 30° with an electric field intensity 2×10^5 N/C. It experiences a torque equal to 4 Nm. The charge on the dipole, if the dipole length is 2 cm, is

(a) 8 mC (b) 2 mC

(c) 5 mC (d) 7 μC

24. A parallel-plate capacitor of area A, plate separation d and capacitance C is filled with four dielectric materials having dielectric constants k_1, k_2, k_3 and k_4 as shown in the figure below. If a single dielectric material is to be used to have the same capacitance C in this capacitor, then its dielectric constant k is given by

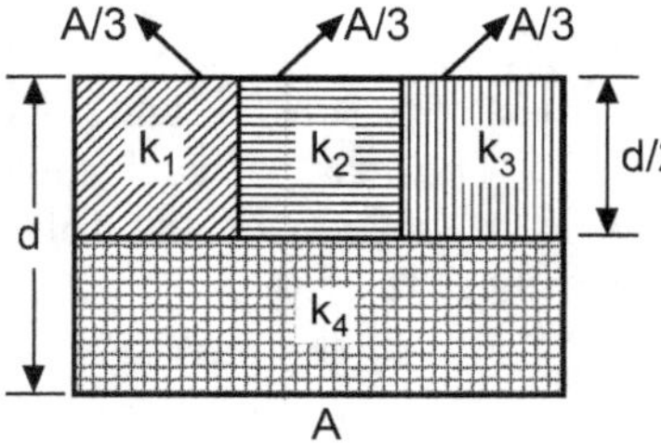

(a) $k = k_1 + k_2 + k_3 + 3k_4$

(b) $k = \frac{2}{3}(k_1 + k_2 + k_3) + 2k_4$

(c) $\frac{2}{k} = \frac{3}{k_1 + k_2 + k_3} + \frac{1}{k_4}$

(d) $\frac{1}{k} = \frac{1}{k_1} + \frac{1}{k_2} + \frac{1}{k_3} + \frac{3}{2k_4}$

25. The potential difference ($V_A - V_B$) between the points A and B in the given figure is

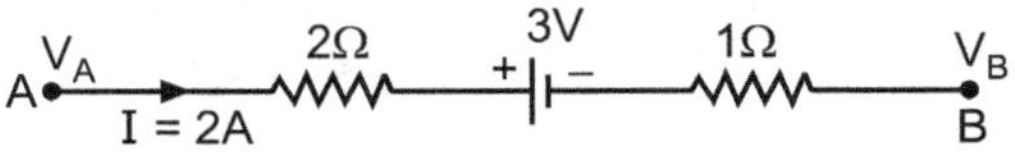

(a) – 3V (b) + 3V

(c) + 6V (d) + 9V

26. A filament bulb (500 W, 100 V) is to be used in a 230 V mains supply. When a resistance R is connected in series, it works perfectly and the bulb consumes 500 W. The value of R is

(a) 230 Ω (b) 46 Ω

(c) 26 Ω (d) 13Ω

27. A long wire carrying a steady current is bent into a circular loop of one turn. The magnetic field at the centre of the loop is B. It is then bent into a circular .coil of n turns. The magnetic field at the centre of this coil of n turns will be

(a) nB (b) n^2B

(c) 2nB (d) $2n^2B$

28. A bar magnet is hung by a thin cotton thread in a uniform horizontal magnetic field and is in equilibrium state. The energy required to rotate it by 60° is W. Now the torque required to keep the magnet in this new position is

(a) $\frac{W}{\sqrt{3}}$ (b) $\sqrt{3}W$

(c) $\frac{\sqrt{3}W}{2}$ (d) $\frac{2W}{\sqrt{3}}$

29. An electron is moving in a circular path under the influence of a transverse magnetic field of 3.57×10^{-2} T. If the value of e/m is 1.76×10^{11} C/kg, the frequency of revolution of the electron is

(a) 1 GHz (b) 100 MHz

(c) 62.8 MHz (d) 6.28 MHz

30. Which of the following combinations should be selected for better tuning of an L-C-R circuit used for communication?

(a) R = 20 Ω, L = 1.5 H, C = 35 μF

(b) R = 25 Ω, L = 2.5 H, C = 45 μF

(c) R = 15 Ω, L = 3.5 H, C = 30 μF

(d) R = 25 Ω, L = 1.5 H, C = 45 μF

31. A uniform magnetic field is restricted within a region of radius r. The magnetic field changes with time at a rate $\frac{dB}{dt}$. Loop 1 of radius R > r encloses the region r and loop 2 of radius R is outside the region of magnetic field as shown in the figure. Then, the emf generated is

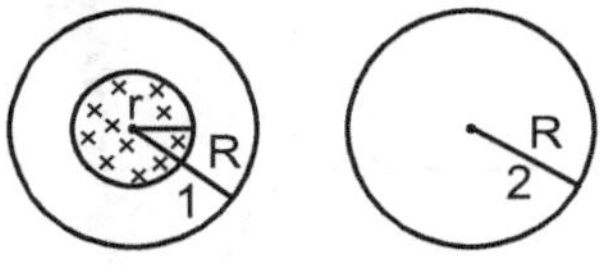

(a) zero in loop 1 and zero in loop 2

(b) $-\frac{dB}{dt}\pi r^2$ in loop 1 and $-\frac{dB}{dt}\pi r^2$ in loop 2

(c) $-\frac{dB}{dt}\pi R^2$ in loop 1 and zero in loop 2

(d) $-\frac{dB}{dt}\pi r^2$ in loop 1 and zero in loop 2

32. The potential differences across the resistance, capacitance and inductance are 80 V, 40 V and 100 V respectively in an L-C-R circuit. The power factor of this circuit is

(a) 0.4 (b) 0.5

(c) 0.8 (d) 1.0

33. A 100 Ω resistance and a capacitor of 100 Ω reactance are connected in series across a 220 V source. When the capacitor is 50% charged, the peak value of the displacement current is

(a) 2.2 A (b) 11 A

(c) 4.4 A (d) $11\sqrt{2}$ A

34. Two identical glass equi-convex lenses ($\mu_g = 3/2$) of focal length f each are kept in contact. The space between the two lenses is filled with water ($\mu_w = 4/3$). The focal length of the combination is

(a) $\frac{f}{3}$ (b) f

(c) $\frac{4f}{3}$ (d) $\frac{3f}{4}$

35. An air bubble in a glass slab with refractive index 1.5 (near normal incidence) is 5 cm deep when viewed from one surface and 3 cm deep when viewed from the opposite face. The thickness (in cm) of the slab is

(a) 8 (b) 10

(c) 12 (d) 16

36. The interference pattern is obtained with two coherent light sources of intensity ratio n. In the interference pattern, the ratio $\frac{I_{max} - I_{min}}{I_{max} + I_{min}}$ will be

(a) $\frac{\sqrt{n}}{n+1}$ (b) $\frac{2\sqrt{n}}{n+1}$

(c) $\frac{\sqrt{n}}{(n+1)^2}$ (d) $\frac{2\sqrt{n}}{(n+1)^2}$

37. A person can see clearly objects only when they lie between 50 cm and 400 cm from his eyes. In order to increase the maximum distance of distinct vision to infinity, the type and power of the correcting lens, the person has to use, will be

(a) convex, + 2.25 diopter

(b) concave, – 0.25 diopter

(c) concave, – 0.2 diopter

(d) convex, + 0.15 diopter

38. A linear aperture whose width is 0.02 cm is placed immediately in front of a lens of focal length 60 cm. The aperture is illuminated normally by a parallel beam of wavelength 5×10^{-5} cm. The distance of the first dark band of the diffraction pattern from the centre of the screen is

(a) 0.10 cm (b) 0.25 cm

(c) 0.20 cm (d) 0.15 cm

39. Electrons of mass m with de-Broglie wavelength λ fall on the target in an X-ray tube. The cut-off wavelength (λ_0) of the emitted X-ray is

(a) $\lambda_0 = \frac{2mc\lambda^2}{h}$ (b) $\lambda_0 = \frac{2h}{mc}$

(c) $\lambda_0 = \frac{2m^2c^2\lambda^3}{h^2}$ (d) $\lambda_0 = \lambda$

40. Photons with energy 5 eV are incident on a cathode C in a photoelectric cell. The maximum energy of emitted photoelectrons is 2 eV. When photons of energy 6 eV are incident on C, no photoelectrons will reach the anode A, if the stopping potential of A relative to C is

(a) + 3 V (b) + 4 V

(c) − 1 V (d) − 3 V

41. If an electron in a hydrogen atom jumps from the 3rd orbit to the 2nd orbit, it emits a photon of wavelength λ. When it jumps from the 4th orbit to the 3rd orbit, the corresponding wavelength of the photon will be

(a) $\frac{16}{25}\lambda$ (b) $\frac{9}{16}\lambda$

(c) $\frac{20}{7}\lambda$ (d) $\frac{20}{13}\lambda$

42. The half-life of a radioactive substance is 30 minutes. The time (in minutes) taken between 40% decay and 85% decay of the same radioactive substance is

(a) 15 (b) 30

(c) 45 (d) 60

43. For CE transistor amplifier, the audio signal voltage across the collector resistance of 2 kΩ is 4 V. If the current amplification factor of the transistor is 100 and the base resistance is 1 kΩ, then the input signal voltage is

(a) 10 mV (b) 20 mV

(c) 30 mV (d) 15 mV

44. The given circuit has two ideal diodes connected as shown in the figure below. The current flowing through the resistance R_1 will be

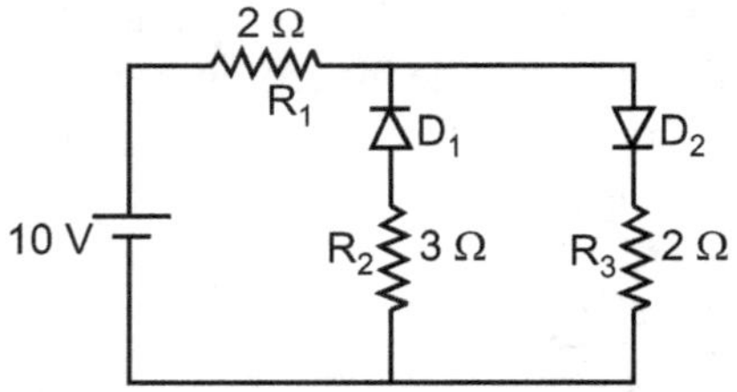

(a) 2.5 A (b) 10.0 A

(c) 1.43A (d) 3.13 A

45. What is the output Yin the following circuit, when all the three inputs A, B, C are first 0 and then 1?

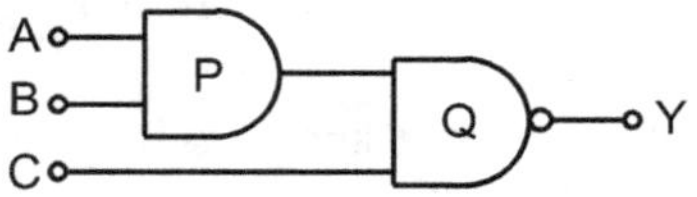

(a) 0, 1 (b) 0, 0

(c) 1, 0 (d) 1, 1

ANSWER KEY

1. (a)	**2.** (d)	**3.** (c)	**4.** (a)	**5.** (c)	**6.** (c)	**7.** (c)	**8.** (c)	**9.** (b)	**10.** (a)
11. (b)	**12.** (b)	**13.** (b)	**14.** (b)	**15.** (b)	**16.** (b)	**17.** (d)	**18.** (b)	**19.** (b)	**20.** (d)
21. (b)	**22.** (a)	**23.** (b)	**24.** (*)	**25.** (d)	**26.** (c)	**27.** (b)	**28.** (b)	**29.** (a)	**30.** (c)
31. (c)	**32.** (c)	**33.** (a)	**34.** (d)	**35.** (c)	**36.** (b)	**37.** (b)	**38.** (d)	**39.** (a)	**40.** (d)
41. (c)	**42.** (d)	**43.** (b)	**44.** (a)	**45.** (c)					

Note: Q.24 - No option is matching.

Correct answer is $K = \frac{2}{3}\left[\frac{K_1K_4}{K_1 + K_4} + \frac{K_2K_4}{K_2 + K_4} + \frac{K_3K_4}{K_3 + K_4}\right]$